1984

CONTENTS

LIST OF CHARACTERS

JOSEPH BARBOUR	*Englishman, later an American citizen*
HILDA BARBOUR	*His wife*
ERNEST BARBOUR	*His son*
MARTIN BARBOUR	*His son*
FLORABELLE BARBOUR (BOUCHARD-NORWOOD)	*His daughter*
DORCAS BARBOUR (BOUCHARD)	*His daughter*
GEORGE BARBOUR	*Brother of Joseph*
DAISY BARBOUR	*His wife*
MARTHA BARBOUR	*His daughter*
ARMAND BOUCHARD	*Refugee from France*
RENEE BOUCHARD	*His wife*
EUGENE BOUCHARD	*His son*
RAOUL BOUCHARD	*His son*
JACQUES BOUCHARD	*His son*
GREGORY SESSIONS	*American gentleman, president and owner of Sessions Steel Company*
NICHOLAS SESSIONS	*His brother*
MAY SESSIONS (BARBOUR)	*Cousin of Gregory and Nicholas Sessions*
AMY DRUMHILL (BARBOUR)	*Niece of Gregory and Nicholas Sessions*
FATHER ALOYSIUS DOMINICK	*Priest of the Church of the Annunciation, Windsor, Pa.*
HANS HECKL	*Foreman in factory of Barbour & Bouchard*
CARL	*His son*
JOHN BALDWIN	*Assistant to Gregory Sessions*

GODFREY BARBOUR
REGINALD BARBOUR
GUY BARBOUR . . . } Children of Ernest Barbour and his
JOSEPH BARBOUR   wife, May Sessions Barbour
GERTRUDE BARBOUR

PAUL BARBOUR
ELSA BARBOUR . . . } Children of Martin Barbour and his
LUCY BARBOUR   wife, Amy Drumhill Barbour
JOHN CHARLES BARBOUR

PHILIPPE BOUCHARD
JULES BOUCHARD
LEON BOUCHARD . . . } Children of Florabelle Barbour and
FRANCOIS BOUCHARD   her husband, Raoul Bouchard

CHANDLER NORWOOD . . } Children of Florabelle Barbour Bou-
BETSY NORWOOD   chard and her second husband, Major
                       Norwood

ETIENNE BOUCHARD
HONORE BOUCHARD
RENEE BOUCHARD . . } Children of Dorcas Barbour and her
ANTOINETTE BOUCHARD   husband, Eugene Bouchard
ANDRE BOUCHARD

MAJOR NORWOOD . . . . Husband of Florabelle Barbour
                           Bouchard
PERCIVAL VAN EYCK . . . . . Husband of Lucy Barbour
THOMAS VAN EYCK . . . . . . Their son
JAY REGAN . . . . Financier
JAMES BELLOWES . . . . Oil baron
ADELAIDE BURGEON . . . . . . Wife of Jules Bouchard
LAND BURGEON . . . . Father of Adelaide Burgeon
ALICE BARBOUR (BOUCHARD) . . . Daughter of Paul and Gertrude
                           Barbour
MISS ELLEN BARBOUR . . . . . Grand-aunt of Joseph Barbour
SQUIRE BRODERICK . . . . . . English squire, employer of Joseph
                           Barbour

Book One: PARTNERS OF DEATH

*"You are Partners of Death.
I want no part in it!"*

CHAPTER I

THE TWILIGHT was like deep pale water standing movelessly over the countryside and the long low hills. It was a medium that held everything motionless and transfixed, not a rigid motionlessness, but a sleeping quiescence, or as though all things had lost the robust body of the day and had become liquid and vaporous dreams, that, should the pale medium that held them be disturbed by even a ripple of air, they would blur together, dissolve, dissipate into silent and spreading rings of water.

There was no definite color in this silent and prolonged spring landscape. All was dim purple, shadowy grays merging into dim blacks, whites spectral and diffused. The meadows, covered by acres of tiny March daisies hugging the soil, were whitish and illusive with a rising mist. The purplish hills were scuttled out at the base by this mist, so that they seemed rather a long baseless ridge of dusky clouds against a western sky that was all dreamlike pale green, cold and unfading. Here and there a lone tree seemed to float on a lonely field, bending its new burden of leaves as if weighed down by a wind too heavy to move. Occasional fences were made of black cobwebs. Over everything was a profound yet vaporous melancholy, drenched by moisture.

The deep hollow lowing of cattle rolled across the meadows, not with the suddenness that attends a more pellucid air, but rather as though it were thunder starting almost inaudibly at a distance and increasing imperceptibly into an all-embracing and imminent sound. Across the meadows came the indistinguishable blur of their plodding forms, white and spotted, dogged and docile. Behind them tramped a buxom milkmaid, her heavy cloak blowing heavily about her, her head bare to the watery coolness of the twilight. Around her jumped a shaggy shepherd dog whose occasional barking sounded thin and unreal. As if their coming were a signal, sudden yellow lights glowed in the dusk, giving evidence of human habitations without making their outlines more distinct.

The cattle had reached a closed gate and milled together patiently, lowing more deeply. The milkmaid opened the gate; she had begun to whistle tonelessly between her teeth. The dog barked irately, dashed through the gate as it began to open. A little boy paused in the road beyond. The milkmaid peered at him.

"Be that you, Martin Barbour?" she called. The little boy politely pulled off his round black hat and quavered an answer. He came to the

3

fence as though with great and fearful resolution, staring at the cattle which lumbered through the gate.

"Still afeared of the poor beasties, Martin?" asked the milkmaid in a jeering but kindly voice. She was an illiterate and buxom wench, but she was unusually shrewd and understanding. "And there he stands, every evenin' comin' from school," she would relate each night to her sister milkmaids, "and frightened to the little heart of him, but standin' like a sojer, he does, and watches the beasties go through glowerin'-like at him with their big eyes. Sort as if he were thrashin' himself inside for being afeared."

Martin clung to the fence, shivering all through his small thin body, but upon his white little face the expression of rigid resolution tightened to one of almost ascetic gauntness. He was terribly frightened; his cold hands sweated on the wet wood which he clutched; he felt his senses swimming and sinking, yet he did not move until the last cow ambled through the gate and started down the road to the barns. Then he stepped away from the fence, not sheepishly before the quizzical eyes of the milkmaid, but quietly and with dignity, as if she understood and had witnessed a scene of acknowledged heroism. As indeed she had.

He stood before her, smiling diffidently, shabby but neat in his tight black coat, country boots and round black hat. His hands were ungloved and raw with cold as they clutched a number of old books. There was about him an air of fear and shrinking, and a self-acknowledged, self-despising scorn of this fear and shrinking, and refusal to surrender to them. He smiled with gentle dignity and sweet pride at the milkmaid. "A perfect little gentleman," thought the girl, as she always thought when encountering Martin. "His folks ain't gentry, but then, he don't seem to belong to them." She beamed at him affectionately, as she dropped the wooden bar of the gate into place.

"Ain't you worritin' your Ma, stayin' out so late at school?" she asked.

"No. Ma knows where I am," he replied in his piping child's voice. He tugged his cap and started away, adding: "Good evening, Miss Susy."

She watched his small figure trudging steadily down the road until it was lost and enveloped in the gathering mist. She shook her head a little with a strange and primitive sensation of melancholy, and her preoccupied whistling, as she followed the cattle, was more tuneless than ever. It was as if she had seen a childish ghost, without a past and without a destination, coming from nothingness into a vague present, and going into nothingness.

Martin could hardly see the road before him as he went on, though long familiarity with it and his quickened breath told him that it was beginning to rise. He curved his footsteps to follow the curve he knew was there. The road was winding behind a very low hill, hardly more ʟnan a rising of the ground. He lifted his small cold face, which was wet with the moisture of the air. The sky was clearing. Between thick and curdled clouds like heavy sea foam a star or two glittered, and the tops of distant hills appeared in the distance. And now a wind rose, weighted with salt coldness and freshness. The mist swirled and twisted over the meadows, became horsemen and charging hosts of spectral vapor sweeping along on an unearthly momentum without sound and without fury. There was something awful in this silent but actively moving panorama, something unconnected with mankind and the earth on which mankind breathed and lived warmly. Martin watched with fear. He hurried a little, involuntarily, then becoming conscious of his hurry deliberately slowed down, sick with fear and self-contempt. "Coward, coward," he said aloud and the sound was almost a whisper. If only someone living and real would come down the road! But no one came, for the cattle were all home from the fields and every man at his hearth. There were only silence and mist, the wet rutted road, the remote and bitter sky. His imagination, acute and terrified, found fresh terrors in the inchoate monsters drifting along on the road before him. His bemused thoughts blended with them, filled his mind with vast and terrible shadows. What, he thought dimly, if his body slowly dissolved so that he became part of the mist and the mist part of him, so that there was no beginning nor end to him, and he drifted away, losing the sharpness of his consciousness, became only a watery dream terrible but unreal? He saw himself peering into cottage windows with vague eyes, drifting by doors opening on golden firelight, forever barred from the warmth and closeness of life.

And so, as he walked, he was no longer a small and frightened boy hurrying safely home, but a universal and diffused agony, voiceless and drifting, its very lack of consciousness only increasing its pain.

The road was steadily rising and gradually the ghosts fell back and the air freshened and chilled. Martin had reached the crest of the rise. He had to pause, for his heart was thundering and laboring, and his breath was quick and short and full of terror. He looked below him. There was no mist, only a slight valley lying in its dim and friendly lights in a pellucid dark air, safe and reassuring. The lights blinked a little like signals, and a dog barked jovially to the right. Over the distant village the very sky was clearer, pointed with stars and trembling with a rising moon. Martin's breath slowed down, became less painful. He smiled a little, tremulously. Then, just before setting out down the road he glanced back over his shoulder down the way he had come.

There lay the mysterious hidden meadows with their cloudy ghosts and monstrous, silent terrors. He felt as one would feel coming out of death into life and security and robust sweetness.

And yet, as he trudged confidently toward the village of Reddish, his home, he felt, as he was to feel during all the course of his short life, that, though he walked and lived in an apparently real and reassuring life with outline and noise and force, the vagueness and shapelessness and chaos of the Things outside life were the only reality, the only terror, the only eternity.

CHAPTER II

IN 1837 the little village of Reddish, near Manchester, presented almost exactly the same appearance that it does today. It is true that there are a few more houses now, and the cotton mills are vaster and busier, and the narrow turning streets sometimes roar with motor cars and smell of exhaust and petrol, and the whine and screech and tinny voices of the wireless sometimes tear the sweet English twilight into quivering ribbons. There is a dance hall now on the spot where the Blue Boar Inn stood in 1837, and the weavers and spinners can bring their lady friends of a Saturday night and dance until midnight and after for twelve pence. But the dancing in the garish cheapness of the hall is very little different in point of gaiety and good spirits than it was almost a century ago, and the girls might have been the same girls who laughed from the windows of the Blue Boar at the coachman and the passengers of the London Stage as that loaded vehicle thundered into the cobbled yard. There are many houses still standing over a century old, lived in contentedly and comfortably, and the new houses, with the exception of some cheap and gaudy little villas beyond Sandy Lane, are built very much on the order of the old houses. The inhabitants plant slips of lilac bushes in their new yards, but the slips are from old bushes and the scent of wet lilacs has not changed. Sandy Lane has changed little, rising from the village and winding gently and drowsily toward the green and rounded hills. When it leaves the village environs it loses itself in pleasant meadows lying under gauzy sunshine, recovers itself as it dips downward to a little stream and crosses an old wooden bridge, pauses for four or five minutes beside sleepy woods, creeps in enchantment by the hawthorn hedges, stops for a space beside Mill Pond to watch the cattle standing in their own reflections under the willows, then gently expires once more into the meadows, never to recover itself again.

In this March twilight of 1837 little Martin Barbour felt that he was reaching security and reality as his feet trudged rapidly down Sandy Lane to the village. The wet trees overhead, just bursting into bud, dripped little cold pellets upon his head, stirred uneasily in a waking night wind. But the air was cool and fresh, not humid and dank as it had been on the meadows. The moon began to brighten as it rose over the fading dim green of the western sky, and suddenly, without warning, a bird cried out once, and then was still. But the sound was so piercingly sweet and poignant that Martin stopped abruptly and waited, tears gushing into his eyes. He waited for several moments, but the ecstatic cry was not repeated, and he went on.

Everything was still silent and hushed, but it was the safe and familiar hush of home. Sandy Lane suddenly made a deep curve about a low stone wall, and beyond the wall the deep green earth rose to a low whitestone house under its tremendous trees. Squire Broderick lived there. Martin hurried a little, for Squire Broderick possessed hounds that were none too friendly and bayed terrifyingly. Martin liked to look at the old houses, and regretted the hounds. Lamplight was beginning to shine from the deep old windows, and he could see the reflection of firelight. Someone must have thrown fresh coal on some of the fires for the great old chimney belched forth red sparks and gray smoke into the dusk. The air was so still that Martin could hear the neighing of the Squire's horses in their comfortable stables and the voices of the grooms. From an upper window came the thin and acrid wail of a baby, the Squire's youngest. The house and all its environs seemed wrapped in safety and peace and warmth and ancient steadfastness, English and immovable.

He passed the little Nonconformist church near the roadway, shining palely in the last dusk. Behind the church were the broken rows of the gravestones, immobile and silent. Martin began to run, then made himself stop, shaking internally.

The dark low shapes of houses began to appear along the lane, the deep small windows burning with lamplight and firelight. Now the houses were side by side behind prim front gardens with little iron fences, and the smell of fires hung in the brightening air. He could hear the creaking of invisible pumps. The sky was swimming in moonlight, and dogs were barking. From the wet earth rose a passionate smell, humid and breeding. Martin inhaled that smell, and felt ecstasy.

Just before Sandy Lane ended abruptly at the Common, the Blue Boar Inn stood at a wide curve in the road, set under bent oak trees. Its casements stood open to the spring night, and through them Martin could see the beamed ceiling trembling redly in firelight, and grotesque black shadows bowing and moving along the dark walls. Laughter, hoarse voices, thumping of sticks, came from the taproom, and the shrill mirth of the barmaids in their white aprons and mob caps. Several horses were hitched up in front of the inn, and they bent their heads patiently, their breath steaming from their nostrils. From the stables behind the Inn came the shouts of grooms and stableboys, and the pungent smell of hay and manure. A maid had been drawing water from the well, and had been waylaid by a groom; they were embracing with singular candor in the shadow of the eaves near the kitchen windows. Someone in the inn began to sing; it was a man's rich voice, rollicking and pleasant, singing an old drinking song. Others picked it up, swelled it, filled it with joy and coarse joviality, until all the night, cool and dark and still, retreated before the living sound. Martin hesitated for a moment or two. Like most reserved and intensely contained people, he was fascinated by color and movement and splendid living and warmth, all those things that have nothing to do with thought and intellect, and the cold bitterness of the mind. Mentally, he stood outside these things, eternally an exile, like the ghosts he had imagined on the meadows, peering in at windows they could not enter, and mentally he suffered. He went on, reluctantly, the singing following him into the darkness.

The Common, which he was approaching, was an irregular oval. Three-quarters of its sides were filled with the crouching homes of workingmen. The dim lights in their windows were like the eyes of waiting wolves. The last quarter of the rim of the Common was occupied by the cotton mill, where most of the men, many of the women, and too many of the children worked. Over the Common, which was ill-kept and muddy and sunken and almost bare, and which during rains accumulated stagnant water, and over the drab old houses, hung an air stifled and gaunt and desolate. Over this place the moon was not so bright, and the earth was not breathing out its fertility. There was only the smell of ashes and decay and hunger and cold hearths and dust and boiling cabbage.

He passed behind the house, came to the third one. He opened the gate of the barren little yard, closed it. There was a light in the kitchen, and a reflection of firelight. He pushed open the kitchen door. His mother, her heavy woolen skirt pinned back over her red flannel petticoat, her black curls crisp and bright under the frills of her cotton mob cap, was bending over the fire. Her sleeves were rolled up, and showed her arms, strong, plump and white. The firelight, leaping, profiled a face vigorous and unsentimental, handsome with the hardy resolution of the peasant. She stirred something in an iron pot, then swung it back over the fire. A cradle stood to one side, bathed in firelight, and in it a baby held up its fat fingers to view them against the flame. The wooden floor was scrubbed and bare, and the fire danced on polished andirons and on the few strictly utilitarian pieces of furniture. On one side of the fire a large, serious-faced, apple-cheeked boy of thirteen or so sat upright on the settle, reading with an air of profound concentration. A little girl of perhaps five sat on the floor at his feet, playing with a cloth doll. The table, with its red cover, was set for the meal with thick plates and pewter utensils. The iron kettle was singing on the fire, the copper vessels hanging on the walls winked like struck gold in a sudden flare-up of flame.

Mrs. Barbour lit several tallow candles on the mantelpiece with a taper. She was muttering to herself; she caught sight of Martin, and an irate light flashed into her eyes, fine eyes, black and sparkling and not too amiable.

"Ah, there, my lad, comin' home at all hours!" she exclaimed. "Look at you, soakin' with the fog! Well, don't stand there gawpin' like a zany. Take off your boots and get you ready for tea."

There was vigor and vitality in her loud, upbraiding voice, but Martin had the impression that all this was not concerned with him at all. He felt that her unusual excitement (for he rarely returned from school much before this hour) was due to something else entirely, and that he had been merely a suddenly opening channel through which the force of her agitation might pour. Yet, he also felt that her agitation was not without pleasure and zest. She seized the black iron pot again and stirred it mightily in her vigorous bemusement, and the room steamed with the odors of onions, kidneys and good rich beef simmering in a brown gravy. Martin's nostrils twitched a little; he pulled off his muddy boots and neatly laid them on the hearth. He had to step between his mother and his brother, Ernest. The latter lifted his eyes so slowly that the act seemed full of languor, but in reality it was the slowness of immense power and enormous coldness. He regarded Martin for a long moment, and during this moment his heavy mouth, sullen and deliberate, moved ever so slightly into a carved line of indifferent contempt.

"When are you going to give up this school foolishness?" he asked. His voice was unusually mature, the voice of one who already knows himself and his capacities.

"Not ever," replied Martin softly, staring into the fire and rubbing his hands. He hated Ernest, as he knew Ernest hated him. Ten years later he would also pity Ernest, but now his hatred made his gorge rise, made his delicate lips tremble and his hands quiver. He knew Ernest despised him, and knew why he despised him. Young though he was, he had such clarity of vision that he could understand why his enemies could feel so toward him.

Ernest shrugged, shifted his big feet, and continued to contemplate his younger brother. The contemplation was full of cold curiosity, indifference and calculation.

" 'Not ever,' " he mocked. " 'Not ever.' Not ever being any good, or doing anything, or getting anywhere. Just lazing over books. How long do you think Pa's going to keep you here, not worth your bread?"

"Now, Ernest, you leave Martin alone," interrupted Mrs. Barbour. But she spoke mechanically. Her face showed no signs of Ernest's words having gone beyond her outer ear; it remained preoccupied and thoughtful. Her black brows were drawn together in a knotted line over her eyes. Tugging abstractedly again at the kettle, she burnt her hand, muttered fiercely, but without a change in her expression. Martin looked alertly at his mother, then glanced at Ernest. But there was no answer on Ernest's face; only his very light gray eyes glowed with hostility.

"You are a great lad," went on Ernest slowly and quietly, each word forming like ice on his heavy lips. "You know how to read and cipher and write a good hand. What more do you want? What can you ever be, with your puling ways and your puny arms? Nothing but a clerk to the squire or the solicitor. But what you can do, you can do."

Martin regarded him in a short silence. This was an old story between the two boys. Usually he ignored Ernest's taunts, merely smiling quietly, shrugging a little, turning away. But tonight something of his mother's suppressed excitement mysteriously communicated itself to him, and his sudden smile was wild and white, and his large blue eyes, opening widely, blazed.

"But I don't want to be like you," he said in a loud clear voice. "Not ever like you, Ernest. That's why I keep on going to school—so I'll never be like you, thinking of money, and getting on in the world, and kicking other people, and snatching pennies. I couldn't bear being like you. I'd rather die."

This show of spirit was so unprecedented, so remarkable, that Mrs. Barbour was jolted from her hot abstraction, and she turned upon her younger son an eye of complete astonishment.

"What's that?" she muttered, then in a louder, harsher voice: "What's all this? Quarrelin' again, you two? I'll knock your two heads together!" She followed up this promise by cuffing Ernest suddenly and vigorously, almost knocking him from the settle, and following up this blow by boxing Martin on the ear with false energy. Only he knew the quick softening of the blow, so that it was barely a slap, but he dodged with extraordinary convincingness. The little girl on the floor roared in sympathy, the baby in the cradle screamed. A black cat, heretofore unseen in the chimney corner, came forth arching and spitting in the uproar.

"As if I haven't enough to think about without you two!" shouted Mrs. Barbour, panting, swinging her short white arms threateningly. "Another word, and out you'll both go, and sing for your suppers! You, Ernest, bring me in some more coal, and quick about it. You, Martin, pick up the baby and quiet her, mind, after waking her up! Quick now. And you, Florabelle, stop that yelpin' or I'll give you a clout you'll remember all your life!"

She glared at them all, her teeth glittering between her rich red lips, her white bosom, more exposed than was usual with the discreet wives of the laboring class, rising and falling passionately. A few more black curls bounced out from under the frills of her cap and framed her warm red cheeks. Smarting though they were, her two sons stared at her peasant handsomeness with open admiration. She was well aware of

their admiration, for she was young and discerning, and tried to mask
her familiar pleasure with renewed shoutings and threats. When they
backed away from her cautiously, she bit her lips to hide a smile, and
returned to her cooking in restored good humor, bridling not a little.
She tossed her head, muttered, clanged her iron spoon against the sides
of the iron vessel.

Growling under his breath, Ernest picked up the scuttle and went out
of the room. Martin lifted the baby, Dorcas, from her crib and sat down
in the corner of the settle, which was still warm from Ernest's body. The
baby was his darling, his plaything; he loved her very much. He perched
her expertly on his thin knee with all the tenderness of a mother, crooning to her wordlessly. She was very much like himself, small-boned and
delicate, with a tiny three-cornered face and large blue eyes and soft
light hair. She felt his love and nestled to him, damp as she was, and
contentedly sucked her thumb. But her eyes were turned upward, shining, fixed upon him. He cuddled the little body against the curve of
himself, smiling downwards. A sweetness enveloped the two children
like a soft aura. Observing them through the corner of her eye, Hilda's
broad face softened, but she felt a twinge. Martin was her favorite,
though she would have stoutly denied it. There was a sultry passion in
her love for him. She turned to the table and began to slice coarse
bread with a tremendous knife. She resumed her muttering, but louder
now, for Martin's benefit. He heard, but continued to smile at the
baby, without, however, missing a word.

"You two!" she growled. "Never a minute's peace. As if a body
hasn't enough to worry about. Fightin' all the time, like two cockerels.
I'll be splittin' your heads, mark my words. There's an end to patience.
You shouldn't listen to Ernest. All he thinks of is guns and gunpowder,
and the like, and don't read anythin' but about guns and such. Like your
Pa."

She paused. "Yes, I know," said Martin softly, still smiling at the
baby and pursing his lips at her.

Hilda shrugged, set down a pitcher of milk with unnecessary vigor.
"You know," she mimicked. "But that don't keep you from fightin' with
him. Not a thimble of sense in you, Martin. Ernest is a born fighter,
but you ain't. You—I always thought you'd be a gentleman. Well, no, I
don't suppose you could ever really be a gentleman; that'd be tryin' to
rise above your station. But you could at least have gentlemanlike ways.
A lad with ways like a gentleman can go far in gentry's houses, writin'
letters and keepin' books. Steward. I always wanted you to be a
steward." She stared at him wistfully, the knife in her hand, her mouth
open like a child's. Still he did not look at her; he was examining the
baby's hands with touching intentness. He kissed the pale little cheek
with infinite love.

"Ugh!" said Hilda harshly, turning to her cupboard and snatching cups from it. "Might as well talk to the cat!"

"I'm sorry, Ma," said Martin gently, turning his face to her. "I'm listening."

She pouted, blinked, tossed her head again with spirit. "That's all very well," she said crossly, pettishly, with a childlike air that even her husband found irresistible. "I try to talk to you, and get the side of your face. And us goin' to America before summer!"

It was out now, and her face shone with excited smiles and her eyes flashed and glittered. The air seemed to crackle about her; the fire rose and roared up the chimney in a rush of yellow sparks and smoke. Martin paled, his expression becoming blank as he regarded his mother intently.

"America," he whispered. He moistened lips that all at once were dry and sick. She nodded her head with quick delight, swooped back to the fire and fell down upon the settle beside him, her face sparkling and dimpling with glee. Her breath blew itself explosively on his cheek, almost with ecstasy. She waited for what he would say with eager impatience.

But he did not say anything; for a long time he fixed his large blue eyes upon her face expressionlessly. She continued to wait, and as she did so she began to frown a little, a small ridge of white flesh rising between her black brows. Her smile began to fade, her lips to open and drop so that her teeth, two small rows of them, showed between them. Her eyes blinked. Then her cheeks reddened as the little boy averted his head and carefully pushed backwards on the settle, away from him, his brother's book. The title flickered in the firelight: "The Origin, Manufacture and Use of Firearms and Explosives." It was an old book, quaintly worded on thick yellow paper with browned edges, and the cover, embellished with curlicues and faded gilt, was thick and dog-eared. After pushing aside the book, Martin stared at it blindly.

"Well!" cried Hilda, and pushed him vigorously with her clenched hand. She flounced upon the seat. "Haven't you anythin' to say, you young calf?"

Slowly, very slowly, Martin shook his head. Tears of misery pushed themselves between his thick fair lashes. He continued to shake his head. Hilda stared at him, dumfounded, her jaw dropping. "Eh," she muttered. She put her hand uncertainly to her mob cap, tucked under the escaped curls. Then an irate light flashed into her eyes and her cheeks crimsoned.

"What a daft little dolt it is!" she exclaimed, offended and bewildered. She sprang to her feet, very lightly in spite of her plumpness, and stirred the pot vigorously. The child Florabelle, sensing her mother's fury, cautiously removed still farther into the chimney corner and peered out from that shelter. Her thick flaxen braids fell over her rosy cheeks and dangled before her, so that the shadow of them on the wall was like hanging ropes.

Hilda was greatly hurt. Her husband was of a dark and sullen disposition, not given to enthusiasms, warm delights and jovial excitements. Ernest was stolid, and contemptuous of hysterias. The two little girls did not count with the zestful Hilda. But Martin was her love, her sympathizer, the one who never failed her in tenderness, gentle enthusiasm, sweetness and understanding. Therefore, his lack of response to her tremendous news not only bewildered her, but filled her with pettish and depressed resentment. She took it out on him by emphasizing the fact that after all they were adult mother and insignificant child, and ordered him sharply to put the baby down and stir the fire, and pull up his father's chair. She felt sore and betrayed.

Still silent, Martin placed the baby in her crib; the child immediately wailed her disappointment. Hilda shouted at her, and both Dorcas and Martin shrank. Florabelle smirked, pleased, in her shelter. She did not like Martin and enjoyed seeing him in disfavor. When her small, shrewd blue eyes caught the firelit glitter of tears on his cheeks, she regarded them with pleasure, a pleasure almost voluptuous.

Martin lifted his head and looked at his mother gravely. He felt very sorry for her, regretful that he had failed her. He began to speak, but before he could say a word Ernest entered the room, sulkily lugging the scuttle. But his sulkiness lightened alertly as he advanced toward the fire; he felt the tension in the air. Hilda glanced crossly at him over her shoulder.

"Ernest," she said, "we be going to America come summer."

Ernest stood, petrified, the scuttle hanging on his hand. His impassive face broke into an expression of amazement, and then, sudden excitement and joy. This mobile and unusual expressiveness surprised Hilda, and she stared at him, diverted, as he turned to her and approached her.

"America!" he cried, his slowness to believe anything at all making his voice rough and hard.

"Yes," replied Hilda grudgingly. She resented this obvious excitement in Ernest because she had expected it from Martin. She shrugged her shoulders; all at once her news became flat, drab and of no importance. It was nothing to her that Ernest was stirred and interested; her audience in the orchestra had failed her, and she did not care for the gallery. She was still sore inside.

Ernest clapped his hands, once and shortly. It was a convulsive gesture, alien to his nature, and therefore the more remarkable. It had an explosive sound, decisive and grim, as if something in him, which had waited since his birth, went on a march toward a predestined place. He turned to the fire without another word, but he rubbed his hands together

in the light of the red and yellow flames, and again the gesture was convulsive and tense, without enjoyment of the physical warmth. His face,
too, was tense, and had in it a sort of dark gloating, and his eyes glowed
with an almost incandescent light. Then a thought occurred to him, the
gloating disappeared, the gleam in his eyes dimmed. He turned abruptly
to his mother, scowling slightly.

"Ma, it's all settled? It's just not one of your—it's just not talk, is
it? We are to go? Pa says so?"

Hilda swung on him, scarlet with anger. "So, my son calls me a liar,
does he?" she screamed. She had a pewter ladle in her hand and she flung
it at him, her breath exploding past her lips in a long "whew!" Ernest,
expert in these matters, dodged and the ladle smashed into the fire. His
expression dark, and now becoming brooding, he picked up the utensil
with the aid of the tongs, and, preoccupied, put it on the table. His heavy
lips were out-thrust, his brow scowling, his movements mechanical. It
was plain that his thoughts were not concerned with Hilda's childish
antics, not in the least; his whole concern was whether her story could
be relied upon. He had had too many experiences with tales born of her
hopes and effervescence, and he remembered, too keenly, his disappoint-
ments and violent readjustments. He did not want to be caught again.

As if her demonstration against him had been some unimportant and
expected act of nature, he turned to her again, impassive once more,
but intent.

"It's all settled?" he repeated insistently. "Pa says so?"

Hilda, who had watched him, frustrated and furious, came to life
with violence. She stamped her foot, snorted, tossed her head until the
curls flew.

"Am I a child?" she shrieked. "Am I a liar, in my own house, before
my own brats? If I am, I'm addled! Send me to Bedlam, chain me up,
call the beadle—!" Martin, on the settle, paled, Florabelle whimpered,
the baby cried.

But Ernest smiled faintly. He regarded his mother for a long moment
with a sort of wry and indulgent amusement. The others might shrink
before her tantrums, be terrified, daunted or appalled. But not Ernest.
He waited. Hilda stopped, glared at him, the whites of her eyes blazing
in the mingled fire- and candlelight. Then, her own eyes falling before
the calm and impassive and waiting eyes of her elder son, she broke
into an oath, stamped madly upon the rocker of the wailing baby's cradle
so that it began to rock crazily. Instantly the baby became soundless with
terror. Florabelle put her thumb in her mouth and sucked it frenziedly,
as she always did in moments of stress. Martin caught the hood of the
wooden cradle, slowed down its wild rockings, and reduced the motion
to one soothing and protective. He shivered a little. Then Ernest, shrug-

ging with a sort of contemptuous resignation, began to whistle softly as he turned from his infuriated mother. But he scowled with uncertainty and disappointment.

In the midst of all this the outer door opened, letting in a flood of cool night air, and admitting Joseph Barbour. As he closed the door slowly after him he glowered at his wife and children.

"What's all the blasted row about?" he demanded irritably. "Heard it comin' cross the Common. Never any peace in the bloody house. What's it about? Eh? What's it all about?"

Hilda swung upon him dramatically. "Mr. Barbour!" she cried with passion, "your son Ernest just called me a liar, me, his Ma! And if you don't flog him within an inch of his life you're no true father! That's all I've got to say!"

Joseph looked from his wife, standing like a queen of tragedy with the ladle in her hand and lightnings quivering about her, and then he looked at Ernest. His glowering looks deepened. He shouldered toward the fire, and as he was thus brought closer to the quiet Ernest he glanced at him furtively, and there was in that glance familiar sympathy and apology. Arriving at the fire, Joseph threw an indifferent look at his two little daughters, and another look at Martin. He was a slight man who seemed shorter than his wife, though in reality they were the same height. He had what the neighbors called a "foreign" look, and in truth there was something Latin about his dark and sultry face, his glowering gray eyes, prominent nose, pointed chin and shock of thick, wavy hair, black and vital. He had a sullen and secretive expression which was not English, and at times his mannerisms, his tendency to violence and furies, his vengefulness and jealousies, his passions and his lustfulness, seemed to bear out his story that his great-grandfather on his father's side had been an adventurous Frenchman who had fled France for political reasons. He had a nervously quick walk, a wiry frame, extraordinarily delicate and mobile hands, and tremendous impatience. He was decidedly no fool.

He took his time before speaking, and rubbed his hands in the glow of the fire. His eye touched Martin who was gently rocking the cradle; a curious expression gleamed on Joseph's face, thoughtful, respectful, impatient. Then he turned to Hilda, who was gathering breath for another storm. His glance stopped her at the explosive point.

"Come now, lass," he said indulgently, "are you certain Ernest called you a liar? I never heard him be disrespectful to you. He'd better not," he added, with a sudden scowl, turning to Ernest.

"I didn't call Ma a liar," said Ernest quietly and reasonably. "I only asked her if everything was really settled about us going to America."

"Oh, so you couldn't keep your mouth shut until I told you to speak, could you, Hilda?" Joseph's voice flogged his wife. Hilda paled; her angry eyes dropped. She put the ladle down, and appeared overcome with apprehension.

"I didn't think it would hurt to tell the lads," she muttered uneasily.

"You never think, lass," said Joseph. Ernest smiled slightly.

"Ma didn't say for certain that we were to go," he said, turning a face so bland toward his mother that she burned white with rage. He quickened, forgetting her. "But Pa, are we going? Is it settled? Did Uncle George send for us?"

"Wait a minute," grumbled Joseph, but he was not ill-pleased. He wanted to discuss this all with Ernest, whom he understood, and who was his favorite, but it was necessary to his dignity to feign reluctance. "Can't a man sit down before being mithered? Where's my chair?" He sat down precisely, for he was neat as well as slight, and there was something delicate about him which repudiated the peasant vitality of his wife. He did not wear the clogs of the average lower class Englishman, for he was a sort of upper servant in Squire Broderick's household, and his clothing, though poor and shabby, draped itself about his body with an air of elegance. Hilda was secretly very proud of him and stood in considerable awe of him. "He's every inch the gentleman," she was fond of saying to her friends.

He pulled off his boots, and deftly Ernest took them, laying them carefully on their sides on the hearth so that their dampness could dry. Ernest's hands were large as well as intelligent, and the boots looked like the boots of a child in them. His every gesture was tender; he loved his father profoundly. Joseph watched him, and his dark expression softened. He glanced idly at last at the baby, clucked half-heartedly to her, threw Florabelle in the chimney corner an affectionate glance. After Ernest, he loved her best. He held out his hand to her, and she bounced from her corner with a shout of glee. He took her upon his knee and began to play with one of her flaxen braids; she occupied herself with playing with the neat plain ruffle of his white shirt. Hilda, subdued, went about the final setting of her table in the background, but once she stared at her family and something deep and satisfied crept into her expression. There was Martin, crouching on the settle and rocking the cradle, the firelight making his hair a flow of fine silver-gilt and outlining the gentle beauty of his profile, and there was Joe, her lord and master and lover, with his slight, well-shaped back to her, his black and wavy hair gleaming beneath the candles, his daughter upon his knee, and there was the powerful though stocky Ernest squatting on the hearth beside his father and looking worshipfully at him. Hard tears burned against her lids.

"Yes, we're going to America," said Joseph quietly. He paused a moment, impressively. Martin, still not speaking, turned his face to his father, and waited, but Ernest eagerly put his hand on his knee. His

heavy young face quivered with a little spasm, and watching him, Joseph
smiled in deep sympathy, something of Ernest's excitement passing
into him. "Yes," he repeated, louder, "we are going to America. Some
time in May, whenever your Uncle George sends us the tickets. You
know where he is, I've told you often enough. Windsor, Pennsylvania
State. So this morning I got a letter from him, and he tells me that he
has things going nice. Three men working now, in his little firearms and
gunpowder factory, and that Frenchy I told you about, Ernest, that
Bouchard fellow, just got his money from France, two hundred pounds,
and bought a partnership with your Uncle George. And now George has
a place for me, too. A real place. No more of this scraping to gentry,
and working your fingers off for a few pennies and a 'thank'ee, sir,
please-kick-me-in-the-backside-sir!' No more of that, for me and my
kids!" He stared from one to the other of the children, his dark gray
eyes brilliant. "No more of that! And money! The damn place is full
of money! In a few years we'll have more than we ever thought of, and
can come back home and lord it over everybody. Gentry, ourselves." He
chuckled, a little hoarsely.

"But, Joe," began Hilda timidly. Her husband flashed a fierce glance at
her, and discerning that she was still in disfavor, she relapsed into
silence.

Then Martin spoke for the first time. "We'll never come back," he
said in a soft and thrilling voice. "We'll never come back, never again."
It were as though he were repeating a litany of grief.

Joseph glared at him savagely. "What's this, you fool? 'Never come
back?' We'll be back in ten years! Think I want to be buried alive out
there among the heathen Indians and the bush and the forests and the
Yankees? England's my home; I'm an Englishman, ain't I? But I want
money. I'm sick of this, here. We'll be back before you've got a beard,
you little donkey." He turned his back upon Martin, contemptuously
dismissing him.

"I'll be glad to see Daisy again," said Hilda, forgetting her disfavor,
and approaching the fire. "It's been more than four years——"

"Will you get on with the tea?" cried Joseph irately. And again Hilda
retreated. Martin, unnoticed, put a thin finger to his cheek and furtively
removed a tear. Joseph turned to him again. "Do you want to be a
servant, like your Pa?" he demanded, exasperated. Martin, unable to
speak, meekly shook his head. But Ernest was impatient that his father's
attention should be called to anyone so insignificant as Martin. He
jogged his father's knee.

"I can't believe it," he gloated, his face glowing, his lips dry. "Oh, I'll
never come back home, I'll never want to! I want to get somewhere;
there's no chance at home. I don't want to wear clogs. It's a new world,
America. A man can do something."

He stood up. They all looked at him. He was only thirteen, but there was something tremendous about his powerful young body, something implacable and invincible in his attitude, something of bitter splendor in the rugged planes of his large face. He was so little given to external excitements and effervescences that now they were doubly striking, and somehow frightening. At least, Martin felt a cold thrill of fear, and Hilda was taken aback. But Joseph smiled, very darkly, somewhat grimly.

"Eh, my lad," he said, nodding his small head. "That's the way to talk. And God willing, you'll get what you want. Oh, there's no doubt you'll get it!"

Forgetting his ill-humor, he twisted in his seat, and smiling, held out his hand to Hilda. "Come here, lass, and give me a kiss." Overjoyed, Hilda, like a child, bounced over to him, seized his head in her warm white arms, and kissed him passionately on the mouth, over and over, until, laughing, he had to struggle with her to release himself. He almost fell into the fire in his struggles, and only Hilda's strong arms, grasping him again, saved him. She was beautiful, hot and flushed, beaming, as frolicsome as a young she-dog. The little girls shrieked, Martin smiled woefully and unwillingly, but Ernest frowned intently into the fire. He heard nothing, saw nothing, of the commotion. His thoughts, his life, went winding implacably through the rosy caverns of the coals, through the golden pathways, by the black and toppling heights. There was nothing else for him, there would never be anything else. A cricket moved jerkily across the hearth, terrified and scuttling. Mechanically, without thinking of it at all, Ernest crushed the creature beneath his foot. Martin saw the gesture, but he also saw more than the gesture. He saw that Ernest had no conscious animosity against the cricket, that his killing of it was mechanical and instinctive. And this lack of conscious animosity seemed to Martin to be a most terrible thing.

CHAPTER III

JOSEPH BARBOUR was a sort of upper servant in the home of Squire Henry Broderick. He directed and managed the grooms in the stable, the boys who cared for the dogs. Also, as the Squire was a great hunter, he had charge of all the guns, which were many, as the Squire had many friends and this was not bad shooting country. Joseph, who had been one of the grooms, had stepped into his brother's place when George Barbour had gone to America four years ago. Surly, independent and eccentric, Joseph was no great favorite with Squire Broderick, but his superior intelligence and high integrity soon became very valuable to him. Moreover, he was an expert with firearms, even better than his brother, Squire Broderick said. The Squire had the best private collection of pistols and shotguns in the country, and they were always in perfect order. Joseph, after considerable mysterious dabblings, and after the Squire had fearfully prophesied that he and his household would be blown to bits during the experiments, had produced an amazingly wet-resistant gunpowder, which caused firearms to discharge cleanly, with less smoke and less danger to the firer. He refused to give up his secret, though enticed financially. It was his hope and his hard ambition. George could use this new and better gunpowder in his little firearms and powder factory in America, in the small town of Windsor, on the Allegheny River, in Pennsylvania State. It was after Joseph's letter about this new gunpowder that George suggested that his brother join him in America. Joseph had not thought of America seriously until George's letter arrived, and then suddenly, as in a vision, he saw vast and dazzling things. He would go.

Joseph was disappointed and irritated by Martin's silence about the coming exodus to America. Every evening he would harangue him, extolling the new country, of which he had very little knowledge, becoming artificially enthusiastic, until he observed Martin's eyes full of tearful pity, and with a volubility entirely out of proportion trying to convince a silent and stubborn audience of the tremendous advantages of the coming journey. His gestures would become extraordinarily large, his language eloquent, his manner buoyant. Ernest became angrily impatient after the first two nights; he wanted hard and definite facts, not eulogies. He liked to hear his father say prophetically: "Time is coming, my lad, when wars won't be fought and won by nations with better men and braver hearts and superior courage. They'll be won by the country with better gunpowder and firearms, even if the men are fewer. Bigger guns, large, swifter bullets. Not men and blood. Wars'll be won in factories." Then Ernest would listen, his glowing eyes turned inwards, his mouth open and smiling. Joseph, watching him, then, would feel a faint uneasiness and jealousy, as if he realized that Ernest saw things beyond his own vision, and went forward into places where he, himself, could not go. It was during these times that he turned instinctively to Martin, who was younger and simpler, yet, paradoxically, more subtle than his brother.

But Martin remained silent. He seemed to retreat behind his flesh, so that it appeared that his outward self was but a deserted and vulnerable outpost a long way ahead of an invincible fortress. Joseph, shouting, could beat down the frail and outer walls with a barrage of words, but he could not even approach the fortress, for it was surrounded by impassable silence. Finally, in exasperation, Joseph furiously gave up, and for several weeks totally abandoned the child. "Ungrateful young dog!" he shouted.

He found consolation, however, in the satisfactory reactions of Hilda, who was delighted at the prospect of seeing her second cousin, Daisy, again. She did not particularly admire George Barbour, a surly man without what Hilda called "family feeling." (He had sent neither of Hilda's little girls a christening present, though Dorcas had been named for his and Joseph's mother.) But the buoyancy of Hilda's character was such that she could find all kinds of excellencies in George Barbour, now that he had offered to send his brother tickets to bring them all to America. Then Ernest's rigid ecstasy contributed to Joseph's complacency, and for the first time he took serious interest in little Florabelle who, without comprehension, took part in the family rejoicing. Only Martin was silent, and helplessly observing the disfavor into which he had fallen, remained as unobtrusive as possible. He avoided Joseph, whom he secretly worshipped. He crept into chimney corners, hurried through wretched meals, stayed outside until twilight drove him home, loitered about his school. Why he despaired and grieved so he did not know, but it seemed to him that he was oppressed by a heavy agony and grief too vast for words, even for tears or thought. He was like a childish Atlas, carrying on his delicate shoulders the tremendous weight of his own unformed emotions. He grew paler, thinner, a big-eyed shadow of himself.

In the meantime preparations for departure went on with elation. Squire Broderick was indignantly disturbed at the idea of losing his best servant, and after persuasion and promises had failed, prophesied dire things for the family in America. Joseph was not moved. He allowed all his secret rancor and contempt for the Squire to manifest themselves, with the result that he was discharged with rage four weeks before the date of sailing. This was very inconvenient and alarming, and might have had disastrous results for the impoverished family had not the Squire, discovering that he could not do without Joseph, sent his eldest son to the Barbour home with offers of forgiveness. This, among other excitements, prevented his parents from discovering Martin's progressive sufferings and emaciation.

Then Squire Broderick magnanimously offered to send Ernest and Martin to school, paying all expenses, if Joseph would remain in his service. For a long time Joseph had had his disgruntled eye on a tenant cottage in the village which Squire Broderick had heretofore seemed unable to rent him; this cottage was now offered to him rent free. Joseph, unusually grave, came home and told his wife of this. They were both shaken, and dazzled. Schools for their children, a tidy little home for themselves. They stared at each other, pale and doubtful. Neither of the two boys had as yet spoken, but Martin's face was brilliant and white. Then suddenly Ernest stood up, ghastly, his features rigid and tormented. He looked from his father to his mother, then cried out, once, very sharply. Then he sat down again, clenched his large hands upon his knees, stared stonily into the fire. Joseph regarded him with vast amazement, as did Hilda. They waited. Ernest did not speak, though Martin had begun to sob softly in his corner.

Nothing more was said of the house and the schools. Nothing more was said of remaining in England. Ernest made no remarks, discussed nothing. He merely prepared for the journey.

Joseph's only living relative was an old great-aunt who lived at the end of Sandy Lane in a tiny house secured by a pension, as she had lost father, husband and sons in the Napoleonic wars. It stood far back from the Lane, hidden under the great shadow of trees. It was all of a hundred years old, with thick walls, tiny sunken latticed windows, squat stone chimneys and square oaken doors. The back windows opened outwards upon a sunken garden full of ancient trees, twisting paths, sun dials, arbors, round flower beds and tangled bushes. It was an enchanted house and garden, where the shade was the thickest, the grass the greenest, the birds more numerous as they thrilled through a silence that seemed palpable. Once the gate, which opened upon the pleasant traffic of Sandy Lane, was opened, one plunged immediately into a profound stillness, where the very sound of sparrows spluttering in their stone birdbaths become loud and obtrusive. The house was swamped in mingled shrubbery, trees and shadow, its west windows opening directly into pale lilacs and ivy, and the very sunshine, trapped here in tiny distorted pools and triangles and misty, shifting blurs, was gauzy and soft with unreality. On the tilted warmth of the stone flags of the garden a great black cat arched and purred and slept, his topaz eyes glinting lazily after the multitudinous birds, and in a sort of tangled arbor old Mrs. Barbour sat through the long summer days and the long twilights, knitting.

Her neighbors, with whom she was only dimly familiar, called her an old witch, but this was unkind, as there was nothing mysterious or malevolent about the old woman. Rather, she was vague and forgetful, with hazy blue eyes, pale, wrinkled face, white hair, plump little body and uncertain gait. She loved birds, and kept several in cages in her sun-drowned kitchen, and endured her cat only because he kept mice away. She never visited anyone except her great-nephew Joseph, and that was only at Christmas. Squire Broderick managed her affairs, as he had been instrumental in securing the pension for her, and she lived a dreamy, half-conscious life, like that of a young child.

Martin was the only one of the Barbours who cared for her. He would sit for hours in her gardens, as in a retreat from an insufferable and untenable reality. He would help her weed the haphazard flower beds, kill slugs, tie up a vine too heavy with fruit or leaves, brush the stone flags of her paths with a broom that was a huge bundle of stiff straw, and feed her birds. He was enthralled by the way the very shy sparrows would allow the old woman's approach, as they squatted on the crumbling rims of the birdbaths, and they would stare at her with brilliant wild eyes, their bodies trembling. He could never get enough of the hollihocks, the marigolds, the primroses, the bachelor's buttons, the lilies of the valley, the small sweet roses on their knotted stems; he never tired of watching the pale, molten light along the edges of the calla lilies, and touching, very gently, the dusty gold of their hearts.

There were no wise conversations between the little lonely boy and the little lonely old woman. They rested in each other. Mrs. Barbour was not always clear as to who he was. Sometimes she called him Nicholas, thinking him, for a moment, one of her long-dead young sons, and sometimes she called him Joseph, thinking he was his father. He answered gently to all the names, not wishing to disturb the vague, tranced light of her eyes. They had no real love for each other in the usual meaning of the word, not even an active affection. But the presence of the boy comforted the old woman, and the presence of the old woman mysteriously comforted the boy. They were like low wind and slow rain together, sometimes not speaking for hours, half-forgetting each other.

Before Martin would leave at twilight, he would follow the vague outlines of his old great-great-aunt into her parlor, where a dim fire would be burning, and he would drink her thin China tea in tall, delicate china cups, and eat a slice of her seed-cake. He never in all his life thereafter tasted seed-cake like this: it had a strange, dim, old taste, spicy and rich, which clung to his tongue and palate long after he had eaten it. Hilda said it wasn't made with good earthly flour and caraway seeds and milk and eggs, but of some bewitched stuff. Then as the hushed pale stars came out over a landscape swimming in a violet mist he would go home, often without a word of good-by, and as he closed the iron gate in the low gray walls he felt that he had left some entranced spot for a reality that was hot and weary and desolate.

As Joseph rarely saw his great-aunt more than once or twice a year, he did not tell her he was leaving England. Likely as not, he told Hilda, she wouldn't know what he was talking about, and would forget it immediately. She would never miss any of them, even if she never saw them again. She would go on, whispering to herself among the flower beds under the trees, feeding her birds, brushing her flags, stroking her black brute of a cat, knitting, nodding, dreaming, forgetting, drowsing in the vaporous light of a sun that seemed unreal in these gardens. A foolish, helpless old woman who nevertheless managed to keep her tiny old house immaculate and filled with forgotten memories, the smell of herbs, the odor of caraway, the small warm hiss of a polished copper kettle on a small dim fire, the songs of caged birds. It was a marvel that she also managed to keep her black, gnarled furniture glitteringly polished, and that she never forgot the ancient tales about it. In one corner of her parlor stood a grandfather's clock of immense age, its wood black and lustrous, its face blurred and faintly gilt. And no matter what she was doing at the moment it struck, she would pause, vaguely smiling, lifting a finger. "Ah," she would murmur, "you see, it still strikes, though your grandfather would say, after it was repaired by our John in '68, that it would never strike again."

Two days before he left England, Martin came to see the old woman for the last time, and to say good-by to her. He felt certain that his good-by would not penetrate through the silences of the large, twilight country in which she lived, nor that, after he left, she would miss him. Nevertheless, he came to say good-by. It was good-by, not only to her, but to the enchanted house, the spring silences, the trees, the birds, the flowers, the damp green grass, the refuge and the peace.

It had been raining for the past few days, but during the afternoon the rain had stopped, leaving the air sweet and tranquil and melancholy. A few carriages were abroad on Sandy Lane, filled with women and children released by the end of the raining. A warmth had crept into the wet English twilight, filling it with clear soft sounds, promise, fragrance, dripping trees, murmurous birds. Martin pushed the rusty iron gate, thrust it, shrieking, behind him, and walked up the lichen-covered flags to the old house. As he always did, he marvelled that the very closing of the iron gate had shut out the sounds of the outer world, and it seemed to him again, for the hundredth time, that he had stepped under deep, transparent water into enchantment, timeless and profound.

Old Mrs. Barbour was not in her drenched gardens this dying evening. Martin found her before the fire in her parlor. The shadows were so warm and dark here that she was barely discernible from them, and she merely nodded to him without looking up, keeping on with her endless, mysterious knitting. Her cap, with its many frills, was rosy with firelight; the skeins of wool slid upon her black silk knees, and falling, were caught by the huge cat, who played with them kittenishly and self-consciously. Her eyes were vaguer than ever, her face more of an expressionless blur. On her bosom the old yellowed lace was caught by an immense cameo.

"Oh, it's you, Nicholas," she murmured. "Sit down, like a good lad, and dry your boots. All covered with mold, they are. The kettle's on, and we'll have a cup of tea before the other young uns come home. Stir up the fire for me; it's gettin' low."

Martin picked up a brass poker and poked the small fire so that it turned into a hot fretwork of black and gold. Mrs. Barbour had already forgotten the tea, and murmured over her knitting, and rocked. Silence gathered in the small room with its black, polished, incredible furniture, and the odor of herbs rose, and the firelight lay on the white flags of the hearth, and the kettle hissed drowsily on its hook. Once the cat yawned, and showed Martin a savage pink cavern behind long white teeth.

The immovable quality of the deep silence was such that when Martin got up and went to one of the thickly sunken little latticed windows his movements did not disturb it. Rather, they seemed a contained motion of the silence itself, enhancing it. The old woman did not look up, the cat did not turn its yellow eyes in his direction, the fire did not rise, the kettle did not hiss louder. He pushed open the window, out upon the crowding lilacs.

A rain had begun to fall again, a silvery, whispering rain, itself increasing the silence. It fell from a sky full of heliotrope mist, fell upon the lilacs that the little opened window was pressing into, and from those cool wet spears of faint purple drew out a piercing and nostalgic fragrance. Martin put his hand out and touched chill leaves running with that silvery water, drew toward him a thin pyramid of flowers and touched his cheek to it. The garden floated with a gaseous mist a little darker than the heliotrope sky, and the trees, mighty and motionless in the drowned gardens, seemed to stand in that mist as in faintly colored water. So standing, they lost clear outline and reality, became dreams in a twilit world of dream which itself swam in cloudy violet.

It seemed to Martin, standing at the little opened window with the leaves and cold wet flowers of the lilac against his thin hot cheek, that he would never forget this moment, this smell, this fresh rain running down his fingers and cheeks, this wan violet light and silence. Its poignancy seemed more than he could bear. Then when a thrush, a single thrush, began to sing, dimly, a last melancholy song in the fountain of trees, he burst into tears. The sweet, faint, unearthly notes, so clear and sad, so thrilling and lonely, poured through him as though he had been mist himself, and their pouring was exquisite pain.

Behind him lay the motionless warm dusk of the room with its low spot of fire, knitting old woman, cat, whitestone hearth, odor of caraway seed and ancient furniture, hissing of a copper kettle that shone like gold.

He wiped away his tears, closed the window gently and slowly. He crept back to the fire, and sitting there on his stool, stared for a long time at the old drowsing woman.

"Shall I light the candles, Auntie Ellen?" he asked at last, very softly.

The old woman, startled out of her dreams, peered at him vaguely over her square spectacles.

"Eh? Oh, it's you, Nicholas. Yes, dearie, light the candles. It's dark, and I was almost asleep. Dear me, the kettle's boilin', too."

Martin touched a wax taper to the fire, then lit the candles on the mantelpiece. They flamed into slender gold in the russet darkness, and a few drops of melted tallow, clear as water, began to slide down them toward the porcelain candlesticks. Martin touched a few drops, let them congeal on his thin fingers, then rolled the milky mass together. Mrs. Barbour, murmuring busily, put down her knitting in a basket, pushed aside the cat, and drew the singing kettle from the fire. From the recesses of the chimney corner she drew forth a canister of tea and a squat blue teapot. Martin carried a small table closer to the fire; it was a round mahogany table with a raised and fluted edge, and was dark red with age. He went to the tall cupboard in the shadows and brought out two blue cups and saucers, two thin silver spoons and two small blue plates. The hot water hissed on the tea, the fire flared up into rosy sparks, and the cat leaned against the old woman's legs, arched and sleek and purring. Outside, the rain sang with a thin, musical sound on the lilac leaves.

"Aunt Ellen," said Martin again in that soft voice that seemed to enhance the quiet, "we are going to America."

The old woman continued to slice, very carefully, the dark richness of her cake. It was not until the fourth and last slice lay on the blue plate that she looked up, confused.

"Did ye say America, Nicholas? America? No, but you be too young and tender to be goin' from your Ma yet. Maybe, when you are a man." She smiled at him tenderly and cunningly, shaking her head as if admonishing a small adventurer who had been dead all of forty years.

Martin, starving for sympathy and understanding, opened his lips. But he did not speak. Tonight, he was Nicholas. He must not confuse and frighten the old woman. He sighed, sat down, and began to drink the delicate pale tea. It seemed to scald his mouth, and the seed cake choked him.

Too wretched to move, he crouched on his stool, long after he should have been gone. The grandfather's clock tolled out a farewell to him, solemnly and in measured sounds, as if it, too, sorrowed because Martin would never again sit in that parlor before that fire. But the fire was almost out, and its dark gold coals fell into coldness and ashes, and the cat slept on the dimming hearth, and the old woman slept in her chair. Outside the rain was louder, falling with hollow and mournful sounds, and it ran, choking, along the ancient eaves. Now a wind was rising, mourning at the latticed windows, and blew down the cooling chimney. It seemed to Martin, chilled and full of despair, that he was the only living thing in a universe that was steeped in vague, shadowy dreams. Slow cold waters of fright and dread rose in him, and though he wished to go he could not get up.

Again the clock chimed, and now the sound was loud and menacing in an almost complete darkness. On the hearth lay two last red coals, burning without heat. The old woman's head was sunken deep on her breast, and the cat whined once and shortly in its dreams.

Martin got up. He felt as if he had been crying for hours, but his eyes were quite dry. In the darkness he kissed the old woman's soft and withered cheek. It felt like old paper under his lips.

When he went, the door closed behind him without a sound and the two red coals winked out, and the old woman and the cat and the clock were left to themselves.

CHAPTER IV

A
S FROM a mighty tilted brass vessel poured the brassy cataract of unendurable light upon the river, the flat lands, the distant hills, the whole world.

Martin had never seen such light, and it hurt his eyes. More than that, it seemed to set something aching frightfully within him. Light like this, so different from the soft and gauzy sunshine of England not only frightened, but oppressed him. His fair skin burned and withered under it; his flesh seemed to melt. He blinked at it, shuddered at it, tried to hide from it under any dusty tree, under the lee of any wooden shack, in the shadow of any stark wall. But he could not escape it; it fumed all about him, and became a personal foe from whom it was impossible to escape. They said winter would come at last, and raised ominous eyes about that winter, but Martin could hardly believe that such a blessing as a winter would finally arrive and release him before he died.

The little town of Windsor on the Allegheny River was a new, raw, big village, only some thirty years old. Thirty years before there had been a handful of farmers in this region; now Windsor was proud of its ten thousand inhabitants. They prophesied that within twenty-five years Windsor would be the State Capital. Less sentimental men, who cared nothing about politics but only about money, declared that Capital be damned, the town would be a city of half a million, bigger than New York, eventually, and would find its glory in vast industrial development. Weren't there tremendous coal mines just beginning to be opened? And where coal was found didn't wealth and business and activity follow? There was no end to the possibilities. Go west, across the prairies, fighting through Indians, crossing those accursed Rockies, wandering through deserts, through strange red country full of burning cliffs and painted rocks? Why? Let those who liked frontiers push them, at the cost of muscle and blood and life, farther toward the hot Pacific. Here, in this State, was to be found every inducement, every hope, every chance for a man who was not a rascal or a ne'er-do-well. All he needed was his hands and his guts and a dash of brains. His fortune was made.

Windsor sprawled in the heat of the valley, dishevelled, dirty, hideous, noisy and exuberant. Most of the streets were just flattened mud roads that rolled in hot golden dust in the summer and seethed with mud in the late winter and spring. Very often the town was flooded with fall rains and melting snow, for the river overflowed and the flimsy wooden shacks and sturdier stone houses stood like queer-shaped arks in flat sheets of gray water. After prolonged rains, when the sun came out, the valley steamed and newcomers sickened and even died in the malarial air. Almost without exception, every sidewalk was made of rough plank boards except in the wealthier section, where neatly placed stone flags kept the ladies' shoes clean. Most of the houses were hastily built of wood, designed for temporary use, the dwellers said. They were almost all unpainted, and there were few gardens and lawns. Tramped, bare brown earth ran from the boardwalks to the high wooden steps of these ugly little cottages where few women bothered to hang curtains at the windows or put a potted plant against the warped glass.

It would have been a frontier town, built only for a day, had it not been for a bourgeoisie section. The bourgeoisie spirit, so jealously brought from England with family silver in wooden chests, made the more intelligent and prosperous citizens build careful, ugly houses of stone and brick, plant gardens, build white wooden fences or low walls, buy watchdogs and monstrous mahogany furniture and turkey-red carpets and tables with marble tops, and sedulously and patiently made creditable housemaids of raw farm and immigrant girls. This solid minority sent to New York for carriages, and bred sleek carriage horses. On Sundays and holidays it lifted their hearts to ride in these carriages through the town, their eyes sparkling as they listened to the jingling of the harness, their women tilting tiny parasols above immense coal-scuttle bonnets also imported from New York, and disposing the flounces of their great skirts about them. This finery, this solidity, comforted spirits that as yet did not feel entirely secure and free from homesickness. And so they buttressed themselves against loneliness and fear with thick walls and planted trees, with great fireplaces and fine tea, carriages and imported silks, immense mahogany sideboards loaded with silver, pianos laboriously hauled to Philadelphia by railroad, with servant girls and wine.

The bourgeoisie section was older than Newtown, as the ramshackle and industrial section was called. It withdrew itself meticulously, allowed no encroaches. It did not care for the river, down which passed water traffic increasingly thick. So between the section of the bourgeoisie and Newtown there lay an empty space, like a pause. This space was owned by the "better element," and they would allow no one to build upon it. It was an open road, but open though it was few of the newcomers felt any inducement to cross it. A branch of the railroad had long been promised Windsor, and through this space, within twelve years, shining steel tracks were to be laid, dividing Oldtown and Newtown more grimly than ever.

Newtown ran, in its rush of shacks and small factories, right down to the river, and as it ran it scarred and twisted, blasted and despoiled. Half of the inhabitants were but newly from Europe, from ancient, ancestral villages of sunken beauty and ivy and scented lanes and flowers, and the other half were but a generation removed. In the blood of all of them ran a love of leisure, of quiet and passionless living, of home and hearthstone. Yet here, in this new land, they ruined and laid waste, building few permanent homes, raping a luxuriant land of all its heroic beauty, laying on it for tens of generations, and even longer, the curse of impermanence, of indifference, of sterility and greed. This could not have been done by men who loved the land, who desired to live here, making a home not only for themselves but for their children's children, and cherishing and keeping alive the many-branched tree of loved tradition. But they did not love this land who gave herself innocently up to them. They did not desire to live upon it, to make a home upon it; they let die upon it all the branches of tradition they had brought with them. And this was because they despised this new land, wished only the things they ravished from her, and had their faces turned inexorably, hopefully, longingly, to the lands from which they had come.

Very few returned, and those who had come for a day lived and died on the new land. But they had placed that curse of impermanence, indifference, of sterility and greed upon it, and though their children and their children's children had forever turned their faces from a Europe they did not know, not even by tradition, this new land held no love for them, no true idealism, no fervency.

Eventually, some of the Newtowners, by sheer greed and ingenuity, and the shrewdness and craft of peasants, would loot enough to enable them to buy homes in Oldtown, "across the tracks," would enable them to marry into tight and haughty families, to swallow in vast gulps the old wine of a delicate tradition. But as they carried the blight of the curse with them, they merely brought to spiritual Oldtowns their innate greed and lack of imagination, their lustful impotence, their ravishing and despoiling hands, becoming the robber barons of finance, the tyrants of vast industries, the corrupters of politics. The diminished ranks of Oldtowners would retreat in silent bitterness to little Southern villages, to small New England towns, to, however, a narrow and steadfast and immortal integrity which would keep alive, even in this maimed land, a soul of dignity and honor and fine living.

But little Martin Barbour dreamed nothing of this, as he shivered under the depression and sickness that this heat and this ugliness, this noise and this confusion had brought down upon him. He had lost the blessed faculty of forgetting. Events of three months ago, three weeks ago, three days ago, all crowded into his mind with simultaneous sharpness, the oldest as clear and clamorous as the newest, so that one merged its colors and its heat and its noises into the colors, heats and noises of all the others, making a vast confusion and an exhausting uproar. Martin was like a man condemned never to sleep, condemned to keep his eyes fixed eternally on all the things that had been in his life, which had blended in themselves the past and the present and the future. He felt all through him a weariness beyond imagining.

There was the last day in Reddish, the crowding into the stage for Liverpool, the sun on blazing water, the great steam-and-sail ship like a scarred black monster at the dock, its rigging, bare now, breaking the burning blue sky into rectangles, squares and triangles, the noise of crowds, the delay, alarms, the roar of voices, the pushing of shawled women, the shouting of men mingling with the hoarse singing of sailors, the false starts, the screams of farewell, the lost luggages, the recovery of them, the red-brown of blank-faced warehouses, the scent of sun-heated wood and the odor of fishy salt air. Finally, the depositing of the Barbour family in the dank steerage with scores of other pilgrims to the end of the rainbow, the deafening crying of children, the pale excited faces of mothers and young girls and the nervous nonchalance of men. The odors of sweat and dirt and beer. And then, through a porthole, the broken line of the English shore drifting down and away, until it was a pencil smudge on a horizon turning an unreal peacock-blue. Six weeks of this, because of summer storms of singular fury, heat, illness, children, wretched discomfort, food that rapidly became unfit to eat, crowding of the sweating steerage passengers, the old man and the two children who died and had to be buried at sea, the everlasting sliding of the great tilted ocean, which at times was a hillside of gray steel, and at other times rollicking sharp-pointed little blue hills. There was little joy or pleasure in this for the steerage passenger far below decks, only grim endurance, only hope that became physically sick and green with nausea. Not for the steerage passenger the cool and wind-scrubbed upper decks, nor the beauty, when the engines temporarily failed, of rushing sails against furious skies, of long rolling moons and the delight of strange marine life, of drowsy reclining in warm sunlight, music, sparkling wines and delicate dishes, and delirious waltzing under brilliant stars. The driven crew might see these things at snatched intervals, might have the bitter pleasure of envy. But the steerage passengers did not have even envy. They had only their hope, and this, too, was at last retched up.

How these things crowded up behind Martin's tired eyes, which even when closed failed to darken them out. There came a gray and watery dawn, but a hot and steaming dawn, when one could look through the small hole and the water seemed quiet and viscous, as if filled with turgid sediment and oil. The ship did not seem to roll and pitch so sickeningly today, but appeared to idle, its rigging limp, its smells, now that the wind had fallen, pungent and putrid, overwhelming the nose with a thick, immovable fog. Martin would never forget the harbor, lying gray and corrugated in that sunless dawn; and then the sun came up, watery and hot and diffused, and the skyline of New York stood out against a pale and palpitating sky, crowded, thick and low and feverishly busy.

There was no railroad to Windsor, but only a lumbering stage, which carried them twenty miles to another stage, and another and another. At this point Martin's memories became nightmare events, none clear, none definite, all rolling together like livid skeins of torture and illness. Rain in the flat valleys, searing sun on the hills, rushing of waters, light too vivid, too unshaded and glaring to bear. Little Dorcas ill and whimpering with fever, and a subdued Hilda, silent and whipped at last, holding the sick child to a trembling breast. Fellow-passengers who had long ago lost the last remnants of common courtesy, who looked on the sufferings of the others with the stupid indifference of personal suffering. Small raucous towns where they changed stages, ugly towns of saloons, boardwalks, fighting men, river traffic, sweat and dust and heat, and that impossible sunlight. Voices with strange twangs to them, faces, English faces, that already seemed to have taken on themselves a thin and foreign patina. Odd bundles of food thrust through the windows of the waiting stages. And that ghastly sense of unreality and untenable strangeness that assails the stranger in a strange land. Later, one or two "Dutch" settlements, with broad-faced stolid women and broad-shouldered squatty men with yellow hair and beards, who, however, seemed kinder than those of their own sort, and often brought fresh milk to the windows of the stage, helped exhausted mothers with babies, chatted encouragingly in guttural voices. "Windsor? Ach, yes, it was but a little more." And again the stage, lurching, pitching, steaming with the heat of the passengers crowded among their luggage, sweltering in the sunlight that never seemed to fail, but even at midnight seemed to lie threateningly along the horizon.

And then storms of incredible wildness and rain and wind and thunder and lightning, mud that boiled up about the wheels, of groaning horses, weird trees seen bending almost to their roots in sheets of red light, the faint moans of exhausted women and children, and the shifting of luggage on the roof of the stage. Endless miles of nightmare in which there was no shelter, only deserts of hills and fields and empty plains.

"I wish," groaned Joseph Barbour through heat-blistered lips, "that we had never left home." Only Ernest did not agree; he had gone through all this rigidly, white-faced, eyes immovably looking ahead. Nothing made him moan, nothing sickened him, nothing tried or terrified him.

More and more confusion revolved in Martin's mind, so that even while he forgot details, did not see them, their accumulated effect made sound and fury in his memories. Windsor at last, in a hot and rainy twilight, and blurred impressions of river and smoke and huddled shacks, hundreds of them, of muddy streets, noise, flaring of lamps and candles, the jingling of harness, shouts, greetings, strange smells, a sullen-faced woman in bonnet and India shawl who was "Auntie Daisy," and a sulky man in a flowered waistcoat who was "Uncle George." And then memories of a springless wagon in which luggage, bursting now at its seams, was thrown carelessly onto a layer of hay on which the children were already deposited, and a long, endless, swimming ride through tunnels of trees arching over a road full of holes and water and mud, and then a falling into a sleep full of sweat and pain, just as a moon, incredibly large and burning and yellow, leapt up behind the low and distant hills.

Closer memories, but pleasanter ones dimmed only a little by wretchedness, of a squat wide house of wood and stone, of rooms, crowded with mahogany and horsehair and pictures and rugs and tables, of hot tea forced through dry lips, of hot soup and boiled beef and bread, of seed-cake and cold pudding, of beds that seemed to swim out to one through a foggy mist, of sinking into feather mattresses like sinking into death. All this, blurred only a little by torment of flesh and mind, accompanied in the distance by the sound of strange children's voices and pushing, wondering faces that did not seem to belong to bodies.

It had taken the Barbour family several days to recover from their journey. And then it was with the timidity of unforgotten exhaustion that they looked about them.

George Barbour, who was rapidly becoming prosperous, lived in a section of Newtown that was sheepishly acquiring some of the amenities of life. The houses in this section were larger, cleaner and more comfortable, and while not built for permanency, were still not built for a month or a year. While no trees nor flowers nor grasses grew here, the boardwalks were swept and kept in repair, and some few windows were draped in coarse laces. Many of the men, like George Barbour, had sent to Philadelphia for furniture, and had set the huge ugly mahogany chairs and tables and beds into their lopsided rooms, crowding them together without taste or comfort. And many of these men, like George Barbour, were cautiously beginning to speak of moving over to Oldtown "one of these days," and speaking less and less of returning "home." They were already beginning to speak of the "trash" in less prosperous parts of Newtown, were already beginning to curse lazy and greedy and incompetent workmen in their mills and growing factories. They sent to New York for flowered waistcoats and frilled shirts and dark red and bottle-green coats, for gold watches and gold-headed canes, for sleek stove-pipe hats and polished boots, for great-skirted, lace-trimmed dresses for their women, and velvet pelisses and flower-burdened bonnets, for the cheaper wines and delicacies, for rings and muffs. A few of them shamefacedly hired servant girls, and considered themselves, audibly, the equal of the "snobs" in Oldtown, who completely ignored them. So many of them worked wistfully and grimly toward the possibility of themselves moving over to Oldtown, not knowing that a more subtle yet stronger barrier than money or locality divided them.

Martin did not like either his Aunt Daisy or his Uncle George, and Hilda, who had had memories of a kinder, simpler, friendlier Daisy Potts, a second cousin, could not recognize this Daisy in this brutal-faced, grasping, overbearing and patronizing woman with her silk dresses, rings of keys, servant girl and mahogany furniture and four-poster beds and new carpets. Daisy Potts had become fatter and more upright, short and condescending of speech, frowning, preoccupied, haughty, rustling about her household, and showing in every infrequent word and in every attitude of her shawled shoulders that she resented the intrusion of her husband's family. She had little to say to Hilda; was harsh to Hilda's children, and did not encourage friendliness between them and her little daughter, Martha, a frail and venomous child with a white face and whining voice, some few months younger than Martin. Martin did not like Martha any more than he liked her parents. She was thin and spindly, with long pointed feet, lace pantalettes, velvet and fine muslin dresses, pale thin hair and protruding blue eyes. Her expression was sly and smug in the presence of her elders, became malicious and mean when with children her own age. It was evident that she despised her cousins, for she stuck out her tongue at the boys, pulled Florabelle's hair and made her cry, teased the baby into shrieks of infantile hysteria, carried false tales to her already prejudiced mother, who resented Hilda her sons. Though she had been born in England, she had the native's contempt for aliens, and called her cousins "dirty Englishmen." She resented the fact that she had to sleep on a pallet in her parents' chamber, while her Aunt and Uncle, and her four cousins temporarily were crowded into her own room.

The meals, consisting of strange meats and stranger vegetables, were served in the overcrowded dining room, whose lace-trimmed windows looked down a short muddy slope to the river. The new family, after one day of attempted friendliness and affection, found themselves silently and miserably choking on their meals under the silent pointed eyes of their hostess. George Barbour, who was planning on squeezing his brother dry of his new powder secret, uneasily tried to warm up his wife's coldness, but her innate stupidity was too strong for her guile. Hilda timidly offered to "help," was harshly repudiated, pushed into an idle and hateful background, in which she agitatedly nursed her baby and grew a little thinner and paler. Her voice grew sharp and hysterical toward her older children; she was terrified that they might offend their aunt, which they did frequently, without intention. When Daisy, after a bad night with George about her stupidity, gave the poor young woman a grudgingly kind word, Hilda burst into joyful tears, told Joseph that Daisy really had the kindest heart, and grovelled before her sister-in-law. For poor Hilda was desperately homesick, bitterly disillusioned. Martin suffered with her. His dislike for his relatives became hatred. He also ached for his father, who had become silent and stubborn and tight-lipped, cautiously and cynically retreating before George's not-too-adroit questions. But Ernest neither hated nor disliked them. He, in fact, hardly saw them. He was tensely waiting, thinking, studying, going down each day to his uncle's little gunpowder and firearms factory, and watching everything. Within two weeks he had won George's reluctant admiration and regard. Soon George was explaining everything to him, and complainingly hinting that "somethin's up with old Joe; why doesn't he tell me what it's all about?" Ernest listened to this, and one day went to his father with suggestions and astonishingly mature advice.

The result of this advice was that Joseph approached his brother one day, after they had sent the women and children from the dining room and had lit their pipes and moved to the empty fireplace. A summer storm was brewing, and through the silent, suspended heat of the air one could hear the rush and hurry of the river. And what Joseph said to his brother was this: He had come all these thousands of miles, and he had not come for nothing. They were brothers, weren't they? They must work together. Joseph must know at once just what he was to expect, and get. He had something that would make both their fortunes, but he had no intention of letting it make George's fortune alone. As he said this, quietly and frankly, he looked full at his brother with his brilliant gray eyes. George said nothing; his flabby ruddy face tightened a little, his protruding blue eyes veiled themselves behind pink lids, and he smoked stolidly. When he came from the factory at night he "dressed" for the evening meal in tight fawn pantaloons, dark red coat and ruffled shirt and polished boots. He had crossed his legs, and when Joseph paused in what he was saying he swung his crossed leg idly back and forth apparently engrossed in watching his boot glitter in the candlelight. Joseph waited; he had all the cards and he could afford to wait. But while waiting for George to speak he glanced idly and indifferently about the ugly room, watching the flickering pools of candlelight on the ceiling, glancing through the window at the lightning.

"What else?" asked George at length, in a sullen voice.

Joseph smiled pleasantly. He must have a little house of his own, nearby, of course. George must lend him money to buy household supplies and furnishings, a very modest sum. George glowered, an angry glare settling in the eyes that fixed themselves with enmity on his brother. But he let Joseph continue. Under Joseph's voice could be heard the children's voices in the next room, the timid laughter of Hilda, the shouts of neighbors as they walked on the boardwalks.

And then, said Joseph, he must become a partner, oh, a very small partner, but a partner. It must all be settled before a notary. Signed and sealed. A share in everything. You didn't think of all that yourself, said George furiously. Joseph, reddening but still smiling, admitted that Ernest had done most of that thinking, and George stared, slack-jawed, unbelieving. Then he remembered that Daisy had called Ernest foxy and underhanded, and he blurted this out to Joseph. But on his lips the words became grudging and admiring, and George found himself prophesying that Ernest would go a long way. Immediately his anger flared up again at Joseph. It was unendurable that his brother should have such a son, and he none at all.

He began to bluster. It was all nonsense. This was a hellish way to treat a brother, who had sent tickets home, and was providing shelter. Besides, what did Joe want? Wasn't he getting ten dollars a week and a home, for just puttering around in the shop and getting on to things? What more did he want? Besides, there was George's partner to reckon with, that Frenchy, that Armand Bouchard. He, George, doubted very much that Armand would listen to taking in another partner, who had no money but only an idea that probably was no good, anyway. He paused, watching Joseph furtively.

Joseph smiled still. Oh, he said carelessly, he was certain Bouchard would not object. He had hinted something to him about the new gun-powder, and Bouchard had seemed eager about it, had himself suggested that Joseph get to work upon it immediately. Speaking of him, Joseph remembered the tiny, avid, furiously active little Frenchman with his oaken face carved and wrinkled, his small kindly eyes so intelligent and amused, his large gestures, his pointed black beard, his courteous friend-liness. Joseph had known almost at once that Bouchard despised and inwardly laughed at George even while he respected his ability as an organizer and contriver of ways and means. "You Englishmen!" he had said with an amiable shrug. "You find all the nine ways to skin a cat, and then invent another. No conscience, no delicacy, no intelligence. But successful, yes. And what virtue!" He and Joseph had conceived an immense affection for each other immediately, and Armand had listened with grave and kindly interest to Joseph's story of a French ancestor. He found Joseph more than a little pathetic, and told his wife, a buxom and gigantic woman, that that George was a pig, a bad-smelling cabbage.

Forestalled about Bouchard, George sat glowering at his feet, puffing violently at his pipe. He hated Bouchard; he might have known that dirty little Frenchman would betray him some way. If the time ever came . . . He lifted his suffused eyes, glaring and repudiating, to his brother. How did he know that the gunpowder was any good? He might take Joseph into a partnership, a very small partnership, mind you, and then after it was all signed and sealed, might discover that the gunpowder was not practicable, not worth making. At this, Joseph grinned a little bitterly. If George had such doubts of the gunpowder, why had he sent for his brother and his brother's family? He knew George too well, he said quietly and gently, to believe that it was brotherly love and kindness. No, George had sent for him because he knew he had something worth while, worth its weight in gold. Joseph's eyes were now cold and bright as ice, and as implacable.

George uncrossed his knee, his face suddenly crimson and swollen. He stamped his foot on the floor. He began to bluster again, this time with real, impotent rage. This was a fine how-do-you-do; no gratitude. This is what a man got for doing his brother a good turn. He should have listened to Daisy; there was a woman with a brain. Now Joseph, to show his gratitude, was proposing to enjoy the profits of something he had not earned as yet. It was a bloody fine business, this. You take a man into your home, give him the best of everything, put up with the noise and the expense and the inconvenience, give him a job at ten dollars a week, for practically no return, and what do you get? This— this blow in the back.

Joseph said nothing at all. He just watched his brother, half smiling, very pale and composed, leaning forward a little with his elbows on his slim thighs, his delicate hands tightly clasped together on his knees. There was something fine-drawn and handsome about his slight body and well-shaped lean head and dark face. Though his clothing was shabby and frayed, he made his brother look a boor. He looked as though he might burst into laughter, bitter and acid.

Suddenly George changed his tactics. He would be generous: after all, wasn't Joe his only brother? He would do the right thing. Look here, suppose he were to give Joe fifteen dollars a week and build him a nice little cottage down the street? There, that was a proposition fit for a prince! And even if the gunpowder turned out to be nothing at all, Joe would still get fifteen dollars a week, perhaps more in time. Now then! He beamed at Joseph, sweating visibly with admiration at his own generosity. His eyes, pale bulbous eyes, glistened as though with tender tears.

Joseph gently shook his head. A partnership, or nothing. Now, he had something to offer. If the gunpowder was no good, then Joseph would allow the partnership to be dissolved. He would then continue to work for ten dollars a week. George knew he was worth ten dollars a week, at least. Look at the work he was already getting from the three men in the shop. He was a good foreman of men.

George's broad red face became cold and hating as he listened. It was the face of a man who would always be Joseph's enemy to the day of his death. But it was a defeated face, and, conscious of its defeat, would never soften to friendliness for Joseph again. Sweat glistened on his forehead, on the upper, shaved lip. George twisted his jaw from side to side, his brutal eyes fixed with hate on the younger man. His broad chest heaved rapidly. He tried one last thing. Suppose he refused entirely, suppose he discharged Joseph. What then? He watched Joseph, but if he expected to see him disconcerted he was disappointed.

Joseph shrugged carelessly. Well, then, in that case, he was sorry, but he had heard of a man who had a large factory in Philadelphia, much larger than George's little place. He would write to him, if George did not wish the idea. He, Joseph, had saved his money for four weeks, and he now had forty dollars. It would more than take him to Philadelphia. And in the meantime, of course, he was certain that Madam Bouchard would house his family for a little while.

The veins started out savagely on George's forehead as he listened to this. His face swelled, turned dusky. He sprang to his feet with an oath, his fists clenched. In a low and violent voice, more frightful than a loud voice, he cursed the little Bouchard, blasphemed, foamed at the corners of his mouth. The dirty little bastard! The Frenchy! The unprintable, the unspeakable! He raised his fists, he shook them in the air, he threatened, vomiting his words into Joseph's face. His teeth glittered, and the neck, above the white cravat, swelled into purple. So! Joseph had done this to him, betrayed him, discussed this betrayal with Bouchard, that ——! They had plotted thus against him, he to whom they both owed everything, their bread, the roof over their heads, their work, their hope of success! They had done this to him!

"We owe you naught a thing," said Joseph, his cool low voice breaking into the savage storm. "Armand put twice as much money into your shop as you did, Georgie, and I know it. He's putting his wits into it, now, too. You'd be naught without him, and you know *that*. As for me— well, you sent for me because you knew I had something valuable. Now I know you are a born cheat. I'll never believe you an honest man again. I know all about you, and I'll know when to watch you. You are a liar and a thief. Hear me, a liar and a thief. Choke that in your dirty throat. And now, if you want me and my gunpowder, you'll make it a full partnership, and I'll pick the notary so that there'll be no cheating, no holes for you to slip out of." He paused, and then repeated, heavily, tiredly: "A liar and a thief. Come, where is your paper and your pen?"

George knew he was beaten. He was not at all a fool, and though he was never to forgive his brother, was always to be his enemy, he knew the silliness of sustained wrath and outward resentment. As he brought out writing equipment and set it on the white-veined black marble table-top, he became cautiously friendly again. That lad, Ernest! There was a lively un, for a fact! A lad to be proud of. Good blood in him. A man could make something of him. It was hard that young Martin was such a milksop, like a lass. And two girls were a hard load for a man to carry these days. How would Joe like to go over to Garnerstown some night soon? Joseph, who had been sharpening the pen absently, looked up in surprise. He was more surprised to see George, whose smiling pink face was beaming, winking his eye knowingly. Garnerstown, repeated Joseph, a little puzzled. There was a nice lass or two there, explained George, still smiling fixedly, but obviously annoyed at his brother's stupidity. Two or three nice houses, where a man could get good whiskey and good entertainment. Joseph stared at him. A faint distaste and disgust twisted his insides. Suddenly he loathed George, not for the suggestion he had just made, but for the sliminess of his proffered offer that bygones be bygones. "Shakin' hands over a whore," he thought with revulsion. He made himself smile, but there was no smile in his eyes. "Later on," he said carelessly. He continued to sharpen his pen. Hilda. Poor little Hilda, in there with that bitch of a Daisy looking down her nose at her! Hilda, whom he loved more than himself. He had to restrain a sudden desire to thrust the sharp point of the quill into George's pink soft flesh at this insult to Hilda. But, God, please God, there would be a day! A day!

The partnership paper was soon written, in plain, short and simple words. Joseph signed it, after George's careful signature. There it was, partnership in the shop. No holes for George to wiggle through in his sleek sliminess. Tomorrow the notary would attest it. And then they would make the new gunpowder.

George wiped his forehead with a large silk kerchief, jingled his gold chains, rocked back on his heels. He was not too dissatisfied. What was done was done. All at once he was overwhelmingly confident and jubilant; it were as though something psychic had whispered to him of the future. He almost trembled with a strange exultation. "We haven't shaken hands on it!" he cried.

Reluctantly, slowly, Joseph put his cold hand in his brother's large hot palm. They shook hands.

And, at the precise moment that they shook hands across the paper of their contract, there came such a flare of lightning, such a bellow of thunder, that the very earth shuddered, seemed to heave, seemed to silence, for a ghastly space, all small earthly sounds into appalled nothingness. And there was another, and still another crash, splintering the air, filling it with an odor like that of brimstone, rocking the houses, blasting distant trees, rolling like great wheels across the hills. It was like a terrible prophecy of doom.

It was for all the world like the uproar of enormous artillery, such as men had not yet dreamed of, or known.

CHAPTER V

W HY SHOULDN'T he love the bloody country, that Frenchy?" George demanded contemptuously of his brother as they walked home together from the little shop. "He had to leave France or lose his head—what a blasted country it must be! He's got to like this hole, or choke on it. Much good it'll do him, the little runt, to hate America. He ain't got a home to go back to, like us."

"Like us," repeated Joseph mechanically. He looked about him. Beyond the river, with its increasing traffic, were flat green fields, vaster than the fields of England, shimmering under evening light that was still brilliant. Beyond the fields, so fertile and waiting and rich, were the hills, fold on fold of bronze velvet, with here and there the living bonfire of some tree touched by early frost. And above these hills spread the tremendous skies, so uncluttered, so majestic, seeming to surrender themselves up to a glory of golden sunset that palpitated from horizon to horizon. Not a niggardly, watery little sunset, this, but a lake of welling light that seemed to rise from some awesome and celestial source. Everything was so large, so open, so vast, and yet in its very immensity so serene and pellucid that Joseph felt an inability to speak for a few moments. Here was something that, though it dwarfed man and his little heats, yet made him feel significant and holy, made him part of the Godhead that had created this and now appreciated it. It made man conscious of his consciousness, made him grateful that he lived so he could know it. This moment of realization was worth more than anything else on earth. For one solemn moment Joseph believed, without putting it into words, that nothing in his past life and nothing in his future life, could be as important, so full of significance, as this moment.

He did not want to speak, hated his brother for speaking. George's voice was like a cock's crowing in a cathedral at the moment the host is raised.

"When I've got two thousand pounds, I'm out of this blasted country," said George. "Not that I'm going back to Lancashire and the rain. The South. Or London, fog or no fog. Where a man can live and enjoy himself. Perhaps, though," he added thoughtfully, "I'd best make it four thousand pounds."

Joseph was silent. He was sick of his brother, sick of his slyness and cunning and brutishness. He knew that George was in some manner afraid of him, and recognized that he often tried to placate him, as if uneasily conscious of Joseph's opinion of him. But Joseph also knew that there was no real regret in George for the loss of his brother's esteem and affection; there was only an uneasiness that Joseph might find out more about him, more that might be dangerous. Like most petty scoundrels, he wanted the respect of honest men, for this respect meant that the honest men were still deluded, still open to exploitation.

"That lad Ernest, of yours," said George, panting a little from their climb up the bare slope that led from their shop. "That lad Ernest. A lively un. Fourteen, isn't he? And, by God, worth twice as much as most men, three times as much as Tom Wilkins! He's got a head on him. Understands. And no whining, though he's there from sunup to sundown." He paused, moistened his lips furtively as he gave Joseph a sidelong look. "He was telling me today about a new idea you and he had, Joe, about pistols. About triggers."

"Ah," said Joseph.

George rolled his lower lip outwards. "Well?" he said with asperity. "We're partners, ain't we?"

"In the gunpowder," reminded Joseph, savoring the situation. "The pistol's not ready, yet. Perhaps I'll tell you about it. And perhaps not." He smiled full at his brother. "One thing at a time, Georgie. There's nothing to show the gunpowder's any good yet. We've got to wait."

They had stopped at a division in the road that led to the two separate sections of Newtown. There was the upper road with many of the holes filled in going toward the houses on higher ground, where George lived, and the rutty, rock-filled, muddy road that led toward the poorer section of shacks, cabins and lean-tos, where Joseph lived, as also did Armand Bouchard.

Joseph wanted to go on, but George uneasily lingered, so his brother began to whistle tunelessly, and stared at the sky.

"Look here," said George, "you and Hilda ain't dropped in to see us for a long time. Daisy was just speaking of it last night."

"Liar," thought Joseph. But he said nothing, merely continuing to whistle; however, he watched George thoughtfully.

"Come to tea, Sunday," George suggested, his voice friendly but a low crimson beginning to creep through the folds of his broad face.

Joseph shrugged. "I'll ask Hilda." He touched his hat with a careless gesture, almost with mockery. "Good night. I'd best be getting along."

He thrust his hands in his pockets and started down the lane, still whistling. As he walked his broken boots kicked up pale clouds of dust, that turned gold in the sunset. His narrow shoulders were hunched up a little, and his thick black hair sprayed out between the lifted collar and the brim of the shabby tall hat. His coat was shabby and frayed, but every button was on the broad sleeves, and the white shirt was immaculate. His tight pantaloons showed legs slim and graceful as a girl's for all their patches. He moved quickly, almost jauntily; almost, he swaggered. A few trees, ragged with yellow leaves, bent over the road, and each time that Joseph emerged from their infrequent shadow into the last hot beams of the sun he seemed consciously to increase his jauntiness, as if he had an audience. The fact was that he was disgusted and lonely, and depressed.

George watched him go. He closed and unclosed hands held rigidly at his side. He despised his brother. His broad face grimaced as if the taste on his tongue were repellent.

"I wonder if he's told Bouchard?" he thought. "The dogs had their heads together all day. They're as thick as thieves, always in each other's house. Their kids falling on top of each other. All except Ernest. I might be able to get around the lad, for all he's as sly as a fox."

As he walked along Joseph's depression lifted a trifle. He began to smile. Trust Ernest to torment Georgie. A clever lad. He could do with this bit of cheer tonight, with Hilda everlastingly crying from homesickness, and little Martin getting thinner and paler all the day, and the little girls whining with the heat. No one could see this country, and all these things, as he saw them. Why, by god, a man could live here! He could grow big, like it. He was sick of this talk of "going home"; that's all he heard. There had been a time when he, too, had talked of "going home," but no longer. There was something here, something he could not as yet define, but it was here, waiting to be taken. None of his family knew it as yet, but he had applied for citizenship.

Citizen. Not a subject. A Citizen. Oh, perhaps it was a lot of bloody nonsense: Englishmen were as free as Americans, even if they were "subjects." But, by God, there was power in a word. The wrong word could make a chap's shoulders sag, the right one could straighten them. Only children and women enjoyed being subjects, for it meant being taken care of, protected. But a man didn't need protection, damned if he did. "Citizen" might make him feel out in the cold, without a ragtag of protection to cling to; it might make him feel that he could win gloriously or fail most miserably, without any great stir on the part of Government or even of neighbors. But it did put his back up; it did set him down hard on his own two feet. And after the first hard jolt, a man liked that. Just as he liked these vast calm skies, the wide cold rivers, the great green hills. These were all indifferent to him, but only in a setting like this could a man enjoy his success, realize that in his own way he was as mighty. A big and terrible land, but the land for a man. The men who made England were not the men who huddled for protection on her little plots of land or dreamt their lives away in small rose-covered cottages. They were the men who left England for large places, places they conquered—tremendous gems that adorned a crown that otherwise would be small and mean.

Oh, this was a mighty land! One probably could never love it as one loved that "tight little isle," but such insular love was only for failures who concealed their failures, like the dead, under flowery mounds of prejudices, habits of mind, country philosophies, protection. One could love only a small place that was familiar and safe and without alarms. No, one could not love this mighty land like that. It was too full of wind for timid lungs, and its mountains were too high for gentle eyes, and its plains too terrifying. But one could reverence it, worship it, die for it as one died for a heroic ideal. And when one succeeded in it how mountain-like was that success, and how as impersonal!

Joseph thought these things, and though he thought without articulate words he felt the lofty impulse of them, felt within himself an icy power and vitality he had never known before. His step lost its jauntiness, but it took on firmness. His slight, delicately knit body became erect. What did Newtown matter, or George, or anxiety, or uncertainty? All that mattered was this heroic Land.

He thought of his sons. Did Ernest, the "lively un" think like this? Joseph, with intense disappointment, suddenly doubted it. All environments were the same to Ernest, provided they did not restrict or interfere with him and his ambitions. He was the sublime egoist, who drew the universe within himself, absorbed it, so that he was both an individual and also the universe. Without words or phrases, Joseph understood the terrible simplicity of his son's mind. All at once he felt afraid, experienced the uneasy fear that the delicate of perception feel when brought face to face with ruthless implacability and oneness of bitter purpose. Ernest, of a sudden, seemed to his father not to be quite human. What did the lad want? Surely, at fourteen he could not fully comprehend what money could mean; he had no experiences behind him to teach him the sweet power that came with money. He could not, surely, know what power meant. Joseph did not know that intuition, or imagination, might take the place of experience. No, he thought, shaking his head, it didn't seem quite human. The lad was down at the shop before any one else in the morning, and his father had to drive him home only a short time before he left, himself.

George had built a small ugly clapboard house for his brother at the edge of town. It was unpainted, and its long narrow front, with its two slits of upper windows and wider door at the bottom, was like a sallow, stupid face, which had been struck into a perpetual expression of amazement. The stone chimney that ran up from the ground on the outside had a slack, drunken air. It was only because of Joseph's strenuous demands that a tree was left standing, and this solitary tree, an elm, stood close to the house at the right, its branches, now golden with frost, sweeping the steep roof. The earth was sunken here in a tiny flat valley, so that a low rise swelled up from its right side, and a low drop sloped down from its left side. Despite the golden elm and the wisp of white curtain at the windows, and the bare cleanness of the brown earth in front of the house, it looked meagre and mean; the three wooden steps rising to the door were steep and narrow. There was a small garden behind the house, which Hilda had listlessly started in response to the urgings of Madam Bouchard, who had the French appreciation of a kitchen garden; in this garden grew a few potatoes, a few hills of beans, a short row or two of corn, a bed of radishes and one of.onions and a square of homely herbs. Hilda had been born and bred on a small English farm, and after she had once begun the garden her old instinct returned and she almost rivalled Madam Bouchard in making her garden yield. Martin helped her, and little Florabelle was not too young to learn to weed. The family kept a goat, for the baby Dorcas had been weaned and it was difficult to secure an adequate supply of cow's milk for her. Beyond the confines of the tidy little garden stretched a tangled wasteland of wild blackberry bushes, scrub, second growth weedy timber and tall dusty grass. Joseph and Ernest had built a rude low fence dividing the garden from this wasteland, over whose hot, lush vegetation the bees would hum like violin notes during the drowsy steaming afternoons.

Heartsick, frightened and homesick though Hilda was, and though her gay dreams of adventure had come to nothing, her homekeeping instinct, rooted in habit, had made her try to give her poor home some semblance of comfort. She had brought her copper kettles with her, and she polished them almost as vigorously as she had always done. They hung on the bare pine boarding of the walls of the high narrow room that served as kitchen, "parlor," and bedroom for husband and wife and the baby. There was a large fireplace, larger than the one in the house on the Common, so broad and high indeed that young Martin could have stood in it with only a slight stoop; the hearth was flagged with rough stones that Hilda scrubbed to a pale immaculateness. The bare floor was of pine boards, and these, and the boarding of the walls, with its black knotholes and resinous rings, gave out a clean turpentine smell. The table and chairs, the low wooden bed, the baby's cradle, were all homemade, of unpainted pine. It would have been a bare and dreary place enough had it not been for the ruddy gold of Hilda's kettles, the china cat and dog and tinkling clock on the mantelpiece, the brass andirons and polished steel stool on the hearth, and the black iron teakettle that sang a low drowsy song on the fire all the time. Hilda had learnt to braid old rags to make rugs, and now a long colorful oval lay on the hearth. Joseph, with sympathetic heartiness, loudly cheered all Hilda's efforts to make a home of this sad place, and by doing so brought the few smiles to a face that had lost a great deal of its color and innocent animal vivacity.

For Hilda was mortally ill of this new land. Its strangeness bewildered her, its heat withered her, the cold indifferent faces frightened her. The food tasted queerly on her tongue, and the deep restless tempo of the town filled her with uneasiness. She was never to feel at home here, but as she was a simple woman, not given to complaining, she bore her simple sufferings with fortitude, except for the infrequent occasions when her sickness of heart made her burst out into gusts of wild fury. These gusts were not followed by smiles and laughter and extra affection as they had so been followed in England, but by a strange pinched pallor of the face and long silence. She saw nothing of what Joseph saw in this immense land, which to her insular ears seemed to be filled with gigantic echoes and colossal movements; she only saw that here she had no friendly gossipy neighbors who would run in for a cup of tea and bread and butter, and complain to her of the mills and of sickness and pending childbirth. There was no market-place here where chickens squawked in pens, and apples stood in heaps and suckling pigs lay, slaughtered, on wooden counters, and where one met all one's friends and complained of the prices. There was no hearty tavern smelling of hops and scrubbed boards and sausage, with long slow sunlight falling through little latticed windows on old black wooden walls and timbered ceiling, with crackling fire, and the polished pewter mugs on the polished bar, where there was a quiet corner so that a woman could have a small glass of ale or porter with a woman friend. There was no soft gauzy sunlight, no grass that was lush and green, no cool, gentle rain, no peace, no comfort, no easiness and no kindliness. Everything, to her sick eyes, was stark and violent, greedy and hasty. Everything was flung up for a day, snuffled at hungrily, tramped upon, deserted noisily; it seemed to poor Hilda that she lived on a highway over which, and all about her, droves of hogs were driven, and when they passed she had the fearful feeling that all she possessed was eaten and defiled, and that the very house she lived in was as insecure as a temporary pen. She was the sort that is rooted to the earth, and when the roots are broken there is no happiness, no security. She cried in her sleep, and Joseph, listening to her, felt as helpless as though he were paralyzed. He told his brother of Hilda's wretchedness, but George, who despised women because of his subjection to his wife, bluffly and impatiently assured him that all he needed was to "give the lass time."

The one thing that sustained Hilda, retained in her for a long time an integrity of hope and living, was her belief that within a few years they would go home. She believed this utterly, though she did not notice that as time passed Joseph spoke less and less of this. But finally, when even she realized that there was no longer any hope, she sank into a dull resignation that was like a drugged existence.

The autumn day was very warm with a smoky languid warmth, and when Joseph opened the door of his new home the heat within seemed to rush at him smotheringly. Hilda did not believe in open windows, and the room smelled of a savory pasty, hot soup and drying diapers. Through two narrow windows on the opposite side of the room the evening sunset poured its yellow light which was full of golden dust specks. The baby crawled on the hearth rug in shrieking pursuit of little Martin who was imitating a singularly ferocious dog; in her homemade rocking chair Florabelle sang childishly to a rag doll. Hilda was slicing bread at the table, and when she saw Joseph her pale face brightened.

" 'Ullo," said Joseph, grinning at his family, and trying not to see how much thinner Hilda was getting. He removed his hat and coat, clucked at the baby, and sniffed the food odors with ostentatious hunger. "Eh? Where's Ernest?"

"He's gone over to Armand's to borrow something," said Hilda indifferently.

"Oh, yes. The new bore." Hilda said nothing to this; she cared not a thing about bores. She spoke sharply to Martin, and the boy picked up the baby and sat down with her. He had grown weedy and taller this summer; his silver-gilt hair hung on his neck in a straight mane, and under the full white lids of his eyes the blueness was shy and sad. Joseph, sitting down with a groan at some distance from the fire, frowned as he furtively studied his younger son. More like a lass than a romping lad. He hated the shop, never came near it after one visit, and shuddered at the sight of guns. But Joseph angrily and mentally repudiated George's contemptuous remark that Martin was feckless. Give the lad time. He was a comfort to Hilda, keeping her company, helping her with the little girls, working in the garden, running errands. Yet Joseph, stirring impatiently on his chair, did not want a son that was a comfort to his mother.

"My word!" he exclaimed suddenly. "Can't you find something sturdier to do, Martin, than rocking the little lass? After all, you are a lad, y'know."

Martin, as if forced to do so, glanced at him timidly. He tried to smile. But before he could speak, Hilda broke in sharply: "Leave him be, Joseph. He's a great help to me. I'd be mithered to death but for Martin."

"That's not it," explained Joseph shortly. "Mithered or no mithered, Hilda, he's just like a lass. He ought to come to the shop sometimes, though I don't want him working there yet. Look here, Martin, why don't you like the shop?"

Martin was silent a moment; he stared imploringly at the dark thin face of his young father. "I don't like the shop," he almost whispered. "I don't like guns, and the gunpowder makes me sick when I smell it. It's not," he added with sudden eagerness, smiling, "that I really hate pistols and shotguns. They—some of them look handsome, so smooth and black and shiny and polished: I like to hold them. But I don't like to think they are being made to kill people with. Why should anyone kill anyone else?" he added with grave simplicity.

Joseph was taken aback for a moment; he frowned, puzzled. Then with a short laugh he reached out and pulled Martin with rough affection to his side. He held the boy's thin forearm tightly, but he shook him as though trying to rouse him.

"Why should any one kill any one else, eh? Ever hear of wars, Martin? You must have heard of them, you've read enough books. Well? Didn't you read why men killed each other in your books?"

Martin, frightened though he was, yet looked down at his father with white earnestness. "No, father, I never did find out why. The British had one reason, and the French had another, and I believe they both lied. And it was the same with the Romans and the Carthaginians. And the Franks and the Gauls."

Joseph's frown deepened, though he felt a shamefaced pride at his little son's astonishing learning. "Go on with you," he said roughly. "I know nothing of this talk about the Romans, and such. They've been dead a long time, I suppose. And as for the Frenchies and Napoleon— why, if it hadn't been for England the little devil would have swallowed up all of Europe. And where would we have been? Think what would have happened if England had made no pistols and shotguns and gunpowder! Why, dammit, you wouldn't be here, now! But because Englishmen aren't milksops there'll be no more wars in Europe. England fought Napoleon so that Europe would have peace everlasting."

"Then why do you and Uncle George make pistols and gunpowder?" asked Martin simply.

Joseph laughed. "Oh, America wants them. By the way, Hilda," he added, turning with animation to his wife, "a Yankee General from Philadelphia wants us to send him our new pistol. Says if it is good he will see we have an Army job. That means," he exclaimed, "that we'll be putting on more men and building a bigger place! Damn it! Where's Ernest? I wanted to talk to him about that new idea we had for a trigger." He glared at the closed door, and fumed. It was some moments before he realized that he was still holding Martin's arm, and when he did notice it he seemed surprised, and frowned again, trying to remember Martin's last words. "Oh, yes, my lad, America wants what we can make. She's got Indians to kill," he added, grinning. "You see, son, the bad Indians are a nuisance, refusing to be robbed of their country peacefully. So, they've got to be killed. And so, we make the shotguns and gunpowder to help kill them with. But, if we didn't make them somebody else would. And I don't fancy starving to death, myself."

He released Martin, patted his shoulder. "Go on with you. Less books and more work. Look here, I heard today that there is a school opening in two weeks down the road, and perhaps I'll get you in there. How would you like that? Looks as if you'll be the clerk in the family, and God knows we need a clerk to keep the books neat and write the letters. Ernest's no good at that, and Georgie is worse. Come, how would you like to be going to school again? For a few years more?"

"We won't be here that long!" said Hilda in the loud, menacing voice in which terror speaks when confronted by a dreadful situation, which it refuses to believe in and consider. She turned from the table and stared at Joseph with strained eyes from which all softness had gone. "We won't be here that long," she repeated, and now her voice had the sound of a bitter cry in it, an anguished refusal.

Joseph did not turn in her direction; he looked at the fire, but when he spoke after a moment he spoke gently and slowly. "A year or two is not long, lass. You must be patient." He must give her time.

Hilda could not speak; she put her hand to the side of her face. After a while she turned back to the table. Oo, this was no way to talk to one's man; men tired of tears and naggings. She must be careful. She loved him so, this Joseph with his narrow back and straight small shoulders and lean dark face. She would die if he went womanizing, as so many men did these days. She had heard from Madam Bouchard, who spoke of these things indifferently, that Georgie visited Mrs. Marsdon and her girls on Shipman Road. Hilda had not recovered from her horror at this news, to the vast amusement of Madam Bouchard. But she could hardly bear this dull aching pain under her left breast, which was like tears that had turned to iron.

Joseph's last words seemed to have infused an air of finality into the room. Florabelle stopped crooning to her doll, the baby stopped her crooning. Martin still stood by his father's side, but his face was averted. His whole body seemed to shake in sympathy with Hilda's silent despair.

Ernest suddenly opened the door and entered the room. He did not enter noisily and vigorously, closing the door after him with a resounding bang. He opened the door almost noiselessly but with a swift decisive movement that used sufficient energy but not an overabundance, and closed it after him with a rapidity which made one expect a crash, but it was as if it were sheathed in velvet.

He had begun to lose the apple-cheeked roundness of early boyhood, and his face was beginning to show the large starkness and cold strength that was to command admiration and fear in his manhood. His eyes were preoccupied, his movements, as he came to his father without a glance for his mother and brother and sisters, controlled and swift.

"Pa," he said, without a word of preparation, "Armand thinks the steel rifled inner tube in a wrought-iron cannon would be practical. He thinks it can be done."

Joseph lifted his brilliant eyes and regarded the severe young face above him with a faint and quizzical expression. Ernest amused him, which Ernest, for all his astuteness, never suspected, though when he saw that quizzical expression it annoyed him as all things he considered irrelevant annoyed him.

"Come," said Joseph, "we have a shop as large as a dog kennel, and you talk of cannon!" His voice was teasing, but proud of his son.

Ernest made a short impatient movement of his hand. "You were talking of it today," he reminded his father with asperity. He would never acknowledge that talk might be idle and merely speculative. If one talked of a thing the talk was merely a necessary preliminary, a laying of plans before action.

"Oh, talk!" said Joseph, bent on teasing. Ernest suddenly pressed his hand on his father's shoulder as if to reach something stern and serious that lay under the lightness.

"I've talked to Armand," he said with a tense quietness. "He's sick of Uncle George's cautious ways and tightness and smallness. He's ready to pull out his money and go into something really worth while with you—with us. Like cannon, and seeing people about Government contracts. He says the Government is looking for someone who can supply arms and gunpowder cheaply. With your gunpowder, Armand says, and someone to go to Washington and tell the Secretary of War about it, the Government might even lend us money——"

Joseph shook off the hand, his face flaring into anger. "What kind of talk is this!" he shouted, half rising from his chair under the impulse of wrath. "Look here, I don't believe Armand said a word to you about doing Georgie in that way, you confounded young rascal, you! I believe that's all your own scoundrelly idea. Wherever did I get such a son! Have you forgotten that your Uncle George sent us tickets, gave me a chance to try out my gunpowder, gave us a roof to cover us and fed us for two months?"

Ernest scowled, pressed his lips together. He was not frightened at his father's anger; he was merely burningly irritated because Joseph was using words and phrases and emotions he considered childish and irrelevant. He flamed with his desire to pursue relevant and important things.

"Yes, yes, Pa," he said, "I suppose that's all so. But Uncle George helped us because he thought you could give him something worth while. But let's not talk about that." He had great courage, but it was a courage

born of what he considered relevant and irrefutable, and not a reckless
or conscious courage. "It's true that Armand did actually say he would
pull out his money and leave Uncle George in the lurch at a word from
you, but he didn't need to say it. I knew it. Words aren't always necessary. And then, when I talked to him about the cannon idea you and
I had——"

Outraged, Joseph remembered his parental authority. "Who gave
you permission to talk about the damned cannon, you young dog!" he
roared. "I suppose you've gone yelping through the town about it like a
Town Crier! Who else have you jabbered with, like the windy bladder
you are?"

Ernest stared at him, turning very white. He was struck to the heart.
When he spoke, after a silence filled with Joseph's enraged panting, his
voice was extremely low.

"Pa, you know that's not fair. I'm not a blabber. I've told nobody
but Armand, and you tell him everything; you've told him about the new
low trigger: I heard you tell him today. So I know you don't really mind
my telling him about the cannon."

Martin had withdrawn from his father's left at the approach of Ernest
at the right side. He stood between his father and brother and the tea
table in an arrested attitude. He was watching Ernest's profile against
the scarlet firelight, and something in its expression despite the largeness
and starkness of the features, filled him with pity. But Hilda, awakened
to interest, was not displeased. It was a good job, she was thinking, that
Ernest was getting a hiding at last, a stiff-necked young un these days,
given not to noticing his mother's existence except when she annoyingly
forced it upon his attention by reason of some trumpery show of maternal authority.

Joseph stared at Ernest's pale face while the boy spoke. He felt a twinge
of shame, and this made him sullen. He shrugged and turned a shoulder
to his son.

"You take too much on yourself," he said sulkily. "Too much for a
lad. You're not a man yet. Why, you really know nothing of firearms
and gunpowder. Just cheap and easy blab. Sometimes you make me
wonder who's master of the damn shop, you or Georgie. And that reminds me," he added threateningly, "I don't want to hear any more
talk about doing Georgie in, hear me? A rascally idea, fit only for
upstarts and cutthroats.

"Now, what I say to Armand is none of your concern, either. After
this I'll mind my tongue. I've puffed you up, treating you like a man instead of the young cub that you are. But I'll not make that mistake again.
Cannon! Government! Secretary of War! Money! Big words coming
from lad's breeches. Little dog trying to bite like a lion."

His volatile anger had blown up and drifted off, and he was already bored by the necessity of maintaining its manifestations. Moreover, he was curious. He allowed himself to smile up into Ernest's pale and rigid face.

"Well, Napoleon, what did our Armand say about the cannon? You might as well tell me the answer, now the damage is done."

A boy less dedicated to an idea than Ernest was, a boy who had less regard for time and more regard for irrelevances, would have become dignified at this, displayed his hurt, and removed himself proudly from his father's side. But Ernest reverenced time, understood only this, refused to waste himself and this moment of his life in unprofitable emotions, which might, at the expense of valuable fundamentals, indulge themselves in pride. So instantly, at his father's words, the rigidity passed from his face, and it became mobile and intent again, full of seriousness and purpose. Yet his father did not deceive himself that he had won an easy pardon.

"He said he did not see why it wouldn't work. It could be breechloading, he says. Old cannon was unreliable; it got stuck, sometimes, and sometimes blew the firers to smithereens. Armand also says that we'd better get to work on it at once, for there'll be all hell to pay in America one of these days because of the slaves down South."

"I hope," said Joseph quickly, remembering Armand's sensitiveness, "that you told him that it's just a new idea of mine that I didn't tell him about because it wasn't clear in my mind yet?"

"Oh, yes. I told him. He said he'd ask you tomorrow about it, and perhaps you could think it out together." Ernest hesitated. "He said to suggest to you not to tell Uncle George about it. Yet," he added cautiously.

Joseph grinned. "He never said 'yet.' And you know it. For a trumpery little Frenchman Armand's got too big an opinion of himself. Where's my pipe?" In grave silence Ernest filled his father's pipe from the packet on the mantelpiece, put it in his father's mouth and lit it with a taper. There was less of affection in all this than there was of the mechanical respect a subordinate gives to a superior. He waited alertly, lighted taper in hand, until he was sure that the tobacco was burning, then he meticulously pinched the fire from the taper and replaced it. Joseph leaned back in his chair, puffed contentedly and looked at the fire. Then he began to speak thoughtfully, as though thinking aloud, while Ernest watched him with pent intensity.

"No, we couldn't leave Georgie out, even if he is an oily, cutthroating scamp. And not because he is my brother. But without his help I wouldn't be in America, and that's straight. Oh, I know all about it not being brotherly love, bringing me here, but that don't alter the fact that if he hadn't brought me here I'd still be bootlicker to Squire Broderick."

"His help was—was accidental," said Ernest.

"You do have words, don't you?" grumbled Joseph. "Well, accidental or no accidental, there it stands. He's always yelping about ingratitude, and I won't give him an excuse to yelp it so that people will have some right to believe him."

"What does it matter what they believe?" asked Ernest, not contemptuously, but in the tone that one uses when pointing out an obvious fact.

"Eh? You're a hard young devil, ain't you? Heart of brass, and soul of iron. Heard that somewheres of a pirate with a turn of mind like yours. My word! I don't care what people believe, but I'd have a sneaking idea that what he would say would be true. No, I couldn't have it on my conscience."

Ernest, who had always known that his father had unexpected honors and softnesses, was yet incredulous at this obvious folly. He could hardly believe that one would discard a blazing opportunity for anything so worthless as a small matter of conscience. It seemed revolting to him, contemptible. And yet, he was not a scoundrel either by design or temperament; parodoxically, it was because he had a large vision that even the small things of conscience were lost in it. To him such indulgence in conscience was feckless or extravagant, to be indulged in only by those who were successful and could afford it. Without loss. He had not as yet heard the theory of the survival of the fittest and the struggle for existence. But he believed in it instinctively. If George were "left in the lurch," abandoned, thrown out of opportunity, it was because he was unfit and inferior by reason of his sly and greedy and malicious temperament, and had no place in plans of great men of immense ambitions. To Ernest, the realist, success was not won by those who possessed pointless vices or virtues.

"He wouldn't stop at doing you a dirty turn, Pa," he said, and hated himself for the inadequacy of his protest. But he knew that he could never have made his father understand. He compressed his lips in despair.

Joseph struck the arm of his chair with an air of finality, and showed that he was about to conclude the conversation and sit down to tea. The firelight was now the only light in the room, for it was twilight outside, a twilight like an infusion of smothering gray smoke.

"No, my lad, I don't care. True, he'd knife me if it would help him get a penny. But I'm not that way." He regarded Ernest with bland complacence, and the boy, increasingly revolted, saw that his father was admiring his own virtue and that this admiration would temporarily sustain him against arguments of logic and reason. He clenched his hands spasmodically, but did not speak. He was confident of ultimate victory.

Perhaps Joseph felt this, and an obscure helplessness suddenly overcame his self-admiration. He stood up abruptly, irritated. He turned to Hilda, who had begun to light the candles on the tea table, and frowned.

"Come, come, lass, Is a man to wait all night for his tea?"

Martin, who had listened in silence the while he had buttered a slice of bread for the baby and had seated her in a tall homemade chair and poured her milk into her pewter cup, suddenly straightened up and looked at all of them with his large blue gaze. He looked at his nervous, handsome young father, his plump mother with her shining cheeks and curling dark hair, at his young sister and the baby, and lastly at Ernest. And his eyes were full of fear.

It seemed to him all at once that there was a danger in the room which would devour them, and that this danger flowed out of Ernest and was a tangibly dreadful thing that he must cry out against. He could feel it like a coldness.

"Stop staring around like a calf, lad," said Hilda irritably, "and sit down." Then she was struck by his expression. "What's the matter with you?"

"I—I feel a little as if I might be sick," he muttered, looking at her with vague fright. "I—I don't believe I want any tea."

CHAPTER VI

THE BOUCHARD FAMILY lived on Garrison Road, about one hundred yards from the Barbour family. Armand Bouchard had built himself a characteristic home; no wooden shacks for him. With the instinct of the French for permanency, his home was of rough stone, hewn from the living rock of the State itself. Though the little house was uneven, uncouth and inartistic, though its thick-walled grayness was sturdy and unshakable, its foundations rooted in the earth, its door was strong against any storm that might blow. It was squat, rather longish, for Armand and his family did not care for upstairs bedrooms, thriftily making the heat of first-floor fires serve to warm sleeping rooms. The rooms were low-ceilinged, the conservation of heat also entering here. But low-ceilinged though they were, the rooms were large and square; no vault-like atmosphere as in other homes during that period, which ran to longitude rather than latitude. The hearths, too, were broad and hearty, scrubbed of stone, vigorous of fire. The house was no more lavishly furnished than the Barbour home, but it was full of lusty cheer, vehement affection, salty optimism and no compromises with reality.

The house was noisy, the inhabitants voluble, seemingly perpetually excited and vehement. Armand was the most excitable of them all, with his carved, nut-like face, vivacious point of black beard, fiery small eyes, yellow-toothed, rather feline grin between his hairy lips. He was a tiny man, but of such energy, speed and vitality that no one noticed his stature nor his shrivelled breadth. His collar and cravat were always loose, so that his brown, stringy neck, small and withered, was open to all weathers and all eyes. In this neck his Adam's apple bobbed continually, even when he was silent. Sometimes he gave the impression of being deformed, for he stooped perceptibly and the "wings" of his back stuck through his thin coat. But this impression was gathered only on the infrequent occasions when he was in partial repose. Once fifteen-year-old Ernest, in a moment of rare facetiousness, put his arm about the little man's waist and lifted him easily. Joseph thought it rather comical and laughed heartily, for Armand pretended to great wrath and helplessness, and his thin childlike arms flailed the air and his wee legs kicked impotently. Armand was almost perpetually amiable and ironical, always patient with a new idea, always eager and sympathetic. Few besides the astute Ernest also knew that Armand was shrewd and bitterly logical, undeceived and undeceivable, opportunistic and miserly. He could be the best of friends, the most faithful, but he could also be most reserved about receiving and giving favors. Ernest admired him even more than he did his father, for he had observed that Armand had no inconvenient honors and twinges, hid no secret subtleties or irresolutions. The boy would feel a current of strength and sureness, vitality and power, irony and implacability, in the little man's presence. He told his father that Armand was a giant midget. Here was a logic he understood.

Madam Bouchard was a woman whose height and bulk would have made at least three of her meagre little husband. Because of her vast bosom and her broad and immense hips, she gave the impression of slowness and sluggishness, but in reality she was as swift on her huge feet as her husband was on his, and her aim with a ladle or a dish, when angered, was little short of miraculous. She was half Italian, with a face as round and large as a shining plate, eyes like black lakes of fire, thick, somewhat sulky mouth. Her three plump chins rested on her chest, for she appeared to have no neck. She was inordinately proud of her one real beauty: glistening black hair with ruddy crests on its waves, which she wore in a tremendous knob at the thick base of what should have been her neck. Armand called her his little white dove, and she called him her little cabbage, for they loved each other dearly. She was ponderously vehement, irritable and suspicious, thrifty and devoted, a disillusioned friend to very few, and given to wild, obscure rages. Her intelligence was the intelligence of a small, quick animal, ferreting, wary and alert. She flavored French cooking with the rich exuberance of Italian cooking, and Armand declared, with some reason, that she was the best cook in the world, even better than his father, who at one time had been chef to one of Napoleon's aides.

She was a cynical but devoted Catholic, and over each bed was a crucifix, and no bedtime was allowed to pass without its rosary. Each Sunday saw the whole family, frail Jacques included, attending high mass in the tiny wooden Catholic church in Newtown, and no Saint's day was allowed to pass without a special remembrance. But hers was an earthy religiousness, as that of Italians is so apt to be, and bunches of dried herbs, knitting needles, pipes, onions, candles and tobacco mingled fraternally on the kitchen mantelpiece with tiny plaster-casts of saints and Virgins To Madam Bouchard, the Saints, and even the Saviour, were intimately and cosily concerned and anxious about the smallest happenings in the lives of the Faithful, and she did not hesitate to invoke them on the most trivial occasions of distress, such as one of Armand's light colds. Raoul's tendency to overeat and suffer indigestion, Eugene's inclination toward bullying, and Jacques' chilblains. To her, the Saints, the Blessed Virgin and the Child Jesus were members of her household, and when she served a particularly delectable dish she would often say wistfully: "Now, if only Saint Francis could have a sup of that, or sweet Saint Therese!" Whether she was dressed in calico, or her one stiff black silk dress, a huge golden cross on a gold chain swung over the vast hillocks of her breasts, and even when she basked in complete repose before the fire of an evening her mighty hands played with that cross and her lips frequently moved in old, half-mechanical prayers.

Being half Italian, she did not believe in the growing French custom of limiting one's family, and could see no connection between the fact that her three boys were only ten months apart in their births, and the lame leg and twisted hip of the youngest, Jacques. Sometimes she suffered sharply when contemplating Jacques, her beloved, and her voice frequently became rough and short when his natural sweetness of character had moved her too poignantly. Then she forced herself to take comfort in sixteen-year-old Raoul's vigor and laughter, Eugene's robust body and ability to take care of himself. Jacques, at fourteen, was bent and thin, with pale and emaciated features and soft brown hair in a mane on his slender neck. He used a homemade cane when he walked so slowly and frequently so painfully, but his face was so beautiful, so often merry and sparkling, that one instinctively felt that here was no sufferer silently pleading for sympathy but a youth who might be envied for some secret and engrossing happiness and contentment.

Raoul was an entirely normal youth, and consequently rather stupid. He was amiable and a little cunning, tolerant and greedy. Seventy-five years later he would have been the football hero of some minor college, for he had great shoulders, enormous vigor and a personality, due to its amiability and gift for leisurely friendship, that would have endeared him to scores of friends.

Fifteen-year-old Eugene was shorter and broader than his elder brother, Raoul, and though his features were actually handsomer than the latter's, his face appeared less attractive, due to the lack of sparkle and gaiety that made Raoul's face so endearing. His eyes appeared smaller, for he narrowed them continually with cold suspicion, and his mouth, though extraordinarily well cut, pouted and was sullen. He was usually reserved of speech, but when he did speak his tone was usually quarrelsome and railing, and often bullying, and at these times his face thickened and reddened as if congested. He was slow and careful and extremely intelligent, with a gift for invention and analysis, and, to his secret shame, he was also exceptionally kind-hearted, and easily moved to a resentful compassion. Only a few appreciated or suspected his many real virtues, just as very few suspected the selfish greed of Raoul. Ernest liked him the best of any of the Bouchards, except Armand, and indeed to the superficial eye there was a great resemblance between them.

Madam Bouchard's three earthly loves were her husband, her sons and her garden, and the garden was not the least of these. She loved the earth with an almost personal and voluptuous passion, and when she felt herself unobserved she would remove her giant boots and sink her bare feet into warm, newly turned soil. At these times a look of tranced ecstasy would come over her face, and her eyes would close, as in some sensual rapture. She liked to dig her mighty fingers into the earth, and when she would pat it about some new plant her gestures were those of a lover. Consequently growing things grew for her as for no others. They grew with a luxuriousness almost tropical in their lush crowding. Her cabbages were gigantic, her carrots like clubs, her potatoes like gourds, her peas great green globes, her turnips larger than a man's head. Her small row of corn grew to an amazing height, and the ears, wrapped tenderly in living silk floss, glistened with healthy milky whiteness. Her kitchen was always aromatic with herbs, and as she loved flowers little less than she loved vegetables, she always had a glass or earthen pot of forget-me-nots, tight rosebuds glistening with dew, or sprays of lavender, on the table during the summer. She also possessed a hardy she-goat who responded to her silent solicitude with floods of rich milk. Once George Barbour had said half-sneeringly, as he looked at the garden and the squat sturdy house of stone: "Anyone would think you intended to live here the rest of your lives!"

Madam Bouchard, in her hoarse, booming voice had replied: "A day or a year or a lifetime: they are all forever." This had puzzled George no end, and only confirmed his contemptuous British opinion that all foreigners were mad when they were not thieves. And indeed, to many of the Newtowners the Bouchard family, with enormous Madam Bouchard and her wall-shaking voice, and Armand, with his sinuous quickness and shrill, piping tones, and Jacques, with his boxes of books and crippled leg and sweet beauty of face, and Eugene with his silences and sullennesses and suspicious glances, were entirely insane, or at the best, "touched." Newtowners, however, understood Raoul, and were patronizingly or genuinely fond of him.

Hilda Barbour would have found her condition much worse and more depressing in this new and bewildering land if it had not been for Madam Bouchard. One day, early in their acquaintance, the Frenchwoman had found Hilda weeping in slow and desperate silence by her fireplace. She guessed the cause immediately, and instead of extending sympathy and consolation she began to upbraid Hilda for not having started a garden. A home without a garden, she said hoarsely, was like a hearth without a fire, a body without a soul. Hilda must come at once, and she would give her some young plants. It was too late, now, for seedings. So Hilda, after sobbing protests, finally went to the Bouchard house, walked in the garden, helped Madam Bouchard with some small weeding, and felt rise within her her sturdy peasant love for the earth, which had, since her marriage to Joseph Barbour, been stifled by petty urban living. She returned home refreshed and almost happy, her apron full of small plants with the cool, wet earth clinging to their roots, and started her vegetable and flower garden. Madam Bouchard during the next few weeks taught Hilda tricks of Continental cooking, and as a consequence garlic-flavored, herb-touched and onion-seasoned dishes began to appear on the Barbour table, to everyone's pleasure except Ernest's. It was his tragedy, though he never suspected that it was a tragedy, that he had no palate whatsoever, and eating to him was a mere tasteless chore to be gotten over with as quickly as possible. It was a necessity, like breathing, and to him as automatic and casual. One ate to live, that was all. He also never acquired a taste for wine, though he later, seeing others' pleasure and deciding that it was an art that enhanced the dignity of success, tried desperately to enjoy it. But though he suffered no ill effects from alcohol, and though he drank copious quantities in an effort to derive some pleasure from it, alcohol was a wry taste on his tongue and nothing else. So Hilda's triumphant production of dishes foreign and exotic in taste aroused no enthusiasm or pleasure in the boy. He could not understand how any one could waste valuable time over a necessity that brought no enjoyment or profit.

One day Hilda complained to her new friend of the impossibility of ever making a home in this vehement and starkly restless country. To which Madam Bouchard replied: "What does it matter where one lives, if one has one's husband and one's children, God, a fire, a roof, a few pots, a bunch of herbs, a warm bed and a garden? And peace?" And she added to herself, silently: "And the greatest of these is peace." But Hilda, looking about her sadly at the ugly disorder and noise of Newtown, at the blazing unshaded light of the sun, at the flat, unfriendly faces of the people, at the hideousness of her little house, sighed. "One can," said Madam Bouchard, "make a home anywhere." And looked complacently at her magnificent vegetable-and-flower garden, and the strong walls of her house. But Hilda, whose happiness depended on old familiarity, on old friends, old tastes, old smells, old skies and old rains, could never understand this. She could endure all this strangeness for the sake of the reward of money, for she belonged to a race that must either have a familiar home or a strange success.

Once Hilda told her brother-in-law, who liked her more than a little, but secretly, that she actually believed Madam Bouchard and her family and husband would not mind staying in America the rest of their lives.

She spoke with affectionate contempt and with a shake of the head. George had sneered and laughed and had replied that it was nothing more than he had expected of these Frenchies, who had no decent country of their own in which to live, but had had to leave what miserable land they had possessed for the sake of their necks. To an Englishman, however, coming from a civilized country of order and intelligence and pleasantness, America was intolerable, fit only to be endured for the profits it offered.

Hilda had expected Joseph's smile and understanding, and it seemed odd to her that when she turned to meet his eyes he was not looking at her, but was regarding George with a most unpleasant expression. His neck had a way of turning crimson when he was either angered or agitated, and though he said nothing Hilda saw, to her surprise, that that neck was a bright and congested red. For some reason this obscurely annoyed her, and for some time thereafter she patronized Madam Bouchard. The only dissatisfaction about this, however, was that Madam Bouchard did not appear to know she was being patronized.

Hilda saw little of her sister-in-law, Daisy, who was building up a little social set of her own from which Hilda was naturally excluded. Daisy was already beginning to talk of moving over to Oldtown, and Hilda, when she heard this, set her lips obstinately and vowed that she would never move over to Oldtown, no, not even if Joseph made himself fifty thousand pounds.

CHAPTER VII

IT HAD BEEN an extremely bad winter, but spring had come at last with a warmth and expansiveness that was like a woman who laughs as she reminiscently shakes her head over a past ordeal.

Here by the river it was simultaneously warm and coolly fresh, for the sun was pouring down in a yellow flood like a cataract and the air, blowing in from the water, still had the chill of frost in its new stimulation. An outward curve of land hid the scarred banks of Newtown, and because of the green fog in the thick clump of willows on that curve even the crowding shacks and ugly warehouses were hidden. Traffic on the river was very slow today, so that the river was a flowing stream of empty bright silver under a sky drenched with light. The banks were still sheets of wet and glistening brownish-red mud, in which bending willows, white and slender and newly green, were fragilely rooted. The opposite shore seemed greener and brighter than this, for the timber had hardly been touched and the trees were taller and more crowded. The tall weeds along the river bank were old weeds, brown and wispy and dead, but tenacious like ancient women; through the dead dryness of these the water shone like liquid quicksilver, restless and moving, and between their ranks the new young reeds were growing: slender green fire.

So brilliant were the air and the water and the awakening earth that one hardly noticed the radiant silence. The birds had returned, and they called in lonely sweetness from tree to tree, as if trying to recall old memories and old friends. Occasionally, with a soft flutter of wings, they blew against the sky, vivid streaks of crimson or fiery blue or shining black. They flashed down to the water, whirled in a spiral upwards, shrilled intensely, vanished into the green shadows of the trees. The water sucked at the banks, muttered to itself, bubbled, eddied, swept on.

The banks sloped upwards, and on the higher reaches of ground flat rocks warmed themselves in the sun and the earth was dryer. Too, grass was pushing up between the rocks and there was a piercing scent of stirring life in the air. It was to this place that Martin brought little Dorcas every fine spring day. He liked to sit sunning himself on the flat gray rocks while she tumbled busily and seriously on the new grass and gathered tiny wildflowers in the cooler shadows of the fringe of trees. Her rough homemade coat came down to her bustling feet and her small face was entirely hidden in the depths of a huge bonnet. Down her back crept a few silken tendrils of golden hair, movingly sweet to young Martin, whose eyes hardly left the child for a moment.

Almost every day when pain and disability allowed, Jacques Bouchard joined Martin on the stones by the river. Sometimes, as Martin and little Dorcas went down the road they would hear Jacques' clear thin hail, and they would wait for him as he came swinging and hobbling along on his crutches, his eager fair face thrust ahead of him like something alive that was tugging futilely to leave the maimed body behind. There he would come, stumbling over the rutty road, his soft brown mane bobbing on his twisted shoulders, his almost useless feet bent grotesquely, his shadow dancing violently about him. But more often Martin would arrive alone with Dorcas on the rocks, for he could never be sure that Jacques would join him. Then he would hear his name called and Jacques would appear, laughing and panting, struggling among the stones down to the rocks. Martin never made the painful mistake of offering to assist the crippled youth, though so understanding was Jacques Bouchard, so subtle of sympathy, that he would merely have smiled wryly at the younger boy and accepted the assistance. Jacques had no false delicacies; he was too intelligent to feel offense at anything.

They would sit together on the rocks in peace and almost complete silence, after Jacques had recovered his painful breath. There was a remarkable similarity between the fourteen-year-old youth and the ten-year-old boy. Both had the same singular sweetness of expression, though where Martin's was touched with confused sadness Jacques' was quiet with peace. Their eyes were both gentle and deep, but Martin's were troubled and Jacques' were tranquil and steadfast. Martin was concerned painfully with the incomprehensible problems of existence, but Jacques appeared to have withdrawn and accepted his withdrawal. In their similarity, their instinctive sympathy for each other, they were a strange young pair in the rough boisterousness of Newtown, for one would never belong and the other had never belonged.

There had never been any strangeness or shyness between them. Instantly, upon meeting, they seemed to have gone to each other across the space of floor that divided them in the Bouchard house. They had not seen each other for several weeks afterwards, but young Martin had felt comforted and sustained through the tormented days of first readjustment. They had met again at Christmas in the Bouchard house, and Martin, almost immediately on entering the big dim room with its conflagration of blazing red fire on the hearth, had gone to the chimney corner where Jacques was sitting toasting new bread. He had sat down on a stool near the older boy, and they had not spoken. But each time their eyes met they smiled. It was strange that the crippled Jacques seemed to be the protector and the shelterer, and Martin, young and straight, was the protected and the sheltered, the hider in the shadow of one who was strong and calm. All about them was the vigorous confusion of holiday, the shrieks of the younger children, the boisterous voices of the men, Madam Bouchard's booming tones that made the objects on the mantel-piece rattle. Chairs scraped, were drawn around the fire in a comfortable semicircle, nuts were cracked, hot spiced wine and whiskey drunk, rich dark cake was passed, the two crying little girls were comforted, voices mingled, laughed, contradicted, roared. But Martin and Jacques sat in a shining little pool of silence, smiling at each other. Over the hubbub, the clink of glasses, the snapping of the logs on the hearth, only these two heard the hissing of the fine dry snow on the board window sills, the roaring of the wind down the chimney.

There were no schools in the section of Newtown where the Barbour and Bouchard families lived, for they were situated on the outskirts of the young city. Moreover, what few schools there were were sketchily staffed, and demanded fees. The newer people in the town were not interested in education for their children, and though Joseph uneasily thought of it in connection with Martin and young Florabelle, he was too engrossed in the desperate struggle to get a foothold to give it concentrated consideration. He had heard of some vague project of building a school in his section, and had contented himself with it. After all, he thought, Martin knew twice as much as lads his own age, in fact, he knew too much for his own happiness and comfort. And the little lass hardly needed a school yet; the less women knew the better, anyway.

And so it happened, very gradually, that winter, that Martin came almost every day through snow and sleet and howling wind and fog and rain to the Bouchard house, where Jacques would be waiting for him with books in both English and French. There by the fire they would sit, gravely reading aloud to each other, gravely discussing. Twice a month newspapers from New York and Philadelphia arrived by stage, and together the two boys would read every item, discuss every event. The question of slavery absorbed them, filled them with pity and terror and indignation. Sometimes they could scarcely speak from horror, and their eyes would well over with tears. The State had reluctantly enacted a law whereby it returned runaway slaves on the way to Canada, and each harrowing and heart-breaking episode seemed to strike at the boys with personal anguish.

To Madam Bouchard, who was not seriously touched by anything or any one outside her household, this seemed touchingly amusing. She had a cousin in Quebec and she said, comfortably, that this cousin complained of the most monstrous winters and subsequent hardships, and she could hardly believe it much of a misfortune if a runaway black were prevented from reaching that desolate land. It was without result, except for a tender smile at his vehemence, that Jacques argued passionately with her as to the merits of freedom, and the injustice of one man owning another's body, no matter the color. She would listen, nodding indulgently, as he related history after history of torture and death and agony, and she would think to herself: "Mon petit looks quite well today. How his eyes shine and how bright is his color!" She had no affection to spare for any one but those of her flesh and her arms, yet because he was such a companion for Jacques, and seemed to arouse him so vividly, she felt something quite close to affection for Martin. She spoke to him warmly and solicitously, hovered over him with more than her ordinary hospitality, cherished him, scolded him, tied the muffler firmly about his neck when he was leaving. Her beautiful eyes melted upon him, and she would pat his thin warm cheek with her great hand. She spoke to Hilda of young Martin, and her immense broad face would beam with gratitude so brightly that Hilda would tell Joseph that Madam Bouchard had the largest and tenderest heart in the world for children. However, had Martin begun to annoy and bore Jacques, Madam Bouchard would have been outraged and inflamed, and her affection for Martin would have turned to the most savage and ferocious hatred. She would have treated him no longer as a child, remembering that she was a woman and a mother, but as an enemy that she would fight and destroy. In fact, quickly discovering that Ernest Barbour was repellent to Jacques, that Jacques instinctively disliked and despised him, she could never spare a word of the slightest courtesy for him, could scarcely endure him. On the infrequent occasions when he reluctantly accompanied his father to the Bouchard house the usually voluble woman would relapse into passionate and menacing silence, though she liked and admired Joseph both for his wit and looks. She would push her chair far back from the fire, overflowing it with her immense bulk, and in the mingled sharp-shadows of firelight and darkness her face and blazing eyes would be fixed with unrelenting hatred upon the uncomfortable Ernest (who pretended to be oblivious to all this). Her hands would clench and unclench upon her gigantic thighs, her breath would be loud and panting. It never occurred to her that all this was enormously ridiculous or entirely out of proportion: where her affections were concerned Madam Bouchard was humorless, and a tiger.

"Madam B. doesn't like you, lad, and that's certain," Joseph had once said to Ernest, with huge enjoyment. Ernest, who was uncomfortable over the woman's attitude only because her vehement and passionate malignancy forced itself by sheer electricity into his preoccupied consciousness, had shrugged. Had he studied the situation his intelligence would easily have guessed the cause of such absurd hatred, but he never spared any thoughts in idle or subtle speculations that had nothing to do with the terrible drive within him.

Martin, with the simplicity of a child, had responded with shy gratitude to Madam Bouchard's exuberant affection. He thought her the kindest and most comfortable of women. Until a certain day. On that particular cold dark winter day Jacques was suffering from a cold. Also, his leg was bothering him severely. Madam Bouchard, watching so fiercely, saw that today even Martin was tiring and distracting to the tortured Jacques, but instead of gently suggesting to the child that he leave and return another day when his friend was better, she pounced on the frightened boy with the savagery of a tigress, thrust his arms into his coat, muttered malignantly under her breath at him as she buttoned the garment, and glared at him so ferociously with her flaming eyes that he became petrified with a purely physical terror. It seemed to him that the very air about her became saturated with a wild and animal odor, such as jungle beasts exhale when infuriated and prepared to destroy. He returned home, and for days was torn between his bitter longing to see Jacques and his active terror of Madam Bouchard. He was firmly convinced that she would annihilate him should he appear again, and was entirely innocent of what had precipitated that monstrous performance. It was not until Jacques had sent Raoul with repeated entreaties that Martin return to the Bouchard house, and then with quakings. But Madam Bouchard received him with such jubilation and affection, such loving scoldings and round upbraidings for his neglect, that he was stunned with amazement and almost convinced that he had dreamt that dark winter afternoon. However, he never again trusted her, was never at ease in her presence, but always watched apprehensively out of the corner of his eye for an imminent explosion. So when spring arrived and Jacques could join him on the river bank he was utterly grateful and relieved.

There they would sit upon the rocks, laughing tenderly at little Dorcas' blundering small feet, comforting her when she fell and wept, playing with her as they would play with a pup, pulling green blades of grass between their fingers, idly talking, sinking into sun-intoxicated and drowsy silences, watching the bright rush of the river, yawning, sighing, humming. There was no barrier of age between them; they were timeless for each other.

Jacques told Martin of Jean Jacques Rousseau. To Martin, bruised and raw and hurt by associations with those who were immediate, exigent and driven by what seemed like an external power, the philosophies of this gentle, half-mad and ideal-tortured Frenchman were as simple as cool fresh water, and as life-giving. Here was the sweet fruit of a simple mind, unexotic and pure, growing on a strong and harmless tree with its ιoots clinging deeply to the earth. He could understand this simply noble thought, which was, however, without heroism, utterly non-combatant, utterly removed, paradoxically, by very reason of its uncomplicated naturalness and harmless animalism, from the very stuff of strong and vigorous and vital life. He did not know that it was an Arcadian philosophy, so divided from reality, so timid and unreal, that it was faintly flavored with preposterousness and absurdity. It was like a group of self-conscious artist-poseurs dressing themselves in flowing garments and dancing chillily under a white moon in a cultivated forest. He was too young to realize this. He, too, was a pilgrim in flight from reality into unreality, and Rousseau was a pillar of gentle fire in the desert.

All he knew was this philosophy comforted and sustained him; it was a voice that spoke in familiar accents in a strange land. It consoled him that there lived people in this terrifying world that were not ambitious and ruthless, cold of eye and dominant, driven and driving, greedy and rapacious. It was a voice like Jacques' hand: kind and steadfast, innocent and quiet.

Martin's religious education had been indifferent. Therefore, he listened avidly to Jacques' stories of the Catholic saints. Here, too, were people removed from reality by mysticism and devotion, people he could understand. They moved through his mind like the gentle plaster figures of Madam Bouchard's mantelpiece come to life, clothed in pink lustre and gilt, beaming at him with their large and mistily brilliant eyes, loving him with celestial smiles, touching him with cool and undemanding hands. He loved them. He listened eagerly to the stories of their lives, tears in his eyes, his heart beating rapidly. He seemed to swell inside with intense and mysterious emotion, so that he wished to immolate himself on some heroic altar in an ecstasy of faith. The wish had in it something of voluptuousness, something of the rapture of copulation. He was not concerned with the center of the Saints' faith; he hardly thought of God at all except as the focus toward which the tide of this delightful catalepsy turned.

Thus it was that Jacques Bouchard and Martin Barbour were as removed from this new world of heat and drive, expansion and power, noise and glory and vulgarity and splendor as if they dwelt in some silver-misted valley of the moon. This was the age of the McGuffey Readers, expanding railroads, widening frontiers, wealth and growth, gold and industry: the age of a new world stretching young strong arms, and if speaking coarsely and without much refinement, at least speaking cogently.

Up and down the Allegheny River new steamboats puffed, flatboats loaded with wheat and machinery and iron and steel floated stolidly by; Windsor's population was increasing gigantically, and the railroad was now promising a branch line by spring. There was talk that a Pittsburgh steel firm was to establish a factory in Windsor, because of the proximity of coal; ten new coal mines had just recently been opened. Already dark-skinned aliens were appearing in the mills and the mines, men with long faces and averted eyes and strange speech. They did not mingle with the townsfolk, but held themselves apart, as if they were either naturally aloof and unfriendly or frightened. It was noticed that they lived adjacent to the mills and the mines, and rarely ventured beyond them; it was also noticed that the mills and the mines had new stores of their own where the aliens seemed to trade exclusively, much to the loud annoyance of the shopkeepers. The ominous significance of this had not yet penetrated the public consciousness, and was not to do so for some time.

In Oldtown, society waxed more and more self-conscious and snobbish and luxurious. More and more carriages appeared on the streets. More and more farm girls, and even girls recruited from Newtown, entered "service" in aristocratic homes in the section of town that was soon to be designated as "across the tracks."

The very air was charged with growth and excitement and exuberance. But Jacques and Martin seemed unconscious of it all. The bright river, the sun-warmed rocks, the baby girl, the fireplaces, Rousseau, days sleepy and heavy with dreams, smiles, hand-touches, sighs: these were their life, and they knew or cared about nothing else.

Less than all things did they care for the gunpowder firm of Barbour & Bouchard, though it held their destiny and the destiny of Martin's children in grim keeping.

CHAPTER VIII

THE GUNPOWDER SHOP was a ramshackle wooden building, unpainted, poorly built, hardly weather-proof, standing precariously, as if perched, on a steep slope of muddy land near the river. The boards that composed it, bare and gray-white and splintering, seemed merely tacked together. It consisted of a large assembling and polishing and grinding room for the pistols and the shotguns, a smaller room full of bottles, glasses and crocks and barrels, where Joseph Barbour experimented, made and prepared his gunpowder for shipment, where Ernest crudely lettered in India ink on white paper the legend that this was Gunpowder Par Excellence, made by Barbour & Bouchard, Manufacturers of Explosives & Firearms, Windsor, U. S. A. (Gunpowder guaranteed to withstand a reasonable amount of wetting— almost smokeless—non-injurious to firer—the World's Best Gunpowder without a Rival.) Another room contained the steam engine that pumped water and operated a small lathe in the assembling room. The steel and iron mill of The Sessions Company in Windsor supplied Barbour & Bouchard with the crude moulds of their firearms. Previous to Joseph's arrival George Barbour had been buying his moulds from a cheaper rival concern of Sessions, Moffatt's, but Joseph, after scornfully examining the product, noting its pitted and brittle quality, its unevenness and careless workmanship, insisted on doing business with Sessions. George had protested bitterly, for Joseph had admitted that he intended charging no more for firearms, made of better steel for some time, until they had steady markets. It did a man no good, he had said, to get a reputation for making pistols and shotguns that were apt to explode in the operator's hands, thus endangering his fingers and even his life, due to brittle air-chambers in the steel, and paper-thin spots. Who cared for reputation? shouted George, who wanted only ten thousand pounds. They couldn't supply guns fast enough, with half the country going west, and the Indians, and the demand for game shotguns from the Southern States. Joseph was an onion-skinned fool to stay up nights worrying whether their guns were about to blow some damned Yankee or Indian or nigger into hell and back; all that concerned him was the money.

But Joseph, with his far inward eye already fixed on a steadfast and dazzling future in this newly beloved land, was passionately firm. He saw that George was not at all interested in permanent markets and expanding business, and hated him for it. He had had many talks with Ernest, and not a few of his arguments and his resolutions stemmed from the boy. It was Ernest who gave him the final and cunning argument that won over George, after many reluctant oaths and protests. Better guns, as well as better gunpowder, Joseph said, while not showing immediate profits, built up a monopoly, so that poorer manufacturers would be forced out of business. Once having all the business, one could charge any price one wished. Give him two years, said Joseph, and their fortunes would be made. And when he said this, Joseph stared at his brother with a startled, almost frightened and curious look, as though he remembered something said by another which he had once repudiated but found that he had been unconsciously influenced by it in everything he did and said.

George had smiled a reluctant, gloating smile at the idea of controlling business and charging enormous prices. So he had consented. He found that Armand Bouchard was entirely with Joseph, and his hate for both of them increased venomously. But, he promised himself, with grim and gleeful joy, there would come A Day. In the meantime, he would use their brains and their sweat; fools like these were born to be victimized by clever men such as himself.

Within two years firearms bearing the insignia B&B had won nation-wide fame. To own a B&B stamped one as a gentleman of discernment and wealth, a connoisseur, an officer, or a competent frontier leader. Orders were coming in from every general store in the country, even from large New York, Chicago, New Orleans, Pittsburgh and Richmond stores. George gloated, grew restless. But Joseph and Ernest, and now Armand with them, had their eyes fixed on Army contracts, though they felt as yet unprepared to angle for them against formidable and old-established firms in New York State. The firm of Barbour & Bouchard, though flourishing, was still too young, its bank balance still too precarious, its pretensions too insecure, to risk any threat of determined annihilation from mightier concerns. Not yet, not yet, they said to each other, their eyes sparkling with wild excitement. But soon, added Ernest. Joseph and Armand thought it wise to purse their lips with judicious indulgence at the boy's quietly spoken prophecy; but oddly, this indulgence seemed immature and childish in the face of this seventeen-year-old's stern lips and fanatic eyes, and bitter driven power. As time went on Joseph respected his son's opinion and intelligence and maturity more and more, and Armand, who had the French respect for intellect under whatever guise or age it appeared, had long ago come to the conclusion that it would not be long before Ernest would dominate the entire firm. It would be folly, he had concluded resignedly and with almost incredulous admiration, to oppose such shrewdness, such insight, such dominance and strength. He guessed, as no one else did, that the subtle and clever and imaginative Joseph was becoming a veritable marionette operated by the invisible strings of the silent Ernest. Ernest employed his father as one would employ a complex and versatile tool, or a brilliant slave. Only Armand knew that almost all Joseph's shrewd and invincible suggestions and ideas emanated from Ernest, who, however, was as yet wily enough to remain in the background and play the devoted son.

Armand did not envy Joseph Barbour his son. He was too clear-sighted for that. Despite the smiling, indolent mediocrity of Raoul, the humorless obstinacy and pettier drive of Eugene, he thanked his God that Ernest was not his son. It would be like having stored thunder and flood in his house, he told his wife.

He was satisfied : Raoul and Eugene worked in the little factory, Raoul indulgently and carelessly, as though he considered the whole concern somewhat amusing, Eugene with slow but religiously tenacious industry, following his worshipped model, Ernest. It was true that Jacques would never be able so much as to polish a bore, but that was insignificant compared to his beautiful face at the table and the fireside. It was like having a saint in the house, before whom healthy family turmoil subsided into peace and harmony. Even careless Raoul was gentle with Jacques, and Eugene, forgetting his arrogance that tried to emulate Ernest's silent strength, became eager and humble before his younger brother.

The American Railroad Company put a branch line through to Windsor, connecting the town with Pittsburgh, and incidentally with New York. In the same month the firm of Barbour & Bouchard moved into a tidy small red brick building recently built, about five hundred yards from its original location, the firm having purchased, for a very satisfying sum of money, all the land from the river bank backwards to Shipton Road, an area conservatively estimated as about two hundred acres, and along the river bank for another two hundred acres. This put the young firm of Barbour & Bouchard into an imposing debt of fifteen thousand five hundred dollars, which knowledge made hundreds of eyebrows to rise in Windsor, and hundreds of dour and complacent prophecies of swift ruin to be made. For by now the town was becoming acutely aware of the Barbours and the Bouchards, and regarding them with amazed and speculative eyes. It was as if a respectably large mushroom had become a gigantic tree overnight. The townsfolk had been too busy with their own schemes and exciting affairs to have devoted much attention before to this young Company, but now they became noisily aware of it.

For two years Ernest Barbour had had a silent plan growing in his mind, a daring and brilliant plan. Or, rather, two plans. And now he proceeded to execute them, boldly, irresistibly, as he always did everything.

CHAPTER IX

THE SESSIONS STEEL COMPANY considered itself an old and historical concern, for it had been established soon after the Revolution. It was originally known as The Sessions Iron-works. The Sessions family had never been members of the proletariat, and had retained a healthy and justifiable hatred of the anonymous horde that came like grasshoppers to devour the crops planted by the competent. The family, originally prolific, had dwindled to two brothers, Nicholas Sessions, the Senator, and Gregory Sessions, president of the Steel Company. Their dead sister, Amy, had married a fool and a wastrel, and had been cut out of her father's will. She had left a daughter, penniless, who presided over the Sessions home in Windsor.

The Sessions Steel Company had lost much of its old popularity among large manufacturers who went in for quantity rather than quality, but those few concerns who had inherited a respect for integrity and workmanship and quality, and who prided themselves in turning out only the best, remained the best and faithful customers of Sessions. America was already thinking in vast numbers, and, as usual, fineness fell, defeated, before the febrile god of Production. However, Gregory Sessions had persuaded himself that he had no yearnings for great wealth, no imperial ambitions, and that the steady and respectable income he and his brother derived from the Company was quite consistent with the estate of a gentleman. It was, he said, enough for him that the mark of Sessions Steel was the insignia of integrity and honor, and that the best manufacturers, though buying in small quantities, bought from no one else. Gregory Sessions, elegant, cynical, lean, smiling and indolent, was the least to suspect his own angry bitterness, his own savage lust for power and wealth. Even to himself he posed as a man slightly bored with business, suffering it only because of the necessary income, and longing to return to his grandfather's England of gentlemen and leisure, quiet, fires and books. Unknown to himself, he had a passionate love for America, and because he resented those who came in hate and greed to this new land, he frequently expressed himself in scorn, amusement and tired boredom when speaking of his country. He detested this thing of figures and heat and furnaces and iron and sweat and dirty arms and naked backs, he said, yet he was secretly and inordinately proud of it, would not allow a piece of steel that did not come up to specifications to leave his factory. He told everyone that it was a matter of personal pride with him, not that he cared a fig for the Sessions Steel Company. Not he! He wished he could be done with it. He was only looking out for a purchaser with a good price, then he would sell and go to England where gentlemen were not engaged in trade. Yet the shipment of one small item of steel that was not of the usual quality was enough to cause him real anguish and rage for weeks on end. It was an agony, he frequently told his niece, to leave his warm, comfortable, spacious home of a morning for the gritty mustiness of his little office, yet he could honestly not conceive of a life without it; he knew every figure in its books, knew every engine, every piece of machinery, every furnace as none of his workmen did. He despised his employees and paid them remarkably well.

It must not be thought that he was a fool and a poseur. He was, in fact, an astute, shrewd, wary, incredulous gentleman of real elegance and intellect. He had been to school in England, France and Germany. He had no affectations; he was merely self-deceived, self-defensive, for he believed that he and his brother were in a fair way, because of ignorance or indolence, to destroy something that had value and worth and dignity. So he told himself that he was no businessman, though in fact he was a startlingly fine one, and it was through his efforts, subconscious and powerful, that The Sessions Steel Company retained its reputation in a growing murk and confusion of hastily and cheaply made products in quantity. His only lack was a knowledge of advertising; he could not make a noise. He believed that good products were their own advertisement, and though this is true in a society that is homogeneous and stable, building up reputations graven in the rock of memory and passed from father to son, it is not true in a society that is in flux, restless, moving, leaving one point for another, and forgetting. He did not know that America was entering a new order, where even gold must be advertised, and the circus "barker" was about to be sublimated in the advertising writer. He heard the swelling tempo of the new and gigantic America, and pretended to despise and belittle it; he was in reality very much frightened over it. It seemed a threat to him against everything that he honored and respected: integrity, the dignity of fine living, peace, leisure, music, good company, solid houses and honorable statesmen, and ease of mind, and even luxury. He hated intensity, and suspected that this intensity led to shoddiness and speed, corruption and rapacity, politicians that were mountebanks and malefactors. The new blood that was pouring into America contained a virus that would change her very features, would transform her soul. And so he stood against it, thinly smiling, indolent, apparently indifferent, and full of hate. Yet something in him, something primitively lustful and eager and ambitious, longed to get into this achingly uproarious fray and be part of it, subjugate it. He hated to see fools seize the prizes, hated his own inertia.

He had more than a suspicion that his brother, Nicholas, was one of those politicians who were part of the new intensity and carelessness and greed, one of the despisers of tradition, one of the hurriers panting at the old machinery. He suspected, with more than a little foundation, that Nicholas was a mountebank and a malefactor, not above bribery, not above corruption and dirtiness. Nicholas was tall, as were all the Sessions males, but where Gregory was lean and elegant Nicholas was stout and impressive. He had the true later politician's personality: bluff, shrewd, friendly, boisterous and democratic, a handshaker, an "agree-er," an element in which the most alien elements could dissolve without explosion, and with the ease of fine oils, blending. He was crafty rather than intelligent, greedy and insatiable, cruel and sometimes vicious, opportunistic and alert. He was making his own fortune without the aid of The Sessions Steel Company, which he privately thought a "fuddling piece of business," not likely to amount to much. Nevertheless, he used it as a good speaking point, for he could call attention to the fine wages paid his workmen (always a good point when talking to workmen), and the aristocratic tradition of the firm, never giving way to shoddiness and cheapness, when talking to uneasy aristocrats who feared for the future. He thought Gregory a fusty, incomprehensible ass, yet used him adroitly in Washington, for he was well aware that his brother "cut a figure" with his elegance and grace and learning and ease in a drawing room. There were die-hard Tories in Washington who still retained great power, and these could be relied upon to succumb to Gregory's charm and breeding and aristocratic traditions. He, Nicholas, had inherited from some obscure ancestor a certain uncouthness of person and speech and manner, a certain brutal forthrightness (which, however, had nothing of honesty in it), and these things were very offensive to the delicate Tories. He used Gregory to placate these Tories, and gloated over his success. Gregory opened doors for him which otherwise would have remained obdurately closed.

Both brothers were bachelors; Nicholas with hints of a dead youthful romance (when speaking to voters of a sentimental turn), and Gregory without any explanation at all. Though neither suspected it, they had one powerful thing in common: a thirst for money and power. Nicholas recognized this in himself, and used every effort to gratify the thirst; Gregory did not recognize it.

Their father had built himself a tremendous stone house with gray square stone pillars on a large rise of ground that, though it was not near the river, did by virtue of its height command a very fine distant view of it. It had gardens and gigantic trees, stables and horses, dogs in profusion, grooms, maidservants, cooks and gardeners. Wings had been added wherever one could be built on without necessitating cutting of trees, and so the house had a rather weird shape without a parallel in geometry. So it happened that the second story of the servants' quarters stared squarely at the first story of the family quarters, due to the fact that the former quarters had had to accommodate itself to a lower level of ground, and because of the proximity of trees, had been added at a right angle. Ivy covered the gray walls in the summer, very impressively, and the trees interlaced over it and about the house, enveloping it in green gloom and slashes of sunlight. It was a house built for many children, and many parties and much gaiety, for the hearths were tremendous, the rooms of a good shape and capacity, the windows large, the gardens, old-fashioned though they were, really beautiful in their informality.

Gregory did not need such a large house and such a retinue of servants, for Nicholas was rarely home. Gregory had only a small and choice circle of friends in Windsor, for he was bitterly exclusive and feudal. However, he would not shut off a single room of the great house nor dismiss one of the horde of servants. His pride lived in every room, walked in every hall. He could not cut it off by so much as a cubbyhole. It was expensive to run, also. Nicholas agreed with his brother, on one of the rare occasions when they did agree, for during the summer he liked to bring (at different times, of course), his Tory Washington friends there to impress them with the order and spaciousness and grace and dignity and fineness which they worshipped, and his more uncouth Democratic colleagues to impress them with his democracy, hospitality, "simplicity of table and countrified life." (No airs, gentlemen, no airs!) When one of his more homespun friends jocosely prophesied that this house would one day be known as a secondary White House, Nicholas protested, but with secret elation.

Gregory despised Nicholas, and Nicholas detested Gregory. Yet the brothers were invariably polite and considerate of each other, respecting each other's privacy of thought and life, listening with apparent deference to each other's opinions. If they argued, they did it coolly and without acrimony. They kept up a tradition between them of brotherly accord and dignity, helped each other, were honest with each other. If necessary, they would have died for each other. For in fundamental things they had much in common, such as their rapacity, disillusion, irony, and hatred for their inferiors.

It was toward this family that Ernest Barbour turned his nineteen-year-old face one fine morning. It was like the turning of the face of destiny, but only Ernest had even the dimmest awareness of this.

George Barbour had done all negotiations with The Sessions Steel

Company himself, and then only through Gregory's assistant, one John Baldwin, a hardbitten and ruthless Man Faithful. George stood in awe of the Sessionses, for they were the feudal family of Windsor, and George had the Englishman's ancient reverence for "gentry" and position. The fame of the family, the fact that Nicholas was a Senator and had been the Mayor, their reputed wealth and seclusiveness and pride, were common talk in Windsor. What the Sessionses did was history, matter for excited talk, even if it were only the purchase of a new carriage or the death or hiring of a servant. Once George, waiting humbly in an anteroom in the Sessions office, had been informed by John Baldwin that Gregory was expected any moment, and George had risen in sheer panic and had fled. Later, he actually did see the great man, who had nodded to him absentmindedly; this nod was enlarged by George into gracious conversation and interest, and not a little flattery. Only his wife, Daisy, believed this, and she was fond of telling her acquaintances for months thereafter that Mr. Gregory had extended a very civil invitation to Mr. George and his family to visit the Sessions home.

Once or twice Joseph Barbour had offered to visit the Sessions factory in George's stead, but this had so horrified his brother that he never again offered it. Had he suggested visiting the King of England George would have thought it hardly more blasphemous.

But Ernest Barbour determined today to visit the Sessions factory.

A lesser young man would have carefully arrayed himself in his best fawn-colored broadcloth coat, his best though most discreetly flowered satin waistcoat, his tightest light pantaloons and shiniest polished boots, would have selected a cane with painful care and tenderly brushed his Sunday "stove-pipe" hat. But Ernest, the frigidly astute, knew better than this. He approached the sooty Sessions factory in his plain dark coat and light brown decent pantaloons and dull boots; he walked in his plainness and respectability with the simplest of dignity and pride. Joseph possessed a sturdy chaise and a smart brown mare now, but even this Ernest did not use. He entered the gritty dimness of the office with an air at once so austere and calm that John Baldwin involuntarily rose to his feet.

"I," said Ernest, looking at him directly, "am Ernest Barbour of Barbour & Bouchard. I should like to speak to Mr. Gregory Sessions."

John Baldwin, as he said later, "was floored." The impudent young pup! he said. And yet, he added, that phrase certainly did not suit young Barbour. He was not impudent; he had stated his name as one would say: I am Bonaparte. Neither was his request impudent; it seemed perfectly natural and proper that such as he should demand audiences with kings. It was true that his features were large and uncompromising rather than refined, and his voice too autocratic and harsh for the graciousness of a born gentleman. But his manner overcame all these, subjugated, for a moment, even John Baldwin. At least that gentleman, without further question, and to his own amazement, found himself announcing Ernest Barbour. Gregory said that he would see the gentleman in a few moments; so John, still under the compulsion of Ernest's will, asked the young man to be seated until Gregory could see him.

Ernest sat down, and with perfect poise looked quietly about him. The room was dim and unaired, and smelled of old papers, dust and mice and coal oil. John Baldwin sat at a splintered desk near the windows, which blazed with the yellow glory of sunlight. Through the golden haze of the glass Ernest could see the swift slope to the river, the bright glitter of the water, the wooden dock that ran out to meet it. A brown flatboat was tied up at the dock and several workmen were rapidly loading ingots and other metal shapes on the broad low deck. From a funnel aft a lazy plume of smoke floated to and fro, seemingly attached to the funnel. There was no foliage in this blasted area, but on the opposite shore the autumn burned in scarlet and bronze and golden trees. Ernest could not see the factory through these windows, for it lay to the side and behind the office, but he could feel and hear its low and steady throbbing and the voices of the men.

The view through the windows was restful and quiet, for all of the pigmy activity of the men on the docks, for the sky was the dark blazing blue of frosty October days, the clouds were extraordinarily pure and white and close, and the river, the same glittering blue as the heavens, carried drowsy flatboats and smaller river craft upon it. But there was no rest in Ernest Barbour, only the repose of one who pauses for a while, grimly, to lay plans and gather strength. He was too discerning and intelligent not to notice the beauty of the river and sky and autumn trees, but this notice had nothing of emotion in it. He appreciated it with his mind, and therefore remained unstirred and untroubled. He was more interested, too, in every detail of the office room, and more acutely in John Baldwin.

He studied that man carefully and thoroughly. John was lean and withered and brown and stringy, but nervously alert. His dark cheeks were sunken and heavily furrowed, his forehead bony, his small bright eyes sunken but agile as a monkey's, his lips splayed and tightened and livid, his nose a prow. He had an extraordinarily large skull, brown and bald, and fringed with a longish edge of black-gray hair, and the effect of this skull, and the shrivelled, sagacious, ruthless face below it was that of a mummy that had come to life. He was only about forty-five, but appeared ageless. He gave the impression of implacable devotion, of an integrity that was not without its malice and its cunning. There was no doubt about his intellect: it showed itself in every deep discolored crease in his face, in the shining gauntness of his immense forehead. A bachelor like his employer, he had dedicated his life to him, not consciously, but because men such as he fasten avidly and immovably on the first object their youth detects. Now he was no longer young, but he clung, and worked as no one else had ever worked for the Sessions Company. He knew the business far better than did Nicholas Sessions, and only a little less than did Gregory. There were no hours too long, no days too tiring, no illness too incapacitating, to cause him to flag. There was less of loyalty in his devotion than egotism.

He did not look through the window with an awakened eye. If he did look, it was with a frown at what he considered the slowness of the workmen. Once or twice he muttered impatiently to himself, shifted his long, cadaverous legs and shuffled his bony feet. The sun blazed on his skull, giving some of its yellowness to it. Then John happened to look up, alertly, to see that Ernest was watching him; he gathered a swift impression that the young man had been so regarding him for a long time. He was annoyed, as if he had been caught partially undressed.

John Baldwin frequently boasted that there was no face that he could not read. But he could not read this quiet and rigid face. It seemed to him that there was no expression whatsoever in those light intent eyes, beyond the mere expression of cold interest. It was like looking at the face of a statue. It gave him, John said later, "quite a turn." His antagonism stirred, and then, amazingly, died away. To his own surprise he felt a sudden surge of interest for the young man, a sudden respect. He was only a beardless brat, after all; but somehow John was not convinced by his own thought. He wetted his lips.

"Fine day," he said.

"Yes. It's getting cool, though," replied Ernest.

"You're English, aren't you?"

"Yes." Ernest smiled. "Any objection to that?"

John's dry mouth twisted. "No. My granddad was an Englishman. Right from the old sod. Baldwin's an old English name. Folks hereabouts don't care much for the English, though. And you can't blame 'em; they never did anything to build up this country, but now they come to grab."

If Ernest was offended he gave no sign of it. He merely listened with that cold interest that had so disconcerted John Baldwin.

"There's lots of building yet to do in this country," he replied after a long pause. "And you mustn't forget that Englishmen were here before your Revolution, and that Englishmen made your Constitution, and that English laws, morals and religion rule your country. In fact," he added, and now he smiled again, coldly, "this is an English country, English language and all. You'll have a lot to be thankful for if only Englishmen come in the future."

John scratched his wiry chin and stared. "Aye!" he exclaimed after a moment, as if struck. "Damned if you're not right! We're already getting in some queer stuff from Europe. But Sessions never will employ such truck. America for Americans. Mr. Gregory says these foreigners are a menace to the country, that they'll make it like ancient Rome, enemies inside the gates. What do you think?"

Ernest frowned slightly. He disliked idle conversation that did not lead to the matter at hand. His mouth jerked with impatience. Nevertheless he replied civilly enough.

"I'm not certain. This country's got to grow. None of us realize its possibilities yet. Look at all the frontiers to the west. Some day they'll be gone, and it'll be one busy nation from coast to coast. But you can't do it on the handful of British descendants you have here, not if every family has ten children. Oh, perhaps you'd do it in a thousand years, but there's something in the air of this country that won't let you wait that long. The air hurries you, makes your blood boil. So, you'll have to call immigrants in, to help you. There's work to do here that your old settlers will soon be too proud to do. You'll have to call in the immigrants, no matter where you get them. Thousands of them; hundreds of thousands of them. To draw your water and cut down your forests and fill your factories. And your cities."

John shook his head ominously. "It'll be a sad day for America."

Again Ernest smiled. He did not answer for a long moment. Then he said: "Cheap labor. That's how we'll grow rich."

"Ah," said John thoughtfully, still staring at him. Ernest held his hat on his knees, sitting upright. He contemplated the scene through the windows so pointedly that John was both irritated and abashed. He was not a loquacious man by nature, and indifferent to the business of other people. But something in Ernest's attitude goaded him, made him force speech.

"So you're the son of Joe Barbour. Never saw him, but heard of him from your uncle, George Barbour." Ernest's eyes for the first time flickered, pointed. Baldwin saw this, gloated a little to himself, though he did not know as yet what had changed Ernest's expression. "You've got a tidy little shop down there, so Mr. Gregory says. You buy a nice piece of our steel. But then, anyone who wants to build a reputation buys our steel. Why haven't you been up here before?"

"There was no need to," answered Ernestly curtly. His pale cheeks had a little dull tinge in them.

"And now there's need, eh?"

Ernest made no reply. He had studied Baldwin and did not underestimate him. He understood him thoroughly. He was annoyed that he found himself wasting time disliking him pointlessly.

The office door opened, and Gregory Sessions called: "Send the young man in, John." Ernest rose, without haste and yet with rapidity, and without a glance at Baldwin went into the inner office.

Gregory, sitting indolently at his wide mahogany desk with his elbows upon it, was slightly surprised at the sight of Ernest. He inclined his thin long head graciously but unsmilingly. Everything about him, Ernest thought, was thin and long and elegant, from his hair, which flowed delicately to his collar and which was faintly waved and gray-touched, to his gaunt, ivory-tinted face and quick, narrow eyes and lips, to his slender pointed fingers and shining, pointed boots. He was dressed in sleek black broadcloth, his broadcloth shirt whitely pleated, his cravat elegantly folded and tied. But what Ernest noticed the most was the fact that even when he was unsmiling his face was carved with lines at once ironical and amused and faintly cruel, and his eyes, sharply blue, were suspicious and cold.

As the young man advanced across the floor toward the desk and an empty waiting chair, he felt vastly relieved. It was as if he had feared something, and finding it non-existent, could breathe more easily and with hope. He had encompassed, within a few seconds, not only Gregory Sessions and his character and possibilities, but the gritty smugness of the office and its air of surety. He knew that the rug under his feet, dusty yet rich, was worn thin, and that if it were not replaced it was not due to poverty but to indifference. Besides, it was the first office he had ever seen that had a rug, and he marked it in his mechanical mind as a very pleasant innovation. He sat down on the chair opposite Gregory Sessions and carefully laid his hat on the desk. The two men, one almost old, the other almost too young, regarded each other gravely.

"Mr. Ernest Barbour, I believe?" asked Gregory at last with elaborate old-fashioned courtesy which even Ernest, the exigent, found agreeable. He could approve of this gracious dallying with unnecessary words, for he felt that Gregory had earned the time for dalliance.

"Yes, I am Ernest Barbour," he answered quietly, looking at the other with his light and steadfast eyes.

Gregory very indolently pushed forward a carved ivory box, long and narrow. "May I offer you one of my Virginia cheroots?" he said indifferently.

"No, thank you. I do not smoke." Ernest modulated his somewhat loud and harsh voice to correspond with the accents that fascinated him. He looked at Gregory earnestly as the latter put a taper in the fire near him and lit a cheroot. "Mr. Sessions, I never waste words. I am here to ask a favor of you."

Gregory raised an eyebrow politely but cynically. That doesn't surprise me, he seemed to think. Nevertheless, he regarded Ernest through the smoke with a well-bred interest.

"The Sessions Steel Company," he said gently, "is always at your service. Barbour-Bouchard, isn't it? A really interesting small firm. It has been my intention to call there soon. I have heard your guns and pistols are singularly fine. I am not a man for firearms, myself, but I have heard reports. Anything I can do——."

"Our gunpowder is still better than our firearms," said Ernest, as if Gregory had not spoken. The faint tinge deepened in his pale cheeks, yet otherwise he showed no agitation. "We haven't developed that fully, due to my Uncle George's—well, carefulness. He started with the firearms, but now we are hoping to develop the gunpowder and a steel bore cannon, breech-loading.

"But I wanted to ask your permission: the Sessions name is famous all over the civilized world for the finest steel. It is like the sterling mark on silver. You have said yourself that our firearms are singularly fine. I now ask your permission to print in small letters on our firearms the legend: 'Made of Sessions Steel.' You will be doing us a tremendous favor, for which we shall always be grateful."

There was a long and pregnant pause. The factory was like deep and throbbing drums through the still air; the sunlight fell into the dusty room, fell over Gregory's head, lay in planes on his carved face like a patina of gold. But Ernest's eyes held Gregory's eyes unswervingly for those endless and fateful moments, held them, commanded them, understood them, allied them with him. Gregory rested his thin long chin negligently on his clasped fingers; he did not move, betrayed no surprise, no wonder, nor, in fact, any emotion whatsoever. He might have been regarding space, for all his expression, instead of a rigid stocky young man in plain and decent clothing, possessing the most rigid and resolute face he had ever seen.

The silence became so prolonged that John Baldwin, who had been listening with unusual curiosity outside the door, ventured to open it a crack and peep in. He saw nothing but his employer and young Barbour sitting there, gazing at each other like basilisks, as if trying to out-stare each other.

Then of a sudden Gregory coughed delicately, and in that cough was a chilly amused sound, as if he had finally seen and understood everything.

"It is I who ought to be grateful," he said gallantly. "You may tell your Uncle, Mr. George Barbour, that I give my full and complete consent to the use of the Sessions name on your firearms. I trust we shall add lustre to each other, as I am sure we must do."

And now he smiled fully into Ernest's face, and Ernest smiled back. When the young man smiled so, there was a singularly radiant quality in his expression, like sun on ice.

"However," continued Gregory softly, ever so softly, "you are no fool, and you know I am no old fool, whatever you thought before you came here. But that was not the real reason, the use of our name, that brought you here. You knew well, damn well, if I may say so, sir, that any firm would be pleased at having its name used on an article of merit. You knew I would give my permission, that if you had written me a simple letter, I would have given my permission.

"And I know that I would underestimate you if I believed that that was the reason you came here. And now, would you mind telling me why you did come?"

Ernest touched his mouth with his hand so that it was partly concealed behind his fingers. He regarded Gregory in silence.

"Of course," said Gregory, smiling his thin, wide smile, "I can see you are very young. In years. But, as I informed you before, I am no fool. I judge no man by his years. I've seen fools in the White House and sages in cradles. Years are nothing. So, I will say nothing about your years except to remark that your Uncle George would not have the vision that I have.

"I saw that gentleman once, only once. But, as I said, he would fix his attention on your years. And the fact that you are his brother's son. So I know well, so very well, that he would not have the audacity even to think of what you have asked me. The idea is yours. And, remembering everything, I can see you have many ideas. I can guess many of them.

"I have only one thing to caution you about: you are not the kind to make mistakes, nor will you be precipitate—however, do not underestimate any one. I hardly think you are likely to do so, but you might. Never eat apples when they are green. But, pshaw, you know all that." He paused. "I am interested. If you have anything to tell me, to ask me, you can be assured of my entire ability to keep the matter confidential." His nostrils dilated a little, and his eyebrows lifted sardonically.

Ernest still kept silent for a long moment. It was not that he was hesitating; Gregory could see that. He was merely marshalling his words into the simplest and most graphic pattern, so that he could speak without confusion. He was not surprised at what might have been considered Gregory's precipitation, his waving aside of formalities and cautiousnesses. His own character, sharp and incisive, brought out these latent characteristics in others. Finally he dropped his hand, and began to speak quietly, and with respect-compelling dignity.

"You are right, Mr. Sessions, sir. I came here for several reasons. I think I can tell you all of them.

"First of all, I wanted to see you. I wanted to talk to you. I had to see the ground. Of course, I know all about the Sessions Company.

That goes without saying. But I wanted to see you. I am satisfied."
(At this, Gregory put his hand swiftly to his mouth to smooth out a
delighted and involuntary smile.) Ernest leaned toward him slightly,
coloring again.

"I know you think what I am saying is presumptuous. But it isn't.
Some day, sir, you will realize that it isn't. In looking over the ground
here I wanted to see if it would be a proper place to advance some of
my ideas. If you had been otherwise than what you are, not receiving
me courteously and civilly, and not understanding everything, I would
have said nothing.

"The time isn't ripe yet for what I have in mind. I am young, I know
that. And you are right about my uncle's opinion of my age. However,
it isn't youth that stands in my way—my father's way—but the fact
that we have little money of our own. My father, who is a great man,
is a lesser partner of my uncle's. My uncle is a cheat: I have allowed
him to go on cheating us, because it would injure my father too much
to know—yet. But my younger brother, Martin, is our clerk, and he
has shown me. I always suspected it.

"It isn't only the cheating. But my uncle isn't interested in what we
want to do. He hasn't allowed us to exploit our gunpowder fully. The
gunpowder, as I said, is far more important than the firearms. My
father and I have ideas for explosives such as the world hasn't seen to
this day. They can't be developed without money; the gunpowder can't
be exploited rightly without money. Neither can it be done while my
uncle is part of our firm. We've got to get him out. We'll get him out.
He doesn't know that we have patented our newest rifles and our gunpowder. I don't suppose he ever heard of patents. We can get him out.
However, he's got fifteen thousand dollars in the business, and has the
land in his name."

"Ah," murmured Gregory negligently. He began to make marks
on a paper with his quill pen; he wanted to escape those resolute eyes for
a few moments. What the devil! he thought. Am I mad to be listening
to this schoolboy chatter? But, by God, is it chatter? I must be dreaming! What does this young devil want? I know damn well what he
wants! The impudence! The effrontery! I ought to kick him out,
wasting my time like this. He looked up at Ernest with a bland smile
at the corners of his mouth. "Go on," he urged gently. He heard himself telling his niece, Amy, of this conversation, saw her lovely, compassionate smile and pretty eyes. Poor girl, she had had so little pleasure
in her life that it pleased him to bring her small and lively tales like gay
little flowers.

"I will bring you copies of our patents," Ernest went on. Behind
Gregory's smile he saw his faint annoyance, his adult incredulity and

amusement. His own face paled, became almost white, and there were bluish lines about his mouth. "You will then see the value of what we have got. I will bring my father. No doubt you think it odd that I have not brought him now, but I must prepare him——."

"For your plan to kick out your Uncle George," interrupted Gregory; his long white teeth glimmered between his spread lips.

"Exactly," replied Ernest, inclining his head without a smile. "He is dead weight on our machinery and our plans. We must get rid of him. But we need money, and prestige. Your money," he said quietly, leaning toward Gregory again, "and your prestige."

He saw the flare of ridicule and amused anger in Gregory's pupils. He clenched his sweating hands, though his face remained calm. Even the astute Gregory did not guess the furious pounding of the boy's heart.

"Your money—and your prestige," repeated Ernest, and now there was something in his voice that made Gregory feel confused and nightmarish, and again, that he was dreaming this whole absurd interview. "Again, you may call me presumptuous and silly, impudent and ridiculous. But you know you will be lying. I am none of these. My father and I have two thousand dollars in this firm. Armand Bouchard has twelve thousand. And the patent on double breech-loading. That is something I induced him to get, just six months ago. I have told Armand about my plans; in fact, he suggested something himself. But he is a Frenchman, and very cautious. He did not believe that you would even see me today, that you would even listen.

"But he promised me, if things went well between you and me today, that he would pull out from my Uncle George and go with us. He has everything to gain. So, all we need is twenty thousand dollars, fifteen thousand to buy out my uncle's share, and five thousand payment on the land. Uncle George paid three thousand on it. We will offer him five."

He stopped, for Gregory had burst out into a loud roar of brutal laughter. He laughed inordinately, throwing his long thin body back in his chair, tossing his head, slapping his gaunt thighs. His face turned crimson; tears stood in his eyes. In his laughter was a contemptuous and malignant sound. "O my God!" he gasped. "O my God! My God!" He shook his head, wiped his eyes with a silken and perfumed kerchief, roared again.

A lesser young man would have risen then with immense dignity and pride, and would have left the room at once. But Ernest did not do this. Gregory's laughter was insulting, but Ernest could overlook such irrelevances as the insult and the laughter. And to him they were indeed irrelevant. So he merely waited, very pale, it is true, but entirely composed and tight-lipped.

Gregory's laughter ceased as abruptly as it had begun, for there had been no real mirth in it, only contempt and impatient anger and ridicule. So now he leaned forward toward Ernest, and the glare in his bright sharp eyes was formidable. But his voice was very soft.

"And is that all, if I may ask—twenty thousand dollars? A mere trifle." You young dog, he added under his breath. "And what security could you offer me for this small sum?"

"Thirty-three and one-third percent of our stock," replied Ernest, through white lips. "You know our product. You will see our patents. I am being generous, for I am desperate. I can't drive hard bargains, yet; you need money to do that. You cannot lose, even if we fail. Property values are increasing all the time. Within ten years the land our factory stands upon will be worth twenty thousand dollars alone, if not more. It runs to Shipman Road, and the railroad will have to cross it.

"I have not come to you without preparation. I have here in my possession two letters, one from the White Gunpowder Company of New York, and the other from the Courtney Explosive Company of Virginia. They both offer us ten thousand dollars outright for our rifle and cannon patents, and five thousand dollars for our gunpowder patent."

Without ostentation, he laid the two letters quietly on the desk before Gregory. All the mirth had suddenly disappeared from the older man's face, leaving it startled and of a somewhat greenish pallor. He stared at Ernest piercingly, caught his lower lip between his teeth. Then he read the letters. He leaned back in his chair, fixedly regarded a spot somewhat to the left of Ernest's ear for a long time. Then still so regarding this spot he asked colorlessly:

"And if your Uncle George will not withdraw?"

Ernest smiled, relaxed. He felt exhausted, but still resolute. He had won! He could feel cold sweat trickling along his spine, and was surprised, by the ache in his muscles, to discover that he had been tense and trembling. There was, too, a faint sickness in the pit of his stomach, and a burning behind his eyes. He had won, but at a cost that even he did not know, and would not know for years.

"He will withdraw," he said in a low and deadly voice. "You see, he is nothing without us. If we are compelled to get out, we will take our patents and our gunpowder. He will have nothing. So, he will take the better part—what we shall offer."

"You young dog," said Gregory, but now he said it aloud. He smiled, but he still did not look directly at Ernest. He seemed a little breathless, and moistened his lips. There was suddenly about him an air of febrile avidity, of one who has seen visions of almost unbelievable things and because of this has been unbearably agitated.

Unnoticed, John Baldwin had crept into the room, and had heard half of this extraordinary interview. It was enough for him. Now he stood by Gregory's elbow, a brown elongated gnome of a man, staring at Ernest.

Ernest stood up. He smiled again, somewhat rigidly. Gregory turned his eyes upon him, and there was a startled expression in them, partly thoughtful and disturbed. Only his mouth remained mechanically cynical.

"Mr. Sessions, sir," said Ernest, "I hope you will consider the matter very carefully. I will bring our patent papers tomorrow. In the meantime, I will draw up our necessary papers and present them for your signature.

"There is but one other thing: your brother, Senator Nicholas Sessions. He is in a position in Washington to help us secure Army contracts.

"I am sure our association will be a profitable one for both of us. I have the honor, sir, to bid you good day."

He bowed neatly and stiffly, like an automaton, and without hurry, and still with that immense dignity, he went out of the room.

After he had gone, Gregory Sessions and John Baldwin stared mutely into each other's eyes for a prolonged moment.

CHAPTER X

IT WAS twilight when Ernest reached Garrison Road. He deliberately
slowed his pace, in order to arrive at the Bouchard house
after Armand. He found it hard to walk slowly, for his thoughts
were like the keen clicking of a rapid machine. There was no confusion in them; part fitted into part, plan into plan. He had taken a
gigantic step; he had more to take. He formulated all these steps incisively, without apprehension, as he walked. He recognized many
difficulties, but he felt instinctively that difficulties must inevitably fall
before will and design. They might annoy, but they could never seriously
delay.

Armand had just come home when Ernest arrived. The little Frenchman lit a pipe calmly, after one look at Ernest's face. His glance had
taken in everything. Madam Bouchard glowered involuntarily at the
young man, but her husband's praises during the past few years had
softened her a little toward Ernest. She had gathered, in her simple
mind, the idea that the fortunes of Barbour and Bouchard lay with
Ernest, and she could force herself to be amiable to one who would make
her fortune. Therefore, after her first instinctive scowl, which Ernest
did not notice, she became very cordial, boomed out an invitation to
supper, which Ernest unexpectedly accepted, absentmindedly, as if he
had accepted in order not to engage in any argument. Raoul and Eugene
had returned with their father. Raoul lounged indolently in the chimney
corner, affectionately teasing his mother and audibly sniffing the bubbling pots. In the firelight his slim dark head was the head of a faun,
with its upward slanting eyebrows and gay and brilliant eyes. He looked
like a courtier, romantic and daring, thought Ernest with disgust.
Eugene, whom he trusted and liked, was absorbed in the task of taking
apart a new type of pistol which a rival concern was making, and as he
delicately removed each part he commented aloud, though no one listened.
He glanced up as Ernest approached the fire, and his usually slightly
lowering but handsome face lightened eagerly, and with affection.
Jacques, still a frail, beautiful-faced saint at twenty, sat in the other
chimney corner, reading. He smiled faintly at Ernest, trying to conceal
his involuntary dislike and distrust. Armand sat before the fire, and as
he had removed his boots and stretched his feet toward the warmth,

the air was pungent with the odor of his sweat, which mingled with the more agreeable smell of brown onion soup and ragout of mutton which were cooking in black iron pots on the fire.

Mama Bouchard, huger than ever, if a little gray, boomed and muttered over her pots, affected to crack Raoul over the head with her ladle, kept glancing absorbedly at Jacques, and stumbled over the swarm of kittens that rolled and scrambled on the hot hearth.

Ernest did not like the Bouchard household. He thought it hot and disorderly and smelly and too noisy. The members seemed to enjoy pointless living, liked to joke boisterously with each other, tease each other, to take an inordinate interest in food and wines and irrelevant comfort. Ernest, who spent his evenings reading everything he could about explosives, firearms, finance, stock markets, commodities, and the history of rival concerns, also concise histories of modern wars and warfare, could not understand how anyone could waste the short hours of life in merely enjoying it. This, to him, seemed the only blasphemy. Therefore, it annoyed him again, as it had done a thousand times, to be received nonchalantly and easily by the Bouchard household, as if he had possibly come for mere desire for their company, for mere pleasure and talk! Only Armand understood.

"Be seated, Ernest," he said gently. Ernest stood, hesitating, looking about him. He distrusted Raoul; he had good reason for that. He could not tell Armand anything with Raoul present. But if he excluded Raoul, even Ernest, who was never polite except when necessary, would have to exclude Eugene. He did not want to do this, for he liked the other youth, and recognized his intelligence; Eugene, too, frequently had clever ideas. But there was no help for it. At the risk of offending Eugene he could not risk any treachery from Raoul. Of course, once Armand was committed to any plan, Raoul would say nothing, but while it was all still in the air Ernest dared not trust him. So he said to Armand in his monotonous and unemotional voice: "I would like to talk to you alone for a few minutes, Armand."

Raoul, who never missed anything, glanced up mischievously from a hungry inspection of the savory pots. His handsome eyes twinkled, his face sparkled with mirthful malice. "What!" he exclaimed portentously. "Are there enemies here?"

Ernest shrugged. He could not meet Eugene's surprised and reproachful eye. "It's not much," he said. "But, as it is a personal matter, I would like to talk to Armand alone."

Jacques, who had not spoken a word, lifted his fair face from his book and regarded Ernest serenely. But Ernest did not look at him. For some obscure reason he feared Jacques, with whom he had not exchanged a hundred words in all the years they had known each other. Jacques annoyed him, but it was also something else.

Armand stood up, diminutive, wry-shouldered and nut-brown of face, and led Ernest into the dank chill of the bedroom that Raoul and Eugene shared. Ernest seated himself on the broad high bed, but Armand sat restlessly on a stool. He waited, smoking. There was only a dim evening light in the room, and the smoke of the pipe circled in it like half-formed ghosts.

"Yes, yes?" said Armand softly.

"I've seen Mr. Gregory Sessions," replied Ernestly abruptly. "It is as I hoped and planned. He is willing."

"Ah," murmured Armand. He made no gesture, but a thrilling alertness sprang from his small body toward Ernest.

"We will hear from him tomorrow. In the morning I am to take the patent papers to him, get his answer. Pa and you, of course, will go with me. I explained everything to him."

"And he has most definitely consented?"

Ernest hesitated for only an instant, but Armand marked it. "Not definitely. But he cannot refuse. Only a madman or an idiot could refuse. He is a greedy man, I could tell that instantly. I could also see that he is dissatisfied, that he will grasp any chance to improve his fortunes. We offer him that chance. He will take it. Nothing could keep him from taking it. I suppose, of course, that he will consult his bank tomorrow. A very cautious man. We will all profit. We can consider it settled."

"You are very sure, my young friend—of everything."

"I never make a move unless I am sure," replied Ernest quietly.

There was a silence, while the smoke rose and drifted. Neither of the men could see the other's face, but they did not need this. Once Armand shook his head in the darkness, half in wonder and amusement, half in gravity. He slipped down from the stool.

"Yes, you are always sure," he said thoughtfully. "It is somewhat bad, always being sure. There is no room for romance there, or enjoyment. Tiens! My remark was foolish. You can see how I trust you when I tell you that I told Martin to take his books home tonight, and be ready for a journey to his uncle's. He looked troubled."

"Martin is a feckless fool!" exclaimed Ernest irritably, making a gesture as though he were brushing aside a fly.

Armand shrugged, spread out his hands. He was standing so close to Ernest that the latter could catch, even in the twilight, the swift gleam of his astute eye.

"Perhaps, perhaps. Who knows? There is scruple there. Even for one such as George Barbour. But your father, our fine Joseph—there will be one to overcome. He must be managed adroitly. Your touch, my young friend, is not always adroit. You prefer the hammer method. Nevertheless, it has its points."

He moved toward the door. "If one is about to guillotine a man, it is most merciful to do it at once, and swiftly. Let us eat our dinner. Afterwards we will proceed to the place of execution."

CHAPTER XI

GEORGE BARBOUR had finally moved over to Oldtown. To be sure, he had been unable to purchase a very desirable spot near the "snobs." His land was on the fringe of town, barely clinging to the end of one of the main streets. But it made up for lack of exclusiveness in the pretentiousness of the house, which was of bright red brick, tall and narrow, with two bay windows, one above another. Everything on the first floor on the outside was iron grillwork and fretwork; the door gleamed with polished brass. Long narrow lawns surrounded the house, well grassed; two iron deer and a faun stood in heroic attitudes near three flower beds. There was a commodious stable in the rear, with two horses and a pony for seventeen-year-old Martha, who liked her two-wheel cart. Daisy Barbour now had three servants, and there was also a gardener.

Joseph Barbour and his family still lived in Newtown, but in a better section. The "barbarians" of Newtown had decided to make an exclusive section of their own, they having come to the final decision that the Oldtowners were definitely not going to admit them to the inner circle even if they moved over to Oldtown. So they made their own society, and becoming richer than many of the Oldtowners, thumbed their noses at the Pharisees. Joseph's house, of course, was neither as rich nor pretentious as his brother's, being a low graystone building of some six rooms, but well built, with a tidy little lawn and a neat garden. Hilda had never dreamt of living in so grand a house, but now it gave her no pleasure. She saw, indeed, how pleasant and secure her life was becoming, how much easier; she saw her closets filling with good linen, her wardrobes with decent and well-made dresses from New York; she was fond of repeating to friends that her husband drove his own carriage. But none of these things were real to her; they were like dreams, without substance, over which she could feel no emotion. She sat at her own table, ordered her household and her one small maid, sewed, knitted, talked, breathed, but without feeling deeply. She lived mechanically, though to the observer's eye she was a plump and handsome woman in her middle thirties, still agreeable to view, and very competent in her black silk dresses and keys. She wore a fine lace cap on her abundant dark hair, which still curled on the thickened nape of her neck; her teeth were white and perfect, and showed in frequent smiles. When she walked briskly through her house her crinolined skirts swayed and billowed and rustled, and her eye was firm and watchful. But inside her, there was still heavy bewilderment and a sluggish pain, which disappeared, and then only temporarily, at the table. All her love for life, her zest, her enjoyment and pleasure, was now centered in food, that solace of the middle-aged. She rarely sprang into angry life as she had done in England; a spoiled dinner caused her ten times the anguish that any crisis in her family could cause her. She had become a trifle bellicose and dogmatic, a petty domestic tyrant not above slapping her two young daughters and her younger son. Once in a great while a dark flame would light up her eyes when she looked at Joseph, but these whiles were becoming rarer and rarer. She consoled her homesickness with geese and dumplings, soups and puddings, jams and sweets.

There was no amity between Hilda and Daisy Barbour. Hilda had no malice, slyness, greed, suspicion nor viciousness. She had simple integrity and honesty, a steadfast attitude toward existence and circumstance. All this did not delude her as to the innate foxiness, stupidity, untrustworthiness and double-dealing of others. Nor was she ready with condemnation. She merely avoided human beings in whom these traits were too obvious, too intolerable. She was terrified of them, blushed uneasily in their presence, stammered, fled. Like her son Martin, they appalled and paralyzed her with an obscure but active fear. So it was that having been disillusioned with regard to George and Daisy Barbour, she avoided them with a sort of terror, shivered behind the curtains on watching them coming up the walk on infrequent visits, had an attack of acute indigestion after dining with them. To her, they smelt dangerous, as they so smelt to Martin. Had they been avowed rogues of majestic accomplishments and large crimes and public acknowledg·ment, it is doubtful if they would have affected her so. Their very vast·ness, in that case, would have obliterated terror. It was the small and secret rogue in them, their hidden but merciless greediness, their small sly eyes, that filled her with mental and physical nausea. She felt like a helpless woman caught in the dark with blood-sucking weasels sniffing invisibly at her heels. Their sniggers, their watchful suspicion, their tight malicious voices, their meaning looks left her staring at them in bewilderment, her heart thumping sickeningly, her throat dry.

Being inarticulate about her emotions, and believing herself silly, she never told any one about this, though Martin would have understood. Had she told Joseph, he would have smiled faintly, and shrugged, admitting her suspicions about his brother and Daisy. Had she told Ernest, he would have grimaced contemptuously, thought her a fool. To him George Barbour was a noxious bug with a nasty bite, that must soon be stepped on and eliminated. As for his aunt, he never saw her except to stare at her with annoyance whenever she spoke in her high and nasal voice. Martha had a chilly and unpleasant effect on all her relatives, even though her character seemed negligible. She was not a talkative young girl, but she had a disagreeable habit of listening to all conversation about her with a slight, knowing smile, as her pale blue eyes slid slowly from one speaker to another. Daisy was determined that her daughter should be a lady, and so Daisy went frequently to Philadelphia to visit friends, and even to New York, now that Windsor had a branch railroad. The girl was dressed elegantly in tilting dresses of the palest blue and pink and green over lace and white satin, and her light yellow hair hung in wooden tubes about her thin, colorless and rather angular cheeks.

It is significant that the George Barbour family made no overtures of great friendliness to any member of the Joseph Barbour family except Ernest. And there was more uneasiness than affection in these overtures. They felt no particular dislike for any other member, either, except Ernest. And him they hated. And abjectly respected. But Ernest was conscious neither of their hate nor friendliness, their uneasiness nor their respect. To him they barely existed, except for the irritation they caused him.

It is also more significant, and instinctive, that both George and Daisy Barbour had come to the decision that Martha must some day marry Ernest. In this way they felt that the future of the business would be made invulnerable, and, too, that they would have nothing more to fear. So it was that Ernest was almost daily besieged with sincere and earnest invitations, that Martha was thrown in his way, where she simpered girlishly, that George slapped him heartily on the back and consulted him, that Daisy beamed upon him and flattered him. Whether he saw and understood these maneuvers cannot be known. It was, however, without a thought or remembrance of them that he walked with his puzzled father to George's house on this night.

He told Joseph so little that it was only Joseph's belief in the young man's integrity and common sense that made the father accompany his son. But this did not allay Joseph's irritation.

"What the devil!" he exclaimed. "This is a rum business, Ernest. You drag me out of the house on a raw night like this on some cock-and-bull story about something important going on at Georgie's." He shivered ostentatiously in his huge warm greatcoat and pulled his high hat down about his ears. He looked younger than Ernest as he walked lightly and swiftly beside him, for he was still slim and agile, still elegant of movement, and graceful. Ernest walked with a certain upright rigidity that was deceivingly mature, and the broadness of his shoulders gave his figure a stockiness that detracted from his height. He walked heavily and quickly, like a man who knows where he is going, and what he is going to do. As he so walked, he kept glancing down at his father, and at these moments the stony harshness of his large features softened ever so little.

"Trust me just a little longer, Pa," he said quietly.

"Damn it, I do trust you, lad!" said Joseph irritably. "But you might give me a hint. What's it all about? Eh? Why don't you tell me?"

Ernest was silent. He knew very well that Joseph would balk violently had he the slightest suspicion, balk sentimentally against his reason. So he said patiently: "I have told you, Pa. Armand and I want to talk over a matter of policy with you and Uncle George. It's in the nature of a surprise. Please wait just a little while. I promised Armand I wouldn't say anything about it until we were all together." Ernest did not wince at all at the lie. Lies, to him, were strong weapons to be used on the necessary occasions.

Joseph snorted, itching with mingled jealousy at his son's implied confidence in Bouchard, and impatience.

"Mystery!" he ejaculated. "Children! I'll bet a sovereign it's some damn foolishness. Why couldn't it wait until tomorrow? And why've you sent young Martin down there with the infernal books?"

Without a pause, Ernest replied smoothly: "It's all about the policy, Pa. We've got to have meetings. We've tried meeting and discussing at the works, but there're so many interruptions and noise, and comings and goings. So Armand and I thought that it would be a fine idea to institute regular meetings between all of us away from the shop. Dignified, and everything. Like other concerns do. Of course, later on, we will have a regular conference room, when we can clean out the trash from another room." (The "other room" was George's present office.)

"Bah!" Joseph was itching worse than ever in his jealousy of Armand. "'Armand and I thought!' I don't suppose I've got the brains to think with you. You and your Armand. I suppose it'll get to the point where you'll retire me, and you and your damned Armand will go on plotting and thinking together. It's been done before by sons," he added darkly.

In the darkness Ernest smiled slightly, and quite involuntarily he took his father's arm in his hand and squeezed it. Joseph was both embarrassed and pleased. To cover this, he grunted, affected to draw away. For some moments they walked side by side, sheepishly. Then Ernest dropped his father's arm and began to talk easily again.

"Perhaps it is all damned foolishness, as you say, Pa. But it's a good idea to begin getting together for discussion. This new policy probably won't meet with your ideas. I'm sure it won't." And again he smiled slightly, and now the smile was grim in the darkness. "That's why I didn't tell you. I wanted you to hear Armand's side, too, before you decide against it."

Joseph felt soothed. He bridled a little. Nothing to worry about. Ernest apparently still felt filial respect, and uncertainty about his youthful ideas. He wanted to bolster them with Armand's arguments. Joseph was flattered, felt paternal and judicious and serious.

"Um," he grunted. "But mind you, lad, if I don't agree it won't do you any good to set Armand onto me, as you seem bent on doing. You might have told me, though."

An actor would have admired the naïve frankness in Ernest's voice as he responded eagerly: "But Pa, I think it's a good idea, and I would have been disappointed had you set your foot down on it without hearing what Armand has to say. If you had set your foot down I wouldn't have gone any further, as you know, and I wouldn't have gotten over it for some time. So, please, when we talk there, be patient, and listen."

Joseph laughed indulgently. He patted Ernest's arm, as he had done when the young man had been a child. "You're still a kid, lad, in spite of your airs. Still afraid of your Pa. God knows why, though," he added, pleased.

And again Ernest smiled palely to himself in the darkness.

A thought struck Joseph. "Say, look here, though. What about Georgie? He's got something to say, y'know. If he don't agree, I'm not sure I will, even if it looks good. He started the thing, and he's got the right to the final word."

"We'll give him," said Ernest softly, "the final word."

"I hope so," growled Joseph. An intelligent man, something in Ernest's voice gave him a quick twinge of apprehension. "I hope so," he repeated more loudly, and there was a sharp question in the words. He tried to see Ernest's face, and for one moment it seemed to him that the young man's profile gleamed in the dusk, white and immovable.

"We'll have some argument with him," admitted Ernest in a candid voice utterly incompatible with that profile. "But, I'm sure he will see reason when we're all against—I mean, we are all in agreement. But, here we are." No one would have guessed from that level tone his relief and the rising of his strength to meet this ominous emergency.

The October night was dark blue velvet against which the huge golden lamp of the moon hung, soft and steady. The air smelled of wood smoke and apples and spicy brown leaves. In the clear and frosty silence the river could be heard, gathering power for the winter, and a wind muttered disturbedly in half-naked trees. It was still very rural and woody around George's house, though distant house lights could be seen through tree trunks. Ernest and his father walked between a row of young poplars to the fretted porches of the high and inhospitable-looking brick house. The parlor lamps were lit, white and a little bleak, as though repudiating the visitors already there, and the curtains were an elaborate frost against the polished windows, the curlicues, touched here and there with a furtive cold glow of a newly lighted fire. Ernest lifted the knocker : the resultant sound, though George Barbour did not yet know it, was the sound of fate.

A trim parlor maid opened the door, neat in her mob cap, white apron and black crinolined skirts. Joseph experienced again the old half-angry, half-subdued squelching he always felt when entering his brother's house. He removed his hat reluctantly, was churlish with the maid when she minced that the gentlemen expected them in the parlor. Joseph followed his son into the vault-like room with its fire snarling grudgingly behind the polish fender, its stiff black furniture with the horsehair seats, its elaborate tables with the India shawls hanging in an attempt of negligence upon them, its globes of glass-enclosed flowers, its sprawling wallpaper of red and immense roses, its hugely flowered thick carpet, its crayon portraits on the walls, its elaborate white curtains which looked as if cut from thick paper, and the polished black glare of a rigid piano between the two high windows. As the room was used only when visitors arrived, the air was chill and repelling, bitterly clean Daisy did not usually open the carved sliding doors for her relatives, and did so tonight only because she was annoyed by their coming and wished to squelch them, remove them from a plane of friendliness. She sat stiffly at one side of the marble fireplace with her daughter, her fat face high-colored and bellicose, her lower lip protruding, her nose lifted, and her eyes pointed. She was short and stout and graying; on her hair she wore a lace cap, and her voluminous gown was a rich dark-red silk. In her ears was a subdued twinkle of diamonds; there were diamonds on her fat red fingers, and a fine chain of gold on her high thick bosom. Martha, mealy-mouthed and slender beside her, kept her pale eyes down, a faint smile on her lips; the wooden yellow curls half hid her cheeks in a very maidenly fashion. Her gown, of pale green silk distended by crinoline, foamed over her white satin skirt; she gazed fixedly at her ankles in their white stockings crossed by the black ribbons of her slippers. George, florid, bluff and aggressive, stood spread-legged with his back to the fire, smoking a rich cigar, his black broadcloth sleek and glossy. He was holding forth loftily and noisily to Martin and Armand. Martin sat in what shadow he could find, a tall and slender youth with his childhood silver-gilt longish hair, his beautiful white-lidded blue eyes fixed on the carpet, his face wearing its usual unhappy expression. On the knees of his light brown pantaloons lay the slim black office books To all appearances he was a painted statue, as removed from this room and its inhabitants as though he were in a trance. Armand, nut-brown and furrowed, sat in his dark brown homespun, smoking, a wry-mouthed gnome who listened, nodded, grimaced a little to himself. His pipe was odorous, the smoke like clouds. Daisy looked at him pointedly, almost viciously, then glanced at her curtains; he appeared to notice nothing. Martha sneezed delicately: Armand listened imperturbably to George. Martha waved her wisp of cambric handkerchief and a vapor of scent rose from it. As Ernest entered the room her thin cheeks flushed and she became visibly tremulous. Daisy smiled, thawed, rose and bustled forward. Ernest bowed stiffly, turned his shoulder to her and addressed Armand:

"Here we are," he said, and smiled. Armand raised his brows, removed his pipe from his mouth. Ernest did not even glance at his cousin. Upon entering the room he had dominated it, so that all the other occupants appeared to have been pushed toward the wall, leaving about him a space vibrant with power and resolution. His rudeness to his aunt nonplussed her, and she stood near him, blinking. Joseph felt a sudden anger against his son, a compassion for Daisy. He addressed her in a kindly, almost affectionate voice; she did not move her face from Ernest's direction, but her gooseberry eyes slid in their sockets and glared petrifyingly upon him. Martin glanced up languidly, and then with a startled expression he concentrated upon his brother as though he had turned suddenly into something affrighting; his whole slender body tensed in the chair.

"Well, here we are," repeated Joseph surlily, shaken by his sister-in-law's repudiation of him, angered anew at this silly mystery. "Now, dash it, what are we here for, anyway?"

"I'm sure," said George contemptuously, shrugging, "it's as big a secret to me as it seems to be to you. All I know is, Joe, that your lad here, Martin, knocks on my door, and acts like a white bunny, and tells me, half-swooning like a lass, that Armand told him to be here at half past seven. So, in he comes, and then Armand comes. And now you and Ernest. It's a rum business."

Ernest had smiled acridly and involuntarily at his uncle's description of Martin, which seemed to him very apt, and then immediately became impassive again.

"Yes, it's a rum business," agreed Joseph with asperity. He sat down gingerly in an elaborate gilt chair behind Martin. He glared irately at Ernest over his shoulder. "Come on, come on! What is it, what is it? Here we are. Open your mouth and stop looking like a bloody hangman!"

Ernest, unmoved, glanced at his aunt and cousin. "I don't think we need the ladies here," he said quietly. "We have business to talk."

"Well, I must say!" exclaimed Martha, jarred from her maidenly pose.

"La!" ejaculated Daisy, who retained many old-fashioned expressions.

George crudely waved his hand dismissingly at his wife and daughter. "Go along with you," he said curtly. "Business is not for women." He was consumed with curiosity; he did not underestimate Ernest. He turned to him in a friendly manner as the ladies rose in a flutter of scent and silk and bosoms, tossing their heads, and left the room. "What is it, lad? Something important?"

"Yes." Ernest regarded him steadfastly. "Very important. I don't think we need to waste time." He turned to Martin. "Martin, open your book to the January entry. The Trenton account."

George stared. His florid face paled a trifle, and his eyes bulged. He removed his cigar from his mouth. Armand tranquilly renewed his smoking, and Joseph blinked his eyes, puzzled and annoyed. Martin, whose fine white hands shook a little, opened a thin book. "Yes," he murmured, without looking at his brother.

Ernest's voice was smooth and urbane as cream. "Tell me, Martin, what is entered there as their paid bill for the last six months before January?"

"Two thousand four hundred seventy six dollars." Martin's words could hardly be heard. A blue vein protruded and throbbed in his delicate white forehead.

"Look here!" began Joseph irately. Ernest lifted his hand without turning to his father or removing his eyes from Martin, and Joseph immediately became silent. He turned in his chair to his brother and was amazed at George's color.

"Two thousand four hundred seventy-six dollars," repeated Ernest softly, almost dreamily. Suddenly his face sharpened, and his voice rang out: "And now, Martin, tell us of the letter you found the other day from the Trenton people, dated six months ago, in which they mention enclosing a draft for two thousand seven hundred and six dollars, in payment of their account."

Martin swallowed visibly, and a febrile tint sprang into his face. He stared at Ernest as if all his will power could not drag his eyes away.

"It's true," he said tremulously. "But there must have been some mistake. It was only that once, after all. It must have been a mistake. I know what you are trying to prove, Ernest, but it was all a mistake."

Joseph looked from George to Armand. But Armand did not return his look. He was intent upon George, who was wetting his livid lips and regarding Ernest murderously. He visibly struggled for breath, his broad chest panting. He clenched hands that were wet and icy cold. His breath, as he exhaled, was almost a groan. When he could finally speak his voice was hoarse.

"You filthy young dog! I see what you're after, curse you. Of course it was a mistake. A mistake, damn you! I've made it up a thousand times. I've——"

Joseph jumped up. He was pale and a little sick. He seized Ernest by the arm, but he might have seized an arm of stone. "What are you trying to say? What is this? Speak up, or I'll cut your throat, even if you are my son. I'll give you a hiding you'll never get over, big as you are!"

Armand smoked placidly, not moving, not speaking. Ernest waited. He was smiling a little, very fixedly. He waited until his father's uproar subsided. Joseph still clutched his arm, but he did not turn to his father. He still faced his uncle.

"You bank all drafts," he said relentlessly. "At the end of each day you give Martin figures of drafts received, which he enters in the ledger. I've always thought it a trifle unbusiness-like and irregular. But no matter. Naturally, we trusted you. It would never have occurred to us not to." He put his hand into an inner pocket and produced a letter. George snatched at it involuntarily, but Ernest adroitly put it behind his back. "Martin found this letter from the Trenton people some time ago, in your desk, the day you were ill, and he was looking for some office paper. It was very careless of you, Uncle George. Martin was puzzled a bit, for the amount mentioned in the letter was not the amount recorded in the books. He thought he had made some mistake, and showed me the letter. He was too innocent to know what it meant. But he never," added Ernest gently, "makes mistakes in unimportant things. I knew exactly what it meant."

A thick silence followed his words. George's face swelled duskily; he made a strangled sound, thrust his finger between his neck and his cravat. Joseph, standing behind Ernest, put his hand to a wet forehead, and his face was haggard. But still Armand did not move; he seemed only mildly interested. Martin found himself unable to look at any of them, and regarded the floor despondently.

Finally George spoke again, in a dwindled and smothered voice. His eyes were glaucous and staring. He looked at Ernest with hate and fury, but he spoke to his brother and Armand.

"Joe, and Armand—you can't believe I'd rob the Company, whatever this bastard says. This viper! This bloody dog! Why, my God! I've built it up. It's mine! I've built it up." His rage suddenly inundated him like a flood, in which he struggled and drowned. "If you believe this, if you can believe this dog, you can all bloody well get out! Out! Out!" His voice rose to a shriek. He struck his breast repeatedly with his great clenched fist, glared at them all with eyes swimming in scarlet. His forehead was dark purple.

Joseph and Martin were appalled at these demonstrations. Martin got up, and going behind his chair as behind a shelter, he clutched it convulsively.

"My God!" cried Joseph, "I never thought a son of mine—, I can't believe it. It—it's hellish. A mistake. What've you got up your sleeve, you devil? Something told me for years—. Damn you, speak up! O my God!" groaned the poor man, sinking into his chair and rubbing his wet forehead with the back of his hand. For the first time Armand moved, regarded Joseph with impersonal and very odd compassion, then again fixed his attention upon Ernest, who stood in rigid silence, waiting. Always waiting. And looking at no one but his uncle. The fire flared up, roared. George's dog, shut out, howled in the darkness.

After a long time George seemed to regain his composure. A thought must have flashed through his mind, for of a sudden the purple began to recede from his face, his eye gleamed malevolently; to everyone's amazement he even smiled. He took a step toward Ernest, one hand clenched into a battering fist, the other hand raised and pointing at the youth.

"I've been testing you just now, you blasted pup. I've been testing you! Oh, it's all right, Joe, it's all right! Let me finish; let me put him in his place, before I bash him in the jaw.

"So you found that letter, did you, you sneak and thief! Well, I'll explain it! I never thought I'd have to, to be shamed and mocked this way. But I'll explain it. That extra money you dare to tell me I stole: know what it was? Commission quietly paid to an agent, a sales chap of the Trenton people!"

He allowed this to penetrate into the consciousness of his audience, the while he glowered at them triumphantly, waited for their grovelling. Joe looked at him in pleading and stricken silence, as did Martin. Ernest waited, unmoved, expressionless; Armand merely waited.

George laughed, shortly and hoarsely, nodded his head fiercely. "I thought that would take the wind from your blasted sails! Commission! You know how we worked for years to get the Trenton trade, and all of a sudden we got it. I got it! By paying Henderson, their agent, a commission—the difference. And by God, I'll go on paying him commission if I have to, just to get their trade!

"And—another thing: any damned one of you can write to any of our customers, ask them—compare their drafts with my entries in the books. And then, show me one penny difference, and by God! I'll leave the whole works in your hands! I'll get out! Give it to you, outright."

He turned to Ernest menacingly, but Ernest's expression was one of tired indifference. Joseph stood up again, stood shaking his head. He looked wizened.

"Say no more, Georgie. It ain't necessary. I'll take the lads home. I'll—I'll make it up to you—someway. I don't know how: it seems to me as if nothing I can ever do will repay you for all this. Ernest—I don't know what got into him. I never would have believed it—. My son. I know he's always had it in for you for nothing at all, and in spite of all your kindness to him. I can see, now, that he's been waiting———."

He stopped. Ernest had turned to him quietly and firmly. The youth's face was almost pitiful, Armand noticed with edified surprise. The hard young eye, so like glittering agate, softened unbelievably.

"Yes, Pa, I've been waiting," he said gently. "I've been waiting to prove to you what a cad and a thief and a rascal your brother is." Again his face became harsh and cruel; he swung upon George, who was advancing upon him. He thrust out his hand, and George stopped abruptly in his tracks. "Rotter!" exclaimed Ernest. "I knew you would lie out of this! Or try to. But you can't! I knew you'd cover your tracks. But explain this!

"When I found that letter I knew it was true what I had always thought of you. I just wondered how far you had gone. So I wrote quietly to nearly all our customers, and asked what they had paid for various shipments."

George's mouth fell open as he stood there. Suddenly he looked broken and ill, and murderously desperate. A white grin flashed across Ernest's face. George caught the back of a chair.

"I found something I didn't expect!" cried the young man. "I did expect to find a difference in price, like this letter. But I didn't! You had covered your tracks. Everything was in order, there!

"But I found something else! Our customers, one and all, mentioned one shipment in every five of which there was no office record, but for which they had paid! In personal drafts to you, my Uncle George." His voice dropped, became soft, almost whispering.

"God!" cried Joseph once, shortly and sharply. Then, dully, brokenly: "I don't believe it! Dear Jesus, I don't believe it!"

Ernest swung on him. "Ask him!" he shouted. "Ask him! Ask him about the nights he stayed down here, to 'finish up work!' Ask Gordon, the foreman, who was in it with him, and who only confessed to me when I threatened him with the police! Ask Gordon! He's ready and willing to tell everything he knows. Gordon's down at Armand's house now, waiting. I would have brought him, but that would have given the game away at the start, and I wanted you, Pa, to see for yourself what kind of a scoundred your brother is, God damn him!"

Emotion in Ernest was so rare, so almost unknown, that this sudden blazing rage of his, his suddenly raised voice, his fierce gestures, had an appalling and arresting effect on his audience. They all stared at him, even George. On the latter's purple lips blood appeared as he chewed his tongue. Joseph swallowed, retched a little, convulsively, swallowed again. He closed his eyes. Martin averted his head, shuddered, then stared at Ernest, fascinated. His gentle mouth trembled, his eyes filled with reproach. Only Armand sat without emotion.

Joseph stirred. He held out his hand to his son. "Ernest," he almost whimpered, "why didn't you tell me—at the start? It would have saved all this.

"Suppose he did steal? Better men than he have done it. And after all, he started our shop; in a way, it's his. Oh, I'm not covering him up, excusing him. But you might have told me.

"I know you, son," he added after a moment, his voice weak and trembling. "I know you. You had something in mind. Out with it! You want something. What is it? You staged all this to get something. And it ain't what it appears to be. What do you want?"

Again an expression of compassion flickered on Ernest's face. That compassion almost undid him, ruined everything he had worked for. Then he stiffened himself. Only Armand saw him stealthily angling for position, and he watched him in utter but ironical admiration.

"I only wanted to show you what he is, Pa," replied Ernest, slowly and gently, his eyes abstracted as he maneuvered. He had it! George had been smashed into silence, into immobility, as he chewed his tongue and flecked his lips with blood, as the congestion rose in his veins. It was not Ernest's desire nor plan that his uncle remain silent. It was his plan to force George's hand, to make him bring ruin down upon himself. Silence was George's refuge, but he did not know it. He knew it later, when it was too late. He knew then, bitterly, savagely, that had he remained silent Joseph would have championed him, that in some difficult and tortuous way, things would have been adjusted. He knew, too, saw, that Ernest had forced him along, had broken his silence deliberately. If he had only remained silent, allowed Joseph to help him!

Ernest approached him a step, faced him without bravado, but with contempt, goading him.

"You called me a thief! You, robber that you are! You, who stole your brother's brains, sold them for your own private pocket. Robbed him! Robbed all of us, of our life and our time and our work! So you could cut a figure, move over among your betters, look down your nose at us, you, who aren't fit to lick my father's boots!

"But your names don't hurt! We know what you are! And we'll let the whole bloody town know. See then what'll happen to you!"

He succeeded. For one moment he feared that he had not, for George remained silent under the lashing. Then he sprang into action. He swung upon Ernest with his fist; Ernest dodged, laughing scornfully. Then George was beside himself. He turned blind; he foamed at the mouth, he gibbered, swung his arms impotently, screamed.

"Get out! All of you! Out of my house, out of my shop! You're finished! I've got what I wanted from you, all of you, and now, out you go, with my foot on your backside!

"If you show your damned faces near me again, I'll have the police on you! Gallows dogs! That's where you belong, all of you, on the gallows!"

He gloated over them, appallingly, murderously. He shrieked with triumphant and malignant mirth. The Day! It had arrived.

"I've waited for this, you bastards, I've waited for this! To put you in your places, to put my foot on your necks. Your brains! Why damn you all, damn your black hearts, your brains were only made for men like me to take and get fat on! I've waited for this day, counted on it, struggled for it. And now it's here. Now!

"Out, out, all of you! With just the shirts on your backs. Back to the gutter, where you started from! I've got everything. Look at it, everything! And what have you? Nothing. Bloody beggars. Get out!"

Ernest listened, drinking it in, smiling. He was white with exhaustion. But he had won. Again. He turned to his father. Joseph listened, unbelieving, to this vicious and savage tirade, to this self-exposure of his brother. And gradually, as he listened, his slender and handsome face hardened and tightened, became thin and almost cruel. His white lips were a slit, without mercy. Only Martin stared at George compassionately, his mouth moving as he silently implored his uncle to be still. He, too, besides Armand, saw what was happening, saw what Ernest was doing.

"You see, Pa," said Ernest mildly, after George had panted into silence. "You see what he is." He regarded George steadfastly. "You've said your say. Now, I'll say mine. And you'd better listen, very, very carefully.

"You tell us to get out. We will. We're glad to. We wouldn't stay, after tonight.

"But, we are going with our brains. You haven't eaten them, though you tried to. For, my dear uncle, you see: we patented our brains!

"Didn't you ever hear of patents? I'll send you a little book on them in the morning. You'll understand then. Oh, you do understand? I thought you did. That makes things easier all around, for all of us. Well! We've got patents, for our gunpowder, our guns, our cannon, our explosives. For everything. And what have you got? Nothing. Nothing but the bare walls of your factory.

"And Armand's got twelve thousand in that, and Pa's got something, too. So, all in all, it appears that you have very little, and it is *we* who have everything. Of course, it was a slight mistake on your part, but I can see by your face that you understand now."

He paused. George looked from one to the other, his head lowered, his eyes wild and hunted. "You dogs," he whimpered, strangled. "You dogs."

No one spoke for a little while. George sat down slowly and heavily, as though his whole body ached intolerably after crushing blows; he sat with his knees astraddle, his head bent forward on his bull-neck, his eyes suffused with blood and exhausted fury, his fists clenched on his knees. There was no shame in his attitude, no attempt to flee to cover, to defend, to explain. He could no longer curse. There was about him the malignancy, the savagery, the brutal lust for vengeance, of some cornered and powerful beast. He looked upon his brother and his nephews, upon Armand Bouchard, with monstrous loathing and detestation and bitter rage. Martin felt shame for his uncle and compassion; he was also distressedly puzzled: he had seen so many people like this, who, cornered in shameful proceedings and guilt, felt neither guilt nor shame but only rage and hate for their uncoverers. He wanted his uncle to show remorse; he felt instinctively that should he do so Joseph even at this moment might champion him a little, might save him from the ruin to which Ernest was inexorably pushing him.

Martin glanced at his father's averted face, at Armand, still unmoved, at Ernest, possessed and implacable. He wanted to say something, to strike a sound into that petrifaction of sound; he felt that every moment he did not speak pushed his uncle down beyond recall. But he could not speak: something emanated from his brother that held all dangerous interruption in a sort of commanded enchantment, that held even unruly emotion pointed in the direction of his purpose. He held everyone inert, unmoving, dissolved of will to do anything irrelevant and merciful.

Finally George spoke, not in a beaten voice, but in a hoarse one of hate and contempt:

"All right. All right. You have me. I could say a lot, but I'm not going to. There's no use trying to talk to bloody bounders like you. What are you going to do? What can you do?"

Everyone relaxed with a faint sound like sighing. Ernest sat down, purposeful and relentless. He addressed his uncle coolly and calmly, as though a casual discussion were under way.

"You have fifteen thousand dollars in this shop. Besides that, you have allowed yourself a salary of nearly two thousand dollars a year. And in addition to that salary your larcenies have amounted to eight thousand to ten thousand dollars. I haven't finished my checking yet, but I will have all the figures tomorrow.

"We are willing to return to you your fifteen thousand dollars over a period of three years, and two thousand dollars extra thrown in for sentimental reasons." He smiled faintly.

George broke. His face swelled to alarming proportions, became purple. Suddenly tears brimmed into his starting and reddened eyes. His thick lips shook.

"My God!" he whispered, looking from one to the other, now, as a man looks upon his executioners. "Seventeen thousand dollars! It's all my work, all my effort, all the years I nearly starved and worked to the bone—. Everything I ever had. I—I planned this for years. It's all I ever had. Everything I built up—." His voice tightened, dwindled. He sobbed sharply, only once, then covered his face with his thick and trembling hands.

Had he mentioned his wife and daughter, Ernest would have despised him completely, might even have withdrawn the "sentimental reasons." But George was sincere; he was utterly undone, utterly broken. Joseph could not endure it. His white face became gray, and twitched. He glanced, not at Armand or Ernest, but at Martin. And Martin looked back at him, distraught with pity. Reinforced by his son's expression, Joseph spoke up in a sickening silence:

"Look here, that's too bad. Seventeen thousand dollars. That's not enough. Seventeen thousand dollars, yes. But say a percentage of the stock. A percentage of the stock," he repeated, turning to Ernest almost imploringly.

"No," said Ernest lightly.

Joseph whipped himself into one of his sudden and volatile rages.

"Damn you!" he shouted. "Who are you anyway, you whipper-snapper, with your sneakings and pointings and your airs? God, I'm not saying you haven't done us all a big service, finding out about—about the losses. But after all, you're not God Almighty. There's others here with things to say. And I say——."

He stopped abruptly, tense though he was with fury. For Armand, small and brown and potent, had stood up with his pipe in his hand, and was regarding them all with his small bright eyes, which were calm and intent and a trifle ironical.

"You are correct, my Joseph," he said in his sharp, accented voice. "Truly correct. There are indeed others here with things to say. And I am one of them.

"This is not an hour for sentimentality. This is the time for reason and logic. You have heard it in the voice of your estimable son. But, you have not heard it with your mind. I must repeat it myself.

"Ernest has given you all a small outline of the whole matter. You may have the details and figures whenever you so desire. And I say now, I, who hold several of the patents and twelve thousand dollars in our Company, that it must be as he says: this man must go." And without looking at George, he pointed the stem of his pipe at him, meanwhile

fixing his gaze intently on Joseph. Joseph, nonplussed, faintly bluster-
ing, turned scarlet with impotence.

"I was not in favor at all of the seventeen thousand dollars," continued Armand easily and softly. "That is a lot of money—for a thief.
He has betrayed all of us. Were he not your brother, my Joseph, but
a mere partner in business, I am certain that you would join with us in
turning him over to justice in the hands of the police. For what he has
done there is a penalty of some ten to twenty years. The law does not
look kindly on larceny.

"However, Ernest and I have decided to be kind, to refund to this
man, this betrayer of his brother and his nephews and his friend, his
original investment and two thousand dollars extra. But there is a condition that Ernest did not mention, but which I will now take the liberty
of saying: For this consideration, and also for the consideration of not
prosecuting him as a thief, he must leave this country, and this within
fifteen days. Otherwise, we withdraw our offer, and prosecute."

"Curse you!" screamed Joseph. "This man is my brother!"

"Do not," implored Armand in a pained voice, "insult my intelligence
any longer, Joseph. I am not a patient man.

"I detest coercion. I left my beloved country because I would not
submit to coercion. But, in the name of reason, and your own interest,
I must coerce you. If this man does not agree to our terms, I not only
withdraw from the Company, but I seek a warrant for his arrest immediately."

Joseph was silent for a long time. He looked from Armand's imperturbable face to Ernest's cold and implacable one. Then he said bitterly
to his son: "I don't understand this. You are my flesh and blood." A
faint flicker passed over Ernest's face. Joseph waited, but Ernest did
not speak. The father sighed and continued: "They say blood is thicker
than water. Not in your case, Ernest. You seem to hate everything that
shares blood with you. You hate your brother, Martin; you dislike your
sisters. Perhaps, some day, you'll hate me, too. Some day," he said,
in a raised and slightly hysterical voice, "you'll do this to me, as you did
it to him."

"You are a fool," interrupted Armand serenely.

Joseph turned to his brother. "Look 'ee, Georgie," he said in a gentle
and cajoling voice such as one uses to a child one considers too severely
punished: "I've got three thousand dollars put by. It's yours. You can
have it. Why, twenty thousand dollars, four thousand pounds, is a
fortune, man! Buck up. Go back to old England, and enjoy yourself.
It's a fortune!"

"That three thousand dollars is also mine," said Ernest. "I object
to my money being turned over to a thief. I refuse to allow it."

Joseph grimaced at him contemptuously. "I have you there, my fine lad! You are not yet twenty-one. What is yours is mine. You are not a man yet."

Ernest, taken unawares, glared with sudden whiteness upon his father. And again Armand interposed, smoothly: "I, too, refuse to allow it. I know I have no authority over your son, my Joseph, but I understand justice. This son of yours has worked beyond the strength of other young men for this money. You shall not defraud him. No, you shall not." He turned to Ernest, whose lips, very pale, were amazingly trembling. "If you are robbed, mon petit, come to old Armand and we shall put this rascal behind the bars."

He picked up his shabby and somewhat grotesque hat. It was too big, apparently, for his wizened body, though his head filled it. He put it on; he was a gnome under a giant's hat. His black hair stuck in oily long strands about his brown, seamed cheeks; his black eyes glittered under the brim. Despite the hat, despite the too-large clothing, the big boots, he looked like a jaunty elf. He made the stupefied company an elaborate bow.

"With all regret, I must leave you. I hope you will not be too hasty, nor too sentimental, my Joseph. I have said my say. I do not change the mind. You will express my regrets to Madam Barbour, my good Monsieur, that I cannot remain even to say good night to her."

And he went out, serene, wizened and small. A moment later Ernest picked up his hat from a carved walnut table, and without glancing at his brother or his father or his uncle, he followed Armand. He found the little Frenchman sauntering easily down the flagged avenue between the naked elms. The bright yellow moon was caught in their branches, was criss-crossed by their black twigs into diamonds and triangles. The air was very cold and still. Ernest walked in silence beside his friend, unable to speak, and Armand hummed to himself.

Finally Armand said, as casually as though discussing the night:

"You have done well, my young friend. Very well. But be careful that some day you do not do too well."

.CHAPTER XII

WITHIN FORTY-EIGHT hours the whole story, liberally garnished, was told over all of Newtown, and a great part of Oldtown, that part that was interested. It was very mysterious, for certainly none of the Barbours talked, least of all George and Daisy, who were crushed under the fall of their fortunes and the family dishonor. Nevertheless, the story got about like fire burning in brush. Somehow, little was said of Joseph's and Armand's part in the affair; everything was Ernest. Men like Ernest are little loved in a world that prefers simplicity and ease, and chooses conservative paths that are not full of exigencies and immediacy and ambition. His very presence made the easy uneasy, the languid conscious of their futile languor, the inadequate aware of their inadequacy. He made the philosophy of both the simple and the complex mere cowardice, mere excuses for incompetence. Worst of all he made the stupid less complacent, less proud of their stupidity. In all the town he had but three friends: his father, Armand and Eugene Bouchard. Of Armand, the astute, Ernest was not too sure.

Therefore, the story did not endow him with a halo of virtue. Eventually even a number of the intelligent, who had despised George Barbour, came to believe that Ernest had actually robbed his uncle, cornered him in a false position, beaten him out of his property and his rights. They hated him with renewed strength, for they feared him, but their reluctant and secret respect for him grew.

When Gregory Sessions heard the story, he called in John Baldwin and told him. The men smiled slyly and grimly at each other. Gregory shook his head, his smile becoming broader. "We were not mistaken in the young man, eh, John? It was a good thing? He will go far. We might as well go with him, especially as he has invited us."

Within a short time the town had another story to electrify it. The Sessions Steel Company had "gone in" with the upstart Barbour & Bouchard. The new rifles and pistols, sleek and black and polished to the envy of those who did not possess them, had tiny letters cast upon them: "B&B. Made of Sessions Steel." The words were an accolade.

It was not long thereafter that the foundry was enlarged and twenty more men, in addition to the regular fifteen, were put on. New machinery, strange and outlandish-looking, was shipped in from Pittsburgh. It made a prodigious noise, and the men declared that it was "better'n human." A new wharf was built near the old one, and sometimes the flatboats stood in line waiting for the cargo of boxes and barrels that were trundled out from the foundry. Barbour & Bouchard now owned the largest "works" in Windsor. Neat advertisements of their products were inserted in large city newspapers, and publications that found their way into the remotest country regions carried dignified engravings and measured eulogies of the new rifles and the "improved" gunpowder. Ernest wrote the advertisements himself; he was almost a pioneer in this art. He conceived a brilliant idea, probably the first of its kind: to every private purchaser by mail of the Golden Quality Hunting Rifle there was forwarded "free, without charge or cost," the choice of a silver-plated watch or "an elegant mantel clock which chimes the hour musically." He had negotiated for the purchase of these articles when he accidentally read in a Philadelphia newspaper of the bankruptcy of a manufacturer of them. The success of his venture was astounding. However, after he had secured sufficient funds to allow of additional machinery, he abandoned the premiums. He used undignified means to an end; but the end secured, the dignity was resumed.

One day in that year, he received a visit from an extraordinarily swarthy but elegant gentleman, who had something vaguely Spanish in his features, which were, however, of an odd mahogany shade. Ernest had appropriated to himself George's office, and he handled all visitors, all solicitors, salesmen and private purchasers. Upon the entry of his visitor, this swarthy and elegant gentleman, he became alert. He closed the door behind the gentleman with unusual courtesy, bowed him to a seat, and carefully closed the window, though the spring air was warm. He kept a special tin box of good cigars for callers of the highest grade and elegance, and instinctively he produced this box and laid it upon his desk. The gentleman, having seated himself, sat rigidly with an almost military dignity, though his clothing was of the finest broadcloth and his cravat of hand-brocaded silk. He had laid his hat upon the desk, and it glimmered sleekly. A perfume, delicate and subtle, wafted from his kerchief as he daintily blew his nose, yet this did not offend Ernest, nor did the hands, golden and effeminate though they were, and loaded with flashing rings, outrage his sense of propriety. He merely waited gravely and attentively for the caller to speak, fixing his gaze on the still youthful face, the brilliant and swimming black eyes and the glittering white teeth.

The gentleman laid his card on the desk before Ernest. "Señor Emanuel Cardonova," was printed upon it in the finest hand-printing, full of curlicues and flourishes. Ernest read it, looked up attentively. The visitor smiled, and there was something so charming in that smile that Ernest smiled back, quickly.

"What can I do for you, sir," he asked. He had hesitated before the "sir," then had decided not to risk the pronunciation of "Señor," in view of the peculiar little wavy mark above the "n."

"I can speak, I presume, in the greatest secrecy, in confidence?" asked Señor Cardonova in a voice like liquid gold, rich and soft. His words were heavily accented, as though covered with velvet.

"I can assure you," said Ernest weightily, "that anything you wish to say will not travel beyond these doors." And he regarded the other man with a firm and resolute eye.

Señor Cardonova smiled just a little, but there was that in the smile which made Ernest's cheek flush ever so slightly. The visitor leaned toward him.

"I have no choice but to trust you, Señor Barbour," he said gently. "It is possible for you to betray me, either now or—later. I have no redress." He paused, smiled more charmingly. "Perhaps," he added. The swimming light in his eye crystallized, became a shining coldness. "Therefore, Señor, I am at your mercy. You have but to accept, or to reject. If you accept, you will profit richly. If you reject, we part like honorable men, with mutual expression of regard, and forget we have met."

"Suppose," suggested Ernest quietly, "that we come to the point."

Señor Cardonova lifted his beautiful hands in an expressive gesture. "You Americans! How precipitate! But you are entirely correct. I will come, as you say, to the point.

"I am from Mexico, Señor." He waited; Ernest's eyes narrowed just a trifle, then became blank again. "You are not too surprised? No, it is not so.

"Señor Barbour, there is a faction in Mexico that is very rich. But it has few guns, little gunpowder. It is a faction that has been vilely insulted and attacked. I need not say how, or by whom. Territory has been torn from my country, unjustly."

There was a long pause, thick and heavy. Ernest's expression did not change except for a slow and deliberate compression of his lips. He still regarded his visitor steadily.

"Not only that," went on the Mexican gentleman, "but my country is in chaos. Our faction desires to control, subdue it, whip it into order and civilization. Our population is strangely mixed: barbarians and Indians and Spaniards. It must be made one, the banditry subdued, law and dignity brought about. For many things, therefore, do we need guns and gunpowder, and ten good cannon."

Ernest swung about in his chair, one strong hand clenched upon his desk, his eyes staring through the window that looked down to the river. His face was like moulded iron. It was youthful, but not young. It had never been young.

"What made you think we could do this?" he asked in his low and monotonous voice. "What made you think we would do this?"

"I did not know, for certain," replied Cardonova softly. "I have merely tried. You have competitors, yes, much larger people. But what they made is not good enough for us. We need the best, guns that will not fail, gunpowder that will fire, cannon that will accomplish. All these things you can give us."

Ernest still stared through the window. He was very pale. "Let me see your credentials," he said, without looking at the other man.

"But with pleasure," murmured the Mexican. He lifted a small black bag he had brought in with him, and which he had laid on the floor between his feet. He opened it, laid upon the desk sealed documents and papers. And quite incidentally he laid beside them a well-loaded, well-polished pistol, which Ernest immediately detected as having been made by Barbour & Bouchard. His mouth twitched for an instant. He lifted the papers, read them carefully, kept glancing up from them to observe the Mexican's serene and smiling face. Then he thrust them back.

"I am promising nothing," he said abruptly. "But, what do you need?"

"Ten thousand rifles, two thousand kegs of gunpowder, ten cannon," replied the other swiftly, and as he spoke his teeth glittered against the darkness of his face.

If Ernest were dumfounded and stupefied at this, he gave no sign. His pale eyes did not waver from the other's eyes.

"That is a large order," he said gravely. "A very large order. It would take some little time to make. Our facilities are not quite in order yet for all this. Some little time. We have on hand," he added slowly, "and can produce in one week, two thousand rifles. It would take four weeks longer for the rest."

The Mexican shrugged, shook his head violently. "Two weeks, only!" he cried.

Ernest stood up, and began to pace the floor measuredly. He spoke, not looking at the Mexican: "You realize, of course, what this means. If we are discovered, you are ruined. And so am I. And more than I: my father, our partner, our whole lives and all our efforts." He stopped abruptly and faced Cardonova. "I will be honest: your offer tempts me, even though," he added, smiling faintly, "we have not yet discussed a price, which, naturally, would be very high. But tempted as I am, it is a fearful thing to risk. We lose everything, while you——"

"Merely lose my life?" smiled the Mexican. "Ah, do not frown, I am not annoyed, nor flippant. I can see very clearly that to a young man like you life is not so valuable as success. My life, you think, would be nothing compared to your ruin. Who knows? Perhaps you are right."

"It would," said Ernest thoughtfully, half to himself, "be treason."

At the word, the Mexican's face became inscrutable. "That is a word," he said, almost indifferently. "And words are for children. Not for men. Especially not for men who make the weapons of death. As you make them. Words are for saints, for the small babies, for women. They cloud meanings, like breath on glass. Let us not," he implored, "exchange words without meanings."

And the two realists faced each other, grim and quiet.

"Your offer?" asked Ernest.

The Mexican smiled subtly. "Exactly twice your customary price." Ernest shook his head; on his forehead there was a dim glisten. "Not enough. It must be three times."

"You," said the Mexican, without rancor and still smiling, "are a thief. That is too high a price, even for honor. And I am not buying honor," he goaded. He knew his man, now, thoroughly. For just a second Ernest's face flickered. "No," continued the Mexican gently, "I am not buying honor. I am not Satan. I am only a poor Mexican patriot who is trying to drive an honest bargain. You spoke of being honest: I believe you desire only your antagonist to be honest, my dear Señor Barbour, for it is impossible for you to be honest.

"I do not hold it against you. Honest men live on charity in their age; the almhouses are full of men who never stole a copper penny. Honest men are the fools and the saints, and you and I are neither."

"You forget," said Ernest with his faint bleak smile, "that I am risking something more than honor: I am risking my future, the future of my father, my brother, my partner. If we are caught, the price I demand from you now will be nothing. It is three times, still. Three times. And even then I cannot promise you."

The Mexican studied him for a long moment; Ernest's expression was unreadable. Then Cardonova opened his bag again, very deliberately, and began to draw from it small oblong packages. He opened them, and soon one thousand gold bills were spread in crisp beauty upon the desk. Cardonova regarded them with adoration.

"Five thousand beautiful American dollars!" he murmured. He touched them with a lover's hand. "How miraculous, how splendid!" He lifted his eyes to Ernest's face, and they were limpid and radiant as though they had looked on ineffable loveliness. "This—now. At the end of this week, ten thousand more. I am weak, I know, but I make this bargain: upon loading, fifty thousand more. And in five discreet banks in New York shall be deposited immediately to your name sixty-five thousand more, to be delivered to you upon the day the shipment crosses the border.

"That is my offer, Señor Barbour. My first offer, my last. It is yours to accept or reject."

Ernest sat down, a little quickly. The glisten had become a glare on his forehead. He stared at the gold as though hypnotized. And Cardonova smiled, smoked gently and serenely, and waited.

Suddenly Ernest put his hand over his face as if to shut out the sight of the gold. Cardonova could see his young lips, livid and compressed.

"There is little risk, if any, except to me," said the Mexican with an artless air. "You will have the money on hand. I am in your power. We are in your power. You can betray us, easily enough. But on looking at you, I knew you would not betray us. Not because of—honor. But profit. And profits are not bedfellows of honor. You are not a man for pittances. There is destiny in you." He waited, suggestively. But Ernest did not stir; the Mexican could still see only those lips, which had taken on a grayish tinge.

"There is little risk," repeated the Mexican. "Boats hired by us will tie up at your wharf, innocently, in daylight. They will be loaded. You will know nothing of their destination. Thirty days thereafter you may claim the money in the banks."

Ernest dropped the hand from his face. He looked drained. "This is a lot of money. And Mexico is poor. Who is helping you?"

Cardonova shrugged, smiled, but his eyes brightened like those of a savage animal. "Ah, Señor, you are asking questions! This is a matter of business, the guns and the gunpowder. You will have your money. That is all that must concern you."

Ernest got up again, and stood by the window. The spring sun on the river was like a blazing white light. Flatboats stood at the wharfs. The foundry hummed, the men sang and shouted in the distance. He put his hand to his forehead, wiped away the sweat.

"You know, no doubt," he said, without turning, "that the Sessions Steel Company holds thirty-three and a third per cent of our stock. You must have familiarized yourself with all this, or you would not have come to me.

"I cannot consult my father in this. Nor our partner, Armand Bouchard. My father is one of those men who have honor, and Armand— he has reason, but this is one thing he would not allow. He came to this country for refuge. No, this is one thing he would not allow.

"But I must consult someone else. I must talk to Mr. Gregory Sessions." He turned to the Mexican, who looked wary and startled. "We can trust Mr. Sessions," he added, and there was something in his tone that reassured Cardonova, made him smile again, very subtly.

Within half an hour they had walked to the Sessions Steel Company, and had been admitted to Gregory's office. Ernest, in an amazingly small number of words, told Gregory the whole story, while Cardonova sat in silence, just smiling, but seeing all things. He was greatly relieved; he had studied Gregory Sessions' face for the past ten minutes, missing nothing, and he knew that here was another realist, above words.

Gregory listened, his lips pursed, leaning back in his chair, his fine hands playing with a pen, his face slightly averted. Then when Ernest had stopped talking, he lifted his head and surveyed both the other men blandly, almost indulgently. He lifted a shoulder; he was a little pale in spite of his smile.

"Of course," he said in his elegant voice, "I can see that we are not to tell Joseph or Armand." He surveyed Ernest's suddenly startled face serenely. Ernest had expected consideration, thought, judicious pursings and hummings. The serenity of Gregory, his manner, which showed that he had not even hesitated, not even thought of refusing, startled him. "No," said Gregory, "it would not do to tell them. It can all be arranged. You must tell them, or I will, that there is a discreet Army purchase, through my brother," he added with an ironical smile, "and nothing is to be said about it. A trial offer, or some such trumpery. We can work all this out better at our leisure, Ernest. Joseph is too innocent to ask many questions, and Armand is too discreet. Armand is a Frenchman, who having smelt profit with a slight taint on it, will say nothing and go ahead, provided he is not insistently asked to sniff the odor. Or offered explanations. The French detest explanations. And rightly, too."

Ernest stared at that smiling and cynical face with its satyrish expression; he suddenly winced when the ironical eyes touched him. He was still young enough to feel a sharp though passing sickness. Then instantly he was ashamed of himself; he was becoming "soft." But: Gregory Sessions, the "old" American, the gentleman! He never liked Gregory after that, and as the years passed he was to hate him. Hate him, he was to think derisively, because he had shown no sentimentality to a young man who hated sentimentality, had betrayed no momentary scruple to a young man who despised scruple!

Within an astoundingly short time all details were roughly arranged. Gregory figured with precision the amount of steel needed, and Ernest figured with him, while Cardonova sat in smiling silence and examined his fingernails and played with his watch chain.

When Ernest and Gregory were alone a little later, Gregory said· "Munitions makers must bargain with strange devils. They are the most neutral people in the world! Wars are nothing to them, as they never are to practical men. Red devil win, blue devil lose. It is all the same to the munitions maker. Panderers to hate. Let the fools hate: the merchant takes his profit, and remains neutral." Which showed, to a suddenly humiliated Ernest, that Gregory was a very astute man, and that he had missed nothing. "You are doing very well, my Ernest," he said, smiling. "But fortune always does well by those destined by her to succeed."

He walked to the door with Ernest, his hand on the young man's shoulder. His slender and elegant figure swayed gracefully beside Ernest's shorter and stockier one.

"You know where I live, Ernest? I have told my niece, Amy Drumhill, a great deal about you. Tomorrow is Sunday. Suppose I tell her you will come to dinner tomorrow, at three? Splendid! At three, then, and we can discuss many things at our leisure."

CHAPTER XIII

IT HAD BEEN six months since George Barbour and his family had returned to England.

No one ever knew what Ernest thought. He professed to think certain things, to agree, to concede, to use hackneyed phrases; he pretended to believe many things, to use the thought processes of others. But he did all this only for certain effects, certain results. What he really thought, what words and phrases he used to himself, what his mental patterns were, no one ever knew. At times, he was an exceedingly fine actor.

He professed to be utterly unaware of his father's new constraint toward him, a withdrawing of the old confidence in some measure. He pretended not to see Martin's long slow glances, nor the turning aside of his head. He listened with his slight smile, which was beginning already to take on itself a certain convulsiveness, to his mother's frank championing of him in the George Barbour affair:

"Well, I must say, Joseph, you don't do the lad justice! Georgie was a rascal, you admit that, and a thief. When I was a girl they hung men in chains for that on the gibbet. Yet, our lad exposes him, and you berate him for it. You ought to get down on your knees and thank him for finding that scoundrel out in time.

"Never mind, Ernest," she would add, turning to him protectively, "I understand. And I agree with you. It was only right. He was a thief. He was robbing us all. We want no thieves about us, do we? You were quite right."

"Of course I was right, Ma," replied Ernest gently. "This world is hard enough for honest men, without tolerating thieves."

Martin rarely cared to attract Ernest's eye to him, or to speak to him. But now he looked at Ernest long and gravely as he said to his mother: "Ernest doesn't care a fig, Ma, for Uncle Georgie being a thief. He's wanted to get him out for a long time; it was luck that played into his hands just in time. But he'll pretend he's agreeing with you about the thieving part, because that's what you understand. You know what they call that, don't you, Ernest? Hypocrisy."

"You always did like words, didn't you, Martin?" replied Ernest, not with cynicism nor immature bravado, but in the tone one uses in boredom to compliment a child. He walked out of the room. "He's a villain," thought Martin despondently, "but he doesn't look like one. I can scarce believe it, myself. But he is surely a villain."

The next day Martin looked for his brother in his office, but he was not there. He went into the shops. The main shop was long and cluttered and dim, acrid with the odor of gunpowder, strong with grease, the air floating with clouds of iron and steel dust from the grinding machines. The wood flooring and even the walls shook with the tremors of the engines in the next shop. The small high windows were open and let in floods of warm spring sunshine, which spilled over prodigally onto mounds of half-finished guns on the floor, and onto the small humming machinery at which men worked, polishing and grinding. Joseph and Armand stood with Ernest near an idle machine, discussing with its operator the reason why it failed to run. Joseph and Armand were oil-stained and odorous, their arms streaked, their faces greasy masks. Ernest had removed his coat, and stood in white shirt sleeves, bending and examining the machine, the sun on his thick light hair, his large face scowling attentively.

Martin disliked the shops. Something in them frightened him. A completed gun frightened while it fascinated him with its utilitarian beauty and smoothness. He was apt to be made ill by strong smells, and gunpowder made his head ache. He was apprehensive of machines; something in their timed and impersonal monotony filled him with a sense of obscure terror. Sometimes he would think: A man could die before them, and spill his blood, or roll in agony, and they'd turn on and on, or roll and reverse, forever and forever, without losing an instant or knowing anything. That anything, even machinery, could be sense-less before anguish and death, appalled him. It was like a nightmare, like a hint of the vast Impersonality and bitter mechanism that waited outside the boundaries of reality for the souls of men. He sweated before the spectre of a dead mechanism that moved in relentless rhythms, that accomplished, created, fulfilled, without life or warmth or desire. He was becoming convinced, to his horror, that God was like this: was some awful Machine that ground on, helplessly.

So more and more he stayed out of the shops, but all his working day in his own stuffy little office was besieged by the malignant voices of the machines, their monotonous, their threatening, their guttural and triumphant voices. He had not been in the shops for a long time, and today they seemed smellier, noisier and more appalling than ever. He walked over to his brother, who was too absorbed in the refractory ma-chine to notice his approach. Ernest's head was almost in the maw of the machine, his fingers pushing and poking tentatively at various springs and bolts and wheels. Joseph and Armand looked at Martin silently, waiting for him to speak. But he was looking at his brother.

"Ernest," he said, raising his voice above the infernal battering of the machines, "Mr. Beveridge has just sent over a boy from the lumber mill to ask you for your answer about Uncle George's house. He wants to know if you have considered his offer?"

Upon George's leaving America, he had turned over his home to Ernest for six thousand dollars, of which Ernest at that time had paid two thousand, and the final four thousand after his negotiations with Señor Cardonova. Two weeks before he had been offered nine thousand by Mr. Edwin Beveridge, who was the superintendent of the Galby Lumber Mills, in which mills Gregory Sessions had a considerable interest. He had expressed his pleasure at the offer, and had announced that he would probably accept it. But something, apparently, had caused him to delay in the closing of the deal.

He did not answer Martin for several moments, and just when Martin, believing that Ernest had not heard him, was beginning very patiently to repeat his words, Ernest lifted his head from the entrails of the machine and said: "I'm not accepting. You might send his messenger back with that, Martin, thanks." He wiped his greasy hands with a piece of old cloth which the workman handed him. He shook his head, glanced at his father and Armand. "We'll have to send it back. It's no good. You'd better get out their bill, Martin, and send them a letter. We'll ship out the machine first thing tomorrow."

Martin was surprised, as was Joseph. "That's a bloody fine offer, Ernest," admonished Joseph. "Nine thousand dollars aren't to be picked up every day, you know. And it's useless to try to persuade your Ma to move over to Oldtown. She's set against it. There it stands empty; you won't even rent it to any one. Are you hoping Beveridge will raise his price?"

"He couldn't have it for twice as much," answered Ernest. It was unusual for him not to look at his father when he spoke to him, but now he seemed very intent on removing the grease from his fingers with the cloth. There was a seepage of dull color into the folds of his pale face.

"Well!" ejaculated Joseph. He grinned. "Not thinking of getting married, be you, son, and living in that house yourself?"

He expected Ernest to smile or laugh; he was not prepared for the bland blank gaze Ernest now turned on him.

"I might be," he answered serenely. "I might be."

"Can it be possible that our Ernest has become a victim of the grande passion?" asked Armand with a somewhat sardonic amusement.

"Not Ernest!" said Joseph roundly. "Not our lad. He's too much sense." He waited for Ernest's belated explanation, but Ernest, having finished wiping his hands, fastidiously put on his coat, which he had laid over a clean workbench. He seemed unduly preoccupied with its buttoning. His expression became infiltrated with annoyance, and ..is color continued to rise.

Joseph was alarmed. He had ostentatiously withdrawn from Ernest during the past few months, and was now dismayed that this withdrawing had robbed him, and not Ernest. Perhaps the lad had already picked some lass, someone not worthy of him. She must be unworthy, or he would have spoken either to Hilda or to himself. With all his knowledge of his son's character, he could still feel apprehensive about the girl Ernest might pick for a wife. "You never know," he would often say, when told of some human inconsistency. He knew that Ernest's acquaintances in the town were very few, his friends none. If he knew any women at all, they were most likely only those that "boarded" with Mrs. Fleury on Chestnut Street. Joseph had no illusions about that part of Ernest's life, and as surely as if Ernest had told him he knew where his son was going on the Saturday evenings when he dressed carefully and almost daintily, mounted his own sleek horse, and rode away. In this, as in all things, Joseph knew, Ernest would be a realist. There would be little of the adventurer in his going "whoring," little gaiety, little laughter, little drinking, little joy or ecstasy. It would be merely necessity. He would go to the rococo house on Chestnut Street, to the house where the handsome young ladies "boarded," as a man would go to a tavern. To satisfy a hunger. Joseph had a very male curiosity, without delicacy, as to just what transpired between Ernest and the purveyor of his satisfaction. He would have given much to know, but he would never have considered asking. Sometimes he thought: the lad's too damn young for that. No, I was married at his age, and Hilda expecting a baby. And Ernest was never young, anyway. Damn it, I suppose I ought to have told him something. There's disease, and everything. But somehow, you can never tell Ernest anything. He looks as if he expected you to mind your own business, thank 'ee just the same.

He knew that Ernest carefully avoided the homes where marriageable daughters were laid out too suggestively reminiscent of a shopwindow. So, thought the alarmed father, it must be some girl not fit to marry Ernest.

"I hope, if Armand's right, that it's no strumpet of the town, Ernest," he said in an angrily warning voice. And was instantly ashamed and disgusted with himself. Having given voice to the words, he knew that his whole thought had been wrong. He wanted to apologize. But Ernest, without replying, walked unhurriedly in the direction of the offices, his father and brother and Armand following. If he were outraged, it was not evident by his expression, which was somewhat thoughtful and slightly annoyed.

Joseph followed his son into the latter's office, and shut the door behind them. Ernest pulled down his cuffs, lifted the tails of his coat, and sat down. Without glancing at his father, he picked up his pen and pulled a pile of bills toward him.

Joseph leaned his hands on the desk and bent forward. "Look here, lad, I'm sorry if I said something to hurt you. I know what you are. I should have remembered. I should have known that if you had any blasted silly notion of getting married, you would have told me." He laughed shortly. "You've got too much sense, marrying yet."

Ernest made a few neat notes on a bill. Then he lifted his eyes, bland light eyes, so without affection or kindness now, and regarded his father tranquilly.

"But I am planning on marrying, and very soon, too," he said lightly. His eyes did not leave his father's face; for one sick moment Joseph fancied he saw something mocking, something malevolent, in those eyes. They were all at once those of an enemy. Joseph could not speak; his hands slipped from the desk and he straightened up. He was bitterly hurt, lashed by jealousy, humiliated. Ernest returned to the bills. "It is Miss Amy Drumhill," he said, after a long moment.

Joseph was astounded. "But you only met the lass two weeks ago!" he cried, incredulity mingling with delight in his voice. "You don't mean she's accepted you already?"

Ernest lifted a shoulder. "Certainly not. I've only seen her twice. But—I like her. She is just what I wish in a wife. There is no use waiting. I shall ask Mr. Gregory Sessions before the month is out. Time enough to speak to her then."

Joseph blinked rapidly. He shook his head. "I doubt that Mr. Sessions will look with much favor on you, lad. After all, he is gentry——"

The sharp convulsion which passed with Ernest nowadays as a smile touched his face. "He's in trade, Pa," he reminded his father. "I thought 'gentry' never engaged in trade. They don't, in the Old Country."

Joseph wondered vaguely why he had never really noticed Ernest's eyes before; or, had he? He could not tell. They were so clear and dazzlingly pale—like something—what was it? It was on the tip of his tongue: ice, ice on a brilliant winter's day. And as emotionless, as merci-less. Yet, they were not entirely without expression; there was mockery, bitterness, irony and greed in them. I would not like to be at the lad's mercy, thought Joseph in confusion. A dim fright rose in him. Surely George must have seen those eyes on that shameful night. But I love the lad, he's my flesh and blood! he thought with a sick pain. Sons shouldn't look at their fathers that way. But he probably looks at every one that way. I never noticed it, though. And all these months he thought that Ernest must have seen that his father was righteously with-drawing a little! He not only had not seen: he had not cared. It was

Ernest who was withdrawing from all who loved him. And frightening them into the bargain. Suddenly Joseph, confused and disturbed though he was, felt a sharp pang of pity for his son. This pity made salt water rise in his mouth. He looked down steadily into those pale and steady eyes with the light of ice in them.

"All the same, I doubt that he'll look with favor," he repeated. "I'm not saying you're not worthy of the lass. But will her uncle think so? After all, she is an heiress." Ernest's face flickered a moment. "To be sure, Mr. Gregory has been more than kind to us. We've gotten on, through him. With that Army contract gotten through his brother. That was a fortune!" Joseph smiled with the delight he always felt when recalling that magnificent piece of luck. "But having you marry his niece is another thing. I was only bootlicker to Squire Broderick, remember. But you can tell, in spite of the trade, that Mr. Gregory has got good blood in him."

Ernest bent his head, carefully examined a bill. "I am not diseased," he said in his monotonous voice. "We're in a fair way to be wealthy. There are twenty thousand dollars in my account. Our shops are growing, and we can't keep up with the orders. I've got to get cheaper hands," he added, half to himself. He raised his voice again. "We're on the way. Soon, we'll be bigger than Sessions Steel. You know what our stocks are worth, today. Only three dollars beneath Sessions Steel. It's almost unheard of. Miss Amy could go far and do worse." His mouth twisted in a faint smile.

Joseph heard himself fatuously asking, like any other sentimental father: "But, son, it's not that she's an heiress, is it? You—like the lass, eh?"

Again, without lifting his head, Ernest smiled, thus making his father feel exceedingly foolish and rustic. "Both, Pa, both," he answered in the light tones he used to inferiors and those who annoyed him. "I wouldn't marry a girl without a brass farthing, no. I wouldn't marry a girl who didn't please me. But Miss Amy is neither without a farthing, nor does she displease me. I think," he added very nonchalantly, as he squinted at the bill, "that Miss Amy could go far and do worse."

"Have you told your mother?"

Ernest glanced at him briefly with that bitterly bright eye. "No, and I don't want her to know of this, either. I suppose I was a fool to say anything."

"To me?" Joseph was outraged. "That's a bad punch, lad!"

Ernest shrugged. "I'm sorry, Pa." His voice became contrite and gentle. "I didn't mean it that way. I only meant that nothing is settled yet, and it is folly to say anything about it." Joseph was not as clear-sighted as Martin. He accepted the voice's inflections, simply; a vast relief flooded him. He was getting to be as imaginative as an old woman.

Seeing witches' shadows. If the lad would only look up, now, with the worshipping look he used to wear when he was a brat in petticoats, everything would be as it was. But Ernest did not look up. He was frowning at the contents of a neat black book.

"The United Mills order is two months old," he said abruptly. "We must do something about it. People won't wait forever, no matter how good your product is. We've got to get some foreigners. I'll speak to Mr. Sessions and Armand about it, again. I suppose you have no objections, Pa?"

"Oh, haven't I?" exclaimed Joseph irately. "And how do you suppose that, my fine young cockerel? Can't you hire American workmen? God knows, you can always get them."

"They want too much money," replied Ernest imperturbably, affecting to be absorbed in the entries in his book. "Too much money. We'll never get along at that rate. We can't afford American labor, when our competitors are hiring foreign labor. When they cut throats, we must cut throats. Or we get out of business. We're not in business for pleasure; only for profits. And I propose that we get those profits as quickly as possible."

"Bringing those poor devils here to work for starvation wages ain't human," his father protested. "I'm down on it. I'll always be down on it. They'll be taking bread from the mouths of native workmen; they breed like rabbits, too, and first thing you know we'll have a nation just like them, and the better people will be pushed to the wall, or out of existence. I'm down on it. We've got to think of other people, too."

The pale line of Ernest's upper lip lifted just a trifle, but that trifle was enough to make the dim fright rise in Joseph again.

"You forget that we are 'foreigners,' Pa."

"No, we ain't. We're the same people. Don't talk like a fool, Ernest. Why, they ain't one hundred years away from old England. We talk the same tongue. Maybe one Government sits in London and the other sits in Washington, but they're the same. The same people. But when you bring those poor devils from Hungary and Prussia and Bavaria, and other outlandish places, you're not bringing the same people. You're— you're bringing strangers. And strangers often get to be enemies. It's human nature. And bringing enemies inside your walls is the best way to commit suicide. We can't do that to America. It's our country. We can't do it to our own people. We've got to think of them, too."

Ernest's pen hand dropped to the desk; he surveyed his father with a long and steady gaze in which contempt was mixed with wonder and surprise.

"Pa, how do you know that these people aren't like 'us'? What makes you think they're inferior?"

When he was a little nonplussed and unready, Joseph blustered. He blustered now. "Did I say they were inferior? I said they weren't the same people. You can't mix oil and water. We—we were free in England, just as America is free. These other poor devils weren't free; they don't know what it means to be free. And that's dangerous, for America. There's scoundrels in America who'll take advantage of these poor devils because they don't know what it means to be free. And that'll be very bad for men who know what freedom is. They won't stand the things the foreigners will stand; they'll be pushed back, to starve to death, or to give up their freedom. And then, this country won't be free any more. You can't bring ideas of slavery into a free country, lad, and have that country stay free. Even if the Government stayed free, the people wouldn't be. They'd have slavery ideas; they'd have the minds of slaves. It's very dangerous."

Ernest rubbed his chin very carefully; the slight smile was on his mouth again. He did not look at his father, but at a little point in space near his left arm.

"I think you're shying at bushes, Pa. We need cheap labor, lots of it, for new mills, to open new territory, to build up our cities. When these wretches get a little money, they go back to Europe. Even if they stay, they aren't noticed by any one. They don't interfere. You are right, they don't know what freedom is, so they'll never get in any one's way, never disturb any one. Every country has a laboring class, and the Americans are too damn uppish to be a laboring class. So we need these foreigners. We've got to have them. Nobody mingles with them except the scum of America, so we'll always have the labor we need. We'll grow it."

"There'll be no end to their coming, until it's too late," warned Joseph, his excitement rising as it always did during an argument. "Men always build dams after they've been ruined by floods, but never before. No, I won't have it. I won't help pull down the country that gave me a start in life."

"Maybe the foreign devils want a start in life, too," said Ernest in his smoothest and coldest tones. "Who are you to deny them? Isn't that damn selfish?"

In one clear flash Joseph saw what Martin had seen. "You don't care about giving them 'starts,'" he replied bitterly. "All you think of is profits."

"And why not? Profits. Of course! What are we in business for?"

"Damn your profits! I won't have it. I've set my foot down!"

Ernest wrote something in his book in his small sharp hand. He spoke, without looking at his father: "We're going to have a little discussion about it, anyway, Pa. We're going to vote on it, Mr. Sessions, Armand, you and I. We're the directors and owners of the Company. So, though I understand just what you mean, and I'm sorry about it, the majority vote carries as usual."

Impotence choked Joseph. "You'd vote against me, lad?" he asked huskily.

There was a little silence. "I'm sorry, Pa. The Company comes first."

"You mean," cried Joseph, "that profits come first!"

Ernest did not reply; his lips were compressed. Hard as stone, thought his father, sickened and afraid. He's got no heart at all. I've brought a monster into the world. Where's it all going to end? He went out of the room, slamming the door passionately behind him, maddeningly conscious that he had been defeated, thrown down, by a slip of a lad. No, he was no lad; he'd never been young and eager and soft like other lads. Joseph's step accelerated. His thin face was dark red with congested blood, his eyes suffused, when he ran up to Armand. The Frenchman heard the rapid running of his partner's tread even above the sound of the machinery, and he turned alertly in the direction from which it came. The workmen lifted dull faces for an instant from their machines. Panting and breathless, Joseph plucked Armand's sleeve, and Armand followed him to a distant wall where they would not be overheard. Then Joseph turned to him fiercely, his hand clutching the other's wizened arm.

"Look here, Armand, I've just had a talk with that damn lad of mine in there! He says you're all thinking of bringing foreigners in here to replace our men. For cheaper wages. Is that true? Damn you speak up! Is that true?"

Armand lifted his thick, wiry black brows over his small bright eyes. He watched Joseph steadily for a long moment. Then he said: "There has been some discussion about it. But only trivial discussion, my Joseph. You have heard it yourself. There is too much excitement in you, my friend. It is not good for men to be excited after thirty. You must calm yourself. We have discussed it, yes. But not too seriously. Why not wait?"

"Oh, you're always for waiting!" cried Joseph with violence. "That's the French in you, playing your sly games quickly and secretly, and all the time telling others to 'wait.' Wait for what? For treachery? For rascals to do what they want to do?"

Armand smiled. He tapped Joseph on the arm with two fingers. "I never believed your story of French blood, my good friend, until now. There is no patience in you, no fox-like watching and maneuvering, no sleek diplomacy; in short, there is little of the Englishman in you. Treachery will rest ill in your stomach.

"I beg of you to calm yourself. See, how you pant! There is too much dark blood in your face, and that is very bad. I may be a Frenchman," and his smile broadened, "but I am also your friend. Truly your friend. And that son in his uncle's room is friend neither to you nor to me.

True, I would not allow my friendship to destroy a profit, but I would do you no treachery. Trust me. There will be nothing secret. When I think of it more, I may disagree with you, vote against you. But it will be openly, and with regrets. I will not play you false. So believe me when I say that nothing yet has been done or decided. The time may never arrive when such a thing will be necessary." He filled his pipe carefully. "So now, you know as much as I, no less and no more."

Still suspicious and fuming, Joseph yet was soothed and almost placated. "Well, I'm glad it's not gone beyond that," he said grudgingly. He was much depressed, however. "I don't know what's gotten into the lad. He tells me nothing. It's only an accident that he told me that he is proposing for Miss Amy Drumhill, presumptuous pup. He never tells me anything."

Armand grunted, cocking his head sideways as he watched Joseph shrewdly. "Your son Ernest is a very wise young man. He never tells anything. He never explains anything, nor asks for explanation."

And that, thought Armand, was very, very wise. He, Armand, had his thoughts about that "Army" contract, that had bloomed so suddenly, so pleasantly, so vaguely, from Mr. Gregory Sessions one fine day. There was something so very smiling and casual about Gregory's words: something murmured about a "test" contract, very private and obscure, but very, very lucrative. But yes, so very, very lucrative. Gregory had been right: Joseph was too innocent, and Armand too clever, to ask questions. All that Armand requested of such a situation was not to be expected to ask for explanations. He required only that others so conduct themselves that they gave the impression of believing that he required no explanations. A man must save his face, and dignity. And explanations were frequently undignified. Not only that, they stood in the way of good profits. He had a very good idea that if he had known the whole story he would have been forced to refuse. For many uncomfortable reasons. No one, then, would have gained anything whatsoever, but would have lost much monetary advantage. Armand did not look gift horses in the mouths, and only asked that he be not asked to. The horse might have many bad teeth, but if he did not see them, why, mon Dieu! the teeth might be perfectly sound. It was characteristic of him that, having come upon something that might smell badly, he held his nose, even in privacy, even in his own thoughts. Especially if his infrequently articulate conscience might have been troubled by the odor. Therefore, Armand had blandly supervised the filling of that stupendous, that most magnificent order, blandly watched the loading of the many innocent flatboats that came out of nowhere and vanished into nowhere, manned by a crew that was as entirely bluff and profane and casual as any other crew.

He was suddenly conscious that while he had been thinking Joseph's irate voice had gone on and on.

"—as cool as a cucumber! By God, I hope the lass has the wit to give him the mitten!"

Armand dexterously swam abreast of the conversation. "But Mademoiselle," he said, "will not be foolish. No, she will accept our Ernest. Or, he will take her. He will always take everything. But some day, perhaps, life will not take him, and that will be a very sad day for our young friend."

"He thinks he's getting the upper hand," said Joseph menacingly. "But, he isn't. He'll never get the upper hand, by Jesus, as long as I've a breath in my body."

But as he began to inspect some finished guns, he was not so sure.

CHAPTER XIV

NONE OF THOSE who knew Ernest, except Armand, would have believed it, but Ernest had fallen in love with Miss Amy Drumhill, so intensely, so all-possessedly, that his mind, for many days, felt as though an earthquake had split it open, letting out thoughts and desires and hopes and madnesses. He carried the inferno within him so deeply, however, so grimly guarded, that his outward composure was not broken at all, and not a flash of his inner lightning could pierce to the surface of his still, bright eye.

It was not a fierce and violent fire that must burn itself out by very reason of its mad voracity. The scars of the earthquake would always remain in him; the very geology of his mind was convulsed, but convulsed by the impact of a glacier and not by a volcano. This mind was like rock and frozen earth, that, having been contorted under frightful pressure, and split under arctic stress, would never regain its old contour. A more tropical mind would have been convulsed by a volcano, would have been turned to fiery fluid, would have run in hot flux, then, the heat subsiding, would have resumed almost entirely its old form. In him, the earth moved and the mountains fell and never rose again.

Amy Drumhill was the only living thing that Ernest Barbour ever really loved. He lived to be an old man, but he never stopped loving her. He was not the kind to be changed or softened by love; it had the strange effect of solidifying his character, strengthening those parts of it already strong, bringing to it the last rigid touch of maturity, grinding away those attributes that were of the least use to his purpose.

But it was not for several years that he fully realized how profoundly and completely he did love her, and how impossible for him it was to rationalize this love, or hold it down. He was to forget many things, many of them very important things, but he never forgot the day he met her.

He had not been overcome by Gregory Sessions' invitation to dinner that momentous Sunday. He had known for some time that the invitation was inevitable some day soon. He and Gregory could use each other too well for them to be strangers. Miss Amy Drumhill had never gone to her uncle's mills, naturally, and though he had not as yet seen her, Ernest was already making plans regarding her. He knew nothing about her, either with regard to her age, appearance or character, but he did know

that her uncles were Gregory and Nicholas Sessions, and that she was
their only niece. Gregory was very uncommunicative about his personal
relationships, and though he gave an air of elegant candor, he really
told nothing. Ernest was vaguely aware that he had another relative,
the daughter of a dead cousin; he believed she was called May Sessions,
but he was not certain. Gregory had mentioned the woman only once or
twice, and Ernest had some idea that she was his, Gregory's, contem-
porary. But when speaking of Amy, even Gregory's cynicism warmed
and softened. Heiress to all her bachelor uncles possessed, she would
be a very good catch, indeed, thought Ernest, coolly, not for a moment
considering himself presumptuous. He had no false modesties; he knew
his full worth, and felt quite fully that Miss Amy could indeed go far
and fare worse. He was also aware that the two uncles must be wooed
and won, also, for he had no intention of marrying a girl who might be
cut from an angry uncle's will.

He went that day to the Sessions house with his mind revolving and
clicking like one of his own machines. The power that was in him welled
out, flooded his whole body, so that his walk became buoyant and firm,
conquering. It was a very lovely spring day, too, soft and bright and
warm, and when Ernest had crossed the rail line that divided Newtown
from Oldtown, and had begun to walk through gracious old streets
sprawled sleepily under gracious old trees, he felt that he had come into
his proper place. He rarely had occasion to come to Oldtown, and so the
dignified old houses, set far back from the walks behind smooth green
lawns and box hedges and syringa bushes, delighted him. He looked
boldly at the distant verandahs and piazzas where the huge flowering
skirts of women billowed and bloomed in bright colors, and from which
came sweet disciplined laughter and gentle, penetrating voices. He
looked at the gentlemen who discussed many things on the lawns, under
the shade of great trees, and felt himself their equal, if not their superior.
He looked at the rich polished carriages as they bowled along on their
twinkling wheels, the coachmen and footmen as rigid as soldiers in their
brilliant uniforms, the horses glistening, and he told himself that soon,
he, too, would have such a carriage and such servants. He looked at the
small, well-dressed boys walking in Sunday decorum with their nurses,
and he said to himself that some day he would have such bright, sturdy
young sons to continue what he had started. The peace, the softness, the
graciousness, the fine manners and old mellowed richness of Oldtown
bewitched him while they invigorated him, and prodded an ambition
already regal and rapacious. The house he had bought from his uncle
would not be at all bad if the gingerbread decorations were removed, a
wing or two added to detract from its angular height, large trees transplanted in a circle about it, a real garden set out, and the stables enlarged.
Money could enrich it, give it a polished old patina and graciousness

He knew obscurely that his aunt had furnished it very badly; he had already begun to sell off the garish and uncomfortable furniture. It would do very nicely. He would buy another half acre of land about it, to give it the dignity of an estate. Very distinctly he saw himself walking up the wide flagged path to the doors, which opened obsequiously before him, and entering dim and polished halls with great, richly furnished rooms beyond. He heard the childish voices of his sons; he saw his wife coming to greet him, a nebulous but graceful female with an indeterminate face. But he could see very clearly that she was a female of refinement and civility, and elegantly clad. She deferred to him, obeyed him, ministered to him, of course, like a privileged upper servant, but he cared nothing as to whether she loved him or he her; she was merely a necessary adjunct to a perfect and progressively ambitious picture. He did not imagine her voice, whether she was handsome or plain: it mattered only that she had brought him the Sessions steel and lumber mills and a tidy fortune.

He had passed the Sessions house a few times before, but never had it looked so beautiful and hoary and noble as it did today, dim gray under bright green foliage, speckled with sun-gilt. There it stood, in its girdle of trees, established, secure and full of gracious dignity. Here were home and peace, comfort and gracious hospitality, urbanity and exquisiteness. Some memory of the old houses in England stirred in him as he walked up the long gentle slope of the lawns to the house. Two of the upper windows, escaping the foliage, burned with the hot yellow sunlight; two large collie dogs romped and barked around the flower beds, and darted about the trees; one of the grooms was whistling in the stables. But these, and the soft, murmurous hum of bees and the drowsy, silken rustle of leaves, were the only sounds in the mellow, shining silence. As Ernest neared the steps, the dogs were attracted to him, and came, leaping and bounding and barking. He was so pleased today that he could be kind even to animals, which he normally disliked. He whistled to them, snapped his fingers at them, called to them coaxingly. They halted abruptly a few feet from him, ceased their barking. Their fringed tails, a moment before uplifted and gay, drooped suddenly; they poked their noses tentatively toward him, their heads lowered a little. He looked into their bright brown eyes, and even he, unaccustomed to animals, read the anxiety and distrust in those eyes. This annoyed him; he renewed his wooing. They did not approach nor retreat nor answer; there was something troubled in their steady and uneasy regard, their fixity, their silence. One could tell all their lives they had been accustomed to love and gentleness and indulgence: they were so obviously bewildered and apprehensive where more experienced dogs would have growled, or attacked. Ernest was still young and boyish enough to be piqued at this lack of enthusiasm on the part of creatures he was prepared to like; his vanity was hurt, where no human being could have hurt it. He reached out suddenly and touched one of the dogs with his cane. The animal shrank, trembled, howled, then turning tail he fled, followed by his mate. They went behind the house, disappeared toward the stables. Ernest, nonplussed, remembered someone saying that "dogs always knew." Damned superstition, he thought, smiling ruefully as he mounted the wide stone steps of the piazza. He began to frown; Joseph, his father, was the kindest and most upright of men, yet he, too, disliked dogs, and they disliked him. Nevertheless, the incident annoyed Ernest. He lost his very human pleasure in his new black suit and shining boots and sleek "stove-pipe" hat. He looked with disfavor on his new malacca cane with its gold knob. Damn the dogs, had they spoiled his day?

But the moment the manservant opened the door and admitted him to a great square hall, polished and dim and cool, he knew that his day was not going to be spoiled. He looked with frank pleasure and appreciation at the delicate white spiral staircase twisting upward through a soft gloom, at the tall black-walnut grandfather's clock ticking solemnly in the friendly silence, at the dimmed long mirrors on the walls. He was led into the drawing room where sunlight gushed with subdued yellowness through white Venetian blinds onto rich dark rugs, delicate rosewood furniture covered with old tapestry, and floors like dark mirrors. He looked with appreciation at the carved tables and crystal lamps, at the silver candlesticks on the white-marble mantelpiece, at the ormolu clock ticking daintily between them in the stillness, at the oil portraits in heavy gold frames that hung on the ivory-tinted walls. Ah, here was all he had ever wanted, everything for which he had worked and driven! The picture in his mind changed abruptly: he saw himself in this house, as lord and master. He forgot his uncle's house. Here was his place, already prepared for him! He knew that Amy Drumhill kept her uncle's house, and he admired, almost with vehemence, the perfection of her keeping.

Gregory Sessions was standing with his niece in the gardens at the rear of the house when informed by a servant that Mr. Ernest Barbour had arrived.

"Come, my pet," he said kindly to the girl. "Our guest is here. Study him carefully. A scoundrel, my love, a very perfect young scoundrel. You will notice I do not speak condemningly, but really admiringly. Anything perfect, even a perfect rascal, is admirable. But what a mind, what an ambition! A veritable Napoleon. Do not mistake me: I am not jeering, nor prophesying. Merely stating a fact."

"I always detested Napoleon," smiled Amy Drumhill, taking his arm and walking with him back to their home. "I cannot see how you can endure him, Uncle Gregory, you, who are the soul of honor and integrity."

Gregory smiled down at her fondly, not with a melodramatic twinge of guilt or conscience, but merely with tender amusement that anyone at eighteen could be so innocent, so undiscerning. Whatever was to become of the girl!

Ernest was absorbed in the study of a portrait when his host and hostess entered. Amy saw him standing there with his back to the door, his feet planted squarely and apart on the hearth rug, his head lifted. She thought, in surprise: what a fine pair of shoulders, and what a large, fine head! But he is quite short—no, he is really quite tall. She noticed his hands, clasped behind him: What big fine hands, so brown and strong! He turned slowly at their entrance: What a heroic face, but how lifeless! thought Miss Amy Drumhill. Yet, not lifeless, on quicker glance, but still and composed and rigid as carved stone, full of power. A slow warmth began to permeate her, and a glow rose to her cheeks.

Gregory greeted his young friend with great pleasure and courtesy. He introduced him to his niece. Ernest took her small soft hand and looked down at her gravely. He saw that she had bright brown eyes, the same brown, flecked with amber, of the unfriendly dogs' eyes, but hers were gentle and shy and welling with soft friendliness. They were set in a small, rather pale face, exquisitely shaped, and her mouth was pale pink and childishly moist. She had a small straight nose with delicate nostrils. Not very pretty, according to conventional standards, she yet had such a sweetness and purity of expression that she was utterly charming. Her light brown hair, smooth and glossy, hung about her cheeks in childish ringlets; her neck was slim and white and childlike, sloping down into small, beautifully formed shoulders. She was tall and very slender, and this, combined with the high but immature rise of her breasts, made her appear much younger than she was. Delicate ivory lace flounced over her shoulders and arms to the elbows, but her immense crinolined skirts were of pale blue silk over white lace petticoats, and when her skirts tilted a little as she walked with her light and swaying step, they revealed lace pantalettes and tiny black slippers with black ribbons. She had pinned several pink rosebuds in the lace on her breast, and the hot sweet scent floated about her entrancingly.

She greeted Ernest in a fluting voice of extreme gentleness. He had seen her but a few minutes when he knew that he loved her, and would always love her. He did not know that the great wave of exultation that swept over him was called happiness, for he had never been happy before, but he knew that he felt intoxicated and shaken, split open and resounding, and that something colossal moved in him and shifted its base. It was not in him to feel humble, but he did feel an enormous and momentary recession in himself, as if something in him was too harsh and brutal to approach her. There had not been many times in his life when he had lost his composure, but he lost it now. Within himself was a great floundering, an agonized attempt to regain footing that was slipping perilously. He had a shameful idea that his uncouth attempts to regain an equilibrium enormously disturbed were visible to both Gregory and Amy; he imagined that they were vastly amused, and his color, always painful and reluctant, rose to the large planes of his pale face. His eye fell away from the serene innocence of Amy's eye; he found himself clutching her hand with prolonged desperation, and when he discovered this he dropped that hand.

"His eyes," thought Amy, her throat throbbing oddly, "are like thick pale glass with a light behind it. You can't see any shadows of what he is thinking in them."

Gregory talked on, easily and elegantly, as they went into the cool white-and-mahogany dining room, but Ernest did not hear him. All the beauty and charm of the house, the luminous green light that seeped through the Venetian blinds of the dining room and lay on the ruddy mellowness of the furniture, the mighty array of silver sparkling dimly on the vast sideboard, the pictures of fruit and game on the walls, the thick soft rug, the table with its whiteness, crystal and silver and flowers, the rustling of the trees outside: all these were suddenly brilliant with a radiance that emanated from Amy Drumhill. He moved in bemusement. He sat down at the dazzling and snowy round table, stared blindly at the exquisite, heavy silver, watched his crystal goblet being filled with a brown sherry, ate a delicate broth as if it were tasteless water, and all in all reacted exactly as most any young man would who had fallen desperately in love for the first time. With this difference: over the frozen chaos of his mind the iron glacier of his will was moving: he wanted Amy Drumhill; he would have her; nothing could keep him from her. It was all settled in him between the soup and the ham and the roast beef. This settled, all uncertainty, doubt, tremors, anxiety, diffidence removed, he could proceed to enjoy and bedazzle himself with the sight and sound of this sweet-faced girl with her fluting voice and gentle smile. He had little palate for table delicacies, but today his very senses were touched and sharpened, become sensitive; each morsel of food amazed and delighted him with its deliciousness. Whoever would have thought there was such cooking in all the world! He had no taste for wines; in fact, he had not the slightest notion of the various kinds he was sipping so stolidly; alcohol was somewhat repellent to him. But today these anonymous wines took on a poignancy and exhilaration on his tongue that communicated themselves to his mind, so that he was filled with a sense of lightness and excitement he had never experienced before. His new sense of power and ease had not come to him until he had reached the ham and sweet potatoes; ludicrously, he found himself regretting that he had not regained himself in time to enjoy the soup.

He found himself talking almost gaily to Gregory; he imagined he was very fluent and casual. But Amy thought him rather stolid if formidable, too reserved and ponderous. She knew he was young, hardly more than a boy, but she had difficulty in believing it. From what her uncle had told her of Ernest, she had been expecting an upstart, a clodhopper-Napoleon, a brutish man with a battering and arrogant manner. She had guessed quite easily that Gregory disliked, if not actually hated, Ernest Barbour, and had been puzzled not only by the association of her uncle with him in business, but by his invitation to him. She had believed, rather ruefully, that one reason for the invitation had been to furnish her with amusement at the expense of Ernest's gaucheries and ignorances; she saw now, with intense and bewildered surprise, that Gregory's dislike for Ernest made him believe that the youth was indeed ignorant and gauche, because he wished to believe it. She was face to face, for the first time, with the peculiar malevolence of human nature that makes a man endow an enemy with all the things that he detests, visible evidence to the contrary. So when Gregory covertly tried to catch her eye, to smile at her with small and meaning malice, to try to draw her into an amused conspiracy against Ernest, she could only twitch her lips nervously and blink her soft eyes. Can't he see that Mr. Barbour is none of the things that he said? her innocent thoughts ran on, painfully. Can I be mistaken? No, I am not. Mr. Barbour is a gentleman; he is not handsome, but he is most certainly compelling. I have never seen anyone like him. George and Eddie and Courtney and Butte are silly barking pups compared to him. He is all of a man, and very civil and dignified, too.

She stared at her uncle with the round and surprised eyes of a confused child. Why? Why? And then suddenly she knew, and was sick with shame. Gregory was jealous of this boy, could have destroyed him smilingly because of his jealousy. He was an old man, secure, rich, elegant, educated, travelled and established, accustomed to gracious living and all the dignities of that living. Yet he could envy, and hate in the envying, a youth of no family, little education, new and still insecure wealth, unacquainted with the mellownesses of life and its graciousness. Why? she asked herself, over and over. She looked from Gregory to Ernest with deep intensity. Ah, she knew now! Her intuition told her that it was because Ernest was young and powerful, and filled with a terrifying vitality. It was this terrible vitality that Gregory envied, for he had never had it, and he was intelligent enough to realize what the possession of this vitality meant. All the softnesses and civilities of his life, all the grace of it, all its elegance and fine gestures, could not compensate for this relentless life-flow, this almost monstrous power. It put him, Gregory, in the shade, despite all the things he knew and all the things he possessed; it made him an old and wizened gnome, with only his wry knowledge to compensate him.

She listened to Gregory's soft baiting of Ernest, knew he was trying to draw him out for her amusement. Her shame for her uncle grew, and with it a still, bright anger. She listened to Ernest's replies; they were intelligent, if not brilliant, profound if not worded with grace and perfection; they were strong with all his strength, dignified with all his natural dignity of character. She was astounded to see that her uncle heard nothing of Ernest's replies; his ears were filled with the ignorances and awkwardnesses and narrowness he wished to hear in Ernest's words. Finally, so stupefied was she at this folly and blindness, that she could no longer eat, and there was a sick taste in her mouth. Her uncle had said that beyond his shops Ernest was an ignoramus and a peasant; she could hardly believe that Gregory could still believe so with all the evidence to the contrary before him. There is something very wrong here, she thought. For the very first time her belief in her uncle's wisdom was badly shaken, and she began to pity him for his obvious intolerance and inability to see. She did not pity Ernest. He had no need of pity, she knew that quite clearly. She was very glad indeed that he was not aware of his host's smiling rudeness.

But in this she was wrong. Ernest was well aware of everything in Gregory's mind. He was not disturbed; in fact, he was darkly amused. His tongue felt acrid with contempt, his eyes narrowed slightly when he turned smilingly to the older man. I am stronger than you, he thought; you are only a posture with a rascally mind behind it. If I have no scruples, it is because they would stand in my way, but you are pointlessly unscrupulous. To him it seemed contemptible to possess a pointless vice, a vice that could not be used, that was not used to large ends. It was a waste of time and energy, and this waste seemed criminal to him. To use malice as a tool was justified; to use malice as a plaything, to wear it like a ring, was disgusting.

I want this girl, he thought, as they all laughed gaily when Amy upset her tiny wineglass, and I've got to beat him down. I can't make him like me: if I tried, he would hate me worse than ever, and I wouldn't blame him. I've got to beat him down at his own game, hold him down. I'm stronger than he; I can easily make him afraid. He looked about him for a moment with lifted head; his shoulders were set squarely, and for a little space he was heroic. Gregory saw this; his Voltairian lips twisted, writhed upwards, paled almost to lividness.

The cold excitement rose higher and higher in Ernest. He would tear down his uncle's house; he would rebuild it into the likeness of this house, bringing to it in the person of Amy all its mellow richness, its serenity and space, its polished leisure and graciousness. He looked at Amy; he stared at her lips, palely pink and moist, and he was seized with such a passionate desire to kiss those lips brutally, greedily, that he sweated in the coolness of the dim dining room. He wanted to press his hard fingers over her white shoulders, to force back her head by the seizing of her shining hair and kiss the tender white spot under her chin. He wanted to devour her, absorb her, to hear her cry out, to soothe her fright and pain with savage tenderness. His hands clenched on the stiff whiteness of the tablecloth, and Amy, turning her pretty head to him at that moment, was terrified by the expression in his eyes as he looked at her. Yet this terror, an instant later, was flooded with a strange delight and excitement; her body tingled, was drowned, became numb, her legs weakening as if prepared to surrender. She could feel her heart rising and swelling, as if it would burst her chest; she wanted to cry, to laugh, to run and hide. Yet when Ernest turned aside his face, as though ashamed of what she might see in it, she was disappointed and deprived. She felt robbed, thrust out into coldness, and her heart seemed full of pain. She wanted him to look at her with that terrible expression again; she waited for it. But he did not look at her again during the meal.

When she rose at the end to leave him alone with her uncle, Ernest watched the slight loveliness of her figure as it swayed toward the door, watched the bobbing and swinging of the childish ringlets and the tilting of her ballooning gown. When the door had closed softly behind her it seemed to him that half the light in the room had gone, and that a bleakness had settled in it in spite of the golden light streaming through the blinds. He sat down again with his host. And so disciplined was his mind that he could remove it voluntarily from Amy, turn it to the business he wished to discuss with Gregory.

He detested the taste and odor of tobacco, yet when Gregory offered him a fine cigar he accepted it, so filled was he with his elation and the consciousness of his own power. The cigar was rich and strong and made him feel queasy, but he puffed at it steadily. He did as Gregory did: sipped smooth port and smoked. He looked at the silver and crystal decanter on the table, at the wine fuming redly in his glass, at the blur of softened sunlight on the rounds of mahogany armchair and buffet, at the glimmer of the carpet and the gilded light that lay in the curlicues of the portrait frames. There was a genial expansiveness in the very atmosphere of the large and stately room; Ernest relaxed, felt more in command of himself than he had ever done in his disciplined life.

He discussed a few minor plans he had, and Gregory listened now, not condescendingly and with amusement as he had listened when Ernest had attempted lighter and more social conversation at dinner, but with intentness and gravity. He leaned toward Ernest, nodding his head slowly at intervals, or pursing his lips and lifting his brows. After these small plans, Ernest spoke of foreign labor.

"As I said before, Mr. Sessions, sir, we must have it. You and I and Armand have talked it all over a dozen times. We are making comfortable profits, yes, but not half as much as we could. I need at least seventy-five more men: I could use one hundred more. I have fifty, now, and we are paying them from eight to fifteen dollars a week. Too much. Our four foremen are getting seventeen apiece. It will be necessary to retain the foremen, as they are skilled in this particular work, and we have trained them carefully. One hundred men—one hundred and fifty men. I must have them at once. And in your mills—how many could you use?"

Gregory studied the ceiling. "I could use the same. Let us say three hundred men between us. Within a year, perhaps you and I could use more. The new labor has been coming in from the Carpathian Mountains: great, sturdy peasants, who can stand smoke and heat and long hours and are used to eating plain and substantial fare. Stanford of Pittsburgh told me only last week that the best men come from Bohemia, Austria and Hungary. Slavs and Cechs. Let me see: I have the figures here." He rose, pulled open a drawer of the buffet, and brought out a small neat book such as Ernest used. He turned pages. "Here are the costs of bringing them here. We can pay by the partial shipload. It is best, too, to bring their families with them if they can come, otherwise the devils get a notion after a few months to return with a handful of dollars to the Old Country."

Ernest studied the figures judiciously, frowning. He followed Gregory's long and elegant finger as it pointed out the various sums.

"If you buy that extra thirty acres, Ernest, that you spoke of last week, that will run your land up to the Galby Mills. Galby's have forty acres adjoining; they could spare about ten, I imagine. We can do as others do, then: we can build shacks for the laborers and their families, set up stores and commissaries. Even a bank, after the shops grow sufficiently. If we get three hundred men, their families will run it roughly up to nine hundred souls. In time we can even furnish saloons for them right on our own territory. Nothing like making everything homelike," he added with a wry smile and a glint of his cold eye in Ernest's direction. "Whatever they make, then, will be returned to us in their food, clothing, rent and drink."

"Something like Russian serfdom," suggested Ernest.

Gregory was surprised; he had not known that Ernest possessed any real knowledge of anything beyond his business. "Ah," he said thoughtfully, staring at the young man. He smiled charmingly. "Ah, hardly like Russia, my dear Ernest. We are a free country, except, of course, for the slaves in the south. Pity we up here can't have the same thing. Four or five hundred husky young bucks would save us considerable money after the first outlay. However, do not use the word 'serfdom.' It has an ugly sound in American ears."

Ernest looked at him directly. He only half believed what he was about to say, but he said it: "It not only is an ugly sound, it *is* ugly. And what we are about to do is ugly, also. It is necessary, true, for us. Our competitors are getting this labor, and we must do so also. It does not detract from its ugliness, however, nor does raising our eyebrows keep serfdom from being serfdom." His lips curled, but his stare remained basilisk-like on Gregory's face. "Of course, I am only a 'foreigner,' myself, and couldn't be expected to feel as sharply about making serfs of other foreigners as you would, you being a native American."

Gregory's genial smile became a little fixed, and over it, like a red flood, swept his congested color. He laughed, leaned back in his chair, but his laugh sounded artificial.

"You are sarcastic, my dear Ernest, but you lack the subtle touch. I could have said that more adroitly. The rapier, my dear lad, the rapier, not the bludgeon. But perhaps you will learn finesse in time." He smarted with rage and hate; he saw he had underestimated this side of Ernest's knowledge and character, and was surprised that the youth could express himself with such cogency. This, however, did not detract from his hate, but rather increased it.

Ernest smiled a little grimly. "I prefer bludgeons to rapiers. They are more honest. But we're wasting time. I will see the Galby people tomorrow. Of course," he added lightly and dryly, "I hope their price is not too high. You will, of course, suggest to them that they don't raise the price on me?"

The dark color increased in Gregory's face. He owned nearly forty per cent of the Galby stock, and he knew that Ernest knew it. He affected to laugh with great enjoyment.

"You don't trust your own shadow, do you, Ernest?"

"Of course not," responded the young man readily. "Why should I? You get nowhere, trusting any one. A few months ago when I asked the Galby people what they wanted for that land they told me one hundred dollars an acre. If it is higher than that, I am sorry, but I won't buy it. I can get the land to the east for eighty dollars an acre, and if I can't get the Galby land I will buy that. Of course, it would make it a little inconvenient for you, as your men would be too far from your own mills and would have to pay rent to me for the shacks I would build for them. That would be unfortunate, wouldn't it? I know you haven't sufficient land adjoining your mills to take care of some four or five hundred people."

There was a little pause. The dark veins rose in Gregory's thin neck above his elegant white collar and cravat; a glare came out over his determined smile. What the hell! he was thinking to himself. A few days ago, my fine buck, a few weeks ago, you would not have dared say that to me. You would have expected a kick in the backside, and with good reason. But I have invited you to my table, my precious scum, and you have taken that to mean I regard you as my equal. Cursed impudence—! But he found himself looking into Ernest's pale and bitterly bright eye, and he was shocked. There was no impudence there, no presumption; only knowledge and contempt. He was alarmed, almost dismayed. He bit his lip in confusion and humiliation, and forced himself to laugh.

"I am sure," he said, with an air of good-humored frankness, "that the Galbys will not raise the price. In fact, I will speak to them tomorrow, myself. Of course, you realize that land values have risen enormously along the river, but the Galbys will do me this favor. They owe me some little matter——"

"Some forty per cent," thought Ernest contemptuously. But he made himself imitate the geniality of Gregory's smile. "Another thing," he said. "I don't like the agent the other factories and mills and mines have been dealing with. I think he's a thief. Besides, the men he has been bringing over have no stamina. Or they are lazy, worthless. I've been thinking it over. Armand's son, Raoul, is a lazy, lounging devil, and he'd be able to weed out other lazy devils by instinct. I've noticed something about him, and that is that if he is not supervised or pushed along he does exceedingly well. He likes responsibility. That is because he is conceited. He thinks he fools me; he thinks I think he is brainless and too light. So he acts up to what he believes is my opinion of him. It amuses me very much." He smiled; Gregory raised his brows and studied him slyly. "But I know he is shrewd and quick, and really far more intelligent than Eugene. So I think we must consider Raoul as our own private agent in selecting our Bohemians and Slavs and Czechs."

"But what does Raoul do in the shops? Very little, I suppose. Didn't you tell me he spent most of his time selling to stores in other towns and cities? Yes. Is he a good salesman?"

"The very best," responded Ernest promptly. "We owe a great part of our trade to him, in the smaller and more remote communities. And yes, even in the larger cities, in the small stores. Raoul believes I think his success in selling is quite accidental, and mostly luck, but I know he sells our goods because he—he sells himself. He could sell rat-traps to rats, and that is no exaggeration." Ernest puffed at another cigar. "Of course, Raoul knows absolutely nothing about the details of our shotguns and pistols and gunpowder and cannon. He can rattle off very glib chatter about them, but he couldn't put a gun together to save his life. He told me the smell of gunpowder gives him indigestion, but I believe it is Madam Bouchard's garlic. Besides, it is a good excuse to keep him out of the shops. He hates the shops."

"And Eugene Bouchard? He is now in charge of the rifle assembling?"

"Yes. Eugene likes tools; he likes intricate things that take patience. He is very stubborn; he calls it being determined. But he never lets up, and always completes what he starts. Sometimes he starts very foolish things, but he will complete them, no matter how disastrous. He is something like our machines, that, if they get started wrong, keep on grinding just the same, until they reach the end or someone forcibly sets them right. But Eugene has very delicate hands, and we owe two of our smaller inventions to him, as you know."

It was rare that Ernest expressed himself in personalities, and Gregory was jarred into reluctant surprise and obscure annoyance. He could not reconcile his own portrait of Ernest with such a cogent and powerful and even subtle insight into the characters and minds of others. "But I might have known," he thought with self-contempt. "Have I grown so old and stupid that I did not realize that such drive and force and strength must also be intelligent, even wise?" But for some reason he liked Ernest none the more for this. He was too much of an egotist to enjoy being proved wrong, even in himself.

"And your brother, Martin I believe his name is? Yes, Martin. He has no liking for the shops either, I believe you once said."

Ernest's face darkened and tightened; he regarded the end of his cigar intently. "Martin," he said coldly, "likes practically nothing, except dreaming with Jacques Bouchard. He is the cripple; you must have seen him about."

Gregory, in a last effort to subdue Ernest, took him into his remarkably fine library, dim with books and dark chairs and darker drapes and rugs. But to his own wry surprise he discovered that he felt on the defensive; all at once his intention to awe the youth seemed childish and absurd. His disconcerted thoughts made him force extra joviality into his voice and manner. He became paternal and almost effusive, keeping his long fine hand on the young man's arm and pressing it appreciatively, and with laughter, at some grimly witty remark of Ernest's. He was not a little pleased when Ernest asked to borrow one or two books. He raised his brows, appreciating the delicious irony of the occasion when Ernest picked *Les Burgraves* and *Notre Dame*. He took out a slim red volume of Voltaire, and briefly sketched Voltaire's career and aims. Ernest was coolly contemptuous.

"I doubt if Voltaire was very well acquainted with the real character of the poor and the 'exploited'," he said. "If he had known it, he would have despised it. I have noticed that nearly all of the signers of your Declaration of Independence were men of intelligence, and many of them were gentlemen. If the lower classes had written the Constitution, for instance, it would have been a Constitution of tyranny and viciousness and stupidity." He tapped the volume in Gregory's hand with a strong hard forefinger. "If Voltaire had written pamphlets about the noble aspirations and rights and souls of baboons in African jungles, a place he never saw, they would have been as true as the ones he did write."

Gregory shook with ruddy-faced and silent mirth. Finally he gasped, between his convulsions of laughter: "You are no democrat, my young friend! I am afraid you will never be a good American!"

"I ask nothing except that I be as—profitable—an American as you are, Mr. Sessions, sir," said Ernest, with a short stiff bow. Gregory stiffened, and stopped his laughter. He stared at Ernest with a rather foolish expression on his face. Then he returned the bow. What the devil did the young upstart mean by that? he thought. He took Ernest's arm again, and led him from one immense bookcase to the other. A week before, Ernest would have been bored and contemptuous, but now his interest was vividly alive. This, too, was a means to an end, and the end was Amy Drumhill.

He announced that he must leave very soon. Gregory rolled up a blind, and they looked out upon the garden. Amy stood at a little distance under the shade of a tree, the filtered sunlight in her bright hair. She was laughing and playing with the collies, who leapt about her, barking, their tongues hanging, their tails vibrating. In her blue dress and creamy lace, she was a figure of almost Dresden delicacy and sweetness; she ran lightly about on the thick green grass, fending off the tongues and paws of the dogs, her small white breast and arms rising daintily from the monstrous flowering of her costume. Ernest and Gregory watched her for several long minutes in silence. Gregory's face had taken on itself an expression of melancholy.

"It is no easy thing, bringing up a motherless girl," he said in a low voice. "I have done my best for Amy. She is a sweet child, and like a daughter to us. I have sent her to one or two good female schools, but not enough to spoil her character." He sighed. His sister, Amy, had been very close to him.

Ernest saw the melancholy, heard the tone of Gregory's voice. He clenched his teeth together in his exultation. Luck and life were with him, as they always were with the strong!

He accepted Gregory's civil offer of a carriage home. Driving through the early evening streets, he asked the coachman to slow down the horses. He was well aware that the Sessions carriages were easily recognized in Oldtown, and he enjoyed the pleasure of watching the "snobs" stare at him and the equipage. He knew he was recognized; he knew very well indeed that within a short time he would receive invitations to other homes like Gregory's.

He was on his way! He was filled with a renewed and savage energy. The world was his, and in the center of the world was Amy Drumhill.

CHAPTER XV

WITHIN TWO months Ernest decided that he would let the matter of rebuilding George's house go. He had come to the conclusion that only one house would satisfy him, and that was the Sessions house. He had become more and more enamored of it; it had entered into him so completely that he felt in exile in his own home, and its plainness and lack of taste and absence of delicacies affronted him. Not having before been conscious of where he lived or how, he was now irritated by his mother's homely housekeeping and ignorance of refinements; the solid comfort of her British menage seemed to him gross and unimaginative. He found himself ludicrously quarrelling with her about her taste in furniture and the utilitarian pattern of her silver and china, and the durable quality of her linens. Hilda was astounded at first, and then highly edified. "Our Ernest is in love!" she announced deliciously to Joseph, who surprised her with his scowl.

"He is trying to ape his betters," he said sullenly.

Nevertheless, both he and his wife were pleased at this display of a very human failing in the formidable youth. Nor were they insensible to the fact that the Sessions seal having been set upon their household had raised them to a high estate, almost into nobility, as Joseph said, trying to make his gratified smile sour. It is true that the gracious Mr. Sessions, who frequently visited the shops, had not as yet extended an invitation to the rest of the Barbours or the Bouchards to dine at his table, or even to call upon him and his niece, but there was no doubting that such was his future intention. He inquired most kindly about Mrs. Barbour and Madam Bouchard. Everyone thought him excessively civil, except Ernest and Armand.

"I never trust a man who believes himself a grand seigneur, and is yet democratic," he said. "Such democracy is hypocritical. It is impossible, my young friend, to know that one is superior and yet maintain the pose of an ordinary man with any sincerity. It is a pose that any simple man must resent."

Ernest regarded him steadily with his pale and implacable expression. "Mr. Sessions," he said, "is not being 'democratic' because he is civil to us. He may think he is playing the grand lord, as you say, but I know who is the better man." He nodded shortly to Armand and walked away.

Armand, smiling a little, murmured to himself: *"L'état, c'est moi!"*

Later he thought: "I balk at shadows," and frowned. Nevertheless, he was very glad that his copy of the partnership contract was safely sealed away in the Windsor Savings Bank. He was also exceedingly glad that he had several important patents in his own name, exclusively. Less and less was he being amused by Ernest; more and more was a wariness and suspicion being infused into his old admiration.

One day Joseph came to him, his face wrinkled grotesquely with his troubled and half-angry thoughts. "Here, Armand," he said, thrusting a sheet of paper into the other man's hand—"read it." He lowered his voice a little. "You know, I gave Georgie two thousand dollars of my own after we got that Army contract. Sent it to him. I thought it was only fair. Now he writes me a letter and thanks me. No, that part isn't important. Read that—that down at the bottom of the page."

Armand read: "You were always a good brother to me, Joe, and sometimes I blast myself that I wasn't a good brother to you all the time. I hope you won't hold it against me for what I want to say to you, now: and that is, watch that lad of yours, Ernest. You're his Pa, Joe, but he'll do you in, so help me God, if he can. It's just his nature, to do people in when he can't use them any more. Just watch him; take my advice. He's got too big a mouth for one man. I always told you that you didn't flog your lads enough, and I hope this time that I wasn't right. But I am afraid I am."

Armand read the excerpt carefully, then handed the page back to Joseph, who was watching him anxiously. For a moment Armand did not speak. Then he said: "It is plain that Mr. Barbour has no love for our Ernest."

Joseph shook his head impatiently. "I do not care about that, Armand. I only want to know what you think?"

Armand raised his brows. "What I think? My friend, a year ago you would have thrown such a letter into the fire, and spat upon it. And have forgotten it. Now you bring it to me, and ask my opinion, in great distress. Why?"

Joseph sat down heavily as though he were very tired, and puffed somberly on his pipe. He began to speak, without looking at the other man, and in so low a voice that Armand could hardly hear him: "I don't know. I don't know. I can't get near the lad. He's like a stranger. I tried to be cool to him after Georgie was kicked out, and I thought he noticed it and cared. But if he noticed it, he didn't care. I can believe now that he was really glad to get away from me, and keep to himself. I thought my being cool would bring him back like a decent lad to his father, but I just opened the door for him to take to his legs."

"Are you," asked Armand, "sad about this—or just afraid?"

Joseph glanced up, his eyes flashing with sudden violence. "Afraid!" he exclaimed. "Of what? Of a slip of a lad? That's an insult to me, and a blasted bad insult to Ernest!"

"In two weeks," said Armand thoughtfully, "Ernest will be twenty-one years old. A man by law and nature. He is no 'lad.' In fact, he never was a lad. My friend, I am not insulting you. I am very sorry for you. I am glad I have no sons who are ambitious. Look you: a year ago I would have laughed with you at this letter. Today, I do not laugh. Why? I cannot tell. Perhaps we are both old fools."

He shook his head a little as Joseph walked away. "I should not have said that," he thought, somewhat ruefully. "It is ridiculous to pretend to be afraid of that Ernest, and it was cruel of me to suggest such a thing to his unfortunate father. Armand, you are not yet fifty, yet you are as malicious as an old woman. And why is that? Because you do not like this Ernest Barbour, and would even break his father's heart to annoy him!"

He regretted his words more deeply later when he discovered that the breach between Joseph and his son Ernest was now almost complete, and a thousand times he was on the verge of confessing his malice to Joseph. But something, he knew not what, kept him silent. Perhaps it was dislike, and perhaps it was something more instinctive.

On Ernest's twenty-first birthday Joseph gave him a gold watch and chain, elaborately chased and of the very best workmanship. Ernest was surprised and very pleased; he examined the watch with care and gratification. Hilda gave him a gold ring, a signet, which delighted him. Martin, who had noted, with great amazement and incredulity, Ernest's recent interest in books, gave him a volume of Shakespeare's plays, elaborately bound in tooled crimson leather and embossed in gold with Ernest's initials. Florabelle, now an engaging young beauty with light blue eyes and flaxen braids about a small head, had embroidered him a number of delicate silken kerchiefs. Dorcas, a frail but beautiful child of eleven, had knitted him a purse and made him a cravat.

Ernest appeared touched at all this evidence of affection. And somewhat startled. It seemed to occur to him with something of a shock that after all he was part of his family, that he shared human flesh and human blood with these loving creatures who had taken such care to give him pleasure, that he was not a formidable stranger to them but a son and a brother, and that, in their various ways, they loved him. And believed that he loved them, also. He saw that they were not really insignificant, and somewhat of annoyances, but individuals. Suddenly he was humbled and made contrite. He looked at his brother and his young sisters with half-ashamed and newly interested eyes. Martin, there, was no fool, in spite of his moonings, and it was contemptible that he, Ernest, had made no effort to set Martin's feet in the right path. Florabelle was a young beauty, and it was in his hands to find her a suitable husband soon, one who would advance her interests and provide for her with all respectability. Dorcas, there, was going to be still more beautiful. He looked at them all with surprise and a little of bewilderment, and wondered where he had been for so long. It was high time that he made plans for those who would one day be dependent on his energy and his bounty, his brains and his strength.

He kissed his mother, and his sisters, who backed away from him shyly and confusedly, shook hands with his brother, and after a moment's hesitation, kissed his father simply and boyishly on the cheek. Joseph swallowed convulsively, and his eyes dimmed. "It's all right, now," he thought, "it's all right. The lad's heart is in the right place. I was a fool." He wondered why he did not feel happier.

CHAPTER XVI

ERNEST WAS not one to make easy resolutions when stirred by emotion, then forget them. Nor did he keep resolutions because he believed it to be his "duty." Duty was a word that never occurred to him. He never forgot resolutions because it was his nature never to make them unless he saw reason for them. And seeing reason, he set himself inflexibly to keep those resolutions.

It was not long before he had persuaded his father to send Florabelle to Miss Cuthbert's Female Academy in Philadelphia, where she would learn "deportment befitting a young gentlewoman, including exercises with the blackboard, mathematics, including algebra, painting, ballroom dancing, French, and performance upon the harp or piano." Hilda was awed at this formidable array of accomplishments. Nothing was too good for the girl. Seamstresses were hired, endless yards of satin and velvet and merino and broadcloth were ordered. Laces by the bolt tumbled upon the chairs and the bed in the girl's room. There were pelisses and cloaks, muffs and bonnets, slippers and petticoats, stockings and chemises all over the place, Joseph declared, pleased at the excitement in his young daughter's pretty face. He cursed when he stumbled over enormous trunks, but was gratified by knowing that they would be well-filled. Raoul Bouchard, handsome and indolent and smiling, newly sophisticated and at ease from his European travels, came to the Barbour house with new regularity, and solemnly assured Florabelle that no Parisian lady of whatever beauty and wealth would sneer at this magnificent wardrobe, though she might indeed envy such a complexion and such hair and such heavenly blue eyes. And Florabelle, dimpling and smiling and blushing, looked at him with the "heavenly blue eyes" and trembled. Ernest, in the background, watched them both thoughtfully, plucking at his lip. Thereafter, he showed more friendliness than usual to Raoul, who raised eyebrows in surprised amiability. He was further surprised when he found his income mysteriously augmented, his responsibilities doubled and his supervision reduced. Then, one Sunday, when Ernest asked him to ride with him, horseback, Raoul was utterly dumfounded. But his distrust did not decrease.

Ernest assured his father that their simple manner of living was a disgrace. A wing was added to the house, and a governess engaged for Dorcas, who was woefully ignorant. Though Hilda protested that she needed another maid no more than she "needed to fly," another servant was engaged. Ernest had found it useless to argue with Hilda about moving over to Oldtown, so he characteristically did the best he could with this house. More land was bought, a gardener engaged, gardens laid out, larger stables, another carriage, more horses, and a collie! "We," he said to his father with his pale smile, "are getting rich. No need to live like beggars any longer."

"Perhaps not," grumbled Joseph, "but you insisting on buying those coal mines because you thought they were such a bargain has left us strapped."

"They are a bargain," Ernest assured him, laughing his short and unmirthful laugh. "Mr. Gregory has chewed his nails ever since for not snapping them up first. His own mines adjoin, and they are not very good. It won't be long before he is buying coal from us, though it will make him sick with vexation. But he knows his own advantage, and he'll buy. He's not one to cut off his nose to spite his face."

"He's been very civil and kind, with his Army contract, and all," Joseph pointed out, wondering irritably why his son only smiled and did not answer. He, Joseph, was feeling languid and tired these days, though he scouted Hilda's anxious suggestion that he "rest" and stop "mithering" so much about the shops. When it was suddenly borne in upon him like a flash of lightning that Ernest had been relieving him more and more of various burdens and responsibilities during the past year, he was made physically ill with fright and dismay and obscure rage. Appalled, he sat back and reviewed everything. How little he knew these days about new orders, prices, salesmen, new customers and new issues of stock! Oh, he knew all about them in a vague and general way from Ernest, but now he recalled that Ernest's voice had been too smooth and too casual, the voice of a subordinate who wished to spare his superior unimportant and tedious details! It was Ernest who conducted nearly all the business, assisted by the docile and silent Martin; it was Ernest who interviewed salesmen and bought and managed everything. Joseph recalled that Armand was often in the office, airily and nonchalantly looking over the books, amiably discussing various matters with Ernest. Now Joseph saw that there was nothing either airy or nonchalant about Armand's conduct. The man was no fool. He, Joseph, was the fool! He had listened, wool-gathering, to the monthly reports, had had few suggestions to offer as they, Armand, himself, Ernest, Martin, Raoul and Eugene discussed affairs and policies and accounts. He had been willing to relinquish more and more. But not Armand! But, he, Joseph, was a lazy laggard.

He began to sweat, to rub his forehead. It was early evening, and Ernest had not yet returned from the shops. Martin, however, had come home with his father. Joseph called him into his bedroom. Once there, however, Joseph found he could say nothing to the young man, who waited mutely for him to speak. Joseph looked into those calm, faintly troubled blue eyes, at the singular purity of the pale features. "He's almost a lass," he thought in despair. "If—if things were not as I thought, he wouldn't know, anyway. He would never suspect any one."

Never suspect any one! Ah, perhaps that was right! Perhaps there was nothing to suspect. Did one suspect one's son? Horrible thought. Suspect him of what? Joseph, sweating coldly and feebly, did not know. But his dim fright and dismay dried his throat, set his pulses to beating as though warned by some secret and rising instinct. "Do you in." Would Ernest "do him in"? How could he? Would he? No, surely never! Not Ernest, his son. He was filled with abject shame. Georgie was a rascal, and was trying to strike at Ernest through Joseph. What had Ernest ever done to cause his father to suspect him? Nothing. And again: suspect him of what?

Nevertheless, ashamed though he was, Joseph, too casually, walked into the office of Ernest the next day and mentioned that there was "some little matter" he wanted to set right in his mind. He asked for the books. As he asked, standing by Ernest's desk, he smiled. Ernest, slightly surprised, looked up. Something in his father's face caused his eyes to point and sharpen. Then for the first time he noticed that his father was much thinner and that his color was bad, faintly yellow and waxen. He saw that his breath was rather short. But more than all these, he saw that the fixed smile was too casual, too amiable. And he knew.

In a quiet voice he called to Martin, who kept his books in a small adjoining office. He asked his brother to bring the books. Then, while waiting he drummed his fingers softly on his desk, his eyes fixed absently on the distance. The silence in the room became palpable. Joseph sat down slowly; there was a rising sickness in him. I am mad, he thought. He stared at Ernest's calm and thoughtful face, saw the strength and compactness of his shoulders, the power in the gently tapping fingers. Oh, I am quite mad, he thought. What has he ever done to deserve this from his father? But, blast it, I have a right to see the books! No sense in him getting uppish because I want to see the books!

Martin brought in the large black books. "Thank you," said Ernest pleasantly. "Sit down, Martin. If there is anything I am not sure about I want you to explain it to Pa, yourself." He regarded Joseph blandly. "If you remember, Pa, this was all run over at our last meeting."

Joseph's thin fingers turned the wide pages. He could not keep them from trembling, nor his eyes from blurring. He heard Ernest's voice quietly accompanying his pretense of looking at the figures. He saw none of them. Frowning, he ran his forefinger up and down the columns, pursing his lips, as if he added and scrutinized. He asked a few halting questions. The sickness was taking such a grip upon him now that he did not know what he was saying. He saw that Martin was watching him gravely, with a faintly troubled expression. Ernest's head was at his shoulder, the light and virile hair touched by sunlight. All at once Joseph wanted to cry. He closed the book.

"Would you like to see the delinquent accounts, too?" asked Ernest, pushing the book towards Martin, and taking the next one. "I can tell you within a few hundreds what is owed us. But here is the book if you wish to see for yourself." Never had his voice been so gentle.

Joseph opened the book and did not see one solitary figure. Ernest talked on, turning the pages and explaining. The door opened and Armand, grimy from the foundry, entered the room. He glanced at Ernest and Joseph, and seemed profoundly startled. Then, forcibly making his expression amiable again, he came up to the desk.

He compelled Joseph's eyes, held them. "Ah," he said, "I'm glad you remembered to look up the Macy account! As I told Ernest the last time, I am not satisfied with the way they have been meeting their accounts." He shook his head smilingly at Ernest. "I'm afraid you have been too kind to these people, my Ernest, so I asked your father to see for himself and give me his opinion."

Ernest regarded him thoughtfully. "Ah," he said. Suddenly he smiled, and looked aside. But there was a gloomy fold about his lips.

What madness! thought Armand. What indiscretion! How can a man be such a fool as this Joseph? But I am not guiltless of this, either. He laid his hand on Joseph's shoulder. "I need you, Joseph. If you are quite done, will you follow me into the grinding room?"

Joseph stood up. He was only forty-six, but he felt feeble and old. Docilely, or as if half-drugged, he left the room with Armand.

Alone with his brother, Martin stood up and piled the books together. He was always desperately ill at ease with Ernest and avoided being alone with him. Ernest rarely detained him, and he was therefore extremely surprised when Ernest said kindly: "Sit down, Martin, I want to talk to you." Martin sat down and regarded him with a disturbed anxiety. His surprise grew when Ernest, smiling with exceptional friendliness, leaned back in his chair as if he had unlimited leisure.

"Martin, you know we are making a lot of money? One of these days we shall be rich."

"I suppose so," replied Martin. His voice was polite but disinterested. Ernest raised his eyebrows with an attempt of humor, and succeeded only in being weighty.

"It does not seem to interest you, Martin. Why doesn't it? Money is the greatest thing in the world. It's power. Think what one can do with power!" I'm not saying what I want to say, he thought, but how can you talk with those blue girl's-eyes on you, as innocent as a baby's? I wonder if he knows the simplest facts of life? He became annoyed, not at Martin, but at himself, for his long neglect of his younger brother.

"Power," repeated Martin softly, as if digesting the word. A slight color stood out on his cheekbones. He looked up alertly at Ernest, and his flush deepened as if with excitement. "Yes, it can get you what you want! I never thought of that! Is any of this money mine?"

Ernest bit his lip to keep from smiling at this naïveté. "Yes," he said in the considerate voice one used to a child, "you have an equal share in this, as you must know. You have your weekly salary, which is only a small portion. But there is the principal—the shops. All the things we are to do——"

Martin stood up, as if his excitement lifted him. He waved his hand as though brushing something aside. "I don't want much," he said. "Not very much. Only enough to—" He stopped abruptly. His chin dropped upon his chest.

"Only enough to—what?" asked Ernest curiously.

Again Martin waved his hand. "It doesn't matter," he said in a low tone. "Except that I might want to go away soon."

Ernest was astounded. He sat forward in his chair, which responded to his movement with a loud creak. "You want to go away? Why? Where to? What would you do?"

"I might want to visit England," replied Martin, not looking at him. Ernest frowned, bit the knuckle of his index finger, a habit of his.

"England! Whatever for? What did England ever do for us? Besides, you can hardly remember much of England. You mustn't listen to Ma's romantic tales. I was older than you and I remember a good deal. There is no opportunity there for anyone. I never want to see the place again."

Martin was silent.

"Oh, come, Martin! Damn it! You never talk to me. Why not? Aren't I your brother? I'm afraid you've been traipsing around too much with that fool of a Jacques Bouchard. It isn't good for sound people to associate with invalids. The invalid's point of view is always sickly and twisted, and you can catch that view just as easily as you can catch the measles. Look here, I'm going to Philadelphia next week on business connected with the mines. Would you like to go with me?"

Martin was silent so long that Ernest began to feel irritable. Then Martin looked at him fully.

"You never cared before what I did or thought, Ernest. Why are you so interested, now?"

Ernest stared at him, antagonistically. But he could not stare down those steady blue eyes. He saw with a sense of shock that Martin's eyes were full of the same expression as Amy Drumhill's eyes; there was the same innocence, the same candor, the same dignified simplicity. He saw that for Martin and Amy life was not complex, full of lights and shades and alarums and secret places and lusts and greedinesses. It was a straight and honest road, and their feet were set on it straightly. He thought without actual words: How free a man could be, on such a road with such feet! He would never have anything to fear or watch. He would never see rascals or cutthroats or any enemies. He would never need to be on guard. And, God, how restful it would be not to be on guard for a while!

"Why am I interested?" he repeatedly absently. "Why am I interested? Why, damn it all, why shouldn't I be interested? We aren't children any more. All this, all this business I—we have built up is ours. We are in this together—inseparable. It is ours! We've got to make plans. Pa won't live forever, neither will Armand. Then it is all ours, yours, mine, Raoul's, Eugene's. It's something that is growing beyond anything we can imagine, and we've got to understand each other."

Martin turned from him abruptly. He spoke in a voice of strange and quiet violence: "I want no part of this. I don't want it. You must not plan on me being in it or wanting any of it."

"Eh?" Ernest could not believe that he had heard aright. His mouth fell open. Martin swung upon him again with something like fierceness. His face became scarlet, and his blue eyes flashed. Ernest stared at him, stupefied.

"I don't want it!" cried Martin. "I never wanted any part of it! It—it's hateful to me, things made for killing and destroying. You always thought I was a fool, just because I never spoke about it. But I know! I know that Army contract was a lie! I know where the guns and the gunpowder and the cannon went to! It doesn't matter, though. But things will go on, and there'll be more wars and more guns and gunpowder, and more blood and death! I can't have any part in it! It won't end, there, either. Jacques says you are too big for just guns and gunpowder. You'll have other things, hundreds, thousands of men working for you! Yes, it's all you! Nothing but you!

"And when you have all that—what? This!" He ran to the window that faced north and pointed through it fiercely. "Look there! Shacks, scores of them, filled with the men that work for you and make you money! Miserable wretches, half-starved and brutalized. Prisoners. Worse than the niggers in the South. Sweating, working, dying in these foundries! And those mines you got for a song—you'll fill them with men like these, hopeless and stamped on and desperate. You—you're like a spider! You'll spread out, and wherever you spread you'll bring injustice and despair and hate and greed and death. There'll never be any luck in you, for you haven't a heart, and you have no mercy. It isn't only the money you want, or power. It's something beyond you. Why, O God, you're a pestilence! And the pestilence won't end when you die— it'll go on in your children!"

Ernest, shaken and enraged, sprang to his feet. His face turned purple. "Why, you damn fool! Shut up! Shut up!" he shouted, beating his fists on his desk. But Martin would not be stopped now. He ran back to his brother.

"You can't shut me up! Because it's all true, every word of it. And you know it. You don't know what love is, or real kindness. You don't seem to feel that these men down there are human beings, with flesh like yours and bellies like yours and blood like yours. They're only living machines to give you your power. You are a murderer! You make guns to kill men, and you kill men who make your guns to kill other men. And what for? You don't know! You just have to go on doing it, for it is you, yourself.

"But I'll have no part in it. I'm going away soon, and forget all this! I'm going away where I won't have to smell the gunpowder and the guns, all the things made to kill. Where I won't have to see you, and the death and the misery you make." He struck the books loudly with the palm of his hand. "Look, if a miracle could occur, these books could be written red, in blood! Everything you touch would have bloody prints on it. Oh, I know that Uncle George and Armand and Pa started it, but it would not have gone far without you. It is all you! And it's you I am going away from."

Ernest sat down slowly, still staring at his brother. His face was livid. "Why, you infernal, you blasted fool!" he said slowly. "You maniac! You've read too many fool books, that's all's the matter with you. Too many fairy stories. 'Blood!' Bah! You should have been an actor. Sing your songs on the street corners! Death—misery—greed—murder! Why, damn you, I haven't any words for you! You put a bad taste in my mouth.

"Look you, you idiot, I am in business. I make what is demanded. I make the best of guns and the best of gunpowder, and the world wants these things. What do I care what becomes of them when they leave this factory? O hell, there is no use wasting words on you. You wouldn't understand the simplest of explanations. How Pa would enjoy listening to you, you white toad! His life's work, in here; he's given the very best in him, and he's rightly proud of it. Damn you, I ought to clout your girl's face!"

Martin put his hand to his head, and his hand was shaking. He gave the impression of not having heard Ernest speak.

"Partners of death," he said dully to himself. "Partners of death. I'll have no part in this."

And he walked out of the room, quickly, as though about to be pursued.

Ernest spat, leaned back in his chair. "I have," he said aloud, staring grimly at the ceiling, "a very fine family. A family of fools!"

CHAPTER XVII

THAT NIGHT, as customary, Martin murmured something about seeing Jacques Bouchard, and left the house earlier than usual. Hilda, who no longer had the young man's confidence, pursed her lips as she embroidered a fire-screen. Ernest was sitting under a lamp at the heavy mahogany table, figuring, frowning and making notes in his neat black book, while Joseph smoked, dozed, stared at the fire, and read the latest papers from Philadelphia. Dorcas had been sent to bed early; only Hilda and Joseph and Ernest occupied the low-ceilinged, comfortable but crowded "drawing room."

A gray and lonely feeling spread through Hilda's plump breast. Her face had lost its old rosy vivacity and brightness, and was pursed, rather florid and sober. In her black silk gown with its immense flounces and spread, her lace cap and gold chains and rings, she was a pleasant picture of a middle-aged matron. But her expression was dissatisfied, as though she were searching wistfully for something she would never find again. She looked intently at Ernest, then at her husband. Joseph, she thought uneasily, was certainly much thinner, almost "puny." Handsome, fine-drawn and nervous as ever, he yet seemed to have broken inside, so that his glance, quick though it was, was irresolute and a little bewildered, and his voice, though sharp and ready as ever, yet had a habit of wavering half through a sentence. "He works too hard," thought his wife anxiously. "And he mithers himself. What can it be? Why doesn't he talk to Ernest as he used to do? Now, they never speak, except to quarrel. And Martin, always with that poor crippled milksop of a Jacques, when he should be with his family. I declare, never was a woman tried so before! I miss my lasses; I wish Ernest had not gotten the idea of sending Florabelle away, even if she was pert and too ready and a minx. I miss her. I never see Dorcas either, with that stiff-backed Miss Prescott pushing her about. I wish we had never come here, money or not! I wish we were still in England, in Reddish!"

She blinked away a few tears, pursed her lips harder than ever, and intricately filled in a leaf. She saw herself wandering down Sandy Lane, over the little bridge, into the dells where she and her children found the very earliest wild violets. And the tavern, with its smell of hops and sausage, and the black walnut panelling, the latticed windows, the long slow sunshine, the laughter and ease and great burning fire

Her friends rose up before her, buxom young housewives, quarrelling and smiling and weeping. She saw the kitchen of the old house, with her pots shining like gold on the walls, and the baby's cradle rocking gently on the white-flagged hearth. Oh, there was nothing like England, dear England! She sobbed aloud, dryly, then guiltily glanced at Ernest and Joseph. Joseph had fallen asleep in his winged flounced chair, but Ernest was regarding her alertly.

"What's the matter, Ma?"

Hilda lifted her embroidery closer to her eyes. "I was just thinking of England," she replied, melancholy. "I think we would all have been better off if we had stayed there."

Ernest grunted. "Living and dying servants, or bootblacks? Ridiculous. You don't know when you're well off, Ma."

"If you mean by being well off, having money, then I'd rather be in England," said Hilda with spirit. "I haven't even any friends here. Not one, except Madam Bouchard, and she is getting peculiar. Joseph has wore himself out, working, and Martin never speaks and is always with that Jacques, and—" She paused, surprised, for at the mention of Martin's name Ernest had scowled and tightened his mouth. "Now," she added resignedly, "what is the matter between you and Martin again?"

"Nothing," he answered. "Are you certain he is always with Jacques Bouchard?"

"Most certainly. Madam Bouchard often speaks of how fond they are of each other, and mentions Martin being there. Whatever made you think he went somewhere else?"

"Oh, I don't know. But Mr. Renfield mentioned seeing him come from the river-way one night, about ten. It was a very bad night, rain and sleet, and Martin had presumably gone to the Bouchards'."

"He can't be courting a lass!" exclaimed Hilda, diverted.

"Not from that direction, I hope," said Ernest grimly. "Nothing but the very poor, Dutchmen and such, and river rats down there, and squatters."

Hilda uneasily turned to the window, on whose polished blackness the candles and lamps of the room were reflected cosily. A light autumn rain was falling, whispering against the glass, and the trees outside rustled lonelily. Hilda, with a sense of refuge, held out her plump short hands to the fire, felt pleasure as a coal dropped and hissed in its bed. She glanced about the crowded room with its red wallpaper and dark-red carpet and heavy, ugly furniture. Then, feeling chilly, she pulled her India shawl about her black silk shoulders. Then she spoke again, musingly:

"I'm sorry it's not a lass. Martin shows no interest at all in females. It is not right. at his age. It is always Jacques."

"And whatever he finds in the swamps near the river," said Ernest. Hilda, suddenly alarmed, looked at him. "The swamps? Are you certain, Ernest? The Bouchards live near the river, still, you must remember, and he may have taken a walk after seeing Jacques."

"On a sleety night, with the river rising? No, Ma, there's something else. But perhaps Mr. Renfield was mistaken, and it was not Martin," he added, with a soothing smile as he saw how disturbed she was.

"Oh, certainly, he must have been mistaken!" she said, relaxing, though still somewhat uneasy. "He took his horse, tonight, though, and he usually walks to the Bouchards. But perhaps that is because it is raining."

She sighed, looked a little bewildered and sad, and resumed her work. But Ernest stared into the distance, tapping his lips with the end of his pen.

But Martin had not as yet gone to the Bouchards. Having saddled his horse himself, he had buttoned the collar of his greatcoat closely about his throat, sprung into the saddle with grace and lightness, and had ridden out into the cool wet quietness of the autumn night. He rode quickly, keeping to the back streets of Newtown, his hat pulled down over his eyes. His longish mane of silvery-gold hair shone with drops of moisture; occasionally he touched his horse gently with the whip he held in his gloved hand. He was tall and slender, and had a fine seat on his horse, though the going became rough and the animal stumbled at times, and slipped on wet and oily ground; moreover, it was exceedingly dark, with a street light flickering dully here and there. In the silence the clatter of the iron hoofs raised echoes.

Gradually the streets became meaner and meaner; an air of poverty and desertion hung about them, and the lights became fewer. No one was abroad, though shrill and drunken voices came from the wretched houses. Martin swung steadily toward the river, whose voice he now heard, hoarse and muttering and sullen as the winter approached. Trees appeared as the streets dwindled, and the darkness thickened. The horse picked his way gingerly on the rough road with its mudholes and stones. He knew his way, for he often came here. He was a fine animal, and resented these excursions. Martin spoke to him soothingly, loosened the reins.

Now only an occasional house was passed. Steadily, they still turned toward the river. In the pallid darkness of the autumn night they could see the water, dull and livid. They passed squatters' shacks, squalid and wretched, the broken chimneys smoking redly, the ground about them strewn with refuse and rowboats, fishing nets and lines, wooden boxes and old bedding, all sodden in the rain. Curs howled dismally as Martin passed; candlelight gleamed through small and dirty windows. The voice of the river was becoming a dull roar.

The squatters' shacks disappeared at last, and now the banks of the river were quiet and lonely, thick with trees and tall dead grasses. A light appeared in the distance between the trunks, and Martin spurred his horse. They came to a small clearing on which stood a low neat house, very small and compact, with a little dock running down into the water. There was a garden behind the house, and other evidences of pride and decency, though it was apparent that those who lived here were poor. There was a dim reflection of red firelight on the small high windows, but this was the only evidence of life in the river-filled silence and darkness.

Martin dismounted, tied his horse to a tree, and started up the wooden walk to the house. A dog barked suddenly and loudly within. Martin reached the sturdy wooden door and struck it three short raps with his whip, waited an instant or two, and struck two slow blows. Then he whistled sharply. He unbuttoned his coat collar, and winced as cold wet drops ran down his neck.

The dog stopped his barking, as though admonished by a whisper. Then the door opened grudgingly an inch or two. A man peered out.

"It is I, Martin Barbour," said Martin. He pushed the door, the man fell back and Martin entered the house.

He stood in a long, low room, the walls of unpainted pine, the furniture simple and sparse. Two wing chairs stood on each side of a gigantic fire that roared like a bull up the chimney. The floor was uncarpeted, but scrubbed to a silken whiteness. In the center of the room stood a small round table, set with a coarse white cloth, on which stood a pewter pitcher of milk, a platter of cold ham, a plate of thickly sliced bread, and a comb of honey. A black kettle hissed and sang on the fire, and the firelight was the only illumination in the room. Despite the evident poverty of those who lived in this plain dwelling, there was an air in the room of comfort and dignity, charm and peace and pride.

A middle-aged woman sat knitting in one of the wing chairs, a woman shapeless and tall and grim-faced, with steel-rimmed glasses behind which blue eyes snapped alertly. Her hair, pale yellow, was thick with white streaks, and caught in a hard knob at the nape of her neck. She wore a white apron over a blue calico dress. Her features, tight and gaunt, bore a Teutonic stamp, and when she said "Gut efenin'" to Martin, her voice was thick with gutturals. She laid down her knitting and stood up, and thus standing she was as tall as Martin, and broad and flat. She smiled at him tightly, but with evident respect and affection.

The man who had admitted Martin helped him to remove his wet coat, clucking concernedly as he did so. He was shorter than his wife, and plump and rosy, a yellow beard hiding half of a pink and twinkling face. He was coatless, and his coarse white shirt collar rolled back from a fat and faintly damp short throat. His feet, in felt slippers, slapped the wooden floor as he carried Martin's coat to the fire. His wife poked the coals vigorously, and the flames leapt upward and devoured the kettle.

"The tea," she said, "you shall haf in a moment."

"It is very wet outside," Martin said, smiling, as he rubbed his hands before the fire. "But I have had my supper, Mrs. Heckl." He glanced about the room, quickly, almost furtively. "Carl has gone? The river is high tonight, and the current sounds swift. I hope he won't have any trouble."

"So we hope," said Hans Heckl, his small eyes bright under their shelves of yellow eyebrows. He, too, rubbed his hands before the fire, but they trembled. A dog approached from a dark corner, a shaggy brute of some unnamed breed; he leaned against Martin's leg, and Martin absently stroked his head.

Martin drew out his watch and frowned at it. "He should have been here. We must wait. Let us pray he was not caught."

"O Gott, do not say so!" exclaimed Hans tremulously. His wife glared down at him while she poured hot water into a blue German teapot. She berated him shortly in her gutturals. Martin smiled. However, he was a little uneasy. He sat down at the little table, and Hans sat with him. But neither could eat much. They listened. Finally Mrs. Heckl, who had been talking steadily, fell silent, also. They waited in the firelit warmth and dimness of the room. The voice of the river seemed to come closer, threateningly, and a wind rattled the small windows. Mrs. Heckl knit determinedly, as though each stitch kept fear at bay; the clicking of her needles and the dropping of coals sounded very loud in the stillness.

Martin glanced at Hans. The latter's face was sweating profusely now, and it was very pale. He kept blinking his eyes, which were full of scared tears. He looked very defenseless, his fat little paunch resting on his fat, spread little knees, and he rolled bread into pills between short fat fingers. He looked at the door steadily, and his lips moved as though he were praying. Mrs. Heckl knitted on, nodding her head as though she were counting each stitch.

"Sometimes," whispered Hans, not taking his eyes from the door, "it iss too much. Each night I wait for the police, but that iss not too bad. It iss this waiting, for mine Carl, out on the river, alone, in the darkness and the rain. And always waiting."

"You haf no strength, Hans," said Mrs. Heckl contemptuously, still knitting. "You haf no faith in Gott. Our Carl is not alone on the river; the gut Gott is with him. He is doing the Lord's work; nothing can hurt him."

"Nothing can hurt him," repeated Martin gently.

Hans' eyelids squeezed together, and a tear rolled down his cheek. Martin watched it slip into the yellow beard. He covered the other man's wet and trembling hand with his thin warm fingers, comfortingly.

The silence deepened, though the rising wind shook the windows menacingly and caused the fire to rumble and flame. The room was bathed in red light, which reflected itself on the shining knitting needles, danced over the white floor, shone on Mrs. Heckl's glasses. The dog, sensing the uneasiness of the men and the woman, walked restlessly about the room, turned several times on the hearth, and sat down. He laid his wolf's head on his paws, but could not rest. He walked about again. Suddenly he stopped, rigid, his head pointing alertly toward the door. Then he growled, low and deep in his throat. Martin and Hans sprang to their feet, and Mrs. Heckl rose slowly, her lips shaking. There was no sound for several moments but the wind and the river; then they heard a soft thumping and bumping at the little dock. Instantly the dog became frenzied, leaping at the door, barking, whimpering. Hans seized Martin's arm, tears running over his cheeks.

"He iss here!" he whispered. He snatched the coat Mrs. Heckl brought him; Martin put on his own coat. Hatless, they ran out into the wet and windy darkness, the gale tearing at their clothing, choking their breath. Their running feet sank into the mud, icy water oozed into their boots, and they slipped several times. Once Martin fell to his knees in the mud, and rose, shivering. They reached the little wooden dock and ran out upon it. The water, which had risen, washed over it and shook it. They had brought no light with them, but they saw the faint cold glow of a muffled lantern at the end of the dock.

A large flat rowboat was tied at the dock, and five dim shapes of men were climbing from the boat. They were voiceless, and their crouching attitudes showed their deadly terror. A young man detached himself from the group and gripped Hans' extended hands. "Papa!" he whispered hoarsely, and chuckled as though with hysterical excitement. "I did it again! I am home, safe!"

The muffled light shone on his face, fair and flushed, shone on his excited blue eyes and glittering white teeth. He picked up the lantern and turned toward his companions, who were huddled together like frightened chickens. They lifted their heads and turned their faces in sick fear toward the light. They were all negroes, two of them strapping middle-aged bucks, one a frail boy and the other an old man with white woolly hair and beard. The old man was blind in one eye, and his cheek was frightfully scarred, as though it had been branded with a hot iron. Their clothing was tattered, and through the tears their dark flesh gleamed, cold and wet. Their teeth chattered audibly.

The feeble rays of the lantern fell over them and behind them, showing the black and restless water fanged with livid foam. The wind, rising fiercely, shook the little wharf, and the negroes clung together, whispering, inaudibly praying. They stared at the three white men, the whites of their eyes glaring with terror.

"Come on, come on," said Carl, grinning at them, and taking the old man by the arm. "We are quite safe, now. Quite safe, my poor fellows." Docilely, like cattle, they followed their rescuers toward the house. The dog had escaped his mistress, and met them with hoarse barks and growls. The negroes shrank. Carl whistled, and the dog came leaping and fawning upon him, writhing in the mud, dancing in circles. They entered the house, and the door was closed behind them, the iron bar dropped. Mrs. Heckl had competently shrouded the windows, and stood, waiting, on the hearth. The newly filled kettle hissed on the flames; a large pot, filled with thick soup, swung on the crane.

The horror and terror of the last few days was still upon the negroes, the memory of the long and dangerous journey on the stormy river stark in their eyes. They shivered, clung together in the center of the room, stared longingly and dumbly at the fire, and did not move. Their rags dripped wetness onto the white floor. They were more like stricken animals than men. The old blind man had begun to whimper, like a sick calf.

"Come here!" exclaimed Mrs. Heckl crossly, jerking her head at the fire. "Don't stand there dripping like pumps all over my floor." Their eyes rolled at her, they dropped their heads, slunk toward the fire. Pity and sorrow twisted her face, but her voice was rough. "Hans, in a minute, take them away and give them the clothes. And hurry. The soup iss hot."

The old negro turned the sightless side of his face to her, and over the bridge of his broad flat nose his one good eye looked at her and filled with tears. Humbly he crouched down, humbly he caught her hand, humbly he pressed his thick wet lips to it. She did not wince, but she turned away as though she could not bear the agony of that sight. She pulled her hand from his grasp.

"Come, now, you will all be sick on my hands," she said hoarsely. "Hans, are you taking them?"

They trooped after him into an inner room, and could be heard scuffling into dry clothing behind the door. Once or twice one of them spoke in a high and whining voice, and another voice answered: "Safe across the Jordan, blessed Jesus!"

Carl, excited and exuberant, slapped Martin on the back. He was a voluble young man, grinning, amiable and fearless. He was shorter but broader than Martin. He kissed his mother resoundingly, kissed his father as fondly, marched about the room, stamped, strutted, related his adventures, roared with mirth, wrestled with the dog, talked endlessly. It was evident that he had been badly shaken for a time, for there was a high note in his voice that came from relaxed nerves. He told his mother that he was starving, that he and his negroes had not eaten for two days, that they had been pursued, lost their pursuers, were pursued again by those eager for rewards for restoring runaway negroes. He laughed again, high and shrill and unrestrained. At last Martin pushed him into a chair.

"You are very tired, Carl," he said quietly. "And everything is not over, yet, as you know. There is still the trip to Auburn."

Carl, sprawling in the chair, snapped his fingers impudently. The warm fire flowed over his strong young body. He yawned, grinned. "That, for Auburn! We are quite safe." He yawned again, slumped in the chair, and went promptly to sleep. Martin stood up, smiling, and threw his coat over him. "Let him rest," he said to the mother and father.

The boy began to snore. Mrs. Heckl poked the fire, set the table with four large bowls and pewter spoons and cups, and poured the hissing soup. The negroes came out timidly, clad in old but warm and assorted clothing. They sniffed the soup, looked, trembling, at the woman, then, as she gestured, they sat down and began to eat with loud noises.

Martin and Hans sat in silence before the fire. Carl snored on, sunk in the profound sleep of exhaustion. The dog laid his head on the young man's feet, and in the firelight his savage eyes welled and darkened with devotion. Mrs. Heckl continued to pour soup, to slice bread, to refill the milk pitcher and cut ham. She moved heavily but swiftly, resolutely not looking at the timid faces and trembling hands of the runaways. Once or twice a black hand touched her calico skirts humbly, as a dog would touch them, but she appeared not to notice. Her expression grew tighter and grimmer.

After the negroes could eat no more, Hans brought a high stepladder and stood it in the middle of the room. He climbed up, pushed against the ceiling, and a trap door opened. Silently, he pointed upward. There were beds up there, and home-made quilts and blankets. As silent as their host, the runaways climbed awkwardly up the ladder. When the last one, the old man, had disappeared above, and had let down the door behind him, Hans carried away the ladder into the other room. Carl still slept. His mother had rolled her gray woollen shawl into a pillow for him, and his yellow hair shone like gold in the firelight.

Martin got into his coat. He laid a thick packet of bills upon the table, and put his hand upon them. "There are eleven hundred dollars there," he said in a low voice to Mrs. Heckl and Hans. He put down a small cotton bag. "And five hundred dollars in gold in this. The gold, as you know, is to be given them when they cross into Canada."

Mrs. Heckl suddenly remembered what another runaway had said of Martin: "Young Massa, he look like these yer angels they tell about in the Good Book." Pious though she was, she had to admit grudgingly that this was so, for Martin's slenderness and height, singular beauty of pale face, and large blue eyes, were other-worldly. If he had passions, there was nothing to betray them in the purity and gentleness of his expression.

"That was all the money I could take from my account without attracting attention," said Martin. "The runners will have to take four hundred fifty dollars apiece, instead of the usual five hundred. Hans, when you come to work tomorrow, find an opportunity to see me alone and tell me that everything has gone well."

Hans followed him to the door, shaking his head, his hand on the young man's arm. "Them poor devils you got in the shops, Mr. Martin, iss hardly any better than these poor black men we got tonight," he said. "Mr. Eugene said to me today: 'Hans, you are a bad foreman. You encourage these men to play sick.' "

A faint hauteur cooled Martin's face. He pulled on his gloves. "Raoul assures me that no matter how hard conditions are for them in this country they are better off than in their own country," he replied.

Hans slowly shook his head again, smiling sadly. "That iss a lie, Mr. Martin. In the Old Country, perhaps, they have no money, but they have a little land, and a cow, and maybe a horse, and some pigs, and a cottage. Maybe the Government force them to serve in the armies, and maybe at times they are hungry. But they do not work so hard, or if they do, they work for themselves on their own land, among their friends and their own people. But here—" He waved his hands eloquently.

"Good night," interrupted Martin shortly. He heard Hans' eager apology, his plea for forgiveness. He did not turn back. His horse was cold, his head drooping, shivering, for the Heckls had no stable. Riding away into the rainy darkness, a deep depression settled upon the young man. They had rescued fifty slaves during the past year, helped them to escape to Canada. Martin knew of the deep devotion that decently treated slaves accorded kind owners; he knew that only those ran away who were desperate from ill-treatment. Only fifty, he thought to himself, with melancholy. It is a handful. Then he thought of the Bohemians, the Czechs and Slavs and Magyars in the shacks near the shops and the lumber mills, and his eyes closed in pain. His loyalty to his clan had made him cold to the foreman, Hans Heckl, but he knew the truth of what the old German had said.

"Cannot men exist without exploiting or killing their fellow men?" he asked himself. "Is there not room for all of us? What mortal sickness of the soul is it that drives a man to become a cannibal? Why cannot he be satisfied with his fire and his children and his garden? Why must he be possessed of something that makes it intolerable for him to have no more than his neighbors?" He remembered something Father Dominick of the Church of the Annunciation had said to him and Jacques a week ago: "All this is because man hates his fellow man, cannot endure to have him enjoy the things he enjoys, cannot stand his smell or his touch, his voice or his breath. He devours because he hates and despises, and not because he is hungry or homeless. He has no wings to lift him, so to reach a high place he must first knock down his fellows and rise on their bodies. When men have love, they devour no more, and they find their brothers not only endurable, but pleasant and pitiable." Then: "It is a mistake to believe that man is a gregarious animal. He is gregarious only when he needs protection from strangers. By nature he is really a solitary, and no creature who is a solitary is kind or just or compassionate. Neither is he civilized. Love alone can destroy the solitary enemy that lives in every man, and make humanity gregarious in a truly holy and noble fashion." Man, the uncivilized, thought Martin, must hunt alone, eat, kill and destroy alone. But he cannot be saved alone. His salvation civilizes him, makes him really human; but he can find salvation only through the medium of his fellow men.

He thought of Ernest, and he believed that the priest had spoken truly. Ernest was a solitary: uncivilized, cannibalistic, predatory. Thinking of his brother, it was ironical that something very like hatred flared in him. But Martin, like Ernest, had little humor.

Through his depression crept a great loneliness. He spurred up his horse; he felt that he had to see Jacques as soon as possible.

Madam Bouchard and Armand, having built their ugly and sturdy house of stone, planted trees and a garden, bought old-fashioned furniture that exactly fitted the long low rooms, could not be induced to buy a more lavish home or to move into Oldtown or into a better section of Newtown. This was their home; it was now part of them, beloved, snug and familiar. The houses of petty artisans and semi-skilled workmen were creeping shoddily about them, to the very borders of their jealously loved land, but they would not move. In fact, Madam Bouchard, a peasant herself, and honest, found her neighbors congenial. Raoul might grumble and Eugene might scowl, but their parents smiled indulgently and looked fondly about the hideous but comfortable rooms.

It was 11 o'clock when Martin reached the Bouchard house, later than he had guessed. Not a light shone in any window, not even the bedroom windows, except the two low broad ones of the living-dining room. Here, however, the light was dim enough to tell Martin that only a candle or two was burning, and the dull glimmer on the window-panes showed that the fire had fallen low. The Bouchards went to bed early, for they were up at five in the morning. Martin knew that only Jacques waited for him, and he was glad. He wanted no others.

He tied up his horse, knocked lightly on the door. There was a scuffling, the sound of a foot being dragged slowly across the floor; the bolt was drawn, and the door opened. Martin, shaking drops of wetness from his clothes, entered the dim. long warm room.

Jacques smiled at him affectionately, as he closed the door.

"It was so long, I was worried," he said in a low voice, with a mechanically warning gesture toward the bedroom doors. Martin smiled; he noticed that his friend's face was pale from strain. He walked to the fire, removed his gloves and warmed his hands. He stood with his back to Jacques, his long, well-shaped legs apart, his greatcoat, with its capes, glittering with moisture, his silvery hair gleaming in the candlelight. Jacques sat down slowly, his eyes fixed on his friend. He showed the strain of the past few hours in his complete relaxation and exhaustion. He had laid out a glass decanter of wine and two glasses on a small table nearby, and now he filled the glasses and offered one to Martin. Martin drank. His face was glowing from exercise, and now the glow deepened to the deep blush of a girl. His almost feminine beauty was like a light in the quiet room. Jacques, sipping his wine very delicately and absently, regarded him as though fascinated, yet completely peaceful and contented.

"It went well," said Martin softly. He lifted up the tails of his coat and sat down opposite his friend. "I was afraid, for the river had risen, and the police have become very strict." Sighing, he averted his face toward the fire, and Jacques studied his fine profile with a strange intensity, almost a sick yearning. "Of course," Martin continued, "Carl will be caught eventually."

"We must then find some one else," said Jacques serenely.

Martin glanced at him swiftly, and frowned. Sometimes the young Frenchman's cool logic and dispassionate words antagonized him. He said: "But it won't be well for Carl. I like Carl. It would break his parents' hearts. If I could only do it myself! But I must think of my father and mother, too. And little Dorcas. Of course, we would find some one else, as you say. But after all, one must think of Carl."

Jacques said nothing.

Martin sighed again. "All we have done is only a drop in the bucket——"

"It cannot last forever, this slavery, Martin. There is already too much agitation in the North against slavery for it to continue very long. You must console yourself with that."

"How can I? Ernest—everybody—is certain that before slavery is abolished there will be a bloody war." He became very agitated. "And we—all of us—will be furnishing arms and gunpowder for that war. It is a terrible thing to have on our consciences!"

Jacques quickened. " 'Us!' " he echoed, in consternation. "We shall have nothing to do with that, Martin! Have you forgotten that by the time a war breaks out we shall have been gone a long time, have left the world outside, be forgotten, ourselves?"

There was a long and very tense silence. Martin did not speak, but continued to regard the fire, his face averted. Jacques, very white, struggled to an upright position in his chair. He leaned toward Martin, laid his trembling, very transparent hand on his knee. "Martin! Look at me! What is the matter? Have you forgotten? Surely you cannot have forgotten? Surely you do not intend to change your mind, and desert me, desert Our Lord, after all your vows and promises?" He was so agitated and frightened that tears sprang to his eyes, rolled down his emaciated cheeks.

Martin laid his hand over the shaking fingers on his knee; he thought to himself that those fingers were hardly as firm and big as little Dorcas' fingers. He tried to smile reassuringly and tenderly at his friend.

"Jacques. You must listen to me, help me, sympathize with me——"
Jacques cried out, once, feebly, snatched away his hand. He covered his face with it, and through the fingers Martin could see that that face was contorted with agonized grief. Finally tears began to ooze between the fingers, but after that one cry Jacques was silent.

Martin reflected miserably that had Jacques reproached him, argued with him, or accused him, he could have stood this easier. But those silent tears, the look of collapse in the frail and twisted figure opposite him, the bent head, struck at him brutally. He knelt down, removed Jacques' hand forcibly from his face, held his wrists in his strong young grasp.

"Jacques," he said earnestly, "you must listen to me. I need your help. You've got to console me." Jacques' face was quiet now, but strained and ghastly. He looked at Martin steadily and mournfully, waiting. "Today, Jacques, I had a quarrel with my brother." Almost word for word, he repeated what had taken place that day, from Joseph's examination of the books to the clash between himself and Ernest. After he had finished, sad resignation passed over Jacques' face, and he sighed.

"So you see," said Martin gently, "I cannot leave, now. I cannot tell you how miserable I am about it. But I must stay. My father suspects Ernest, and no doubt he is right. I do not know, for I have never seen anything. But he is so treacherous and cold-blooded. And now my father is very sick; any one can see it. And he is frightened. If I leave now, God knows what Ernest will do. He is capable of anything. Anything. Of ousting my father, and robbing my mother and my sisters." Incredibly, Martin said this in all good faith and belief, for in his idealistic and other-worldly mind Ernest had taken on the proportions of a monster. Rarely had Martin seen the world logically and truly and understandingly. He had the mind of a recluse, a child and a saint, and was fanatical and deluded to a high degree.

"But," said Jacques feebly, finding nothing ludicrous in Martin's simple suspicions, "Father Dominick has expended so much effort and trouble to get us into the monastery in Quebec. Everything is arranged; we are to be accepted just two months from today." He turned aside, bitterly. "Of course, you being a recent convert, you cannot realize how frightful this is. But one who has been born in the Church can understand."

"You are being very cruel!" cried Martin, distracted. "I have given up everything! I will have to give up my parents some day, perhaps very soon, when I enter the monastery. Think what it will mean to them! They are not at all religious, and never attend any church in this country, but they are rigid Protestants. What they call 'Popery' is a frightful thing to them, and it will break their hearts when they learn that their son has become a 'Papist.' But you don't understand, Jacques. You couldn't. I will give up more than you, for your mother will be proud. So, knowing what sorrow I am going to cause Pa and Ma, I owe them a duty, now, to shield them against my brother."

"Your duty is to Our Lord," said Jacques, through white lips. "Father Dominick has told you that. You must choose between your unbelieving parents and God." He seized Martin's shoulders in his shaking hands. "Martin, don't desert Our Lord! Don't desert me! I will have to go alone, and without you I should surely die! You speak of your parents: you know that the only way to salvation for them is through your prayers and sacrifice for them in the monastery. Do you not owe them that duty?"

"But I shall enter the monastery!" said Martin. "It is only that I cannot go until I am sure my father is well again, and able to fight Ernest. It will only be a little while. Of course, you cannot go alone, and I only ask you to be patient. Do you not understand that it is a terrible disappointment to me, this delay? Cannot you realize that I hate the world, and want to escape from it? You were born in the Church, and have always had peace and comfort, but I have just come in, and cannot get close enough to it to satisfy me. It is a refuge to me, the only joy I have ever had in my life. Every moment I stay here is unendurable. To me, the monastery is like the old home of my great-aunt in England, with the wet lilacs and the rainy twilight and the fire and the latticed windows and the silence. Peace. You must believe me when I say that this delay is more of a sacrifice to me than it can be to you."

Jacques wrung his thin hands together, and was silent. He could not tell Martin that he was filled with fear, fear that each day's delay, each hour's dragging, might snatch Martin from him, restore him to the world, shut the door of reality forever between them. He was more intelligent than Martin, and more astute; he had none of the dreamy enchantment and exalted devotion of the recent convert. The French blood in him was both subtle and cynical, running cool with logic, and he was well aware that there was more than a little of unreality and tenuous mysticism in Martin's transports. He lived in terror that the gauzy curtain, spangled with its glittering symbols and signs, might lift, and Martin discover that the world was very close after all. He knew, quite coldly, that had he not been a cripple he would never have wanted to run away as he had now decided to do; his flight was from his own impotence. But Martin was sound and strong, and Jacques more than suspected that there lay passions in him that the right touch could arouse. It was from these passions that Jacques wished to withdraw him, for they were his enemies who would take Martin from his friend. Once together in the monastery, neither passionate devils nor desires could ever separate them again, and Jacques would be safe, forever in possession of his love. So though he said to Martin, stubbornly: "I must go alone," he knew that he could never do this, for Martin, relieved of his presence, might be relieved of his enchantment also, and might never see him again. Without Martin, he would never have thought of entering a monastery. Martin, to him, was beloved booty with which he would flee to the fortress of religion.

So as he wrung his hands together, his lips moving in agony, he was sick with terror. Like many of his countrymen, he was a fine actor, and his acting was all the more intense and convincing because he was emotionally involved. Martin could not endure this grief. With an ardor so innocent and childlike that it would have moved one less emotionally engrossed than Jacques Bouchard, he reiterated over and over, a score or more times, his affection, his faith, his impatience over the delay, his promises. When he had finally driven away the look of despair on Jacques' face (and in truth Jacques was finding it a little tedious to maintain that look), Martin was totally exhausted. He promised Jacques to see him the next evening, earlier than usual, and was astonished, upon the door closing behind him, to feel a flood of relief, a sense of release from something hot and exigent and smothering, something that clutched. He was struck by the similarity of this sense of release to that which he felt when escaping from Ernest's proximity. So astounded was he at this thought that he paused with his hand on his horse's neck, preparing to rise into the saddle. Everyone clutches, urges, seizes upon, he thought in his bemusement. Cannibalism. This word in association with Jacques appalled him, made him shake his head as though trying to rid himself of a stupor. And all he asked of any one was to leave him free, never to grasp him, exhaust him with exigencies! He rode away rapidly, and spurred his horse so fiercely that the surprised animal rose once on his hind legs and circled half about. Martin was frightened, and angered, and more than a little confused.

Jacques had closed the door behind his friend, and had bolted it. He had stood in silence, his hand still on the bolt after he had shut it. The candlelight, falling upon him dimly from a distance, threw his shadow on the door and the ceiling, so that it became a monstrous, deformed caricature of the twisted body huddling below it. Moment after moment went by, and Jacques stood there, still with his hand on the bolt, his emaciated cheek pressed to the wood, as though it had closed between him and something beloved, inexorably. The deathly bitterness of his realization seemed to creep into the most vital parts of him, so that he felt mortally ill. He shuddered. His bent legs became weak under him, so that he slipped slowly to his knees, his cheek still pressed to the door. He fumbled in a pocket and pulled out a rosary, tried to pray. But his fingers felt cold as ice, and completely numb. Finally, the beads slipped impotently from his fingers and rattled onto the uncarpeted floor. He stared at them stupidly.

"Why!" he said aloud, as though in amazement, "they are only glass and gilt, after all!"

He fell on his face, writhed, bit his fingers, groaned. And then lay still, his body thrusting in agony against the door, as though it would burst the wood and escape. Or pursue.

CHAPTER XVIII

MARTIN ARRIVED home after midnight, wet, aching and depressed. He found his father alone, sleeping beside a fire that had fallen very low. The room was cold, and had an empty, airless smell; the candles had begun to gutter, throwing wavering and rising and falling shadows over the walls and floor and ceiling.

Martin was surprised to see his father up so late. He tiptoed to a position in front of him, peering at him anxiously in the dim and uncertain light. But poor as the light was, he saw that Joseph looked extremely ill and broken; his skin was stretched with a yellowish cast over his high cheekbones, and his mouth was livid. Apparently he had not shaved that day, for a purplish shadow spread over his chin and under his throat. As he slept, he breathed with a curiously rasping sound, and his arms, hanging over the sides of the chair, swung like those of a dead man. His thin and vital hair was full of gray patches.

Martin knew that his father must have sat up waiting for him. So he laid his hand gently on Joseph's shoulder and shook him. "Pa," he said in a low voice. Joseph started, moaned, moved his head restlessly as if in pain, then opened his eyes. He stared blankly at Martin, standing before him, and to his confused vision his son took on the height and aspect of an archangel, silently waiting. He pulled himself upright with evident difficulty.

"It's late, lad," he said hoarsely, rubbing his eyes with the tips of his dark, thin fingers. "Oh, yes, I've waited for you. A rum time to be coming home," he added, glancing dourly at the clock. "Can't you leave that crippled fellow alone for one night?"

Martin's lips pressed themselves together, but he said nothing.

"A fine pair you are, you and Ernest!" Joseph continued, in the strained voice of a sick man. "One can't rely on either of you! Ernest with his close mouth and scheming and conniving, and you with that humpback! A man might as well have no sons."

"Pa, you are ill," replied Martin, with quick concern and gentleness. "Let me help you to bed. Tomorrow, I'm going to ask Dr. Fisher to see you. You'd best stay home and rest." He took his father's arm. "Let me help you to bed."

Joseph, with an oath, wrenched his arm away. "Blast it, I'm no more ill than you are! All this petty-fogging business! I'm in the prime of my life." His voice rose menacingly, as though his words were intended for other ears, too. "Damn it, I'm not fifty, yet! I've got a long way to go."

Martin regarded him gravely and thoughtfully.

"Who said you didn't have a long way to go, Pa?"

"Nobody!" Joseph exploded. He struggled out of the chair, stood up, swayed for a moment. Martin, careful not to enrage him, did not put out his hand to steady him. "But you and your mother, and that damned Frenchman, and your scheming brother—all of you whining: 'You'd best see a doctor! You're very ill!'" His voice rose higher, shriller, full of hysterical rage. "What do you want of me? Are you trying to get me to peg out, all of you?"

"You're being very foolish, Pa," said Martin quietly. "And you're upsetting yourself. Please come to bed. What you wanted to say to me tonight can keep, can't it?"

"No, it can't! That's always been the trouble with you, Martin, shilly-shallying, leaving everything for tomorrow, pretending that every-thing'll be all right if you leave it alone. But it's never all right! Things've got to be settled——"

Martin smiled patiently. "All right, then, what things? Let us sit down, and talk about them."

They sat down, and Martin tried to break up the dull coals into a blaze with the poker. He threw on fresh coals, and the fire brightened. Joseph shivered, huddled his body forward on his chair, trying to get warm. He kept rubbing his chin with a shaking hand. Martin turned to him. "What's bothering you, Pa? If I can help you, please tell me."

Joseph's hand fell slowly and slackly to his knee, and then lay there, like a leaf that has been caught on a ledge. His shoulders, thin under his coat, sagged. He stared at Martin with empty eyes. Then, very slowly and heavily, he shook his head, blinking.

"But, Pa, you must have wanted to ask me something, tell me some-thing, or you wouldn't have waited up for me. What did you want to tell me?"

Yes, what? thought Joseph stupidly. It was too late. He had not wanted to ask or tell anything. But he had been deadly frightened all day and all night; he had wanted Martin to come home, so that he would have an illusion of safety. Martin always understood things that stiff-necked brother of his never understood. He understood without words. Any-way, his mere presence would have been sustaining, for he had calmness and quietness, and a serenity that often comforted his father, though he could not understand it. Had he come home at nine, or ten, Joseph would have said nothing, would only have smiled, talked to him desultorily, and gone to bed, a little relieved. But he had waited and waited, and it was past midnight, and it seemed that when one waited until midnight one should have something to say, in all truth. But what could he say? Could he say: I think your brother is a rascal, and will rob us all some day and throw us into the street? What shameful words, and how untrue! Could he say: I feel that I am going to die soon, and I am afraid? But this too would be a lie. A sick irritation began to smoulder in him.

But though the thoughts had been put into crude, harsh words in his mind, hardening there like rock that has been molten but is now cooling, and though he repudiated them with silent fury, a distillation of them filtered all through him, and his fear started up again. But it was a vague fear that floated like mist over the rock-like thoughts that he refused to see or acknowledge.

"Damn it," he said weakly, "do we have to make a special occasion of it, just because I was feeling a little off color, and lonely, and wanted to talk to someone besides your mother? So I waited for you, thinking you'd be home at a decent hour, and then I fell asleep and your Ma went to bed herself. Come, come. Don't sit there! In about five bloody hours we've got to get up again. A man gets no peace, anywhere."

He went up the stairs slowly, with the helpless and abandoned movements of a sick child. Martin watched him go. When he heard the bedroom door shut after his father, he poked the fire into a blaze of last heat and fury, blew out the candles, and went upstairs himself. The house had been enlarged during the past year, and Martin had a bedroom to himself. In emulation of the saints he had been introduced to originally by Jacques Bouchard, he had furnished his room severely, so that it was more than a little chill and cell-like. He never had a fire, and there were no rugs on the floor, no curtains at the windows. The bed was narrow and hard, with no canopy, no fringed and flounced counterpane. On a bare table stood a simple, undecorated oil lamp, and beside it was a stiff chair; in one corner stood a homemade bookcase, full of Martin's many books. Over his bed he had hung a very bad print of the Sistine Madonna, and had silenced Hilda's violent protests and accusations of "Popery" with the specious story that the print was a present from Jacques. He had smiled at her warning that he was never to let his father suspect that such a thing was in the house.

He always entered his room with a sense of austere satisfaction, but tonight it struck him that the air was as dank and chill as that of a cellar, and that it was utterly cheerless. He shivered as he lit the doleful lamp, and waited while its bleak white shadow fell on the boarded walls, the cold wooden floor and the hard narrow bed. His depression had given way to a profound emptiness of emotion, which was partly due to the unceasing demands on his emotions during this night. Standing there in the middle of the room, irresolute and exhausted, he thought to himself that he could not bear these blank walls and coldness and dreariness. He threw off his coat, ran downstairs, and came up again with an armload of wood, paper and a scuttle of coal. Within a short time he had a roaring fire. The chimney had never been used since it had been built, and there was somewhat of a stench in the room for a little while, but Martin, sitting close to the fire and rubbing his dry and dusty hands, felt cheered and confident again. The sense of escape and relief that he had felt when leaving Jacques came back; it seemed to him that something within him stretched cramped muscles, breathed, looked about and laughed a little. He forgot entirely until the next day that he was supposed to enter a monastery very shortly.

When the room felt sufficiently warm, he started to undress. Then he heard a faint knocking at his door. He opened it, and little twelve-year-old Dorcas stood there in her chemise, a candle in her hand.

"What are you doing up at this hour, child?" he asked softly. He saw she was shivering in the darkness and coldness of the hall, so picked her up and carried her to the fire in his arms. She put her small arms about his neck, and cuddled her face against his. A thrill of tenderness and love passed through him. He rubbed the girl's cold feet in his warm hands, as she chattered in a whisper, and perched kisses on his cheek and chin.

"I heard the awful noise you made, Martin, bringing up the coal. And I wanted to talk to you. I feel so lonesome."

He smiled down at her. How beautiful she was! he thought. The blue eyes were dark and brilliant, the lashes bronzed, the fair hair like threads of rippling gold. Her complexion was not bright, like Florabelle's, but pale and lustrous, and there was a deep dimple in her left cheek. She was a very slight child, delicately and exquisitely made, and she had a trustful and innocent air that was very touching. Between the brother and the sister was an intense affection, stronger than it had been when Martin was a young boy with a small baby to mind. He held her very close to him, her head on his breast, and he began to rock her with meaningless crooning sounds. The warmth, the comfort of his presence, and his arms, soothed her so that she fell asleep, and he continued to rock her. The heat of her body mingled with the heat of his; her little white hand slipped from his neck; her breath touched his cheek like a feather.

Holding her so, and rocking her, Martin became conscious of a still bright joy in him, which made him strong, drove out forever all chill and doubt and indecision as to what he should do. His sister needed him, looked to him for protection and affection. Besides, he loved her so!

For the first time in his life he did not feel afraid; he was powerful and ardent, sure and firm. When he carried the sleeping girl back to her bed, it seemed to him that he carried all that was beautiful and warm and living in the world.

CHAPTER XIX

ONE BEAUTIFUL spring day Ernest rode over to the Sessions Steel Company to keep an appointment with Gregory Sessions.

Ernest was jubilant. His jubilation did not show itself in excitement, nor even by a sparkle in his light and implacable eye. He neither hurried his horse nor betrayed other signs of exhilarated impatience. But there was a dusky flush on his face, and when he walked into Gregory's office his step rang confidently. He greeted the older man, flung his gloves on his desk with a flourish. Gregory smiled, raised his eyebrows slightly at these unusual demonstrations.

"Ah, the spring air has finally permeated the iron, eh?" he asked indolently. "What it is to be young! Is it a matter of the heart?"

Ernest's exhilaration was such that he was not annoyed at this chaffing.

"No, money," he answered, with his convulsion of a smile. He lifted his coattails, sat down and crossed his legs. "Money," he repeated, his smile broadening as Gregory's became a little thin and acid.

"Money," said Gregory thoughtfully. He snapped his fingers. "Like that."

Ernest snapped his fingers also. "Yes, like that."

"Am I to presume that you are here to borrow money, Ernest? That is astonishing. I understand, from the bank, that Barbour & Bouchard are doing extraordinarily well, and that you ought to be millionaires within half a dozen years." This recalled to his mind that he still owned thirty-three and a half per cent of the Barbour & Bouchard stock, and a sense of satisfaction pervading him added cordiality to his voice. "I cannot believe you are here to borrow money? It is I who should borrow money from you."

"Nevertheless," said Ernest, "I want to borrow money. From the bank. You are one of the directors of the bank, and I expect that you will approve my note." He leaned forward, closer to Gregory. "For seventy-five thousand dollars."

"Seventy-fi—! You are mad, my dear boy, quite mad!" Gregory pulled his long and elegant body upright in his chair, and looked irate. "Of course, it is out of the question! But I am curious. Whatever do you wish seventy-five thousand dollars for? God help us!"

"Our balance at the bank is well over that amount," said Ernest, unperturbed. "I shall have to withdraw twenty-five thousand, however, to add to the seventy-five I intend borrowing. The other fifty thousand is to remain in the bank for emergencies. I shall expect, of course, to pay the bank six per cent interest."

Stupefied, Gregory stared at him, clutching the arms of his chair. His expression was that of a man who contemplates a maniac. Ernest laughed a little, lit one of Gregory's cheroots and smoked it for a moment, though the taste was obnoxious to him.

"I want," he said, "to buy the Kinsolving Ammunition Works. Old Mr. Kinsolving wants to retire. He has no sons to leave the business to. He wants to travel. I heard just a rumor of this a month ago, and I've been talking to him. He wanted one hundred fifty thousand dollars for the business. That includes everything, naturally, patents and all. Finally, after prolonged argument, he agreed to take one hundred thousand dollars. Cash."

Gregory came out of his stupefaction a little. "Very nice of him, I must say," he remarked ironically. His thin face suddenly was suffused with angry color. "Of all the damned nonsense! What do you want that business for? Haven't you enough to do? Do you want to plunge us into bankruptcy? Hell, you talk like a child! I'm amazed at you, Ernest, I really am. Ammunition! Why, it's all over town that Kinsolving is just one step ahead of the sheriff! And you propose— Damn it, lad, you are wasting my time!"

Ernest listened quietly, smoking. Then he said: "You are one of the directors of the bank. No matter how you decide, the others may decide in my favor. If not, I shall go to Pittsburgh or Philadelphia and get the money. Armand and my father are quite in accord with me. However, I wanted to give the bank this opportunity. I believe in doing business in the home town.

"You have said many a time that I am no fool. Please recall your incredulity and annoyance when I first approached you for that measly twenty thousand. But you see that I was justified, that I knew exactly what I was doing. And I know now what I am doing.

"It is true that old Kinsolving is on the verge of bankruptcy. If he weren't, the business would cost me twice as much. But he is about to go bankrupt because he is incompetent and old. Perhaps you aren't aware that he holds many valuable patents, one for an exploding cannon ball that is still, I admit, in the experimental stage. But his best patent is a percussion cap for guns, a device using a highly explosive powder for the setting off of a bullet charge. I have investigated it thoroughly, and I am now of the opinion that it is far superior to the Forsyth percussion cap, which Robsons-Strong of England manufacture. Besides, they still use the black gunpowder, whereas we have just patented my father's latest invention: an almost smokeless powder.

"Of course, the business is run down. It will need a lot of building up.

But with Barbour & Bouchard behind it, with new machinery, work-men, our reputation, our money, it will not be hard. We make the arms: we can make the ammunition. I have it worked out in detail." He laid a sheaf of long papers before Gregory, then fixed his eyes intently on those of the other man so that Gregory stared back as a bird stares at a snake. "Look these over, Mr. Sessions, sir. And I am sure that you will be quite in agreement with me."

"You are quite mad," Gregory repeated. His voice was dull and absent, and his expression heavy and hostile.

Ernest smiled. "You do not believe that, yourself, sir. I do not believe you underestimate my—business ability. When I speak, I generally know what I am talking about. I always have things prepared, settled, worked out in my own mind, before I say anything about them. With all unexpected events allowed for, we cannot fail to profit by this." A crafty look narrowed his eyes, widened his mouth. "I have taken an option on the business. That was a week ago. This morning, Mr. Kin-solving informs me, he received an offer from Burbank Summers Com-pany for twenty-five thousand more than I offered. Mr. Kinsolving," added Ernest, "hopes that I shall not be able to raise the balance of his price.

"It is my plan to give the bank six notes at six per cent. That will give us six years to repay the seventy-five thousand. I have allowed generous time. But I expect to repay it within two years.

"Now, Mr. Sessions, what do you say?"

Gregory fingered the papers on his desk. He was experiencing mixed emotions. Never had he disliked Ernest so much as he did at this minute. He positively abhorred him. It would have given him great satisfaction to have refused so finally that the young man would not have been able to float his loan anywhere. He would have given a great deal to see that confident look destroyed, that cold equanimity broken. He felt toward Ernest at that instant like an enemy, full of malevolence and hate. He could not have explained why, and was more than a little contemptuous of himself. But there it was. The young ass made a man's gorge rise. On the other hand, Gregory felt a sudden certainty that the Kinsolving business in the hands of Barbour & Bouchard would be enormously successful. And he would share in that success. Already he was reaching a bank balance that he had never dreamt of in the most wistful moments. If Sessions Steel had helped Barbour & Bouchard, how much more had Barbour & Bouchard helped Sessions Steel! The price of the Sessions stock had tripled in the last three years. But how ironical it was, how bitter, that he could not thwart Ernest without thwarting himself; he must choke on his hate to fill his pockets. He must agree, assist, when he would have given five years of his life to refuse. But he would not give profit.

He asked a few surly questions, and was both enraged and excited at the answers. Finally he said grudgingly: "Do not count too much on this. But, after deliberation I may decide to approve your notes. Of course, it's a lot of damned nonsense. Gambling." He bit off the end of a cheroot with delicate savagery. "I don't know why I don't throw you out. I'll go over these papers and talk to John Baldwin about the matter, and let you know. Tomorrow."

Having made his furious decision, his mood changed, became genial. His look of the elegant and fastidious satyr came back into his face. Again, he became affectionately paternal and chaffing.

"It is almost a week since you visited us," he said. "Amy was remarking on it. Why not return with me? I shall be leaving very shortly." Ernest, without a change in expression, calmly accepted. "And Ernest, I expect my brother, Nicholas, next week. It will be his first visit home in nearly two years, and I dare say he is returning now only because he is hoping to be re-elected in the fall. He has to do some campaigning, become just a rustic home boy again, for benefit of votes. You remember, you were in Philadelphia when he was here last, and he was much annoyed. This time, you two shall meet, I hope. He has expressed himself as delighted with the way things have progressed."

"That is very civil of Senator Sessions," said Ernest in his level voice, a voice so even and unemotional that Gregory's sharp ear could not detect if there were the slightest satirical timbre in it. But he had an irately uneasy feeling that there had been. He shook his head, pretended to be serious. "I don't know what Nicholas will say about this."

While Gregory finished up his last few pieces of business, Ernest talked to him desultorily. Then just before they left the office, the young man said: "My father respects you, sir. I am going to ask a favor of you." He paused, while Gregory regarded him quizzically. "I wish you would suggest to him, in a very roundabout way, of course, that he make a will. As you are a director of the bank, he will not think it interfering of you to suggest it."

While he had been speaking he had been staring at the end of his cheroot with composure. Finishing, he looked at Gregory fully and calmly.

"Ah," said Gregory, surprised and curious. "A will. He has made no will yet, you are certain? What is the matter? Is he no better than he was?"

Ernest paused a few moments. "He will not," he replied deliberately, "get the slightest bit better until he does make a will. I know. Once he has made a will his mind will be at rest, and he will not be so—so absorbed in what is troubling him."

"You have no suggestions, of course, as to what you would consider—fair, in the will, have you?" said Gregory, with a sly smile.

"None at all, none at all," answered Ernest equably. "It must be left to my father's judgment. I suspect, however, that a will would leave his share to be divided between Martin and myself, with due provision for my mother and sisters. I only want what is right."

"You are a most extraordinary young man!" exclaimed Gregory, much diverted. But he could hardly believe what he had heard. "After all, nearly everything that has been accomplished has been your doing. Do you think it fair that you should only share equally with your brother?"

"I am only conjecturing," Ernest pointed out, smiling faintly. "My father might have other plans. Let him do as he wishes, so long as his mind is at rest."

"Ah," murmured Gregory, watching him thoughtfully. "This is a lot of pay for a father's peace of mind. Besides, may I ask, if I am not too presumptuous, what a will would do for his peace of mind?"

"He doesn't trust me," said Ernest. "A will would make him feel as an animal trainer feels when he gets his beast safely behind bars." He smiled again, a smile of utter and rueful candor. But Gregory was not deceived by that smile. He recognized it; he used it often enough himself. He smiled internally.

"But Martin does not particularly care for the business, does he?"

"No." Ernest hesitated, then told Gregory of his quarrel with his brother during the last autumn.

The carriage arrived for them, and they rolled toward the Sessions house in a heliotrope spring twilight.

"Next week I shall send Raoul to Europe," said Ernest. "I expect a great deal of difficulty with my father, again. He has not been reconciled to our importation of labor last year, and always holds it against me. Says I hypnotized all of you into agreeing."

"Yes, I remember," reflected Gregory Sessions. "He was quite bitter about it, was he not? It is strange to find one who is himself a foreigner objecting so strenuously to the coming of other aliens. A passionate patriot."

"Pa believes that he is interested in the maintenance of the democratic ideal, which oppressed peoples will not understand," said Ernest cynically. "But what he really is afraid of is the stranger himself, his oddnesses and strangenesses."

"I suppose so. All ideals are founded upon fear, from religion to democracy."

They were driven up a long smooth slope of road, and reaching the top, preparatory to gliding down the opposite side, they had a vast, long low view of the river, cold cobalt in the twilight, the shores dark and formless. Above the river, in the west, the day had flung her green scarf, and it seemed to blow in immense winds against the gloomy heavens. From somewhere in the gathering darkness a boat blew a deep and melancholy whistle, drawn-out and lonely. To the left Windsor was a thrown cloak of sequins, glittering brighter as each moment passed. The air had turned cold, and the wind that came up was fresh and astringent, full of moisture and the smell of earth.

"The world is very beautiful," said Gregory musingly. "And at night one cannot see the scars we have put on it."

Ernest was silent. Everything about them was so quiet as they approached the broad street on which stood the Sessions house that the sound of the carriage wheels was sharp and harsh in the ear.

"I forgot!" exclaimed Gregory, with animation. "Did I not tell you that my cousin, Miss May Sessions, is visiting us? She cannot endure Windsor, you know, and lives with her mother's sister in New York, though she was born here. A very gay lady. She visits us because of duty, I know, though she professes to be fond of Nicholas. I confess that we do not always agree, for she is opinionated and determined, and something of a bluestocking. My poor Amy, who is only a bird, finds her a trifle oppressive."

Ernest scowled to himself. He had wanted Amy alone that evening. The night was not too cool for a walk in the garden. He had much to say to her. Now, the evening was to be spoiled by the presence of a maiden lady with masculine propensities. And a bluestocking, by God! He had half a mind to excuse himself and go home. Then he thought of Amy, and told himself that the presence of the hangman would not be too bad if she were there. The very thought of her was like a warm fire, a quiet room full of roses, a frail staircase twisting upward into restful dimness. She was all the things that do not tire men, that lull them and soothe them. He remembered the innocent steadfastness of her eyes, and it recalled Martin to him, and the things he had thought of these two whose feet were set on a straight way, without deviousness and craft and enemies. There was nothing weak or tenuous about Amy, in spite of her innocence and quietness. She was as strong as a silken thread that can support a man, and he believed that nothing could ever move or shake her from a purpose she believed just and true. He knew, also, that she had bright swift angers but no pettinesses.

He was ready to declare himself, and he believed that she would not refuse him. But first he must secure Gregory. When the note was safe and approved, he would ask Gregory for permission to press his suit with Amy. Perhaps no later than tomorrow night. He clasped his hands together tightly, and his heart beat a little faster. He had never seen any one like Amy, and silently, in the darkness, his mouth formed the shape of her name. When the carriage rode up the driveway, he was sweating with impatience to hear her voice, to see the luminous brown of her sweet eyes. He had never so much as kissed her hand, but he had kissed her lips a thousand times in uneasy dreams. Because of this uneasiness, he had spaced his visits farther apart. There was no use in a man tormenting himself until he had reached the well.

A low rosy fire burned in the grate in the ivory drawing room, and candles quivered in yellow pools of light on the mantelpiece, the table and in sconces. Before the fire, in huge-skirted, dark silk dresses, sat two young ladies, embroidering, their ringlets hanging over their grave, flushed cheeks, their white hands glittering with rings. They rose as Gregory and Ernest entered.

"Ah, my dears!" exclaimed Gregory affectionately. "I have brought a guest, for dinner. Amy, my love, I hope the headache has gone? May, my dear, you do not know this most remarkable young man, but I am certain you have heard of him from Nicholas: Mr. Ernest Barbour. Mr. Barbour, this is my young cousin, Miss May Sessions."

Ernest was astonished. He had expected a middle-aged spinster with the traditional spinster's appearance, all angularity and sourness and spite, with perhaps the suspicion of a mustache on the drawn upper lip. But he found himself staring at a very handsome and lively young woman with auburn ringlets and bright, sparkling eyes, full of mischief and a touch of malice. She was smaller but plumper than Amy, and gave an effect of constant animation. Her figure was charming, full-bosomed and slender-waisted. Because of her color, which was brilliant and warm, she seemed to possess much more life than Amy, who had more repose and reticence. Her ringlets bobbed and danced, her eyes bobbed and danced, her whole beautiful little body seemed to bob and dance. She wore a dark gown of russet silk, and about an extremely white and lovely throat she had clasped a necklace of old gold and garnets. When she spoke, her hands moved and fluttered, opened and shut, waved and sank. As she either laughed or smiled almost constantly, the observer had an opportunity to admire a very fine set of small and glistening teeth between her red lips. Her manner, face and figure and voice were so charming that one was apt to overlook the sharp and pointed intelligence of her expression, the wary, meaning glance of her eyes, the alert and slightly suspicious angle of her pretty head. She could not have been more than twenty, but her air of sophistication and ability to take care of herself made her appear several years older than Amy instead of scarcely two.

Disconcerted, Ernest was glad to turn from this lively and intriguing little vision to the poise and smiling calm of Amy Drumhill. She lifted her eyes to his, so gentle and kind and trusting, and as he took her hand May Sessions became nothing more than background, a rather chattery background, but still only background, and there was only Amy with her sweetness and grace and shy glance.

May talked to her cousin, Gregory, very animatedly, as they went into the dining room; she hung on his arm, twisted her gay little head upwards toward him, and her garnet earrings danced with a red light against the whiteness of her cheek. She had a clear and ringing laugh, very fascinating. Amy and Ernest followed a few steps behind, and to all appearances May had forgotten their existence. But even as she chattered to Gregory she was thinking in pleased astonishment: Whoever would have thought that any one like that could be found in this moldy, poky old town! What shoulders, what an expression—quite Napoleonic! And what a posture and chest and figure! Such masterful eyes, and what a firm handclasp! Something tells me, May, my love, that your visit will be extended and very interesting. There is no one, even in New York, to hold a candle to him! And quite a wealthy young industrialist I believe, too! How I adore these men who do things, even though I am a dyed-in-the-wool little Tory, as Nicholas says!

As they sat at the table, she tried to capture and hold Ernest's attention by the sheer will of her voice, the movements of her shoulders, the flash of her laughing eyes, the sparkle of her teeth and the bewildering gestures of her little white hands. She was very amusing and had a sharp wit, swift and stinging. When she laughed, everyone had to laugh with her, no matter how puzzled or resentful they might be, for her laughter was compelling and very sweet, if malicious. She deliberately set herself to fascinate Ernest. She had no particular plans as yet with regard to him, but she meant to subjugate him as she had done scores of others. His polite smiles as he regarded her, the permanent furrow between his pale and steady eyes, his air of grave attention, excited and drew her, almost against her will. Moreover, she was vexed; she saw that she did not interest him, that he merely regarded her as another pretty woman in a world full of pretty women. She determined to make him acknowledge that she was unique and all-conquering. What she would do then when he reached that desirable state she had not yet decided, but the idea thrilled her suddenly as nothing else had ever thrilled her.

As the dinner went on, rage gathered behind her smiles and laughter. It was evident to her experienced awareness that Ernest was in love with Amy, and that Amy, if not yet in love, was quite close to it. But she is such a slow puss, thought Miss May Sessions, that she wouldn't recognize a declaration if she heard one. A silly rustic maid, who is so quiet and graceful because she has nothing worth while to say! She will be fat at thirty, and have two chins and at least eight children, if she is lucky enough to get a man to have her. But she will probably die a spinster, for she is a born old maid, with her vapors and silly timidities, and never a thing to say for herself.

Miss May saw very clearly that Ernest was an intelligent man, so being a shrewd young woman she addressed intelligent questions to him, and listened to the answers with an air of astonished delight and humility. She knew she was pretty enough not to need to disguise her quick mind;

in fact, this mind was like the tang of soda in whiskey. Her face was so lovely, her color so brilliant, her smile so fascinating, her voice so musical, that her intelligence, if used judiciously, did not frighten a man but whetted his curiosity. A bluestocking with a white bosom and dimples and bronze ringlets! What an intriguing combination, full of startling possibilities!

So she allowed Ernest to know that she was a graduate of Oakwood Female Academy, that she had studied two years in France, that she had a fine knowledge of literature, music, painting and politics, that she had won a gold medal for poetry, and an award for a treatise on early Greek science. Then when he gave signs of being oppressed by these formidable accomplishments, she adroitly made him believe that she considered them much inferior to his own vast store of knowledge of more important things. All these, she seemed to say with an airy and feminine wave of her hand, are only baubles. Please enlighten me as to what is really important and splendid. The result was that Ernest, though he rather disliked the young woman, was somewhat dazzled and flattered. He explained everything very gravely, looking into those long-lashed and welling eyes opposite him, and finding a vague pleasure in the moistness of the half-open red lips.

"Really," she said with a sigh and a melancholy drop of her eloquent shoulders, "I am quite despondent. I see that I actually know nothing!" And she regarded him with a pensiveness that yet had a sparkle in it.

Amy merely smiled, murmured when directly addressed, presided unobtrusively in her place as hostess. When she looked at May her smile became a little uncertain, as though May made her feel a trifle uncomfortable and inferior. As for May, she ignored Amy almost completely, as one ignored a superior servant who was allowed to sit at the family table, in the background, serving and solicitous of the comfort of her superiors. When Amy asked her if she would have another cup of tea, she answered with impatient pettishness, and when the cake was offered a second time she pouted adorably and shook her head with very pretty childishness and a flurry of ringlets. Gregory found her delightful and amusing, and Ernest soon found himself intrigued and stimulated. He laughed all of a dozen times during the course of a meal, and May guessed that she had scored a triumph, for his laughter had a reluctant and grudging sound.

Watching her, no one would have suspected her chagrin and jealousy and anger. The meal had hardly been finished before she had decided that she was madly in love, and that she would have no other man but Ernest. And to think that that puling Amy dared push her pale face between her and the man she wanted, dared to insert the murmurous sound of her timid voice into their sprightly conversation! It was too odious. too infuriating. She, May, would soon end it, and put the white-faced little cat into her proper place! How dared she look at such a splendid creature as this Mr. Barbour, who deserved a lively, handsome and intelligent little wife! And one who would bring him a fortune.

So when Amy gave the signal to her to rise and accompany her from the room so that the gentlemen could be alone with their wine and cigars, May pouted, tossed her head, arched her white throat mutinously. "No!" she exclaimed, with the childlike manner she could so easily assume when she desired, "I want to talk to my sweet old cousin, Gregory! You bad old Amy, you, wanting to take me away from him! You go on with that haughty Mr. Barbour there into the drawing room, and Greg and I will come in a few minutes!"

Both Gregory and Ernest were enchanted by this pretty little play of word and gesture and pouting red lips. Besides, Ernest was only too desirous of being alone with Amy for a short time. A soft spring rain was already whispering outside, so the garden was out of the question. He gave Amy his arm, and the instant he felt her soft hand on his sleeve May Sessions vanished into the limbo of things-that-do-not-matter. He led her out of the room with a sensation of hidden but passionate tenderness, and their eyes meeting, they could not take them away, but entered the drawing room in that manner.

Gregory, alone with his young cousin, turned to her with smiling affection.

"Well, puss, what is it?" He was surprised to discover that her impish expression had vanished, and had been replaced by one of contempt. "Eh, what is the matter?" He laid his hand on hers; she snatched it away, pettishly.

"Oh, Greg, you are so blind to what is right under your nose! Can't you see? Amy is setting her cap for that young man; it is so very plain!"

"What!" bellowed Gregory, turning crimson, his eyes glaring upon her. "Are you mad? He wouldn't dare!"

"Dare! Tish, how you do go on, Gregory! He is a young man who will dare anything. For money. Cannot you see that he believes Amy is an heiress? He must believe that, for his kind of man does not marry penniless chits. They always look for money, to further their ambitions. How you talk! One would think that you consider him presumptuous. It is Amy who is presumptuous!"

Gregory stood up, his face still crimson, his hands shaking. He looked as though he would gladly strangle his charming young cousin.

"You are lying! I do not believe it! A man cannot look at a woman without every female for five miles around believing he wants to marry her. It is ridiculous! Amy! And that low-born English servant! That's all he is, in spite of his high-and-mighty ambitions and greediness and rascally schemes. Why I—I could ruin him! I could put him back in the gutter——!"

He paused, choking impotently. May, smiling and dimpling, was fanning herself with her perfumed kerchief.

"How silly you sound, Cousin Greg. You could do nothing with him. Or to him. I am no silly little fool like Amy. I well understand all that has taken place. It was in my own interest to understand, for ain't I your heiress? Doesn't everything belong to me, after your and Nickie's death, by the terms of Cousin Aaron's will? I like money, too. I wouldn't be a Sessions if I didn't, in spite of our breeding and family, and owning a bed that George Washington slept in when he visited great-grandfather in this very house. We all like money. We'd be fools not to. So I know exactly how much we owe Mr. Barbour, and I know that he owes us nothing. So please do not shout empty threats. I know, too, that you don't care for any one in all this world but Amy. Well, if you love her so you will do what you can to save her from unhappiness. If Mr. Barbour marries her and discovers that I, not Amy, am the heiress, he will hate her and make her life wretched. You must do something as quickly as possible. It is quite evident that she is touched by him; but I know that it is still her fancy and there is time to save her."

Gregory sat down very slowly, staring at the door through which Ernest had passed. He was alarmingly white, and looked suddenly old and shaken.

"Amy," he muttered. He clenched his fists. "If he hurts her, I'll kill him!"

May trilled deliciously. "Oh my, Gregory, do not be so dramatic, like a play! Men do not kill each other nowadays. The law doesn't like it. If you just drop a hint to him that Amy is really penniless, and living on charity in our house—my house—I am sure he will drop her like a hot coal. I may be only a female, but I do understand gentlemen. They are all alike, whether they live in Windsor or in New York."

Gregory pressed his fist against his teeth, still staring at the door. He looked very sick and full of fear. And hate.

"Yes, of course, I'll tell him. I never thought—— It is all my fault. I think you are wrong, May. If she wants him, and he wants her, knowing she has no money, she shall have him! Amy's happiness is more to me than anything else in the world. He'll go a long way. In a certain respect, he is a good catch for her. But he is unscrupulous, a rascal. Almost a mountebank. God! I don't know what to do!" He covered his face with his hands.

"Rascals, and men almost mountebanks, sometimes go a long way. They might even become President," said May, smiling. "Fine, virtuous men very often have to beg in their old age. I have seen this so many times! If Amy got Mr. Barbour, it would be a feather in her cap, and quite a load off your mind, my dear old Greg."

"I should have got her married off to some young man of family and money," muttered Gregory, without lifting his hand. "It is all my fault. I wanted to keep her with me for awhile. But I did wrong."

"Fie!" exclaimed May lightly, but with some compassion. "Most of our friends here in Windsor are becoming as poor as old cheese. And young gentlemen, even if they have money of their own, do not like to play King Cophetua. It would have been hard to marry Amy off satisfactorily."

"Are you advising me to allow her to marry that—that English bumpkin—if he wants her?" asked Gregory, with some curiosity.

May shrugged. "He will not ask her—if he knows. I am certain of that. But he ought to know, for her sake as well as for his."

"Ah," said Gregory thoughtfully. He watched her for a long moment, and she met his eyes serenely and squarely, the dimple appearing and disappearing in her bright cheek. "You are a minx, May, but I do not think you are cruel. Nevertheless, you are a minx." He stood up. "I believe you are quite wrong. It will not be hard to find out, and I will do it at once."

She rose in a swish and flurry of silken petticoats, and ran round the table to him, where she took his arm, her small gay face a little anxious "Gregory, please. If he does not ask her, after hearing of this, and you are certain that he would have done so, otherwise, you will not hold it against him? I have always loved you, Greg, much more than I have loved Nicholas, for Nicholas loves his platitudes for all he is a really savage beast. But you have no platitudes. You are very fair, and you will acknowledge that if he does not speak for Amy, you would not have spoken in his place?"

His mouth and nostrils tightened, and he moved as if to shake off her hand. But she forced herself in front of him, taking him by the lapels of his coat. "Gregory," she said earnestly. "Please, Gregory?"

He shrugged, tried to smile. "What a realist you are, May! It's unbecoming in a female. But you are quite right in this: in his place, I would do exactly as he will do. I will not hold it against him."

They went into the drawing room, together, where Amy was sitting in the glow of firelight and candlelight, her hands in her lap, her face, which was uplifted, radiant. Ernest was leaning against the mantelpiece, and looking down at her, was talking softly. They both started as Gregory and May entered the room.

CHAPTER XX

ERNEST FELT that everything was with him, tonight, when he led Amy from the dining room into the drawing room. Here everything was warm and dim and intimate, the fire a fretwork of red and gold on the hearth, the candles burning in an aura of gold. When Amy sat down before the fire, he thought he had never seen anything so lovely and exquisite as this girl, with the pure high sweetness of her expression and her perfect dignity. He stood, looking down at her.

He experienced a sensation of complete satisfaction and peace. Everything was complete. He had never seen awakening love in a woman's face before, but he saw it in Amy's, and it touched him profoundly. He felt quite humbled and contrite, and yet invincible. It was all so beautiful: this girl, the love he felt for her and the rising passion, the charming grace of the room, the old house, and everything that these things meant. He could not dissociate Amy from her home; somewhat banally he thought: She is like a pearl in its proper setting. His infatuation embraced the house and all the things in it. Without Amy, the house was nothing; without the house, Amy was disoriented, out of joint in his mind. He could not conceive of them being apart; the house was a body, and she was a spirit, he thought extravagantly.

Yet through all his extravagance, like a wool thread through cloth of gold, ran the sober and satisfying thought: Everything is to be hers, the mills, the mines, the foundries, the fortune in the bank and in stocks. It is a fortune! No doubt her uncles will give her a sizable dowry, just to begin with, and we shall live here together in this lovely house. I have seen larger houses, and newer houses, in Philadelphia and New York, but they were nothing compared to this. And Gregory is an old man, and his brother is old. In the normal course of events I shall soon be managing the mills, and when they die it will all be mine!

The excitement of his thoughts made his face glow, fill with expression. He bent down toward the girl, whose cheeks colored.

"Miss Amy," he said in a low voice, "how much I owe to you and your kindness! I was a—a barbarian, until I met you. You have introduced me to a new world, of music and books and fine living. How can I ever thank you?"

A fluttering rose in Amy's throat, and she felt tears in her eyes. She regarded him gently.

"Oh, Mr. Barbour, you are too kind! I am sure I have done nothing for you at all! But gentlemen frequently become so absorbed in business or in their professions that they have little time to cultivate music and literature. It is we women who must keep them alive, and ready, for the time when gentlemen can spare a few moments for them. They are only graceful things, after all, merely decorations. But you are interested in much more important matters."

"I was a barbarian," insisted Ernest. But he smiled, just a trifle smugly. He bent down and poked the fire to a brighter blaze. When he stood up his face was red and slightly agitated.

"Miss Amy, do you find me completely intolerable?"

The question was so abrupt and unexpected that Amy, used all her life to graceful circumlocutions, to polite innuendoes and suggestions, was taken aback. Her face turned scarlet with embarrassment; she did not know where to look. Then, meeting Ernest's eyes, she could not look away again.

"I am sure," she almost whispered, "that no one could find you at all intolerable."

"I am glad of that," he said, in a voice almost as low as hers. "You make me very happy, Miss Amy."

He drew a deep breath. He was about to burst out with his proposal when he suddenly remembered that gentlemen do not first approach a young lady, but ask her parents or guardian for permission to sue for her hand. He became almost sick with mortification. What a boor she must think him, how gross! It would serve him right if she rose and left the room haughtily, and never spoke to him again. But she did not do this; instead, she was regarding him with the brightest of expressions, and her soft pink lips were parted as though she waited eagerly. Fascinated, overcome, he looked into her eyes, and thought confusedly that he had never seen anything so radiant, so exquisitely trustful. Why, he thought, humbly, she loves me!

The thought was so shattering, so full of splendor and joy, that he felt that he was about to burst into tears. He forgot everything, everything, except that he loved this girl and she loved him, that he could have her as soon as he wished. He took her hands in his and kissed them, his lips shaking. He could feel the trembling of the small white fingers in his. All at once he was afraid, afraid that he might some day hurt her, that he might not be what she wanted. He released her hands with an aching reluctance. The devil with etiquette! He would speak, now!

The door opened at this very critical moment and Gregory and May Sessions entered. May bounced and glided coquettishly to the fire, and stood before it, fluttering her kerchief before her face. Gregory came behind Amy's chair and touched her head with his hand in a caress of great tenderness. But he looked at Ernest, smiling genially. He thought:

I pray to God he has had sufficient decency and decorum not to speak to her yet!

He said: "Ernest, you were a little precipitate this afternoon, about the loan of that money. Also, I did not have time to go over those papers. I shall be at the bank most of tomorrow, and so, if you care to, you and I can adjourn to the library and discuss this fully."

Ernest thought exultantly: "Luck is surely with me! I shall convince him of my worthiness tonight, and ask him for Amy."

They both formally begged the ladies to excuse them for a while, and permission being graciously given, they left the room together. Gregory was feeling distinctly sick; he had seen Amy's radiance, the soft color in her face. He felt that she followed them with her eyes, and he knew, with deep pain, what she was thinking. I can almost pray, he thought, that he will not be as I would be. Half an hour ago I was ready to knock him down for his presumption; now, remembering my poor Amy's face, I only hope he will be presumptuous!

The library was lit only by a great fire, and Gregory took some moments to light the candles. A cold premonition was on him; he wanted to delay what he must finally face. Ernest laid an envelope of papers on the immense mahogany table with its clawed feet; there was about him a serene and confident air, as though he had realized everything he had ever desired. In the light of the candles his face looked strong, yet young, and incredibly handsome; it was as though a stone face had come to life. The premonition lightened in Gregory; surely, if he loved Amy like this he would never give her up, even if she hadn't a solitary penny to her name!

They sat down, and Gregory poured two glasses of brandy, and put a gilt box of cigars on the table. "Now, let us see those papers," he said in an almost affectionately bantering voice. He glanced humorously at Ernest with his hard bright eyes, his lips lifting in a faintly satirical smile.

Ernest had never talked so well, so to the point, so pungently and convincingly. He was fighting, not only for his ambitions, but for Amy, also. So well trained and disciplined was his mind that he could put her face out of it, and concentrate on the matter at hand. Fighting for her, he forgot her in the fighting. He spoke with an adroitness rare with him; everything became clear, confident, irresistible. There is no failure in him, thought Gregory bitterly. He will always get what he wants. He listened to his guest with a grim surprise, watched the flash and play of expression on a face that was usually implacable and expressionless. And as he watched and listened, something in him became colder and harder with fear. He turned the papers over mechanically, nodded mechanically, smiled when he considered it expected of him. And heard and saw absolutely nothing except his own sick thoughts.

suddenly at the clock on the mantelpiece. They had been ...ost an hour, and he had said nothing! Forcing himself to smile, ...laid aside the papers. Ernest, in the midst of a telling argument, stopped abruptly, frowning somewhat. Gregory yawned elaborately.

"You have quite convinced me, Ernest," he said. "But convincing the other directors is another matter. However, I will take these papers to them tomorrow, and discuss it at length. Another glass of brandy?"

Ernest accepted, expanding. Disliking the taste of alcohol as he did, he felt he could endure it tonight. He sipped the brandy, stared raptly at the papers on the table. He did not see Gregory clasp his hands, lean forward toward him. He did not see the wrinkling of pain on his face.

"You have not visited us for some time now, Ernest." He made his tone casual and exceedingly friendly. "Of course, it is rather dull here, with an old man and one young girl. But we are changed, now. May is a lively young lady, and will brighten up this quiet house. Amy has been kept like a nun here, and I am hoping that May will enliven her, show her what it is to be young."

"Miss Sessions is to remain some time?" asked Ernest politely.

Gregory carefully cut the end of another cigar, threw it meticulously into the fire before answering. And when he did answer he did not look at Ernest.

"Oh, yes, she will remain. Probably for a long time. Maybe permanently. After all, you see, this is her home. She was born here, her father and mine were born here. Her father was eighteen years younger than mine, and married rather late in life. When Nicholas and I die, this house will belong to her. Everything will belong to her, our mills and foundries and mines. Our fathers were very devoted; they built up the Company together. May's father died two years before mine died, and my father's will left all he possessed to myself and my brother, and upon our deaths, to May. We are her guardians, and in addition to her already large fortune left to her by her father, she will, as I have said, have ours."

He paused. He affected to be deeply interested as to why his cigar did not smoke well; he frowned, muttered, brought out his penknife and trimmed it again. He knew that Ernest had not moved so much as a finger, nor turned his head, nor uttered a word, yet, without visible movement, Gregory could feel that he had become rigid. There was more violence in this silent rigidity than in an open cry or oath. Gregory put the cigar in his mouth and lit it; he prayed that the young man did not see how his hands were shaking. He sighed deeply.

"My sister, Amy, was cut from my father's will entirely, so my poor little Amy, here, has absolutely nothing. My father enjoined Nicholas and myself to protect, guard and cherish May, and allow not one cent of income derived from his property to be diverted to Amy. We respected him very much; we would never go against his wishes."

There was a silence. Finally, Gregory forced himself to look at Ernest. The young man sat in his chair like a statue; his face was deadly pale, the hands on the arms of the chair were clenched. But his expression was quite calm, his eyes straight and piercing as ever, as he regarded the older man. A horrible sinking sensation struck at Gregory's stomach, as though he were about to be sick. He made himself smile, picked up the papers as if to resume his survey of them.

"I don't know why I tell you all this, Ernest. It cannot be of the slightest interest to you. I don't usually make a confidant of any one, but I have been worried lately as to what will become of my little Amy when I am dead."

He stopped. And waited. Waited as he had never waited for anything with such frightful intensity before, not even when he watched by his dying father's bedside. Now, he thought, he will speak if he intends having her without a penny, having her just for her sweet self. Surely, he will speak if he will have her. My God, let him speak! I shall never forget her face tonight, when we came in the room: God, let him speak!

But Ernest did not speak. In fact, he looked as though he couldn't have spoken if he had tried. He had turned his head ever so slightly, and was now staring directly at the fire. His face was gray stone, carved and still, over which the firelight cast a specious change of expressions. At one moment he appeared to be smiling slightly, at another, to be grimacing in torment, at another, as if he had become ill. Gregory thought: Poor devil, it is as if the firelight shone on his soul, on his mind, and brought out their expressions through the thickness of his flesh. Even in his own pain, he was full of the strangest pity for this very young man who had gotten everything he had wanted, but this.

If I do not speak, he continued to himself, this will become rather shameful. We know each other's thoughts. He opened his mouth to speak, and was horrified that his voice, when it emerged, was hoarse.

"Of course," he said, "Amy will probably be married by the time I die, anyway." He smiled, and so dry were his lips that they cracked painfully when the smile spread them. "I am aware that she has had proposals, and it is only a matter of weeks until she accepts one."

Ernest stirred, turned his face. As though by some acute sixth sense, Gregory knew what an effort these movements cost him. Throughout his own muscles he could feel the strain and the pull, the heartsickness of the struggle, the terrible battle of the will.

"I am sure," Ernest's voice said, expressionlessly, formally, "that Miss Amy has not wanted for suitors. You are only in the prime of life, sir, and I believe you are worrying yourself unnecessarily." His voice stopped, dully.

Suddenly Gregory hated him. His pity was burned to a cinder in the flame of his hate. He half rose in his chair with an impulse to crash his t heavy young face with the unreadable eyes. He fell back, and pa. But Ernest was not looking at him, so he was spared this final shame. He felt a cold drop on his cheek, and was objectively amazed to discover that his forehead was wet with an icy sweat. With hands that shook visibly, he poured himself a large glass of brandy and gulped it down. Drawing the glass away from his mouth to set it upon the table, he stopped halfway in the gesture, and stared at Ernest. Ernest was calmly looking at his large gold watch. As he looked at it, he pursed his mouth judiciously, and frowned.

"It is almost eleven! And I have accounts to check over before I go to bed." He stood up, quite without an effort now. The life and light had left his face, but he was quite composed and inscrutable. Gregory laid down his glass and stood up also; he felt that eternities passed between each of his movements. His whole body ached as if it had been held in an intolerable strain through many hours. The two men regarded each other steadily. If you say what you would like to say, it will make it impossible for us to meet again, ever to have business with each other again, Ernest's cold eyes seemed to say. In the bright blue of Gregory's eyes something flickered like the flash of a snake's head. You have shamed me and my house, struck at a sweet girl's heart, said Gregory silently to him in reply to that silently projected thought. And then, suddenly, his face became ironic, satirically bitter: You have done what I would have done! You have done what I did! May your portion be as happy as mine has been.

They went back to the drawing room together. Each felt as though he were going to his own execution. To the enormous, soul-shaking relief of both of them, they found the room empty. The ladies had retired. The ormolu clock on the mantelpiece tinkled softly, eleven times, in the warm, candle-lit silence. Ernest looked about him, and it seemed that something exceedingly, unbearably, painful opened in his chest. He felt as an exile might feel.

He and Gregory said good night very formally, but they did not shake hands. One of the grooms had brought Ernest's horse from the Sessions Steel office when he had driven away with Gregory in his carriage. Now the horse was brought for Ernest. Gregory did not offer his carriage as usual.

The sound of his going had not yet died away when Gregory thought to himself, with a sudden surge of hope: "He has not decided yet. It is too great even for him to decide immediately. My God, I would not be in his shoes tonight!"

CHAPTER XXI

HILDA BARBOUR was sleeping uneasily.

She dreamt that she was suffering a great pain in her breast, and she thought, panting, in her dream: "I cannot endure this. Please, make it stop!"

But the pain did not stop, and now she discerned that it came rhythmically, in beats, dully yet ponderously. Like a heavy pulse. And she thought: "The pain is like footsteps." And somehow, realizing this, her pain seemed to increase, to leave her body and flood her mind, so that there was no release or end to it. She found herself sobbing, pleading with the owner of those footsteps to stop his endless, his eternal, marching back and forth through her brain and her thoughts. But he kept on marching, and finally she thought again: "It is because I know him and can't help him that it hurts so."

At this point she woke up, as if the pain had become intolerable, and found herself crying into her pillow. It was still dark, but as her windows faced east she could see a faint grayness in the eastern skies. In this half-darkness the heavy chairs in the bedroom, the posts of the bed, the mahogany wardrobe, took on nebulous and sinister shapes. Beside her, Joseph slept lightly and restlessly, and mechanically turning, she put her hand gently on his forehead. It was hot. Her heart sank. It was almost always hot in the morning, now. In the sick surge of her anxiety she momentarily forgot her dream, and then it came back to her most vividly. Her hand paused on her husband's head as she listened. Faintly, very faintly, yet dully, came the sound of footsteps marching back and forth over a carpeted floor; they never stopped: Hilda counted them, ten steps forward, ten steps back. She sat up in bed, concentrating. They came from Ernest's room.

She slipped cautiously from the bed, pulled her woolen wrapper over her ruffled cambric nightgown, stepped into carpet slippers, threw back her braids. She crept into the hall and listened. The footsteps sounded louder now. She moved down the hall to Ernest's door and knocked softly. The footsteps stopped. There was a long and humming silence. Downstairs the grandfather's clock boomed somberly, four prolonged strokes. In the room she had left Joseph moaned uneasily. But there was nothing but silence from Ernest's room. Hilda bent down and looked through the keyhole. A candle was burning on the table; it was sunken deep in serried rings of pallid wax, showing that it had been burning many hours. She could see nothing of Ernest but a hanging hand; however, from its position—turned toward the door—she knew that he was standing up and that he was facing her. The hand was not clenched, but because of something in the position of the fingers, the tensity of the knuckles, she knew it was the hand of someone who was in terrible distress. It fascinated her, that eloquent and suffering hand; it disarmed her also, in its utter helplessness, and yet she felt a little ashamed, as though she had come on her grown son quite naked. She knocked at the door again, shivering, for the hall was drafty and cold. After a long moment she heard steps approaching the door, and it opened just a crack.

"Well, Ma?" Ernest whispered, somewhat impatiently.

The sight of his hand, however, had given Hilda courage. She was no longer afraid of Ernest; he was just her lad, needing comfort. She tossed her head, pushed open the door pettishly, and bounced into the room. "Nonsense!" she said. "You wake me up, with your trampin', and now you want to know what I want!"

Ernest closed the door after her, and turned to her slowly. He was still fully dressed; his greatcoat and hat were thrown carelessly over a chair, with his gloves and his cane, and he was still in his coat. But his cravat was untied, his collar loosened. Over his chin spread a dark stubble, and his hair was disordered. His expression, even at that hour, was as impassive and calm as ever, but Hilda saw beyond the expression, saw the purple circles about his eyes, the strained brilliance of them, the white dents about his nose and mouth, the pinched nostrils. Her heart flowed out to him. Why, he's still just my lad, in petticoats! she thought, almost bursting into tears. Because of this, she was not cowed, as usual, by his formidable and impatient manner.

"What is it, Ernest? Can't you tell your Ma? I'm still your mother, lad."

He smiled, or rather, his mouth jerked convulsively.

"I've got a toothache, Ma," he answered in an indulgent voice. He regarded her almost fondly. Short and plump, wrapped in dark wool, her round face rosy and unwrinkled, and the black braids hanging over her shoulders, she looked young again.

He was palpably waiting for her to go. But she tossed her head again, said "pish!" and sat down deliberately. She studied him shrewdly.

"Toothache! You don't look it! If you had toothache you would have been yelpin' for help long ago. I know my men-folks. And you're not even undressed. Toothache doesn't hit one until one is in bed, almost asleep. And this candle: look at it, been burnin' for hours." She paused, leaned toward him in tender pleading. "Son, you ain't a man to me; you'll never be that. I can see in your face it's somethin' else. Let me help you."

Something chillily hostile crept into his expression; he stared at her steadily. Then he smiled again, almost with affectionate contempt. Even before he spoke she felt hopeless, as if a door had been shut inexorably in her face.

"You can help me, Ma, by going back to bed. The—the toothache's stopped now, and I'm going to undress and try to sleep. If you'll let me," he added.

She bounced angrily to her feet. "You are the most stiff-necked young devil I ever saw! Well, I'm not goin' back until I know you're goin' to bed!" She scurried to the bed, threw back its satin cover, folded over its blankets and quilts, and as she did this she muttered to herself. Ernest watched her helplessly. She swung upon him. "And I'm goin' to get you a cup of hot milk and a hot brick. It'll help you, if you have a toothache."

All the muscles tightened and hardened in his face. She went to the door, and he followed. After she had gone over the threshold, he said in a low voice: "Ma, don't come back. I don't want milk. I don't want a brick. All I want is to be alone." She started to speak, but he cut in deftly and brutally: "I've got to be alone. Otherwise, I'll leave this house. I insist on my privacy." And he closed the door firmly and silently even as she stared at him.

Hilda crept back to her warm bed and uneasily sleeping husband. She was very desolate. She felt that she had lost a son, that the man in the room she had left was a stranger. She huddled close to Joseph, pressed her cheek against his thin hot shoulder, holding his nightshirt in her hands, as though seeking protection. And she thought suddenly, painfully: There's no comfort for women in men!

Left alone, Ernest blew out his candle. The guttering light, since his mother's invasion, seemed obtrusive. He was given a specious sense of solitude and privacy in the darkness. He went to the window and looked out. This particular window faced large flat meadows and fields, but these fields and meadows were merely formless darkness meeting the formless darkness of the sky. The gray light had vanished, and the night itself was not so black as this coming dawn. But as Ernest watched dully, a long low line of fire ran between earth and sky, dividing them, and the ragged edges of it shot upward into the rosy fringes of the morning.

A heavy sense of amazement possessed him. Was it possible that the endless night had passed? It had seemed to him that everything in the universe had stopped, halted, ceased to be, during that night, that time itself had been suspended, and there was only himself in the cloudy chaos. But he saw before him now the evidence that nothing had stopped but himself, that all things had gone on implacably, heedless of him. He thought abstractedly: it is morning, and they'll be calling me for breakfast, and I've not even been to bed.

The trees outside were still leafless, but birds had returned and their awakening calls and whistles were shrill and achingly close. He heard a faint groaning in the attic above; the maids were beginning to rouse themselves. There was a dim quivering thunder in the air, and a train whistled long and thinly as it rushed away from the dawn.

The conflict in his mind had dulled it, as lashing whips will eventually anesthetize the flesh they sear. Now his thoughts, orderly and marshalled, could parade over this calloused area without torturing it.

His first sensation when Gregory had informed him, not too delicately, of Amy's position, had been one of profound and bitter disappointment. It had disrupted his thoughts, thrown him into disorder. He had felt routed, utterly dispersed, confronted by something he could not yet face and overcome. He was not quick to readjust his ambitions, the trend of his thoughts; he lacked facility of emotion. As he never had alternate plans, and built all his hopes and determinations on one premise, he lacked the flexibility of mind of those who wisely provide themselves with alternatives. This cast of mind of his was well suited to the attainment of success, but badly tuned to those inevitable defeats that even the strongest natures must sometimes acknowledge. His disappointment had been so catastrophic that he was submerged in it; he could experience only one emotion at a time, so felt no immediate grief at the probable loss of Amy Drumhill. He had gone back to the drawing room with Gregory, and had looked about the lovely, ivory-tinted, crystal-brightness of the room with a feeling of frightful loss. It is safe to say that he did not think of Amy actively until he arrived at his own home, went upstairs to his room.

The disappointment was lifting slightly by this time, and his emotions could concern themselves with Amy. He had begun to pace his room with a slow frenzy.

Once he stopped, stupefied with amazement. Going over the scene in his mind with Gregory, he recalled that the older man had been hinting broadly that he would not be averse to Ernest's suing for Amy's hand. Remembering this, his amazement grew. He had been concerned all evening with ingratiating himself with Gregory, adroitly getting the latter into a position where he would have found it impossible to refuse. And Gregory, in the end, had tried to force the issue, to thrust Amy into his arms! Glaring about his room, Ernest had rubbed his head, in stupefaction. For a few moments a fire of gratification ran through him.

Then he thought: A penniless girl who would bring him nothing! That house, the land, the mills, the foundries, the mines—they were not hers, and if he married her, they would not be his. A penniless girl, with ␣ly the gloves on her hands and the clothes (bought with the coin of ␣ity) on her back. For a little while it did not occur to Ernest ␣us-minded that he was, to give up Amy. His desires had fastened on her, and though he looked at her with bitterness, something of anger and disillusion, he did not at first intend to relinquish her. Had Gregory known this, he would have been astounded.

No, he did not at first intend to give her up. The thought did not occur to him, for he loved her. Even in his desperate disappointment, he loved her as much as ever, and even as he thought of her in the new light of her poverty, something warm and soft and tender glowed in him. Brine burnt his eyes.

He sat down, overcome and weak. He covered his face with his hand, shielding it from the candlelight. But—a penniless girl! He had worked so hard, so passionately, so strenuously, so mightily. It was wrong, very wrong, to have fallen in love with a girl who could bring him nothing at all, no dowry, not even a carriage or jewels. He would open his home and his arms to a woman for whom he would have to provide in cold coin. Inevitably, there would be children, but they would not run through the wide cool halls of the Sessions house, would not play on the lawns and in the gardens. He tried to visualize himself in a strange house, with Amy and her children, but his vision had so crystallized itself in another environment that he could not make this alternate true. It remained tasteless and unreal, and he regarded it heavily, without appetite. Even Amy, while he still loved her, did not stir that appetite. But still, he did not yet think of relinquishing her.

He began to pace again, a heavy nausea dragging at his vitals. He stood by the window, staring out. Due to his own orders for steel, the Sessions plant was working the past few nights. Against the black curtain of the night he could see the dull scarlet glow hovering over the chimneys of the mills. The glow taunted him, sickened him, filled him with an irreparable loss. Had Amy died when he was about to take her, he could have felt no greater grief. He struck his fists together in desperate anguish. He had lost everything—a stranger would inherit all he had built on, all he had confidently seized beforehand.

Up and down the room he had marched, while the candle dwindled more and more, and the drops of it hissed. The fire had long since died, and an ashen chill stole through the air. He glanced at the bed, and thought, sadly, that he would never be able to rest in it in peace again. He thought: If I could only cry, like a woman! But he was conscious, all the time, of the restless prowling of his obstinacy and his ambitions: they still would not let go—they still looked for a way in which he could have what he had desired.

He fell into his chair once more, exhausted. He put his hand abstractedly into his pocket, and his fingers closed about a little filmy kerchief he had carried about for a long time. Withdrawing it, he regarded it with a worn and twisted smile. He held it to his nose, and a faint odor of jasmine floated up his nostrils. The odor brought Amy vividly before him, her soft bright eyes, her parted eager mouth, her white throat and soft little bosom. His hands clenched on the kerchief, and in the candlelight his harsh large face was suddenly transfigured, softened into a touching tenderness. His lips moved as if they were tasting the sweetness of her innocent mouth; involuntarily his arms lifted, stretched out to embrace the vision. "Amy," he said, aloud.

As if his voice had been an evil shout to break a lovely spell, the vision was shattered. But the hunger remained. He jumped to his feet, paced feverishly. He could not endure the girl's absence; he could not endure his arid longing. What did it matter, after all, if she were penniless? He had a thousand times enough! With Amy, all things were possible. Why, damn it, he would have a dozen mills such as the Sessions; he would have mines that dwarfed the Sessions mines! He would have the world! All that he wanted now was Amy. The devil with anything else —these puny things could be had by dint of his strength and his planning. Strange thoughts for a young man like this, and in later years, remembering, he could hardly credit that he had had them.

All his exhaustion fell away from him; he was uplifted, exalted. His heart began to beat very fast; he paced rapidly, in a delicious disorder. Everything was solved, everything was settled. There was only Amy. And the sooner he had Amy the sooner this delight would come to stay. Feeling confident and strong, and suddenly refreshed, he went to his huge mahogany desk, pulled out paper, whittled his pen, plunged it into the brass inkwell. He wrote:

"I have the honor, sir, to sue for the hand of your niece, Miss Amy Drumhill, and ask your permission to press my suit with her." With flourishes, he signed his name: Ernest Louis Barbour. He folded the letter, addressed it to Gregory Sessions, Esquire.

So inflexible and ponderous was his mind that had he gone to bed then, with the letter written, his resolution made, nothing would have upset his will again. In later years he was to look back on those few minutes following the writing of the letter, and wonder. How different his life would have been! How different, his children! Posterity had hung on those minutes, a whole dynasty balanced on them. Perhaps a world had been different if he had gone to bed then. Just the mere act of taking off his boots, blowing out his candle, lying down under the quilts, would have changed scores, perhaps multitudes, of lives.

But he did not want to go to bed just yet. He had never felt so wakeful, so intense and feverish. A light sweat had come out on his body, and he was conscious that he was trembling a little. He seemed to feel Amy's very flesh in the room, virginal and soft; at any moment he expected to turn and see her, waiting and smiling. All at once, he needed air, floods and currents of cool fresh air, and he ran to the window.

He flung out the window, breathed deeply. The night was very still, and now he was conscious of a faint throbbing against it, like beating wings. The Sessions mills. Pouring out steel—for him. Making wealth —for him. He saw the flare of its fires. Slowly, very slowly, his hands dropped to the sill; his eyes could not leave the flare, could not turn from it. A coldness ran over his body, and a taste of salt spread over his tongue. Only last night he had stood like this, and had looked at those flares, exultantly. Only last night, he had stretched out his hand greedily, had clenched it as though it grasped. Only last night his heart had beat with impatience and anticipatory joy. Only last night, he had been on the very edge of all his ambitions.

And as he stood there, becoming colder and colder each moment, feeling heavier and sicker, the light dying out of him like a febrile flame that had had very little to feed upon, Amy's face dimmed, dissolved, passed away. And for the first time another face stood before his. The face of May Sessions.

He remembered now, with a sort of profound shock, that she had looked at him provocatively, challengingly, admiringly. She had looked at him as the whores he had frequented had looked at him. So familiar had been that glance that he had passed it over, mechanically. But now it returned, significant. It had not been the look of a pretty woman who merely wanted to flirt: it had been full of desire and invitation. She had smiled and coquetted, she had simpered behind her fan, she had laughed at him and prodded him and shaken her ringlets at him. When he had stared at her fixedly, he had been surprised to see her blush like a school-girl, for all her sophistication. Her face had been the face of a woman seized with hunger.

"By God," he said slowly and heavily, aloud, "I could have her if I wanted her."

And then he had stood there, gazing blindly out into the night, for a long time.

When he finally moved, it seemed to him that his flesh had frozen, become stiff and old, that something had twisted upward like a wisp of smoke in him, and had vanished. Slowly, as if propelled against his will, he went to his desk, and picked up the letter he had written to Gregory Sessions. He turned it over in his hands, over and over, dully, with empty eyes and a face that was suddenly sunken and full of furrows and white dents. And then he picked up the candle in one hand and ignited the letter. He held it, staring at it, while it was being consumed, until it was but an edge of whiteness rimmed with charcoal. He put down the candle, but still held that edge. Then he dropped it, watched it flutter to the floor.

He took a few turns up and down the room, lightly, almost staggeringly. It was at that time that his mother knocked at his door, and he had stood beside the table, beside the murdering candle, listening, breathless, hoping she would go away. And she had peered through the keyhole, seeing his hanging hand, that eloquent hand that said everything his mouth would never say to any one.

CHAPTER XXII

ON THE third day Gregory Sessions said to himself: "He will not come. He has decided against her."

He looked at Amy's serene smile and tranquil expression, and he knew that she had no suspicion as yet. But a week passed, two weeks, three weeks, and the smile became slight and automatic, and when she thought herself unobserved her expression was bewildered and pinched. At the end of a month, when spring became summer and a pall of heat lay over the valley, Amy's face had lost its color, become white and translucent as a moonstone. She seemed to lose vivacity and spirit, and though she never complained, Gregory noticed that she moved slowly and heavily, as though weighted down, and that she frequently stood at the windows that looked out on the drive. But if anything, her smile was sweeter, if more uncertain, and her low, steadfast voice was gentler. May uneasily insisted upon Amy accompanying her on drives and small social visits, and with a sort of anxious remorse, tried many expedients to restore life and pleasure to the stricken girl.

No one mentioned Ernest's name. When Gregory mentioned Barbour & Bouchard, he carefully skirted about that name, sometimes going into elaborate circumlocutions. Had Amy been of a suspicious nature, she would have suspected something, but being unsuspicious, it was not hard to deceive her. May and Gregory aligned themselves together to save the girl's "face." If May felt some natural feminine contempt that her young cousin had not been able to bewitch a man into forgetting her fortuneless state, she did not show it by the slightest glance or word. Being intelligent, she was able to achieve the nice balance of forcing Amy out on calls with her and hiding her real pity and regret. She cleverly scolded Amy for her pale face and "vapors," irritably demanded to know the reason, fretted and upbraided with great skill. Gregory, following her clue, threatened the doctor, bought extract of iron in a large bottle, pretended annoyance. And Amy, looking at them with her bewildered eyes, betrayed, heart-breakingly, the piteous relief she felt that they had not suspected her humiliation.

Alone, or with May, Gregory cursed Ernest with passion and hatred. He swore that he would never permit him to enter his house again, that he was a low-born upstart possessed by a Napoleonic devil, a nincompoop without culture or civility or respectability, a mere presumptuous, impudent and uneducated peasant. And to think that a man like this dared repudiate Amy, whose great-grandfather had been a cousin of the Virginia Fairfaxes, an officer on Washington's staff, a signer of the Declaration of Independence, a descendant of the Earl of Sussex! It was intolerable! He, Gregory, no longer believed in democracy: democracies exalted no men, but levelled the highest to the state of the lowest. "The common denominator of the barnyard," he said. In democracies, one's inferiors not only dared aspire to climb to one's elevation, but arriving there, insulted one, spat in one's face. Such a system of government was insupportable, to those who were by right of birth, fortune and culture entitled to occupy the high places in peace. He expressed longings for England, where a nice adjustment had been made centuries before, and where no one had the audacity to question a régime that had Nature, herself, as protagonist. In England, he said, such as Ernest Barbour would not only not have aspired to Amy's hand, but would not have dreamt of aspiring. A good booting would have been his punishment had he dared to look at her or touch her hand. But in America, we had tavern equality, where miscellaneous beer-dregs polluted the fine wine of high-born and gentle blood.

May would listen to all this, her dimples appearing and disappearing with faint cynicism. She would fan herself thoughtfully and think: "Nevertheless, my dear cousin, I shall marry him!"

A few days after that humiliating night, Gregory had almost, for the actual space of two minutes, decided to veto Ernest's request for the loan. With this veto, the other directors would have doubted, wavered, finally, respecting the Sessions acumen, would have refused. A discreet word to the banks of Philadelphia and New York, and the loan would have been turned down unanimously. Gregory formed in his mind his message to the banks: "After all due consideration, careful and secret investigation of Barbour & Bouchard, though showing apparently sound assets and fine credit rating, etc., etc., leads us to the belief, due to certain phases of character of the owners, the spirit of doubt in their ranks, and certain animosities, that the loan would be badly advised."

The Sessions name on such a message would have been the seal!

Gregory gloated over this unwritten message; he gloated over Ernest's face when the loan was refused. His gloating rose to a frenzy of hatred. He actually picked up his pen to write his veto to his bank.

And then he burst out laughing in self-contempt, tossed the pen from him so that it rolled off the desk and fell to the floor with a derisive clatter.

"You know you can't do that!" he said aloud, to himself. "It would destroy your own future profits!" He felt sick with his self-disgust, sick that he could gloss over for the sake of profits an insult to the only thing

᷁e loved. But he was also realist enough to know that the approval of the loan was the act of a sensible man. Only idealists and other fools could afford the luxury of righteousness and indignation. He went down to the bank, approved the notes, argued with a few cautious and suspicious directors, beat down opposition, signed the approval with large flourishes. A few days later he received this polite and cold note from Ernest, written in his neat, harsh hand: "I have learnt that had it not been for your kind intervention and insistence, your championing of me and belief in me, the loan would have been refused. I have the great honor, sir, of proffering my sincere thanks and lifelong gratitude."

Gregory's first reaction when he received this note was that he was about to have a stroke, his second, profound and shattering mirth. He howled with choking laughter, struck his thigh, threw himself back in his chair, shrieking. He carried the note to his cousin, for he recognized in that young woman a very salty realist. She read it, and smiled broadly. She said: "What irony! The young man is no fool." When Gregory, stopping his laughter suddenly, stared at her in surprise, she added: "I suppose this is his first attempt at humor." And joined Gregory in his renewed hilarity.

But a month later he became uneasy, for two reasons. Amy had lost much weight, and there was in her face a certain transparency that betrayed failing health. She hardly took the trouble to speak except when a direct question was put to her. Daily, she became more languid, yet restless, as if her body craved relaxation but her nerves refused it. She did appear to be utterly heartbroken; but it became very plain that she was also now ill with humiliation. She had had time to think, to brood over Ernest's loss of interest, his shameful desertion of her. Once when his name was inadvertently mentioned, a wave of scarlet swept over her face, and she looked as though she had suddenly been robbed of the power to speak. Feeling her shame and mortification, she began to creep furtively about the house, unable to look the servants and her uncle and cousin in the eye; she flushed, trembled, avoided all human contacts. Her behavior was that of a woman who has been publicly disgraced for deserved reasons. This was the first reason for Gregory's uneasiness, but not the more important.

The second reason was that he daily expected the arrival of his brother, Nicholas, and retinue. The rooms were all ready, extra servants engaged, and an accelerated air in the house. Though more than a hint had been written to the Senator by his brother about the possibility of a military contract being awarded to Barbour & Bouchard, Nicholas had remained blandly noncommittal; in fact, he had not replied to the first half dozen hints at all. Finally he had written: "I must see into this myself, when I return to Windsor. After all, there are more things to the awarding of a contract than a Senator's predisposition, my dear

Gregory." Now he was coming home, and among the things he would decide would be the possibility of an army contract for Barbour & Bouchard, and the subsequent accruing profits to the Sessions Steel Company. And at this time, this most important of all times, Amy must become lovesick (poor Amy, my little lamb!) and drive away the one person who would be able to impress Nicholas. Armand Bouchard was able, but Nicholas suspected "foreigners." Joseph Barbour, Nicholas would probably feel, was too erratic and excitable: he would not inspire respect from Nicholas. As for Martin Barbour, Raoul and Eugene Bouchard—Gregory grimaced. What weak rods they were! The brains of the company resided in Ernest, Joseph and Armand, but Ernest held the possibility of a military contract in his own hands. So, because of Amy's "lovesickness," the contract might go a-glimmering. Thinking this, Gregory's irritation rose, and he was rather short with Amy. Her timid, humiliated expression deepened into fright, and she ran from him. He cursed himself, fumed, felt his irritation become an ugly sense of wrong, knew himself to be cruel and unreasonable to the only creature he loved and who loved him, hated himself for this, and felt a renewed if loving resentment against the girl. Women, he thought angrily, cannot keep their boudoirs even from the counting house and the Senate chamber. Damn it, the girl had driven away Ernest Barbour, just when Nicholas returned!

He thought it over, biting his lips. Then he conceived quite a clever plan from his sincere desire to alleviate the girl's sufferings and his wish to bring Ernest and Nicholas together. He knew very well that he could not approach Ernest, except on the most cold and formal of footings, until he was reconciled with him, and Nicholas had a particular hatred of cold and formal footings, except when he deliberately created them himself. But other people's affairs, especially when they collided deleteriously with his, aroused his impatience and his ire. No, the contract business had to be discussed genially and informally and intimately in this very house, if anything were to be accomplished.

So one warm dim summer evening Gregory sent for his niece. She stole silently into the library, a too-slender, white little ghost in her huge and filmy skirts, her glossy ringlets clustered childishly about her pale cheeks. She looked at Gregory with frightened eyes, sat down, regarded him silently, and waited.

He began to pace up and down the shadowed twilight of the big library, affecting great agitation and distress; she watched him, her eyes following him mutely. Finally he stopped before her, bent over her, his hands on the arms of her chair, and kissed her forehead gently. She did not stir for a moment, then she leaned her head upon his shoulder as though she were very tired. He stood up, averted his face.

"Amy, my love," he began hesitantly, "I must confess something to you, and afterward, beg your forgiveness. I should have told you before, but I did not think it important. However, I mentioned it to May, only today, and she expressed the opinion that I should tell you, in order that we all might refrain from punishing too much a young man whose only fault was his very natural presumption. After all, May said, no man coming in contact with Amy could help loving her, and it was really too harsh to deprive this certain young man of the pleasure of her society and the society of his other friends here because of something outside his will."

For a few moments an expression of stark bewilderment settled itself on Amy's face, then she suddenly flushed crimson. Her mouth fell open as she uttered a faint cry; she half rose in her chair, then fell in it again. She clasped her hands tightly in her lap, and fixed her eyes passionately on her uncle. Meeting those eyes, he felt a momentary shame.

"Amy, my love, the last time Ernest Barbour was here, you will remember that he accompanied me into the library, leaving you in the drawing room with May. We had been together here only a few moments when he impetuously asked me for your hand." He stopped; Amy had put her handkerchief to her lips with a sharp gesture, and over the filmy bit of lace her gaze widened, deepened, filled with tears.

He affected to laugh uncomfortably. "Naturally, my pet, I refused. What else could I do? Here was a man who not only was low-born and under-bred, a boor and an upstart, but also a scoundrel, a mountebank of the worst order. He had attained his success by reason of skullduggery, cheating, treason, ingratitude and greed. I found it quite easy to silence him, for I knew that you had no regard for him whatsoever, that a lady of your breeding and your blood would have been outraged at the very suggestion. My first impulse was to kick him down the stairs. And then, I pitied him. For it was very evident that he had a sincere attachment for you."

He stopped again, for Amy had suddenly begun to cry into her kerchief, deep, long, wavering sobs. Her slender shoulders huddled and shook, her ringlets fell over her face. But there was release in her weeping, release from intolerable humiliation.

Gregory's voice broke with real feeling when he continued: "I knew such a man would never make my darling happy, that he would break her heart, bring her shame and mortification and grief. So I not only refused, but forbid him to speak to you. Being low-bred, he arrogantly said he would speak to you anyway, and I replied that my niece, my dutiful Amy, would refuse him at my command, knowing that I would never recover if she made a bad match, and that, she, realizing that I am an old man and have no other thing to love and love me in all the world, would never leave me until I felt able to relinquish her."

He knelt down beside the weeping girl, drew her head to his shoulder.

"Amy, my dearest, you would not leave your desolate old uncle until he was quite willing to give you up into the hands of someone he would feel was worthy of you? Amy, I am an old man, and I have not so long to live: if you married against my wishes, married someone unworthy, someone detestable, I would never be happy again. Promise me, my love, that you will marry only when I give my consent?"

She clasped her hands about his neck, and sobbed: "O uncle, you know I would never leave you, never!" He could feel the trembling of her light body; he kissed her over and over with a sort of remorseful passion.

"Ah, my darling, you will leave me some day with one worthy of you. And I shall be happy. How else could I be, but happy?" She shook her head slowly and with a sort of painful grief. "Yes, my love." He tightened his arms about her, and let her cry out the poison of her humiliation and the bitterness of her love. He fixed his mind on what May had really said, that Amy's fancy only had been touched, and not her heart. He hoped so, by God, he hoped so!

After a while her sobs grew easier; she wiped her eyes, and fixed them, in all their luminous innocence and pity, on his: "Uncle Gregory, he— he was not too hurt? You were not too—harsh? He—he did not look too distressed?"

Gregory hesitated. Now, this was all damnation! What should he say? If he said Ernest was utterly cast down, her pity might indeed ripen into enduring love; if he said Ernest was philosophical, she would be ill from mortification. So he said, picking his way as a man picks his way between sharp stones: "One cannot say. I would say, however, that he had a sincere regard for you, but he is too impatient, too gross, to linger over ground he knows will never be his. Nevertheless, May says that I am being too harsh to him. I had told her of his admiration of our home, and his pleasure in it, and she believes it is cruel to deprive him of the only means to culture of a sort that is open to him. Also, she says, it is very humiliating to you to allow him to form the idea that I have permanently banished him because you are so lacking in sensibility and decorum that you might form an attachment for him, against my wishes.

"So she advised me to ask you what to do, and abide by your wishes in the matter."

Amy wiped her eyes, smiled feebly, colored a little.

"You are perfectly right, Uncle Gregory, and dear May, too. We—we must not be cruel. I think it would be nice if we invited him to dinner, to meet Uncle Nicholas."

"Do you think so?" he asked humbly and doubtfully, but inwardly gratified. How easily women could be swayed through vanity or love! But through love more than through vanity. One had only to appeal to their affections, their tenderness, their mercy, and the creatures ran to floods of warm water. Precious fools!

It was finally arranged that Gregory should write a note to Ernest inviting him on the evening of June 21st to attend a dinner in honor of Senator Nicholas Sessions. While writing the note, and hoping that it was as cool and formal as possible, Gregory, on an impulse, suggested that Ernest also bring his brother, Martin. This addition, he believed, made the note more impersonal. He thought about Martin Barbour as he folded the note and rang for his butler's young son. He had met Martin many times, had talked to him briefly and pleasantly. He recalled the young man's excessive and almost womanish good looks, the clear and straightforward blue eyes. (No murkiness, there!) A strange pair, those brothers. He intrigued Gregory, who discerned in him the voice, the features, the dignity, the manner and bearing of a gentleman. He spoke with pride and a touch of hauteur, was courteous but without intimacy. There was a curious detachment about him, a dreamlike quality, very irritating, Gregory guessed with amusement, to one of Ernest's exigency. At times, he was stony-faced, wore an air of deliberate imperviousness. Yes, a very odd and irritating young man. Familiar of a cripple. Probably lived in a world of roses and enchantment and moonlight and impossible gossamer creatures. Gregory shrugged, sealed the note. He enjoyed odd people, for he detested mankind and liked to laugh at it.

CHAPTER XXIII

When Ernest received the note in his office, he turned it over and over in his hands, absentmindedly. So the old boy decided to call quits for his own advantage, he thought. He threw the note from him, contemptuously, shrugging. He felt very tired these days, full of an unemotional heaviness. For a long time he stared at the note, as it hung on the edge of his desk; he slowly rubbed his face with his hands. Then he recalled something, and smiled grimly. He picked up the note and went to the door of Martin's small office and opened it. The evening was hot and dim, presaging a storm, and a lamp stood on the plain table where Martin worked at his books. The dull yellow light fell on his bent head and grave face and steadily moving hand. He glanced up, when he became aware of his brother, and waited, not speaking.

Ernest tossed the note to him, smiling again. Martin looked at it suspiciously, not picking it up, as though it might contain something hurtful, having come from his brother's hand. A glimmer of amusement flickered across Ernest's impassive face. Of course, he thought, he will refuse. But I wonder what fantastic excuse he will offer?

Martin read the note thoughtfully. Then he glanced at Ernest; an unusual animation expressed itself on his features. "Isn't Senator Sessions the great Abolitionist? Didn't he make that stirring speech in the Senate last session?"

"Yes, I believe he is the one." Ernest regarded him curiously. "He has no slaves of his own, naturally."

"Why are you so cynical? Why can't you believe that persons might be actuated, occasionally, by honorable and kindly motives? Do you believe there is no good in all the world?" Martin's voice rose to the thin edge of hysteria, and he flung his pen from him with Ernest's own gesture. He bounded to his feet, ran to the window and stared through it, as though the sight of his brother excited him to intolerable frenzy. He clenched his hands at his side, and to Ernest's amazement, he trembled.

"You are the damnedest fool, you know," said Ernest quietly. "Of course I believe there are good and disinterested persons in the world. There are Pa and Ma, for instance—and you—and—oh, countless others, I suppose. I wish you'd stop making me out to be a stage bogeyman," he added irritably. "I'm not, really. Where you got the daft idea is beyond me. Gad, you're an ass!" He went toward the door. "You will want me to refuse for you, of course?"

Martin was silent for a few moments. He seemed to be struggling with the vestiges of his former hysteria. Ernest's irritation rose furiously, and he doubled his fist. What a feckless fool it was, to be sure! Full of womanish vapors and all kinds of nonsense. A fellow couldn't talk to him without him flying into weird excitements. Martin turned to him just as he was about to leave the room.

"I—I want to go. I want to see Senator Sessions," he said in a low dull voice, not looking at his brother. Ernest, after his first stare of surprise, went out without comment. He was surprised, once he was in his own room, to discover that he felt nauseated. His tiredness overflowed him; he glanced at his desk with a sudden loathing and distaste. Where was this all getting him? Where was he going? There was his father, who watched every move he made with the darkest and the most ridiculous suspicions. There was his brother, who lived in fantasies and thought him some Popish demon. There was old Armand, who accepted, even sought, intimacies, but gave none himself. Raoul and Eugene— Raoul was a crafty, smiling, indolent fool, and Eugene was too slavish and unquestioning in his admiration. There were others he knew slightly in Windsor, young and greedy men like himself, whom he could not trust, young gallants who chased women and foolish other pleasures, dull and arrogant dolts who sneered at him. There was absolutely no one else. Except Amy.

His feeling of sickness increased. It was as though his will, which had put Amy forever out of his life, was a stone wall against which he, himself, beat his head impotently. The will seemed beyond him, outside him. He could see it in his mind's eye, impervious and unbreakable. Someone came into the room. It was Eugene, carrying a pistol.

"Ernest! Look at this! See, this little trigger—this hook! I've got the pistol loaded: I pull back this little catch. Try it! There! You see, it won't fire! And so simple, too, not like the safety catches Colt and the rest have been making. You can see that it is so close to the trigger that it can be flipped off and on almost with a single motion."

The two young men discussed this latest invention of Eugene's eagerly. Of course, said Ernest, it was a little too flimsy; it could easily get out of order. The trick was to work it out so that the catch would be firm and strong, yet light, easy of manipulation. Yes, Eugene agreed, his father had said the same thing. It would take some working out. Now, it could be done this way— He talked on, rapt, his long strong finger with its blunted tip pointing and demonstrating. Ernest found himself watching him, almost sadly. Eugene did not as yet interpret his inventions in terms of money. His innate miserliness and cautious frugality had not yet made themselves felt. He was a scientist, in a laboratory. A neophyte in a monastery. One of the (what did Martin call it?), yes, one of the Partners of Death. But a dedicated, serious, curiously innocent young partner. He turned out his inventions as a bee made honey—impersonally, industriously. He was sturdy, rather stocky, not unhandsome, a little grim and heavily grave, but virile. Probably a virgin, too, thought Ernest. There was something chaste about him, in spite of his strength and his infrequently bullying manner with others. There was also about him the simplicity and single-mindedness of the peasant.

"We ought to be hearing from Raoul, soon," said Ernest, as Eugene finished speaking. "Three hundred men for us this time, Eugene! We've got to get the Kinsolving works under way. We can't forget those inevitable notes, you know."

"My father was saying he hoped we had not bitten off more than we can chew," said Eugene. But his voice was not uneasy. He was like a child when he spoke of such matters. "But no matter; you, you cannot fail, my Ernest."

"Why do you say that?" asked Ernest, obscurely annoyed. "I'm only human, you know. Why shouldn't I fail as well as better men?"

Eugene smiled with affectionate cunning. He tapped Ernest on his arm with his finger. "Do you know what you are, my Ernest? Destiny. You, and maybe a few others, in this grand country. There is destiny in you. Yes, destiny. This is a country for destinies, like yours. That is why you cannot fail."

"You French!" grumbled Ernest, as they went together into the factory. "The most fanciful race alive. That's why you stomached a Napoleon as long as you did. He appealed to the actor in you. And speaking of fancies reminds me: what the devil has your Jacques done to my brother, Martin? He always did have a white liver and womanish ways, but he's gone clean daft, now. Has Jacques been telling him some terrible Popish fairy tales?"

Eugene's bland and friendly expression disappeared. He glanced at Ernest with a furtive coldness. "Of course, you English could not understand Jacques," he said stiffly. "Jacques is a saint. It is well for your brother that he knows Jacques. Jacques has the influence of heaven in him; I have never heard him utter a hard word or say a cruel thing. To know him is to know one of God's own angels. If Martin's spirit has been impressed by him, it is because God has blessed him."

"There is something here I don't quite understand," thought Ernest. "You can go only so far with these people, and then you see they are unfriendly strangers at heart, if you try to go all the way. There is no trusting or understanding them."

"There is no trusting or understanding them," thought Eugene. "They make light of the most sacred things, and become solemn over trifles that do not matter."

Joseph, irritably supervising the sluggish work of the Magyar laborers in the powder room, glanced with some sullenness at his son. "I tell you, I can't stand these fellows. They make my gorge rise. Lazy brutes. Hell, though, it's not their fault; it's ours. Yours. For bringing them here."

"Now what's the matter?" asked Ernest good-naturedly. He turned with a frown and sharp gesture to the laborers, who suddenly acquired speed. "You don't step on them, Pa. They don't understand kindness. They've been clouted all their lives and kicked in the breeches. Come on, there, you, you big fellow with the red hair! We haven't all day. Come, come on!" His voice crackled like a whip, and the laborers began to roll barrels and shovel the acrid gray powder with zeal. "There, Pa, that's how to do it."

"I'm not a—a Simon Legree," growled Joseph.

Ernest laughed. "So you've been reading that book of Martin's, eh? Damned rot, that's what it is. Written by a sentimental old fool who probably never saw a blackamoor in her life."

"You're a hard devil," said his father, with an odd glance at him.

Ernest went in search of Armand. The Frenchman seemed a little somber. He filled his pipe while Ernest discussed some matters, and then he said, fixing his small bright eyes intently upon him: "Look you, my Ernest, unless we secure those military contracts you have spoken of, we are quite ruined. I am not certain that it was wise to accede to your wish to buy the Kinsolving works. As it stands now, it is a—a white elephant on our hands. Nothing is being produced there, for you refuse to hire American workmen, and those four foremen you have retained are standing idle, waiting for supplies and men."

"Within a month we shall have three hundred men, Armand. Big, powerful devils. The foremen understand foreign labor. The supplies have been ordered. In the meantime, the factory is being put to rights, the machinery being repaired. Within two months we shall be running day and night. I am positive of this. As for the military contracts: I tell you, we shall have them before the summer is over. Tomorrow, Sunday, I am invited to meet Senator Sessions."

"I hope your golden hopes are justified," said Armand, shrugging. "I have stood with you at all times, my young friend, even when my better judgment shook its head. I must admit you were right. But you cannot always be right. Everything I have is in this work. I have no money besides. If we sink, go into bankruptcy, I am a ruined man."

"We shall not lose," said Ernest. He walked away. "I shall not lose," he added to himself. But there was no ease in his thoughts. His father was obviously ill; his fevered flesh seemed to be consuming itself, brightening his eye, making the bones ridge themselves visibly under his skin. He would not rest, however, and Ernest, knowing his suspicions of him, dared not suggest that he rest. And the military contracts: he had to have them, that was all. Without them, he knew only too well, they were, as Armand had said, "quite ruined."

Damn it, everyone leaned on him. He was sick of it.

But tomorrow he would meet Senator Sessions at last. The military contract must be obtained. There could be no ifs or whens about it: it must be obtained. He would not allow himself to think of any alternative. It was victory or ruin.

It was characteristic of him that, concentrating on the business he must do the next day, he entirely forgot Amy and the pain it would cause him to see her once more. He forgot Amy, indeed. But he did not forget what he must do, and he did not forget May Sessions.

CHAPTER XXIV

WHEN ERNEST and Martin arrived at the Sessions house the next day, they found the grounds filled with laughing and chattering groups of strangers.

It had been very hot lately, but today was balmy and soft. The air seemed to have a material quality like silk, and the breeze appeared to move it visibly. The great trees sprayed gigantic green fountains against an intensely blue sky. The leaves darted and leapt and glittered in a rain of light. Cloud shadows rippled over the broad and sloping lawns; the wind shook the flowers in their beds, swirled the many-colored skirts of the women, so that they looked like delicate tops, bent back the broad-brimmed straw hats and showed dozens of pretty faces and tossing ringlets. The strong gray-stone house was alternately sparkling with speckled sunlight or drenched in rushing shadow. The grass turned silver as it bent, became vivid green as it sprang upright. Everything shone, danced, shook, sparkled, quivered with color, laughed, in a day that ran and warmed and trembled with radiance.

The two collies came barking and tumbling to meet them. Ernest had so far won their tolerance that they greeted him with pleasant reserve. Turning to Martin, however, they joyously flung themselves upon him, worrying his boots, licking his hands, laughing at him with their soft brown eyes. He was awkward with most animals, so spoke to them with an amusing courtesy, which delighted them. Their enthusiasm embarrassed him; he knew nothing about dogs. But, evidently, they knew him. They adopted him, fought for his attention fondly, staged sham battles for his mirth as they preceded him up the broad pathway. "The dogs," said Ernest with a wry amusement, "seem to like you, Martin."

Martin, who disliked and feared strangers, was chilly with terror. He marched straight ahead, not glancing at the hilarious groups under the trees, but watching them furtively out of the corner of his eye. His pale face was flushed; he kept his head bent. This social excursion was dreadful to him. In all the city he knew only the Bouchard family well. For others he had a stony reserve and suspicious fear that antagonized them.

The delusion he had of his brother made him feel amazement that certain people hailed Ernest with evident pleasure, called laughing remarks to him, promised to speak to him later. He, himself, hurried along, a little ahead of Ernest, fearful that the latter might stop and wholesale introductions ensue. This is something he could have endured only with inward agony. He glanced back at Ernest incredulously. He had more or less vaguely imagined that his brother was always grim, that others regarded him as he himself regarded him. That a woman or two should flash a smile of invitation, a man wave a hand, another call, seemed impossible for him to grasp.

When they had been children together his emotions toward Ernest had been a mixture of distrust, astonishment, respect, shrinking and slight affection. He had avoided clashes, feeling himself both the weaker and the one in the right. Ernest intruded violently upon him by his very presence in the room, injuring the timid feelers of his personality. But in later years his attitude underwent a slight change. His distrust had deepened, his astonishment had given way to bitter expectations of the worst, his respect had disappeared, his shrinking increased, his affection died. He had also developed a hysterical intolerance toward him; he found himself flying into hectic rages at the slightest disagreement, the slightest encounter, with Ernest. At times the hysteria and rage became aggressive, so that Ernest fell silent before them, even retreated. Martin, the gentle and the kind, was the most astonished and regretful of men at these uncontrollable demonstrations of his unconscious hatred. But they remained, nevertheless.

He was secretly ashamed of the fear he felt as he walked toward the house he had never entered before. He held himself stiffly and ungraciously, so that many a girl and woman, intrigued by the glimpse of his extraordinary good looks, told her neighbor that "that was the most haughty young man!"

In the small and pretty grove to the left of the house tables had been set out, tables stiff with the shiniest of damask linen, centered with bowls of bright flowers, heavy with silver. Servants went to and fro between the house and the tables, carrying covered silver dishes, tureens, platters and cups. Wine pails appeared on the grass at each table. The blowing and speckled shadow of the trees danced on the linen, drew sparks from the silver. Laughter rang over the lawns; girls, fluttering in their billowing yards of crinolined dresses, darted behind trees, pursued by their swains. Under the shade of one tremendous oak the dowagers sat in their mauve and violet and black silks, fanning themselves, smiling benignly at the youth and gaiety about them, gossiping none too kindly behind their black lace fans. From the house, through the open French windows and doors, came the sound of a piano and the voices of a girl and a man in a sentimental duet.

"Lovely house, isn't it?" asked Ernest, as Martin hesitated at the stone steps. At his question, Martin glanced up, and then over his shoulder. His smile was nervous and artificial. "Yes, it is. I wonder how soon I can see Senator Sessions?"

"Senator Sessions? What on earth do you want to see him about?" Ernest rang the bell; the sound disappeared through the open door into the dim wide coolness of the hall. Martin did not reply. The butler came forward, greeted them ceremoniously, led them toward the second drawing room. Martin's heart throbbed painfully. Through the drawing-room archway he saw what he thought was a multitude of critical strangers, all waiting with secret smiles to be amused at him. There were, in fact, only about a dozen young people in the room, besides Gregory Sessions and the Senator. A girl was playing the piano: it was Amy; the sun, which poured through the window, bright in her soft brown hair. The girl who was singing was May Sessions, in a green-striped silk, a wreath of jade flowers in her dark-red curls. Beside her sang the youthful tenor, very elegant and sentimental. The other young people sat about on little gilded chairs, flirted, flashed their eyes in the golden dimness, fluttered their fans, whispered extravagant nonsense to each other as the duet pursued its carolling way. Whispering together in a discreet corner sat Gregory and Nicholas Sessions. Catching sight of the new arrivals, Gregory whispered hastily to his brother, and the two men came forward, smiling genially.

"Well!" exclaimed Gregory heartily, as though he and Ernest had parted only yesterday, and the best of friends, "here you two are at last! Nicholas, this is Mr. Ernest Barbour, and this, Mr. Martin Barbour. Gentlemen, my brother, the Senator!"

> "Each wish of my heart,
> Shall sti-ll-l verdantly cling!"

sang the duet. There came an enthusiastic clapping, the rattle of fans. A hubbub of voices. And near the doorway, Ernest solemnly shaking hands with his host and the Senator. Martin, bright of color with nervousness, also shook hands, murmured something chokingly, fell miserably silent.

So this, thought Ernest, oblivious at the moment of the girl at the piano, is Senator Sessions! This tall and florid man, with Gregory's long and slender legs and vigorous mane of hair. But the slenderness ended at his torso, which was slightly swollen under the satin waistcoat. His posture, his manner, his voice and his words, were all elegant, but compared to Gregory's elegance they seemed vulgar and affected, as though Nicholas were merely copying his brother. In Nicholas, Gregory's fine-drawn geniality and courtesy became bluffness, a too-frank camaraderie, a democratic expansiveness and patronage, that were in themselves the very essence of vulgarity. His voice boomed with rich pleasure and urbanity; his handclasp was firm and warm and affectionate, his manner full of open friendliness. All these things deceived most people, subjugated, charmed and entranced them, made them adoring and compliant slaves. But Ernest pierced beyond them ruthlessly; he pierced beyond the high complexion, the beaming smile, the handsome and glowing features. He saw that though the small bright blue eyes glittered jovially, they had a certain coldness and porcine wariness. They were sunken under the drooping cowl-eyelids of the brutal and suspicious man. Though Nicholas was evidently a man who loved opulent and luxurious living, was probably the best of dinner companions, he had no true friendliness nor kindness in him. There was avarice behind the smile, voracity in the heavy folds about his mouth, selfishness showing its dull clay through the glaze of his manner. Gregory Sessions was one who recognized his own occasional rascality, because he was intelligent. His brother, being less intelligent, lacked this insight into himself. At times, he actually believed that he meant his florid sentimentalities. He was the perfect politician.

"I have heard much of you, Mr. Barbour!" exclaimed the Senator. (He appeared to speak exclusively in exclamation points.) "Frankly, one of my reasons for returning home was to know you! I have heard so much, indeed, yes!" Knowing the value of a direct and open eye, he stared down with evident pleasure at the young men. Already he was under no misapprehension as to the relative positions of Ernest and Martin; after a few slightly fixed and glazed glances at Martin, he concentrated upon the other brother.

"You are very kind, Senator," said Ernest, with an air of gratification.

"I have so little time! But I have heard so much of your—your genius, your acumen, your—ideals, that we must get together, we two, just we two! and have a little conversation alone—eh?"

"Nothing," said Ernest ceremoniously, with a short, stiff bow, "is nearer to my desires."

Senator Sessions beamed; his smile took on itself the faintest hint of a grin. He placed his hand familiarly on Ernest's shoulder. Gregory watched, slightly smiling. Martin, as usual, had tried to efface himself against the wall.

"Tomorrow," continued the Senator, "I must go to Philadelphia. Politics, my dear Mr. Barbour, politics! The elections this fall, you know. A bad feature of democracy is that even a politician, after several years of faithful service, must periodically convince his constituents of his worth. Dashed short memories they have, eh?"

"Or perhaps long ones," interposed Gregory, with a quirk of his eyebrow. The Senator boomed out into his rich laughter at this acid sally, then turned off his laugh abruptly as Amy and May came toward them. "Ah, my dears," said Nicholas, "what lovely music you two birds have been making! May, my love, I have never heard you sing better."

"How excessively civil of you, Nicholas," said May, mockingly, dropping him an elaborate curtsey. Her dimples frolicked in the bright color of her cheeks and her eyes sparkled with vitality and spirits. She tapped Ernest on the arm with her fan, very archly: "Mr. Barbour! Is it possible that you forgot me? If so, you are the first man who ever did so!" Ernest, surprised and flushing, found himself laughing involuntarily. No one could help laughing when May desired him to; there was about her such an air of gaiety and slyness. Ernest was grateful for her ability today, for it made the awkward moment of meeting Amy again slide smoothly on a wave of laughter. He could actually turn to her, smiling, actually take her hand. It is true that the smile became a little fixed, and a sick pain stabbed at his throat, but his expression remained mirthful, quite automatically.

"It is so pleasant to see you again, Mr. Barbour," Amy was saying. Her sweet face was tranquil; her eyes met his with a puzzling pity, but their gaze was direct and kind. Her hand lay in his, cool and faintly throbbing, and when he glanced at it an instant, he saw the beating of the delicate blue veins in the lace-veiled wrist. Her billowing yellow muslin gown brought out golden lights in those steady brown eyes and in her glossy light-brown hair.

Ernest murmured something to her, what, he never knew. He only felt, with terror, the rising of a sense of acute illness and faintness. He could not let her hand go; he clung to it, pressed it, felt a fierce ache behind his eyes. This was far more dreadful than he had expected; he was appalled by the strength and relentless power of his own emotions. He had not known that he had loved the girl so. He stared at her soft pink lips, and was seized by such a passion to kiss them that his desire subtly communicated itself to her, and she drew back, gently disengaging her hand from his. Thin red welts rose on its whiteness from pressure of his fingers. But she still looked at him with sweet kindness and compassionate dignity.

"I must help him to forget me," she thought. There was a certain integrity and rigidity in her nature that could obliterate emotions she did not desire, and now there were only pity and kindness in her for the unfortunate young man. She said: "We were hoping you were not ill, Mr. Barbour."

For a moment Ernest could not reply. He had turned very white, and veins had risen in his neck and on his forehead. He stood perfectly still, but the fiercest battle of his life was trampling all over his secret defenses; if he could have spoken, if Amy had not turned from him slightly just then, he might have thrown everything over, have taken what he desperately wanted. But he could not speak; she had turned away. He looked up to see May Sessions regarding him with an odd mixture of mockery and compassion.

Gregory, vaguely remembering that Martin was present, looked for him. That young man had pressed so closely against the wall that he was a full four feet from the others. His misery was so evident that Gregory wanted to burst out laughing. May, being the closer to him, he said: "May, my love, this is Mr. Martin Barbour, Mr. Ernest's brother. Mr. Barbour, this is my cousin, Miss May Sessions."

May made her slightly malicious and ceremonious curtsey, bouncing up from it like a pretty toy on springs. She glanced up at Martin coquettishly, and exclaimed, with a fine disregard of taste: "Gracious! What handsome gentlemen Windsor does produce, to be sure!" Martin rewarded her with the reddest blush she had ever seen, bowed stiffly over her hand, glanced over her head in the most abject panic. His expression was the precise one of an animal looking for an escape. And his eyes, slightly wild, fell on Amy, who was regarding him with her usual gentleness and understanding.

And at that very instant, the thing that Jacques Bouchard had feared and dreaded, the thing he had agonizingly prayed might never happen, did happen. Martin fell in love with Amy Drumhill. His panic disappeared, his color receded, his heart amazingly steadied itself as if he had laid a strong hand on it. He dropped May's fingers, turned from her to Amy. Gregory introduced him. Martin took her hand, held it strongly, as if he knew her very well. They both recognized their own gentleness and timidity in each other, their own simplicity of mind and straightness of uncluttered thought. There would only be trust and honesty and faith. Amy's thought was that in turning from Ernest she had turned from violence and obscurity and bitter selfishness to kindness and clarity and truth. It was as if Martin was a mirror in which all the only faintly suspected qualities of his brother were ruthlessly shown. A feeling of rest and peace passed over her. Quite to their amazement, they found themselves walking out of the room, walking down the long hall, going through the back door, going down to the garden. Ernest and May, Gregory and Nicholas, had, in the meantime, become submerged in a frothy sea of gay skirts and ringlets and fans, bounded in a circle by fawn coats and elaborate cravats. Only Ernest and May were aware of Martin's and Amy's escape. It had been so easy, so natural, after an incoherent murmuring which no one noticed particularly. But Ernest, smiling, laughing at May, was struggling with a sick rage and confusion.

The gardens were very quiet, for most of the guests were already assembling at the tables, the first warning chimes having rung. They were laid out in a rustic and charming manner, with flagged and uneven paths overgrown with green fungus, trees heavy with golden summer, peonies in pinkly riotous beds, roses bursting over white-painted trellises, marigold, pansies, bachelor buttons, dahlias, sweet williams and phlox all mingling in a joyous bewilderment, disregarding the formalities of better-behaved gardens. Amy laughed with happy inconsequence under the lankiness of tall hollihocks, looked at Martin with gentle courtesy as he made some remarks near a giant clump of ragged golden-glows. The grass was long and thick, the wind bending the flowers all one way, so that they were like an uneven and colorful army in deep genuflection, tossed Amy's ringlets, swept under the multitudinous fluffiness of her petticoats so that they billowed and spread, made the trees momentarily roar and turn their lighter undersides up. Alternate shadow and blazing sun rushed over the gardens, so that their color assaulted the eye one moment with unbearable brilliance, and the next dimmed them until their hues became almost drained and cold. Gray-white pigeons fluttered against the wind, filled the air with their cooing. The two collies tore around the side of the house and leapt upon Amy and Martin with extravagant affection and noise. Amy, with much laughter, defended herself help-lessly against the assaults of the wind and the dogs. She pleaded for help from Martin, turning her tinted face and dancing brown eyes upon him, pushing her blowing ringlets aside with one hand.

Martin, struggling with the wildly delighted collies, thought he had never seen anything so lovely and so tender as this girl. He was not confused, nor made inarticulate by his feelings for her. They seemed to strengthen him, on the contrary, making him sure and strong, easy and quiet. There was such simplicity and directness in her, such lack of affectation, such gentleness. And as they went on together, an old faint misery in Amy suddenly disappeared. When she lifted her head and glanced up at Martin, meeting the steady shine of his almost beautiful blue eyes, she felt utterly at peace, strangely comforted. There was a childlike confidence in the unconsciousness with which she rested her hand on his arm. His voice seemed to her infinitely reassuring and familiar. By the time they turned back toward the house, she was not in love with him, but she loved him, though she did not know it as yet. She had been in love with Ernest, and that condition had brought with it uncertainty and pain, excitement and breathless confusion, exquisite joy and bitter longing. These she would never experience with Martin, but she had something infinitely better and surely calm.

When they went back to the emptying drawing room, Amy heard Ernest laughing loudly, but with enjoyment, and she thought content-edly: "I could never have made him laugh like that, as he does at May."

Amy was the first young woman to whom Martin had spoken in familiarity and with pleasure. Heretofore he had run from women, utterly disconcerted and terrified, though a strong but unrecognized instinct in him had tugged at his vitals, urged him to return. He had had curious, and, to him, shameful thoughts about them. He had tried to deify them in his mind, identifying them with the pallid and sexless female saints of his newly adopted religion. But in spite of this, there were times when a powerful longing and appetite rose in him, a sweet yearning that made his flesh weak. The blood of sturdy Englishmen would not be repressed; under the lash of his secret and contemptuous cry of "lust!" this blood seethed and became full of fever. He might drive his hungry thoughts from the scene of this sweet shame, but they returned like starving dogs at the scent of a doe. At other times he looked at women with loathing, hating them for the madness they stirred in his body. So he had avoided them, encouraged his terror of them. In this, the sad and impotent Jacques had abetted him, his arguments eager and fervid and full of latent terror.

But now that he had met Amy he was full of contentment and joy. He said to himself: "I love her," and was amazed that no feeling of shame or degradation followed. He seemed suspended in golden enchantment, in which everything was right and simple and beautiful. Not for one instant did he remember Jacques Bouchard, and the fact that he had been planning to enter a monastery.

When he and Amy rejoined the others, he was no longer afraid of them. He looked victorious and self-possessed, so much, indeed, that Ernest could not stop staring blankly at him.

They went out onto the lawns, found their table. It was a large round one centered with pink roses and trailing green vines. In an arbor to the side of the house several musicians were playing, gentle, sentimentally soft music. The wind rushed in a golden current through the trees; a hubbub of voices and laughter, of callings to and fro, made a bright confusion.

May, Amy decided fondly, was at her best. It was as if that young woman had brought out from some place of reserve all her wit and her cleverness, her charm and laughter, her gaiety and impudence, and sitting in the midst of them picked them up one by one, holding them high for admiration. If she seemed too lavish with them, displaying them too quickly and eagerly, it was because she realized that she had little time, and that a pause, a flagging of interest, would turn a bored eye from her upon Amy again. She was like a circus showman who must rivet interest, keep up a constant ululation, entrance, absorb, enchant and fascinate, so that prospective customers would not leave her in ennui for a rival showman. One with an observing eye would have detected a slight desperation in her arts and tricks; she seemed to dance wildly before Ernest, trying to hide out the sight of Amy with the lifting and fluttering of fan-spread skirts. And she succeeded so well that she kept him laughing, so much so that he could scarcely eat. Laughter was new and strange to him: he was surprised that he enjoyed it enormously.

He came back again and again to May Sessions, as a very thirsty man comes back again and again to a well of good water. His pale face was full of color; he even amazed himself by saying witty things that had no irony in them. May's wit sharpened the wits of everyone about her. When they all laughed at her remarks, an expression of mingled tiredness and gratification crept about her eyes and smiling mouth.

Even Martin laughed. But his was the reserved and suspicious nature of the recluse, the nature that despises easy laughter and suspects a too lavish gaiety of being "light-minded." He laughed at May Sessions, but secretly despised her, felt a very agreeable sensation of superiority. The others laughed with her, and looked at her with pleased gratitude. So as the circle knitted itself more closely, more eagerly, about this pretty dispenser of gaiety, Martin withdrew, smiling serenely still, but withdrawing. He turned to Amy. She was smiling at May, but when Martin spoke to her she blushed a little, looked at him with gentle attention. They talked together in low voices, as they sat side by side. Neither was very talkative, and what they said to each other was inconsequential and widely spaced by understanding silence. Martin blessedly lost, for a time, his passionate self-preoccupation, his aching awareness of his own body and face and hands. When he spoke, he spoke with eagerness and anxiety, as though to reassure himself that Amy was all he had thought her, that she liked him, that she understood what he was trying to say. He found everything delicious: the air, the wind, the flash of silver in the sunlight, the gay colors of the women, the laughter, the rich food, the glance of friendly eyes. They all intoxicated him; he looked about him, thinking: I am happy. And smiled like an amazed child.

Gregory, happening to glance at Martin and Amy, thought to himself in astonishment: How alike these two are! The same innocence of expression, of unworldliness and gentleness and timidity and kind simplicity! And they would both impress others as having weakness of character and no will. This is probably true, but they could both be strong and resolute and unshaking enough if they were doing what they thought was "right." Nothing could move them, then. Not even God in His heaven, and all the seraphim, or all the devils in hell. What inconvenience they could cause others! I'm not sure I like these soft characters that turn to stone at unexpected times.

Another thought occurred to him, and he stared at them with open curiosity across the table. He noted their contentment and serenity, the understanding smiles they gave each other, their air that they were quite alone and pleased to be in that condition. What if—! By God, the girl looked happy again, as if she had come home, into a safe place. And the young man looked alive for the first time in his life! What if—! But the girl was penniless, and if things went on as they were going, Martin would have little money, either. Ernest would take damn good care of that. And then another thought occurred to Gregory Sessions, and it was so stupendous, so delicious, so full of hate and pleasure and malice and joy, that he burst into a roar of laughter, and threw himself back in his chair. What a joke that would be! The others regarded him with open-mouthed surprise. The conversation had become serious for a moment, and no one could understand the laughter. Seeing their blank faces, he stopped laughing abruptly, and apologized. "Only a thought I had," he explained. Ernest resumed what he was saying, and Gregory listened courteously. But the delighted laughter lurked in the corner of his eyes.

With the coffee and the cordials everyone relaxed. There was a coming and going between the tables. Long yellow shadows mingled with the tree-shade on the grass; the wind had died down a little, and only the tops of the trees rustled in golden light. The western windows of the house were already ruddy and hot, its gray walls drenched in brightness. Some of the guests were already leaving, coming to the table of their hosts to say their laughing good-bys; carriages were already appearing on the driveway, their wheels twinkling in the beaming sunset light, their horses sleek under polished harness. From the town came the loud clangor of the bells of the First Reformed Church calling sinners to worship in a harsh and domineering voice, and then the low, almost timid but musical bells of the Church of the Annunciation. The young city stretched herself, yawned, sighed contentedly in the last warmth of the golden day.

Gregory and Nicholas and Ernest were talking together with increasing seriousness, their elbows on the table as they sat sideways, in order to face each other. May listened also, her sparkling and intelligent eyes going from one face to another; she was not speaking now, only listening, and comprehending much. Her fan moved slightly and steadily, throwing reflections on her pretty face. Ernest was skirmishing mentally for position. He knew that his natural directness would be offensive to Nicholas. He could be direct with Gregory, and openly ruthless, for Gregory was no hypocrite if occasionally a smiling rascal. Gregory was amused, almost delighted, when caught shrewdly, appreciated an eye that could not be deceived. But Nicholas, though also a rascal, hated ruthlessness that did not disguise itself in graceful hypocrisy, was terrified at a straight coming to an inevitable point; he preferred circumlocutions, mental starings at an innocent sky, roundabout approaches, delayed arrivings at a position he had refused to recognize until arrival. He had the politician's necessary deference and respect for public opinion; he knew the success of a politician was not in the honest and intelligent support of a competent minority, but in the support of the average man with all his pious hypocrisies, his timidity, his hatred for definite issues, his love for pleasant generalities and sticky platitudes. So, in his very successful attempts to win this vast majority, their color had flowed into his personality, infusing it with their own dislike of quick decisions, ruthless conversation, bitter reality. Once, Gregory had told his brother that the tragedy of being a politican was that one lost his own soul and acquired a perfect menagerie of little monkey-souls to take its place. A politician had to be all things to all men, and as the majority of men were simians, a politician eventually became a simian, too.

While Ernest skirmished for position, Nicholas gravely affected to be entirely unaware of this, and Gregory watched, delighted. May listened, sometimes smiling faintly. Amy and Martin had pushed their chairs back from the table and were again softly absorbed in each other, utterly oblivious of anything or any one else. And Nicholas waited with an air of grave innocence to be wooed.

Ernest proceeded cautiously. He knew that a too-quick word would send the timid and tender moralities of the Senator into a wild retreat. He knew that Nicholas was waiting for the proper and discreet approach to the thing for which he had returned to Windsor. So Ernest began by praising the growing and robust vitality of the town. A few more industries, an expansion, building—and Windsor's population would more than treble itself in ten years. He infused into his voice a sectional enthusiasm and eagerness, a provincial patriotism.

Nicholas sighed gently, glanced about him with the expansive manner of a contented paterfamilias, the simple landowner, shook his head slightly.

"And then," he said in a melancholy voice, "we shall have a veritable roaring metropolis."

"But also great prosperity, wealth," suggested Ernest, smiling.

"But my dear young man," said the Senator, with a pained but gentle expression, and a glance for approbation at the silent others, "we shall then have destroyed what is the greatest charm of this little city: its simple faith, its innocence, its modest way of life, its hardy nobility, strength. The simple things, the simple life! Ah, that is truly beautiful —the very spirit of a young and devoted country."

This, thought Ernest, with a wry mouth, is a very dangerous rascal indeed. I must be careful. He studied the Senator carefully, and despised him. Why, his thought continued, the scoundrel actually believes he believes this! I wonder just how disappointed he would be if I pretended to take a hint and said nothing more? He glanced at Gregory; the latter was regarding him with uplifted and pointed eyebrows, uplifted and pointed mouth of silent and delighted mirth. There was something almost fiendishly satyr-like in all those pointed, thin and lifted angles, something pitiless and objectively amused.

"But the spirit of this country is growth," Ernest said respectfully. "We cannot help but grow. Or, if we try to delay its growth, merely for love of an old state, we are really unpatriotic. Don't you think so? We cannot help but grow; we must help America grow."

"Ah, that is true, also," agreed the Senator, with the gracious and benevolent gesture of a man who is not afraid to admit himself out-argued.

"So, we are all doing our share. I flatter myself I have done my share. It is little enough to do for a country that has given us refuge and hospitality and kindness." Ernest resolutely kept his eyes from Gregory now, but he knew, without seeing, the broadening of his ecstatic smile.

"You speak very nobly, young man," said the Senator, returning to his customary bluff heartiness. He winked. "I hope your politics are as circumspect, also?"

"I am not a Whig," answered Ernest, smiling.

"But not too much of a Tory, I hope?" The Senator shook his head, pleased. "Neither Whig nor Tory: just American. Simple American. But are you not an Englishman?"

"Yes. But we are citizens. American citizens. Have been, for the past three years or so. And very proud to be, I assure you.

"My vision of America, Senator, is not provincial. I would like to see America expand, become the greatest of nations. And how can she do that? By conquest? We hope not, for that is the dishonorable way. By industry? Yes! Peaceful conquest of the world's markets. We, all of us, must help so. And I believe I have already helped. I am sure that you know a little of my—our—activities——"

"Yes, I believe Gregory mentioned a few," said the Senator with a vague but benevolent smile.

Ernest could hardly restrain a grimace. He paused. Dare he mention the fact that the Sessions Steel Company owned thirty-three and one-third per cent of the stock of Barbour & Bouchard? No, not outright. That would offend the Senator. So he said: "What I have been able to do has not been entirely without help. As you may know, Senator, Mr. Gregory helped me considerably, first by money and then by approving my notes for the purchase of the Kinsolving works."

"You acquired the Kinsolving works? But how very rash, young man! Is this not too big for you?" The Senator affected concern and surprise.

"No, sir. I believe in the future of America. I believe in the future of Windsor. Nothing is too big for such a country and such a city. Perhaps I am overly hopeful, but I think not. You see, what we make is the finest in the country, quite possibly the finest in the world. America has the right to that. America has the right to acquire our arms and our ammunition for her army." He looked full into the Senator's narrowed eyes and nodded with pretended mystery. There was a long silence.

"What do you mean?" asked the Senator at last, with great naïveté. "You cannot mean military contracts!"

"That is precisely what I mean," said Ernest soberly. He struck his fist on the table. "Military contracts."

"But that is impossible, that is preposterous, young sir! You cannot know the situation. The National Powder Company has been getting all the military contracts for the past twelve years, and has the confidence of the War Department, due not only to their ability to produce large quantities of good materials, but by proving their trustworthiness in guarding valuable Government secret patents. The War Department would oppose any bid from any other company. This Company employs a number of ex-army men whose loyalty has never been questioned. You, you know, are really a new and almost unknown concern, though I grant you that more than one rumor has come to me of the superiority of your arms and powder.

"The officers and owners of the National Powder Company are very old and faithful men. They have the respect and trust of all Government officials."

Ernest listened with passionate care to this. All the time the Senator was speaking, he had been watching his face, its bluff frankness of expression, its appearance of sober sincerity, its manly gravity. For the life of him, Ernest could not read now beyond that face. His own lips tightened grimly.

"I have set my heart on military contracts," he said quietly. "It will be the end of a dream if I do not get them. Men may serve their country in many ways, in politics or on the battlefield, or in supplying necessary supplies as honestly as possible. I can supply the Government with the finest of arms, the best of powder. We hold patents which I believe are superior to Government patents. We have been offered thousands upon thousands for them. The National Powder Company practically begged us to sell them our new smokeless powder."

Nicholas listened with an air of paternal seriousness and affection. Then he appeared to sink into deep and sober thought. He played with the stem of his cordial glass. He frowned, twitched his lips, sighed. Ernest, impatient and a little frightened, presently glanced at Gregory. The latter's face was inscrutable; he still seemed to be enjoying an objective comedy.

Finally Nicholas stirred weightily and said very slowly, as if thinking over each word before speaking it: "It is possible, though I do not say probable, that when the National Powder Company next bids for its annual contracts in September, a whisper in the right place to the effect that a new but substantial company holding valuable patents, and able to produce and deliver any amount of superior arms and ammunition, able, into the bargain, to underbid the National Powder, may have an interesting effect. This rumor would undoubtedly reach the National Powder, who are no doubt aware of your existence and the possibility that you may eventually become their strongest competitor. They will send gentlemen to see you, who, after a lot of anxious hemming and hawing, will offer you a consideration. What that consideration will be I am not in a position to say, but it ought to be a share in the business. What bargains you may drive then, young man, I leave to your acumen and judgment, which I hear are prodigious."

Ernest held his eye steadily. "The National Powder Company is not a large concern. They have old equipment. A better company ought to be able to underbid them, or arrange a very nice settlement with them. Is that what you mean?"

"Exactly." Nicholas smiled brilliantly.

"And the whisper? The rumor that might bring this about?"

Nicholas waved his hand loftily, his expression bland. "Oh, that. Any gentleman of position in Washington can start that whisper in exactly the proper place. After all, one must have the best interests of the Government at heart."

There was a long pause. Martin had begun to listen, his wide white forehead wrinkling in mingled perplexity and suspicion as he looked from Nicholas to Ernest, and back again. But Ernest turned to Gregory. The latter faintly nodded, faintly grinned. Ernest heaved a deep and satisfied sigh, sat back in his chair. He moved his head in May's direction, and she, too, nodded, her dimples flashing in and out of her cheeks. To his pleased surprise, she seemed genuinely and generously elated at his success. She leaned toward him and whispered; he was obliged to bend his head to her ear, after a glance at Gregory and Nicholas, who had begun to argue as to the merits of their own cigars. He thought as he listened to May: I have won!

May whispered: "It is my birthday on Thursday. I am having a small party, only a few friends. I may expect you?"

He looked into her eyes very gravely. "Assuredly," he said, as if she had proposed something of tremendous importance in which he concurred.

Martin was saying eagerly to Nicholas, in his usual breathless and hurried fashion when speaking to strangers: "I have a copy, sir, of your speech last winter in favor of abolishing slavery. I want to tell you, Senator Sessions, that that was the noblest, simplest, most comprehensive speech I have ever heard!" He stopped abruptly, red of face and confused of eye.

No flattery is too humble for a politician, and Nicholas was quite touched at this tribute to his eloquence. "Ah, you are interested in the slavery problem, sir? So am I. A nefarious business, young man, a nefarious business! A grave situation will eventually be created, in which arms may be taken up in a righteous cause against the Southern States. I hope not, I sincerely hope not. But unless these States will be brought to realize the un-Christian, the inhuman cruelty of slavery, we may have to bring it to their realization with iron and powder and steel."

"Great-grandfather Prentice was a slave trader," said Gregory idly.

"Posterity," thundered the Senator, turning crimson, "is not responsible for the crimes of past generations, my dear Gregory."

Everyone, even Amy, laughed a little; only Martin did not see the humor of it. He was still gazing at Nicholas, his face full of innocent anxiety.

"I hope there will be no war, sir," he said. "That would be frightful. Almost worse than slavery. I do not think it advisable, or right, for men to kill even to save other men."

Nicholas delighted in human beings like Martin. They are effortlessly swayed by argument, because they cannot usually detect fallacy and hypocrisy; if a man speaks to them loudly and incisively, appealing to their simple and uncomplicated emotions and integrity, they will believe him utterly. It had surprised even Nicholas to discover that the bigger a mountebank or blackguard a politician is, the easier he can convince the pure of heart and the unsmirched of soul. Children, he had thought to himself, are easily taken in by plausibility, by rascality that, having no scruples whatsoever, can speak with authority.

"Dear Mr. Barbour," he said somberly, "have you forgotten that God allowed Christ to be killed in order to save other men? Have you forgotten that freedom has sprung from the blood of the faithful, that democracies are built on the graves of the brave? If we have a war, which I pray we shall not, I think the young men of the North will realize it is a holy war, a just war, a war blessed by God."

"Perhaps," said Martin in a low and almost terribly earnest voice, "you are right."

His brother was annoyed. The old scoundrel had no right to put such ideas into Martin's head; he would believe any wickedness or stupidity if it were suggested to him in fine and noble words. He spoke with unusual impulsiveness, and abruptly: "No wars are righteous, sir. I must disagree with you. Perhaps they are necessary, at times, to prevent invasion, to put down would-be internal destroyers. Men must defend themselves, and so must nations. But except for these occasions wars are brutal and stupid."

Immediately, he could have bitten off his tongue. He had spent hours placating and wooing this old buzzard, and now, on a silly impulse, had put his foot in it. Gregory was staring at him in delighted surprise, May's eyes had widened, Amy was regarding him with softness, and Nicholas' face had swollen to the bursting point. But Martin said, turning to his brother with a bitter look: "If you believe so, why do you manufacture the materials with which men can kill each other?"

This question seemed so childish to Ernest that he colored with embarrassment, did not know where to look. Then he saw that all the others, except Amy, were waiting maliciously for his reply. So he turned his back full on his brother and said to Nicholas, with an unpleasant smile: "My brother appears to think that we manufacture armaments out of sheer hatred for humanity and depravity of soul."

May thought: What extremely bad taste! And regarded him with admiration. Martin had become scarlet, Amy gazed at Ernest reproachfully, Nicholas fumed, and Gregory seemed more delighted than ever. He nodded imperceptibly to May and Amy, and the girls rising, the men were forced to rise also. Twilight, warm and duskily blue, was setting down over the house and its grounds. Almost all the guests had gone, and the sky was a clear and distant heliotrope. The wind had died, and except for a faint and melancholy rustling the trees were still. A robin's evening song, one long cascade of pure and mournful notes, ran down the pellucid curve of the evening like silver drops. Someone began to light candles and lamps in the house, and one window after another began to glow.

"What a lovely day this has been," said Amy softly, looking at her relatives and guests. "It could not have been more perfect." Everyone concurred. Ernest and his brother were invited to supper later, but refused. Nicholas still appeared to have been wounded, and wore an aggrieved expression. Ernest decided to leave him to the adroit ministrations of his brother. So he said good night, with formality. In the dusk Amy's face was like a pearl, and May's eyes had a warm flash. Their dresses had lost color, and had become soft clouds about them.

Ernest and Martin walked down the drive together, without speaking. At the end of the drive an irresistible something made Ernest glance back.

Amy was standing alone at the top of the rise, watching them go. She was only a dim pale shadow, quiet and lonely. Seeing her, the old sick pain tore its way through Ernest, and he stopped abruptly. Martin walked on a few steps, then turned and waited, curiously.

For a long, a very long moment, Ernest looked up at Amy and she looked down at him. The trees and the grass had faded almost into obscurity about her; she was a ghost in the gathering darkness. But behind her the house had come to life, its windows shining, its walls beginning to shimmer in rising moonlight. And Amy's figure faded into the dusk.

By a sheer and terrific effort of his will, Ernest lifted his eyes from that silent shadow under the trees, and fixed them on the house. And as he willed himself to look, the pain left him, and he stared at the house, not as an exile, leaving never to return, but as one who expects to come back soon, in triumph.

CHAPTER XXV

IN SEPTEMBER, Ernest Barbour married May Sessions. It was an extremely "fashionable" wedding, due to May's dimpled insistence. Her friends from New York and Philadelphia trooped into Windsor like a flock of noisy and colorful birds of passage, making the more sedate and conservative Oldtowners appear very dull and drab by contrast. Everything was very lavish and gay, rich and expensive. The month was still warm, golden with early autumn, exactly right for lawn fêtes and dances, lanterns and long tables heaped with dainties. May, in a wedding dress of old ivory satin, countless yards and yards of it over the new enormous hoops, was, everyone said, a beautiful bride. Her veil, of French hand-made lace, was like a large cloud over and about her; her round gay face, so bright and vivid, shone through it like a rosy moon. She wore her cousin's gift, a string of delicate and exquisitely matched pearls, and her bridegroom's gift, a bracelet that was a thin hoop of icy diamond fire. Everyone spoke of her vivacity and laughter, her untiring pleasure in everything, her happiness and effervescence. She seemed to bubble, to bounce, to run and laugh constantly. There was no doubt as to her happiness and even joy, and her passionate love for her husband. As for Ernest, he seemed to have thawed and relaxed from a grim and formidable human machine to a young man who laughed almost with ease, joked with comparative strangers, and appeared quite the fond bridegroom. At any rate he eyed May with affectionate and indulgent smiles, seemed grateful for her ability to make him laugh, and showed her every consideration and kindness. Despite himself, he was caught up into the gaiety of the occasion; also, having succeeded again, his air was touched with that of a conqueror. For, not only had he married the Sessions heiress, but he had secured a very important military contract from the War Department. Only Gregory Sessions knew what craft and bullying, determination and sweat, none too subtle threats and hints, pressure and tenacity, Ernest had brought to bear on the National Powder Company, which was a group of simple and honorable old men who had nothing but the weak shield of their integrity to defend themselves against these implacable weapons. And only Gregory knew the part of Nicholas Sessions in this.

At any rate, after five agonizing weeks, an agreement was signed between the National Powder Company and Barbour & Bouchard, for the consideration of one hundred thousand dollars, whereby the National Powder Company undertook not to solicit military business, Barbour & Bouchard to turn over to them a certain per cent, possibly twenty per cent, of the military business that Barbour & Bouchard obtained. But even the innocent officers of the National Powder Company knew that it was only a matter of time until Barbour & Bouchard would absorb them completely.

Amy Drumhill, in turquoise silk and ivory lace, was her cousin's only attendant. Something softly vital and eager, Gregory noticed, had gone forever from Amy's gentle face, but these had been replaced by a certain serenity and contentment which puzzled him. At any rate, her color had returned, and she seemed to enjoy the wedding and its festivities. Martin, after strenuous pressure had been exerted on him by his parents, acted as his brother's best man.

Hilda was overcome and subdued by all the magnificence of this wedding; the bride, though all that was affectionate and kind, did not win her peasant confidence. Ernest had bought her endless yards of mauve silk in Philadelphia, a fine rich quality she had never suspected existed, but she had had it made up into a gown by a local dressmaker, and the result, though impressive, was of a mode at least five years old. Her buxom and middle-aged figure looked, Ernest thought irritably, "stuffed," and her color was too florid and coarse for the delicate color. For the first time in his life he was ashamed of his mother, who was unaffectedly what she was in the midst of the elegance of the other ladies : a hearty and uncertain and humble creature terrified by her betters.

Joseph, darkly feverish and full of sullen pride, was obviously a very sick man, almost emaciated, his eyes sunken and burning with his obscure disease. But his slight and upright figure was fine, even elegant, in its sleek black broadcloth, and his thick and vital hair was almost completely gray. He was, he said with a glower, not afraid of these "blasted snobs," but he was wretchedly uneasy. Despite their estrangement, Ernest was proud of him; he would have given a great deal to have been at peace with his father. But there was no approaching him. Sometimes he looked at his elder son with something hideously resembling hatred.

Beautiful little Dorcas, astonishingly like her brother Martin, was May's flower girl. Everyone exclaimed over her beauty, the young ladies affectionately, the young gentlemen banteringly. Her long, pale gold hair hung in silver-touched ripples over her white muslin dress, almost down to her knees. She had the face of an exquisite, rather serious wax doll; it had a dreaming, unawakened quality that was infinitely touching. She endured the lavish petting she received in an agony of shyness, clinging to Martin whenever she could, and when he was not about, turning to Eugene Bouchard, whose large and awkward simplicity and gentleness toward young things had gained her confidence. He was never bullying or rough to Dorcas, and always subdued his rather grating voice when he spoke to her. Raoul, elegant and happily at ease with the grace of a French courtier, charmed all the ladies, who swore he broke their hearts, flirted, drank, was indolently and delicately impertinent, and squired Florabelle Barbour, home from boarding school. There were several points of resemblance between the pert and vain and pretty young girl and the mocking, egotistic and entrancing bride, and they loved each other from the start.

Ernest, busily engaged in the complexities of his new undertakings, could spare only two weeks for a honeymoon. They went to New York. Upon their return, they occupied large and renovated apartments in the Sessions house. May's bedroom, almost octagon-shaped, with many windows, had gray painted walls, silken curtains of old rose, and a rose-hued carpet. Gilded mirrors and gilded candle sconces added brightness to the room. She had a lounge of gray-brocaded satin, and a multitude of little gilt chairs upholstered in satin damask colored yellow, pink and silver. Her huge bed was draped and canopied in heavy lace. Ernest's room was all dark mahogany, crimson and dim blue, the windows heavily draped with fringed curtains. Their sitting room was full of velvet, heavy chairs with involuted curving arms, the front legs painted black and mounted with small bronze rosettes or ormolu, and equipped with rose cushions tufted with buttons. The great fireplace, of black-veined marble, was looped with red velvet and ball fringe. May acquired a new personal maid, and insisted that Ernest have a valet.

Ernest was very pleased with his bride. She amused him, made him feel indulgent and constantly on the verge of laughter. When he returned home at night, her gaiety and pretty coaxing ways, her witticisms, tender solicitude, hurryings to and fro to minister to him, diverted and soothed him. She seemed full of variety, and while she was often pettish and a little sulky, she never whined or nagged, but could spring from her moods to laughter and teasing. He had discovered that in spite of her real intelligence and sophistication, she was curiously innocent, and he enjoyed teaching her. He had only hoped that in marrying the Sessions heiress she would not bore him; to have her amuse him, to have her make him fond of her, was more than he had ever hoped for. And fond of her he was. He even liked her feminine bullying; he prepared to be very content, for not only was his marriage successful but his business affairs were progressing satisfactorily.

As he came home very late at night, partly by design in order to avoid the first awkwardness of living in the same house with Gregory and Amy, he ate most of his meals with May in their sitting room. The evenings were getting chilly, and it was infinitely delightful to him to sit at a dainty table shining with white linen and silver before a great red fire, and sip wine and coffee after a rich meal. May, opposite him in a rose velvet and lace peignoir, her black eyes twinkling, her dark red curls bobbing about her cheeks of pink damask, never seemed so inviting, so lovely. She diverted him with vivacious tales, waited on him as a mother waits on her child. When she looked at him her eyes shone with a steady and lambent light. Sometimes her love for him embarrassed him, made him feel uneasy.

Once a week he ate the evening meal with his parents in Newtown. In contrast with the luxury and fine living of his new home, his old home looked ugly and heavy to him, utterly without taste and dignity. He nagged Hilda constantly about the hideous furniture, the clashing of colors, the crowded living room, the glaring wallpapers and violent rugs, and the knick-knacks that gave an air of disorder to every corner. Even when Joseph, who had at first listened with a disagreeable smile to this haggling, burst into a fury on one particular night, it did not quiet Ernest. As for Hilda, she alternately stormed, jeered, became elaborately sarcastic, and wept.

Ernest was beginning to take his family very seriously, for he was ashamed of the house they lived in, the simplicity of their daily life, their disregard for elegant niceties, their lower middle-class lack of affectation. Dorcas, however, was a growing pleasure to him. He preferred the more voluble and lively Florabelle, who was fond of him, but Dorcas' beauty affected him to the point of tenderness. He was solicitous about her education, personally choosing her governess; he brought her yards of delicate velvets and laces and silks from New York, and, at Christmas, gave her a beautiful white ermine cape and hood. "Damned if he doesn't act as if he's the father of this family!" Joseph growled one night to his wife. But Hilda was pleased and touched at Ernest's serious attempts to mould and guide his people, however he irritated her. She wore the tasteful shawls of his choosing, was proud of the garnet necklace he bought her, rubbed perfumed beeswax on her hands because he complained of their red coarseness, tried to infuse a little refinement in her ready and forthright speech. But she would not change one thing in her house, nor forego her kitchen, where she supervised and scolded the kitchen maid with something of her old vigor. "Now, laddie," she said once to her older son, "you can't make a silk purse out of a sow's ear, so you'd best leave me be."

One source of secret satisfaction to Ernest was a change in Martin. Hilda reported that Martin did not go to the Bouchards' nearly so much, and that when he did he returned earlier and seemed agitated and vaguely distressed. He began to take interest in his clothing, admired Ernest's new suits, seemed almost anxious to please his brother, discussed cravats with him very seriously, even accompanied him to Philadelphia upon one occasion to buy a coat and some shirts and two or three hats. When Ernest reported the latest styles, Martin showed an almost amusing intensity of interest. Dressing better, he was actually theatrically hand-some; his posture improved, and his natural grace and ease of movement were intensified. He talked more pleasantly, seemed less afraid of every-thing, even accepted invitations to parties at the homes of the "snobs" in Oldtown. Ernest, surprised and pleased, curbed his tongue, made himself as agreeable as possible, and told himself that he'd make some-thing of Martin yet! He was flattered and touched when Martin showed pleasure at being invited to dinner at the Sessions house; he was more pleased when Martin formed the habit of dropping in unexpectedly, and joining Ernest and May, Gregory and Amy, in the family drawing room. "He's almost human, after all," he said to May one time. May admired Martin's good looks, was not above flirting with him in a sisterly and affectionate way, not above bullying him amusingly. Only she and Gregory suspected the reason for Martin's change, and she had her rea-sons for not enlightening her husband as yet. She cultivated her brother-in-law, put him at ease, tormented him until he laughed in spite of himself, and tried to show him, subtly, that life could be very pleasant. The climax came when Hilda reported that he had demanded comfortable furniture and a rug for his room.

It would have pleased Ernest had Gregory found another home for himself and Amy, and left him in complete possession. But even he had to admit that this was unfair. It was he who was the stranger; however, he told himself that the house would belong to May in the future. His contempt and dislike for Gregory were increasing; he found that it was only by a violent effort of his will that he could control himself now in the face of Gregory's silent and sardonic laughter, his lifted eyebrows, his ironical smiles, his knowing glances. The young man was earnest and sober, little given to humor, and Gregory's satire, his pungent and mali-cious witticisms, his pitiless if elegant jeers, antagonized him. He always felt at a disadvantage before this slim and steely wit, this adroit mental stepping, these stinging little rips in his vanity. Moreover, he suspected that Gregory disliked him as much as he disliked Gregory, and this mutual knowledge did not add to the ease of the Sunday dinner table, where the family met in its entirety, and of which Martin was now a frequent member. Gregory, however, was pleased at the arrangement; he would not have had it otherwise. He could thus keep avidly in touch with the developments in the affairs of Barbour & Bouchard; it gave him a sensuous thrill to hear of new orders, higher prices, rising stock prices. Moreover, life with Amy had been a little dull; May was a con-stant delight and comfort. She had brought life and laughter to the house, and both of these Gregory loved.

Absorbed in the many aspects of his life, which was full of clamor and excitements, pleasures and mirth, conjugal titillations, increasing wealth, Ernest had little time to think of Amy, or to indulge in the stabs of pain

ʹᴱe knew would come to him if he stopped to think. When he sat opposite her at Sunday dinner, or occasionally at dinner through the week, or Sunday breakfast, he forced himself to look at her as from a great distance, resolutely marching to and fro like a sergeant before his private line of thoughts, keeping them in line, disciplining them. Each time a thought writhed or groaned, he tramped it down, shouted at it, stopped its mutterings with the iron blow of his will. He was done with all that; he had a pretty wife of whom he was truly fond, and he had the world besides. He succeeded so well that sometimes weeks on end would pass without him giving her more than a casual thought, even on Sundays; he even criticized her sincerely to May because of her frequent languors and apparent lack of interest in important things. "Of course, if she does not take care, she will be an old maid, and that will be an unfortunate thing for others, as well as for herself," he said once to May. "She doesn't seem at all interested in young men."

May had smiled at this, had looked at him with covert sharpness. She was too astute to be deceived, and she knew that Ernest was not safe yet. When she criticized Amy to him, she did it delicately, and with expressions of affection and concern for the girl. She professed to worry about her lack of beaux, confided to her husband that she was afraid that poor Amy did not attract gentlemen. These excessively refined and delicate girls rarely did. They were, said May daringly, a little too female. A woman must have just the littlest dash of masculinity to appeal to men, a little meeting them on their own ground before a timid and pretty flight back into femininity. The result was that Ernest was gradually becoming annoyed with his wife's cousin, found her gentleness and silences, her sweetness and light voice, irritating. It was an obscure irritation, a sort of goad, and even May was not astute enough to guess the reason. When once Ernest burst out in a sort of frenzied annoyance to the effect that he wished Amy would get married and "clear out," May felt only a glow of pleasure and security and contentment.

Everything was going splendidly, with the long, high and steady sweep of the lives of the triumphant, until one brilliantly icy and snowbound day in March.

CHAPTER XXVI

IT WAS an exceptionally lovely morning. The snowfalls had been heavy lately. Through the long and latticed windows of the dining room, draped in their rich crimson velvet, one could look out into the garden, an enchantment of trees blazing with crystal, bushes filigreed mounds of white, black sparrows fluttering above the ice-filled bird-baths, long and undulating stretches of pure and burning whiteness. The sky was dark blue and dazzling, polished by the wind, and the sun poured out of it in a flood of colorless radiance.

Never had Ernest felt so alive and happy as he did this morning, look-ing at the cold and frozen gardens from the security of this warm, firelit and pleasant room. The white linen, the shining silver, the steaming coffee, the syrup-soaked flapjacks, the little spicy sausages simmering in hot gravy, the thick cream and yellow butter, the tall mounds of biscuits, the platters of thinly sliced ham, all seemed to him to be blissfully perfect. He shook out the huge folds of his napkin, smiled contentedly at Gregory, pleasantly at Amy, fondly at his wife. Everything seemed bathed and outlined in light; everything was just as it should be. He could have sung in his happiness and delight. He even made a pleasant remark to the butler as the latter passed him ham and biscuits, though as a rule he dis-liked the old man, whom he suspected of patronizing him as the son of an ex-servant.

He thought it was only part of the perfection of everything that Amy looked so glowing this morning, that she laughed so easily and with a faint suggestion of joy and excitement. He thought it was only natural, on such a morning, that Gregory was kinder, more considerate, listened with more seriousness to Ernest's remarks. Even when Amy exchanged glances of extraordinary vividness and soft exaltation with her uncle, when she laughed catchily once or twice, when her eyes suddenly filled with tears, he still thought it was only part of this most delicious morn-ing. Everyone was affected by it, he thought, even the collies, who had come out now and were deliriously romping in the deep white snow. From the stables came the virile neighing of the horses, sniffing the sharp and intoxicating air. May, too, looked excited, and just a little pale, though her eyes flashed almost feverishly, and she laughed even more than usual. But that was because she had a secret which she had not as yet told her husband, or any one, except her doctor. She was now almost four months pregnant. She did not particularly care for children, but

her condition overjoyed her. She felt that it was the closing of the last
door between Ernest and his old love, and that she was safe at last. If
only it would be a boy!

They were all drinking their last cups of coffee in a state of blissful
repletion, when a little silence fell. Ernest, preoccupied with his pleasant
thoughts, felt a sudden tenseness in the atmosphere. He glanced up. Amy
was looking softly from him to May and back again. She was smiling,
and her eyes were bright with tears.

"What on earth is the matter with you, Amy?" asked May in a drowsy
voice.

Gregory cleared his throat, sat up. "I think," he said, with a smile,
"that Amy has something to tell you both. Go on, my love, tell them,"
and he looked down at her with a moved expression.

Ernest stared; May stared, diverted. Can it be she is engaged? she
thought. But to whom? Can it possibly be——? No, that would be
incredible.

Amy tried to speak, could not, touched her eyes with a wisp of a handkerchief in her trembling hand, smiled, then burst into tears. She sprang
up from her seat in a flutter of pale blue silk, flung herself on her knees
beside May, and buried her flushed face in May's plump little bosom.
May was annoyed, but amused. She lifted Amy's face gently, smiled
down at it, then was moved in spite of herself by its wet radiance. "Why,
I believe the child is in love!" she exclaimed, touched. Suddenly she was
delighted, made almost dizzy by her delight. She pressed Amy's cheek
again to her breast, smiled over the girl's head at her husband. Was it
the reflection of the sun on the snow that made Ernest's face so suddenly
white and cold?

"Well," said Gregory, smiling, "if Amy cannot tell you, I will. Last
night, Ernest, your brother, Martin, asked me for Amy. After consultation with Amy, and finding her of the same mind, I consented. So, in
May we are to have another fine wedding, and I am to lose both of my
girls to the same family."

Ernest's first sensation was that the whole bright room tilted, table,
silver, walls, blazing windows, smiling occupants, and the next, that he
was going to be horribly sick, right there before them all. The intensity
of his emotions appalled him. He felt that all his senses had become one
swirling flood that struck him squarely, roared over him, smothered him,
threw him down. Then, as this flood ebbed, he felt as if he had been
bludgeoned over the head, stunned, deprived of all sensation. All this
happened in the space of a few seconds; he was too concerned with his
frightful fear that he was about to be horribly sick then and there to
experience despair. He struggled with it, hearing a distant hubbub of
laughter and voices; it passed; its place was taken by a veritable anguish
of mind and body.

He felt a movement on his face, and knew he was smiling. He even believed that he shook hands with someone—probably Gregory. His eyes were clearing, and the sun blazed pitilessly into them so that he blinked. Someone spoke, and he was dully astonished to hear his own voice saying: "This is a delightful surprise! What foxes you two were to steal such a march on us!" And all the while there was chaos in him, crashings down, wounds and tearings, bitterness and grief. Through it all, like an arrow tipped with poison and death, flew one thought: "I love her. O God, I love her. I never stopped loving her. Amy. Amy!"

Everyone laughed and chattered, and Ernest smiled and answered. He was even able to control himself enough to accept another cup of coffee, to put in sugar, to stir it, to sip it, smiling benevolently all the while at his wife, at Gregory, at Amy. I cannot endure it, he thought. She is going to marry Martin, that feckless fool. Suddenly he indeed could not endure it; the most dreadful hate he had ever felt for any human being convulsed him when he thought of Martin. Martin! Had it been any one else he might have suffered it, but God! this was too much. Like a mad hunger he was seized with a desire to kill; only blood-letting would ease him. Scarlet clouds began to swim before his eyes, and his hands suddenly clenched themselves on the edge of the table. Shudders swept over him visibly, but Gregory and May were teasing and kissing Amy, and he was not seen.

All at once clarity returned to his vision, and he could see Amy. She was sitting very close to May, who was holding her hand and occasionally kissing her cheek. Gregory had his arm about the back of her chair, and as he teased her, he played with her glossy ringlets. Her sweet face was shyly glowing; she looked from one to the other with wet eyes, smiled, murmured, laughed at Gregory's teasing. May glanced at her husband; how cold he looks, she thought, forgetting her old jealousy of Amy and wishing Ernest would show some enthusiasm and real pleasure. She felt quite resentful; his indifference, she believed, had already affronted Gregory, who studiously avoided looking at him. After all, Martin was his brother, and it was a fine match all around. Perhaps, she thought, with a stronger access of resentment, Ernest was already thinking, as he had done for himself, that Amy was a penniless girl and could bring his brother nothing. Nothing, indeed! Nothing but a fine old name, breeding, dignity, gentleness, good blood and such sweet prettiness! All at once she said to herself, with a sort of grim satisfaction: She shall have my mother's diamond necklace and her ruby ring! They will be my wedding present to her. And Nicholas and Gregory *must* give her some sort of a dowry, Uncle Aaron notwithstanding! Penniless, indeed!

And all the time the apparently detached and indifferent Ernest was looking at Amy with such held passion that his eye-sockets ached with the straining, and there was a ripping agony in his chest, and he was saying over and over in himself: "My darling, my darling. Oh, my God, my darling, how I love you! How could I ever have forgotten you, or not wanted you, even for a day?" Only another horrible suspicion that he might burst into tears controlled him from an impulse to cry out, to scream, to beat his fists on the table, to say dreadful and unpardonable things. And Gregory, feeling a quite unaccustomed pity and understanding for what he had seen for just an instant in Ernest's eyes, still avoided looking at him. Then as he chaffed Amy, and played with her curls, he thought: It serves him right. I am glad to see someone suffer as I did. It serves him right. Damn him, I hope he chokes on it! He had his chance. Men only have one chance. Nevertheless, his pity survived even his dislike and obscure desire to avenge himself.

He told himself at last that the poor devil had suffered enough. He stood up, and Amy stood up also, laughing, half-crying, wiping her eyes hastily. Ernest found himself on his feet, and the muscles of his face ached with his smile. He had suddenly turned quite red, and his breath came fast.

His will was gone, his control gone. He wanted only one thing, now. He stepped around the table, put his hands on Amy's soft warm shoulders and turned her to him. She looked up at him in smiling surprise, her pink lips parted, her small white teeth shining between them. In her bright brown eyes was the most innocent and trustful of lights.

"You are going to be my sister," said Ernest, with a slightly wild smile. "So, I think it is quite proper if I kiss you." And he drew her closer to him, bent his head, and even as the girl made a faint sound of astonishment, perhaps even dissent, he kissed her full on her lips. He held that kiss, pressing his mouth so fiercely against hers that her teeth bruised his lips, and she strained backwards away from him, the muscles of her white throat leaping out plainly in the light. Her hand fluttered to his arm, to push it away, then, as if deprived of strength in an instant, it fell away, fell to her side and swayed there, and her ringlets dropped in a mass down her back. She seemed to swoon in his grasp.

May was staring at them, slightly frowning, a forced smile on her lips. Really, after that indifference, Ernest was trying to repair matters too vulgarly. But men were frequently vulgar, seizing any occasion whatsoever to kiss a pretty girl. It is odd that May did not see the truth for several minutes.

Gregory thought: I must keep on smiling, I must keep on laughing for a little while longer. If I do not, there will be no repairing the damage. So he laughed and said banteringly: "Amy, if you don't stop kissing that gentleman this instant, I shall tell Martin, by God I shall!" And he, still laughing as if it were all a pleasant and exuberant joke, took Ernest by the shoulder. It looked a casual touch enough, but his strong lean fingers bit into Ernest's shoulder, brought him back to sanity as nothing else could have done. He released Amy so suddenly that she stumbled a little. All the color had gone from her face; her white lips had patches of stung red about them, and her eyes were wide and strained. It was her face, more than anything else, that brought the sickening truth home to May, that made her feel as if her mouth had filled with acid. For several seconds she thought her pain was not to be endured, that she would die of it before them all.

She stood up, very pale. Her dimpled vivacity had left her, and she stood there, so dignified, so composed, that she seemed taller than she was. Gregory, turning to her, was struck with admiration and surprise. But she looked directly at Ernest, at his gray face, his twitching mouth, and he looked back at her.

"Martin," she said, "is coming for dinner today, as usual. And as the engagement will have to be announced soon, the wedding taking place in such a short time, we might as well invite our best friends, just a few of them, to call this evening. Amy, my dear," she continued, turning with that new poise and dignity to her cousin, "will you please make out a little list immediately? I shall then write a few short notes, and send them by messenger at once. Of course, most of them will probably drop in later anyway, but I prefer to have them all together. Tomorrow we can make plans for a very formal announcement, but tonight I am sure that you will like a few of your friends to be here, to tell them intimately."

There, thought Gregory, is a woman! Without another word or glance toward any one, May literally swept from the room, her lace cap bobbing on her curls. But before she quite reached the door, Ernest was there before her, opening it, and when she passed through, without lifting her eyes to his, he followed her.

He followed her up the great dim twisting rise of the stairway, past the grandfather's clock striking in the warm and silent gloom of the hallway, past the stained glass window on the first landing. Her voluminous petticoats and skirt swayed and flowed behind her on the stairs; her hand was steady on the banisters, and she did not look back nor speak. The swish of silk was the only sound in the stillness. When she reached her bedroom door, Ernest opened it for her, and let her enter. She walked to the middle of the floor, expecting him to follow, but she saw that he had stopped on the threshold. His color was that of a very sick man's.

"Ernest," she said in a steady and tranquil voice, "please come in, my love. I have something to tell you."

He came in. Her heart misgave her, and she smiled forlornly. He looked so like a small boy who had committed some enormous sin. She took his arm with a faint resumption of her old coaxing air. "Do sit down," she said. But he walked away from her and went to the window, and stood staring out of it. Then she saw that he was indeed a man, and that she could not use the arts she would use with that small boy. She saw that he was desperate and overwrought, that he had reached a state of madness in which he might do anything. She had never suspected that he possessed this sort of violence; she must save him from it. Her heart lifted on a wave of tenderness. She did not go to him, not one step, but stood in the center of her large and pretty apartment, with the fire burning so low and cosily on the marble hearth, and she said simply and quietly: "Ernest, I am going to have a baby."

What she expected she did not quite know, but she did not expect that he would remain unmoving at the window. His hand was on the drapery; it tightened a little, but that was all. She seized the back of a chair, to keep herself from falling, to help her to recover from the sensation that she had received a blow in the stomach.

"Ernest," she said again, raising her voice a little, but keeping it gentle, "did you hear me, love? I said, I am going to have a baby." She swallowed convulsively. "I hope it will be a boy," she added.

Then he turned. He came toward her slowly, very gray, almost like stone. But his eyes were quite steady and calm.

"I hope so, too," he said. And took her hand.

CHAPTER XXVII

MARTIN WENT to see old Father Dominick. He was much disturbed in mind. Being a new convert, he was not quite sure as to what penalties, if any, might be inflicted upon him for the "sin" of changing his mind and turning to worldly things. But he was resolute about one thing: sin or no sin, excommunication or no excommunication, he loved Amy and he intended to marry her.

He did not believe that any one had ever been so happy before. It was not a wild and clamorous happiness, full of anxieties, doubts, fears and disturbances, like a stormy day that was slashed at intervals by brilliant and fateful sunlight. His happiness was as still and clear as a summer dawn, and as quiet. It seemed to run all through him like bright water. His timid, haughty and gentle nature, so resolute and kind and simple, so strong when stirred by his idealism, so suspicious of the exigent and the commanding, was like a soft-colored, faintly melancholy landscape touched all at once by a pure and unshaking light. He had the innocent passion of the very young and untouched man for Amy, but more than this, he had tenderness and protectiveness, a feeling that with her he was safe from the ugly laughter of those he did not understand, their gibes and their satire, their cunning and their cruelty. The love he had for her was a coat that covered his nakedness, kept out fear. She was so much weaker than he, so dependent and trusting and loving and tender, so just and wise in her innocence, that he became strong by protecting her, grew mental muscles that heretofore had been flaccid, developed a backbone that had had the bad habit of becoming fluid at crucial moments. Besides this, she had been a surgeon's hand that had removed cataracts from his eyes, given him sight to see the loveliness and desirability of life. He did not as yet have courage to admit to himself that his old vision had been false and distorted, morbid and full of death. But he did feel delivered and released.

Somehow, even the shops ceased to bother him as they had done. Everything but his happiness had become unimportant. He promised himself, however, that he would not always be so heedless of his duty, that Amy would help him find out what he must do. Because she had not seemed to find much that was repulsive in the making of armaments, his antagonism modified itself. Because she had found admirable qualities in the inexorable Ernest, he searched for them also, and was quite humbly contrite to discover that Ernest was not a fabulous monster after all, though he still had serious doubts about him and could not bring himself to trust him. Because Amy found pleasure in dancing, in little gaieties and laughter, in songs and flowers and the company of others, his austerity relaxed, and he enjoyed them also, not with full acceptance, to be sure, and not without self-consciousness, but with some symptoms of pleasure. The world, he discovered, was really very agreeable as well as grim. He and Amy had veritable orgies of talking; not shy with each other as they were with others, their voices stumbled eagerly over each other's; they interrupted, exclaimed, cried out, gesticulated, laughed with an exquisite sense of complete harmony. They found themselves in each other, and were inexpressibly enchanted by the finding. At other times they did not speak for hours, merely holding hands and walking silently, or just glancing at each other at intervals. He had given himself to Amy in an ardent surrender of all that he was. Sometimes he was faintly disturbed when he thought he detected something in her that was a little sad and uneasy, a little wistful and unsatisfied. It was as if she thought of something, then, that had nothing to do with him, but was like the memory of pain.

Ernest had made a kind and generous gesture. He announced, as though impulsively, that his wedding present to the bride and groom would be George Barbour's house. Hilda and Joseph, who had fallen abjectly in love with Amy, announced that they would furnish the house as the young couple desired. Before he had made his decision, Ernest had visited the closed and shuttered house and had walked through the empty rooms. On that tormented night a year or more ago he had furnished this house in his mind, after he had told himself that Amy was worth the sacrifice of the Sessions house and the Sessions fortune. And now, the day he decided to give the house to Amy, he walked through it, very slowly. He stood by the windows she would stand by, and imagined what she would think of the various views. The western windows, because of the height of the land, overlooked the crowded basin, looked at the river. Here Amy would see the red sun of winter setting in a crown of fire; here she would watch the wan and timeless light of the stars. These windows would be gray and streaming in autumn rains, while she sat at this black marble fireplace and knitted, her small feet on a hassock, her children playing on the hearth. She would see the river, fiery blue or white with cold; she would see it flame into crimson, run like hot gilt, become mysterious under the moon. These windows would be a permanent frame, in which the changing pictures of the seasons would be presented, one by one, for her pleasure. And each picture, wild with storm, green and quiet with summer, radiant and fresh with spring, black and white with winter, would be seen through the glass of her moods. What would she feel, when she looked at this present picture, at twilight? The sun had gone, but the western skies were a cold peacock-blue, a frozen and motionless lake, on which sailed bright golden little ships, winged with fire. Above this lake and its ships was a dark and bitter strip of cobalt blue, merging into a paler tint as the sky rose to the zenith. The river ran like liquid iron, dim and strong, under the heavens; the basin on this side was adrift with a spectral fog, so that the buildings on it were mere blurs. The grounds about the house were steep though not long; they were bounded by a circle of really fine elms, still naked and brown, and thrusting distorted branches upward in the pale light, so that they appeared to have been caught in a writhing posture of torment. The whole scene was so lifeless, so cold, so infinitely melancholy, that Ernest, the exigent, the realistic, could not move from the window. His sick and desperate grief was an enchantment that had temporarily opened his eyes; he felt that the scene was part of him and he was part of it. His consciousness flowed out and mingled with it, drawing back its sad and fateful and hopeless essence into him. This sensation that his personality was disintegrating, flowing out mystically, returning with a burden of mystery, like a tide bringing in strange flotsam and jetsam to the shores, was so unique to him that he was appalléd. He found places in himself, abysses and currents, thoughts and longings, yearnings and bitternesses, that he had never suspected could have been found in any one, much less himself. Consequently, he was completely absorbed in these new sensations, fascinated by his ability to feel so intensely that it seemed to him that his heart was shaking from the impact of it.

Finally he turned away, faced the dark chill room. "Yet," he thought, "I would not do anything different from what I have done. I would do it over again." He promised himself, as he left the house, that his rein of discipline would never relax in the future, that a man has no business to indulge himself in fancies and vapors and melancholies. He had work to do.

So steadfastly did he adhere to this that he could speak to Amy, who had avoided him for some time, with impersonal and brotherly affection, looking at her with a vague though friendly eye. He could speak to Martin with more than ordinary intimacy and consideration. And these were not mere affectations; he could actually control his thoughts and his emotions, bend them to his will. But even as he did so, he knew that his love for Amy was a violent prisoner that might burst its prison at any time, devastating and destroying all that he had built in his life. He did not make the mistake of calling himself a sentimental fool; he was too honest with himself for that. So he recognized the danger in which he stood, and slowly and laboriously he built up a wall of determined indifference and cold resistance against it. The fact that he was sincerely fond of May, that she diverted, amused and coddled him, loved him passionately, helped him to control himself; it was not that this control was based on honor and a sense of duty toward her—it was based purely on his strong instinct of self-preservation and a desire to continue the pleasant relationship with his wife. Moreover, the thought of the first of his children excited him. They would inherit the dynasty he would build. They would live in this house for which he had sacrificed a glory and a splendor and a delight; they would love this house as he did, and perhaps sacrifice themselves for it as he had done.

Perhaps it was because of some subconscious desire to make Amy happy, some recognition of the fact that she had loved him, that he cultivated Martin so assiduously. He encouraged Martin to express ideas about the laborers in the shops, affected to consider very seriously the halting of the importation of labor, pretended to feel horror at some of Martin's passionate accounts of slavery in the South. Martin found himself, though still distrustful, telling his brother something of what he had done to help escaping slaves. He watched Ernest anxiously as he told these things, but Ernest's face, to his relief, expressed only thoughtful concern and interest, and even sympathy. But Ernest was thinking: My God, what foolishness, what criminal lack of common sense! And what a position we will all be in if he is caught at it! I've got to put a stop to all this. He tried to get Martin to tell him the names of his confederates, but Martin, suddenly wary, suddenly unconsciously warned, refused to tell. Ernest looked at that handsome, that resolute and anxious face, and hated him. And at the stirring of that bitter hate, the prisoner behind the wall was aroused, and cried.

But one thing Martin guarded from everyone, and that was his conversion to "Romanism." It was sacred to him, though he wore its mental garments uneasily, as he would wear a strange uniform to which he must become accustomed. And now that he was going to marry Amy a veritable chaos was tumbling and thundering in him, a condition that no one suspected at all behind what Ernest called his "frozen face." But that "frozen face," as disdainfully termed by Ernest, was merely a window behind which Martin, in his vehement desire to protect himself from exigencies and situations with which he could not cope, drew opaque and characterless blinds. Behind the blankness, he could conduct his struggles, indulge in his despairs, fight out his fights, without fear of the pointing curiosity of others.

So he went to Father Dominick in his little shabby cottage behind the little shabby brownstone church. The priest, who was of French extraction, was very short, very round and fat, very bald, very genial, very subtle and kind, and exceedingly intelligent. When he led Martin into the closed dankness of his small and hideous parlor, he expressed his jubiliation and thanks for Martin's recent gift to the church of five thousand dollars. "And that," he said, ringing a small bell violently to summon his old housekeeper to bring in coffee and fruit cake, "with your other gifts, my dear Martin, will enable us to start building our new church. Do you realize, my son, that you and Mr. John Slattery of the Tanneries are the only rich men in Windsor who are Catholics? And Mr. Slattery is sometimes remiss— Ah, well. He has a large family, and families frequently make men greedy. It is well that you have no family, will never have one, for your gifts to the unfortunate must certainly draw heavily on your resources. What the Sisters' Hospital in Garnerstown would have done without your fifteen thousand dollars is something I cannot endure thinking about. They have ten new beds now, and can afford a good doctor on the staff. But tell me," he said with animation, as he lavishly sugared his coffee, "how is our dear son, Jacques Bouchard? I noticed him at Mass last Sunday, and he looked excessively ill. What an affliction! But how beautifully borne! And what a face—like an angel's, so patient and purged of all wickedness."

Martin was silent. In the gloom of the parlor, the happily chatting priest, who had few visitors, did not notice his silence. He drank his coffee with noisy enjoyment, stuffed whole slices of cake into his mouth, mumbling over them. What he said was naïve and enthusiastic, with a sort of childlike simplicity, but there was none of this simplicity in his small and penetrating eyes. Replete at last, he wiped his hands on his handkerchief, beamed upon Martin, and prepared to bestow on him his entire attention.

"And now, I presume, you are come to tell me that you are leaving at once for Quebec. Ah, what a privilege to leave the world, not when one is old and broken and disillusioned, but with youth and ardor and strength undiminished, ready to be poured out in service to the Lord!" He sighed, beamed again, then seeing Martin's face, sharpened his eyes upon it, his smile fading. Martin stood up, took a turn about the room, then began to speak, his foot on the fender of the little lurking fire, his profile outlined in dim crimson.

"Father, I came today to tell you I can't go to Quebec. I came to tell you that I love someone, that I am going to marry her." He did not turn toward the priest, but waited for his answer. This did not come; the dimness increased in the room, the fire snapped in discouragement. Finally Martin turned to him. Father Dominick's face was impassive; he was regarding Martin intently. Impulsively, Martin went to him, stood before him. "Please understand, Father," he said desperately. "I couldn't go. It wouldn't be right. I do not want to go."

The priest took his eyes from Martin's face, stared steadfastly at the floor. He began to frown, plucking the coarse stuff of his shabby pantaloons between his thumb and finger. He spoke, without looking at Martin:

"Are you certain of all this? Are you sure it is not a passing infatua
tion in which young men frequently indulge? Will you not regret this?"

"I will not regret it! I love this girl. She is Miss Amy Drumhill——"

He stopped, for the priest was gazing at him in astonishment and
wonder. The gaze lasted for several long moments, and as it did so a
subtle change came into it. It became speculative, obscurely excited, exceedingly thoughtful. The priest began to speak, slowly and carefully,
still regarding Martin with that odd expression: "You must be certain,
my son. When you first came to me with Jacques Bouchard, asking me
to help you both to enter a monastery, I was certain that Jacques had a
vocation. Of you, I was not so sure. That is why I made you wait a year
before writing to Quebec. Even then, I had a few doubts. Finally I
decided that I was in error, that you indeed had a vocation, that you
had never been of the world and would never be of it. But I see I was
wrong.

"Do not look so distressed, Martin. Better men than you have been
mistaken. And it is well that they have discovered this in time. I can see
that you are afraid that you have done something heinous. Not so, my
son, not so. God does not wish the services of those who cannot give
them willingly. Besides, there are more ways than one to serve God.
The good father, the good husband, the faithful and pious head of a
family, also serves our Lord. God has been good and merciful in pointing out to you before it is too late that you really have no vocation, and
that you can best serve Him in the ways of the world." He stood up and
waddled over to Martin, and took his arm. "Go, my son, and marry Miss
Amy Drumhill. I have seen her, in her carriage, and have heard of her.
A fine lady, a truly great lady. She will bear your children in the fear
of the Lord, and bring you happiness. But there is one thing you must
remember. Though she will probably insist upon a Protestant marriage,
you must not forget that you are a Catholic, and there must be another
marriage by a Catholic priest, and your children must be Catholics."

Martin was almost incredulous in his relief and joy. "You mean,
Father, that I have your blessing?"

"Most certainly. But tell me, what does our dear son Jacques Bouchard
think of this? Is he not most terribly disappointed?"

Martin turned aside. "I have not told him," he said in a low voice.

"Has he not suspected something?"

Martin hesitated. His expression lost its animation and joy. "I think
he has. Yes, I am certain he has. But I haven't told him yet. But now, I
can. I'm going to him now."

CHAPTER XXVIII

THE BOUCHARD family was just finishing its evening meal when Martin arrived. He was greeted with exuberant affection by everyone, except Eugene, who was reserved with Martin for Ernest's sake. Madam Bouchard issued booming orders to the fat maid to set another place for Martin, and she herself lumbered to the kitchen to see what delicacies her larder held. Armand, who despite his prosperity still removed his boots at night and toasted his socks before the fire, sat in his huge chair, smoking, a small brown gnome whose sharp eyes gleamed and flashed even when he was silent. Feeling at ease in the unaffected and unselfconscious household as he never felt in his own, Martin ate and drank and listened and smiled and commented. Raoul had not returned from his second European foraging for new laborers for the voracious mills and factories of Barbour & Bouchard, and there was a definite gap in the atmosphere.

Jacques, who had finished his meal, moved his twisted body back to the table in order to sit with his friend, and his mother, encouraged by this, slyly heaped a plate with small cakes and filled another cup of coffee, and pushed them in front of her beloved son. She knew that he would be absorbed in Martin, and would eat mechanically, thereby acquiring another supply of nourishment.

"You have not been to see us for four days," said Jacques softly, his face glowing with affection and contentment as he looked at Martin. But he did not speak so softly (he could never speak so softly), that his mother did not hear.

"That is true!" she exclaimed hoarsely. "How you have been neglecting my Jacques! He watches by the window, like a girl, for you, and will not eat, and languishes. Assassin!" she added playfully, giving Martin a push on the shoulder. But her fiery eyes were not playful, and her smile had something fierce and threatening in it.

Jacques smiled indulgently at Martin, as though begging his patience with his mother; but Martin, sick with uneasiness, saw that his smile was also self-conscious and significant.

"You forget, maman," he said to his mother, putting his thin arm partially about her enormous waist, "that Martin is a busy man, and I am just a useless bundle of bones eating up the family substance."

"Tiens! You eat no more than a sparrow, my Jacques!" Madam

Bouchard raised her voice to a shout and glared upon her son with great
ferocity, but the hand that touched his head was tremulous and tender
with pain. Her face, so huge and dark and sullen, with its enormous out-
thrust underlip and hint of mustache at the corners of the upper lip,
turned upon Martin. "Tell me, is he not fatter? Does he not look
better?"

"Yes, he looks very well," answered Martin, forcing his dry mouth
to stretch itself to a smile. But Jacques, with the alertness of one who is
always afraid, always watching for the thief, saw that Martin's forehead
was faintly damp and that he was quite pale as though tormented with
anxiety. There was a sick thrust of fear in the cripple's stomach, a tightening of his emaciated muscles. He stared at Martin earnestly, noted
that though Martin brought the coffee cup to his lips he did not drink,
did not touch the food he turned with his fork. A lump that threatened
to choke him rose in Jacques' throat. He moistened lips hot with a sudden fever of terror. He panted a little, and his eyes rolled about the room.
How to get alone with Martin, take him away from this press of family,
force him to allay his desperate fears? Ah, a new case of books had
arrived that day and was waiting to be opened in his room: he would take
Martin there at once on this pretext. But before he could gather his voice
strongly enough to speak, Armand was talking to Martin.

"Has Joe been to his doctor lately, Martin?"

"No, he will not go, though Ma begs him every day," answered Martin, anxiously. "He says we are mollycoddles, that there is nothing at all
wrong with him. But he eats nothing, and we hear him groaning in his
sleep at night. His color is very bad, also. We think it must be his liver."

Armand shook his head slowly, regarded the fire and smoked, and made
no further comment. He had seen the mark of death on Joseph's face.
Martin, watching him with apprehension, waited for him to speak again,
then seeing that he would not, pretended to drink his coffee. He dared
not risk meeting Jacques' eyes again; each time that he had done so the
steadily shining light of love in them, the eager smile, were more than he
could bear. He was also painfully aware, with surprise, that the light
and the smile had become annoying to him, that they were like hands
seeking to clutch him tightly, that there was something morbid in them.
He was shocked at these thoughts, tried to feel touched at Jacques' evident joy and contentment that he was there, and succeeded only in rous-
ing a passionate thought that he would give anything to be out of that
house. Then he remembered that he had come here to disrupt Jacques'
entire life and throw it down, and he was ill with anxiety and remorse
again.

Eugene, aloof but courteous, asked him something about the new military contracts; it was but a polite inquiry, and Eugene was quite aware of
the fact that he knew a great deal more of the business of Barbour &

Bouchard than did the self-absorbed and removed Martin. When Martin replied, vaguely and uncertainly, Eugene regarded him mildly but with inner contempt and pity. What a child it is! he thought, and looked at Martin's fine slender body and length of limb with a certain wonder and perplexity. And then his dark and stolid face warmed, and he smiled at Martin with sudden affection. Martin's fair hair and blue eyes, his posture and slight gestures, reminded him of little Dorcas, who was his especial adoration.

Jacques finally was able to separate Martin from the family and take him into his own room. Once there, he was on the point of bursting into hysterical recriminations, accusing Martin of neglect and indifference, when he remembered, with a tightening of his shaking lips, that words frequently brought things into the open that might have lain harmless in the silent darkness. Words, he thought, were a fatal precipitant. So he forced himself to smile, poked ineffectually at the fire, and surrendered the poker with a weak laugh to the stronger hands of Martin. Martin knelt on the stone hearth, vigorously stirred up the short thick logs; the fire, turning to a sheet of resinous yellow, flung a glaring light into the room, bathing Martin with a flame like lightning. Never, thought Jacques, clasping his thin hands convulsively together, had he possessed such splendor, such beauty, such decisive strength. Involuntarily, one of his hands began to steal out, to touch Martin's shoulder, then Jacques, becoming aware of his own gesture, sharply withdrew his hand, and turned crimson. A wave of heat, of ecstasy, of fear and love, ran fiercely over his maimed body. His heart began to beat with strange insistence, as though aware of something he himself did not know as yet.

Martin stood up, the fire stirred to his satisfaction. But he did not turn to Jacques. Instead, he stood there on the hearth, his head bent, his eyes fixed on the flames. Thin muscles began to throb about his mouth.

"Sit down, Martin," said Jacques, leaning over the arm of his chair to pull another chair into place beside his for his friend. But Martin did not sit down. He turned to Jacques; now his back was to the fire and Jacques could not see his face.

"Jacques, I must tell you something," he said hurriedly. "I had to tell you, tonight. Not to tell you was lying. My God!" he added, his voice tight with despair, "I don't know how I am to tell you!"

It has come, thought Jacques, and darkness fell over his eyes. It seemed to him everything stopped inside him, that reality had dropped away and left only him and this mortal anguish that ran through his chest. The muscles of his throat closed, and his mouth dropped open. But Martin saw only that he appeared to be very calm, in spite of his whiteness, and he took courage. He sat down beside him, leaned over the arm of his chair eagerly.

"Jacques, please understand. I've been to see Father Dominick. I told him. He says it is all right, and gave me his blessing. There was no use, he said, in forcing yourself to take up a vocation for which you were not fitted."

"You are not going with me?" Jacques whispered. He had begun to pant a little, as though his chest were incased in slowly closing bands of iron.

"No, I can't, Jacques. I have no vocation."

"You had a vocation a year ago, six months ago." The whisper had become almost inaudible, and now Martin saw that his friend's face was covered with a gleaming damp film, and that his skin had taken on a bluish tint. Impulsively, he took Jacques' hand and was horrified at its icy coldness, its wetness and rigidity.

"Jacques, please try to understand," he pleaded, hating himself. "I was mistaken." Jacques' eyes fixed themselves on his unmovingly; there was death in them, and the expression of one who looks at his executioner. Martin wet his lips, forced himself to go on. "But now I find it was all a mistake. It wouldn't be right to do it." He had meant to urge Jacques to go to Quebec, himself, but somehow this now seemed intolerably callous to suggest. "Please forgive me. You wouldn't want me to do anything that was not right, I know."

He wanted to drop his friend's hand, but Jacques' fingers, cold and trembling, had fastened themselves convulsively on his. A faint chill. a thrill of something he could not define, shot through Martin, and sweat broke out between his shoulder blades.

"What are you going to do?" asked Jacques, and now he spoke almost in a normal voice. Martin was enormously relieved and grateful. He smiled. Jacques was behaving much better than he expected; he had been a fool to waste time in anxieties and apprehensions.

"I am going to be married," he said, coloring a little. "To Miss Amy Drumhill. You know, Mr. Gregory Sessions' niece." The mere mention of Amy's name was enough to warm him and hearten him.

He had been prepared for surprise and indignation on Jacques part; he had been prepared for expressions of coldness and contempt, for arguments that tried to turn his mind back to the old arrangement. He had even been prepared for the fine-drawn, high-pitched rages that he knew Jacques could whip up on occasion. But he was not prepared for what did happen, and his shock was all the greater.

For Jacques had uttered one keen thin cry, as though he had been knifed. And then he huddled in his chair, sinking down into it until he seemed only a heap of maimed bones and broken shoulders. A sort of disorder, disintegration, fell on him, a wildness and confusion, a dispersing. His face became a ghastly mask superimposed on that shapeless heap of bones, a mask thrown carelessly and haphazardly upon it. From it, his eyes, dilated and glared in agony upon Martin. The firelight flamed upon him, throwing everything into shadow and vagueness but that mask and those eyes, and the bluish hands clutching the arms of the chair.

Then before Martin, appalled, could speak again, Jacques' broken body had struggled from the chair, and he had flung himself at Martin's feet. He was clutching Martin's knees, that mask, convulsed now, and streaming with tears, raised to Martin. There was a deathly strength in the hold of his arms; he sobbed, he grovelled, he beat his head on Martin's knees. He would not let go; his arms were steel. But had they been only child's strength, Martin could not have moved. Jacques was saying such strange and dreadful things. No, no, he was moaning, anything but that, Martin must promise him anything but that! He would die of it, just thinking of it. He must not marry. See, he must stay here, with Jacques, who loved him as no woman could love him, and he would promise, in the name of God, in the name of Mary, that he would never reproach him for breaking his promise; he would never speak of it again. He, Jacques, would be Martin's slave—anything, O God! anything. But he must not marry. Please, he must not marry. He smiled through those tears, a child pleading for his life before an upraised axe. No, Martin must not marry! He would promise anything—do anything. They could go away for just a little while, if Martin wanted it, and talk and think and be together as they had once been. He had not long to live—he knew it. Just a little longer, and Martin would be free. Mercy. Mercy. He grovelled, crawled, moaned, in an abandonment of all dignity, an abandonment of all human pride, that the English Martin found shameful.

And then he collapsed in a heap, suddenly silent and lax, as though he had died. The fire crackled, roared, moaned uneasily. Through the thick oaken door Madam Bouchard's loud boom came only faintly.

Martin could not move; a cold paralysis lay along all his muscles. He told himself that he dared not move, or he would be violently sick. But he began to shudder slowly and heavily, and he could hardly breathe. He was too innocent, his life too narrow and removed from the turbulence of living, to guess the full import behind Jacques' agony. But his instincts of fear and flight were aroused and screaming in him. A sudden dull horror possessed him; he would have given his life to have been removed from that room, from the mad grasp upon him. He would never come again! Never again! He never wanted to see Jacques again. Chills of loathing increased his shuddering. He could think of nothing but escape, nothing but flight. This was a nightmare. Soon he would wake up and be safe, and alone.

The thought was so piercingly sweet, so desirable, that he moved his feet involuntarily. But Jacques held them, his face pressed to them. The movement of his own body, however, aroused Martin to coherent thought and reality. He looked down at that broken heap, at the wretched maimed body, at the grotesque legs twisted on the floor, at the terribly humble head on his feet. Pity assaulted him, disgust for himself. Poor Jacques loved him, was afraid that his marriage to Amy would separate them. How foolish, how silly. This poor broken creature, who would never love a woman nor have a woman love him!

He bent down and gently disentangled Jacques' arms. He had no difficulty now—the arms fell from his legs as though they were dead. Martin lifted him as though he were a child, put him in his chair. Jacques' head fell on his chest; his eyes were closed as though he had fainted. But behind his eyes the strange and dreadful things went on.

"Jacques," said Martin gently, bending over him, "I won't ever leave you, even when I am married. You will visit us, and we will come to see you. Nothing will be changed. There will just be three of us, instead of two. You don't know Amy, how sweet and kind she is. She understands everything."

Jacques had begun to sob again, as though he had not heard, silent sobs infinitely pathetic and desperate, as though he had given up all hope. He did not look at Martin, and his eyes remained closed. Timidly, he groped for Martin's hand, brought it to his wet lips and kissed it, very humbly, and let it go. There was something of renunciation, of leave-taking, in the gesture.

Martin heard himself incoherently promising, consoling, urging. The sickness was on him again, but his pity impelled him to comfort his friend. And Jacques sat with closed eyes and sunken head. silent now, unmoving, as though he were sleeping after a shock.

Martin sighed and moved away a little. Jacques was breathing regularly; once he moaned and shifted himself, as if finding a more comfortable position in which to sleep. Martin, holding his breath, moved back to him, bent over him anxiously. He was assured, with vast relief, that Jacques had fallen into a sudden sleep of exhaustion. He brought a blanket from the bed, arranged it gently over Jacques' knees and legs. Then, sighing again, he tiptoed from the room.

The door closed softly behind him. The minute it did so, Jacques' eyes opened, deep and sunken. He did not move so much as a finger, but he stared into the fire for a long time, more than an hour, until the logs fell apart in the last blaze of light, and the room began to chill.

CHAPTER XXIX

MARTIN COULD not force himself, during the next few days, to see Jacques. Finally he went to Father Dominick and told what had taken place between him and the young Frenchman. The priest listened intently, and as Martin proceeded, his eyes narrowed, became thoughtful, fixed themselves curiously upon him. When Martin had finished, he muttered to himself: "I had thought as much. What a singularly innocent young man this is!" And he became even more curious, almost incredulous. However, he said with great kindness and concern: "It frequently happens that cripples are touched with selfishness. Their lives are necessarily narrow and circumscribed, and whosoever they love becomes unusually dear to them. I suspect that our poor young friend is jealous." And again he stared curiously at Martin.

He advised him to remain away from the Bouchard house for a little while. In the meantime he, the priest, would visit Jacques, try to make him understand, try to help him take a more unselfish view of the matter. Martin was enormously relieved. Everything, he was sure, would now be all right. When he had gone the priest shook his head, made a wry mouth, and thought: "A terrible business. A very terrible business. It will be better if they never meet again, for some day our poor Jacques might not be able to contain himself, and will give his friend a very great shock."

In a few days he reported to Martin that Jacques was unexpectedly calm and reasonable. He had listened to everything that the priest had said, had smiled a little, agreed, begun to talk of other things. But he had not asked that Martin come to see him. Martin was perplexed and hurt at this, and was very uneasy for the next two weeks. But when he encountered Armand, the latter was as casual and friendly as ever, so Martin came to the conclusion that Jacques was merely sulking or trying to recover. He told himself that he missed Jacques, and was ashamed that he could not believe it, that he felt delivered and released, and inordinately happy. All things had been so wearisome to him, so pale and unreal; only his dreams had had substance. Looking back at his dreams, he was amazed that they had ever satisfied him, and he came reluctantly to the conclusion that he had been under a sort of enchantment that had robbed him of living.

He had had no idea that things could be so pleasant. Gregory Sessions seemed to have taken a great liking to him; this was no delusion on Martin's part, for Gregory found something touching in this young man's eagerness and ardor, simplicity and integrity of outlook. Gregory had never been like this, even when he had been young, and had met it in all his life in only three persons, his sister, Amy, her daughter, and Martin. Like Ernest, he thought somewhat enviously: how peaceful it must be to see things straightly, never to set snares to catch your own feet! But at other times he came to the conclusion that such an attitude of mind was similar to the unconsciousness of a very young child's mind. It was because Martin had never really recognized and accepted reality, he thought. He knew that only two kinds of men have such unconsciousness, the fool and the ascetic, and sometimes he wondered which Martin was.

Gregory, too, found life exceedingly enjoyable these days. Martin had served up a piquant situation, unwittingly, for his pleasure. There was Ernest in love with Amy, so much in love that each day he seemed to become a little more flat and pale of cheek and harder of eye. Gregory delighted in watching the unending fight behind that eye and iron forehead; he delighted in the torment with all the exquisiteness of a Torquemada. He knew Ernest too well to fear that he would destroy everything for a mere passion, so his pleasure and hatred could glut themselves without apprehension. He told himself that it served Ernest right, that he was suffering as poor little Amy had suffered, but he was sufficiently self-analytical to realize that the truth went deeper than that. It was characteristic of him that he was amused at the result of his own probing of his own mind.

Amy chose the furniture Hilda and Joseph bought for her. Her taste was simple yet perfect. The house Ernest had given Martin was not like the Sessions house, long broad rooms with delicately frescoed wall borders and wide fireplaces. The rooms were longitudinal and none too light, with high narrow mantelpieces. It was, she said, a "shouldering" house. So she chose rich yet delicate colors that brightened the darkish rooms, replaced the black marble fireplaces with white marble, had the hideous wallpapers removed and replaced them with papers painted in soft tiny nosegays or long pale stripes. Her furniture was simple dark mahogany, with none of the satin damasks and plushes and tufted cushions of May's preference. Gardens were set out in old-fashioned beds, to soften the girdling grimness of the elms about the land. Ernest declared that the house had entirely changed its character; he was lavish with praise. He looked at Amy's happy rosy face, listened to her laugh, smiled at her soft chatter, all with an affectionate blandness that hid everything but a faint knot between his eyes. He helped May choose the brocades for the windows, and the rugs, and quarrelled with both young women good-humoredly when they questioned his taste. During all this, he would glance up and look at Martin, and be alternately amazed at the splendor of his brother's face and carriage and contemptuous of his simplicity. At other times, his hate was like poison in his mouth.

Ernest's marriage had been important, and a little serious, in spite of May's gaiety and fashionable friends from New York and Philadelphia. After all, wealth was marrying wealth, and it was a noteworthy occasion. More than a little stateliness and serious thought had entered into the ceremony. But in the case of Martin and Amy it was very different. To be sure, it was more than likely that Martin would share equally in the fortune that Joseph Barbour would leave, and there was nothing to indicate that Ernest would inherit the major share; but nevertheless the impression was abroad that Martin had little and would probably have very little more. And Amy was a penniless girl, who could expect nothing in the way of a substantial dowry from her uncles. So in their marriage there would be a childlike pleasure, simple laughter, unreserved affection, joy and lightness. Everyone could enjoy himself without thinking of the fortunes involved, and how to install himself solidly in the regard of the young couple. There was exquisiteness and delicate gaiety in this marriage, something touching and sweet.

The marriage, by Nicholas' request, was put ahead two weeks, as he was about to begin his electioneering, so the last weeks were a flurry of merriment and excited protests, dressmakers and tailors, cooks and furnishers.

It was only two weeks before the ceremony when Jacques Bouchard committed suicide.

CHAPTER XXX

IT WAS a lovely and tender spring evening when Jacques Bouchard decided to put an end to his life. It was a Sunday night, and everything was still and filled with rosy and violet haze. Even Oldtown was less raucous this evening, and the church bells rang in clear and lucid peals over the whole city. Over black massed trees the skies were like a wide and dreaming meditation, and the air was full of a sweet movement.

Armand Bouchard had just purchased a fine open carriage, capable of seating five people. It was a solid vehicle, not too expensive, but heavy with fringe and gay and black leather, silver harness and brightly painted wheels. Armand had hired a youth to take care of the new fat dappled mares, and their gray tied tales bunched over haunches that gleamed and rippled, and their manes were as fine and soft and curling, Armand declared, as any woman's hair.

It was such a fine evening that nothing would satisfy the family but a drive before darkness came. But Jacques, at the last moment, decided not to go. His mother protested, threatened, pleaded, but he gently urged that he was tired and would rather read or sleep. She announced she would remain with him, but with rare peremptoriness he refused her company, declared it would distress him if she deprived herself of the pleasure just for his sake. There was a lot of room, he said. Why couldn't they stop by and take one or two of the Barbours for a drive? He turned his gentle and penetrating eyes upon Eugene, smiling. Eugene flushed darkly; it annoyed while it obscurely pleased him, that Jacques had guessed his adoration for little Dorcas.

So Madam Bouchard, grumbling and scowling, lit the candles and the lamps, and then they all went off on the drive, leaving Jacques entirely alone in the house, for the two maids had gone to church.

Despite the warmth and loveliness of the evening, a few embers lay on the hearth, and Jacques sat before them, regarding them fixedly for a long time. His face was impassive and motionless, but all at once slow tears fell from his eyes, rolled unheeded over the crooked rise of his chest. Then, when a pale cool curve of silver which was the new moon shone through the window, he rose, got paper and pen and ink, and wrote two short letters. He laid them on the table near by. He then fumbled for his crutch, climbed painfully up the stairs to his room. He went to his high chest of drawers, and drew out a long black pistol. On its side was stamped: Barbour & Bouchard. With great calmness, almost absent-mindedly, he examined the chamber, saw it was filled. He went to his bed and sat down upon it, and looked through the open window at the brightening curve of the moon.

At the opposite side of the room was a low stand covered by a fine cloth of exquisite linen and bordered with hand-made lace. On this stand stood a tall and elaborate silver crucifix. Before the crucifix stood a low unlit candle in a red glass holder.

Jacques looked away from the moon, and looked at the crucifix. The room was almost dark, but a faint gleam was on the silver. He stood up and dragged himself heavily to the little altar, the pistol in his hand. He lit the candle before it, and stood watching the golden flicker make a haze in the darkness. For a long time thereafter, he gazed at the crucifix, at the distorted silver countenance and the tiny silver thorns on the bleeding head. Then he said: "But You knew nothing of this."

Then he put the pistol to his head, and still gazing at the face of Jesus, he pulled the trigger. There was a single barking roar, a fall, and then silence. The candle flickered on serenely, the agony on the face of the crucified man became more distinct as the light became stronger, a thin and acrid scarf of smoke twisted in the golden and diffused radiance. And on the floor lay Jacques Bouchard, face down, in a dark and widening pool, the pistol fallen from his hand. The light did not fall on him; he lay in shadow.

CHAPTER XXXI

ERNEST AND GREGORY had also gone for a drive that night, but May, who had not been feeling very well lately, remained at home. She was languid these days, and preferred to rest and sew and read and drowse. She had never had more than a casual affection for the Sessions house, but since her marriage it had become infinitely dear to her, every room poignant with peace and contentment, every old wall beloved and cherished. Here was home, full and complete, impregnable and whole. She liked to be alone, as she was now, listening to the faint crackle of a newly lit fire, imagining the sound of Ernest's voice, conjuring up from the silence the running beat of her children's footsteps. She liked this soft and mellow candlelight, the shine and glimmer of the furniture, the dark faces of the portraits on the ivory walls. Through the open windows, thrust out to the night, she could hear the deep burbling of the frogs in the pool at the foot of the gardens and the taffeta murmur of the trees. Martin and Amy were still out in the gardens, though it was almost ten o'clock. May wondered drowsily if Amy had remembered to take her shawl, but even this could not occupy the delicious and sleepy peace of her mind. "I am a terrible chaperon," she thought contentedly.

Then Martin and Amy came in, laughing together, Amy wrapped in the depths of a soft blue shawl. May looked at them and smiled; she loved them, for their faces reflected the happiness she felt. "It is shamefully late," she said fondly. She wished Martin liked her more, and was amused at the shy distrust he had for her. But nothing, she thought, could be nicer nor more elegant than his courtesy. She glanced at the serenity of Amy's face, listened to her low laugh, and told herself, as she had done a hundred times, that it was purely her silly fancy that something vital and eager had gone from the face and the laugh.

There was a sound of carriage wheels, and voices. May heard Ernest's voice, and a flush seemed to rise about her heart as it always did when she heard him. Her drowsiness vanished, and she sat up. She did not see that Amy had turned her face in the direction of Ernest's voice, and that a sort of white listening look came out upon it.

Ernest and Gregory came into the room, talking loudly. But May, glancing at them, stopped smiling. They were very pale and seemed a little breathless, for all they greeted Martin and Amy and herself with great heartiness. Something has happened, she thought, coldness running over her. When Ernest bent over her and kissed her forehead, she stared at him sharply, but she could not read his expression. Gregory had rung the bell and ordered wine; he was talking inconsequentially to Martin. Then Ernest, still bending over May, whispered in her ear: "My love, please take Amy out of the room with you. We have something to tell Martin. Now, please don't disturb yourself. It is nothing of consequence, except that Jacques Bouchard has been taken ill, and wants to see Martin. You know how fond Martin is of the poor devil, and we want to break the news to him easily."

"Oh, poor Jacques," said May, who had seen him once, and had not cared for him. She gathered up her fine sewing, and lifted her heavy body reluctantly from her chair. "Amy, my pet," she said, "I am feeling a little too tired. Will you come with me and help me undress? You know, Gladys has gone to her sick mother tonight, and I am all alone."

The two young women left the room together. When the door had closed behind them, Gregory stopped his rambling talk abruptly. Martin was surprised; he turned to Ernest. His brother, he noticed for the first time, looked pale and concerned, and not a little grim.

"Martin," he said, "have you quarrelled lately with Jacques Bouchard? About anything at all?"

Martin's expression became blank, then on an instant, it turned crimson, then paled again. "Why do you ask that?" he stammered. Then, as Ernest did not answer, but only regarded him with piercing steadiness, he cried out sharply: "What is the matter? Is something wrong with Jacques? I shall go to him at once!"

But Ernest blocked his way. "No," he said harshly. "There's no use now. Eugene's just been over at Pa's, and we had stopped by. Jacques," he added, watching Martin's white face and starting eyes intently, "killed himself, about two hours ago."

There was a short sick silence. Then Martin exclaimed in anguish: "I don't believe it! It's just one of your lies, Ernest! I don't believe it! Why should he kill himself?"

"You might answer that," said Ernest contemptuously. But he appeared breathless and not a little frightened. "Here. Here is a letter he wrote you. Eugene found two letters, one to you and one to his mother. He had the sense to pick yours up and conceal it, and to bring it to me." He tossed the letter onto the chair by Martin's side. Gregory, slowly sipping a glass of wine, watched them both absorbedly. There was something here he did not quite understand, but nothing in the world would have removed him from that spot short of an earthquake. "Why don't you read the letter?" asked Ernest, raising his voice, for Martin stood in the attitude of a sleep-walker. Finally Ernest took him by the arm and shook him violently. "Read the letter!" he shouted.

Like a hypnotized man obeying the commands of the mesmerizer, Martin picked up the letter. He turned it over, dully, in his hands. Then he lifted his glazed eyes to Ernest. "You opened it," he said tonelessly.

"Yes, I opened it," said Ernest in a flat tone.

Martin blinked; the letter shook in his hands. He bent down so that the candlelight could fall upon it. He read:

"Dear Martin: Please forgive me. Please do not blame your kindest and dearest of selves. It is not your fault that I can't live any longer. But I could not bear to think of sharing you with any one else, or having you love any one else. I am selfish and wicked, and in doing what I shall do I have put myself beyond the reach of God's mercy. But even that is not as bad as having you leave me. I have only one more thing to say, and that is that I wish you to have my silver crucifix from France, and my garnet rosary. Forgive me. Pray for me, if you can. Your friend, Jacques."

The letter was like a thunderbolt passing through Martin. He fell into the chair. The letter dropped through his fingers onto the carpet. In the silence that followed, the faint sweet chime of the ormolu clock rang out, ironically, and the candles flickered in the slight wind that came through the windows. Suddenly Martin put his hands over his face and began to sob dryly.

Ernest bent down, picked up the letter, and threw it, with a grimace, into the fire. "What a foul mess!" he said grimly, and for an instant nausea stood out on his features. He glanced at Gregory, who lifted his eyebrows and shoulders expressively. "Come on, Martin, be a man. This has got to be faced. What do you know about all this? You've got to tell me. God knows what the mad fool wrote in his letter to his mother. He might have accused you of anything. And there's always the police. My God!" he added with suppressed vehemence and passionate disgust. He spat in the direction of the fire as though there was a vile taste in his mouth.

Martin dropped his hands; his face was white and haggard, his mouth bitten. He began to speak almost in a whisper. "It's all my fault. I killed him." He twisted in his seat and faced Ernest. "It's all my fault!" he cried shrilly, his eyes a blue and terrible blaze. "I killed him! I was all he ever had, and I was going to leave him." He stood up, disordered and trembling. "I'm going to his father and his mother, and I'm going to tell them that I killed Jacques!" He stared about him, blindly.

"Christ!" said Ernest between his clenched teeth. He grasped his brother by the front of his coat, and literally flung him back in his chair. "You god-damn fool!" he went on, standing over him and panting. "Have you no sense at all!" He paused, stood up, tried to regain normal breathing, but his broad harsh face was suffused with an almost apoplectic color. He looked at Gregory as if for help, as if calling upon him to denounce, with him, this infernal and atrocious fool. But Gregory looked back at him, without expression. Go on, you devil, thought Gregory. Go on, thinking about the danger to your precious shops, and your ambitions. You'll find some way, trust you! to save everything, and wriggle things through, but in the meantime you can sweat, and be damned to you! And he waited, gleefully, to see in what manner Ernest would "wriggle through."

Martin, dazed and broken, huddled in his chair. He had been thrown into it so violently that a thick lock of his pale yellow hair had fallen over his face; his chin was sunken on his chest. He did not move.

Ernest drew a deep breath, and the purplish color faded from his cheeks, very slowly. He seemed to brace himself, to straighten his wide shoulders, to draw back into himself all his tremendous will and strength. He put his hand on Martin's shoulder, pressing it as though to command his attention through the haze of grief and despair, and began to speak, very slowly and distinctly.

"Listen to me, Martin. You are not responsible for Jacques' death. He was a cripple, and cripples are never quite right in their minds. He was bound to do this sooner or later. It is not your fault. You had a right to your own life, and it was selfish and stupid of him to think that you did not. It's too late to do anything for him. Damn it, I'm sorry for the poor wretch! But it's too late. You've got to think of the living. You've got to think of Armand and Madam Bouchard. You can't hurt them more than they've been hurt. It would be cruel for you to do so."

He paused; his quiet and insistent voice, however, had had its effect. Martin was listening; he had raised his head, and his piteous eyes were fixed on Ernest's face as though he found salvation there.

"If Jacques knows anything now, he is sorry," went on Ernest, holding Martin's eyes with his. "Sorry that he caused you all this grief and worry. And he would want you, more than anything else, not to add to his parents' misery. You've got to think of them. Think how they would feel to have you bursting in upon them, like a maniac, like someone escaped from Bedlam, accusing yourself of having killed their son, and raving like a fool! Would that help them? Would a lie bring Jacques back to them? If you were so stupid as all that, how do you think Pa and Ma would feel? No, you've got to think of others, Martin."

Gregory regarded him with satanic admiration. Bravo! he thought.

Ernest waited for what Martin would say. Tiny drops of moisture stood out upon his forehead under the crest of his light and vital hair. He wet his lips. Martin was gazing fixedly, now, at the floor, at the ashes of Jacques' letter. Then he said, hoarsely and dully: "You are quite right, Ernest. I can't hurt them any more. Jacques wouldn't want it."

"That's the way to talk!" said Ernest. There was about him a great and weary relaxing, as if after intolerable strain. He pulled out his large linen handkerchief and mopped his forehead. Gregory saw that the back of his strong hand was wet. Again, Ernest put his hand on Martin's shoulder. "Spoken like a man," he said.

"But," said Martin, as though he had not heard his brother's remark, "there's one thing I can do. I can do what Jacques would want me to do: keep my promise to him. I can't marry Amy now. I'll do what Jacques would wish; I'll go alone to the monastery."

"What!" shouted Ernest, his face wrinkling, his eyebrows jerking as if he had not heard aright, had thought he had heard something incredible.

"What!" exclaimed Gregory, aroused now, and advancing.

Martin nodded his head heavily. "I should have told you all before, Ernest, and this is the price I must pay because I didn't. Amy knows. I told her. A long time ago I became a convert to the Roman Catholic Church. Jacques and I intended, a year ago, to go to Quebec, to enter a monastery there. It was all arranged. And then—," he stopped, his voice dwindling in anguish.

Ernest and Gregory regarded each other in stupefaction. "God!" whispered Ernest at last, and his mouth fell open. Suddenly Gregory was convulsed with his silent, red-faced and crumpled mirth, and his suffused eyes stared at Ernest with an unspeakable comment. Then he began to cough thickly, as though choking.

"A Papist?" said Ernest at last, turning to Martin, and speaking dazedly. "You became a Papist? What the hell for? This is quite beyond me. Am I dreaming?" He rubbed his forehead.

"You're not dreaming," said Martin miserably. He made a despairing gesture. "It's all over now. I can only do this one thing for Jacques. I can't marry Amy. You—you've got to tell her, Ernest. I just couldn't. Tell her good-by for me. I'm going, tomorrow. To Quebec."

He stood a good two inches taller than Ernest, but there was something so pathetic and bewildered and broken about him that he appeared to have become a boy again, overcome with the miseries of an adult world.

"You can't do this thing to Amy!" exclaimed Gregory, sober and alarmed enough now. "By God, I'll kill you first! You can't do this thing to Amy! Martin, for God's sake, don't be such a fool!"

"Do you think this is easy for me?" cried Martin passionately. "Do you know what it means to me to give up Amy? The only peace and happiness I have ever had have come from her! Do you know what it means to have had others all your life jeer at you, think you a dolt, laugh at everything you say, turn away from you in contempt? That's what I have had—from everyone but Amy." He turned fiercely upon his brother. "I've never said anything, wanted anything, suggested anything, but you have made me feel like an idiot, or worse! You've actually made

me believe I was an idiot, too. You seemed to have the strength to overcome me, to close my mouth. And all the time you were wrong—you
were stupid and vicious and blind. People like you can always silence
those who are gentle enough, or cowardly enough, or courteous enough
not to fight you. To give you the consideration you never give others."
He waved his hands in a distraught gesture. "We can't fight you. We
can only retreat, back away from you. You have weapons we haven't got,
because we have some pity and kindness. We—we believe in some things.
But you believe in nothing, except yourself. You laugh at everything;
nothing is sacred to you. And to you, we who do believe in something
are ridiculous." He stopped, unable to speak for his anguish. Then he
went on, more quietly, but more heavily. "Only Amy understood what
I feel. I was happy with Amy. But, I've got to give her up. I owe that
to Jacques."

Gregory, in violence, turned to Ernest demandingly. Ernest had been
listening, inscrutably eyeing his brother. He had been thinking only one
thing: he dare not do this to Amy, my darling! He dare not. I'll see him
dead first, the impossible imbecile. He shall not do this to Amy!

He took Martin by the arm, held him tightly, commanded his attention
again. He said, very earnestly: "Martin, listen to me. Please. I'm not
going to say, now, that I'm sorry. For a lot of things. I'll tell you that
some other time. I suppose we just didn't understand each other. But
now we've got to talk about Amy."

He paused; he gathered strength again, invincible strength, fighting
strength, for Amy. He was desperate; he could be wily now, coaxing,
placating, wheedling, grovelling, humbling himself, for Amy. He could
see her stricken face, bewildered, agonized, not understanding. It was
like a white flag to his will and dogged obstinacy. He was full of a quite
intolerable pain.

"Martin, don't you see? Don't you see that is just what Jacques wanted
you to do, to give up Amy? That is why he killed himself before you
married her, instead of afterward. He wanted to ruin your life, and
break Amy's heart. He wanted you to be unhappy. He hated Amy, killed
himself so that she would lose you.

"At the last, he hated you, too. Poor devil, his mind was as twisted
as his body. He couldn't really have had any affection for you, or he
wouldn't have done this, to make you miserable, and keep you from
Amy. But he timed it exactly, so that you would do as he wanted you to
do, without thinking, giving yourself no time, breaking off everything so
that it would be too late if you ever came back to your senses. Martin,
don't let a dead man's hand kill you, too. Don't let someone's selfishness
and hate spoil yours and Amy's life. You've got to think of Amy. She'd
never get over it. And that's what he wanted, too. That was his revenge
on the poor girl for taking you from him."

He paused again. Dare he fling the truth into Martin's face, the truth that leered behind that monstrous letter? He knew his brother's austere innocence, and something unknown in him held him back from speaking. But he told himself that he would speak, if his present argument failed.

However, Martin's dazed and listening face gave him hope. Martin was looking at him with pathetic intensity, as if trying to pierce behind the words to find if he were sincere. Perhaps he was half convinced, for he turned to Gregory with touching bewilderment. "Mr. Gregory, do you believe him? Is he telling the truth?"

"Yes, Martin," replied Gregory gravely. "It is quite true. You can believe him. Jacques Bouchard evidently hated you at the last. But at any rate, even if he did not, I am sure that he would not want you to hurt poor Amy."

CHAPTER XXXII

To Ernest's unspeakable relief it was discovered that Jacques Bouchard had left nothing in his letter to his mother that might lead any one to blame Martin for his death. He merely begged forgiveness, said his pain had become more than he could bear any longer, and left a few instructions as to his meagre possessions. However, for some years, Armand had been depositing large sums of money for him in the local bank, and Jacques stated that he wished one-half to be given to the Church of the Annunciation, and the rest to the Fund for the Abolition of Slavery.

Madam Bouchard was like a wild beast deprived of her young. She, said Armand sadly, "howled like a wolf," day and night. Nothing could comfort nor soothe her; when the priest attempted this, she spat in his face and cursed God, then, in an access of grief and remorse, she grovelled at his feet, begged his pardon, implored him to pray for her and for her dead son. Her agony was all the greater because Jacques could not be buried in consecrated ground and had not received the Last Sacrament. But Father Dominick was priest of a Church that knew how to temper the wind to the shorn lamb, and was all things to all men, and he was able to give her a measure of peace.

A week after the funeral Ernest Barbour called upon the priest. He informed him who he was, with great stiffness and disdainful courtesy. But his rigid Protestantism suspected all sorts of sinister intentions and furtive obscurities in "Popery." Martin's revelation of his new faith had alarmed and disgusted him; God knows, he thought, what will be the end of this—Romanism was dark and subtle, and had a strange hold on its adherents. He was apprehensive of this "hold" on any member of the family, and he had a vague suspicion that he must deliver Martin from its clutches. That infernal monastery business! Pah!

Father Dominick received the stiff and impassive young man without revealing any surprise he might have felt. He knew instantly why Ernest had come, and he smiled a little to himself. So he talked artlessly and frankly, had coffee and thin French petits fours served, shook his head over Jacques, and asked candidly after Martin. Ernest was reassured; there was nothing crafty nor subtle about this pleasant, fat little man with the agreeable smile and gentle laugh. Moreover, he appeared to respect and admire his visitor, for he spoke with enthusiasm about the phenomenal growth of Barbour & Bouchard, and confessed that he was an excellent marksman and owned a B&B rifle, himself. Ernest was surprised; there was nothing of the Spanish Inquisition here, nothing sinister and devious. He found himself telling the priest of his recent discovery that Martin had become a Catholic, and then, cautiously and with an effect of carelessness, smilingly remarked that Martin had told him that at one time he had intended to enter a monastery.

His cautiousness did not deceive the priest, who smiled inwardly again. So he said frankly: "Ah, yes. Martin once thought that he had a vocation. I hardly believed it, but he seemed so sincere about it that I considered that I might have been mistaken. I am afraid," with a sigh and a covert eye on Ernest, "that our poor friend, Jacques Bouchard, might have persuaded him that he had a vocation. But that is over, now."

Ernest's relief showed amusingly in his face. He knew a great deal about Martin's temperament, knew how unstable and changeable it was, how unsure under strong argument, how simple and trustful and kind. He had been afraid of the grasp of "Popery" on his brother's emotions, afraid that somehow it would seize him, spirit him into some unknown darkness, leaving Amy bereft and abandoned at the last moment.

With apparent innocence, the priest went on to say that Martin had told him he intended to marry Miss Amy Drumhill, and that he had given him his blessing. Ernest's relief increased, and he smiled upon Father Dominick almost brilliantly. Seizing his advantage, Father Dominick became serious, and told him that he had explained to Martin that, as a Catholic, he must follow any Protestant or civil ceremony with a Catholic one, and that all children resulting from the marriage must be Catholics. "I thought," he said with a faint smile, "that I should tell you this, Mr. Barbour, in case you might, in ignorance, attempt to influence your brother against these laws of the Church."

Ernest, the Protestant, winced a little at "the Church," but he was so blessedly reassured that he said with light indignation: "Whatever made you think sir [he could not say "father"], that I would at any time try to coerce or influence my brother against his private beliefs?"

Father Dominick could not help smiling broadly, and Ernest, coloring, had to smile with him. "I see," said the priest, "that I was quite mistaken, and have done you an injustice." And then, suddenly, without preamble, they laughed together, almost uproariously.

When Ernest was about to go, he drew out a cheque for a very respectable sum and laid it down on the rickety little table. "What is this? A bribe? And if so, for what?" asked the priest, taking it and noting the amount with intense pleasure.

"It is not a bribe," said Ernest, his lips twitching in amusement. He added with candor: "Perhaps it might have been. But it is not, now. Call it an expression of relief." And again they laughed together, and parted with promises of continued acquaintance.

Martin never knew of this visit of Ernest's. Had he learnt of it, he would have gone into a passion of shamed indignation and resentment. He had gone to the priest in anguish, accusing himself of causing Jacques' death, and even after Ernest's arguments, had pleaded to be reassured by Father Dominick that he would not need to do penance by renunciation of Amy. He could not endure going to the Bouchard house, where everything reminded him of Jacques. The last two years were becoming dim in his memory, and he recalled only the very young Jacques and the contentment and affection he had always felt when with him. But Madam Bouchard sent for him frequently; looking at Martin, whom Jacques had loved, seemed to bring her son closer to her, and she would sit, unspeaking, merely staring at Martin as she rocked, her flabby huge hands on her mountainous knees, and tears streaming down her immense flat face. Several times she embraced him, sobbed incoherently in his ear, wet him with the flood of her weeping. She wanted him to accompany her to the cemetery, refusing the offers of her husband and Eugene; it gave her release and comfort to see him kneeling on the lonely grave and saying a brief prayer. So this was Martin's humble penance for the part he had had in Jacques' death.

CHAPTER XXXIII

ERNEST PUT Eugene Bouchard in charge of the Kinsolving works, provided him with an astute assistant who had been the former treasurer of the concern. Raoul returned with an avalanche of Magyars and Germans, Slavs and Czechs. Tremendous activity went on in and about the factory, and flatboats and freight cars arrived with the newest and most formidable of machinery. And Ernest paid off his first note ruefully but with undiminished trust in himself.

He had always been stocky and well built, his long torso set solidly on well-shaped legs, but now he became almost lean, and a certain hawk-like look came out on his large features. He began to look driven and exhausted, and gave the impression that something would not let him rest. Gregory suspected, with pleasure, what it was, and knew that though Ernest might come to the very edge of breaking he would never break.

Then, three days before the marriage of Martin and Amy, Ernest abruptly announced that though it would cause him untold regret not to be at the wedding, the outbreak of the Crimean War presented an opportunity he could not overlook. He must go to England, interview Strong and Robsons, persuade them of the superiority of his steel-bore cannon and other patents.

"You mean," said Martin slowly, with a strange expression, "that we are now to sell our munitions to be used in a war?"

"Why, of course," answered Ernest impatiently. "Did you believe that the beginning and end of armaments was squirrel-shooting?" And he walked away. Martin did not argue; he said not another word. But the strange expression came out on his face whenever the subject was mentioned.

"So," thought Gregory, "he's running away." He was disappointed, for he had promised himself some really exquisite enjoyment. However, he did not try to dissuade Ernest from his plan: there was too much profit at stake. Ernest was in a ferment, however, quite distinct from the misery he was experiencing in his private thoughts. He needed to take some competent person with him to England, for, if his offers were accepted, he would need someone to oversee the manufacturing of Barbour and Bouchard munitions in a new shop there. He could not take Eugene, now deep in the Kinsolving works, and struggling to grasp the business; he could not take his father, growing more pettish and irritable and feverish as the weeks passed; he could not take Armand, for many reasons. "If I only had the right kind of a brother," he thought bitterly. "He and Amy could come with me, on their honeymoon, and he could be left there when I returned to America." But Martin was out of the question. The only one left was Raoul, Raoul the handsome and the indolent, the smiling and careless. But he knew so damned little! Then Ernest took him in hand, and reinforced by the threats and promises Armand made his son, beat, in the space of five days and nights, a vast store of knowledge and information and technical matters into Raoul's perplexed and anxious brain. Raoul, excited, now, and feeling tremendously important, sweated and struggled, went into the shops, smeared himself with black grease, tore his clothes, blistered his hands, forced his indolence to become concentration, and emerged, after those thundering five days, exhausted but triumphant. He then slept twenty-four hours without awakening. Ernest was none too sure of the results, but consoled himself that he would also have three or four weeks to continue the finer points of this education aboard ship. Raoul, who had always detested and hated Ernest in his smiling, lazy fashion, had conceived an immense respect and admiration for him. The fellow knew so damned much, and had such a monstrous will-power and drive! Partly to tease his unflagging driver, and partly to see his real reaction, Raoul, after the terrible five days, said: "If I do everything so very correctly, *mon cher,* and you are proud of me, you will not look too frowningly upon me as the future husband of your little Florabelle." And watched Ernest with narrowed eyes, smiling but alert.

"Bah! She is still just a chit," said Ernest. But he smiled with great good humor, struck Raoul on the shoulder, and talked of something else. "I think I am beginning to see that he so intended this from the beginning," thought Raoul, astonished and delighted. And redoubled the tired beating of his brain. When Florabelle returned from her school for the wedding, he told her of that conversation, and Florabelle, coquettish and blushing, but frank, announced herself as very willing to take Raoul for a husband. "You're quite the handsomest thing in the world," she added, with schoolgirlish candor.

Gregory Sessions, deprived of his main enjoyment, for Ernest and Raoul were leaving barely two days before the wedding, still would not be entirely deprived. Ernest was eating his last supper with his wife and her cousin, and was very preoccupied (Amy was dining with the Barbours). May, pale and despondent, her dimples entirely absent, could hardly touch her food. Ernest had reassured her a hundred times that he would be back the middle of July at the latest, two weeks at least before the baby was expected. But she was not comforted.

"I cannot see," she said querulously, "why you cannot delay your going for three days longer, considering that it is your brother who is marrying my cousin."

"I have told you, my dear, that I cannot," replied Ernest, forcing a strained patience into his tired voice. "The *Mayflower* is the swiftest packet between New York and Liverpool, and if I miss it I will be delayed more than two weeks. And if I lose that two weeks, I cannot be back in time. Every moment counts over there." He patted her cold hand as it lay flaccidly on the table near him. "Lift up your chin, love. It won't be long."

"If I could only go with you," mourned his wife, laying her cheek for an instant on the back of his hand.

"Ah, but you are too precious now, to risk such a journey," he answered lightly, looking at her broodingly with his exhausted eyes.

Then Gregory, who had been waiting impatiently for his enjoyment, said: "Yes, it is really too bad. But it can't be helped.

"Ernest, I want to tell you something. Once," and his face did not flicker as he regarded the younger man, "I told you that Amy was penniless, that not one cent of my father's money could go to her. The mills, the shops, this house, the stock: these all belonged to May. However, there was no stipulation that any private funds of mine and Nicholas' could not go to Amy." He smiled with an affectation of generosity and delight. "You have made no objection to your brother marrying a girl without a dowry, whatever you might have thought about it. So, I know it will give you tremendous satisfaction to know that Amy will not be without a dowry." He paused, and looked full at Ernest with a bland and open smile, as though inviting his surprise and happy anticipation.

He knew Ernest too well to fear an open demonstration that would overthrow the dish that held all their fruit, or would strike mortally at May. But he had expected, perhaps, a flicker, a sudden pallor, a dilation of the eye. However, none of these came. Ernest looked merely interested, pleasantly so. If his fingers tightened on his fork, or his throat thickened, Gregory did not know it.

The older man was disappointed. But wait, he thought, you don't know everything yet! He continued to beam archly. "No, indeed, she shall not be without a dowry! On her wedding day," and he paused portentously, "I shall present her with a sheaf of railroad bonds which will, in ten years, be redeemable for thirty thousand dollars. And that is not all: with our own money, left to me by my mother, we bought, ten years ago, 40 per cent of the Galby Lumber Mills, and 5 per cent of the stock of the Pittsburgh Steel Company, which, at that time, was merely a minor concern. The mills, and the stock, are worth, I should judge," and he cast his eyes meditatively to the ceiling, "at least one hundred thousand dollars. Pittsburgh Steel is one of our foremost mills, now. Of course, we shall leave May a small portion of this, as a token of our regard," and he bowed to her affectionately, "but on our death Amy will inherit the major part. So, in fact, Amy is not a portionless girl, but an heiress."

He had looked forward to this punishing of the man who had almost ruined Amy's life, and he had anticipated the torment all the more because he knew that Ernest dared not make a sound nor show openly what he was feeling. But he knew with great accuracy that Ernest's heart had taken a sick plunge, that his hands and feet had turned cold. He knew all this, though Ernest remained impassive except for two pale blue lines that sprang out like brackets about his lips, and the deep wrinkle that suddenly appeared on his forehead.

There was a long stunned pause. Then from May's throat came a faint flutter that might have been a choked cry, or a low laugh. She had put her handkerchief to her lips, and was looking over it at Ernest. She drew away the handkerchief, and there was a faint stain of blood on it as though she had bitten her lip.

"I am sure," she said faintly, "that this is very splendid for Amy, and more than any one could expect, Gregory." But she looked at Ernest.

For a long moment Ernest regarded Gregory fixedly, not a muscle moving in his face. Then he slowly turned his face to his wife. He saw the ghastly tint of her complexion, the anguish in her bright dark eyes, the stain on her handkerchief. His expression changed very slightly, and he took her hand, held it warmly and tightly. And again turned to Gregory.

"Your generosity, sir," he said in an even and disciplined voice, "is too much. I can only thank you for my brother."

And they looked at each other as over the flash of daggers. I shall never forget this, thought Ernest; I shall never get over his bringing out that look in May's eyes. His real affection for his wife was sharpened by his pity and rage almost to the keenness of love, and could he have struck Gregory dead by a touch he would have done so.

Gregory was silent. He had not bargained on hurting May so brutally, for he was fond of her; in some obscure fashion he thought she might have felt a little irony, also, for he knew she loved wrynesses. He saw, now, that love has no conception of irony, and is no enjoyer of wryness. He had struck a sick woman who could not defend herself, and he quaked a little with self-disgust and angry remorse. His anger rose from the fact that he had been deprived of his enjoyment by his regret, and that he had not waited until he was alone with Ernest.

Ernest stood up and offered his arm to his wife, and in silence they went to her room. Once there, he held her tightly to him, kissing her hair, her forehead and her pale mouth. He said nothing, but she was comforted, and put her head on his shoulder like a tired child.

CHAPTER XXXIV

THE WEDDING was simple but lovely, and after it, in secrecy and happiness, Martin and Amy went to Father Dominick's study and were remarried there in accordance with the rites of the Roman Catholic Church, with only a dim lamp to add gaiety, and the old housekeeper and sexton as witnesses. Martin had pleaded secrecy for the sake of his parents, especially for his father, who had suddenly taken a turn for the worse, and had not appeared at the shop for two weeks. Then they went back to the house so prettily furnished and ready for them, and walked into it, at midnight, hand in hand like children. "I am so happy," said Amy, in her young husband's arms. I am so happy, she repeated to herself, at dawn, laying her cheek against his shoulder as he slept. And she felt an utter peace and contentment, as though life had fulfilled itself. If there was no ecstasy in all this, she realized it only subconsciously, and just as the sky brightened she fell asleep, holding Martin's hand.

Ernest prowled about the deck of the packet that wedding night, alone and in silence, watching the bright, broken chaos of the moon's path on the tilting and rushing water. When the moon stood at midnight, it became very cold. A ship's officer passed and repassed him, at first curiously, and then with pointed glances. "First night out, and I can't sleep," said Ernest to him. The man stayed for a moment's inconsequential remarks, then went on.

Ernest was feeling absolutely nothing, he discovered with some dull surprise. Not an emotion stirred the vagueness that lay over all his senses like a fog. It was not long after midnight, when he found that he was shivering with cold and dampness, and that the ocean was particularly lonely and uninviting. I'm a damn fool, he thought, smiling sheepishly to himself, and went below to his room that he shared with Raoul. Raoul had gotten well drunk that first night out, and was fast asleep in his own bed. Ernest went to bed, and was instantly asleep. His last conscious thoughts had been that his bed was deliciously warm and soft, and that he wished May were lying beside him.

During the next two weeks he was full of curiosity about returning to the country of his birth. He had not given England half a dozen thoughts during the past years. But now he was full of stories to tell Raoul. He remembered gauzy English sunshine, the long slow days, the quiet winters, the homely fires, the English voices, customs, kings and villages. He remembered the old stories of British might and conquest, indomitable courage and dogged relentlessness. He remembered the stories of Nelson and Wellington he had heard from his father, and old grandfather, who wore knee-breeches and lace at his cuffs to the day he died, and kept snuff in a tiny silver box with the lion and the unicorn embossed on the cover. Strange, he had not thought of the old man once since he had left England! But all at once Ernest was before the fire on a howling wet night, a lad of seven or eight, and his grandfather was sitting in the chimney corner, rigidly dressed in his old-fashioned knee-breeches, his hands and chin on his cane, and he was telling Ernest about his service at Waterloo, and old Boney, and Wellington with his nose and his mighty voice. He had a ball in his leg, and limped. He was almost illiterate, and a prevaricator into the bargain, but his speech had vividness, and he conjured up before the young Ernest's eyes the mud and terror and thunder of Waterloo, the white plumes of the cavalry in the rain, the drums, the blazing trumpets, the guttural screams of the Germans, whom he hated for all their aid to England, and the Union Jack that fell, was torn from dying hands and lifted aloft again, only to fall once more, to rise, to fall and rise, until the terrible day was over and victory gained. The young Ernest had thrilled and trembled, had panted, had glowed and hardly breathed. Ernest had forgotten all this, but as the ship turned eastward steadily, he said to himself one morning: "I am an Englishman!" and was wryly astonished at his saying this and the lift in his pulses as he said it. He was excessively amused when he found himself humming "God Save the Queen!" but he kept on humming, half derisively.

Raoul was diverted at this belated patriotism. He could hardly be expected to share Ernest's shamefaced love for England, and said: "Your Queen Victoria is a fat little pig with a German swine for a husband."

But Ernest was bemused in memories of Sandy Lane, and three children trooping behind a young Hilda with a baby in her arms down to the meadows where the tiny spring daisies made a white carpet on the dark wet earth, and where the cattle, released, lowed contentedly under a sun caught in a tangle of golden mist. He had visited his father's great-aunt not more than a dozen times, but he remembered with sudden vividness the thralled silence of her old sunken gardens, and the smell of her lilacs in the rain. The call of the cuckoo, the smell of hawthorn, the low green hills with the sheep grazing upon them and sending out plaintive calls under the evening skies, the still, small blue ponds and lazy streams, the thatched roofs and white walls of farmhouses, the gray little Norman church sunken in its ivy, the rutted country roads and the oaks on their knolls: all these came back to him poignantly, and he was homesick. He felt that he had left behind him noise and confusion, heat and vivid light, comings and goings that were like drum-beats on his weary consciousness. He promised himself that he would take time to go to Reddish, and walk down Sandy Lane once more, and see if his father's great-aunt still lived in her enchanted house and garden.

But he never went there, for he had no time. Strong and Robsons received him with British reserve, modifying it, to be sure, when he informed them that he was an Englishman, but still reserved. They were suspicious and skeptical about the patents, argued endlessly, promised nothing, grumbled, delayed, hummed, murmured, consulted, objected to being rushed, assumed heavy dignity in the face of Ernest's urgent argument. Having become accustomed to the staccato of American business and American lack of deviousness and weightiness, he was mad with impatience. From saying "they" when referring to Americans, he began to say "we." In the end, after nearly three months of battering at these suspicious and stolid British minds, an agreement was reached, whereby Raoul was to supervise manufacturing in accordance with Barbour & Bouchard patents. "Of course," said Mr. Edwin Robsons, "this war will not last very long. But one can never tell about future wars, and it is best to be prepared."

"No," agreed Raoul artlessly, "one can never tell—with the British."

The British gentlemen were none too trustful of Raoul, the Frenchman. Of course, one had no quarrel with France, these days! But one was well aware of the French character: treacherous, slippery, smiling, grasping, unsentimental and cruel. Mr. Strong hinted as much to Ernest, who enjoyed retailing it to Raoul. "I think," said Raoul, thus astonishing Ernest, who had not suspected quite so much insight, "that it is the unsentimental part that they cannot forgive. For the British are everything else of which they accuse us: treacherous, slippery, grasping and cruel. And worse than all else, they *are* sentimental. One cannot," he added, shaking his head sadly, "forgive that. Perfidious Albion!"

"I would hardly call them perfidious," said Ernest, somewhat annoyed. Then he smiled. "Rather call them astute. The English just jump the way the cat jumps, and that is why they are invincible. They shout that they defend the underdog, but to unprejudiced eyes it seems that they make a mistake and champion the top dog."

He had never been to London before, and it seemed grimy and ponderous, slow and soot-fogged, still and gloomy, as it sprawled along the yellow Thames, its ancient towers drifting like darker shadows in lighter mist, and its old clock booming hollowly over wet roofs under lurid red sunsets, its drab inhabitants creeping along under masses of umbrellas, its dispirited horses and trundling drays and wagons and shabby carriages. It was a depressing place, for all its hugeness, in comparison with the blazing springtime of New York and Philadelphia and Chicago. Ernest shivered in the damp dripping early fall weather, crouched over niggardly fires in unspeakably grimy hotels, ate dank lax kippers for breakfast, and drank abominable coffee, shrank from contact with moist linen in tomblike bedrooms.

Yet, as the weeks went on he discerned something here, something impregnable and secure, unshakable and indomitable, rooted and strong. Where had he heard:

> "For London is a man:
> There's power in the air?"

Yes, there was power here, ponderous exigency, force, glacial determination that crept, never hurried, but always arrived eventually with annihilating weight. He felt, all at once one gloomy morning, that he was blood and sinew of this spirit that pervaded London. And he knew it was this transplanted spirit that had so enchanted him about the Sessions house, the same quality of fastness, of fortress-like impregnability, of rooted might, of security unmenaced by changing years.

He walked through the streets that Dickens knew, and bought curios for May—an India shawl of bewildering design, a necklace of turquoises in old silver, yards of India muslin and a dozen pair of silk stockings. He watched a detachment of cavalry parading before it left for the Crimea, and the brilliant red coats, the strong lithe bodies, the tossing white plumes, the lances, tipped with flags, held at rest, the coal-black horses, all stopped his breath, and the shattering white blaze of the trumpets shook him to the bones. "I am sentimental, as Raoul says," he thought, sheepishly, and was a little surprised to discover that this made him more than a trifle proud that he shared this sentimentality with the thronging thousands who shared his blood. He was part of a crowd that watched Queen Victoria pass in her carriage, a little dumpy woman with an arrogant face and hard, obstinate chin, and he found himself cheering with the rest.

Old Mr. Robsons liked Ernest cautiously. "There's stuff there," he said to his associates. He invited Ernest to his hideous tall old house with the snarling and lurking little fires at the end of dark and musty rooms, and introduced him to three tall and lanky daughters with head-colds. He was visibly depressed when Ernest mentioned having a wife. However, he recovered, and gave Ernest a very important hint.

It was because of this hint that Ernest found himself crossing the channel one raw September morning, in a gray wet dawn that was only a few degrees drier than the choppy water on which the little vessel rolled. By the time he reached Paris, after a torturous trip on an old train, he had a severe cold. This did not prevent him from going to see Schultz-Poiret within an hour of arriving in Paris. They occupied an incredibly dirty suite of offices on an incredibly dirty street which was veiled in sheets of rain. Ernest presented a sealed envelope from Strong and Robsons, and was immediately made welcome. For four hours he talked, steadily becoming hoarser and more feverish, and at the end of those four hours an agreement beyond his hopes had been reached. Mr. Schultz, who spoke the better English of the partners, had even allowed himself to be enthusiastic over the patents and the powder. "Some day," he said, "we shall have trouble with our neighbor over there," and he nodded his head eastward. Ernest looked suspiciously at the Teutonic cast of his face, but said nothing.

Schultz-Poiret were delighted when Ernest informed them that Raoul Bouchard, "our French member of the firm," would supervise the manufacture of munitions in France as well as England (Ernest made a wry grimace as he hoped Raoul would be adequate). His trip back to England was a fog of fever, sneezes, aches and coughs and exultation. He went directly to bed with a poultice on his chest, a pile of handkerchiefs on his pillow and a hot brick at his feet, and put Raoul through his paces again, for the hundredth time. Ernest looked at that face, so merry even when it tried to be serious, and uttered a despairing prayer to his private gods. Then relaxed to indulge a fine case of influenza.

One morning, two weeks later, when he was able to sit up, a pile of mail arrived for him from America. There was a letter from Gregory, informing him that May had presented him with a splendid son on August 3rd, as yet unchristened, and that May was doing exceptionally well. There was a short note from Eugene, asking him to tell Raoul that their mother had died on August 12th of a stroke. "I cannot," wrote Eugene simply, on paper suspiciously blotted, "tell him myself."

And there was an inky, badly written and incoherent letter from Hilda, informing him that she had taken Joseph to New York to consult a famous physician, who had issued a sentence of death. Joseph had cancer of the stomach, and could not possibly live to Christmas.

CHAPTER XXXV

HAD ERNEST been morbid or mystically inclined, he would have felt some grim significance at Gregory Sessions' greeting when he arrived home on October 4th.

On the way across the ocean, still weak from his recent illness, he had struggled under a weight of depression and sadness and anxiety such as he had never experienced before. This seesawed between exultation in his accomplishments in England and France, which had been beyond his hopes, and a passionate and excited desire to see his wife and son. His physical strength, which heretofore had kept emotions and thoughts in check, was depleted, and therefore could only partially control them now, and his mind was assaulted by a thousand sensations and morbidities and febrile excitations and melancholies that it had never known before. He loathed this being victimized by himself, and his efforts to regain stability exhausted him mentally and physically. He tried to focus nearly all his attention on his books and papers, spent hours struggling to put them in order, worried determinedly about Raoul's lapses in knowledge. But each time, his father's face sprang out on his inner vision, and his stomach turned over in a roll of bitter nausea. The last years dissolved from his memory, and the young Joseph came out, strong and wiry and vital, irritable and humorous, affectionate and proud. Then his pain would be so great that the pen would snap in his tensing fingers, and cold drops would come out on his forehead. If possible, his longing to see his father was stronger than his longing to see May and the boy.

During the slow railroad ride from New York to Windsor, he forgot everything but his personal affairs. He had neglected, in his haste, to send a telegram announcing his arrival, and therefore there was no one at the station to meet him. He hired a cab and rattled home through the quiet evening streets. Windsor seemed to have stopped in time, to have lain under enchantment until his coming. The air was chill, the trees almost leafless, and it was hard to tell whether it was spring or fall. When he was driven up the drive of the Sessions house, and saw the dim bulk of it nebulous against the dim sky, with the yellow lamplight superimposed on that unreal mass like rectangles of brilliance, he could hardly realize he had been away. But something lifted in him, was comforted. Here was security, changelessness, monotony that was like cool steady

water on a fevered surface. He sprang almost lightly, and with eagerness, from the cab. The butler had heard the approaching wheels, and
came running out to seize Ernest's bags; and Gregory, reading his
newspapers alone in the library, heard the commotion, and came into the
hall as Ernest entered the house.

And then occurred an incident of grim significance which Ernest
would have detected had he been superstitious or mystically inclined.
For Gregory said no word of greeting, but came forward, alert and excited, tense and sharp. He took Ernest's hand, looked at him in the warm
lamplight that shone from the lamp on the newel post, and said quietly,
swiftly: "Success?"

There was a pause. Then Ernest answered: "Success."

It was like a passport, the password to a challenge. The passport and
the password to his life, in which, in spite of himself, everything else was
relatively unimportant. He saw it all very clearly, and sickened momentarily in the seeing. Only twice more in his life was he to have that
clarity of vision, during which he stood off at a distance and watched
himself as though propelled and driven by some external force over
which he had no control. Why, he thought suddenly, I am not free at all.
I'm the most bound of slaves. Then he said: "I want to see May. And
my son."

"Of course! Of course!" Gregory was jubilant and expansive. "My
dear boy, how thin you are! You never let us know anything. You never
tell us anything! Come in! No, you must first rest. Goodwin, coffee
and a light supper for Mr. Barbour. Now, sit down, boy, sit down!
Five months! A lifetime! Your supper will be served right here in the
library, where we have a good fire tonight."

Ernest was surprised to discover how exhausted he was. He let Gregory lead him, talk to him, arrange him. It was good to be home! "Where's
May?" he asked.

"Upstairs, nursing your son and heir. Goodwin will tell her. Ah, here
she comes, now!"

There was a light rush of feet on the stairway, a cry, a rustle of skirts,
a gasp, a sob, and May had flung herself upon his knees, had clutched
his head to her breast, was dropping tears all over his face, kissing him,
sobbing, laughing, scolding, smoothing his hair with her soft and trembling hands. "Oh, why didn't you send us a telegram! Ernest, my love,
how ill you look! You have been ill! And you never told us!"

"Softly, pet," he answered, laughing. "Let me see you! Prettier
than ever, but aren't you a little plump?"

May was indeed much plumper, and something in her figure reminded
him of Queen Victoria. The thought of this warmed him, renewed in
him the sense of agelessness and security of home. May's ringlets had
been gathered into a shining bun on the top of her head, and two smooth

red curls lay on her white shoulders. There was about her a comfortable
humor in place of the old gaiety, a staidness that captivated him. Goodwin brought in his supper, and May, alternately scolding and caressing,
laughing and weeping, arranged the familiar dishes on a little table,
opened his napkin, and would have cut up his breast of chicken had he
not rebelled. She poured rich and steaming coffee from the old chased
silver pot, lifted the silver covers of the dishes and looked at the contents
severely, coaxed him to eat, and stood over him like a mother over a
delicate child. To his protests that he would not eat until he saw his
son, she replied that he would not see him until he had eaten, so laughing,
and to please her, he ate. Never had he felt so secure, so loved and
wanted, so safe. He felt that he had left the storm outside, and though
it waited for him, and he must fight it again, he had gained a shelter.

After that first question, Gregory asked him no more about his business in England and France. It was enough for him that Ernest had
been successful. Details would come later. Now he could relax, be
friendly and welcoming, pleasing and laughing, watching May's clucking and pretty ministrations. He felt no animosity toward Ernest tonight,
only a kinsman's affectionate and approving regard.

No one had mentioned Joseph. Ernest had not wanted to ask, as yet.
What he was bound to hear, he knew, would blast the happiness of his
homecoming. And yet, when he shrewdly noticed how May and Gregory
skated skillfully away from any mention of Ernest's family, except for
a loving remark on Martin's and Amy's contentment, his heart began to
beat heavily. He saw them exchange swift glances. And a sort of sick
terror tore through his chest again, and he could not ask. Time enough
for that; in the meantime, he must see his son.

He went upstairs with May. Her step was a little slower and heavier,
and she had lost the little bouncing spring that had been so amusing.
She panted a trifle as she climbed the stairs, holding up her hooped and
tilting skirt with one hand, and the warm pink blood rose up through her
plump white throat and breast, and ran into her cheeks. In a few years,
thought Ernest fondly, she will be quite fat, and he reached up and
pinched her creamy little forearm as she climbed ahead of him. The old
gay May with her bounce and gaiety had amused and intrigued him, and
he had been grateful for the laughter she gave him. But in some way this
plump young matron with her merry eyes, sedate ways, competent little
airs, pleased him much more. She had always used perfume of a somewhat exotic blend, which Ernest had not liked, remembering the scented
and furbelowed ladies on the furtive streets. He was pleased to discover
that May no longer used this perfume, but exhaled, instead, a clean sweet
odor of orris root.

The largest guest chamber had been converted into a nursery, and a
fat cheerful young nursemaid had been engaged. A warm rosy fire

burned on the tiled hearth; flounced and draped white curtains shut out
the cool night; the baby's crib was all flounced and draped in voluminous
white lace, the rug a soft blue, the furniture simple and painted in an
ivory tint. The room smelled of soap, of freshness and sweetness. The
little nursemaid, in blue and white, a German immigrant girl, curtsied in
an old-fashioned way when Ernest entered, and retired to a little distance, all blushings and flutterings. May, with a finger on her lips, led
Ernest to the crib, and tenderly lifted up the veil of lace. He looked down
at his son, now two months old, and saw what seemed to him a pink and
shapeless little bundle of round face and minute doubled fists. What he
had expected he did not know. He had seen very few babies, and not with
a conscious eye. But he had had some vague idea of a largish, boisterous
child, with a grin and possibly a shout. In short, a child of about
eighteen months.

"He's frightfully small, isn't he?" was the first question he asked.
May, who had waited, beaming, for exclamations of pride and joy, was
electrified with indignation. "Small!" she exclaimed, so loudly that the
baby stirred, whimpered, and thrust his thumb in his mouth. "Small!
I declare, Ernest! Dr. Winston said he was unusually large for a first
baby. All of eight pounds at birth, and now he weighs fourteen, and
only two months old!"

Ernest laughed. He felt somewhat flat. The baby lacked character,
he thought, with that little yellow fuzz on his head, and the round flushed
wet cheek. Then, aware that May was glaring at him and bridling, he
poked the child tentatively, arousing May to a shriek of protest. But
Ernest did not hear the suppressed shriek: his son's hot damp fingers had
curled about his own finger. He felt a sudden contraction in his chest.

"He's hideous," he whispered, glancing at May.

"He's beautiful!" she answered, but she smiled, and laid her cheek
against her husband's arm.

They went downstairs, their arms about each other. The child had
not yet been christened, May said, as they entered the drawing room
where Gregory waited for them before the fire. She had thought of
naming him Godfrey James, after her father, if Ernest approved.
He stared at the fire thoughtfully for a long time, and gradually
his face became pale and heavy. He turned to May, and took her hand
gently.

"I would like to call him Joseph, after my father, love," he said.

No one spoke. Gregory, uncomfortable, affected to be absorbed in
cutting the end of a cigar. But May looked back into Ernest's eyes, and
her own eyes filled slowly with tears. She lifted his hand impulsively,
and pressed it against her cheek.

"You may tell me now," he went on. "How is my father?"

Gregory coughed gently, lighting his cigar. "I have called for the carriage," he answered quietly. "I think it best we go to your father's house, tonight. We hoped you would return—in time."

"Then," said Ernest, in a low voice, a muscle twitching in his cheek, "he is dying."

May put her handkerchief to her eyes.

"If you had not returned for another month, Ernest, you would not have seen your father alive," said Gregory, very gravely. "But come, here is the carriage." In the stillness of the autumn evening they heard the crunching of wheels on the gravel.

Neither Gregory nor Ernest spoke much on the way to the Barbour house. To Ernest, huddled in his seat, the world had become echoing and desolate, a tormented place. Everything was empty, from the cold black sky to the distant iron gleam of the river under the lights on the shores, from the smell of dry and faded leaves crisping under their wheels to the mournful chirping of crickets, from the chill whisper of the wind to the distant bellow of a train.

Gregory coughed that gentle, preliminary cough. "You may find your father changed a little, Ernest," he said.

"Changed?"

"Yes. It seems he has a grievance against you. Probably imaginary, but sick people are often imaginative. He has, I am sorry to say, the delusion that you are waiting to rob your brother and your sisters after his death, and he is fighting death, when he would be better dead, in order to fight you. Cancer," he added thoughtfully, "is a frightful disease. Nothing can alleviate the pain very much. The doctor has expressed himself as amazed that your father lives from day to day, with a perforated stomach and frequent hemorrhages. He says he is living by sheer force of will. Each day he asks when you will return. Perhaps, now that you are here, he will let himself—go. That will be the best thing of all."

Ernest did not speak. Gregory could not see his face in the darkness. He was disappointed a little. "I am certain," he said tentatively, "that your father need have no fears of you. I wonder where he could have gotten that idea?"

"I don't know," said Ernest, after a long pause. He had pulled up the collar of his greatcoat, and not only was his face hidden but his voice was muffled.

"He has seen your baby once, I believe. He said he was the image of you at your age, and appeared to be quite affected. I believe he said something about leaving him his father's watch, which his Company commander had presented to him after Waterloo, for distinguished conduct." He turned his head alertly. "Did you say something, Ernest?"

"No, nothing."

The Barbour house came into sight abruptly through the thin trees.

In spite of the lamps burning in the windows of the lower floors, the building was singularly desolate-looking tonight. The bleak wind eddied the dead leaves about the walks, and spoke in melancholy around the eaves. A dull smudge of crimson smoke wavered over a chimney. But for all the lamps and the smoke, the house looked abandoned, completely deserted. Had there been no answer to their knocking, Ernest would not have been greatly surprised.

A new maid, unknown to Ernest, led them into the living room. It struck him with dull surprise to discover that the room was crowded with people, some sitting before the fire, some standing in groups, and whispering. There was Amy, shawled and pale, her sweet face grave and sad under her bonnet, her gloved hands in her lap; beside her stood Martin, his hand on her shoulder, his head bent as he talked inaudibly to her. There was Florabelle, home from school, eyes red and swollen, curls in disorder, crouching at one side of the fireplace and weeping. There was Eugene, with a white-faced little Dorcas on his knee, and there was Armand, slowly pacing the room, his head bent, his face and posture that of a man who had aged rapidly. Martin had sent for Father Dominick, and the priest was there, though he was not certain that he would be admitted to the presence of the dying man. John Baldwin was there, Gregory saw with surprise, and an old German, evidently a foreman from the shops, and a young man whom he called Carl; both were strangers to Gregory, but Ernest's eye touched them with dull recognition, indifferent and haughty. There were several other clean but shabby men there, unmistakably workmen, with dark foreign faces and queer, unreadable eyes, men who must have loved Joseph to come where they must inevitably see Ernest. Ernest did not know any of these workmen, but he knew they had come from his shops, and he made no more acknowledgment of their presence than he would have noted work horses in a stable. Hilda was not in the room. The door stood open to the high narrow hall, and once or twice the thin wisp of a groan floated down it.

When Ernest and Gregory entered, everyone turned troubled and saddened faces to them. Martin, flushing, unable, as usual, to look Ernest directly in the eye, shook hands with his brother, turned his head aside when Ernest asked after their father. Armand shook hands, and Eugene, not rising from his chair, and John Baldwin came up, gravely, to express his sympathy. But Ernest found his way to Amy through the workmen, who parted as he came forward, and he took the trembling hand she offered him. She looked up at him, sadly and compassionately. But, as if they had parted only yesterday, she said: "How is the baby? Isn't he beautiful?"

Ernest could not speak. He dropped her hand slowly, and turned to the fire. In a world become two-dimensional, she was the only reality to him then, and he stayed near her for as long as he could. They did not speak to each other, but imperceptibly they drew together, involuntarily. Yet they did not look at each other, but only at the fire. Finally he broke the dim enchantment, and went back to Gregory and Martin, who were whispering near the door. Martin seemed quite composed, but he dabbed his eyes occasionally.

"When can I see Pa?" asked Ernest abruptly. "And where is Ma?"

"Ma's upstairs, with him," answered Martin. "The doctor's there, too. He—he won't live the night out, the doctor says. It is a good thing you came home in time. We can go up when the doctor comes down. That is what we are waiting for."

"I didn't know," said Ernest in a tight voice. "I didn't know!"

"No one knew," said Martin gently, looking at him steadfastly with his blue eyes. Ernest gazed at him stonily for a long moment; then he said: "You don't know what I mean," and turned away from him.

The room was hot, and the still air of it seemed to choke him. Yet he had nowhere to go. He must wait like these others. He walked about. The workmen, abashed and deathly frightened of him, formed and re-formed in their huddling groups to avoid colliding with him. They wiped wet faces with red and blue kerchiefs, and exhaled odors of sweat and crude soap and tobacco. One or two had fortified himself with a generous amount of beer. Ernest sickened. Yet he controlled himself, so that he did not glare upon them. Finally, Armand joined his pacing. The older man put his hand on Ernest's arm, and there was something in that touch that seemed to hold down a knotting and writhing in himself. He remembered that Armand had had his grief, too, in the loss of his wife and son, and he stopped, ashamed.

"Armand," he said, "I'm sorry I didn't say something before. It was a shock to hear about your wife. Raoul took it hard."

"That is what I wanted to ask," answered Armand quietly, and again Ernest was ashamed. "Raoul, I believe, loved her best of all, though she loved Jacques above either of her other sons. Perhaps it is best that Raoul was not here."

"Raoul is in Paris, now," said Ernest, and made himself sketch, in a few words, the result of his journey. Armand listened; finally he smiled a little, as though wryly amused. "I had not expected any success at all," he confessed, "but I might have remembered you." He sighed. "My cousin, from Quebec, a newly-made widow, is keeping my home for me and Eugene." He fumbled for his pipe in his pocket, and then, finding it, did not draw it out. "You remember what a good Catholic my little Renee was? Yet she requested, with her last words, that she be not buried in consecrated ground, but beside Jacques, just outside the wall of the cemetery. You Protestants," and he shook his head with a twisted smile, "would not understand the pure love and sacrifice of that!"

The air became close and stuffy. The workmen found that their discomfort in the presence of Ernest overbalanced their concern for Joseph and they began to drift away. At midnight, only the family remained, with the exception of Gregory, John Baldwin and Father Dominick and Pierre. Amy had removed her bonnet and shawl, and her soft hair was combed back, showing her fair forehead; she had persuaded Florabelle and Dorcas to go to bed. When the two young girls were leaving the room, it seemed that Ernest became really aware of their presence, for he called after them: "Good night, my dears." But they were too involved in their grief to answer, and they went out with bent heads.

It was Amy who went to the kitchen and persuaded the maids to make coffee for those who kept sick-hearted vigil in the living room. There was utter silence upstairs, though occasionally a faint footstep creaked overhead. No one spoke, merely sipping the hot coffee or adding lengths of wood to the fire. The lamps burned yellow, flickering slightly in the draft from a window. Amy sat near the fire beside her husband, and her profile was illuminated by it. Though it was sad, it was also serene and contemplative, the mouth steady and quiet, her eyes fixed on the fire, her hands in her lap. Ernest, watching her under the shadow of his hand, thought with a sense of shock: "This is not the Amy I first knew! She has grown much older." He continued to watch her until at last all reality outside of her faded, even his father dying upstairs faded, and there was only Amy in an aura of light, swift-burning fire. Then after a long time he noted a slight distortion in her figure, and a queer thrilling numbness ran along his nerves. He could endure, now, the thought of her being Martin's wife; but he could not endure it that she should be carrying Martin's child. He dropped his hand from his face with a little gasp, as though he could not breathe.

There was a dim thin cry upstairs, the quicker sound of footsteps, low voices, a deep groan. Then the doctor and Hilda came down the stairs; the doctor's arm was about Hilda, who was sobbing in tight anguish. Everyone stood up as they entered the room. Hilda's graying hair (Ernest was shocked to see how gray it had become) was roughly twisted in a large knot on her neck and her comely face was blotched and wet with tears. She went to Ernest immediately, clung to him, kissed him, sobbed over and over: "O Ernest, Ernest, Ernest!"

"Mr. Barbour," said the doctor, "is conscious now. He won't be—for long. He has asked that everyone here come upstairs at once. I don't approve of it," he added primly, "though I don't suppose it will do much harm."

They went up the stairs in silence, Ernest and his mother leading the way, Martin tenderly helping his young wife up the stairway. Has he no sense? thought Ernest. She ought not to be coming up here, in that room! He glanced down at Amy, who was holding her skirt up with one hand, her other hand on her husband's arm; she was looking up at him with grief and compassion. But Martin seemed oddly composed though grave.

The sick room was hot with firelight and candlelight; there was an air of confusion in it. Joseph was lying high on a mass of ruffled pillows, and his breath had a snoring quality. He lay with his eyes closed; he was horribly emaciated, and his flesh was the color of wet clay. Ernest, seeing him like this, seeing the lax skeleton-like hands on the coverlet, listening to that breathing, became sick with shock. This dwindled man, whose still vital hair made a black-gray and untidy blotch on the white pillows, this dying man, could not be the ironical and irascible Joseph whose accumulated wealth had confused and troubled him, who had found no peace anywhere. In that lightning-flash of thought, it was suddenly clear to Ernest that his father had possessed a singleness of thought, a simplicity of living, such as Martin had; it was suddenly clear to him that all the family, except himself, was of that singleness and simplicity.

He knew, even before his father opened his tortured eyes and looked at them with the terrible listlessness of the dying, that this death was not going to be easy, and that in some way he was involved in it. He looked at Hilda, who had gone to the high white bed and was kneeling beside it, sobbing; he looked at the dark faces lit by the firelight, the crowding faces, the sad and troubled faces, and something made his heart beat intolerably fast as though confronted by danger. He wanted to slip away to the fire, but he had hardly reached it when Joseph opened his eyes and looked at the group at the foot of his bed. His gaze slipped over them, exhaustedly, without desire or recognition; he was looking for someone. He caught Ernest's shadow near the fire, and his head moved slowly in that direction. Ernest stood before the fire, silhouetted against it, so that its dull crimson enlarged his figure, lay in planes upon it, gave his large face and head a sinister air. He knew his father was awake and looking at him, but he could not move. It was as if his flesh had become a prison of ice in which he was helpless.

"So, you're back?" Joseph's voice was hoarse and broken, almost whispering.

"Yes," replied Ernest at last, quietly and steadily. His own voice broke the appalling enchantment on him, and he came to the bed and stood by its side, looking down at his father. "Yes, I'm back, Pa." He tried to smile.

The dying man peered up at him; there was a strange gleam lying over his distended eyes. Ernest thought: he hates me. And it seemed to him all at once that that hate was a piteous thing from which his father must be saved, if he were to have peace. If he could only have died before Ernest's return! If Ernest had not had to see this clay-colored ruin with the eyes so terribly alive, the picking and restless hands! "Yes, Pa," he repeated, and forced his stiff lips to spread into a smile. A cold wetness ran between his shoulder blades.

A strange gloating smile came out on the ruin that was Joseph's face. He turned his eyes upon Martin. "Bring me those papers on that table yonder, lad," he said. Martin brought them, a thin sheaf of papers closely covered with Joseph's handwriting; he slipped them under the claw-like fingers. The fingers closed on them fiercely. Joseph looked at those at the foot of his bed. The gleam came out again in his eyes, hating and triumphant. He moved his head in Ernest's direction, without looking at him. His voice came stronger.

"Look at him! That's my son, Ernest! My son! Do you know what he has been doing? He has been waiting for just this minute. For years and years he has been waiting." He tried to sit up, fell back. Hilda had stopped her low sobbing. "Joe!" she cried. "Joe!" She struggled to her feet. In the dim dancing light she looked at Amy, who was crying, at Martin, at Armand, at Gregory. "He doesn't know what he's talking about—Joe!" she cried wildly. Fear sprang out over her blotched face; she implored the others with one upturned and shaking hand, and with the other hand she grasped Joseph's cold fingers. Martin left his wife and stood by his mother. She leaned against his shoulder and sobbed. But Ernest merely waited, watching his father impassively.

The gloating look had gone from Joseph's face, but it had become sombre and grim. "Aye, I mind what I'm doing, lass," he said in a hoarse and dwindling voice. "That's why I wanted you all here: to see that I knew, and be my witnesses. And there's Mr. Gregory here, who's a notary, and can sign and witness things, and say that I was in my right mind. So there'd be no conniving and cheating, no double-dealing and foxy lawyers." His voice fell; he panted, twisted on his pillows, and at the edge of his livid lips there bubbled a line of tiny red beads.

"Lass, do you stop your crying for a minute." He regarded his wife with exhausted mournfulness. "I've got only a little time, and I've got to speak. I've got to speak, for your sake, and Martin's, and the lassies'."

He lifted a finger and pointed it at Ernest, still without looking at him, but commanding the eyes of the others. "Yes, look at him. My son. Who's waited for this time. Waited to rob his brother and his mother and his sisters. When I wasn't here to protect them. To take the bread from their mouths and throw them into the streets. To——"

"That, Pa," broke in Ernest, steadily and quietly, "is a lie. And deep down, you know it is a lie. Why you are saying all this, I don't know. I don't believe you know. But you do know that you are lying."

"Ernest!" exclaimed Martin sharply, outraged. He moved a little, but just then Ernest looked at him, and there was something in that look that paralyzed him.

"So, I am a liar, eh?" whispered Joseph. He was staring at Ernest, now, with malevolence, and was again smiling. "You can call your father on his deathbed a liar! But that will only show them all what you are. And you know I'm not lying. You know you're a thief and a rascal, and have just waited for this!

"I made a will, three years ago. You—and Martin—you were executors. Everything—in your hands." His voice thickened, strangled. "I trusted you, then. But I know I was wrong. Martin is a simple lad. Sometimes I've thought he was calf-brained, for all he knew of—things." (A dark gleam stood on Ernest's face for a moment.) "Yes, I see you know what I mean. Martin is a simple lad. Any bright rascal could twist him around his little finger. Make him believe anything. And I knew it would only be a matter of time until my poor lass, here, and my little lassies, and this lad, would have nothing, be penniless, perhaps be shipped back to England, like poor Georgie, with a capful of pennies. And he, my fine Ernest, would have the field to himself, have all the money, everything I've worked for. That's what he would connive to do——"

"That," broke in Ernest again, loudly and clearly, "is a lie."

"Ernest," said Gregory, shocked and stern. "Remember——"

"Ernest," murmured Armand, shaking his head.

"Ernest!" sobbed Hilda, heartbroken.

Only Amy was silent. But she was gazing at Joseph steadfastly.

Ernest turned to them all with an abrupt and furious gesture.

"You know he is lying, all of you! And you'd let him die, lying! You'd let him go on repeating it, until he began to believe it himself! But I'm not dying; I've got my life to live. I've got a wife and a child, and all the years I've put into the shops, and the things I've done. I've got sacrifices behind me, and God knows what work! I've got to go on living, remembering that you all let my father die, lying. I've got to live, smudged by a filthy lie! Damn you all, do I care what you believe? But I've got a son, I'll have more sons, and I'll not have them dirtied by this lie!"

He doesn't care if we believe this "lie," thought Gregory. It's something else. And he regarded the young man in silence, curiously.

Ernest turned to his father again, almost savagely. "You are too ill to know what you're saying. You don't believe it, anyway. For God's sake, if you must die, die in peace, without that on your conscience. I've known for years that you didn't trust me, suspected me. But I thought that all this was only on the top layer of your mind, and that underneath you didn't believe it. How could you believe it? What evidence did you have? Your brother, George? You know, yourself, what he was. Other things you call my 'conniving'? That's business, Pa, business. That's how fortunes are made. I've made fortunes for all of us. You'd not have one-tenth, one-hundredth, what you have today without me. My God!" he added, his voice breaking, tightening, "you know all this!"

Joseph had listened; his whole ruined face seemed alight with mockery. He jerked his head feebly in Ernest's direction, the while he gazed at the others.

"You've heard him. But you, Martin, and you, Armand, and you, Mr. Gregory: you all know the truth. You know if I'm lying. He calls it 'business.' He'd call it business, robbing his mother and his sisters and his brother. I tell you," and he struggled up from his pillows, a mad light glaring from his eyes, "it's always been 'business' with him. The lad's not human!"

Hilda forced him back on his pillows, where he lay gasping, his eyes rolling. The doctor appeared at the bedside, forced some mixture between the panting lips. While this was going on Ernest faced the group at the foot of the bed as a man would face silent accusers. There was Gregory, inscrutable as ever, Armand, thoughtful and grave, Martin, with conviction written all over his handsome and sensitive face, and Amy. And she looked back at him steadfastly, gently. The fire crackled, the lights dimmed and flared, and Joseph struggled for the last time against the death that had him by the throat.

Joseph won again, for a few minutes. He waved the doctor aside. He lifted the sheaf of papers in a clenched fist. "I've got it all here!" he continued in his hoarse whisper. "All here. Written down, word for word. I've left everything to Martin and his mother and his sisters. All I have. All my bank money and my stock, my interest in the shops, my patents. Everything. And for him—" and his eyes rolled on Ernest, "nothing. Fifty dollars, that's all. I've done it, to protect all of them. Protect them from him!"

As if a freezing wind had blown through the room, everyone stiffened. Everyone stared at the dying man, as if fascinated. Then Hilda cried out in haste and disbelief: "No, Joe, my love, you can't do that! This is our lad, too, our Ernest! Our own bonnie lad! Joe, Joe! God would punish you for this!" She reached across the bed and seized Ernest's hand, trying to pull him closer to his father. "Look, Joe, you know you are wrong. He would not rob his own flesh and blood. It is the sickness in you that puts such a thing in your mind. Martin! Tell your Pa it isn't true, what he says about Ernest," and she turned her twisted wet face to her younger son imploringly.

But Martin said nothing. He looked down at his hands, which were clenched about one of the bedposts; his knuckles whitened swiftly in the lamplight. But he did not look up. Hilda's mouth fell open, then she turned from him, visibly shaken, her mouth slack and an expression of dull horror and incredulity on her features. "Armand, tell Joe that it isn't true about Ernest. And you, Mr. Gregory. Tell him, as God is your witness."

Armand looked over the footboard at his friend, very sadly. "No, my Joseph, it is not true, what you say. Ernest would not do this thing to his mother and his sisters."

Gregory spoke with quiet sternness: "You have let your imagination run away with you, man. But if you do this thing you will only hurt those you wish to protect. Ernest has given all of you what you have today. If you do this thing to him he may withdraw from everything, and I assure you that the interests of your family will suffer."

Then Ernest said, slowly and heavily, as though he spoke from a core of sickness: "Let him do what he wants to do. I don't care. If it will ease his mind, don't torment him: let him have his way."

Joseph twisted himself convulsively on his pillows to face his son. His face, wet with a deathly sweat, wrinkled and contorted itself grotesquely: "What do you mean, eh? by that? Do ye think I'll be turned aside by that hypocrisy? What do you want, eh? What do you want by this?"

Ernest looked down at him impassively; there was a livid flash in his pale eyes. "All I want, Pa, is for you to realize that what you have said is a lie. I want you to know it is a lie. But you know it already."

And he walked away from the bed, away from the firelight, and sat down in the shadows of a distant corner. He sat quietly, his legs crossed, his arms folded across his chest, his large face a white and expressionless mask in the semi-darkness.

Joseph struggled valiantly against the mortal exhaustion that was dragging him down. "Pen!" he gasped. "You doctor, you, Armand, you, Amy! Get a lass up here from the kitchen. Four witnesses. You, Mr. Gregory, you are the notary. You'll sign. My new will. You—will destroy the old one. Pen! Pen! For God's sake, hurry!"

"Are you sure you want to do this, Joe?" asked Gregory sternly. He began to sharpen a pen, but he did it so slowly that his fingers barely moved. The doctor went downstairs to call a maid.

"I'm—sure," Joseph panted. "God! The pen! It is sharp enough——"

"Ink," said Gregory, after a long slow stare at the dying man. Martin went to a chest of drawers, brought back the ink. He did not look at his brother, though he passed within three feet of him.

"Sign!" shrilled the dying man. "All of you!"

"We must wait until another witness is brought in," answered Gregory gently. Under the smooth and elegant crest of his gray hair his high and sloping brow was shining with moisture. He continued to sharpen the pen. And now Armand looked at him, and what he saw made him stare intently, without blinking. He saw that someone else was having a race with death, and hoping death would win. Hilda was kneeling again by the bed, her head on the same pillow on which Joseph's head lay. She was finished with crying, and her eyes, dark with anguish, glared blindly about her.

The doctor and the housemaid came in. The girl was shrinking and whimpering. They all stood about the bed. Gregory dipped his pen into the ink; somehow, it appeared, his fingers shook and the inkpot fell from them upon the floor, emptying itself. "Damn!" exclaimed Gregory. "Will someone please bring me some more ink?"

But the doctor raised a warning hand as he leaned over the bed. For

Joseph, after a convulsive movement of ecstatic agony, had fallen back against his pillows. The black pits of his eyes had closed; he lay, hardly breathing, except for faint gasps. The doctor opened the slack lips wider, put a pellet upon it, gently held the jaws shut with his hand. The pen rolled upon the white counterpane, staining it, rolled down upon the floor. Martin picked it up, stood with it in his hand, helplessly.

Ernest could not see his father from where he was. He could see only the group about the bed in the red and dying firelight. A flame darted up and revealed the shining spheres on the bedposts. And then he saw, through the crowding bodies, the lax and fallen hand of his father in the firelight, a white, shrivelled and waxen hand, suddenly slack. From the fingers slowly fell, like large leaves, the sheets of the will. One by one they fell, as if even in unconsciousness Joseph was reluctant to relinquish this will, and they lay on the carpet in a quiet heap.

Then, seen by no one but Ernest, Amy detached herself from the group about the bed. She bent down behind her husband, and her hand, slim and swift, darted out and secured the sheaf of papers that Joseph had written. Ernest watched her expressionlessly. She crouched, backed silently away from the bed, clutching the papers. She continued to back away, her skirts tilting and swaying, her hair falling over her cheeks. She reached the fire, turned swiftly and noiselessly, rolled the papers into a thin tube and thrust them between two glowing logs. They caught fire, flared up a little, and showed her crouching there, as if cold and trying to warm herself.

Then, after long moments had gone, she turned her head slowly and looked at Ernest over her shoulder, the firelight on the right plane of her face. Across the space of the room, across years and distances, across forever, their eyes met steadfastly, and held.

Joseph lived for nearly a week longer in a state of mingled suffering and unconsciousness. During his periods of awareness he was so preoccupied with all the nuances of his dying that the small world he was about to leave was consumed and forgotten as his will was consumed and forgotten.

When he finally died, there was no grief for him. His friends and his family looked at each other in pale and haggard joy that he had been released at last. Not the least part of their joy was the fact that no longer were they, themselves, to be tormented by the sight of his torment; but this no one, except Ernest, would acknowledge.

Once or twice during Joseph's last days alive Martin and his sisters had made weary search for the unsigned will. The girls finally gave up searching, but Martin, tenacious and grim-mouthed, continued to look until the very day of his father's death.

CHAPTER XXXVI

JOSEPH'S OLD WILL was found and probated.

Four weeks later, at a stockholders' meeting, Ernest was elected President of Barbour & Bouchard; Armand, Vice-President; Gregory Sessions, Chairman; and Martin, Secretary. Joseph's death had left a starkness in the atmosphere, but no one spoke to Ernest of the last days of his life. He had become much older, and in spite of endless work, stouter. He assumed everything; nothing was too small for his consideration. He and Martin had inherited equally, but he acted as though he had inherited all. As the head of the family, he directed its activities down to the most insignificant details, until May complained, only half-humorously, that Hilda Barbour had regained a son and she had lost a husband. She had cause for complaint, for Ernest spent at least half his time with his mother and sisters, and visited Martin frequently at his new home. All through the affairs of his family, private and financial, ran the current of his decisions and his autocratic plans. Martin was helpless before him, becoming more haughty and timid and suspicious, yet dependent; Hilda, broken and hopeless, left everything to him, and the girls feared him more than they had feared their father. Dorcas was actually terrified of him. Only Florabelle, with her impudent, pretty ways, her roguishness and red-lipped poutings, her flippant and tinkling laughter, sometimes opposed him. He liked this fragile and feminine opposition, and indulged her sheepishly; she was quick to take advantage, proud that she could sometimes win him over, and once or twice flaunted her influence over him in public. She loathed study and application of any sort, and thought for a time that she could coax Ernest into allowing her to remain at home after her father's death, on the plea that her mother needed her; but Ernest could not be moved, and she returned to school in tears. A few weeks later, Dorcas followed her sister to the same school. Ernest put up the Barbour house, which he had hated and which he hated still more now, for sale, and sent his mother to live with Martin and Amy.

His energy poured itself out like a cataract. "He has a finger in every pie," said Gregory to his associates at the bank. "One day Windsor will be famous because he lives here."

"Of course," Martin said to his wife and mother one evening, "the last will of Pa's was not valid, without signature, but I wish we had known what—other bequests he had had in it. We might have had the pleasure of doing some things as he had wished, if not all. It is very strange that nothing was ever found of it."

"Perhaps it is all for the best," said Amy gently, meeting his troubled eyes with an expression of tenderness. "I am certain that many things in it would have made us all feel very badly. Things about Ernest. It was not signed, as you say, and being so, it is better it was never found."

He went to her and knelt beside her chair, and put his head upon her breast. He was desperately tired these strenuous and confused days in which the drive of his brother was like fist-blows on his mind and body; he was very frightened, also, and suffering mentally.

"Amy, darling," he said, "I cannot go on, like this, with our arms and our explosives killing men in the Crimea. I feel like a—murderer."

"What do you want to do, love?" she asked, putting her hands on his head and looking down into his face with her gentle smile.

"I want to withdraw. I want to leave it all. We have enough. More than enough. I'll take nothing from—from the shops. No profit from blood and death. We have this house, and what your uncle gave us. We can buy a small farm, and live simply by ourselves. Tell me that would satisfy you, Amy."

Amy was silent for a while. Upstairs, in their tall, narrow nursery, lay her twin children, Paul and Elsa, two months old, seven months younger than their cousin, Godfrey James Barbour. Amy was no fool, and had, since she had become a mother, developed her latent Yankee respect for money. If Martin did as he wished, they would live very modestly indeed. It seemed to her with sudden clarity that this would be a heroic and silly thing for him to do. She could understand a woman's shrinking from munitions making, for women were expected to be horrified at war and its bestialities. But she could not understand a man feeling so. It violated certain of her beliefs in the hardnesses and the power of men. So, though her expression was soft, she asked hesitantly:

"But what of your mother's share, Martin?"

Martin glanced uneasily at his mother, who was dozing over her knitting.

"Ma, I suppose, will want to keep it," he answered doubtfully. He sighed, running his fingers through his fair thick hair, and stood up.

"And the children, love? Must we not think of them, too?"

Martin turned the sudden blue blaze of fanatical eyes upon her. She had seen this blaze only a few times during her life with him, and each time it was as though her husband had been transplanted to another dimension where she could not follow, which she could not understand, and which clove them apart. At those times they became strangers, looking at each other across abysses. Or through thick glass against which sound was annihilated, speech silenced, however they might make gestures or move their lips.

"The children!" he cried. "Don't you see that I would want to do this particularly for the children? I can't have them taking profits as partners of death, either. I can't have their whole lives made easy at the cost of others' lives. Fine houses and fine clothes, servants and carriages, bought with blood! Amy, can't you see this?" He looked at her imploringly, almost desperately.

His emotion and his words seemed extravagant to her, and she was distressed at what she considered her treachery in not feeling as he did. She could understand that he could feel this way, could even understand the processes of his thoughts. She could even know that any arguments were impotent against his conviction of right. She was in the sad state that afflicts most tolerant people: comprehending emotions that were alien to her nature and feeling sympathy for them, while feeling in herself that they were quite wrong and more than a little absurd.

"Yes, Martin, I can see what you mean," she replied softly. "But perhaps you are a little hasty—perhaps there are things you have over-looked——"

"How can you say that, Amy?" he exclaimed despairingly. "It's as clear as day. We make munitions, guns, powder, cannon, explosives: and what are they made for? To kill! There's no getting around that. They are made to kill! And now there's a war in the Crimea, and men killing each other with our powder and our guns and our cannon. Fine phrases and what Ernest calls 'common sense' can't get around that one simple fact. Facts are pure and fundamental, but men try to muddle them with phrases and long arguments and pleas for tolerance and patience, and all the time the facts are there, like earth under snow. We are wholesalers in death, and I can't, for my peace and my sense of honor, have any part in it.

"For years I've wanted to get out. Then Pa was ill, and I felt that I—I had to protect Ma and the girls from Ernest——"

"But how silly!" cried Amy involuntarily.

Martin made a gesture almost fierce for him. "Amy! Let me go on. For years I've wanted to leave. I haven't kept much of the money I received from the shops; I've given most of it away—I've told you how, and why. At the present time I have less than four thousand dollars altogether in actual cash. I refuse to take any part of the stock and money Pa left me, and I've already told Ma that it's to be hers and the girls' as soon as it can be arranged."

Amy had turned white to the lips. She saw her children in their cribs, and something like sternness tightened the lines of her sweet face. "Martin, you shall not do that! The children! I cannot allow you to do this!"

He had never seen her like this before, so white and stern; there was anger in her brown eyes, also. He was moved by all this, and he took her cold hand and kissed it. But the white severity did not relax on her face, and her eyes commanded him.

"Amy, my darling, please try to understand," he pleaded. "I am not robbing my children of anything but dishonor. We have enough, more than enough. Why, your bonds are giving us an income of more than two thousand a year. It is a fortune, love! An honorable fortune. We are rich.

"Amy, Amy! Please try to understand me! Don't you love me? Would you have me go on in this unhappiness, hating myself, hating living, hating everything connected with the shops? You speak of the children—but how about me? Is my happiness nothing to you at all?"

Amy gazed at him steadily, seeing the bitterness and anguish in his eyes, hearing his despair. And her expression softened, saddened. She sighed.

"Yes, Martin, your happiness is everything to me. I can understand what you mean, and I sympathize with you. But I can't feel that way, myself. Someone must make munitions; sometimes munitions are very necessary. Nations must defend themselves, and sometimes they must fight for the right, too. But I can see that you can find no justification in this business. So, whatever you wish, for the sake of your happiness, you must do, and I will do it, too. And I will try to feel that you are right."

Nevertheless, she went quietly to her uncle and told him. Gregory was incredulous and aghast. Forgetting his niece's sensibilities, he broke into a furious and contemptuous tirade against Martin. What a fool! What an imbecile! He was a snivelling brat in man's breeches! He should be confined as a danger to society! Was there ever such monstrous senselessness, such stupidity? He had a wife and children, and he would beggar them in his folly. He overwhelmed Amy with expressions of compassion and promises that Martin should not be allowed to do this thing.

"I am so confused," confessed Amy, in tears. "Uncle Gregory, you mustn't attack him that way. He feels he is right, and that his happiness depends upon doing what's right. I have come to you only because you are older and wiser than Martin and I, and because I thought you might persuade him to reconsider by offering him arguments I can't think of, myself."

"Damn these fools who will be heroes and martyrs!" ejaculated Gregory. "I can well understand ropes and stakes and wheels, now! Amy, my dear, go home, and I will talk to Martin tonight."

But he found Martin encased in the fanatical obstinacy of the simple and unworldly man who is convinced of his righteousness. Gregory's fury and arguments, pleading and ridicule, were only light winds blowing against a steadfast tree.

"But how are you going to live?" he cried at last. "On your wife's money? On the dowry I gave her when you married her? On my money?" His fine and elegant face twisted in a sneer. "Of course, Martin. an American would understand that no honorable gentleman lives on his wife's money. But you, being an Englishman, might not understand that!"

He saw, to his surprise, that he had at last found his Achilles' heel, for Martin winced and colored. "Perhaps Englishmen, Mr. Gregory, do not distinguish between a man's money and his wife's money. Perhaps Englishmen believe that what is one is the other's. You, apparently, do not believe that. However, I have four thousand dollars of my own, and I'll buy a small farm with it, and Amy may keep her money for herself and her children. I promise you I will not touch a penny of it."

Gregory was shocked. "Do you mean to say that you would subject my niece and her young children to the rigors and hardships of a small, poor farm, without comforts and decencies? My niece, who is a gentlewoman, a lady, and has always had the best of everything?"

"My wife and my children," replied Martin coldly, "will share whatever life I choose to live. If Amy wishes to have a servant or two on my farm to assist her, I shall have no objection, seeing that she will be paying for it with the money you have pointed out to me is not mine."

Gregory turned to his niece, who had been listening in pale silence.

"Amy, I cannot allow you to live such a life. You must come home, with your children. There is always a place and a welcome there for you."

And Martin turned to his wife, also, and waited. He said nothing, but looked at her steadily and gravely.

Amy bent her head and wiped her eyes. Then she rose and going to her husband, she stood at his side, and looked at her uncle. "Wherever Martin goes, Uncle Gregory, I must go too," she whispered. "He may be wrong—I don't know. But he believes he is right, and he has a right to happiness, too, and wherever he goes I shall go."

Gregory stared at them bitterly, his face wrinkling and pulling.

"Very well, then, Amy, you have made your bed and I suppose you want to sleep in it. But listen to me," and he shook his finger almost under Martin's nose, "you could not have chosen a better way to play into your brother's hands. Oh!" he exclaimed in a livid fury, "I can tell you that there will be one who will not try to dissuade you! He will offer you no arguments, nor urge you to use some intelligence! Go to him; tell him what you have told me, and leave your mother and sisters at his mercy! Turn back your money to him, the money your father left you, the money belonging to your wife and your children, and see if Ernest refuses it!"

He had not counted much on this last appeal to fear and distrust, to simplicity and unworldliness and lack of understanding, but he saw, from

Martin's changed expression that he had struck home. It did not take him long to capture this advantage, to advance the most vehement and absurd of arguments, to appeal, again and again, to Martin's fear and suspicions and sense of duty. When Gregory, at midnight, finally went home, he left Martin in a pathetic state of irresolution, despair, confusion and anxiety.

The next day the poor young man, in a quite dreadful state of mind, went to see Father Dominick. For a full hour, in that dark, musty little parlor, he talked, argued, pleaded for understanding and advice. And Father Dominick listened, half incredulous, half sad, and wholly ironical. He saw that Martin was in the deplorable condition of the idealist caught in a world of realism, that for such an idealist there would never be peace except in flight into himself, into fantasy and mysticism and gentleness. The world, to this idealist, bristled with swords, on which he would continually impale himself. He had no armor, no shield, for the faith he had adopted was full of earthly realism and tolerance. In mediæval times he would have found his place, but in this civilization he had no place. He was no builder of Utopias; he was merely naked in a society that went masked and armed, and his plight was exceedingly piteous, if not absurd. Father Dominick had extolled and prayed to the saints; he had taught their lives to thousands of men and women and children. He had wept over them, dwelling tenderly on their patience and sweetness, their steadfastness and faith, their idealism that fire and sword could not shake. He had urged his parishioners to emulate them. But now, face to face with such a character, he was helpless, and a little inclined to smile, not too sadly. For some moments he indulged in silent irony at his own expense.

But he had little to offer Martin except vagueness and sympathy, kindness and patience. Martin, he said, must be very careful that he was doing the right thing. Of course, he added in a melancholy voice, a man must always follow his conscience, for that was something he had between himself and God. Money, he said, was all things to all men. To the fool it was an executioner, to the good man it was ability to alleviate suffering, to the tyrant it was a sword, to the miser it was a prison, to a king it was an army, to the wise man it was power, to the slave it was freedom, to the avaricious it was heaven and earth and hell. Money was not to be despised. One should be very careful. So Father Dominick, with a large gesture, left it entirely to Martin's conscience. And the young man left the priest's house in a state of worse confusion than ever. Facts, which had seemed to him so simple and unshakable, became tenuous.

He had nowhere to turn, no firm hand to grasp, no understandable voice to hear. The two natural fortresses of men, wife and priest, could not help him. One had given sympathy and tenderness, and the other had advised patience. But they would not stand beside him, fighting; they left the battle entirely up to him. Never had he felt so lonely. He even tried, in his desperation, to make his mother understand, but her horror, her bewilderment, her utter inability to grasp what he meant, left him more despairing than ever. Once, when alone at the cribs of his children, he whispered to them: "If I do this, will you blame me some day for robbing you?" He could hardly make himself believe that they were his children, for he felt as helpless and as unsure as they.

His old suspicions and distrust of Ernest returned with renewed force. Gregory, he decided, was quite right: Ernest would seize upon this chance to enrich himself. He found himself watching Ernest, as the brothers worked together in their new and larger offices, and among their four new clerks, and he began to wonder if Ernest knew anything about it. And more and more he convinced himself that without himself in this place his mother and sisters might indeed be robbed of their inheritance. His handsome face thinned and his blue eyes began to look haggard and sleepless. He no longer spoke of it to Amy; between him and his wife had always been great gentleness, love and sympathy, and he still felt these things in Amy. But he also felt that she was helpless, and could only wait in silence for what he must decide himself.

One summer evening he went down to the river. He sat down on one of the flat stones along the bank, where he and Jacques Bouchard had sat so many times. It was very quiet down here, in the coming twilight, with the white willows mysterious pale shadows behind and about him, the wide river before him, running with long, thin glimmers on it like quick-silver, the far shore a dim blur and the sky a clear high arch of mauve light, shading, toward the west, into a heliotrope-rose. A few lights began to glimmer like small lamps of gold on the farther shore, the river darkened and its voice quickened, and a couple of black flatboats floated lazily down with the current. There were few houses near by, and Martin felt isolated and quite alone.

The stones were still warm from the sun, and the air was still as clear warm water. Martin had come here to think, but he found he could not think. His mind became quiet and almost numb. The heliotrope sky, the single song of a robin behind him in the trees, the stillness and peace, filled him with nostalgia. All at once he was back in his great-aunt's enchanted garden among the wet lilacs and the scented mist and the song of the thrush, and the memory twisted in him like pain. He thought: Why, I've never really left that garden! I'm still there. That's why I can't understand what they all mean, here. That is why everything is so confused and hot and full of enemies. If I could only go through that gate again! Even sound was softened there. It's across the ocean, and I'll probably never see it again, but my mind is still there, and my soul, too. I've never been able to face what they call "life," and perhaps it's my fault. But what they call reality seems stupid and harsh to me, and without reason or mercy.

He looked at the silent sky and he prayed simply: "Father, help me. I don't know where to turn, or what to do. I thought I knew what the right was, but I've been deafened by arguments. Perhaps I am a fool, as they say. Perhaps I've always been a fool, and not a man. If I have been, show me. If what I have wanted has been good, help me to achieve it."

When he went home, in the darkness, he was not exactly comforted, but the heat of confusion had abated in his mind.

CHAPTER XXXVII

ARTIN SENT a large check to the Society for the Abolition of Slavery.

"Please apply it to your funds in the fight for the liberty of the negro," he wrote. "God bless you in your great work, especially in your effort to keep the Territories free, particularly Kansas."

He was fanatical about John Brown, whom Gregory had called a "bloody villain." "I thought," he said sarcastically to Martin, "that you believed all blood-letting vile, and the means of blood-letting viler, yet here you are praising a man who shoots down other unarmed men for nothing more than that they differ from him in opinion. But, perhaps, you find what he does excusable because he prays both before and after doing it."

"He does that in order to keep new Territories free," answered Martin. But he was now more confused than ever. Could murder ever be holy? Could wars ever be just? And if murder could be holy and wars just, then the arms whereby the first was committed and the second waged could not be unholy, nor the making of them reprehensible. His confusion increased, and he could do nothing.

One day, when he was more confused than ever, and could hardly keep his mind on the work of supervising the two clerks assigned to him, he had a visitor.

His office was beyond Ernest's, and to reach his office any caller had to pass through the larger, outer room. A clerk came to Ernest and announced that one of the men from the shops wished to speak to Mr. Martin. The workman was admitted, and as he timidly sidled toward Martin's door, Ernest halted him.

"Just a moment, please. Aren't you old Hans Heckl's son?"

The young man stopped, scarlet-faced and more than a little frightened.

"Yes, sir, I am," stammered Carl, twisting a length of waste cloth in his oily hands, and coloring still more deeply. Ernest regarded him curiously.

"Is something wrong in the shops? You're in charge of the barrel loading, aren't you? Is it necessary to disturb Mr. Martin about anything?"

The young man was too simple to be wary. "It—it isn't about the shops, sir. It—it's something else."

"Mr. Martin," said Ernest, "is too busy to be bothered about small personal matters. Besides, I handle everything dealing with the men. You had better tell me what it is."

"It's personal, sir." Carl's agitation had become terrified misery. He even took a step or two, backwards. "If Mr. Martin is so busy, I'll see him some other time." He turned and fled toward the door. Ernest raised his voice. He was smiling.

"Don't run away." Carl stopped on the threshold like a young bull halted in flight, and irresolute. "I want to talk to you. Don't you and your father live down by the river? Haven't you a number of boats you hire out on Sundays and holidays?"

"Yes, sir." Ernest's smile had reassured him, for it seemed amused and pleasant. Ernest was a bogey to the hundreds of men who worked for him, and had he been the devil, himself, his appearance could not have agitated them more. But Carl felt his courage coming back before that smile, which made his employer's face assume a certain boyishness and charm. He tried to smile back and as he did so he looked directly into Ernest's pale relentless eyes, which had no smile in them whatsoever. A cold thrill ran along Carl's nerves.

"Aren't you the young man who is always taking two or three weeks off, about every two months?" asked Ernest. He looked good humored. "I remember, now, that your father keeps coming in to see me and asking me to take you back. It's against my principles, of course, but you have a good record, so I always oblige him." He waited. But Carl said nothing; the color had gone from his face, and Ernest watched him intently. The young man's sudden and curious pallor interested him; he saw that his hands were shaking, also. He saw that his eyes had filled with terror and suspicion.

"Well, now, Mr. Armand Bouchard is in charge of the shops. Why don't you see him? No, wait a moment. I suppose you may see Mr. Martin. But you must remember that all matters pertaining to the shops must be taken up with Mr. Bouchard or myself." He waved his hand dismissingly, and Carl fled past his desk into Martin's room. When the door closed behind him, Ernest sat and stared into the middle distance, frowningly.

One of the clerks, who had a small desk near the outer door, cleared his throat timidly until Ernest glanced at him in annoyance. "If it may please you, sir," he stuttered, "I'd like to say something about that man and his father. There's stories about them——"

"What?" asked Ernest with affected impatience.

"The young fellow, there, sir, goes on long journeys down the river, in a boat. My brother, he has a house near the river, and one night, late,

he heard oarlocks, and it was a bright night so he went out, curious-
like——"

"Ah, curious-like," murmured Ernest. But he was listening with odd
attention.

"Yes, sir, curious-like. There was a moon, shining on the river, but
there wasn't a sign of a boat on it, out where it was bright, so my brother
went soft down the banks, behind the trees, watching. And a big boat
came by, with three sets of oars, hugging the banks and slipping along
as well as it could against the current, very slow, for they were afraid, it
seems, to use the oars too much. My brother saw that there were six men
in the boat, bent over, as if trying to hide themselves. He followed them
along the bank, and they finally got to the pier that runs out from the
Heckl house, and they jumped out of the boat and scrambled real fast
to the house. A man stayed behind, fastening the boat, and the moon
came out, brighter than ever, and it was that young fellow there, Carl.
My brother couldn't see the faces of the other men at all, for they ran
so fast, and dipped down behind bushes and such, but he did see that
Carl."

"Well," said Ernest impatiently, as the clerk stopped, "is that all?
Didn't your brother investigate further?"

"No, sir. He was afraid. You know, there used to be river robbers
along these parts, and sometimes they creep up on lonely houses, yet.
And my brother didn't like the looks of things, so he went away, glad
he was still alive and not seen."

Ernest grinned. "Carl doesn't look particularly ferocious to me," he
said. "He's a German, and Germans are usually docile and timid people.
And I can't believe that old Hans and his son are up to anything very bad.
Your brother, I am afraid, has been drawing on his imagination." He
held out a sheaf of papers. "Check this up at once, please."

But when the clerk bent his head over the papers industriously, Ernest
sat motionless, frowning and biting his lip.

When Martin saw Carl, he was startled. He motioned his own two
clerks into the small office they shared beyond his office.

"What is it, Carl? Don't you know you ought not to come in to see
me so openly?" His voice was sharp, but his expression was kind, so
Carl did not feel much apprehension.

"I'm sorry, Mr. Martin. But I've tried to see you for a long time, and
couldn't. And you haven't been to see us lately, either. And now, I just
had to come here, for things are so bad——"

He came closer to Martin, and lowered his voice. His long fair face
flushed, and his light blue eyes began to flash.

"Awful bad, Mr. Martin. I had to tell you."

"What's the matter?" Martin was alarmed, and he glanced uneasily at the shut door of Ernest's office. "Didn't the last lot get through all right?"

"Oh, yes, sir. They're in Canada now. It isn't about—them, that I came. Mr. Barbour, have you ever been over to the place where the Kinsolving shop men live? You know, they built them a lot of shacks on the grounds, and they put a big fence around them, and the men and their families never get out. They buy from the company stores—everything—and they don't get money. It's something new, worse than we've got right here around the shops. They get little pieces of paper for so much, and they spend it in the company shops, like money. But that ain't the worst——"

Martin had turned very pale. "I didn't know anything about it," he muttered. His eyes fixed in horror upon Carl Heckl. "Are you sure? Oh, I've been a selfish fool! But are you sure? I've never been over there, to the Kinsolving works. I knew that Raoul Bouchard had brought back a boatload of men and their families, but I thought things over there were as they are here. Bad enough, God knows, but the men are free. My God, do you know what you are saying, Carl? You are saying we have slaves here, white slaves! This is intolerable. I can't believe it. Even Ernest—I mean, no one would do this thing to these helpless men and women! The Government wouldn't stand for it——"

"The Government's standing for it all right, Mr. Barbour. Whether it knows or not, I don't know. But that ain't the worst.

"If they get sick, they can't call a doctor. If they get real bad, the foreman calls a doctor for them, and stands right there all the time. When they die, they can't even have a priest. They die like dogs, sir," and Carl's eyes filled with tears and his nose reddened. "And then they ship them out like dogs, in boxes. They never get out, unless they die. They work twelve and fourteen and more hours a day, and the only life they've got is in the company saloon. Oh, yes, sir, they've got a saloon down there, where they spend their little pieces of paper that ain't money. They drink themselves blind and drunk, and so their wives and children half-starve all the time."

"But my God!" cried Martin under his breath, "there are hundreds of them! If they wanted to leave, they could. No one can force them to remain behind that fence if they don't want to." He shook his head. "I can't believe it. Hundreds of men. Why, they could overwhelm half a dozen foremen in a few minutes——"

"Oh, no, they couldn't, Mr. Barbour," replied Carl grimly. "You see, the foremen have got guns. And worse than that, there are ten men patrolling the fences all the time——"

Martin sprang to his feet. He was aghast, his face sick and working. "How do you know all this?"

"Well, sir, one of the men got away, in the dark, over the fence. It was a miracle. He ran down to the river, thinking he could get a boat and get away. But he was sick, and his hands were torn from the fence. He got into one of our boats, and couldn't go any more. My father found him there in the morning, half dead with fever and chills, and bleeding. He brought him in, with me helping him, and then he told us. He's home there now, and you can see for yourself if you want to. They can't keep *you* out of there."

They stared at each other in a long and shaking silence. Then Martin went to the window and looked out. Far over the thinning trees of autumn he could see the high thick chimneys of the Kinsolving works, fuming against a chill and colorless sky. He turned abruptly. He seemed changed, stern and drawn, but his eyes were steady as iron. He opened his wardrobe door and took out his coat and hat and put them on. Carl watched him.

"You go back to your work, Carl, and say nothing. I'm going out—there. I've got to see for myself."

He waited until Carl had been gone for nearly five minutes, then he called his clerks, gave some instructions, and went out into Ernest's office.

"Going out?" asked Ernest casually, raising his brows.

"Yes." Martin did not glance at him, but continued toward the door.

"Will you be back?" Ernest called after him.

Martin stopped abruptly at the door. Then, after a long moment or two he turned and gazed at his brother strangely. "I don't know," he answered slowly. "I—don't—know."

He had been gone only a short time when Ernest wrote a brief note, called a clerk, and asked him to take the note to the Sheriff's office. Within half an hour two bulky constables arrived, and then Ernest sent for Carl Heckl, and his father, Hans.

CHAPTER XXXVIII

SINCE ITS renewed activity Martin had not visited the Kinsolving works, which still operated under its old name. Therefore, he looked about him intently as he walked along the boardwalk that surrounded the building.

Ernest had spoken of secret patents and industrial thieves, so Martin had thought nothing of the high strong wooden fence with its pointed palings. It formed a wall, its joinings caulked. Now he studied it, computing its height to be at least ten feet. Moreover, it sloped inwards quite a bit, so that one climbing from the inside would have a difficult time. All at once the fence became sinister to Martin, and his imagination, already stimulated, ran away with him. His heart was beating thickly when he arrived at a strong iron-and-wood gate set in the wall. There was no outside handle, and when he pushed against the gate it resisted his efforts as easily as though he had been a fly. He noticed a bell, and pulled it with violence. It rang angrily behind the gate. He expected the gate to be opened within a few moments, but it remained shut. Then he noticed that near by was a small wooden building, not more than four feet square, with a pointed roof, and from this building had emerged a short, thick man with a black beard, the rough clothes of a workman, and fierce, suspicious eyes. Martin saw that he carried a heavy club.

"And what would ye be wantin'?" he asked, in a rumbling, Irish voice, coming up and looking Martin up and down impudently.

Helpless anger, almost hysteria, began to rage through Martin.

"I want to go in there," he said peremptorily. Under stress, he lost his usual timidity and shrinking from encounter with others.

The man stared at him again. It was evident that he had not the slightest idea who he was. But it was also evident that his appearance and his clothing were beginning to impress the watchman, for his manner became more pacific and respectful.

"I can't let you in there, sir, unless I know who you are. That's orders from himself."

"And who," exclaimed Martin with tight fury, "is 'himself'?"

The watchman's eyes narrowed with suspicion again. He lost a little of his respect, and his hoarse voice was somewhat contemptuous when he answered: "Now, then, who would be 'himself' but Mr. Barbour? Ye're no townsman, or you'd know that without me tellin' you."

"Why is the gate locked? Why can't any one go through as they do at other shops?" Martin demanded, after a pause. It occurred to him that he might get more information if he concealed his identity for a few moments longer.

The watchman laughed abruptly. "And be stolen out by robbers? There's Government contracts agoin' on in there, my fine bucko, and we've got to watch. Nobody gets in there as have no business inside."

"But how do the workmen get in and out, from their homes?"

Again the watchman laughed, now brutally. "They goes in, sir, but they don't come out, unless in boxes." The amusement disappeared from his uncouth face. "But what would ye be askin' me these questions for? Is it business you have inside? And if it is business, what might your name be?"

Sudden wild impatience ran along all Martin's muscles, a veritable fever to get inside these walls. His worst suspicions were aroused. His pale face flushed and his hands clenched.

"I'm Mr. Martin Barbour. I must go inside at once. Open this gate!" He had a confused and sweating feeling that behind those wooden walls hopeless men were waiting for his deliverance.

The watchman's mouth fell open. Then he recovered himself and grinned slyly, shaking his head. "Ye'll not be gettin' around me with such a tale, me lad. If ye were Mr. Martin Barbour, I'd be knowin' you, for ye'd been here before. I'll need a better story than that."

Martin tried to control his trembling. "Mr. Bouchard is inside, isn't he? Go and tell him that Martin Barbour wants to come in."

The sneer left the watchman's face; he regarded Martin with uncertain uneasiness. He cleared his throat, as he sidled around Martin to the gate. "Ye'll be understandin', Mr. Barbour, if you are Mr. Barbour, that it's my duty I've been doin', and no offense meant? Orders is orders." As he fitted a big iron key into the lock he glanced over his shoulder at Martin with anxiety, and still unallayed suspicion.

Martin was astonished that, after turning the key, the watchman did not thrust the gate open. Instead, he rang the bell sharply, three times. A moment or two later there was the sound of a heavy bolt on the inside being withdrawn, the grating of a chain. Then the gate opened ponderously about six inches and another face peered out suspiciously. Under other circumstances Martin would have laughed, but now his alarm grew and he realized how grave this situation was. The watchman jerked a thumb over his shoulder in Martin's direction, and one sharp eye on the other side of the gate examined him intently.

"There's a gentleman here that says he is Mr. Martin Barbour," said the watchman. "And says to tell Mr. Bouchard that he wants to come in."

The eye continued its scrutiny. Then, abruptly, it was withdrawn, the gate closed and the bolt was shot.

"What now!" exclaimed Martin, becoming more feverish. The watchman, facing the gate, shrugged deprecatingly. "Ye'll have to wait, sir. It's orders."

Martin fumed. The flush had receded from his face and had left blotches on it. He began to pace up and down, hardly able to control himself. The watchman followed him furtively with his eyes. His uneasiness was growing.

A long time passed. A carriage drove up, and two important gentlemen in black broadcloth, tall black hats, and carrying significant little leather bags, alighted. The watchman ran forward obsequiously to assist them. Their bearded faces were lean and sharp and cruel. "Ah, Mr. Judson, Mr. Stanton! Your foot, here, sir, where it's not so muddy!" The two strange gentlemen glanced at Martin alertly, with long, narrowed eyes. The watchman, beaming, saw an opportunity to recover good favor, if the stranger were indeed Mr. Martin Barbour.

"Ye know Mr. Ernest Barbour, Mr. Judson? Mr. Stanton?"

"Yes, of course," replied Mr. Judson impatiently.

"We've met him a dozen times in Washington, and three times in this mill," supplemented Mr. Stanton, who was evidently meticulous.

"Would ye be knowin' Mr. Martin Barbour by sight, too, sir?"

Mr. Judson frowned thoughtfully, looked at Mr. Stanton, who shook his head. "No," said Mr. Judson, "I've never met the gentleman."

"I, sir, am Mr. Martin Barbour," said Martin. He had approached the two gentlemen. They gazed at him in incredulous astonishment; his face was scarlet and his eyes were a blue blaze of shame and anger.

"I'm sure there was no slight meant, sir," stammered Mr. Stanton, at last, coloring in embarrassment. He held out his hand. "I'm happy to know you, sir."

Mr. Judson was slower to recover equanimity. But he was thorough in his attempt to cover up the situation. "Indeed, yes, it is a pleasure!" he exclaimed heartily. He, too, held out his hand. But Martin turned away, swinging on his heel, and went to a little distance without a word.

The two gentlemen, discomfited, regarded each other, and shrugged uncertainly. The watchman approached them, whispering hoarsely. "He says he's Mr. Martin, Mr. Judson. But I ain't never seen him before. He's been a-shoutin' to get inside, but we've sent for Mr. Bouchard. I can't let him in till I know for sure."

"Of course not, my man," muttered Mr. Judson.

"Quite right," added Mr. Stanton.

The watchman opened the gate, rang the bell, the bolt was withdrawn, and after a preliminary scrutiny, the Eye allowed the gentlemen to step inside the walls. The gate shut again and the watchman, half apologetically, locked his side.

Another galling interval elapsed. Martin paced back and forth. A light chill rain had begun to fall, and the approaching evening mingled with the smoke of the mills so that the atmosphere became acrid and gloomy with fog. From the unseen mills behind the walls came a steady and prolonged rumbling. Martin, shivering, pulled up the collar of his coat. The watchman tentatively offered him the shelter of his little shack, but Martin coldly refused. At last the inner bolt snored again in its socket, the watchman sprang agilely to unlock his side, and the gate opened grudgingly, then wider. Eugene himself stood there, frowning. In the dimness of the approaching evening, he looked singularly like Ernest, as though his attachment and admiration had helped to mould his body in conformance with the outlines of his friend.

"Martin! Diable! I did not expect you! Why was I not told? Come in, it is so very wet! If I had only known you were coming——"

He seized Martin's arm, and tried to be cordial as he pulled him through the aperture past the grovelling watchman. "Ernest was here this morning and said nothing. How extraordinary this is! You have not been here before? No. This is really too bad, on such a day! And to have had this inconvenience with the guards! It is too appalling." His harsh voice expressed his regret, impatience, annoyance and sympathy. "Let us hurry. I have business visitors, a Mr. Judson and a Mr. Stanton. You must meet them at once." He regarded Martin curiously and with increasing impatience. One never knew what to expect of him. He was so exceedingly singular. And now he was being more singular than ever, for he was withdrawing his arm from Eugene's grasp.

"Eugene," he said quietly, "I didn't come here to visit you, or meet strangers, nor to see the shops. But I've heard stories about—about your workmen. I—I wanted to see for myself."

Eugene stopped and stared at him incredulously, blinking in the gray dusk. The rain ran down his face, which was broad and brown, and which began to screw itself into knots as he tried to comprehend.

"What did you say? Stories? What stories? See for yourself? What is there to see?" He made a helpless gesture. "You mean, Martin, that you want to see the men at work?"

"No, I want to see how and where they live."

This sounded like madness to Eugene. He could not cope with this impossible situation, and so could not speak, his features wrinkling and working in his perplexity. "Eh," he muttered at last, and wiped away the rain that dripped into his eyes.

"You wouldn't understand, Eugene," said Martin sadly. "But I've heard that the men were prisoners, with their families, that they never got out, that they had no attention when they are ill, no priest when they were dying, no money, only some scraps of paper. That they were slaves, white slaves, in bondage, like the black men in the South."

After a long moment of stupefaction, Eugene stammered: "It is you who do not understand, Martin. You must remember that we have Government contracts here, secret patents. We must protect ourselves from spies, from vandalism, sabotage. Many would like to know our patents. They are exceedingly valuable. So, we keep the men and their families incommunicado, to protect ourselves——"

"You are not always filling Government contracts, Eugene," Martin said with increasing sadness. "And even if you were, this imprisonment would not be necessary. I do not remember hearing that the National Powder Company ever enslaved or locked up their men, and they had Government contracts, too. Nor have I heard of any other company giving men worthless paper, denying medical attention, imprisoning women and children. It's frightful! I've never heard of anything so frightful! It must be against the law. If it is, I want to know it."

Eugene tried to control his crawling impatience, his passionate desire to burst into oaths of annoyance. He tried to smile.

"Of course, it's not against the law, Martin. You have most certainly been hearing fairy tales. We give the men what we call 'scrip.' You see, they are ignorant wretches, Slavs and Poles and Germans, who are as innocent as children and would not know how to handle sums of real money. They would probably waste it or drink it up. So we provide them with scrip, which is the value of their wages, and provide stores on the grounds wherein they are certain to get their money's worth. We provide them with better homes than they ever had in their own countries, and as they are a provincial people, close-knit, they prefer only their familiar friends, so feel no hardship in not associating with outside strangers. When they are ill, we provide doctors at our own expense. We provide burial. So," he ended with a smile, "we are not slave-owners or drivers. We are really excessively kind to our workmen and their families. But you must have known of this condition for a long time. It is not new with us. After all, you have an equal interest with Ernest."

"I didn't know!" exclaimed Martin passionately. "It's my fault, too! Your arguments are like Ernest's: they sound reasonable and just and valid. But I can't be fooled this time, Eugene! In spite of your arguments. I *know* there is something wrong here. How about the children? Do they go to school? No?"

"They are peasants," said Eugene coldly. "They are unteachable. Learning would do them no good. Beasts of burden."

"That is a lie, Eugene! They are human creatures, with souls and minds. Not beasts. You have no right to imprison them so. Your arguments are false. There is something most terribly wrong here, and I'm going to see for myself."

Eugene shrugged; his heavy mouth became sullen and contemptuous. "We do not see eye to eye, Martin. I assure you that I am not a monster. The original idea, of course, was Ernest's. I believe he studied the mills in Pittsburgh, and came to the conclusion that it would do very well here, also. But I, myself, am convinced that this is very good for the men, to be protected so, and that you must remember their origin and their stupidity, and their ignorance. They must be protected like children, and we must also protect ourselves." The rain was running down his neck now, from his uncovered head, and he cursed Martin to himself.

"Yes, I can easily see that this would be Ernest's idea," said Martin bitterly. "It sounds like him. But these men have children, and their children will have children. We have no serfdom in America. You can't confine these people forever! It is slavery! No government, even for the sake of patents, would have it so. And you give them no money. Oh, I can see a thousand holes in your arguments! You take back the scrip you give them for their wages in your stores; you allow them nothing for savings, for little decencies and pleasures. And I can well imagine how much and the kind of medical treatment you allow them! If they want to leave, to look for work elsewhere, to find better living conditions, you keep them here, like chained animals——"

"Why do you say 'you'?" asked Eugene contemptuously. "Your profits, my good Martin, come from this, as well as ours. Your family is fed and comforted by this, your carriage moves on this, your bank account thrives from it, your luxuries and pleasantnesses are derived from this source. And your children's inheritance comes from these mills and the labor of these people." He tapped Martin on the shoulder with insulting familiarity. "Think it over very carefully, my Martin."

The rain had become stronger, pelting and cold, and a wind was beginning to lash it vigorously. On this side of the wall guards patrolled, armed with rifles. Martin could see them, gigantic, uncouth men with brutal faces, moving doggedly back and forth, pausing occasionally, to spit tobacco juice or stare about them. They wore a sort of military uniform; their greatcoats ran with water, and the visors of their caps streamed with it. These men had been immensely diverted by the sight of their employer standing arguing in the rain with this strange and vehement young man. As it was now definitely dusk, they began to light lanterns, and carried them to and fro in their patrol, their boots splashing in growing puddles.

The factory stood at some distance, squat and bulky, a shapeless black mass of buildings with immense and towering chimneys which smeared stains of black and dull crimson against the darkening sky. Lights began to burn sullenly in the black walls of the factory, and the noise of the machinery quickened, became guttural thunder, as if everything were hurrying against the night. Between the factory and the walls stretched a desolate space, all flat mud and gravel, with here and there a low heap of slag or rusty iron or other débris. This flat level was pitted with shallow puddles now, which riffled with the rain. There was nothing but ugliness and desolation here, from the grim factories under a dark gray sky to the sheets of rain and its cold bleak splashing. Far to the left was another fence, lower than the main fence, and Martin could see the tops of low houses above it.

Martin was oblivious of rain and cold and the fact that his hat brim ran like eaves. He had forgotten himself and his own sensations. When aroused by injustice, cruelty or exploitation, he lost all fear, became bold and passionate, immovable and implacable. And in this implacability was something of Ernest's implacability. But Eugene Bouchard was acutely aware of his own discomfort, and he became angrier. Martin had not answered his last argument, but had stood, regarding him mutely, his face pale and stark in the increasing dimness.

"Look you, Martin, let us go inside. I am drenched completely. My visitors will think I am quite mad. If you must argue, come with me and dry yourself, and after I have disposed of Mr. Judson and Mr. Stanton, we will continue our argument in peace and comfort."

He started to move away in the direction of the factories, but Martin stood obstinately in his tracks. "No, Eugene, I did not come for visits or arguments. I came to see things for myself. Leave me alone. I will walk about until I have seen everything."

"You'll get lung fever," protested Eugene, but his expression was such as to lead one to believe that such a culmination had a lot in its favor. "Well, I, at least, do not wish to get it. I will be in my office for another hour, if you want anything."

He walked away, clumping solidly through puddles and mud, his hands thrust in his coat pockets, his large head bent between his shoulders. Martin looked after him for a moment. He had no really active dislike for Eugene Bouchard. He knew that Eugene imitated Ernest unconsciously, and that his harshness and roughness, his assumed coldness and relentlessness, sat on him uneasily at times. He had distinctly seen a flash of discomfort and embarrassment on that broad brown face during the argument. Martin had read much of the innate cruelty and sadism of the Latin, but he suddenly doubted that even a Latin could be so icily cruel, so remorseless and brutal as his own race, which stemmed from the Teuton. He remembered that the Latin laughed, but never tried to justify himself; he remembered that the Teuton and his stems never laugh, but always try to justify themselves. He thought the latter the greater immorality. Martin grew quite a bit older as he stood there in the gathering darkness and the rain, and he felt considerably more humble. Some measure of his single-hearted fanaticism passed from him in that short space of time, and his eye seemed to him to have grown larger, and sadder.

"Ernest," he thought, "is like a blight on everyone's life. He's blighted Eugene. He blighted Pa, though I don't believe he meant to. He has blighted me, and he'll blight his wife and his children. And I don't believe he consciously means to! He can't help it; he's like a plague, or a cyclone. But I can't," he added to himself with resolution, "let him go on blighting the lives of hundreds without trying to do something about it."

He turned on his heel and walked toward the lower fence. The guards watched him curiously. Very strange conduct for a Barbour and a gentleman! Martin arrived at the fence, and discovered himself confronted by another gate. This, however, was obsequiously opened for him by another watchman, who offered to escort him, an offer that Martin declined.

He found himself at the end of a short travesty of a muddy street, nightmarish, muddled and distorted, heaps of helter-skelter wooden refuse, crazily lining wood sidewalks and mudhole roads. Here and there in the leaning wrecks a yellow light burned bleakly. Wisps of smoke came from low chimneys and mixed with the foggy rain, so that the air was almost unbreathable and acrid. There was little sound here, on this street, besides the bitter rumble and splash of the rain, and the distant growling and clashing from the factory. Behind some of the shacks were chicken coops, and as Martin walked down the street very slowly, he would now hear the quarrelling and squawking of chickens and the dim hopeless wailing of little children. Once or twice the shrill voice of a woman rose, nagging and hysterical and violent. And the rain came down steadily, filling the mudholes with treacherous slimy pools, and the foggy, smoky air stung his lungs. He stumbled along, for it was almost too dark to see clearly, and there were no lampposts. He noticed that not one blade of grass was to be seen, not a single garden, not the smallest of shrubs or trees. Here lived and suffered and endured a veritable abomination of poverty, hopelessness, dirt and pain. The weight of his depression and sorrow and rage were too heavy in him to be articulate, even to form themselves into conscious thought. He felt as if he were carrying a burden too heavy for breath and heart to stand. He had feared much, but not so much as this. His feet seemed to lag, to be borne down, and he had a sudden horrible thought that he was going to fall into a mudhole and drown, right there in the midst of this welter of broken shacks and mud and rain and darkness and desolation.

He was far enough along now to see that still another street lay at right angles to this one, a street no more attractive, and bounded, as was the other street, by the imprisoning wooden wall. He had almost reached the intersection when from one of the houses soared a searing cry of agony, shrill and penetrating. So sharp and high was it that it seemed scarcely human, but as it was repeated again and again, with increasing force and crescendo, he was able to control his suddenly thudding heart long enough to recognize that the cries came from some suffering child. Interspersed with the sounds of resistless anguish came the hoarse, sobbing voice of a woman, apparently trying to offer sympathy and help, and a chorus of frightened cries from other children.

Martin found himself in front of a shack of rough, unpainted boards, stained and running with water. A dim lamp burned in the one window that faced the street, a rude, uncurtained window. He stumbled through a hole of water and mud, and went to this window. He could see inside quite clearly. He saw a room whose walls and floor were of unpainted pine; it was not a large room, and its smallness was cluttered. Two rude beds almost filled it, and a number of home-made chairs. There were two or three large wicker boxes in the corners, heaped with rags and unidentifiable objects. A small iron stove fumed smokily in the center of the room. There were at least five small children crowded about the stove, and in one of the beds lay another child, tossing and screaming, throwing up its hands and legs with drowning gestures, while a slatternly woman, shapeless and haggard, tried to hold it down by force and voice. All the children were crying in sympathy, shivering in their inadequate clothing. The yellow lamplight glimmered on the pale and emaciated faces and arms, on the woman half lying on the bed, on the tortured child struggling to escape its agony.

Never in all his life, in England or in America, had Martin seen such a sight of poverty and despair. He ran to the sagging door, beat upon it passionately. The crying children stopped their wailing, but the agonized screams of the other went on and on. There was a stumbling and a movement inside, and the door was dragged open, revealing the weeping, dishevelled woman, and behind her, the crowding faces of the children, their mouths open, their eyes peering anxiously. The slightly warmer air rushed out, fetid and smoky, and Martin gasped.

"Let me come in!" he exclaimed.

The woman barred his way. He could see her dark, foreign face, her black eyes, her dragging black hair. She was staring at him with dull perplexity. He put his hand on the door, thrust it from her grasp and entered the room. The woman burst into exclamations, gestured excitedly, wrung her hands, glared at him. He looked pitifully at her terrified face, and noted the sunken cheeks, the empurpled broken lips, the eyelids swollen with tears. He looked at the children, who, shrinking from this apparition, had run behind the stove. Even the screaming baby stopped her cries and stared at him from the bed with a twisted, wizened face and bloody mouth.

He tried to smile, but his lips felt thick, and he was afraid that he was about to burst into tears. He tapped himself on the chest. "Barbour. Mr. Barbour." Now he could smile, encouragingly. He knew he must be a strange sight, drenched and mud-stained, his hat and hair running with water, and his face pale and wild. No wonder the poor woman continued to glare at him with open terror, backing away from him toward her children, who rushed from the stove to cluster about her calico skirts. "Barbour," he repeated, and held out his hand.

She blinked like a stupid animal. The name evidently meant something to her, but his appearance more evidently did not. So, he turned from her in despair and went to the bed. The woman shrieked, leapt forward, reached the bed the instant he did. But he bent over the child, and the lamp shone on his face. Then something in his face, so steadfast and so calm, so almost beautiful, and so kind, seemed to reassure her, for she burst out again into a torrent of guttural sounds, and began to weep. She pointed to the baby, who had resumed her screams of anguish. The child threw her limbs about, clutching at Martin's hands with clawlike fingers, glaring at him with mad baby eyes, her mouth open and vibrating with her screams. He felt the burning and emaciated grasp on his hands, and very gently he began to examine the child. But he could ask no questions, and looked at the mother helplessly. She comprehended, turned the child on her side, and touched the ear. Martin now saw that back of the ear was a great red swelled place, humid and hot, and he knew what was wrong. Unless aid was gotten for the little one immediately, she must die. "My God!" he exclaimed, "can no one speak English here?" He looked at the children. The eldest was a boy of about ten, and he looked at Martin hesitantly. "I can. Little bit," he muttered, frightened.

"Thank God! Look here, boy, run out there to the watchman. Send him to me. Tell him Mr. Barbour wants to talk to him right away."

The boy, after one long stupefied stare at Martin, ran out into the rain and darkness. Within a few minutes he returned with the Irish watchman from the main gate. The panting man was much amazed and disgruntled, but his voice and manner were obsequious. He shouldered aside the woman as he tramped, wet and muddy, into the room, and stood before Martin, his hat in his hand, his club tucked under his arm.

Then for the first time Martin realized what a blessed power money was, how it could command and save, soothe agony and destroy fear, raise up and rescue. He had thought of it as something inherently evil and sinister, and here it was, an angel of mercy in robes of light! Its power rushed through him, making him feel stronger than he had ever felt in all his life, and he knew, instantly, what it was that he must do! All his confusion left him, left him free.

"I want a doctor," he said curtly to the watchman. "At once. Tell him a child here has a very bad ear, and is suffering. Tell him Mr. Barbour wants him at once. Now, run!"

The watchman hesitated, though he scraped respectfully. "But Mr. Barbour, orders is that the Superintendent must give the word——"

"Damn you!" cried Martin, to his own astonishment, "is the Superintendent named Barbour or am I? This is my factory, not the Superintendent's! And I want the doctor or you'll get the sack tomorrow!"

The man ran precipitately. Martin returned to the bed. He made the woman understand that he wanted warm water, and when it was brought he wiped the child's stained face and hands, and gave the little one a cup of cold water. So gentle was he, so tender, that the baby's screams dwindled to whimpers, and once she managed a smile so piteous that he could scarcely endure it. He continued to talk to her soothingly, and for a few incredible moments she actually slept with her cheek against his hand. Her mother crouched on the opposite side of the bed, and the children stood about her. They all looked at Martin as they would have looked at a deliverer or a god.

The child awoke, sobbing, and had begun to scream again, when the watchman returned with a young and shabby doctor with an amazed expression and incredulous eyes. Though Martin had never seen him before, he had seen Martin in his carriage many times, and recognizing him, was overcome with trepidation and embarrassed nervousness. He examined the child with his fine thin young hands, and then gave her a crushed tablet in water. Then standing up, he turned to Martin and shook his head. "She ought to have had a doctor before this," he said. "I'm sorry, sir, but it's septic ear. They do operations on it, now, but it's very dangerous, and almost always fatal. But I think it's even too late for that, Mr. Barbour."

Martin looked back at him steadily and quietly. "Look here, nothing must be spared for this child. She must have everything. How about a hospital? Nurses? A doctor from New York or Philadelphia?"

The young doctor shook his head slightly. "Our hospitals aren't— aren't very good, sir. Pesthouses of infection. It's the crime of the nineteenth century, that no one has ever done anything about our hospitals. Worse than prisons, and not much cleaner. Mr. Barbour, sir, you can't realize what is going on in the world! Only a doctor knows. And we're helpless. Our hospitals aren't fit for dogs, and no one tries to do anything about it. We have no adequate nursing, only women who are little better than outcasts, drudges and drunken slatterns. Every doctor knows what is needed, but the poor ones are helpless, and the rich are indifferent. Wealthy people can have the best in their own homes——" He gestured helplessly. "For the poor, they can get along by the casual help of nature, or die. Sometimes death is best for them. Hospitals sometimes prolong their suffering, or kill them quicker." His young face became hard and twisted with bitterness.

The child had fallen into a drugged sleep, moaning and restless. Across her bed the two young men regarded each other steadily and sadly. Then Martin said, after a long time: "Doctor, you don't know what you have done for me. But some day I might tell you. In the meantime, everything must be done to save this child. Food, comforts, care, nursing—everything. Nothing must be spared. Perhaps, after all, some of us can make this world a little better for her to live in than what it has been."

"It's bad enough now, God knows," sighed the young doctor. "But I'll tell you what we can do: if we can get this child out of this—my sister, who keeps house for me, can nurse her in our own home. She hasn't really much of a chance to live, but perhaps we can make her more comfortable. We could call Dr. Montrose, if you wish; he has done some operations on ear cases, and has had only a fifty per cent mortality. People in New York send for him. You'd like Dr. Montrose.

At that moment Ernest was reading a note from Eugene, which had been sent by messenger. In it, Eugene informed him that his brother had visited the Kinsolving works, and he, Eugene, did not like the look of it.

CHAPTER XXXIX

THAT EVENING Ernest said to his wife: "My love, I am very sorry, but I am afraid that if you go to the Culverts' dinner this evening, you must go alone. I will take you, of course, and call for you. But I am having a very important and unexpected visitor tonight. I didn't know until this afternoon that he was coming, and it is necessary to receive him at once."

May was disappointed. She had finished nursing her child only a few months ago, and was already in her third month of pregnancy with another child. She coveted and cherished every moment of freedom she now had, so protested with some indignation. Gregory, who had previously declined the invitation, offered to escort her in Ernest's place, and the offer was accepted after much head-tossing, pouting, recriminations and tears. When she had finally dressed and was about to leave, she tapped her husband on the shoulder with her fan. "I'm sorry for your visitor, my dearest," she said, dimpling knowingly. "Ah, you're no sphinx to me, Ernest, for all your smoothness!" And went out, laughing.

Ernest sat before the bright fire in the library. He lit a cigar, smoked it meditatively, and stared at the coals on the hearth. The clock was chiming nine when the butler came in and announced Mr. Martin Barbour. Ernest nodded. When Martin came in, Ernest did not rise heartily as usual, but remained in his chair. From his seat he regarded his brother in silence with his light and inexorable eyes. And Martin looking down at him, felt a ripple of warning all through his body.

"I see," he said quietly, "that you know."

There was a pause. Then Ernest indicated with his cigar a chair on the opposite side of the fire. "Sit down," he said. Martin sat down.

"I suppose," Ernest went on smoothly, "that this could not wait until tomorrow, at the office?"

"No, it could not. In fact, I am sure that when I am finished, you will be glad I didn't wait until we were in the office. But, now that you know, I am going to tell you what I am going to do.

"Some time ago, after the Crimean business, Ernest, it was my intention to withdraw from this business." He paused; a dark gleam passed over Ernest's features, but he showed no other sign of any emotion. He, himself, was studying his brother, observing his pallor, his worn and agitated expression, his nervousness and exhausted manner. Martin, regarded him, in turn, very earnestly. "I couldn't stand the business any longer, this making of guns and explosives to kill other men. I couldn't bear the thought of my children profiting from death.

"I told Mr. Gregory about it; I told Amy; I told Ma; I told Father Dominick. Mr. Gregory objected violently, Amy was willing for me to do what I wish, Ma didn't understand at all. But Father Dominick advised patience." Again that dark and subtle gleam passed over Ernest's face.

"I thought, Ernest, that Father Dominick was wrong. After awhile I became confused. I didn't know what to do. Everyone seemed against me. Sometimes I suspected I was a fool, and at other times the whole world seemed out of joint, or hungry, like a beast." The memory of those months of indecision and torment upset him even now, and he stood up, restlessly. Ernest was intently engrossed with the end of his cigar; he might have been alone for any indication he gave of having heard Martin.

"And then," Martin continued, "I saw what Father Dominick had meant when he advised patience. There were so many things— But today, I discovered what I wanted to do, what I must do. I went to the Kinsolving works, as Eugene, I see, has already told you. I went because I had been told of the conditions there." A sort of horror went through him at the memory of that hour in the mud and darkness and rain, and the anguish of the dying child. "But they were much worse than I had expected. But you know that, too."

He sat down again, leaned toward his brother, as though he were about to make a last and despairing plea. "Ernest, you know all about conditions there. And yet, you can sit here, before your fire, in comfort, with the rain shut out and a good dinner eaten, and money in the bank, and not feel ashamed. You can even enjoy these things that the misery and enslavement of others have brought you. You can sit there like a stone!" And his voice rose almost to a cry. "Like a stone! You haven't any heart. You never had one. Why, I can remember you stepping on crickets, absentmindedly, as if it were part of your nature to crush helpless things, and you couldn't help it. Sometimes you looked at me, as you did at others, and I had to think of those crickets running around on the hearth at home! And these people out there, dying, imprisoned, cold, sick and helpless, are just crickets to you. Yet, I can't believe it! I don't want to believe it! I want to believe that somewhere in you there is something mortal, something that can bleed. I want to believe that you will do something about all this——"

"And what," asked Ernest softly, regarding the fire placidly, "would you like me to do?"

Martin felt sick and hopeless, but he went on: "Release these men and their families. Don't enslave them. Give them money, not scraps of paper. Don't let them die like chained dogs out there in the cold and the rain. Give them enough to live on. Let them go."

Ernest laughed a little, very softly, as if in gentle amusement. Now he looked at Martin directly, and in his pale eyes the pupil seemed pointed and extraordinarily bright. "You'll never grow up, Martin. You'll never grow out of the little Eva rôle, will you? Do you forget we are men, and that we are engaged in a great industry? Fortunes are not built on brotherly love and charity. They're not even built on fairness. Nothing is ever created except by labor and blood and iron. Races aren't won by keeping horses fat in stalls; fields aren't plowed by letting the plowman sit with his boots on the fender and his chin on his chest. Roads aren't built and mountains tunnelled and frontiers pushed back by people who drowse in rocking chairs; all these things have been done and are being done through suffering.

"But I've told you these things so many hundreds of times! I'm sick of it, now. We're building up an Industry, and other men are building up Industries, and this whole country is going to be made to grow, and grow strong and powerful, by Industry. Somebody's got to suffer for it. Even die for it, if necessary. But Industry has one great virtue, which you have overlooked: it destroys only the worthless and the superfluous. It doesn't eat up the best, as other things do. It is a big cow that doesn't need hay and fresh grass and good corn; it can get along very well on sawdust and chaff. And that," he added with cold contempt, "is what those laborers of ours are: sawdust and chaff. They'll never be anything else; their fathers were never anything else. Wars and famines and plagues used to destroy them. But we've found something better for them than these—Industry. They at least live, and eat. But I've told you all this before.

"The main thing that I can see, of course," and he laughed again, "is the 'imprisonment' idea. I am afraid you don't understand. Don't you know that any man of them, by just saying the word, can leave any time he wishes to?"

While he had been speaking, Martin had grown paler and more hopeless. He sighed, half covered his face with his hand. "I suppose there is nothing I can say to persuade you," he said, half to himself. He dropped his hand. "Yes, you've told me all this before. You can make it sound so plausible. But lies and cruelty can be made to sound so, and that confused me at first. But they don't confuse me now.

"Yes, I suppose if any of those poor men really wanted to go you would let them go. But where would they go? They have not a cent. You've taken care of that with your scrip and your company stores. They would starve. I can see that you've built a higher wall about them than the wooden one out there.

"So, now I come to what I want to do, what I must do. I'm not going to withdraw from this business. I've an equal amount of stock with you. But you can outvote me, for Armand and Eugene and Raoul and Mr. Gregory are always with you. Either you hypnotize them, or they are like you. I don't know. So, it is my intention to stay with the Company, to return to those poor men a part of what they have earned. I shall deposit two-thirds or one-half of all my dividends in the bank for these men, so that when they wish to leave they can withdraw a certain part of this money in proportion to the time they have worked for us. That will be considered their savings. When each man wants to leave, he can, with money in his pockets.

"I shall also provide sufficient doctors for them, and have a small hospital built right on the grounds. Father Dominick will help me. These people are Catholics, most of them, and it shall be a Catholic hospital, endowed by myself and others whom I can interest. We can get brothers to nurse the men, nuns to nurse the women and children. Oh, I know it will take every cent of my dividends and profits. Every cent. But I don't care! I don't want a penny for myself or my children. For every man you knock down I'll raise up a man. I'll save every child you leave to die. I'll feed every wretch you make hungry. I'll free every laborer you put behind your walls." He stood up again, and a sort of splendor came out over him that struck even Ernest. His face glowed. and his eyes were again a blue and passionate blaze. He looked invincible, even triumphant, unafraid, co-ordinated and of a powerful oneness. He was no longer the irresolute, silent, withdrawn dreamer that had had Ernest's contempt, for it was only when he was concerned with himself that he was such a dreamer. In the midst of the black boil of hatred that seethed and bubbled in Ernest there stood a sudden and reluctant admiration for such heroic folly, for such sublime imbecility. It seemed incredible to him; in another, he would have doubted sincerity. But he did not doubt Martin's sincerity. It was just such a thing that Martin would do; his whole life and nature pointed to sacrifice and heroism, idealism and superb idiocy. To fantasies such as justice and love, straightness and simplicity, honor and gentleness, compassion and peace. People like this, thought Ernest in one clear and luminous flash over that black boil of hatred, are dangerous. They must be destroyed, if the world is to survive.

But nothing of what he thought showed in Ernest's continued and casual placidity, in his languid smoking of his cigar. He continued to smoke, while Martin stood there, and he still went on smoking until the glow went out of Martin's face and became pale resolution. Then he stood also, putting his hands under his coat-tails and staring at the fire. He might have been about to discuss the most insignificant of matters. Even his voice was quiet and indifferent. But he did not look at his brother while he was speaking.

"Today," he said, "our stock, common, closed two points higher than it did yesterday. I'll buy your stock from you, all of it, at today's market price, though it may open lower tomorrow. I'll buy your bonds from you at today's price. I'll pay you these amounts over a period of three years, twice yearly. And I'll expect that you will immediately give me your resignation as Secretary of Barbour & Bouchard."

And after this, there was a long and, to Martin, a terrible silence.

His mind, incredulous, refused to believe what his ears had heard. He felt within himself a great dark tumbling and crashing, a falling, a sensation that he had been violently thrust from solid ground into treacherous space. His eyes, staring at Ernest, became protuberant and glazed, and his mouth fell open. But he was more astounded and horrified than frightened. There was a whirling in his head. Scraps of what he had heard his father say, what he himself had thought of his brother, dashed incoherently in his mind like sparks in darkness: "—try to get control"; "—and rob"; "—cheat your mother and sisters"; "—be the whole blooming show, and not leave even a scrap for the rest of you." But still he could not believe; still he was incredulous. He could only stare, speechless, at Ernest, and now Ernest looked back at him, blandly, relentlessly.

Martin struggled to speak, and when he finally succeeded, he could only whisper: "So that's what you've been waiting for, and planning for, all this time! To force me out, just as Pa said you would try. I'm in your way, and now you'll force me out." He made his voice stronger, and it was hoarse and shaking. "But you can't force me out! I'm staying. I'll try to undo all you do, and you can't stop me! I've got to stay for the sake of Ma and the girls, too. You can't force me out! I've got as much interest in this business as you have." For the first time in his life he was gloating triumphantly; he laughed in his brother's face. Something of Ernest's own expression, fierce and exultant, sprang into his eyes. Their mutual hate, so long concealed, now stood between them, and they saw it and recognized it openly.

Then Ernest smiled, as if deeply amused. He nodded his head. "I think you'll get out," he said softly. "For, if you don't, Hans and Carl Heckl go to prison for helping slaves to escape to Canada. They seem very fond of you. They won't tell your part in the affair. But, if I do not have your resignation at once, and your promise to sell me your stock, they go to prison for very long terms. I shall see that the terms are long."

Martin, suddenly ghastly, sat down abruptly. Ernest, still smiling, sat down also.

"They're good, simple men," he said. "They don't know how to lie. In fact they were so proud of themselves that they confessed everything.

Carl was defiant, but the old man was quite crushed, when it was all over. I talked to them privately before the constables came, and they refused to speak of you or say anything of you——"

Martin's eyes were suffused, and he was breathing loudly. He remembered, with self-hatred and despair, what he had confided to Ernest a couple of years before, in his innocence and impulsive trust. He might have known he would be treacherous! Oh, what folly to have trusted him! Better to have trusted a water-mocassin, the devil himself. To have betrayed himself was bad enough, but to have betrayed the Heckls who had trusted him was immeasurably worse. Sweat glistened on his white face, and his lips were livid. God forgive me for a fool! he thought in his despair.

He looked at Ernest. There was no relenting there, nothing that a man could appeal to, or touch. Any idea he had had of appealing for mercy, for consideration, died at birth. Martin felt as if he had come to the edge of an abyss. He saw Hans' face, old and terrified and shrinking, his trembling hands; he saw Carl, young and defiant; he saw old Mrs. Heckl, and winced. He had brought these to the mercy of a hyena, a lion. God forgive me! he said again, and did not know that he spoke aloud. He was overcome. Everything he had ever done was in ruins; at every step he, and only he, had committed irreparable follies. And he had dragged others into his follies with him. He became sick with his self-loathing.

Then after a long time he said slowly and haltingly: "You are trying to blackmail me to get out. You think that I will give up all I have planned to do if you threaten me with the imprisonment of those two poor men. But you can't get me out; you can't threaten me. I won't give up what I have planned to do. I'll talk to Hans and Carl as soon as I can, and I know that they will agree with me that it is better that two men go to jail than hundreds be in prison and hopeless."

Ernest was still smiling, and his amusement seemed to increase. "I am afraid that if you insist this way, there'll be three men in prison, not two. It wouldn't be just for those two to accept the penalty alone, would it? Their associate, you see, must go to prison with them. And I'll send him there, too."

"You would send me to prison?"

"Of course. My dear Martin, you're always mouthing about justice. Yet you would have me do something very unjust. And sending two men to prison, and allowing their associate to go free, would be very, very unjust. You must agree with that."

But to his surprise, Martin had begun to smile. It was a pale smile, and grim, and the lines about his mouth were blue.

"If I asked you, Ernest, to think of Ma and our sisters, you would laugh at me. If I asked you to remember I am your brother, that we had

the same father and mother, you would laugh louder. But still, I do⌐
think you will send me to prison. You can't be reached by common h⌐
man appeals such as reach other men. But you can be reached anoth⌐
way. I don't think you'll send your wife's cousin's husband to jail.
don't think Mr. Gregory will stand for your sending his niece's husba⌐
to jail. May and Mr. Gregory are arguments you can't get aroun⌐
though, of course, you wouldn't think of poor Amy."

A most extraordinary change had come over Ernest's face at t⌐
mention of Amy's name. At first, there was stupefaction following t⌐
shock of something remembered; it was almost as though he were sa⌐
ing to himself, in incredulity and amazement at his own singlemind⌐
relentlessness: I had forgotten that! In my determination to do t⌐
thing, in my inability to see anything but the object to be attained, I h⌐
forgotten that! I had forgotten Amy. My mother, my sisters, my wi⌐
and my children, Gregory Sessions—everybody: I would not step do⌐
for all of these. But I had forgotten Amy!

In his agitation and shock he stood up, abruptly. Martin smiled bleak⌐
to himself; he had hit Ernest there when he had spoken of May a⌐
Gregory! A sense of returning power came to him. But he could r⌐
control his trembling. He looked at Ernest, standing there before t⌐
fire, his fists clenched at his side. There was a disordered air about hi⌐
as if he had been struck vitally. I have him down, thought Mart⌐
amazed. For the first time in my life, I have him down!

He began to speak, slowly and carefully, to the silent man on ⌐
hearth.

"There can never be any peace between us after this. We can nev⌐
meet again, as friends. I don't think I could ever stand seeing you
speaking to you again. It's all over between us. I've known all my ⌐
what you were, but I didn't really believe all of it until tonight. Now
can't bear to be in the same room with you, or looking at you. I'll g⌐
He stood up, also, and buttoned his coat. Ernest gave no sign that ⌐
had heard him or was conscious that he was there. He was extraor⌐
narily pale, as if he had suffered some profound shock.

"So, I'll resign from Barbour & Bouchard, if that is what you wi⌐
But I won't sell you my stock or bonds. And I'll resign only on yc⌐
promise that Hans and Carl will be released at once. I'll go on with ⌐
plans, with the exception of the hospital. I'll build that hospital near ⌐
gates of the Kinsolving works. And something tells me that you'll
the sick out from behind those wooden walls of yours. I'll spend ev⌐
cent of my dividends on these people you have oppressed, and you ca⌐
stop me. I'll see the Mayor, or even the Governor, about some things, t⌐

"Tomorrow, I'll send you my resignation. And I'll tell Ma that ⌐
still behind her and the girls, watching to see that they aren't robbed.'

Ernest stirred; he turned to his brother. He was quite calm.

"I shall expect your resignation tomorrow morning. I'll see that Hans and Carl are released tonight." His voice was heavy and listless, as though he had lost interest in the whole matter.

Martin went to the door. On the threshold he stopped, and turned.

"I'll never have anything more to say to you. But I want to say this: You can't shut your strong doors tight enough to keep out the disease you're breeding down there among your laborers. You can't close your windows close enough to keep out the malaria you're creating in your swamps. There aren't bolts strong enough to protect you and your children from the wild dogs you're setting loose. Every child that dies down there from hunger and neglect threatens the life of your children. Every woman you make husbandless and homeless makes your wife's bed the harder. You poison their water and the water will seep through the ground to your own wells. You can't keep out the misery and the ruin you are making." His voice became eloquent with prophecy, the great glow came out on his face again. "You're making death for others, but you're making it for yourself, too. Mentally and physically, you're making death for yourself and your children, and your children's children. You are breaking down dams, but some day the water will drown you, too. And your children. You can't sow the whirlwind, and build a house strong enough to stand in it!"

"The door," said Ernest, "is to your right, and straight ahead."

CHAPTER XL

MARTIN TOLD Amy what had taken place with such passionate simplicity, resolution and sadness that she was moved and shaken. She shuddered when he told her of the child he had rescued; she exclaimed faintly when he described the street bounded by the wooden walls. And when he had finished, she burst into tears, went into his arms and kissed him. "You have done the only thing it is possible for *you* to do," she said, and even Martin missed the significance of her accent on the last pronoun. Later, she said: "It doesn't matter what others say about you, Martin: you must not let them confuse you or turn you aside again. According to your lights, you are right. Don't let yourself be betrayed. Whatever you do, I am your wife, and whatever you decide is my decision, too."

Sometimes she would watch him as he covered paper with figures, sighing and combing his light thick hair with his fingers, and her eyes would fill humbly. Never had she loved him so much; never had she so appreciated and valued him for what he was. It seemed a privilege to her to be his wife. When he told her that he wished she would never go again to the Sessions house, she felt ill with grief, but her voice was steady when she told him that she would respect his wishes. He had, he said gently, nothing against May and her little boy, and she could come to their home as often as she and Amy desired, but he did not want his wife to come into contact, however trifling, with "that man." When he spoke of his brother with loathing and heaviness, Amy was silent. She was too clear-sighted to blame herself for any emotion she had for Ernest; it was something inevitable, she thought, something to be endured, like wind or rain or darkness or cold. She had no control over it; she would have thought an exercise of conscience stupid, like the beating of drums to call attention to one's own ambush. Or, she would have thought it self-dramatization.

Martin was determined to sell the house he lived in. It was impossible for him to endure it any longer. His first impulse had been to return it to Ernest, but he thought of something better. It would be his planned hospital. In the meantime, he looked about for another home.

Gregory Sessions, outraged and vituperative, came to see him. But before he could even say more than a few words, Martin stopped him. He looked at the older man with such new sternness and resolution that Gregory was struck into silence. "I don't want any discussion with any one about this," said Martin. "My life is my own to live, and I must live according to the rules which seem right to me. I, too, Mr. Gregory, have a right to happiness and peace."

Martin moved about alertly and with vitality. He had so much to do. His strength seemed to himself to be prodigious. Life flowed and pounded in his body, and he never tired. He was exalted, not feverishly, but with growing power. One night when he knew that Armand and his sons would be at home together, he went to see them. Armand's cousin from Canada had changed the ugly old house so that it had a sprightly and knowing air of more modern comfort, but Armand seemed less at ease in it than he had been in its former genial gay disorder. He looked like a nut that had become dried out with age, so that its kernel had lost its juices and flavor. Browner, more wizened than ever, somewhat more silent, more twisted, he sat before his fire, booted, not bootless as of old. He smoked cigars now, for the sprightly cousin objected to pipes. But Eugene and Raoul were more satisfied in the new cleanliness and primness. They could bring their friends here without imagining that these friends were making odious comments to themselves.

They all received Martin with rather surprised reserve and embarrassment. They glanced furtively at each other, smiled uneasily at the visitor. Armand recovered almost at once, offered Martin a seat with grave courtesy, inquired about the health of his family. He knew that Amy was expecting another child, and he had always admired her, and had been touched by her steady gentleness and soft manners. Raoul had been polite enough, but there were derisive lines about his sparkling eyes and smiling lips; Eugene was inclined to be sullen and restive with Martin, muttered something about business outside requiring his attention.

"Please stay, Eugene," said Martin with such earnest sadness that the other young man was startled, and sat down again. Even Raoul became serious. As for Armand, he removed the despised cigar from his mouth, and waited.

Martin looked from one to the other for several moments before he spoke. They saw how pale he was, how much thinner. They saw that his eyes burned with weariness and unshakable courage.

"Before I came here," he said, "I was already convinced that it was hopeless, that I would be wasting your time and mine. But I felt that I must leave nothing undone, and neglect nothing.

"You know what has happened. Except for being a large stockholder I am no longer connected with your Company. But because I was once a member, and am still a stockholder, I wanted to make a last appeal to you. You know why I left the Company; you know the intolerable conditions that forced me to do that. You know what I am doing now. I can't believe you are made of stone, without feeling and mercy. I can't believe that profits are more to you than the lives and rights of other human beings. I can't believe that you would take money that has cost the life of a child. I can't believe you can enjoy something that is bought with misery. There are three of you against one man. Perhaps two men, if you count Gregory Sessions. But he has not so much to say. But the three of you might be able to do something.

"So, I am asking you, though I feel it is hopeless to ask, to change things. To have a little mercy. You, Raoul and Eugene, each have a dog that you are fond of and take care of. You would fight the man that would kick them. You shelter them and feed them and protect them. Are men less than dogs?"

There was a long silence. No one looked at Martin. Armand regarded the fire, and Eugene and Raoul stared at the floor. Then Eugene, still without looking at Martin, made an irritable gesture. "What are we to do?" he asked with asperity. "We are in business. We have competitors. We have large Government contracts because we have underbid everyone else. If we do not continue doing what we do, we cannot exist as a company. To employ American workmen, even to treat our foreign laborers as we would have to treat American workmen, would ruin us. We are not responsible for this industrial situation. The roots are deeper than our house. They lie in the whole system. We must do as our competitors do or go out of business.

"Yes, the roots lie deeper than you suspect. The only cure is in the prohibition of these laborers being brought to America for this purpose. Then, of course, if they are stopped, we can absorb what is here. Things generally tend to get better. Conditions would improve for these people, and they would soon be demanding as much wages as our American workmen. But so long as there is no restriction on their coming, and our competitors can bring in as many as they like, we can do nothing to improve the condition of things. We must run with the wolves if we are to survive. We must get these people for ourselves, however much misery it costs, or how many American men cannot make a living."

"Eugene has said it exactly," said Armand thoughtfully. "And I can see that you have not given this point of view much serious thought, my Martin."

Martin regarded them in silence for a long time. Then he said, almost in bewilderment: "You are right. I overlooked something. The cure, as you say, is the stopping of this importation of foreign labor. You have given me something to think of, to try to cure. So, after all, I haven't wasted my time in coming here." He stood up. "Still, you are not guiltless, any of you. Barbour & Bouchard has a lot of influence in America. You could start the movement against foreign labor if you wanted to. But you won't. However, I'm grateful for the help you have given me already. I suppose I ought not to ask any more favors."

Armand went to the door with him. He put his hand on the young man's arm. "Martin," he said kindly, "I wish you would move more slowly. I wish you would consider many things. The newspapers are already commenting on what you have done. I am certain that you understand, now, that we aren't the sole culprits, that, in fact, we are also victims. Too, you are prone to look on the dark side of things. Human misery is no new story. Exploitation of man by man is history. You cannot reform the world." He patted Martin's arm, and laughed a little grimly. "Remember what the world does to its reformers. And its saints. Nevertheless, I admire you. You believe in something, and that is very enviable."

"I believe that every man has the right to live," said Martin bitterly.

Armand shook his head. "No, he must earn the right to live," he replied. "No man has the right to anything, neither to breathe nor to eat, unless he has earned it. The world owes nothing to any one. But we owe the world a great deal." He poked Martin's chest with one small brown finger, like a twig. "Go on, my Martin. You have a vision. Perhaps you are right; perhaps you are wrong. But at least you have a vision. In a way, I, too, have a vision. I shall get enough money so that my dear fellow men shall never have me at their mercy again."

Amy's cousin, May Barbour, was exceedingly disturbed by the whole situation. But she could get no satisfaction from Ernest. He forbade her to enter Martin's house again. But Martin had probably forbidden Amy to enter the Sessions house! May exclaimed in consternation. She set her red mouth mutinously. The silly men, she said, could have their quarrels, but she would not abandon Amy. Amy, she insisted, no doubt needed every friend she had now. Ernest might frown and thunder and curse, but she would see Amy, either in this house or in Amy's own house. She would not abandon Amy, however much their husbands might quarrel. To her surprise, Ernest suddenly backed down, became milder, grudgingly admitted that perhaps she was right.

So May called on her cousin, and was not at all nonplussed at seeing Martin, who treated her with every courtesy. She had the good sense not to discuss the situation either with Amy or with Martin. Her sprightliness, her chatter of her coming child and Amy's coming child, her laughter, shrewd gaiety and kindliness, vivacity and cheerfulness, did Amy considerable good. Amy reproached her for not bringing little Godfrey James with her. May shrugged. "I despise children," she said with disarming frankness. "It is very annoying that I am about to have another. But what is one to do? It is fortunate that I have an excellent nurse for Godfrey James: I hardly need to see him more than once a day." She studied Amy with sympathy and concern. Amy looked tired and pale and sad, and her brown eyes were enormous in her quiet face. But she had about her an air of reserve-strength and steadfastness that May respected. She demanded to see the twins. They were brought downstairs by their nurse, handsome and pugnacious babies with fierce blue eyes and hard red cheeks. May felt a pang of envy. Little Godfrey James was frail and silent and timid; sometimes he trembled without cause. She thought of how he liked to be seated in a big chair and listen to her play on her piano; at those times he smiled with such sweetness and infant radiance that she often burst into tears for no reason. Thinking of her child, she no longer envied Amy her roaring babies. "They have eyes just like their father," she said, and knew this was only partially true.

Martin loved his children passionately, but he was ill at ease with them. Their robustness of voice and body bewildered him. They crawled over him with astounding vigor and disregard, poking his ears and his eyes with tiny hard fingers. He was a deer that had fathered a pair of lion cubs. One could not tell one child from another, so almost identical they were. But Amy claimed that Paul was getting larger than Elsa every day, and that he was showing his sex in a new tendency to bully his sister.

One day Armand said to Ernest: "Martin is preparing his house as a hospital. What are you going to do? There is considerable strange talk, also, about the dividends he is depositing for our men. Are you planning on trying to stop this in some way?"

Ernest laughed shortly. "Stop it? My dear Armand, do not be absurd! Of course, I shall not stop it! Why should I? It is a great help to me. We can reduce the amount of scrip we give the men and there will be no complaints. They will show no desire to leave us; in fact, less than ever. For, you forget that my dear brother has arranged it so that the longer they are in my employ the more money they will receive when they leave. I think it is all a very excellent arrangement." He paused. "As for the hospital business, I shall put a stop to that. Any man who takes advantage of it, of course, shall be given the sack. And I have given orders not to admit any doctors to the grounds except Dr. Withers. That will spike *that* business."

He waited for Armand's usual wry comment, and was somewhat surprised that Armand merely walked away without speaking.

Martin went to the Governor. The Governor was a kindly man, but bored. He had read the newspapers, and on principle he disliked reformers. However, he received Martin courteously and with friendship. He listened attentively to what his visitor had to say, and his face was thoughtful. Finally he said: "I grant you everything, Mr. Barbour. The situation is abominable. But what can we do? After all, as you admit, the men can leave at any time. You have generously supplied them with funds when they leave. There is no law we can enforce to prevent these people from being brought to this country like slaves in wholesale lots. For some time there has been agitation in Washington about this, but so far nothing has been done. At the present time slavery in the South seems to be occupying everyone's attention. Perhaps after that is out of the way Congress can take up this alien labor affair. There is already a small lobby in Washington that you might investigate. Lobbies are always grateful for funds. Now about the doctor and hospital business: Barbour & Bouchard are a private concern; they have Government contracts; the land is their own. This is a free country, however paradoxical that may sound to you, I admit, and no one has the right to demand admittance to the grounds of Barbour & Bouchard, nor to trespass, however humanitarian his object. You are dependent on the consent of your brother, or other members of the firm, to give aid and comfort to the poor men inside their walls. From what you tell me, and from what I have read, I doubt very much that you will get that consent. To be sure, the men could leave the grounds and apply to you for medical help and hospital treatment, but who is to tell them that there is such a thing outside for them? They are so ignorant, so stupid, really, so sunken and submerged, that they would never know, or if threatened, which is quite possible, they might not accept even if they did know." He stood up, and Martin had to rise also. "No, my dear Mr. Barbour, I am afraid that if you are to accomplish anything you must walk a little softer. Exhortations, however just and eloquent, attempts at force, however righteous, always antagonize your opponent to the point where even reason has no chance with him. I advise you to use other methods. Softer, softer." He continued in this strain.

To Martin, it seemed that justice and mercy were always doomed to be thwarted and destroyed by something euphemistically called reason. It seemed strange to him that when something so obviously outrageous occurred that even the most stupid man must admit it required righting, there was a great deal of talk about law and trespassing, due process and respect for the rights of the strong, and the unjust. Law and reason, he was coming to believe, were continually being invoked to protect the haves against the have-nots, the robbers against their victims. He returned to Windsor in a state of much confusion and helpless wrath.

He went to see Father Dominick, less to seek advice than to find comfort. He did not know that the priest knew his brother, so attached little importance to the former's cryptic remark "that perhaps something could be done." So, he went to Washington in a last desperate hope that perhaps his wife's uncle might give him some encouragement.

In the meantime, Father Dominick visited Ernest at his office. Ernest received him with great, if wary, cordiality. He pressed cigars on him, inquired as to his health, laughed and joked with him, treating him in every way as a welcome visitor. Nothing could have been blander than the priest's expression, but he missed nothing of Ernest's gray stoniness of complexion, the light and unmoving implacability of his eyes, the grim wide mouth and strong short nose, the harshness behind the geniality. "Warmth rests uneasily on him," he thought.

He approached his object leisurely. He did not want Mr. Barbour to think he was intruding, but Mr. Martin Barbour had come to him in a state of much distress. He, of course, knew all about the whole matter; it was much to be regretted. Misunderstandings and enmity between kinsmen were an abomination in the sight of our Lord. He came today to Mr. Barbour more as a peacemaker than one impudently offering advice or suggestion. After all, Mr. Martin was a communicant of the Church, and entitled, therefore, to her protection and assistance. What he, the priest, had in mind, therefore, was a little—just a little—forbearance. He would not attempt to question the justice or injustice of the quarrel. He was interested only in peace, in an amicable settlement that would give both sides of the quarrel satisfaction. Now, Mr. Martin told him that Barbour & Bouchard had refused him permission to send a doctor within the gates of the Kinsolving works, had refused to send the sick to his hospital. This was very distressing.

There was a pause. Ernest said nothing. He had merely fixed his eyes upon the priest, and he still waited, utterly without facial expression. Father Dominick cleared his throat. And now, he pleaded with a smile, he really must be forgiven for offering a suggestion. Mr. Martin had the resolution and inexorable determination of a righteous and single-minded man. He would never give up; he would never relinquish what he had in mind. He would, like all his prototypes, eventually move mountains. And the movement of mountains, the priest pointed out delicately, is never accomplished without a great many casualties and other unpleasantnesses. There was nothing the just man would stop at to bring about what he considered justice. Carnage was an item to him. The eruptions of volcanoes were puffs of smoke. Heaven and earth might roll up like a scroll, but he would not see it; all he would see were his object and his simplicity of purpose. Simplicity of purpose, Father Dominick again pointed out, was a terrible thing. It was like the force of armies fused into one sword, that was irresistible. Nothing could withstand it. The end was inevitable: Martin would secure at least part of what he desired. It was the better, the more graceful, the quieter, the easier thing, for Ernest to concede a little. He had, said the priest, come out with the spoils, after all. If Ernest would concede the point of allowing his brother to care for the sick and injured of the Kinsolving works, and the other factories, he would not only secure the esteem of his fellow citizens, but would also be doing himself a benefit. Half-sick and injured workmen were notorious time-and-money wasters.

Ernest was still silent, but there was a faint and satirical smile on his mouth.

Father Dominick became momentarily interested in a hangnail. There were, he went on, more people to be considered than just Ernest and his brother. An increase in enmity, more uproar, more threats and struggle, would be very distressing to many others. Weren't their wives cousins? Hadn't he and Martin the same mother, the same sisters? Women, especially, the delicate and sensitive creatures! must be dealt with gently. And how they deplore quarrels between their men! It veritably breaks their hearts. And now the priest looked at him blandly, waiting.

Ernest's face had darkened, become heavy and sullen. He played with his watch chain and stared through the window. Finally he said slowly: "There is much in what you say. As for myself, enmity between my brother and me is an old story. I wouldn't care what happened between us. But, as you said, there are—others." He laughed shortly. "Yes, I can see your point in many ways.

"You may inform my brother, if you wish, that I will no longer object to my men being treated by his doctors either in their houses or in his hospital, and that once a week any doctor chosen by him may enter our grounds."

The two men regarded each other kindly. But the priest read the question in Ernest's eyes: I wonder, you crafty priest! how much you know? Father Dominick smiled to himself with more than a little irony.

Father Dominick called upon the Martin Barbours, and was disappointed when Amy informed him that Martin had gone to Washington. He was, however, too triumphant, too pleased, to retain his news, so he told it to Amy. He sat before the pleasant living-room fire, with the sun streaming in a broad path through the high windows, a baby on each knee, and beamed paternally upon Amy, who had acquired a deep affection for him. The babies crawled over him, tugging at his collar, thrusting fingers into his eyes and nose, clutching his hair, exploring his pockets. Between the fat scrambling legs and arms his face peered out good-humoredly at Amy, a round red moon shining with laughter.

Amy was delighted. Her eyes sparkled through tears. How pleased dear Martin would be! She confessed that she did not share his passion for social justice and all the other things he was so intense about, but she understood what he meant; she understood how he felt. He was so good, so truly noble. Her love for him made her sweet face luminous, and the color in her lips grew warmer.

Father Dominick began to talk of Ernest. At the mention of that name a faint and subtle change came into Amy's expression.

"In all my life," said the priest genially, "I have never met a truly godless man before. There was always just a little spark— Mr. Barbour is a revelation to me, though I have read of his kind. A truly godless man. A man utterly without God. And yet," he added, catching a twin deftly as it was about to dive to the floor, "I like him! I do not really know why, but I like him!"

CHAPTER XLI

MARTIN ARRIVED in Washington late in the afternoon. The train was late, and none too clean. Consequently he was tired and covered with soot and grit. He was also hungry. He had no intention of bursting in upon Senator Sessions demanding supper and sleeping accommodations, for he had the uneasy reserve of the shy man who is afraid to ask favors for himself. So he discovered a small and shabby hotel near the station, rented a dusty room, washed away the greasy soot as best he could, and had a supper served to him. He found the cold smoked ham surprisingly good, the sweet jams delectable, the chicken hot and fried and delicious, and the coffee quite exceptional. He had not been too hopeful on the train, but the food fortified him, and he felt his new sense of power flowing back.

He had no particular curiosity about Washington. It was a small city, he knew, not much larger than Windsor, and very beautiful. Perhaps it was the ashen airlessness of the early winter day, he thought, which seemed to give the rumor of beauty the lie, for so far he had seen only deadness and dinginess, few people, and uninspiring streets. But the amount of negroes surprised him. They were freemen, he knew, but not at all like the humble, servile, childlike and grateful wretches he had saved and shipped to Canada. These negroes were impudent and slovenly. His own particular waiter sniffed audibly at Martin's tip, though Martin had considered it exceedingly generous. He asked the waiter to call a cab for him, and when the man had been gone an unreasonable length of time, he was forced to put on his hat and coat and go downstairs to look for a cab, himself. He found his waiter lounging in the hallway talking amorously to a mulatto maid. At Martin's angry glance he did no more than stare insolently, finish the sentence he had begun, then drag himself reluctantly to the outer door. He opened it an inch and announced indifferently that it seemed like there was no cabs around this evenin', no sir! Martin went out himself. There was a light rain falling, and a vivid light, lying on the dingy poor buildings along the street, gave an air of desolation to the scene. A cab trundled dolorously toward Martin, drawn by one disconsolate horse, and he hailed it. As the door of the hotel closed behind him, he heard the negro say something about that "damned Yankee."

This incident agitated Martin out of all proportion to its importance.

He felt unnerved, almost wounded. When he heard his own breath, hurried and short, he had to smile, though a little sadly.

The cab rolled leisurely down Pennsylvania Avenue. Martin was interested at the breadth of the street, the vague flash of white buildings illumined by flickering street lamps, the long wide streets radiating off the avenue. The rain had become a drizzling pall; when a few red beams of the setting sun thrust themselves through twisted dark skies, they lay on the wet roofs of houses, so that the roofs seemed to run with fire. Hardly a soul was to be seen anywhere, except an occasional languid negro carrying baskets. Then the rain came down again with renewed chill fury, and the windows of the cab streamed with gray rivers. The dankness penetrated into the vehicle, causing cold threads to run up and down Martin's legs. The horse clop-clopped through the deserted streets, splashing up showers of muddy water.

The cab stopped before a tall narrow brick house with grilled balconies, grilled lower windows and tall narrow stone steps. There was a glimmer of rosy firelight on the stiff white curtains at the bay windows, and the light of a lonely street lamp glittered on the polished brass knocker on the door. Martin knocked on the door, and up and down the quiet, rain-running street the echo boomed with a faint and hollow sound.

The manservant who opened the door and took Martin's card informed him that Senator Sessions was at dinner with two guests. Martin said he would not interrupt, and was conducted to the library, a narrow lofty room, dark and chill, with a red fire lurking behind polished fenders. He sat down in a black leather chair near the fire, and looked about him timidly. It was a typical bachelor's room, without imagination or beauty, all black walnut and leather, gloomy books in gloomy tall bookcases, dark rugs and narrow windows, heavy sombre tables with claw feet, and brass lamps with round china globes painted with dim purple flags. A foreboding of defeat came to Martin, and he sighed heavily. He thought to himself: I am frustrated everywhere. Everywhere I am regarded as a fool, or worse. At the best, I get vague promises. Men are dying and suffering and being cheated, and I am advised to have patience, or to walk softer—softer! Rome, they say to me, wasn't built in a day. But it takes less than an hour, sometimes, for a man to die.

From somewhere across the damp cold hall outside came the faint boom of men's voices and laughter, the distant clink of silver on china, the short bark of a dog. Martin became more and more apprehensive. He stirred the fire vigorously, but the coals merely glowed without much warmth. He surveyed the result with discouragement.

He realized with bitter clarity, now, how silly this whole expedition might seem to the Senator. Nicholas Sessions, though vaguely fond of Amy, liked her less than his cousin May. He had seen more of May than

of Amy; besides, his niece was not the type to appeal to him. Martin was
the kind he could deceive very easily, but Amy was not. May, too, read
him without delusions, but she had such a whimsical and indulgent way
of reading him that he felt no offense, but rather enjoyed her mischievous
penetration. But Amy had a manner of looking at him with her clear and
steadfast eyes that made him resentfully uncomfortable. May had also
been his hostess for two years in Washington, and he had been gratified by the comments made on her by his friends and colleagues. He
felt uncomfortable with Amy, and though he always treated her with
avuncular affection, was generous as to her dowry, answered her letters
with more or less promptness, and presented each of her babies with a
golden christening cup, he was not inclined to regard her affairs with
real concern. Martin he recalled on rare occasions, with a slight pleasure
which had more than a little to do with the young man's apparent acceptance of him as a crusader for the rights of the oppressed. Martin was
more than a little aware of Nicholas' vagueness and real indifference
with regard to him and to Amy, and he was not relying at all on the
relationship to secure any assistance. In fact, he thought heavily, he
would have felt easier if Senator Sessions were a mere acquaintance.

A door was opened across the hall; light streamed out from it, warm
and smoking. Voices and laughter boomed like an explosion into the
dank coldness. Three men crossed the hall and entered the library.
The butler scurried into the room, lit another lamp or two, set down a
tray with a decanter of brandy on it and four glasses.

"My dear Martin!" exclaimed the Senator affectionately, as he advanced toward Martin with warm, outstretched hand. "What a pleasant
surprise! Why did you not let me know? How long are you remaining
in our fair city? Is Amy with you? No? You are looking splendid!"
He shook Martin's hand vigorously, clapped him on the shoulder, assumed the heartiest and most paternal of expressions. He put his arm
about the embarrassed young man, and turned to two strange gentlemen.
The color rushed suddenly into Martin's face. One of the gentlemen was
Mr. Stanton, whom he had met at the gates of the Kinsolving works.
Mr. Stanton bowed with an assumption of indulgent irony, but he was
exceedingly uneasy as he greeted Martin after Nicholas' introduction.
The other gentleman, an ungainly, shabby-looking man of indeterminate
age, with an ugly but striking bearded face and extraordinarily penetrating eyes, looked at Martin attentively while Nicholas performed the
introductions.

"Mr. Lincoln," boomed the Senator, "is almost certain to be our next
President, Martin. Martin," he added to Mr. Lincoln, "is much interested in the slavery question, also. Gives a great deal of money to an
abolitionist society. And that," he added grinning, "is the best and only
real test of a man's sincerity."

"I am sure, then, my dear Senator," said Mr. Lincoln genially, "that your sincerity has been put to the proof."

Nicholas laughed loudly, but his smiling face was exceedingly red. "Sit down, gentlemen, sit down! Brandy, gentlemen, of course? A gentleman, as you know, brags about only two things: his liquor and his horses. So, when I tell you that this brandy has not its equal anywhere, you dare not accuse me of vulgarity."

"Nor question your always unimpeachable veracity," added Mr. Lincoln. And again Nicholas laughed loudly, the color congesting in his face. Then for the first time Martin noticed his eye, and was startled at the steady baleful gleam of it. It was most evident that he hated Mr. Lincoln. As for Mr. Stanton, he merely listened to everything, smiled with a flash of small white teeth through his bearded lips, murmured polite inaudibilities, and saw everything. He looked steadily from Nicholas to Mr. Lincoln and back again all the time, as though he were a trainer calculating which of two powerful horses would win the race, and trying to determine which to ride.

Mr. Lincoln, who was unusually tall and lanky, settled his long body into a chair at the opposite side of the fire. He was a fluent talker, and his voice had a pleasant timbre for all its back-country flavoring. His clothes were badly cut, and looked sadly in need of brushing and pressing; his cravat was tied carelessly, and as he talked he had a farmerish habit of rubbing his right ear. His ugliness, Martin decided, was almost grotesque, but at times there was a flash and a gleam in it, a smile, that made it beautiful in a strange and compelling way. He had not been attracted to Mr. Lincoln, for he thought him too acid, for all his smiles, and he was afraid of people who could smile and thrust at the same time. It was, to him, like treading on treacherous ground. But now he saw, with surprise and confusion, that Mr. Lincoln's eyes were both sad and immeasurably kind, and that when he turned to Martin for his embarrassed comments on a remark of Nicholas', he listened with the sweetest of courtesy and gentleness. The eyes, Martin decided suddenly, belonged to a man who would never be cruel or brutal, exigent or ferocious. He had almost decided with a rare impulsiveness to mention the object of his visit to Mr. Lincoln, when Mr. Stanton abruptly reminded that gentleman that they had an engagement with Senator somebody-or-other in twenty minutes.

When the door had closed after the visitors, Nicholas said, as he helped himself to more brandy: "What do you think of Mr. Abraham Lincoln, Martin? As I said, he is almost certain to be our next President. I can smell the way the wind blows."

Martin, who had heard May confidently assert, dozens of times, that Nicholas would be the next President, asked naïvely: "But I thought you were to be, sir?"

Nicholas laughed, the florid coloring deepening in his broad face. "Sometimes it is best not to be President, Martin. I wouldn't take the job if I were drafted for it. Not for ten years, I wouldn't! As I said, I can smell something in the wind, and I don't like it. Let Mr. Lincoln, or anyone else, go polecat hunting. Not me!" Over the glass of brandy, he grinned at Martin. It was a fixed grin, and Martin, all at once, saw that it was cunning and unfriendly. And worst of all, he felt with abrupt sharpness, the unfriendliness was directed at him. He was alarmed.

"But tell me," said the Senator, with animation, "why this unheralded visit? Why did you not let me know? You, of course, are staying for a few days? Here, with me?"

"No, sir, I am not staying. I am taking the midnight train back to Windsor. I suppose I should have let you know, but everything has been so disturbed——"

The geniality went out of the Senator's face, and it became vague and smooth. "Ah, yes," he murmured. "I believe I recall something—" He put down his glass and stared at it. Martin, faintly frightened, leaned toward him eagerly. "Mr. Nicholas! I can see you have heard about it—all. And I knew—I know—that you would realize why I did it, and sympathize. And approve. What else could I do under the circumstances? You, of all people, who have been so much interested in slavery, have crusaded so strongly against it, even declared that the North would not hesitate to go to war to free the slaves, you understand! I thought to myself: Of all men in the world Mr. Nicholas would understand and approve."

Nicholas cleared his throat. He knew what he should say, but he could not bring it out yet. He was so good at this sort of thing; he knew so many sonorous phrases, so many lofty sentiments to express. He knew the exact gesture to use in this case, the exact opening of an eye, the exact expression and posture. But he could not forget that this young man was married to his niece, to whom Gregory had persuaded him to give a reluctant dowry, and that the dividends which were being "thrown away" counted up to a devilish large sum of money. If he had not been a member of the family, the sonorous phrases would have come easily enough, garnished with pious and appropriate sentiments; but it was a devilish large sum of money! He was not incredulous, as were the majority of people, about Martin's sincerity or sanity; he had met many such zealots, though none whose zeal was so damned expensive. Nicholas fleetingly reflected that few zealots had much cash, and he wondered if it were not a case of cause and effect. He liked zealots: where would a politician be without them? But his normal affection for this particular one was tempered by the thought that he was a member of the family, and that it was a devilish large sum of money to be going out of that family. Then he recalled abruptly that Martin's renunciation of the money had been given lavish space in many influential newspapers, and that he had not done Nicholas any harm whatsoever! He remembered with considerable pleasure that one newspaper, a radical but powerful one, had emotionally called to its many readers' attention the fact that Martin Barbour was the nephew of that dauntless defender of liberty and the rights of man, Senator Nicholas Sessions.

Still it was hard to strike the proper note when he replied to Martin: "Er—I believe I understand, Martin. I understand, of course, why you did it. Hum. I suppose I must say I approve." He made a vague gesture, smiled, ran his tongue along his inner cheeks. But in spite of himself, his tone was lifeless, his smile disagreeable, for all his efforts.

Martin sat back heavily. He put the back of his hand to his forehead. He was silent.

Nicholas was annoyed. This would not do at all. He could be ready enough to sound lofty sentiments when it came to anything else but money—his and his family's money. He saw that Martin had been repulsed, and he wanted to hold him. A zealot, even a family zealot who threw away good cash, was very valuable to a politician. He saw himself introducing Martin tomorrow to his colleagues, the more radical and wild-eyed ones whom he had not yet convinced of his sincerity. With these, his influence in the Senate was unpredictable in its possibilities. He could hamstring Lincoln if he were elected; he could ruin him. He could be the power behind the throne! Remembering this, he infused his manner, with no effort now, with cordiality and affection and warmth. He patted Martin on the knee.

"Martin, I have seen many men. But only two have been sincere. You are one of them. When I read what you had done, I could hardly credit it. Even tonight, I could not credit that any man had such faith in his own ideals as to pay cash for them. It—it was—Christ-like! Impossible! Sublime! Glorious beyond understanding or belief! I assure you, Martin," and his voice became solemn, eloquently shaken, "that you have done something that will awaken the nation to a new consciousness of its duty to its fellow men. You have given us all a new and heroic concept of the just life. You have given us an ideal. An ideal! Something that is bound to awaken the universal conscience, make the world a greater and a sweeter place in which to live!" His voice dropped, trembled as if with suppressed tears and humility, and he stood up, apparently overcome. He stood with his back to Martin, a strong man moved to emotion, trying to compose himself.

Martin's face had become radiant with a white light. "Mr. Nicholas, I knew you would understand! But I am afraid that you overestimate what I have done. It is very little. There is so much more to do, and it seems almost hopeless. I admit that I felt pretty hopeless when I came here tonight, myself. But I came because I thought—I knew—that you would help me. In a way, this situation in the North is as bad as the situation in the South. It has even greater peril for liberty and progress, and a decent regard for the rights of men. Slavery that is openly acknowledged is dangerous, but its very openness restricts it. But slavery that is unacknowledged and furtive, practiced in secret, cannot be controlled. It is like denying a pestilence, and so doing nothing to stop it, until life itself is destroyed. And that is why you, and only you, can help now."

What the devil! thought Nicholas, still trying to control the emotion of a strong man with his back to Martin. The idea that Martin was plotting fresh and perhaps more dangerous idiocies alarmed him. But he controlled his impulse to swing on the young man too abruptly. He allowed himself to sink, overcome, into his chair, to cover his face with his hand. Behind that refuge he need not be hypocritically harsh with his facial muscles.

"Tell me," he murmured. With his free hand he pulled out his handkerchief, blew his nose.

"Mr. Nicholas, the whole thing is wrong and unwholesome and menacing. Bringing this ignorant labor here in large lots to be exploited for the sake of larger profits. It is intolerable to American ideals and fairness, not to mention the inhuman side of it. It must be stopped. You have influence in the Senate. I understand there is a lobby against it, also, in Washington, but a very small and almost unknown one. But the whole thing comes down to this: the importation of alien contract labor must be prohibited by law. Appeals to decency can do nothing. Only the law remains. And that is why I have come to you. You can advance this law, introduce it, force it through, if not at once, in the near future. You can sponsor it; you have eloquence and power. With your help, it will pass."

So astounded was Nicholas that his hand fell from his face. He stared at Martin with the protruding eyes and open, slack mouth of utter stupefaction. His expression was one of complete imbecility, of entire inability to believe what he had heard. His eyes began to blink rapidly over their glaucousness.

Then, as he finally comprehended that Martin was not joking, but was in deadly earnest, dark color rushed into his face and fury into his eyes. His face was like the blank front of a secret house, whose windows and doors have suddenly and violently been thrown open to emit evil countenances and obscene voices, that could not longer be restrained inside. There was an enraged shouting within him, mingled with exclamations of incredulity. Was this man a fool? Was he actually appealing for this preposterous help to a man whose main income was derived from the very thing against which he was asking punitive measures? Was he actually so blind, so stupid, so devoid of common intelligence? It was all very well for him to cast lustre on Nicholas by his own self-denial, but to ask Nicholas to share in his lofty imbecility was insulting as well as incredible. It was like asking a wolf, whose jaws were already running with the blood of sheep, to help in the giving of protection to, and the saving of, the very creatures that sustained him. This innocence unnerved as well as astounded Nicholas. There was something appalling, something almost indecent, in this innocence, something contemptible. For one wild moment he thought that Martin was maliciously baiting him, that he was deep and dangerous, perhaps in the pay of enemies.

Then, in spite of all this, in spite of his screaming incredulity, he realized, with shock, that Martin was indeed innocent and simple, sincere and faithful. His reason repudiated this acknowledgment, but the evidence was before him. He gaped at Martin as at the denizen of a strange and out-of-focus world, strayed into a planet where ferocity was respectable and wickedness sanctified. He shook his head repeatedly like a man who has been struck with a heavy instrument. Such innocence, such unworldliness, such lack of ordinary perception, stunned him, tore his mask from him, left him aghast.

Finally, before Martin's puzzled and questioning expression, he saw his danger in his unmasking, and he violently pulled himself together. His efforts were visible. He was like a Frankenstein monster laboriously co-ordinating its movements. He made himself smile, though the muscles of his face ached. Martin only saw that he had become livid, and that the folds of his face were moist.

"What makes you think, Martin, that I would—that I could—do this?" he asked in a voice that shook without conscious design.

Martin's perplexity grew. The answer seemed obvious to him, and he smiled deprecatingly. "Why, sir, it is very plain. You have put yourself on record as against any kind of exploitation, as against slavery. You have defended the Constitution, have led debates in the Senate against injustice and greed. Who else is more capable than you to lead the crusade against alien contract labor?"

Nicholas poured himself another stiff glass of brandy with a shaking hand, and gulped it down. And then another. He began to sweat, his collar became too tight. Then he said, through a pleasant and dulling haze: "You overestimate my—er—my talents and my influence, Martin. I can see your point. It—it is very well taken. Very well, indeed. I—sympathize with you. Believe in you. But you must understand how things are, a little.

"Laws are not rushed through after sudden and unannounced introduction. The way must be prepared for them, the ground made ready. It is true that there is a small and poverty-stricken lobby here agitating against the importation, unrestricted, of foreign contract labor. But the people are as yet unaroused about it. There is a lot of preliminary work— Newspapers. Articles. Speeches. Remember, Martin, that a situation is not coalesced into a proposed law until long after the public at large has agitated for such a law, has perceived the need of it. Legislators cannot themselves introduce a law out of a clear sky. The public is a jackass, suspicious and easily bewildered. The legislator is like a musical instrument on which his constituents must blow a certain air before he can sound it. So far, the public, as I have said, is unaroused, unaware of this need you have proposed.

"Of course, there is another way. And that is by deliberately educating the people into seeing a need they never suspected existed. It can be done, and has been done. It takes a tremendous lot of money, paid committees, the impressing of newspaper editors, public speeches and agitations, fanfare, constant pounding at the public consciousness. This is a prodigious undertaking, vaster than a single man can undertake, too expensive even for a millionaire. And I am afraid that you would not be able to convince millionaires.

"No, there is only the slower, the deeper and the more natural way: the self-awakening of public awareness, the spontaneous demand of the public. On that you must hope and rely. You must have faith."

He stood up. He no longer wanted Martin to remain for display to his colleagues; he might say something that would be impossible for the Senator to live down. Laughter had killed stronger than he. Moreover, the very sight of Martin infuriated and frightened him. He could not see the last of him soon enough. It was like having a dangerous explosive in the house.

Martin was astonished when he found himself in a cab in the rain bowling back to his dingy hotel. He came awake through a cloud of bemusement. He remembered that the Senator had at the last been hasty though effusive, fluent in protestations against a departure that seemed to occur all by itself, full of messages for Amy and Gregory and May, expressions of affection for the children, lavish and meaningless promises and consolations and sympathies, agreements that perhaps he did have considerable that needed his attention in Windsor. Beaming smiles, handshakes, more promises, laughter booming and loving, exactions that Martin would take care of himself and let his uncle know— And then the rain and the cab and the closed door and silence, except for the sound of the wheels and the clop-clop of the horse through the dark and silent streets. The silence was what awakened Martin, brought him to himself with a start.

"Why," he exclaimed aloud, "he threw me out!"

Then all at once he burst into loud and dreary laughter. He shouted with it. The cabby heard it, told himself philosophically that his passenger was drunk. He had suspected it, the way the bigger man had led the younger and slighter to the vehicle, talking constantly and consolingly; the younger man had seemed more than a little dazed, had been deposited, like a piece of baggage, on the seat.

"I've been thrown out!" shouted Martin inside the cab. And he laughed and laughed until he could laugh no more, and the merriment had gone from his voice and only the dreariness remained, like a desolate whisper.

CHAPTER XLII

WHEN MARTIN told Amy the result of his interview with her uncle, he was astonished at her passion of anger against Nicholas. She trembled with her private suffering at Martin's humiliation; her indignation galloped away with her close family feeling, and she surprised herself by her unsuspected command of what Martin, sadly smiling, called her "strong language."

"But then," she cried, "Uncle Nicholas was always a rascal!"

"You knew that?" he asked, incredulous.

"Of course, darling. All of us knew. Uncle Gregory knows; May knows. Why, May has made fun of him a thousand times! She can take off his hypocrisies to perfection, and his bombastic speeches and gestures. He's too much of a hypocrite, though, to be a really big scoundrel." She pressed his head fiercely to her soft young bosom with a jealous and maternal passion of protection; she kissed his face and lips over and over, as though she were a mother kissing away tears. She knew, instinctively, that the tears were there, though they were not visible. Oh! she thought passionately, Who could hurt him? Who could have the heart to hurt him so!

"Uncle Nicholas," she went on after a moment, "never really cared about slavery, Martin. That was just a pose of his. All the poor black people in the South could be lashed or shot to death, and it wouldn't stir a hair of his head. I wanted to tell you that, but it seemed so necessary, I thought, that you should believe in someone. You see, all Uncle Nicholas cares about is that slavery might some day threaten his own profits, because a Northern industrialist might not be able to compete with Southern industrialists who employed slave labor without wages. Then, too, he has a personal grudge against a Southern Senator who blocked his appointment to the Supreme Court. So, you see, all the pretty roads lead right back to Uncle Nicholas."

"What a starry-eyed fool you must think me!" said Martin with bitterness.

"Darling, you must not say that! I think you are the best and finest of men, the kindest and truest. It is not your fault that you are Daniel in the lions' den. It is not your fault that the world is so wicked and stupid that it cannot understand an honest man."

Then she told him, triumphantly, of Father Dominick's message. Martin was immediately elated. But he was also puzzled. "I did not know that Ernest knew him," he said thoughtfully. "But how good he is to do this for me! I remember that he said something about not giving up hope, but I thought it was just his way."

He temporarily forgot his recent humiliation and disappointment. He was overwhelmingly busy. First of all, he bought a farm within four miles of Windsor, a little farm among softly rolling foothills, not very fertile but with tight buildings upon it. The house, of rough whitestone, was commodious and comfortable, well built and sturdy, large enough for a family of eight or more. There were big gardens behind it, both fruit and vegetable, an apple and cherry orchard, an acre of peach trees and another of pears. The hills in the summer were folded soft green velvet, intersected by quiet narrow streams that bore tiny plumed islets upon them. The farm was well stocked, and there was a flock of guinea-fowl that delighted the children with their anxious "pitty-querks!" Martin looked over the stock with satisfaction : three cows, ten hogs and their litters, six horses, one hundred chickens. Amy expressed herself as delighted, said nothing could be more perfect. If she lifted her skirts very high and tiptoed about fastidiously in order not to soil her boots in the mud, she maintained a bright and shining smile. If she was anxious because her time was close for the birth of another child, and she was wondering about obtaining adequate help and medical attention in this quiet and isolated place, she did not disturb Martin with these worries. She had appointed herself the keeper of his cheer, and for a long time never relaxed in this duty.

Martin was exceedingly hurt because Hilda promptly refused to accompany him and Amy "into the woods." Since Joseph's death she had become anxious and querulous, forgetful and irritable, keeping to her rooms in Martin's house and nursing what she considered some grievance against Amy. Amy never found out what it was, though she felt the antagonism of her mother-in-law. Hilda, too, had developed an extravagant fondness for little Godfrey James, Ernest's son, and was fond of relating loudly at all times, especially after Amy's babies had been unusually obstreperous, stories of his tractability, sweetness and good breeding. She knew, of course, of Martin's quarrel with his brother, and of his withdrawal from the Company, and was brutally tactless and outspoken about the matter. It was then that Amy created the grievance, for one day she said clearly and quietly to Hilda, in Martin's absence: "Mother, this is my house and Martin's. You are our guest here, and we love you. But it is not the part of a guest to speak so to her host, and wound her hostess like this." Hilda never forgave her for the twinge of conscience she inflicted upon her. Hilda considered herself of an age when she should be spared a conscience, and her many disabilities and sorrows remembered. So she took out her restlessness and sense of guilt and annoyance in more subtle but more galling ways. She complained that the children disturbed her, treated them indifferently before their parents, scolded them whenever she thought Martin or Amy might hear her. It was unfortunate that neither Martin nor Amy saw her devotion to the babies when she was really alone with them, and how she kissed them and wept over them.

The truth was that poor Hilda felt usurped and useless, ill in body, sick in mind and heart, torn with unending longing for Joseph, finding no interest or real pleasure in living, not even in her food. She had always been vivacious and vigorous, mistress of her household, a good-natured and competent scold and mother and wife. Now she had been relegated to the chimney corner, she thought; no one wanted her or needed her. Night after night she whimpered like a child into her ruffled pillows, and stretched out her empty and trembling arms for a body that was not there. Night after night she went over the deathbed scene, and bitterly blamed Martin for his refusal to protect Ernest against the accusations of their father. She perversely thought that in this Martin had made his father's death harder, had alienated Ernest long before the quarrel. She was the type of lusty woman who is wife and lover first, and mother only incidentally. Deprived of her lover, she found only irritation in her children. Had she been childless, she would have been happier.

The "girls" were not sure which was their home. Florabelle decided, finally, that hers was with her favorite brother, Ernest, for May was fond of her and liked her to occupy the best guest chamber whenever she desired, during school holidays. But Florabelle's several years at school had become quite enough, more than enough, and there was now the problem of her permanent home. Then there was Dorcas, who said her home was with Martin. But she was a delicate girl, and had had scarlet fever the last winter. Amy was doubtful that she ought to be far from refinements and the vicinity of her doctor.

So it was finally arranged that Hilda and the "girls" were to live in a small but fine little house near Ernest. He had vaguely considered bringing his women-folk to live in the Sessions house, but May exclaimed: "God forbid!" with astonishing frankness. Florabelle, she said, was a love, and she adored her. But she was also stubborn and given to pouting for days at a time. Dorcas was too silent and reserved, too unsmiling and proud and suspicious. "She gives me the vapors," said the candid May, who was envious of the girl's beauty. As for Hilda! May raised pious eyes and hands to the ceiling. It would be, she informed her laughing husband, just one cat-and-dog fight after another.

Martin, approached formally through an attorney, consented to pay one-third of the price of the house, and one-third of the cost of its upkeep and the maintenance of its inmates. These things ate deeply into his funds, he observed anxiously to himself. "Well, the girls are so lovely that they are bound to be married soon," said Amy consolingly. She privately cancelled half of her large order for new clothing; she was fond of fine gowns and laces and furs, and this was a real sacrifice. She sturdily decided that the new baby would not droop and pine because he could not have yards and yards of hand-made French lace on his dresses, and that one narrow border of tatting would do as well. So she tatted the borders herself. They would not entertain so much in the country, she told Martin, so really would not need three maids. One cook and one housemaid were more than enough. Also, one carriage.

A few months ago Martin would not have noticed nor heeded such deprivations, or, if he had, he would have thought it only right, the expected thing for Amy to do. But now he said somewhat sadly: "I am robbing you, my dearest."

"Do you think," asked Amy, "that all of these things together are worth your happiness?"

One day, three days before the removal to the country, Gregory called upon his niece in great agitation. He was realizing afresh how much he was attached to her, how much he really loved her and her children. He came to her without irony or sarcasm; he came in real perturbation and anxiety.

"Is it possible that he has converted you to his madness, Amy?" he asked, walking rapidly to and fro in the dismantled parlor, and kicking aside scraps of paper as he did so.

"Please, do not call it madness, Uncle Gregory. You hurt me so. No, I have not been converted. As I told you before, I can see it from his point of view, but I cannot feel it. I confess I would not do it, myself. Perhaps I am stupid in believing that one man cannot set his shoulder against the world and move it all by himself. He has to have help. Martin feels that no one will help him, so he is giving all his own strength. He has to do it; he is compelled so by his own nature." Her voice became very low. "And then, perhaps, it is we who are blind and mad and stubborn, and not Martin, as you seem to think. Perhaps it is we who lack understanding."

Gregory irritably waved aside her last words. "Yet, not believing in it, you allow him to rob you and your children without a word of protest, and in fact, even encourage him?"

"Uncle Gregory, it is the duty of a wife or a husband to do all in her or his power to make the other happy. Children, money, position, the respect of one's friends, friendship itself: these are absolutely nothing compared to the happiness of the one you have married. They should not even be considered for a moment. If it would give Martin happiness to give everything away to put us down in a log cabin, to surround us with poverty, then it would be my duty, and my own happiness, to let him have his way without a murmur from me."

Gregory was moved. "I believe you·mean that, my love. It seems incredible——" Then his violence renewed itself. "But you are elevating a self-appointed reforming fool to a dignity he doesn't deserve! There is nothing to be gained by all this, except jeers and deprivations and loneliness and anxieties. Martin is no great hero, no Savonarola, no Martin Luther or Moses or Voltaire or male Joan of Arc, though perhaps he considers himself such. He's just another tilter at windmills."

Amy forced a smile to her tired face. She rose and laid her hand on her uncle's arm. "Well, then, if he is just a tilter, I can carry his sword, and keep it from getting rusty. But you have not seen the babies for two weeks——"

Gregory sighed, then made himself smile also. "Where are the rascals? They're the prettiest things I've ever seen, Amy, twice the size of little Godfrey James. Ah, there's a puny little mite, God help him! Not much stamina there, or strength. Do you know, I'm beginning to think he looks oddly like your precious husband, my love. Much more so than do his own children. I hope to God we aren't going to have another reformer in the family! God knows this one is hard enough to bear." He growled: "All this talk of 'happiness'! I wonder if these self-appointed little Messiahs know what unhappiness they cause everyone else who is unfortunate enough to be connected with them!"

When the babies were brought to him, he held them on his knee and struggled to keep them in order. They had begun to walk now, and insisted on moving floorwards over his legs, his arms, his knees and his stomach. They were like an eight-limbed octopus, restless, hard-fleshed and vehement with strength and brassy of lung, and as hard to hold. Gregory exulted in them, rescued his watch a dozen times, choked on his pulled cravat, blinked his poked eyes, and laughed at their smiling mother over the welter of them. When they had been carried away, roaring, by their nurse, he said, with a little hoarseness in his voice: "Don't take them away from me, Amy. Damn it, I never meant to say this, but my own home is becoming intolerable to me! I have no complaint to make of May, except that she is becoming dictatorial and a little too managing; but damned if I will be able to put up with Ernest Barbour much longer without sneaking into his room some night and murdering him. No, truly, Amy," as she laughed enjoyingly, "I'm a man of few attachments, and you and your children are the only things I care a copper penny for in this whole world."

"We are not going far," said Amy, putting her arms about him, and pressing her cheek to his. "You can drive out in half an hour. And you know how we love you, how welcome you will be, dear Uncle Gregory."

He looked down at her, and it seemed to him that she was her mother the sister he had loved. He remembered, too, how much he had hated the man his sister had loved; yes, he was a rascal and a mountebank, but she had loved him. Then he remembered the night the message came, that she had married him, and how enraged their father had been, cursing his daughter and swearing she would get not one red penny from him if she starved for want of it. He could have done something then, thought Gregory; he could have softened the terrible old man, turned him back to his daughter, for his father respected his opinion. But he had not done it: he had been so outraged and bitter against her. Finally it was too late, Amy died, and then their father died, and there was the will and the baby girl. He thought suddenly: If I had spoken to my father, if I had softened him toward my sister, Amy would have married Ernest Barbour, and those babies would be his. The idea struck him so forcibly with its possibilities, that he could not help asking Amy: "Are you sorry, my love, that Ernest—that I did not want you to marry Ernest Barbour?"

Amy was startled. She looked up into his eyes. She did not know why he was asking, but she felt with sudden intuitiveness that should she hesitate, show the least sadness or faintest regret, she would hurt him beyond repair. So she said quickly, smilingly: "Of course not, Uncle Gregory! That is all gone and forgotten. I was just a chit, then, not knowing my own mind. And I do love Martin. Only *I* know how much!"

But he was still uneasy, gnawed by an obscure discomfort he could not name.

It was a raw and windy day when Martin's young family moved to the country. The trees were still bare, the ground wet-brown and running with cold water, the barnyard and gardens dismal, the chickens half drowned, the house still dank from unoccupation in spite of the roaring fires the maid had already built on every hearth. Against a pale jade evening sky, cold and cheerless, the hills were dark and irregular mounds and ridges. The meadows and fields ran from the house, dipping and rising to meet the hills, and the rail fences sagged gloomily in the muddy earth, which was still entirely without color, and full of miniature lakes and rivers. Just as the family arrived, depressed and damp, a cow set up a mournful lowing in the barn, and this hollow sound, combining as it did with the cold strong air, the utter lonely silence, the desolate meadows and the dark hills against the green sky, sent an icy wave of melancholy over Amy. Her hoops swayed gingerly over the muddy ground; she was carrying one baby, and the cook carried another. The gardener brought up the rear with several wicker suitcases and bags. Amy was already exhausted, and the weight of the child on her arm and body was dangerous. She looked up at the house as she approached it; it would be comfortable enough and homelike after awhile, she told herself stoutly, but just now it had a lowering air against the pale and livid sky. The curtains were not hung as yet, and the windows scowled at her bleakly. Her heart sank lower and lower as she stumbled up the muddy path; she had dropped her heavy skirts, now, and they dragged in the brown slime. Martin had been unable to come with her, for there were some last details to attend to in the city house. The beds for the hospital were already being brought in.

The maid opened the door as Amy approached it, and she could see the heartening glow of a fire beyond her. Amy dropped the baby with a gasp into the maid's arms, and the girl burst into loud exclamations of indignation. "Now, ma'am, you come right in to the fire, and I'll make you a cup of tea, that I will, and while cook starts supper in the kitchen I'll attend to these two poor little dears! The idea, a lady in your state carrying a big rascal like this! It is a shame and a disgrace, I do declare!"

The cook and the maid exchanged condemnatory and significant glances over Amy's bent and trembling shoulder; they did not particularly care for Martin, and with others of their class had freely discussed what he had done. The consensus of opinion was that he was a maniac to say the least, and a fool into the bargain. Amy they respected and admired, for she had no active interest in them, nor anxiety about their class, as Martin had. So her manner was always impersonal and indifferently kind, while his was always thoughtful and courteous. Her attitude, they thought, stamped her as a great lady, while his, so touchily conscious of them, so concerned for them, betrayed his more plebeian origin.

Everything was not yet in order. The babies were carried, scolding, upstairs, and Amy sank into a chair before the fire. She rubbed her hands exhaustedly in the warmth, glanced about her, shivering. Tables were still piled together, cushions heaped on chairs, pictures leaning against the dark walls, the windows livid and desolate rectangles in the dimness. A mahogany mantel clock, standing on the floor in the nearest corner, suddenly chimed sturdily in the silent and dreary room. Amy laughed weakly, looked at her dry and dusty hands, listened anxiously for the rattle of china and the heartening hiss of water on tea. But the kitchen was still silent. She could hear cook and the maid talking hoarsely together upstairs; one of the children had begun to cry. Amy remembered that the beds were still unmade, heaped with linen and quilts and blankets, and the thought of her bed, still stripped, its springs revealed cheerlessly, the mattress in the corner still wrapped in paper, overcame her. She began to cry, whimpering like a tired child, and childishly she wiped her wet eyes on the corner of the shawl she had not yet removed. "I am so tired," she whispered, looking at the jumbled furniture and the flowered rug which was scattered with sawdust and unpacked small boxes.

All at once she was sick with homesickness and helpless despair, not for the home she had left, not even for Martin, but for the Sessions house with its great fires and marble fireplaces, quiet lofty halls and chiming clocks, deep soft rugs and bookcases, rooms shining with candlelight, the subdued coming and going of maids, the distant smell of a delicious supper, the warmth and inviting comfort of the bedrooms. Her tears fell faster, became sobs and little cries. If she were just in her old bed, a girl again, without alarms and worries, without the burden of young children, without fear and anxieties, her life uncomplicated and serene and pleasantly dignified, all things and dreams before her, and someone, someone she loved, coming tonight!

Then she pulled herself together sharply and said aloud, as she wiped her dust-and-tear-streaked face: "This is all such nonsense, pitying myself this way! I am just tired and a little ill, and it is so silent here, so lonely, and everything so muddled. I'll be splendid again, tomorrow, after a good night's sleep."

She rose and went to a window. It afforded a wide view of the valley and the hills. But her heart sank again; all was pale and leaden sky, dark ridges, wet and colorless earth. Not a soul was to be seen, not a sound to be heard, except the dismal clucking of chickens, the melancholy throbbing of frogs in the pool at the foot of the garden.

Amy leaned against the cold window-pane and struggled with herself. The mental conflict seemed to extend itself to her body, and all at once she was alarmedly conscious of quick hot pain. "It can't be!" she thought. "Not for at least another month!" Terror rolled over her, filled her with sick weakness, set her knees to knocking together and sweat to break out over her face. She stumbled back to her chair, fell into it. The pain was more intense now, like the plunging of knives into her vitals. She cried out, again and again. The footsteps and voices still sounded dimly overhead; no one heard her. A grotesque fear swept over her that no one would ever hear her, that she would die alone in this place, away from her friends and those who loved her. She staggered to her feet, clutching her tortured body in her wet hands; she began to scream with terror and agony. A mist fell over her eyes, and everything danced before her: the red fire, the piled furniture, the pale rectangles of the windows. She heard someone screaming on and on down a dark tunnel, and she seemed to be dragged along that tunnel by the power of that screaming.

There was a startled confusion above. She heard that. But she also heard the outside door open, and three persons, entire strangers, came into the room, a tall lean old woman in a gray shawl and black bonnet, a short stout old man with a yellow beard, and a young man, tall and fair and strong. She stopped her screaming, but her eyes and mouth remained open and vibrating.

"Mein Gott!" exclaimed the old woman. She came forward, peering in the dusk. "It iss Mrs. Barbour, iss it?" She let the lightning flick of her old eyes pass over Amy. Instantly she became competent, understanding. Amy had a last impression, before the mists closed down upon her entirely, of being lifted, of a crooning voice in her ear, of confusion, voices, searing pain, a delicous mattress under her, cries, and prolonged sailing screams. Then total darkness.

At midnight, her second daughter, Lucy, was born. At dawn she awoke to find Martin, haggard and spent, sitting near her bed, in the hastily organized front bedroom, with the old woman. Through peaceful drowsiness she felt his kisses, his pleas for forgiveness; she heard him tell her faintly that the old people were Mr. and Mrs. Heckl, the young man, their son, Carl; that they were to occupy the tenant cottage down the lane and run the farm. Amy had one dim moment of weak amusement; it was so like Martin never to have told her this until now. She was grateful for the aid and comfort and competence of the old woman, who had most assuredly saved the baby's life if not her own, and somehow, as she fell asleep again, she felt safe with this woman near her, safer than she had ever been with Martin, whom she had had to protect, and would always have to protect, against the impaling points of life

CHAPTER XLIII

ONE MONTH later May's daughter was born, a dark-eyed, triangular-faced little creature who was named Gertrude.

Ernest had expressed a desire for another son, but he conceived a sudden, and to May, an absurd, passion for the little girl. He totally forgot Godfrey James for the time being; nothing was too good for the new baby. A cry from her in the nursery sent him leaping upstairs with more agitation than a mother would display; he discharged, with much violence, a nursemaid whom he suspected of a minor carelessness. When, at the age of one month, she developed a slight indisposition, he returned from the office at noon, unable to concentrate in his anxiety. To visitors, he would say: "My daughter!" as though he had no other child. When she was three months old, he bought her a fine fat pony and a cart, in which May was forced to ride, awkwardly carrying the baby. He started a bank account for her with a staggering deposit, though he had not done this for his son. Before very long, all Windsor rang amusedly with stories of his passion for his daughter, stories none too kind nor sympathetic. Ernest cared not a jot for this, probably never heard of it. He was immune to the dangers of ridicule, now.

Early in the year, Florabelle Barbour married Raoul Bouchard with great pomp and ceremony. Six weeks later, over her mother's protest and with Ernest's approval, Dorcas married Eugene Bouchard, with less pomp and ceremony. Florabelle was fond of Raoul, fascinated by his handsomeness and gay manners, but she was sicker of her mother's querulous discipline and prim, old-fashioned notions. Florabelle was pert of tongue and flippant of manner, two things that caused Hilda to utter dire prophecies of her ultimate end. It was to escape the constant scolding, reprimanding, regimentation of her home, that Florabelle married Raoul so precipitately.

Armand gave Raoul a fine large new house in a good quarter of Oldtown, where Florabelle proceeded to set up housekeeping in a grand style. Within an incredibly short time her soirées and dinners were famous for their food, conversation, gaiety, music, and the lustre of the guests. Having married a Frenchman, she archly furnished her new home with elaborate, frivolous French-style furniture, all tufts and brocades and dainty-colored damasks, pale gray walls and frescoed ceilings rose-silk hangings and pale primrose or blue rugs, pallid paintings of gay ladies dressed in Empire fashion, white carved commodes and gilt-framed mirrors stretching from floor to ceiling, spindly tables with delicate bow-legs and rosettes and leaves and blossoms, an ivory-colored piano and little gilt chairs. She would say to a new guest: "Ah, you see, dear Raoul is French, and my house must be in accord with his nature!" Raoul smiled, bowed, showed his brilliant white teeth, and cursed his pretty wife amiably to himself. He was too indolent, or too good-natured, to tell her what he thought of her furnishings, and how he loathed them, shuddered away from their pastels and gilt and carvings, kicked them savagely in private. Raoul's idea of a fine and comfortable home was the peasant's lusty idea: great stone fireplaces in which a man could stand upright, iron vessels with flavorsome contents bubbling and steaming on the fire, high, mighty featherbeds like vast apple pies, bare scrubbed floors, low, comfortable rocking chairs well cushioned, sturdy plain tables spread with checked or white cloths, thick plain silver, pewter cups, strong, plentiful wines in earthenware jugs, brass andirons, and a hooded cradle on the hearth. But he was really too fond of Florabelle to dismay her by telling her this; she was such a dainty little thing with her blond ringlets and sparkling blue eyes, dimples and tiny elegant white fingers, small plump breast like a white dove's, and a manner at once peremptory and coaxing. Had he told her what sort of home he preferred, she would have been horrified and disillusioned, almost broken-hearted. After all, he thought, she was a fine young lady from a fastidious female academy, where coarsenesses such as his desires were never mentioned, and everything was spun sugar, graciousness, politeness and silver filigree, tinkling of pianos and handling of fans, tilting of hoops, singing in high sweet sopranos and painting on china.

There was an awkward time when it was anxiously discussed as to how Martin and Ernest were to be kept apart at Florabelle's wedding. Florabelle had no love for Martin, said "pish!" with much pretty impatience and head-tossing whenever Martin was mentioned, and declared it to be a bore. Once she frankly suggested that he not be invited, but this aroused such horror, even in the indolent Raoul, that she poutingly dropped the subject. She did not like Amy, either, and thought it still more of a bore that her sister-in-law must be present. There was something in Amy's calm, her clear and straightforward eyes, her sweetness, integrity and lack of affectation, that aroused active dislike in the young Florabelle. She could not understand why everyone thought Amy such a great lady, and spoke of her with such respect. She, herself, thought Amy very plain and pale, without vivacity and those social graces taught at the female academy, which she had been assured were totally devastating to gentlemen. When she mentioned this to May, and her always-indulgent elder brother, she thought she discerned sympathy in May's faint smile and averted head, but was not at all prepared for the gust of livid anger that burst over Ernest's face. He sternly forbade her to criticize her elders, and stalked huffily from the room. Florabelle, in tears, turned to May for consolation, but May's expression had become rigid and cold as snow.

No one, whimpered Florabelle, ever saw Martin and Amy these days, anyway. If Martin was in town, he was at his old hospital, but Amy was always buried in the country with her babies and the chickens and the cows. Why, she had only seen her little niece, Lucy, once in all these weeks!

But Martin and Amy were invited, of course. They accepted, as was to be expected. But events saved the anxious ones the fear of a meeting between the two brothers, and spared them a lot of embarrassment. For Martin took quite ill with a sort of cholera a week before the wedding, sufficiently ill so that Amy would not leave him. The wedding present arrived safely, however, a small, modest little boudoir clock of old silver, all cupids and roses and leaves, with a piquant face of silver-gilt. Florabelle, daughter of Joseph, "bootlicker to Squire Broderick," turned up her pretty tilted nose at this gift, and hurried it out of sight. When May, with frank disapproval, called her a little upstart, and pointed out to her that Martin and Amy were now comparatively poor, and that the gift was in excellent taste though inexpensive, Florabelle merely tossed her head, pouted and wept because her sister-in-law was so harsh to her!

With Dorcas, it was an entirely different matter. She had a passion for her brother Martin that was deep, silent and almost fierce. Sometimes when she looked at his thin face, so worn and tired, so gentle and invariably kind for all its anxieties and the bewilderment that frequently stood upon it, she ached wildly with her pity and her love. She loved Amy deeply, partly for herself, and partly because her sister-in-law was so obviously devoted to her husband. At first, she had been inclined to be bitterly jealous of Amy, but no one of real perception could have been resentful of her for very long, and now her devotion to her was only less than her devotion to Martin. Martin's children had a share in her passion, and hardly three days passed in succession without her driving out in her own smart little buggy to the isolated farm.

Dorcas had grown very tall, taller than her sister, quite as tall as Ernest, and was not much shorter than Martin. Where Florabelle was petite, vivacious and dainty, all flutters and laces and perfumed kerchiefs and dancing ringlets, Dorcas was long of body and limb, silent, dignified, almost unsmiling, moving with slow and quiet grace, dressing in rich plain stuffs and dark furs and wide, untrimmed hats. Her beauty had become even more extraordinary than was expected. Strangers stared unbelievingly at the slim oval of her face, her clear white skin, her red, beautifully shaped mouth. Her dark blue eyes with their bronze lashes, her smooth silvery-gold hair in a great roll coiled on her long white neck, her tall, exquisite figure, her long and transparent hands, were incredible in their splendor.

Almost everyone was fond of Florabelle, but few people liked Dorcas. She had so little to say, was so cold and reserved, so without social arts, so evidently indifferent to the necessity of pleasing. She was shy, not with Martin's fearful and uneasy shyness, but with a shyness born of her real and inherent aversion to people. She had no genius for friendship, in fact, she had no friends. Many said disparagingly that she was cast in her brother Martin's image, but this character-likeness was in a measure superficial. For where he was silent because of an agony of embarrassment, she was silent because she had no desire to speak to those whom she felt were not in sympathy with her; where he was kind, she was polite; where he was simple and straightforward because he was without deviousness and guile, she was so because she despised others too deeply to take the time to be complex and illusive. Where he was apprehensive and weak, she was strong, for she had the courage of unspoken scorn. But she had his own passion for justice, hatred for abstract exploitation, contempt for craft and greed, indifference to money. Martin could be deceived by noble words, but no one could deceive Dorcas. She did not have his mercy and compassion, his keen sympathy for suffering and misfortune; but not even Martin suspected this, for she was constantly in his hospital, helping with the sick, tireless of body, ready and strong of hand, always attentive and efficient. (There was something of her brother Ernest in this phase of her character.) She saw there was suffering in this hospital, and coldly accepted it as her duty to help alleviate it. But much of this sense of duty lay in her desire to please Martin, to see him smile in gratitude, to have his confidence. Like Amy, she had a fierce desire to protect him and shield him, to stand between him and a reality that he sometimes painfully glimpsed and found unbearable.

It was a distinct shock to Martin when Dorcas told him quietly one late summer evening that she was going to marry Eugene Bouchard. He was deeply disturbed, and looked at her in apprehension and bewilderment.

"I know," said Dorcas in her quiet voice, "that you can't understand this, Martin, for you have always said that Eugene was much like Ernest. But he really isn't. He is very gentle and good to me, very honorable and true. And I love him very much. I believe I have loved him all my life."

Amy put her arm about the girl in silent understanding, but Martin rubbed his head in pale confusion. Then he said heavily: "I have never disliked Eugene, in spite of everything. I think he would be all right, if it were not for his aping of Ernest, and his attitude that Ernest can do no wrong and is all-wise and omnipotent. He—he is quite simple-minded about Ernest. He doesn't know that Ernest is blighting him, really

destroying him, eating him up as he tries to eat everyone up. I have noted
that though he unconsciously quotes Ernest, his nature is really against
what he is saying. Perhaps, Dorcas, you help save him from hardening
into a smaller mould of Ernest."

"Ernest will do no eating-up if I can prevent it," said Dorcas, with her
cold and lovely smile.

Ernest was proud and fond of Dorcas. Moreover, he respected her,
as he did not respect Florabelle. But he also thought her a little repellent
and pathetic. He wanted her to be married from the Sessions house, as
Florabelle had been married, but she refused. She would be married in
her mother's house, she said. Then the old impasse about Ernest and
Martin arrived tiresomely again. As the day approached, Ernest saw
that no act of nature was going to relieve him this time. Martin, from all
reports, remained healthy. Ernest finally confessed to Dorcas and to
May that he simply could not endure meeting Martin face to face, to have
to carry on the farce of smooth relationship. It would be, he said, too
much of a strain. Dorcas was to be given in marriage by Martin, so he,
Ernest, was not really necessary at all. He would remain in the background, watch the ceremony with himself unobserved, then quietly elim-
inate himself until the bridal couple had gone away and the guests had
departed. Though even Dorcas protested, everyone was finally convinced
that his decision was wise, though the necessity was exceedingly tedious

Martin gave his sister a bracelet of old gold set with exquisite opals,
her birthstone. Amy had chosen the gift, and May, who examined it,
said with all sincerity that it was the most beautiful thing she had ever
seen. "But then," she added a little jealously, "Amy's taste was always
irreproachable." She and Ernest gave the bride a string of magnificent
shell-pink pearls, "a quarter's dividends," Ernest had said, more than a
little ruefully.

Eugene was more thrifty than his brother, Raoul, and hoped until the
last moment that either Ernest or Armand would present him with a
house. But Armand remained bland, and Ernest, silent. Both of them
knew he had saved frugally for years, and had at least three times the
money that Raoul, the careless, had. Eugene personally possessed, in his
own name, ten per cent of the Kinsolving stock. Finally, when matters
were becoming embarrassingly acute, Armand offered the young couple
a home with him. The Canadian cousin, he said, could remain as housekeeper, and Dorcas and Eugene could refinish and refurnish the house
as they would; the expense, Armand added mischievously, watching
Eugene's dark and cautious face, to be entirely his son's. Eugene, after
consultation with Ernest, who assured him smilingly that the arrangement would be very economical, accepted with a gratitude surlily shadowed by his unspoken disappointment that a house of his own had not
been offered him.

After Dorcas' marriage, the problem arose as to what to do with old Hilda. She was bitterly set against going to live "out in the bush" with Martin, and May was still candid in her refusal to live under the same roof with her mother-in-law. So Hilda's state was pathetic, to say the least. She shut herself obdurately in her house while the debate raged outside. Of course, it was decided, she could not live alone. Her sons and her daughters-in-law came and went, argued with her, waved their hands helplessly. For nearly three months the argument went on, with Hilda, behind her curtains, grimly enjoying the new commotion about her, and the unwonted excitement.

Then, when things were really becoming desperate, Florabelle discovered that she was pregnant. She immediately subsided into a helpless and childish condition, wailed for her mother, longed to be girlishly free of the responsibility of a household. Raoul, good-natured and bored as ever, suggested that Hilda come to live with them. He was privately pleased at his own suggestion : he thought that for the first time a decently sturdy meal might be served on the frivolous table, and a secretly longed-for substantiality of living be restored to his existence. So Hilda, needed once more, and in triumph, packed up and went to live with Florabelle. There she scolded and managed, bustled and arranged, dictated and cooked, fought with the daintily aproned maids, and behind the silly gilt and damask and frescoed façade of the household built a sturdy background of stone and brick.

CHAPTER XLIV

FLORABELLE's and Raoul's son, Philip, or Philippe, was born amid great excitement, much running about with cologne and smelling salts, much screaming, tears, lacy pillows and ruffles, perspiring maids and nurses and two eminent doctors. It was Christmas, and the house was decorated with holly and hothouse flowers from the Sessions conservatory, and there was still a litter of papers and boxes and ribbons in the rooms when the young Philip Bouchard decided to make his entry into the world.

Four months later, Dorcas presented Eugene with a son, a handsome child they called Etienne, after Eugene's grandfather.

"The family," said Gregory bluntly to his cousin, May, "has become just a breeding kennel." May laughed with enjoyment; she always relished a little indelicacy. Besides, she was carrying, with much resentment, her third child; when he was born, they called him Reginald. Five months after his birth, Amy bore her fourth and last child, John Charles Barbour. He was born in September, 1860. Three months later, Florabelle, with much more fortitude than before, produced Jules, and Dorcas, six months after that, bore a sallow little daughter, Renee. Eleven children now composed the Barbour and the Bouchard families.

After Gertrude's birth, May accused Ernest of losing interest in her darling, Godfrey James, or Frey, as she called him. Ernest denied it conventionally, but he was indeed almost indifferent to his first born. In some vague and uncomfortable way, the child reminded him of Martin. He became deeply involved with Reginald, who was plump and robust, and rosy as a peach, but Gertrude remained his love and his passion. The little girl returned this love whole-heartedly, and May, subtly pushed aside, was tormented by a jealousy of which she was ashamed.

The young matrons were so busy, their husbands so occupied with the gigantically increasing business, that Martin and Amy, on their isolated and lonely farm, were rarely visited except by Dorcas. And now, she, too, was bearing children. Therefore, months passed without any one visiting Amy, alone with her homesickness and babies, having no companion but old Mrs. Heckl, seeing no friends whatsoever.

Martin, with the single-mindedness of the reformer and the altruist, lived and breathed only for his hospital. Father Dominick directed many of its activities. Its dozen beds were almost always filled, its two doctors having as other patients only those who were employed by the Kinsolving and the Barbour & Bouchard shops. Father Dominick had interested a few of the more affluent members of his parish, and by heavy and continued pressure, had induced them to part with money for the hospital.

It was, for that time, a model hospital. It was in charge of two Sisters of Charity, intelligent, middle-aged women from Canada. The other attendants were youngish and sober young women, clean and competent, who endured with silence and indifference the slurs and slights put upon them by the townsfolk. Many of them were German women. The doctors were young, one of them being the physician who had saved the life of the child that Martin had rescued. Though the theory of asepsis was as yet unknown, the hospital had remarkably few fatalities, even after serious operations; there was little gangrene, very little infection. The hospital was lavishly supplied with linen and blankets, the newest operative equipment, the newest medicines, the newest theories. "Why," exclaimed one lady who had inspected the hospital, "it is actually as clean as my kitchen!"

Martin called it Sisters' Hospital. He was proud of it, felt satisfied and contented. But it was taking nearly three-quarters of his dividends. Consequently, as it was a practically free hospital, he was obliged to canvass with grim anxiety and determination among the Catholics of Windsor, and even among the wealthier Protestants. With the latter, he had very little success, first because they considered hospitals pest-holes of infection and degeneracy: ("Anyone with a decent respectable home doesn't need a hospital!") and secondly because they were dourly suspicious of anything that smacked of "Popery."

It had been Martin's intention not to restrict the hospital to patients from the Company's shops, and their families, but to admit any one in Windsor who needed hospitalization. In discussing it with Father Dominick, he said: "Of course, those who can afford it must be charged a fee in accordance with their means, and those who have nothing must receive equally good care without charge." But in two years only eight patients from the "outside" were admitted and treated, and only three of these could pay the modest charge.

Quite incidentally, he was the reason for increased wages among the laborers of the Kinsolving shops, and even for the increase given to other laborers in the other shops all over the city. For Barbour & Bouchard were forced to raise wages as an inducement to their better employees. They had kept these men without any increases for years, for very few of them were able to accumulate sufficient funds to take them elsewhere. But now Martin had deposited a fund for discharged and quitting workmen, and to keep the better class, wages had to be raised.

He went about his work, grave and absorbed, returning to the farm at night so exhausted that he could barely smile at his wife and children. The two youngest, he hardly knew at all. He was unaware of, or indifferent to, the fact that he had become a storm center; that arguments about him, debates, quarrels, even fist-fights, took place in Windsor. He was a fool or a maniac, or a hero and an angel, according to the convictions of friend or antagonist. He did not hear the furies of laughter, the exclamations of contempt, the words of friendship and admiration, of which he was the cause. All he saw was his work. It gave him a joy beyond anything he had experienced to see a man's life saved, to see a child eased, a woman's agony decreased.

The farm, run by the Heckls, was self-supporting, which was a great mercy, for Martin had begun inroads upon his wife's income, and even the principal. This aroused such apprehension in Gregory, made him so aghast at its possibilities, that he came post-haste to see Amy, and in a great rage threatened that not another cent of his or Nicholas' money would go to her if the depredations upon her small fortune were not curtailed. He was seriously frightened; he saw Amy and her children, whom he loved, reduced to dire circumstances, to mere farm laborers sinking into the mud of monotony and poverty and hardship. He saw that Amy was pale and thin, smiling as if it were a difficulty, that she was already overburdened by the care of four children and a household, with only two women, and one of those an old woman, to help her. Remembering her guarded childhood and girlhood, the money, schools, jewelry, clothing and care he had given her, it infuriated him to see how careworn she had become, how roughened her delicate small hands, how drooping and tired she was when he caught her off guard. But to his shouts, oaths, accusations and epithets, she said with dignity: "You may leave your money to any one you please, Uncle Gregory. That does not interest me at all. But if Martin needs my own money, I shall give him as much of it as he wishes, even to the last cent."

"And what of your children, ma'am? Will your wifely devotion be enough to let you contentedly watch them starve?"

In spite of her effort to speak, Amy was silent and white with sudden fear. She looked at her children playing on the hearth, at the baby in his cradle, and involuntarily her worn hands clasped tightly together in the lap of her dull woollen dress. It was evident that she had considered this very thing very often, thought Gregory with grim satisfaction. With more pain than he would admit even to himself, he studied her profile against the fire, saw how pinched it was, how patient and wearily sweet her mouth, how heavy her eyes. And yet, in some way, her girlish prettiness had given way to beauty, and though she looked older than her twenty-seven or eight years, much older than May who was her senior by almost two years, there was a dignity about her, a chiselled-down and refined quality, that was infinitely moving and lovely. Gregory remembered a spiteful remark that May had once made of her cousin, that she would be old and fat at thirty, and he smiled bitterly to himself. May was well on the way to fatness, if not to age, and Amy was growing more serene and beautiful, more transparent and finer, as she grew older. She is a great lady, as her mother was, and my mother, he thought.

"Amy, my love, bring your children and come home, just for a little while," he said impulsively. She smiled, sighed, kissed him, shook her head.

That night she said quietly to Martin: "Dearest, Uncle Gregory was here today, and threatens to cut me entirely out of his will if any more money is taken from my principal for the hospital. Please, Martin, let me finish. I knew you would say it does not matter, but it does. After all, if Uncle Gregory leaves me considerable money, that will give you more for your work, also."

The result of this was that Amy's income was also swallowed up into the voracity of the hospital and the bank funds, though the principal remained untouched. The little family, in order to preserve the principal, was forced to curtail its expenses even more stringently, and the cook was therefore dismissed, leaving Amy with the entire household of children and work upon her hands. Mrs. Heckl, though strong and wiry, had her own work of butter-making, cow-milking, garden tending, preserving, chicken care, sewing and cooking, in her own small house, and could give Amy only one or two hours' assistance a day. Gregory, visiting his niece two months later, was overwhelmed at the sight of her. She looked extremely ill and exhausted, and the children were casually dressed and none too immaculate; the house, itself, had a film of gray dust upon it. Amy had her arms deep in a tub of gritty suds when her uncle arrived, and her thin face flushed scarlet at the sight of him.

This was too much for Gregory. In a cold grim voice he gave Amy two choices: either she would return home with her children until Martin could be brought to a decent regard for his family, or he, Gregory, would wipe his hands clean of her, never visit her again, and she and her children could go to perdition, or starve, for all of him. His voice was harsh, almost brutal, as he spoke to her, but inside he was aghast, full of rage and hatred for Martin, as he looked at her bedraggled skirts, her ill-combed hair, her sunken cheeks, her brown eyes grown cavernous, her lips a faint purplish outline in her gray drawn face. But though she cried silently at his ultimatum, she said with quiet majesty: "I'm sorry, Uncle Gregory, but I can't do as you wish. I can't leave Martin: how could I? I love him. I can't take his children from him. I can't destroy his belief in himself. He thinks that I am better than I am, that I am willing to sacrifice myself for a principle and an ideal, and how can I tell him that his wife is just a greedy woman who wants comforts and luxuries and

silks and jewels for herself? More than anything else in the world I
want his love and respect, I want him to feel that he has one person at
least who stands with him."

"Amy, my God! I never thought you would begin to mouth silly
platitudes! I never thought that you were a fool! Don't you remember
how we used to laugh at Nicholas, have contempt for his hypocrisies and
high-sounding periods that meant nothing at all? Have you lost your
sense of humor? Or do you think that you have to stand by a bad bargain, for pride's sake?"

She was silent for some minutes, then she said in a low voice: "Uncle
Gregory, vicious people and hypocrites have brought platitudes into dis-
repute. But it's not the fault of the platitudes. They remain. They're
true. False people make virtue sound disgusting and contemptible to
intelligent men, but we are just as bad if we can't pick the false people
off virtue just as we pick bugs off plants." She smiled sadly. "I'm not
really platitudinous, Uncle Gregory. And I wouldn't stand by a bad bargain; life is too short for that. Pride doesn't enter into it. The only thing
that matters is that I love Martin."

A nasty sneer lifted Gregory's upper lip. "Aren't you protesting just
a little too much, Amy? If you have said that once the last five minutes,
you've said it at least three times." He added with cold meaning: "You
are a hypocrite."

But sneers and arguments could not budge Amy, and Gregory went
off, swearing that he would never come to see her again, and that if she
wished to see him it would be in her old home. Amy watched him go,
tears running down her impassive face. She was too tired to resume
her work. The children were crying in the frowsy yard, and the baby
was screaming upstairs. But she could not leave her chair yet. She stared
mournfully and emptily before her, seeing the order and luxury and quiet
and peace and spaciousness of the Sessions house, remembering her
pretty dresses and the glossiness of her well-kept ringlets and the whiteness of her hands. Now she looked at her hands, and sighed, felt her hair,
and noted its unkempt roughness. But finally her soft mouth set itself
rigidly, as it had a habit of doing lately, and she rose heavily and started
to work again.

Gregory had heretofore told May and Ernest little of Amy's condition,
but this night he could not contain himself. He was flaming with hate and
grief and fear. May listened, horrified, looking from him to her husband
and back again. Ernest said nothing, but faint bluish dents appeared
about his lips. However, he finally said calmly: "It is Amy's affair.
Apparently she knows what she is doing. She is a grown woman, after
all."

But May quietly went out to see her cousin, taking with her one of her
own maids. Conditions were even worse than she suspected, but being

a young matron of resource and little given to useless exclamations, she lifted her hoops a little higher, tucked up her wine-colored merino skirts over her petticoats, wrapped a towel about her dark-red curls, rolled up her sleeves above her white plump elbows, and set to work with the maid, over Amy's feebly laughing protests. Within a few hours the house was gleaming, if shabby at the corners and edges, the babies were scrubbed, fed and asleep, Amy was resting on the worn sofa in the parlor, and May and the maid were busily mending clothing, while Mrs. Heckl worked over the stove and the pots in the kitchen.

May did not reproach her cousin. She talked placidly of their children, of the latest fashions, of the imminent threat of war. When she spoke of their husbands, it was with ease and indifference, and then only casually.

'When the weather is better," she said, "I will bring my babies out to see their little cousins. It will do Gertrude good, this fresh country air. She is not a strong child, you know, and is so wild and dark and thin, like a little gypsy." She sighed a little. "How strong and rosy and noisy your children are, Amy! I only wish mine were. Often I think mine are not normal, Godfrey James being so frail and timid. The child becomes sick whenever Ernest scolds him; he has such a delicate stomach, anyway. He actually runs from his father; I found him under the bed one day. And as for Reggie: he's only a baby, but what tantrums! Sometimes I think he will have a fit!" Then she added with pride: "But, did I tell you? Godfrey James is a real little musician, even if he is hardly six. He won't go out to play unless I drive him out; he likes to stay in the drawing room and strum on the piano. He can pick out little tunes, and he can even make them up! Ernest pooh-poohs it all, and frowns like a graven image, and says the boy is a mollycoddle and ought to be out fighting with other little boys; I am afraid Ernest has little regard for music, or any other of the arts. But he shall not frighten Frey out of his music!" She looked at Amy with a sudden obstinate grave face, and repeated, as though she were vowing to herself:

"No, he shall not frighten him out of his music!"

CHAPTER XLV

L IKE AN ABSCESS beginning to "point," all things were drawing to a focus as it was rapidly being conceded, even by the most conservative, that armed conflict between the States could hardly be avoided much longer.

The financial panic of 1857 had not blotted out the memory of the "war" between Pro-slavery and Anti-slavery settlers in Kansas. Even the Mountain Meadow Massacre in Utah stirred only a brief and violent horror, that soon subsided to the fearful and intense contemplation of the dark storm that began to mount into the national skies. When Hinton Rowan Helper's *The Impending Crisis* was published, a sort of dim frenzy fell upon Washington, in which all lesser issues of the day were obscured.

Then in 1859 John Brown raided Harpers Ferry, West Virginia, captured the United States Arsenal, and killed five men. The effect on the country was as though two opposite factions had been gathered in a great arena, watching a conflict between opposing gladiators; everyone was tense, pinch-faced and breathless, though the conflict seemed more or less formal and unexciting. Then suddenly one gladiator made a thrust, a deadly thrust: confusion fell upon the opposing gladiators, and they fell back. The spectators, already at a high pitch, rose in their seats with a great cry, standing aghast, but ready for violence. From them emanated disorder, fear, bewilderment, hatred and confusion; they looked about them with red eyes, waiting a signal to fall upon their neighbors. But the moment was not yet ready, and the spectators sat down again, trembling, on the edge of their seats, watching once more the gladiators resume their formal and prosaic fencing.

Ernest Barbour and the other members of the Companies knew that war was coming. They thought of their military contracts, and though they shook grave heads at each other, they gloated in secret. As far as Ernest was concerned, he was not interested in the causes of the impending war, nor was Raoul or Eugene. But Armand, remembering the bloody days in France, was uneasy. He had, he said querulously to his sons, seen enough dead men to last him all the rest of his life. He was mildly against slavery, but, he said, he did not believe all the black men in the country were worth a drop of a white American's blood. When, a short time after Abraham Lincoln was elected President of the United

States, South Carolina seceded from the Union, Armand declared that this State was only acting in accordance with her constitutional rights, if she considered the Union detrimental to her interests. For this opinion of his, he was ostracized from the society of his friends both in Oldtown and Newtown, a condition which he found reminiscent of his youth in France. Ernest, who considered Armand's expressed opinions very bad indeed for the prospect of continued military contracts, impatiently and angrily took the old man to task. But to his amazement, Armand suddenly flared back at him with brittle savagery and cried that he was now old enough to think less of money and more of truth and justice. "When I go out of the world," he said contemptuously, "I want to have a good taste in my mouth, instead of a sour." He added: "Let me feel virtuous once more, my Ernest, for the last time," and smiled with more bitterness than Ernest thought appropriate to his words.

"I cannot see how a debated question, on which many good men are divided, has anything to do with virtue," he said.

"But if it were a matter of money, you would soon see where the virtue lay, would you not?" asked Armand, with a cunning sidelong grin that revealed his yellowed teeth through his beard.

Ernest was not disturbed. He merely smiled. "That is not hard to see even now," he answered. "If there is a war, we shall have some fat military contracts. We are in the business, and have nothing to do with questions."

He was pleased about many things. The first petroleum well had been opened in Titusville, and he had been one of the first businessmen to take an option on the surrounding property. Already men were drilling on the properties, very slowly, to be sure, for Pennsylvania ground is rocky and grim, but Ernest felt that they would bring in vast amounts of oil. He had spent several days out there, watching the painful drilling, the rumble and steaming of the engines, the rhythmic rise and fall of the "bits." His shops were already developing a high explosive to "shoot" the well when it was ready.

Now that the rumor of the approaching conflict had burst in the air, Ernest went to see Senator Nicholas Sessions in Washington. Nicholas was more cordial and effusive than ever. He admired the young man, often told him it was too bad that he was born in England, that he was a born politician, and might have been President some day. He had acquired the mechanical gratitude of the politician, and did not forget that Ernest had been more than lavish with party and campaign funds, and that he had, in fact, dragged Sessions Steel from desuetude and dry rot, had bolstered its weakening timbers with the strong iron clamps of his genius. Ernest, he remembered, was responsible for his own increased power and luxury, his own immense fortune. Moreover, Nicholas was fond of his cousin May, appreciated her frank realism and witty candor.

He had also acquired something of Ernest's passion for little Gertrude, and had secretly left a large share of his fortune to her.

Ernest was brief about his visit. A new armaments company had sprung up during the past five years, which, while it did not as yet seriously threaten the strength of Barbour & Bouchard, was reputed to possess very formidable patents. The president of the company was one Angus MacIlvain, a Scotsman, who had British patents, one of which, it was rumored, was a seven-chamber repeating rifle. He was trying to get this rifle patented in the United States, and if he were successful, Barbour & Bouchard would certainly have something to worry about, especially if a war should actually come.

"You want me to keep The MacIlvain Arms from bidding, eh?" asked Nicholas. "And how am I to manage that, pray?"

"Easily," replied Ernest smoothly. "You see, old MacIlvain's son, Robert, is running for State Senator on the Democratic ticket. Now, you see, it is very simple: he's old Angus' only son, and the apple of his eye. You, Senator, are a Democrat also, and due to the peculiar circumstance that you support Lincoln, and stand behind him, according to the papers, in spite of being a Democrat yourself, this gives you strength with both parties. So, I am wondering——"

"If it could be arranged to swap old Angus' son's election, through my support in a State gone Republican, for the patent for the repeating rifle?" Nicholas' smile was sour but admiring. "What makes you think old Angus will agree to this swap?"

"There is only one thing that a Scotsman likes above money," said Ernest, "and that's public honor. I think he will trade."

"And you will proceed at once to manufacture repeating rifles, eh?"

"Not at all. We would have to scrap our present machinery, and I haven't gotten my money's worth for it yet. I would just hold the patent for a couple of years, or so, and if I thought it justified, I would then have new machinery made. Besides, things have been very bad, lately, and I have thousands of rifles already made. I would dispose of them first."

Nicholas was doubtful. "The war outcome may depend on the repeating rifle," he said. "I don't know whether or not it would be treason to withhold it from the Government."

Ernest smiled, rose, put his hand on Nicholas' shoulder. "Let me worry about the treason, Senator," he said.

"I should imagine, my dear Ernest, that you have had that worry more than once," Nicholas grumbled. "Well, I'll think it over. Perhaps in a month or two, I'll send for young MacIlvain, and have a talk with him."

"That will be too late," Ernest replied decisively. "It must be seen to at once. You forget that the British, especially the middle class, tend to sympathy with the South, and once war is declared, or definitely in the offing, nothing short of assassination will get that patent from old Angus. I have reliable information that he is about to withdraw it from the Patent Office as it is."

Nicholas detested being pushed, and he burst out irately: "All right, then, do it yourself! Use my name if you want to, but do your dirty work yourself! After all, you are an Englishman, and you ought to get down to business with MacIlvain better than I can."

Ernest laughed. "I am an Englishman, Senator. And Angus is Scotch. The Scotch like us little better than do the Irish. No, only you can handle this. Will you let me know within the next two weeks?"

One month later Ernest filed the plans for the repeating rifle in his iron safe, locked the strong door, and dusted off his hands.

On April 12, 1861, Fort Sumter was fired upon by Confederate troops, and the War Between the States burst like a blinding shell into the fields of peace.

CHAPTER XLVI

THE WAR between the States came like a personal agony to Martin Barbour.

"It is not necessary to kill men to save men!" he cried, over and over, to Amy, and to Gregory, who had forgotten his vow never to come to this house again.

"I am not aware," said Gregory cynically, "that this is a war to save any men, even black men. Of course, I read only seventy-five per cent of what Lincoln says, so I may have missed something. Perhaps you can tell me if he has declared this a holy war, for the express purpose of invading the South to free black savages and give them the status of civilized men."

"Of course, he hasn't said anything of the kind!" Martin exclaimed excitedly. "But that is the real purpose of the war, to remove this blight from our civilization, this monstrous degradation of men by men."

"I thought," said Gregory, "(but please correct me if I am wrong) that all this fighting was to preserve the Union. But you, perhaps, are privy to secret councils, and if so, I apologize for my ignorance."

Amy was mortified at this baiting of her husband, and somewhat sharply she said to him: "Nothing is ever so simple as you believe it is, Martin. You only see one clear issue, but there are many in this war, as there are in all things. It is deeper than slavery, deeper even than the right of the States to secede. It is compounded of all the ignorance and jealousy and hate and greed and stupidity in our country today; it is made up of sectional patriotism and provincial senselessness. Yes, and the idealists aren't free from blame, either, for they have fomented ill feeling between the North and the South, and have frothed all over the place over problems they know nothing about. It's easy to be virtuous about your neighbor's failings, when you haven't the slightest idea of his reasons for these so-called failings."

"Amy!" Martin was aghast, deeply hurt. Gregory laughed loudly. "Martin is a stylite," he said. "And stylites don't get around very much. Come down off your pillar, Martin, and travel about a bit."

But Martin was too busy in these days to be much troubled by gibes, though Amy's defection depressed and bewildered him. His was the type of spirit that can endure anything from a stranger or enemy, but cannot stand the slightest opposition or sharpness from one it loves.

He was rapidly becoming very poor. All his income and practically all of Amy's was being swallowed into the hospital and the bank funds for the laborers. Moreover, he had extended his operations into a swarm of lesser charities. Missionaries, free schools, orphan asylums and prisons absorbed what small crumbs remained. The farm was poor, and though Hans and Carl brought to it the knowledge culled by generations of workers on poor land, and made every yard of earth yield beyond belief, the crops were barely sufficient to support the family, pay taxes and buy seed. But they stood behind Martin like monks behind an angelic abbot, and if old Mrs. Heckl grumbled, or Amy sighed audibly, they were outraged. They would have gone hungry to please Martin, to help him, and could not understand the selfish female nature that could find no pleasure in hardship and poverty for the sake of Martin. When Mrs. Heckl protested at the selling of the last two sides of bacon, pleading Amy and the children, they were horrified, refused to listen. But Mrs. Heckl ran and told Amy, and Amy, who would endure anything but depriving her children of food, came out across the fields to the smoke-house, confiscated the meat, and brought it back to the house herself. There was about her such still anger, such cold white fury, such bitter silence, that the two devotees could not say a single word, and tactfully refrained from telling Martin.

Amy was no saint. She was approaching the point where even her steadfast affection for her husband, her desire for his happiness, would break. She looked at her children, in their patched clothes and rough shoes, and set her mouth. Paul and Elsa were seven years old, almost eight, and had not yet gone to school. There were no schools in this isolated section, and not even within four miles. Nor could she afford a governess for them. She taught them herself, but she was so crowded with work, so exhausted after this unusual and strenuous effort, so wearied from the prolonged nursing of the baby, that she could spare the twins only an hour or less a day, and then only when she had to sit down to sew or knit for them. It did not matter to her that she was aging before her time, that her shoes were breaking at the seams, that she had not a decent gown to her body, that her nails were black and broken, and that her bones ached constantly; but she was coming to the point where she would not have her children suffer any longer. Sometimes she dared not speak to Martin for fear of the rage that would burst from her mouth; sometimes she had to leave the room, trembling, pleading weariness. Sometimes, in fact, she almost hated him. She did not want to have May or her sisters-in-law see her condition, and so discouraged their visits. She found May's shocked expression unbearable, and Florabelle's uplifted eyebrows, smirk and dainty shrug almost impossible to stand in silence. Once she saw Florabelle frown delicately at the shabby rugs and fastidiously lift her skirts from contact with them, and something close to a homicidal impulse rose in the gentle Amy. Worst of all to endure was Dorcas, who observed everything, sympathized with nothing, but instead wore a certain smug expression of rectitude which testified to her opinion that Amy was doing nothing that was not her duty to do.

For several long weeks after the war had commenced, Martin wandered about in a sick and absent daze, talking to no one, not even to Amy. Finally he wrote to Nicholas and offered his hospital to the wounded. To his amazed and almost incredulous delight, the President wrote him personally, thanking him for the offer and promising to take advantage of it. Not a month later the hospital was crowded with the wounded and dying soldiers, and Martin was again taken out of himself, and was happy. He took food from the larder for the soldiers, dainties such as home-made jams which Amy had put up herself. So, she took to hiding delicacies, caching them away like contraband.

She was never quite certain when the change of attitude about the war came to Martin, but she did notice, eventually, that he spoke less and less of its wickedness and futility, and more and more confidently of the great good that might come out of it. He began to speak of Sacrifice in rounded periods, and Amy, who was sick to death of the word, which seemed to her the ugliest in the whole language, was filled with apprehension. At last Martin suggested to her that she might fill her spare time rolling bandages and knitting socks for the soldiers. "Spare time!" Martin thought Amy had never looked so strange, so white, and her eyes had never blazed so upon him. But after that first exclamation, she said nothing, merely rose quietly and left the room. Nevertheless, she did not roll bandages. Mrs. Heckl, however, was prevailed upon to do so.

One day Martin came home and told his wife that Carl had enlisted. He spoke quietly about it, but his handsome face was alight. Amy, suddenly weakened, sat down abruptly.

"But, Martin! Old Hans cannot manage this farm alone! And this is all we have to live on!"

"Amy." He took her hand gravely, looked into her eyes. "My dear, you must try to do as other brave women are doing: the best you can. Other women's husbands and sons have left their farms and gone to war, and the women have taken their places as best they could——"

Amy rushed into a wind of hysteria. "In the fields? Do you want me to work in the fields, Martin? Do you want me to do the milking and the threshing and the weeding and the hoeing? Is that what you want?"

"Amy! Did I say so? I shall get you a young boy, under military age, to help you, as soon as possible. But you must try to get along as best——"

However, he found he was speaking to empty air, for Amy had fled. He remembered, troubled, that more and more she was fleeing like this from his presence, as though she were carrying a dangerous bomb outside before it exploded.

A deep loneliness and heavy melancholy were settling upon him of late. Amy never reproached him, never complained, but he felt that a chasm had opened silently between them. He could not understand it; simply, he could not understand it. When he spoke of the hospital, she was silent, where she once smiled. When he elatedly told her of some injured man making an almost impossible recovery, she pressed pale lips together and continued sewing; once she had shared his elation, or at least appeared to share it. A sick suspicion came to him that perhaps Amy had never really felt about things as he felt about them. Why then, he asked himself, had she ever consented to do as he wished? It did not occur to him, in his simplicity and single-mindedness, that a person might do some things against all his desires, all his deepest impulses, merely for love. He could not have imagined himself going against his convictions even for love. That would have seemed to him hypocrisy and self-betrayal. He loved Amy with all his heart, had once felt that there was nothing devious or secret between them, and could not believe that she would be either hypocritical or self-betraying for anything or any one.

She and Martin had reached a place, thought Amy in despair and cold pain, where they could no longer continue without an explosion that would be irreparable. In terror, she realized that she could remain silent very little longer, that passions and wraths and indignations, perhaps even brutalities and greedinesses she had never suspected in herself, must burst out from her like wild beasts escaping from behind bars. She could not hold them back much longer. I am not a saint, nor a heroine, she would think despairingly. I am a woman, with a right to comfort and happiness, and security for my children. He has no right to subject me to this! But I am much worse: I should never have consented in the first place. I thought I was doing it for his happiness, but it surely won't make him happy to know that I have lied all along, that I have hated and loathed all this; it won't make him happy when I scream into his face that I must go home to comfort and warmth and peace and dignity, or go mad. I have been very wrong, God forgive me!

One night she reached the breaking point. "The young boy under military age" was a loafer, and useless. The woodbox was empty, and the weather was still chill and damp with early spring. The baby developed a cough and fever, and Amy remembered that there was a load of washing to be done, that Mrs. Heckl had not had time to do. She was feeling ill, herself, and all at once, she burst into cries and screams that brought Mrs. Heckl running, pale as a ghost.

When Martin returned home, he found his wife in bed, quiet now, with resolutely closed eyes and bitten mouth. Mrs. Heckl was pottering about with the evening meal, and the children were subdued for once.

Martin went directly to Amy, took her hand, murmured sympathetically, kissed her cheek, and wondered wretchedly why she did not look at him. He had so much to say to her, and finally he burst out with it impulsively:

"Amy, darling, look at me." He laughed a little, drearily. "You won't have many more chances. Amy, please tell me it is all right, love. You see, I enlisted today. I'm a Captain, now, in the Quartermaster's Corps, with the Third Division. I leave day after tomorrow. I'm not fighting; only helping with the supplies, and things, bringing up the rear, helping——"

He stopped suddenly, for Amy was sitting bolt upright in bed, red blotches on her white face, her eyes staring at him wildly, her mouth open and gasping. He was frightened by her expression, tried to put his arm about her, but she recoiled.

"Amy! Please, love! I won't be in danger. You know I would never bear arms, that I would never kill. But this is different, being in charge of the food supplies, and so on. Such as blankets and medicines, tools and horses. I—I had to do it, darling. Everyone else was going. It was my duty——"

But she had burst into laughter, loud and shrill, a little savage, quite terrible, and not to be controlled.

CHAPTER XLVII

MARTIN'S FAMILY was stupefied at his enlistment. They had no sooner heard of it than May and Florabelle, Dorcas and Hilda, called for their carriages and descended upon the frowsy little farm. They found Amy alone with the babies, working in the garden in the pale spring sunshine. She stood up as she heard the twittering of voices and the swish of silk coming up the broken walk, and her female relatives had a horrified glimpse of her, tall and thin and mud-stained, her skirt bedraggled, her hair in a loose swinging braid down her back, her hands black and moist with earth, her face with its fine pale skin drawn and weary in the disillusioning light.

"Why, she has become a slattern!" thought Florabelle with smug disapproval, forgetting her lowly origin, and feeling exceedingly superior to this daughter of "gentry" and prideful aristocrats. Dorcas felt a sudden uneasy doubt of her adored brother's wisdom, when she saw Amy, and for the first time a real pity for Amy and indignation against Martin made the color rise high in her smooth cool cheeks. May exclaimed out loud compassionately, and ran to her cousin with outstretched and perfumed arms, overcome with anger, her hoops tilting vehemently, her red curls spilling from the blue silk bonnet that matched her blue silk dress and dark blue shawl. As for Hilda, plump and gray and bellicosely florid, she stopped short, folded her black silk arms upon her bosom and said loudly: "Well, I must say! Charity begins at home. Seems to me that Martin has lost his good sense, if he ever had any!" And tugged her black shawl angrily over her shoulders.

But the children, running to meet their grandmother, were sturdy and brown, with cheeks like wine-saps and eyes that blazed. Their clothing was shabby, even ragged, and the twins were barefooted in the warm spring earth. They leaped about her, tall Elsa and Paul, and fat little Lucy, like boisterous puppies, thrusting their muddy fingers greedily into her reticule for the sweetmeats she always brought them. She bent over them, grumbling and scolding, her bonnet rattling with jet, and kissed them roughly and soundly. "It's a shame and a disgrace!" she shouted. "I'll give Martin a piece of my tongue!"

They had not seen Amy since Christmas. At that time the earth and the garden and the house roof had been covered with snow; fires had burned high on the hearths, the candles had glowed on table and mantel, and the sky had been low and gray over smoking chimneys. But the spring sunshine revealed all the shabbiness of house and grounds, the sagging fences and dusty windows, the oozing earth, and the ashes in the fireplaces, the grimy rugs and scarred old furniture. The four female visitors stood in the disordered parlor, looking at each other, aghast, making an island of themselves of hoops and shawls and ribboned bonnets and velvet reticules, perfume eddying from them, their bracelets jingling. Florabelle shrank from the children's dirty hands, Hilda, with renewed scoldings, tried to brush them off with her kerchief, Dorcas kissed their soiled hard cheeks. But May held her cousin's rough hand, and could not speak for the tears in her throat; however, her dark eyes burned and welled, and her lip trembled.

All of the women had come to scold Amy roundly for her weak acquiescence in Martin's latest folly. Only Hilda and Dorcas were alarmed for him personally. Florabelle thought he was making himself "ridiculous," while May was outraged at his treatment of her cousin. But looking at the tight pale grimness of her once soft mouth, at the still bitterness in her once gentle eyes, none of them could speak of Martin yet, they could only look upon Amy with pity and concern. Even Dorcas thought Amy excessively foolish in allowing Martin to absorb the very sizable income from her dowry.

Amy explained, simply, that she could offer them nothing but some indifferent tea, as Mrs. Heckl was ill with rheumatism and had not baked for several days. However, she said, she had some good wine which Gregory had brought her, and she produced it and four chipped glasses. The ladies sat gingerly on the dusty furniture and sipped the wine, which was beyond their expectations. Then May, unable to contain herself, burst out: "Amy, I can't forgive Gregory for letting you come to this, and not telling me!"

"I don't know about that!" said Hilda sourly. "Seems to me it's Amy's fault as much as Martin's. Of all the silly things, and all that money, too!"

"Suppose we don't talk about that," Amy interrupted, smiling. But her expression warned them off. "I know you have come to shout at me for letting Martin enlist. I am sure, if you will think about it for a moment, that you will remember that nobody 'lets' Martin do anything. He does what he thinks is right." The faint twist of her lips as she said this was indescribably wry.

"Raoul thinks it is absurd!" said Florabelle.

"Eugene," said Dorcas hesitantly, "thinks you might have done something, Amy, but I suppose you understand Martin best. I only hope that nothing happens to him," and her voice broke.

"I don't care what happens to him!" cried May, the muscles rising in

her white throat, and her hands twisting her handkerchief violently.
"But I think it outrageous for him to reduce my cousin to this! Perhaps
it is best that he is going away; maybe Amy might have some decency in
her life, and some comfort." She swung upon the others passionately.
"He is your son and your brother, and——"

"And he is my husband, May," broke in Amy's voice, cold and incisive.

After awhile they went away, dissatisfied and discontented. When
they had gone, and the children were outside again, quarrelling over the
candies their grandmother had brought them, Amy sighed. She had not
told any of them that Martin had already gone; he had left that duty to
her. "I couldn't stand seeing my mother cry, and Dorcas, too," he said
simply. "Eugene and Raoul and Armand aren't my friends any more;
you can't run with the hare and hunt with the hounds, and they can't be
Ernest's friends, and mine, too. So, I won't need to say good-by to
them." But Amy, today, had not had the strength to tell them.

Sitting there, her tired hands slack on her mud-stained knees, she
remembered the last morning she and Martin had been together. She
had not slept much the night before, and the baby, John Charles, had
been restless, too. She had watched the windows become gray, and finally
blue with the early morning sky. She had gotten up to help Mrs. Heckl
with the fires and the breakfast.

A terrible constraint had grown between Martin and Amy since the
night he had told her of his enlistment. Neither could leap over the abyss
whose bridge Amy had destroyed with that wild and uncontrolled laughter. Amy felt internally frozen, and beneath that icy crust raged
things she dared not let come to the surface. Martin had been frightened
by that outbreak from the controlled and usually soft-voiced Amy; he
had seen something in her face and her eyes in the space of a few seconds
that was strange to him, and savage and fierce, like something primitive
fighting for survival, something terror-stricken. The Amy he knew had
gone, and it was a hating stranger who had looked at him. He was still
bewildered over it; he was almost afraid to speak to this shadow of Amy,
for fear it might turn its face upon him and show him again that
stranger's face. In Catholic mythology he had once read of a demon
driving out a woman's soul and taking its place in her body, and though
he smiled a little sadly to himself at the memory, he thought it somewhat
appropriate.

Then the morning of his going came, and the abyss lay between
them, bottomless. During the past few days they had talked very little,
and then only quietly, as if afraid of disturbing something that had best
not be disturbed. Martin had talked only of business matters. He had
left the affairs of his hospital, the bank funds, his charities, in the joint
care of Amy and Father Dominick. He did not add that he had left his
will also, in the priest's care.

On his last morning at home, Martin was heavy with grief. He watched Amy timidly as she moved about the table, but she did not glance at him. He was afraid of her white grim face, and he could see the bony line of her tight jaw. Moreover, the fact of his fatherhood had come home to him very closely, and he could not get enough of his children. He held the fat baby, John Charles, on one knee, and Lucy on the other. The twins stood at his side, jabbering, demanding to know just what exactly he was going to do in the war : Was he going to kill lots of wicked Rebels? Would he bring them a Rebel gun when he came back? If the war lasted long enough, would he let Paul go with him as a drummer boy? And could Elsa nurse in a hospital? The twins, who had always been a little reserved with him, instinctively guessing that he lacked their brand of robust vitality, stared at him with blue and shining adoration. He had justified himself in their eyes. Lucy tugged at the brass buttons on his new dark blue uniform, and the baby pressed his round face against Martin's chest in order to bite one of the shiny things. He kissed them repeatedly, holding them closely to him, and Mrs. Heckl, coming back and forth with the breakfast, thought the sight a beautiful one. She thought Martin looked like a fair angel in uniform, with his children about him.

Then had come the moment of parting. Amy and he stared at each other for a long minute, then, with a cry, Amy was in his arms, clinging to him, sobbing incoherently yet dryly, holding him, clutching his arms. Finally, he had to push her away. He ran out of the house, and got onto his horse. Amy rushed from the house, came flying down the path, clutched his reins, looking up at him with a distorted face. "Don't go, Martin, don't go!" she cried, over and over.

He carried that memory of her as a sort of comfort and renewed joy, into the Army, into danger, and finally into death. She loved him still, and that, at the end, was all that mattered.

Thinking of all this, as she sat by her cold and ashen hearth this spring day, Amy began to cry silently, wiping her eyes on the edge of her apron. Something crackled in her bosom, and she withdrew a letter she had received that morning from Martin, sent from Washington. She re-read it, her tears staining it.

"I'm not trying to be a hero or a reformer, Amy, dear," he had written, "but I do believe it is the duty of everyone to save and not to destroy, to conserve and not to devour, to speak gently, and not brutally, to be merciful instead of cruel. To set himself against viciousness and treachery, wherever he may find them, to fight injustice and hatred, because they are enemies of mankind. You would not think I was making a gesture if I jumped into the river to save a life, or ran into a burning building to drag out a victim. Yet a man who speaks out against injustice and cruelty, greed and hatred, is ridiculed, even though he is really trying to rescue men and women and children from dangers more deadly than water and fiercer than fire. Ernest always called me 'feckless,' but I assure you it requires more than ordinary courage to take that epithet in silence and continue doing the very thing which has called it out. It takes courage to be yourself, though Ernest would say it requires only money. So, in doing what I am doing now, I feel that I have done the thing I must do, not even sure it is right, but certain that it is not cruel and not for self-gain."

CHAPTER XLVIII

MORE POIGNANTLY than suffering, even than death, the scarred land affected Martin. Men died, and were buried, and their suffering was over, but the land stood there mutely under the hot autumn sun, blasted and desolate. To Martin, there was something infinitely pathetic and terrible in this mute immolation of earth to the hatred of man. It was an accusation against him, silent and frightful; it was the evidence that betrayed his eternal ferocity, his inability to live at peace either with his fellows or with the earth from which he had come. It proved again that he was Nature's outcast, Nature's pariah, a white, forked animal that left a scorched trail of destruction wherever he trod, a creature from whom all other creatures fled, gentle or wild, bloodthirsty or ravenous. He was the abomination of Nature, the cannibal, to whom all things, including his brother, were prey. He was the monster who killed for pleasure as well as for hunger, destroyed wantonly because of his innate perversity, a mad beast against whom the innocently savage and the humble and the timid had no defense whatsoever.

Bringing up the rear with his supplies, Martin rode for days in the autumn sunshine, his horse sweating under him, the water running down his face from under his broad-brimmed hat. He looked about him at the burned fields which spread on each side of the dusty, rutted road. The crops had been destroyed by a marauding section of the division to which he belonged; he passed houses gutted and black from fire, the chimneys standing alone and sooty in the midst of the broken ruins. Where crops had been inadvertently spared, they were rotting in the hot sun, or were trampled down. Orchards stood silently on low hillsides, their red leaves hanging, their fruits, overripe, hot and decaying, dropping slowly, one by one, into the white dust beneath them. The doors of blackened barns hung open, showing the empty interiors; here and there a dried hog-wallow showed the imprints of vanished animals. Not a horse or a cow stood in the brown meadows. Once they passed a small farmhouse newly abandoned; the gardens behind it were ragged and boisterous with color, and a child's swing swayed a little under a big old tree. A bucket still stood on the lip of a mossy well, and birds fluttered thirstily on the brim. Faint blue hills fumed in the distance; overhead spread the wide blue heat of the skies. But on the earth were desolation and destruction, silence sweltering and empty. The cavalry made the only sound, as it escorted the Quartermaster's Corps and the supplies; the jingling of harness and spurs, the hoarse singing of the men, the ribald shouts, the velvety clop-clop of the horses in the clouds of golden dust, the roll of wheels, were the only things that broke the oppressive and abandoned stillness. Once a noisy string of cawing crows rose blackly against the hollow flame of the heavens; once buzzards sailed low and silently, as if they knew that death rode below. On and on, over the withered and ravished earth, yellow-brown as though seared by a conflagration; on and on, over land that had revolted passively and speechlessly, in drought and heat, in blackened trees and blasted meadow, in shrunken muddy streams and burned hills, in sandy erosions and dusty gullies.

A few times they passed ancient log cabins squatting low in an area of littered ground. The haggard faces of the sun-bonneted women and children struck at Martin. He was Captain of his detachment and in spite of his men's scowls and half-audible mutters, he stopped the train and gave bread and meat and flour to the poor creatures. They accepted only after prolonged coaxing, and then without thanks. They looked after the train with expressions of stupid wonderment and perplexity. Conquerors who were kind and merciful, who smiled gently, were quite new. A few of the older children essayed to shout "damned Yankees" after the train, but the shout was without true conviction or spirit.

Martin was not popular with his men. They had a vile name for men who hated bloodshed and killing, who disliked ribaldry and dirtiness of all kinds. They would have applied it to Martin, had it not been for the edge that could come through the mildness of him, his obvious strength and height, the quiet steadiness and command he could infuse into his voice. But because he was also kind and considerate, forbearing and gentle, they felt a contempt for him, and he had a hard time to maintain discipline. Not being their kind, he gave orders that were received with only slightly concealed resentment. This puzzled him, for he heard other officers issuing harsh commands that were instantly carried out, with automatic cheerfulness and acceptance; he knew his own orders were mild, and issued only when necessary. So he could not understand the obvious ill-will and sullenness of his own men. The whole thing depressed him, made him withdraw more and more from friendly communication with those under his command. He had not yet learned that the whip and the boot and the sword are the only languages the majority of men understand, and that justice and compassion are incomprehensible.

Following up the devastating Army that went before, his sadness increased, and also his anger. Surely, he thought, it was not necessary to lay waste and induce misery among women and children, in order to free slaves and preserve the Union. It was robbing Peter to pay Paul. One day a company passed them, going in the opposite direction, with a detachment of prisoners. The ill-will his men nourished for him was not decreased when he forbade them to harry the prisoners or taunt them.

Long hot days, brown and sweltering, over the blasted earth. Friendless and avoided even by his brother officers, Martin drew more and more within himself, and his shyness made him appear haughty and secretive. Finally he was left entirely alone, and the only words that passed his lips were orders. He would look sadly ahead at the rising and falling blue backs, listen to the good-natured and ribald talk of the men, and feel himself utterly outcast.

They were in enemy territory now, and must keep a sharp lookout. The laughter began to leave the men's voices, and their faces drew tighter and grimmer. What they did not as yet know was that their rear was being cut off, that a circle was closing in about them. But one morning, just before dawn, they were bloodily apprized of these facts.

Martin, sleeping uneasily on the warm dark earth, under a tree, was aroused by a volley of shots, by screams, shouts, uproar, mad runnings to and fro, the thin shriek of wounded horses, and blasts of red fire in the dimness. He stood up, staggering and dazed, tried to call out through parched lips. He was one of the first to be struck down. He felt a searing blow in his chest, another in his arm, and was unconscious before he hit the ground.

He was awakened by his own torture after what seemed eons upon eons of singing black emptiness in which he crawled, dying of thirst. Something brilliant was burning against his eyelids, and as he painfully lifted them, he saw it was the sun pouring down from a brazen void. All about him was the most profound silence he had ever known. Through the heat-mist of agony, he saw that he was lying half under a gutted wagon, his head exposed to the sun and innumerable insects. Not a human sound was to be heard; not a moving thing to be seen, except the ominous sailing of lowering buzzards. All about him were trees drenched in light, their leaves vividly clear and green; his sharpened eyes saw every blade of trampled and stained grass.

He knew he had been left for dead. He knew there was no hope for him. He knew he was about to die. And he thought of nothing except his thirst and the agony in his chest. He listened to the hot and dazzling silence about him. Once he called feebly.

And then after a dark period, he awoke again, and thought of Amy. And the thought of her was like a cool hand touching him, a cup of cool water. She had been angry with him for something, but she had forgiven him, and she loved him. Contentedly, he thought: That is all that matters.

He was about to die, but he did not think of God. He thought how blessed it was that the twilight was coming, and how good it was to be cool and without pain. He closed his eyes, and sighed.

It amazed him all of a sudden to find himself in a dim and heliotrope world, smelling of rain and trees and earth. He found himself standing before a low white gate in a low white fence. Suddenly he was enormously excited and filled with joy. He opened the gate, began to walk up a winding path of flagstones, covered with green moss. On each side were drooping trees, heavy with moisture and evening; between them he saw flower-beds small-globed with dew, and he could smell their piercing fragrance. Everything was twilit and still and at peace. He passed the familiar old sun-dial, and he told himself that tomorrow he would stand by it again and read it by the sun. And now, at a little distance, he saw the old, low white house with its chimney and latticed windows thrown open to the evening. He saw the trees clasped above it, saw the little black kitten rolling on its step. He saw the skies, mauve and misty, with here and there a star beginning to sparkle faintly in them. And then, all at once, with a sensation that was both pain and ecstasy, he could smell the lilacs, dripping with crystal water.

"There has been a storm, and now it is evening, and the storm has gone," he thought. He hurried toward the house. The door opened, as though he were expected, and his old great-great-aunt stood on the step, wrapped in her white shawl, nodding and smiling at him.

"You are late, Martin," she called to him in her thin and piping voice. "But never mind, my love. Better late than never."

CHAPTER XLIX

"IF THE war lasts two or three years more, I shall be worth three million dollars," thought Ernest. He looked through his office window with complacency. "What shall I do with it? Travel. Hum. I don't know. I'm not much interested in seeing strange places, for the people never change except in dress. Their stupidity never varies; their incompetence never becomes competence. The same dull eyes and heavy mouths, the same flat voices and silly words. Build a bigger and showier house? I'm not interested in that; I've got the finest house in all the world! I'm not afraid of poverty any more; I've got a golden wall that nothing can ever blow up. But I don't care about the things that other men care about: assorted women and fine wines and horses and queer ways of making a fool out of yourself. Nor do I care about collecting paintings or bric-a-brac or jewelry or statuary; I don't know anything about them and don't particularly want to know. I've got more than enough money for my children, even for Gertrude. What then, do I want with more money?"

He smiled a little sheepishly to himself, for he knew the answer. Over that sheepish smile his eyes pointed brilliantly with something oddly like hate and triumph. Power. There was nothing like power. A man could never have too much, if he understood what he was getting. Power to set your heel on the neck of a world you loathed because of its stupidity and vicious brutality and animal-like treachery, its weasel-soul, its tiny vices and tiny virtues. But best of all, Ernest said to himself, power gave a man the inestimable right to be himself, to be what he was, without apology or hypocrisy.

Strange that it should take power, money, to be simply yourself! As if your own personality was like a prisoner that could be freed only upon an enormous bond, that the mere right to do as you pleased, say what you pleased, eat, laugh, sleep, think when you pleased, must be purchased with a ransom. There were some people, ruminated Ernest, who declared that a man was free only when he had a gigantic fortune or absolutely no money at all. In either case, he could be free. But if a man were not either penniless or immensely rich, he was in bondage to his fellows; he must live, or pretend to live (which was worse) in accordance with the rules their stupidity dictated; he must learn to mouth their words. (Like eating their vomit, thought Ernest disgustedly.) He must trim down his soul to fit their measurements, which was almost as bad as expecting one to cut off one's flesh in order to please one's tailor. He must pretend to accept their god, or be in danger of worse than the hell fire they promised: their hatred and fear, their suspicion, and their ability to inflict a thousand little septic wounds. Not to be rich, or penniless, was to be chained in a vast monkey-cage, helpless against ferreting fingers, squeaking tongues, indignities and dishonoring.

Ah, he thought exultantly, he had power, now! Why, if he killed, he would be immune! He could rob, cheat, destroy, play the traitor or the idiot, say what he wished, do as he wished, and at the worst the world would smile indulgently and think him a little odd! If it reproached him at all, it would be with the manner of a doting mother, who begs lenience for her precocious offspring. One need not be a recluse, running away from the world, to be free of it: one only needed to be very rich. Wealth was a strong door: it kept out everything.

At this point in his thoughts, an unpleasant memory rose in his mind. "Strong door. You cannot close your strong doors tight enough——" Who had said that to him? Martin. He shifted irritably in his seat. Martin, that feckless fool, whose silly idealism had led him right into the pit of death, had destroyed his wife's happiness and his children's security—— Martin, whose life was like a house without doors and bars, open to every evil and mental pestilence that was abroad.

The thought of Martin suddenly became so intense, so compelling, that he turned suddenly in his chair and stared at the door; had Martin entered then he would not have been at all surprised. It seemed to him that Martin's personality invaded all the air, the very air he breathed, so that the essence of his body and his mind were pervaded by the etherealized substance of Martin's body and mind. It was like, he thought, two streams of water merging and losing individual integrity, or two cells dissolving into one.

He jumped, startled, for the door was indeed opening. It was a shock to him to see Gregory Sessions entering, and not Martin. He laughed shortly. Gregory came in, and looked at him in surprise. "I was thinking about my precious brother, Martin," said Ernest in apologetic explanation, "and I'm damned if I didn't almost expect him to come in! Just as though he were waiting in the outer room—— The most curious sensation——"

Then he stopped, abruptly noticing for the first time that Gregory was exceedingly pale and disturbed, and that in some way he had grown perceptibly older; his face seemed to have withered and shrunken together.

"Is there something wrong?" he asked in a changed voice.

Gregory slowly lowered himself into a chair; Ernest, in amazement, saw that his hands were shaking as he withdrew his handkerchief and touched his forehead with it. Then he looked up and regarded Ernest strangely.

"Perhaps, if I were superstitious, I would say it is very probable that Martin did come in," he said hoarsely. He swallowed with difficulty. "They've just posted the latest notice of the dead and the missing and the wounded on the courthouse wall. I was passing there—" Ernest began to rise out of his seat as though propelled by some outside force, and his lips shrank, turned livid, twisted in his face. Gregory nodded; he looked aside, his cheek muscles visibly falling inwards. "Yes," he added heavily, "Martin's been killed. His brigade was ambushed, hundreds slaughtered, the stores carried off." Ernest was standing now, his arms swinging like dead arms at his sides. Gregory got up, as though the seat had become intolerable to him, and he began to pace up and down the room, his hands behind his back, his head bent upon his chest. "Amy," he said. "She probably knows now. Telegram from Washington. Amy, my poor little Amy! My God, what can we do for her now!"

Then, without shame or apology or an attempt to hide it, he began to weep. They were an old man's tears, slow and painful.

"He was," said Ernest stonily, "always a fool."

"You can say that, even now, when he is dead?" asked Gregory, his voice strangling in his throat.

Ernest made a violent and aimless gesture. "Yes! Even now! He was always a fool! There was no reason on God's earth why he should have gone, no reason for him doing that, or any other of the cursed things he did! There was no reason for him to die, to desert his wife and his children! But he must cut a figure, he must go forth on a crusade, he must tell the world that he is a little Jesus and a hero, better than other men, choking on his ideals and his own stupid holiness!" He stopped, for it seemed to him that his heart was in his neck, smothering him with its thick salty bulk and its terrible and thundering beat. He felt blindly for his chair, fell into it. His arms dropped like marble upon the desk and lay there, spread out, the palms upward. He stared before him, swallowing convulsively, moving his head slowly from side to side, as if in agony. "This will kill my mother," he said dully.

"Your mother!" screamed Gregory, springing to the desk like a lean old tiger and leaning upon it toward the younger man. "What about Amy? This will kill Amy! Damn you, have you thought about Amy?" His bared yellow teeth gleamed between his purplish lips with hate.

Ernest did not reply for a moment, as if he had not heard. Then, without looking at Gregory, he said in a low voice: "But Amy loves me."

There was a long and frightful silence. Then Gregory whispered, trembling: "Are you mad?" And then, over and over, in a sinking whisper: "Are you mad? Are you quite mad?"

Ernest put his hand to his eyes, and spoke from behind it, in a dead but very quiet voice: "No, I am not mad. And you know I'm not. You've known all the time that she loves me. And that I love her. It is too late in the game, Gregory Sessions, for you to be a worse hypocrite than you are. But it doesn't matter now. This won't kill Amy. It will shock her terribly, perhaps overcome her for awhile. She was fond of Martin, loved him in a way, the way a mother loves a child. But only you and I know what she had to bear. There are her children, too. We can rescue something from the wreck for them, now. We can really do something for Amy and her children—" He dropped his hand and regarded the shaking old man before him emptily. And waited.

"If you hurt Amy, after all this, I'll—I'll kill you," said Gregory simply.

Ernest moved his head in sick disgust. "Don't be a fool, sir. I'll never hurt Amy again. I don't think any one can hurt her. Even this won't, very much. She is beyond any of us. But now she is in a position where we can help her."

He got up, and touched the bell on his desk. His chief clerk came in alertly, on long shabby legs. "Bring me my coat and hat, please," said Ernest curtly. When the man had gone out again, Gregory cried: "Where are you going? What are you going to do?"

"I'm going to Amy. At once."

"No!" Gregory ran like a youth around the desk, seized Ernest by the lapels of his coat. He shook him with a savagery that even he realized was impotent and brittle. "You're not going to her! Haven't you hurt her enough? Do you know you broke her heart when you married May? Do you think I didn't know, that I couldn't see every thought behind her poor face? You killed her, then and there! But you're not satisfied, you want to stamp on her now! You're not going! I won't let you go!"

The clerk returned with the coat and hat. His long gray face was impassive, and there was no knowing what he had heard. If he felt some surprise at seeing his employer in the grip of old Mr. Sessions, he did not show it. He merely held the coat for Ernest to put his arms into. Ernest snatched the garment from him, motioned with his head for the man to leave. When they were alone again, he said to Gregory: "Please don't tear at me like that, sir. And stop threatening me. It sounds silly; like a tenth-rate play. Do you think you can stop me? Do you think anything you have to say can stop me or change my mind? Don't be a fool!"

But Gregory clutched him more desperately than ever. "What are you going to do? What can you possibly say to her? It's not your place to go to her; do you want to ruin her more, put a scandal on her? Do you want slimy tongues licking her? Haven't you done her harm enough already, without making her open game for any dog to hunt?"

Ernest shrugged him off so violently that he almost fell. The younger man's eyes were literally full of flame, and his face was as rigid as granite. "You are a worse fool than I thought you! Get out of my way!"

"May! Your own children! Can't you think of them? You have no right to do this! It's my place to go—I'll go with you——!"

Ernest snatched up his hat. "Why, damn you!" he said quietly and slowly, "you are a reprobate as well as a fool! What did you think I was going to do?" He spat. "Get out of my way! I'm going to her, because I'm the only thing she really loves, because I'm the only one that can help her now. Don't worry, you yellow old dog, we won't talk of love! I'm going to her, to bring her, and her children, home. To the place where she belongs."

Gregory had taken his arm again, but Ernest flung him off, ran around the desk, and went out.

Gregory stood where he had thrust him. His mouth was open, and he was gasping. His face was the color of saffron. "There are things a man can't overlook. In very decency. Things a man can't overlook. I've come a long way with him. He's always been respectful and full of deference, the vicious devil! Because we could use each other, but he could use me more than I could use him. No one could ever use him, curse him! But there are things a man can't overlook, if he wants to keep on calling himself a man. This is the end——"

But he knew that he lied. And this knowledge, this knowledge of himself, made him retch. His sensation of helplessness before Ernest was almost voluptuous.

Finally he went home, thinking how he could tell May. When he arrived, she was in the nursery, and he sent for her to come downstairs. When she saw his face, she was horrified. But he said quietly enough: "May, my love, we have just heard that Martin has been killed——"

"Oh," said May faintly, and sat down, the color running out of her plump and dimpled cheeks.

Gregory took her hands and held them tightly. It was so terribly necessary to him for her to believe what he was about to tell her.

"Ernest and I—were together—near the courthouse, when we heard about it. It was posted on the wall. Naturally, he said he would go to his mother at once." He swallowed, tensed himself. "Florabelle's house, as you know, is on the way to—to the farm. So I suggested to him, that after he told his mother, he go on to Amy's, do what he could, and then bring her and the children home. No doubt Florabelle will go with him to get her."

May burst into tears, put her lacy handkerchief to her eyes, and rocked, stricken with grief, in her chair. "Oh, poor Amy! My poor darling! And how good of you, dear Gregory, to think of bringing her home! My poor darling, this will break her heart! After all she has had to endure, too. But perhaps Ernest should have come home to me, first, and I would have gone with him-- A man never knows what to say to a poor woman in these circumstances."

"No, my love, he should not have come home first. Remember, he had to see his mother. His first duty was there; Martin is her son, remember. And it was my suggestion that he go without delay to Amy, and bring her home. I confess I wasn't up to it, myself. So I came home to tell you, so you would have time to prepare. After all, there are four little children."

May jumped up, the need for action practically overcoming her grief for her cousin. "Of course! I must open the bedrooms at once. Let me see! Amy can have the rose bedroom, across from mine. It is just big enough for her and the baby. Lucy and Elsa can share Gertrude's room; it's very big and sunny. Three little white beds side by side—" She wiped the last tear from her eyes. "What a noisy household we shall be, with all these children! I'll have to get two more nursemaids, and Heaven knows where they will sleep!" She sighed, smiled ruefully. "I'm afraid none of us will have much peace with a household of babies! Well, it can't be helped, and I'll be glad to have Amy with me, you know that, Gregory."

She hurried up the stairs. Gregory stood immobile for a few moments, then he ran from the house, calling for his carriage.

CHAPTER L

ERNEST, ONCE in the street, slowed down to a firm but casual walk. He mounted the steep narrow street to Endicott Road, walked down it to the Endicott Hotel, where he found a line of hacks. He engaged the roomiest one, and was soon being driven down the quiet back-country road which was called Quaker Highway. He had not yet left the confines of the city, however, and the houses that stood back from the road were large and elaborate, with great grounds, newly planted trees, gardens and stables. This section was called Quaker Terrace, and was rapidly becoming the most exclusive section of town, for it was little travelled, with all the advantages of city life and the quiet and dignity of country living. Later on, when the city had long overtaken it, swallowed it and digested it, excreted it thereafter in the form of slums, it was called Quakertown, though only one Quaker family, the Benshaws, ever really lived in it.

The hack stopped at the fancy-grilled iron gates of a tall, narrow-fronted red-brick house, with white porches all around it in a wooden lace of fretwork, white cupolas and useless turrets, thin windows at least eight feet tall, like slits in the walls of a fortress, and a high broad door with a fanlight above it. The autumn sun was warm, and a nursemaid in cape and hood sat on the round seat about a tree, watching two babies tumbling about on a spread rug on the brown grass.

Ernest got out of the hack, leaned over the iron gate, and whistled softly. The nursemaid rose with a startled cry, then recognizing the whistler, her eyebrows arched in surprise, and she came running respectfully.

"Where is Mrs. Barbour?" asked Ernest peremptorily.

The girl stammered: "Mrs. Barbour, sir? Why, I believe she is in the drawing room. She was there about half an hour ago."

"Damn," muttered Ernest. He looked at the girl sternly. "See here, my girl, I have something to tell Mrs. Bouchard that I don't wish Mrs. Barbour to hear yet. Will you please see if you can find Mrs. Bouchard, and tell her I am waiting out here for her? I have only a moment or two to spare. Step along, my girl, step along!"

The nursemaid fled respectfully. Ernest opened the gate and moved around to the side of the house, where he could not be seen from the south windows. He did not have long to wait, for Florabelle, wrapped in a gay blue cape, came out of the side entrance. In the sunlight, her light golden hair turned to threads of fire. She glanced about anxiously, then seeing Ernest beckon around the side of the house, she ran up to him. She was a diminutive and dainty little creature, and the top of her head hardly rose above his shoulder.

"Ernest! What on earth is the matter? Is May ill? The children——?"

He kissed her forehead gently. "No, love. No one is ill. It is much worse." He paused. "Martin has been killed. We have just heard."

She cried out, faintly, paling; the cloak fell open, showing her white and throbbing throat. But she did not cry, as he had expected. She merely looked shocked.

"Oh, poor Amy!" she exclaimed in a subdued voice.

"Yes, poor Amy indeed," replied Ernest gravely. "I'm going to her now, and am taking her and the children home with me."

At last tears came into Florabelle's pretty blue eyes, and one of them spilled over onto her round soft cheek. She said: "Is May with you?"

"No." Ernest spoke carefully. "She has quite a lot to do to prepare the house for Amy and the children, so she has sent me to get Amy."

"Let me go with you, Ernest. Wait, and I'll just put on a bonnet——"

"No, Florrie. You will have your hands full with Ma. Go back and tell her, as gently as you can. It will be very hard on her, at this time, just after her influenza."

"But—" Florabelle paused, and seemed doubtful. It appeared a little odd to her that Ernest, who had been Martin's bitter enemy, should be going to comfort his widow, to bring her home. And all alone, too. The more she thought of it the stranger it became to her, and her smooth white forehead knotted a little as she tried to puzzle it out.

Ernest patted her shoulder. "Now, run back like a good girl, and tell Ma. I'm not up to it, myself. And tomorrow, after Amy is settled, May would like you to come to see her."

Florabelle's artless face cleared, and standing on tiptoe, she kissed her brother's cheek. It frightened her that his flesh was cold to her lips, and she looked at him sharply. She was not a very observing young woman, and it occurred to her for the first time that he was quite ghastly, and that there were dark ridges under his eyes and about his mouth, giving him a most haggard expression. She was greatly touched. It was evident to her that Martin's death had hit him deeper than any one would have suspected, and she burst out crying in sympathy.

Ernest was not ill-pleased; he had seen that Florabelle had scented something puzzling, and her attention being diverted relieved him. He went back to the hack and was driven rapidly away. Alone, his mouth fell open a little, as though there were a pain in his chest, and he began to sigh at intervals, over and over, audibly. Once or twice a tremor ran over him, and he shivered as if with cold. But he was not thinking of his dead brother, nor of the very likely possibility that a bullet made by

Barbour & Bouchard, fired by a rifle made by Barbour & Bouchard, had killed him. If it had occurred to him, he would merely have shrugged, for he was not the man to indulge in whimsical and sentimental philosophies.

During the past several years he had not seen Amy more than five times. And in all those years she had never entered the Sessions house. He had seen her, alone, at Dorcas' house, and at Florabelle's house. Martin, apparently, had been too much engrossed in his work to accompany her. He had, however, never seen her children, but he thought of them a great deal. Because they were of Amy's body, he sometimes thought of them as being his, and the poverty into which their father had forced them agitated him with impotent rage.

Ernest had been aghast at Amy's appearance the last two times they had met. It seemed to him that she had become emaciated to the point of transparency. Almost, he could see the fine thin bones of her face through her pale clear skin and delicate flesh. Her figure, too, had become thin and fragile, but retained outlines of roundness and grace. He looked down into her eyes, so shining-brown, so limpid and steadfast, and he saw the purplish hollows under them. But she had smiled as though she had last seen him yesterday, and her expression, full of courage and fortitude, dared him to pity her. When he took her slender hand he could feel the stiff hard calluses upon it, and the roughness of the skin. Her gown, he noticed, was old-fashioned, and did not have the wide spread of hoop that all the ladies were wearing now; it was of brown wool, and obviously home-made. Yet he thought her more beautiful than ever, the sweetest and loveliest woman he had ever known. Once, he remembered, May had said that she was insipid, and once or twice he had tried to believe it, remembering her quietness and gentleness, her lack of aggressive qualities. But he saw that May had been mistaken, and he had been a fool sneering at sour grapes. For he knew that Amy was a great lady, serene and poised in the midst of intolerable hardship, and remembering her intelligence and insight, he knew that she had never been hypnotized by Martin's beliefs, that she had never believed in them. She had followed him, sustaining him, knowing that his happiness depended on her acquiescence, and she had loved him enough to let him find peace in his folly.

He remembered all these things about her, and he sighed over and over, until he, himself, heard his sighs and was wryly amused at them. He clasped his hands firmly upon the head of his cane, and said aloud: "Yet, I would do as I did. I would not do it differently if it were given me back to choose." After a few moments he lifted his cane, and surveyed the knob, which was a round piece of gold hammered into the likeness of a puckish face. He addressed the face ironically: "Am I a liar? For once I don't know!"

But as the hack began to travel more slowly down a narrow, winding and rutted road, began to lurch and pitch like a small ship at sea, the desolation of the unkempt countryside seemed to creep through the very seams of Ernest's consciousness. This was a poorer part of the country, with shacks crowding near the road, chicken runs and hog wallows, tipsy fences and wash-lines, screaming children and barking dogs. Slatternly women came to the doors as the hack rumbled past, and a mule, in an ironical spirit, he-hawed after his half-brother, the horse. The autumn sun had gone behind a cloud, and the sky was full of brownish gray mist; the trees were bare, writhing emptily in a sudden wind, and a few red leaves swirled up from the dusty earth and rattled against the windows of the cab. But it was near sunset anyway, and in the west there was a wild and sullen glory of dull scarlet. In the distance, the hills, low and rolling, were mounds of dun-colored fog, turning slowly to copper at the tops under the sunset. The harvest was in, the fields and meadows denuded and brown, blowing with straws.

"What a Godforsaken place!" thought Ernest. He looked about him at the shacks and the occasional child or woman with detestation, forgetting that the desolation and the hopelessness were partly due to the fact that most of the men were gone, and those they had left behind them sick and listless with fear. "How has Amy endured it this long?"

Now they reached a narrower side road, and the hack turned into it reluctantly. All shacks disappeared. On each side of the road stretched the bleakness of dead fields, which ran sluggishly to meet a dead sky. The meadows were not fenced off: there was something prairie-like in these long stretches of unbroken earth, and the rumble of the hack wheels made a hollow echo in the profound cold silence. Then in the distance Ernest saw a group of low buildings, a large building which he guessed was the house, behind it barns and stables, and at a distance of a quarter mile, another but smaller group of buildings.

The hack jogged along, pitching and tossing, so that Ernest gathered a few minor contusions. But now that he saw the place where Amy and her children lived, he began to sweat with agitation and nervousness, and he beat out a tattoo on the floor of the hack with his cane. Once he tapped against the glass to attract the driver's attention, and shouted: "Faster! Faster!"

A low, broken picket fence surrounded the house, and the gate stood open on rusty hinges. Prepared for something very bad, Ernest was appalled at the true picture. His eye quickly gathered in the frowsy gardens with the long unkempt grass, the darkness of the windows in spite of the twilight, the silence and desolation of the grounds about the house. As over abysses of space lonely cattle lowed mournfully, and a calf bawled from the barns. "Could it be possible that she has already gone?" thought Ernest. He got out of the cab, told the driver to wait, and ran up the dusty path to the door. He stumbled over a child's shovel and bucket, saw a headless doll in his way, heard the barking of a dog inside the house. It was definitely twilight now, and the whole world was full of gray silence and utter ruin and hopelessness. He knocked savagely upon the door, as though that very act would give life to this lifeless scene. A wind rose with a gale-like force, rattled the windows and the door loudly, swirled dust into his nose and eyes, tore itself through the denuded trees to the right of the house.

Several long moments passed, then from inside the house came the lusty cries of a child, the hushing voice of a woman, then slow footsteps. The door opened a crack; Ernest put his hand against it and thrust it open ruthlessly. The woman fell back with an alarmed and croaking exclamation; he saw she was an old woman, tall and stooping and emaciated, with pale blue eyes behind steel-rimmed spectacles. She had evidently just lit a lamp in the room behind her, for it threw a bleak dim light over the shabby furniture and the worn rug.

Ernest glanced briefly about him, missed nothing, then said to the waiting old woman, who was blinking her eyes at him with mingled apprehension and perplexity: "I must see Mrs. Barbour, at once!"

The old woman clasped her hands before her, and she began to weep, silently, bending her head forward upon her chest. Then she closed the door behind Ernest, went to where a few dull coals burnt upon the hearth, and stirred them up. Ernest followed her, striking his legs impatiently with his cane. She looked up at him through the rain of her tears, as he stood beside her. She knelt there upon the hearth in an attitude of utter abandonment to grief and despair.

"Didn't you know, sir, that Mr. Martin has been killed?" she asked in a guttural voice. "We just got a telegram this morning." She put her gnarled old hands over her face and sobbed convulsively.

"Yes, I know," said Ernest, with a forced attempt at patient gentleness. "That is why I have come. Is Amy—is Mrs. Barbour in a condition to see me? Will you please tell her I have come to take her home?"

The woman dried her eyes upon the edge of her apron, began to rise laboriously. Ernest, to his own surprise, found himself helping her, his hand under her elbow. She muttered hoarse thanks, the muscles of her face twisting as she fought for self-control. She remembered social amenities then, and politely offered Ernest a seat.

"It iss not my way, to be so like a child," she apologized, wringing the fringes of her shawl between her trembling fingers, and looking at him imploringly. "But Mr. Martin, he was so like an angel, so good and kind— It iss more than we can bear. My Carl, he iss gone, too, my son, and there iss only my old husband and myself. But we thought if Mr. Martin was near him, nothing could harm him, God would not let anything harm Carl. And now there iss only that poor lady upstairs, lying on her bed so white and cold and still, like the dead, and the poor children—" She sobbed dryly, pressed her shaking lips together, apologized again.

"It may be she will not see you, sir," she said deprecatingly. "But, I will see. What iss your name, please?" she asked simply.

Ernest opened his mouth, then closed it again. He had the oddest conviction that if he told his name Amy would not see him. He could not understand how he knew this, but he believed it implicitly. He studied old Mrs. Heckl curiously, for now he knew who she was. It was apparent that she did not know him. He cleared his throat and said: "My name isn't important. Please tell Mrs. Barbour that her uncle has sent a friend to bring her home, with her children. That will be sufficient."

Mrs. Heckl's face flashed into a thin joy. "That will be very good, sir! To take her home, to her friends and her people! That iss where she should be, and not here, with only an old woman to care for her." Then she shook her head with sudden doubt. "But iss he not there in that house, that man?"

"Who?" Ernest lifted his brows at her and the corner of his lips jerked in spite of himself. The old woman's cheek had flushed a dull red, and her eyes were flashing; she had clenched her hands in her apron, and the fabric was twisted.

"That man! That wicked man, who was so cruel to Mr. Martin, and to mein Hans and Carl, and all the poor people in his shops! That rich wicked man God will surely find and punish some day!"

Ernest's expression became bland and smooth; his eye pointed brilliantly as it always did when he felt either hate or derision or contempt.

"Come, come, my good woman, I'm sure Mrs. Barbour would not want you to express your opinion of her relatives to strangers! And now, if you please, I would like you to take my message to her."

Her color deepened with mortification, but she curtseyed in silence, and left the room. He heard her heavily mounting some stairs in the rear. The clock chimed on the mantelpiece, and a coal dropped.

Then another door opened, there was a babble of childish voices, and three children spilled into the room, a tall boy and girl of about seven, and a child between them, probably not much more than three. They were hauling the baby by its fat short arms, and it was doubling up its knees, so that it could swing over the floor. The girl was scolding the boy, prophesying dire results to something she called the baby's "sockets," and he was jeering at her, jerking the baby so that it swung clear of the floor, shrieking with joy in the process.

They did not see Ernest sitting by the fire until they reached the hearth. Then they were so startled that they dropped the baby, who fell with a fat crash and a shout of pain and rage. Quite automatically, not removing her eyes from Ernest, the little girl whisked the baby to its feet.

brushed off its rear, pressed its roaring head to her flat childish breast. The little boy stood there on the hearth, his legs apart, his hands on his hips, and merely stared with more impudence and astonishment than fear.

"Who are you?" he demanded loudly, in a fresh boyish voice.

Much amused and interested, Ernest stared back at them.

"Not so fast," he answered. "First, you must tell me who you are."

"I guess that's only polite," admitted the little girl, when the boy glanced at her for her opinion. "Well, sir," said the boy, putting his sturdy brown legs still farther apart, and holding his head at a high and cocky angle, "I'm Paul Barbour, and this is my twin, Elsa, and this is our little sister, Lucy, and upstairs in mama's and papa's room is our little brother, John Charles. He can't hardly get around by hisself yet. And," he added, "who are you, now?"

"I," smiled Ernest, "am your uncle. Your Uncle Ernest. Ever hear of me?"

Paul frowned, glanced again at his sister, and shook his head after she had shaken hers. "No, sir, we ain't never heard of you. We got an Uncle Raoul, and an Uncle Eugene, and an Uncle Gregory and an Uncle Nicholas and an Uncle Armand, leastways, he ain't really our uncle—Uncle Armand—but we call him so. But we never heard of an Uncle Ernest."

Ernest still smiled, but his mouth tightened. "Well, then," he said lightly, "I'm just a new discovery. You see, I'm your papa's brother."

"Papa didn't have no brother," replied the boy abruptly. But the little girl reached out and plucked his sleeve. Still keeping his eyes fixed on Ernest, the boy leaned backwards while his sister whispered in his ear. Then he frowned.

"Are you *that man?*" he demanded.

So, that's what they have called me, thought Ernest wryly. He said aloud: "I'm sure I don't know, Paul. You see, I've been quite a distance away, so I suppose your parents haven't told you much about me." He paused. "I'm not really very bad, you see. I've got two little boys of my own, your cousins. Haven't you heard of Godfrey and Reginald, and your little girl-cousin, Gertrude?"

Amazement shone on the children's faces, and they burst into an excited chorus of exclamations. Was he Frey's and Reggie's and Gertrude's papa? Was he Auntie May's husband? They swarmed about him, incredulous, but warm with sudden friendship. The baby, Lucy, leaned against his knee; the twins stood side by side, breathless and eager, on the hearth, staring at him.

How strong and brown and handsome they are, thought Ernest enviously, almost painfully. No one would ever have suspected them of being Martin's children. All three of them had fiercely blazing eyes, choleric and intolerant, short belligerent noses, big generous mouths a bit on the sullen side, and vital hair, curling and medium brown. Their bodies were stocky, like his own; their legs were like his, also, well-made and well-planted, as if they owned the ground and no foolishness. They had square shoulders, tensely held hands, proud if insolent carriage, "cockiness" and independence, pride and angry courage. Looking at them, Ernest felt a sudden kinship to them, closer than the avuncular one, almost as if they were bone of his bone and flesh of his flesh. He had never felt this way toward either of his young sons, and even his passion for Gertrude did not have it in this strong tide of blood-feeling, this complete understanding and body-sympathy. Strange that his own children should seem more like Martin's, and Martin's children more like his! This realization shook him profoundly, and he looked back at his nieces and nephew with an expression of passionate concentration.

All at once, in the midst of this flow between the man and the children, which the children themselves unconsciously recognized, it occurred to him that they did not appear like offspring who had just heard of their father's death. So he asked cautiously, while he lifted little fat Lucy to his knee and began to stroke her gleaming curls: "Where is your papa, Paul?"

The boy bridled, smiled, glanced at his smiling sister, and nodded: "My papa's in the war. He's fighting the wicked old Rebels, and he's going to bring me back a gun. Why aren't you in the war, Uncle Ernest?"

Ernest bit his lip to hide his amusement. "Well, it's this way, Paul· you see, a number of us must stay at home to make the guns and the cannon and the powder for our soldiers to use. That is what I do: make guns and cannon and powder."

The little girl suddenly tugged again at her brother's sleeve, and he leaned backwards to listen to her whisper. His expression changed, became doubtful. "My papa says it's wicked to make things to kill people with," he said. "Papa says soldiers are wicked men, murderers. He went to war, but he isn't going to fight," he added with such open and child-like regret that Ernest's amusement rose to a high pitch. "He's just going to help people get something to eat, and because this war is kind of good, freeing the slaves, and everything." His voice became more and more doubtful, more and more regretful. The little girl's face, so like her twin's, also showed this regret.

So, thought Ernest with obscure and elated satisfaction, Martin's idealism had not tainted the healthiness of his children's minds, for all the apparent intensity of his efforts. Perhaps it was just as well that Martin had died. For his own sake. He would never have had any peace as his children grew older, for he would always have been in conflict with them, trying to silver-plate the strong iron of them, trying to make hands, that grasped and were made to hold, carry olive branches tied with blue ribbon. He would have tried to make marching feet walk softly, tried to tune hearty rough voices to gentleness. Yes, far better that he should die this way, far better for his children, too.

There were slow footsteps on the stairs in the hall, the murmur of old Mrs. Heckl's voice. It was apparent that she was bringing Amy down. Hearing that voice, the children turned and ran toward the door, shouting at the top of their lungs: "Mama! It's Uncle Ernest to see you! He's Frey's papa, and Reggie's papa, and he makes guns! Mama, can we have a gun if Uncle Ernest brings us one?"

Ernest heard a great cry from old Mrs. Heckl, he heard a faint one from Amy. He rose swiftly, went to the door with the speed and silence of a cat, and entered the hallway. Again, he had the oddest conviction that Amy might even now run from him, hide away from him. The instant he left the room, the outer door opened and Gregory entered, panting with haste. He hid himself in the shadows.

The hall was dimly lit, and in that pallid and uncertain light Ernest saw Amy, stopped upon the stairs, her hand on the banister. She wore a loose white wrapper, and her thick brown hair hung over her shoulders and back in the disorder of grief. He saw her face, white to ghastliness, the black circles under her eyes, the agony in the expression of her colorless mouth. Below her stood old Mrs. Heckl, staring at him with an almost ludicrous face of hate and terror, her lips apart, her eyes dilated. The children, puzzled and still quivering with their eager excitement and vitality, stared up in sudden silence at their mother.

Ernest came to the foot of the stairs, and ignoring the old woman and the children, he held up his hand to his sister-in-law. She looked down at him in mournful fascination, saw his large pale features, saw what he dared not say.

"Amy," he said gently. And he went up a step or two, and took her hand. It was cold and rigid as stone, but she did not remove it. He stepped down, still holding her hand, and she followed, as if sleep-walking, still regarding him with that vacant yet agonized expression. Her loose white garments trailed behind her; her hair rolled on her shoulders.

Old Mrs. Heckl suddenly snatched the children from Ernest's proximity as from the path of a deadly and ferocious beast. She gathered them almost completely in the folds of her dress and apron, backing away from him, like a hen sheltering chicks from the shadow of the hawk. Over their heads, she glared at Ernest.

But he saw only Amy, whose hand he held, who was following him as he walked backward into the living room. Neither noticed Gregory, near the doorway. Ernest closed the door and drew Amy to the fire. She stood there, obediently, as if drugged. He put his arms about her, slowly, gently, and she let her head fall on his shoulder, as if she had found her true place. He held her so for several moments, not daring to breathe lest he disturb her, and then he bent his head and touched her hair with his lips.

He had experienced in life, and was still to experience, triumph, elation, exultation, passion and satisfaction. But even under the tragic circumstances that had brought him to this house, he experienced what he had never yet experienced: a great flame of joy, of utter surrender to something that was at once too terrible for passion, too gentle for it. It made his blood burn and sting in his veins, made his throat knot painfully. He had never felt such piercing sweetness, such tenderness, such devotion and love. He had always been able to control himself, but now he did not want to control himself. He wanted the tides in him to carry him along wherever they would, to break down his self-discipline, to blind him to everything but the immediate present and its ecstasy. It seemed to him that all his life, all his consciousness and experiences, had been created only to flow into this minute, or like building stones, had been quarried only to be built to this apex. Without this moment and this apex, they were meaningless; because of them, they had acquired pattern and purpose.

Yet his habit of control was such, possessed such automatic power, that when Amy stirred, his arms dropped of themselves from her body and fell to his sides. But his breath was unsteady, his face dusky. He led her to a chair. She began to sob dryly, in short coughs, shrinking in her chair, and shivering. Her body shuddered, her clothes trembled in the feeble light of the fire. Ernest pulled a chair beside hers, and leaned toward her.

"Amy," he said, and then, "Amy, my love, my poor girl."

She looked at him, stopping her sobs abruptly; it was as if she really saw him for the first time. She seemed to realize many things, things that would have taken years to remember, and to repeat. She moved away from him a little, remembering these things.

"He was so good, so very, very good!" she wailed, and in that wail was the thin and bitter sound of accusation. He was so good, said that accusation, and you hated him for it, and you drove him out. You blackmailed him and threatened him; you laughed at him, not only to yourself, but to all your friends, so that he became the universal fool in cap and bells, and everyone was against him, ridiculing him, leaving him so lonely and friendless. All his life you were his enemy, said her anguished eyes, beating him down and driving him away, and he had never harmed you, was incapable of harming you.

"Amy!" he exclaimed sharply, involuntarily, "don't look at me like that! Whatever else passed between my brother and me, I never denied that he was sincere and gentle and kind, that it was impossible for him to be dishonest or vicious. I never denied that he was 'good.' Will you believe me when I say that I am sorry, frightfully sorry, that he has gone? I swear to you, Amy, that I would give ten years of my life to bring him back to you!" And in that moment, he believed what he said. His voice was loud and firm with sincerity, and the tense misery and accusation began to die out of Amy's eyes. They filled with tears; she averted her head, and cried like a child.

"He was too good for me," she sobbed. "He was too good for any of us. No one understood him, except me. But even I could not feel any real sympathy for what he was trying to do. I was too greedy, too indifferent. I tried to pretend to be what I wasn't, and I don't think I really succeeded. Sometimes he would look at me so sadly! But, O God, I really tried! I really tried to be what he wanted me to be! And now, it is too late. It'll always be too late."

Ernest was silent, helpless for the first time in his life. He took her hand again, held it gently. He saw the broken nails, the calluses on the small palm; he saw the throbbing of the blue veins in the delicate wrist. He could hardly hold himself back from putting his lips fiercely to those veins, from pressing the little palm to his cheek. He glanced at her; she had stopped her sobbing, and was regarding him with a sort of stark terror that electrified him.

A thrill ran along his nerves, and the blood hummed in his ears. His glance dropped from her face to her slender white throat with its transparent hollow; the wrapper fell away loosely, showing the gentle rise of her breasts. Suddenly he was aware that she was trembling violently, and that her hand, at first tensing and drawing away, had relaxed, and the fingers had closed about his. He looked at them in the swimming, firelit silence, then, very slowly, he lifted them to his lips and kissed them.

For a moment she did not move; he even imagined that her fingers responded, pressed against his mouth as if hungry for his touch. Then she snatched away her hand with a cry, and stood up so abruptly that her chair fell back from her. Ernest stood up, also, shaking, and she turned upon him with a strange excitement, her face wild, her gestures disordered.

"Please go, Ernest! You can't help me. No one can help me. I don't know why you came! Why did you come? It isn't because you are sorry. Did you come here to torment me? Please go! And never come back! Never, never! I never want to see you again!"

"Amy," he pleaded, "forgive me. I forgot. I promise you I'll never forget again. Forgive me, Amy. O my God, this is impossible! It should never have happened. Amy, it never happened! Believe me, I came here to help you, to take you and your children home with me, where you belong. You have a duty to them, too. Now that I have seen them I want to help them. I feel that they are my own flesh and blood, nearer to me than my own children. Let me help them. Let me help you. May is waiting for you—the rooms are all ready. She—she sent me here for you, Amy. Come home, with your children."

She regarded him with an almost idiotic incredulity. "But I can't live in the same house with you, Ernest! I can't do that to Martin. Or to my children, or to May. I owe it to Martin to remember the promise I made him. You were his enemy, the only real enemy he ever had in the world, and you, his brother! Do you think I can be friends with his enemy?" It was evident that she was nearing the breaking point, for she had begun to gasp, putting her hands to her breast.

"It isn't like you to talk that way, Amy," he answered painfully. "You always saw things straightly, without false sentiment. If I had wanted to be a real enemy to Martin, it would have been easy. I could have forced him to give up his stock at the price I wanted to pay; I could have sent him to prison, with his confederates. But I didn't. Believe me when I tell you that Martin disliked me more than I disliked him, that, when we were younger, he refused to be friends with me, though I honestly tried, at times. I'm not apologizing for anything, or explaining anything. I feel sure you know these things yourself. But you are trying to hurt me just so you can hurt yourself. Is it conscience, Amy? Are you trying to injure yourself because of something you can't help, and I can't help? That is stupid. You owe it to your children to take them from this place.

"Are you afraid of me, Amy? I promise you, my darling, I'll swear to you——"

"On what?" asked Gregory's voice, smoothly and coldly. He came out of the shadows.

Amy gave a faint scream of fright, and Ernest fell back.

The two men stared at each other, everything down between them. The hatred of years spurted between them. Across the flow of their mutual detestation, released now, they could see each other's nakedness, unclothed by hypocrisy and social politenesses. What Ernest saw only increased his contempt, but what Gregory saw appalled him, for he realized he had never fully known what an enemy this was, what an implacibility stood there.

Then Ernest lifted a shoulder, turned his back and regarded the fire.

"I suppose," said Gregory, "that an appeal to honor would have no weight with you?"

"None at all," agreed Ernest indifferently. "Besides, who are you to talk about honor, anyway?" He glanced over his shoulder at the old man with such infinite disdain and knowledge that Gregory winced even in his anger. "And why this talk about honor? I have done nothing but offer Amy a decent home. She knows in her heart that she has nothing to fear from me." He took his foot off the fender and began to button up his coat. He could not see Amy's face, for she was pressing it against her uncle's chest, her hands clutching his coat.

"But this is ridiculous!" exclaimed Ernest, turning hot and sick. He flushed with mortification.

Gregory ignored him. He was talking to Amy. "My love, I—I sent him here to bring you home. Then I went to May to tell her the sad news, and ask her to prepare for you and the children. Then I followed him here—to help him bring you. But on the way I began to think, and it seemed impossible for me to live under the same roof with him any more. Things—became unbearable. And I thought of having all those children there, and I remembered that I am an old man, now. So I decided this: the Henthorns are leaving to live in Philadelphia, and they are willing to sell their home here. I intend to buy that home, and you shall live with me, keeping my house, and there will be plenty of room for the children." He held her to him tightly, for her knees were bending weakly under her. "And in the meantime, until the house is ready, I shall stay here with you."

He moved his head in Ernest's direction. "Unless, of course, you wish to remove your wife and children, and let Amy and her children and me live in her old home together. It is still my property, and will be, until my death. But May was born there, and her children, and she loves the house. I couldn't force her out. It must rest with you what to do. Will you leave, or must I?"

Ernest picked up his hat, examined it minutely, then put it on his head. He looked at Gregory, then at Amy, who still would not turn to him. He shook his head in slow negation.

"I'll stay," he said briefly. "I've given up a lot for that house. I'll stay."

CHAPTER LI

THE NEW house in Quaker Terrace was like Paradise to Amy, after a long gray-brown muddy Purgatory. Merely to be near town, to see carriages drawn smartly after spanking horses, to hear voices and see faces of plump and prosperous women, to walk out in neat boots and not sink into mud, to trip out in the widest and most sweeping of hoops and not bedraggle them: all this was heaven enough. But again to have a carriage, as smart as any one's, to drive into town and see the shops, to finger velvets and laces and silks, to try on the newest bonnets, to sit in friends' parlors sipping delicate China tea and eat seed-cake and glacé fruits while one shook one's ringlets dolefully over the war, to know that one's little children were snug in their nursery in the care of efficient nursemaids, to know that a good cook was presiding over the kettles and pots in one's kitchen and that eventually a dinner would be served on gold-traced Haviland, and that at one's place one would find frosted crystal and heavy shining silver and a stiff white napkin: all this was ecstasy upon ecstasy.

Amy had been brought to her new home in a state of grief-stricken apathy that Gregory feared would not pass. Not even he, and perhaps only Ernest, guessed that half her apathy and sorrow was the sick probings of conscience, and that her loss would not have been half so terrible had she not remembered the few days before Martin's departure. I failed him; I sent him away sad and wretched, feeling that he hadn't a friend in the world, she thought over and over, staring into her sleepless nights. If for the past year I had only had the courage and the fortitude and loyalty I started out with! O my God, I began bravely enough; I never said a word against what he wanted to do until nearly the end when I should have gone on as I had begun! But I became small and petty and cruel; I had accepted the sacrifices with promises to uphold them cheerfully, and then when they turned heavy I became bitter and poisoned all his dear life! Oh, if but for one week, one day, I could bring you back, Martin! Even an hour, a minute!

Worst of all was the thought that Martin had sacrificed his whole life, all the joy and ease he might have had, to bring comfort and mercy and justice into the lives of the oppressed, and had failed at the last. For the Government was filling the hospital with the wounded, and there was no place for the shop-workers and laborers. Due to some entanglement of red tape in the matter of the bank funds, the payments had been temporarily stopped. Father Dominick had been removed to another city, and had left the administration of the funds in the hands of his successor, who was to co-operate with Amy in the matter. But Amy was still unable to do her share, and the new priest was a fussy and meticulous individual who declared he must "study" the whole matter thoroughly before carrying out the terms of the will. What Amy did not know as yet was that Gregory had quietly held up the probating of the will and had stopped the funds; he was looking for a way to restore the income from the Barbour & Bouchard stock to Amy. He had already taken charge of Amy's dowry, and the income was again flowing smoothly into her account at the bank.

Since his open rupture with Ernest, a change had come over Gregory. For one thing, he was rapidly aging. He leaned more and more upon John Baldwin and the latter's assistants; sometimes he would not arrive at his office until noon, and about every two weeks he remained home for a day, playing with Amy's children, walking, resting, reading, or merely talking with his niece. He had suddenly come to the conclusion that he needed no more money, and that he had lost the taste for it. His greed had become dulled and tired; it was as if he had sat down at a table with a friend and had eaten too much of food that was both indigestible and impure. He had discovered the casual friend to be a most bitter and implacable enemy, and the food had made him violently ill. He knew that he would never again want to gorge, and that his diet must be simple for the rest of his life. Another change took place in him: his cruel irony softened to a gentler and sadder pessimism, and his old malevolent laughter, silent and red-faced, became kinder. He rarely mentioned Ernest to Amy, and when he did so his face became dusky and brooding. But his remarks were always indifferent and casual. Only once did he speak of Ernest with feeling, and then he said: "He did me the greatest service any man has ever done me: he showed me what I was. And it frightened me." He told himself that he didn't hate Ernest, but that he abhorred him. And this was very near the truth, except that he did not add that he also lived in terror of him, not for what he might do to him, but for what he might do to Amy. He's a mad tiger on the scent of his female, and he won't let up until he gets her, he thought. But worst of all, Amy isn't really on the run; she's helpless against him, but though she is hurrying away, she is looking back in spite of herself. All Gregory's life now seemed to be on guard, sleepless and watchful, about the house he had filled with Amy's children. He shall not hurt her, he said over and over to himself. He shall not have her and destroy her. He shall not bring misery to his wife and his own children. But as he looked from his watchtower at the "mad tiger" prowling impotently below, he felt an exultation that had nothing whatsoever in common with the paternal emotion of protectiveness.

Amy eventually tried to carry out the terms of Martin's will, but at every turn she met mysterious obstacles and delay. She was assured by Gregory and the other bank directors that everything was all right, but that there were "little matters" to be adjusted first. This puzzled her, and frustrated her. Gregory told her fondly that such affairs were too much for the female mind, to which she replied with a smiling sidelong look that made him chuckle. When she insisted that she must begin at once, the directors dolefully laid before her masses of books and papers and ominous-looking documents that made her sag with helplessness. She finally agreed to allow Gregory to adjust the affairs, and eventually manage them. With the strangest feeling that she was doing wrong, that Martin was at her elbow with a sad face, she gave Gregory power of attorney. She could not explain this feeling even to herself; had the thought of distrusting her uncle, of suspecting him, entered her mind, she would have been outraged.

During her greatest months of grief, she could not rid herself of the thought that Martin's life and sacrifices, his ideals and hopes, had all been water poured into sand. The thought became a specter, an obsession she could not rid herself of, try as she might by throwing open the clear windows of reason. It was without effect that she told herself sadly that everyone lives in vain, and that there is no real success anywhere. So besieged was she by her sorrowful regret, that when Nicholas returned to Windsor for a visit he was quite startled out of his pomposity by his widowed niece's mournful face and eyes. Moved for once from his hypocrisy, from his almost automatic phrase-making, he questioned her. When she had finished telling him, with tears, of her sorrow for Martin and his sacrifices, he thought in silence for a long moment. Then he said with sincere gentleness: "My love, you are quite mistaken. A long time ago Martin came to me and told me of the sacrifices he was about to make. He asked me—er—at that time, to suggest some way to him whereby a law could be passed to prevent the bringing into America of alien labor; he asked my help. I wasn't able to do anything at that time, as I told him. But I told him of the small lobby that had already started in Washington against this very thing. As you probably know, he contributed quite a lot of money to this lobby. It is getting stronger; it is beginning to bring this—this outrage to public attention. There is already considerable agitation among native-born Americans. Amy, it may take ten, twenty, even thirty years, for the movement to become powerful enough to pass a stringent law against alien contract labor. But pass it will. There is no stopping it. When Martin investigated the lobby, it was about to die of anæmia; his efforts, over a period of years, and his money, his constant interviewing of Congressmen and politicians, revived the lobby, strengthened it, brought it to the attention of those who will profit by its activities. So, you see, my love, though Martin has passed away, doing his duty (which ought to be some compensation to you,—h'm) he is the man who started a small snowball at the top of the mountain, and though he has not lived to see it, the snowball has become a glacier too tremendous and gigantic to be stopped.

"And in other things, too, his influence is felt. Clean hospitals, free hospitals and medical care, good nursing, mercy, social conscience, regard for one's fellow men, decent living conditions and wages and protection for workers: all these owe a great deal to Martin, and to the few others like him. Nothing strong and ardent and good, however small, is ever wasted. It's like that snowball, growing bigger and heavier, and moving glaciers. Forests are begun with seeds, ma'am, and the seeds Martin has planted may take a long time to become trees, but they will become trees, eventually."

He was quite amazed and pleased at this rare ardor of his, this really sincere ardor, this astonishing altruism. He felt exceedingly virtuous, for he had thought that he had lost all real ability to feel sincerely long ago; he told himself that he had made the best speech of his career. He spent many days thereafter trying to recall it and write it down. But coldly transcribed, artfully written for effect, it lost its splendid glow and heroic simplicity.

It accomplished one thing, however; it eased the ache in Amy's heart. For she knew it was quite true. Very carefully she went through Martin's desk, reading every scrap of paper. She was amazed at the letters written him, by those he had helped through his dozens of activities in politics and propaganda, of which he had never told her. She was ashamed and humbled by this, as though they were mute reproaches, mute accusations that there were many things which he had kept from her, fearing her lack of sympathy and trust. She made promises, vows, that she would be a good steward of what he had left in her hands.

Fortified by this vow, released from much of her sorrow and regret, she found time to enjoy her new leisure and peace and comfort. To be sure, evidences of the war were all about her; the husbands of many of her friends had appeared briefly in the glory of blue and brass buttons, mustaches heroically curled at a fierce angle, and then had disappeared. She had talked with young men who were reported dead two weeks later; she had smiled and flirted in a mild, matronly way with other young men, who were later returned to Windsor blind and crippled, horribly mangled, old men whose youth had been blown out of them in a few short weeks. She had even been led, for just a little while, into the universal hate against the "Rebels," who had widowed her and left her children fatherless. But on the whole the war did not touch her too sharply; she was too far removed from the lower welter of humanity from which the common private was dredged to feel war as it really was, full of agony and hunger, despair and terror. Too, the North's prosperity was not abating. Barbour & Bourchard, opulent with military contracts, grew richer and richer. It was a fad to roll bandages and knit, now; an important pleasure to meet at friends' houses to do these things for "our boys." It was not too bad even to visit the clean hospital Martin had built, and look at the clean young men in their clean shirts in the clean beds. In the South, the women suffered as poignantly as did their men, deprived themselves of the little they had left, stood heroically steadfast in the dark winds of hatred and fear and bitter grief. But women like herself, daughters and wives and sisters of Northern industrialists, might know grief, but it was cushioned by security and ease, carpeted with luxury. They wept in unthreatened homes, comforted by that greatest of friends, Money. Their warm houses were hushed about them, and even sorrow must be shod in velvet before it was allowed to enter the canopied bedrooms. They might be widowed, but they had strong-boxes and secure bank accounts. Their doors were too heavy, too carefully guarded, to allow one cry, one starving hand, one dying face, to penetrate.

Martin's life had been like a bright and evanescent light upon her, not fierce and searing, but more like the shining of a moon at its full. Its passing did not leave her cold and lost, as the removed light of the sun would have done. It began to leave in her memory a sweet wistfulness, a not-unpleasant sorrow, a quiet happiness. She had loved him, loved him still, as one might have loved a pensive dream of some luminous man-angel. Gradually, as time went on, his humanity faded, his misty stature increased, and she remembered and loved him as one would love a fabulous and unearthly creature seen only for a brief and beautiful moment. This was partly due, perhaps, to the fact that Martin's personality had not impressed itself too strongly upon her, and at times, in hours of self-analysis and reproach, she understood that at the last he had withdrawn from her into complete loneliness, feeling instinctively that he had lost her sympathy and trust. Sometimes, thinking of the loneliness of him, she endured some keen moments of real and intense suffering and bitter self-hatred, and for days nothing she could do relieved her grief.

CHAPTER LII

HILDA'S GRIEF at the loss of her son became heavy half-stupefaction for a long time. Even her scolding of her children and grandchildren became dull and absent. The color left her face, and its pallor was accentuated by the engorged small veins that were like red hairs upon it. She waddled about efficiently enough through the large and ornate rooms of Florabelle's house, supervising, berating and managing, but it was a visible effort for her. Her lower lip, always slightly protuberant, but in her youth red and moist and inviting, was now faintly purple and thick, thrusting itself outwards as might a sullen child's. The glance of her once-vivacious eye was heavy and opaque, and sometimes for hours on end she was silent, shutting herself into her room. She hardly noticed her grandchildren, and sometimes refused to come downstairs when her children called. She had always been too quick and emotional to develop the stamina that withstands the shocks of sorrow. Wounded, she was broken, and withdrew, her vitality poured out as from a shattered cup. Her hair, massy still, turned pure and lifeless white.

But Dorcas was broken-hearted. The death of Eugene could hardly have caused her more grief. For a long time she lived in the cemetery where Martin's body lay under wide green elms. When Amy came to that grave, Dorcas would flee, crying wildly. Her family was much disturbed, for she was about to bear her third child, who, when he was born, was named Honore. She had always had the reputation of being "deep" and secretive; her open suffering, her lack of attempt to hide her terrible sorrow, impressed her family as the grief of a more volatile nature would not have done. She withdrew from the bedroom she shared with Eugene, and for months she slept in the small chamber opposite, alone. Eugene would hear her sobs and cries night after night, but when he would tap gently on her door she would subside into a throbbing silence, pretending sleep. Once she cried out at him frenziedly: "I've lost the only friend I ever had!" She looked at her husband's suddenly pale face and saddened eyes with the bitter, half-regretful grief of a sadist. Then she flung herself into his arms, and cried for hours. But she never again said what she had said. And after that night, her sorrow seemed easier for her to bear.

When her nephew, little Honore, was four months old, May gave birth to her fifth child, a little boy they named Guy. And Florabelle Bouchard, two days before Raoul became a gay and debonair Major in the Third Infantry, produced Leon. There were fourteen children in the Barbour-Bouchard families, now, all handsome and well-bred, and more or less charming.

Raoul's enlistment was taken somewhat as a joke. Ernest openly accused him, with amusement, of being bored with domestic life and his elegantly casual duties as ambassador-at-large for Barbour & Bouchard. Everyone laughed, but Raoul knew, as Ernest knew, that there was much of truth in this. Raoul was the born adventurer, not the rugged type, but the silken, philandering, gracefully lustful sort. He was careful not to expose himself to much danger or hardship. He spent much of his leave in New York and Washington, where pretty ladies were plentiful and there was a great deal to drink, and a great many gay parties to attend. He was the type of Frenchman that is constitutionally unfaithful, even while his real love is entrenched in his wife and family. Scandalous tales began to drift back to Windsor, from which Florabelle was carefully guarded by her family. Only Ernest did not reproach Raoul, and that, thought Gregory contemptuously, was probably because he was himself engrossed in a rather sticky affair with one Mrs. Lydia Turnbull, the wife of an artillery captain. As Ernest serenely made no attempt to conceal his latest amour, the family was kept strenuously busy "protecting" May, who knew all about it, and was kept busy, in turn, concealing her knowledge from her relatives. She smiled placidly and gaily as always; kept up the front of happy domesticity. And in truth, she was not too disturbed; she knew Ernest's affections were not really involved. Her real fear lay elsewhere, in the new and charmingly smart house in Quaker Terrace. Nothing had occurred to justify her ever-watchful terror; nothing was ever said, ever communicated to her by the lift of an eyelash. But the fear was there, immovable, self-recognized.

She knew that Ernest rarely if ever saw Amy. Amy never came to the Sessions house. When May called upon her, she never mentioned Ernest. She knew very well that since Martin's death, eighteen or more months ago, Amy had seen her brother-in-law only once. But the fear stood there still.

Ernest was all May wished in a husband: considerate, courteous, fond and interested. He was affectionate to her, engrossed when he was at home, in his children, especially in little Gertrude. When he spoke of Amy, it was only very casually, and with the most brotherly of sympathy. His attitude toward his wife had not changed at all since their marriage, except that it had become more friendly and intimate, confident of her sympathy and laughter. But May looked at him mournfully and thought: He is a stranger. He has always been a stranger. We,

Gregory and I, have done very wrong. He has always loved Amy, and probably always will. But she hugged the thought of him fiercely to herself, hoarded every word he said, was secretly elated each time she made him laugh. He was her husband, and that fact was a strong bolt behind which she could rest in peace, even if it were an uneasy peace. She adored him more than ever; every word and glance of his, every touch of his hand, had power to thrill her as it had done at first. Sometimes she felt that her love for him was a tangible power that nothing could successfully assail. She did not confess, even to herself, how much her safety lay in Amy's hands.

Then, in spite of all his care to avoid danger, a stray ball finally found the gay and indolent Raoul, and on the third of February, 1863, he died in a wretched Washington military hospital, still smiling, but a little regretful that he must leave a jovial world so soon. His fourth child, François, was born in an upper bedroom just as the muffled bell rang below for the messenger who was bringing the telegram announcing his death. They kept the news from Florabelle for nearly a month, and even then the pretty, dainty little thing almost died. Raoul had given her love and protection, gracefulness and ardor, tendernesses and gaiety; his serious lacks of character were quite forgotten by the inconsolable little widow. As for Armand, he sucked in his brown and withered lips at the death of his son, and the lips remained so, sunken, sucked in, until the end of his life. As Raoul had happily died intestate, the Court appointed Ernest Barbour administrator of his estate.

In January, 1865, Dorcas bore her last children, twins, whom she named André and Antoinette. And May, in July of that same year, bore her last child, too: little Joseph, or Joey. The family was now complete.

Except that Florabelle, in August of 1867, with the approval and urging of her brother, Ernest, married one Major Edward Norwood, a middle-aged but gallant bachelor, who owned, they said, "half of Windsor" and a fortune in Western silver mines. After this marriage, Florabelle bore two children, one year apart, Chandler and Betsy Norwood.

CHAPTER LIII

AMY HAD been restive for some time over the slow progress, or rather lack of progress, in the settling of Martin's estate. Here it was, July, 1863, and the hospital was still precariously existing on the small sum donated by the Government for the care of its own wounded. The bank funds, of course, had been stopped a long time ago. But what went on behind the high walls of the Kinsolving works, and now behind the new walls that surrounded all the shops, did not as yet concern Amy. She supposed, in those cases, that the men were taking care of matters. At any rate, a vagueness possessed her when she thought about it, for she had never been in real sympathy with the idea, and still subconsciously resented the misery it had once brought upon her and her children.

However, she received a visit one day from the Mother Superior in charge of the hospital, and from her learned the state of affairs in the Windsor hospital, and the Garnerstown hospital. The nun also told her that no payment had been made to the County orphan asylum, in accordance with Martin's will. Various other permanent charities had received no donation for two years. Amy listened to all of this, wincing under her self-reproach. Here she had been luxuriating in her new home, sentimentally thinking of Martin and utterly ignoring his last wishes! A still bright anger burned in her when she remembered what she now knew was Gregory's deliberate procrastinating, and this anger did not grow less at realizing he had done this for her own benefit.

It was a hot and breathless day, but she called for her carriage, put on her hat, opened her white parasol, and started for the bank. She knew her uncle would be there, for it was his "day" to be present. But when she arrived, she was respectfully informed that "Mr. Gregory" had gone out into the country to look over some mortgaged property the bank had recently acquired, and would not return.

Amy fumed with impatience and impotent anger. She left the President's office in a flurry of hoops and head-tossing, ignoring his invitation to rest awhile in the cool dimness of the room. She emerged into the stony quietness of the bank and started for the street door. But before she reached it, it opened and Ernest entered.

He was still dazzled by the heat and brilliance of the summer day outside, and so did not see her at first, but she saw him at once. It seemed to her that all her blood rushed in a dark and chokingly hot tide to her heart, and her knees trembled weakly under her. She had seen him three times during the past year or so, four times in all since Martin's death. Two of the times she had seen him in Florabelle's house at Christmas, and then only in a room full of people and for just a casual, friendly moment. Once she had met him at a ball given for a soldiers' benefit; she had been in charge of a booth, and he had bought a cravat from her. May had been with him, and they had all laughed a little, joked a little, indifferently, for exactly three minutes. Then Ernest had excused himself, and had left May behind with her cousin. But though May came often to the charming white-pillared house in Quaker Terrace, she came alone or with her children. Everyone in the family, even among their more intimate friends, knew that there had been "something" at some time between Gregory and Ernest, and it was tacitly understood that no questions were to be asked. Gregory and Ernest met only with the greatest and coolest formality in their respective offices, and at the bank. Socially, they avoided each other. May often packed up Amy's children, of whom she was quite fond, and piled them into her carriage for a day at the Sessions house. But Ernest had never yet entered Amy's new home, and no one questioned why this was.

This was the first time since Martin's death that Amy had accosted her brother-in-law alone, and for one disordered moment she thought of turning and running. But he had already seen her. He had stopped short for a single breath, staring at her across the white marble space between them. He had actually hesitated, she saw. And then, smilingly, coolly, he came forward to her and held out his hand. She looked up into his face, and could only think that it was much changed, graver, thinner, lined; his hair, too, light though it was, and still thick, was noticeably gray at the forehead and temples. During their past casual meetings she had been too confused, too hurried, to see much; now, she saw it all, clearly, vividly. He was thirty-seven and appeared much older, for his body had become lean and compact and somewhat stiff, and the moulding of his large, arrogant features was harsher and bolder. She saw that his pale and relentless eyes had narrowed, and that through their lids they darted out coldly and watchfully. The aura of power about him had increased to a formidable degree; always forbidding, he had acquired a presence that aroused fear, distrust and respect. His broad shoulders, the posture of his unusually large head, the dilated nostrils in his short and powerful nose, the certainty of his step and carriage, struck vividly and breathlessly upon Amy. His grasp on her hand was strong and warm, possessive, and it seemed to her that fierce electrical shocks, burning and weakening, ran from that grasp up her arm and flowed into her body. He was smiling down at her in the friendliest way, and into his implacable eyes came something hot and passionate, though wary.

"Well, Amy," he said, still smiling, still holding her hand.

"Well—Ernest," she answered, with a flutter in her voice.

She stood there before him, the color high in her cheeks, quickening and fading and quickening again; the redness in her gentle mouth was as fresh and moist as that of a young girl's lips. Her eyes, clear and lambently brown, shone with a light of their own under the wide and drooping shadow of her white straw hat with its floating ribbons. Her dress, yards upon yards of filmy, cloudy muslin ruffles draped over her hoops, was tied at the slender waist with pale blue ribbon. In her white gloved hands she carried her ruffled parasol. Despite the moulded sadness of her expression in repose, the cast of maturity upon her pretty features, and a certain nobility in the directness of her eyes, she did not look like the mother of four children, and a widow. Her integrity and straightness of mind gave her an appearance of untouched youth. Yet Ernest, the observant, thought that in some way she appeared to be much older than the woman he had gone to comfort that wretched autumn day a long time ago.

After their first inane words, they were silent for a few moments, smiling foolishly at each other. Behind those foolish smiles chaos rushed along like storm-ridden clouds. Ernest had waited very patiently; he had seen Amy many, many times from a distance; he had contrived this seeing. And had waited, knowing that this moment must come some day at last. So his embarrassment was not so great as hers, though now that he held her hand, stood close to her, watched her breathing, and her consternation, his hunger started up and stood astride of him like a starved beast. And with it the strange old feeling, mad and incredulous, that it was preposterous, unbelievable, that she should not belong to him. The sense of furious outrage, of monstrous deprivation, went leaping all through him again.

Yet he dropped her hand easily enough, and led her to a seat along the side of an empty marble wall. The bank had few customers, for it was noon, and very hot, and the cashiers yawned behind their brass grills. They were languidly diverted at the sight of Mr. Ernest Barbour talking so earnestly and inaudibly to Mrs. Martin Barbour near the wall, and tried, out of sheer ennui, to hear what was being said.

Yet what he was saying was inconsequential enough. He was telling her of a day her children had spent in the Sessions house; "my house," he called it. He related a tale of one of Paul's enormities, which caused Amy to blush, and laughingly apologize. She put her lacy handkerchief to her lips, and looked over it at him with laughing eyes; behind it, her lips shook. Something was singing all through her body, a sort of airy ecstasy, a dancing along her nerves, that had nothing whatsoever to do with the silly little tale. It had been a long time since she had felt this excitement, this mysterious and shameful urge. She was sitting down and Ernest was standing before her, leaning toward her, his hand against the wall at the side of her head. Through the corner of her eye she could glimpse this hand at stolen moments; its size and breadth, the largeness of the knuckles, the bluntness of the fingers, were all vividly remembered by her. But never had she wanted so terribly to kiss that hand, to hold it against her cheek, humbly, surrenderingly; she had to clench her own hands to control herself, while she lashed herself with her own contempt. But the desire remained, and it was like the heat of close fire over all her flesh. She thought with real horror: "If we were alone, now, I don't know what I would do. I don't know what I would do—!" When she glanced again at his supporting hand, she had a frightful perception of acute and imminent danger, and a cold thrill ran over her body.

She glanced up, shivering. It occurred to her all at once that she had not heard Ernest's voice for some moments. His posture, his closeness, gave her a cornered and conquered sensation, at once helpless and intoxicating. But it was his eyes that finally aroused her to realization: they were looking down at her, their paleness glittering and devouring. His heavy lips were parted, and she could see the moist shine of his strong white teeth. Her instinct recognized the lustful male look, and it brought her upright, abruptly.

"Well, I must go," she said suddenly, and it seemed to her that she was babbling insanely. "I came to see Uncle Gregory, and he isn't here, so I must go home, for the children are so boisterous and uncontrollable until they have had their lunch, and the baby had a little fever this morning, and I promised Elsa—" And so on, in the pointless chatter of fear and confusion.

Ernest still looked down at her with that look that alternately terrified her and filled her with ecstatic languor. He did not say anything, did not move. Then, after a long time, he removed his hand from the wall, stood up slowly. He half turned from her, stared at the distant bronze door. His profile, jutting, rudely carved, was outlined against the dimness. He said indifferently, without looking at her: "I am a director here, now, and perhaps I can help you."

In a saner time he would have been the last person in all the world to whom she would have told the reason for her coming to the bank today. But she was not entirely sane just then; to her profound cold horror she heard her babbling voice go on and on, telling everything, from the terms of Martin's will, to the deliberate delay in the carrying out of the terms, from her uncle's procrastination to her own anger and determination to see that the will was fulfilled.

Ernest listened, still not looking at her, his face slightly averted. His expression was that of any courteous, mechanically interested director of a bank listening to the complaint of a client. When she had finished, miserably, he was silent for a little while, and then said thoughtfully: "If you wish, I'll look into it for you, though I am certain that your uncle is proceeding with all possible discretion and competence——"

"Oh, yes, yes!" exclaimed Amy, hot-faced with confusion and mortification. "Please forget I spoke of it. It isn't fair to Uncle Gregory. I'm sure he can explain." She stood up, almost crying in her nervous embarrassment and agitation. "I don't know what possessed me——"

He smiled, almost imperceptibly, and secretly. "Of course," he agreed in a soothing voice. He offered his arm. "May I help you to your carriage?"

When she had gone he walked into the President's office and asked that the papers pertaining to the Barbour estate be brought to him. He was still studying them at five o'clock. At that time Gregory returned unexpectedly from the country, and came into the office.

He stepped back when he saw Ernest. "Pardon me," he said formally, and would have gone out but Ernest lifted his hand. "A moment, please, Mr. Gregory. I have something here I would like to talk to you about. Something that has been hanging fire a long time, and ought in all decency to be settled, considering this bank is in the position of joint administrator. Will you come in, please, and be seated?"

An hour later, Gregory, livid-faced and pinched of mouth, said: "You're not really interested in justice being done, either to your dead brother, whom you persecuted shamefully, or to those he helped. What is it, then?"

Ernest folded the papers, put them away in their envelope. He smiled slightly, and said, without glancing at the old man: "Say I am interested in justice as a pure thing in itself. Or say, as a director, I am interested in business being settled and over with."

Gregory pushed himself painfully to his feet; every muscle in his face was twitching, and his voice was a little strangled. "Say, instead, that you are interested in Amy."

"Amy?" Ernest blandly lifted his eyebrows as if in surprise. "What has Amy, except as a client, got to do with the business of this bank? After all, though you are her uncle, I hardly believe she would forgive you for interfering grossly in her affairs, even to the extent of embezzling funds, though you might plead it was for her sake. I don't like embezzlement; it's a nasty business. Authorities don't like it. I hope, now everything is straightened out satisfactorily, that your niece will be satisfied."

Gregory went home. The twitching of his face extended to his legs. He could hardly get out of the carriage when it arrived at the house. Amy was quite alarmed at the sight of him, led him into the library and poured him a glass of brandy. He watched her as she pampered him, and thought that though she was in her thirties, she was lovelier

than ever, with a matured gentleness and poise that was infinitely soothing. He did not underestimate her; he knew she looked too straightly,
was too logical and realistic, to be insulted with hints and innuendoes.
So, after he had rested a little, had put his feet into the house slippers she
had brought him, and had relaxed under the cool smoothing of her hands
on his forehead, he said, trying to keep his voice steady: "Amy, my love,
were you at the bank today?"

The hands on his forehead halted a moment, then she said calmly:
"Yes, Uncle Gregory, I was. I went to see you, but they told me you
were not there." She put her fingers on his eyelids, and he wondered if
it were really true that they trembled ever so slightly. "But, it isn't important just now. Please rest."

"But it is important, Amy. Did you see Ernest while you were there?"
He gently put aside her hands. He looked up into her face piercingly. A
faint color rose on its cheekbones, but she did not glance aside.

"Yes, I saw him." Anxiety wrinkled her forehead. "Why do you
ask, Uncle Gregory? Did he say—anything—to you?"

"Yes. He had called for the papers pertaining to Martin's estate, and
when I dropped in for a few minutes, he insisted I remain and go over
them with him. Did you, ma'am, ask him to do so?"

She had turned excessively pale. But she answered steadily: "It is all
my fault. I am such a fool. I did not ask him to do anything about it,
Uncle Gregory. To do so would have been an insult to you. But I
haven't seen him for some time, and it was hot, and I was disappointed,
and I didn't seem to have anything to say to him, and I am afraid—I
babbled——"

"I see." Gregory's voice was quiet and thoughtful. He stared before
him for a long while. As clearly as though he had been there he recon-
structed the scene. It seemed to her that he repudiated her, and a dry sob
rose in her throat. She pressed her palms together and looked down at
him piteously, as though begging his forgiveness.

"Sit down, Amy, I must talk to you," he said steadily but faintly.
When she had pulled a low chair near him, and was regarding him pleadingly, he went on determinedly, not looking at her for fear he might
falter and save her the pain he must cause her for her own sake.

"I must tell you something. Perhaps I should have told you before.
I see now that I should have told you. It would have saved many unpleasant things. But better now than not at all.

"Amy, I am sure you will remember the night we introduced Ernest
Barbour to May. It's a long time ago. But I am sure you will remember."

"Yes," she whispered.

"Ernest Barbour," he went on, wondering desperately how to proceed, "has always felt for you, from the first moment he met you, something which he no doubt calls love. If he has ever cared for any one in

his crafty life, he has cared for you. He still cares. Amy, you know that?"

"Yes. I know that, Uncle Gregory." The color flushed into her face again, and to his despair and self-reproach he saw the sudden brightening of her eyes, the involuntary lift of her expression.

"But what you don't know, ma'am," he said bitterly, "is that he refused to have you. On that night, a long time ago, I offered you to him, and he refused to have you."

She cried out, faintly. Then she stood up, her cheeks red with shame.

Gregory nodded. Then he drove the knife home, as a surgeon might drive it, to reach an abscess. "You see, Amy, he was under the impression that you were our heiress, and when I told him the truth, he was terribly shocked. Shocked, because he really loved you, if you can call it love. He had been about to propose to you, and when I told him that, he did not. I knew you cared for him, so I as much as offered you to him, outright. You know the rest. Within the year he married May, who was the real heiress. I lied to you, ma'am, if you will remember. Because you seemed to be guessing the truth, and I couldn't stand for you to be hurt and humiliated.

"Yes, he loved you. But he loved you less than he loved money. And to this day, he loves you less than he loves money and power. If he had it to do over again, he would do as he did, even though he knew that he would always love you."

She had grown quieter and paler as he had talked. When he had finished, she sat down again, facing him. Her expression was quite calm, and only the peculiar drawn brightness of her eyes betrayed anything of what she was feeling.

"He is a coward, a welcher," said Gregory. His lips felt numb and thick, and there was a strange tearing in his chest. "If he had been all a man, he would have abided by his decision. He had made his choice. But now he wants to eat his cake and have it, too."

She moistened her mouth, and after a few moments was able to ask in a low voice: "Why do you tell me all this, now?"

Gregory was silent for so long a time that she began to believe he had not heard her. Then he answered: "Amy, you know why I have told you."

"I believe I do." She stood up, trembling a little. She walked to the door. "Paul and Elsa are waiting to see you, Uncle Gregory. I believe it's something about a boat for Paul's birthday. I'll send them in, while I see about dinner." She went out, closing the door softly behind her.

Gregory sighed, relaxed in his chair. A faint grin, bitter, half-regretful, and wholly sad, stretched his lips. "I've finished you now, Mr. Ernest Barbour," he whispered aloud.

He had done the right thing, he knew. He knew very well that Amy had too clear a vision to be sentimental, that eventually, she would have given in. She loved Ernest Barbour too well to have withstood him much longer, now that he was definitely after her and would not be denied. She would have been helpless, with more than a little of her own consent.

Gregory, himself, had lived too long, too far removed from impracticalities, to have considered such a surrender shameful or reprehensible. Had it not been Ernest Barbour, he would have told his niece frankly not to fight against the only thing in life which has true validity, true splendor and satisfaction. But—it *was* Ernest Barbour. And he, Gregory, had waited many, many years just for this.

But still, the old sentimentalities that encrust the race had their last little moment with him. He whispered: "He would have hurt her. He would have devoured her and ruined her." And knew that he lied, and was disgusted that he could lie so to himself, and he an old man. "There is May," he persisted, to that disillusioned self, and had to wince.

He raised himself painfully and laboriously in his chair. He said aloud: "Nothing could have stopped her, now that he's at her heels. Nothing but shame. I've given her that, poor child. He'll not get around that. He'll never get around that! I've done you in, Mr. Ernest Barbour. I've had the last word, after all!"

He began to cough thickly. He thought, in a confusion: I'll not put off going to the doctor any longer. I ought to have gone a long time ago. This pain—but of course it's just my age—it's just my stomach. A slight indigestion. He coughed again.

The next day he was unable to return to his desk. He had no desire to, however. Hour after hour, he sat in his library, or walked in the garden with the children, or talked to his niece. All desire had left him, for everything. He could not feel sad even over the fact that he did not regret the loss of his desire. He was like a numb and drowning man who indifferently and slowly releases the edge of a spar, finger by finger, while the waves grow larger and blacker and more imminent. Like that drowning man, he felt that the struggle to live, to breathe, to fight, had become insupportable.

One night, in his sleep, he released his last dim hold on the spar, and the waves sucked him down.

CHAPTER LIV

MAY INSISTED that her cousin, Gregory Sessions, be buried from his old home, where he had been born and where he had lived the major part of his life. Amy consented, for only she knew how he had missed the Sessions house, and how hard he had tried to accustom himself to the new house in Quaker Terrace. It seemed little enough to do for him, to let him lie once more in his old home, to let the green light from the trees shine in upon his dead face. Besides, she was too grieved to offer any objection to anything.

So, in this emergency, the old promise to Martin was forgotten, and Amy entered the Sessions house for the first time in many years. Even in her grief, it was soothing to enter here, where everything seemed to remember her, and where she remembered everything. She slipped away from the crowded groups talking whisperingly in the drawing rooms, and went all through the house, with the exception of the bedrooms. But her old bedroom, she discovered, was not being used at present, and she went in, closing the door behind her. It was just as it used to be, even to the ruffles on the high deep bed and the canopy over it. To be sure, she reminded herself, the ruffles were new, as were the ruffled curtains, but someone had decided to keep the room as it had been. The sunlight poured through the open window, lying on the thick dark-red rug, on the white and virginal bed, the pale ivory walls, the polished mahogany dresser and high-backed chair. Crystal candlesticks dripping with rainbow prisms still stood on the mantelpiece. Of course, it was all a little prim and old-fashioned: Great-grandmother Pierce had brought most of this furniture from England one hundred twenty-five years before. But it was simple and fresh, and, to Amy, full of innocent peace. She sat down upon the bed, then dropped her head to the fat ruffled pillows. She had not slept much during the past two nights, and her eyelids were raw and burning from tears. But it was so silent here, so comforting, as though the room had arms that had enfolded her, a consciousness that had remembered her, and she fell suddenly into a profound sleep.

When she started awake, the windows were rectangles of shining blue sky, but the sun had gone. The air that rushed through the room was fresh and scented, but unseasonably cool. For a long moment Amy was utterly disoriented. She was back again in her old home, **a young** girl. Time had doubled on itself, had returned her unscathed and un-wounded to her prim, soft little bed, as a tide brings back the jetsam it has carried out. She sat up, pushing back her disordered hair, struggling with the curious enchantment that seemed to lie over her. She had slept here for the last time the day before she had left it forever as a bride. Then all the years had come between, husband and children, death and sorrow, hopelessness and pain. They had run like swift water between herself and this room, frothing and thundering. But the water had gone, and she had crossed the narrow space of Time and was back again in her old bed, with the old simple peace upon her. Oh, if it could be true! she thought, lying back upon the pillows, pressing her cheek into them. If I only were as I was once, with Uncle Gregory waiting downstairs for me to join him at dinner, and the collies racing on the lawns, and my new gowns in the closet, and no complications, no sadnesses, no tirednesses waiting for me outside. But things were not so simple as all that, more was the pity. One came back to the old places, but one was not the same. Strangers with borrowed memories came back, strangers who had no right in the old places that waited for the old familiars. She, herself, with all the burdens of life upon her, her very face changed, experiences carved upon her mind, was an intruder in this room where a young girl had slept and dreamed.

She sat up again, sighing. A fleecy white rug lay across her legs. Someone, she thought, startled, had come in upon her and had covered her against the cool fresh breeze. She was a little annoyed, disliking the thought that she had lain in defenseless sleep while someone had looked down at her at leisure; it was almost like being caught naked. It was undignified, if not humiliating.

She rearranged her hair in the old, slightly bleared mirror which had once reflected the fresh smiling face of a young girl. Now it reflected the face of a tired woman in her thirties, thin and worn a little sharp, whose eyes were heavy from crying and lost sleep, whose cheeks were pale and drawn. It was surely not the face of that young girl! Even the eyes were not the same. Suddenly she thought: I've never been happy one moment since I left here!

"No, no!" she exclaimed aloud, in panic, dropping her hands from her hair. Surely she had been happy in her marriage! That first year or two of gentle understanding and contentment and companionship—nothing could ever change that or spoil its memory. She recalled Martin's un-varying kindness and sweetness, his consideration and faithfulness in all things, his simple love that she had not fully appreciated. "He was too good for me," she said in a dull voice. But, surely she had been happy in her marriage. If the last years had been gloomy and bleak, tight-lipped and lonely and desperately resentful, the fault was hers, not Martin's.

She went to the door and opened it. The room was still bright with the reflected light from the sky and the green thick trees; the white soft bed waited under its ruffled counterpane and canopy; soft light poured along the rounded curves of the chairs and dresser. On the swept hearth a load of small logs waited in their basket, and the brass tongs and poker stood ready. But the hall outside was dark and chilly and silent. From the rooms below there rose the dim murmur of respectful voices, May's sudden faint sobbing. But Amy looked back at the room of her girlhood as she stood on the threshold that led out into the dark hall and her present life. When she finally closed the door, she felt as though she were shutting in some part of her life that was gone forever, some part of herself she would never know again.

Gregory was buried in the family plot where his parents already lay, his sister, Amy, and his uncle, May's father. Martin was not buried in that plot; he lay beside his father at a little distance. It was a hot still day when Gregory was buried, the trees heavy and warm with summer, the shadows clear black and sharp on the vivid green grass. Amy watched them lower the coffin into the earth, heard the solemn words "Whosoever believeth in me shall never die," and knew suddenly, without question or doubt, that Gregory was not really in that coffin, being lowered into that moist black ground. Where he was, she did not know, but she did know that he was not here, would never be here. She carried this comfort back to her home with her, a strange, weird comfort that sustained her for many days until she had become accustomed to her grief

WHEN GREGORY'S will was opened, it was discovered that it had been newly written. May Sessions Barbour, of course, inherited his share of the Sessions properties and interest, including the stock and the bonds. His share was much larger than had been estimated. Ernest, figuring rapidly, was pleasantly surprised to discover that his private liquid assets were some hundred thousands above his original estimate. He had known for some time that Gregory had the controlling number of shares; now he, through May, had this control. It was all his, this larger share of the mills, the mines, the wells, the lumber yards, the foundries, the fleet of flat-boats on the river, and the controlling interest in the bank, which carried with it the Chairmanship. The bank, in its way, controlled the financial destinies of the town. Ernest had often imagined this moment, when he would be the most powerful man in Windsor, perhaps in the State, but its full sweetness and richness of flavor was greater than his expectation. To be sure, Senator Nicholas Sessions was a partner in all these enterprises, a lesser partner; but as he was never actively engaged in the management of them, and as May would eventually inherit his share also, he left everything in Ernest's hands. Thus Ernest had absolute power in all dealings.

He knew some moments of intoxicated exultation. He was still under forty years of age, and he was the richest man in the State, surely the most powerful! He had always wanted a subtle hand in State, and even national politics: now Senators would be errand boys for him! A few weeks after Gregory's will had been probated, Ernest invited the Governor and his wife for a week's visit, an invitation which was immediately and graciously accepted, though Ernest had assured the Governor that the visit would be informal and quiet, because of Gregory's recent death. Once, Ernest had a moment of grandiloquence, and said to himself, aloud, in an exultant voice: "Eugene once told me I was a man of destiny, and by God! he was right!" He was immediately embarrassed by this childishness, but the impression remained with him, a secret intoxicant.

Gregory had left seventy-five thousand dollars from his private liquid assets to his niece, Amy Drumhill Barbour, and lesser bequests, notably fifty thousand dollars to John Baldwin. None of the children of either Amy or May was specifically mentioned, except little Godfrey, Ernest's son, for whom Gregory had lately acquired a secret affection. He left the child five thousand dollars with which to purchase "the best possible violin." May, in soft tears, thought this excessively touching, but Ernest, looking at his oldest son, set his mouth grimly. He was not so sure of the purity of Gregory's motives; he knew the old man's subtleties too well. And hated him, dead though he was, rich as was the fortune left to May.

Not a penny was left to any charity whatsoever.

Nicholas Sessions gave Ernest, whom he increasingly admired, power of attorney. Nicholas and the bank had been made joint administrators of the will. Thus Ernest had the handling of Amy's legacy as well as all the rest.

Amy was the only one who truly mourned Gregory Sessions. May had been fond of him, in a humorous cousinly way, but her real attachment was for Nicholas. At times she had thought Gregory exceedingly unfair to her husband, and though Ernest was too astute, too indifferent, to disparage him to May, she had gathered that Gregory had been more than a little prejudiced. After the first numbness wore off, and Amy found herself lonely and desolate in a house full of servants and children, she could hardly endure it. Her female relatives suggested that she take Paul and Elsa, now past ten years old, on a sea voyage; Armand and Eugene, who had always liked her, and considered her a grande dame, visited her often with Dorcas, urged "a change of scene" upon her But two months after Gregory's death, Amy fell ill from worry and grief, developed a sort of low fever, and was confined to her bed for five weeks, nursed in turn by May and Dorcas and Florabelle. Everyone came, even Hilda, except Ernest. He inquired politely enough about his sick sister-in-law, sent her flowers and brotherly messages, but seemed little interested. He had waited a long time; he could wait a little longer. But not too long. May told him that Amy was much changed in every way, and she shook her head when she told him. But Ernest, who loved Amy, knew that to him she would never be changed, not even in old age, not even in death.

CHAPTER LVI

A MY RECOVERED. She had grown very thin, so that her height seemed to have increased. She moved more slowly and in a more stately manner, though her poise had always been remarkable. She was very lonely, for she was too intelligent not to be bored by children, however much she loved them, yet she shunned visitors, never visited, herself, except for a brief call or two upon the widowed Florabelle and Dorcas. The first snow was already upon the ground, lying thinly upon the gardens; she would sit by the large French windows of her own sitting room, warming her feet by the fire, and looking out upon the white silence of the earth. She rarely read, did little sewing; she seemed to be thinking, absorbed in her mournful and lethargic thoughts. When the children rushed in upon her she received them with gentle smiles, kisses and touches, but seemed glad when they had gone out again. Warm life appeared to be suspended in her. Sickness of mind had succeeded sickness of body.

Tt was just after Thanksgiving, when the sky was gray and still, the snow deep and dimpled and carved into drifts by a recent wind, that Ernest called upon her with papers from the bank pertaining to her legacy, which demanded her signature.

He asked the neat maid who admitted him not to announce him; she led him to the door of the little sitting room where Amy spent her slow days. He knocked gently, and at her faint command to enter, he opened the door and stepped inside the room.

She had been sitting there, thinking of him, as she always did, night and day. She had been sitting quietly enough, her feet on the fender, her white woolen morning robe loosely belted about her, but within she had been crying out, running to and fro, as she was always doing. But by some odd power of telepathic communication, the memory of Ernest, the very feel of his personality, had been intensely upon her, so, that when he entered, standing by the door for a moment after he had closed it behind him, she was not surprised, only bemused.

"I was thinking about you," she said simply, in a voice that sounded as if it came from some distance. The next minute realization flooded in upon her, and she rose to her feet, clutching the robe about her.

The pretty, informal room was very dim and warm, except for the pale white wall of the windows that looked out upon the snowy gardens. A fire burned red upon the hearth, and a canary in a golden cage whistled near the window plants.

Ernest looked at Amy intently as he advanced slowly toward her across the soft primrose carpet. Yes, he thought suddenly, with a sort of sick pain, she has changed a great deal, my poor Amy, my darling. He did not at first see her expression of repulsion and anger, even fear. He stopped a little distance from her, and then, as the fire leapt up a little, he saw that expression. Something cold and warning ran through him.

"Well, Amy," he said quietly. He laid his leather letter-case upon the table, kept his hand upon it.

"You should not have come here!" she cried out suddenly, in a voice shrill and tight. She retreated a step from him.

Now his own voice sharpened. "Why not? You aren't very hospitable, or even courteous, Amy! Your Uncle Nicholas has given me power of attorney, so I am virtually the administrator of your legacy. You have been ill and unable to attend to business, so I have brought the necessary papers to you today for your signature. I am sorry to say that this matter could not have waited. Otherwise I assure you that I would not have come today."

He could see that she was swallowing convulsively as she listened. She had put her hand to her throat as though it pained her. He moved a chair near the table, and said, more gently: "Please sit down here, Amy, and sign these papers. And then I will go at once, if that will give you pleasure."

She bent her head. Very slowly, as if enfeebled, she moved to the chair and sat down. He dipped his own pen into the ink for her, handed it to her. He turned the papers as her trembling hand put her signature upon them. When it was all done, he folded the papers and began to put them back into the case. Not a sound had passed between them during this interval, though once their hands had touched, and Amy's hair had brushed his sleeve. Then she said, still keeping her head bent and away from him: "You could have sent someone. Or you could have brought someone with you."

He finished the methodical putting away of the signed papers before he spoke. Coals dropped upon the hearth in the silence. A flutter of wind flew by the windows, and a tree outside snapped in the cold. Ernest bent over the table and pulled the straps of the case into place. Then he asked softly:

"Why do you hate me, Amy? Because I dare to love you?"

She stood up, supporting herself with her hand upon the table. She looked at him directly, and in the gloom her eyes flashed like fire.

"No!" she cried. "Because you dared not love me!"

Ernest's head jerked up; he moved a step toward her and stared at her. And she stared back at him, bitterly, contemptuously. There was another silence between them, but now it vibrated. Then, very slowly, Ernest half turned from her and looked at the fire.

"I see," he said. "So he finally told you."

She gave a faint and smothered cry, and struck her hands together in a sort of frenzy. All her poise, her control, were gone. "Oh, why did you do that to me? Why did you hurt me so, all these years? I—you—both of us, ruined Martin's happiness; I wasn't the wife to him that I should have been! Because of you. Because money was more to you than loving me. When you left me and I married Martin, I thought I could be happy; for a time I really was happy—I think. But I couldn't forget. I—didn't know, or I might have forgotten, made myself forget. That's what I can't forgive my uncle—not telling me then. Not for my sake, but for Martin's." She put her hands over her face, crouched a little, sobbed aloud. "All those years, my years and Martin's years, wasted and ruined. Because you were a coward, and greedy. Because nothing meant anything to you, but money and power. And you're still a coward, and greedy. You have what you sold me for, but you are what Uncle Gregory said you were, a welcher. You won't leave me alone. You won't leave me to any little peace I might be able to feel eventually."

All the sufferings of years, all the humiliation, the full realization of what she was herself saying and the truth of it suddenly revealed to her, stood in her tearing and choking voice. When she had finished, she put her hand to her head, sobbed heartbreakingly, without shame or control, a broken and distraught woman. Anguish had done away with all observances of niceties, all masks and proprieties. It would not have touched her if the whole world had heard what she had said. She was beyond all self-respect, all pride.

Ernest watched her without moving. Many things had shaken him, but never like this. The blood stood congested in the veins of his face, and his hands were clenched at his side. Once he moved his large head as though what he was seeing and hearing had become too unbearable for endurance.

He put his hand on the mantel-piece and turned from her when she had finished.

"I can't say anything," he said heavily. "What is there for me to say?"

She had stopped sobbing, and was feebly wiping her eyes. "Nothing at all," she whispered finally. "Nothing at all." She paused, then resumed eagerly, almost fiercely, in a louder voice: "Except this: knowing everything, would you do what you did over again?"

He dropped his hand from the mantel-piece and turned to her in amazement. She was looking at him passionately, quickened with hope. She was begging him to save her pride at the very last, to rescue her from her humiliation, to give her the comfort of self-respect. She was asking him to give her strength and courage, fortitude and resistance, again. For one moment his love for her was strong enough, selfless enough, to make him want to give her all this, at a terrible cost to himself. For one moment he wanted to bestow this comfort, to restore to her her very strength against him. How terribly he wanted this, with her pleading face and brightened eyes so close to him, her hand outstretched in her last hope!

Then Ernest, the gambler, played what he felt was his greatest stake. "Do you want me to lie to you, Amy? Do you want me to tell you that I would do differently if I had it to do over again?" He said this simply, regarding her directly and steadily.

For a long moment her face was as blank as though he had struck it unexpectedly. Her eyes blinked almost idiotically, and her hand fell to her side. Then, before she could fully realize what he had said, and what it meant to her, before she could even recover herself a little, he had taken her in his arms, and was kissing her violently, upon the lips and throat and hair, as though the hunger of years could no longer be controlled. He was saying hot and incoherent things in her ear; his arms were crushing her. All through her weak body went a sensation as though she were drowning, and she struggled feebly, her hands fluttering at his arms, her head thrown back.

At last her hands fell slowly, her struggling stopped, and in the room was a deep warm silence.

CHAPTER LVII

M R. LINCOLN had long ago been assassinated. The War was over and Reconstruction had begun in the South. Ernest had purchased five large cotton mills in two Southern States, and was buying the newest machinery for them. He also bought a vast tract of land in Tennessee. Armand and Eugene had long ago come to the conclusion that Ernest always knew what he was doing, and beyond a few eyebrow liftings and light shrugs they said nothing. But May was edified.

"What are you going to do with that old trash?" she asked. "You are surely not going to add dirt-farming to your list of enterprises, are you?"

"I might," he answered, smiling, and tugging at the richness of her still beautiful curls. "You ask too many questions, Puss."

"Well, of course, I've only brought you half a dozen mills and foundries; I've only restored to you fifty per cent of the Barbour-Bouchard stock which the Sessions Steel owned! Not to mention items such as this house, and the lumber yards and the twenty per cent of the Kinsolving stock that Gregory owned in his own name. However, these are probably so small that they do not give me a right to be interested in your manipulations."

Ernest laughed. "But I am a very remarkable man!" he said. "All these things, with which you purchased me, are really below my real price. But you, as a woman, are so charming, so sweet and clever in yourself, that I let myself be bought very cheaply."

May laughed also, but she never forgot those words: "All these things, with which you purchased me." Yes, she had purchased Ernest; she had never regretted the trade. But love, she thought with unusual bitterness, was a curse; it made you drive mad blind bargains, which, though intrinsically valueless, were necessary to your very life. She had had no rest since her marriage. She had borne Ernest five children, had secured his confidence and his affection, had loved him devotedly, lived only for his comfort and his amusement. She knew she was not a dull woman; knew that only she had the power to make him laugh and relax, look upon problems with a humor he otherwise would not have had. She had never bored him. Yet she knew that he did not love her, that even in his passion she was playing proxy.

She was too intelligent and reasonable a woman to be silly and jealous.

She had been too fond of Amy to cultivate hatred for her. Perhaps, she thought wryly, this was because she had never lost hope that Ernest might love her some day as she wanted him to love her. Now, she was losing hope, and as her hope waned the red star of hatred began to rise in the darkness it was leaving behind. She told herself a thousand times that Amy had done nothing wrong, had not lifted an eye or hand to attract Ernest, had not shown by any sign that she cared for him. She tried to believe that Amy's sense of obligation and affection would prevent any flirtation, however mild, with the man who loved her. She would surely have honor—! Honor, thought May ruefully. In her place, if I loved him, would I have honor?

Amy had never been a woman to visit constantly, and since Gregory's death her excursions abroad were fewer than ever. May rarely saw her, except when she herself visited the house in Quaker Terrace. And now that her own hope was dimming, becoming colder and sadder, she visited Amy less than ever, rarely sent the carriage for her children. On the occasion of her latest visit she had thought that Amy looked exceptionally well, suddenly blooming in her middle thirties as some women do, but that her manner was a little distrait and preoccupied. She had seemed relieved when May had prepared to go, and May imagined that she had winced a little under her warm cousinly kiss. She had stood beside the carriage while May had settled herself, prattling humorously as always, and when May had looked down at her for a last smiling good-by she had been startled to see that Amy's eyes were full of tears. On the way home, May was suddenly amazed at her own surge of bitter instinctive hatred for her cousin, an emotion of which she was at once ashamed.

May knew that Ernest's affair with the buxom Army widow was over and done with. She thought that if he had begun another affair she would know of that also. But what she did not know was that when Ernest wished a matter to be secret, it was a secret indeed. So, May began to feel some contentment and some hope that her husband was done with all his straying.

Two months after Florabelle Bouchard married her gallant Major, Nicholas Sessions succumbed to cerebral hemorrhage, and the balance of the vast Sessions fortune passed into May's hands, and through hers, into Ernest's.

CHAPTER LVIII

GODFREY JAMES BARBOUR, though fourteen years old, was still known as "little Godfrey," or "Frey."

It was not that his stature was so small; he was only an inch less in height than his robust cousin, Paul Barbour, one year younger. But he was exceedingly slender, not gaunt, but so delicately made, so almost exquisitely made, that he appeared shorter than he was, and frailer. He carried himself well, however, and gracefully. His hair was very fair and curling, his eyes a soft bright brown; he had the Barbour nose, short and rather square, but he had not inherited his father's belligerently distended nostrils. His mouth, flexible and well colored, was his most beautiful feature. In fact, as Ernest sometimes said with disdain, he was a beautiful boy. His beauty lay not so much in the contours and coloring of his face, but in a certain lofty nobility of expression, a certain width and height of brown eyes, a certain attitude of his long and slender head. Sometimes his father, disgruntled, told his mother that the lad was getting to look uncommonly like Martin, and he hoped to God that the family wasn't going to be afflicted by another martyr and idealist. But the truth was that it was only in his external coloring that he resembled his dead uncle, and then he did not have Martin's blue eyes.

Godfrey, or Frey, as she called him, was May's darling, her Benjamin. When he was at home, he was never far from her. She often laughed at him, poked him, rallied him, amused herself with his seriousness and only slight humor, and understood him only a little. Sometimes she scolded him, like a "Billingsgate fishwife," Ernest said. But more than all these, she loved him, and if her face was frequently humorous when she talked to him, her hand was gentle and had in it something fiercely protective. She was rarely impatient with him, though she was not instinctively fond of children (in fact, rather disliked even her own). But her patience with Godfrey was remarkable. She was never too hurried, too tired, too irritated, to listen to him, to sit down and draw him to her, to touch his cheek and hold his hand while he stammered out what had been troubling him. While she listened, her face would soften, glow, bend toward him attentively. Sometimes he puzzled and annoyed and worried her, for he was silent and secretive, dignified and inexplicable, given to wild little rages that had in them something of despair. He never played as other children played; he was apparently afraid of his contemporaries, and actually seemed to suffer when forced to be with them. But though she understood him only a little, she knew when he was distressed, though not why, guessed his lostness, though not the reason, sympathized with his obscure pains without knowing their source. If sometimes, even with her, he felt helplessly alone, her smile and voice, her touch and love, comforted him.

May knew that the boy disliked and feared his father. When he had been a very little child, he had frequently run from Ernest, even to the extent of hiding under beds. When Ernest, in impatient affection, had lifted him upon his knee, had tried to engage him in talk, the child had sat in petrified silence, like a caught bird shivering under a hand that tried to be kind. Like that bird, he had been unable to move in his terror, had merely fixed his bright distended eyes upon his father's face in a sort of deadly fascination. It would have astonished Ernest had he known that to his little son's vision he appeared almost monstrous, like a strange and dangerous animal, that his eyes had seemed to shine with ferocity, that his breath had seemed hot, his teeth gleaming savagely, his voice rough for all its attempt to be gentle. It would have astounded and disconcerted him to know that the very young Godfrey dreamt about him at night, enlarged and frightful, like something out of the dreams of the pagan Teutons: gigantic, emerging from thunders and mists, riding on winds, a Wotan that bestrode mountains and carried lightning in his hand.

His first conscious memories in childhood were not connected with sight or taste or touch, nor even with hunger or pleasure or greed. They were connected with sound. Sounds to him had personalities, even if they were merely the creaking of a shutter in the wind, the rush of trees at midnight, the snapping of wood in intense cold, the iron ring of winter nights, or the metallic falling of summer rain in the pool at the foot of the garden. The song of the robin at evening seemed more real to him than the bird; notes struck on the piano keys were more alive than the hands that evoked them. He early discovered that all things had a rhythm peculiar to them and to them alone, and sometimes lying awake at night he tapped out on the wall near his bed the rhythms of low wind, cricket, or rattle of casement. When a sound with a steady rhythm, or an odd cadence, came to his attention, he was elated; his tapping out of it gave him a sensuous satisfaction, almost voluptuous. He came to love certain rhythms, hate others, be irritated by some, made restless by many. Sometimes May, lying awake also at her husband's side, heard that low steady tapping on the wall, for she slept in the room adjoining, and for years she was puzzled as to what made it. When Godfrey told her, she did not quite understand, but she thought it very touching. She bought the boy a drum, something which Ernest assured her he would not care for. But Godfrey seized on it with cries of joy, much to Ernest's pleasure and surprise. Thereafter the rhythms pulsed through the house and the gardens, strange running rhythms, slow dolorous rhythms, rhythms that danced and hopped like little old-fashioned figures, rhythms that seemed to fold hands in prayer, to rise in triumphant ecstasy and victory.

One day May and Godfrey were sitting alone in a little arbor in the garden, she embroidering, he tapping on his drum. Neither had spoken a word for some time. May dropped her needle, and looked down at the young boy at her feet. His head was bent, and a shaft of sunlight, coming through the lozenge-shaped slats of the summer house, gilded his fair head until it seemed to blaze with light. She studied his delicate profile, the long fair lashes, the faintly flushed cheek, the beautiful dreaming mouth. All at once she was afraid; he seemed to have been removed far from her, where she could not go. He was only a little boy of seven at the time, but she felt that he had gone from her, and that if she did not speak and break the enchantment, he would not come back. It was quite absurd, she knew, but she put her hand tenderly on his head and said: "My darling, why do you sit there dreaming so, just tapping on your drum? What are you thinking about?"

He had a nervous, self-conscious color that had a habit of rising and falling in his face when he was spoken to. He looked at his mother in embarrassment; young though he was he knew her sympathy for him was connected only with her love, and not her understanding.

"Why, I'm just making sounds," he answered. "The sounds I hear. I'm trying to make the same sound." He regarded her seriously. "Everything has a sound, Mama. Even you have."

May was quite edified. "Have I, now! Show me how I sound."

He regarded her with increasing seriousness, while she struggled not to smile. Then, still looking at her, he began to beat out a rhythm on his drum. She was like a score that he was following. He beat out a rhythm that was quick and light, somewhat erratic at moments, sometimes dancing and fast, sometimes slower and softer, followed by swift tapping sounds like rapid and laughing speech. But under all this he struck a steady and sober rhythm, unchanging and steadfast, if a little monotonous.

May had often confessed that she had no ear whatsoever for music. She could use a piano passably, ballads and light sonatinas and simple melodies, but she performed them almost playfully, with an air of apology. She had attended scores of concerts in Boston and New York, as a necessary polish to her education. But she never really liked music, and could rarely tell one symphony from another. So Godfrey's rhythmic beating appeared only a jumble of mechanical hollow sounds to her, without individual meaning. She wrinkled her white brow as he finished and waited for her comment, and tried to look intellectual. "Very, very sweet, my lovie," she said at last, bending to kiss him. "You are really quite clever."

But the next day she called him into the drawing room, sat down at the piano with him beside her on the bench, and began to teach him what she knew of music. He had been strumming for most of his short life on that instrument, and she was astonished to find that he could play quite well, already, if utterly without technique or clarity. He played, of course, by ear, and it was exceedingly difficult for her at first to make him relate the notes on the written page to the sounds his hands evoked. "Dear me," she thought irritably, "I'm pretty much of a fool. I should have paid some attention to this long ago. Now I've got to unravel all the bad things he has picked up, himself."

But she enjoyed the teaching. It was not until the boy had acquired everything she knew that she thought of professional teachers.

And at first, she had taught him only because she wished to give him pleasure, and not with any dream or thought of the future. But one day, as she watched his beautifully shaped small hands evoking from the piano keys an exquisite impromptu melody, watched the ecstatic absorption on his lifted face, she thought humbly, with a sudden clarity of vision: He shall have his music. He shall have his life.

Godfrey had never heard an orchestra; in fact, it is doubtful if he knew such a thing, dedicated wholly to music, existed. Two or three times a year he heard the band concert playing in Sessions Park, on Fourth of July, Thanksgiving Day, and a time or two besides in the summer. The musicians were not very skilled, and leaned heavily on the brasses and the drums, which was all very well on the side of noise, but not very subtle. However, to music-starved Godfrey James Barbour, the blared marches, the sentimental melancholies, the dolorous nocturnes, were exquisite. He would wiggle his way as closely as possible to the bandstand, and would stand there, gripping the criss-cross slats of its platform, staring up at the leader or closing his eyes in ecstasy. Sometimes, when a particularly poignant passage stole out through the noisy jumbled confusion of the drums and the horns, tears would roll down the boy's cheeks, and he would press his meagre chest against the hands that gripped the slats, heavily, as though the self-induced pain relieved the transports in him.

But this was before May had taught him all she knew of music. Introduced to Bach and Beethoven, to Mozart and Gounod, listening to May's description of them as played by an orchestra, conjuring them up with remarkable fidelity by the aid of his intense imagination, Godfrey soon found his beloved brass band intolerable. May remembered all her half-forgotten hours in music halls; she would play, for Godfrey's benefit, a few bars of an overture, then explain, with quite commendable color and accuracy, how the horns came in here, or the flute there, how the melody whispered here, rose triumphantly there. Here would be the hushed murmur of drums, like meditative voices heard at a distance, here a harp would sing thinly, like rippling moonlight, here a 'cello would add depth and poignancy that would be almost unbearable, here the violins would emerge, like supple dancers with strong sweet voices, or a theme would burn softly and clearly, like tapers ringed with light. She would play sections of symphonies, and before the boy's startled and radiant eyes abysses would open, spanned by rainbows, or chaos would tumble before him, blinding him with darkness or light.

May found a sudden, tremendous and exciting happiness in this teaching of her young son. She found that her life had become regulated and staid, placid when not anxious about her husband, somewhat petty and circumscribed. In teaching Godfrey, in watching the white light upon his face, the trembling of his lips, she became aware of old dreams and joys, old glories and majesties, old feelings that beyond the rim of a narrow earth splendors stood veiled and imminent, which she thought she had forgotten in the welter of a fat trough. For some time she felt the old delicious restlessness, the old mysterious urge of the spirit, the old sensation of ecstatic waiting for a vision. She told herself a little drearily that these were all lies, the vagaries of an awakening adolescence; nevertheless, she felt that nothing else in the world was so beautiful, so satisfying, so close to God. All the things she had come to accept as truth, as validities proved beyond a doubt, seemed flat and stupid to her, like empty prairies without hills or valleys. "What does it matter if you know at last that two and two are four?" she thought. "Does it make living more endurable or more beautiful; does it make miseries easier to bear if you know a relentless formula? Two and two make four. But that's not an axiom that stands in the presence of God."

One day, on an impulse, as she sat with Godfrey at the piano, she held up four fingers and looked at him quizzically. "How many fingers have I up, Frey? Four. Don't you believe it! There's no end to my fingers, there's no end to what I can do with them! I can save with them, kill with them, be kind with them, steal or play with them, destroy or love with them. Those are the real fingers, all the thousands of things they can do; and you can't count them, love. So, you see, when you say these are four fingers, you lie. Some day the world will try to teach you that they are only four fingers after all, but if you believe that, you will lose your soul."

Godfrey had listened gravely. At the end he had nodded his head. "Did you understand?" cried May irritably, wondering, herself, at this irritation.

"Yes, Mama." And she wondered for a long time if he did. But one day he said to her, quite unexpectedly, several months after that episode: "Mama, Papa believes that you only held up four fingers, doesn't he?"

May was quite startled. She regarded Godfrey in silence for a few moments, then she pulled him to her, kissed him passionately, tears in her eyes. "Yes, love, Papa always believed that there were just four fingers."

"Then, he lost his soul, didn't he, Mama?"

May put him from her a little and looked into his face blankly. "Perhaps he did, my pet, perhaps he did." Then she pushed him away and smiled. "You mustn't carry metaphors to a bitter end, sweet." She paused. "In fact, never carry anything to a bitter end."

May bought him a thick volume of the lives of famous composers written in a simple and clarified style; it was also copiously illustrated with fine engravings both of the composers and scenes from various operas. It was, to Godfrey, as though he had entered a dark, uncertain room and had thrown open vast windows upon the heavens and the earth and the mountains and the seas. He sat at the piano, playing sections of themes, selected arias, fugues and concertos, and it seemed to him that he sat in the midst of heroic and terrible figures, among confusions and majesties, in a world peopled with angels and Odins, monsters and demons, fairies and giants; he heard winds of terror and rage, cries of agony, voices lifted in the lofty measures of faith and prayer.

CHAPTER LIX

M AY WONDERED how professional teachers could be introduced in conversation with Ernest without causing too much of an uproar. But Ernest himself gave her an opportunity very soon.

Godfrey had been attending Windsor's newest and most exclusive boys' school ("A few Pupils will be Instructed by an English Gentleman, Formerly Schoolmaster at Gloucester Boys' School, London, under the Patronage of H.R.H. the Duke of York"). The English Gentleman, incidentally, had been en route to Chicago, but he had sadly miscalculated the vast distances in this new country, and found himself in a distressing state of embarrassment in Pittsburgh. He found friends in that city, and at their home met a lady from Windsor, who prophesied a fine future for him if he would condescend to consider Windsor, and promised all sorts of assistance. He had no other choice; his new friends were very generous, and he had soon rented a tall narrow red brick house, gloomy and sombre, with vault-like parlors, high narrow windows and black marble fireplaces, furnished accordingly, and there he opened his school for a few "selected pupils, the sons of gentlemen."

Ernest, who was no snob, and despised "gentlemen," if they were fools, equally with paupers, if they were fools, at first objected to sending Godfrey to Mr. Glendenning's school. He called at the school, upon May's insistence, and interviewed the exquisite former schoolmaster. When he returned, he told May that the man was only "shabby genteel" (using his half-forgotten English vocabulary) and that it would not surprise him if he turned out to be a former barber, footman, butler or valet. "His Oxford accent doesn't ring true to my English ears," he said. But May insisted; the only other private school was filled by very vulgar people, she protested. So Ernest, who had been privately considering sending Godfrey to a military academy in Washington, relented temporarily, for May's sake. But he was never satisfied, and was waiting until the boy was twelve to separate May from her darling.

As he went over a sheaf of bills one night in his library, he thought of this. May was keeping him company, reading by the fire. He glanced over at her, frowning.

"*Must* Frey learn Greek, my love?" he asked.

"Why, of course, Ernest! All gentlemen learn Greek! I thought you knew that."

"Who said I wanted 'gentlemen' to take my place, when I've pegged out, ma'am? I can't see how Greek is going to help Frey run our expanding businesses. By the time he is twenty-one, I expect we'll have a finger in every pie in the country. How is Greek going to help Frey get the better of his competitors?"

"I don't think he will ever get the better of any one, my sweet lamb," thought May sadly. She answered her husband evasively: "Knowledge never hurt any man, Ernest. You can't know too much. Besides, as I said, all gentlemen know Greek."

"Now, May, I'm not going to get 'bluff and hearty,' and swear that I want no puny gentlemen about me! I'm not that big a fool. I've never pretended to be a gentleman, and by God, I'll knock the man down who calls me one! And that's not democratic bravado, either. But I've no objection to Frey being a gentleman, if he is more solid and practical things besides. But look here, ma'am: Glendenning reports that he's actually an imbecile when it comes to plain figuring, and that the simplest mathematical problem is impossible for him to grasp! And he will handle millions some day!" He paused, and bit his lip. "May, you're making a mollycoddle, a milksop, out of your son."

"That isn't fair, Ernest. Have you ever considered that some men aren't made to grasp business problems? Just as some men will never be musicians or artists of any kind." In her agitation, she dropped her book and went over to him, and leaned against his desk. "Ernest, I've wanted to talk to you. We have three other sons, and from all signs, Reggie, at least, is going to be what you want. Guy will probably be it, too, the cheerful imp! even though he is hardly four, and little Joey looks like a little business man even in his cradle! Why can't you spare Godfrey, Ernest? Why can't you let him do what he wants to do?"

Ernest's face darkened. "And what is it that the lad wants to do, ma'am?"

"Please don't take that heavily sarcastic tone, Ernest. Please listen to me." She pulled a chair beside him, laid her white plump hand on his knee, and looked at him imploringly. "You know, I've taught Frey all the musical knowledge I possess. But now he needs professional teachers. Wait, Ernest, please! He needs professional teachers, the best we can get, the best schools of music. You see, Ernest, our boy is a genius. A composer. Only the other day, he played a little composition of his own, and I declare that I thought it was something of Beethoven's. He is a genius! He must have his opportunity——"

Ernest pushed her hand off his knee with suppressed violence.

"What nonsense! 'Genius'! Out of the clear sky, too! Genius doesn't fall from the air, ma'am. I've heard nothing from him but a lot of idle strumming, and moon-gazing. Now, I don't pretend to understand music, or care for it. I think I would have known, however, if Frey had

had something worth while. But you can't persuade me that a girlish, puling lad like that, with no more gumption than a whining cat, is a genius!"

"But you never pay him any attention, so how could you know? But I do know——"

"Just what do you know about music?"

"Not a terrible lot, Ernest, I admit. I never liked it. But I have heard enough of it, even if you haven't, to distinguish good music from bad. I am familiar with all the better operas, and I've heard most of the symphonies. I don't need to remind you that I can play the piano and the harp, also, and sing rather creditably. I have known musicians, too——"

"And just how many real composers have you known, ma'am?"

May smiled, a little triumphantly. "I met Richard Wagner in Munich, my pet. Did you ever hear of Richard Wagner? I thought not! But he has composed some rather nice operas, at least they are thought well of by discriminating people. And I met a number of others, too, at Paris soirees and in salons, but I won't embarrass you by mentioning their names." Ernest grinned unpleasantly for a moment. May went on: "So, I think I am a little qualified to pass on the merits of a musician. Frey, right now, plays better than I ever did; he loves music passionately. And now he is composing it. So——"

"I see. You now expect me to play the crass boor, and shout down music and ridicule it, don't you? I am the new rich, so can't be expected to know anything of the finer things of life. The burly, checker-vested business man, who crushes delicate things in his big beefy fist. But you can't pin that caricature on me, pet. It won't fit. I admit there are many things I don't understand, and I'm not going to be a fool and shout that they really can't amount to anything or I'd know about them. I'm not even going to say that because they are not rewarded by lots of money they must be, at bottom, valueless. I'll go a step further, and admit that there are probably a lot of things that are really more valuable, in the long run, than commerce and business and industry and government. I expect that a great picture or book or poem or opera will live longer and be remembered with more pleasure than men of my kind and the things we build. But after all, this is a practical world, and if a man can't live by bread alone, he damn well can't live without it! And you can live without pictures or books or poems or operas. They are just—just decorations on a sturdy house, and in a pinch we can get along without the decorations, providing we have the house.

"Now, in my case, I've built up something I'm proud of, crass and materialistic though that may sound to your delicate ears, ma'am. I've trebled, quadrupled, your original fortune, if not more. I'm not quite forty, and I started from scratch, and I'm now a millionaire several times over, and I've made others millionaires. too. I've created industry;

I've trebled the population of this town. I'm the friend of Governors and Senators. I've built immense factories and given thousands employment. I've pushed inventions and exploited them. I'm part of a stronger America that has no time as yet for decorations. America would be poorer without me.

"And the time is coming when I will have to put all this into the hands of others. My sons. And you want to take my eldest, and make a damned long-haired, cravat-flowing musician out of him!"

"Don't be tiresome, Ernest. I grant you everything you say. I'm proud of you, and I love you. But you've heard that before. But now we are talking about Frey. I am willing to compromise with you: I will take him to the Bouillon School of Music in New York; Monsieur Bouillon is a great composer in his own name, and lives only for music. Tyros, pretenders, poseurs, mediocrities, are his abomination. I will have Frey play for him, play his own little composition, and I will abide by his decision. If he says that Frey is a mediocrity, then we come home and nothing more need be said about it. We will all forget this. Frey will be persuaded to study more practical things. But if Monsieur says that Frey is a genius, and will some day be a great composer if he has proper instruction, I will leave Frey at his school."

Ernest regarded her sullenly, his large head bent forward like a bull's.

"Nonsense," he said, after a moment, returning to his desk. "I don't want to hear any more about it, ma'am. And now, will you kindly explain this bill——"

May had paled, but her lips had hardened, grown thin with her desperate determination.

"I know, Ernest," she said in a low, trembling voice, "it is because you hate Frey. You don't want to help him, to encourage him to develop his potentialities. And it isn't because you are so interested in training him for a business that you know, yourself, he will eventually despise, and for which he is absolutely unfitted by nature. You just want to thwart him, make him suffer."

"What a fool you are, May!" He had flushed heavily, and was staring at her with baleful hostility. "I admit that your coddling of the lad, your turning him against me, has made me a little cold to him at times. You would probably say, unsympathetic. But hate him! My own flesh and blood. I'm not sentimental, really, about flesh and blood, as you damn well know, but he's my son, my first born, and if he weren't such a damned little ass I would be proud of him. But I have you to thank for making him an ass. And now, leave me alone! I've work to do, and I'll listen to no more folly." He picked up his pen and wrote furiously. "My God, why couldn't I have had children like Amy's!"

May had grown still paler at the mention of her cousin's name, and something bitter and glittering came into her round dark eyes. "Like

Amy's," she repeated thoughtfully. "Yes, I can see why and how you would prefer children like hers. I have nothing against Paul and Elsa, except that they are brutal little savages; not very intellectual, either. I can see, too, why you might like Lucy, who falls all over you and hugs you and kisses you in her cunning little childish way—for the small silver you give her! And John Charles might appeal to you, too. He's only a baby, but I saw him enjoying pulling a butterfly apart a few days ago. But you're not going to pull apart my butterfly, Ernest."

He pushed back his chair savagely and stood up, glowering, red-faced, at her.

"Will you be quiet? I never heard such a pack of drivel in my life! I won't have this quarrelling over a puny brat, who hasn't even the courage to double his fists. I'm tired of it. Put him in skirts, and be damned to both of you!" He had never talked so to her before, and something became still and very cold in her resolute heart. I'll never feel the same about him, again, she thought. But she faced him silently, waiting for him to have done. He had clenched his hand upon his pen, and in his rage he was breaking it, snapping it, as though he would have liked to do the same to his wife. "You've made him a milksop, a whiner, a hider behind petticoats. And I'll have no more of it, by God! Next week he goes to General Smith's Military Academy in Washington, and let's see if they can kick and punch a little guts into him there, and make a man of him. Or kill him, trying."

He stopped, panting, all the veins in his face congested and swollen. But in spite of his rage and resentment, he was more than a little sobered by May's waiting silence, her white cheeks and steadfast eyes. Something in those eyes, fearless and uncowed, reminded him forcibly of Amy's eyes, recalled to him the kinship of the two women. He had never noticed any resemblance between them before, but now he was quite shaken by the sudden likeness. She showed nothing of the real shock and despair she had experienced at the mention of the military academy, except for the convulsive and involuntary wringing of her hands.

"No, you won't send him to that school," she said quietly, wondering dimly about the sick pang in her chest. "I won't have it. Not if I have to take him away from here, myself, and leave you. They'd really kill him there—kill him, inside. I won't have that; I won't have you murder him. Ernest, I've asked you for very little, and I've given you a great deal, all my love and faithfulness and devotion. But I've come to realize that you owe me something." She took a step toward him, forced him to look at her because of the strange white significance of her manner. "Yes, you owe me a great deal. And because of that, I'm insisting that Godfrey shall have his chance to live, without your hand on him. Yes, I'm insisting on that. You see, you owe me a great deal."

Ernest, disturbed and startled, tried to bluster. "What do I——"

Then stopped. What does she mean? How much does she know? he thought rapidly. He fixed his eyes piercingly on her face, so close to his, so pale and unwavering, so oddly sad. And then, for one of the few times in his life, he felt pity. He pitied his wife, felt a mysterious sorrow for her, a sinking regret. It went all through him, seeming to weaken and dissolve all his flesh, relaxing his harsh expression, making him turn aside, finally, as though he could not look at her any longer. He played with the articles on his desk for a long moment, lifting and setting down his brass inkwell, rubbing his thumb along his paper knife, carefully and mechanically pushing together into their proper places the fragments of his destroyed pen.

It was some minutes before he spoke, and when he did, his tone was milder, attempting to be indulgent. "Yes, perhaps I do owe you something, May. You've been a good wife, not a gadder or gossip or fool, like most men's wives. Perhaps I've been a little hasty. I'm willing to meet you half way about the lad."

May sighed, so loudly, so deeply, that the sigh was almost a sob. Ernest heard it, and again the weak, dissolving pang of pity went through him. But he could not look at her, yet. "All right, May. Take him to your French jig-dancer, and see what he says. But mind: if he says music is a waste of time for Frey, there's to be no more nonsense." He sat down, pulled papers toward him and began to write upon them rapidly. He waited for May's bubbling little laugh, with which she always ended small altercations between them; he waited for the warm whiteness of her arms about his neck, the warm pressure of her cheek against his. Strangely, he suddenly wanted this more than he had wanted anything for a long time. But he heard nothing, felt nothing. After awhile, he heard the clock chime ten in the hall, heard the distant throbbing of bull-frogs in the pond. Though he tried to prevent it, he turned almost involuntarily, smiling.

But May was not there. The place where she had stood was empty.

CHAPTER LX

MAY'S FIRM BELIEF in the idealism of M. Henri Bouillon, his imperviousness to money when accompanied by vain stupidity and mediocrity, was a little naïve. In his really very fine school of some two hundred pupils, there was a high and rigid standard of excellence, unceasing demand and inflexible discipline, for the gifted students, and an ease, a suave flattery, an indulgence and humoring of the mediocrities, which formed about one-third only of the student body. Considering that M. Henri Bouillon had the French lack of aversion for cash, this spoke astonishingly well for his possession of ideals and reverence for music. He had discovered that seventy-five per cent of the mediocrities were extraordinarily rich, and fifty per cent of the talented pupils extraordinarily poor. It also spoke exceedingly well for him that one-half of the poverty-stricken youths received free tuition and board at his school, offerings laid at the feet of an art he profoundly worshipped. His wife, who was an idealist, often protested at his admittance of some young fool who wanted even more adulation than his father's money to gorge his conceit, but Monsieur Henri said wryly that if he did not admit wealthy fools he would also not be able to admit poor geniuses. "Art is a glorious mistress," said this practical Frenchman and artist and composer, "but like all mistresses she demands sustenance." When his wife pointed out that geniuses have died in garrets, and thus glorified forever these fetid dens under eaves, he replied: "But how uncomfortable! Nothing is worth dying for, not even art. And I cannot see that a comfortable bed and a delicious ragout, just touched with red wine and garlic, would be deleterious to inspiration. To me there is something just a little precious, a little affected, in self-immolation to anything."

May brought little Godfrey to him, was admitted to the great man's untidy study; she was soon thereafter ordered out, and she retired with some apprehension, leaving her little son with Monsieur Henri and a vast and dusty piano. She sat in the musty and disordered ante-room, listened to the faint notes which Godfrey produced. He was playing his own composition, and May, listening, suddenly decided, with humiliation, that she had been mistaken, that Ernest had been right. She was about to enter the study again and retrieve her offspring, when Monsieur Henri bounced out of the room, slammed the door behind him, and confronted

May. She stood before him, her gloved hands clasped unknowingly together, her wounded eyes upon him: a plump and pretty woman in her dark red velvet and plumes.

"Madam," said Monsieur Henri, "your son is almost a genius." And he touched his eyes elaborately with his handkerchief.

For a moment cynicism twisted in May. "Is he, truly? Monsieur Bouillon, we are very rich, as you probably know. We could afford to indulge Godfrey, even if he had only a little talent. But we do not want that. I have made a bargain with my husband that if the boy is not really talented, I will bring him home."

Monsieur Henri, a huge and shapeless man with a spade-shaped beard, glowered at her terribly. "If he were a street urchin, I would snatch him from you and teach him myself!" he shouted, assaulting her with his lightnings and his rage. "Madam, you are a fool!" He flung himself with such solid violence into a chair that it teetered precariously, and groaned. "It is not what he played, nor whether he had composed it or not, nor even his technique, which is vile, Madam. How I would like to lay my hands on his villain of a teacher! And what a crime to subject a child like that to female monsters who have a faint knowledge of the difference between flats and sharps! No, Madam, it is not all these that tell me the truth. It is your son, his face, his eyes, his soul!"

So Godfrey James Barbour was left at the school, after Madam Bouillon had assured May that the child would be as her own, his health guarded, his other studies not neglected. If Madam would not object, would see reasonably, she suggested delicately, and with such gentle modesty that May loved her, there was a boys' school just around the corner, a small, semi-private school, conducted by the good Brothers of St. Joseph. They would not use any subversive means to convert the little garçon to Catholicism; there were many Protestant boys there, even Jews, and their teachers were excellent, dedicated. "And such a choir!" she exclaimed. "An inspiration itself, in the beautiful little chapel. But Godfrey need not attend, though Henri approved of it, as part of the musical education."

CHAPTER LXI

H E REMAINED at the school nearly five years.

For the first time little Godfrey was happy. Before this, he had lived in a disjointed, disoriented world, that had faced him like the distended quills of a porcupine. He had lived among strangers, whose voices were too harsh and near and loud, whose eyes were too avid with curiosity, whose touch was a shock and an affront. He had loved only two people, his mother and his sister, Gertrude. And only May had given him complete tenderness and sympathy.

But life, apart from his mother and his sister, had been almost unendurable for young Godfrey. He never questioned the misery of his existence, or wondered why it was; he merely accepted it as one accepted a congenitally twisted leg or a clubfoot. Sometimes, watching the happiness and gaiety of other children, he was struck with amazement that they could be so at ease, so unrestricted, so free from the iron sadness and malaise that afflicted him. Sometimes, he thought it sheer pretending, unable to believe in such lightness, in such casual acceptance, in such complete adjustment to reality. Even at eight, or ten, he was not an innocent boy, in a more subtle and wider meaning of the word, and his modesty masked an angry but timid conceit, a cold aloofness, a distaste for too much closeness, a shrinking and a hauteur before attempts at intimacy, a somewhat cynical if frightened sadness.

At the Bouillon school, among the gifted pupils, he met others almost exactly like himself, and naturally joined their unintimate, reserved and haughty brotherhood. His face, as he grew older, took on itself that certain congested look about the nose and eyes, that classic indifference, which distinguished them from the others of the mediocre student body. Yet even in this brotherhood of friends who were not friends, he formed no close attachments. These youths were like small asteroids belonging to one constellation, revolving closely together, crossing each other's path, shining upon each other, but each pursuing his own silent and lonely orbit.

He knew that his father was wealthy; he knew practically everything about him. But perception in his case, acute and painfully intense though it was, was born of his fear, distaste, and real terror of Ernest. They were a bitter light in which he saw his father—naked. Had he loved him, he might have been blind. But the extent of his father's fortune, the immensity of his holdings and enterprises, did not exist as realities for him.

Even the boy's passion was intellectual, and the adoration he had for Monsieur Bouillon was based on his full appreciation of his teacher's genius. There were twelve other teachers in the school, each a master of some particular instrument, and an artist and composer in his own right. But Monsieur had a selected small class of his own, in which were all those he considered superlative, and Godfrey was a member of this class.

When he came home for infrequent visits, he was wretched. He felt his father's eye on him constantly, felt his personality even when he was not in the house. Sometimes it seemed to him that Ernest was like a pervading gas in the atmosphere, from which he could not escape and which he must perpetually breathe. When Ernest tried to approach him, to find some little platform to stand on with him, distaste was like a vital sickness in his body. He never tried to explain this aversion, for it was too profound and instinctive. He could not even pity his father, for terror destroyed any compassion that might be born in him. When he saw Ernest's hurt, his fright increased, dreading new displeasure as revenge.

The house was always full of cousins, he thought wretchedly. He particularly could not endure Paul and Elsa; he knew that Paul despised him, and he despised Paul in return. He knew that Elsa was "sweet on him," and this offended him, even outraged him. Her red cheek, her bold, aggressive eye, her robust handsomeness and loud, arrogant voice, her practicality, exigency, earthiness and uncompromisingly simple acceptance of realities, revolted him. He thought of her as a heifer, smelling of hay, which was somewhat unfair, as Elsa was by no means a fool or unastute. He hated Lucy, with her cunning, coaxing ways, her plump rosiness and greedy eyes. He disliked the noisy, relentless children of his Aunt Dorcas little less; Florabelle's children, silent and frail, aroused in him some distant feeling of compassion and softness. They looked so defenseless and bewildered in a world too much for their weakness, their thin, uncertain hands. They were like the wan, undernourished children of London slums.

By the time he was sixteen he had written a concerto, a few simple sonatas, and one or two nocturnes. The concerto had been without M. Bouillon's approval, for he felt that the youth should confine himself to simpler things that did not require orchestral cooperation. "Time enough for symphonies and operas and concertos," he said, fuming. "But the little cabbages, the toddlers, always want to write epics or operas before they know what a triolet or a nursery song is; they scorn simplicity, the pure gentle beauty of an exquisite phrase or an uncomplicated theme, though Shakespeares and Beethovens have not scorned to use them. It is the babes who want to climb the mountains, and the wise men who know the hills."

Later he wrote to Ernest Barbour: "I can do no more for your son. My friend, M. Georges Lorenz, of Paris, who is world-renowned, as you doubtless are aware, will receive him at my insistence. From his hands young Godfrey will emerge ready to take his place in the world of music."

Ernest read this, contemptuous and gloomy. Let the lad once go to Paris and his father would lose him forever. He would no longer exist for Barbour-Bouchard, nor would Barbour-Bouchard exist for him. His family would know him no more than if he had been deposited in a cemetery. Almost as bad as a monastery, he thought sourly, and his gorge rose as it always did when he thought of Martin in connection with his son and recalled their physical resemblance. He struck his hand heavily on his desk, sent the butler for May. This time, he said to himself, he would have his way.

May came in. Nearly forty, she had grown pleasantly buxom, her lace cap was pinned on dark-red hair threaded thickly with white. No longer did it bounce in curls about her cheeks, but was smoothly combed to the top of her head in a tight roll, the cap covering it. Her complexion was still beautiful, her eyes sparkling and vivid as in her early youth, her throat plump and white. She had become philosophical as she had grown older, and had decided that wisdom began and ended with the acceptance of the half loaf.

"Yes, love," she said cheerily, smoothing the front of her straight black silk dress, and plucking up and out the crushed buoyancy of her bustle. "Dear me, how that lint from that wool does stick! Yes, Ernest?"

He tossed her the letter. Hypocritically, she pretended to read it through to the end, though she was well aware of its contents. She laid it down, beamed upon him.

"That is very splendid! Think of it! I was right about Frey, after all. Do you think he is a little young to be going to Paris? I thought, perhaps, when he is seventeen, this spring——"

"He is not going to Paris at all, ma'am!" he said grimly.

May pretended bewilderment, though her heart tightened.

"But, Ernest, he needs it. He needs this final help. M. Bouillon hinted something about this a year ago. When Frey leaves Paris, he will be a real composer——"

"I don't want a damned composer in the family!" shouted Ernest. "I want a son who can take his place in his father's affairs. Now mind, I don't want the old arguments about him not being fitted. A man only needs to go hungry to be ready and fit for any work. I want him; I've got some training of my own to give him. While he's learning to live, he can play around with his music if he wants to. He can write his ballads and sonatas for amusement, but the real world is out there, and he's got to pull up his breeches and get into it. I've been patient; I've let him do as he wants for five years. Now, it's my turn."

May sat down, laid her arms along the chair arms, and regarded her husband steadily. "No, Ernest, it's still Frey's turn. He's got his life now, out of your grasp, and he's not going to turn it back to you. He has a right to his life, just as you had a right to yours. You did as you wished, though you alienated your father, and might have estranged me, also, if I had not loved you quite so much. But you allowed no one to touch your life. You were stronger than Frey is, and had resistance. He has very little; if you press on him too much he'll snap like thin silver. If you force your will on Frey, he'll die——"

"Pack of blasted nonsense, woman—nonsense! You talk as if the lad is a frail bit of trailing arbutus, or a lily in a dell. He won't die, learning how to manage millions in money and thousands in men. Why, he's got to learn! Otherwise the money'll spill out of his hands like water. He hasn't the slightest understanding of it, you know that. God, when I think what I would have given——! Look here, ma'am, I've been more than fair. You asked me for four years; I've given five, and not a complaint. Now, I'm finished. I've done my share. I've humored both of you long enough."

"Humored us? Ernest, Frey's a genius, not a dilettante. Music is his life and soul."

"I'm sick of this talk of souls! Let's have done with it. I've been reasonable. Now it's my turn."

May went on quietly, with a kind of desperate tenacity: "You've still got Reggie and Guy and Joey. You don't need Frey. And you're not going to get him."

Ernest glared at her blankly, incredulously. "Are you defying me, May?" he bellowed unbelievingly.

She rose, clasped her hands together before her, pressed the fingers one into the other in her inner agitation. But her expression was calm, unshaken.

"You may call it that, if you wish. Frey isn't a child any more. He has a right to his choice. And I am with him. He'll go to Paris——"

"Against my commands? Against my express commands?" Ernest could not believe that he was actually hearing this. His face flushed darkly and his eyes glittered down upon her in fury.

"Ernest, you are being tedious, and very noisy, shouting like this. I've never disobeyed you before; I've always reasoned with you, and when your reason was better than mine, I've always given in. But this time I'm not giving in. With or without your consent, Frey is going to Paris. I'm not penniless. And if you become theatre-ish, and threaten to cut him off with a shilling, he won't mind. And I won't mind. He wouldn't think of money, but as I said before, I'm not penniless."

The eternal inflexibility of female nature astounded Ernest. Dumfounded, he stared upon a wife heretofore complaisant and humorously yielding, reasonable and placating; in a few moments she had become impervious as stone, not to be moved, not to be broken. He could not believe it; his fear of impotence roiled through his veins. He dared not be impotent! He dared not yield, even in the face of this implacability. Surely he dared not yield to a woman! Frey, as an individual, was forgotten; he had become an abstract issue, to be used like an iron hammer to smash this stony image.

Ernest forced himself to relax, to unclench his hands, to lower his voice.

"You forget, ma'am," he said, almost quietly, "that he is under age, and I am his father. Take him to Paris; send him to Paris. I'll bring him back. By the law." He picked up M. Bouillon's letter, and deliberately tore it to shreds before his wife, as though it were a living thing, as though it were flesh, as though each tearing sound wounded her, and he enjoyed so wounding her.

May had become white as death. She trembled violently, and the flesh about her upper lip and around her pale mouth turned bluish. Her eyes became brilliant and distended as though a light had been turned upon them.

"To save Frey's life, Ernest, I would destroy my happiness, and yours. Not only mine and yours, but Amy's."

A deadly silence, imponderable yet weighty, fell between husband and wife at the mention of that name. The last shred of the destroyed letter fell from Ernest's fingers as though they had become paralyzed. A livid tint suddenly flowed over his features.

May sighed; she appeared to have grown older, to have become ill. But she went on resolutely, turning her head slightly from her husband, as though she could not bear to look at what she had brought about: "You have forced me to say this. You gave me no other choice. God knows I wish it might have gone unsaid. Now there'll never be any straightness between us again. Pretense that all is well sometimes helps us to maintain cheerfulness, to make life endurable. All this will make it impossible for either of us to be happy or casual or friendly again. I'm terribly sorry. I'm sorry for you. But I'm so awfully sorry for myself! I wanted to keep on pretending. Now you've robbed me of my pretense, that made my life comfortable. But I'm glad to give it all, for Frey."

"May—" The one word seemed dragged from him by a sort of torture.

"I don't care any longer, Ernest. I'm not asking you to give up anything. I'm not going to watch you, or condemn you, or nag you. I have my own pride, too. O my God, don't apologize, don't promise! Don't pity me—I couldn't bear it! If you do, I'll never forgive you; I'll—I'll leave this house forever! All I want you to understand is that if you prevent Frey from going to Paris, I'll sue you for divorce, and in order to get the children, to get Frey, I'll prove you an unworthy father. I'll bring Amy into it, cousin or no cousin, children or no children."

"May." His voice trembled, hoarsened, and his face, as he approached her one step, looked crumpled and seamed. "May, my love, you wouldn't do this to me, this horrible thing, this blackmail—I'm not thinking of what you have threatened—a divorce or any such silly thing —I'm thinking how terrible it is that you have said this to me. In my way, I've loved you. I still love you. But—Christ! how could you hurt yourself so—bring yourself to this point——"

"I'll do anything." She retreated a few steps. "Anything!" Her face shone with a white exaltation. "Anything to save his life. You can't stop me, Ernest. If you try, it's your own disaster. And Amy's. Now everything is gone in all the world for me, except Frey. And I'll never give up."

She turned and went out of the room, walking steadily, unhurriedly. She even went into the nursery, where the two young boys, Guy and Joey, slept heavily. She even put her hand on Joey's head, and wondered with automatic uneasiness if it were her imagination that his head was hot. There was an epidemic among the working men's families in the flats along the river in Newtown, and it was spreading like mud through water. So far it had not touched Oldtown, though every mother here was sick with apprehension.

Still moving automatically, May covered the restless little feet, lowered the light, drew in the shutters. She closed the door softly behind her.

She went into her own room, almost running now. She closed the door as if pursued. She turned the key, locking it, for the first time in all her married life. Then she leaned against the door, panting, drooping, and utterly undone.

She crept to her bed, threw herself upon it, fully dressed, and stared blankly at the wall that shimmered with pink fire-reflections. Her eyes tormentedly, dully, followed the twisting vines of the paper that appeared and disappeared as the rosy light waxed and waned. It seemed to her at last that she must follow this pattern forever, relentlessly, through wild terror and death, a sort of running through twisted passages, to keep behind her some monstrous agony and destruction.

She heard a faint sound. The firelight shot up; by its illumination she saw the handle of her door turning, turning. She watched it, holding her breath. It fell back into place, and turned no more.

Then she heard Ernest's door close. For some reason that last sound gave strength to the pursuing agony, and it pounced upon her vengefully. She pressed her face into the pillows.

Book Two

I AND LAZARUS

"The Government of your Country! I am the Government of your Country, I and Lazarus. Do you suppose that you and half a dozen amateurs like you, sitting in a row in that foolish babble shop, govern Undershaft and Lazarus? No, my friend, you will do what pays us. You will make war when it suits us and keep peace when it doesn't. When I want anything to keep my dividends up, you will discover that my want is a national need. When other people want something to keep my dividends down, you will call out the police and military. And in return you shall have the support of my newspapers, and the delight of imagining that you are a great statesman."
MAJOR BARBARA—*George Bernard Shaw.*

CHAPTER LXII

Gertrude was reading aloud in the summerhouse:

"Our birth is but a sleep and a forgetting;
The Soul that rises with us, our life's Star,
Hath had elsewhere its setting
And cometh from afar;
Not in entire forgetfulness,
And not in utter nakedness,
But trailing clouds of glory do we come
From God, who is our home;
Heaven lies about us in our infancy!"

"O pooh! That's stupid!" exclaimed Elsa Barbour, flouncing on the summerhouse seat until her blue-striped foulard rustled satisfyingly. "It sounds like Philippe. So that's where you got that, Trudie!" She reached out quickly and snatched the book from Gertrude's hand, though her cousin unsuccessfully tried to retain it. She thumbed through the pages back to the flyleaf, and laughed with malicious triumph. "There! 'To dear Gertrude, on her seventeenth birthday!' But he overlooked the 'love and kisses, from her Philippe!'"

"Don't be tiresome, Elsa. Give me back my book." Gertrude's dark colorless cheek was suddenly red with embarrassment and annoyance. "If you don't like Wordsworth, the others do. They're not all barbarians."

"I don't like it. Sounds so milky, to me," said sixteen-year-old Lucy, grinning. She was a smallish, plump young girl, with a pretty rosy complexion, rather tiny sparkling eyes, the color and shine of black-raspberry jelly, a big red mouth showing small white teeth set far apart in pink gums, and a mop of dark chestnuts curls tied with a red ribbon that matched her gay red dress.

"I think it's pretty," protested little ten-year-old Renee Bouchard, who loved her cousin, Gertrude. Even in childhood, Renee's face was not young; it was very narrow, sharp and bony, sallow and uninnocent. She had a prominent nose, with a long ridge in it, fleshless and acquisitive, and a wide, pale mouth pressed tightly together. Her eyes, long and narrow, never opened either in great joy or laughter; the pupils had an unpleasant habit of sliding quickly from side to side. Beautiful blond

Dorcas, her mother, never was consoled for Renee's lack of comeliness, nor could be reconciled to the Indian-straight, lank black hair that always escaped its ribbons, and the lean, stringy young body that was never to be graceful. Dorcas contented herself, therefore, with her handsome Etienne, her distinguished Honore, and her beauties, her darlings, the twins, Andre and Antoinette, so rosy and blond, so exuberant and affectionate.

At eighteen, Elsa was a coquette, but a sly and anxious one. She was not courted for herself, nor her handsomeness, though she was a comely girl, big and vigorous and full of vitality, her dark blue eyes bold and vivid and blazing, her mouth red and full, her short, dilated nose straight and well-shaped, her hair dark and full of deep, shining waves. Her figure, though verging, as her Aunt May said, "on the goddess side," was yet youthful and symmetrical, and her manner was forthright and breezy. Yet, she was not popular among the men she liked, though she had a large number of suitors, attracted by the glow of the Barbour wealth. It is true that her widowed Mama was not as wealthy as Aunt May's husband, and Uncle Eugene, and Aunt Florabelle, but she was very comfortable, and it was rumored that Elsa and Lucy would have large dowries. Elsa, however, though not intellectual, was shrewd and sharp, and was not to be had, just yet at any rate, for her money alone. She wanted romance, secretly desired it, in spite of her bluff and common-sense personality.

Elsa had no subtlety, and made no secret of the fact that she ardently desired her cousin Godfrey's favor, and she did not shrink from urging upon her cousin Gertrude her brother Paul's preference for her. It was her hope, more or less evident, that some day she would be Godfrey's wife, and Paul would be Gertrude's husband. In that way, she thought, more or less aloud to her mother, and her sister, Lucy, everyone would be happy and the Barbour money would be kept in the family. It was an itch to her that her sister, Lucy, was already engaged to a New York gentleman of some twenty-four years, handsome, gallant, wealthy, and with a most fetching little black mustache. (He was eight years older than Lucy, not at all to Amy's taste, but of a prominent family.)

The four young girls (including Renee, whom Lucy pettishly referred to as "that nosy child, always underfoot wherever grown-ups are"), were sitting in a white, ivy-covered summer house situated on a lower slope of the Sessions grounds. Elsa was clumsily working on lace to be used as pillow-borders, Lucy was embroidering napkins for her trousseau, Gertrude was reading aloud, and Renee, at her feet, was trying to weave a basket of raffia.

A translucent green light filled the summerhouse, like airy water, spangled with the yellow, diamond-shaped light of the sun falling through the lattices. It lay on the girls' young faces and bright silk dresses and

flashing needles. Gertrude sat upright, a little primly, her back sup
ported by an octagon wall. She was not a pretty girl, many said; she was
slim and tall, not graceful, but inclined to a touching and youthful
angularity, for her shoulders were thin and wide, her hips unfashionably
narrow, her movements swift and a little jerky, and, oddly, though she
was really very repressed, very self-controlled and poised, she yet often
gave an impression of wildness and dim, passionate bewilderment. Her
hair was straight and without shine, and framed her small, colorless face
like a cloud of dusky smoke. But the bones of her face were delicate
and fine, and the contour of her cheek-bones, especially, seemed to shine
through the clear dark skin like ivory. May said that her daughter had
her grandmother Beveridge's eyes, wide, a little distended, restless, with
a bright, startled expression in them. But they were singularly beautiful
to discerning people, their hazel tint appearing to be an intense black
when she was moved or intensely excited. Her mouth, too, though almost
without color, had a lovely shape, and when she smiled it was as if that
small face burst into a living radiance, quick and intelligent.

She was not very fond of her girl-cousins, and privately thought them
singularly stupid, but May had brought her up well and she concealed her
impatience with them perfectly. Renee touched her; she thought the
ugly child pathetic, and she was gratefully aware of the fact that Renee,
at ten, surpassed Lucy and Elsa in wit and subtlety. Sometimes, when
she talked to Renee, her rather cold voice warming, she felt that the child
understood to the very uttermost nuance. Sometimes the seventeen-
year-old girl and the child exchanged involuntary glances of faintly
contemptuous amusement when Elsa and Lucy were present. The robust
exigency, the blatant inquisitiveness, the greediness, the lack of reticence,
of the two sisters, were an ache along their nerves. Sometimes Gertrude
felt that their strong, undelicate hands seized on her roughly, and proceeded to handle her, turn her, examine her with a crude and childlike
curiosity. "I feel like Gulliver in the grasp of the baby Brobdingnagian,"
she once told her mother. She was not unconscious of the fact that Elsa
and Lucy privately thought her a rather "poor stick," and not very
bright. They thought her breeding a sign of lack of character, her reticence cowardice. When she failed to respond to a vulgar frankness, they
considered her exceedingly dull, or prim, or patronizing. Elsa, who
adored her twin brother, Paul, could not understand his slavish infatuation for Gertrude, but as he seemed set upon her she had decided that he
would have her, though she struggled to the end. Too, the greedy Elsa
could not endure the thought that Paul, whose share of their mother's
fortune would necessarily be modest, might be "cheated" out of the vast
inheritance that Gertrude would some day possess. She, herself, had
a passion for Godfrey, and lovingly decided that when she was married
to him she would cure him of his "music-nonsense," thus assuring her

own happiness and gratifying her adored Uncle Ernest. For the sake of all these agreeable advantages, she cultivated Gertrude, whom she rather despised, and was almost constantly at the Sessions house.

Because Wordsworth had been unsympathetically received by Elsa and Lucy, Gertrude closed the book gently and laid it beside her on the cushioned seat that ran along the inside of the octagon-shaped summerhouse. She folded her small dark hands in her lap and smiled down at Renee.

"Child! What a mess you have that basket in! Here, let me take it. I'm not much better than you, but I think I can find the end you are fishing for."

"I don't know why she bothers," said Lucy, flouncing pettishly, and favoring her young cousin with an unpleasant downward glance from her small, shining eyes. "I'm sure no one would want that ugly thing, anyway."

"My Mama wants it," said Renee, regarding Lucy with a swift balefulness. "She has no sewing basket, and she told me she would like a raffia one."

"Your Mama," instructed Elsa, with a grown-up and final air, "was just trying to be kind to you. What hideous colors you have in it! Purple and green! I think it uncommonly awful."

Gertrude set her lips for a moment, then said coldly and quietly: "And I think it uncommonly pretty. It's commodious, not like the silly little gilt things that ladies use for sewing baskets. You've got sturdy little brothers, Renee, always wearing out their stockings, and I'm sure your Mama will find this big enough for all her yarns. If you have time, I'd love one for my birthday, darling."

Renee favored her with a sad, somewhat whimsical smile, but said nothing. Gertrude put her hand impulsively on the untidy black head, as if in protection.

"There," she said. "Here is the end. Don't you think a little yellow would be nice here, between the purple and green? There, that's just the color." She compared the raffia critically.

"O heavens!" Lucy sat forward, looked at the contrast, and burst into loud laughter. "How appalling! Gertrude, I thought you had a little taste! Elsa, do look at the mustard-yellow that brat is going to put next to the purple!"

"Vile," was Elsa's uncompromising verdict.

Renee looked at them with intense contempt and dislike. "I think both of you are vile," she said. "My Mama says you girls have no breeding, and I believe it."

"Oh, Renee!" exclaimed Gertrude in a shocked voice. But she smiled a little, irrepressibly. Lucy's and Elsa's hilarious expressions faded, were replaced by disagreeable smirks.

"Your Mama," Lucy blurted, "is not a lady. My Mama is. My grandma was a Sessions, and my grandfather was a gentleman. But your Papa is a French peasant, who had to run away from France because they were going to arrest him for goodness knows what. And your Mama——"

"Is my father's sister!" said Gertrude sharply. Her voice shook with anger. "And your father's sister! I am ashamed of you both, Elsa and Lucy. If you can't be nicer to poor little Renee, and be ladies, I'm sure that I would prefer that you don't visit me so often——"

"Indeed, ma'am!" cried Lucy, bouncing so violently to her feet that her sewing fell to the ground, where Renee surreptitiously rubbed her black boot against it. "Well, I'm sure, my lady Gertrude, that it's not *my* wish to come here! I come because Elsa asks me to, and because she's sweet on Godfrey, and she wants you to marry Paul! Though, I don't see why any one would want Frey, or you, either, ma'am, with all your airs and high-and-mighty ways, and——" Her small black eyes sparkled with rage, and her breath expelled itself gustily from her furiously red mouth.

Elsa calmly, and without hurry, kicked her sister in the shins, and the young girl's enraged howling filled the hot summer quiet with clamor, and her painful dancing shook the frail wooden floor. She kicked back, after a moment, with a savage turmoil of skirts, but Elsa swung her legs dexterously onto the seat, and shrieked gleefully into her sister's face. Gertrude had burst into a sweet hysteria of laughter, and Renee, laughing helplessly, rolled out of the way of Lucy's boots, which were ardently seeking Elsa. Lucy, to facilitate her efforts, had lifted her skirts and multitudinous white ruffled petticoats very high, and showed lengths of plump, white, agitated stocking.

"I'll kill you!" she shouted. She panted, breathing fire, then dropped her skirts. Her hands, curved like claws, sprang at her sister, pulling her hair down upon her shoulders, ripping open the blue stripes that covered her plump bosom. Elsa, exhausted, weak with laughter, rolled about on the seat, fending herself as best she could. But when one of Lucy's nails found her cheek, and dragged a thin red wake behind it, Elsa's laughter abruptly ceased, and her big florid face became ugly and contorted with sudden rage. She was much larger than Lucy, and with one swing of her strong hand she swept the younger girl to the floor in a riotous confusion of skirts and waving legs and disordered hair. Gertrude had pulled her own legs up beside her, and Renee was standing on the seat, jumping up and down and shouting with excitement, and egging the sisters on.

"Girls!" said a shocked, half-laughing voice from outside, and a shadow fell into the green light of the summer-house. "Girls!"

The mêlée suddenly quieted. Lucy, on the floor, burst into savage sobs, and Elsa sullenly mopped her bleeding cheek. "Nasty little cat!"

she said, as May entered the enclosure. "I'm sorry, Aunt May. Some one ought to break Lucy's neck."

"What a noise!" exclaimed May, amusedly, but trying to assume a severe expression. "You aren't children, to be fighting like this, Elsa and Lucy. You, Lucy, a young engaged lady——"

"I know, Aunt May," said Lucy, scrambling to her feet, and beginning to mop her wet eyes. Then her face crimsoned with fury again, and she stamped her foot. "But what can you do with a jealous old maid, who can't get a beau herself, and who kicks you out of sheer mean feeling? She's just jealous of me, because I'm going to be married soon, and she's an eighteen-year-old hag, already on the shelf."

"Pooh! I wouldn't have your girl-faced Oswald if he were the last man on earth," replied Elsa, touching her cheek tenderly. "He's been cultivating mustaches for years, and they aren't any bigger than a wisp, after all."

Lucy began to dance frenziedly. "His name isn't Oswald!" she screamed. "It's Percival! And he's a man, which is more than you can get, for all your big eyes and your flirting!" She clenched her plump white fist suddenly under Elsa's nose, and the older girl involuntarily backed away. "Don't you call him Oswald again, or I'll—I'll——"

May watched and listened with a faint smile in which there was a subtle cast of cruelty. Amy's daughters! She glanced at Gertrude, who had formally risen at her mother's entrance, and now stood in silence, her head a little bent, her expression absent and cool. She is a young birch, thought May. Gertrude's dress, pearl gray striped in darker gray silk, clothed her like a sleek second skin from throat to hip, and from there was draped elaborately over a bustle in the back, thereafter to fall behind in a crisp, fashionable cascade. The dress showed every young, delicate line and curve of breast and slender waist and smooth, narrow hip. Above the close plain neckline rose the smoky coils of her hair, the fine small oval of her face. No, she is not a pretty girl, thought her mother for the thousandth time, but she is very fascinating, and that is a great deal better. She is also a lady, makes Elsa and Lucy look like farm girls.

May sat down, still smiling, and fanned herself with a thin cambric handkerchief, which, as she waved it, dispensed an invisible mist of rose-odor. Her plump, still-smooth face was scarlet, the gray-red of her hair bursting into little spirals about her hot moist cheeks.

"Gracious, isn't it a warm day! Too warm, I'm sure, for fighting, girls. Lucy, do sit down, and Elsa, put down your legs. You're naked to the knees. Renee, darling, do stop jumping up and down in this heat; you'll have a fit. Here, let me tie your ribbon: it's hanging half-way down your frock." She restored order with her good-humored, pleasant voice, with its affectionate and amused undertone. Lucy pointedly sat at the greatest distance possible from her sister, who glowered at her constantly. Renee docilely permitted her aunt to pat and fold and tie her into coherence and neatness, her narrow eyes sliding sideways upon her in sly adoration. Gertrude sat down again, clasped her hands in her lap. With May's coming, she had become silent, and a little stiff, as though ill at ease.

Tying Renee's hair-ribbon, May glanced at her daughter with maternal censoriousness. The glance was affectionate enough, but, as usual, had in it a slight irritation and antagonism.

"I'm sure, Trudie, that if you had been aware of your duty as hostess, the girls would never have gotten into such a quarrel," she said, trying to make her voice light and succeeding only in making it a little malicious.

Gertrude colored a little, pressed her mouth together, but said nothing. Mama knows she is unfair, she thought with bitter and cynical passion, and that just makes her more unfair. She stared broodingly at a diamond of sunlight on the floor.

" 'Tain't—'tisn't—Gertrude's fault," said Renee stoutly, twisting her hair out of her aunt's hand as she swung her head around to see May. "She was just reading the prettiest poetry, and Elsa said 'pooh!' and teased Gertrude, and then she and Lucy made fun of my raffia, and Gertrude said——"

"Renee! How do you expect me to tie your ribbon if you jerk so? Besides, you talk too much for a very little girl, and I'm sure you didn't try to help any, jumping up and down and clapping your hands and shouting like an Indian."

A look of pleasure passed over Renee's dark and narrow little face. "Andre and Antoinette like me and Honore to play Indian for them, and we pretend to scalp them, and Antoinette yells like everything, the silly thing——!"

May gave her a good-natured little push. "There, do sit down like a civilized child! I've got something to say to the girls, and if you're very good you may listen quietly, and then we'll go to the house and have punch and iced cakes and cream." She beamed at the older girls, and then withdrew a letter from a fold of her mauve silk dress. Above the delicate, rather trying color, her plump hot face looked too florid and middle-aged. But her neck was still round and white, and her bosom full and shapely. Her round eyes still had their girlhood twinkle and mischief, her small mouth its dimples and ready laughter. If, in the presence of others her face was frequently drawn and sad, as though she momentarily forgot a determined rôle, she made up for it immediately in brighter gaiety and humor. Only Ernest, and his daughter, Gertrude, felt the hard strain behind all this, and were ill at ease in consequence, Ernest with good reason and understanding.

"I've just received another letter from Frey," she announced viva-ciously, glancing about the little circle, and becoming pleased at the happy sensation she produced. Gertrude lifted her head sharply in that strange, gently wild gesture of hers, Elsa glowed and sparkled for all her big-ness, and Lucy smiled politely. Frey was no favorite of Lucy's. Renee bounced on her seat and clapped her hands delightedly, not that Godfrey had ever particularly noticed her, not that she had cared much for him, but because of the joy she knew that Gertrude was feeling. May unfolded the letter impressively, removed a little sealed slip of paper. "Here, Trudie, is dear Frey's usual note for you, though I still do not see why he seals it. As if I would read it! And now, I'll read my letter aloud to all of you.

"He says: 'Paris grows more wonderful each day, particularly now that it is spring, and the plane-trees are in leaf, and the sky is so pure and blue. It is so easy here, so friendly and full of laughter. Every one eats and sleeps and drinks when he chooses, and there is no tightness or harshness anywhere.

" 'I walk down the Bois, and look at the chestnut trees, and I think of home, and how the leaves must be coming out, so green and spreading, and the way the shadows and the sun run over the lawns and dance on the pool in the garden. And the old gray wall at the back, with the moss and the ivy on it, and the frogs at night under the moon, and my own room with the windows flung out and the wind coming in. And then I'm homesick just a little for all of you. [May noted, with a pang of sad tenderness, that the 'all of' had been inserted between the 'for' and the 'you'.]

" 'But I know you aren't interested in my silly thoughts, and want to know how I'm getting on. Mama, we are to have a concert in the Acad-emy of Music tomorrow night, and the opera orchestra is to play. Three compositions of the students are to be played, and one of them is mine! My Prelude in C major! It is a great honor, and my master thinks I may win the Grand Prix. You cannot realize what this means to me and for my future! It is the beginning of all your hopes for me, all that I want to be, all that I can be! Monsieur Edmund Brisson, the conductor, declares it the equal of anything similar of Mozart's, and as he is the most brusque and ungracious of men, this is delirious praise.

" 'Mama, darling, how can I ever repay you—' " May halted abruptly. Her voice had thickened and trembled as she had read. She cleared her throat, blinked.

A tense and shining look had come into Gertrude's beautiful dark eyes. Elsa was smiling politely, but with a superior lift to her brows. (Dear silly Frey, and his foolish, frittery music! When we are married, he'll forget all this nonsense!) Lucy was bored, and though she tried to smile, her eye, fixed on Elsa, had an evil glint in it. She thought Godfrey the most stupid of silly boys, and the most tedious, and was not always tactful enough to conceal her opinion from his mother and sister. (Dear Uncle Ernest should have strapped some sense into his conceited head when he was a brat. Paris for the likes of him! I bet it's just the French girls he likes so well, and not his absurd piano-playing!) Her smile became a little leering, a little cunning.

"Well, I am sure you girls aren't interested in Frey's opinion of his Mama," said May, now openly wiping her eyes. "So, I'll go on with the rest of the letter: 'Thank Papa for his last check; it was more than generous. I'm sending Reggie and Guy a box, and there is something in it for Joey, too. Tell the girls that rose and blue seem to be the colors in Paris this year; at least, that's all the women seem to be wearing on the streets. And parasols as big as pancakes, and all frills.'" (Godfrey had made a painful point of consciously observing these phenomena for the dutifully remembered benefit of his sister and cousins.)

"That's absurd!" broke in Elsa in her loud, somewhat strident voice. "Mama's latest copy of *Les Modes* definitely states that blue and rose are out, and it's all yellow and heliotrope this year."

"And parasols are quite large, because the hats are so small, for all their plumes," added Lucy, thrusting out her lip contemptuously. "Does he say anything about basques, whether the neck is high or low, or frilled or plain, this summer?"

"I'm afraid," said May, "that dear Frey is talking through his hat. It's just his way of trying to be normal, poor lamb, and making an effort to do what is expected of him by us foolish women."

"Why should he do what any one expects?" demanded Renee shrilly.

May regarded her whimsically. "'Out of the mouths of babes and sucklings—,'" she murmured. "Renee, my love, I'm sure I don't know. If you guess the answer you'll be wiser than any one on earth."

"Oh, Mama, do go on!" exclaimed Gertrude impatiently. She wanted to get away alone with her own little note.

May pursed her mouth and scanned the pages in her hand. She was still very kind-hearted, and she felt sorry at the sight of Elsa's eager and hungry expression, her parted lips into which a brighter color had come. The girl, thought May, trying to stifle her sympathy and compassion, looks almost beautiful just now. I believe she really loves Frey. As if my darling would ever look at the great noisy creature. Poor thing! So she dissembled, and pretended to read:

"'Give Elsa my love and tell her that I shall soon answer her most interesting letter. Assure her I have not forgotten her, but I am a frightfully bad letter-writer. So she must forgive me, and not forget me until I come home for a visit next Christmas.'"

Tears sprang into Elsa's brilliant blue eyes, softening them, giving them an almost touching gentleness.

"As if I could ever forget him!" she cried passionately. "Dear, dear Aunt May, can't you tear off just those few little lines and give them to me?"

Gertrude smiled thinly, and a little acidly. She looked at her flustered mother with a touch of malevolence. Mama must eventually learn not to lie like that, even to Elsa, even to give her some foolish pleasure. It was wrong, and an insult to Frey. She felt an edge of anger.

"Darling," stammered May, "I'm really sorry! But there is something on the back that is very, very private. You understand, dear?"

Elsa was fiercely disappointed, but May's manner was so gentle, so strangely soft, so almost appealing, that the exigent girl was mollified and touched.

"Of course, Aunt May. I suppose I should not have asked——"

May could not bear those drenched eyes, that tremulous mouth. She bent over the letter again. "Frey goes on to say that Paris is still quite sad since the War. After all, it only ended a short time ago. They have draped the statue of Alsace-Lorraine in black, and there is such poverty— It was really very hard for Frey, having to come home when the war broke out—and losing nearly two years."

"How inconsiderate of the Germans!" exclaimed Lucy ironically. "They should have remembered Frey and his music."

"Dear! That is so unkind," said May indignantly. She had no humor where her Benjamin was concerned.

"Papa says Barbour-Bouchard made millions, just millions, out of the war!" shrilled Renee excitedly, beginning to bounce up and down again on her seat.

Lucy lifted her head alertly. The sun shone full into her eyes; they had widened, and showed themselves what they really were, not black, but a dark pointed blue. "That's nothing to brag about, Renee," she said, and her voice was strangely harsh and changed. May, looking at her in surprise, was struck. She had never before noticed any resemblance between the dead Martin and his daughters, but the resemblance had sprung out now, evanescently, tenuously, on Lucy's suddenly grave young face. "It ain't anything to be proud of, you kid, to know that your money comes from stuff that blows men you have no quarrel with into little bits. There's no pleasure in getting rich at the price of the lives and blood—of others."

"Why, Lucy!" May was quite astonished; she felt a qualm. Surely she had misunderstood Lucy, after all. She was something more than just a hoyden.

"You don't have to worry," said Gertrude, with a fine cool contempt. "Your Mama's profits from the stock go into the Martin Barbour Memorial Hospital, so there's no odium on you."

"Lucy's just envious," Elsa informed them in a bored voice. "She doesn't give a hoot for 'lives and blood.' She's just thinking of what she could do with the money."

May caught her breath hastily, expecting another furious outburst from Lucy. But to her increasing astonishment, the girl was silent. The look of Martin was fading from her face, but it was still just perceptible. There was a sort of dignity about her silence, as though she had not heard what her sister said.

May rose. "Well, darlings, it becomes hotter and hotter. And it is almost dinner time. Renee, I believe I saw your Papa drive up with Uncle Ernest, to take you home. Shall we go to the house and have our punch and cakes?"

CHAPTER LXIII

MAY AND the four young girls climbed up the long green-golden slope of the lawns toward the house, carefully lifting their skirts and avoiding the croquet hoops.

The upper windows of the great gray house were sheets of steady fire. Light turned the ivy to bronze, made the chimneys ruddy. The white shutters blazed. From the stables came the whinney of horses; over the dull red hoofs of the house and its outbuildings a flock of pigeons were flying, carrying light on their wings under a sky of burning cobalt. Robins hopped on the thick grass; shadows like plushy indigo stretched far and thin from the bases of the immense and scattered trees. The west was a passion of throbbing scarlet radiance.

As she climbed, a little breathlessly because of her increasing stoutness, May looked up at her house, and experienced, as always, a sense of benediction, a peace and enfolding. The pain might never completely leave her heart, where it had taken its place that night of the quarrel with Ernest, but at least it eased a little, became bearable, before the security, the beauty and steadfastness, of her home. These always remained.

Gertrude looked up at the house where she had been born, and worshipped it silently. Sometimes she felt that it was a larger heart, holding in it all the larger things, the deeper and realer things, that her own heart was too small to hold. It was the vault that held her memories, a gallery full of pictures, an album containing faces and costumes, colors and prints, of all her life, some of them painted and vivid, hardly dry from the "bath" of emotion, some already dim—the poignancy vague. Some of them were confused, the lights and shades uncertain, and still others were sharp with bitterness and warped with tears. But this album of a house had from her a passion which was like her father's, and she felt that it had a personality, vigorous and defined, that pervaded every room, every hall, every floor, as blood pervades every cell. When her parents lightly spoke of marriage to her, she was full of silent enraged protest, and sometimes, a terror. Leave her home? Never. Oh, never!

She knew that something was amiss between her parents, not that they quarrelled, were discourteous to each other, cold to each other, or even formal. Nor did they seem bored by each other's company. They were exceedingly kind and considerate, listening attentively and with apparent pleasure when the other spoke, exceedingly polite in even the smallest matters, looking at each other with the fond interest one bestowed on near and liked relatives. She remembered earlier years, before Frey went to Paris; she recalled that her parents then often quarrelled with fury, that her mother wept stormily, her father raged and stamped, doors slammed, shutters banged. After this came laughter and affection, father and mother reappearing arm in arm, and the air, released from tension, seemed all the warmer and the sweeter, all the closer. Now they never quarrelled, and for all their kindness and courtesy, Gertrude felt a strange coldness between them, as though they had discovered that they were in reality not husband and wife, but brother and sister. The girl knew that her father never entered her mother's room, and that her mother entered her father's room only in his absence, to attend to some duty there. Gertrude's knowledge of the marriage state was still somewhat vague, a threshold she could not approach without shrinking, but she knew there was something wrong. She had seen the double beds in the houses of her friends' parents; she had seen the familiar ease between the husbands and wives, and recalled a similar ease that had once existed between her parents. It was gone, gone with the quarrels and the storms, the tears and the laughter. May smiled, sometimes laughed, joked a great deal, but Gertrude, remembering the vivacious turmoils of old laughter, recalled that it was gone. Uneasily, and selfishly, she wished everything were "all right" again; she disliked inexplicable things that disconcerted others not in the secret. She had once confided this to Frey, when he had come home from Paris because of the War; he had merely stared at her with the bright coldness of indifference, declared she was too fanciful, and turned away. Gertrude, stubbornly sure she was not mistaken, had begun to watch her parents, carefully noting the inexplicable thing between them, until it became an obsession with her, a compulsion to uneasiness and irritability. She resented this small dimness on the warmth of her home; also, she felt that her father was uneasy, too, and she blamed her mother for it.

She was thinking of this as they all entered the cool wide gloom of the hall. With a tense tiredness of the nerves she thought: "Papa is home, and now I'll have to watch him and Mama, and try to find out what it is. And it won't really be anything, and it'll be everything. Funny how a word or a gesture, the slightest bit below or above the usual, can be so significant, so compelling, so strange, that it can make you unreasonably happy or unreasonably sad. Mama will say: 'Home early, love? I'll ring for tea immediately,' and Papa will kiss her forehead and ask her if she found it a tedious day, and he will tell her a little scrap of news about the shops and they'll laugh, and the tea will come in and Mama will pour, and every one will be bright and affectionate. And there the Thing will be, destroying everything, warping everything, like a—like a leer on a nasty face in a room full of normal people."

"Home early, love? I'll ring for tea immediately," said May brightly, as she entered the library where Ernest sat with Eugene. The Venetian blinds shut out the glare of sunlight that lay on the grass, and only a green, watery-bright light filled the quiet room. Gertrude and the other girls followed her, Gertrude watching with that hateful compulsion, Renee struggling eagerly to get past her to her father. The child succeeded, almost knocking over her cousin in the rush, and bounded like a dark, bony young pup upon Eugene. She flung her arms about his neck, kissed his brown cheek, shouted in his ear, and pulled his cravat to one side with her feverish hugs.

"Mon Dieu!" exclaimed Eugene, laughing, and disengaging his young daughter's arms. "Your arms are like razors, ma petite. And look at your frock! Your Mama will be annoyed with you. And your hands!" He pulled her to him and kissed her tenderly. She was his favorite child; let Dorcas love her two older sons, and the blond-angel twins: this child was flesh of his heart. He tweaked her ear, continued his scolding, smoothed his roughened gray hair. The years had not widened him, padded him, as they had Ernest; he had grown thinner, withering slowly and brownly, to his old father's image. Armand lay beside his wife in the cemetery now, and Ernest, unconsciously struck by the resemblance between dead father and living son, sometimes called his friend "Armand."

Gertrude ran silently to her father's chair, and as silently sat on the arm of it. He turned his face to her, kissed her without speaking. Gertrude glanced from him to her mother: the Thing, like a gauze veil that was barely visible, hung between them.

"Do not get tea for me, May," said Eugene, struggling to sit up with Renee's hanging weight still on his neck. "You know I detest that beverage. Besides, it is dinner time. My landau will be here in a moment, and I will take this young savage home. No, May, we cannot stay for dinner. Dorcas would be excessively annoyed. She detests disarrangement of plans."

"Dorcas is entirely too rigid and inflexible," said her brother, annoyed. "She is a slave to chalkmarks, and never allows for human fallibility. A school-marm of a woman."

Eugene laughed, but a line of vexation appeared between his small brown eyes. He pulled Renee's slipping ribbon awkwardly into place, and said nothing.

"Well, my dears," said Ernest, smiling at his two nieces. Lucy, after she had kissed him with a flurry of skirts and flouncing of curls, collapsed on a stool near his knee, and Elsa had kissed him heartily, and sat on the other arm of his chair. Lucy looked up at him, pouting her lips and adoring him; Elsa looked down at him, absently straightened his cravat, and adored him. But Gertrude sat silently, without motion, her hand in his. Her fraility and delicacy made her look like a soft gray cloud temporarily taking a human shape. May, sitting down at a distance from them all, thought, with irritation, that Gertrude had no expression at all; sometimes the girl was as blank as a stone.

"Your cheek is scratched, Elsa," said Ernest.

"A cat did it," she replied serenely. Lucy flung up her head, flushing, then bit her lip. Gertrude's hand slipped deeper into her father's warm grasp.

"A letter came from Frey today, Ernest," said May, beaming. (As if there was something determinedly affable behind her face, thought Gertrude wearily.)

"Yes? What does he say?" Ernest puffed on a cigar which Gertrude had just lit for him. The veil lay on his face, now, like a faint gray web.

May was very animated. "He is coming home for a visit at Christmas. He is to have a composition of his played at a concert." She pulled the letter from her pocket, read the part.

"Splendid!" said Eugene. "(Renee, my heart, you are choking me.) You are to be congratulated, May, on giving the world an apparent genius." He seemed genuinely interested and understanding. Gertrude saw a luminous pale flash on her mother's face, and the smile she gave her brother-in-law was a little pathetic.

"I hope it is received well," said Ernest. His words seemed forced, as though he had thought it over and had carefully picked the exact phrase, and was wondering if it sounded as wooden as he felt.

"The composition? I am certain it will be. The Master would not have permitted it to be played had he had any doubts," said May, with an increase in her determined affability and vivaciousness.

Elsa caught Ernest's eye and winked crudely. She was somewhat discomfited when this little pleasantry was not returned, and a little frightened when her uncle's expression tightened and hardened against her. She felt affronted; she knew very well that Uncle Ernest did not approve of Frey's silly music-making, that he was bitterly disappointed in his eldest son. There was no need of his making faces at her like that, as though she had committed a crime, she thought resentfully. (Elsa, thought Gertrude drearily, is a pig. How can Papa abide her?)

Lucy was more astute, and kinder. She detested Frey heartily, but she loved her uncle, and her placating of him was much less hypocritical than Elsa's.

"Frey will make us all feel like country dolts one of these days," she said. May, surprised at this unexpected appreciation of her darling, stared at her in surprise. Off guard like this, the smiles gone, one saw the bitter lines of sadness in her plump face.

"Thank you, dear," she said gently.

Ernest smiled, pulled one of Lucy's curls from its coil. Restored to good humor, he looked up at Elsa.

"Paul says to tell your mother he will be a little late tonight, Elsa. He is going over some books; we are not yet certain that young Reynolds is entirely straight." He became animated in his turn. "You may also tell mother, my dears, that Paul is doing splendidly at the bank, and if he continues so, which he will, there is no knowing how far he will go. The President was just saying this morning that he is one of the most efficient and capable young men he has ever seen. A natural-born banker."

The gray web was over May's face now.

"How nice," she murmured. She surreptitiously fingered the letter in her pocket.

Ernest spoke to his daughter. "Oh yes. Paul wishes me to ask you what flowers you prefer for the Stantons' party, Trudie."

A pinched, slightly blue look appeared about Gertrude's mouth.

"I don't care," she answered indifferently. (How she hated the thought of going to another party with Paul! During the last six months, some diabolical scheme seemed to have been afoot to couple her with her cousin. All her other beaus had drifted away; sometimes a sick and terrified thought assailed her that her father had let loose a subtle rumor that there was an "understanding" between his daughter and his nephew. She worshipped her father, but she was aware of his relentless power. But oh, please God! he shall not do this thing to me! I will not have Paul, even though Papa pushes me right into his arms. I'll get away somehow! Mama will help me! Mama hates him, too!) Thinking this, she turned eyes wide and dark with fright upon her mother, and May looked back at her with a sharp steady gaze.

"How can you be so indifferent?" demanded Elsa incredulously. "The Stantons' lawn fête is going to be the event of the summer season. Sometimes I think you are quite bloodless, Gertrude. Why, Lucy and I just can't sleep nights trying to decide what we'll wear." She was suddenly diverted. "What are you going to wear, Trudie?"

"I hope, her new white satin from New York," smiled Ernest. His eyes were pointed a little, as he fixed them on his daughter's face. "I confess I know very little about ladies' gowns, but this one is something special. I could not help noticing it particularly when she showed it to me. And the pearls your Mama and I gave you on your birthday, darling. You will be quite the belle of the ball."

"Gertrude!" Elsa's and Lucy's voices blended together in a faint shriek of indignation. "You never told us of your white satin! You must show it to us at once!"

"I don't like it," said Gertrude, forcing a thin smile. (How could she like it, after her father had said, only a few days ago, that Paul would be completely enslaved when he saw her in it. Oh, I loathe him! I detest him! I wish he'd die!) The terrible, sick trapped feeling assailed her again like a real hand upon her mouth.

"I think it a little mature for Gertrude," said May. "I would prefer she would not wear it just yet. Her pink-sprigged muslin, perhaps——"

"It would make an excellent wedding dress," said Ernest casually.

Elsa clapped her hands delightedly. "Then, of course, Paul mustn't see it, yet," she said, with an arch and teasing glance at her cousin.

Gertrude stood up. A cold sheath was over all her slight body. "It doesn't matter if Paul sees it or not," she remarked in a preoccupied voice. "Mama, shall I see if Guy and Reggie are preparing for dinner? And look in at the nursery at Joey?"

May regarded her gravely. "Yes, my love," she answered in the gentlest and saddest of voices. I've escaped Ernest, she thought mournfully. Will Gertrude escape him?

She thinks she's too good for Paul, thought Elsa, with hatred. With her hoity-toity ways! And her pale dead face, and that dull hair! How can he possibly look at her? It isn't just the money she'll have; he really wants her. He's wanted her since we were all children. I can't understand dear Paul at all.

Gertrude moved toward the door. She heard the quick rat-tat of hoofs in the driveway; she stopped dead, halfway to the door. A shaft of sunlight blazed into the hallway, blinding her, but she stood still, hardly breathing, her heart rioting in pain to her throat. She put her hand to it.

"What's the matter, dear?" asked May. The girl turned slowly; a radiance stood upon her face, in which her eyes swooned and her lips parted.

"I—I think it's Philippe," she murmured chokingly. She looked about her, dazed, then was out in the hall with the swift movement of a bird. A very young man was crossing the threshold into the hall, a tall, exceedingly thin, dark young man, with thick, longish black hair and black eyes that began to burn when he saw his cousin. All his movements were rapid and jerky, full of nervousness and angry vitality, and his face, thin almost to gauntness, and brown, had an Indian look about it.

"Trudie!" he cried, and seized her hands. He stared down at her, smiling a little wildly, and breathing as though he had been running.

May appeared in the hallway from the library. "Philippe! How nice! You are just in time for dinner. How is your Mama?" She advanced upon him, smiling cordially. She almost loved him at times; Florabelle's son reminded her in many ways of Godfrey. Philippe had emerged from a pale and colorless childhood into this sudden dark restlessness that was beginning to disturb the Barbour household.

"Mama is very well, thank you, Aunt May," replied the youth, struggling for formality, and succeeding only in looking as radiantly dazed as Trudie. "She sent me to ask if you and Uncle Ernest would dine with us on Sunday. Grandmother, Mama says, is becoming impossible," he grinned, showing blazing white teeth, "and Mama thinks Uncle Ernest might be able to control her."

"Dear, dear," said May, smiling. Old Hilda was becoming very obstreperous with age. Her new son-in-law, Major Norwood, had the soldier's heavy lack of imagination and stubborn stolidity, and these were like a thick wall in the flood of Hilda's frequent furies and increasing petulance. Meeting this wall, catapulted against it violently, they frothed and foamed, became turgid and uncontrollable. Ernest was frequently called upon to restore peace to a harassed household.

Philippe, becoming aware that he was still holding Gertrude's hand, dropped it as though it had begun to burn him. A pulse was beating visibly in the girl's slender throat; the beauty was still out on her face, like a spring morning. They all went into the library. Eugene, who had spied his landau coming up the drive, was standing up, making his goodbys, and Renee was bounding about him, her hair flying. She looked very much like her cousin, Philippe Bouchard, and perhaps this fact had endeared her to Gertrude. The youth greeted his relatives with nervous formality.

Eugene smiled at Raoul's son. "Bon jour, Philippe," he said, and shook his hand. He liked his nephew very much.

Ernest smiled also, but with a bleakness. "How is your Mama, Philippe?"

More nervous than ever, he stammered out his mother's message. Ernest laughed shortly. "We'll be there," he said. He glanced at May, shook his head humorously. "Ma still has a lot of fight in her. She makes Florrie miserable."

Elsa stared at her cousin with open derision and dislike. How could Trudie like this dark-skinned, skinny, piddling boy, younger than herself! A jumping-jack if there ever was one, always reading and writing poetry, or running to his awful Catholic Church! Wasn't there something said once about him becoming a priest, or something equally dreadful? Then why doesn't he go off, and do it, whatever they did in such a case? To be sure, her Papa had been a Catholic too, but he had been a convert, and no one had really taken it seriously. And she and Paul and the others had been baptized in the Catholic Church, but Mama never urged them to go to Mass, or anything, and the priest was scared of her and let them all be. No, no one in *her* home took this business seriously, but the French were so odd, and so intense about everything. Really, she quite disliked the French. Lucy, who thought Philippe an ugly brat, had not replied to his greeting. They were practically the same

age, but she was an engaged girl, and therefore, by that right, and the
right of her mature femininity, was really older, she thought.

"Mama Barbour is quite old, you must remember, Ernest," said May,
absently pulling and twisting Renee into shape again. "Must you really
go, Eugene? Renee, my pet, give your Aunt May a kiss. Tell your
Mama that you must remain to dinner the next time you come. Tomorrow night? Capital!"

Elsa and Lucy exchanged grimaces at this. When Eugene and his
daughter had gone, Elsa was loudly shocked at the time. In the midst
of flurry, runnings back for a last word, swirling of petticoats and skirts,
reddening of cheeks, shouted last good-bys, cries and scoldings, Elsa
and Lucy also departed for home. May's invitation to dinner had been
polite, if feeble. (She still remembered Elsa's face upon receiving the
pretended message from Godfrey.) But Elsa, with passionate regret,
told her that her mother had expressly asked that the girls return home
that night for the evening meal.

A quiet like that following a clap of thunder fell on the house upon
their departure. May laughed a little. "What exuberance," she said
mildly.

"I like a little life in young people," replied Ernest, a trifle ill-naturedly.
May still smiled with a sort of bright determination, but made no
reply.

"Gertrude," Ernest went on sharply, "would be better off for a little
of their life." He turned on the girl. She and Philippe were standing
close together, not speaking, but just looking at each other. "Trudie!"
said her father, raising his voice.

The girl actually jumped. "Yes, Papa?" she answered, turning to him
with a bemused expression. How beautiful she looked, all at once,
thought Ernest angrily, with a lowering glance at his nephew.

"Didn't your Mama ask you to see about the boys, and Joey?" he asked.
Gertrude fled, as though she had been struck. Philippe looked after
her for a long moment. His tall, angular young body appeared as though
it had been turned, in the midst of tremendous animation, into stone.

"Let us go into the dining room," said Ernest abruptly.
And stalked out gloomily, leaving his wife to follow if she wished.

CHAPTER LXIV

THERE IS some brutality, some atavism, in us that makes us hate the old and the sick," thought Ernest, as he drove alone to his sister's house to see his mother. "We forget that we have loved them, that they are our flesh, that many of our joys and our sorrows are theirs, also. All we see and remember is the sick face that resents our health, the heavy legs that trip us up, the tedious drag on a sympathy gone sour like a wine that has overfermented. Sometimes the old get our strongest hatred, and we come to wince at the sound of their nagging voices, the sight of their bleared eyes, the presence of their obstinacy and childish obstreperousness. And when they are dead, we hate them worse than ever, these horrible creatures, not sublime, not noble, but just stinking clay, threatening us, gloating over us."

Suddenly he remembered that his old mother was no fool. Did she know how her children regarded her: as a querulous burden, a bore, a hindrance, a repulsive old beldame, a tiresome responsibility that had once been useful but had now outlived its usefulness? He wondered Perhaps that was what was making her so outrageous these days, the knowledge that the children she had borne, nursed, thrashed, loved, tended, and reared, now hated her for the one crime of not being dead. All at once he seemed to see her, a frightened old woman at bay, unwanted, repellent, strident-voiced and peevishly bewildered. I don't want to die yet! she seemed to cry out at him in a thin high terror. Why do you push me to my death with your wills and your eyes? "Poor Ma," he said aloud, with a rueful smile. The coachman turned around enquiringly.

But Ernest's sympathy had veered again to his favorite sister, Florabelle, by the time he arrived at the big, brightly lit house on Quaker Terrace. (Through intervening trees, across long quiet vistas of damp lamplit lawns and paths, he could see the far distant light of Amy's house.) Florabelle's house was always too warm, hotly lit, over-furnished, with its heavy velvet drapes, dripping fringe, cluttered corners, crystal chandeliers, ornate lamps and gilded picture frames. When she had married the solid and unimaginative Major Norwood, the soul of conservative and heavy tastes, she had thrown out all her gay "French" furniture and had gone ponderously Victorian. Pretty still, plump now, as well as small, her cheeks still dimpled and bright, Florabelle lived, as her mother shrewdly said, "in a fluster." Her flutterings had become flusterings, and even her clothing partook of this confusion, so that her veils were always blowing about her hats, her bangles and chains clashing together, her curls escaping from their blond coif, her petticoat peeping out, gloves dropping, reticule slipping from her hands, furs slipping, ear-rings falling; she was always in a hurry, her pink cheeks glowing warmly and her voice sharp with strain and excited petulance. To be sure, she had six children now, two of them mere babies, Philippe, barely seventeen, being the oldest. She had a swarm of servants, but they had caught her flustery ways, her confusion, her tendency to leave sentences excitedly unfinished, her habit of starting a dozen things at once and finishing none. So the house looked like its mistress, and confusion ran riot in the heat and the brilliantly lit rooms and the stuffy ornate atmosphere, and there seemed always to be a child crying in the upper regions or a quarrel going on downstairs among the servants. Ernest often wondered how Major Norwood stood all this. But the Major seemed utterly unperturbed, sat solidly reading his papers and smoking in the midst of a very mob of noise and runnings to and fro and cries and exclamations, frenzied young wife and romping children.

He either enjoyed it, or was deaf to it, Ernest thought. Nothing ever excited him. He loved his pretty Florrie, was fond of Raoul's children, was dutiful toward them, and adored his own babies. He felt that he had much more than an old bachelor deserved; actually, he liked to hear children's voices, having become sick of the musty silence of bachelor quarters and lonely hotels. Those loud rioting voices, the energy, the spirits, the laughter, the scufflings, the fights, drove out from him the fears that had besieged his middle-age with threats of loneliness, lovelessness, and death. He became almost young again, and was grateful both to Florrie and her children.

Florabelle was surprised to see her brother, and before she could recover herself she exclaimed crossly: "But I said Thursday night! Oh, dear, those children again. Do come in, Ernest! Kiss me! I'm glad to see you. Major! Major, love, here's Ernest; I don't know what I'm going to do about Mama!"

"How do you do, sir?" said the Major, rising, and allowing a welter of newspapers and cigar ashes to slide to the floor. He was a tall and florid man, with simple clear blue eyes, a military haircut, a clipped gray mustache, and, despite a slight paunchiness, still possessing a soldier's bearing and erectness. There was about him a freshly scrubbed look, partly due to the bland naïveté of his expression and the crisp neatness of his clothing. Ernest had long ago dismissed him as not being very bright, but he was "harmless," and so he liked him as he liked all simple people who never interfered with him.

The Major was about to sit down again in his soft leather chair, but his wife bustled him hastily out of it, shoved her brother toward it and into it, complaining incessantly as she did so in a high sweet voice. The Major, uprooted, glanced about helplessly, as though he were in a strange house and were wondering if he dared sit down, then, finally deciding he might, he cautiously lowered himself into a horsehair, mahogany rocker. He disliked horsehair; it bit through his trouser legs. He began to·scratch, surreptitiously, while he beamed upon his brother-in-law.

Ernest firmly refused tea, wine, cigars and cake. "Dear me," said Florabelle crossly, "you never want anything when you come here."

"If you want to, you can send it up to Ma and me after awhile," he answered, taking her hand and patting it. "Sit down, my love, your face is very red and hot."

Florabelle plumped herself down with gestures of dainty despair, waving her handkerchief, and raising her pretty blue eyes to the ceiling as if overcome:

"You have no idea what I suffer with Mama!" she exclaimed. "The Major says I am an angel of patience!"

"Where is she now?"

"Locked up in her room, as tight as a drum. Diggs puts her tray on the floor by her door, and after he has gone she deigns to open it, and eats every bite, then puts out the tray again. I knock and knock, and send the children, and I cry and plead, and she sits behind her door like a— like a graven image, and never answers. It's been almost three days now. She won't even let the servants in to make her bed or clean up, and with this hot weather and everything, and one has to watch things so for— unpleasant things—things that breed in dust, and you know Mama was never too tidy in her later years—" She stopped abruptly, out of breath. "I don't know what to do," she resumed in a burst of emotion. "I can't stand the strain, with all this house and the children and the servants. After all, I've had Mama for seventeen years, and it does seem that I ought to be relieved occasionally. There's Dorcas, so selfish and secretive, staying away from us in case we ask her for something, or a favor, and Amy, a widow, without any one, and Martin was Mama's favorite son, and May," she added spitefully. "I'm really surprised at May! But now she seems so cold to me, when we were so fond of each other once. I can't see why May——"

Ernest examined his fingernails. "What is it this time?" he asked casually.

"How should I know! A week ago it was Jules' impudence, then Leon's slyness, then Francois' screaming. The week before it was offense because I disagreed with her about the discipline I was using on Chandler and Betsy. Mama is so indulgent to the children, though I can't remember she was ever indulgent to us. Sometimes I think she hates all the children except Philippe, and she only likes him because she really had the rearing of him, I being so weak after he was born, and because she says that he looks like Pa, though that's ridiculous, for Philippe looks just like his father's family——"

Three little boys, aged about twelve, ten and eight, respectively, came into the room to bid their mother good night. They were all very dark and wiry, slightly undersized and colorless, with long thin faces, black eyes and puckered mouths. Ernest always thought of Armand when he saw them. He privately thought them excessively ugly. He terrified them, filled them with suspicion, and they were always quiet and subdued when he was present, even lowering their rather shrill and exigent voices to whispers, as though in the presence of a danger.

He shook hands with them, with Leon, the "deep" one, with Jules, the sly one, with Francois, who was given to silent and violent hysterias (he used to have "fits" when he was a baby). Their similarity never failed to amuse him. He might have been friends with Leon, had the child encouraged him, for there was a somber intelligence in his deep-set, somewhat sullen eyes, and wit showing in the flexible lines of his puckered lips. But Leon never encouraged him; he maintained a precociously mature reserve.

As though she were subconsciously made aware again of their ugliness and big stiff ears, Florabelle said absently: "Betsy is more like a cherub every day, and Chandler is the handsomest little boy in Quaker Terrace. There, kiss Mama, and Papa, dears, and Uncle Ernest, and go to bed. Where's Nurse? Upstairs? Well, go at once to her."

Jules kissed his mother, balked at the Major and his uncle, and led the little procession out of the room again; the children walked Indian-file, which enormously amused Ernest, and he burst out laughing. The little boys did not heed this laughter, though Jules' ears turned fiery red.

"You're always laughing at them, Ernest," Florabelle remarked, annoyed.

Major Norwood stood in great awe of Ernest, and had a tremendous reverence for him. He had a vague idea that Ernest considered him negligible, if good-tempered, and was always earnestly trying to prove to him that he was quite wrong. So he asked seriously: "And how is business, sir? I see by the papers that your military contracts were renewed, in spite—er—of the trouble about those patents in France during the war—er—between France and Prussia, and shipping the explosives——"

"Yes, the contracts were renewed," replied Ernest pleasantly.

The Major sweated with the strain of his efforts and pleasure at Ernest's amiability. A moisture came out over his blue limpid eyes, and he leaned toward the younger man.

"And the French Government no longer suspects you of implication in Monsieur Schultz's dealing with the Prussian enemy, sir?"

"No, indeed. Though Schultz lost his head over it, I believe him innocent." Nothing could have been blander than Ernest's face.

The Major made a regretful clucking sound, and shook his head. "Such tales the papers do make up! Libel! Sir, the law is very inadequate about libel. Something should be done——"

"Only small fry are concerned with libel," said Ernest, smiling.

The Major became quite excited, and his eyes flashed blue, honest fire. "But, sir! They actually stated, in editorials, that it was at your suggestion that Schultz negotiated with the damn Prussians for the sale and shipping of munitions out of France into enemy territory! That is outrageous! Surely, you are not going to let it pass? A gentleman in your position?"

"Let the dogs bark," said Ernest. He suppressed a small yawn and glanced at his watch. The Major sank back into his chair, his broad face still flushed, his eyes still flashing. He bit the end of a cigar with great vigor, shook his head, and muttered: "Damn lying yellow sheets!" Nevertheless, his simple heart was wounded; he suspected that Ernest had snubbed him, and he shrank a little.

Ernest stood up. "Well, I'll run upstairs and see Ma now." At that moment Philippe came into the room, carrying a book and a basket of peaches. He started when he saw his hated uncle, who he knew hated him in turn. But there was a French courtesy in his quiet greeting. Ernest muttered a reply; the amiability had quite gone from his face. Philippe kissed his mother. "Good night, Mama. I'm going to my room, now." Florabelle looked up at him affectionately. He reminded her acutely, in some ways, of his father, whom she had loved more than any one in all her life. "Mind you, don't throw the peachstones on the floor, as usual," she warned him, patting his cheek.

The youth shook the Major's hand, bowed formally to Ernest, and left the room.

"He's such a student," said Florabelle fondly. "He's been reading for hours in the library, and now he'll read for an hour or two in bed, before going to sleep."

"I'll wager it isn't anything practical that he's reading," said Ernest acidly. "Florrie, I've told you over and over there's a place for him in the bank, or in any of the shop offices at any time, and if you had a grain of intelligence you'd insist that he start at once, instead of finishing his silly school. After all, he has your estate to think of, and your present affairs. The sooner he becomes familiar with them the better for every one."

"I don't see you forcing Frey into the business just yet," replied Florabelle maliciously, glaring at him. She was pleased when he colored. "Well, Ernest, Philippe isn't Godfrey, and he knows his duty. He is quite willing to go into the shops or the bank when he is eighteen, but he wants to finish at St. Therese's; he has hardly two more years."

"Well, all I wish is that the family had more lads in it like Paul," replied Ernest. He left the room without another word, and went upstairs to the second story.

"Paul!" murmured Florabelle viciously to her husband. "Everything is Paul! He's trying to force him on Trudie, and the girl despises him, and no wonder. I don't like her, but I sympathize with her just the same. But Ernest always did have a weakness for that branch of the family—" She nodded, gloatingly.

"My dear!" whispered the Major, aghast, with a glance at the empty doorway. "He may hear you! After all, it's only gossip——"

Ernest tapped on his mother's door. There was no answer. He rattled the knob. "Ma," he said impatiently. There was a faint creaking inside, the sound of slow heavy footsteps, and the door opened.

"Come in," said Hilda somberly. "So there you are, you rascal. I knew they'd send for you when they'd had enough."

Ernest glanced about the room with distaste, his distended nostrils quivering. "The devil, Ma, why don't you open a window?" He flung open the windows, his arms entangling themselves in the dusty curtains. The room smelt, but the warm night air, pouring in, cleansed and purified it.

Hilda had brought her own furniture to Florabelle's house, and the hideous old mahogany bed and bowed chest of drawers, rocking chairs, commode with its china pitcher sprawling with pink roses, filled the smallish room chokingly. Her own dark red rug covered the floor; beloved old paintings, dim behind rococo gilt frames, covered the walls. Though, of course, there was no fire, Hilda had evidently been sitting before the grate, for the chair was pulled close to the fender. A sweetish-sour odor hung in the air, mingled with essence of peppermint. Old Hilda was fond of lozenges. She had evidently just finished a snack before bedtime, for a demolished tray stood on a dusty table beside the rumpled bed. She had lit only one candle (she disliked lamps) and its hot feeble rays smouldered on the mantelpiece.

Hilda sat down on her chair near the fireplace, bolt upright, for all her stoutness, and folded her hands in her lap. Her handsome old face, a fat ruin now, had set itself in belligerent lines, the under lip sticking out like a shelf. Her white hair was untidily bundled under a dingy lace cap, but her black bombazine had a ruffle of white at the throat.

"Well, can't you sit down?" she demanded, raising her voice.

Ernest leaned against the mantelpiece, after frowning at its dust, and smiled down at his mother.

"What's all this nonsense about locking yourself up in this room like a child, Ma? Do you realize how unpleasant this is for Florabelle? After all, she has a houseful of servants and children to take care of, and she can't very well spend her time——"

"Taking care of a silly old woman!" growled Hilda. "Go on, say it. I don't mind. I've had worse things said to me." She seemed to crumple a little. "I'm not beholden to Florabelle like a pauper. I've my own money. She gets her share of it, and the brats do, too, on birthdays and Christmas, and other times. So, because I'm not beholden to her, I think I'm entitled to my moods, too. God knows she's got enough of 'em herself. I never saw such a flutter-budget in my life. She gets worse as she grows older. It's enough to drive that poor man down there mad."

She glared up at her son, full of pathetic fight. I'm not needed any more, but don't dare to say that to me! she seemed to cry soundlessly. Ernest felt uncomfortable, examined the nail of his index finger minutely, and then bit it.

"You aren't helping to keep him from going mad," he said. "Major Norwood is an innocent, and I believe you are making his life disagreeable. Florrie has her faults, no doubt, but avoidance of duty is not one of them. She'd be only too glad to let you help her, and advise her, if you didn't go at it hammer and tongs."

"But she lets it get like Bedlam!" cried Hilda desperately. "She—" She stopped abruptly, for Ernest was looking about the bedroom with elaborate significance.

"If this isn't Bedlam, I'd like to know what it is, Ma. Filthy. Smelly. Before you lecture Florrie on her housekeeping, you might try keeping this room neater, or at least letting the servants in."

Hilda burst into tears. She rocked herself to and fro in her tremendous old rocker, as though moving in the rhythms of grief, covering her face with her kerchief. "It's not all this at all!" she sobbed. "It's deeper than this. I'm lonely and miserable, and——"

"Lonely with a houseful of children, and your own daughter?" cut in Ernest. "And in the same city, your son, and another daughter, and all their children? God knows, we've always made you welcome——"

Hilda snatched her hands from her face, which was now contorted and empurpled. Her old eyes, sunken in nests of fat wrinkles, blazed upon him. "Made me welcome! D'ye think I want to be made welcome? If you do, you're a worse fool than I thought you, Ernest Barbour! Mothers of real children are never 'made welcome,' any more than a mother makes her children welcome. Like—guests, or relatives you don't like. I'm not a relative; I'm not a guest. I'm your Mother! And I might as well be a dog without a penny——"

"Don't keep harping on the money Pa left you, Ma," said Ernest distastefully. "We know all about that. We realize you aren't a pauper."

But Hilda, broken-hearted, had begun to weep again. "No one wants me! No one cares whether I live or die. You'd all be glad if I pegged out; I know you! I'm a nuisance, a mithering old woman who ought to know better than going on living. If I tell Florrie that she's spoiling the little ones, she gets uppish and snaps my nose off; if I tell her she's hard on the old Major, she tells me I vexed my Joe in the old days." The tears ran down her face, filling the furrows, running over her lips, and like a child she tasted the saltiness of them with the tip of her tremulous tongue.

Ernest gazed over her head, frowning, drumming with his fingers on the mantel. "You're always pitying yourself, Ma. We want to make you happy. What do you want? Within reason, we'll give you anything you want."

Hilda was silent. She tugged at a pocket in the fold of her dress and pulled out a crushed handkerchief, which she applied to her eyes and nose. The fight had gone out of her; her old hands trembled, and she looked sick and beaten. Ernest pursed his lips as he looked down at her, and when she finally glanced up and saw his face, a sort of wild fright seized her. She waved her hands in agitation, as though to ward off something. "I wish we'd never left home!" she cried.

Ernest had to smile, though a little thinly. "Just listen to yourself, Ma! Aren't you being a little silly? Would you have had us remain in England, servants and bootlickers and grooms? We're people of consequence now, the richest family in Windsor, one of the richest in the State, and the country. All in thirty-odd years, too." His voice became more and more the voice of one who speaks impatiently to a child. But Hilda's eyes had begun to flash, her breath to come quickly in loud gusts.

"I'm not proud of it," she answered in the loud portentous tones of a woman who speaks courageously and in truth. "I'm not proud of it, Ernest Barbour. I've waited a long time to talk, and it's roiled in me until I can't abide it any longer. I've got to speak.

"What has all the money brought us? Look at your own face in that glass there, over the mantel, and see for yourself! Is it the kind of face you'd want your daughter's husband to have, the kind he'd show her on the wedding night? Ask yourself! It isn't even the face of my son. It's the face of a scoundrel, a highwayman. And that's all you are—a highwayman. You drove your Pa down to his death, you made his last years miserable, with your connivings and your treacheries. He couldn't even die peaceful because of you. Night after night," and now her voice broke, grew stern with sobs, "I heard him crying in his sleep, and it was always Ernest doing this and Ernest doing that, and where was it going to end, and making money from Englishmen dying in the Crimea, probably shot down by guns made by us and sold underhand to the Russians. Your Pa never was much for the munitions business, not in wartime, anyway, and it set badly on him. He talked easily about it, the killing and all, but it gave him nightmares; he tried to be hard and brave and easy-like about it, but it killed him. No, don't you dare interrupt me! I'm not finished yet!

"He was afraid of you. Yes, he was afraid of you. Afraid because he knew you were cruel and had no heart in you. I didn't agree with him about Georgie—I thought you did right. At first. And then I saw that you really weren't upset because Georgie was a thief; you always were a thief, yourself. All you wanted was to get him out of the business so you could manage it yourself; he was in your way, and what he had was worth something, and you wanted it. Poor Joe knew it; he was cleverer than me. I never was a clever one to read the dirty minds of rascals. And because he knew all this, and was afraid of you, and tried to hate you, it killed my poor Joe. You made me a widow, Ernest Barbour, and before God, you'll answer for it!"

She stood up suddenly, so suddenly that the chair swung back and fell over. She faced her son, trembling violently, her livid old face streaming with tears, her eyes beating upon him with contempt and denunciation.

"Don't be a fool, Ma," said Ernest sharply. He moved away from the mantel a little, putting a few steps between himself and his mother. "If you insist on talking like a damn fool, I'll go. I came down here to see what I could do for you——"

"Do for me?" she almost screamed, as though in astonished outrage. "Do for me? What could you ever do for any one, you scoundrel? What have you ever done for any one, except yourself? Who have you ever served, but yourself? Who have you ever loved, but yourself? Look you, it's no time for fancy words now, my lad. Out with it! Who have you ever cared for but yourself? Amy? Amy, your dead brother's wife? Ah, I know all about that, my fine cock! Thanks to all the money you've got, you can't go anywhere without being seen——!" Her voice ended in a choked gurgle, for Ernest had put his hand savagely over her mouth, and was holding her in a grip like iron.

"Quiet!" he whispered. "Quiet!" as she struggled impotently. Over the rim of his hand she glared up at him in her rage and detestation. Even the balefulness of his light and distended eyes, the murderous and silent violence of his expression, could not daunt the desperate old woman. She tugged at his hand, sunk her nails into it, wrenched it from her face. Every one of her facial muscles twitched with palsy under her livid skin. In a deep mad silence mother and son regarded each other with hatred.

Hilda's panting, like a gust, filled the room. "I'll never forgive that," she whispered at last. She put her handkerchief to her lips, and as she did so a strange glazed expression settled over her glittering old eyes. "I'll never forgive that," she said aloud. She dropped the handkerchief, struggled for self-control; she put her hand to her head, and began to speak again to Ernest, who had gone to a window and was looking through it at the night.

"I've seen you for what you are," she said, in a low, almost meditative voice. "I thank God for that. I can go on with what I've got to say. You're not my son any longer. You're a devil that's gotten into my lad's skin.

"You've helped us all to money, not that you cared whether any of us had it or not. But you were pulling it after you, and so we were caught in the edges. But what has it given any of us, I ask you? It killed my poor Martin, who never hurt a fly, and who was an angel if there ever was one. And you drove him to his death, too, just as you did his father! You killed Martin. Aren't you proud of that? Yes, I think you are proud. You made all his poor life wretched, and ended up by killing him, just as if you'd pulled the trigger yourself. You tried to rob him, and when you couldn't you killed him. And sometimes I think you killed old Mr. Gregory, too."

"You're mad," said Ernest softly, without turning. "You ought to be in Bedlam."

Hilda nodded her head, fiercely smiling. "Perhaps so. But there's no Bedlam and no gaol that could hold you. The law can't touch you; it never does touch murderers and robbers as big as you are. It'd be like trying to chain the Black Plague. You are a plague! But God remembers; God will reach you some day. You can't keep Him out, Ernest Barbour. You've got a reckoning with Him, for all the lives you've spoilt, all the lives you're still trying to spoil, even your poor daughter's life, and your poor wife's, and Frey's, and Amy's— You can't shut God out; your doors can't keep Him out!"

Ernest turned to her. "You're a silly old woman," he said, apparently without rancor or much interest. "Like all old people you talk too much. You're abusive and foolish. Because you've become so cantankerous, no one wants you about. I'd advise you to mend your ways. None of us is going to put up with you much longer."

He left the room, walking firmly.

Hilda stood where he left her for a few moments, then fumbled blindly for a chair. Rigors ran over her stout old body. She sat on the edge of the chair, her hands, palms upward, on her knees. They were short, fat, warped palms, that had known hard work for four children. They were hands that had thrashed them, tended them in babyhood and illness, loved them. But she did not look at her hands, which pathetically expressed more than any words could say. She lifted her eyes, brimming again with a sharp saltiness like blood, and fixed them on an old daguerreotype of the young Joseph Barbour, which stood upon the mantel. She began to whimper, like a lost and whipped child.

"Joe, lovie, that was our son, Ernest, talking to his Ma with such a face and voice! That was the lad we were so proud of, walking him down Sandy Lane, a little toddler, holding his hands so he wouldn't fall. Do you remember, Joe, how we picked the daisies for him? Even then he snatched at things! But he was so pretty, such a red-cheeked little lad, and you said that there was nothing you'd not do for him, and you just a lad yourself!"

She sobbed aloud, terribly. Something seemed to wrench in her breast, tear away. "That was our lad, Joe, talking to his mother with that face, like a devil's! Remember when I carried him, and he was so vigorous even then, in my womb, and we'd sit in your old aunt's garden, with the trees dripping around us, and we'd plan for him, when he'd be born? And I was so glad I was having him, your son, Joe.

"O God in Heaven, why do we have children? Joe, why did we have them, to hate us at the last? We bring them here, and love them, and give our lives for them, and all we can hope for is that they won't hate us before we die. But they always do—they always hate us!"

She struck her palms silently and frenziedly together, in the strength of her grief. She turned and stared at the door through her tears.

"Ernest," she whispered brokenly. "My son, come back to your Ma. I love you, my lad, even now, I love you——"

Ernest was talking to his sister and her husband in the reception hall as he pulled on his gloves and waited for his carriage.

"There's no doubt that she needs attention," he was saying casually. "She's not responsible. I'll have Dr. Benjamin stop in tomorrow and see her. There are places, fine private places——"

A dull thud from upstairs shook the ceiling for a moment. They all stared at each other, paling, frozen. Then Florabelle, with a faint cry, gathered up her skirts and fled up the stairway. Behind her ran her husband and brother. A fine high singing suddenly began to pierce Ernest's brain, like a string drawn tightly; he was wet with sweat when he arrived at his mother's door a pace behind his sister.

Hilda was lying in a huddled mound upon the floor, her face turned to the ceiling, her eyes glazed and open. Ernest glanced over Florabelle's shoulder at their mother, and he seized her shoulders suddenly and swung her into her husband's arms. She collapsed in them without a sound. The children, aroused by the strange noises, began to peer through the open door, their long white nightgowns touching their brown toes, their puckered mouths open. From the nursery came the wail of the disturbed babies. The lone candle flared with a sickly yellow light as the draft struck it.

Ernest knelt beside his mother. He looked at the open slack mouth with the bloody bubbles at the corners; he looked at the glazed dead eyes. Then he opened up his own large handkerchief and spread it gently over her face. He stood up. Major Norwood had begun to weep silently, for he was a kind-hearted man, and had borne his old mother-in-law no grudges, and the grief of his wife unnerved him.

"My mother," said Ernest in a thick, expressionless voice, "is dead." He put his hand to his eyes, as though a light dazzled them.

François, who had had fits when he was a baby, began to scream.

CHAPTER LXV

Ernest, after he had conferred with President Marlowe, of the bank, stopped in at Paul's tiny private office. On the glass door there was neat black lettering: Office Manager. Ernest smiled. The lad was doing very well, very well indeed. Next year he would be a vice-president. Paul had a flair for finance, had the natural-born banker's sharp incisive look, cold pointed eye, brisk cynicism and complete disbelief in the integrity of human beings. We'll make him President, yet, thought his uncle, tapping lightly on the door, then entering.

Paul was sitting at a scarred black desk going over some books with a nervous cashier old enough to be his grandfather. The young man's face was puckered disagreeably; the old man was crouched in his chair, wetting his lips and trembling. But Paul's expression cleared and lighted at the sight of his uncle. He dismissed the cashier with a wave of his hand, and the old man struggled to his feet, pale as a spectre; he bowed and scraped first to Paul, then made a deeper and more terrified bow to Ernest, and fled like a rabbit.

"He's got to go, Uncle Ernest," said Paul, rising and smiling at Ernest, and extending his hand. Ernest shook it. "Old Sedley's been with the bank for ages," he said. "What's the matter this time?"

"Carelessness. Old age. This is the third time. The amount isn't much, but it takes effort to untangle things. He's got to go. In forty years he ought to have saved enough to live on during the few years more he's got to live."

Ernest sat down. He laid his cane and hat and gloves on Paul's desk. He noticed that, as ever, the desk was neat and meticulously arranged. He loved order, and this additional evidence of the likeness between himself and his nephew gratified him. Paul sat down. He was taller than his uncle, and well built, looking much more than his twenty-two years. He was much handsomer than Ernest had been at his age; he had the short belligerent Barbour nose and distended nostrils, a fair clear skin, dark blue eyes and vigorous light brown hair. He kept his face clean-shaved. His manner was alert and vital and hard; yet, he was sentimental at times, which did not displease Ernest, who knew that sentimental people are usually without mercy or gentleness.

There was nothing of his father about him, thought Ernest. Nor, really, anything of Amy, except the fair smooth skin and a certain grace-fulness that occasionally imposed itself on the big strong body. He said aloud: "We can't throw old Sedley on the street, Paul, though I don't suppose many people would care. But there's something foolish in the air these days, something they are beginning to call 'a social conscience.' Old Sedley was kind to me when I was a raw lad. No, we just can't throw him out. I suggest we give him a month's notice and a check for two hundred dollars. That ought to settle the old women and satisfy Sedley, too."

Paul made a brisk note of this suggestion, nodding respectfully as he did so. "It's very kind of you, Uncle Ernest. Not many would think of that. I suppose it would be pretty terrible to throw old Sedley and his wife into the almshouse without a little warning, and something to help pay for their funerals. After all, we aren't barbarians; sometimes it pays to have a feeling for the unfortunate."

Ernest bit the corner of his lip. Then he said: "Yes, I believe in being kind. We don't owe Sedley anything; what are forty or more years of service, anyway? He got paid for them, a regular salary, enough to keep him in bread and jam and tea and provide a shawl occasionally for his old wife."

Paul glanced up sharply, but Ernest's face was smooth and bland. Paul felt uncomfortable and undefended for a moment. Sometimes Uncle Ernest made remarks that were very ambiguous; he, Paul, could not always tell whether he was laughing at him or not.

The young man lit a thin long cylinder of paper and tobacco, a very fashionable thing called a cigarette; all the young men smoked them: they were quite a craze. He offered Ernest one, was refused. Paul looked at his cigarette doubtfully; he wondered if his uncle would ap-prove of him even more if he stopped the habit. He always wanted to please him. This was not hypocrisy; he really worshipped Ernest, con-sidered him the wisest, keenest, most marvellous of men, and nothing pleased him better than to have some one remark on the resemblance between them. Ernest read his thoughts, and smiled indulgently, and with affection. "But don't let my likes and dislikes affect you, Paul. Be no man's imitator. You have a right to your tastes."

"Uncle Ernest," said Paul, after a moment, wrinkling his eyes through the pleasant smoke, "I've been racking my brains lately about all that money from Barbour-Bouchard stock going into that hospital. Can't we possibly get around my father's will? I've looked over the will carefully, hour after hour, and I've come to the conclusion there might be a loop-hole——"

Ernest's pleasant expression faded, and he regarded his nephew with some sharpness. "I thought you'd be around to that presently, Paul. Yes, I know, myself, of a number of loopholes. I thought you'd find them. You've got a good mind, and it was inevitable. I don't blame you at all, mind, for resenting all those thousands and thousands in dividends going into the hospital. I realize that it sucks in every penny of the income from the stock. That's because your father made the policy of the hospital, that those who can't pay were to have precisely the treatment that the paying patients were to receive, and that even the paying patients were to be charged the smallest possible fees. Your father," he added wryly, "was a very charitable, a very kind man."

"I think it is folly!" cried Paul, flushing to the roots of his hair with his heretofore-suppressed anger and resentment. "Charity begins at home. At least, if we're going to sink every cent into the damned hospital we ought to get a little return from it. I suggest raising the cost of treatment, and treating no one free of charge. There are loopholes——"

Ernest raised his hand abruptly, and Paul subsided, breathing heavily.

"As I said before, Paul, there are loopholes. I saw them before you did. Your mother saw them. She could have changed it all long ago. But she didn't. She believes she owes it to your father to do as he wished. Nothing," he added with a sternness that puzzled Paul, "must ever be done in that respect against her wishes, against her belief that she is carrying out your father's will. It is a great comfort to her." His voice became preoccupied.

"I don't see why——" muttered Paul sullenly.

Ernest picked up his cane and struck the desk with it quickly. "There are many things you don't see yet, my dear lad. If you attempt anything against your mother's wishes, during her lifetime, I'll wash my hands of you. Even in talking about it, you displease me very much."

Paul turned a bright red, but he did not hasten with the apology and assurance that Ernest expected. When it came to money, even affection and respect became reserved in Paul. Ernest sympathized with him, was pleased at what he read in the young man's face. But he did not relent. "Remember what I've told you," he said harshly, and stood up. Paul had to rise, also. He stood there, immovable as a rock, his expression heavy with his sullenness.

"You're not starving," went on Ernest, his ill humor vanishing. He smiled, poked his nephew lightly with his cane. "Your Mama is worth over half a million, nearer three-quarters of a million, in her own name. The railroad stock her uncle left her has quadrupled in value, and will go still higher. Railroad stocks are worth gold these days. You're not starving."

"But there are four of us children," said Paul involuntarily, and was covered with embarrassment at this slip of the tongue.

Ernest laughed. "By the time your Mama dies of a good old age, her holdings and cash will be over a million, maybe two million. Besides," he

winked, "when you marry I'm going to give Trudie ten thousand shares
of Barbour-Bouchard stock, as a dowry. And some day you'll be President of this bank, if I have anything to do with it. What the devil's the
matter now?" for Paul's expression had become gloomy.

"Uncle Ernest, I can't get close to Trudie. She holds me off. She
won't let me speak to her. After all, she's twenty, old enough, God knows,
to be married. But she won't let me speak. I've contrived, but I've not
been alone with her for over a month." His face became pink and moist
with anger and distress, and there was a struck expression in his eyes.
"I love her, Uncle Ernest! I've got to have Trudie; there'd never be
any one else for me, even if she died, or married some one else, or refused
me. I've loved her ever since we were children. I'd kill any one who ever
came between us—" His voice choked, stopped. He turned away with
a fierce gesture, as though he were trying to hide an overwhelming
emotion. "I'd have Trudie, and no other, if she didn't have a cent," he
said with strangled bitterness, his voice breaking.

He loves her as I loved his mother, and still love her, thought Ernest
compassionately. He clenched his hands about his cane, remembering
the young Ernest who had lost his love and who never recovered from
it. He felt that in defending Paul, in deciding that Paul should have his
love, he was making it up to that young Ernest. Paul was not to have
those sterile years of devouring misery, of unending hunger.

"Remember, faint heart never won fair lady," he said, taking the
young man rallyingly by the arm. But Paul did not respond, did not
turn. He had thrust his hands in his pockets, and his head was bent.
Ernest could see the hard angle of his jaw, the pale lips. "Paul, Trudie's
just an imaginative chit. All girls are silly. You're too solid to be the
delicate knight of her dreams, and all girls dream of dainty knights on
white horses. Maybe you're a little too precipitate. You lack finesse."

Paul's muscles tightened under his hand. "To hell with finesse," he
said in a hard voice. "I'm a man; I don't play games. I'm not going to
cavort with songs around Trudie. I want her, as a man wants a woman.
You're trying to say that perhaps I frighten her. No one could ever
frighten Trudie. She may be frail and look as though she'd break in
my hands, but she isn't. She's not afraid of me, except that she's afraid
that she won't get away from me. There's no nonsense in her; my hurry,
my exigency, if you'll have it, doesn't wound her maidenly feelings.
She's not being coy with me. She just doesn't want me. She hates me."

Ernest scowled; he forced Paul to face him. "What do you mean by
that? The girl doesn't hate you. I've told her a dozen times that I want
her to marry you. But I've let her take her time. She's the only daughter
in the family, and I prefer her to all of my other children put together.
I'll miss Gertrude more than I can tell you. That's why I haven't pressed
her. But now I will! Are you satisfied, now?"

But Paul's bitter look did not lighten; his suffused eyes looked at Ernest cynically, almost with a sneer. "No, I'm not satisfied, Uncle Ernest. You forget Philippe Bouchard, my nice little cousin."

Ernest dropped Paul's arm, and his face blackened. "Philippe? That jerking French manikin? God, you're a fool! I thought better of you! My girl wouldn't look at him; you're insulting her! He's younger than she is, and he amuses her. He's all over the place, as if he had St. Vitus dance. Trudie wouldn't look at him, I tell you. What damned nonsense have you got in your thick head?" His voice rose to a shout, but behind the shout, behind his fury, was a nausea. What a fool he had been! He should have watched. I didn't know, he thought.

Paul turned to him with some eagerness. "I know Trudie's your favorite, Uncle Ernest. Because of that, I thought perhaps they, she and Philippe, might get around you, and do me out of her. But if you'll set your foot down— I'll have her if I have to take her by force, Uncle Ernest." He smiled, as though to deprecate his own extravagance, but his eye did not smile.

Ernest put on his hat and pulled on his gloves. A purple tinge had seeped into his face. He did not answer Paul's smile. He started toward the door and Paul followed. "Look here, Uncle Ernest, don't push things too far. Just lay down the law to Trudie. Tonight, I'll see her, if you'll help me. We'll settle this tonight."

Ernest regarded him gloomily, and in silence. I needed no help with your mother, he thought, almost with contempt for the young man. But then, he added to himself, Amy loved me. The purple began to recede from his skin, and he laid his hand on Paul's shoulder, pressed it. "I'll help you," he said quietly. "Come to dinner, if you will. Get your hat. My carriage is outside."

They drove toward the Sessions house in a deep violet dusk. They did not speak for some time. Ernest moved his large head slowly from side to side, somber with his enraged thoughts. The streets were quiet, and the horses' hoofs rang through them, echoing. Every one was at dinner. The houses stood steeped in an evening mystery, the trees hanging heavily with quiet, their upper branches still faintly ruddy from a sun fallen behind the river. They drove along the river road, past the factories and the docks, past the squatters' cabins. The river was the color of iron, and the sky was cobalt above it. Autumn was already chilling the air. The river road, broad and smooth, now called Riverview, had become a fashionable site for the homes of the new-rich, people who were still ostracized by an Oldtown society growing shabbier and shabbier with integrity and pride, with the years. The last of the squatters' cabins had disappeared, and now great homes stood among new young trees along the road. Lamps were lighted in broad bow-windows; glimmers shone on white columns and wide porches. Smooth lawns, rolled and neat, with iron stags and dogs upon them, ran up to white steps. Each house had its private little dock, with a boat or two tied up to it. Prosperity had come to a section once low muddy banks and flat, sun-warmed stones. Something must have brought this vividly to Ernest's memory tonight, and he saw the thin white birches and willows along the river, the stones between them, and the sun bright blue upon the glittering water. He saw a little fair boy and a baby girl playing on the stones, and a crippled youth laughing near them. He had seen them like this a thousand times, from the dusty windows of the little red-brick factory, that had now become a series of huge shops, loudly bellowing to the night.

"I remember when this was just waste land," he said aloud, and suddenly, to the silent young man beside him. Paul listened politely; he glanced without interest at the great new houses and the tamed river, smooth dim gray under the failing light. Waste land, he thought. Probably bought for a song. The old codgers had struck it rich, without much work. Luck, and a new land. But he, and the young men like him, had to sweat blood for every penny.

"Your father," went on Ernest, in an odd tone, "used to play down there, with your Aunt Dorcas. Your Uncle Eugene had a brother, a cripple. Jacques Bouchard. Your father and he were great friends. They lived in a little world of their own; Jacques died in it. Sometimes I think your father died in it."

Paul's lip twisted. When did all this happen? A thousand years ago! It was an old, uninteresting story, dead and stale; he wished his uncle would stop his reminiscing. The issue about Gertrude was too near and hot and troubling. Ernest glanced sideways at him, and smiled wryly to himself, not without sympathy. (He thinks I'm becoming an old bore, talking about the past. He doesn't know that there is really no past, that it keeps intruding into the present, with all its old pains and emotions. It's more important than the present.) He had not thought about Martin intently for many years, but suddenly Martin was everywhere, more real, more vital, than his son sitting so stolidly in this carriage. Poor wretch! thought Ernest suddenly, with such intensity, such aroused feeling, that he was astonished and amused at himself. Poor wretch! he repeated. And as if this acknowledgment of his brother were a secret enchantment, his whole personality was suddenly assailed by the essence of the dead man, so that he felt unstrung through all his mind, and even his body. Then, this was followed by the most colossal sense of loss, of utter emptiness, as though he had been drained of everything, of integrity, of personality, of reality, of substance. It was the strangest feeling, and somehow terrible.

I'm getting old, he thought. He turned to Paul. "We own half the mines in Pennsylvania," he said. Paul answered something, something that was loud and strong and pleased. I don't know, thought Ernest. I don't know.

The carriage had left the river, was rolling again through quiet streets toward Oldtown. They crossed the tracks. Night had closed down; the air was full of smoke and the chirp of crickets. He, Ernest, had stepped on a cricket once, on the hearth of the dingy old house in England. Martin's face shone before him with the light of the fire on it; he had seen the crushing of the insect, and his face had been full of a wild terror. As though I had stepped on him, thought Ernest. Now that was very odd! I wonder why I never thought of that before?

Paul was asking him something. "Godfrey? Oh, he's not expected until next summer. He's completing his symphony in Paris. He had hopes that it would be played in New York the following winter." Ernest's voice was noncommittal, smooth with polite conversation. "Reggie, of course, is doing very well at Harvard; I have fine reports of him. One of the youngest freshmen. I'm hoping that he will forget his religious nonsense there. It was all that damned Amish woman's fault, the nurse he'd had. Missionary, by God!" Did Paul remember the nonsense about him not wanting buttons on his clothes? That was eight—ten years ago! It was still a family joke. "Where are your buttons?" Signifying, of course, that the one questioned had lost his wits. Guy? Ernest frowned. Not doing so well as one could wish at his school in Philadelphia; too much spirits; always wanted to play. At fourteen, he still played pranks. But "little" Joey—ah, there was a lad after a man's heart. Ten years old and a profound business man, careful of every penny. (Damned sneaky little miser! thought Paul viciously.) Never happier than when in the shops, said the "little miser's" father, grinning slightly.

They rode up the drive. Through the trees the lamps of the house shone out at them brightly. They could see the new gaslights in the large drawing room; they had a bleak white light which Ernest did not particularly care for. They spoiled the house for him.

Fires had been lighted in the house, and the warm quiet air was very grateful as they entered the hall. How quiet the house was these days, with only Gertrude and Joey home, the three other boys away. The rooms were full of a before-dinner hush. May was reading by the fire in the second drawing room. She wore glasses now, and when her husband and nephew entered the room, she removed them, laid them carefully between the pages of her book. She smiled at Ernest as he kissed her forehead. She smiled at Paul, as she gave him her hand. She did not like him at all, but she smiled at him.

"It is too bad that we did not know you were coming to dinner, Paul," she said, and her round merry eyes with the wrinkles spraying out from them had a clear brilliant spark. "Trudie is dining with your Aunt Dorcas tonight. It is Etienne's birthday, and I believe there is a little party afterwards——"

And she smiled again, as she laid her book aside, and looked at the fire

CHAPTER LXVI

IT WAS Etienne Bouchard's birthday, and his parents were making a little party for him. He was fifteen today, and felt quite a man. He knew he was extremely handsome and graceful, very much like his Uncle Raoul, who had been killed in the War between the States. In the clear dark pallor of his right cheek there was an extraordinarily deep dimple, very fascinating, and he had clear, dark, beautiful eyes, like a girl's. Everything seemed clear about him, from the brow that rose straightly to the line of his thick black curls, to the lines of his fine smiling mouth and sharply cut nose. Nothing was blurred or distorted in his face, or irregular. Nothing of his English mother lightened or made phlegmatic the quick lively play of expression on his features. He was all French; the warm gaiety of the southern Provinces ran frothing in his actor's blood. For Etienne was a born actor, and a calculating rascal into the bargain, for all his charm. Slight though he was, and not very tall, his exuberance and vivid temperament made up for his lack of flesh and stature.

He was given to bullying his fourteen-year-old sister, Renee, who adored him; he scolded her violently one moment, was lavishly affectionate the next, so that the poor young girl was in a constant state of apprehension or delight. But he did not bully Honore, the broad, rather short thirteen-year-old brother, with his irregular distinguished face and ponderous quietness and thoughtful glances. Etienne frankly admitted that Honore was the "bright" one of the family, and by this admission usually captivated his audience, as though in some way he had added lustre to himself and made Honore faintly ridiculous. And in some mysterious way, when the brothers were present together Honore looked like a distortion of Etienne's good looks, the perfect nose pulled a trifle too long in his case, the smiling mouth made crooked, the clear brow heightened ludicrously until the hairline seemed to retreat precipitately, the beautiful dark eyes stretched up and out, giving them a decidedly Celestial appearance. Yet, in spite of this, after the ludicrousness faded, Honore seemed to gain in distinction and Etienne to become too obvious and too florid, a little too colorful; he reminded one of a male dancer with timed gestures and artful postures.

Eugene and Dorcas had given their son a handsome gold watch on his birthday. Dorcas had added her English caution to Eugene's French parsimony, and so a gold watch was an event in the family. They still lived in Armand's ugly stone house in Newtown, using the same heavy, ugly old furniture, even to the old-fashioned stove and Dutch ovens in the flagged kitchen and the high deep French beds into which one crawled after using a stool to mount upon. Dorcas, who was growing niggardly as she grew older, might have carried her thrift into the kitchen and dining room, but here Eugene's French love of good food and rich food held up an abrupt hand. Nothing would do him but the finest sauces, the best wines, the juiciest joints and hams, the heaviest silver, the handsomest plates, the choicest coffee and sweetest butter. "The cousin from Quebec" still presided over the kitchen, and in spite of Dorcas' uneasy hints, she spared neither cream nor herbs, wine nor eggs, in her cooking. Nor would Eugene stand for sleazy linens on his bed, nor thin towels or shoddy blankets. He was quite willing to do without elaborations and elegances, but he demanded the best in necessities. So the family of children, while never beautifully nor elegantly dressed, wore the most expensive of plain and comfortable clothing, ate richly, and slept under down beds. Nor was their learning skimped, Eugene employing a well recommended tutor for his two older sons, a governess and nurse for Renee and the twins. If there were no pictures on the dark drab walls, no ornaments on the mantelpieces, no lace curtains at the windows, or ruffled counterpanes on the beds and gold-and-crystal bottles on the dressers, there were bookcases crowded with books, the finest of pianos in the dark drawing room. Never was Eugene too tired or too busy to talk to his children, to instruct them, to listen to them, to answer their endless questions with the gravity he would give to any adult. They repaid him with serious devotion and bottomless love. He did not believe in idleness: the boys made most of their own toys; each had his own section of the garden for which he was responsible, his own horse to groom and tend. Etienne and Honore had accompanied their father frequently to the Kinsolving works (now five huge buildings brawling without ceasing) and at the respective ages of fifteen and thirteen had really formidable knowledge of the making of munitions, and an understanding of labor. Renee had her responsibilities, also, caring for her own room and helping with the twins, making her clothing and learning to cook, as, Eugene said, " all thrifty, well-bred French girls do."

Etienne, the elegant, was already, at fifteen, ashamed of his ugly, unpretentious home. It did not matter to him that his father was a millionaire; he wanted evidences of this happy state in beauty and indolence, pleasure and money in the pocket. His allowance of one dollar a week infuriated him; boys with less affluent fathers received anywhere from five to fifteen dollars. On his birthday, he had gloomily expected a dollar. The advent of the gold watch, elaborately engraved, sounding the hours, the quarters and the half-hours with a fairy chiming, with his name etched inside the thick yellow case, and further garnished with a ponderous chain and a garnet charm, stunned him. He could not believe it; his first thought was that "the old man must've gone soft all of a sudden." His next was emotional gratitude. He had it in and out of his pocket a dozen times during the course of the little party in his honor. He dangled it before the envious but noncommittal Honore, whose hands itched for it. He opened the case and let Renee and his little brother, Andre, and his little sister, Antoinette, put their ear closely to it to hear the sweet far tinkling of the quarters and the half hours. (The twins were handsome ten-year-olds, blond and plump and good-tempered and dimpled—Dorcas' "angels.")

Etienne sat among his presents, his lighted birthday cake before him. He blew it out, very earnestly trying to extinguish all fifteen candles at the same time. He succeeded, and looked about him proudly, awaiting applause. A mighty fire roared on the immense, old-fashioned hearth; candelabra on the mantel and on tables near the walls filled the great crowded room, with its stone floor, with a warm and golden light. Etienne, his cousins, Gertrude Barbour, Philippe, Jules and Leon Bouchard, his brothers, Honore and Andre, his sisters, Renee and Antoinette, his two especial friends, David Benshaw and Harold Lansbury, and his parents, all sat about the enormous round dining room table set with its thick white linen cloth and heavy silver and steaming birthday dinner. None of his other cousins were invited, for Francois was ill, and Etienne had no liking for Paul and Elsa, Lucy and John Charles Barbour, nor even for Gertrude's brother, Joey.

Etienne loved to be the center of admiration and importance. He had an actor's passion for excitement and drama. His parents, and Philippe, Leon and Gertrude, were highly edified at the mystery with which he invested his unopened presents, the slow, calculated gestures with which he opened them, while the younger children wriggled on their chairs with impatience and implored him to hurry.

Jules, who, at sixteen, was like a prematurely old gnome, had given his cousin a fine new saddle for his horse, brave in light-brown leather and heavy silver harness. Leon, fourteen, "the deep one," had long ago guessed Etienne's wistful love of elegance, and had brought him half a dozen gorgeous cravats, very theatrical in a sober decade that leaned heavily toward simple black. Philippe gave him a signet ring, heavy gold and garnet, engraved with his initials; Gertrude presented a travelling case fitted with silver, for Etienne was going to a preparatory school in Boston in a few months. Honore gave a set of Shakespeare and Milton and a prayer book, all bound in old vellum and stamped in gold. The twins had combined on a pair of ebony military brushes, and the two especial friends had facetiously collaborated on the best of Swedish razors against the day he would begin to shave. Etienne was quite overcome by all this magnificence. He had never received such lavish gifts before. But best of all he loved his gold watch, and after that, Philippe's signet ring, and then the cravats. However, he had sufficient imagination (the actor's imagination), and natural sweetness of disposition, to be the most touched at the present from "the cousin from Quebec," which was a rosary of ebony and old silver. It was not new; it had been in her family for generations, had belonged to her mother, and her mother's grandmother, and the gift was a personal sacrifice. Etienne kissed her tenderly and lingeringly for this, though she was an old woman and her skin was flaccid and dry to young lips that already liked the feel of warm firm flesh. And, despite all his artifices and unconscious strivings for effect, there was no hypocrisy in his kiss.

After the ceremony of the presents, Etienne beamed about the table, his handsome face glowing and shining with pleasure and affection. He sat like a sultan among offerings. Dorcas, smiling at him from her place, thought him as beautiful as a dark angel, even more beautiful than the twins, her darlings. Eugene, touched, pressed his son's hand swiftly, with an unusual display of Gallic affection. Under the shelter of the heavy tablecloth Gertrude's hand lay in Philippe's, and the burning of her eyes was due to something more than the wine and Etienne's joy. She looked about her vaguely, suffused with a sort of dreaming ecstasy. She had never thought this great lopsided room very pleasant, after her own lovely old home, but tonight it had a patina of soft radiance that bewitched her. She loved every one. Her heart was beating with deep hot strokes like cymbals, and a shiver of slow delight quivered along her nerves. In a little while she would walk home with Philippe, disdaining carriages, and he would tell her again that he loved her, and they would plan for the day when they could be married. (Philippe, though only just nineteen, had already been graduated from the University in Philadelphia, and was working with his Uncle Eugene in the Kinsolving works.)

Renee's allowance was only fifty cents a week, and she had nothing of her father's French thrift in her. Each Friday she discovered that she not only had not one cent, but was usually in debt to the shrewd and placid Andre. (Andre's favorite cousin was John Charles Barbour, and the two ten-year-olds ran a mutual bank between them for the benefit of their acquaintances and less foresighted young cousins.) So, when the time arrived to buy Etienne a birthday present, Renee had no money, and her agony was very great. But Dorcas believed in making a child suffer for irresponsibility, and was adamant to her daughter's frantic and tearful pleas. She also warned her other children not to lend the helter-skelter, rough-haired Renee any money. So, Renee, in despair, was reduced to giving her brother her treasure, a gold holy medal, which had come from Rome and was guaranteed to have been blessed by the Pope. No one, except Etienne, realized what this sacrifice had cost the girl, and he had the delicacy to accept it in private from her trembling and soiled little hands, and to kiss her feelingly for it. It meant nothing to him, for Etienne was anything but religious, though he loved the ceremony and the beautiful ritual of his Church; his secret admiration was for Voltaire, not that he understood much of that great man's subtlety and fiery lightness of wit, but because he adored his dramatic boldness, his gay courage.

Warm with the memory of Etienne's kiss, Renee sat and glowed at her brother. Then she looked at Dorcas. She never tired looking at her mother, whom she thought the most beautiful, the wisest woman in the world. She respected Dorcas more than she respected any one else on earth, even the priest, and her mother's lightest command, her least stern glance, was enough to whip the girl to instant action. But she did not love her, though she would have died for her. All her love was for Eugene, all her idolatry; after Eugene, came Etienne. Honore was too much like his mother to awaken much affection in his older sister. For once, Renee was too overcome to chatter loudly as usual.

The dinner over, they all surged in a body toward the fire. The younger children sat on the hearth. There were nuts and tiny, rich little French pastries, glacé fruits and sweets, and black hot coffee. Preserved ginger, clear as amber, and frosted with sugar, was passed around in old Madam Bouchard's hammered silver compote. Eugene sat with his plump, fair little daughter Antoinette on his knee; Renee had twisted herself upon the arm of his chair, and was laying her dark thin cheek on his graying hair at intervals. Andre hammered steadily at the nuts; they flew all over, and there was much scrambling for them, and much laughter. Jules was straining, in the firelight, to read one of Etienne's new books. Philippe and Gertrude sat on the ancient settle in the chimney corner, and whispered together. Dorcas, sitting smiling and erect, like a quiet golden goddess in her dark blue draped dress, watched her niece and nephew uneasily. She was well aware of Ernest's plans for his daughter, and she wondered what he would say to this. But she was too indifferent, too self-centered, to disturb herself overmuch. She pulled her gaze away from the young lovers in the corner, and serenely concentrated upon her family. Eugene, more in love with his beautiful wife than ever, could not keep his eyes from her. How elegant she was! What a lady she was! And how like that *pauvre* Martin, except for that slight hardness (he called it resolution), about the jaw, the slightly pinched nostrils, which his infatuation could not call selfishness, and the faint coldness of her eyes. But she had her brother's natural dignity, his gentle manner, his sweet and luminous smile. She was delicately strong, Eugene decided for the hundredth time, where Martin had been weak. He wondered, sighing a little, if it were really true that Dorcas had grown just a trifle cold, the slightest bit unfeeling, since her brother's

death. He missed a certain responsiveness in her, a shy yielding. It was
as if, since the tragedy, something had been stunned in her, some soft
distant core had petrified.

Eugene's attention was suddenly diverted to Gertrude and Philippe,
and he was alarmed and annoyed. He felt that he was being treacherous
to Ernest to permit this in his home. He was fond of Gertrude, and
loved Philippe almost as though he were a son. But he had the innate
French cynicism about love-marriages, and in addition thought Philippe
too young for Gertrude, though the boy certainly was mature, and, in a
way, much older than his cousin, Paul Barbour. And certainly much
more subtle, much finer and swifter of comprehension! But that,
Eugene decided, was because of his French blood. But all this did not
matter. Loyalty to Ernest was the first and only consideration. If Ernest
wished to marry his daughter off to that brutal young Britisher, he,
Eugene, would not permit anything in his home that would jeopardize
his plans. On the contrary, he would help further those plans, however
he disliked them personally.

"Philippe!" he called. "Why do you hide yourself? Come here; I
wish to talk to you."

"Papa's Roland is calling you, Philippe," whispered Gertrude, with a
wry smile.

Philippe pressed her hand, and they looked into each other's eyes.
Then the young man got up and went to his uncle. He sat down beside
him. Renee glanced swiftly at Gertrude; she was only fourteen, but
she was filled with a hot pity for her cousin. She left her father and
went to the older girl and sat down beside her. She put her hard brown
young fingers over Gertrude's, and pressed them. Gertrude, the haughty
and reserved, felt no resentment at this silent invasion of her thoughts,
this unasked-for understanding. On the contrary, tears came into her
eyes, though she smiled. The younger children screamed, laughed, quarrelled and scrambled on the hearth, and Dorcas sat, cool and aloof, and
saw everything, and cared for nothing but her family.

Eugene gravely offered his nephew a thin cheroot, and lit one for himself. Etienne and Honore, Jules and Leon, seeing this, suddenly lost
their boyish looks, and inconspicuously gathered around, their faces alert
and interested. The Business of the Family, they knew, was about to be
discussed, and they were vitally interested, even Etienne, who acted out
Hamlet and Othello, Romeo and Julius Cæsar before his mirror in his
bedroom, even Leon, who hated everybody and could not endure the
proximity of any one, except Jules.

"I did not have the opportunity to tell you, today, Philippe," said
Eugene, gratified at all this interest among the boys of the family, "but
your Mama came in possession today, along with the rest of us, of
several thousand shares of the new United Utah Railroad. Thanks to

your Uncle Ernest. They did not cost much, for no one believes that California can be united with the East by rail. But your Uncle Ernest's judgment can be relied upon. We expect those shares to be selling at fifty dollars or more, within ten years. At the present time it is planned for this railroad to run from San Francisco to Ogden, Utah."

Philippe considered this a long time. "But the cost of labor will be enormous," he said doubtfully. "You couldn't drag our Easterners out to the Rockies and beyond. Why, they're barely more than Territories!"

Eugene smiled, his brown face shrivelling into seams and wrinkles. He tapped Philippe lightly on the knee. "But we have a solution! We're going to bring in thousands of Chinese, and Irish, to build our railroad! Your Uncle Ernest is leaving tomorrow to consult with the President of the United Utah, and to tell him what we have done, ourselves, and our friends in Pittsburgh, with imported labor."

"Chinese?" Philippe looked disturbed. "And what will you do with them afterwards? Ship them out?"

"Out? I do not know. Perhaps. Perhaps not. They can breed us cheap labor. Besides, it is terrible work that, in the mountains. Many will die. But these are yellow men, and no matter how they live here, they will be happier than in their own land, where they have floods and famine and cholera."

"But the Irish are not yellow men. They are white." Philippe was still uneasy; he regarded his uncle with deep gravity.

"The Irish? I do not know these Irish. I have seen none, except our three watchmen. But they are begging to come. We will give them the opportunity."

"I do not like Chinese in my country," said Philippe in a preoccupied voice, as he stared at the fire and frowned.

"In your country? Ah, I forgot. You were born here. You are an American." Eugene smiled. "Do not worry. This America of yours is big enough for all men."

"It won't be, long, with all these brought here," persisted Philippe morosely. "It is wrong. You must persuade Uncle Ernest not to do this. I feel it will have bad results."

"How?"

Philippe hesitated. "Uncle Eugene, you can't have a successful nation if it is divided. And by that I mean divided in tradition, race, philosophy and way of life." The young man sullenly poked the fire. "To bring in those Chinese, Uncle Eugene, is an act of treason against the people of America, against my people. And Uncle Ernest ought to be made to see this. He has no right to despoil my country."

Eugene stared fixedly at the toe of his foot, as he moved it before the fire. His face took upon itself, imitatively, the hardness of Ernest's face, and Philippe smiled a little to see it. He knows I am right; he feels the same way, he thought, but his confounded loyalty stands in the way of his sense of decency and his reason. He doesn't know that he is being loyal to a wolf.

"You are too young to see all sides of the question," said Eugene at last. All at once he looked tired. He glanced about the warm sturdy fastness of the big room, filled with the children and their laughter. His children would never forget these nights, this house, he thought. Here was tradition, rooted in simplicity and strength and the fundamental things of pride, security, intelligence and peace. And home. Home in America. His blood rose in irritation. "Despoil your country? Do you think I would allow such a thing? These Chinese shall be shipped out immediately after the work is accomplished! You are only a child, Philippe!" Nevertheless, he felt scratched and sore. He tugged a pipe from his pocket, his father's pipe, and lit it. As he sat there, irritably puffing, he looked like Armand, a younger Armand, come to life again before the old fireplace.

Philippe spread out his hands in an eloquent French gesture, shrugged, and said, after a moment: "We have enemies inside our gates. Men like Ernest Barbour. These are the destroyers. Perhaps I was wrong. The poor Chinese cannot do us much harm. But men like Ernest Barbour can always do us wrong. He's a pirate. An industrial pirate. I suppose some people would consider it very fine to have immense industries; but anything immense finally overshadows the smaller things. If he and his kind are not stopped, we are going to have industrial minds and an industrial civilization. I can't imagine anything less imaginative or beautiful! Or anything more dangerous to the development of individual life."

Dorcas, who was apparently lost in her own quiet and serene thoughts, glanced at her husband and nephew with a sudden vivid flash upon her face. "I've heard that before! It sounds very much like Martin, Philippe! Your Uncle Martin." She loved no one outside of her children and her husband, but this resemblance of Philippe to Martin aroused her, made her look at him intently, and with a softening in her eyes. "He hated Ernest," she added gently, and her lashes were wet.

"Oh, Martin was a fool!" Eugene glanced with annoyance at his wife.

"Was he a fool, Uncle Eugene?"

Eugene puffed at his pipe, took it from his mouth, and glared at it. "Who knows?" he muttered. "Diable! This is no world for saints."

Dorcas laid her hand on her husband's knee. The gesture was very eloquent. But she looked at Philippe with an odd and speculative expression. It was as though she were looking at him for the first time. But Philippe did not see her.

"Uncle Eugene, what are you—we—going to do if the strikes in the coal mines spread to our mines?"

"Eh? Our mines? I suppose Ernest—we—will do as the other owners do. I suppose we will call in private detective agencies."

"There's been plenty of blood-letting in those mines," warned Philippe. "They've been shooting down the miners, and even the women and the children. You can't drive men to the last inch, and over, without having them turn on you. Blood will run from both sides."

"Canaille!" muttered Eugene impatiently. But he was uneasy. Canaille! That is what they had called his father and his friends, when they had so desperately, and so futilely, opposed tyranny and greed. The guillotine had done good work in those days, and his father had had to run away to escape it.

"Canaille, Uncle Eugene? Words never defeated justice for very long. No wonder Uncle Ernest wants to bring the Chinese in!"

Eugene muttered again. Out of the corner of his eye he regarded his nephew. What had Ernest against this fine boy, this dark, nervous, restless boy? Was it because there was something in him that reminded him of Martin? No, Martin had never had this fire and energy. He thought of Paul Barbour, with distaste. Ernest had imagination: it was strange that he preferred Paul to Philippe. It was very cruel to the little Gertrude, sitting there so tense and silent in the chimney corner, and never taking her eyes off her young lover. It was shadowy in that corner, and her figure and face were nebulous and indistinct; but the light of the fire shone in her eyes and they gleamed steadily and beautifully.

The carriage was arriving for the two "especial friends," and also the Norwood carriage, for Philippe, Jules and Leon. Eugene was surprised when he saw Philippe bundle his two younger brothers into the carriage, and instantly guessed the reason why he did not go with them. When Philippe came back into the house, Eugene said carelessly: "I have called the carriage, and I shall take Gertrude home. Do you wish to accompany us, Philippe?"

They were standing in the hall, after the last good-bys, Dorcas and Eugene, Philippe and Gertrude. Gertrude had a cloak over her slim shoulders; her hair was covered by the soft flame of a scarlet-silk scarf. There was upon her the mysterious wild-soft manner that was so peculiar to her, and her face had a gleam upon it.

Philippe looked blank for a moment; he turned to Gertrude. The light had gone from her; she was touching her cheek uncertainly with her hand in a familiar gesture that never failed to awaken tenderness and fierceness in Philippe. The gesture was so lovely, and so pathetic. Philippe thought rapidly. The servant was already helping Eugene into his greatcoat, and Dorcas was holding his hat. The carriage wheels were already grinding the gravel. Then Philippe turned to his uncle. He had taken Gertrude's hand.

"Uncle Eugene," he said softly, "we don't want you to take Gertrude home. We want to walk home together." They stood side by side, these young resolute things, and regarded their uncle steadily.

"Absurd!" Eugene pretended irritation, but his innate kindness tormented him. "It is late, and damp. There's a fog coming from the river. It will not be good for Gertrude, to walk through the damp and the mist. It is a long walk."

"Nevertheless, we wish to walk home together. Alone." Philippe had turned pale. Both he and Gertrude looked hunted, but steadfast.

Eugene, hat in hand, glared at them with rising irritation. They were making it very hard for him. Dorcas, withdrawn once more in her serene indifference, gazed at them idly. The hall lamp shone on their colorless young faces, their stern young eyes. "You are not very polite, Philippe," she murmured.

Philippe turned to her with a little passionate gesture. He did not hope much from this cool and selfish woman, who always protected herself, at all costs, from the anxieties and trials of others. "Polite!" he cried. "How can I be polite, when I know all this plot? All this plot to keep Trudie and me apart? We have nothing but enemies. Uncle Eugene is our enemy, too. They want to kill us——!"

Gertrude spoke up now, in a clear high voice. "Philippe and I are going to walk home, alone. We don't care for what you think is your loyalty to Papa, Uncle Eugene."

"No!" Philippe cried out desperately. "We aren't going to pretend, and contrive and sneak and plot! We know what it's all about. It's Paul Barbour. But he's not going to have Trudie. We are going to be married, just as soon as we can, and to hell with what Uncle Ernest wants, or any one wants!"

A faint look of distaste came upon Dorcas' face. She seemed to withdraw from them into her English reserve, but in reality she did not move a step. But Eugene looked angry and grave at the same time. He was really frightened.

"This is none of my business, what you and Trudie wish to do, Philippe. That does not concern me. You must discuss it with her father. I am merely offering to take Gertrude home, as it is damp, and will soon be raining. All this wild talk of marriage and defiance is very silly. In a few years, you can discuss the subject calmly, with the persons concerned." He turned to Gertrude and held out his hand imperatively. "Come, my child. It is getting very late."

Gertrude did not move. Her eyes were distended; she looked like some terrified creature that had been cornered by dogs. Philippe felt her hand grow cold.

"Gertrude is going with me," he said in a suddenly quiet voice. "You can't stop us, Uncle Eugene. And you really don't want to stop us."

"This is my house!" shouted Eugene, but wincing inside. "I won't have such folly starting from here. What her father wants is what she must do, silly boys to the contrary. If she walks with you tonight her father will rightly reproach me for lack of duty tomorrow. There is more in this than what you see, you boy just out of the schoolroom!"

"I think," said Dorcas coolly to her husband, "that is none of your affair, Eugene. I can't see why you agitate so about a matter that is not your business. Ernest is quite capable of managing his daughter. Gertrude is not a child. If she wishes to walk with Philippe, she is entitled to walk. You have done what is expected of you, and it has been refused. That is all you can do." She turned to Philippe and Gertrude. She seemed utterly detached, utterly indifferent to their problems and their distress. But she felt some pity for them. "Why do you not be a sensible girl, Gertrude, and remain here for the night, as you often do? After all, it *is* damp, and you were never too strong."

Gertrude's courage had come back. "Thank you, Aunt Dorcas, but I'm going with Philippe. We have things to talk about. I'm sorry to hurt your feelings, Uncle Eugene, but I really am going with Philippe."

They went out together, past Eugene, who appeared stupefied, past Dorcas, who struggled with sensations of mingled annoyance and amusement. The door closed behind them. Eugene turned to his wife with a mute gesture. She had begun to laugh a little, very softly. Her eyes were sparkling; for a moment he thought she gloated.

"How you hate Ernest, Dorcas!" he exclaimed involuntarily.

She helped him off with his coat, still laughing. He could see the reflection of her face in the dark hall glass. She had never frizzed her hair into bushy "bangs" over her forehead, as was the style, and the pale gold waves framed her cheeks, outlined her head, with an almost artificial beauty.

"Yes," she said serenely, "I do hate him. I loved Martin so very much."

CHAPTER LXVII

I<small>T WAS</small> indeed very damp outside. But it was not raining. A bronze moon, shedding no light, hung threateningly in the black sky. Spectral mists, drifting and rolling, came in from the river, which was hidden. All the trees were empty; they stood in mysterious and contorted attitudes, and their cold trunks dripped livid drops of water. Everything was so lonely and so silent, so very sad. Gertrude and Philippe walked slowly together up the rise from Eugene's house to the road. There were a few shabby houses scattered about, and dim lights twinkled in them. A dog barked gloomily. They reached the street that ran above the rise and looked back. The mists were parting a little, and showed the river, black and swift; the moon hung over it, and orange ripples broke into planes on the water. A steamboat whistle sounded, a melancholy roar that lay on the night rather than disturbed it.

The street was deserted; the cobblestones shone in the feeble and flickering lamplight. Mean little houses stood on each side, shutters tightly drawn. Smoke hung in the air, and the walk was gritty underfoot.

Gertrude coughed, and pulled the cloak closer about her. "It is indeed very damp," said Philippe, alarmed. "We should not have insisted, perhaps."

She held his arm, and pressed it against her side. It bruised her young breast. She did not mind. Their shoulders rubbed together, stayed together. They walked down the street, forgetting everything, their faces turned to each other. The lamplight shone on Gertrude's face; her eyes were as deep and shining as a pool.

"Eighteen months!" cried Philippe, "it is not too long!" They stopped in the shadow of a clump of leafless trees, and they pressed their lips together, their young bodies welding into one in the embrace.

"Too long," said Gertrude at last. They went on; heat throbbed in their heads, their hands, their hearts. Their whole bodies were on fire with it. Philippe heard a faint sound; he glanced down at Gertrude. She was crying.

"I'm afraid," she said simply. "I'm afraid we'll never be happy. Something will happen to us, Philippe. I know it."

"Your father? That is foolish, Trudie. In eighteen months I'll be twenty-one, and take over the management of my father's affairs. Uncle Ernest can't throw me out. I have my father's share of the business. Then we can be married. Your father can't do anything, then."

Gertrude sighed. "Papa can always do anything he wants," she said. "I should not be talking so about him! I've always loved him so, and I've been his favorite. It is so terrible to hurt any one you love!"

"But what has he against me?" demanded Philippe, for the hundredth time, and with increasing bewilderment. "He has told me I am no fool, that my father's affairs will be safe in my hands. He has taught me himself, in the bank. He has praised my progress with Uncle Eugene. He has talked of sending me to the mines for experience there, and the wells near Titusville. Mama is his favorite sister; she consults him in everything. So what has he against me? Why does he prefer Paul Barbour, that brutal ox?"

"He doesn't like you, my darling," answered Gertrude sadly. "Your —your character annoys him. He cannot reconcile your real ability with the fact that you can laugh so easily. He just dislikes you. We all dislike others without definite reasons, and Papa is no exception. Just as the French hate the Germans, and the Christian hates the Jew, and the Turk hates the Armenian. It is something rooted in character, mysterious and without explanation. Besides, he wants me to marry Paul. Paul, he thinks, is like himself. What Papa does not know is that I am like you, and you are like me." She pulled the cloak about her and began to cry again.

"I'll make him like me at last, Trudie," he said in despair, as he wiped her tears with his own handkerchief. "I know he distrusts me. We see things so differently. Perhaps I quarrel with him too much, contradict him too much. But he told me he likes young people to be independent. He—he's so damned nasty to me, Trudie!" His voice ended in a youthful tremor.

"But Frey got what he wanted," she reminded him eagerly, becoming strong as he became more distressed. "And Frey hasn't half your spirit, darling. And he hasn't near so much as I have. And Papa gave in, eventually. He sees reason after awhile, though it takes him a long time to get over what he wants, himself."

"That is so," said Philippe, struck. "Every one in the family bet that he wouldn't let Frey go. But he did. We've got to remember that. I'll try, Trudie, honest I will. If he likes Paul's type, I'll be a take-off of Paul. I'll out-Paul him." They laughed shakily.

"If you do," cried Gertrude, "I'll never marry you in a thousand years! A real Paul is bad enough, but an imitation would be impossible." She became interested. "There you are, Philippe. I don't like Paul. Why? He's never been anything but kind to me, and anxious to please. He's handsome and industrious, and intelligent. Dozens of girls are always languishing around him at every party. But he's devoted to me. He's worked very hard, and he's risen on his own merits. I know he will make an excellent husband. Then why don't I like him? There you are! It's rooted in our characters." She beamed at him, with such an artless pride in her unravelling of the problem that he had to stop and kiss her again.

They walked on together, their bodies seeming to cling through their clothing, their eyes shining with a bemused joy. Sometimes they walked for hours like this, not speaking. Streets passed them slowly and emptily, like gray, dimly lit caverns bored into the night. They did not see them. A late carriage rolled by them, splashed them from a shallow puddle, but they did not notice it. Drops of moisture collected on Gertrude's head, rolled into the folds of the bright scarf; her cloak became damp. But she was no longer cold and frightened. She was looking up into the intense and smiling face above her, and kept looking, until all her senses seemed floating in the light of joy. She had dropped her skirts, and they dragged in the wet and the grit and the mud, and though this was one of her favorite frocks, she had gone beyond caring.

"And to think," said Philippe loudly, "that I once planned on being a Trappist monk!"

Gertrude had started at the sudden sound of his voice, and then what he had said struck them both as exquisitely ludicrous at exactly the same moment. They burst into shrieks of laughter. Gertrude smothered her mouth in the folds of the cloak; they rocked helplessly in each other's arms. When they finally could control themselves, they were sobbing weakly and tears were on their cheeks. Some one had thrown up a window irately, and was bellowing at them from the darkness.

"They'll be calling the constable," sobbed Gertrude, when she could catch her breath. Philippe seized her hand; they ran madly through the silent streets, which shone with a leaden lustre; their heels beat upon the uneven pavement, also slimily moist. Their shadows raced after them, gyrating under the street lamps, twisting about them like strips of darkness. Somewhere aroused dogs began to bark excitedly. They stopped, gasping. They could hear distant carriage wheels on a far street. Every house was shrouded and dark. Water slowly trickled along eaves, and their breath steamed on the wet air. Suddenly a bell from a far church tower began to strike the hour, churning up the hollow air and sending it, mourning, through the night. "Eleven o'clock," said Philippe aloud, with disdain. "And Windsor fast asleep! Trudie, we shall go to New York on our honeymoon. Maybe we'll live there some day. You have no idea how splendid, how incredible it is! It never sleeps. We are just being buried alive, here."

"There is no excitement, it is true," Gertrude admitted, as they walked more sedately now. "Outside of a few little skirmishes with the die-hard Oldtowners who still won't accept our family. But even that excitement is going: there are only three Oldtown families who don't recognize our existence, and they're wavering. I hear Jules has been invited to the parties given by that little Endicott girl, and we actually received an invitation from the Sandringham family yesterday."

"They can't hold out against our money," said Philippe, with a sneer.

Gertrude lifted her shoulders slightly. "Money is a wonderful thing," said the daughter of Ernest Barbour. "Papa says so, and I believe him. Mama was always well-to-do, and so she depreciates the value of money. Never mind, dearest. We all have plenty, so we can afford to sneer at it."

But Philippe would not acknowledge her sarcasm. "It makes me afraid," he said stubbornly, "when I see that money can buy everything. Practically everything of value. I'd like to believe there are a few things it couldn't buy. I'd like to believe there are some things that are inviolate."

She pressed his arm against her breast. "Money couldn't buy me, Philippe," she said softly. He looked down at her, almost with distress. "It might break you, though," he said. They began to walk fast, as though hurrying away from something. "Oh, I'd like to believe there are things money couldn't buy!" repeated Philippe with passion. "Things accessible only to honor and love and integrity and ability. It would take the slime off living. Most of the time I feel dirty. When I was at school in New York the boys toadied to me because of my father's money. At college, the richer students tried to get me to join their silly little fraternities and athletic clubs; they told me that 'of course' I would not want to associate with 'nobodies.' So I looked them in the eye and said 'Of course not!' They blackballed me, after that. It was all very dirty. And foolish. And impossibly silly. It makes me sick, knowing that the things I want, and am willing to work for with all my heart and my soul, can be bought without effort on my part."

"You wouldn't want to be poor, Philippe?" Gertrude was smiling at him indulgently.

"No, you silly pet. Who would? But I'd still like to feel that I'd have to buy many of the things I want with something else besides money."

"But there are so many things," said Gertrude softly, looking up at him radiantly. "Health and love. And peace. They have to be bought too, but not with what you have in your purse. Grandpa Barbour died of cancer, and his money couldn't save him. Grandma Barbour wasn't very happy, when she was old, and she was very rich. It is true that being poor wouldn't have saved Grandpa and Grandma, but being rich didn't save them, either. And, as I said before, money couldn't buy me. But what you are could, Philippe."

Again they stopped for a last kiss, a last passionate straining together. They were approaching the Sessions house. They could see its lights on the rise in the distance. They trudged up the long slope toward it.

"I'd like to do something," said Philippe meditatively. "Something outside of the family business. Something such as Frey is doing. But

I have no talents. I used to think, before I loved you, that I would enter a monastery, or become a priest. I think I should have done it, become a priest, if it hadn't been for Mama marrying again. Major Norwood is a Protestant, and any little flavor of Catholicism there was in our household disappeared when Mama married him. I'm the only one in the household that goes to Mass even once a year. And even Mama smiles a little now, when I go. Once she said: 'But isn't it all nonsense, dearest?' As if God were ever nonsense! Though sometimes, seeing things as they are, I almost believe He is!" he added bitterly.

Gertrude was silent. They were dangerously close to a dark place which they had agreed they would never approach again. Philippe looked at it miserably. Then he, too, fell silent.

The lights were all blazing in the library. They could see them through the blinds. They tiptoed to one of the long tall windows, and peered through a crack. Though it was after eleven, Paul Barbour sat with his uncle before the fire. It was too evident that they were waiting. For Gertrude. Philippe did not see the significance, but it suddenly occurred to Gertrude, and she felt giddy with fear. She withdrew precipitately, pulling Philippe with her.

"Paul and Papa are waiting for me," she whispered. The light from an upper window shone on her face; it was quite white. "I can't see Paul, tonight. I don't want to." Philippe was surprised to find how she was trembling. The dogs in the stables began to bark, and from the shadows on the blinds Gertrude saw that her father and cousin had risen, and were waiting. She picked up her skirts and ran around to the rear of of the house, down the steep little slope to the back door. Philippe followed. Gertrude tried the back entry door that led into the kitchen. It was open; she had not expected this, and a sharp breath was exhaled through her lips. They crept through the little hallway, and silently opened the door. The kitchen was blazing with hot friendly light; the stove glowed redly, and three of the women servants, the cook and two chambermaids, were sitting at the kitchen table sipping coffee, eating cakes and gossiping. They cried out, startled, as Gertrude and Philippe entered, then rose, red with embarrassment.

"Good evening, Mrs. Battle," said Gertrude, smiling at the cook. "Good evening, Jane and Edith. My father has a visitor, and I'm so rumpled and soiled and tired that I don't want to see or be seen——"

"But, Miss Gertrude," protested Edith timidly, "your Papa gave me express orders that when you returned I was to tell you to go into the library at once." She smoothed her apron, and regarded Gertrude anxiously. "I should lose my place, Miss Gertrude, if I didn't tell him you had come home."

Gertrude stared at the girl, her eyes very dark and wide in her pale face. Then she turned mutely to Philippe. He took something out of his pockets: three five-dollar gold pieces. He laid them on the table. The women blinked at them, audibly sucking in their breath.

"No one has seen Miss Gertrude come in," he said easily. He smiled at the servants; his white teeth flashed in his brown face. All at once he was his father, irresistible, charming, fascinating, the courtier. The cook and the maids might have resisted the money, after a titanic struggle, but they could not resist Philippe with his dancing black eyes and the cleft in his cheek that was almost a dimple. They yearned at him adoringly. The cook thrust the money toward him. "Go on, Master Philippe," she said, grinning. "We wouldn't say nothin' about Miss Gertrude if she didn't want us to. Would we?" she demanded with a fierce frown, as she turned upon Edith. "Why, no ma'am," she stammered. She and Jane regarded the money wistfully. Philippe pushed it forward again.

"There, this is just a present for you and the girls, Mrs. Battle. Not a bribe. I know you are all above bribes. But I haven't forgotten the cookies you used to make for me, and the way Trudie and I used to tease the girls. Buy yourselves something with the money."

The maids snatched up their gold coins, Mrs. Battle deftly slipped hers into her apron pocket, and muttering something about needin' butter, she went into the scullery. Gertrude and Philippe kissed each other swiftly, again and again, then Philippe slipped out into the hall, and Gertrude heard the door closing after him.

She looked about the bright empty kitchen. The brick stove exhaled waves of pleasant heat, and the lamps on the table and on the shelf near the pantry blazed through polished glass. The copper vessels on the walls shone like gold. She was conscious of great fatigue; there was a trembling in her legs. She removed the wet red scarf from her hair; the moisture had soaked through, and her hair was a mass of damp ringlets against her pale cheeks. Her skirts were bedraggled, dark at the hem with mud and water; she dropped them out of her hand and they fell soggily about her feet. She shook out her cloak, and the water splashed upon the stove with a hissing sound. Then, gathering up her skirts again, she opened the door that led into the butler's pantry. It was all dark and quiet there, smelling of soap and herbs. The whole house was quiet. Somewhere a door opened, and Gertrude heard the impatient loudness of her father's voice. The door closed again, and the voice was lost.

She slipped into the dining room, then out into the great hall from which the library and the drawing rooms opened. The staircase twisted up dimly, a wide spectral stairway, and the grandfather's clock boomed the half hour. The lamp on the newel post burned with a faint and uncertain light. Gertrude's heart began to beat very fast; the library door was still shut but any moment it might open and she would be caught. She lifted her skirts high about her slender ankles and was about to bolt for the stairway when she heard footsteps descending with a soft hissing on the carpet. She shrank back under the stairs; it was the butler. He opened the library door and the light gushed out into the hall, accompanied by wisps of smoke.

"I am sorry, sir," said the butler, "but Miss Gertrude has not yet returned."

Ernest shouted an oath. "This is a fine thing, a girl staying out half the night!" he said.

"Perhaps she is going to stay overnight at Uncle Eugene's," suggested Paul in a disappointed voice.

"That might be. But stay until midnight, Paul. Then if she isn't here we'll know she is going to stay over there. She often does, especially on disagreeable nights. If Eugene hasn't brought her home by twelve, you had best go."

The butler discreetly closed the door. He turned toward the kitchen. Gertrude squeezed herself against the wall under the stairway, holding her breath. She was shaking with an absurd terror. But the butler passed within three feet of her and did not see her. The dining room door shut behind him noiselessly. Gertrude dared wait no longer. She pulled up her skirts about her knees, bent her head and plunged for the stairway. Never had she gone up so fast, even in her childhood. It seemed endless, like a stairway in a nightmare. When she reached the top she was faint and sick and trembling. She reached the door of her room, then halted. She had a feeling that she would not be safe there, that her father would soon be doing a little investigating on his own. There was a light under her mother's door. She tapped on it lightly, turned the handle, and entered.

May, ready for her bed, was sitting before her fire in ruffled nightgown and maroon dressing gown. Her red-gray hair hung in two neat plaits on her plump round shoulders. She removed her glasses self-consciously and put aside her book, and regarded Gertrude with surprise.

"My dear! Did you know your father is waiting for you downstairs, with Paul?" Then she became aware of the fact that Gertrude had closed the door swiftly behind her, and was leaning against it, panting, and that her clothing and hair were in a sad state of dishevelment. Her surprise and apprehension quickened at the glimpse of the girl's face in the firelight and lamplight; it was pale and drawn and there was terror in it. "What on earth!" she exclaimed, rising and advancing.

Gertrude glanced fearfully at the door, put her finger to her lips, and turned to her mother. May took the girl's hands; they were icy cold and tremulous.

"Mama," she whispered, "may I stay here tonight with you?"

She had not asked this since she was a child, overcome with mysterious night fears. May peered at her keenly, looked at the door, and comprehended. She drew her daughter to the fire, made her sit down.

She picked up an edge of the heavy wet frock and shook her head reprovingly. "The prettiest thing you have had for a long time," she murmured. Gertrude still sat and trembled on the edge of her chair, her body rigid. "You'll catch your death," went on May. "Luckily there's some hot chocolate left in the jug." She went to her bedside table where a neat silver tray stood holding a silver jug and a cup. She poured out the still steaming liquid and brought it to Gertrude. The girl made a faint negative sign, but upon May's silent insistence, she drank. And immediately felt better. May sat down.

"You know," she said, keeping her voice low, "your agitation is all out of proportion to the cause, Gertrude. In fact, it's silly. Your Papa isn't a dragon, and Paul isn't waiting down there to devour you. You are a young woman. You have your own mind and your own will. I can see very well that you don't want to marry Paul; it is easy enough for you to say so. No one in all this world can make you marry him if you don't want to."

"Oh yes, Papa can," said Gertrude, in a faint high voice. "You know he can, Mama." She wrung her hands in her lap. May's brows drew together and her lips tightened. She turned and gazed at the fire.

"I thought you would always do what your Papa wanted, Gertrude. He was always fonder of you than of any of his other children, and you were devoted to him." She was sorry immediately when she said this; it was like striking a terrified child who had appealed for help. She was ashamed of the little pinprick of malice that had made her say this to the poor girl. Gertrude knew what had occasioned this speech, and she knew that her mother regretted it. She smiled twistedly.

"Papa has changed toward me the last year," she said mournfully. "It's always about Paul. Papa is beginning to harden; he hardly speaks kindly to me. I know it isn't because he loves me less, but I am opposing him, and he'll get harder and more inflexible until I give in. And it breaks my heart. And I'm so afraid that I will give in, just to have him love me again! Just to have him stop looking at me so sternly, and not answering when I speak. I can't bear it." She began to cry. May had turned to her and was watching her with an inscrutable expression. But she was full of pity and a sort of ironic appreciation.

"You're not a booby, Gertrude. You're not soft and spineless. You don't have to give in. It's Philippe, isn't it?"

A bright flush ran under Gertrude's tears, and she nodded. May's face become somber and grave. "He's only a boy, still, Gertrude, and younger than you. Of course, it is so little younger— And Philippe is so mature—" Her voice was preoccupied. "But it will be years, my dear, until he can marry you. I like Philippe, and like his mother. And before he went to Paris, Frey became quite attached to him. I believe they carry on quite a correspondence. I never could understand what Ernest had against him. I'm not advising you," and involuntarily her tone hard-ened, remembering. "You've always taken all your troubles and prob-lems to your Papa, and made me feel out in the cold. So, at this late day, I'm not going to advise you to turn against him and defy him. You must use your own judgment. It is your own life. You are a woman now. You must make up your own mind as to where your happiness lies, and I hope you will have the courage to stand by your decision."

Gertrude was silent. She thought of the long years of her childhood and girlhood, when she had resented every sign of affection her father had given his wife. Childishly, she had indeed excluded May, running always to her father. She had an insight, now, into the pain she had given May, and was bitterly sorry for it. Finally she spoke in a shaking voice: "Mama, I'm awfully sorry. You are quite right. I was a little selfish pig." She held out her hands, the tears splashing down her white cheeks. "But I'm coming to you, Mama, now! Please help me! I haven't any one else."

May took her hands, pressed them in her own, and smiled. She drew the girl down to her and kissed her cheek. But the years had run a cleft between them, and the soil was washed away. Instinctively, she would help Gertrude, but there would be more of duty in it than love.

"Of course I'll help you, child," she said lightly, putting the hands aside with a gentle gesture. "But we must look at this from all sides. Paul is the son of your Uncle Martin, whom your father hated with all his might. You have often heard him mention Martin. Perhaps what he said has unconsciously affected your regard for Martin's son."

"No, Mama. It is true that I have often heard Papa speak contemptu-ously of Uncle Martin. Almost as if he hated him, as you say. But I remember Uncle Martin quite well, before he went away. You used to take us to that dreadful farm where he lived. He was so gentle and kind to us all. I never heard him say a hard thing. And he was so beautiful, like one of the angels in Renee's Catholic books. Or in Papa's Dante's *Paradiso*. We all loved him very much. Even Frey wasn't afraid of him. So it isn't what Papa has said about Uncle Martin that has kept me from liking Paul. It's something else."

May listened thoughtfully, and with some curiosity. The vagaries of the sexual selection never failed to amuse and intrigue her. "But why, Trudie? He is far more of a man than Philippe, and looks much older. He is very handsome—they say. There is nothing at all negative about him, and one cannot call him a fool. He does everything extremely well, and will soon make himself a fortune. In fact, many people say that he is made in your father's image."

"Oh, no, Mama. No! He is not like Papa, except that—except that you feel he'll have his way with you, just as Papa does. That you can't resist him. It would be like trying to resist a wall of lava. When he is near me I feel weak, as though all the resistance and strength has gone out of me, and I'm so frightened. Sometimes I'm so terribly afraid that I'm not strong enough to stand up against Paul and Papa, both. If it were just one of them——"

May smiled again, that faint ironic smile, as though she were thinking that the scales were beginning to balance at last.

"You have quite an imagination, Trudie! I'm sure Paul isn't as formidable as all that. He can't kidnap you. I assure you that your Papa won't throw you into the street if you persist in refusing Paul. He might browbeat you and refuse to speak to you. But he loves you better than any one, still. And eventually, he will come around. At least, I believe so. And here is another thing, Trudie: Philippe is a Catholic, and an ardent one, I understand. I know he was always at church when he was a child—it was quite a family joke, along with Reggie's buttons. Didn't he always say he was going to be a priest? Well, then, how is he going to marry you, his cousin? The Catholic Church does not permit marriages between cousins."

Gertrude's small white face became angular with the pressure of emotion upon it, and she seemed exceedingly distressed, as though she had been forced to look upon a dangerous place again. "Philippe and I have talked about all that, Mama," she said painfully. "A long time ago. And Philippe has decided to leave the Church." The memory of those long, sad, anguished struggles was too strong in her memory to be recalled without agitation, and she stood up, the wild fragile look upon her, once more.

"Leave the Church?" May's eyebrows rose and her forehead wrinkled. "Philippe? He must indeed love you very much, Trudie, if he can give up his Church for you. I understand that's a very terrible thing for a Catholic. Is he happy about it?"

"I don't know. I don't know," Gertrude whispered. "But it was his own choice. He chose, himself. I told him I would not try to influence him. And after a month, he came to me and said he loved me better than he did his Church."

May suddenly lifted her head alertly. "Hush!" she murmured. "Some-one is coming." And footsteps indeed were coming down the hallway toward the door. Gertrude recognized them as her father's. She glanced about her wildly, seized her skirts and fled toward the bed, crouched beside it, shut from a view from the door. Ernest knocked.

"Who is it?" called May, rising and advancing toward the door. She opened it. Ernest stood on the threshold, frowning and annoyed. He glanced beyond his wife, and saw only firelight and an empty room.

"I thought I heard Gertrude's voice, my love," he said. May held the door. He had not stepped into this room for years. He hesitated, glanced at the white arm that barred his entry. Quite irrelevantly, in spite of his annoyance, he wanted to enter that room again, to be invited to sit before that fire. But May was looking at him with a pleasant smile, and the arm still barred him.

"I'm sure you were mistaken, Ernest," she said, as if surprised. "I didn't hear her go to her room. Besides, she always comes in to say good night first. But surely you remember that she was to stay at Dorcas' tonight? Don't you recall her mentioning it?"

"Did she?" Ernest looked baffled and angry. "I forgot. And I've been keeping Paul waiting down there." He looked again at the room through the half-opened door. He wanted to suggest that he would like to come in and discuss Gertrude with his wife. But he did not have the courage. He felt foolish standing there, like a stranger outside his wife's door, barred out, like an importunate and improper stranger. Anger rose hotly in him, but whether it was against May or the situation, he could not tell. His voice was sharp and curt when he spoke again. "I'm going to New York tomorrow, May, and I'll be gone before Gertrude comes home. Please tell her for me that she'll have a week while I am away to make up her mind to obey me. I'm sick of this nonsense. Paul's sick of it, too. She's old enough to be married, and I expect her to think about a Christmas wedding."

"She's quite young, yet," said May. She thought suddenly of a young and piteous Juliet who had pleaded youth, and the memory of the sorrow she had felt for the tragic heroine during that play was absurdly poignant.

"Nonsense. All her friends of her age have been married long ago. She's practically an old maid. I won't put up with this any longer. Playing about with a silly romping boy like that infernal Philippe! Please tell her what I've said."

"I'll tell her," said May, smiling sweetly. "Good night, Ernest."

He had turned away, and now he turned back. Husband and wife regarded each other steadfastly through the twelve-inch opening. The light from the room fell on Ernest's face and quite-gray hair. He looked tired and haggard, but indomitable as ever. But he also looked lonely, and the light implacable eyes were almost pleading. "Good night," May repeated, and closed the door softly in his face. Forgetting her daughter, she pressed her cheek against the wood of the shut door, and stood there for a long moment. When she turned away, there was a moisture upon the wood.

Gertrude stood on the hearth, biting her lips, her hands clasped rigidly together. May put her hand gently on the girl's shoulder. "We must not speak aloud," she whispered. "And it is very late. Undress as quickly as possible, and we will go to bed. Now, no more talk, tonight! Take off that poor ruined frock, and get under the covers."

CHAPTER LXVIII

AMY OFTEN thought that she had mothered four total strangers, a different species altogether. Once her pretty housecat had found four motherless little puppies and adopted them. Amy watched the incongruous family and told herself that she and her children offered as strange a sight.

Her three older children were taller than she, and John Charles, fifteen years old, was well on the way to overtopping her. They were all big-boned and squarish, hearty-voiced and brutal and bluff of manner, exigent and selfish, cynical and high-tempered. There were a few times, clear in her memory, when she seemed to be able to meet Lucy on equal ground and understanding, but Elsa and Paul and John Charles were alien to her. Nor could she find, except in Lucy, any resemblance to Martin, and even then, Lucy's resemblance was faint and nebulous.

In her cousin May's children, Amy found the same substance that formed herself, the same delicacy of perception, the same mental pattern. For Godfrey James and Gertrude she felt a real maternal love, and the alienation that had grown up mutely between herself and her cousin caused her the more pain because she was separated from the two children. In Reginald's fanaticism she found a flavor of Martin, in Guy she discovered her old youthful gaiety and delight in living. But Joseph, or Joey, repelled her amusedly; he was so like her John Charles, so like his cousin Andre Bouchard. She called them The Three Bankers, with as much apprehension as laughter.

The estrangement between May and Amy had been complete for nearly two years, and May had ceased her visits entirely to her cousin's house. Gertrude, though she loved her aunt, had also ceased to visit her, because of Paul. When Lucy had been married, nearly three years ago, the families had met in the house on Quaker Terrace, but even the wedding had not eased the strain. Amy, lonely among her savage young aliens, Paul and Elsa and John Charles, sat for hours in her own little sitting room, or worked in her garden, or read or walked, her only joy stemming from Ernest's visits. Her whole life now revolved about those hours with him, so that everything else became unreal, was like a pasteboard background beyond which was nothing but the bare props of existence. No one realized the insecurity, the danger and the psychic dissatisfaction of her life, the unreality of it, better than did Amy, but

she seemed helplessly caught in it, without the will to extricate herself.
She lived for her love as a drug addict lives for his morphine, and spent
herself in the two dimensions of it, trying not to think too much. She
realized that there was plenty of gossip: old friends were visiting her
more and more infrequently. She hardly subscribed to Ernest's casual
impatience and declarations that if one refused to discuss a certain
thing with others, or appeared unware of it, it remained below the surface, and unprovable. But danger and gossip, ostracism that extended
only to her, jeers and whispers, insecurity and loneliness, still seemed
a small price to pay for the only thing that mattered to her. Not even
the vague fear that her children must one day suspect, if they did not
already, could frighten her for more than a few moments.

She was feeling unusually lonely and depressed one damp autumn
day, as she sat in her sitting room looking out into the garden. The
grass and the denuded trees, the earth and the distant wall, were all of
one uniformly brown tint. A few soaked red leaves lay on a garden
path, their edges curled up, and the cups they made full of livid water.
Mist wound its way over the muddy ground, seeming like a cold exhalation from the earth itself. The skies were gaseous; everything dripped,
though it was not raining; long trickles of water ran down the tree trunks,
hung on their shining bare branches, water dropped from the eaves,
water lay in the little puddles everywhere. Even the canaries in the warm
little room were silent, and the only other sounds were the melancholy
dropping of water outside and the dropping of coals inside.

Amy was all alone, trying to read. Elsa was somewhere in the house,
listless as she always was on inclement days. She is twenty-two, thought
her mother, sadly, and still unable to find another interest besides Godfrey Barbour, though he never writes to her and she has not seen him
for two years. Amy, who had loved silently and miserably for so many
years, could sympathize with this mute agony that waited and watched,
and could sustain itself on the bitter crumbs of second-hand messages
and anecdotes. And half of the messages are lies, thought Amy mournfully, because May is really too kind-hearted to hurt poor Elsa. Sometimes she wondered if it would not have been kinder to have killed this
hopeless and wretched passion which the big red-cheeked girl felt for
the delicate pale young man. "It is so incongruous!" exclaimed Amy
aloud. She felt a sudden sharp resentment against Ernest, who encouraged Elsa to hope; he made no secret of the fact that he wanted Elsa to
marry his son. "Knock the silliness out of him," he said once. But Amy
could not find anything that was not grotesque in the thought of such
a union.

She had half decided to send for Elsa (for none of the children were
allowed in the sitting room of their mother without special invitation),
and had tried to arrange in her mind a number of subjects on which she

nd her daughter could meet pleasantly, when she heard the front bell ing. She wondered, without much interest, who could be calling on uch a day. When the maid knocked discreetly, and announced Miss Gertrude Barbour, Amy turned quite pale with surprise and pleasure.

Gertrude came in, wrapped in an enveloping waterproof cape of black roadcloth, a hood over her head. Amy rose, and approached her with miles and outstretched hands. "My dear Trudie! How delightful! Do come to the fire, child. Bertha, take Miss Gertrude's cloak and umbrella and dry them in the kitchen. Trudie! How pleased I am to see you!"

She kissed the girl's cheek; it was wet and chill under her lips. Then vith her hands on Gertrude's shoulders, she held her off and beamingly regarded her. Gertrude forced a smile; she looked rather wan and colorless in her brown wool dress and closely buttoned basque. Her ustreless dark hair lay smoothly but lankly on each side of her clear pale cheeks. Amy saw that there were smudges of violet under the dark eyes, and that the girl's lips looked pinched and cold.

"I'm so pleased, so happy, to see you again, dear Aunt Amy," she murmured in her restless way. She regarded Amy intently. Her aunt never seemed to grow older, she thought heavily. Her eyes were so limpid and brown, her skin so fresh, her bright brown hair so shining in ts smooth waves and high piled roll on the top of her pretty head. Her lark blue wool frock, with its touch of lace at the throat, made her look young again. She looks much younger than Mama, said Gertrude to herself. She kissed Amy again. She loved the sweet odor of rose that came from Amy's flesh and clothing; it seemed more a part of her very personality than an external fragrance.

She sat down in a chair Amy drew for her to the fire. She waited, her small delicate hands in her lap, as Amy ordered tea. She stared at the fire, with such a quiet hopelessness that Amy was alarmed and touched. Pretending not to notice anything wrong, Amy assumed a sprightly tone and asked after May, and the children. She poked the fire, made a small joke, and laughed. Gertrude smiled painfully; her lips trembled.

"How nice of you to visit a dull old lady!" said Amy, taking the girl's hand, and holding its slight coldness between her warm palms. "Elsa and I are just not on speaking terms on days like these. I believe she is moping upstairs in her room. Shall I invite her to join us?"

"Oh no, please, Aunt Amy!" Gertrude came to life in agitation. "I came to see just you." She began to wring her hands desperately on her knee. She looked at Amy, who had become gently grave, and her distress was so marked, so pathetic, that the older woman felt alarm.

"My dear," she said softly. "What is it? Is it some trouble? Can I help you? If I can, please tell me. You can rely upon me."

"I know I can. Oh, I know I can, Aunt Amy!" Gertrude began to

cry; the tears gushed from her eyes, fell over her cheeks. She did no
wipe them away. She merely implored her aunt with hands and eyes
and Amy's alarm increased.

"Tell me, Gertrude." She assumed a voice of firm quietness, an
again took one of Gertrude's trembling hands. It felt suddenly clamm
and increasingly cold.

Gertrude gazed at her blindly, then averted her face. "But, how ca
I? I don't know where to begin, what to say——"

"Suppose you don't 'begin,' Trudie. Suppose you just start right out
I don't need preliminary explanations."

"But it is so horrible, to insult you this way!" cried the girl, her han
writhing in Amy's strongly retaining grasp. "I must have been mad t
think that you might want to help me, that you would listen to me in
sulting your——"

There was a silence, after Gertrude's one sharp sob. Her chin ha
fallen on her chest, and her hair, loosened, half covered her haggar
young face. Amy still held her hand. Her own face had become grave
than ever, and sadder.

"It's about Paul, isn't it, darling?" Her voice was very gentle an
tender. "Yes, I know. And you've come to tell me today that you don'
want to marry him, and that your Papa is urging you into it, and you—
Trudie, how did you imagine I might be able to help you?"

"I didn't know!" Gertrude turned to her wildly. "I didn't know! Bu
I thought you might understand. I thought in some way you might help
I didn't realize how it would be insulting you——"

Amy dropped her head a little and studied the hand that held her ow
with such a desperate thin grip.

"It isn't insulting me, love," she said softly. "I understand how yo
feel. I always thought it—quite wrong. But your father assured m
that you were willing, that you were quite fond of Paul. I didn't know.

"He lied! Aunt Amy, he lied! I—I never liked Paul. Forgive me
he's your son. But I never liked him. I don't mean he isn't—excellent
and all that, and that he isn't a really fine person. But I don't want him
He's not for me. I—I love Philippe, and we want to be married. An
Papa is forcing me to marry Paul."

"Forcing you? How horrible!" Amy stood up, agitated herself. Sh
had become pale, and the tensed bones of her face showed in a hard wa
through her flesh.

Gertrude clung to her dress; Amy looked down at her pitifully, breath
ing very hard in her indignation and real horror.

"Yes, Aunt Amy, he's forcing me. Of course, I know he can't dra
me to Paul and marry me outright to him. But—there are other ways
You—you don't know Papa—" For one moment a faint smile, like
gleam, passed over Amy's eyes. "But Papa has so many ways. You can'

resist him. It's like fighting a mountain of iron. It just stands there, and after awhile, it bears down on you and crushes you."

"Does Paul know how you feel about him, Trudie?"

"Yes. I've told him. Dozens of times. He either laughs, or gets angry. He doesn't believe it. He says he loves me, and he can't understand what difference it makes if I don't love him."

Amy listened to this thoughtfully. "Yes, I can see that Paul would say that. Paul is something like your father—he wants something and is outraged or contemptuous if any one opposes him. My children never did have much sense of humor. I admit that Paul is very egotistic, too; he believes that his own desires are more important than any one else's. Your own father only believes that as he is the stronger, the weaker ought to yield without so much fuss."

"And they usually yield," said Gertrude with despair. "I can't hold out against Papa much longer, even though I'd rather die than not marry Philippe. That's why I've come to you, Aunt Amy. I—I thought perhaps you might talk to Paul."

"Talk to Paul?" Amy smiled wryly. "What good would that do? Paul and I have never been—congenial. I have a suspicion he thinks me a weakling. At least, we can never meet, even at the table, without clashes. Besides, he would be very indignant if I tried to interfere with what he would call his own business. However, I will speak to him. But I have a still better plan than that. It might be successful."

Gertrude, flushed with hope, sprang to her feet. She seized Amy's arm. "What is it? Do you think it would be any good? Please tell me!"

Amy put her arm about the girl; her throat thickened with compassion. "I can't promise too much, darling. But I think, I really think, it might have a good chance. Trust me to do what I can."

Gertrude, laughing and smiling now through her tears, wiped her eyes. A faint color had come into her face. "I will trust you! I do trust you! It's—it's like a new life in me."

Amy sat down. "Does your Mama know you have come to me to ask for help?"

"No. I didn't tell her. You see, Mama thinks that I ought to be strong enough to oppose Papa, and keep on opposing him. Sometimes," and her expression saddened, "sometimes I think Mama is just standing back and watching Papa and me, as she'd watch a play. Sometimes I think she wouldn't care if Papa beat me down."

"But how unjust of you, Trudie. Your Mama isn't that sort at all."

"Aunt Amy, you don't know. One night I asked her to let me sleep with her, because Papa and Paul were waiting for me and I wanted to hide. She did let me sleep with her, and told Papa I was staying with Aunt Dorcas for the night. But she said that I'd always gone to Papa with everything, and it was a little late——"

"I see." Amy was very grave. "I see." To herself she said wretchedly: So May is even making this poor child pay for Ernest and me. I did not think it of her. And yet, it is only human. "Trudie, your Mama has much on her side. I think you have hurt her feelings for years. Try to understand that. But I am certain that she would do anything at all to keep you from being unhappy."

Gertrude started fearfully. The door was opening, and Elsa after a hasty knock thrust her discontented face into the room. "May I come in for a moment, Mama? Oh, is that Trudie?" She smiled, her expression lightening.

"Come in, lovie," said Amy, pulling another chair toward the fire. Elsa, without a glance at her mother, came beaming into the room. Her dark gray woollen dress was untidy and none too immaculate, and her pretty shining hair was disarranged and uncombed. There was a smudge on her big, well-shaped nose, and her hands were soiled; it was evident that she had been digging in the conservatory recently. She had grown quite plump, and this exuberance of flesh and her unusual height, made her appear much older and much more matured than her twenty-two years. Too, her fresh and blooming complexion, big white teeth, and general air of hearty earthiness, made her look like some wholesome, big-footed peasant girl. She sat down between her mother and Gertrude, and she made the girl appear fragile, colorless and too delicate by comparison.

"Well!" she exclaimed loudly. "I haven't seen you for an age, Trudie! And the weather's been so bad that I haven't felt like visiting, myself. But how is everyone at home?" A deeper tinge came into her face "Have you heard from Frey lately?"

Gertrude smiled her rather thin and satirical smile. "We are all as well as ever. Did you know we expect Frey for Christmas, after all? Mama got a letter from him yesterday. She said she was anxious about it, and was wondering if he were well. His letter was a little incoherent and excited. We think he might have good news for us. Of course, Papa says he was probably drunk." She laughed, a little hysterically, as though relieved from some enormous strain.

"But how silly. Frey hardly ever drinks anything," said Elsa indignantly. Her color was very high, and the big capable hands that folded and unfolded a fold of her dress were trembling slightly. "So he is coming at Christmas?" She smiled brilliantly. "How awfully nice for— for all of you."

Amy watched, pityingly. She sighed. What irony, she thought, that her children had fallen in love with Ernest's children, and the latter would not be had by them. If only Elsa were not so big, so bouncing, so utterly impervious to delicacy, so utterly lacking in subtlety. Poor girl. It was probably the fragility of Frey and Gertrude that attracted such lustiness.

such arrogant crudeness, such loud-voiced hunger. Why, she thought
with whimsical melancholy, Frey and Gertrude would be squashed like
bugs under the weight of Paul and Elsa, or be lost, like Gullivers, in the
hands of her young giants.

Gertrude, her terror lifted, was quite willing to be more amiable to
her cousin. She chattered of Frey, his prospects, the praises of his
teachers, repeated little anecdotes from his letters. And Elsa listened,
brooding with delight upon the girl, her massive shoulders hunched
toward her, her big lighted face intent.

She said, with an elaborate carelessness: "I haven't written to Frey
recently. I'm so afraid he'll be cross with me. Did he—did he mention
me in his last letter?"

Gertrude hesitated; Amy turned her calm face to her. "Why—yes, I
believe he did," lied Gertrude, embarrassed. "He—he said he had quite
a lot of things to tell you. About Paris."

Elsa smiled again. It was like the sun, that smile, shining and content.
Can she really be as blind as that? thought Amy compassionately, her
heart aching for her daughter. Or does she, like all of us, believe what she
wants to believe? The lies are so obvious; only stupidity or love could be
taken in by them. Sometimes I think, in Elsa's case, that it is both.

"Oh, Paris," said Elsa. "I would love to see Paris." Amy regarded
her with surprise. "Windsor is so dull," went on Elsa, "it makes all of
us dull, also. It is strange that we make our environment out of the stuff
of ourselves, and yet it chokes us, sometimes, as if it were a foreign
element we couldn't breathe. As if," she hesitated for words, "as if our
environment was like the air we breathed out, a sort of exhalation, that
it wasn't wholesome to use again." (No, thought Amy, with renewed
surprise, she is not stupid. I wonder why she never talks so, to me? Do
I oppress her, as Ernest oppresses his children?) Elsa, having concluded
her speech, frowned; she never could find the exact words, and it infuriated her. "You know what I mean," she added, with a lumbering, helpless wave of her hands. "You know—as if our environment, our civilization, was dung."

Gertrude colored, Amy laughed, at this forthright description. "Yes,
Windsor is dull," agreed Amy. "But I never thought you considered
it so."

"What is there here for me, for any one?" asked Elsa surlily. "We'll
all be a pack of old maids, Trudie and me and Annabelle Shirley and
Mary Anne Stimson and Adeline Liggett—all of us. Because our beaux
are looking in New York and Baltimore and Philadelphia and Pittsburgh
for wives. It's just an accident that Lucy met her Oswald, and she had
to do that in New York." She rose, yawned and stretched, her gray stuff
frock pulling up over her petticoats with the soiled flounces. She looked
like a rosy great child, yawning so. She dropped her arms. "I'll be glad

to see Frey again," she added. "I wish I could go back to Paris with him." She looked at Gertrude as she said this, and deep within her blue eyes a spark started, and grew. Gertrude, feeling ashamed of her pitiful lies, glanced away.

Tea was brought in, and cakes. They ate and drank, snug in the golden firelight, the autumn day lowering more than ever outside. It was raining heavily, and the windows were awash with gray streams. The bare trees outside were spectres, writhing and drowning in a wall of water.

When Gertrude rose to go, she felt as if she were about to leave a snug harbor to sail out again into storms and distresses.

CHAPTER LXIX

ERNEST, AFTER a comfortable little dinner alone with Amy in her sitting room, looking about expansively, smiled at her, and sipped a very small glass of sherry. He still detested the taste of alcohol, and only the little fillip the sherry gave him made him drink even this modest amount.

Paul was detained at the bank, as it was the first of the month and the books were usually gone over at this time. John Charles was staying overnight with a friend, and Elsa, also. On these visits of Ernest's, things were always neatly arranged in this fashion, without discussion, seemingly occurring in the natural train of events. If he guessed by what anxious contrivance, what humiliation, what secret self-detestation, Amy arrived at these satisfactory arrangements, he pretended bland ignorance. He could not help seeing the flush on her face when he arrived, her silence and stiffness. But after awhile she always became herself, gentle, laughing, understanding and tolerant, eager to please him, courting his good temper and his affection.

Amy had arranged an exceptionally fine little dinner this night, which tempted even Ernest's casual appetite, and made him express unusual praise. She also looked exceedingly charming and youthful in her dark green velvet gown, elaborately draped and decorated with sparkling crystal buttons. At her ears glittered the rosy fire of diamonds, and her slender white hands with their delicate tips were ringed and braceleted. He noticed again that there was not a single strand of gray in her polished hair, not even at the temples. His love had made her bloom, regenerated her whole body, glossed her flesh.

He began to tell her of his recent visit to New York and Washington. He had had luncheon with the President. "Mr. Grant, or rather, General Grant, is a very amiable and simple man," he said, "sturdy, unimaginative as are all soldiers, thinking himself very subtle, and remarkably easy to deceive. Soldiers are always very conservative, for they have deep faith in authority and are disciplined. I consider him a very fine President."

"But they say he is quite stupid, really a cipher," replied Amy. She had mastered the supreme artistry of conversation, to be able to think her own thoughts and yet make intelligent remarks.

"Precisely, my dear. And that is why he is such a good President! What the devil would we want with a President who had a will and notions of his own? God knows what sort of follies he would have up his sleeve, what arrogances. He might even get the idea that he could be a leader, or a reformer, leading the nation on to 'higher and better' things. And get himself into a fine tangle with Congress, thus dividing and upsetting the country. What we need in a President is a simple gentleman to sign papers and add dignity to public affairs, a nice conservative gentleman who has no dreams of social reforms, and is quite satisfied with things as they are, one who loves his garden and likes children, rides horses sedately, grows a beard in order to look benign, and presides over Congress like a very benevolent and amiable deity."

"I wonder," said Amy thoughtfully, "what would happen to this country if we accidentally elected someone like Lincoln again, a real leader? God knows we need one in these times."

"Nonsense. Congress is capable of managing everything, and capable of being managed—by those who are really in power." Ernest smiled slightly. "If we had had a President with 'notions' around September, 1869, we would have been ruined. He might have stopped that corner in gold. There's been a lot of so-called 'labor agitation' these last couple of years, too, and a President who had social delusions might have encouraged the dogs in the mines and the factories, might have made the financial panic we are just digging out of now the excuse for miserable 'labor' legislation and 'protection.' We don't want kiss-mammies in the White House, full of brotherly love and indignation. This is a practical world; there's no place in it for putting axioms into practice and setting up the Kingdom of Heaven down here. There are hard-headed men behind Congress, capable of managing things without nonsense."

"And without mercy," murmured Amy. But Ernest's sharp ear caught the remark.

"Without mercy? What does mercy mean? Sloppy sentimentality? Impractical ideals that split into shavings on the first contact with reality? Mercy, my dear, is always the enemy of progress, for progress demands strength and courage and uncompromising resolution. Virtues are all very well for parlor ornaments, but you can't carry much water in them."

"And what do you mean by progress? The greatest good to the greatest number? Or the greatest profits to the few at the cost of the greatest misery to the many? I don't call that progress, Ernest. I call that exploitation."

But Ernest merely grinned. "I see you have been reading the nasty newspapers. I'm surprised at you, Amy. Why don't you read a little biology, instead? Really a fascinating subject; I've just discovered it recently, and found that Nature expresses all my ideas. Not that I'm a crusader, even for Nature's very excellent methods; I merely want to mind my own business."

Amy poured more tea. "What is this I hear about the Knights of Labor? I understand they are actually boasting of a fifty thousand membership."

Ernest grunted. "Just discontented cattle, second generation Magyars and Prussians and Irish, and Czechs and Bohemians, whose fathers were damn glad to come over here in cattle boats and work fourteen hours a day in mills and factories and mines for more to eat than they had ever had before in their lives. But feed a dog and he thinks he is a wolf. Impudent rabble! They were starving in their own countries, and utterly hopeless. We bring them over here, put them to work, put roofs over their heads, pay them all they are worth, and once the edge is off their hunger, and they have cleared their mouths of their food, they begin to yelp for more. Even if they can't eat any more."

"Didn't Oliver Twist ask for more, too?" Amy's smile was faintly satirical.

"Oliver Twist? Who the devil is Oliver Twist?"

"You would not know, Ernest. He's only a character in a novel."

"A novel, eh? Well, I leave the novel-reading to you women."

Amy rose and went to a small rosewood bookcase, and came back with a thick book in her hand. She laid it playfully near Ernest's cup. "There, it's by your own countryman, Dickens. I'm sure it'll bring memories back to you of the place your mother used to call 'dear old England.' Oliver Twist is in there. I have an idea it might do you some good to read about little Oliver."

"Oh, Dickens is another one of your social reformers, full of thunder and lightning and indignation." Ernest turned the pages disinterestedly. "I'm surprised his books are ever published in England. But then, there's been a lot of fool labor legislation in England recently. Filthy sentimentality!"

"Yes, that's true."

Ernest looked annoyed. "Some fools even prophesy that the day may arrive when labor will have something to say in Government. I hope not. I'm sure not. That would be a calamity." He frowned. "Do you know why I went to Washington, Amy? Well, there's been a lot of scurvy agitating lately about the importation of foreign labor. There always was a little yammering, but no one paid much attention. Now it's gotten worse, due to those Chinese we brought in to build the Western railroads. There's even a lobby in Washington, very vocal. So I went to Washington to see a few of my friends there, Senators and Supreme Court Judges. Gentlemen. They assured me I had little to worry about." He laughed shortly. "Amy, all things are for sale in Democracies."

"Including honor."

"Including honor." He sipped the last of his sherry. "But honor always was a cheap commodity."

In a lesser man, she thought, what he had been saying would have sounded like bravado. But there was not even cynicism in his calm statements.

"With all this foolish agitation about 'trusts,' now. Hamstringing industry. The health of a nation depends on the robustness and health of industry. The bigger the industry the bigger the nation, the greater the expansion, the more employment, more money, more power. When giants build cities there are always places in it for the dwarfs. But crippling and hog-tying giants never increased the stature of little men. It is as foolish as telling a farmer with one thousand acres not to plant more than his neighbor with ten acres, in order that the first shall not sell more nor profit more than the last. Or denying the first the use of the railroads because the little fellow cannot afford to use them. You don't build up civilizations with the smallest stones; you don't raise forts with pebbles. Business should be allowed to expand to any size. When tables are loaded for the giants there are always lots of crumbs for the pigmies. But you don't agree with me?" He smiled, and put his hand over hers as it lay on the cloth near him.

She laughed lightly. "My dear, I have never once agreed with you in all my life!"

She rang for the maid, and the small table was carried out. Ernest poked the fire, relaxed into the comfortable chair Amy pulled forward for him. He was in an amiable mood, she saw, with satisfaction.

"Ernest, I want to talk seriously with you, about Paul and Gertrude."

"Eh?" He turned to her alertly, and suspicion sharpened on his face. "Yes? What about them? I suppose Paul has told you that they are to be married the day before Christmas?"

"Yes." She gazed at the fire. "But I am not satisfied. From many little things I have heard, I have put two and two together. I am convinced that Gertrude does not want to marry my son."

He flushed angrily. "What do you mean? What have you heard? It's all nonsense. Of course she wants to marry him! Girls get notions, but marriage knocks them out of their heads. Gertrude has known for years that I wanted that marriage."

"But she doesn't love Paul, Ernest." She turned to him calmly, though inwardly she was tense. "Believe me, I know."

"How can you know?" He lifted a shoulder in contempt, and she colored with humiliation. Then again he was suspicious. "Look here, has May been talking to you?"

"No."

"Gertrude?"

"No."

He paused. "Amy, you are a poor liar. So Gertrude has come whining to you." His face became gloomy and disgusted.

"Ernest, suppose the poor child did ask me for help. Isn't that sufficient to show you that she doesn't want Paul——?"

"She doesn't know what she wants," he replied violently. "She thinks she wants that jackanapes, Philippe, but I know what is best for her. Paul is exactly what she wants; he will make her the best of husbands. What can a girl know of men? Don't be romantic, Amy!"

"I'm not romantic, Ernest. Put Paul is my son, you know, and I want him to be happy. He won't be happy, marrying a girl who hates him. Love doesn't come with marriage. Marriage is a hard thing, and unless love is sturdy enough, and determined enough, the marriage will fail. If Gertrude and Paul marry, their chance of happiness will be non-existent. I'm thinking of Paul, too. I am surprised that he wants Gertrude, knowing how she feels toward him. I'd think he'd have some pride——"

"Bah. He's set on Trudie; that's all he cares about. A year or two, and she'll be fond enough of him. He's ideal for her." He turned to her, and to her surprise, he laughed. "Look here, my pet, are you under the impression that I am whipping Gertrude to the altar and Paul? Don't be silly. She's old enough to know what she wants; if she really wanted that jack-in-the-box she'd fight for him, and oppose me sturdily enough."

"You forget," said Amy quietly, "Gertrude loves you, poor child. You are breaking her heart."

For an instant he looked touched, and gentler. "Yes, Trudie has always been my pet. In all her life we have never disagreed, until now I hope she understands that it is because I love her so much that I want this marriage. I wish she would trust me to know what is best for her."

He rose, began to pace up and down the room, his hands under his coat-tails. She watched him gravely. He was very gray, now, and broader than ever; he even had the suggestion of a paunch. But power had thickened and strengthened him; the large pale face was as ruthless and crude as stone.

"Ernest," she said softly, "I wish you would do something for me. For Gertrude and Paul. I wish you would stop oppressing her in the many ways you have of oppressing people. Give her time. Tell her she has two—three—months to make up her mind, and that after that time, if she is still determined not to have Paul, you will listen to any other suggestion about Philippe. After all, he is really a fine boy, Ernest, and I can't understand what you have against him, your favorite sister's son. But you might also tell the poor girl that in all fairness she is to give Paul a chance, that she is to soften her mind to him, consider him without prejudice, to cultivate him and try to find qualities that might please her. Tell her that you are trusting her to be fair, and that for the next two or three months you won't mention marriage with Paul to her."

He stopped, swung on his heel, and from across the room stared at her. Those pale relentless eyes flickered, stared, regarded the carpet, returned to her. She wished she could read what went on behind them, but they were closed as always to any penetration. His face became like a smooth mask. She was not deceived. She knew he was giving plenty of consideration to her suggestion, but she distrusted the other reservations he was forming in his mind. When he approached her, seemingly having reached a satisfactory solution, and smiling, her distrust increased. Ernest, compromising, Ernest, smiling, was a man to be watched, and suspected.

He sat down, looking extremely expansive. "Amy, your idea has its merits. Suppose I promise you that I shall tell Gertrude just what you have suggested. Suppose I do as you advise. And suppose, after two or three months, she decides to take Paul—will that please and satisfy you?"

Her suspicions became full fledged, but she could not see the ambush for all her intent searching. She felt it was there. But she had to be content. Perhaps in this case, she might be mistaken. She smiled, held out her hand to him.

"Yes, if Gertrude is satisfied, if she chooses that way, I'll be satisfied."

CHAPTER LXX

ATHER ALOYSIUS DOMINICK was now Bishop Dominick of the Philadelphia diocese, and occupied a handsome house behind the city cathedral. He had grown exceedingly plump, florid and genial, deeply concerned with food and the spiritual, not to say material advancement, of the Church. His favorite meal was breakfast, which, coming after ravenous hours attendant on Mass, was really his heartiest meal. He sat down to monstrous platters of bacon and eggs, gigantic cups of coffee, mountains of toast and jam, pitchers of thick wrinkled cream. His first savage hunger satisfied, he liked to look out upon the smooth lawns, now bronze with autumn, and watch the distant street.

He was mildly interested when a station cab drew up near the carriage stone and discharged a sleek broad figure of a middle-aged man; there was something vaguely familiar about that figure, he thought, as the owner marched solidly up the walk toward the house. He moved the curtain a trifle: he must have seen the man in newspapers. Yes, that was it. Photograph of whom? After a puzzled moment, the Bishop rose with a gasp, wildly rang his bell, mopped his face with a napkin.

Within five minutes Ernest Barbour was seated across from the Bishop at the laden breakfast table; fresh platters of bacon and eggs were appearing, fresh cups of coffee, another pitcher of thick clotted cream. "I should have been a priest," said Ernest, breaking a golden-orange egg with a silver fork.

It was the pleasantest, and the most filling, of breakfasts. The Bishop was very gay, full of ruby laughter, sly jokes. He had a habit of poking his companion with the blunt end of his knife or fork, to point a witticism. A dozen times he expressed his pleasure at this surprise visit. "It's been years!" he exclaimed reproachfully. Now, what the devil does he want? he asked himself. I'll wager it's something unholy. When Satan visits a priest he doesn't come as a penitent. But Ernest spoke of nothing except the Bishop's unchanged appearance, comfortable circumstances, happy table. And I'll also wager, continued the Bishop to himself, that this visit bodes no good for some poor wretch.

After the breakfast they went into the study. Ernest joined his host in a glass of wine and an excellent cigar. "One thing I like about the Papists," said Ernest frankly, "is that there is no sanctimonious nonsense about them. They recognize the truth about human nature, and, for the sake of the immortal soul, will allow a few minor sins."

"That is why the Church will still be standing when all your Protestant little churches will have murdered each other," replied the Bishop. "Protestantism forgets that men are men, and that there are appetites that it is better to wink at, provided that certain duties are observed. We don't strain at a gnat and swallow a camel, nor swim in an ocean and drown in a puddle."

They smoked contentedly for a moment or two, then the Bishop, closely observing the fine gray ash accumulating at the end of his cigar, said: "Of course, you did not seek me out at this late day, Mr. Barbour, for a mere social visit. I do not underestimate you that much. Now, I expect to spend the next few hours very pleasantly with you; so, suppose we come down to business and you tell me just why you have come? Then, that over, we can continue our visit."

Ernest laughed so heartily that he displayed almost all of his well-preserved white teeth. He liked the direct approach as much as ever. So, without preliminaries, he said: "Have you been in communication at all with the Bouchard branches of our family?"

"Yes." The Bishop seemed faintly surprised. "Mr. Eugene Bouchard is very charitable—lately. In the past he has been quite thrifty, but lately he has been more than kind. Let me see: it is only six months ago that he visited me here, and we had a pleasant visit. He brought three of his children. Etienne? Honore? Renee? Yes. I could wish for a little more devotion, according to the reports of Father Regan, in Windsor, from the Raoul Bouchard branch, but of course, there are circumstances. However, I have had hopes for young Philippe Bouchard. Several years ago he came here to me, as he had heard I was an old friend of the family. He said it was his intention to study for the priesthood, and when I examined him it did seem to me that he had a vocation. Of course, he was very, very young at that time, hardly more than a boy. Surely he is not more than twenty or so, now? He wrote me regularly for years, and I had high reports of him from the priest. After all, the Bouchard family is very prominent," went on the Bishop candidly. "So, I followed all their activities with interest. But for the past year or so young Bouchard has not followed up our correspondence, and Father Regan says that he has not seen him at Mass for some time. He investigated, left messages, but it appears that the boy has avoided him." Interest sharpened on the Bishop's fat face. "Is it possible you can tell me why?"

Ernest carefully put the tips of his fingers together.

"I don't know. But isn't it a rule in your Church that cousins may not marry—first cousins?"

"Yes." There was a silence, while comprehension, cynical and acrid, began to gleam in the Bishop's eyes. "You have a daughter, Mr. Barbour, and our young Philippe wishes to marry her?"

"Precisely. And I don't wish him to marry her."

The Bishop was silent.

"Oh, I've nothing against the boy, personally," went on Ernest with a broad-minded gesture. "After all, he is my nephew. But I have other plans for Gertrude. Besides, I don't approve of marriages between cousins——"

The Bishop looked at him directly, and now there was no amusement in him.

"Didn't I hear a rumor that your daughter was to marry your dead brother's son, Mr. Barbour?"

There was the smallest pause. "Yes," said Ernest blandly. Their eyes met and held. Then the Bishop turned just a little aside.

"I see," he murmured. He tapped his fingers thoughtfully on the table. "I am disappointed in the Barbour branch of your family, your brother's branch. He was a devoted Catholic, and his children were baptized in the Church. However, they have drifted away. Laws of the Church would never affect them, I know. It is very sad." His big florid head bent a little. "What did you expect of me, Mr. Barbour?"

Ernest answered readily, and coolly: "I think it would be well to recall young Philippe's duty to him. As you say, he was once an ardent Catholic. And probably is, still, at heart. If he marries Gertrude, he will eventually be very unhappy, after the first excitement, remembering he has 'sinned.' He will make Gertrude unhappy, too. But I'll be frank with you. That is not the real reason I want this marriage stopped. I have other plans for my daughter."

"So you enlist religion on your side? Isn't that a strange ally for you, Mr. Barbour?"

Ernest smiled. "I've heard of worse allies," he answered evasively.

The Bishop stared at him without disguise or apology for a long moment. I wonder what men of his kind think? he asked himself. I expect their thoughts would make unusual reading in the literature of Hell. He felt a little sick. Finally he stood up, stout and impressive in his clerical black, and his face was not friendly, but remote and sad. Ernest had to rise also, irritably aware that something in this priest repudiated him, reduced him to an insignificant stature.

"I'll write to young Philippe," said the Bishop, "and ask him to see me. He will come, I know. I'll do what I can to bring him back to Mother Church, and show him his duty. But not for your sake, Mr. Barbour! Not for your sake! This is a matter between Philippe and his God. You have nothing to do with it."

Bitter fire had flashed into the fat old man's eyes, and his heavy pendulous lips shook with some obscure passion. But Ernest guessed that that passion was more human than divine. There was an awkward pause. It had been Ernest's intention to invite the Bishop to join him in a remarkably fine dinner at his hotel, and to spend a few pleasant hours with him. But even he did not have the effrontery to offer this invitation now.

They parted coldly, and with embarrassed ceremony. Three days later Ernest sent a check for a startling amount to the Bishop, "my belated contribution to your many worthy charities."

And three days later Ernest received a formal letter from the Bishop thanking him for the check. "I know," he had written, "that you will be pleased to hear that your money will be used in our Missions to the lepers."

CHAPTER LXXI

FLORABELLE WAS in the midst of a dishevelled attempt to settle a dispute between the hysterical François and his governess, when Gertrude Barbour was announced.

"Oh dear, oh dear!" exclaimed the frantic and upset Florabelle, giving François an agitated push, and immediately goading him to fresh screams and stampings. The governess, a prim Irish girl who had "served the gentry in England," raised her eyebrows, folded her hands on her dark-blue lap, and assumed a suffering expression. Gertrude, rosy and dark, furred richly against the chill autumn winds, came into the little sitting room as onto a scene of explosions, confusions, and disaster. François was shrilly screaming, and Florabelle was alternately slapping him and trying to soothe him. Though he was eleven years old, he appeared much younger, due to his slight body and small stature, but the brown little wizened face was, in spite of the tears and cries, not young at all. The little sitting room had not been tidied as yet, though it was almost noon of a Sunday morning, nor had the shades been opened to admit the bronze sunlight. Candles burned on the disordered small tables and on the mantelpiece, and books, papers and trinkets lay scattered about in the utmost confusion. A great fire roared behind polished bars, making the dark room uncomfortably warm.

"Oh, there you are, Gertrude!" ejaculated the harassed Florabelle, glancing over her shoulder at her niece. "Dear me, do find a chair! What a time to come—! I'm sure if I had expected you—! Is something wrong? You must pardon this mess, with François and all, refusing to eat in the nursery with the little ones, because he thinks he is too old now, and kicking Miss Callahan in the shins—! Do sit down, Gertrude, and stop looking so lost. Is that a new seal jacket? You are looking well. Will you have coffee? We've just been having some, the Major and me, but he's gone out to see if the new mare— François! Will you stop pulling my ribbons?" added Florabelle with a shout and a resounding slap. François obliged by a kick and a shriek. His exhausted mother burst into tears. She looked very young sitting there in her light rose peignoir, her fair curls falling over her plump shoulders. Her face, though cross just now, was flushed and fresh, and her blue eyes were as unblemished as a child's.

"My God, take him out and smother him!" she cried, utterly overcome, and Miss Callahan, thus given authority to do as she would like to do with François, boxed his ears with ardor, looking, as she did so, as though she had done something which was good for her soul, seized the scrawny arm of the little boy in no mean grip, and hauled him, struggling and kicking, out of the room. His screams ran like tattered streamers behind him, became fainter and fainter as he was dragged upstairs, and were reduced to inaudibility by the closing of a door.

"Gracious, did you ever see such a fiendish child!" cried Florabelle, wiping her eyes and shaking her head. "I can do nothing with him. No one can do anything with him except Philippe. The Major is such a coward; he always runs. But, you didn't tell me if that is a new jacket? I can't say that black becomes you so much, with your sallow skin, Trudie, and your hair. Why on earth doesn't your Mama take you to Dr. Brewster? He's doing wonders in building up young ladies who are too thin; iron and such. You look as if you are about to go into a decline. Will you have some coffee?"

"No, thank you, Aunt Florrie," replied Gertrude in a soft voice. "Where's Philippe?" she asked.

"Philippe? He's out in the stables with the Major. The new mare isn't doing so well. She's about to foal," added the forthright Florabelle, who called reticences in the presence of unmarried young ladies "stuff."

The bronze sunlight had disappeared, and had taken with it all the warm browns, the golds and the scarlets, of the land, leaving an earth robbed of color, and desolate. A hollow silence lay over everything; when a horse neighed, or a dog barked, the sounds had an unreal and dreamlike quality. The house and the stables seemed gray and unsubstantial, and the ground, when walked upon, showed a white and broken frost-glaze, crackling underfoot. Houses and trees in the distance were hung like darker shadows in a vague mist, and near at hand the trees showed naked and twisted boughs painted with the bright glisten of frost. The air was cold, yet damp, and one's breath floated near at hand, like a small cloud.

Gertrude ran over the frozen earth, her narrow small black boots leaving little white tracks behind. She picked up her dark red skirts as she ran; the seal jacket blew back under her arms, and her hair, loosened, was like soft smoke about her ardent young face. She peered in the carriage house; no one was there. She heard Philippe's voice in friendly altercation with a groom, and went toward the stables. She found him there, demonstrating to a newly hired stable boy the proper way to curry a horse. He was coatless and hatless, his white shirt sleeves rolled up; he was currying the horse with vigor, and the boy stood idly by, watching with assumed interest.

"Philippe," said Gertrude, entering the stable. The youth swung about swiftly, and at the sight of Gertrude his dark lean face sprang into life and joy. "Trudie!" He dropped the currycomb, seized her hands, and looked at her with delight and amazement. The stable boy, interested now, gaped.

They went outside, went behind the stables, where they could be alone with only the desolate autumn garden around them. They went instantly into each other's arms. Philippe pressed his warm palms to Gertrude's cheeks, looked down with passionate eyes into hers, tenderly kissed her parted lips. They could not speak for a few moments; they could only hold each other, smile, cling together. A great content and happiness gathered in them, a sense of completion. Philippe's eyes, usually so intensely dark, had warmed to a deep and lustrous brown, shining with tenderness, and he held Gertrude against him almost fiercely.

"My sweet, my sweet," he said, tilting up her chin so that he could kiss her again and again, over and over.

"Philippe, darling, I've got such good news," Gertrude was able to say after a few more minutes. She began to cry, laughing and smiling through her tears. "Papa called me into the library last night, and do you know what he said? He said that if you and I still thought we loved each other after three more months, we could marry with his consent! Isn't it marvellous? Oh, I've never been so happy!"

Philippe was astonished, overwhelmed with joy. He held Gertrude off from him, so he could look unbelievingly at her. "Is it possible? He meant it? Gertrude—thank God! I—I can hardly believe it. Everything smoothing itself out so, after all our worries. It doesn't seem quite right, to have things happen so easily. Why, Trudie, do you realize how happy we'll be, planning openly, and waiting just a little while longer, after all these years—" He stopped abruptly, and in a strained voice added: "It seems too easy. All of a sudden, it seems—ominous. Things don't happen like that. Not when they're connected with your father. Forgive me, sweetheart," as fear and apprehension flashed into her face, "but it doesn't sound like your father. He was so set on your marrying Paul. He doesn't give up that easily. Are you certain you understood him?"

"Yes, Philippe! He did say that. Oh, now you've frightened me," and the agitated girl, already overwrought, burst into stark tears. Her thin shoulders became convulsed, and she regarded him piteously and with terror.

He was instantly upset and remorseful. "Trudie, dearest, forgive me. How could I say anything like that? It was actually—vicious. But it was so sudden. Why, only last Monday night, when he and your Mama called on us, he gave me a look that curdled my blood, and every remark that he said that night seemed directed at me, and sharp as hatred. He can be the nastiest of any man I ever saw. He sat there and talked constantly of Paul's superiority in every way to every young fellow in

Windsor, and hinted what he was going to do for him, and sneered at me obliquely until even poor Mama uneasily guessed there was an undercurrent. And I got colder and colder and sicker and sicker, because of you, Trudie, and seeing the way he hated me, and I remembered what a simple old nun had told me when I was a little shaver—about hate being a real poison that could injure the person you hated, or a sort of lightning that could burn up his blood. I really became quite afraid, and felt dead with hopelessness. I saw he thought I was standing in Paul's way, and he was so set on Paul. And then all of a sudden you tell me he has relented, and is quite willing for us to marry——"

"But Philippe, he is!" Gertrude's vehement cry was as much to reassure herself as to reassure Philippe, for a cold ring had begun to tighten about her heart, strangling it. "He said so. You can't mistake what Papa says. He's never ambiguous. He means what he says. Besides, he wouldn't hurt me with a lie. He—he was gentle when he told me, and kissed me, and looked a little sad, when I cried and laughed together. And then, I was so excited, and felt so loving toward him, that I kissed his hand—it was around my neck—and he jumped when I kissed it. And then he kissed me, and said, over and over: 'Remember, I always want your real happiness, Trudie, my darling. Always remember that, whatever happens. No matter what you might think, your happiness is first with me.'"

"It doesn't seem possible," marvelled Philippe. He looked down into her pale pinched face and eager mouth, and was full of remorse and tenderness. "I'm always saying the wrong thing, sweetheart, aren't I? I'm always so careful about accepting things too quickly; that's the French in me. But I believe now; I believe it is all right." He lifted her hands (such little cold hands! he thought) and kissed them. She pressed them to his lips as if to draw his warmth into her shivering body, and smiled so tremulously.

"It is all right, Philippe. Please believe it." Her eyes widened, became intense and strained. "Why, if it wasn't all right, I'd die. I'd die!"

In the library in the Sessions house, Ernest paced restlessly and gloomily to and fro. He could not rest. He stopped, started again, paced endlessly. The great door opened noiselessly, and May entered. He regarded her somberly, without speaking. And she stood there quietly, watching him for a long moment before she spoke. When she did it was in a quiet yet penetrating voice.

"Ernest, I've been married to you for twenty-three years, and I don't know anything about you. I've never known what you were thinking, not one single solitary thought. Trudie came to me last night, and told me what you had said to her. She was almost crazed with joy, poor child."

Ernest turned his back to his wife, and stared through the window. She advanced a step; her hands were clenched together before her, and there was a strange expression on her middle-aged face, which still retained its girlhood dimple.

"Ernest, I thought I'd done all I could do when I locked my door against you. But I realize now that I can do more." Her voice rose, become loud and portentous. "Ernest, if you hurt Gertrude, if you break her heart, I'll leave you. One roof will never cover us again. Either you will leave this house, my house, or I will."

When he finally turned around, she was gone.

Ernest picked up a newspaper he had been reading. There was an important little announcement bracketed on the front page: "We are glad to inform our readers that Bishop Aloysius Dominick of the Philadelphia diocese of the Roman Catholic Church, is to visit our city within the next few days. He is well remembered and loved by our Catholic readers, and even our Protestant readers will recall him as Father Dominick, pastor of the Church of the Annunciation, this city."

CHAPTER LXXII

FLORABELLE NORWOOD was exceedingly indignant when Ernest attempted to impress upon her most forcibly that there was really no official engagement between his daughter and her son. There was to be a three-month trial period, in which the young people were to consider all phases of the situation, to look at other girls and youths of their acquaintance, to judge each other deliberately, not to monopolize each other exclusively, but to attend all parties to which they were invited where they would meet their contemporaries, and to retain, in public at least, a merely cousinly relationship.

Florabelle professed to be insulted, and it was only after prolonged kindly and tolerant reasoning on the part of the Major that she finally acknowledged that Ernest might be showing common sense. "After all," she admitted, "Ernest was quite right in saying that perhaps Philippe was a little young to know his own mind; boys are always younger than girls. Though I have come to love Trudie like a daughter, and just couldn't think of any one else for Philippe. She is getting to be quite passable; a little more flesh here and there, and brighter clothes (her mother does dress her so spinsterish) and she would be rather distinguée. Never pretty, of course, with that skin and that perfectly lustreless hair, and sharp shoulders, and those funny, sort of bewildered gestures of hers, but in time she would be rather fascinating, as so many plain women are."

Ernest held his daughter strictly to her part of the bargain. He would have felt less uneasy had she shown a little disinclination, but she obeyed him with such radiance, such joyful alacrity, that he began to avoid her, and a bluish pinched expression appeared about his nose. She was amiable and gay to Paul, who had been taken into the secret by Ernest, and went with him to many of the early winter parties of their friends. Paul had been warned by his uncle not to speak of marriage, or even affection, to Gertrude, but at all times to exert himself to be charming and gentle, unexigent yet unobtrusively always at hand. "In other words, old-fashioned words, woo the child," said Ernest. Paul, who had the wiliness of a real love, followed instructions, and Gertrude found, to her conscience-stricken astonishment, that Paul was not at all bad, and at times a pleasant and interesting companion. He was always sympathetic, never demanding, yet maintaining a virile independence which prevented him from being servile, and caused her to respect him. Heretofore he had imposed, or tried to impose, all his demands and opinions and beliefs upon her; now he listened, and discovered how delightful, how enlightening it was, to listen when a beloved woman talked freely to one without reticence or fear. His assumed gentleness became sincere; he cultivated to its full extent his very slight sense of humor, and even made a few witty remarks, which Gertrude found entertaining. As Ernest had restricted her days and evenings with Philippe to two or three a week, she would have been lonely, and would have spent the empty hours in thinking about Philippe and brooding, if it had not been for the adroit and quite casual visits of Paul. After a lonely and dissatisfied day, Gertrude was quite surprised at the pleasure and relief she felt when Paul "unexpectedly" called in the evening, with various exciting suggestions about theatres and rides and visits to informal parties. His suggestions were always offhand; he had abandoned his old possessive and stringent attitude. When they attended dances together at the homes of friends, he was careful not to ask for more than one or two, leaving Gertrude to fill her program as she wished. Sometimes she would not see more of him than a distant glimpse, flirting with other girls, for the entire evening.

Once or twice, half apologetically, half archly, she hinted of her "understanding" with Philippe. Paul seemed quite sympathetic, said something light and easy, and changed the subject. He appeared entirely disinterested. "Paul," Gertrude told her parents, "is evidently taken by Belinda Lansbury; he does nothing but dance attendance on her at every party."

"He could do worse than Miss Belinda," said Ernest. But May said nothing. She only watched. And as she watched, some cold and deadly suspicion began to grow in her that her husband was playing a game, and Paul with him. What the game was she did not know, but she was alert, fearful and militant. But, she told herself, it was like watching in a dark forest, not knowing what tree hid the enemy.

In the meantime she herself had other worries. Godfrey's letters from Paris were becoming fewer, and those few sounded constrained, incoherent. Once or twice he would fill pages with wild assurances of his love for his mother, his promises, vehement and passionate, that she would not be disappointed in him, and that he was sure she would always "understand." The next letter would be short and cold, merely acknowledging checks, or commenting on the weather, or repeating that he would try to be home for Christmas. Again, May felt that she was surrounded by dark trees and jungles, utterly confused, yet conscious of menace. Reginald, fortunately, was having good, if reserved, reports sent home; his letters were always ceremonious and correct, yet lifeless. He never mentioned friends; it was evident that he had none even in that gay and social University. He never forgot to send his love to each member of the family in turn. "Copybook sentiments," sneered Ernest. Guy wrote home, gay, effervescent letters, mostly "dunning" his mother for small extra sums of money; he was witty and sprightly, and seemed to May, who still had a high regard for laughter and the bright virtues attendant on it, to be the most intelligent of her children. She was of the firm opinion, and perhaps rightly, that no one with a sense of humor is a fool, and that while many excellent people did not possess this endowment, the majority without it were dolts, and dangerous to society. However, she would have liked to have had a few good reports from Guy's school, instead of the reserved notes from the headmaster, if only to placate Ernest, who was certain that Guy was a "wastrel." Too, she was worried about Joey, who was a secretive, though not sly, boy. It was painfully evident that his love for his mother was more than indifferent, and that he worshipped his father. He would look at May, when she spoke on even the most casual subjects, with a sidelong knowing expression and the slightest and most faintly contemptuous of smiles. He had nothing to say to her; he avoided her. Big and heavy-bodied, small and sharp of light eye, obstinate and ponderous, tenacious and dogged, bad-tempered and sullen, he caused his mother many heavy-hearted hours. It was so evident that he thought her trivial and unimportant, and found her gentle lectures, to the effect that while money was very good it was not the supremest good, rather puerile. He moved among the members of his family, deliberately unaware of them, never asking about the absent ones nor making himself agreeable to his sister, and becoming alive only when his father was with him. It was becoming more and more obvious that he really hated Gertrude, because of Ernest's attachment for her, and he sometimes would not speak to her for days, though passing her in halls and meeting her at the table.

Sometimes May, sighing, would think: "If I had only had Godfrey! How happy I would have been. Or Godfrey and Guy. But how much happier I would have been if I had never had any children at all! Not one of us, Amy, Florabelle, Dorcas or myself, has had any real joy from our children. In spite of the sentimentalists, children are no comfort in grief, no companions in loneliness, no consolers in illness, no hope for the future. Flesh of our flesh, they are often stranger to us than any real stranger, and become our enemies."

But knowing this, she could not free herself from her anxieties, her exhausted alertness, her love and worry and great fear for all her children.

CHAPTER LXXIII

IT WAS two days before Thanksgiving. The weather had been very inclement, snowing one day, sleeting the next, raining the next. It seemed that the sun had not shone for weeks. Everyone was affected by the atmospheric depression, and went about gloomily and lifelessly.

May, who was expecting a visit from Florabelle, had dressed herself in a fine new gown of black wool trimmed with black velvet, and elaborately draped. Her gray curling hair, with dark bright stains of red shading into it, was piled high and frizzed over her forehead in the latest fashion. She wore her grandmother's old garnets set in ancient gold, and the deep dim fire sparkled against her ears and at her throat. She fixed an expression of good temper and serene amiability upon her plump dimpled face, which sagged at the chin and the lower areas of her cheeks. Dressed in her best, jewelled and faintly perfumed, she had considered this a duty she owed to her family because of the dreariness of the weather. "You all have such bad manners," she complained to her gloomy husband and lifeless daughter and sulky young son. "You leave it to me to keep this house from being a morgue."

Joe was tinkering with something in a remote attic. "Probably counting his miserly savings," said Gertrude, somewhat spitefully. Gertrude, in dark green velvet, which did not enliven her colorless face in the least, sat near the window where she could command a view of the rain-drenched, dead-leaf-cluttered, drive. Everything seemed to weep, the skies, the brown soaked earth, the empty trees.

"Dear me, Trudie, you are very disagreeable today," said May, who was busily crocheting lace. "Do come away from that chilly window and sit near this delightful fire. You look so wan and tragic."

"I feel tragic," said Gertrude miserably.

May smiled; Gertrude did not see that smile, or she would have been surprised at the irony and sadness and bitterness of it.

"Tragedies aren't external and apart from life, Trudie," May went on gently. "They aren't visitations. They're part of living, just as the pleasures are. And most of the time they don't even disrupt life for very long. We learn, eventually, to receive tragedy like an inevitable and permanent guest, make a place for it in our living, adjust ourselves to it, compromise with it, and then go on, quite calmly, quite accustomed to what once seemed impossible to bear."

"Oh, you make me hopeless with such resigned talk!" cried Gertrude passionately. "It's—so dead, so—so awfully *old!* Like not fighting, because you are a coward or not young any more. I—I'd *never* accept tragedy; I'd die fighting it! I just *won't* make room for it, or even acknowledge that it can exist in my life—" She broke off, her face wild with despair and fear.

"Dear me, how unnecessarily vehement you are, Trudie." May glanced at the agitated girl mildly. "And how absolutely ignorant. I suppose all this excitement is just because Philippe didn't call last night. Heavens, just because he misses coming one Wednesday night, no doubt because of the perfectly terrible sleet storm we had, so dangerous to horses and carriages and even to walkers, you begin to act like a tragedy queen. In a few minutes your Aunt Florrie will be here with a perfectly common sense explanation, if she even remembers there needs to be one. After all, you must remember how it was last night. I'm sure I wouldn't have wanted my worst enemy to be out in it."

As if driven to look for comfort, Gertrude came toward the fire. She seemed much shaken, and there were humble tears in her eyes as she regarded her mother eagerly. "Mama, perhaps I am a fool. Perhaps you are right. Of course, it was so awful that Philippe had better sense than I have, and decided to stay home. But somehow," and she wrung her small thin hands together, "I've been so afraid lately! It's been like a cloud over me. Being afraid. Like waiting for something dreadful to happen, that will kill me inside, even if I don't die outside."

May lifted her head sharply and gazed at her daughter. After a moment she said, very gently, though her throat dried in speaking: "You mustn't be fanciful, darling. The weather has been so bad that it has depressed all of us. Every time I hear the doorbell ring I'm certain it is a herald of disaster. But I try to be cheerful." She smiled, a little fixedly. "It is our duty not to be overcome by weather. A duty we owe others who have no regard for manners."

Gertrude huddled her slight body on a big chair near the fire. She shivered visibly, pushed back her hair. "Dear Mama," she murmured, with a ghost of a smile, "you believe good manners overcome every evil under the sun, don't you?"

"I'm sure they make all evils more bearable," replied May, laughing. "But aren't those carriage wheels I hear outside?"

In a few moments, Florabelle, accompanied by the wizened and gnome-like François, came into the room. She was all ribbons and furs and bangles and chains and curls, all agitated gloved hands, lifted eyes, exclamations and heavy perfume. "What perfectly horrible weather! Darling Trudie, kiss your auntie! May, you look like a grand old dame in that black wool and velvet—so distinguished! I brought François— do you mind? I hope not, for I couldn't leave the house without him.

Such a nuisance, crying and screaming, pretending he has such an affection for me all of a sudden, when all the time he didn't want to stay in the nursery with Chandler and Betsy. But I can't do a thing with him! There now," she cried, seizing on the silent little boy and tugging his clothes into place, "do stay neat and run upstairs to your dear little cousin Joey. Where's Joey, May?"

"In the attic. He's in a bad mood today though, Florabelle. I'm not sure that little Frank will be welcome. However, go on up, my dear, and see. And if your cousin is rude, just come down again here to us." She laid her hand for a moment very kindly on the boy's shoulder, and he smiled his strange and twisted smile. He was very fond of May, and she always felt compassionate toward him.

Moaning a little, Florabelle allowed the maid to carry away her astrakhan jacket, muff and hat. She stood revealed in a gay bright blue gown, elaborately puffed and gathered and draped, with lace cuffs and deep lace collar. Her curls were piled high, and cascaded down very fashionably about her cheeks, which were rich with color. When she moved she tinkled faintly, and her bangles clashed. Unrestricted now by the jacket, the perfume eddied from her in almost visible waves. She stood before the fire, preening and smiling and rubbing her short plump fingers.

"What a pretty gown," said May. "I haven't seen it before. Is it new? I thought so. And how very becoming, with your hair and eyes and complexion."

"I like color," replied Florabelle complacently. She shook out a flounce. "It's so enlivening. I can't understand why Trudie wears such dull old-maidish things."

"Perhaps it's because I'm a dull, old-maidish person," said Gertrude, with a faint smile.

"Well, I always thought you were a born little spinster," Florabelle informed her candidly. "You never did seem to have the beaux I had when I was a girl. Gracious, the house used to swarm with them whenever I came home from school! Dear Papa used to say that he fell over young gentlemen whenever he turned around suddenly. I had a dreadful time at cotillions—absolutely crushed. I could never wear a ball gown more than once or twice. Just a wreck afterwards. And the brothers of the girls at school were just too impossible! The headmistress often said, because of the boys' visits to their sisters, that it was looking more like a young gentlemen's school instead of a young ladies'."

She laughed and sat down. And immediately broke out into renewed exclamations. "Do you know those new horrible Grimshaws, May? The ones from Pittsburgh—new-rich? Well, they are positively too impossible. Climbers. Dreadful people, really, pushing into everything. They think that because they made a few million dollars in that ghastly

Pittsburgh they can come here to little Windsor, which is so exclusive, and simply *force* themselves upon our notice. I've received three elaborate invitations during the past month, and of course, just ignored them. Nobody at all will have anything to do with these people. You know, they built that frightful place in Mayfair, thinking if they pushed their way into a fashionable suburb it would help them into society. But nobody sees them or visits them or looks at them."

"How lonely it must be for them, poor things," murmured May. She regarded her sister-in-law with an ironical gleam in an eye that could still dance.

"Lonely? But they deserve it, May! How tiresome you can be. Who cares if they are lonely? They ought to stay with their own class. That is just the trouble with America——"

"Yes, we do see odd families coming into society these days," said May serenely. "I remember how tight our set was when I was a little girl. We allowed no families who had become rich recently to enter our houses. No tradespeople. But it was very silly. And ignorant. We must have been a little comical, with our airs and graces and exclusiveness."

"How you do run on, May," said Florabelle pettishly. "But we simply can't have nobodies, rich nobodies, and so vulgar, pushing into society."

She continued to rattle on with great vivacity, reducing her audience, finally, to complete silence. May crocheted placidly, occupied with her own thoughts, occasionally coming to the surface to smile amusedly at Florabelle and to murmur something inaudible. Gertrude sat and waited, her hands clenched on her thin knee, the veins beating in her throat. But she was more at ease. If anything had gone wrong with Philippe, this gushing well would have flooded forth the information long ago. She stared at the golden fire restlessly, building pictures among the coals that covered the flame with a black fretwork.

All at once the sound of a name brought her abruptly upright.

"And as for François," Florabelle was sighing, "he is such an odd child. Sometimes I think he will never be able to go into things like Philippe and Leon. But none of my children are strong, except Chandler and Betsy. Sometimes I don't think my dearest Raoul would have lived long even if he hadn't gone to war. Now weather never bothers me, but Philippe is feeling so badly today that he didn't even come downstairs to breakfast or luncheon."

"Philippe ill?" Gertrude's voice sounded as though it had been squeezed in pain from her throat. May put down her knitting and looked concerned.

Florabelle lifted her eyes despairingly. "Ill? I suppose so. A small cold, but it always seems to make him sick for days. But I warned him last night, knowing he isn't very strong, not to go out in that sleet."

Gertrude could not speak; she could only gaze at her aunt.

May bent over her needle as if intent. "We rather expected Philippe ourselves last night," she said, "but concluded when he didn't come that the weather was too bad. How foolish of him to go out. Unless it was very important." Not in the very slightest were her last words raised as if in question.

"Important?" Florabelle was a trifle shrill with ridicule. "*We* didn't consider it important. It is really too bad that I gave in to dearest Raoul and had the children baptized Papists. But I was so young at that time, and so much in love. No one will ever know how much I loved Raoul. He was my life! Why, when I got that awful telegram, I thought I'd die, too. Everything went black and dim, and I said to myself: 'I'm dying. Raoul is dead, and I am dying, too.' And I was so glad. But time heals all things, they say, and I'm not unhappy now. The Major is one of God's gentlemen. I tell you, May, no woman could ask for a finer husband, so considerate, so kind, so protective. And he treats me like a daughter! Of course, it's foolish, but I must admit——"

"What," said May in a gentle but incisive voice, "has the fact that the children were baptized Catholics got to do with Philippe going out in the sleet last night and taking cold?"

Florabelle felt as though she had received a shock. She blinked confusedly at May, her mouth opening in its childlike, somewhat stupid manner. "What? Going out in the sleet? Dear me, May, you do jump from subject to subject! Really, it's quite disconcerting. I always believe in following a conversation to the end, not jumping around like a frog in a puddle of words. Out in the sleet? Oh, yes. I wish you'd let me finish what I was saying about Philippe. Well, as you probably know, that tiresome priest or bishop who used to live in Windsor but now lives in Philadelphia (though Heaven knows what he would want to come back here for, even for a visit, after Philadelphia), is staying with the present priest of the Annunciation Church. He was a great friend of the family; wasn't his name Dominick? At any rate he married Raoul and me, and baptized the children. Silly, I thought it, but I was so much in love! Well, he is here, and he wrote a very polite little note to me, recalling himself to my memory—really the most civil and elegant note—I never thought priests were schooled in gentlemanly language, but this one was exceptional. He also mentioned that he had been much interested years ago in Philippe, and that he would like to see him as soon as possible. He mentioned last night, and suggested that Philippe call on him, saying it was quite important. Now what on earth could he want to say to Philippe that was important? Philippe used to be so devout, always running to church on Sunday—for Mass or something barbaric like that, though I don't exactly know what Masses are. Really, he used to drive me frantic, running out at six or seven in the morning, sometimes every day. He used to make something he called Novenas, too—so silly. Once he even said that he would be a priest. (It's a pity Papa didn't live to hear that! And it's a wonder he didn't turn over in his grave, anyway. Papa hated the Papists so.) But Philippe got over that." She smiled at Gertrude archly. "I think we have dear Trudie to thank for that! But dear me, child, what an extraordinary color you are! Like clay. I don't approve of this immoral rouge so many woman are using these days, but I do think just a touch— Gracious, I hope you are quite healthy, Trudie. I wouldn't want Philippe to be burdened with a sickly wife."

"So," said May, clearly and quietly, "Philippe went to call upon Bishop Dominick last night, in the sleet." To herself she said: Oh, may God never forgive you, Ernest Barbour! May God never forgive you!

"Yes. Please don't interrupt, dearest May. It is so tedious. He went out, though the Major and I laughed at him and warned him. But he was determined on it. And he was looking so badly even then, so pale and sort of set. I remarked on his appearance, and pointed out that he ought not to go, in that awful weather. But he went. He was gone such a long time. I waited up for him. And when he returned, he looked worse than ever. A little wild and breathless, and I knew right away that he had taken cold! He could hardly breathe, and when I went to him, very upset, he waved me away, as if he couldn't speak, and ran up the stairs and locked me out. I tapped and tapped, and finally he groaned: 'Mama, *please* leave me alone tonight!' And I knew more than ever, from his hoarseness, that he had a very bad cold. Really, that bishop was positively wicked, inducing the poor boy to go out in the storm, and I've a good mind to give him a piece of my mind, very lady-like of course, but a terse little note——"

Gertrude stood up. She looked about her in a disoriented and frenzied way, as though tortured. "I think, Mama," she said in a high voice, "that I'll run upstairs and see how Joey and François are getting along."

May half started to her feet, the lace slipping from her lap. "Darling," she said, and the word was a cry, full of compassion and suffering. But Gertrude looked about her again, as if trying to orient herself; she put her hand to her cheek in her old, wavering and pathetic gesture. Then turning swiftly, she ran out of the room. May sat down; nausea climbed into her throat.

Florabelle was much concerned. "Is Trudie ill, May? Really, she doesn't look at all strong. Very frail and anæmic. Why don't you take her to Dr. Brewster? Or give her Blaud's Pills? They say they are excellent—create good red blood. It is so necessary to married happiness that the wife be healthy. I wouldn't want Philippe— But you are not looking well, yourself, May. I don't believe you get enough fresh air. Now the Major believes in exercise, even for ladies, and pooh-poohs the idea of it not being very genteel to have rosy cheeks like mine, and we walk for hours, truly hours, every day. Why don't you and Trudie do that, too? It would build up the girl."

She chattered on in a cloud of phrases and exclamations. May no longer crocheted. She sat in stony and rigid silence, staring at the fire. The chatter was like a welcome wall between her and Florabelle, giving her privacy. Once or twice her pale lips moved, as if in imprecation or pain. She had no knowledge of time or of any one but herself in that room.

All at once Florabelle jumped up animatedly. "Dear me, it's almost five o'clock! No, never mind tea, May dearest, though I must say you have never been this forgetful before. I've always said you would remember decorum even on your deathbed. Gracious, how dark it is getting! And where is Trudie? She has been gone almost an hour."

The clock chimed a slow and melodious five. May regarded it, stupefied. Then she jumped up with the swiftness of a young girl, and without a word to the surprised Florabelle, she ran out into the hall after ringing the bell for the maid. She met the girl in the hallway. "Miss Trudie—?" she murmured, through a thick and closing throat.

"Yes, ma'am," stammered the maid, frightened at May's face. "But she said it was all right. She said I was to tell you at five o'clock that she had just gone to see a sick friend, and not to worry."

May clutched her arm. "Did she order a carriage?"

"No, ma'am. She said it wasn't far, and not to bother."

May's hand fell from her arm. Florabelle, curious, was peering out into the dim hall. "What is it, May? You look so strange——"

May turned and forced a smile to pale lips. With a wave of her hand she dismissed the maid. "I just remembered something," she said easily, leading Florabelle back into the drawing room. "But it seems that Trudie remembered, and has gone to do it, herself. It's a surprise," she added with an arch lifting of her brows. "I am so forgetful, lately! It is such a comfort to have Trudie about, to remember."

"A surprise?" repeated Florabelle, diverted. "A party?"

"Well, not exactly. You—you'll know about it very soon, I think. If it comes out correctly. As I hope it will. But Trudie didn't wish to disturb us, we were chatting at such a rate. Trudie also has manners," she added, smiling whimsically. She regarded her sister-in-law affectionately. "Florabelle, that is really the most becoming dress! Where did you say you bought it? Well, now, I might have known it wasn't a Windsor product. It simply screams Paris."

"Seventy-five dollars," said Florabelle proudly, turning slowly about to give May every possible view. "I always say it pays to buy good things."

May sent for François. She helped the chattering Florabelle into her jacket, loudly admired its excellence. Will she never go? she thought desperately. But finally Florabelle went in a flutter of words and ribbons and veil and skirts, scolding François constantly as they went out of the house to their carriage. The door closed behind her in a last confusion of messages and hand-waving. May went back to the drawing room. The house lay in deep pre-dinner hush, though the faint rattle of silver could be heard at a distance. May heard Joey's voice upstairs.

For a long time she stood there on the hearth, gazing at the fire. She touched her forehead. It was quite cold and wet. The muscles in her cheek twitched convulsively. Once she put her hand to her breast, and gasped aloud. The clock ticked on, chimed the half hour. May still stood there. The fire began to burn itself out, and the room fell into shadow. She did not light the candles. The clock struck six. And the outer door opened and Ernest came into the house, his greatcoat and hat covered with crystal drops.

May went out into the hall to meet him. Her legs felt stiff and cold. Ernest started to greet her when she appeared, but something in her manner, something in her face, revealed in the dim hall lamplight, made him stop, dead and pale.

"Ernest," she said in a low and terrible voice that broke in the speaking, "Florabelle was here. She told us about Philippe, being called by that bishop who is visiting Windsor." She paused, and her effort to regain her breath ended in a groan. She approached him a step, and he stood there, not moving, only staring at her as at an executioner. "Ernest!" Her voice was a cry, dreadful to hear. "What have you done to our child? She has gone, out of this house, hours ago, after hearing what Florabelle said! What have you done to our child, Ernest Barbour?"

"Trudie? Gone?" he whispered painfully. He took his hat off. His hair gleamed almost white in the lamplight.

"Gone." She seized him by his damp coat. "Where is she?"

He put his arm about her convulsively. "Trudie!" he muttered, looking over her head. "My God! My God!"

She had begun to sob aloud, in a sort of agony. She pushed his arm aside, and fell back from him. "Don't call on God!" she screamed. "Don't dare call on God—you! You—you'll bring a curse down on us, calling on God! You—you monster!"

He stood there and looked at her. His face was in partial darkness, but his eyes had turned to fire. He wet his lips. He flung out his hands. Then, wheeling on his heel, and without another word, he opened the outer door and went out into the drizzling darkness of the night, to look for his daughter.

CHAPTER LXXIV

IT HAD BECOME brownish yellow and smoky, the wet and drifting air, and slow steady rain was falling. Gertrude, wrapped in an old gray cape, voluminous and shabby, the hood pulled over her head, let herself out the back door. She ran through the garden, her boots sinking into the oozing yellow mud; she brushed by the bare hedges, and showers of water splashed over her. Her foot sank deeply into the mud near the birdbath, and she had to stop a moment to release it from the sucking mire. She leaned her hand against the cold wet marble of the bath, and pulled her foot loose. Only then did she become conscious that she was panting, and that every breath hurt her chest. She leaned against the bowl, her head bent and drooping, as though she were faint; her sick eyes followed the jagged black crack in the marble, stared blindly at the white limestone deposit at the bottom. "O God," she said aloud, without passion or vehemence.

She skirted around the garden, followed its slope, opened the fretted iron gate, red and wet with rust, and emerged onto the semi-private road that ran below the Sessions grounds. The house had sunk behind the rise; there was no longer any danger of detection. The slight gray-cloaked figure was more like a wraith than flesh and blood as it skimmed swiftly down the road toward one of the main streets. A scabrous-looking cab with a disconsolate horse stood at the corner, its driver sullenly squatting on his seat, the rain beating down upon him and running from his drooping mustaches. He came to life with a sort of incredulous animation when Gertrude ran up to the cab and began to tug at the door. She got in; he picked up the reins, and the vehicle began to move. "Where to, Miss?" he shouted down at her.

"Ten, Quaker Terrace," she replied, leaning forward. Even through the streaming glass he could see her eyes, enormous and dilated. The cab jogged through the deserted streets, passed wide soggy lawns covered with soaking red and brown leaves, the houses at a distance looking exposed and dreary. Hardly a soul was out, and only an occasional umbrella shone with a wet and livid light as it bobbed down the walk. Here and there a cab splashed by, the horses running with water.

Gertrude sat upon the seat without moving, her hands clenched on her knee. She stared before her, not even blinking. Her mouth was a sharp line of pale violet in a face of clay. The interior of the cab reeked with the odors of rotting old leather, dust, and feed and dampness. She never forgot that sharp and acrid stench; it filled the emptiness in her skull where thoughts ought to have been. But there were no thoughts at all, only the humming emptiness and the smells of the cab. Once or twice she did glance through the window, watched the streets slide moistly by. Once or twice she drew a sharp breath, and held it. But still she could feel nothing. She closed her eyes and fell into a sort of swimming dream.

The cab jarred to a stop. They were standing before Florabelle's house. Gertrude pulled her cloak about her, stepped out of the cab, and paid the driver. She ran up the slimy walk to the house, tugged at the knocker. It echoed with a hollow sound through the dripping quiet. A maid answered, admitted her.

"Is Master Philippe home?" asked Gertrude in a low and breathless voice. She dropped the hood on her shoulders, and water ran from it.

"Why, yes, Miss Gertrude," replied the maid, surprised and puzzled. "But he's ill, in his room. He doesn't want to be disturbed. Shall I tell him you are here?"

Gertrude was silent for a moment. Then she shook her head. "No. I'll go upstairs, myself. Don't disturb him. I—I'll just look in and see how he is. His mother is visiting my mother, and she said he was not feeling well, and that is why I came. If he's asleep, I won't bother him."

She turned, gathered up her rain-soaked skirts, and ran up the stairs to the second floor. When she neared the top, a violent shudder ran over her flesh, and she felt mortally cold. Softly, without a sound, she went down the dark hallway to Philippe's room. The door was shut, and there was silence behind it.

She put her hand on the door handle and stood there in the darkness, holding it, gazing at the door. A long time passed; she distinctly heard the musical chiming of the French clock downstairs in one of the deserted drawing rooms; she heard the rattle of coal as a maid replenished a fire. She heard a faint altercation from the direction of the nursery on the third floor. But from behind the door of Philippe's room she did not hear a sound.

Almost without will, she turned the handle slowly. She could hear the wild and frightful beating of her heart, the throb of it in her throat. The door opened without sound.

The room, where Gertrude had often played with Philippe when they had been children, was full of the dim afternoon. The windows were pale rectangles in the gloom, and she could see the bare arm of the elm outside, like a jagged black bone. All the room was in shadow except for a little table near the white bed; the table was covered by a lace cloth, and on it stood a silver crucifix; before that crucifix burned a single low candle in a red cup. The light rose and fell, striking a chair-arm here, the gilt of a picture there, the glitter of an andiron before the small muttering fire.

But Gertrude saw these things only as accents on agony. For kneeling before the little altar was Philippe.

He knelt, perfectly motionless, his long young body stiff and immobile, his head bent. Gertrude closed the door soundlessly behind her. She ran to the youth, knelt beside him, held his head in her arms, pressed it to her small breast. She knelt there, holding him so, her lips against his forehead, her eyes dry and staring. And the two young creatures clung to each other as if death threatened them.

Finally Philippe moved; Gertrude drew him closer. "Never mind, darling, never mind," she whispered. But he lifted his head, and they looked at each other. Philippe's face seemed to take on age; it had wizened, and was the color of the sky outside. His mouth was bitten, and there were red flecks at the corners. But all his anguish stood in his eyes as he regarded his cousin.

"Trudie. Trudie, dearest." He spoke painfully, in a voice thick and hoarse from exhaustion and suffering.

'Yes, Philippe. I know. I know."

'I've prayed, Trudie. I've prayed so hard. For God to forgive me. But I don't get any answer. Father Dominick—he said it was a sin against Mother Church, that our marriage wouldn't be a marriage in the eyes of the Church, that I would be excommunicated. Thrown out, down to hell. Never allowed to enter the Church again. Lost. Sinning against God, against the Holy Ghost. A mortal sin. And dragging you down with me, Trudie. Down, and down. Ruining you, when I love you so!"

She knelt beside him, her head leaning, now, against his shoulder, holding his hand, so cold and lifeless, against her young breast as if to warm it. And she looked steadily before her at the crucifix and the shining candlelight. She was young and inexperienced, but she knew, profoundly and without words, that before the mysterious power of the gods human speech was only a voice in a wind, and reason itself was a shattered lamp. Humanity was impotent against that power; its fighting arms threshed air, its eyes could not see. But there the power remained, and the blood became water before it. Love, triumphant over life, triumphant even over death, was a torch blown out.

But what am I? she thought. What am I, compared to this torture he is enduring? As long as I am here, as long as I am in the way, he'll never get over it. If we marry, he'll never be happy, never in all the world. We could have been, if that priest had not sent for him; if he had not brought it all back to him. He might even have forgotten, after awhile. Men do forget their gods, in time. But he'll never forget, now.

She put her lips gently to his cold and sunken cheek.

"You are so tired, darling. Do lie down on your bed. And I'll stay right with you. I'll hold your hand. And we won't talk. Not yet, for a little. We'll just be together."

Obediently, he struggled to his feet. He leaned upon her, his legs sagging, as they moved toward the bed. He fell upon it heavily. She removed his boots, and drew a blanket over him, lifted his head to a pillow. The room became darker and darker; the candle fluttered in a draft. But Gertrude sat beside her cousin, holding his hand, and smiling down at him. And slowly his hand became warmer; the eyes that stared so fixedly, so terribly, at her, became dim and soft, began to blink. Finally, they closed; he sighed; turned his head toward her as a child turns to its mother. He slept. His tormented face was at peace.

She bent over him, kissed his forehead, his lips. She kissed his hand, before laying it down. Then she stood up. He moved a little, and his lips opened. She stooped, hoping to hear her name from him. But he only whispered: "God. Jesus. Mary. Forgive me."

The room became darker and darker. Gertrude pulled her hood over her head. The sleeping youth sighed, sighed again, sank deeper into sleep. The candle, as if triumphant, became brighter and stronger, and the crucifix became alive.

Gertrude turned to the altar, and stood looking down at it for a period that seemed endless to her. Then, bending down, she blew out the candle. Philippe stopped sighing, and a profound silence settled like water over the room.

She went out and closed the door behind her.

CHAPTER LXXV

PAUL BARBOUR was just preparing to leave the lonely lighted vastness of the bank when the door of his office opened and Gertrude entered. He was astounded; he regarded her unbelievingly, not able to say a word. She stood there before him, smiling, in the shabby gray cloak and hood that ran rivulets of water. Under the shadow of the hood her face was ghastly.

"You seem surprised to see me, Paul. I suppose you wonder how I got in? Well, I did have quite a time with the watchman at the door, but I finally convinced him I had to see you."

"Trudie!" He had found his voice. "What the devil are you doing here? Is something wrong at home?"

"No." She pushed back the hood; he saw that her hair was disordered under it. He saw all the fine delicate bones under her flesh, as though she had become suddenly emaciated.

"Sit down, Trudie." He was a little grave. "You are not looking very well, my dear. And out in this weather, too. Is it something I can do? I can't help but see that you are very much upset. Will you let me help you?"

She sat down. The smile was hung on her lips as though carved forcibly. He thought her expression a little wild and strange. Pity did not come easily to him, either by nature or deliberate self-training, but he felt a distinct pity for the girl. He stood near her, leaning against his desk, but he did not touch her. She looked up at him, breathing quickly, the wildness increasing on her face. And he regarded her steadily in return, concerned and almost gentle.

She began to speak; her voice was very light and breathless, as if she were trying to inject a little humor into it. Paul had little subtlety of imagination, but as he listened to her voice, he watched her face, and he thought with a thrill like pain that the combination was heartbreaking.

"Paul, you like me, don't you? You wanted to marry me once, didn't you? Perhaps you do, still. It would please Papa very much. Papa likes you, and thinks you quite remarkable. Paul—will you marry me? Now?"

He was electrified. He stood up abruptly, his blue eyes blazing in the glaring gaslight.

"Marry you, Trudie? Do you know what you are saying? Marry you! My God, I've wanted to marry you since I knew there was such a thing as marriage!" His voice broke, incredulously. "But I can't believe it! It seems impossible!" But still he did not touch her, though his tense hands twitched, made futile gestures.

"You may kiss me," she said faintly. And closed her eyes as she lifted her ravaged young face. But he did not kiss her. After a long minute, she opened her eyes and stared at him blankly from sunken sockets. He was gazing at her intensely; his large strong features were working with emotion and understanding.

"Please tell me, Trudie dear," he said gently. He bent over her, took her icy hand and held it in his big warm palms.

She began to smile again, but above her smile the tears flooded out in anguish. She began to speak, with great difficulty. "Paul, perhaps you knew, but Philippe and I were going to be married. You see, I can't lie to you. But now he—he would rather not marry me. I—I think we both discovered at the same time that it would be a mistake. A really awful mistake. I——"

"Why would it have been a mistake, Trudie?" he asked softly. And held her trembling hand more tightly.

She moved her head a little as though tortured. "Well, you see, Paul, it was his religion. About cousins not marrying. He decided he wanted me, anyway, and we talked it over, years ago. It was all settled. And then that—that priest came. He used to be Father Dominick—you remember? He visited your home when we were all children, and before Uncle Martin died in the war. And it all came back to Philippe, that in his Church it was a sin for cousins to marry——"

The high color in Paul's cheeks had receded. He looked at Gertrude penetratingly, and his expression was both grim and grave.

"And so," he said, "he decided not to marry you?"

"No! It wasn't that, Paul! But I decided not to marry him. I couldn't make him so unhappy. I thought it best that I go away, make the decision myself, and then he would have some peace again, and forget——"

He dropped her hand abruptly, turned and walked to a window. He stood there, with his back to her. The light of the room fell out into the darkness and showed the long rods of the steely rain in a circle of bleak illumination. He was horribly shocked. Ernest had not told him this part of their mutual secret. He had merely hinted at some strategy he had in mind that would separate Gertrude and Philippe, and had advised Paul on his behavior and attitude toward the girl until the separation could be arranged. But this is monstrous! thought the young man, shaken as he had never been shaken before. He saw it all clearly, and was really appalled. It did not seem possible to him that any man could be like this, and for the first time he experienced a violent revulsion against his uncle. My God! his outraged thoughts ran on, how could he hurt his own child so? It's inhuman—it's beastlike!

He had a sudden impulse, out of his pity and indignation, to turn to Gertrude, to reveal the whole thing to her, to urge her not to give up Philippe, but to fight for him, against his Church, against himself, against all the mysterious and ominous things that assailed his mind. For the first time in his life he experienced the hot and blinding glow of altruism, of true tenderness and mercy and love. For the first time self was obliterated in that glow, like a shadow.

He actually turned to her, actually opened his mouth to speak. And then his mouth closed. The glow vanished; he was thinking rapidly and clearly once more. Would it be best for Trudie, even if she succeeded? Would it be good for her to marry a man who for one moment could hesitate between her and "superstition"? Didn't that prove him to be a weakling and a fool? Paul, who had never had any faith whatsoever, looked at this manifestation of it with incredulity. It seemed like grotesque folly to him, something out of the Middle Ages, something that smacked of dungeons and martyrs and stakes and sorcerers and in- cantations. A glimmer from a fantastic age when men saw demons and angels, and went on murderous Crusades. He could not orient it with the nineteenth century, with machinery and banks, industry and demo- cratic government, Darwin and railroads, electricity and telegraphs, scientific facts and bonds and explosives and steamships. Horror flashed into his thoughts. He recoiled mentally from a power that seemed unholy and disgusting—a power emanating from the hidden places in men like a dead effluvium, a psychic disease that could destroy and warp and devour its host. Horrible! he thought, more and more appalled. Philippe's not stupid; I've got to admit that. If this Thing can attack people like Philippe, people with education and intelligence, what can't it do to simple folk and children? No wonder Uncle Ernest says that reli- gion must be abolished before men can be free! Paul felt a little giddy; his cold and factual mind was attacked on all sides by a sensation of dis- torted fantasy, of terrible supernatural things in ambush.

Gertrude was sitting where he had left her. Her head had fallen for- ward on her chest; her whole attitude spoke of exhaustion, defenseless- ness. Out of his amazement and repugnance, he said aloud: "But it sounds so impossible, Trudie! Are you certain you quite understood Philippe?"

"Yes." She lifted her head and looked at him steadily, hopelessly.

He was silent again; he chewed the corner of his lip and scowled at the floor. He no longer blamed his uncle; Uncle Ernest was quite right. That fantastic boy was certainly no husband for Gertrude. Trust Uncle Ernest always to be right, even in this! And now nothing stood between him and Gertrude. He could marry her, restore her to health, a normal life and normal love.

He felt a touch on his arm; Gertrude was standing at his side, her hand on his sleeve. "Paul," she said simply, "will you take me away to someone now, and marry me? Tonight? Right away?"

He put his hand over hers and held it tightly against him. "Tonight, Trudie? But doesn't that sound silly? We don't have to elope." He smiled. "I'll take you home now to your Mama, and tomorrow we'll make all arrangements——"

"No! You'll marry me tonight, Paul, or never! Never! I mean it. If you don't marry me right away, I'll go away myself, out of Windsor, right this night." He tried to smile, but when he looked into her eyes he stopped smiling. "Don't you see, Paul, I've got to do this for Philippe? So he'll have peace? So there's no recalling anything, and going over the misery again and again?" She was gasping loudly. "Or have you changed your mind about me? You told me once that you didn't care whether I loved you or not. I don't love you. But if you'll take me away I'll try—I'll try so hard——"

"But Trudie, love, what will your father say?"

"He's always wanted me to marry you, Paul. He won't care. He'll be glad."

"But people like us just don't do these things, child."

"What do I care what we do?" Her voice, her gestures, her manner, were wild and desperate and full of agony. "I'm thinking of Philippe. I'm thinking of tomorrow! I couldn't face tomorrow, hoping there might be a chance, when I know there'll be no chance. And even if there were, making Philippe suffer!" She clutched his sleeve. "Is it because I've offended you, speaking so of him? Hurting your pride? But you've always said you wanted me no matter how. And I've promised you I'll try to love you. You won't regret it; I'll try to forget Philippe. I'll be a good wife." She began to whimper, like a distraught child. "Take me away now, Paul, and marry me."

"All right, Trudie. But let us send for your Papa and Mama. to see us married tonight, if you must have it that way."

"No! I don't want them! I can't stand any more words—I can't stand faces and voices and talk!"

"But this is a mad, mad thing to do! Like a ditch-digger and a housemaid. A sneaking, secret marriage." He was silent for a few moments. "Well, if you must, you must, Trudie. Judge Bainbridge will marry us. God, what will he think when we burst in on him at dinner this way!" He reached for his coat and hat where they lay across his desk. "The newspapers will make a Roman holiday of this."

CHAPTER LXXVI

T HE MARRIAGE did indeed create a furore in the newspapers and among the friends of the Barbour family. May issued formal announcements: "Mr. and Mrs. Ernest Barbour announce the marriage of their daughter, Gertrude, to Mr. Paul Barbour, of this city, her cousin." When the excitement was at its height, with one or two reporters from New York, Boston, Philadelphia and Washington present, the news exploded that Mr. Philippe Bouchard, member of the wealthy Bouchard family, had left for Montreal, Canada, in order to enter a seminary to study for the priesthood.

Rumor had been flying about that both events were cause and effect. Gertrude, the heartless flirt, had jilted one cousin to marry the other. ("Whoever would have thought it!" exclaimed countless friends of the family. "That anæmic plain little thing, with no life in her, no color! Why, we all thought her a born old maid!") But May, with an eye on the prostrated Florabelle, declared that her daughter had never been engaged to Philippe Bouchard, who, by very reason of being a professing Catholic, could not have married his cousin. Fastidious May loathed this necessity of satisfying the hungry dogs of scandal, but upon realizing that it had to be done, did it vigorously. She even called the reporters into the Sessions house, served them coffee and sandwiches and cake, thus flabbergasting and enslaving them, and told them a story in which truth and fiction were dexterously mixed. Gertrude, she said, had been privately engaged to her cousin, Paul, for some time, and a large marriage was scheduled for the day before Christmas. But the young couple had frequently expressed themselves as disliking the thought of a large and tiresome wedding, and on a lark, "more as a prank," said May, smiling with indulgence, "the naughty young creatures had run off on impulse and had gotten married. Mr. Barbour," continued May, "was really very much annoyed at the whole irresponsible business, and was still rather cool to the gay silly children, but we all hope that he will soon be reconciled to the informality of the affair." Then May, remembering countless columns she had idly read in women's books and magazines railing against the ponderous and exhausting social pageant of fashionable weddings, with its attendant weariness on the part of the young bride, the irritability and confusion of the groom, rivalry and heartburnings and enemies made, "money poured out like water," merely closed her eyes, and quoted at great and fluent length. This much impressed everyone, who began to think more respectfully of the scapegraces; the newspapers became very pompous and asked their readers if this sensible act was not to pave the way for simpler and more dignified society marriages, "where all is not fuss and feathers and vulgar jewels and too much rich food," but a return to the days "of our fathers, who were rugged and simple and strong, not effete like their elegant and spendthrift descendants of these days." Gertrude and Paul were commended by the press as young folk who remembered the old pioneer stories, and because they were unaffected and modest, in spite of the vast wealth of their family, had resolved to set an example that others might very well follow.

Then May, determined and a little haggard these strenuous days, turned her attention to the hysterical and vituperative Florabelle. For days she had refused to see any one, the poor, foolish, heartbroken woman, but having in some measure recovered her strength, allowed May to be brought into her bedroom, whereon she broke into cries and screams and sobs and reproaches: "That horrible little beast of a Gertrude of yours! Jilting my darling that way, and driving him away from his mother into a dreadful priests' place! Leaving me forever!"

"You know that's a lie, Florabelle," said May quietly. "Philippe told you the truth. You didn't want to believe it. Now, I'll tell you something else. You remember that day you told us of Bishop Dominick's message to Philippe? Well, Gertrude left us, you remember? and went directly to your house, where she saw Philippe and had a talk with him. And he told her that he couldn't marry her because she was his cousin, and the poor girl begged and begged, heartbroken, but he would not listen. I don't blame the boy; he believes in that religion of his, and who are we to fight faith in any one? So Gertrude, in her bewilderment and sorrow and hurt, went to the bank to find her father. You know what a favorite she is with Ernest. They told her he had gone to the bank. But when she reached there he had left for home, but Paul was there. And Paul, who is really the finest of young men, sympathized with her and comforted her, and asked her to marry him. And on impulse, because she was so hurt, she decided to marry him. At once."

(And after saying this, May closed her eyes and said to herself: God forgive me!)

But Florabelle was comforted. May had well known that pride and money are the greatest comforters of grief, and so she had given Florabelle pride. Recovering as much as possible after the loss of her son to his religion, Florabelle whispered mysteriously to her friends that "all had not been told," but that her Philippe had really been very cruel to his cousin, Gertrude, and had chosen his Church at the last moment in preference to her. So very soon after May's visit, she dressed herself in elaborate black, as one who mourns, called for her new carriage, and went to visit Gertrude. Sitting in the drawing room with the pale and silent girl, Florabelle wept over her, commiserated with her, shook her head, became faint, and sent Gertrude scurrying for smelling-salts. Gertrude held the salts under her aunt's nose, as she knelt beside her. Florabelle, recovering somewhat, looked at the little hand that held the bottle: it was, as she said later, "like a poor little bird's claw, so thin and bony and trembling."

Paul and Gertrude remained at the Sessions house, temporarily, until Paul could decide where he wished to buy a home. He had half decided on a section just opening up, tentatively called Roseville, quite near the river, but on an elevation. Several fine homes were just in process of being built, already sold, some for sale. Gertrude and Paul had driven out to look at one especial house, sentimentally called Robin's Nest, a dignified and restrained structure of light gray stone, with broad low rooms, deep old trees and terraces. The house, when bought, was to be Ernest's wedding present to the young couple, and Gertrude's dowry was to be an income of one hundred dollars per week until her father's death, with an increase, Ernest said with a sly smile, of fifty dollars per week for every child. May had promised to supply all furniture and linens, and to staff the house.

Nothing, thought the contented Paul, was wanting in Gertrude. No young bride could have been sweeter nor more docile. Of course, he thought, she lacked life and vigor; she had a habit of sitting quite still for hours, not with a serene and restful stillness, but in a sort of half-expectant trance, like a statue. Her hands would lie empty, palms up, curled upon her knee, in a curiously helpless or defenseless attitude, her head a little bent, with a wing of the dark lustreless hair cloudy about her small colorless face, her eyes partially closed as though she waited for something in a dream. She had always been noted among her less friendly friends as "a piece with a sting in her tongue," but now the sting had gone, temporarily at least, and when she spoke it was in a faint distant voice, gentle and abstracted. Marriage, May's friends told her, had certainly improved Gertrude. She was not near so nervous or jumpy, not near so wild of eye and quick of speech, though, of course, she had always been a perfect lady. But she seemed so dignified now, they said, so reticent, so properly matronly, knowing her place in the company of older and wiser matrons. And May, listening, smiled politely and agreeably, with pain tearing her heart.

Within a few days after the sudden wedding, Amy called at the Sessions home for the first time since Gregory's death. The cousins had not met for nearly two years; the social paths of each, these days, did not cross, for Amy had gone into virtual retirement, and if May ever saw Amy at a distance she was careful to avoid her. Between the two lay a horizonless area of silence.

May was sitting alone in her morning room, sadly and heavily going over household accounts, when Amy was announced. Gertrude was up-stairs in her own large bedroom which she shared with Paul. The house was full of sunny morning quiet, the early snow deep and white over the grounds and trees.

May's first sensation when her cousin was announced was a thick and trembling fury, a feeling of outrage, a "rising of her gorge." The pen fell from her hand, and, rolling over her neat black book, left a smeared trail behind it. But after a moment she said, calmly enough: "Please show Mrs. Barbour in." And while she waited, she clenched her hands together and locked her teeth and stared out into the snowy garden.

Amy came in, vital and poised and smiling, sleek in brown sealskin sacque, toque and muff. Her clear skin was flushed with cold and her quiet brown eyes sparkled from exercise, for she had walked from her own home. She looks like my daughter, thought May bitterly and with hatred. But her own face was calm and smiling, if cold with reserve.

She rose. "How nice, Amy," she murmured. Her heart was beating with unbearable force, and her throat threatened to close.

Amy smiled, hesitated. Does she possibly think I can kiss her? May asked herself in outrage and repugnance. But what shall I do if she holds out her hand? Dare I refuse to shake her hand? Dare I acknowledge openly to her that I have reason to refuse? Dare I humiliate myself so?

But Amy did not offer her hand. Her smile became a little fixed as she loosened the neck of her sacque. "I had to see you, May," she said, a trifle breathlessly. "Do sit down, Amy," said May. The two women sat opposite each other, but though they sat in the same room, hardly five feet apart, the horizonless area of silence still lay between them, un-touched, desolate, concealing things they both knew were there but which neither dared openly acknowledge.

Amy was silent; she gazed steadily at her cousin, and then into her gaze came a sort of helplessness, a distress. The slender white hands on the muff trembled. But Amy had never lacked courage; the color did not increase nor fade in her face, and she did not flinch. Nor did her voice shake or waver when she spoke:

"May, I had to see you. Alone. I wanted to tell you that this marriage was as much a shock to me as it was to you. I never thought it would occur. You see, I knew Gertrude liked Philippe Bouchard. I thought it was settled between them. And then, when I heard that she had married Paul, I assure you I was utterly amazed." She paused; her eyes implored May to understand.

"Just what," said May in a clear cold voice, "are you trying to say to me, Amy?"

Amy dropped her head, and one hand began to smooth her muff, over and over. "I'm sorry Gertrude married Paul," she said sadly. "I never was so sorry for anything in my life. There are things I don't understand, about this. But I am sure that whatever they are, they are very, very wrong. But I had to come, to find out if Gertrude was not too unhappy. I couldn't rest, until I knew she had chosen, herself, and that it was all going to be for the best."

May did not answer. And after a long time Amy looked up. Tears were standing in May's eyes. But there was no softening in her face.

"O God!" cried Amy sharply, pinched lines appearing about her nose, "she is unhappy! The poor child!" She stood up in her agitation. "I can't bear it! Something awful's the matter! Let me see her, please let me see her!"

Contempt sprang out upon May's face. "What could be the matter? What makes you think Gertrude's unhappy? It is true that Gertrude preferred Philippe, but he decided he could not marry her, because they were cousins. Gertrude always knew that she might marry Paul some day. And so, she married him."

They regarded each other across the bitter silence for some moments. Then Amy sat down again. She turned her profile to May, and the latter could see the cords straining in her throat. She could see the wet lashes. But nothing softened in May; the rigidity spread from her heart over her whole body, so that she seemed, finally, not to feel anything.

"Paul's my son," said Amy at last, very quietly, as though she were thinking aloud, "but I've never felt there was anything between us but the accident of birth. My children are not like their father, my poor good Martin, and they're not like me. I've never been able to touch them; and I'm certain that they don't love me in the slightest. It seems incredible, but a long time ago when Paul first began to speak of marrying Gertrude, I was against it. I love Gertrude," she went on simply, still not looking at her cousin. "I love Godfrey, too. Even Reggie and Guy have seemed closer to me than my own children. Yes, I was against the marriage. I felt it would be very bad for Gertrude. If I had known about this, before it happened, I would have done all I could to prevent it."

There was a strange and empty pause. Then May, with a pale and malignant smile, said: "This is very odd, from Paul's mother. Mothers don't usually talk so of their children. But I am certain that you underestimate Paul, and do him a shameful injustice. He is really very excellent; in the long run he will make a better husband for Trudie than Philippe could have done. I assure you I am quite satisfied, so you need worry no longer."

Amy turned to her, and again the two women regarded each other steadfastly. Finally, Amy asked without emotion: "May I see Gertrude, for just a moment?"

"Yes, certainly." May was cool and courteous again. "She is upstairs in the big bedroom. Where Gregory used to sleep."

Amy stood up. We can never be friends, of course, thought she, sadly.

It is quite terrible. She did not know what to say. Naked hatred, now, stood between the two women; it wore Ernest's face. They recognized it; neither was hypocritical enough to pretend that it was not there for any one to see. Amy walked out of the room without a backward look.

She went up the broad twisting stairway. And as she climbed the stairs, running her hand lightly over the balustrade, she said to herself: This is a stairway of pain! How many, many times I've gone up it this way, feeling as I feel now, that life was a sick misery and not to be endured! And when that purple light fell on my hand then, as it does now, through that window, I can remember I felt the same, that it was the light of death and I wished that I could be dissolved in it.

May sat rigidly by her desk after Amy had left the room. She listened; everything about her seemed to listen. She heard Gertrude's door open; she heard Gertrude's joyful, shaking cry: "Aunt Amy!" Then the door closed.

May still sat so, and then, quite suddenly, she let her head fall upon the desk. After a little, she began to cry, slow and tortured tears that scalded her eyes and her cheeks. But she was not crying for Gertrude.

CHAPTER LXXVII

A WEEK BEFORE Christmas Ernest sent for Paul. As he had parted casually enough from his uncle at the breakfast table that morning, Paul knew that he was not being summoned to the Barbour-Bouchard offices for mere pleasantries. Ernest greeted him cordially; his expression always became amiable when he saw his nephew.

"Sit down, Paul. I want to talk to you. Here are some of your favorite tobaccos. Help yourself." He smiled at the young man. How can any one help liking him, wanting to do anything for him? thought Paul, charmed by that rare and agreeable smile. He thought his uncle rather pale and reserved since the marriage, though he well knew that Ernest had not been displeased at the precipitate ceremony. Nor could it be that Gertrude troubled him, for though she was somewhat quiet and absent she had acquired a certain sweetness of manner, had lost all of her old swift abruptness and fragile wildness, and seemed to depend more than ever on her father's affection. But no one, thought Paul without resentment, ever knew what Ernest was thinking.

With a shortness that reminded Paul of Gertrude's lost shortness, Ernest went on: "I want you to put in your resignation at the bank, Paul. On January first I am taking you in here. As my assistant," he added, fixing Paul with his relentless eye. "After all, you will have to manage Gertrude's share." He paused, and his big mouth became heavy with cruelty. "You will probably have to manage Godfrey's share, too. And Reginald's. And Guy's. I've never hid from you what weaklings and fools these three are. Joey's the only one I have any hopes for. I've lost hope that the others will ever amount to anything." He moved a paper knife, stared at it. "Eventually, you may take my place here. I intend to train you for that eventuality."

Paul made no reply. Ernest looked up at him. The young man was pale, and the line of his jaw showed under his skin. But something in his expression made Ernest smile and say with amusement: "Is it possible this does not surprise you? Were you expecting this?"

"Yes." Paul lit his cigarette. "I hoped for this. I expected it. Would you want me to lie about it?"

Ernest was more amused than ever. "Well, aren't you going to say anything more? About 'cheating' my sons out of their birthright, or some such stuff?"

"No. I wouldn't be cheating them. I know, for instance, that their share would be intact in all that you have, even if they weren't active in the business. They would simply draw their income from the stock you would leave them. Gentlemen of leisure. Frey would live in Europe, where he seems to like it. Guy would play. Reggie—well, he's the unknown quantity just yet, though he hasn't shown much interest in business matters. Joey. Well, Joey is dogged and obstinate and keen on the money, but he will make a better banker than a business man. I have an idea you've thought of him in connection with banking. He's got a shrewd head for finance. Like John Charles, the Shylock! But no imagination, no daring. You're not a man, Uncle Ernest, to be offended at the truth.

"But just what am I to expect? You say, 'take my place.' 'My assistant.' Just what does that mean, in plain English?"

As he had done hundreds of times before, Ernest studied him. He weighed the audacity, the greed, the ruthlessness, of the face before him. Imagination! the young brute had said. Yes, practical imagination, the kind that builds bridges and suborns politicians, scuttles the honesty of Presidents and builds vast industries, sets loose whispers of wars and makes the chimneys of mills blaze, grinds Civilization into the face of the wilderness and establishes dynasties that are greater than Law and more powerful than the foolish honor of the tender-hearted, or the filigreed thrones of kings. But he had no real craftiness, Ernest observed. What he would get he would get by sheer force and brutal hammering, if negotiations failed. He still had a certain hesitancy before the final implacability, but that would pass, swifter than it had passed in Ernest, who had had a gift for irony. Paul had no irony. Men who retain irony are not to be trusted, thought Ernest. They can't always resist an impulse to tickle themselves. He, himself, had not always been adroit, but that was because he had despised adroitness as an exercise in time-wasting subtlety. He had consciously avoided it. But Paul did not know that such a thing as adroitness existed. He lacked patience. But he was strong enough not to need it. He still had a faint conscience, but he would soon lose it. Ernest firmly believed that men without humor never retained consciences.

Paul, he reflected, was an opportunist, not the colorful adventurous opportunist, but the savage kind. In time he would be completely rapacious. He lacked the drive which Ernest candidly recognized in himself. Instead, he had a conscious and insatiable greed. Which would serve practically as well, said Ernest to himself. Nor would he exult in power, as Ernest did, an exultation which was like the joy the elephant felt when he discovered he could uproot trees. But this needed a certain amount of a more subtle sort of imagination, which even the elephant possessed, but which Paul would never possess. Paul was like a belly that would never be filled, but which he would try all his life to fill. But he's less intelligent than I, went on the older man's reflections, so he'll never be troubled with indigestion. Damn it, I'm getting subtle in my old age! I've certainly been unconsciously developing humor, which is as destructive as cancer.

"What do I mean?" he asked aloud. "Just what I said. I intend to leave Gertrude more than half of my private fortune, and half of my stock in Barbour-Bouchard, and the Kinsolving works, the lumber mills, the mines, the oil wells, the railroads. I might even do a little better. You can, of course, be President some day. Joey, as you have quite cleverly said, will naturally turn to the bank." He paused. "May, naturally, will probably not be so generous with her own private fortune. If she dies before me, that will settle itself. If she survives me, she can leave it where she wills. I don't imagine she'll leave much to you."

"I'm not worrying about Aunt May's money," said Paul, smiling.

"You're a cool young devil! Yet I think you're a liar. If May left you and Gertrude out, you'd be mad as hell. Even if you had practically everything else."

All at once the vastness of what he was being given shook Paul. The poorest of the family becoming the first and the greatest!

"Christ!" he exclaimed, reddening. "I don't know what to say, Uncle Ernest! Except that I think you won't be sorry!"

"I'd better not be!" said Ernest, his mouth twitching. But Paul was desperately sober. He began to walk up and down the room, thinking heavily. Ernest watched him. He's not half so bright as young Jules, he admitted to himself, nor one-tenth so clever as young Honore. The Bouchards will be ones to reckon with, eventually. Jules will finally be as savage and subtle as a Spanish Jesuit, and Honore can smell opportunity before it turns the corner. These French have wit and brains and cunning; we British are no match for them in these. What we get we get by sheer weight. I'm counting on Paul's weight. As I counted on mine. The monkey is brighter than the elephant, but the elephant can still fight tigers and pull up trees.

"Sit down, Paul," he said. "You've got to get back to the bank. But I wanted to discuss this where no one else would hear. By the way, I expect you to visit the coal mines immediately after Christmas. There are a lot of disorders there lately; I want you to look over the situation. Labor disorders are like smallpox; they spread. Eugene tells me that the Kinsolving works are beginning to mutter. Some of my business associates tell me that they are afraid; but that's because they've got yellow bellies. There's no need to be afraid. All we need is a strong hand. The trouble with America is that there are no masters here. I propose to start the fashion in business. That's why I'm sending you. I've already got a dozen William P. Scott detectives out there, and they'll stand no nonsense. Look over the place, and order more detectives, if necessary. I'm putting it all into your hands.

"It is strange that during financial depressions and panics there are no strikes. The dogs are only too glad to have jobs to feed themselves. But let them satisfy the first edge of their appetites and they get cocky. I think the best thing is not to let them satisfy the first edge. I am weighing an idea to reduce wages in the mines; you can use that as a threat. That might make them think as much as they can think with their donkey skulls. But do what you think is best. A great deal depends on how you go about it."

"It is a lot of responsibility, Uncle Ernest. I know next to nothing about the situation. I'll do nothing hastily, though. Sometimes if you just sit like a rock and do and say nothing things pass over and there's no need to do anything after all."

"Spoken like a Briton! But this is not England, Paul. People do things here, and if you sit and wait, sometimes you discover you're sitting on dynamite and the fuse is about to reach it. By the way, I'm taking you to Austria next summer. There's a Company there, Skeda, which might need a few modern suggestions about armaments. Europe, for the next fifty years or so, is going to be a very good field for munitions. Especially France and Germany and the Balkans. Bismarck's given the Germans a national feeling, as well as unity. There'll be no stopping the Germans, now. They've tasted blood. It takes little to make a German drunk, and blood is his quickest intoxicant.

"And then there's South America. I think we've all been forgetting South America. Our nearest neighbor, and she might just as well be on the moon, as far as we are concerned. Next year we'll go there together, you and I, and impress on those homesick Spaniards the duty they owe their new country to buy and make munitions."

"In other words," said Paul, "if there are no markets, you make markets."

"Of course. Business is a little dull these days. And we are singularly handicapped. We can't advertise. We can't suggest a nice little war, and then offer our patents or our arms. And yet, we've got to do business. And Fear is our best salesman.

"Your Uncle Raoul was one of the best salesmen I ever employed. But that was in the old days, when we concentrated on squirrel-shooting. We had a small tidy little place then. But we've got a monstrous mill here today, and we can't keep it running making pop-guns for little boys. Last week, as you know, we laid off over half our men in the two foundries. America's the damndest place for munitions! Not a fortress along thousands of miles of border. There's Canada over there; but you might as well whistle up an alley as suggest Canada as a formidable neighbor. It's been tried, but it's no good. It was quite cleverly suggested in Canada recently that America had a lot of sly thoughts and half-plans about annexing her. And do you know what happened? Canada shut down her one and only munitions plant, and thumbed her nose at us! Worse than that, she decided to import her next batch of rifles from England. That was a nasty kick in the trousers!"

Ernest laughed, but Paul could see no occasion for laughter. He looked annoyed. "Has it been suggested very forcibly over here that Canada would make a nice meal? What about the Monroe Doctrine? Couldn't some interest be stirred up in that? People have been very patriotic since the Civil War."

"Oh, that's an old story. Every once in a while it's dusted off and brought out of the cupboard. I'll admit people are beginning to show some interest, but it's still very little. However, some really creditable anti-British rumors are being set loose. They've been received with quite an encouraging amount of interest. Especially in cities with large German populations. It's a slow process, though; blood is thicker than water after all, though it's a damned nuisance. More and more people, it is true, are beginning to talk about the Monroe Doctrine, but it's mostly from those who know very little about it. Just recently a New York paper reprinted the Doctrine and explained it, and ridiculed its application to Canada. However, there's one comfort: the people who spread rumors, the people who can be counted on to relay fear, the people who are easily stirred to hatred and attuned to war, never read newspapers.

"For a long time nothing was said very much about the old American Revolution. But lately some good work has been done about reviving it. Have you seen the latest school textbooks? Here, I have a copy in my desk. Quite inspiring reading. A lot of spirit. I've a number of friends in Washington, and there is nothing half so good as a politician with a new check in his pocket. Give me half a dozen politicians with flannel heads and bottomless pockets, and I don't care who runs your churches. Well, anyway, the new textbooks are very good. Within twenty years there ought to be a well-defined anti-British sentiment. All the schools have to do is beat the drums and sing about George Washington and Valley Forge and Paul Revere and cruel King George, and you won't have to talk about the Monroe Doctrine! In fact, it would be a good idea to bury it!"

"But what about the Hessians? They were Germans."

"Oh, that's being very neatly handled. Just poor mercenaries impressed by British savagery and greed into a war they knew nothing about. They're not being played up very prominently. It's all Cornwallis and the Indians and Boston and the burning of the White House about 1812. Of course, the French enter into it, too, and that's really being delicately managed. You can't offend the French."

Paul had listened, full of absorbed interest. He asked: "But in the meantime, you still have the military contracts, Uncle Ernest?"

"Of course. But this year's orders for arms were almost insignificant.

However, we've had large orders for explosives; the railroads are going ahead at a merry rate. It's fortunate that munitions are now only one of our activities. But I've always thought of it as my pet; munitions can be made into the most gigantically profitable enterprise if properly managed. And I, and my competitors, intend it to be properly managed in the future. In the meantime, we live very comfortably."

Paul was silent. Then all at once, a strange thing happened to him. He saw a clear, dazzlingly brilliant winter day, all snow and vivid blue sky. He and Elsa stood on the snowy doorstep of the shabby farmhouse, heavily encased in coats and scarfs. Their father, Martin, was standing near them on the wooden porch, and he was saying to an old man, Uncle Gregory: "You can't change my mind. It's blood money, and it's going out into the hospital as usual to help stop blood. I wouldn't touch a penny of it." He raised his voice, and cried, almost shouted: "That man's a scoundrel! He's a beast!" Seven-year-old Paul was curious. He said: "Papa! Who is a scoundrel?" Martin turned; his fair face was flushed and his blue eyes fiery. But he smiled at his little son. "Your Uncle Ernest, my love."

Paul had forgotten that scene entirely, but at this moment he remembered it vividly. But more vivid than anything was his father's face. It floated before him with the blazing winter sun upon it, and he could actually see the flash and passion of his eyes. They dazzled him, even in memory. He recalled all the old stories of the enmity between his father and his uncle. He was much shaken.

He was startled when he heard a chair scrape. Ernest was standing up and glancing with a frown at his watch. Paul gathered he was being dismissed. He stood up.

"Paul, how is John Charles doing at the bank lately?"

"Very well, Uncle Ernest." Paul's face began to pale, his voice to recede. "Of course, we can't tell just yet. After all, he's only been there three weeks. But even though he does small routine things he's showing an aptitude. We have hopes for him."

"It's too bad he didn't want to finish school. But he's a fine lad, and he's got his head set right on his shoulders. Think he can take over a window within a year?"

"Positively. He's bull-headed, but as you say, he's got all his wits. And he thinks, eats, talks, lives, nothing but banking. He's dragged out all my own books from the attic."

"Well, he and Joey will probably run the bank together, eventually." Ernest smiled. "Your Aunt Florabelle has already been speaking to me about putting Jules in the bank after he finishes school. A fine boy; silent as the grave, but knows what he wants. Your Uncle Eugene thinks Leon will do better with him." He laughed. "Did you know Etienne wants to be an actor?"

They walked to the door together, Ernest's hand affectionately on his nephew's shoulder. But once at the door, Ernest's expression darkened, became uneasy.

"Paul." He hesitated, then resumed with difficulty: "How is Gertrude? I mean, when you are alone together? I confess I don't like her looks, these days. She's getting thinner, and I notice she eats little. She also avoids her Mama and me, as if she didn't want to be alone with us."

Paul turned slowly, and fixed his eyes on Ernest's. A faint cynicism, a shadow of thin fine cruelty, moved over his large and rugged features. But all he said was: "Trudie? But she's splendid! I think all the excitement has tired her, and she's a little disappointed that we haven't had a honeymoon yet. I've promised her one in the spring, however." He pulled on his gloves. "Please tell Aunt May I'll be a trifle late for dinner tonight. It's nearly the end of the year you know, Uncle Ernest."

When he had gone, Ernest closed the door slowly behind him. A cold knife-edge of dislike inserted itself in the strong door of his affection for his nephew. Why didn't he tell me? he thought. What did he mean by that expression on his face? Was he daring to mock me? That young jackanapes?

He went back to his desk, and as he sat down he was besieged by uneasiness and an undefined distress. He saw his daughter's hand as he had seen it at breakfast holding a fork over a plate of bacon and eggs. He remembered that the fork had seemed too heavy for those thin transparent little fingers. They had trembled, he remembered. And somehow, he had not wanted to look at her face.

He rang the bell on his desk furiously. His secretary raced in, full of apprehension at the peremptory summons. "Haven't we anything from Garfinkel's about receiving that pearl necklace from Tiffany's yet?" he shouted angrily. "It's only five days to Christmas, and Tiffany promised to send it to Garfinkel a week ago!"

"No, Mr. Barbour, it hasn't come yet," said the frightened chief clerk. "But, if you like, I'll go down at once to Garfinkel and tell him to send a telegram to Tiffany's in New York. I'm sure it'll come soon, though. They understand it's for Miss Gertrude's Christmas present."

"I should have gone to New York for it myself, instead of bothering with that fool of a Garfinkel. But I wanted the clasp changed, and that's why I sent it back through him. Yes, go on down there and see what can be done."

He took up his pen and irately pulled a pile of letters toward him as the man went out. But he could not work just yet.

He could only see that little trembling hand holding the heavy fork. And beside it, unnoticed, the pearl necklace.

CHAPTER LXXVIII

M AY HAD tried for days to find Paul alone, where she might talk
to him without Ernest's suspicion or Gertrude's knowledge.
She found the opportunity tonight. He had gone, after
dinner, to the little back parlor where Gregory had kept
boxes of old books and accounts. He had brought some
books from the bank, and had carried them to this unused small room;
the library oppressed him, for some reason, and his bedroom did not seem
to him the proper place for his work.

May followed him into this room. He had just sat down and spread
his books upon a scarred old black walnut table, and lit a lamp and
trimmed his pen, when his mother-in-law came in softly, closing the door
behind her. He frowned uneasily; he did not like May and knew that
she had no liking for him in return. But he stood up courteously and
offered her a chair. Before she was quite seated, he had already resumed
his own chair. He picked up his pen, frowned at it, and signified in every
way that he was exceedingly busy. But he was also curious; he wondered
what the old girl wanted of him.

She smiled benignly, and studied him furtively for a few moments,
gauging what she could from that handsome face with the almost
pouting lower lip, the short square nose and averted eyes.

"Paul," she said, and she tried to make her voice affectionate, "I've
wanted to talk to you alone for a little while. This is the first chance I
have had. After all," and she laughed gently, "you and I are more than
mother-in-law and son-in-law. You are also a blood relative. My cousin
was your grandmother, you know."

"Yes." He was more amiable now, and returned her smile. "What are
we, Aunt May? Third cousins? What a mixed-up family we are!"

"Your grandmother, Paul, was a lovely young lady. I remember her
quite well, though she was a grown woman while I was still a little girl.
It seemed to me that she was the most beautiful thing in the world. Her
eyes were violet-blue and she had chestnut curls hanging down on white
shoulders, and a small short nose. Do you know, I've often thought that
you looked much like her."

"My mother has said that before," answered Paul, pleased. He put
down his pen, and regarded May with more graciousness.

Her face changed, and she leaned a little toward him. "Paul, I want you to tell me something. Please don't shut your mind away from me. This is so important. Lately I've thought you somewhat depressed and irritable. And I've had an idea it wasn't just business. Won't you tell me what it is?"

He looked away from her, sidelong, angrily. His native wariness and suspicion jumped up, alert. In all his life he had never had a confidante, with the exception of his twin, Elsa, and even with her he had been watchful and reserved. He could not break the habit of a lifetime, a congenital habit, so easily. It was not his nature to trust any one, to believe any one simple and selfless, so he began to wonder, as he sat in stubborn silence before May, just what she was "getting at," and what she hoped to discover or gain.

And yet, bewilderingly even to him, he wanted to speak. May had risen from her chair in great agitation, and was now standing beside him. He glanced up at her sullenly, and his heavy lips parted a trifle. She clasped her hands together and bent over him.

"Paul! I'm Trudie's mother. Remember that; she is my child. What is wrong with her? I know you feel it, too, and as you are her husband, you ought to be able to tell me. I can't stand seeing her so, Paul, so silent, such a dreadful color, so docile and lifeless. As if—as if part of her had—died——"

He moved his head a little; the movement signified thick and impatient pain. He lifted his hand to make a gesture, then the hand fell to the desk again. "She cries in her sleep," he said, and was alarmed at what he had said. A dark wave of color washed over his face, and he glared at May angrily.

"Oh." The sound, coming from May's lips, was like the sound one makes when struck violently in the chest. She moved back to her chair like an old woman, and sat there, haggard and white, gazing at him. The young man got quickly to his feet, clenched his hands behind his back, and began to walk up and down the room. He could not restrain himself now; he could not have kept himself from speaking. He stopped abruptly in front of May, and she saw the twitching muscles about his mouth.

"There are other ways of doing things!" he exclaimed, as if the words were forced from him. "You don't need to sneak about—in personal things. Business is different. But not when it concerns—when it concerns girls like Trudie——"

There was a silence. Then May said softly: "Oh, then you know, Paul?"

"Yes. But I didn't know until just before I married Trudie. Only an hour before."

"Paul!" The cry from May was full of horror. "Trudie doesn't know?"

"No."

May was silent a moment. "Paul, I told Gertrude's father that if he hurt her I would leave him, leave this house forever——"

Distaste made Paul wince, and his expression became cold once more. "Leave Uncle Ernest?" This was blasphemy; Paul felt degraded at the thought that a woman of his family could become depraved enough to consider leaving her husband! There were certain women that did abhorrent things like this, but one did not speak of them in mixed company or before the females of one's family. He was amazed that May did not realize the enormity and shame of her own words; it astounded him that her face was quite calm and steadfast. Perhaps she was not herself? Females frequently were not "themselves."

"Certainly. And I intended to do so. Then when Trudie married you, and I learnt in a roundabout way that she did not know her father was responsible for it all, I knew I could not leave him. To do so would enlighten her, and probably do terrible things to her. So, I am staying, for her sake."

Paul picked up his pen and began to tap his desk with it, gloomily. He said nothing. He still seemed offended as at an appalling breach of taste.

"My dear," said May gently, after a few moments, "perhaps it might turn out well, at last. Be good to my poor child. We, her parents, can do nothing for her now. It lies in your hands."

He was touched in spite of himself, as he was always touched at any reference to Gertrude. A rare animation flashed indignantly into his eyes. "Be good to Trudie? My God, I love her!" And ashamed again of his emotion, he clamped shut his mouth and the line of his jaw sprang out.

I was mistaken, thought May. He is not like Ernest at all. But Ernest will eventually corrupt him as he has always corrupted people. It's as though he were afflicted by some frightful disease which he involuntarily gives to others. She sighed. Paul had covered with his hand the part of his face that was turned to her, as if to shut out her eyes. She put her hand on his shoulder after she had moved beside him again; she pressed that shoulder, and forced into her voice a humorous lightness and affection.

"And eventually, I know that Trudie will love you, Paul. Fancies—— change. Gertrude was always reticent and never had the silly flirtatious love affairs that young girls have, and Philippe—he was her first fancy." She paused. Paul gave no sign; the shoulder was unyielding under her hand.

She moved toward the door. "It is too bad, my dear, that you aren't going with us to New York to hear Frey's symphony. We shall miss you."

Paul dropped his hand. He was already disgusted and apprehensive because of his involuntary outbreak. He scowled, as May turned at the door.

"I think it mighty peculiar that he doesn't want to come home for Christmas," he said.

"But, my dear, if you remember his letter, he says that there are final matters to be arranged and details to be seen to. After all, he only arrived in New York this morning. Yes, this morning! And the concert is to be given December 28th. Frey *is* a little difficult sometimes, but he must have a reason for requesting us not to come to New York until the day of the concert. After all," she added with a placating and humorous smile, "it is the artistic temperament, perhaps."

"Artistic temperament! Just plain ugly selfishness." All Paul's inherent dislike of his cousin roughened his voice. "Mark my words, he's been up to something."

The idea of the cold, dreaming, aloof Godfrey being "up to something," amused May. She laughed almost gaily as she went out. But before she closed the door they both heard a loud authoritative voice. "Elsa!" exclaimed Paul, bright with pleasure. He got up, closed his book, and followed May back into the family living room.

They found Elsa planted squarely on the rug before the fire. She had declined to remove her fur cape, and its dark richness was flecked with snow. Her round fur hat, set straightly on her head (no coquettish tilts for Elsa!) was rimmed with melting whiteness. Her hands were still thrust through her muff; she had refused a chair. She stood there on the hearth, buoyant, rosy, dominating, and dripping. Standing there, big and broad-shouldered and vigorous, she was like a wholesome Amazon. She bent down and pecked May's cheek, and bestowed a hearty and smacking kiss upon her beloved brother's mouth. Then she stepped back and looked at him. Her face was smoother than Paul's, and slightly smaller, but otherwise the two faces were identical, from forthright, slightly choleric blue eyes to square and aggressive chins.

"Do sit down, Elsa," said Paul.

"No. I've only a moment or two."

"Are you alone, my love?" asked May, seating herself near the faintly smiling and silent Gertrude.

"Alone? Of course! I love to walk out in the air and the snow and the wind and the night. Hardly any one is out, the poor sickly things, and it is so nice to walk quickly through the deserted streets. I love it."

"That's why you have such hard red cheeks," smiled Ernest. He had laid aside his paper, and seemed pleased that Elsa had come.

"I'll never have to paint my face, that's certain," replied Elsa complacently. "No, Aunt May, I don't want to sit down. I really must rush back. Mama is quite alone; John Charles is out tonight, too.

"I just wanted to tell you that I'd like to go with you and Uncle Ernest and Trudie to New York to hear Frey's music. Why, I haven't seen Lucy for ages! She hardly writes since her little Thomas was born. I've just got to see him. So, I've written today and told her to expect us all on December 27th."

May flushed, but her voice was quite equable as she replied: "But, my dear, we've already arranged to stop at the Astor Hotel——"

"Stuff! Why, with Trudie's own sister-in-law in the city, your own niece, Aunt May! I think it quite insulting. Lucy would be insulted, too. After all, she has an eighteen-room house, and just a legion of servants, and her dear Percy Van Eyck has a fortune that makes ours look like two cents. Please don't be obstinate. You know that Lucy has invited all of us dozens of times, and Uncle Ernest is the only one who has taken advantage of the invitations." She swung on Ernest. "Has she, or has she not, the most gorgeous home in the world, Uncle Ernest?"

He smiled, raised his brows. "It is quite commendable," he said in a casual voice, to tease her.

"Pshaw, you always were a torment, Uncle Ernest!" She thrust her damp muff playfully into his dodging face. "You know it is magnificent. I didn't believe it at first, but the Van Eycks are really the cream of the élite in New York. When I was there I felt like royalty, being Lucy's sister. Mrs. Van Eyck, Percy's mother, is a regular old dowager, and, Uncle Ernest, you must know her brother, Jay Regan? The financier?"

"I know him slightly," said Ernest, with a wink at Paul.

"Do stop teasing me! I remember now that he spoke of you. Quite civilly——"

"I'm sure I'm grateful," said Ernest.

"Tush! Everyone in the whole country, probably in the whole world, knows you. Well, Lucy's home on Fifth Avenue is just a palace. I could see that even Mama was impressed, and you know how Mama is: so unimaginative. Nothing ever impresses her much. I believe she wouldn't notice it if our house were turned into a log cabin overnight."

"I wouldn't think of inconveniencing Lucy," said May. "And on such short notice, too. It is not only imposing and rude, but——"

"Dear Aunt May, please don't be so formal. Besides, I've already written to Lucy."

"And very wrong of you not to consult me first." May seemed really annoyed.

"Nonsense." Ernest moved irritably in his chair. "Tempest in a teapot. Perhaps Elsa was a little hasty, but I'm sure it is very thoughtful of her. Lucy's hospitality will be much better than a hotel's, and I, for one, am pleased at the arrangement. Lucy is nothing if not hospitable."

All the color had gone from May's face; her lips were so compressed that they were just visible as a straight white line. She glanced from

Ernest to her niece and thought: So Frey is to be sacrificed to these young beef-eaters, too! But not my son! Not my son, my darling!

Ernest had begun to tease Elsa about Godfrey. "Don't be a hypocrite, my girl. You don't care a damn for Lucy's baby. It's Frey you're after! Well, no doubt he'll find you a bouncing big armful. You eat too much."

Elsa had turned decidedly red, but her eyes sparkled. "I do not! Besides, majestic women are quite the thing now. I'm sure I'd like to see Frey. I've been pretty bad, not writing to him as much as I should have done, but I'm hoping he will forgive me. But New York is so marvellous this time of the year. I adore the shops. Lucy says the shopping center is moving up from Fourteenth Street, Aunt May."

"Indeed," murmured her aunt.

During all this time Gertrude had not spoken one word, not even to her young husband, who had seated himself near her and had placed his arm along the back of her chair. She was looking into the fire; its redness shone on the small triangular face, vividly lighting the new weary patience of the colorless mouth, the transparency of the pinched nose, the long thick lashes that hid the still and heavy eyes. The dark cloudy hair was loosened childishly over her forehead and cheeks; her little hands, open and palm up, lay defenselessly on her sharp young knees.

When Elsa spoke to her loudly, she jumped, and turned bemused and frightened eyes to her cousin.

"Dear me, Trudie, whatever are you dreaming about?"

Gertrude smiled, and to her father that smile seemed enormously pathetic.

"I'm so sorry, Elsa. I know I've been quite rude. But to tell you the truth I was trying to decide what to get Mama for Christmas. Even at this late day I haven't decided yet."

Elsa made her good-bys. She was in high good humor, and excited. May accompanied her into the hall.

"What's the matter with Trudie?" asked Elsa in a stage whisper that carried quite easily to the ears of those in the drawing room. "Is it possible that she is already enceinte?"

Ernest glanced furtively at his daughter. Her face had turned quite sick.

CHAPTER LXXIX

REGINALD AND Guy Barbour arrived home from their respective schools the day before Christmas. Guy was overjoyed at his release, and even the dour Reginald, or Reggie, condescended to relax. Reginald, being neat and orderly, did little to disrupt the routine of the household, but one might have thought a whole school of youths had been let loose, to judge by the noise and excitement Guy created.

"Imagine you going off and marrying that stuffed shirt, Paul!" he said with winning candor to his sister. "I thought you were all for Philippe. Say, did I tell you Philippe can jump aces and spades over the best jumpers at school? And he's gone to be a priest! Well, all I can say is it's beyond me. Maybe you jilted him, eh? I wouldn't put it beneath you quiet pusses."

Reginald, the gloomy and reserved, expressed himself in very measured terms, in a voice and manner suggestive of a middle-aged clergyman: "Paul Barbour is most certainly not the man I would have chosen for you, Gertrude. There is not the slightest touch of godliness in him. But this age is all for the things of the world, so I suppose he has his place in it."

At this, Gertrude smiled her first unforced smile since her marriage.

"You both do Paul a sad injustice," she said. "But remember, boys, he's not only your cousin, now, but your brother-in-law."

"That won't make him loosen up any," averred the frank Guy. "Last Christmas he gave me a pair of brushes that began to shed hair practically immediately, like a mangy dog. Now they're as bald as an egg. He's liable to give me a gold-plated watch fob that'll turn green within twenty-four hours, this year. Where's the bright green chain he gave you last Christmas, Reg?"

Reginald smiled involuntarily. He so rarely smiled that he seemed like a stranger when he did so. "I gave it to our bootblack," he said. "But I believe he thought very little of it as I found it in the hall wastebasket the next morning."

While his brother had been speaking, Guy had been studying with interest his sister's pale drawn face and heavy eyes.

"Say, you're not going to have a baby already, are you?" he demanded.

It was Reginald, not Gertrude, who blushed furiously. In fact, Gertrude laughed when she saw Reginald's color and expression.

"What ideas you do get for a boy, Guy!" she exclaimed.

"What an immodest thing to ask a lady!" said Reginald, with a black and censorious glance at his younger brother.

"Blah! What's immodest about a baby? You're an old woman in pants, Reg. Say, Trudie, do you know what they call old Reg at his school? I have it direct from Chetlow, whose brother's with Reg. They call him Rainy."

"Rainy?" Gertrude was diverted. "What for?"

Reginald's color had become purplish, and the fire in his eye was dangerous and ugly. For one moment he was startlingly like his father. He jumped at Guy agilely, but that gay youth bounced blithely out of his clutch and shouted at Gertrude as he dodged in a corner: "Old Rain-in-the-pants! And I dare Reg to tell you why!"

Gertrude blushed, laughed uncertainly. Reginald was able, by a dexterous move, to capture his brother, and began to cuff him with an enthusiasm not at all in keeping with his usual poise and dignity. Guy returned the assault with interest, and the two youths fell to the floor with a great clatter, and began to roll over and over together in a welter of flying arms and legs. Gertrude pulled up her slim legs and skirts upon the window seat and watched the noisy fight with a large amount of pleasure. Seated thus, her thin arms hugging her shins, her chin on one knee, she looked young again, and almost happy, for her sunken eyes sparkled amusedly, and she laughed.

The boys brought up in a mighty crash against a wall, causing the fall of a picture. They rose, dusting themselves off, roaring threats at each other. Reginald was more dishevelled than Guy, for his dignity had suffered much and his coat much more, and though he laughed as did Guy, there was a sullenness about his expression when he stopped laughing.

The three young people were in Guy's and Reginald's bedroom, a large old-fashioned room with sturdy walnut furniture and a large hooded fireplace in which a hearty fire burned. Outside, the gray and snowy December day loomed in shadows through a slow blizzard.

The two boys were exceedingly fond of their sister, whose marriage had secretly shocked them. Guy had a light regard for his brother Godfrey; Reginald had contempt for him. Guy disliked young Joey; Reginald ignored him. Both were continually surprised and offended at Gertrude's love for Godfrey. In this was mixed a little jealousy.

It was an old habit of Gertrude's to spend hours with the boys in their room, listening to Guy's eager, malicious and amusing stories, sympathizing with the uneasy gloominess of Reginald. Sometimes they would have their tea there together, sitting before the fire, Guy dropping crumbs all over the sturdy but shabby carpet.

Each year the sprightly Guy had a new and passionately enthusiastic ambition. This year he had decided he must go West. The Eastern world, he remarked airily, had become effete and enervating. It was all cravats and decorum, silk dresses and sentimental songs, carriages rolling sedately down smooth streets and old gentlemen strolling with gold-headed canes. The East was dull and dead; the life had gone out of it. Safety had eroded it and it was acrid as dust.

Tea had been brought in, and Guy gestured lavishly with a piece of cake. He was going West, where one could see the simple aborigine, see the wide stars at night, ride a horse over endless prairies, feast one's eye on color in the Painted Desert, rub shoulders with the raw shoulders of Nature, know life again, exuberant, and strong-flavored, and where— "—Men are men," cut in Reginald with a short laugh that had in it something suggestive of a snort.

"Papa wouldn't consent to that, Guy," said Gertrude, after the short tussle resulting from Reginald's words had come to an end.

"Oh, I'll manage him," said Guy loftily. "I'll just tell him I'm tired of dull life in the East, among a lot of cut-throat, blood-sucking industrialists——"

"Those are just words." Gertrude shrugged and sipped her tea with more relish than she had had for weeks. "Just name me one of those cut-throat, blood-sucking industrialists——"

"The old man," replied Guy blandly. "Didn't you know he was nothing but an old pirate? Oh, he's no worse than the rest of them, but he's pretty bad."

Reginald was silent. Gertrude, uncertain whether to be amused or annoyed, looked at him tentatively. He had a long dark face, which later on would become cadaverous; his long upper lip fell from his short nose to a mouth that was a straight and uncompromising line. His eyes, dark and slow and inclined to sullenness, moved under heavy and hooded lids. He had thick straight black hair sleekly combed and longish. Ernest had once said his second son was as lively as a corpse, and this was no very great exaggeration. Reginald disliked loudness and sprightliness in clothing, and in pleasure or study, at church, school, the homes of friends, summer or winter, he wore sober black broadcloth and simply tied black cravats. His body was long and thin, somewhat slat-like, his boots always well polished on long thin feet. His air was invariably decorous and dignified, cold and reserved, and, at times, censorious.

Guy was startlingly different from his favorite brother. His coloring was Godfrey's, but he had none of Godfrey's classic beauty of feature and austerity of expression. "Impish" best described his blond flushed face with its deeply indented dimples on each side of a smiling mouth. Even in rare repose, or sleep, or anger, the dimples cleft his cheeks deeply. His lively blue eyes lost much comeliness because they were rather slit-like, tilting upward at the outer corners, from which sprayed deep laughter-wrinkles. This gave him a slightly Oriental look, and added its share to a somewhat cunning expression. His fair hair curled luxuriously all over his head in shining waves and ripples, an asset of which he was frankly vain. His good looks, added to a disposition malicious and gay, boisterous and fun-loving, generous and apparently frank, endearingly untrustworthy, made him legions of friends. Incorrigible and time-wasting at school, blithely managing to get through his classes without learning anything, he was yet far more intelligent than Reginald, who was the joy of his professors.

Before Gertrude could protest at Guy's light sketch of their father, Joey came in. ("He always smells food," Guy would say disgustedly.) However, upon seeing his young brother, Guy became quite animated and friendly.

"Just in time for the last of the cake!" he exclaimed. "God, that kid gets bigger and heavier every time you see him! I bet he weighs as much as I do!" Guy, though he might have wished for a few more inches in height, was more than a little proud of his slight gracefulness and agile dancer's body.

Joey surveyed the remainder of the cake with a sullen and cunning look. But without commenting, he picked up a slice and munched it. Guy, affectionately smiling, thought his young brother exceptionally repulsive. He knew that Reginald at times was deeply antagonistic to the ten-year-old boy, and that this antagonism took the form of indifference and avoidance. His own antagonism was apparently more good-natured, but in reality it was tainted with malice and smiling detestation. He watched the boy eat; the heavy jaw and mouth moved slowly, almost sensually, as he rolled each delicate morsel of cake over his tongue and against his palate, savoring it. The pleasure in his expression was almost obscene, thought Guy behind his indulgent smile. There was also cruelty in that expression, as though the cake were a living thing that he was crushing between his teeth. While he ate, his eyes, small and shrewd and gleaming, studied his brothers and his sister, slowly and separately. He gulped, and the cake slid down his throat. He glanced at the last slice. Gertrude put her hand over it.

"No, Joey. You know what Mama said. Not so near dinner time."

He pushed her hand away, pinching it as he did so with abstracted brutality. "Shucks! Why shouldn't I?" He stuffed the other piece in his mouth. But before he could swallow it Reginald fetched him a blow across the back of his head that flung him forwards like a stuffed pillow, and he would have sprawled headlong had not Gertrude caught him with her thrown-out arm. "Reggie!" she cried protestingly.

"That'll teach the young scoundrel to pinch you," said Reginald, glowering, and nursing his stinging hand. "Head like a paving stone!"

Joey, rescued from a landing in the fireplace, roared, thrusting his sister backwards from him. "I'll tell Papa, see if I don't!" he screamed. "You're nothing but a white-livered, shamblin', pious yokel, with a heart like mashed potato and no guts!" He aimed a kick at his brother's long thin legs. "You're a corpse, but you don't know enough to lie down!"

Gertrude stared at Reginald blankly and indignantly. The youth colored violently, made a feint at Joey which the latter ducked dexterously. But Guy laughed with delight, slapping his shapely thighs. "Papa's little echo, Reg!" he exclaimed. "He must have been listening to the Old Man behind curtains. I've heard him say that about you half a dozen times." He gloated upon them all with relish, even malice. But there was something even in that malice that did not arouse antagonism and anger. "Look here, Joey, stop yelling. You'll have the maids sweeping in here in a body. I've got something capital for you for Christmas."

Joey ceased his roaring abruptly, like a stream of water shut off with great suddenness. Instantly he eyed his younger brother with that narrowed and gleaming stare, full of cunning and unchild-like contempt. "'Capital!'" he snorted, moving away from Reginald's purple-faced proximity. "Bet it didn't cost twenty-five cents! You never have any money. Just fritter it away on nonsense. You'll come to no good; end up in the gutter. You're a natural-born blackguard and ne'er-do-well!"

"Papa's little echo, Guy!" reminded Reginald with a short and unpleasant laugh.

Guy laughed with some discomfiture. But he seemed determined not to take umbrage today.

"Joey, you have no right to repeat things," said Gertrude, sad for her young brothers. "Papa doesn't always mean what he says. Fathers sometimes have a lot of worries and say things they do not mean——"

The boy regarded her disagreeably. He finished chewing the cake that had precipitated all this, and swallowed it audibly. "Well, Pa don't think so very well of you either, Miss Gertie! I heard him telling Ma it was a wife's duty not to look like a sick cat most of the time, and that you weren't adding anything to Paul's joy in life. Not that I think much of that couch-cushion, but——"

Guy and Reginald glanced swiftly at Gertrude, and for one moment, in the ashen dusk, they saw her face. What Reginald saw made him rise with sinister swiftness, bent on Joey's annihilation. But Guy, with his dancer's dexterity, waltzed the lad behind him and rushed him toward the door. "I'll take care of him," he cried, over his shoulder, and the door banged after them, leaving Reginald, darkly flushed and breathing heavily, standing on the hearth, and trying not to look at his sister. "Vicious little brute!" he muttered. He straightened his black cravat. "I suppose I ought not to have called him that. No one has the right to call any one else violent names. But sometimes he makes me forget myself—" He sat down, peeped furtively at Gertrude. She sat in rigid silence, her head bent a little, her hands clasped in her lap. Something in her attitude made him ache intolerably, forced him to say with unnatural impulsiveness: "Trudie, did Pa—did any one—force you to marry Paul?"

Gertrude lifted her head slowly. He could feel, rather than see, the hollowness and pain in her eyes. "Force me, Reggie?" she repeated gently. "What a strange idea!" She reached over and laid her hand for a moment on his knee. His dark, saturnine face was quite miserable. "Dear Reggie, everything is just as I wanted it, believe me. I admit things have been—confusing, and I have been so lonely. I'm glad, so very glad, that you and Guy are home, and perhaps we'll bring Frey back with us, and then we'll all be together again."

He was silent. Her colorless gentleness frightened him. This was not the spirited, somewhat erratic young girl of last summer, with her sweet wild jerkiness of movement and gesture, sudden lifting of lids to show eyes of uncertain brilliance and amusement, quick irritability of tongue and nervous impatience. He put his hand over the cold little fingers on his knee, and could not say a word for some time. When he did speak, his voice was restless and somber, and though he did not speak again of herself, she gathered, from his words, that what he was saying had stemmed from his unquiet fears for her.

"Trudie, I haven't told any one this, but now I'm going to tell you. Pa, as you know, wants Guy and me to go into the business with him when we leave college. But I'm not going. I don't want his money; I don't want anything he has to give. I've heard rumors in the family that Uncle Martin wouldn't have anything more to do with the business, finally, because he thought munitions making was wicked. I understand how he felt, but I don't feel just like that. It's just that I'm not interested in money. I don't want it. A lot of money, millions, from any source, seems wrong to me. I can't believe that God meant any man to have great wealth, such as Pa has. You can't get it honestly. But even that isn't the important thing. I believe it was intended for us to live simply and frugally, quietly and nobly, not in great cities and congested areas, but in country places, on the land, meditating and working, and literally earning one's bread with the sweat of one's brow." He studied her uncomfortably and suspiciously, afraid of ridicule. But the little fingers on his knee were steady, and conveyed to him nothing but love and sympathy.

"I want to go back—to the Amish people, Trudie," he almost whispered, with a glance over his shoulder which betrayed the instinctive fear all Ernest's children felt for him.

Gertrude did not speak for some moments. Her thoughts had run unwillingly to her father, and automatically, as in her childhood, her loyalty to him, her adoration for him, turned her from Reginald. "The Amish people, Reggie? But what extraordinary people they are. Impossible; truly they are. Aren't they something like those awful Quakers? This all comes from that frightful Amish woman who used to teach you prayers and frighten you half to death with stories of hell-fire." Involuntarily, she remembered her father's sarcastic comments after the "Amish woman's" dismissal, and his tormenting question: "Where are your buttons, Reginald?" She disliked herself for smiling in the darkness. But really, poor Reggie was quite absurd, thought her loyalty to her father. "Money, dearest, is not to be despised. You've never done without it. You're just a boy, and can't understand yet what money means. You've always had everything you wanted, and I assure you you wouldn't enjoy working on the land, as you call it, at all. Aunt Amy has told me what she suffered when Uncle Martin took her to the farm, and how horrible it all was, and how lonely——"

Reginald was bitter with disappointment in her. "Lonely!" he cried. "What else am I now?" He stopped abruptly. He had no words to go on. His inarticulate tongue turned thick in his mouth, and he felt like crying. She fixed her eyes searchingly on his face; the fire had risen a little, and its rosiness touched his mouth, dark and somber and tormented and bleak. Bleak like the faces of the stony farmers who lived in the Pennsylvania hills, having a quality of gauntness in it that was more of the spirit than of any bodily hunger. She saw, all at once and with a kind of shock, that Reginald was of such stuff as those dour farmers; he was of the frugal, stripped gauntness of the Amish folk, to whom money meant nothing at all, neither a thing of power nor the purchaser of luxuries and ease. For they were constitutionally unable to realize what power and luxuries and ease could mean; it was beyond the comprehension of their particular turn of mind. Their happiness, their fulfilment in living, their peace, lay in other things. She sensed these things dimly, but they seemed distasteful and gloomy and acrid to her. Nevertheless, she understood that Reginald was driven, not by an ideal, but by his peculiarity of temperament. And she understood that a man might change his ideal, but never his personality. So she said, not with sympathy, but with comprehension: "However, dearest, you know best what you wish. Of course, Papa will be very disappointed. Frey—it was quite a blow. He has hoped you and Guy would make it all up to him. But if you can't, you can't. It will be quite difficult, however, to convince Papa that it will be impossible for you, not because of some freakish idea, but because you are just naturally unable to do what he wishes. I'll help, if you want me to."

His thin and gloomy face, still young and not yet entirely rigid, flashed into a relieved and grateful smile. "You do understand, don't you, Trudie? Do you really want to help me? Well, help me to convince Pa I don't want to go to New York with all of you this time. I—there's someone I want to see upstate. I practically promised——"

Guy, in the meantime, had taken Joey into the hall, and had succeeded in calming him to some extent with soothing flattery and humor. He implied, without actual words, that Reginald was something of an ass. No one, except Ernest, ever felt affronted by the boy's gay hypocrisies: he never meant them to be taken seriously, for they were utterly without viciousness, if tinged with malice and self-seeking. Joey, however, was not to be taken in by such gaudiness, and his surliness returned.

"Oh, I know what you're after, Mister Guy!" he said contemptuously. "You want me to lend you some money."

"That's it!" agreed Guy with disarming good temper and effrontery. "You're a clever little chap, Joey."

"Never mind that stuff," said the preternaturally adult Joey. "You can't get around me with your smooth tongue. You can get around Mama and little old Gertie with it, but not me. No, sir! I'm not going to lend you any money. I lent you two dollars last Thanksgiving for Gertie's birthday present, and you haven't even paid me the interest on it yet, though you promised it all to me on December 1st, when you got your allowance."

"On my honor, Joey, I forgot it——"

"Your honor? You ain't got any. Besides, I don't care a fig for honor, yours or any one else's. What I care about is the money I saved out of my allowance, and from birthdays and Christmas. Money's what counts. And you've got two dollars of my money."

"Don't I always pay it back, Joey?" Guy still smiled, but his gorge, quick and deadly, was rising, and his slender white hands became fists, for all they rested negligently on his hips. "This is the first time I ever forgot."

"I want my two dollars," replied Joey with contempt. "If I don't get it back on January 1st, I'll ask Papa to get it for me."

"You wouldn't do that."

"Wouldn't I, though! Well, that's all I got to say. You can borrow money from any one else for Christmas presents, but not from me. And I don't want none of your measly presents. Just give me my two dollars, and fifty cents, for interest, and forfeit for not paying back on time. After this, I'll know better than to lend my money to rascals and spendthrifts like you——"

Reginald was just in the midst of trying to enlarge on his reasons for going to live with the Amish people when there was an anguished roar from the hallway. Gertrude, startled, started to get up, but Reginald laughed. "It sounds as though Guy didn't succeed in getting a loan from Joey," he said. "In a way it serves Guy right. I've been giving him practically all my own allowance, and he got rid of it and his, too. For his own sake, I'm not going to give him any more. It just encourages him in his prodigal ways——"

The door opened and Guy appeared, a little pale, but still amiable. The roars dwindled down the hall, descended the steps. Guy, coming toward the fire, held out his hand for inspection. "Look at those knuckles! The kid's got a jaw like the jawbone of an ass. But it was worth it!"

"Oh, Guy!" exclaimed Gertrude, distressed. "You know Joey'll tell Papa, and then there'll be such trouble for you. Why didn't you ask *me*, if you need money?"

"Well, how could I? I've got everybody's presents but yours; I ran out of money. I only wanted five dollars from the little animal."

"But Guy, you know Papa has expressly warned us, dozens of times, that we were not to borrow from each other. You know he heard you borrowed from Reggie, and you didn't get a penny for three months. Besides, I'm a married woman now, and I could have let you have all you wanted."

"You're sweet, Trudie, but——"

"My Christmas present to you, Guy, was a twenty-dollar gold piece. What would you say if I gave it to you now, instead of on Christmas?"

"And mine," said Reginald reluctantly, "was a five-dollar gold piece. That makes twenty-five dollars. I know I ought not to let you have it ahead of time, but I'm weak, like Trudie. Try to make it do until you get your allowance. And if you owe Joey anything, pay it back to him before Pa gets home tonight."

Guy, light-heartedness restored, was all the gayer for his brief and deadly rage. He related his interview with Joey, and exaggerated it delicately and with such wit that Gertrude, and even his brother, laughed to the point of tears. But Gertrude was still apprehensive about their father's anger when Joey would have an opportunity to revenge himself on his brother by telling Ernest.

"Don't worry about the Old Man," said Guy airily. "I've figured out a way to get around him. He's always roaring that we don't take any interest in business, and are just utterly worthless. Well, I'm going to tell him that I don't care about going to New York to listen to Frey's pretty little music. I'll tell him I want to go with Paul to the coal mines and see how things are run. That ought to bring him around."

"Doesn't that seem a little far-fetched, dear?" asked Gertrude, smiling. But Reginald, who had at first listened with indifference, sharpened to quick attention toward the last. He stared at his brother searchingly, his eyebrows knotted over his deep-set and lustreless eyes.

"Far-fetched? I don't think so. I'd like to see the mines. Strikes are going on down there. I'd like to see them, too. I've been reading the newspapers at school." The youth nonchalantly inspected his fingernails, yawned. Reginald's attention became stronger and more fixed.

"Do strikes interest you?" he asked slowly.

"Perhaps they do." Nothing could have been more casual than Guy's voice.

"But how strange!" exclaimed Gertrude, diverted. "What for? Strikes! Don't the men fight dreadfully? I've heard Papa talk. I think something ought to be done to show those miners their places."

"Perhaps," agreed Guy indifferently. He surveyed his sister with the blandest of expressions.

But Reginald said nothing at all. But he thought: So Pa is to have only one of us after all. Joey. He watched his brother. But Guy is so elegant, almost like a girl. How strange that I never noticed before that he has a really hard jaw and straight mouth. But that is because he is always smiling; perhaps it is just to hide what he really is. However, Reginald could not convince himself of this. But he also was too young to reconcile Guy's light-heartedness and gaiety, his impudence and grace and activity and frivolity, with any great depth or purpose. He finally gave it up, puzzled. Reticent himself, he never probed into the minds of others, and regretfully decided that perhaps he would never know the solution to the mystery.

They talked until the winter dusk had become definite darkness, and until the crunching in the snow below warned them that their father and Paul were arriving. They had not bothered to light lamps, or to turn on the gas, and the warm dim-red glow of the dying fire made for intimacy in the heavy shadows of the room. One by one the coals were dropping onto the hearth, and now they could not see each other, and only occasionally caught the vague outline of a gesture or the movement of a shadowy face. Then loud and clear the dressing bell chimed through the pre-dinner hush of the house. Guy bounded away alertly, anticipating dinner, followed by Reginald, who had no desire to meet his father in the halls. Reginald did not close the door after him. Gertrude remained behind, reluctant to leave the quiet darkness of her brothers' room. She knew she ought to go to her own apartments, partly to meet Paul when he came upstairs, and partly because it was time to change for dinner. But she could not move. A heaviness lay along all her body, and her legs felt like iron. She began to shiver a little.

She heard Paul's footsteps, muffled by the carpet, coming up the stairs. She shrank back against the fireplace and held her breath. Why, she did not know. Her mother came out of her own room and encountered Paul in the hall. He greeted her courteously and asked for Gertrude.

"Why, she must be in her room," replied May. "She was in the boys' room all afternoon, but now I hear them splashing in the bathroom."

Paul was more cordial than usual with his aunt. He detained her in the hallway near the door of the room where Gertrude sat in shrinking silence.

"Aunt May, I've just decided today to buy the house in Greenville. It ought to be ready for us by early summer." His voice sounded exultant and young, for all its native weight and inflexibility.

"How nice," said May warmly. "Trudie will be so pleased. Of course, it is quite a way out, but then, Windsor is bound to grow that way."

"I hope not," said Paul decisively. "I like privacy. I have told Uncle Ernest a dozen times or more that the whole locality about here is rapidly going down, but he hardly believes it. Why, there is that wholesale butcher living practically next door! Within fifteen years this house will be the center of a slum."

"How very unpleasant." May's voice was still determinedly light. "I shouldn't like to think that my old home was decaying. But things do change, don't they?"

She left him, went down the stairs. Gertrude could very plainly hear the rustling of her dress, the swift fall of her still agile feet on the carpet.

There was the dimmest of light-glows in the long hallway. Paul evidently caught his foot on the frayed edge of the hall carpet, for he stopped directly in the doorway of the room where Gertrude was crouching, hidden. He muttered something; I should speak, thought Gertrude. Her mouth felt dry and thick and paralyzed. But this is absurd, her wild thoughts continued. But her body shrank farther into the darkness about the fireplace. She could see Paul's dark, almost formless bulk in the pale rectangle of the doorway. She knew he was peering in, absently. She held her breath; her heart beat with a sickly sensation, and she felt herself gyrating mistily, with only that half-formed shadow a fixed spot in a place of flux. And all the time her thoughts intoned over and over: This is very, very stupid of me.

Paul went on to their own apartments. She heard him call her name, then the door closed after him. She relaxed; her legs sagged, and her forehead felt wet. Her heart seemed to sink into a bottomless pit.

She began to shiver again.

CHAPTER LXXX

ERNEST WAS edified, and not a little secretly pleased that his frivolous
and airy young son, Guy, apparently seemed to be beginning to
feel an interest in his father's vast enterprises. He was also,
knowing his son, somewhat skeptical. But Ernest was not one
to look too deeply into intrinsic motives: sometimes, he considered, the less probing one did the better. "Of course," he said to the
annoyed Paul, who had not much patience with his young brother-in-law,
and was bitterly jealous of all Ernest's sons as potential heirs to what he
considered rightfully his, "of course, Paul, I realize it is probably just a
fad on his part. Guy is always after something new and exciting. He's
under the impression the coal mines, now that the strikes are on, ought
to be very romantic places. It won't do him any harm to see things in
the raw. Might sober him up a bit."

"I doubt it," replied Paul dourly.

So only Ernest, May, Gertrude and Elsa went to New York. May had
no illusions that Ernest had softened toward his oldest son and was going
to New York solely to hear him make his debut in the Academy of Music
on Fourteenth Street. He had been contemptuously silent for years in
the face of May's reading of Godfrey's letters and the enthusiastic comments of his masters. He had sent checks, paid bills, in that averted
silence. It was as if he had given Godfrey up, and paid his bills as one
paid up a hard debt. But May, in bitterness, saw that so far as Ernest
was concerned, Godfrey, as a significant individual and a son, had ceased
to exist. She did not have to hint overmuch, therefore, to discover
Ernest's real reason for going to New York. It was to see his friend,
Jay Regan, Senior, the great financier, and also to discuss with him the
possibility of selling to the newest American pirate, James Bellowes,
his interest in the Pennsylvania oil wells in the vicinity of Titusville.
May knew, from overhearing conversations between Ernest and Paul,
that Bellowes was exerting pressure on Ernest either to sell him the
wells or come in with him in the most infamous exploitation that had
ever disgraced the history of American business. Ernest, as director of
the railroad that did most of the oil carrying for the Bellowes combine,
was in a peculiar position. He was in the anomalous and dangerous
position of being a potential and deadly competitor of the biggest customer of the railroad, and the other directors were becoming restive and

apprehensive. He had reached the point where he must decide to remain a competitor and enter into a war of titans for the control of oil, in which his chances were barely hopeful, but in which profits beyond any of his imaginations were the reward of victory, or sell, or combine his oil wells with Bellowes. The latter would enrich him, also; but it would be his first compromise, his first yielding. However, even his egotism was not sufficient to allow him the luxury of a battle for the battle's sake and some adolescent idea of never-give-up-the-ship. He was perfectly willing to give up the ship if he were promised a share in the victor's loot.

Better to yield gracefully, with an enormous profit, and gain the friendship of this basilisk, this almost unhuman creature, that stood at the head of the oil industry. Ernest was not vainglorious nor really conceited: he saw nothing ignominious in becoming a vassal to such a formidable king, especially when an oath of fealty could be so pleasantly profitable. "Only the little man can afford glory," he said to Paul. And so his journey to New York was for the sole purpose of yielding, after allowing himself to be persuaded, and bringing back with him, as reward, the friendship of the basilisk and an agreeable profit.

He was too indifferent to May's feelings, or at least pretended to be, to allow her to believe that the journey to New York was for the purpose of hearing Godfrey's symphony performed. There was something brutal in his openness on the subject; he yawned ostentatiously when Godfrey was mentioned. It was probable that he took a sadist's pleasure in May's obvious pain and sadness; he was almost elated at the distress that stood starkly behind her serenity and poise. When he spoke of Godfrey it was with lightness and cruel indulgence. May thought: He has become my poor boy's enemy. It would please him to see Godfrey ruined. A great part of her distress was due to the fact that in the face of all this, she could not hate Ernest. She was also extremely alarmed because he had been indifferent to Reginald's fumbling request that he be excused from going to New York, and had not listened to his stammering explanation that he "wished to see someone, and it was very important." A servant, explaining some petty future absence, would have gained more attention from Ernest than did Reginald. He had seemed to be attending, but his brutally indifferent manner, his apparent boredom and disinterest, had seriously upset May. Was another of his sons about to cease to exist for Ernest? she thought, terrified, mentally rushing in protection to the side of her second son. It was all because of Paul! her frantic thoughts ran on, and she glanced at Paul, reading his paper, with hatred. In a voice louder than usual, and edged with fear, she attempted to gain Ernest's attention by arguing with Reginald about his decision not to go to New York. But Ernest's attention could not be gained.

Therefore, when Guy requested that he be permitted to go to the coal regions with Paul, May did not protest very much. It was such a relief to her to see Ernest warm into interest toward her third son, and smile upon him with real pleasure for the first time in years. Her complacence grew at the sight of Paul's evident discomposure and annoyance. Joey, ill with a slight cold, was not to go to New York; he seemed quite resigned.

It was a dark and snowy morning when Paul and Guy set out for the coal fields. Paul, more annoyed than ever, was heavily silent. Their accommodations on the train, though first class, were none too comfortable. The coaches stank of kerosene and wood smoke. The oil lamps had been lit, and flared into a yellow and uncertain gloom, swinging back and forth overhead with the motion of the train. The plush seats were gritty, the windows steamed and ran into little sooty puddles on the ledges, and each time the door was opened by the conductor a gale of bitter wind and snow roared through the coach.

Paul, huddled in his fur-lined coat, had brought office books and papers with him. He pulled his hat down over his eyes and went to work. Guy, slender and clean and young, sat beside him. Paul had told himself that the boy would probably be an infernal nuisance, and this was no time to be dragging brats about with one into the wild violence and wretchedness of the coal regions. He could not understand Ernest; what the devil had come over him to dream of allowing a little numskull and idiot like Guy to accompany him, Paul, as if he were going on a holiday? He would not understand it! This was going to be grim business; he was Ernest's deputy in one of the most serious disorders that had ever struck the coal centers. He was literally the messenger of life or death, and what his decisions were would have an immense effect on the attitude of capital toward labor for many years to come. Whatever he would do would have a detonating result. And all this was given a ludicrous quality by his being forced to take with him a brat barely out of short breeches. It was taking on the air of a hilarious outing, big brother taking little brother to the fair for a Christmas treat! It was intolerable. Intolerable and ridiculous. His gorge rising to an unendurable point, Paul glanced sidewise at his companion, the full enormity of his position occurring to him for the first time.

He was a little disconcerted at the sight of Guy's profile. It was a young and handsome profile, fine-drawn and sharp, almost dainty in its cleanness and smallness of feature. Guy had removed his hat; his fair curls and waves gleamed in the yellow lamplight. But his expression was what suddenly engrossed Paul's attention: it was so tense, almost rigid, and yet composed, as though he were thinking thoughts no "brat" had the intelligence or the right to think. Especially not Guy, the spendthrift and the caperer, the laugher and the jokester, the player of practical jokes, the riotous jackanapes. The deep dimples made clefts in his cheeks, yet oddly did not detract from the rigidity of his expression. Paul felt quite a shock. He did not like the look on the boy's face; the cool acidity of his jealousy began to stir without words, as though it instinctively felt the presence of a smiling enemy who had suddenly grown formidable.

"What's the matter?" he asked, infusing into his voice a note of surly ridicule. "Got a belly-ache?"

Guy smiled. But he looked straight ahead, and not at Paul. "No," he said.

Paul pulled his hat irritably. "I still can't see why you took a notion to go with me?" he went on, shouting over the noise of the wheels. "What's behind it all?"

"You've asked me that before," replied Guy.

Paul colored at this cool impudence. He disliked Guy more than he disliked any of his other cousins, and it would have given him much pleasure to slap the youth. "That's true. But you've not given a sensible answer. You said you've 'read the papers,' and wanted to see what was going on. Couldn't you have kept on reading the papers?" His heavy lip curled, and he tried to smile as one smiles at a precocious but secretly hated child.

"No," answered Guy, still staring straight ahead.

Paul bit his lip. "This is a lot of damned nonsense," he said, viciously infuriated at the futility of what he was saying. But Guy was silent. The dimples made him appear to be smiling faintly. But he was not smiling.

"Perhaps you aren't aware that we aren't to stay at some luxurious hotel," went on Paul. "Pittsville is only a wretched little mining town, with a drummers' boarding house, a saloon, a few company stores and a dancehall and miners' shacks. You won't find things very pleasant, especially now. If you think you are going on a holiday, with lots of romance and excitement, you are going to be sadly mistaken."

"Did I say I expected things to be pleasant?" Guy turned to him, and now his face had the smooth blank quality of his father's face when he felt particularly hostile and brutal. "I don't mind where we stay. I'm not a girl." He paused. "Why can't you let me alone? You feel there's some mystery in my wanting to go to Pittsville. Perhaps there is. Perhaps there isn't. But I'm a human being, and I've a right to my thoughts and motives. You're not paying my fare, you know. I think Pa took care of that." He smiled slightly. "It's no money out of your pocket, though I imagine you might feel it is." His eyes were like a thrust into Paul's face.

Paul turned white with rage. His expression became quite ugly with it. For one teetering moment he was on the verge of striking the youth beside him. He saw that he had underestimated Guy, and his hatred became stronger as it was goaded with apprehension. Ernest needed only one son to show interest and wit and cogency, and his natural paternal vanity would do the rest. And what of him, Paul? He had been working for months on the supposition, the growing hope, that he would be the heir to what he was by nature qualified to inherit. He was giving all his time, his life, his ambitions, his sweat and his very flesh. Was all this to be jeopardized by a little dancing ninny? Especially one who guessed all he had been thinking and planning, and who, serene after all in the knowledge that he was Ernest Barbour's son, was laughing at his brother-in-law? Real fright, real suffering, mingled themselves with Paul's rage. It became imperative to him to discover the reason behind this "child's" determination to visit the coal regions. He could not yet believe that intelligence and mature interest were behind it. So he controlled himself, clenched his teeth on his rage. He returned to his papers, waiting to find out what he knew he must know if he were to have any peace. He had a dogged mind, and the books he had brought with him were engrossing and familiar, so he was able to push his new apprehension away from him. But it lurked at a distance and his whole consciousness began to be pervaded with a singular malaise, as disturbing as it was new.

He did not speak to Guy again for some time. The youth had brought nothing with him to shorten the gritty hours of travel. He had the seat near the window, and he stared through it for a long time. Compared with the tall and bulky Paul, he was childlike of figure, immature of face and development.

As the train ran toward the foothills the snow became rain. The little villages and lonely farmhouses huddled drearily under a sky of wet iron. At noon they came to the foothills, gray and dim purple in the rain and rising fog. The engine began to climb, thundering and puffing under the strain. The flat land fell away; they were in a sea of hills, black, snow-patched, cold and implacable. Here and there a ridge of pines marched away from them; the snow patches became more frequent, lying like scabrous spots on the dark hillsides. The rain splashed and rattled and ran over the windows.

Toward evening the hills became wilder, blacker, more snowy, for they had left the rain behind. The engine struggled more and more. Pine forests bristled over the tops of the shifting hills; the valleys ran with water. Snow had begun to fall again, dropping silently. Through its moving haze a hilltop shouldered and disappeared; the train roared over a bridge, and Guy caught below a glimpse of icy black water between floes of ice. The air, even in the closeness of the train, became colder and fresher.

Hour after hour had gone by, and nothing had passed between Paul and Guy though they had eaten together. Guy had become exceedingly restless; his quicksilver temperament made itching sensations about his bones and an ache in his back. He was too young and too volatile to be able to keep his mind relentlessly on one thing no matter how important to him. There was something of his father's character in the way he could decide upon a matter, consummate all details in his thoughts, and then lay it aside, completed, except for the mere mechanics of action. For the whole past hour he had peeped furtively at Paul, alternately admiring that savage concentration and feeling contempt for it. Finally he felt that any conversation at all with Paul was preferable to this sodden silence between them. But Paul showed not the slightest inclination to speak to him. I've put a bee in his bonnet, thought Guy, not without satisfaction. He's got the wind up, and he'll have plenty to think about. Whatever made Trudie marry him? I thought it was all settled about her and Philippe? His fatigued thoughts grew sharper at the thought of his cousin, Philippe, of whom he was very, fond. Philippe, the subtle and nervous, the quick and supple, who had something of Guy's own volatile instability of temperament and was so clever and full of a swift radiance of color. Guy recalled that Gertrude had written to him saying that her father had practically consented to her marriage to Philippe. And now, the mystery. Overnight she had married Paul Barbour, the favorite of his uncle. I'll bet, thought Guy cynically and with unusual bitterness, that dear Papa had a hand in this mess. Thinking this, he glanced again at Paul, and it seemed to him that his whole slight and graceful body expanded in a surge of hatred. Trudie, married to this conniver, this contemptuous potential robber of Ernest Barbour's children, who had not even the decency to be subtle about it!

It was nearing sunset now, and the hills were giving way to the mountains. In the distance, through the thinning snow, Guy caught glimpses of some terrible black majesty, lonely and towering. Higher and higher rose the solemn ridges; the snow was twisted and deep upon them. The train ran like a furtive little animal through empty valleys and over yellowed floods.

The western heavens, gloomy and purple, suddenly changed. A crimson slash opened in them. The sun, a round and scarlet ball, pushed itself through the opening. Instantly the landscape became a scene of terror and splendor. Against that lake of cold fire the mountains thrust, black, gaunt, ribbed with snow. The sun poured on this cloudy chaos like a red cataract. Pine forests huddled below, the tops coppered, the valleys sinking down under fog. Brighter burned the lake of fire, and against that ruddy background the mountains rolled wave on wave, black and red and frightful, disappearing into moving walls of mist.

Now it began to get dark; now the mountains were merely darker shadows against a gloomy and gaseous sky. A faint roaring passed the windows as a wind rose. The engine was heavily laboring, and the thick boiling steam and smoke could be seen as the train rounded curves. The flickering yellow light of the lamps made the interior of the musty car the more dreary. Nearly all of the few passengers had left the train before this at various stops, and only one or two men besides Paul and Guy sagged wearily on the dirty cushions.

Fatigue fell like a blow on Guy, and he went to sleep, through which he was uneasily conscious of the monotonous clicking of the rails and the kerosene-flavored chilliness of the coach. His head fell smartly against the window, and he awoke with a start, hungry, stiff and aching. The train was slowing down; he could see nothing through the windows. Only his own reflection and the reflections of the lamps glimmered on their blackness. Paul was restrapping his luggage after replacing in it the books and papers which had engrossed him all day. His profile seemed swollen with vengeful hostility and contempt; he still did not look at Guy.

The conductor appeared at the door, holding a lantern and swaying on the threshold. "Pittsville!" he bellowed. Guy stretched and yawned, full of depression. He was still only a boy; what he had come to see with such relentlessness and determination seemed silly and yet overwhelming to him, as though he had no part in it and could not possibly ever have any part. As he shivered in the dank and penetrating chilliness of the coach, he longed for his home passionately, as a child would long. What on earth was he doing here, with Paul, that bounder, in the wild and desolate coal regions? He could well imagine the laughter of his father, and for a moment he felt apologetic toward his cousin.

The train, steaming, puffing and churning, lurched to a stop, and through the window Guy could see the dreary station with its lantern swinging in the wind and snow. A group of men clustered together on the platform, wrapped in sheepskin coats. In the startling silence that followed the grinding of the train, Guy could hear the bellowing of the wind; in the lantern light huge icicles hanging from the station roof glittered and dripped. They alighted, and the wind seized them. As they struggled with it, the train went on without them, puffing and groaning, and its lights blinked off into the night. Snow stung their faces.

Dizzy and vague with fatigue and depression, Guy was aware of the men surrounding them. They evidently knew Paul, who had been here once before. They talked to him rapidly, in hoarse tense voices. One was the Superintendent, a Mr. Wilkes, another was an engineer, Mr. Bronston, and the remainder were foremen, detectives, and the chief detective. The wind flayed their rough red faces, which seemed to glower in the lantern light; their voices sounded large and diffused in the wind. Guy caught a word here and there: "State Militia— situation getting worse—

the dogs—had to shoot two Hunkies today. The Governor'll be sorry
for this! Anarchy. What does Mr. Barbour say? The Crowder Mines've
given in, and it makes it god-damned hard on the rest of us! What does
Mr. Barbour say? Mr. Barbour—Mr. Barbour—Mr. Barbour—" Then
a hoarse expletive: "They hung four Mollie Maguires yesterday. That's
the way to deal with the bastards!" Paul listened, holding his coat about
his throat.

Guy became aware of a sudden silence. They were all regarding him
incredulously, finally conscious of his presence. Big hulking men staring
down at the slim and shivering youth. Then they stared at Paul, their
mouths opening, unbelievingly. "Is this kid with you, Mr. Barbour?"
asked the Sheriff, astounded.

Paul glanced at his cousin with an annihilating eye. "Yes. He wanted
to come. Gentlemen, this is Guy Barbour, Mr. Ernest Barbour's son."

The men were petrified. After a long moment one or two of them
pulled uncertainly at their hats and caps. "Hullo," said Guy in his clear
high voice. He felt ridiculous, and undefended. "Glad to meet you,"
mumbled a few appalled voices. "Master—Mister Barbour."

His presence seemed to oppress them and stun them. They glanced at
each other, more and more astounded. Then they led the way to several
hacks waiting at the end of the platform. They walked softly and
lumberingly, staring in a dumfounded way. The Chief Detective said to
Paul helplessly: "The only place for you, Mr. Barbour, is Miz McCloskey's roomin' house, and it ain't overly nice. You and young Mister
Barbour, there——"

"Don't worry. It'll have to do," replied Paul shortly. "We're not here
on a holiday, you know."

They climbed into the hacks and lurched away over an unseen but
rocky road into the icy and screeching darkness. To Guy, numb and aching and exhausted, it seemed that they travelled and swayed and hurled
back and forth for hours. He sat with Paul and the Sheriff and Mr.
Wilkes and Mr. Bronston. The dead and bitter air was soon laden with
the smell of bodies and the reek of whiskey, the smell of sawdust and
manure and dirt and filthy blankets. Guy could see nothing at all, not
even the faces of his companions. His feet rested on hard objects which
he knew were guns. The men shouted above the unending wind, the
rattling and groaning of the hack, the cursing of the driver.

From the pressing of the bodies about him, Guy guessed they were
climbing.

He peered out. The snow had stopped, and between clouds like flying
black rags the moon poured out, glacial and savage. Vague looming
bulks crowded and shouldered against the sky—the broken ridges of the
foothills. They passed mountains of slag, and the wheels of the hack
gritted over layers of cinders with a crushing and desolate sound. They

passed shacks, with a dim light here and there like a dull moan in the wild night. Once or twice a starving dog howled. They passed coal tipples, gaunt and skeleton-like, like giant gibbets against the moon. Guy, looking, felt a cold and deadly horror in his chest, a sick dropping in his stomach. The coal regions. Men lived here, and were dying here, now, because they had gone mad with hunger and cold and desolation and despair. Outside of the wind, the occasional dog, the crunching of the wheels, there was no sound, though where the clefts appeared in the hills there was an occasional moving and bobbing lantern light, like a feeble candle in a black and freezing and formless hell.

Paul was listening to everything his companions were telling him. The Militia had been called out today; the Governor had been forced into it, though the bastard had shown it was entirely against his will. But what could you expect of a man whose grandfather had been a miner, himself? That was the trouble with this country! The speaker had an Irish brogue, and his clothing stank of old tobacco and beer. But now that the Militia was out, and there had been some hangings and shootings, they'd soon have the dogs on the run. They were dying like flies, anyway—starving. The women were as bad as the men. One of them had clubbed a detective. But his companion had finished the bitch. They'd had to kick the kids around a bit, too, what with their throwing rocks and coal at the detectives, and setting dogs on them. Mr. Wilkes and the Sheriff and Mr. Bronston laughed hoarsely.

Paul said nothing. A hot sick sweat had broken out across Guy's shoulders. I'm going to faint, he thought. But he did not faint. Instead, he began to gasp a little, silently, stiffly, in the darkness. And then, swiftly and gigantically, it seemed to him that a fiery red glow was flowing toward him from the sky and the earth, the black hills and the mountains of slag, and when it focussed in him it became a brilliant and burning incandescence of hate. I hate him! he thought simply, and not childishly, and the face of his father stood before him.

Then he became aware of a certain awkwardness and loudness in the voices of the speakers. It occurred to him, with an almost hysterical amusement, that it was because he was there. Each man had begun to speak boastingly of his particular exploits in the work of subduing the desperate miners. He could not see their faces, but he felt them turned to him. Then the Superintendent asked him concernedly if he had enough blankets, and apologized that he was unable to have Mr. Barbour and Master Barbour stay overnight with him at his own house in the lower valley. "The bastards burnt it up for me two days ago," he said savagely.

The hack was steadily climbing. One of the vehicles climbed ahead, and another scrambled behind. The moon was riding higher, pouring down a cataract of polished steel over the black rounded hills and narrow clefts that were tiny valleys. Even in summer this must be a desolate

place, thought Guy; there were no trees about at all. There was a settlement of shacks huddled here, built of clapboards, with low leaning chimneys and windows like holes. None of them were lighted. Yet somehow
Guy knew that men and women and children slept behind the sagging
doors. They passed a saloon, mean and drab and badly lit; there was no
one inside but the bartender, and there was a gun lying across the bar.
Now they were leaving the small settlement behind and were skirting the
bottom of a hill. The noise of the cinders under the wheels was a constant raw scraping of the nerves, and the air that seeped into the hacks
was acrid and deathly cold. The moon showed scabs of snow here and
there.

They rounded the hill. Perched halfway up its side was another shack,
a little larger, a little better built than the others. A light, bright and
almost cheerful, burned against the formless darkness of the hill. The
Sheriff, seeing this shack, burst into obscenity, and snatched up a gun
from under Guy's feet. Each man in the hack came to tense life. "That's
where that goddam traitor, Buzak, lives! One of our own foremen, too!
Didn't he shoot down one of our detectives yesterday, Bill? I been
lookin' for him everywhere. His woman and kids must still be up, curse
them!"

The gun was in the Sheriff's hands; he poked aside the curtains of the
hack, and then the thin iron silence of the night was shattered by a splintering crash. Instantly the light went out in the shack. There was a prolonged stillness after the shot, as if all the hills had sucked in their breath
in horror, and were holding it. Then, as the hack crawled on, the long
and jagged red scream of a woman ran after them, a horrible sound of
anguish. The Sheriff relaxed, chuckled, dropped the gun. The men
made uneasy sounds. Paul, stiffening against Guy, said angrily: "See
here, we want none of that unless it's necessary." The scream of the
woman was becoming a high, gibbering madness. They rounded the hill
completely, and the shack was lost, and there was only the night and the
screaming growing fainter and fainter, yet the more terrible.

Then Guy spoke for the first time since he had entered the hack.
"You are a good shot, Sheriff," he said, in his clear boy's voice. "And it
was a good gun, too——"

The Sheriff, made uneasy by Paul's sullen and angry silence, responded
eagerly. "Kind of you to say so, Mister Barbour." He chuckled in-
gratiatingly. "It ought to be a good gun! It's one of your Pa's forty-
fives!" He patted it with gloating affection. "They shipped in twenty-
five yesterday. Best in the country! The old MacIlvain was considered
mighty good, but it can't compare to these here old forty-fives of Barbour-Bouchard."

The hacks crunched to a stop, and Guy could see that they had arrived
at a dismal and biggish house built of clapboards. The windows glared

empty and black in the moonlight. There was a smudge of red smoke lazily vomiting from a chimney. Two militiamen, guards, paced back and forth around it, guns over their shoulders. The snow was thicker here, and there was a little path of beaten ice over it, from the feet of the soldiers. Everyone got out of the hacks. The Sheriff hailed the guards boisterously, and they sauntered toward the group of men, grinning. They were brutal-looking creatures with broad empty faces.

The Sheriff opened the house door, and they all trooped in. "Miz McCloskey!" bellowed the Sheriff. Someone lit a lamp. They were standing in a small square hall, indescribably filthy and bare, the board floor scarred and soiled with tobacco juice. The kerosene lamp which had just been lit swung gauntly from the ceiling. A stairway ran up into reeking gloom. A woman appeared at the head of the stairs in an old-fashioned and frowsy mob-cap and hideous frayed dressing gown. "I'm here!" she shrilled in a rusty voice. "Lands sake, Sheriff, I thought you'd never come, so I went to bed! Come in, everybody!" She came clumsily down the stairs. The ghastly lamp shone upon her face. She was old and gaunt, withered and cunning. Her speech, her gestures, the glance of her fiery little eye, were at once impertinent and fawning and servile. Granddaughter, daughter and widow of miners, her sympathy ought naturally to have been with her kind, but it was not. Not because of a delusion of superiority, but simply because of greed. Nor was she hypocritical; greed had induced in her case, as it often does with her sort, a vicious loyalty to the masters and a malevolent hatred for the members of her class. She would have betrayed the latter gladly, without a conscious expectation of reward, and totally without a sensation of treachery.

She grinned at the assemblage of men, as she stood on the last step. Her yellowed teeth were like a broken fence between her withered lips, and her long out-thrust jaw was like a narrow spade. She clutched her gown about her with talons.

"Ma'am," said the Sheriff, "this here is Mr.—Mr. Brundage, like I told you, come from downstate from Mr. Barbour. And this young man here," indicating Guy, "he's sort of—sort of secre'ty to Mr. Brundage. Name of Miller." He turned to Paul and Guy. "Guess Mrs. McCloskey'll put you up fine and dandy, sir. You'll have the big room next to mine. It's got two beds in it, ain't it, ma'am? Fine! I'll call you in the mornin', sir, and we'll go out to the mines. And Mr.—Miller, too. Mrs. McCloskey," he added heartily, beaming on the beldame, "is the best cook in these parts, and you'll find no fault with her breakfasts."

"Now, you go on, Sheriff!" she exclaimed, bridling and simpering. "But come, gentlemen, it's quite nippy down here, and I've got a right nice little stove a-burnin' in your room." They trooped after her; the splintered board stairs were gritty under their feet; the long wavering light of the lamp followed them. The cold persisted, following them like a wind. She flung open a leaning door and showed them the hollow wood shell of a drab, half-empty room barely lit and warmed by a tiny pot-bellied iron stove. The chill here was hardly less than in the hall below. Two iron cots with dingy quilts stood in the center of the room, and a broken chest of drawers, two rockers, a table and an oil-lamp, made up the rest of the furnishings. And over them all was the fine black patina of coal dust that nothing could eradicate.

When Paul and Guy were alone, Paul began to unpack a few of his articles and lay them on the chest of drawers. The austere silver brushes glittered in the dim light—the stove crackled. Guy sat down on the edge of his dubious cot and stared blankly at his own bag. He shivered. He had removed his hat and his bright curling hair showed threads of gold. He looked pathetically young, and frail, a light dancing figure collapsed on a sordid dust-heap.

"I hope," said Paul grimly, without turning to face him, "that you're enjoying yourself. I hope you are not too disappointed."

"I'm not." Guy's eyes were bland and his voice high and calm. "It's pretty horrible, though." He took off his coat and opened his bag. A silence fell between them again as they prepared for bed. Fastidious Guy examined the straw mattress and the sheets and blankets. He pulled them back into place, put his shoes on again. It was apparent that he did not intend to sleep under the bed clothes, but on top of them. He laid out a woollen afghan that May had insisted he take with him. Without looking at Paul, and with apparent indifference, he said: "I think I know your game."

Paul was so astounded at this remark that for a moment his bent back remained in position, petrified. Then he swung about on his cousin with rage. "What the hell do you mean by that remark?" he shouted. "My game? What game?"

And then he stopped, abruptly. For from out Guy's small dimpled face Ernest's eyes stared back at him, baleful, opaque and implacable. Those eyes were like a fist in his chest. "My father," Guy said, "is a very remarkable man. I know it, too. But even a remarkable man can make mistakes. He thinks you're the best he's got. He doesn't know what a big lumbering donkey you are. My father thinks he is founding a sort of dynasty: that's the Englishman in him—family, money, tradition, father-to-son business. But he's picked the wrong man to carry on the dynasty; he's made his first mistake—in you. You're no Empire-builder; you're no Atlas. You're all bulk and push. But Pa didn't get where he is just by bulk and push. He's got something else. For a bright man, Pa's showing his age. You've got no imagination. No vision. Ever hear of vision, Paul?"

Paul, more and more astounded, more and more enraged, felt the thick black blood swelling through his throat and into the veins of his head.

He stood there, his big body shaking with restrained explosions, his face swollen and empurpled. He opened his mouth, but no sound came from it.

Guy casually snapped his fingers, and smiled. The baleful look in his eyes took on a derisive shine from that smile. "But perhaps," he continued lightly, "Pa expects the vision and the cleverness to come from the Bouchards. I don't think he could really believe you have any. He can't really not know that there's a weak flabby place in you, Paul. A place like the one in your Pa." He paused. "You see," he added conversationally, "Pa thinks that you're like him in lots of ways. He looks at me, and thinks he sees what he calls a jackanapes. But I'm really more like him. More like him than any one else in the world. What I want, and what he wants, are entirely different. I'm looking out of a different window. And looking out of that window, I see you. And I know what you are, and what you are after." Under his cousin's very nose, he lay down and stretched out, turning his back. "But you'll see. I'm not going to let you get it. I'm my father's son, after all."

Rage alone was not now petrifying Paul. It was fully aroused fear, the sickening consciousness that his suspicions were justified. This malicious little dog, this little terrier! Many times before he had experienced blind rage, but never before had he wanted to kill. The desire became a veritable ecstasy, a yawning, head-swinging ecstasy. It actually propelled him toward his reclining cousin with extended hands, for he was caught in the most overwhelming instinct of his species. When he suddenly realized what he was about, his knees turned to shaking jelly, and for one moment all his other thoughts and hatreds were lost in the black pit of his real horror. He stood there, trembling, gasping.

Then he turned away, sat down heavily upon his bed, and stared somberly before him. He began to speak in a thick strained voice. "You're a little ass, Guy. You're just a kid. I—I have no game. You forget that I'm part of Barbour-Bouchard now. I'm going to do my best to help your father carry out what he wishes. If you're really going to show some interest at last, I'll help you. I'm your sister's husband, and I've got to take care of her share. My father helped build up this business too." He drew a heavy breath. "I don't want to rob you." And because of his horror, he believed this.

Guy turned over slowly, and the lamp glittered on his handsome teeth as he grinned. "Who said anything about 'robbing'?" he asked.

And across the little space between their cots, the cousins stared at each other, and the cold mountain wind shook the bare window-panes. They were alone here under the most fantastic circumstances, this powerful young man and the boy. Then suddenly Guy, exultant, saw the grotesqueness of the situation, and he burst into wild thin laughter, and rolled in spasms upon his bed.

"My father," he cried, "would have killed, if he had felt that way!"

CHAPTER LXXXI

WHEN GUY awoke the next morning he discovered that Paul was already gone. He was amused at this, but satisfied. He had had no desire to accompany his cousin anywhere. He saw that much snow had fallen in the night, and long velvety folds of it made soft terraces on the black hills. A clear thin sky shone overhead. There was not a sound, except for the distant closing of a door and a woman's shrill voice. Moreover, the room was bitterly cold, and Guy huddled under his coats. He stared at the ceiling fixedly; the dimples in his cheeks gave him the effect of smiling boyishly. But he was not smiling. His eyes had in them a certain pointed slash of pupil which was more than a little savage. After a long time of staring, he began to whistle under his breath, and sprang out of bed. The whistle rose to loud singing. "After the ball is over, ta ta ta tatata!" He danced about the room as he pulled on his trousers; after he had laced his small and dainty boots he danced again, with curvettings and pirouettes, with swift light movements full of grace and buoyancy. His fair bright hair fell back from his face with a faunlike flow, and his features seemed sharpish and puck-like and a little unhuman. When he had been a child, old Hilda had called him "fey." She had seen a wild laughter in him, a cruelty in the gaiety, a bitter brightness that no human flesh could touch. Only she had known that in spite of that gaiety and brightness and laughter, the dancing and the grace, he was more like his father than any one in the world would ever be. People said of him, as they said of Ernest: "You never know what he is thinking."

He flew down the rickety stairs three at a time and landed at the bottom as lightly and boundingly as a cat. A dingy door opened from the hallway and Mrs. McCloskey, still in dressing gown and cap, thrust her gaunt and cunning face through the aperture. "Land sakes!" she ejaculated angrily. "Was you aimin' to shout the house down?" As youthful Mr. Miller, secretary to a more important man, she disdained him. "Come on in the kitchen and eat your break'as. I ain't got all day. Coffee's cold, but I don't guess you'll mind that."

He followed her into a filthy and ancient wooden kitchen where a coal stove fumed sullenly and the coal dust and dirt were thick on the one narrow uncurtained window. On the corner of a wooden table, scarred and ingrained with grease and more dirt, she had laid his breakfast.

The coarse white china was none too clean, and the tableware was of bent pewter. She poured out lukewarm coffee for him; it made him slightly nauseated as he smelt it. She thrust discolored sugar in a paper sack under his nose. On his plate she deposited two slices of fried "sow belly" and a thick stale slice of gray bread. This done, she retired to the stove, folded her arms on her sunken breast, and regarded him malevolently over her pointed shoulder.

"I don't think I'm hungry," said Guy, turning his smooth face toward her.

"Hah!" She wrinkled her face hideously at him, and fiercely nodded her head. "You don't like my victuals?"

"Oh, it's not that." He smiled at her, and the lightness of his eyes took on an innocent deep blue tinge, and the dimples made him look like a fascinating girl. "But it was a long journey yesterday, and my stomach's upset."

Even Mrs. McCloskey could not withstand that beautiful smile and ingratiating voice. She humped her shoulders, growled under her breath, and then exclaimed that she guessed she could give him an egg if he wanted it, and she had a couple of biscuits still hot in the oven. While she prepared this treat with unusual alacrity, Guy talked to her in his gay light voice, and she began to shout with laughter. He was telling her an amusing, and entirely fictitious story, about Paul, and she was sufficiently close to her ancestry to enjoy a story at the expense of her "betters." The malice on her face made her more repellent than ever; as she squatted before the stove and fished inside for the biscuits, she rocked on her haunches in an ecstasy of enjoyment. When she gave him the egg and biscuits, and "found" some butter, she said, looking down at him with a leering and broken-toothed smile: "You are the prettiest young un I've seen in many a day!" A rank odor emanated from the long emaciated body in the frayed and matted dressing gown; he could see the sprouting whiskers on her spade-like chin. But he sparkled up to her as though she were an object of delight. She put her talons on his burnished and curling hair and wound a tendril or two over soiled fingers like bones.

"Tell me," said Guy, lavishly spreading butter on his biscuits, and helping himself prodigally to large portions of apple butter which Mrs. McCloskey had also "found" in her larder, "are the miners starving much?"

"Starvin'?" Her gritty voice descended to a contemptuous growl, though she continued to play with his hair. "Yes, and dyin' of it, and good riddance to the scum! Yesterday some hussy came a-beggin' at the back door with her brat on her arm and I threw dishwater in her face!"

"Why?" asked Guy innocently. "She had done you no harm."

"Why?" The talons paused on a lock and with unconscious viciousness jerked it smartly. "Scum, that's why. Strikin'! Fightin' their bread and butter. Destroyin' law and order! That's what: destroyin' law and order! We got to have law and order. That's the law."

"Yes, I suppose so. It is rather defying law and order to ask for enough to eat, isn't it?"

"Eh?" She peered down at him suspiciously. "You ain't ribbin' me, are you, young man?"

"I? Not at all. I'm just agreeing with you. You see, having the kind of father I have, I've got a great admiration for the law. It's so—so convenient. Isn't it?"

She scowled at him, confused and suspicions. "Your Pa? Was he a miner?"

"No. But he had something to do with the mines."

"Railroad man?"

"Yes, I think you could call him that. Railroad man. But tell me, Mrs. McCloskey, how did you really come to hate the miners? You look like a mining man's wife, yourself."

"I told you, they're scum. Ain't that enough? Quarrellin' with their bread and butter. Tryin' to run the mines, and tellin' the bosses what *they* want and what *they'll* do. 'Tain't right nor decent. Impudent, that's what. If they don't want to work, they don't have to, but they ain't got no right to stop other folks from workin'.'"

"So you've been reading the Constitution, too, Mrs. McCloskey?"

"Constitution? What's constitution?"

"Never mind. You know it without reading it. That's called intuition. You are a very smart woman, Mrs. McCloskey."

She simpered hideously, though still suspicious. "If you ain't the beat-ingest young un! Want some more coffee?"

The snow was already flecked with the black dust that seemed to hang perpetually in the air when Guy left the boarding house. The militiamen on duty watched the slight quick figure mounting the side of the western hill, its coat collar upturned and hat well over the eyes. It was a boy's figure, small and lithe. The militiamen grinned at each other, puzzled.

Guy reached the top of the hill, and stood in dazzling sunshine. He paused and looked around him. The hill descended to a narrow and jagged valley, white with snow, which was divided by the oozing black seepage of a narrow stream. On each side of the stream were small clapboard shacks with thin leaning chimneys languidly throwing off thin wisps of orange smoke against the pale and shining clarity of sky and hillside. Here and there the remains of broken picket fences staggered partially around a shack. Behind one or two shacks a bleating goat was tethered. The new snow was barely polluted as yet either by dust or foot-step, though Guy did see the scuttling figures of some bent shawled women darting in the rear of the shacks. But no children nor men were visible. The slopes of other hills broke up the landscape beyond the valley, scarred irregularly by the shafts of the mines.

Guy had never been in a mining section before, but he knew instinctively that such a region was noisy and active. But though railroad cars stood on sidings and the tips were gaunt and black beams in the white winter sunlight, there was no sound at all. Not even a militiaman nor a prowling detective was about. Guy was disappointed; he had been led to believe that the strikes in this region were particularly desperate and violent.

He heard a shot, sudden and sharp and reverberating through the shattering white hush. He struck off in its general direction, his legs and feet rapidly becoming soggy and wet; soon he was sweating as he waded through the snow. He reached another narrow valley and another double row of silent and smoking shacks. He went on. Finally he arrived at the steep slope of the last hill and struggled up it. Reaching the top, he looked down.

The feet of the gathering hills formed the crude and smaller end of a great funnel. In this irregular circle or pit were crowded at least one hundred men. Another two hundred or more were scattered on the hillsides, their shabby clothes black blotches against the whiteness. They looked more like mis-shapen, pathetic and enormous ants than men, for they moved with continual restlessness, and their bodies were bent, their heads turning from side to side. In the center of the hundred at the bottom, on a box or large stone, stood the man whose voice Guy had been hearing. He was haranguing his fellows with passionate gestures, movements up and down of his long ragged body, and the rising crescendo of his sharp and assaulting voice. He seemed to be having little success, however, for the miners remained apathetic. They said nothing, made no sound whatsoever, yet their attitudes, the very aspects of their huddled sharp shadows on the trampled snow, showed despair, irresolution and defeat. They made no individual movements, except to blow on their numbed hands and languidly stamp their freezing feet on the ground. Here was no violence, no fury and hate, but only men who were hungry and bewildered. No Militiaman or other stranger was in sight, and no one lifted his eyes to see that small watching figure on top of the hill.

There was a sudden pause. The speaker had come to the end of his speech. Not a man spoke, there was no murmur of applause nor dissent. Then there was a quick and violent disturbance among the men on the eastern slope, and a man ran down the hill to the bottom. His movement was like a torpedo lashing through still water, and electrified his companions. He reached the bottom, pushed aside the other speaker and leapt upon the box. The men on the slopes began to run down, crowding closely about this man who was about to speak. Now a murmur rose from them, excited and expectant. It was a throaty murmur, partly of hope and partly of pleasure.

He lifted up his arms in a dramatic gesture, and again they were silent. The air was so clear and transparent that Guy could see him very distinctly. He was a tall broad man of about forty, with fiery hair uncovered in the sunshine. He had a broad and fiery face, irascible and fierce. This was John Glenwyn, a Welshman, a miner by birth and heritage and instinct, who had left Wales during the last disorders in the collieries there. A bachelor, a hater, an idealist and a fighter, he had the raw and catastrophic eloquence of his kind; they called him a firebrand, both because of his hair and his tongue. At that time he was both detested and hunted by the mine owners, and he was forced to live cautiously and furtively. But he was always mysteriously imported when a strike was about to collapse, and never failed to lash the strikers into action again, usually a mad action full of violence and narcotized loss of the instinct of self-preservation. Nor did he disappear when the fury ran screaming through the region; having great personal courage and a natural lust for struggle and combat, he could always be found where the blows were the thickest and most unrestrained. Hate was native to him, a vigorous force which would have been impersonal and dangerous in a man without a vision. But he had the vision: that of social justice, and the hatred became a hammer that could not be resisted. "The only difference between me and the bosses," he would say, grinning and showing his wolfishly white teeth, "is that they love money and I don't. That's all." It was true, for all its apparent obscurity: John Glenwyn was totally penniless, though he could have been quite otherwise.

Guy had heard of John Glenwyn, and remembering descriptions of him, he knew this man was he. He crouched down in the snow near the top of the hill, in order to be less conspicuous.

John began to talk in his heavy and resonant Welsh voice, which seemed natural to these naked hills and grim skies. He seemed to be speaking easily, without overmuch vehemence or drama. But every word carried, and not a man moved. They watched John's slightest gesture, swayed from side to side in time to his voice.

"Well, boys, they've got the Militia out on us now. They've hung some of us. They've got the soldiery now to shoot us down. Because we're starvin'. That's the biggest crime in all this world: to be hungry, men. It's the sin the vicars talk about, that God don't forgive. It gives the Law the right to shoot you down or hang you, shut doors on you and beat your wives to death and let your babies starve. You ain't got the right to live.

"Perhaps they're right. But we don't believe it! We believe we're hungry because they're lyin' to us and cheatin' us. This whole damn world's full and overflowin' with milk and honey, and they won't let us have a share in it, and summon up the law and the soldiers to keep us from tastin' what we've worked for. There's enough for every man and his woman and his babies; God don't play favorites. But we ain't got the law—because we ain't got the money. Just a matter of pounds and pence, my friends, and naught to do with God's will, though the parsons say so."

He had been speaking with a hoarse wry humor, a "gallows humor." There was a dull and guttural roar from the men. No longer were they apathetic, lost, and bewildered, as though disoriented, as though wondering what had happened to them and what they were doing, idle out upon the hills in midday. John had pulled the ropes of their slack and hanging sails, had opened them to winds, and once again they knew where they were going and were alive once more with the thought of their destination. He had beat the drums in their foggy and purposeless dawns. He was giving them the joys of anger and courage. Enlivened and aroused, they milled about him, shouting, reaching up their hands to him, laughing, fiercely nodding heads, and spitting. He smiled down at them with grim satisfaction.

"Sometimes, lads, we think the law is all wrong, that there's something bloody well daft about such law. We don't think the good God in heaven meant us to starve, even if the blasted parsons nod their silly heads, like punch-and-judies, or the dummies them chaps talk through on the stage. We're willin' to work. Look at our hands! We're patient, and we don't want no rows with the law. But we come to a place where we ask: Is this all there is to livin'? Just the mines and the sweat and the blood and the darkness and not havin' enough to eat, and the consumption that gets in our lungs from the dust, and never seein' the sun, and not knowin' every time we go down the shaft if we will ever come up again? Never gettin' away, like bloody lifers, unless we get drunk—in their pubs!

"Right there in the Good Book it tells the bosses not to muzzle the ox that treads out the corn. But they do muzzle us! We tread out the corn from sun-up to sundown, but they got our jaws tied shut and not a grain goes into our gullets.

"Maybe it's us that's barmy, lads! Yes, maybe it is! Like the ox. Knee deep in corn all ready to eat, and we starve in it! Because we let a puny handful of greedy men put a muzzle on us! Why, we're strong— we're powerful—we can stamp out their guts if we've a mind to! What's the matter with an ox that lets himself be muzzled when he could have a share in the corn he treads, if he'd just make up his silly mind he wants that share?"

"He's right, boys, he's right!" shouted a hoarse-voiced and grizzled miner with a frightful burn-scar on his right cheek. The men roared again, and now there was a sullen menace in their roaring.

The wry humor had gone from John's face. There was a savagery, a fury, out upon it, a brutal passion.

"Two days ago Tim Murphy, here, sent for me from the Trudell mines to come and talk to you lads. 'Help us, John,' said he. 'The lads are losin' their silly hearts. They're lettin' a few Barbour guns put the fear of hell in 'em. If you don't help us, they'll be runnin' back to the mines with kicks in their behinds, and sayin' thank'ee for each kick.' And so, I came. I came out and saw everythin', and says I to myself: 'They can't stop now. They don't dare stop.'

"Lads, you can't stop! Not for your own sakes, but for your kids. Want them to live like you? Want them to die like you? Ain't they worth a little guts, a few bullets, an empty belly? Are you men or pigs?

"You might lose this fight. What of it? But our kids'll remember! And because we fought, they'll carry on the fight. And they won't lose! Because of us, they'll know they've got a right to live, and a right to some part of what we dig out of the earth. We'll say to 'em: 'Our hands bled on our picks and our feet got cut on the rocks, and we never saw the sun. But we fought for you, to give you the right to live like men, to share in what you bring out of the bowels of the earth.'

"We've got to remember that right for ourselves, too. We're fightin' for our share, and we can't stop the fightin', for it's a just fight. We dig the coal—we carry it. It's our strength that puts it in cars to be hauled away and burned in houses and factories and mills and palaces. It's our labor that makes wheels turn and trains run. We, Labor, have made the earth and the good things that are in it! But have we inherited this earth we have made? No! By the Holy God, no! And why? Because we've been too addle-brained to realize that this, the earth, is ours, not theirs, that it is ours to claim and theirs to fall under our fists!

"Remember that, when you want to run whimperin' back to the skirts of your women with a foot in your behinds. Remember that, and you'll bring around a day when the bosses'll have to listen, either because our voices get strong enough, or—," and he paused ominously, looking at the breathless men with fierce and sparkling eyes, "or we got the guns!"

A deep hush followed his last words, then from the throats of them all one shout burst out, violent and enraged. It was a short shout, like an explosion, but after it had stopped, itself, the hills threw it back as though armed camps in hidden valleys acclaimed it and saluted it.

Guy had been crouching in the snow during all of John's speech, his folded arms on his knees. He had listened, intent and motionless. Once he had thought, smiling ironically: There's a man only Pa could appreciate! When the shout came he stopped smiling, and the thin and savage slash of pupil gleamed in his light eyes again. Then he heard a furtive, hissing, hurrying sound on the other side of the hill, crunching footsteps, the sliding of hooves, the rattle of arms. Swiftly yet cautiously, he scrambled up the four feet to the top, lay flat and looked over. At least fifty burly men, afoot and on horseback, armed with clubs and guns, were climbing rapidly and with deadly purpose to the top of the hill. One of the men, on horseback, was Paul Barbour, and he held a vicious-looking pistol ready in his hand.

Guy saw all this in an instant. He rolled over, rolled down a few feet, scrambled upright, and throwing up his arms into the air began to shout and scream warnings to the miners below as he raced down to them. He knew it was hopeless and was sick with the realization, but at least they had had a warning and a few might escape or make ready.

The miners, startled and suddenly frightened, looked up at the slight figure racing down to them, screaming and pointing backwards to the top of the hill. They stood in black and frozen groups, faces ghastly, eyes lifted, mouths dropped open. The apparition was too sudden, the noise too unexpected, for their slow minds to grasp it all quickly. They began to mill in panic; a faint terrified sound exhaled from them in their breath.

But John Glenwyn realized at once. He shouted, attracted their scattering animal eyes. He stamped, screamed. "Run, damn you, run!" he yelled. "Hang together and they'll mow you all down in a body! Make it easy for 'em to slaughter you like sheep! Scatter! Each man for himself! Run, curse you, run!"

His voice, jagged and lashing, roared through them like an electric current. They seemed to leap into the air; they darted and burrowed, dashed and scrambled, scuttled up the sides of the far hills, their bodies like struggling black beetles against the whiteness of the snow, which they were raising in clouds about them. John Glenwyn did not try to save himself; he jumped and stamped upon his box, throwing his great arms about, his fiery head like a leaping torch in the bitter sunlight. He screamed without pausing, urging the miners to fresh and desperate speed; his voice, stentorian and powerful, rang back from hilltop to hilltop. He was alone now, the space cleared about him, and most of the miners were halfway up the hills and moving with such speed that they made poor targets. Guy, exhausted and crumpled at the bottom of the hill, suddenly saw what John was about. His dancing figure, his height, his vehemence, his shouts, his agitated red hair, would attract the attention of the attackers for a few precious seconds longer, would give another man or two, slower than the rest, a chance for life. Moreover, his uproar would warn the attackers that their presence was known, would make them hesitate, gather together, hastily reorganize themselves and change their old plan of attacking swiftly and suddenly, without warning. This, again, would add a few more precious minutes. By now they had had sufficient time to reach the brow of the hill, but they had not done so. They were still hidden on the other side, and were completely silent.

Many of the miners, moving in a diagonal direction, had disappeared around the curve of the hill to the right; some of them, having climbed with incredible speed, had almost reached the top. John, shouting below, warned them to throw themselves down at the top, to roll down the other side. Guy, lifting himself slowly to his feet, could look at nothing but John Glenwyn. The boy, fascinated, moved as though by a supernatural and awed terror, could see nothing but this shouting man with the flaming hair and beating arms. And then he saw also that he was laughing and that upon his crimson face was a mad, exultant ferocity, the ferocity of a Titan who could meet red death with glee and contempt.

The attackers, massed together and cautious, appeared at the top of the hill. Guy, in affright, glared up at them. He was only a boy, and he was afraid. He suddenly realized that he would not be recognized, that he and John, as the only stationary targets, would be the first to die. He cried out, lifted one thin young arm in a desperate and futile gesture. Then, as if realizing the strength of John Glenwyn, he turned to him, flung himself toward him through the snow and rutted earth. Less than half of the miners were still in sight on the opposite hillsides.

Guy did not want to die. He was not of the stuff of which heroes are made. Whatever the mysterious motive, whatever hate or contempt or rage against his father, or sense of angry justice had brought him here to this place, he was not aware of it now, nor caring. He was terrified; he wanted to escape. He began to run and slide down the hill with heedless and increasing speed, screaming, glancing back and up over his shoulder.

Two shots rang out, almost simultaneously. And as they did so, Guy leapt into the air, arms and legs flung out, grotesquely, like a bounding dancer's. As he fell to the earth again his legs buckled under him, he sank to his knees, collapsed abruptly in the snow on his face. He writhed once, violently, then lay still.

John Glenwyn, too, did not move again. He, too, lay, face down, in the snow, which was slowly turning red.

CHAPTER LXXXII

IT SEEMED impossible to May, on the train to New York, to escape the exigent ministrations of Elsa and the sound of her loud and confident voice. She was beginning to forget her usual compassion and tolerance for the girl, and was developing an active dislike. She found that her facial muscles ached from her forced smiles, and that she could hardly keep impatience and sharpness out of her own voice. Finally, feeling cowardly, she suggested to Elsa that Gertrude was looking wan and tired, and so diverted the avalanche of officiousness and affectionate solicitude upon her distressed daughter. But really, she thought to herself, emergencies arise where even maternal affection goes under. Now she could talk to Ernest in peace. He had been sitting composedly reading his papers, undisturbed by the feminine confusion about him. When May, a little sharply, though smilingly, demanded his attention, he laid aside the papers and looked at her with a smooth and friendly expression.

"Really, Ernest, you might listen to me a moment. I realize, of course, that your journey to New York has nothing to do with the fact that your eldest son is making his debut at the Academy of Music. Naturally, you are too great and important a man to care about such trifles——"

He smiled. "Come, come, my dear. Why excite yourself? Remember what the doctor told you about your nerves. You are quite red in the face. But what was it you wanted to say?"

May still smiled, but her breath was jerky and uneven. She touched a handkerchief to her lips and forehead and jerked her stole about her neck. "I wanted to talk about another one of your children. You remember him? Guy? Your third son? Perhaps you have forgotten." Tears smarted in her eyes.

"What about Guy?"

"I don't like that idea of his going into the mining regions. Less and less do I like it. I realize it is too late to talk of it now. I don't know why I ever consented, however. So foolish, a child like that. Why, he isn't quite sixteen! Just a boy. Wherever he got the notion——"

"I'm sure I didn't give it to him."

"But, so foolish! Didn't you see that, yourself?"

"Foolish? No. Guy didn't deceive me at all with his fine talk of 'taking interest.' He's got a notion, but he's a secretive little devil. And hard as rock and smooth as tanned leather. Yes, he's got a notion. It *is* interest, in a way, but not the kind he wanted me to believe it is. I won't pretend I know what it is. I'm curious to find out, though. When he comes back, I'll find out. He's no fool. Yes, he's better than I thought. I think we can make something of him, eventually."

"What do I care for that?" May's voice had become passionate. "All I care for is his safety. I don't trust Paul. He doesn't like Guy, and he'll let him wander into all kinds of danger."

"You think he might shoot him accidentally?" Ernest laughed. "I agree with you that there's danger there, and roughness. Guy won't find soft beds and pleasant speeches and good dinners. He'll learn what life's all about; he'll see some of the things his father saw. Rawness. He'll find there're sterner things in this world than not having enough pocket money. He'll see that men can get so hungry and desperate that they'll die fighting for a little food. It won't hurt him at all. Perhaps put a little seriousness in his head. Perhaps," he added thoughtfully, "it'll help his notion grow. Damn it, I almost don't care what kind of a notion it is, so long as it's a real one, and he's got the guts to fight for it. And sometimes," very slowly, "I think a notion of his might be real, and that he has the guts." He settled back in his seat, smiling with unusual satisfaction.

"And sometimes," said May unwillingly, "I think Guy is much like you. He has your eyes."

"Perhaps." Ernest's satisfaction increased, made him amiable.

May, still heavily anxious and unaccountably depressed, glanced about the ornate gilt and crimson plush of the private car. Vaguely, she recalled that she detested plush; to her, it never seemed quite clean. Her anxiety became the sharper and the closer as her glance slowed over the gilt fixtures. She was not impressed, as the Barbours were, by private cars, personal maids, valets, plush, ornateness and oppressive, dusty and untidy luxury. She thought to herself that the private cars in which she occasionally travelled with Ernest resembled nothing on earth so much as circus cars. The painfulness of her thoughts, and her anxiety, made a web of hairlike wrinkles spring out over her plump cheeks; in the bright winter sunlight she looked haggard and tired, and her eyelids, once so white and full, were like sallow bags over the tired brilliance of her eyes. The hair under the trim bonnet was quite gray. She kept blinking, and occasionally moistened the puckered dryness of her lower lip. Ernest watched her furtively from under the hand he had lifted to shut out the sunlight that poured through the small windows. When she spoke again, staring before her absently and not looking at him, he dropped the hand. His expression was very odd for him: both compassionate and gentle.

"It means nothing to you, of course, Ernest, that Frey's about to justify all I have believed of him. You don't care about that. You would prefer it if he were like Paul." And now she looked at him directly. "You've never pretended otherwise. You've not lied about it. But it is poor comfort to me; sometimes I think I would rather you had lied."

"May, believe me when I say that if it happens as you think it will happen, and you are happy, it will make me happy, too. Can't you believe that?"

Her eyes, as she looked at him steadily, suddenly dilated, darkened with bitterness. "Yes," she said, "I can believe that. It would be such a relief to you!" And she turned her head away from him.

Ernest's secretary, who was with the party, discreetly knocked at the door. He brought in a sheaf of papers for Ernest's attention. Ernest extended his hand for them calmly, glad of the interruption. May's maid followed on the heels of the secretary to remind May that it was three o'clock and time for her afternoon nap. Elsa, seeing the slight commotion, rose from her place with Gertrude at the end of the coach, and came forward briskly, swaying from side to side with the motion. May, who had been about to refuse the nap, said hurriedly to her niece: "Darling, you must excuse me. I am so tired."

"Of course," said Elsa. "I will help you. I can do it better than that girl."

Helplessly, May silently cursed her good breeding, which would not allow her to insult Elsa as she so heartily desired. It's my nerves, she thought severely. Yesterday I thought what a really good girl she is, and how pathetic and affectionate, and truly intelligent, and today I believe I could cut her throat. I'm becoming quite abominable.

Elsa was already assisting the maid and the porter to prepare May's couch. May, resigned, was about to leave Ernest when he said, glancing bemusedly through the window: "Each time I travel this way I remember that I took this very route by stagecoach, a thousand years ago. Stagecoach! How damnable that was! Days and days of torture, mudholes and craters, rain and sun, thirst and dust, aching back and bruised legs, and grimy sweat."

May, already standing, looked back over her shoulder at him. "My great-great-grandfather Sessions made the same journey in his own coach." As she lay down on the couch, and Elsa and the maid fought simultaneously to make her comfortable, she said to herself: That was petty. And it's very funny, and embarrassing, that that is the sort of thing that can impress him! But it was very petty. Yes, I am really becoming abominable. She closed her eyes, but the lashes did not meet. Between them, for a long time, she watched Ernest. The pillow under her cheek showed a dark spreading circle of moistness.

Elsa sat near May, reading and yawning. Her great legs were spread out, so that a deep purple velvet hollow lay between them. May thought her feet enormous. The sunlight rippled over her thick hair, and her large dominant face was the face of Brunhilde. Between chapters she would pause, stare into the empty distance beyond the windows. It was then that a shining look came over her big features, a look of ecstasy, and she trembled slightly.

Gertrude, alone now, looked mournfully from the rear of the coach at her father. She knew that the old eager confidence she had had in him, the faith and trust, the ease, were gone. Since her marriage to Paul she had not been able to approach Ernest with any naturalness. This situation was almost agonizing to her, but some hidden instinct kept her from attempting to change it. She lay back in her chair. The window was dusty. Her fragile forefinger traced a letter in the dust without her conscious exertion. She looked at it. It was the letter P. She stared at it a long time, with dry fixed eyes.

Twenty-four hours later they arrived in New York. Lucy Van Eyck's carriage, resplendent with two coachmen in uniform, was waiting for them. They drove through the blue and white glitter of the wintry New York streets, and the morning air had a zest in it. The hour was still early; only a few drays and heavy wagons lumbered and crunched over the blazing snow, though occasionally the sweet jingle of sleigh bells rang festively from the quiet residential streets. The intense dark blue of the sky and the white clouds were reflected brilliantly in every high window; the shops glittered; icicles hung from eaves like lances of crystal. Omnibuses lurched by, crowded with early workers. Lower Fifth Avenue, decked with small shops like a dame scintillating with bracelets, brooches and ear-rings, looked gay and vivid, for the sidewalks were already thronged with scuttling thousands, who turned into Fourteenth Street like overflowing rivers. This was the heart of the shopping district; sales were afoot, post-Christmas sales, and clotted masses of women were feverishly and belatedly buying presents for forgotten friends and relatives, or exchanging presents found undesirable. Carriages were already lined up against the curbs along Fourteenth Street, Fifth Avenue and Broadway; the harness dazzled the eye as it caught the sun, the horses tossed their heads and exhaled clouds of white steam and stamped their hoofs. May caught a flash of an elaborate black velvet and sequin gown in the broad window of Arnold Constable's, and made a mental note to visit the store later in the day. Driving up Fifth Avenue, leaving the shopping district behind, the streets became quieter and more sedate; the shops thinned out. Magnificent dwellings lined themselves up along the thoroughfare. Upper windows were still shrouded in rippling pale silk, but there was activity below in the areaways. Servant girls were already rushing in and out with baskets, and altercations were going on between cooks and vegetable and meat men. The sun, growing higher and warmer, was beginning to melt the snow; it was forming soft flabby patches on the street between which ran writhing black water.

Gertrude, looking unusually small and wan and dark, huddled under the thick fur rugs; she watched the passing streets dimly. May, in spite of her anxiety and excitement, could feel pleasure in the swift flow of the great city and anticipation of a long shopping orgy. Elsa, vigorous and exuberant, bounced about continually, dragging the rug from May's knees, apologizing, rearranging, exclaiming, laughing, clapping her gloved hands, settling her bonnet which always fell awry, and showing her delight, excitement, feverish joy, with the lack of restraint of a passionate and healthy child. Once Gertrude glanced at her slowly, and May was quite struck by the expression of her daughter's face, so tired was it, so contemptuous, so languidly brutal. Dear me! she thought, disturbed, it is true that Elsa is extremely tiresome—and wearing—but it is hardly right to hate some one like that without real provocation. Ernest, however, seemed pleased and amused at his niece's bouncing pleasure in the city; he pinched her hard and blooming cheek and rallied her. "You are a handsome piece, Elsa," he said, gratified at the resemblance to himself in her features.

She laughed heartily. "I only hope Frey thinks so, too!" she exclaimed.

May glanced involuntarily at Gertrude; Gertrude's eyes became brilliantly pointed with hate and malevolence as they fixed themselves upon her cousin.

"If he doesn't, he's an ass," said Ernest. It would be nice to have this girl for his daughter. She would put strength into the vinegar of his son's blood; she would give him children, Barbours, vital and strong and forceful as herself.

They arrived at Lucy Van Eyck's house, a quiet but dignified four-story residence on Twenty-third Street and Fifth Avenue. It was of whitestone with narrow balconies, and enormous arched windows rippling with gray silk shades. Ernest had been here before, but not May or Gertrude. "Lucy," he said as he helped May to alight, "has done herself well." The butler and two men servants rushed from the house to assist.

They entered a great square hall panelled in mahogany, from which a squarish and solid staircase, ivory-colored, stolidly marched to the second floor. Lucy, plump, affectionate, sharp-eyed and smiling, greeted them in a rose-colored morning gown. Her husband, Percival, a tall narrow young man, insipid and fair and kind, and "not too bright" (to quote Ernest), stood by her side. His light silken mustaches hid his weak and pretty mouth. But he was all elegance, soft voice, sincerity, true graciousness and hospitality. Beside him, Lucy seemed more than a little common, with her forthright expression, small sharp sparkling eyes, loud authoritative voice, plumpness, high color and arrogant manner. She loved her Percival, but she thought him "a poor helpless lamb that I have to watch like a child, and guide and scold."

She kissed Ernest with a resounding smacking report, assaulted May's cheek in true matronly style, and greeted Gertrude with a sudden dropping into reserve. She shook her dark curls at Elsa with a knowing smile, and in the midst of her chatter and exclamations told her sister frankly that she needed some decent clothes, that she positively looked a fright. Gertrude smiled for the first time in two days.

Before the guests were allowed to eat their late and waiting breakfast, they must inspect the big house from kitchen to store-room, especially the nursery, where young Thomas sat in his crib playing with his toes. He looked much like his mother. Percival demurred gently at this imposition on the guests, but Lucy silenced him with a competent wave of her hand. The young man trailed disconsolately and apologetically behind the inspecting party, murmuring every now and then. Finally, Ernest, who liked the simple and the none-too-bright better than he liked the more intelligent and troublesome who might get in his way, engaged him in a pleasant and interested conversation as they went downstairs again.

Lucy expressed herself as quite offended that "little Godfrey" had not chosen to call upon her, or to remain at her house since he had arrived in New York. "Imagine!" she exclaimed when May mentioned her son's address. "On Seventh Avenue between Thirteenth and Twelfth Streets! Why, that's the artists' neighborhood. Really quite dreadful people, many of them so poor they are living, men and women together, four and six in a single room."

"I'm sure Frey wouldn't associate with any one who was really dreadful," said May smoothly, disliking her niece.

"How do you know that?" demanded Ernest brutally. "He never had an ounce of discrimination in his life."

May colored, though her smile was determined. Ernest enlarged on his theme: "I don't know why it is accepted that 'artists' must necessarily be fools. It seems to me that if a man has keenness enough, and intelligence enough, to give sound or substance to what he has seen of other men or things, his faculties of discernment and wit and competence develop in proportion. An incompetent man is an incompetent 'artist,' no matter how many silly women gush over him and declare him a genius." May shrugged. "Of course, my dear, that is only your opinion. You haven't met any artists, you know."

Elsa lavishly buttered a slice of bread and bit into it. "Frey isn't an artist," she said in her confident voice, which settled all things. "He just thinks he is. That's his way of playing. But I'm sure he is realizing now that his playtime is over."

Ernest laughed. "I'll give you the biggest diamond in America for a wedding present, Elsa!" he said.

May stood up. Her color was still high and she was trembling. "My dears, you must excuse me, but my head aches slightly. Gertrude, if you are quite finished, may I speak to you before I lie down?" And May, poised and controlled as ever, swept from the room followed by Gertrude, who had left her breakfast almost untouched.

"Well," remarked Lucy, "Aunt May is a good example of Mama's epigram that a true lady is a woman who knows how to insult you thoroughly without offense."

"She hasn't insulted me," said Elsa. "I know she shudders at the idea of me marrying Frey. But that's a weakness of women with sons."

After breakfast Ernest excused himself on the plea that he had an engagement with Mr. Jay Regan, and must keep it immediately.

CHAPTER LXXXIII

MR. JAY REGAN, financial baron extraordinary, had offices on Wall Street that were sumptuous if old-fashioned. He lived behind a battery of attendants and secretaries, through which the visitor must pass as through an armed camp. The camp was polite enough, but frankly suspicious. However, when Ernest Barbour appeared, there was a great presenting of arms and salutes and dipping of colors. The Praetorians formed an escort to conduct him to the aide-de-camp, who thereupon conducted him to the tent of the General. Presenting the visitor, the aide-de-camp saluted, clicked his heels, and smartly retired.

"What are you afraid of? Assassination?" Ernest asked, laughing. "Each time I come you have added another couple of captains, brigadiers, and a detachment of lieutenants."

Jay Regan grinned. "Of course I'm afraid of assassination! Didn't some idiot, who claimed I had ruined him, charge my men outside, waving a gun? One of your guns, too, we found out later. A little out of alignment, or it might have blown me inside out. There's a bullet hole just two feet over my head. Look at it," and he pointed to a black scar in the red mahogany panelling behind him.

"Tut, tut," said Ernest. "I'll have to see about that alignment."

Jay Regan was an immense man, six-foot-three in stocking feet, broad and tremendously paunched in proportion, his gigantic round head set squarely upon shoulders like beams. He was quite bald, but his sandy eyebrows were bushy to make up for it. Below those eyebrows were pinpoints of ambushed eyes. A full white-sandy mustache half-hid his broad mouth, which was savage in repose. His nose was of the type of Ernest's nose: short, broad, belligerent, with distended nostrils. He had arms like Goliath's, thighs like small kegs. One had a sense of shock when observing his hands, which were long and thin and white and delicate, like a woman's, with nails pale and smooth as mother-of-pearl. Cruel hands. "Pickpocket hands," he would say, himself, with enjoyment.

Original paintings of the old Masters were his hobby. Over his head, just above the bullet hole, was a fine Rembrandt, all passionate ochre and blazing jewel-points and curve of fine gold and black-brown shadow. Over the fireplace, leaping with ruddy flame, was a Rubens. His palace on Fifth Avenue was an art gallery. His son, a replica of himself, young Jay Junior, shared his obsession for beauty, and a great part of his business trips to Europe was spent in searching, stealing, bribing, cajoling and intrigue, in order to enlarge his father's private galleries.

Mr. Regan was very glad indeed to see Ernest Barbour. He thought him one of America's truly great men. He admired him. "There's a fellow utterly without a conscience," he would say heartily. "Not a gentleman, of course, and not a man I'd care to have marry my daughter. But for all of that, a great man."

He pressed brandy upon Ernest. "Well, what have you come to New York to grab this time?" he asked genially. "Railroads? You'll have to fight the Vanderbilts this time—and you haven't got the ghost of a chance. Even the Goulds are going to drop out; interested in copper now."

"I'm interested in copper, too. I've got options in Montana. Got them for practically nothing. Need that for our new type shell. I'm not dealing with the Goulds; I don't need to. What I do need is manganese. I don't propose to do mucn business with Germany, and just at present the Russians don't like me. But I've got options in South America. The damnable part of it is that the manganese is almost inaccessible there, so I'm helping finance a railroad into the territory. When that's done, I can tell Germany to go to hell. I never liked the buggers, anyway."

"You'll like them better, later on. They've got an eye on all of Europe, since Bismarck. Maybe it won't be tomorrow, but eventually Europe will be a good market for your munitions. So don't curse the Dutchmen too much. Am I too inquisitive, but what have you been doing lately? Seems to me I've heard you mentioned quite nastily a few times in the papers, both here and in Europe. According to some reports, you've turned into a Machiavelli—manufacturing wars so there'll be a market for your munitions."

Ernest smiled. "A munitions maker," he said, "dare not make himself too conspicuous either by defending himself, or advertising. Munitions making is one industry in which advertising, voluntarily or involuntarily, would be fatal. I am condemned to a very private life. But, you've asked what I have been doing. Well, I'll tell you. A little."

He sipped the brandy. He considered it a "gentleman's drink," and his pretense of enjoyment had by now become second-nature.

"You remember, I worked for years trying to do some business with Japan, but she preferred to struggle along with other concerns in other countries or make her munitions herself. The Japs have great inventive ability and patience, and eventually, laugh if you will, they'll be formidable competitors in trade with every Western nation. You're not laughing? You are a wise man. We've got to watch Japan. There's a ferment there. White men's officiousness, in the name of civilization, will make a yellow wrath out of Asia. You can't teach your neighbo:

such gentle embellishments as trade and Christianity and agreeable inter-
course without infecting him in the process with ideas. When you teach
him to play nicely with you he'll soon begin to wonder if he can beat you
at the game. When the white man 'civilizes' what he considers the
inferior races he either annihilates them in the process or makes them his
enemies. So, while it is too bad that the Jap won't be a nice boy and stop
with our virtues, but will learn our vices and how to surpass them, we can
still get our profit out of him before he realizes what we are doing to
him."

"I detest philosophers as a rule," said Jay Regan. "But a rascal like
you can make something worthwhile out of philosophy. But go on."

"You remember that the feudal tenure was practically abolished in
Japan comparatively recently. Sakuma Shozan, Yokoi Heishiro and
Omura Masujiro, were all fine men. I admit it myself. Under them, the
Japs might really have become civilized, according to Western standards,
and might have learnt to be great instead of becoming the yellow wrath
which they will become within the next fifty years. They were true
patriots (if you like patriots), liberal, tolerant, intelligent. They hated
all that makes civilizations: cruelty, war and exploitation. But as men
for me, they were very bad. How are you going to civilize a nation unless
you teach it how much it needs munitions? Protection against other
races that might get hungry and ambitious.

"There was Kumoi Tatsuo who had no illusions about the white man's
'freedom' for the masses of people. A good sound old conservative,
Kumoi Tatsuo, and no nonsense about him. A good old samurai—no
democrat. He had the first essential necessary for true leadership—he
despised the people. So he plotted with his fellow samurai and the three
great liberals were assassinated. A very nice man, Kumoi Tatsuo—
we'll be able to do a lot of business with Japan in the future because of
him."

"You didn't, by any chance, have anything to do with the successful
uprising led by Kumoi Tatsuo?"

Ernest smiled. "You credit me with omnipresence. Japan is still
practically a closed country. But I have been informed by Skeda in
Austria that the arms shipped by them via Russia got through into Japan
with a minimum of difficulty. A few more shipments, and Japan will be
able to attack Korea."

"And Russia, of course, is being helpful in permitting the transportation of arms through her territory?"

"Everyone is helpful if properly approached. Of course, there has
been some uproar and a lot of threats in Russia since it was discovered
that arms were being shipped into Japan. They didn't accuse Skeda; they
accused me. Absurd, of course. It is true that Skeda has a lot of my
patents, and we exchange ideas and suggestions, and I own a consid-

erable portion of Skeda stock—but it is silly to say that I am behind the feudal revolt and agreeable to the conquest of Korea."

"Oh, we understand that. I can see that your feelings are badly hurt."

"Yes, as I said, the Russians don't like me just now. I don't like them. They stole a shipment of arms intended for Japan, and never offered to pay for them. Our newest type of rifle, too. Well, after Japan gets tired of the old samurai, or is convinced he is really harmful, there is a man called Saigo in Satsuma. Nothing like controversy to aid civilization. You see, I am interested in civilizing Japan, also. Peace is no civilizer. I have hopes for Saigo. There is also Russia, Japan's only significant white neighbor. The Russians are barbarians: Skeda reports they have rebuffed all their attempts to approach them. We could be of considerable help, but you can't teach stupidity anything, not even an awareness of danger." He smiled. "There is Japan, beginning to learn that self-defense is the first law of conquest, and here is Russia, thinking that her whale-bulk is a protection. I prefer the white race, but an armaments-maker must be tolerant."

"I see," said Mr. Regan thoughtfully, studying him with his pinpoints of eyes.

"However," went on Ernest calmly, "I have not lost all hopes for Russia. Within a short time she is bound to declare war against Turkey. The Serbs hate Turkey; the Slavs of Herzegovina are due for an insurrection against Turkey, too. Austria is playing a little fast-and-loose game with the Turks: at times she looks indulgently at them even while they violate her territory and the frontiers of Croatia; then she becomes stern and refuses to allow them to land arms on their own territory at Klek. A little conciliatory game known in vulgar circles as now-you-see-'em-and-now-you-don't. Austria's not up to it; she ought to study John Bull, who is a master at that kind of business. Only England seems to know when it is safe to look and when it isn't. Well, anyway, the Balkans furnish armament makers with a sort of first-class laboratory and experimental depot. There're always opportunities there to try out improvements in cannon and guns and powder. Skeda informs me they've shipped a tremendous cargo of powder to Turkey, and a huge shipment of cannon to Austria. Mussulmans and Christians: a nice pot of stew that'll keep the fires burning in the Balkans for many years. And between the two of them it's hard to know which is the worst rascal. I believe I prefer the Turks: they don't smear honey on their crimes. So long as the Hungarians can keep on hating the Servians and loving the Turks, and so long as we have Klapkas and Count Andressies and Abdul-Kerins in the Balkans, the cause of aggressive peace is not lost."

"It seems to me," said Mr. Regan, "that you are playing a little game yourself, a little stinker known as playing both ends against the middle."

"Pardon me, *for* the middle," replied Ernest.

"I'm no villain. I'm a business man. The world needs armaments and I supply them. The very best, too, mind you. And like all business men I must stimulate a market; that's my legitimate right. I'm infringing no law. Men will fight; it's a law of nature. And I supply them with the means to fight. But blast it, I don't need an advocate, not even myself. The trouble with this world is that it's too damn full of sentimentalists and fools, who live with their guts instead of their brains. I'm no worse than a bloody usurer like you."

Regan shouted with laughter. "A usurer? That's good, very, very good. But here we sit like a pair of ninnies, congratulating each other like stage villains on our villainies. You're a bold devil, Barbour. I like you immensely."

"That's capital, but I detest being called a villain. I wouldn't mind so much if I really were one. As I said before, I'm a business man." He looked exceedingly annoyed. "I detest sentimentality. I could name you a handful of real villains, including yourself, who could give me worthwhile lessons in everything, not excluding mayhem."

"Come now, let's not pout like a pair of girls. Here, have some more brandy. As I suspected, you don't really like brandy, do you? So don't force yourself to take it; it's seventy-five years old and meant for a man with a palate. Villains? A villain, my dear Barbour, is a man who fails. So I owe you an apology. The last time you were here you asked me if I were going to grant that loan to France. My answer now is that I'm not. Too precarious; she's still too weak from the war. Too bad, too; I like the French."

"I don't."

"Why, half your family is French."

"Nevertheless, I don't like them. Perhaps it's the Englishman in me. Oh, you called me a provincial once. Perhaps I am. But I don't like the French."

"Like all Britons, you don't like any one but yourself. But you don't like the French because you don't know how to live. The French do. They have a thousand means of satisfaction and zest in living; you haven't. You have only one way. Making money."

"Power," said Ernest quietly. He leaned forward and put his clenched fist on Regan's desk. The other man leaned back in his chair, smiling indulgently and with a touch of understanding derision. "I've always wanted power," said Ernest. "When I was a lad in school in England, the other lads hated me. I never knew why. I was a quiet little beggar, never ran from a fight, always behaved myself. I was not twisted or crippled or defective, and I had no halt in my tongue. I never lied nor cheated; never bothered to. But the lads hated me. Why? I never knew. I don't know now. And then we came to America, and I avoided the lads. I did not go to school. But still, every one hated me, from strangers to my own brother. And I never knew why. I soon saw that if I hadn't the protection of laws those who hated me would soon finish me off. I won't say I didn't care; I did care. Nobody likes to go around feeling like a leper. So in self-protection I hated back. And I've done a good job of it. I've got the thing that's a boot in the face—power."

Regan was no longer smiling. "Just the other day I heard a Jew say that very same thing."

"Then the Jews and I have much in common. The reply to hatred is power. Not kindness nor surrender nor placation. Power. It's the only thing dogs understand."

Regan was silent. The pinpoints became sharper, more incisive. And curious. He did not like Ernest Barbour. Now, understanding him, he liked him even less. He lit a cigar, and spent quite a little time in the operation. Then, without looking at the younger man across the desk, he said: "No, you have really nothing in common with the Jews." He puffed carefully at the cigar. "The trouble with Americans is that they hate ruthlessness, even while they admire and envy it. Even when they are ruthless themselves, they are careful to explain it as something else."

The large planes of Ernest's face moved in the convulsion that was his smile. After a moment he stood up.

"Wait a minute, Barbour! Don't be so damned abrupt. Are you going to see Bellowes? I understand he has sent for you. I want to go with you, if you don't mind."

"Sent for me? That's imperial, isn't it? No, I don't mind if you come with me. But I assure you I can handle Bellowes, oily or not oily."

Regan chuckled. "I'd never call Bellowes oily. There's a man who's your match, Ernie Barbour. And he also serves as an example of what I have been telling you about American ruthlessness. He hasn't had time to justify himself yet. But when he has sufficient money—or power—and when he has settled his private grudge against the world, and exhausted himself, then he'll set to work to disclaim his ruthlessness. Just at this time he's the most vicious dog that ever smeared his poison saliva over another dog's meat so it can't be eaten, except by himself. But mark my words: before he dies he'll be one of America's saints. So, he's called you in for conference. Friend or enemy? Would you mind telling me which?"

"It all depends on the price he offers me."

"Damn you, you're not even cynical! I hate cynics, anyway: apologists. Well, I'd like to go with you." He rang for his secretary. "Look here, didn't I read something lately about your boy, Godfrey, being a musician, and having something or other played at the Academy?"

"Yes." Ernest's voice and face were smooth. "Tonight: at the Academy. I believe it is his first symphony. That's really why I'm in New York at this time."

Liar, thought Regan without contempt. "How remarkable this is, my dear Barbour! You must, of course, have my box. Mrs. Regan and I were to dine with friends, but this is much more important, and we must go to hear this symphony. Mrs. Regan is quite a patroness of the Academy. And will you dine with us at home tonight?"

"I am not alone. Mrs. Barbour and my daughter and my niece are with me."

"Splendid! We'll be honored, I assure you. Charming lady, Mrs. Barbour. All the Sessions were charming. May we expect your son, also?"

"No. He is too busy getting ready. After all, it is an occasion for him."

"Yes." Regan became thoughtful again. He had put on his smooth silken hat and his thick fur-lined coat. He picked up his cane and gloves. They left the offices together. "Why the devil don't you move to New York, Barbour?"

Ernest smiled. "You gave me the answer yourself. I'm a provincial."

CHAPTER LXXXIV

JAY REGAN found Ernest's cold and impassive habit of stilted speech rather amusing; he also amused his friends by repeating his ponderous witticisms. But the greatest amusement he and his friends derived from Ernest Barbour was the latter's complete and unapologetic implacability, his brutal lack of reticence concerning the aims and progress of his traffic in armaments. It was as if he said to them: "This is what I shall do—this is my plan. You might call some men indiscreet if they told as much as I do, but you can't call me indiscreet. You see, I am afraid of nobody." So, while they laughed at him, they did not do it to his face, nor among those who might repeat their laughter to him. There was hatred inextricably mixed with their derision, and though most of them had fortunes exceeding his, there was also envy.

The American robber barons, heavy with loot, were already becoming ashamed of their own fierce lustiness, their crude robustness, and looking with embarrassment at their black finger-rims, were already sheepishly admiring the cool and listless elegance of a white-handed Europe. They were already beginning to reject from their society members who found nothing to be ashamed of in their titanic lack of refinement. The better established of these were tentatively speaking of their London "town houses," and patronizing their fellow Americans. In uncertain voices, gradually growing stronger, they joined their European friends in denouncing American ruthlessness and greed and exigency, and refused to know the "new-rich" who were vulgarly shouldering them. A slow but steady pro-Britishism was beginning to grow among these satiated robber barons, and they were beginning to speak deprecatingly of all things American, even to the extent of joining in the thin and derisive laughter of their European friends.

These were the people who found Ernest Barbour disconcerting. An Englishman, he was yet more exigent and greedy than they. He made no pretences of elegance; he was distinctly not a gentleman, nor did he affect any refinements. Worse than all else, he had no patriotic loyalties, either to England or America. He was the real cosmopolitan, the real man-without-a-country, the real outlaw. Had he been at all wistful about England, or had he been vigorously, loudly, vocally loyal to America, they would have forgiven him. His complete unawareness that certain sentimentalities were expected of him won their endless enmity. There was something about him that frightened them. They suspected a superior strength, beyond shamed intimidation, beyond opinion. He was sufficient unto himself : he showed no signs of needing anybody or desiring anybody. This made them envy him, though he was still not as rich as most of them.

When they spoke to him of England, he smiled contemptuously and said: "There is nothing there for any one. America is the best of all countries." And yet, when they became lyrical about their own country when among themselves, he remained silent. They could not understand him. Finally they told each other that they accepted him only because of his wife, "that charming May Sessions."

If Ernest were curious as to why Jay Regan was accompanying him to the Apex Oil Company and the office of James Bellowes, owner, organizer and exploiter, he did not advertise it. It was his theory that apparent indifference was the unbearable reply to an antagonist, and that under its influence the most astute of men will betray himself. He knew that Jay Regan wanted him to express curiosity, and that that curiosity would strengthen Regan's reticence. Because he refused to express curiosity, he irritated Regan, who soon enlightened him obliquely.

"Did you know that Vanderbilt is one of the new stockholders in the Middle Oil Company?" he asked.

Without showing much interest, Ernest replied: "Are you also one?"

Regan chuckled. "Did I say I was? But I want to tell you, it'll eat up all the little men. Even the big ones. Why, even Charles Brett and Company have sold out to the Middle. What have you to say to that?"

"Only this, that I can't be threatened. I still own one-third of the stock in Jack Bellowes' Crusade Oil Company." He paused. "It would ruin Jack Bellowes if I threw my stock on the market. I've backed him, too. Yes, it would quite ruin him. Besides, I don't like his big brother, James. I never like sharks, when they go to Sunday school and pray earnestly. It's always been my theory that competition is necessary to industry."

"How much will it cost James Bellowes to change your theory?" Regan grinned.

Ernest smiled. "More than he expects," he replied. His reply jolted Jay Regan, who would have preferred a little cynicism. "And I like Charles Pitts, who's President of the National Transportation Company. You know, he's pipe line ally of the Pennsylvania."

"Um. Well, you've got your match in James Bellowes. Some day, Rockefeller will have to notice him. He's got practically all the refineries sold or leased to the Middle Oil Company, except yours. And brother Jack's. Don't fool yourself that you'll be able to hold out, with your loyal-heroics to the National and to Jack."

"Did I say anything about 'loyal-heroics'? I have my price. It is up to James Bellowes to meet it. If he doesn't, we'll lead him a dance. And I'm not at all sure he'll call the tune, either."

Feeling a little foolish, but also obscurely outraged, Regan asked: "Did you ever hear of ethics?"

Ernest turned his bland pale face to him and stared at him with his colorless eyes. "No, did you?"

Goddam Englishman! thought Jay Regan. He smiled serenely. "You're a sharp one, Barbour. You mentioned you had a price. Would you consider me impertinent if I asked approximately what it is?"

"Yes, I would. Besides, why should I tell you? You are also a stockholder in the Middle. All I can say is that I own a lot of wells around Titusville, that Bellowes needs the railroad of which I am a director, and from which he has received nearly five hundred rebates, and that I own stock in the Crusade Oil Company, and that I believe that competition can fill many pockets. No doubt, you'll have a word or two with James Bellowes before he sees me, and you can tell him what I've told you."

So Jay Regan, smiling and fuming, knew that he had betrayed himself, and cursed his own tongue. He glanced at Ernest with eye-points like fire, to see if the other man were smiling triumphantly to himself. But Ernest's face was still smooth and pale and bland.

"In other words, you mean that you'll sell out Jack Bellowes and his Crusade Oil Company, and Charles Pitts of the National Transportation Company—if your price is met?"

"Yes."

"If you ask too much, the Middle will refuse. You know that?"

"Yes. But I wouldn't like to see the Middle refuse. I believe in sweet accord between business men. I wouldn't like to see the Government poke its hand in the stew; governments always make messes out of nice quiet little family stews. We've given five hundred rebates to the Apex Oil Company, or call it Middle Oil Company—both stink as bad under any name. Pretty thin ambush, I call it, too. By reason of those rebates Bellowes has been able to cut the throats of his competitors. I know one or two Senators who might get quite overwrought if they knew all of the truth."

"Do you think you can intimidate Bellowes?" demanded Regan incredulously.

"Do you think Bellowes can intimidate me?" The words were egotistic, but the voice and the face were not. Regan fumed. He poked his cane viciously into a low snowbank as they walked down narrow and crowded Wall Street.

"You're nothing but a blackguard of a blackmailer!" he growled.

"I," said Ernest tranquilly, "still own one-third of the Crusade Oil Company, and I still know a few politicians."

The full impact of what he had been hearing fell upon Regan and he stopped short in the busy street and stared at Ernest. "You actually mean you are going to *force* Bellowes to *buy* you out? Why, my God! he's called you in to try to make you *sell* out!"

"It'll be quite a surprise to him, then, to see that I'm quite willing to sell, won't it?" asked Ernest pleasantly.

Regan could not refrain from saying, stunned as he was: "You are actually demanding to sell! Is it possible you don't realize what you hold in your hands at the present time?"

"Yes. But this time I'm not after money as much as I am after something else."

"Oh, a trade, eh?"

"A trade."

Jay Regan showed no delicacy whatsoever in frankly abandoning his companion in the offices of the Apex Oil Company and going into Bellowes' office for an agitated conference before the oil man saw Ernest Barbour. Ernest sat down serenely, and waited. He folded his hands on the top of his gold-headed cane and smiled to himself. He liked the Apex Offices, and always enjoyed being in them.

He had not been here for some years. The offices had not changed except to acquire a rich, glowing patina that had flowed over old mahogany. It was as though Time were an expert old housewife armed with oiled rubbing cloth and careful brush. Even the shabbiness that comes with use was yet sumptuous and full of mellow dignity; it had a warm sheen. There was a portrait of James Bellowes, James Duggan Bellowes, to be exact, hanging on the wall over a deep fireplace. It was a dusky and sallow face, severe and bitter, with a wide thin cleft of a mouth that spoke of immovable obstinacy and more than a little brutality. Ernest thought that for so dour a man brutality was a sort of luxurious sensuality, a savage ecstasy of the mind. In the small and narrow eyes, intent and coldly fierce, was a mummy stare. The man had a large family, yet about that portrait hung so emaciated an air, such sterility, polar frigidity, that it was almost impossible to conceive him in the process of begetting.

Beyond the tall old windows the winter snow had sifted down; an even white rim lay on the windowsills. Someone silently turned on the gas, and the bulbous chandeliers burned with a soft and mellow light. An old clerk crept up to Ernest and whispered obsequiously that Mr. Bellowes would see him now. He led the way to a carved and discolored oaken door behind which old James sat in unshakable silence, as unhuman and merciless as death.

He sat at his gigantic old mahogany desk across what seemed to Ernest half an acre of darkly glimmering floor. The light in the room was diffused and gentle; the huge clock boomed with lofty urbanity. Behind its polished grate the fire leapt and danced, glimmering over the furniture, then falling again.

Nearby sat Jay Regan, with the faint cynical smile under his mustache. James Bellowes did not greet Ernest. He watched his approach in utter silence, and did not speak even when his visitor sat down. He sat behind his desk, thin to impossible fragility, watchful, straight and rigid. In spite of his fragile appearance, brittle and tense, he was a living and immortal strength.

The two men regarded each other intently, pale eye to eye, implacability face to face with implacability. The regard went on for some moments. Then a faint flicker passed over Bellowes' gray face and a sharp pallid flash disturbed his lips.

"I am glad to see you, Mr. Barbour," he said in his dry and grating voice. "And I am glad to hear from Mr. Regan that you are prepared to come to terms with me."

"I am a reasonable man," replied Ernest. "And my time is valuable, too. I am glad to hear Mr. Regan has spoken for me. What have you to offer?"

Bellowes' long face turned grim and sour.

"In your section of the country I patronize your railroad. We do business together. In spite of our business relationships you are operating a refinery of your own, selling oil, shipping it on your railroad. A very ambiguous state of affairs, Mr. Barbour, a very ambiguous state of affairs. I do business with you under the pleasantest of relationships, and you cut my throat by competing with me. Do you call that fair?"

Ernest did not reply for a moment. Then he said very carefully: "Mr. Regan has told you what I have to say. We are not discussing fairness; only business. So I must ask you again: What have you to offer?"

Bellowes did not answer. He pulled toward him a paper and studied it intently. He had gray corded hands and thick wrists. A good hangman, thought Ernest.

Again Ernest spoke, slowly and distinctly. "You need our railroad. You can't do business with Charles Pitts. He's a stubborn man. As I said before, I'm reasonable. I can sell him out, put you in the way of ruining him. I can throw my stock in your brother's business on the market. You need me; I need you."

At the mention of his brother a sort of spasm passed over Bellowes' corpse-like face; then it relaxed once more into its rigid immobility. He raised his eyes with all their cold ferocity shining in them, and fixed them on Ernest.

"I will give you fifty thousand shares in the Middle Oil Company, and forty thousand in the Apex Oil Company, for your refineries and your wells."

There was another silence. Jay Regan pursed his mouth in a soundless whistle. Ernest put the corner of his right index finger in his mouth and bit it reflectively.

"And," went on Bellowes, "you will carry out your agreement with regard to Pitts—and my brother." He sighed thinly. "Poor Jack; I used to rock his cradle!"

For some odd reason or other, Ernest thought suddenly of Martin, whose cradle he had rocked. He studied Bellowes openly; he thought: He is obscene! He said: "That part is satisfactory. Now, I must ask something else.

"Your Senator Ford is a meddler. He is agitating for an alien contract labor law. That would be very bad, for me. And for dozens like me. Then there is Senator Winslow, a worse meddler, for he is a fanatic. He has introduced a bill, which, should it pass, would keep America from ever entering into any military agreement with a foreign nation, would forever prohibit alliances for mutual—protection. He is doing a lot of waving of the Monroe Doctrine. Now then, nations are coming closer to each other. We have steamships that annihilate distance—we have the cable. Nations are no longer isolated, and cannot maintain a policy of isolation. A nation that persists in isolation is in a dangerous position. Winslow would put America into that danger. You have more than a little influence. I want both Ford and Winslow stopped. I want their mouths shut."

Bellowes put his long pallid fingers carefully together, and over the bony tent they made he stared at Ernest without a change of expression. "It is a pleasure to do you this favor, Mr. Barbour. I have already written to Senator Ford about his alien contract labor agitation. Tomorrow I shall write to Senator Winslow about his bill. I consider it very unpatriotic of him."

After a prolonged moment Ernest rose, and gathered up his hat and cane and gloves. He turned to Jay Regan, who had been watching him blandly.

"I must ask," he said, "that you reconsider your refusal of a loan to France. Schultz and Poiret have just received a large armaments order from the Government."

Regan said nothing. Bellowes looked from one to the other of the two men and a pallid smile touched the corners of his lips. Regan's face turned scarlet, and then he smiled. He rose also.

When they were out once more in the narrow sunlit street, swarming with its feverish brokers and messenger boys, Regan said: "You have me to thank for the very excellent exchange you made with Mr. Bellowes."

Ernest's mouth twitched. "Thank you," he said, and there was no perceptible irony in his voice. Regan laughed. "He didn't like your reference to fanaticism in connection with Winslow. They belong to the same church. Bellowes is very devout, you know, very pious."

"He only needed that to complete him," replied Ernest.

CHAPTER LXXXV

WHEN THE Barbour family arrived at the Academy of Music with their host and hostess, Mr. and Mrs. Jay Regan, and the latter's daughter, Miss Alice Regan, the large auditorium was already filled. The great crystal chandeliers were sparkling like hanging baskets of diamond frost; the great crimson curtains were looped about the gilded boxes and hung over the stage. The high ceiling gleamed with gilt knobs and curves. A tremendous crowd filled both the orchestra and the balcony, and every box was crowded with occupants. The musicians were already in their places, and the discordant wails of their tuning, the bump of their instruments, the thin glittering notes of the harp, mingled with the festive roar of the audience. Everywhere was movement, colorful and sparkling; here and there the gleam of a white arm or shoulder, the red or blue or green shimmer of a gown, the toss of a feathered head, the flutter of bright fans, the flash of eyes and jewels, the motion of black-coated, white-cravated gentlemen, the agitation of a program, the foam of lace, the white brilliance of a smile. Everything was in a ferment. Everyone was vehement and excited, full of laughter and gay anticipation; voices flashed from row to row, accompanied by nods and the wave of a hand. Pretty bare white backs leaned forward energetically, swayed, returned to place. The fashion and wealth of New York sat in the orchestra and the boxes, or moved from row to row exchanging laughter and jokes, or like a tide rose into the boxes and ebbed away. The air was very warm, and before long the audience sat in a mist of perfumes.

May wore a Worth creation purchased that very afternoon, a deep crimson velvet elaborately draped and bustled and banded in rich black seal. It was cut very low in front, and displayed her still pretty plump white throat and chest and bare arms. She had put on her old garnets and wore the garnet ear-rings. Her small fat white hands flashed with diamonds and rubies, and on her hair, mingled dark red and gray, was perched a tiara of blazing blue diamonds. Her right wrist burned with broad bracelets of the same stones. Gracious, smiling, discreetly rouged, perfumed, and wielding a fan of black lace embroidered with garnets and diamonds, she sat in the Regan box and acknowledged the surprised nods and smiles of old friends below in the orchestra. Ernest thought she looked exceptionally well, and he was proud of her, and proud ᴊf the fact that members of families with great names greeteᴅ with real pleasure and without patronage. It did not disturb him to see how their faces changed slightly when they saw him, and how distrustful and wary was their renewed attempt at cordiality toward him. In fact, he was slightly amused. It was enough for him to see how they greeted May; he had never felt so strong an affection for her. He did not sit in the Regan box and sentimentally think: Nearly forty years ago I was a penniless immigrant boy. His arrival, his success, was to him the expected and inevitable thing. One did not marvel over the expected and the inevitable.

Gertrude pleased him tonight, also. She was dressed in a long-sleeved, high-necked gown of bottle-green velvet banded with black velvet, draped with dignity. She wore no jewels, except the diamond Paul had given her. Her slim body sat upright in the gilt chair, and her dark cloudy hair and colorless cool face, while not at all pretty, had distinction. She made even her mother, who had no plebeian ancestors, seem almost dowdy. Ernest, the Englishman, thought to himself that his daughter looked quite the patrician. The Englishman was unshakably strong in him, and though he would have denied it with fury, he had the Englishman's reverence for aristocracy and birth. And so he looked at his daughter, with her wan face and immobile expression and pale lifeless hands and slim throat, and he was grateful. There had been no exchanges of affection or confidence between them for a long time, but tonight he broke open the wall she had built about herself and leaning forward, he touched her hand. She turned her face to him; and he had a faint shock. He had thought her expression serene. He saw now that she was only rigidly entranced, and that she looked at him from deep within herself with eyes like a cry. Even when she smiled at him, and turned away, he still felt the shock, and his head fell forward a little on his heavy neck. I am imagining things, he thought, and shook his head faintly, over and over. But he did not touch Gertrude again.

Mrs. Regan, short and fat and amiable in black lace, was very vivacious, jerking her gray curled head about acknowledging acquaintances below. Miss Alice Regan, conscious perhaps of her father's origins, sat in state with a very refined air, and inclined her pale blond head regally. Jay Regan, who had dined and drunk too well, fought with a tendency to go to sleep. He talked loudly in consequence.

Elsa, in heavy rose satin and brilliants, with a long rosy feather in her piled hair, was excessively florid. Had she been dressed in black velvet and white ermine, with here and there a pearl or a diamond, she would have been magnificent. But Elsa was not distinguished for her taste in dress, and thought her rose satin devastating. As it was, she resembled a huge blooming cabbage-rose more than anything else, and her fine vivid complexion, which May thought vulgar, did nothing to add refinement to her appearance. Elsa's voice, loud and more than a little husky, attracted the attention of people as far as four rows away in the orchestra below the box.

May was gracious and smiling enough, endearing herself all over again to the Regans with her sympathetic air of interest and gentle attention. But she was trembling inside; it seemed to her that every bone in her body shook in its sheath of flesh. There was a thick lump in her throat and her hands were wet and icy. Between smiles and laughs and remarks, she studied the program. First was Beethoven's Fifth Symphony, followed by a concerto by Mozart, and then at the bottom was printed: "The Academy of Music is pleased to introduce at this time a distinguished young American composer, unknown as yet to American audiences though newly acclaimed in Paris: Mr. Godfrey Barbour. His First Symphony, called 'The Mountain Symphony,' will be played tonight." Then followed extracts from the opinions of French critics, all laudatory, some extravagant, and a brief résumé of the life of Mr. Godfrey Barbour and the schools of music in which he had studied.

May read the program over and over. Sometimes her heart swelled, and tears burst into her eyes. She winked them back. When she smiled again, the smile was radiant and tremulous. She gave Ernest the program and he read it impassively, returned it to her without comment. For a moment or two she decided that she hated him. But when she accidentally glanced at Gertrude, her daughter smiled whitely, and May saw that her hands were shaking. Mother and daughter drew closer together than ever before in their mutual agitation and terrible excitement.

There was a disturbance at the velvet curtains behind the box, and a tall broad youngish man with thick black mustaches, and an immense, arrogant-faced woman in early middle-age, and dressed in the most execrable taste, entered the Regan box. The gentlemen rose. The newcomers were Mr. Vanderbilt and Mrs. Urlich. The lady had a hoarse contemptuous voice, lavish diamonds, and arms and hands like a butcher's. Her mauve lace and satin gown, her feathered hair, set off her dark-red face and darting small black eyes, sharp as jet. Ernest, who respected birth and not money, was not overly cordial to the guests. He did not like Vanderbilt, who had worsted him in a little railroad business. He particularly hated arrogant women of no great handsomeness. So, before the guests were seated, he had already sat down again.

Mrs. Urlich liked Ernest Barbour, and even while she talked rapidly in her hoarsely rippling voice, she eyed him with those jet-like eyes that had little glittering points in them. Ernest had presented her with only three-quarters of his face and it was impassive, utterly without expression. The lady privately thought him fascinating, and considered his wife a smiling fool, who had nothing but good birth to recommend her. So she boomed at him, and as he continued to remain impassive she wanted to cut his throat. She fanned herself vigorously, emitting, as she did so, a prostrating effluvium of rose perfume, and Jay Regan leaned respectfully over the back of her chair. Her huge thighs were round and glossy under the mauve satin.

"I refused to believe, at first, that that dear young man was really your son, Mr. Barbour! I would rather expect him to be an excellent business man! But when I was finally convinced, I simply had to come over and congratulate you! I tell you, all of New York is humming with his name! America has so few real artists, that we all feel grateful to you."

May glanced triumphantly at Ernest, who sat impassively and faintly smiling. His arm hung over the back of his chair, and it swung a trifle.

"Let's hear what he's got to play, first," he said, "before we judge."

Taken aback, Mrs. Urlich glanced at May, whose steady smile became a little fixed. "Ernest," said May, fanning herself agitatedly, "cannot believe that a son of ours could be anything but an industrialist!"

"Pardon me, May—'anything but a fool,'" said Ernest in his monotonous voice. And as he said this he looked at his wife blandly.

A sickening silence fell in the box, against which the uproar below was like a crash. Then Mrs. Urlich burst into violent and enjoying laughter.

"What a delicious creature you are, Mr. Barbour! So excessively witty! I declare, you'd be invaluable at a dinner!"

However, it was apparent that neither May nor Gertrude thought Ernest a wit. May had turned as pale as Gertrude and bluish lines sprang out on each side of her faint smile. The diamonds on her fingers splintered into sparks because of her trembling. The Regans smiled also, but with discomfort. Good-natured Mrs. Regan was on the point of tears, in her sympathy for May.

Mrs. Urlich looked up. The jet eyes almost disappeared in the red flesh about them. She glanced sidelong at Mr. Vanderbilt, who was pulling his mustaches. She rose, and the perfume flowed about her rustling gown.

"I am sorry you are thinking of returning tomorrow," she said cordially. "I would so like to have you all for dinner tomorrow night."

May murmured regretfully; the fan hid half of her haggard face. Gertrude murmured, Elsa heartily expressed her disappointment. Ernest said nothing. He merely smiled. When the guests had gone, May moistened her lips behind her lace handkerchief and did not look at her husband.

But the auditorium was darkening. A silence fell, broken only by random whispers and the rustle of a program. The color and sparkle of the audience faded to a dim, restless sea. The conductor struck his score, lifted his baton. Beethoven's Fifth Symphony dawned on the warm per-

fumed air like the voice of a celestial host. The horns of the orchestra were disks of gold in the darkness.

Ernest soon saw that May had been quite truthful when she had said
she knew little about music. Part of her inattention was due to her inability to enjoy music, and part to her own agitation. She kept touching her
lips with her fan, then fanning herself vigorously; in the half-darkness
of the box her diamonds winked. She moved on her chair as if it burnt
her. Occasionally she sighed, a long and quivering sigh. But Gertrude
sat utterly without movement, her long pale hands clasped in her green
velvet lap, her profile pure and expressionless. Elsa fussed with her
bangles and chains, and kept preening her large handsome head.

Ernest was not the type of new-rich that affected to despise music
because he did not understand it. Neither did he feel superior to it. He
was merely untouched. There were no great calms in him, no super-
worldly ecstasies and majestic movements, and he recognized this very
clearly. It was necessary, he said to himself, for a man to feel like the
musician in order to understand his music. Nevertheless, though his
emotions were undisturbed (which he knew was all wrong if one wished
to appreciate music), he felt a sort of admiration for such lofty perfection, for such unhalting flow of sound. Had there been a break, a flaw,
an uncertainty, his ear, trained to catch breaks and flaws and uncertain-
ties in the speech of other men, would have caught them in this symphony. The fact that he did not pleased him tremendously. He admired
Beethoven for his perfect workmanship, his grasp, his scope, his masterful precision. Such things were pleasurable to hear in themselves; master
of technique himself, he felt an almost sensual enjoyment in discovering
technique in another man, no matter what the medium.

He was surprised to discover that Jay Regan was completely absorbed
in the music. The satirical cruel face, with its shining bald head, was
entranced. Behind his reserve something entirely foreign to Ernest's
knowledge looked out, unguarded. The long white slender hands, the
pickpocket hands, were clasped together on the balustrade, and the attitude of them was both exquisite and arresting. As the music proceeded
the jaw dropped and softened, the hooded eyes blinked, the mouth
twitched. So, he's got that behind his mask, thought Ernest. He's less
invulnerable than I thought. And his anxiety about the French loan
relaxed triumphantly, and with more than a little contempt.

The symphony moved on, infinitely moving, almost terrible in its
beauty. Feeling warm, Ernest mopped his face and moved his neck
uncomfortably in his collar.

He began to think of what he had accomplished that day. He
chuckled. He was unaware that Regan glanced at him with a fury suddenly become like the rage of a disturbed wolf. Mrs. Regan looked at
him with distressed surprise. May, almost weeping, bit her lip.

At length, after eons, the symphony swelled to a close. There was wild and prolonged applause. Possibly a dozen people in the audience had understood the music.

The lights were brightening, and the orchestra stood in the pit, bowing in response to an applause becoming scattered as the audience rose to rush into the lobby for the intermission. The aisles were choked, the backs of the audience teeming and uproarious. Before rows and rows of empty seats and surging·backs the musicians bowed and bowed.

Ernest left the box with Regan for the intermission. Regan was surly, and disinclined to talk. As the two men stood in the lobby, hiding themselves in a corner, Regan kept glancing at Ernest with an almost threatening eye. They did not return until the orchestra was tuning up again.

Ernest found Mozart had less perfection than Beethoven, and did not like him. Besides, though he would not admit it even to himself, he was becoming infected with the excitement of the others in the box. His discomfort grew; he gnawed the nail of his right index finger. His pale eyes moved restlessly in their sockets.

The lights went up again. May, suddenly as white as paper, suddenly as rigid as ice, dropped her fan with a·clatter upon the floor and leaned forward. Her hands clutched the red plush of the balustrade, and the veins rose in her throat. Sympathetically, Mrs. Regan laid her hand on the other woman's arm, but May did not feel it. She was looking at the manager who had come in from the wings.

"Ladies and gentlemen," said the manager in a high and lilting voice. "the orchestra will next play for you the First Symphony, the 'Mountain Symphony,' of Mr. Godfrey Barbour." He paused; there was a ripple of polite applause. "I am not going to take your time to tell you of this symphony. You are the audience; you are the judges. On you the fame and fortune of this young American composer rest."

"No American ever composed anything fit to listen to," said a woman's clear piercing voice below the Regan box. "Except, perhaps, Stephen Foster."

"O God," whispered May. She was shaking visibly. Gertrude leaned toward her mother, put her slender arm about her shoulders. May shook her off as if in agony. "Where is Frey? Where is my boy?" she whispered over and over.

The lights dimmed, the conductor raised his baton. The symphony began.

The first movement, the allegro, was disappointing. It was a perfect movement; the technique was faultless. It was as brilliant as the cold shooting of stars on a winter's midnight, but as completely without fire or significance. A purely intellectual movement, one to delight a mathematician. The best and the worst of Godfrey Barbour's music was in it:

it was bad and good simultaneously, for the same reason. It was as beautiful and as dead as a crystal image, swift and lifeless, intellectuality without splendor, perfection without glory. Its very intellectuality betrayed its lack of substance. It was abstract mechanics without a meaning.

May listened to it without hearing it; her bare back was moist with cold sweat; a constant tremor agitated her diamonds. Regan sat with his elbow on the balustrade, his hand covering his secret mouth. He listened with intent and polite attention. He heard the icy pyrotechnics of the movement and was amazed at the minuteness of detail.

But Ernest was dumfounded. The technician was astonished at this technique. He did not hear the emptiness of it; he heard only the precision. What a mind for detail! he thought. Ernest felt quite an unusual excitement, a gratified pleasure. His son was not a fool, after all! What a delicate mechanic! What an exquisite inventor! He came close to being as happy as he had ever been, in this realization.

The first movement ended. Regan turned to Ernest. "It's perfection," he said quietly, "but it's not music." His wife looked puzzled, but Ernest understood.

"It is perfect," echoed Gertrude, turning to May. But May's eyes were closed; there were tears on her cheeks, and her lips were white. Elsa, who had been bored to the dozing point, giggled.

"But, it is not music," repeated Jay Regan.

"Well, what is it then, Papa?" asked Miss Regan, considering her father extremely rude. He glanced at her over his shoulder. "It's a problem in abstract mathematics, brilliantly solved," he answered.

But the largo was beginning. The audience had listened to the allegro in perfunctory silence, as they might have listened to a lecture that had not touched them. But after a few minutes of the largo they became interested, glanced surprisedly at each other, sat up. Even those who did not understand music nor care particularly about it were jolted upright.

There was no technique here, no careful pruning and polishing and mechanical lighting; no brilliancy without warmth. There was no perfection. The allegro movement, the first in the Mountain Symphony, brought to mind nothing whatsoever pertaining to mountains, except, perhaps, icicles glittering in the sun and patches of glazed snow, which was not, however, what Godfrey Barbour had meant to convey. But from out the dark-and-light chaos of his uncertainty, the frightened lack of discipline, the gigantic loss of control (as though he were trying to manipulate forces too great for his feebleness), had emerged a colossal form. He had become an involuntary rider of Titan's horses, a dainty and precise dancer whose sparkling platform had become an earthquake. All through this dark-and-light, these shifting bases, these thunders and rolls and flame-drenched oceans, these abysses struck open with the hammer of Thor, these burstings apart of space and explosions of matter, the white and terrified face of Godfrey Barbour seemed to shine. He was a child who had involuntarily evoked ruin.

When the movement reached its conclusion, the audience sat, a little stupefied. They had accepted the splendor of Beethoven indifferently, as one accepts a sunset or a majestic panorama to which one has become apathetic through familiarity. They took Beethoven for granted, even his glory. But here was something new, someone close to them, someone alive, and not in legendary time. Nothing that a god can do astonishes, but a man who approaches the gods is an object for marvelling and worship. The orchestra was actually beginning the scherzo when the audience broke out into a delirious riot of applause, stamping, shouting, waving of fans, cries and shouts. Many stood up, clapping madly, laughing with feverish excitement.

May, in the Regan box, wept hysterically. Gertrude and Elsa put their arms about her. Mrs. Regan twittered incoherently to her daughter. Jay Regan said nothing, and now his hand was completely over his mouth as he stared at the orchestra. "My son! My son!" May sobbed over and over. But Ernest sat in silence, his heavy face as impassive as ever, his fingers slowly playing with his watch-chain. He knew, now, that he would never own his son again. Not with that in him! The young devil! he thought, and listened contemptuously to the uproar of the audience.

The audience became quiet enough to listen eagerly to the scherzo. They were not too disappointed. A dozen dainty dancers moved prettily over glassy mirrors and bowed elegantly to their own images. There was no sprightliness here; the dancers formed angles and rectangles and triangles and precise circles all in the best and most intellectual taste. If there was any lifting of skirts it was to form a glittering parallelogram. An equation was worked out in tights and spangles. True sportiveness was absent in this studied prettiness.

"How delicate, like lace!" exclaimed the kind-hearted little Mrs. Regan. Elsa, who had no liking for tiny shoes twinkling with paste, made a grimace. The audience, gratefully and emotionally remembering the largo, applauded vociferously.

When the manager was finally shouted onto the stage, he could not make himself heard for the roaring. He pleaded; he gesticulated. Finally, laughing, waving his arms, he returned to the wings and dragged out of them a slender, smallish young man, blond and terror-stricken, pulling-away, confused and scarlet. "Maestro!" screamed some young men in the balcony. May stood up in spite of the hands that tugged at her. She leaned over the balustrade. "Frey! My darling, my darling! Frey, it's Mama! Frey, dearest, Frey, Frey!" But Godfrey, overcome, bowing, his handsome face twisted with his terror-blighted smile, did not hear her. May beat her hands on the balustrade, she laughed and shrieked together, she sobbed. People in the rows below looked up at her, and many of them smiled and cried in sympathy. All at once the heat in the vast auditorium became intense, and agitated as though by scorching winds.

It was an ovation. The audience went completely mad. The orchestra climbed up beside the young man and stood around him like priests about their high-priest. Many of them, true artists themselves, had privately thought the symphony very bad, but they were infected by the general insanity and uproar. They joined in the applause. No one knew just when Godfrey disappeared, but when the musicians left the stage Godfrey was no longer on it.

CHAPTER LXXXVI

WHEN THE Barbours finally fought their way through the crowds to the back of the stage, they were pounced upon by the manager, who greeted them with a mixture of rude excitement, obsequiousness, rage and hysteria. He screamed something incoherent to the effect that Mr. Godfrey Barbour had left without a word, just disappeared, and a thousand people clamoring to meet him, really important people who were donors and patrons, and this was insupportable and not to be countenanced, this insult to the donors and the patrons, and a large deficit last year, and didn't he understand that an artist, no matter how acclaimed and great, must be polite and ingratiating to the donors——

Ernest remained at least four feet from the excited and infuriated and despairing man, but when his eye finally caught that wandering and glittering eye the uproar stopped, and the manager stood in a state of suddenly suspended animation, his mouth hanging open, a photograph snapped in the midst of wild activity.

"Did my son leave any message for his mother, or me?" asked Ernest calmly.

The photograph resumed life, but in a more subdued form. "No! Yes! I don't know! Oh, this is not to be explained or forgiven! There has been arranged a party for him, one hundred distinguished guests, who can raise the Academy to magnificent heights or close it in bankruptcy, and Mr. Godfrey Barbour, a newcomer, a stranger, an unknown, dared insult these guests who could help him and the Academy so, and now everything is in ruins, everything lost—" He sobbed aloud. May stood watching him like one in a dream, her dry lips parted.

"A message?" repeated Ernest in a loud and commanding voice.

The clamor stopped. The four Barbours and the manager stood in the cold and shabby dressing room, the door closed. In the hall outside was the deep roar of an impatient mob.

The manager put his hand to his head. "A message!" he muttered. He lifted his head and stared at Ernest wildly. "Yes, he gave me a little note! Before the performance! Perhaps it is for you. O my God, how could he do this thing to me, to all of us, who have brought him forward, introduced him—" He fumbled in his pocket and withdrew a crushed envelope, which he fiercely pushed into Ernest's hand.

The three women crowded about him as he opened it. May leaned against his arm, overcome. There were only a few lines, and they were addressed to May. "Mama, darling," Godfrey had written, "I don't want to see you at the Academy after the performance, whether it is good or bad. There will be too many people, too much of a crowd. But I want all of you who attend the performance to come to my rooms on Seventh Avenue immediately after. You will understand why when you arrive."

"The young fool," said Ernest irately. He thrust the paper back into his pocket. "Well, I suppose the only thing to do is to call the carriage and drive over to his rooms."

"Oh, dear," murmured May faintly. She was very white. Elsa supported her with her strong arm. Gertrude stood in silence, the long folds of her ermine cloak falling over her dark green velvet gown, her pale face without expression.

The door opened, showing a mass of moving heads and excited, curious faces. Lucy appeared, stout and competent, escorted by the disheveled Percival. The pressure outside catapulted them into the room.

"Dears!" exclaimed Lucy with vigor. "What a time we had leaving the orchestra, struggling with the crowds! But where is Frey?"

"Frey," said Gertrude quietly, "has invited us to his rooms on Seventh Avenue. He wanted to avoid the people, and no wonder! Will you come with us?"

Lucy stared, her eyes shining like bits of black raspberry jelly. "How odd! Certainly Percy and I will come! But then, all artists are modest! Gracious, he'll make a fortune out of this! Or do artists ever make fortunes?"

"You'll have to ask an artist," said Ernest. "Ladies, if you are ready, we will go."

The snow was falling when they went outside, thick and soft as cotton batting. Most of the people were still inside the Academy, and the street was almost deserted. The Van Eyck carriage was called, and the family got in. Lucy and her husband followed in the Regan carriage, which had courteously been offered to them. They rolled without a sound on the soft white cushion of new snow to Seventh Avenue. The streets were quiet and empty, almost every window dark and bleakly reflecting the flickering street lights. No one spoke. May leaned back in her seat under the fur rug, and her eyes were closed. Even Elsa was silent.

May was thinking with bitter fear: It is not like Frey, my little Godfrey, to want the family about when I am there. It must be that he knows Ernest will be there, too, and has something to show us or tell us, and he believes he will be safer among a lot of us than just alone with Ernest and me. It is Ernest he is afraid of. He must have seen him in the box.

By the time the carriage reached the shabby neighborhood of Seventh Avenue and Twelfth Street, May was physically ill with apprehension and anxiety. When the vehicle stopped before a gloomy narrow house, four stories tall, with narrow windows like slits in the red brick walls, and a cluttered half-dozen of steps hemmed in by brownstone sides, May was hardly able to leave the carriage. The snow still fell, steadily, with a sort of implacable indifference. On the very top floor a feeble light or two burned expectantly. Ernest pushed open a shabby oak door with stained glass insets about a dirty uncurtained panel of plain glass, and they trooped into a gritty hallway with bare floor and narrow dirty stairway winding upwards in a dimly lit silence. The stairs were uncarpeted; their boots echoed on the bare wood. The ladies lifted their heavy velvet skirts and climbed laboriously. Elsa's feather had been liberally snowed upon, and curved back over her big head ludicrously. Ernest followed in gloomy speechlessness, his lower lip thrust out, his cane tucked under his arm like a sword-sheath.

They seemed to climb indefinitely in that dreary, partially lighted silence. May began to pant. Ernest offered his arm, but she refused it with an exhausted motion of her head. When they reached the fourth floor a door opened and threw a beam of yellow light into the narrow hallway. Godfrey, still in his overcoat, but with no hat on his bright and handsome young head, greeted them with a smile. He seemed unable to speak. The smile on his narrow long face was fixed and twisted with fright. May saw at once. Everything else was forgotten: her darling was terrified.

"Frey!" she cried in a heartbreaking voice as she reached the doorway. She threw her arms about his neck, pulled his face down to hers, burst into broken cries. "Frey! How you have frightened us! Frey, darling, why did you run away? When it was all so beautiful, and everyone was so glad! My darling, let me see you, let your Mama see you, after so long!"

"Let us go inside, first," said Ernest ironically.

"Mama!" cried Godfrey, and there was as much fear as affection in his voice. He clung to his mother as they all went inside the drab and chilly apartment.

It was a dreary place in a dreary house in a dreary neighborhood patronized mostly by unarrived young artists and those who would never arrive. The dull red paper on the wall, the scarred oak woodwork, the Brussels rug on the floor with its faded roses and leaves, the small coal stove smoking in the center of the room, the mended curtains, the old-fashioned worn horsehair furniture, the table with its china-globed lamp and feeble light, the books heaped helter-skelter on the floor under the windows with their torn shades, the dusty and rickety old piano heaped with paper and portfolios, all were dusted over with the gray patina of poverty and the hopelessness of dozens of others who had lived here before Godfrey.

Nobody could speak for a minute except Elsa. "Well!" she ejaculated. "I must say this is a terrible place, Frey!" She turned to her cousin, who was still shrinking behind his mother, and her large handsome face lightened, became radiant. "What on earth possessed you to come here! Dear, how extremely odd!"

"Ghastly!" exclaimed Lucy, fastidiously lifting her skirts again and glancing about the room. Her Percival, embarrassed, coughed to remind her of her manners, but she ignored him.

"Darling," whispered May, turning paler than ever, "why on earth did you come here? You can't be staying here!"

"Yes, Mama." Godfrey's voice trembled. He glanced furtively at his father, who stood in the center of the room and was calmly and thoroughly taking inventory of everything it contained. "I—I don't know how to explain— It's so hard."

Gertrude went to him, and kissed his cheek. It was damp and cold under her lips. "What does it matter, Frey?" she said gently. "If you work here, if you are happy here, what does it matter? I'm sure it is quite good enough. But you ought not to have run away. With everyone applauding so, and waiting to acknowledge you, and everything. Oh, it was so beautiful, your symphony! What does anything matter compared with that!"

"Speak to your father, love," said May faintly, disengaging her son's rigid and clutching arms.

Ernest turned his smooth pale face to his son as the latter approached him hesitantly. He and Godfrey were almost the same height, but the young man seemed much shorter because of his slenderness and daintiness, his narrow face and girlish figure and his haughty yet diffident manner. He did not look his father in the face as he extended a visibly shaking hand, soft and white and transparent as a girl's. "Papa—" he began, and could say nothing else. Ernest took his hand, shook it. He smiled heartily. "What the devil, lad!" he exclaimed. "Why did you run away? Why are you here? You made a success, a splendid success! And you ran away from it! That's no way to do.

"Let me look at you. Not much meat on those bones, is there? I thought France would fatten you up. Look up, lad, look up! Nobody's going to bite you, damned if they are. I don't like this simpering business of running away from people who want to honor you and toady to you. You'll never get anywhere that way. But look here, have you met Percival Van Eyck? Lucy's husband? Speak up, to all of us, your mother and Trudie and Elsa and Lucy and Percival. What's got into you?"

His voice boomed cheerily in the gritty and desolate room. The others, becoming infected by Godfrey's tremblings and visible fright, glanced at each other uneasily. May fixed her eyes upon her son with an imploring and anguished expression, and put one hand to her heart.

Godfrey, aroused by his father to a cognizance of the others, bowed to them formally, smiled a little. His lips trembled continually with a faint fluttering. He was like a bright and fragile bird caught in a pair of crushing hands. Elsa's hands, thought Gertrude, as Godfrey, in his circling, reached his cousin. Elsa was a little taller than the young man; her buxom rosiness, her great vitality and bouncing health seemed to envelop him. Simply, without a smile or a simper, she bent her head slightly and kissed him full on the lips. Her arms went about him as if in protection.

"Frey," she said, and her hand touched his cheek. "Frey." When she released him, there were tears in her eyes.

"Please sit down," said Godfrey, after the greetings. He spoke feebly. They found seats. The ladies in their jewels and ermine and furs and velvets and feathers looked incongruous in that shabby and dreary room. "I haven't anything but a little wine to offer you," he continued, trying to smile. "I just moved here yesterday. I've been busy."

"Of course, darling," said May, crying out as if to throw him some of her strength.

He looked from one to the other and wet his lips with the tip of his tongue. Behind the white and delicate handsomeness of his face terror dodged about. He clenched and unclenched his hands on his knees. Ernest, folding his own hands on his cane, watched him. All at once his face thickened with brutality and malignancy. Gertrude, waiting, felt her heart begin to beat ominously. How ridiculous, she forced herself to think, for all of us to be sitting here like this, staring at poor Frey, who is dying by inches! I wish I could say something, but there's a ball in my throat. It's all a dream of course, a silly absurd dream, sitting here, staring at Frey, in this dreadful room.

"Don't you think, lad," said Ernest suddenly, "that all this is a little strange, not seeing you for an age, and then coming here to find you in a den, and you looking as though you are scared out of your wits? Don't you think you owe us an explanation?"

Godfrey was silent. The hands on his knees suddenly fell open as if something thin and vital in him had shattered.

"Never mind explanations, Frey!" laughed Elsa tremulously. "Just tell us you are coming home with us tomorrow, and we'll all be satisfied."

In the silence that followed her words, Godfrey drew a sharp and audible breath. He struggled upright; he was trying to evoke a courage he never had, and succeeded only in becoming desperate. He glanced at his mother, and the expression of suffering on her face, her evident comprehension that something was very wrong, unnerved him. He glanced at his father, and winced so openly that on any other occasion the involuntary gesture would have been amusing. He looked at Elsa, and her robust bloom seemed to sicken him; his eye slid dully over Lucy and Percival. But when he reached Gertrude and looked at her, his expression steadied, his mouth tightened, as though she had spoken encouragingly to him. He spoke to all of them in an almost inaudible voice, but he looked only at his sister, whose smile was steadfast and gentle.

"I want to give you an explanation. That's why I've asked you here. But it seems terribly hard. I'll have to skip a lot of it. I came to New York a few days ago, and I've been busy——" He drew a deep breath and plunged on, his terror rapidly increasing as though he were running from something trying to overtake him.

"Yes, darling!" cried May. Ernest glanced at her briefly. His lips had turned pale and his nostrils were distended.

Godfrey still gazed at his sister.

"I'm not going—home!" he said, incoherently. "I can't go home! For more than one reason. I'm going to stay in New York, to work. I—I've got another symphony half finished. There's nothing for me in Windsor. I mean, nothing that can help me with my work. I—yes, the symphony was a success tonight, but it is the first thing of mine to be performed here. I—I don't like the largo. The largo," he continued, more and more incoherently, and now flashing his strained brown eyes from one to the other with increasing dread, "isn't good at all. I want to delete it. I don't care what the critics say— It isn't any good. I've got a better largo partly written, and then I'll——"

No one spoke, even when his strangled voice was silent and he visibly struggled. They merely stared at him, fascinated, infected by his own terror. Coals dropped in the little stove, and the mended curtains swayed in a draft. Gertrude, bemused and cold, thought of a bird beating its wings against a closed window, dying. Frey! she cried out to him soundlessly. Don't be so frightened, Frey!

Ernest stirred. His expression had become more and more brutal, and his eyes had contempt in them.

"You've got something to say to us, haven't you?" he asked loudly. "Well, be a man, and say it! No one's going to murder you. Be a man."

Godfrey turned to him and glared at him, his terror without a mask full on his face. His throat worked; his hands worked. Suddenly he sprang to his feet and ran to the end of the room. "Simone!" he cried.

He stood aside. A woman about thirty years of age appeared in the doorway. She was much taller than Godfrey, and very much fatter. She was luxuriantly made, with deep full breasts and broad hips. Her cheap black silk gown, draped and rustling and badly made, could not conceal the abundance of her flesh. Her reddish hair was elaborately curled and twisted, and false brilliants winked in it. Below the hair was a bellicose and florid face and snapping yellow-brown eyes, a curved nose and a thick painted smile. On her pudgy hands, none too clean, were other false brilliants. Her whole air was common, vulgar, aggressive and bold. And frightened. Her fright made her stare belligerently at the guests, though her smile pulled her red lips wide apart to show really excellent white teeth.

Godfrey lurked behind her. An impersonal observer might have thought this extremely funny. No one in that room found it funny. They merely gazed at Simone with blank faces, and blinked a little.

"My wife, Simone Renard," said Godfrey faintly, and seemed to dissolve behind her.

There was absolute silence for a long moment or two. Then May rose slowly, with a distraught expression and looked about her blindly. Gertrude stood up also and put her arm about her mother. Elsa merely sat, the bright strong color sinking from her face. Lucy and Percival turned and glared emptily at each other. But Ernest stood up slowly, without any expression at all, and with only a dusky tint appearing about his mouth to show that he heard what Godfrey had said.

"Your wife?" he repeated, almost politely, as one repeats a phrase which has not seemed clear to him.

"Yes," replied Godfrey, dodging from behind the silent big young woman. His voice was fainter than ever.

Ernest glanced at his wife, hatred like points in his light disks of eyes.

"Really," exclaimed Lucy helplessly. "Percy, my love, I don't believe any one wishes us here now, so would you mind taking me home?"

No one noticed the flight of the Van Eycks. May had sat down again. In some way Godfrey had been induced to stand beside his wife, and she held his hand. Her eyes glinted, and though she pressed her young husband's finger the look she kept flashing upon him was bitter and menacing. Then she turned to Ernest and said in a hoarse, painfully accented voice: "I am not so very, very bad, M'sieu Barbour. Your son lived at my father's pension. He was very lonely. I taught him French and he taught me English. A very lonely young man, very unhappy. My parents are respectable, so you must not be too disturbed. I helped him with his music. I have the very good voice, also. I wish' to come to America to sing here. In concerts. My little Godfrey promised that he would help me. Would you wish to hear me sing, M'sieu?" she added, with mockery.

Ernest said nothing. He leaned on his cane, his torso bent forward slightly. He still looked at his son, and then he turned from him with a gesture of disgust.

May lifted her head, looked about her dazedly. Then her eyes fastened upon Simone, dilated, filled with tears. An expression of almost piteous pleading came out upon her face, as if she begged someone to assure her that what she was experiencing was not real. She wet her lips, and the cords of her throat strained as though every word cost her physical anguish as she spoke:

"No, no, my—my dear, you cannot be 'bad' at all. Not if you love my Godfrey—" She looked at her daughter in agony, at her son, and then again at Simone. "I am sure—I know it must be—all right. Perhaps if we—" Her voice sank, dropped to a whisper, was no longer audible. She wrung her hands, and Gertrude, unable to bear the sight of such misery, closed her eyes as on an internal spasm. Simone showed no emotion whatsoever.

As she gazed at Godfrey, studying his imploring face, his terror, his incredulous expression, all these things showed on her own face and Ernest read them. He pursed his lips; he inclined his head as though he saw something he could respect and deal with. He almost smiled.

"My poor little one," said Simone at last, sighing, and taking her husband's hand. "How can we live without money? Not your little Simone, I am devastated to confess. And it is very evident that your Papa will give us no money. How, then, shall we live?"

"Simone!" he pleaded distractedly. "You said nothing of money before. If it is money you wish, I shall make it——"

"How?" she asked gently and reasonably. "You are only a child."

He glared at her blankly. He looked much less than his twenty-four years. His mouth worked. Simone shrugged, sighed again, turned from him with pity, to his father.

"He is only a child," she repeated.

"Oh, of course!" assented Ernest ironically, with a significant undertone. But Simone did not seem embarrassed. She merely smiled. And waited.

Godfrey looked about the room distractedly. His wandering glance fell on his mother. He made a faint whimpering sound. Gertrude regarded him steadily, with great quietness. He did not see Elsa yet at all. When she loomed up beside him and faced Simone, he could only blink at her dully.

Elsa, tall and broad as Brunhilde, said to her cousin: "Come home, Frey. Come home with us." Her voice trembled with pity, indignation and love.

"And that," said Ernest, "was what I was about to suggest, myself. When this lady," indicating Simone with a wave of his hand, "is ready to leave this—place, I will make arrangements with her about her little—reward. Of course, none of it shall be given to her until she sues for a divorce. And, in the meantime, on Godfrey's promise that he will forget all this music nonsense and return home with us and try to make a man of himself, we will take him with us to Lucy's house——"

Godfrey had listened to all this stupidly. He saw his life taken competently into the hands of his Wagnerian cousin and his father; he saw the flash between them, the faint smile, the sudden indulgent smugness of Elsa's mouth. He was too austere and cold and selfish of temperament ever to have had much emotion or passion, too shy and self-centered ever to have learned the ways of other human beings. Therefore, when he looked at his father and Elsa with new clarity, he was horror-stricken and filled with frenzy; they were as suddenly alien and incomprehensible and dangerous as creatures from a world never approached by him. And their danger was all pointed at him. All at once he was overwhelmed with loathing and rage, so new to his character that they drove deeply into the virgin places of him like the shining blades of plows. They scarred him and turned him over, this loathing and this rage, set him afire, made him mad, tore his roots from the cool and sterile soil in which they had lain all his life, and tossed them out into the burning sun of reality. He forgot the defection of his cunning wife, forgot he was ridiculous and abandoned, forgot his mother, and thought only of his danger and his despair and his frantic need of escape. He even forgot his life-long terror of his father, and his hatred.

"No!" he cried. "I'll not go home with you! I'll never go home with you! You can't buy me off; you can frighten others, but you can't frighten me any longer. I've done with all that!"

He stopped abruptly, panting. An evil and brutish look started across Ernest's face.

"Why," he said, with dull wonder, "you scurvy little dog!" And struck his son across the face viciously.

At that sound, May and Gertrude stood up abruptly.

"Ernest!" May cried out. "Frey!"

Ernest swung upon her. "Get out," he said in a low voice. "Get out!" He turned to Elsa. "Take them away; get them out of here. I've got to take care of this, myself!"

Elsa hesitated, then when she saw his face she caught her aunt by the arm. "Aunt May, let us go. Uncle Ernest can take care of what is to be done very well without us——"

"Frey!" cried May, trying to release her arm, trying to go to her son, who stood with his hand against his struck cheek.

"Get out," said Ernest again, and involuntarily his fist doubled as he commanded his wife with glittering eyes.

"Mama," said Gertrude through pale dry lips, "let's go. We can see Frey tomorrow. Tomorrow, Frey—," she repeated, glancing at her brother pleadingly. "Tomorrow?"

Godfrey had been completely demoralized since his father's blow, but now, at the sound of his mother's voice his scattered wits and courage came back. For one of the few times in his life he felt pity for someone besides himself, experienced the new emotion of wanting to help someone else, wanted to give protection to another who desperately needed it. His pity and love made him strong, made his courage stiff once more, made a sort of exhilaration run along his nerves again. He looked at his mother gently, pitifully.

"Go on, Mama, go home," he said quietly. "I'll see you—tomorrow. Please go home," he repeated, and under his quietness May, even in her misery, heard his urgency.

"Tomorrow, darling," she whimpered, trying to smile at him, to give him the assurance of her support no matter what happened. Then Gertrude took one of her arms and Elsa the other, and the three women went out.

Ernest watched them go; after they had closed the door, he stared at it for a long moment. Then he turned to his son, who had not moved. On Godfrey's white cheek the imprint of his father's hand stood out in red welts. But the young man stood there, thin and pale, and completely resolute, as though despair had given him immovable courage. Simone, smiling ever so little, seated herself negligently in a chair, began to play with her chain. Her glance, indolent and amused, passed between father and son; the spectacle seemed to give her some enjoyment, quite detached and impersonal.

"Now, then," said Ernest. "Now then."

Godfrey tightened the muscles about a mouth that tried to tremble. But he said nothing.

"For the last time," Ernest went on, trying to keep his voice calm, "I tell you that this is the end. You'll come home with us tomorrow, or you can make up your mind never to see any of us again. Is that clear?"

"Yes, it's clear," said Godfrey.

The eyes of the two men met and held. Suddenly it occurred to Ernest that in all his son's life he had never met Godfrey's eyes fully before; at all times they had shifted away from his, and he had caught only half-glimpses, as one catches glimpses of the shape of a deer in a thicket. Now he saw them, brown, and bright with terror but also shining with the courage that terror can finally bring. But he also saw his son for the first time, and something seemed to tell him that never had he really touched Godfrey, and that never would he touch him. Martin had looked at him like that once or twice, even out of the extremity of his fear. The last night he had ever spoken to Martin came back to him; Martin had had such a face as Godfrey's, and such eyes. Martin had always eluded his brother, and then, when forced to see him, cornered by him, had looked at him directly, terrified by him, yet knowing that

Ernest could never reach him, could never pass into the dimension that protected him.

The most curious sensation of impotence came over Ernest. He knew now that in spite of everything he had never conquered Martin. And he knew that he would never conquer Godfrey. He might strike him down, he might kill him. He might drive him off, might forget him. But never would he conquer him. He had fought and overcome the strong many times, but he knew now that he had never overcome the weak.

He heard himself saying tonelessly, out of his impotence: "I suppose your mother means nothing to you? I suppose you don't care whether you see her again or not?"

Then Godfrey, still looking at him, said: "I don't care what happens. I'm not going home with you. You needn't lift your cane to me. You can't change anything. No matter what you do to me, you can't change anything." He paused. "I never want to see you again. I hoped that I would never need to see you. If it hadn't been for my mother, I would never have come back here. All my life, I've wanted to get away from you. You—you made me sick," he added simply.

And again their eyes held. Finally, it was Ernest who looked away.

All at once, quite suddenly, he was no longer enraged. All at once, he was only tired to the point of collapse. The strangest feeling came to him, as though he had lost something, and as though the loss was causing him intense pain and grief. There was a dry taste in his mouth, a sort of turning away of his whole mind and spirit in a weariness not to be endured.

"I'm going away now," he heard Godfrey's voice saying. Surely, all his life he had heard Godfrey saying that! "I'll see my mother again, sometime. You can't prevent that, even if you try. I'm not sorry this happened. It's so good to get away from you at last!"

The young man went into the bedroom, came out with his hat and coat. Then, without looking at his father or his wife again, he went out of the room.

Ernest listened to the sound of his son's footsteps going down the stairs. He strained to hear their last echo. And then there was no other sound for a moment or two.

Simone got up, shook out her sleazy dress. She was still smiling a little.

"So, that is all, M'sieu," she said. Ernest looked at her but he did not seem to see her. "And you will not forget your promise to me?"

Ernest stirred. He sighed, picked up his hat. He put it on his head. "No," he answered. "I will not forget."

CHAPTER LXXXVII

Lucy herself opened the door for Ernest when he arrived home. He did not notice that her face was white, with traces of tears on it. She murmured something to him about Gertrude and Elsa having put May to bed, and that she wanted to see him for a moment. He made a vague, almost distraught gesture, but she followed him.

He went into the drawing room. A fire had been kept up, and its handful of coals burned gold and red behind the grate. A single lamp glowed on a teakwood table, shone softly on all the crowded confusion of a Victorian parlor. Ernest stood before the fire, his hand on the mantel, his head bent. He kept drawing deep hoarse breaths.

The velvet curtains that separated one room from another stirred, and Lucy, in a lacy cream dressing gown, her hair on her shoulders, entered. She was crying distractedly. Ernest put up his hand. "I'm not interested in anything else, Lucy," he said to his niece. "I've got my hands full."

But she came up to him. "Uncle Ernest," she said brokenly, "you've got to listen to this. It—it's very terrible. When I came home I found a telegram from Paul——"

"Paul?" He turned to her rapidly. "Paul?" If he had been pale before, he was ashen now.

"Yes. You see, Uncle Ernest, he wanted you to get the news first, before everyone knew it. Before the papers knew it, and Aunt May heard. So he sent it to me." She handed him a sheet of yellow paper, covered her face with her handkerchief and sat down.

Ernest slowly smoothed out the paper. He read the telegram:

"Lucy, am sending telegram so you can tell Uncle Ernest and others won't know immediately. Guy shot and killed this morning by miners during riot. Am bringing body home at once." It was unsigned.

Very carefully Ernest refolded the yellow paper, bent, pushed it between the coals. Lucy slipped the handkerchief from her face. She stood up and went to her uncle. But he stood regarding the fire, which was flaring into a fan of swift light. It burst over his face, which seemed to have shrivelled into gray folds.

"Uncle Ernest," whimpered Lucy, touching his arm. He put his fingers over her hand.

"Thank you, my dear," he said, "for not alarming your aunt. She has had a very—exciting night. We must, of course, leave for home as soon as possible. I'll have to have your help. You may tell her, if you wish, that you have had a telegram that Guy had to return to Windsor, with a sudden illness."

"Won't you tell her, Uncle Ernest?"

"No, I am afraid I can't. This—is a little too much, for me."

"But won't she think it odd that the telegram was sent to me, instead of to you?"

"True. I don't seem able to think very clearly, Lucy. True. I can see no way out of it, unfortunately. I never thought I was a coward."

"Uncle, I think you had better sit down," said Lucy in alarm. "Let me pour you some brandy." She began to cry again. "Oh, how terrible this is! Poor little Guy! How could it have happened? It is like a dream, not real at all——"

Ernest, having sat down, laid his arms along the arms of the chair. His chin fell on his chest.

"If you intend to return to Windsor, Lucy," he said, "I would prefer that you waited until we left. I would rather May did not know about it at once, and if you came with us she would suspect something immediately."

"Yes, certainly, dear Uncle." She wondered at his very calm voice, his thoughtful expression. Was it possible he was not very much disturbed, she thought resentfully, all her instincts offended.

"And to hear of this, to have this happen, just when Frey has made such a success, when everything is so wonderful——"

Falling coals rattled in the fireplace. Ernest did not move. His arms still lay along the arms of the chair. Lucy could see the dull sparkle of the signet ring on his little finger.

Lucy sobbed aloud. "Poor little Guy! Poor little Guy! And Frey, too, married to that awful woman! How dreadful to have children! Oh, dear, dear me, how shall I tell Aunt May? I really can't do it—her heart will break——"

In response to her ring a sleepy and resentful maid brought in a silver tray with a decanter of brandy and a glass. Lucy poured the glass full of the amber liquid and held it out to her uncle. "Dear Uncle Ernest, please drink this! It will do you such good."

He glanced at it and waved it aside. "No, thank you, Lucy. I always hated it. This is one time when I need not be polite and drink it down."

Percival Van Eyck, who had lurked in the upper hallway, too kind-hearted to have been present when his wife broke the news to her uncle, now came downstairs timidly, to offer his condolences. Lucy glanced at him with tearful impatience; Uncle Ernest was certainly not the kind to bear the condolences of kind fools with any good grace, she thought. But to her surprise Ernest seemed touched when Percival stammered out his broken and sorrowful words. Perhaps it was because it was so evident that this young man, who had never seen his wife's cousin, could be overwhelmingly affected by the griefs and the calamities of others. Nor was it mere sentimentality; he was genuinely distressed by the sorrows of absolute strangers, and Lucy often declared that it was a good thing that he had married a woman with sense or certainly his inheritance would soon have been dispersed in a thousand charities.

The three sat together drearily, in silence, in chill and gloom, until the morning silvered the sky over the houses opposite. For over an hour Ernest had not spoken; he had half hidden his face with his hand, while Lucy, not his wife or his daughter, had sat in silence beside him, and Percival, sad and sleepy and dishevelled in his dressing gown, had poured coals frequently upon the fire.

It was definitely light when Ernest said quietly to his niece: "I would like to send a telegram, Lucy."

A servant was aroused and came downstairs carrying a lamp. Ernest sat down at the secretary and wrote quickly yet without hurry, a telegram to Paul in Windsor.

"Give orders all miners be evicted from company houses, and driven from county. Hire all detectives needed. Leaving for Windsor today."

Lucy and Percival watched him write, watched the motion of his steady hand, the squareness of his compact shoulders. His impassive face was as quiet as ever.

The servant was just carrying out the message when the raucous voices of newsboys sounded down the silent snow-filled street. "Twelve Knights of Labor killed in riot in Pennsylvania coal regions! Son of Armament King murdered by striking miners!"

The voices were like the voices of avengers, enormously loud and threatening in the deserted morning quiet. Every house rang back the shouts; windows began to open and voices to call in return. The yellow street-lamps were dull flares in the white glare of the dawn.

Then Ernest went to the window and, holding aside the draperies, looked out. The newsboy, passing slowly and shouting, waving his papers fresh from the press, saw this face, gray and immobile, with fixed eyes, against the glass. The boy paused hopefully, made a gesture. There was no answer. The fixed eyes looked at him and did not see him. The boy passed on, shouting.

Book Three

THE FIRST CHESSMAN

*"Our first chessman is Stupidity, in the terrible
game we play against mankind."*

CHAPTER LXXXVIII

AMONG THE many things, and they were many, which Jules Bouchard ("the Jesuit") detested was his cousin, Paul Barbour.

He was thinking of Paul one morning as he sat in his small office in the bank. He could afford to take time off to think, for he worked swiftly and smoothly and without effort and accordingly had plenty of opportunities to think at leisure.

His thoughts about Paul were not pleasant, but the brown narrow face of this twenty-one-year-old young man was inscrutable. He had a small narrow head, bony-looking under the sleek black hair, and a high narrow forehead. His cheeks, mouth, prominent nose, and pointed chin, all had a wizened and puckered look reminiscent of old Armand Bouchard. His ears, stiff and large, protruded from the side of his head. His eyes were usually puckered and narrowed and gleaming, but when he infrequently opened them wide it could be seen that they were full and black and very brilliant. He was not more than five feet eight, but because of the stringy slimness of his body, his litheness and swiftness, he appeared taller. Though not at all vain about his appearance, he was invariably dressed in the finest and most conservative style, with never a wrinkle or a bulge or a badly tied cravat. He had feet almost as tiny as his mother's, and his boots glittered like mirrors. Ernest, with affection and distrust and appreciation, and a little touch of derision, called him "that dried young eel of a Frenchman, that Jesuit!"

Jules was a complete stranger to everyone in the family except Ernest and his brother, Leon. Only these two could see even a little way behind the withered brown face, the hooded and averted eyes, the polite coolness, the smooth infrequent speech, the more infrequent smile, the courteous reserve. Jules despised most people, was indifferent to the rest, hated only a few, of which the chief was his Uncle Ernest, respected only one, which was also Ernest, and loved in all the world only his brother Leon. If Jules, the secretive and the supple-minded and the subtle, had any confidant, it was Leon, and even Leon did not progress beyond the little ante-room that stood before his real self.

Jules was now one of the vice-presidents of the bank. He was respected for his ability, for his alertness and swift decisions. It was impossible for him to do anything badly, and even though he had decided that banking was not for him he gave it the best he could, which was considerable.

His thoughts having come to a head, he tapped the bell on his small polished desk, and when a clerk replied he asked that his brother, Mr. Leon Bouchard, be sent in to him. Then he waited for Leon, nervously yet smoothly turning a pen over and over in his long bony brown fingers.

Leon, "the deep one," came in. He was much like Jules, except that he was broader of face and shoulders, and slightly shorter. He was inclined to plumpness, and later on would have a soft paunch. Moreover, his complexion was lighter and pinker, and his face had a surface merriment at times which had nothing to do at all with the static quiet brutality of his mind. Jules, when necessary, could use hypocrisy as delicately as a spice, but Leon considered hypocrisy a waste of time and preferred the thrust of a short wide knife.

"Good morning, Leon," said Jules, as politely as though they had not seen each other for at least twenty-four hours, though it was only two hours ago that they had had breakfast together and had driven to the bank. "Sit down. I want to talk to you. Is that door closed?"

Leon tried the door, shook it, sat down. "Well, what is it?" he asked. "What has the Jesuit got on his mind this morning?"

"Nothing sacred, you can be sure. Besides, don't call me a Jesuit. It reminds me too much of poor Philippe. And he's been running through my mind this morning very prominently."

"Philippe? But he is perfectly well. You know Mama just got a letter from him yesterday, saying he was quite splendid. God! A leper island! There must be a taint of insanity in the family! But why Philippe?"

"I don't know. For some reason whenever I think of our nice Uncle Ernest I think of Philippe. I don't know why. Unless it is because Philippe once had an infatuation for Gertrude. I've been thinking of Gertrude. She's quite conspicuously enceinte now, poor girl. And for some strange reason, thinking of Philippe has led me to Uncle Ernest, then to Gertrude, then to that bull-on-skis, Paul. I've done some thinking about Paul, quite a lot of thinking."

"Well, that's more than he ever does—think."

"Don't be so sure, my Leon, don't be so sure! These Aryans may be dull and slow-witted and hammer-like and thickly powerful and may not think often. But when they do think—God help us! It's a convulsion of nature. Whereas when we think, it means nothing at all. We've already worn ourselves out thinking, and have made a complete circle of the world and left no more impression on it than the whisk of a feather. Thinking, Leon, can certainly polish the mind, but it also wears it down to a very bright but brittle shell. Like very old silver that's been rubbed for generations."

"Did you ask me to come here to listen to your philosophies? Remember, it's the first of the month tomorrow and I've got more god-damn books to go over———"

"The trouble with you, Leon, is that you are all exigency. To be successfully exigent you must have brains, or you are just a noise and a nuisance. Sometimes I don't think you have much brains. Uncle Ernest is the perfect type of an exigency that had brains. But don't try to be Aryan like him. There's too much Latin in you. Which leads me back to Paul Barbour, who is a blind man's mailed fist."

"All right, you are now back at Paul. I'm exhausted, following you. What about Paul?"

"This: Uncle Ernest is the kind of a man who would defraud and rob his brother without any conscience, on the theory of let the best man win. He would have no illusions that what he was doing was correct and gentlemanly and guiltless. But he would not care. The ethics of the thing might be very clear to him, but I believe that he would enjoy doing it for that very reason. The conscious villain, and pleased over it. Greedy and rapacious, and bland about it. But Paul, there, is quite different. He wouldn't even see the ethics. He wouldn't even know that you had a little right to live, and that what you had belonged to you. Uncle Ernest would recognize those facts, and enjoy taking from you what you had— a case of dog eat dog. But Paul would not recognize that you had any right to live, or any right whatsoever to what you have. In fact, he would resent the fact that you dared try to retain your property if he wanted it. He would become your enemy, if you remained stubborn. He sees what you have, and develops a voracious appetite for it, and goes after it, smashing you in the process if you are so impolite and silly as to get in his way. Juggernaut in trousers."

"It's very nice, hearing family history so early in the morning. But what has this to do with the books waiting out there for me?"

"More than you think. Because, if we don't watch out, there won't be any more books with our name in them."

"I see now where you get your reputation of silence: you babble on but you never really say anything. I suppose I'm pretty stupid, but would you mind telling me everything?"

"I'm disappointed. Haven't you ever studied Paul?"

"Studied him? You mean, do I think he is a burglar? Yes. I think so. But how can he burgle us?"

"He'll find a way. He already resents the Bouchards. He sees what we have, and is very indignant that we have anything. Soon this pouting-bear-that-walks-like-a-man will decide that he ought to have it, and nothing will stop him, unless———"

"Unless what?" Leon's saffron face had lost its specious look of amusement and had become threatening.

Jules leaned back gracefully in his chair and delicately touched the fingers of his left hand with his pen. He studied his brother thoughtfully.

"Did you ever read about the ancient Roman gladiator combats, Leon? They'd arm one gladiator with breastplates and helmet and put his legs in armor and give him a shield and a powerful short sword. He was usually the heavier and the stronger man, and the more brutish. And they'd give the other gladiator, the lighter, swifter, more intelligent one, just a net and a spear. No armor, just nakedness and a net and a spear. And they'd set them fighting to the death. And usually the man with the net and the light feet and the quick brain would win."

Leon hunched up his shoulders and sank his neck into them. He glowered at the floor and bit the corner of his lip.

"Metaphors are very nice and vivid," he said, "but the trouble is that they are not practical. They don't tell you how to go ahead. I admit that I've watched Paul, but the thought of danger didn't really occur to me until just now. And now, I see it very clearly. How are we, with net and nakedness, and just the spear of our relationship to Uncle Ernest, to get around that boulder, Paul?"

"It is necessary in a campaign to review the past and study all circumstances. Let us begin with Uncle Ernest's children, who would naturally be his heirs. There's Frey, who's thrown off everything pertaining to his father, and now calls himself Godfrey Sessions. He lives in France, on what he gets himself from his compositions and on what Aunt May sends him out of her own funds. I have heard that he has said he will never return to America while his father lives. And you can be sure that none of Uncle Ernest's money will go to him.

"There's Reggie, who's married that Amish girl and gone to live on a farm, and declares he wants nothing of his father's money. There *are* people like that, I understand. He rarely comes to Windsor, and never when Uncle Ernest is at home. There was Guy, of course, but he was just a kid, and he's been dead for years. So, we don't need to count him at all, though I would have felt easier about Paul if the poor little devil had lived. (Incidentally, I have just learned that the Snedlow incident cost Uncle Ernest a cool five hundred thousand dollars, to shut up the miners and keep him out of prison. That was a ghastly thing: after driving the miners out of their shacks, so that they had to go to the next county and take shelter with friends or put up tents to keep them out of the snow, to set fire to the tents and the shacks and kill fourteen women and children! That's carrying revenge a little too far.)"

"There's no proof that it wasn't an accident."

"Perhaps not, but it stinks. Besides that, there's not the sign of a proof that Guy was shot by the miners. They didn't have one solitary gun among them."

"What are you trying to say?" asked Leon uneasily. But he did not want an answer.

"Nothing. We were talking about Paul. Well, that leaves only Gertrude, who is Paul's wife, and enceinte, poor creature, with what will probably be a little monster, considering his father. And Joey, the ape. We can count Trudie out. Joey, of course, will be president of the bank some day, now that Paul has practically become Uncle Ernest's Prince of Wales. Joey's a born banker, and will probably make this bank give birth to a dozen little ones. So, in one way, we can count Joey out.

"The whole trouble is this: Paul has evidently counted the Bouchards out. He doesn't think much of me, and you, and François, and Etienne and Honore. Naturally, he feels he has nothing to fear from Philippe; and Renee is a girl and Andre and Antoinette are just brats yet, and there's little danger from our half-brother and sister, Chandler and Betsy. Etienne is looking at the stage, ever since he carried a spear in 'Cleopatra' last winter in New York. I believe he said something about being promised a part in 'Ben Hur' in a few months. Probably as one of the horses. But he's no fool; he's got our French eye for the cash, and I believe Paul underrates him. However, a man can't think of togas and Hamlet and balconies in New York and keep his mind on his business in another city. Honore will probably have to watch Etienne's share. That brings me to Honore, who'd like to insert a knife in Paul's back, also. As for our own dear little brother, François, he'll never be any good so long as he thinks he is a poet. By the way, did you read his last sonnet?"

"Yes!" said Leon fervently. "But never mind François."

"So, everything finally rests with me, and with you, and with Honore. I talked to Honore last night, as I have talked to you today."

There was a little silence. Leon resumed his glowering at the floor. Jules negligently cleaned his nails. Then he sat up swiftly, putting away his little gold penknife.

"How would you like to take my place in the bank, Leon?"

Astonished, Leon lifted hard black eyes. "Take your place? But splendid, of course. I think I have a better head than you for banking, Jules. But what will you do?"

Jules stood up, pulled down his immaculate sleeves. "I'm going to see Uncle Ernest, at once. Tonight, you and I shall go to Uncle Eugene's and have a quiet little talk with Honore."

"I see," said Leon slowly, as he stood up also. He glanced at the closed door. "By the way, you know we have an enemy in our camp. John Charles."

"Yes. He does good yeoman service for his brother, doesn't he? And he hates our insides. I've caught him watching us. We've got to be cautious, for he'll report every move to Paul. Sly, sullen devil! Don't even think about what I've told you, Leon, if you're within six feet of him. He can read minds."

"If I'm not mistaken, that's his shadow that's been passing and repassing that door ever since I came in here. Look there, now, on the glass! I can see his bullet head——"

Jules moved swiftly and silently to the door and pulled it open abruptly. A shortish broad young man of his own age stood there, nonplussed, slowly reddening. He had a crest of stiffish light hair on his head like his Uncle Ernest's, and he also had light malevolent eyes and big features in which there was a certain coarseness. He was a caricature of what Ernest had been at his age, without Ernest's intelligence and real implacability. In place of the implacability, he was stolidly, unoriginally brutal.

"Hello!" he said, finding his voice. "I've been looking for you, Leon. Someone was asking for that Truesdale entry."

"Truly?" Leon's voice was cool and impersonal as velvet. Jules stared down at his cousin with a mixture of contempt and politeness.

"I didn't know you had charge of the 'T' entries," said Jules.

John Charles flashed him a glance of hatred. "I haven't. But Mr. Knight asked me if I knew where Leon was, and as I had seen him come in this direction I came after him myself, to tell him he was wanted."

He walked away stiffly, his ears red, his shoulders seeming too square and big for his rather short sturdy legs.

"You see?" said Leon to his brother.

"I see. Apparently the sooner I act the sooner we will be safe. Remember: Don't think around old Johnny. He reads minds."

CHAPTER LXXXIX

WHEN JULES arrived at the Barbour-Bouchard shops he was greeted with great cordiality by Paul Barbour. Paul had a new office which formed a barrier between the public and his uncle's office. He had surrounded himself with clerks who kept him informed of the smallest details of the business.

He shook Jules' hand, and showed his big white teeth in a friendly grin. "Well, what can we do for you, Jules? Anything wrong at the bank?"

"What could be wrong? No, I came to see Uncle Ernest."

There was a little pause. Paul was taller and bigger than his cousin. He thrust his hands in his pockets very negligently, but there was nothing negligent in the eyes he fixed on him.

"Uncle Ernest?" His tone became regretful. "Lord, I'm sorry! He's busy in there with a very important client. It may be hours."

"I'll wait." He glanced about Paul's office. "You have plenty of chairs here. You won't mind if I occupy one?"

"Not at all. Not at all! But I warn you, it'll be hours. Perhaps it would be better if I told him later that you had come, and I can then make an appointment for you. I can let you know in a few days——"

"Thank you. But I'll wait. Leon's taking my place at the desk until I come back. Besides, we're not very busy."

He sat down without a chair having been offered him. Paul stood, irresolute, just barely frowning. When he turned again to his cousin, Jules' face was brownly inscrutable and composed.

"Very well, then, Jules. But I am afraid you are going to have to wait a long time." He called a clerk by the touch of a bell. "Mr. Johnson, will you please tell Mr. Barbour that Mr. Jules Bouchard——" he glanced at Jules and the faintest sneer pulled at his mouth, "Mr. Jules Bouchard wishes to see him when he is at leisure."

He glanced at Jules sharply. "But wait, Mr. Johnson. Jules, are you certain that this isn't something I can handle instead of Uncle Ernest? Won't you tell me about it?"

"I will not," said Jules quietly.

There was a small silence. Paul nodded to Mr. Johnson. "Mr. Jules Bouchard, Mr. Johnson, would like to see Mr. Barbour when he isn't busy."

"Mr. Jules Bouchard begs to inform Mr. Barbour that it is a matter of the deepest importance," added Jules solemnly.

The clerk was highly edified at all this, and looked exceedingly pleased. "Yes, sir, Mr. Bouchard," he said, bowing, and hurrying away.

Paul's large fair features had become suffused. He was struggling with himself. Jules' eyes were wide open now, and innocent, brilliantly black under the full lids. "Jesuit!" thought Paul with ferocity. "I'd like to know what he's got up his sleeve. I'll ask John Charles tonight."

Aloud he said, trying to regain his pleasantness : "I heard that Major Norwood had very little insurance on the warehouses that were burned last week. I also heard that he lost a great deal when the Union Atlantic Railroad failed. So, I am wondering if Aunt Florrie is embarrassed at all. If she is, I will be glad to buy any amount of Barbour-Bouchard stock that she owns. At today's prices."

Jules' mouth puckered slightly, but his expression otherwise remained innocent. "But that is very kind of you, Paul. However, I am glad to inform you that my mother is not at all embarrassed." He added, to himself : What a boor !

Paul had recovered his heartiness. "That is good news, then." He paused. "How is Leon doing at the bank ?"

"Splendidly."

"John Charles speaks of him very glowingly."

Jules did not answer.

"And how is Philippe ? Gertrude was just speaking of him this morning, and wondering how he was."

Jules regarded him fully. "That is very strange. Gertrude visited my mother yesterday and while there she read the letter we received from Philippe."

Paul colored violently. "She probably forgot," he said with indifference.

The door opened and a gentleman emerged with a brief case. Paul rose, greeted him with great respect. While he was doing this, Ernest appeared at the door and nodded pleasantly at Jules. "All right, Jules. I'll see you now."

Jules, imperturbable as ever, rose and went into the office. He closed the door carefully behind him. Ernest had already seated himself. He regarded his nephew with amusement. "What's the matter ? Is what you have to see me about so important that you are afraid of spies ?"

"Yes, I'm afraid of spies," replied Jules calmly. "Or, I should say, a spy."

"Oh, nonsense. But sit down. How is your Mama ? And everyone else ?"

"We are all splendid." He paused. "But Paul believes we are financially embarrassed. He offered to buy Mama's stock in Barbour-Bouchard."

Ernest raised his eyebrows. "He did, eh?" He studied his nephew. He had a high respect for him, though the young man rarely failed to amuse him. His amusement rose from a sort of acknowledgment of his subtlety, his devious ways and silences, which Ernest read without too much difficulty. He had often thought regretfully that Paul could do very well with some of that imagination and supple-mindedness. Nevertheless, probably because of his understanding, he did not trust Jules in the least.

The events of the past four years had changed Ernest considerably, had whitened his hair, had plowed his broad and heavy face, had made him at once leaner and more compact. But they had not made his expression more mobile or revealing. Across the polished space of his flat desk he continued to study Jules.

"I hope," he said slowly, "that your Mama will consult me first before selling any of her stock."

"She won't sell," said Jules. He flicked a white speck from his black broadcloth knee. "Uncle Ernest, I won't take up much of your time. It is this: I want you to take me out of the bank. I want to come in with you."

"With me? Extraordinary! I thought you were doing well at the bank."

"Nevertheless, I want to come in with you."

Ernest chewed his nail thoughtfully. "This is very unexpected. But where could I put you, Jules? I thought you had quite enough of the mills and foundries when you spent that year with your Uncle Eugene in the Kinsolving works."

"I didn't have enough. But I had sufficient to work out something."

"Ah. Would you mind telling me what is behind this?"

"Nothing, except that I feel I can do better in the mills."

There was a silence. Without trying to disguise his close scrutiny Ernest went over his nephew, feature by feature. He looks more like old Armand every day, he thought. But he is closer than Armand, and hasn't one atom of his kindness or amiability. At the end of the long scrutiny he knew exactly why Jules had come. And was not at all displeased, but only amused. It might not be a bad idea, he continued in his thoughts. Paul has the force and the obstinacy, and Jules has the wit, the imagination and the adroitness. They'll balance each other, watch each other. Only Paul'll have to take care, or at the end he'll find only eggshells in his basket. This French serpent is by nature a sucker of eggs. Ernest was very pleased at all this. Paul frequently annoyed him and irked him; he felt quite a malicious pleasure in anticipation of the effect of Jules' introduction into Barbour-Bouchard. Latin brains and Teuton force:

it would be edifying to watch them in juxtaposition, especially when spiced with hatred.

"But just what do you think you can bring to the business, Jules?"

"This: during the year I worked with Uncle Eugene I studied everything. The cannon we make would be all the better for a better steel. What we have now crystallizes too easily, and is too brittle. Crumbles after considerable use. Moreover, steel is going to be in tremendous demand eventually, for use in street-car tracks, rails, bridges, buildings——"

"Buildings?" interrupted Ernest.

"Yes. I believe a time is coming when steel will be used in tremendous quantities, especially for tall buildings. Iron doesn't meet requirements. But the steel we have now is not good enough, and is too expensive to make."

"Go on." Ernest had not thought the usually secretive Jules could make so long a speech nor speak so clearly.

"I've worked out something in steel. I didn't speak of it before, for several reasons. They've got something like it in England now, and I admit I got an idea from that source. But what I have in mind is a little different. Just enough different——"

"To get by the patent laws?"

The saturnine grimace that pulled Jules' mouth was usually what passed as a smile with him. "To get by the patent law," he agreed. "England has already patented her own new steel. But, frankly, I believe what I have in mind is better, though based in part on the English patent."

"Very, very interesting." Nothing could have been more patient than Ernest's voice. But the cigar he had been smoking died in its tray. "Would you mind giving me an idea what this new steel is?"

"Not at all." Jules lowered his already low voice. "But, of course, this is in confidence, Uncle Ernest?"

Ernest smiled. "Do you think I might rob you?"

But Jules was not embarrassed. He went on, as though Ernest had not spoken: "My plan is to produce steel by the decarburization of molten gray iron by air-blasts, which will oxidize out and carry off the carbon, other impurities, and the silicon. Then it can be cast into ingots."

Ernest dropped his eyes and fixed them on his desk. There was a long silence. Jules, anxious himself now, watched his uncle's face. He could gather nothing from its heavy smooth powerfulness, its total absence of mobility. "You have the formula?" he asked absently.

"Yes."

"What makes you think it is practicable?"

"I am certain of it. I've studied the English formula very carefully, and the steel is already being produced there."

They smiled at each other slightly and simultaneously.

"I've heard of the English steel," said Ernest. "Your formula will have to be—ah—very adroit, very clever, if it can evade the patent rights and also retain the qualities of the English steel. May I see the formula?"

"Why certainly, Uncle Ernest. I shall be very glad to work it out in your presence in the Sessions mill—when I have been established there."

He stared at his uncle coolly, his narrow brown face calm, the sunlight glinting on the sleek thin hair that covered his well-shaped, small bony skull.

Ernest burst out laughing, with acknowledgment and approval. "You don't trust God or the devil, do you, Jules? But that's perfectly all right. I admire you for it." He put a fresh cigar in his mouth, and Jules lit it for him. "Thank you, lad." He puffed at the cigar for a few moments, and regarded Jules through the smoke. "Of course," he added genially, "I understand perfectly why you wish to come here. I don't hold it against you, Jules; in fact, I admire you for it. A man's entitled to all he can get. You have proved that you will get what you want. But you're not a bulldozer. Some people—are. However, slyness is frequently better than bulldozing. You don't mind if I call you sly, do you?"

"Not at all," replied Jules courteously.

"Sometimes slyness is called adroitness and quick-wittedness. However, I knew you'd prefer a simpler if less polite definition. You're a sly devil, Jules. I like sly devils."

"Paul," said Jules, smiling faintly, "is strong and competent."

" 'Brutus,' " added Ernest, " 'is an honorable man.' "

He got up and began to walk up and down the room, his hands behind his back. Without looking at Jules, he spoke slowly: "Paul is my daughter's husband, the father of my grandchild. He'll naturally inherit most of what I have. I want you to understand that clearly. Sometimes it is better to make issues very clear, so there'll be no misunderstanding, no pot-shotting, no guns in the dark. My son Joey will own most of the bank stock. That's taken care of." He stopped and swung on the silently listening Jules. "What, then, do you expect to get from this?"

Jules examined his narrow oval fingernails minutely. "I have sent my formula to the patent office. Just the other day." He raised the full brilliance of his eyes to Ernest's face.

"Ah," said Ernest reflectively, after a pause.

He sat down. "Jules," he said, "you may enter the Sessions Steel mills tomorrow, if you wish."

CHAPTER XC

THAT NIGHT Jules and Leon went to see their cousin, Honore
Bouchard.

The three young men felt a trust and a camaraderie for
each other that nothing was ever to destroy. They had other
brothers, whom they scarcely noticed, and other cousins, whom
they noticed less. They understood each other, respected each other,
had mutual aims, mutual opinions and mutual affection. And oddly, they
liked each other's mothers. Honore was quite his Aunt Florabelle's
favorite, for though he was somewhat unwieldy of manner and phrase,
and a little too sober, Florabelle found something sadly reminiscent of
Raoul in her nephew's imperturbable courtesy, his occasional wild gaiety
which contrasted grotesquely with his usual unyouthful stateliness, and
a certain gallantry that he wore eternally like a jewelled dagger. She
often said that she felt she could "trust" Honore, completely forgetting
that she had never been able to trust Raoul. As for Jules, he was his
Aunt Dorcas' favorite. She was very fond of the young man, and he
was the only one among her numerous nieces and nephews that she
could endure. She knew he admired her, for this middle-aged woman
was still beautiful and calm and coolly serene, so different from his
flustered little mother with her untidy graying curls and fluttering ribbons and peeping petticoats.

Both Leon and Jules liked and respected their Uncle Eugene. They
sensed his real kindness under his rather sullen and abrupt mannerisms.
Sometimes he would look at them with tired eyes in a brown-gray face,
and his expression would be sad and gentle. They knew his integrity,
and though having none of this commodity themselves, they could not
help reverencing it in their uncle. They believed him implicitly, respected
his judgment, invariably acted on his advice. When they asked him
for it.

Tonight, they were not to ask his advice. In this particular instance
they distrusted his integrity. What they were plotting together could
not be entrusted to a man who would have denounced them indignantly.
Besides, though each knew exactly what they were plotting, they had
not spoken of it frankly to each other. Their French subtlety filled in
their silences.

Jules, the usually unsmiling and silent, was almost gay this evening.
He chaffed his Aunt Dorcas; he knew that she loved his chaffing. Leon,

the exigent, forced himself to be considerate and polite. Dorcas found him less objectionable than usual. Jules could be witty and ironical, and even Eugene laughed heartily several times during the course of the evening meal. Afterwards, Jules and Leon retired together to Honore's room, upstairs in the old, big and still ugly house. "Do not you three go to your plotting too vigorously," Eugene called after them, smiling, but a little uneasy. He liked his nephews, but he decidedly did not trust the supple Jules. He said to his wife: "Jules is an intriguer. The others only follow. He is a natural courtier and plotter, and Richelieu would have found him invaluable."

When the three young men were alone, Jules told Honore of his interview with his uncle that afternoon. Honore listened intently and somberly, but his eyes glinted. "Good!" he exclaimed. He was a stocky young man, dark and handsome and heavy-faced, with calm features but intensely vivid eyes. "And today I secretly sent away my formula for the new explosive."

"You are certain your father knows nothing of it?"

"Nothing!"

"Very good. Things are certainly going well. The old devil smells what we are about, and it seems to amuse him. If we get what we want, and outwit that horse-in-a-cravat, old Ernest won't lift a finger to save him. What a man he is! You must give him credit."

"I still don't believe he'd allow us to strip Paul, Jules."

"Certainly not. He'd protect his interests. But he wouldn't keep him from losing the surplus. He got where he is by taking other people's surpluses. He admires bandits. He believes in letting the best man win. Spoils-to-the-victor idea. He loves victors. Yes, you've got to give the old devil credit."

"But he's still Ernest Barbour. You must remember that. I doubt even the three of us could outwit him one single time."

"Who said anything about outwitting him? We're out to gain his acknowledgment, tolerance and amusement. He likes to be amused. And the only way to amuse him is to let him see you outsmart someone else. Even Paul. He likes his joke, does the old dog."

"I hope you're right, Jules," said Honore dubiously. He seemed uneasy. "It isn't easy for me to deceive my father, I can tell you."

"Easy?"

"I mean, I hate to do it. The dear old boy will get an awful shock when it comes out that I've patented my new explosive over his head and under an assumed name."

Leon flashed his brother a slightly contemptuous smile. "Your father, Honore," he pointed out, "admires Uncle Ernest. And you can be sure that when dear Uncle Ernest expresses his amusement and admiration at what you have done, your father will soon be convinced that you have been pretty astute and smart."

"Exactly," said Jules.

Honore lifted his big shoulders in a resigned and melancholy shrug. "You are very clever, Jules," he said.

"We shall need all our cleverness," Jules replied smoothly.

Honore had brought up a bottle of wine and three glasses. He filled them carefully and soberly, pursing his lips as he did so. The three young men lifted their glasses. The lamplight shone on their faces, all brown and secretive and dry, Jules' crafty and hidden, Leon's coarse and ironical, Honore's somber.

"A toast!" said Jules. "To Bouchard and Sons!"

"To Bouchard and Sons!" echoed Leon, smiling.

Honore drank the toast in silence.

CHAPTER XCI

SINCE THE various debacles in his Uncle Ernest's family, Paul had felt very safe and complacent. Minor irritations rarely affected him, for he ignored them. Consequently, Guy having been removed as a very formidable threat to his complacency and prospects, and Frey banished, and Reginald repudiating all his father's wealth, and he, himself, married to Gertrude Barbour, and Joseph Barbour a youth only fifteen years of age and away at school, Paul had considered himself secure. The subtle things that make for real happiness, though not in his life, he did not miss. All his thoughts and desires were centered on the acquisition of money and the exhilaration of success, and having these he did not miss less concrete and more tenuous things.

Gertrude did not "bother" him, as women usually bothered their husbands, and Paul was grateful for this. She never had any tantrums, any whimsicalities or visible melancholies; she was never temperamental and exacting, incalculable and petty. The new fine house in Roseville, which he had named Robin's Nest, was perfectly kept, artistically furnished, splendidly run, dignified, quiet and formal, with tall cool rooms and curving dim staircases, white marble mantels and mirrors, parquet floors and severe polished mahogany, high French windows and stately gardens. So carefully was it built, so precise its design, in such good taste its every room, that fifty or more years later it was still the pride of its owners. Gertrude, silent, faintly smiling, colorlessly dark and patrician, never in a hurry, never upset or querulous, never disordered or annoyed, was the perfect mistress of this house. There was never any fluster here. Two guests or twenty: it was all the same, the servants moving with precision and without flurry, the meals excellent, the service not to be bettered. It never occurred to Paul that a man could ask more of his wife, more warmth and tenderness, passion and laughter, storm and sweet reconciliation. He loved Gertrude as he had always loved her, and he never bothered to inquire much if she loved him. He took it for granted: she seemed contented and serene, no longer nervous and tense and erratic, as she had been before their marriage. At first she had seemed tranced and almost stupefied, had cried in her sleep, had often turned from him with involuntarily wild and timid gestures. But this had passed. Everything was as it should be now. A child was expected, and Paul hoped desperately that it would be a boy. He had little hope for any more children, for Gertrude was apparently not prolific, this being the first child after nearly five years of marriage. If he needed anything more to solidify his position, he would have it in his child. He knew that Ernest had already established a large trust fund for his coming grandchild. Paul had already decided to name his son after Ernest. "Let the Bouchards try anything after *that!*" he would say to Gertrude, in contemptuous triumph.

So everything had been going along satisfactorily until the sinuous arrival of Jules Bouchard in the Sessions Steel mills. Paul's first reaction, after fear and uncertainty, had been outrage. That slippery Frenchman daring to insinuate himself into something that was not only beyond his powers but really none of his business! His mother was a stockholder in Barbour-Bouchard, but naturally inactive. Paul felt not only rage, but affront. He had demanded of his uncle the reason for this, and Ernest, looking at him with his pale round disks of opaque eyes, had answered coolly that Jules had satisfied him as to his sincerity and ability. Those eyes had frightened Paul more than the words, more than anything had ever frightened him before. He had gone home, sick and shaken and bewildered. "Why!" he exclaimed passionately to his wife, "I believe your father is treacherous, as well as cruel and malicious! I heard that before but never believed it. I do now! It's like being at the mercy of a—a Nero, or something. He's been raising my expectations, with actual promises, mind you! and showing me all kinds of favors, and consulting and advising me, and putting his arm around me, and now he does this! I suppose I'm not courtier enough," he added bitterly.

He was so distressed, so pathetic, that Gertrude felt pity and a sudden affection for him. She kissed his flushed cheek upon her own volition, something she had never done before. It surprised and startled Paul, and he suddenly realized that perhaps he had missed something in his married life. He actually clung to her, with a rising of hope and relief in himself, and he listened with eagerness to her insistence that he was imagining things, and that, really, her Papa was only being fair in giving Jules a chance. After all, Jules' mother was his own sister, and his favorite. "Papa," she said, bravely looking her lie in the face and simultaneously denying and acknowledging it to herself, "never was treacherous to any one. If he promised you something, he will certainly keep his promise."

Paul, wishing to believe this, was half convinced. However, he threw himself madly into his work, giving himself up to it with fever and grimness. No hours were too long for him, no detail too small, no work too tedious. Ernest watched this, smiling to himself saturninely. Nothing like greed to spur a man either to heaven or hell, he thought. He did nothing to reassure Paul, who had become a little diffident and suspicious when with him. He could easily have turned Paul's misery into peace, but the sadistic spot in him needed its tickling, even at the expense of those whom he cared for and planned for.

Guy's tragic death had affected him more than even Amy suspected. He had shown little evidence of it, except in the savagery of his treatment of the striking miners. When the railroad men had struck in West Virginia, in 1877, it had been by Ernest's orders that the militia had fired upon the strikers and killed over a dozen. He was responsible for the riots that took place thereafter, the desperate and murderous fighting between the soldiers and the strikers. When the news of the massacre was brought to him, he said only one word: "Good!"

Yet he did not believe in the slightest the story that Paul had told him. He knew very well that Paul had shown exceptional wiliness in giving that story to the newspapers. What an ironical joke it would have been to the world had it known that the thugs Ernest Barbour had hired to kill the miners had killed his own son! He was not at all sure that Paul himself had not fired the shot that killed Guy; Paul's distress, his real anguish, betrayed this possibility to Guy's father. But Ernest knew there were places where it was not well to tread, and he knew that should he force Paul's confession, if confession there might be, he would no longer be able to have him near him. Besides, Paul had saved him from world-wide derision and taunting laughter. For this he was more grateful than the uneasy Paul ever suspected.

There seemed little satisfaction in things nowadays, Ernest would often think morosely. His oldest son, Godfrey, had repudiated him and had been repudiated in turn; he had even committed the unpardonable crime of shedding his father's name and taking his mother's. If Ernest would ever have forgiven him, this act of his made that impossible. Guy was dead. Reginald, who had never seemed one of the family, anyway, had become a stranger, dour and rigid and removed. There was left only Gertrude, and Joey, who was away at school.

His home was silent and deserted. There were the same rooms, the same careful burnishing, the same beauty and delicate dignity, the same warmth and spaciousness. Yet, somehow, it had taken on an air of dark brooding and arid desertion; something bright and comforting and lofty had gone from it. It had become just a darkened shell, full of echoes and silences. Certainly the Sessions house had become strange to him; something hostile, something inimical, stood in every room and faced him darkly and obscurely. He no longer found comfort in any part of it. He felt himself an intruder, and every object became stiff and unfriendly when he approached it or even looked at it. Moreover, the gleaming surface of things had been lost; at times the silent rooms looked almost shabby.

Perhaps, he thought, this was due to May's attitude. He and she were all alone in the house, except for the servants. They had never been alone before. There had been Gregory and Amy in the beginning, and then the children. But now there were only these two. And between them was a silence and emptiness wider than the house. May no longer appeared at breakfast; he ate alone in the great dining room at the end of the mahogany table. The servants moved in a hush, and he could hear them whispering behind doors. The clink of his china and silver echoed back from the panelled walls, and in the winter even the fire seemed to lurk uneasily behind its polished bars. But at dinnertime May appeared, perfectly and carefully dressed and discreetly jewelled, presiding over the silver tureen and polished teapot. She had aged very much in the past four years, and her face and eyes were sunken. But her smile was gracious, her voice composed, her glance calm and steady. At the dinner table she and Ernest talked of the most casual and trivial matters, not awkwardly or even just politely, but with the manner of cool and pleasant acquaintances. Ernest watched his wife furtively during these agreeable exchanges. He remembered his mother's prolonged and sultry furies, her ominous silences, her passionate resentments and hostilities. He was still not accustomed to the ways of gentlefolk and the manners of great ladies; he never ceased to admire his wife. Over the agony he knew was constantly in her, she could smile amiably, converse pleasantly, listen with interest, even to the one person responsible for most of her suffering. But he dared not approach her with any word of intimacy, any look beyond mere friendliness; he knew he dared not do that.

He also knew that she spent most of her time writing to her three sons, especially to Godfrey in Paris. But of Godfrey she never spoke to her husband. At first he thought that it was because of a delicacy toward himself; finally he became convinced that she would have been outraged, overcome, had he spoken of Godfrey to her. He could not speak to her of Reginald, whom he had literally kicked out of his house. He could not speak to her of Guy. No, never of Guy. Sometimes, at dinner, when he would involuntarily think of his murdered son, he could eat no more, but would push his plate from him, and then sit staring heavily at nothing at all. He never knew that May guessed what he was thinking, and that her suffering increased accordingly.

He found it difficult these days to visit Amy. More and more often he arrived at Amy's house only to find Elsa, paler and very silent, firmly and bitterly rooted in the room. She had little to say to him, though her voice was as affectionate as ever when she did speak. Sometimes she would sit and gaze broodingly at her mother, with something close to disgust in her restless eyes. At twenty-seven, she considered herself a hopeless old maid. In the morning her eyes were often pink and rimmed. She had loved, and still loved, her cousin Godfrey with all the force of her ardent and exuberant nature.

Amy, as usual, understood everything without words. Without her, he could scarcely have borne with stolidity what he had to bear. When he looked at her, and she smiled gently, or touched him, or said something casual, he was inordinately comforted. "I never understood what a great lady was until I knew you—and May," he would say to her.

She would smile with a little wry humor.

"Being a 'great lady,' my dear Ernest," she would say lightly, "has its advantages. It does so help, to behave as though disagreeable things did not exist, and as though insupportable things had not occurred!" She added: "Sometimes, it is possible to persuade even yourself that everything is exactly as it should be. A harmless but necessary way of making life endurable."

Once she said to him: "It is so nice, dearest Ernest, that you are not a gentleman. You have no idea how really honest you are!"

And he did not know whether to be pleased or affronted.

CHAPTER XCII

ONE NIGHT, when Gertrude was in her eighth month of pregnancy, she had a frightful dream.

She dreamt that she was lying in her bed at night, as she actually was at the time. There was moonlight outside, a cool white cataract of light that poured over the spring trees and seeped through the Venetian blinds, striping the quiet dark room and all its objects with silver and black. She could plainly see the distorted shadow of the newly leafed trees on the blinds, and could clearly hear the throbbing of tree-toads in the motionless midnight silence. She dreamt that Paul was lying beside her, as he really was, and that she could discern his low and rhythmic breathing.

Then she saw that someone was standing in the room, between her and the windows, a dark tall form with bent head. She sat up abruptly, and felt all through her body the ominous loud pounding of her heart, the roaring of her blood. Her throat felt as though a thin iron band were tightening about it. A sick horror churned in her, a sensation that something dreadful, something too enormous to be borne, had happened somewhere, was connected in some way with this quiet dark figure between her and the lighted windows.

She cried out: "Who are you? Speak to me! O God, can't you speak to me?"

The figure stirred, came toward her without visible movement. Then she saw that it had a wan light on its face and she could see its features. It was Philippe. Never had she seen such a face, such deathliness, such torment. But worse than all else was the sudden agony in her chest, the swamping anguish. She screamed out, madly, over and over, over and over, beating her hands together, screaming his name: "Philippe! Philippe! Philippe!"

A blindness passed over her eyes, and through its dark waves she felt herself being shaken, heard someone call her. The blindness passed, and she found herself lying on her pillows. Paul was bending over her, calling her, shaking her gently. He was very frightened. His one thought was that her time had come upon her prematurely. It was not for some moments that he remembered that she had been calling Philippe.

"What is it, my darling? Are you in pain?"

She stared at him; he could see the brilliant distended eyes in the semi-darkness. Then she turned from him slowly and her eyes rolled about the room. All at once a convulsion ran over her body; she seized Paul wildly, she burst into convulsive sobs.

"Philippe! Something has happened to Philippe! I know it! He was here only a moment ago!"

She clung to him, her hands clutching him, tearing at his nightshirt, his arms, his hair, his shoulders. But when he tried to draw her to him, she thrust him off. And all the time she sobbed and groaned, and looked about the room. Her face was terrible, her long black hair dishevelled about it, and falling over her pillows.

For a moment Paul was silent, still gently holding. At last he said with difficulty: "My darling, there is no one here. You have been dreaming."

Her cries and sobs became more and more anguished. Servants, awakened, stirred and murmured apprehensively in their rooms above. Paul was sick with alarm. Gertrude still struggled with him fiercely, but finally, as though suddenly stricken, she subsided, and lay against his chest. He held her with tender firmness, smoothing her hair, pressing her face against his body. Her moaning became softer, yet more agonized, harder to endure. He said nothing, but over her head he stared into the darkness, bitterly and sadly. He began to sigh deeply; his hand continued to stroke her head, and he still murmured soothingly to her.

Finally she grew quieter; the sobs were farther between. At last she slept in his arms, her cheek against his chest. But even in her sleep she whimpered a little. Paul did not sleep again. He lay gazing steadily at the dusky ceiling until it was morning.

When it was time for him to get up, Gertrude still slept, her face drawn and gray and small upon her pillow, her hair tragically strewn about it. He tiptoed softly from the room and ate his breakfast downstairs alone. He felt quite stony inside, quite motionless.

He had been gone an hour when Gertrude awoke. She dressed without haste, went downstairs to her breakfast, and then called for her carriage. She wrapped herself in a concealing broadcloth cloak and put her plumed black velvet hat on her head. Her maid, a young German girl, protested affectionately, assuring her mistress that she looked very ill and ought to remain at home. But Gertrude, smiling a drawn and twisted smile, was driven away.

She went to her father's house. Ernest was just recovering from a combat with influenza and was still at home. Both he and May were surprised and alarmed at this early visit from Gertrude. But she assured them calmly that she had to do some shopping in town, and that she was going to call upon her Aunt Florabelle. May, apprehensive, studied her daughter's clay-colored face with its pinched bluish nostrils, its tremulous and livid mouth. "Why, my dear child, you must go to the doctor!"

she exclaimed. "And if you insist on seeing Florabelle first, I will certainly go with you!"

They drove away together in Gertrude's carriage. There never had been much spontaneity between mother and daughter, very little confidence. It was only because Gertrude was really distraught that she told her mother of her dream. May, concerned and exceedingly alarmed, listened intently, seeing nothing but her daughter's tortured face, her purple and bitten lips, hearing under the slow, unhurried words, the real terror and suffering. At the end, she looked at Gertrude's misshapen body only half concealed by the cloak. Her own expression was full of despair and apprehension.

"But, my dearest," she said, "it was only a dream, after all. This is really very silly, going to see Florabelle to ask her for news of Philippe."

"I know it was Philippe. I know it," said Gertrude's soft monotonous voice, in which there was something relentless. "I've got to know. Otherwise," she added more loudly, "I'll go mad."

May was silent. Under the fur robe of the carriage her gloved hands twisted and twisted. Once her lips parted suddenly, as though she found it hard to breathe.

The very instant the carriage turned into the driveway of the house on Quaker Terraces May knew that something was most frightfully wrong. The house looked quiet enough in the spring morning sunlight, its lawns greening visibly, yet through a sudden nightmare mist of horror, May knew something was wrong. It was all unreal, glaring, ghastly, and she had a feeling that at all costs she must stop Gertrude from entering that house. She cried out something peremptorily, and the coachman, surprised, pulled in the horses. May turned to Gertrude. Her voice was trembling when she spoke: "See, my darling, no one is up yet, except the servants. The whole household is still asleep. The blinds are all drawn. It would be unkind to disturb your aunt at this hour."

Gertrude gazed at the house; the windows, shining in the sunlight, were shrouded in pale gray silk, shirred and fringed. But there was a stricken mute look about it, as though it had opened its mouth in a soundless scream. No one was about; the front door stood ajar. The house and its grounds seemed to stand in an awful nightmarish sort of trance.

"This is really very stupid of me," thought May distractedly, over the thudding of her heart. "I'm letting my imagination run away with me."

Gertrude said clearly: "Please drive in, Michaels."

It was Gertrude, after all, who had the strength to get out of the carriage first. May followed, lifting her heavy skirts high, as she found she had a tendency to stumble. Gertrude had not bothered to pull the bell, but had stepped into the hall. Everything was quiet inside, full of sunshine on old polished red mahogany panels and Turkey-red carpeting. A picture frame on the reddish walls caught the sun on its scrolled gilt. But there was not a sound.

In that silence the slight noise the women made on entering the house seemed like an uproar. The library door opened and Major Norwood thrust a dishevelled white head and tear-stained face into the brilliance of the hall.

"Is that you, Jules and Leon?" he asked faintly. "You were a long time returning home. You'd better go up to your mother——"

He stopped abruptly when he could distinguish the visitors. They regarded the Major fixedly, unable to move. Then he uttered a sort of whimper, held open the door leading to the library, and with a mute pathetic gesture invited them in. Gertrude asked no questions; she did not hesitate or make a sound, but walked steadily into the library, her mother following. He closed the door after them. Then, still standing by it, he burst simply and unaffectedly into tears.

"Of course," thought May numbly, "this is all a ridiculous nightmare. Such things don't happen in the customary movement of events. Or, do they?" She seemed more upset than Gertrude, who had moved near a table and stood there tranquilly, her concealing cape falling in motionless folds about her tall slight figure. Nothing could have been calmer than her face, though it looked marble-opaque in the dimmed light of the library; nothing could have been steadier than her distended eyes.

"Dear Major," murmured May, "what is wrong? Is Florabelle ill?"

"How can I say it?" the Major cried, dabbing at his cheeks with his silk handkerchief, and shaking his head. "It is too terrible. We have sent for the boys. They ought to be here now. Poor Florrie is in a condition! Her heart is broken, her poor tender little heart," he added with such pathos that the sentimentality was forgotten. "She will never get over this, my dear May! Never get over it! He was her love, her favorite."

Gertrude laid her gloves carefully upon the table and loosened the neck of her cape. May went quickly to her side. But Gertrude did not glance at her.

"It is Philippe, isn't it, Major?" she asked in her clear light voice.

"Yes," he answered, blowing his nose and blinking the kind and foolish tears from his eyes.

Gertrude drew a long slow breath, but her calm expression did not alter.

"He is dead, isn't he?"

"Yes, my love, dead. I do not know, I really do not know, what we are to do——"

Gertrude sat down rather quickly. Her hands folded themselves in her lap. She stared at the floor. There was something appalling in her calm, her lack of outward emotion. But May began to cry, as she stood by Gertrude's side, her hand on her shoulder. Naturally, her grief was less than it had been at her son's death, and so she cried as she had not cried then. But her sorrow was for her daughter and not for the dead man. Finally she said, through her tears: "Darling, this is very dreadful. But you must remember— There are so many things for you to remember—" her voice trailed away vaguely.

The Major sat down and covered his face with his handkerchief. His broad shoulders heaved.

"May I go upstairs to poor Florrie?" asked May, drying her eyes.

"Ah, no, dear May. She is not in a condition to see any one. Her maid is with her, and the doctor. We have sent for Jules and Leon. I have sent a telegram to Chandler's school, and we expect him this evening. Betsy, the poor child, is in the nursery, crying her little heart out. François is no use at all, and he has been put to bed. Florrie will not even see me, her husband. I believe they are putting her to sleep."

"But what happened? What is it?" asked May faintly, becoming alarmed at Gertrude's long immobility. The shoulder under her hand hardly moved with the slightest breath.

"It is so horrible," wept the Major, looking at her pathetically with his simple wet blue eyes. He looked like a child himself, in spite of his bulk and his white hair. "It came this morning, the letter from Bishop Dominick. So kind, in spite of being a Roman and a priest! He wrote to us himself, and said he will come to see Florabelle soon, and sends his blessing and assures us of his sorrow, and says he will pray for us and for poor Philippe. It seems," he added in a breaking voice, "that the poor boy died on the leper island to which he had asked to go. I believe it was cholera, or something equally dreadful."

May averted her head. Gertrude still did not move. Her hands had relaxed and lay on her knees flaccidly, like dead hands. May dared not try to see her face.

"Will they send his body—home?" whispered May.

"No, he is already buried, the Bishop said. Nearly a month ago. It is such a long way off, that island, and ships only call once a month. They brought the news back." Something seemed to occur to the poor man, for he stopped his weeping and looked at Gertrude and May with round wide eyes. "It is very strange, but it just occurred to me. The Bishop said he was sure that Mr. Ernest Barbour would be particularly affected to hear of his nephew's death because of his deep interest in Philippe, as expressed on a certain day in Philadelphia, before the poor boy went to Montreal——"

"No! No!" cried May shrilly, before she had time to prevent herself. And then stopped, her hand against her lips. Then she caught Gertrude's head in her arms and pressed it convulsively to her breast, as if to prevent it from seeing something too hideous to be borne.

The Major was dumbfounded, through his grief. He regarded May blankly for several moments. "What—what is it?" he stammered at last, blinking. "What have I said? That it was strange that the Bishop should think Mr. Ernest might be affected? But it is strange, is it not? I was not aware— Mr. Ernest did not seem to like Philippe, and Philippe —but pardon me, ladies," he added with pathetic courtesy, "I should not say this——"

Gertrude pushed her mother away from her firmly but gently. Her face still had not changed, though there were purple clefts about her lips and patches like bruises under her shining eyes.

"I think—I understand, now," she said in a bemused voice.

"I don't see how we can bear it!" exclaimed the Major, weeping again. "To die all alone out there, without a friend."

"Come home with me, my darling," sobbed May, distraught, and taking one of her daughter's hands. "Don't think, my love. It—it is not what you think— What can I do? Darling, do not look like that! See, it is your Mama, who loves you— You must remember your baby, darling. You must not let yourself be upset. You owe it— Come home with me."

"He was such a fine boy," said the Major hoarsely, "such a fine boy Such brilliance, such kindness, such devotion to his mother. Whoever would have thought it, when he was such a sturdy little fellow, running about, and laughing, that some day, on a far away island, among lepers, that the cholera would kill him——"

"No," said Gertrude in a loud and ringing voice. "It was not the cholera that killed him. My father killed him."

"Darling!" said May. "You must not say that! You must not! Don't look like that, Gertrude! This is your Mama! See, it is your Mama kneeling here beside you, crying for you. Your Mama! My little girl! Look at your Mama, kneeling here," and indeed, the poor woman knelt in a welter of petticoats and furs beside Gertrude's chair, trying to hold the stiff body in her arms, trying to draw down the stiff head upon her shoulders. "Trudie, sweetheart, you are killing me—I can't bear it——"

"Madam!" exclaimed the Major, overcome with remorse. He forgot his grief and tried to induce May to rise. But she clung stubbornly to Gertrude, who did not move. "I am a cad, Madam, a cad! A blackguard, only a blackguard! I should have remembered Gertrude's— Ah, I ought to be shot!" he added with fervent self-hatred.

May laid her gray head upon Gertrude's knees and sobbed helplessly, with a sort of relaxed anguish. She felt the thinness of them under her cheek; once or twice she turned her head and pressed her lips against them. Her arms clung to Gertrude's rigid legs. All other sorrows, other griefs, seemed nothing compared to this, this torture she suffered for her daughter. Could she have died to save Gertrude this, could she have given up anything in her life then, she would have done it with joy. This was worse, she thought wildly, much worse, than giving birth, much worse than seeing your child's dead body; nothing was worse in all the world than seeing your child being torn to tatters in front of your eyes, watching it die fragment by fragment, in an ecstasy of torment too great for sound. If only Gertrude had died when she was born, or yesterday, an hour ago——

"O God," she groaned deeply, as though she were dying herself. "O dear God."

She heard a faint far sigh. Gertrude was stirring. "Don't cry so, Mama," she was saying quietly. "Nothing can help me—or Philippe, now. Please take me home. I want to see my father," she continued in a curious voice. "I must see my father."

There was the sound of hurried footsteps and agitated voices outside. Jules and Leon had arrived. They burst into the library, full of questions and anxieties. But when they saw Gertrude standing there, with such a face, they could not speak or move for several moments.

CHAPTER XCIII

ERNEST WAS just coming down the stairway from his room when Gertrude and May entered the hallway from outside.

His peculiar instinct, that always warned him of danger, made him stop halfway down and grip the banister; the hairs on the back of his neck bristled, and a cold tingle ran down his spine. Gertrude stood at the foot of the stairs, staring up at him, and he stared down at her in return, in rigid silence. As for May, she stood slightly behind her daughter, and said nothing, made no gesture at all. Her attitude was fateful, waiting.

Through the pounding warning of his aroused instinct, through his apprehension, through his awareness of an awful danger, a horror, in fact, Ernest felt that this young woman waiting for him at the foot of the stairs was no longer his daughter. It was not Gertrude's face lifted up to him; it was not Gertrude's eyes fixed on him. Only the recognition of him was there; Gertrude had gone.

"Trudie!" he exclaimed, his voice thickening in his throat. But he did not take a step down toward her.

"You've killed Philippe," she said loudly and clearly.

"Killed— What do you mean?" He wondered if it were his voice that he heard. Everything was rising and falling about him in sickening waves. He could see the purple and orange light that fell through the windows splashing on his own hand as he still gripped the banister.

"I know it all, now," said Gertrude, in that odd automatic voice, which was without inflection. "You sent him away. To die. He's dead now." She flung out her arms with a surrendering, a convulsive gesture. "And I'm dead, too. You've killed me, as well as Philippe."

The tip of Ernest's tongue shot out and furtively wet his pale dry lips. He turned to May. She stirred only slightly.

"When we went to Florabelle's," she said in a low, almost indifferent voice, "we heard that Philippe had died on that leper island." She paused, and he saw her eyes on him, dark brilliant circles in the whiteness, without mercy or any other emotion. "And there was a letter from the Bishop—" She lifted one hand a little, let it drop back to her side, heavily.

Very slowly, Ernest put his hand to his head. It was only for a moment; he seemed to move his strong legs apart, to brace himself for a terrific blow. He went down the steps, three more of them, and extended his hand to Gertrude.

"Don't talk like that, Trudie," he said gently. "I'm—sorry, for Philippe. But remember, I'm your father. You are upset. I would never have hurt you, or Philippe—" He went down two more steps. "My darling."

But she jumped back from him, and her face was quite terrible. "Don't touch me! You've killed Philippe! You are a liar! A vicious liar! You've tried to kill all of us, Frey and Guy and me! You killed Philippe." Suddenly she burst into horrible dry sobs, and again she flung out her arms in that convulsive gesture. "You killed him, and you killed me. All these years, since he went away, I haven't lived. I haven't remembered one day from another. I haven't lived at all since the day Philippe went away. Went away, because you made it impossible for him to stay. Lying, cheating, wicked man! You wanted something, and it didn't matter to you if Philippe died to give it to you, or I died——"

"May! Stop her!" exclaimed Ernest. For the first time in their married life, May saw distraction on her husband's face, saw that he was distraught and trembling. "Take hold of her, May. Can't you see how she is—? Can't you do something but stand there? She won't let me touch her. Don't stand there like a fool! Do something!"

"Why should I?" asked May coldly and bitterly. "Why should I save you from what you deserve?"

There was an abrupt silence. Then quietly, calmly, without passion, Ernest said to his wife: "Curse you." He ran down the remaining stairs very quickly, and took Gertrude by the arm, very firmly, his fingers crushing into her flesh through the cape. To soothe this girl, to calm her, to hypnotize her, he put into his voice, his manner, his grip, all the strength and power he had ever had. And she looked at him blankly with her strained, half-mad eyes, trying to pull away from him.

"Trudie, my love," he said gently, insistently, as though speaking to someone under a blanket of anæsthesia, "listen to me, only a moment. Try to hear me. My darling, if I had known this was to happen, I would have given my life to prevent it. Do you hear me, Trudie? I didn't send Philippe away. I had nothing to do with his going. You say foolish things, Trudie. That is because you are—not well. But when this is all over, you will be ashamed. You will know then, as you have always known, that your father loves you more than any one else in the world, that he would give his right hand to save you from pain— Trudie, do you hear me, dearest?"

There was a great, an almost mortal anguish in his chest, and a cold sweat burst upon his skin. But his hand did not relax upon the thin arm he was gripping, that was trying to pull away from him.

For a moment after he had stopped speaking Gertrude continued to stare at him blankly. Then all at once a wild, almost childlike smile broke over her face. "You are such a liar," she said, wonderingly.

There was another little silence. Then Ernest sighed. May had never heard such a sigh in her life, and something, in spite of herself, turned over in her breast. Ernest's hand left Gertrude's arm, and fell slowly to his side again. But he continued to look into her eyes, sadly, gently, pleadingly. And those eyes of hers repudiated him, stripped him, defied him to reach her again.

"Let me take you upstairs, my love," he almost whispered, for he had seen a certain spasm in the muscles of her face, and a deadly alarm ran along his nerves. "Let me help you upstairs. You must lie down. You must think of your baby——"

Then she burst out laughing, tearing, strident laughter, and struck her hands together. "My baby! Do you think I care about my baby! Do you think I care about anything at all except Philippe."

She stopped, and her face changed again, as though she had heard something frightful a while ago and was just beginning to realize what she had heard.

"Philippe! Philippe!" she cried suddenly, in a tone of mortal shock. A spasm of rigidity straightened her upwards to what seemed like unusual height.

And she turned and ran toward the hall door, her arms flung out before her. She actually reached the door, half opened it, then crumpled, all at once, as though shot. When Ernest reached her an instant later, he saw that she had fainted.

He picked her up in his arms and ran with her to the stairs. At the foot he paused; her head was fallen back, and on her open lips there was a faint line of foam. But he did not look at her; over the body of his daughter, over her face and hanging arms, he looked at his wife.

For a long moment their eyes were fixed on each other, and then May stepped back very quickly. Ernest went up the stairs with his daughter. May heard his rapid footsteps going down the hall, heard him carrying Gertrude into the room where she had been born.

There was another little silence. Then Ernest sighed. May had never heard such a sigh in her life, and something in the state of herself turned over in her breast. Ernest moved her arm and fell slowly to his side again, but he continued to look into her eyes, sadly, gravely, pleadingly. And those eyes of hers repudiated him, stripped him, defied him to reach her again.

CHAPTER XCIV

THE DOCTOR, shaking his head, murmured something about "very frail constitution," and returned to the bedroom. Two nurses were summoned from the hospital, the hospital which Martin had built and endowed. They would not allow even May to enter the room, from which came an endless, monotonous moaning. She sat by the closed door, very quiet, unmoving. The nurses found something unbearably pathetic in the sight of this silent, stout, middle-aged woman sitting there as though she were blind and only half-conscious. Downstairs, Ernest sat with Paul, his son-in-law.

In the afternoon Dorcas arrived, after having visited her stricken sister, Florabelle. Her liking for her brother had not increased with the years, but when she saw him the selfish coldness in her relaxed and warmed. She sat beside him, holding his hand. She said comforting things to him, and he listened, apparently, but she realized, sighing, that he did not really hear her. Paul walked up and down, running his hands distractedly through his hair. At every sound from above he ran to the stairway, and peered up, straining and listening. Then he returned to the living room and began his walking again. They could hear the steps of the nurses above, the low voice of the doctor. Once in a while they heard a shrill and ripping scream, convulsive cries of agony. At these times Ernest caught his head as though he would like to tear it from his neck.

This went on all day, and into the twilight. No one thought of eating. The servants tiptoed about, whispering. Some of them had heard what had taken place between Ernest and his daughter, and they repeated it to each other, gloating. None of them felt any sympathy for him, but many expressed their pity for May and the suffering girl dying in the bed where she had been born.

At twilight they heard a door open, and the doctor came downstairs, pale and haggard, almost weeping. Ernest got up and ran to him, speechless. He shook his head. "She's conscious now," he said. "She's asked for her mother." He paused. "The baby will live, perhaps," he said gently. "It is a little girl."

Dorcas, crying, came to stand beside her brother. She took his arm. "And Trudie?" she faltered.

The doctor spread out his hands significantly. Paul had come up to him, and he put his hand on the young man's shoulder. "You may go up, Paul," he said.

Ernest moved a little. "Hasn't she—asked for me?"

"No, sir. I'm sorry. Women—like this—usually want only their mothers and their husbands. I'm sorry. My dear sir," he added in consternation, "you had better sit down and try to rest, at once!"

At eight o'clock that night Gertrude Barbour died, without struggle, without even a murmur from the depths of her apathy and pain. But Ernest, sitting with Eugene and Dorcas in the living room, was not told for over an hour. And then he was told as he stood in the old nursery where his children had played, with his granddaughter in his arms.

The news was brought to the Norwood family, and Jules received it. He went upstairs at once to his brother's room. This house, too, was dark with mourning, and Florabelle still lay prostrate in her room with her husband beside her.

Jules opened Leon's door. That young man was lying on his bed, his arms folded under his head, staring gloomily at the ceiling. As Jules entered, swiftly and silently as was his custom, Leon sat up. Something in Jules' manner made him stare at him alertly.

Jules sat down, neatly crossed his thin knees. He returned his brother's regard steadily, and with somberness.

Then he said: "Gertrude died tonight." He paused, and carefully removed an imaginary thread from his sleek broadcloth. "The baby is a girl."

There was a silence. Then: "Ah," said Leon.

The brothers continued to look at each other.

A WEEK AFTER Gertrude's funeral, Amy sent for Paul, who had
not called upon his mother since his wife's death. He came,
silent and haggard and cold, and sat opposite her in her little
sitting room. But she saw that he would not look at her. She
was full of pity and grief for him, and at last she laid her hand
on his knee. He did not say anything, but after a moment he moved his
knee from under her hand. She sighed.

"Paul," she said gently, "if you would like it, I will be glad to move
out to Robin's Nest and keep house for you."

He did not reply for a moment, and then he said, not looking at her:
"Thank you. But I've already talked to Elsa, and she is coming to me."
He paused. He lifted his eyes and looked at her with such hatred, such
bitterness, that she felt a shock of illness and astonishment. "You've
made it impossible for Elsa to live here any longer with you. And as
for myself, I don't care to have you in my house."

Amy, unable to speak for a few minutes, sat rigidly in her chair. She
was nearly fifty, but seemed much younger in spite of her sad face. Her
hands lay in her lap, but the cords rose in them after her son's words.

"Why?" she asked quietly.

Paul stood up, shrugged, and went to a window. Then he turned to her
and said, with contempt: "I think you know why."

Amy picked up her filmy handkerchief and touched her lips with it.
"I see," she replied gently. "You know about it."

He made an enraged gesture. "I've always known about it. For years.
I've heard whispers and laughs, behind my back. I've always known it.
And always detested you for it." He paused, breathing in a disordered
fashion, then continued with fury: "You've asked me before if you could
do anything for me. You can. You can never let Uncle Ernest know that
I know. Because—because if he knew I knew, it would make it impossible for him to have me with him any longer."

"And knowing this for years," went on his mother's soft voice, almost
abstractedly, "you never felt like telling me before?"

"No. Why should I? I had other fish to fry, and I didn't want anything to occur to keep Uncle Ernest from taking me in with him."

"And what makes you tell me now?"

"I can't help it! I suppose I should have kept my mouth shut. But—

well, things have gotten a little out of hand with me, lately. And then, to realize that my mother is a light woman——"

Amy looked at him gently. "I see," she said again. Her voice was full of pity. "Poor Paul."

He was astonished. He lowered at her suspiciously. But he had never understood his mother and he was no nearer understanding her now.

"And you're sure this will make no difference in your relations with Ernest, Paul?"

"None. Why should it? Unless you tell him I know."

"I won't tell him." She hesitated and said, once more, "Poor Paul."

A few days later, in pale silence, Elsa left her mother's house and went out to Roseville, to Robin's Nest. Then when John Charles, sullen and heavy-lidded, informed his mother that it would be convenient for him to live with Paul, in order to keep him informed about things at the bank, Amy said, as she always said to the puzzling and the unbearable and the sad: "I see." So Amy was left alone in the house on Quaker Terraces. She had never thought it was possible to feel so lonely, so desolate. Ernest had not come to her since Gertrude's death, and she had a feeling that he would not come again for some time. Sighing, she thought that she had never been like this, not even when she had lived on the farm ages ago. Remembering the farm, she remembered Martin. And sighed again. Life, she thought, was a tragic and useless business.

Two weeks after Gertrude's death, May spoke to her husband for the first time since that event. She informed him, very quietly, that she was leaving him, and was going to live with Reginald and his wife in the country, for a few months, and then was going to join Godfrey in Paris. Joey, she said, was so attached to his father that she felt it would be unfair to take him with her. She said all this without emotion, almost indifferently. She had lost much weight, and the folds of her shrunken skin made her appear quite old. Her hair had whitened perceptibly, and it was only underneath that there was any vestige of the bright dark red of her youth.

Ernest received this news impassively, without a word. One night he came home and was informed by the excited butler that Mrs. Barbour had gone. Ernest walked upstairs and entered his wife's room for the first time in many years. She was not there, now, to forbid his entrance. He sat down in her own chair by the empty fireside, and looked at the smooth bed. There was not even a breath of scent to tell any one that she had ever lived and slept in that room. Everything was polished, with glossy repellent surfaces, as though no one had ever touched it. Every trace of May was gone, and the doors of her great polished mahogany wardrobe swung open to show the dark and empty interior. When Ernest got up to go he glanced in the mirror above the dressing table. He thought to himself: That's an old man's face. He went downstairs and walked all through the house, the Sessions house. And as he walked, he said to himself : This is the Sessions house. It's not mine at all. It only tolerated me, this house I've worked for. And now it doesn't tolerate me any more. It's like an empty house with all the furniture removed, and even the walls hate me.

It was one of the few sentimentalities of his life. But then, he thought wryly, a man should be allowed to be sentimental once in a while. However, he could not rid himself of the weird feeling that the house, which had been his, was once more the Sessions house, and even the fact that he lived there all alone could not alter that insistent and gloomy fact. He looked at the dark portraits on the ivory walls in the drawing room, and the faces, all Sessions faces, regarded him with sombre affront. Once he had a ridiculous feeling that Gregory Sessions walked behind him, smiling.

He went out to Robin's Nest more and more often, where he was received with the lavish affection and sincere pleasure which he had never received in his own house from his own children. Paul had named his little daughter, who had had a severe struggle to retain her life, Alice Sessions Barbour. She lay upstairs in a great new nursery, attended by the most efficient of nurses, a tiny blue-eyed little thing with a fluff of pale red hair. She reminded her grandfather of his son, Guy. When she was christened, Ernest gave her a gold christening mug with her name engraved upon it.

Elsa worshipped her. She actually wept when Paul refused permission for her to teach the child to call her mother. But Elsa was very happy these days. All her old ease and affection for her uncle had returned, now that she was removed from her mother. Her old exuberance came back much to the disapproval of the nurse, who finally had to refuse to allow Elsa to jog her niece violently. Elsa knew that she would never marry; she knew she would never stop loving Godfrey, of whom she never heard anything.

When Paul and Elsa suggested to their uncle that he come out to Robin's Nest to live, he did not refuse as promptly as they had feared. In fact, he seemed to be thinking the matter over. Certainly it was no pleasure for him to live in the Sessions house any longer, with Joey away at school and only at home in the summer. (He was thinking of it as "the Sessions house" almost always, now.) Moreover, as Paul pointed out, the section was becoming "run down," and the house, though immaculately kept up and painted and polished, with lawns still velvety and trees trimmed and green, seemed to be acquiring an air of desolation and dilapidation. But, though Paul's hopes became stronger, Ernest had not the slightest intention of leaving the Sessions house.

He had not seen Amy for four months now, and she had not written him nor had he written her. But he was beginning to act a little oddly now, when at home. He would sit at the end of the great mahogany table, and look across its vast circular width for minutes at a time. Years ago the whole family had sat there, Godfrey and Gertrude, Guy and Reginald, May and himself and young Joey. No one but he sat here now, in the silver and mahogany and ivory emptiness of the room, with the vast ivory candles burning in their candelabra on the sideboard and the walls, and the butler making the only other human being beside himself in all that shining and polished vastness. But these days, as Ernest looked fixedly across the table, he began to smile a little. As though someone sat there and spoke to him.

Then, five months after May had left him, he did the most audacious thing of his life: he sued May for divorce.

CHAPTER XCVI

ON THE SURFACE it did not seem so very audacious, even in 1882, when divorces were extremely uncommon things and severely criticized. Ernest Barbour's wife had obviously deserted him, and refused to return to her home, and so he was suing her for divorce, a deeply injured and saddened gentleman. But in reality, his suit for divorce against May Sessions was a dangerous thing, audacious to the point of foolhardiness and effrontery. He was gambling everything on the hope that she would keep her mouth shut with regard to Amy, that she would not contest the divorce and bring countersuit, naming her cousin. If she did speak, did bring countersuit, he knew his losses would be terrible. In the first place, hostile newspapers and politicians had never let him forget that he was a low-born English man, that his entry into society had been accomplished and facilitated by his marriage to that great lady, Miss May Sessions. He had gained a great deal through the friends of the Sessions; even the President had been a younger friend of Gregory's. He needed the politicians who accepted him because of the Sessionses, especially since the late labor disturbances, the growing sentiment against the importation of alien contract labor and the increasing distrust of the people for powerful industrialists. They would, after the first shock, forgive his divorce, but if they felt, in the event that May talked, that the late Miss Sessions had been grossly ill-used, they would never stop until they ruined him. Then, in the second place, Amy would be so shamed that she might have to leave the country; his relations with Paul would come to an abrupt end, though he had no illusions that this would be because Paul would feel outraged at the revelations. In fact, Ernest had a faint idea that Paul knew all about his uncle's relations with his mother. Then, there was his granddaughter to be considered.

All these things Ernest Barbour chanced when he sued his wife for divorce, gambling on the possibility that she would not contest the suit, would not name Amy in a suit of her own. He knew his wife extremely well, and sometimes, during the weeks that followed the astounding news, he felt quite secure. But at other times, remembering May's anger, which could be violent on occasion, remembering her integrity and courage, her contempt for scurvy subterfuge, her almost blatant lack of fear where honor and name were concerned, he was not so certain as he would have liked to be. Besides, after he had filed his suit for divorce, he was puzzled that he did not feel more relief. Instead, an uneasiness he could not name, a sort of heaviness, grew on him.

When May was served with the papers, living as she was on a remote and austere farm with her son Reginald and his young, stern Amish wife, her first reaction was incredulity. Next, she was stunned. And after that, prostrated. She took to bed, in the narrow, boarded comfortless but immaculate bedroom which she occupied, and stayed there for nearly two days. She did not cry nor complain, nor do anything except gaze at the pineboard walls and the candlewick bedspread which covered her. Then she got up, dressed, and went to Paul's house. Reginald, dour and silent and dark as ever, with neat buttonless clothes and short black beard, drove her to the station, where she took the branch line. It was a ride of about two hours. She arrived at Paul's house in the late evening, just after dinner. Paul and Elsa were surprised to see her, and with some embarrassment made her welcome. They had not yet heard of the divorce proceedings. Elsa forced her to eat a portion of dinner, then carried her off to see her little granddaughter, then triumphantly assigned to her the best guest-chamber. Both she and her brother were eaten up with curiosity regarding May's visit, and were highly excited by her pale drawn face and red-rimmed eyes. But Elsa, alone with her aunt in the guest-chamber while May removed her wraps, could get nothing out of her except her usual kind well-bred remarks and praises for the care of the baby. They went down to the living room together, where Paul was waiting in a highly nervous condition.

May sat down and said, quietly: "Your Uncle Ernest is suing me for divorce, Paul, on the grounds of desertion—and cruelty," she added with a faint twisted smile.

"A divorce?" Paul had turned a peculiar sickly yellow. "A divorce?"

"Yes."

Paul and Elsa looked at each other, both thinking the same appalling and terrified thoughts.

"I am thinking of fighting it. Yes, I am certain I shall fight it," went on May. "Unless, of course, he agrees to drop the suit."

Shocked, full of fear, enormously upset, Paul got up and paced the hearth rug. He thought: Then, this is the end for me. For, of course, she will bring mother into it, and then— But, of course, she'll bring mother into it! How else could she fight it? Elsa, thinking the same thing, sat in miserable silence, watching her brother.

"Would you mind telling me how—how you will fight the suit, Aunt May?" asked Paul, standing in front of her and looking down at her wretchedly.

May smiled drearily to herself, and twisted her handkerchief about her fingers.

"Don't be frightened, Paul," she said kindly, "I'll avoid a family scandal."

Paul turned crimson, and Elsa colored also. "Look here, Aunt May," began Paul, stammering, flooded with a weakening and profound relief. He stopped abruptly, for May had burst into tears. They comforted her, but over her bowed head they looked at each other in triumphant elation. Their pleasure increased when she said she would not stay more than the night, but would return to Sweetcold the next day. It was not until she had gone that they began to wonder why she had ever come to them.

Amy, alone in her house, read the news a few days later in the newspapers. She could hardly believe it. Then, overcome, intensely moved, she sat down and wrote to Ernest, begging him to withdraw his suit. It never occurred to her that May might fight the case and bring her name into it. Remembering her cousin and her love for her husband, her devotion and kindness, Amy became ill with pity and indignation. She waited a long time for a reply from Ernest, but he did not send one.

Then, to everyone's amazement, May set sail for France just two days before the suit was tried. Her attorney appeared in court and curtly announced that his client had decided not to appear and not to contest the suit. Within the hour Ernest Barbour was granted a divorce from his wife, May, and suitable property settlements were signed and sealed.

He walked out of the courthouse through a thick cluster of questioning newspapermen, and went home, to the Sessions house. But for some reason, he could not bear it there. He saw Gertrude's face in the hallway at the foot of the stairs; he saw his son Guy leaping like a faun down the hallway; he saw Godfrey at the silent closed piano; he heard Reginald's low doleful humming behind the door of the room he used to occupy. And in the drawing room, sitting before the fire with her embroidery, he saw his wife, not as she was now, but a young gay May, with dark-red curls tossing coquettishly and a huge hoop-skirted dress all lace and satin. He went upstairs again to May's old room and sat in her chair, his head on his chest. The whole house was empty, full of faint and hollow echoes. The early winter ivy, robbed of leaves, tapped the window. It was very cold, for there was no fire in the room and he had not lit a lamp. The window-glass rattled, and he heard the rush of the dry leaves on the dead grass below. The dry and ashen desolation of the evening seemed to permeate him and disintegrate him.

He thought: I have driven all the Sessionses out of their house. I'm a stranger here, but I'm in possession. Then, without reason, he remembered May the night he had returned from England, when Godfrey lay in his cradle in the now empty nursery. He remembered her laughter, her kisses, the smell of her warm young flesh, the feel of her cheek against his, the touch of her curls. He got up quite suddenly and went downstairs again.

Three months later he brought Amy into the Sessions house as his bride.

CHAPTER XCVII

HONORE BOUCHARD secured his patent on his prismatic powder and the machine he had invented to compress it. He turned it over to Ernest Barbour for fifteen thousand shares of stock in the firm of Barbour-Bouchard and ten thousand shares in the Kinsolving Arms Company. Jules Bouchard sold his steel patent to the Sessions Steel Company for eighteen thousand shares of stock, and was made general manager of the Company. Soon thereafter Honore was sent abroad by his uncle to compare the American powder with the new prismatic brown and smokeless powders which the Belgians and the Germans were manufacturing. Honore learned the methods of manufacture, changed the formulæ only slightly, and returning to America patented his new explosive. England heard of the new powder and bought one hundred thousand barrels of it.

Honore suddenly had a brilliant idea. Why not manufacture revolvers and other arms so accurately and uniformly that the parts were interchangeable? Within three months the Kinsolving Arms Company was sending sights, barrels, mainsprings, triggers, to all arms-users in the country who wished to repair their weapons. For this idea he acquired five thousand more shares of the stock. When he perfected new machinery which increased output three times, he was made assistant to his father, Eugene Bouchard.

Only a few months later the Sessions Steel Company sent Jules to Europe to observe armor-plate factories, for America was now considering armor-plated battleships. He returned with such revolutionary, such magnificent ideas, that his uncle was tremendously excited. Not only this, but Robsons & Strong, and Schultz-Poiret, had granted the Sessions Steel Company licenses for the use of their processes in making the plate. Ernest, accompanied by Jules, visited the Gonegan Steel Company in Pittsburgh and the Middleton Ordnance Company, and these companies joined the Sessions Steel Company in the manufacture of armor-plate. The Sessions Steel Company secured the government orders for this. Hardly a year later Jules invented a new steel, based on a new German patent.

Jules was not devoid of even more brilliant ideas than those of his cousin, Honore. Why not issue catalogs in various languages, advertising powder, plate and munitions? Within a short time Compagnie des

Acièries de Windsor and Compañia de Acero de Windsor were doing miraculous business. The Russians placed tremendous orders, alone, and Schultz-Poiret reported sales exceeding imagination.

Honore proved to his uncle's and father's satisfaction that the hand-made rifles and pistols made by the best artisans were vastly inferior to the weapons turned out by his newest invention, an amazing machine. Heretofore hand-made weapons had been considered superior to machine-made weapons. Ernest pointed out they were still cheaper to make than the machine-made type. Honore set to work on improvements, and soon the machine was cheaper than the hand. He also suggested to Ernest that the latter advise wealthy governments to sell their obsolete arms to poorer nations, and buy the newer types as they were invented. Honore visited Turkey and sold the army six hundred thousand rifles. He had a very hard time, for there was a certain etiquette to be gone through, a certain smoothing of officials who were not averse to accepting a little gift or two. Honore used bribery to good effect, and the orders were placed.

In the past there had been growing a formidable rival to Barbour-Bouchard, Robsons & Strong, and Schultz-Poiret (those three good friends), in Essen, Germany. This was a firm known simply as Kronk. Germany, whom Ernest called the "surly hog of Europe," had grown arrogant since the Franco-Prussian War, and was excessively proud of Kronk, who was reported to be making the best cannon in the world. The Russians bought in prodigious quantities, as did other nations, and Barbour-Bouchard and its friends felt consternation. Kronk was even more unscrupulous than they; its agents swarmed everywhere, bribing ambassadors and other officials. It was all-powerful in European courts, gathering together representatives from every nation to secure orders for cannon which they would use to murder each other. Kronk, all-sufficient, refused even to receive Ernest Barbour to discuss negotiations, until Jules' latest steel patent was dangled before it. Thereafter the greatest accord ensued. The three good friends were now four, and the peace of the world was delivered into their ruthless hands. With great insouciance and speed they sold their products to both sides of any international argument, the wealthier side securing the best and the latest and turning over its older and obsolete arms to the munitions manufacturers, who in turn delivered them to the poorer antagonist for neat sums. "We are," said Ernest, through a dozen foreign newspapers, "not concerned with controversies. We are businessmen only, meeting a demand adequately."

When a great English newspaper pioneered in denunciations of "these dealers in damnation," Ernest issued a statement to the effect that "we are neutral; we cannot take sides. Private emotions and principles, nationalism and patriotism, greeds and injustices, in any nation, are none of our affair. The abolition of armaments dealers will not abolish war, which is older than cannon and rooted in greed. If men cannot have cannon, they will use rifles; if they cannot have rifles, they will use the bow and arrow. If they cannot have the bow and arrow, they will use their fists. The first step in the abolition of the armaments dealer is the abolition of war, which all my patriotic enemies will agree is preposterous." And again: "Peace is an absurd dream. While one man has one thing more than his neighbor there will be hatred and war. It all resolves to cupidity, and all the fine phrases, the noble ideology, the patriotic fervors, the holy indignations and righteousnesses, will not change this basic fact. To blame the armaments dealer for war is to put the cart before the horse." And he, who was a private and enormous contributor to two of the most militant patriotic societies in America, said for publication: "The foolish patriot is the clown of the greedy statesman. He is usually very articulate, and has all the clichés and the platitudes on the end of his tongue. The people love noble phrases, which relieve them of the necessity for thinking. If you are really looking for enemies, look at your patriots, and, beyond the mouthings and gesturings of these innocent mountebanks, look for the statesman who adds up accounts behind the beating of the drums."

The great English newspaper conceded much of this, with honest reluctance. "But," it said, "it does not relieve the armaments dealer of guilt, in that he supplies the weapons for stupidity to do murder." To which Ernest replied contemptuously: "We have no reply to sentimentality." And again: "Profits have nothing to do with emotions, which are the luxury of the incompetent." On a certain occasion he said: "Hatred is not to be despised. Nothing grows in the marshes of peace. Strife is, and always has been, the promoter of civilizations and the destroyer of barbarisms." He regretted this later, when it was extensively used by his enemies as proof that he instigated wars with "the noble phrases he despises, for his own private gain."

In the meantime Jules and Honore Bouchard were threatening the peace of mind and happiness of Paul Barbour. He, himself, by the exercise of innate force and inability to see obstacles, had accomplished as much in his way as had Jules or Honore, but it was less spectacular. It never occurred to him that Ernest might appreciate his efforts and successes as much as the more flamboyant accomplishments of his cousins, and he was tormented by his anxiety. He desperately wanted glamour to attend what he accomplished, but he was naturally too laborious and painstaking of character to add this color. He naïvely believed that because his work lacked drama and excitement and color it was not seen by his uncle, and he literally bit his nails in a very fever of apprehension. His hatred for and envy of Jules, especially, caused him sleepless nights in which even his vehement grief for Gertrude was forgotten. (Being of the turn of mind that can think intensely only of one thing at a time, the pressure of his sorrow was relieved by the profound and active irritation of his fear and worry.) Jules had by far a more sinister and subtle appearance than did his more stolid-appearing and slower-mannered cousin Honore, and lacked Honore's effect of impervious integrity. His eyes were quicker and darting, "like the tongue of a snake," thought Paul with loathing, and his whole body seemed swift and agile and supple, like a snake's body. His silent attitude, his ever-watchful face, his faint secret smile, alarmed and infuriated Paul. He appeared always to be engrossed in some subtle and treacherous plotting, and when he spoke, his words, innocent and courteous enough, gave his audience a slight sense of shock, so incongruous were they with that dark countenance and those "licking" eyes. Paul's old distrust of "the Jesuit" grew to a sort of mania of hatred, an insanity of suspicion and detestation, an almost uncontrollable desire to do murder. Before all this, it would never have occurred to him to humiliate himself in an attempt to placate Honore; he had always scorned the Bouchards, and the very idea that he might one day try to win the friendship of a lesser member of that family would have made him shout with contemptuous laughter.

But he did try to placate and win the friendship of Honore Bouchard. Though his imagination was not intense, his instincts were very strong, and he smelt a very vivid but hidden danger. Jules, he felt, was the dangerous one, the greater menace to his ambitions and desires; but he also felt that strength and protection lay in Honore. So, for the first time in years, he visited the home of his Uncle Eugene, put on his frankest and friendliest manner, assumed a geniality he had unconsciously picked up from Ernest, and wooed Honore. Honore was not too surprised; he had been warned by Jules that this might happen. Jules had laughed cuttingly about it, as he had made his prophecy, and as Paul sat opposite him with such a naïvely ingratiating face, Honore felt pity for him, remembering Jules' laughter and cruel expression. He was also embarrassed for Paul, as well as sorry for him, and his conscience, which he had inherited from his father, stirred uneasily. Jules, he thought, smiling stiffly at some pleasant remark of Paul's, was really a vicious devil, cold and corrosive as some deadly acid; if he had been here tonight he would have gloated behind the thin dark mask he wore over his real face. How he would laugh tomorrow when Honore told him of Paul's attempts at placating. And then, of a sudden, Honore, though burning with shame for Paul because of the latter's humble words and manner, decided not to tell Jules. His resolution was not seriously disturbed, his determination not at all moved, but he was genuinely sorry for Paul and was sad that he must some day hurt him mortally. Sitting there, with his fixed smile beginning to hurt his facial muscles, he suddenly thought that he was being treacherous to Jules, and between his alarm at this and his pity for Paul, he was very uncomfortable indeed. When he found himself promising to have dinner with Paul at his home some night the following week, he was aghast. Now he must tell Jules, and hear his merciless laughter at Paul, and after that he would spend a frightful evening with Paul, wondering to whom he was being treacherous, and all in all succeeding in being actively miserable. Before Paul went he was violently cursing his "softness," and accordingly his manner at parting was so suddenly abrupt and brusque that Paul left in perturbation, which, when seen by Honore, disturbed him more than ever. A dozen times or more that restless night he told himself that Paul had wooed him because he was afraid of Jules, because he knew that Honore was one of the heirs of Eugene Bouchard, the partner of Ernest, and because he childishly hoped that he might succeed in splitting the combine of Jules and Honore and Leon, and that in the end, should he succeed, his old patronizing manner toward Honore would return. But all this realization had little effect at the present time upon Honore's uneasiness and wincing compassion for him.

And Paul, always the expedient, and now desperate, turned his mind to the placating of his mother. It never occurred to him that he did not need to placate her: he knew he had insulted her grossly, had literally shut the door of his house to her. Reasoning from his own point of view, he thought that she would feel resentment against him, would desire to humiliate and hurt him, as he himself would desire to humiliate and hurt any one who had affronted him so outrageously.

Amy's unexpected marriage to Ernest had jolted her children so profoundly that it was weeks before their slow minds and preconceived beliefs could take in what had happened, and could accept the fact. They had always had a poor opinion of their mother, whose whimsicalities and unpredictable amusement had aroused only the contempt of their tenacious and humorless minds, and the distrust of their simple stolidity. Besides, as Paul had told his sister Elsa a hundred times, "men did not marry their mistresses." They accepted the phrase with their smug simplicity, their naïve belief in the authenticity of their own conclusions. When events calmly refused to live up to these conclusions, they were so upset that it seemed as if the wildest disturbance had occurred in the complacent house of their minds. It was a long time before they could adjust themselves, during which interval they felt indignation, outrage, bewilderment and incredulity. Then Elsa settled down to a bitter acceptance, John Charles laughed shortly, Lucy became amused and expressed a shrugging admiration for her mother, and Paul felt a violent apprehension as to what Amy's attitude toward him might now be. So, to Amy's grief, mortification, compassion and distaste, he courted her good will.

He was much elated and relieved when she received him with her old calm affection and interest, her old concern for his welfare, her old un-complex kindness. She conducted the interview as though nothing whatsoever had ever happened between herself and her son. He did not see a great lady who was suffering because of him; he thought he saw a simple woman who had not had the backbone to be offended or resentful and was only too glad to be accepted again by her son and through his condescension able to feel respectable once more.

John Charles, showing marked signs of the Barbour expediency, blandly announced to Paul that he intended to take up his residence with his mother in the Sessions house. He smiled at Paul's suddenly suffused face, packed without any appearance of embarrassment, and moved. To Paul's intense shock and rage, he saw that his younger brother had calmly become his enemy, not from any personal change in his attitude toward him, but from a certain something which Paul felt was the more menacing and disturbing.

After three years, he was still actively grieving for Gertrude, he was constantly fearful of Jules' and Leon's and Honore's increasing influence and power, he was more and more aware of his brother's impersonal enmity and implacable growth in importance. Also, he had failed, through no fault of his, in a mission with which Ernest, not with much hope, had intrusted him in Washington: that of exerting sufficient influence, bribery and coercion to prevent the passage of the Alien Contract Labor Law. He had gone, armed with all the Barbour prestige, power, political influence and ability to suborn integrity, and he had failed. Though Ernest amusedly assured him that it was not his fault, that it was bound to pass because the people were demanding it vociferously, that there were too many influences behind the bill to prevent its defeat, Paul again reasoned from his own character and believed that his uncle was beginning to despise him and that he would never forgive him.

Then, completely if temporarily demoralizing him, his Uncle Eugene Bouchard died, quite suddenly, and Honore Bouchard, as one of the executors of his father's will and one of the heirs of the dynasty, took on the suddenly giant stature of an enemy who had appeared deceptively small in the distance, but who had now approached within a few paces.

CHAPTER XCVIII

ONLY HONORE BOUCHARD knew why his father died, and he never told any one, not even his mother, not even the woman he was to marry, not even the priest whom he visited at long intervals.

One morning, as Honore was experimenting in the factory on a new explosive, which he believed would be ten times as powerful as the one Barbour-Bouchard now manufactured, a clerk approached him and told him his father wished to see him. The British had recently been experimenting with "cordite," which they fondly believed was a deep dark secret. The formula was guarded with ferocious care, yet in some way, with which only Ernest Barbour and his nephew Jules were acquainted, the formula had become known to Barbour-Bouchard. The "mystery" cost Ernest over half a million dollars, which he did not regret. The formula had been turned over to Honore, who was now testing it. Already Barbour-Bouchard, on the strength of the discreetly broadcasted hint in Russia that the Company was in possession of the secret of British cordite, had received enormous advance orders from that country for this explosive. Honore had in mind a certain process by which the power of cordite could be increased, and within a few days Barbour-Bouchard expected to begin the manufacture of this "black plague."

Honore felt some irritation at being called away from his work, and he merely brushed off his clothing and hands sketchily and went into his father's office. The young man walked with a peculiar "sea-going" gait, because his strong short legs were slightly bowed, and he had a manner of thrusting his reserved and handsome square face a little ahead. When he came into Eugene's office, Eugene sniffed audibly at the acrid smell that attended his son.

"It gives me the most atrocious headache, Honore," he said, but he smiled. "You must not concern yourself," he added, as Honore frowned with a quick anxiety, "I am always having headaches. Sometimes I think I am having the *petite mal*." He spoke in French, the language he always used to his family, and which they used in return.

Honore sat down and scrutinized his father earnestly. His irritation at being brought from his work disappeared. It was not his imagination, then, that told him that his father was failing. Eugene had grown perceptibly thinner, and his face, always dark, seemed to be disintegrating and falling away behind the sallow seamed skin. Honore, his alarm quickening, saw how bony his father's forehead had become, and how it shone with a smooth yellow lustre, like a skull. His lips were purplish, and livid about the edges, and his nose appeared unusually prominent and pinched. His hair, once Indian-black and wiry, was harsh and almost white. For a long time his family had been uneasily noticing these things, but Eugene had scoffed, first with amusement and then with annoyance, and insisted that his health was most excellent. Today, Honore, with a sick plunge in his chest, told himself that death was impressed indelibly on his father's face.

He exclaimed, forgetting everything else: "You are ill, my father! You must go away and rest! You must think of my mother, and all of us."

At the mention of Dorcas, Eugene's expression changed for an instant. Then he smiled his kind reserved smile and shook his head. "I am growing old, my child, that is all. Old age is a disease for which there is no cure. It is true that in myself I do not feel old, but unfortunately I cannot convince my flesh that this is so." Again his expression changed, darkened and became stern. "But I did not call you in to me to discuss my sensations, Honore. I called you here to demand an explanation from you."

"An explanation? For what?" Honore was still searching his father's face with anxious eyes, and spoke absently.

"For this strange alliance between yourself and Jules and Leon."

Honore was jolted to attention. He came completely to the surface, and eyed Eugene with great caution and intentness. "Alliance!" he repeated, with apparent bewilderment. "What alliance? Who has been telling you this story?"

"What story?" Eugene's eyelids narrowed and a gleam shot from them. "What makes you think there was any one to tell me a story? Ah, my Honore, you are not so subtle! You are too honest, in spite of a relentlessness you are trying to cultivate and which I observe with sorrow." He paused. "Now, you must tell me about this alliance. I am most interested."

"I do not know what you are talking about!" exclaimed Honore, coloring.

"You know precisely what I am talking about!" replied Eugene angrily. His breath shortened, and the livid tint deepened about his mouth. Father and son glared at each other like two aroused antagonists. Then, after a few moments, Honore shrugged, became sullen.

"I cannot understand all this," he said. "Jules and Leon are my friends, as well as my relatives. Our personalities are congenial; I have always been closer to them than to any other members of my family, with the exception of you and my mother. But, you are surely not objecting to my friendship with my cousins! You are surely not objecting to Jules and Leon?"

Eugene, a little taken aback, plucked at his lip. "But, certainly not! I do not know whether you are being subtle in this, Honore, or simply childish. I am exceedingly fond of Leon, especially, though I candidly admit that I neither like nor trust Jules. Few people do, and I am sure that Jules himself would be the last to be surprised at this. Your Uncle Ernest has called him a Jesuit, but even Ernest, who has named him aptly, never saw more than one or two Jesuits in his life. I have! And I see how exquisitely the name suits Jules. He is subtle, expedient, suave, crafty and conscienceless. The real Jesuit uses these things to serve his Church, and so feels justified, as probably he is. But Jules serves no one but himself. I see that he loves his brother, and also loves you. But I do not doubt that should the occasion arise, should the pressure of greed be great enough, he would betray both of you, coolly and efficiently."

"You apparently do not admire Jules, my father," said Honore, with the satirical dryness that distinguished him.

Eugene made an irate gesture. "My feeling for Jules has nothing to do with it. Body of Christ! you force me to blurt out what I have heard, like a child who can be trusted with nothing! Paul Barbour was here to see me this morning."

"Ah, I see!"

"I do not admire Paul Barbour. Jules, that phrase-maker, has called him a boulder on cannon-wheels! That is very apt, uncomfortably apt. He imitates, probably unconsciously, his Uncle Ernest. Now, Ernest's power is always conscious and directed, but Paul's is unconscious and directed only by his desires. You see, I listened to Paul, not because I liked him and was prejudiced in his favor, but because, knowing Jules, I saw that there was a great deal of truth in what he was saying. He told me that you and Jules and Leon were uniting, very competently, in an alliance whose sole purpose is the securing of control of Barbour-Bouchard and the ousting and ruining of himself. He gave me proof. Naturally, I was horrified. I detest treachery above anything in all the world. Not only was the whole thing dangerous and untenable, but it was also repulsive. Perhaps I am sentimental in my old age, but I was more concerned with the treachery. Success, the worth-while things in life, are never obtained by treachery and scoundrelly tactics——"

There was a little silence, then Honore asked quietly, lifting his eyes steadily and looking piercingly into his father's face: "Are they not?"

Eugene's mouth fell open slightly, then his face was suffused by a tide of purplish red. An expression of acute mental and physical distress twisted his features. He stood up suddenly, then caught hold of his desk. His breath was short. Honore, alarmed for him, stood up also.

But Eugene was not enraged. "You are quite right, Honore," he said painfully. "Quite right. I am becoming sentimental, because I am ill and old. And I am frightened. A great deal—of this—what we have all become, never rested easily with me. I—I have been led, not because of the unscrupulousness of—any leader—but because I must really have been weak. I suffer from inertia. Even my ambition was merely the spinning of a top set in motion by some one else. I suffered, and I perversely thought my suffering was weakness. I see that my acquiescence was the real weakness. I—I am blaming no one, not even myself. I was made so. At a certain time in life a man ceases to blame himself or any one else. It is the life. But I would spare my sons that suffering. You— none of you are of the stuff of which the Anglo-Saxon is made, that combination of brutality and viciousness, justification and morality. I want no 'alliance' that will lead any of you to my distress, my ignominy, my foolish regret. No man of any honor could endure the thought of such treachery——"

Though Honore was full of compassion for his father, he could not help asking: "Could Uncle Ernest endure it?"

The color slowly subsided from Eugene's face, and he sat down as though every bone in his body ached. His head dropped a little. "Yes," he murmured, "Ernest could endure it. I understand you. He would be amused, and admiring. He would say: 'Cocky young devils, let's see where they are going!' And if he thought you were unscrupulous enough, rascally enough, his admiration would grow, especially if you showed wit, which you no doubt do, and he would actually help you. But, God! what am I saying—" and he put a thin brown hand to his forehead.

Honore sat down, exceedingly moved, for he loved his father very much. After a little while, he said, very gently: "I will not dodge adroitly, my father. I will be frank with you. Jules and Leon and I have discussed all this for a long time. Jules holds a large block of stock, now, in the company and its subsidiaries. His family, his mother, hold a large block; he will have his share too, some day, of that. Leon holds stock. I and my brothers and sisters are your heirs. Your holdings are enormous. We have talked all this over. And, with justification, we have come to the conclusion that Paul Barbour, ingratiating himself as he is doing with Uncle Ernest, will, after Uncle Ernest's death, be the controlling power in Barbour-Bouchard. He is dogged; he has no fierceness or vehemence, but he has the weight and the solidity of boulders. He is not clever, but we have seen that he is out to take from us what is ours, and to destroy our opportunities, make us mere figureheads in the Company. Our 'alliance' was merely self-defense." He paused. "And in the natural course of events our self-defense has become a deadly and irresistible offensive. As you would say, 'it is the life.'"

Eugene rubbed his forehead, still concealing his eyes. "I can see your point of view, yes. And in the main, I do not quarrel with it, knowing it to be mostly true. But I can also see that Jules is not truly concerned with mere 'justice.' He is very obviously using you, for he knows such an appeal would have weight with you. No, he is not concerned with justice. He is cruel and rapacious."

"You would object less to this plan of ours if Jules were activated by 'justice' only?" demanded Honore with involuntary impatience.

Eugene dropped his hand. "Yes," he said simply, "I would. You observe," he added with his painful and whimsical smile, "how old I have become!"

Honore got up and began to walk the floor, his hands gripped together behind his back. "It is very odd to think of justice or any other virtue in connection with the making of armaments!" he said with a sort of plaintive contempt.

An odd expression, subtle and darkening, stood in Eugene's eyes. "So, you feel that, too!" he muttered, too inaudibly for Honore to hear. He said aloud, withdrawingly, "you must not speak childishly, my son. There is no question of virtue in the mechanical business of barter and sale. A fair product at a fair price." He was bitterly conscious of quoting some of Ernest's recent newspaper statements. "Your Uncle Ernest has provided the better product, so he has become the wealthier and the more powerful man. Virtue has not entered into it——"

Honore whipped about, very suddenly for a young man of his sober character. "No, it has not! Oh, I am not blaming Uncle Ernest; I admire him, for a man of force and genius. But it has not been all fair business at a fair price, and I am certain that you know this, my father. Armaments are something beyond mere innocuous business. Quite coolly, I realize they are a nefarious one. But I do not care for that. Our business, our wealth, our profits, flourish on death. A very nasty idea, to any one who is weak-stomached. We grow fat on blood. I am very willing to grow fat that way, and have my profits, but that does not blind me, any more than it really blinds Uncle Ernest, even when he has been most reasonable and logical in his newspaper statements. Only you, my poor father, have been blind. Perhaps willingly so, for you could not endure looking. Forgive me, but I must speak, and you must hear.

"You have known of the work our representatives, and Jules, have been doing in Europe, the 'war scares' they have incited, the newspapers they have suborned and filled with lies, the setting of one nation against another, all to stimulate the purchase of armaments. You know how we, and others like us, have served two masters, with good profits from both. You know that we have been responsible for wars in Europe, and that our chief business is to play on hatred and greed and fear and prejudice. In the terrible game we play against mankind our first chessman is Stupidity. Uncle Ernest knows all this, and he says blandly: 'What of it?

Our profits are enormous. All things are justified in the name of profits.'
He is only what the French mean when they call a man a cynic——"

Eugene struck his hand violently on his desk, livid with something else
besides rage. "Yes, I know all this!" he cried in a voice so strained that it
was almost whining, like a drawn violin string. "You are a young fool
to think I did not know! Am I not Ernest's partner, can I not read! But
Europe must always fight; the peoples are so dissimilar; they are natural
and hereditary enemies. It will always be so, as it was in the past. It
needs little stimulation over there for one race to hate another, I assure
you. I have lived there. So, we cannot condemn—ourselves, too much
for that. We can, without much strain on our consciences, take the profit
that must inevitably go to someone. Sometimes, though, I have thought
Ernest might have been just a trifle too clever——" His voice sank into
one of dull reflection, as though he had begun to talk to himself. "We,
through Schultz-Poiret, sold guns and explosives to both France and
Prussia in '70, to both Turkey and Russia, and——" Again he struck
his hand violently upon his desk. "But, Europe is like that, and I do not
care! No one of intelligence could care. C'est la guerre. But, in America,
it is different——"

"Is it?" countered Honore swiftly. "Is it?"

The tense fist on the desk opened as though the owner had received a
mortal blow. Eugene's eyes seemed to sink in their sockets; as if a
hollow had opened up behind them. "What do you mean?" he asked in a
low hoarse tone.

The single-minded Honore could not be stopped now in his own
momentum. He went on rapidly and incisively, leaning on the desk
with both his hands: "Germany has no nickel, or very little, father. You
know that. And little or no copper. And you must know that Barbour-
Bouchard, through its copper companies, is shipping this metal to Germany. Why? You must ask and answer that, yourself. Is it to make
shells to kill Frenchmen? Pooh, puny little foe! Who is the only real
juicy meat in Europe? England! The British Empire! Ah, there is a
foe worthy of German ambition and greed. But Germany cannot do this
alone, for there is Russia who hates her, and France, who still has a
poodle-bite. Germany must have help from some nation full of power
and wealth and limitless resources. And who is that nation? America!"
Eugene lifted one hand as though in a feeble attempt at defense, and then,
not making a sound, he let the hand drop.

"O my God!" exclaimed the young Honore, with a fierce gesture, "is
it possible that you, partner in Barbour-Bouchard, could not know this!
How wily, how clever, how devilish that man has been! But it does not
seem possible! My father not know this! How splendidly, how majes-
tically, you have been deceived! Yet you must have seen in the news-

papers, those nice big ones controlled and owned by my nice Uncle Ernest, all the subtle anti-British propaganda, the sneers, the suspicions, the planned jealousies, the implications, the increasing references to the American Revolution and the new prominence given to accounts of England's sympathies and assistance to the South during the Civil War. You must have read the editorials, full of lofty indignations and accusations; you must have read the taunting paragraphs and the distrust openly expressed. But perhaps you did not know, my poor father, that Robsons & Strong, our associates and our business friends, are doing the same thing in England, in English school textbooks and newspapers and magazines, that we are doing here. Against America! They are doing as we are doing, using politicians who can become lyrically oratorical, after discreet transfers of stock. They are doing as we are doing, suborning educators and patriots, inciting the foolish, simple people with lies and hatreds and filthy patriotism. They are doing as we do, dispensing fear and hysteria. They have bought their government, as we have bought ours.

"And, you know for what purpose, do you not? You surely must know why Americans have become so friendly with the Germans, why German is taught in the primary schools these days, why the Kaiser is spoken of affectionately in the newspapers, why German trade is encouraged and stimulated, why actually, in many schoolrooms, an etching of the Kaiser hangs side by side with etchings of Washington and Lincoln. Surely you must know why all things German have become interesting and accessible, and why our people are becoming more and more conscious of Germany, her musicians and her heroes, her scientists and her poets. Her publicists are everywhere! Paid for by Barbour-Bouchard, by Robsons & Strong, and, most probably, by Schultz-Poiret——"

Eugene, with the face of a madman, struck the bell on his desk. "America!" he cried, in a strange muffled voice, as though he were choking on blood. "America, who helped us, and gave us refuge! The Government that trusted us, encouraged us, relied upon us!" A clerk ran in with a white face, for Eugene's voice had penetrated beyond his office. "Call my carriage!" cried the poor man, beside himself. "America! You are a liar, Honore, a foul liar! I do not believe you! You lie!" In his native language he called his son foul and unspeakable names. "No, do not touch me, you swine, you liar! I do not believe you! I cannot have been so blind, such a fool, that even a child, a miserable youth, must enlighten me! Mary in Heaven, I shall kill that man, that cursed Englishman! Where is my carriage!" He stamped and screamed. Honore, terrified, appalled at what he had done, tried to hold him and control him. "How he has deceived me, knowing me for the imbecile I am! I might have known that he, who deceives everybody, would deceive me! Heart of Jesus, where is my carriage!"

The next few minutes, to the trembling and self-loathing Honore, were a succession of ghastly blurs, in which Eugene lashed about when his son and his clerks tried to hold him. Honore implored him to take him in his carriage, but Eugene, snatching the whip from his coachman's hand, slashed savagely at his son with it. He was driven away, still brandishing the whip. The clerks assembled in the offices, aghast but enjoying, and whispered together, conjecturing what had caused this sudden madness in Eugene, and expressing the wildest theories, none of which came even remotely near the truth.

Honore, now too ill physically as well as mentally to return to his laboratory, sat at his father's desk, trying to control his violent trembling, wetting his lips, covering his face with his hands, cursing himself with the deepest fervor and sincerity. Mother, he thought, will never forgive me for this. He is sick, he doesn't know what he is doing. God, what will he say to Uncle Ernest, what will be the outcome of this? God curse me!

But when the carriage arrived at the Barbour-Bouchard Building, Eugene was found lying on the cushions in a broken grotesque attitude, and when they lifted him up they found he was dead.

Archbishop Aloysius Dominick read of Eugene's death in the newspapers and sent a telegram of condolence to the widow. He thought to himself, sadly and grimly: "Not only does that man deal out death to the world, but he also deals out death to those about him."

CHAPTER XCIX

GODFREY SESSIONS, self-absorbed, delicate and selfishly remote from reality, knew nothing of his mother's complete despair and wild grief when she received the news, both from Florabelle and the newspapers, of Ernest's marriage to her cousin, Amy. He had his lessons, his friends as selfish and chill and absorbed in themselves as he, his concerts and his pale arctic excitements. His demands on his mother were rigorous, for he had an exceptionally large amount of self-pity, and she must constantly encourage, soothe, cajole, pet and sympathize with him, share his indignations no matter with what sadness she observed how petty they were, pretend to a passion she did not feel for music, suffer the visits of his friends and entertain them, though even her inexperience saw how mediocre and stupid many of them were, how utterly ill-bred and boorish and whiningly predatory for all their reverential talk of their "art." Godfrey was a pouter; when the smallest thing displeased him or the smallest obstacle demanded a part of his immediate attention, he flung himself about in distraction, emitting loud wails and bitter denunciations against a brutal and greedy world. He was erratic and childish, complaining and melancholy, brooding and icily passionate by turns, sometimes not speaking to his mother for days if she displeased him in the least or gently criticized the more atrocious of his friends.

But when the name of her son, Godfrey Sessions, appeared more and more frequently in the French newspapers, when more and more of his compositions were played by great orchestras, then May felt that she was repaid for her devotion and financial outlays and sacrifices, and even for the crushing loneliness of her days and the scalding tears of her nights.

When she received the news of Ernest's remarriage, Godfrey remarked with the icy rage that was so much a part of his character: "I expected no better of that beast and that woman." He dismissed the subject with that phrase and a single gesture. He was much perturbed and affronted that May could not dismiss it so. Really, his actions and his expression implied, she was being very tedious and annoying, with her weeping and her broken words and her hand-wringing; could she not see that she was causing him irritation and impatience? Pouting and tossing his head, he packed a small portmanteau and retired to a nearby little hotel for nearly a week, with great dignity and offended manner, giving his mother to understand that he would return only when she was sure she would no longer annoy and bore him. He expected to hear from her within two days at the most, but after six days when he still had not heard from her, he returned, prepared to forgive if she showed sufficient contrition and signs of behaving herself. He found May silent and haggard, but kind and considerate as usual, and he was too selfish and petty to know of or care for her torment and anguish. However, she never felt her old complete devotion for him again, and while she pitied him for his constitutional blindness she knew that she was more alone now than she had ever been before in all her life.

May's income was lavish enough for her to afford an immense suite in a family hotel on the Champs-Élysées, a hotel noted for its vast lobby with black marble pillars, thick dark red carpets and gilding, crystal chandeliers and wide stately curving white marble staircases, and expert servants. She employed four servants of her own, a chambermaid, a personal maid, a coachman and a valet for Godfrey. Each day she drove in her Victoria down the Champs-Élysées and through the Tuileries Gardens and the Bois, her parasol tilted over her tiny hat, her eyes interested and smiling mechanically. She still loved beautiful objects, and her suite was exquisitely ornamented and furnished by herself. But eventually, she observed to herself, there is a saturation point even in buying, and when one's wardrobes are filled to bursting with fine garments one seldom has the occasion to wear, and one's house is perfect in every detail, one simply can't shop any longer. And after awhile one tires of travelling about Europe and listening to music, music, music, until one's brain dances in a maze of bars and notes, and symphonies become something which one finally endures with intense distress. She had few acquaintances, even among American residents, and though she gave to charities and tried to interest herself in the wretched and the indigent, and entertained Godfrey's "unspeakable" friends, her boredom and loneliness became a physical agony. She was in that state of mind when the news about Ernest arrived, and thereafter she went about in a sort of numb stupor, in which everything she did was automatic and life became only a vague gray dream of grief and pain.

She suddenly realized that though Ernest had divorced her, and though she had allowed him to do so, he not even being chivalrous and kind enough after nearly thirty-four years of marriage to give her the privilege of divorcing him, she had believed in her heart that he had a deep affection and regard for her, more than he realized himself, and that a separation from her would bring him to his senses, where he would acknowledge that he was too old for passion and needed her companionship and good-tempered understanding more than he needed satisfaction in "love." She saw now, with what anguish and deathly despair only she knew, that she had discounted his love for Amy too much, and that even a man in his fifties might remember old passion and need old love. I cannot live any more, she thought simply, from the depths of her suffering, everything is dead for me. But I do not blame him; I blame myself, and Gregory. Gregory should have understood what sort of man Ernest was, and I should never have married him knowing he did not love me.

The tragic deaths of Gertrude and Guy had not caused her half this grief, and she understood only too well that her leaving Ernest after Gertrude's death had been the pathetically childish desire of a middle-aged woman for the consolations and tendernesses of a beloved husband who had turned cold and indifferent. But there was no chance of that now. With indifference and complete forgetfulness of her, Ernest had finally married the only woman he had ever wanted. What shall I do now? she asked herself. And went about asking over and over, until it became a chorus to the terrible days and nights: What shall I do now?

She heard from her friends and relatives in America very often. She was much distressed at hearing of Eugene's death from a heart attack, for she had always liked him because of his innate kindness and integrity, which few people suspected, and because she had been one of two or three others who had any idea of the constant uneasiness and vague distress in which he had lived. May, however, had never liked Dorcas; she had always maintained that: "Dorcas is, I grant you, a very ladylike person, but hardly, considering her antecedents, a lady." May suspected the true aristocracy of delicate, dignified and exquisite women whose fathers had been laboring-class nonentities. A true aristocrat herself, she well knew that thoroughbreds are not normally born of plow-horses. Nevertheless, though recalling Dorcas' indifferent coldness and inability to feel real sympathy or tenderness or compassion for any one outside her immediate family circle, she felt great sorrow for her. She wrote her a long and affectionate letter, forgetting her own private sufferings, for she knew that Dorcas' husband had been her whole life. She received no reply to this warm and generous letter, and she was not hurt, understanding grief too well. But she was exceedingly shocked to receive, a few months later, a black-bordered letter from Florabelle telling of Dorcas' death.

"Dorcas died, I do believe, when Eugene died," wrote the voluble Florabelle. "She had never been the same. Even her children did not interest her. Of course, I visited her a great deal, and tried to comfort her, and recalled my own sorrows to her, and how bravely I bore them, as the dear Major said, and how I refused to be completely cast down, to the extent of forgetting my dear children and all my obligations as a wife and mother, and the duty I owed my long-enduring friends and the community at large, to wear a brave calm face in the midst of misfortune, to remember that sorrow is our common lot, and trouble our daily companion, and—" May, with the tears on her soft withered cheeks, skipped several paragraphs of this very hastily, and arrived at the short and final information that Dorcas had contracted the influenza in the winter, developed lung fever, and had died within twenty-four hours.

Florabelle later wrote that Etienne, "who is really too handsome for words, dear May, even if he is my nephew and I ought not to say so, had secured a minor but substantial rôle in a fine play in New York, and sent home dozens of favorable press notices. It was rumored that he was to go to London within a year with the same company. And do not think at all that Etienne is a fool, for he is really very sharp, and he and Honore are hardly on speaking terms any longer because of the terms of Eugene's will, which made Ernest and Honore, who is nearly three years younger than Etienne, joint executors. Etienne demanded to see all the books and accounts, and went over them all minutely, and it was only after long persuasion and pressure on dear Ernest's part that Etienne consented, as one of the major stockholders, to vote for Honore to become president of the Kinsolving Arms Company. I honestly believe that if he had not been offered the part in that play he would have wanted to be president himself, but dear me, these men are so tiresome with their petty jealousies. As for Renee, the ugliest, scrawniest, gangling, dark-faced old maid imaginable! I never could see that she even had the fine eyes everyone remarks upon, and she is so wild-mannered, so strange and flyaway, and careless about her clothes, that, dear May, you must forgive me, she reminded me of poor Trudie just a little, though, of course, dear Trudie had a sort of small fine elegance that big stringy Renee never had. Andre and Antoinette are living with me now, and that horrible hideous old Bouchard house is being pulled down. And I do believe, and isn't it delicious? that my own dear Leon and Antoinette are becoming quite serious about each other, and she is so lovely, that child, like Dresden china. Andre is one of Leon's assistants in the bank, and Leon thinks very highly of him indeed. My darling Chandler is doing excessively well at Princeton, but declares himself deeply interested in that most dreadful place, the factory. And my dear darling Betsy, at nineteen (and a beauty, I do declare, almost as pretty as I was, so my dear extravagant Major insists), will any day announce her engagement to the Major's nephew, Henrik. Of course, Henrik is not too wealthy, but his father, Johan Van Ryn, was a descendant of Rembrandt's cousin, and the family is impeccable. The Major declares he will give the young couple a present of seventy thousand dollars when they marry. Did I tell you that Francois has just had a volume of poems printed, in the most elegant red morocco you can imagine?

"Did I tell you in my letter last week that I have seen your Reggie? He was in Windsor, on heavens knows what business, but I saw him on Evergreen Road driving the most atrocious country carriage, with his wife. Heavens, what a pair, like those old Puritans we read about in

school, Reggie with a wide-brimmed black hat and the blackest beard!
and black flapping pantaloons and long black coat, and his Amish wife in
her bonnet and shawl! They had their two little girls with them, lovely
little creatures, and it is such a shame to dress the little fairies like that,
in those hideous bonnets and long dragging skirts. Simply caricatures,
dear May. You mentioned that Joey seldom writes. Well, he is in the
bank also, now, as you probably know, working side by side with Dorcas'
Andre. John Charles is second vice-president at the bank, and resents it
very much that he is subordinate to Leon. I always detested John
Charles. They do say that it won't be many years before Leon is president. And at the next meeting of the stockholders, it is certain that my
wonderful Jules will be elected president of the Sessions Steel Company.
If only my sweet sainted Philippe were here! But one must remember
one's blessings, I suppose, and my other children are all a mother could
desire. The Major calls me Cornelia and her jewels.

"A few days ago I saw Elsa in her carriage, shopping, and your darling
little granddaughter Alice was with her. I asked for a photograph of
the child, as you suggested I should, and when I secure one from Elsa I
shall send it to you, though I still don't see why you feel you cannot ask
for it yourself. Alice is now nearly six years old, and all dark-red curls,
the way yours used to be, though we all thought she would be a blonde,
like me and Dorcas, and the prettiest dark blue eyes. How sad that she
does not know her grandmama! Elsa is very stout, and unfriendly, I
suppose on account of Jules, for Jules and Paul haven't spoken to each
other in a social way for over two years now. And Elsa, though she is
barely thirty-five, has considerable gray hair. She is the type of woman
who grows old quickly.

"We rarely see Paul, except at a distance at soirees and receptions and
parties, and he, too, is stout and getting somewhat gray. Such an unpleasant young man, not at all agreeable, at least, not to me, his aunt.
However poor mild Martin could have been the father of such as Elsa
and Paul and John Charles is quite beyond me. Why, Martin was as
meek and sweet as new butter!

"Lucy and her husband were in town for Christmas, bringing their
boy with them. Thomas is a great boy now, nearly ten years old, and
not a Barbour at all. Lucy has turned out to be a very pleasant young
woman, and New York has certainly improved her, for she is amiable
now and interested in the family. However, she is quite stout and losing
her looks."

There were more pages of this. And then, at the bottom, very cautiously for the indiscreet Florabelle: "I do not see much of Amy, but she
is looking very well, for a woman of her age, and a grandmother. Ernest
came alone to dinner last night, for John Charles and Joey have not been
feeling very well lately, and Amy couldn't come, and one has to be so cau-

tious these days, with all this typhoid about, and the newspapers screaming that Ernest is really responsible for it all, not attending to the shacks of his workers and draining off the swamps down near the river where they live, and so many of them dying of the epidemic. Ernest himself isn't looking any too well, and is quite thin. He works entirely too hard, we think, and his hair is quite white. He is showing his age, I am sorry to say."

May put down this letter, as she did all the others, with the feeling that she had come an exhausting way through tangle and brush and hot sterile stretches just to reach an unsatisfying oasis where the water was bitter and scalding and the date-palms heavy with dust.

CHAPTER C

MAY RECEIVED a ceremoniously autographed copy of *Poems of Melancholy* by her nephew, François Bouchard, "elegantly bound in red morocco," stamped in gilt. She was too kind and gracious a woman, even in her thoughts, to lay the book aside with a smile: she was not only curious as to what François had written, but also conscientious. She had always been a little sorry for François, thin and brown and neurotic, with his feverish black eyes and thick black hair and dry brown lips which he was continually wetting. He was "the Jesuit" forgetting his cruelty and becoming afflicted with a sort of inward St. Vitus's dance.

The poems were not too bad, but embarrassingly amateurish to the eye of an adult mind; in places they were exceedingly turgid, grandiloquent, heavily despairing, or banal. But there were a few lines that caught May's attention, amazing her, making her wonder that such a youth as Francois, innocent and egotistic, could have written such a thing:

> "O tell me not that memory is life!
> It is but death,
> Aware of itself!"

And that is what my life is: "death aware of itself," she thought, with grief-stricken and astonished realization. She put the book aside, as though it had burned her. O God, if I did not have any memories! If I did not remember the children around the dining-room table where my father ate his dinners: Frey and Gertrude, Reginald and Guy, and Joey! Christmas dinners, with the turkey and the ham steaming on the table, and the silver bowls of nuts and apples and sweets, and the fire on the mahogany panelling, and the even rim of white on the window sills, and the snow falling and falling and the frozen trees snapping! And the sleighbells out on the drive, and friends and relatives arriving with bundles and baskets, and everyone laughing and shouting and stamping snow from his boots, and kissing, and turning hard cold red cheeks to be kissed—all the things that make home, and which nothing can ever replace. And Ernest, standing with his legs apart, back to the fire, young Ernest, middle-aged Ernest, old Ernest, but always the Ernest I loved——!

Her restlessness and despair were worse, now, for it was Christmas again, Christmas in Paris, with a long gray rain falling and splashing hollowly in the gutters, and carriages sliding by and umbrellas and alien voices. Godfrey, as usual, was absent, for his Second Symphony was to be played in the Opera on Christmas Day and he was busy attending rehearsals, unaware of time or mother or obligations, or even food and sleep. He would not be home, even for dinner, and May was allowing her servants the day off and intended to eat her lonely dinner in the great drafty dining room of the apartment-hotel. After that, she would drive to the Opera and hear the symphony, though her weary mind and tired body shuddered at the prospect.

As the ormolu clock on the black marble mantelpiece in her living room chimed one o'clock, May sighed, and began to consider whether to wear her black velvet or her dark blue gown, and whether pearls or diamonds were the more suitable. The rain ran in quicksilver streams down her silk-curtained windows, and she could hear the clop-clop of horses drearily trudging through the rain on the street below, and the rumble of carriage wheels. The fire had become low, and seemed to lurk sulkily behind its bars. She could hear the clock ticking loudly, the run and pelt of the storm, the faint dropping of coals, her own breathing. And nothing else.

All at once she thought: I am a lonely old woman in a strange house in a strange country among strangers, and the strangest of them all is my son! Not even he wants me, and there is not a soul to care whether I die in this room this very moment or not. And I have not been a bad wife or a bad mother! I have loved my home and my children and my husband, and brought to them humor and tenderness and understanding and charity. And in my old age, in spite of all the maxims and the proverbs, I have been left alone, an old woman with tears splashing down on her plump bosom, and a lonely dinner waiting for her downstairs in a lonely empty dining room, prepared for her by strangers.

She wiped her eyes and told herself despairingly that she could not attend that symphony. Godfrey would not know whether she were there or not, and he never asked her opinion of his compositions. And yet, she could not stay here, alone! She rose to her feet, filled with panic in the rain-darkened room, and clenched her hands to her heart, breathing heavily.

There came a loud shrill peal from the door-bell, splintering the silence into jagged fragments. May was so startled that she dropped her handkerchief, and her heart began to race. It could not be Frey, and it certainly was not any of her very casual acquaintances, who would not think of a lonely old woman on Christmas Day who apparently had wealth and position enough to entertain herself. She went to the door, for not one of the servants was in the apartment, and opened it herself, her knees trembling.

A tall, gaunt, rain-drenched young woman stood there, with great black eyes in a thin sallow face, rain-wet black hair streaking about her bony cheeks, hat tipped drunkenly over her forehead, the plumes running with water, and her badly fitting coat so hastily fastened that two large pearl buttons were riding up under her chin without the detention of the buttonholes opposite, now occupied by other buttons. Her boots were already leaving wet stains on the red carpet, and behind her, astonished but polite, lurked a small bellboy pulled lopsided by the weight of a vast and untidy-looking portmanteau, seemingly about to burst at the fastenings. The whole air of the young woman was one of febrile and haphazard forgetfulness, as though she found clothes an intolerable nuisance, out necessary, she supposed; she had a breathlessness which one suspected was quite common to her, and the manner of an absent-minded innocent who found life just a little too much at times, too exacting and exasperating.

May stared, blinking and incredulous. "Renee!" she burst out at last in a faint voice.

"Yes, Renee. How are you, darling Aunt May?" And the wet and astonishing young woman planted a vehement and very damp kiss on May's cheek. "I just arrived in Paris this morning, to spend Christmas with you, and—well, here I am! Darling Aunt May, kiss me again! You haven't changed a bit! Oh, bother, yes, boy—garçon—put the bag down anywhere. Anywhere! Aunt May, have you a franc? Let us get rid of this little wretch!"

In a mist of confusion, May led Renee into her own bedroom, helped her to unpack and change to dry clothes (the while Renee jerkily and vehemently chattered), and thought: She will, of course, sleep with me. What on earth will Frey say, and he so sensitive, and Renee so nerve-racking and noisy and talkative and untidy, but the dearest girl!

But when Renee, in wrinkled dry clothes consisting of a hideous shapeless black frock with crushed drapery at the back and a twisted white collar none too clean, and big black boots badly in need of cleaning, and sleek straight black hair confined sketchily in a net, and two huge pearls in her big brown ears, was sitting before the fire and sipping hot sweet coffee, the room no longer seemed desolate and abandoned, the fire crackled redly, and even the rain added a warm and protecting touch to the wintry afternoon.

She chattered on in her loud jerky nervous voice, seeming to run with febrile violence from one subject to another like one pursued. Her great dark eyes, soft and shimmering and heavily fringed, added beauty to the long thin colorless face with its big colorless mouth. Her long bony hands, with their prominent knuckles, gestured continually with motions oddly foreign. But May, smiling and happy and relaxed, thought what

a pity it was that no one ever had realized what intelligence and kindness and understanding integrity lived in the plain, almost "horsey"
face; and that should someone take the care to dress the poor girl appro-
priately, perhaps in dark red velvets and severe smooth broadcloths, and
pile the sliding hair high in shining swirls, Renee would have been decidedly distinguée. Then, behind the swift animation, the almost convulsive energy of Renee's face and manner, May, used to sadness herself,
saw sadness and pain, and remembered that Renee had worshipped her
father. And now she had neither father nor mother, and was keeping a
lonely house for her brother Honore, who was too busy to know she was
alive. "It is just a small house," Renee was saying, with her strained
laugh that revealed her square white teeth, "on Crescent Road, you know,
one of those new things with dormer windows and long dreary doors
and wooden fretwork and belfries. Only eight rooms, and three servants,
but then, it is big enough for Honore and myself, and has two extra
bedrooms, for when Etienne comes home, which is not often, and brings
a guest."

Renee had come to England with one of her few friends, quite unexpectedly: "But then, it was so lonely at home, and I couldn't bear
another Christmas without my—Papa; and now this Christmas there
won't even be Mama— And I thought, 'why not go over to Paris and
see dear Aunt May and Frey?' and so here I am! Oh, Anita won't mind;
she's going to Scotland, where she has a great-aunt and uncle, and I
couldn't bear to think of Scotland, after England. England was bad
enough—" She smiled broadly, but May again saw the loneliness and
fear and grief behind that smile.

"Stay with me, dearest Renee," said May impulsively. She took the
girl's warm bony hand and held it in her trembling palms. "I'm a foolish,
self-pitying old woman, but I'm lonely, and I've always loved you, my
dear. And Frey—he'll not even notice you're here, unless you like
music— You do? Then he'll be captivated and you'll hear enough music
to satisfy you all the rest of your life."

Renee's smiling face suddenly changed to horror. "But how dreadful
I am, Aunt May! I haven't told you: Joey and John Charles are very ill
with typhoid fever, though Joey was believed to be getting better just as
I left four weeks ago! But John Charles was very low, and Aunt Amy
was taking care of them——"

"Joey?" May's face went gray and pinched, and a sickness rose up in
her. "Joey? But he must be better, or I should have heard!"

"Of course! He was getting better four weeks ago. But it is such a
terrible epidemic, and the people all say it is Uncle Ernest's fault, which
is ridiculous, though he absolutely refused to do anything about the
water supply for his workmen, and it is so marshy where they live, and

the doctors have been warning that if he does not do something the epidemic will spread and nothing will stop it. But he says 'Stuff and non-sense'—you know Uncle Ernest."

"Yes, I know 'Uncle Ernest,' " said May through pale lips.

"And then when Joey and John Charles took it, and others took it, he had the water supply attended to, but it was too late. The Philadelphia papers are just screaming for his blood, and he's suing one of them, and now even the New York papers are dancing like dervishes, and there's an investigation."

May, suddenly prickling all over with deadly fear, rang the service bell. When an attendant came she wrote a cable with hands that were cold and shaking. It was addressed to Ernest, and asked to be informed of Joey's condition.

This done, she sat down and tried to concentrate on Renee's chatter, but a dreadful presentiment was upon her, and her whole body shivered and became icy. I shall be violently ill if I don't control myself, she said over and over in her thoughts, trying to listen to Renee. Her hands would clasp themselves together convulsively and she would swallow dryly to keep from screaming aloud.

Then, crossing her own cable, a cable from Ernest arrived that night just as May began to light the lamps and the servants were returning.

It read, briefly: "Joey died this morning at ten o'clock. John Charles died three days ago." Only that, no attempt being made to soften the blow, no concern shown for the mother of his son.

But May, in her own agony of grief, forgave even this, for in Joey's death Ernest had lost his last hope in his children. His son had died almost by his own willing and his own hand, just as Guy had died, and Gertrude had died.

RENEE ATTENDED May with devotion during the month's illness that kept the poor woman in bed. She was suffering from shock, nervous breakdown and grief. Her condition was such that she ceased to care for Godfrey's feelings, as to what his sensations were with regard to Renee's arrival and residence in the apartment, and the inconvenience and disorder and confusion that illness brought with it.

But to her languid amazement, she discovered that after the first upheaval and indignation, Godfrey settled down happily to the new conditions. It is true that for several weeks he was very distant and formal to his cousin, and avoided his home ostentatiously, not appearing for meals, and showing, when he was obliged to be there, only the faintest solicitude for his mother and very little consideration for Renee. His entire unspoken attitude was that he considered the whole thing, including his brother's death, a fiendishly designed plot to disarrange his tranquillity and disturb his comfort. He walked about with an indignant manner and a lofty resentful face. However, he had controlled his first hysteria, and was very silent and dignified, making no trouble at all, and keeping his friends away.

Renee tried kindness, humor, placation, interest in music, patience and smiles, without any result save blank stares and curled lips. Then one night, after leaving May's bedroom and seeing that her aunt was asleep, she encountered Godfrey sulking in the living room, a blank score and a pencil upon his knee. He made as if to get up and flee as usual at the advent of his cousin, but she suddenly placed her strong young hands on his delicate shoulders and forced him roughly back into his chair. Then, standing over him as he blinked below her, and keeping her voice steady and quiet, she said: "You are a pig. Only a pig. Not even the shadow of a man. Only a pig." And she looked down at him with her beautiful eyes suddenly fierce with contempt and vivid with disgust.

Then she went away, walking firmly, to the kitchen, to supervise the preparing of the menu for the next day. She did not look back at Godfrey, huddled and astounded in his chair.

Godfrey went out and did not return for three days, in which Renee frantically lied to May about his whereabouts. On the third day he returned, and Renee met him in the hallway. Her face was very pale and thin. her eyes shadowed with sleeplessness and anxiety. When she saw

her cousin, her expression lightened with passionate relief, followed instantly by another expression of scorn and anger. She tried to pass him,
but to her surprise, he took hold of her arm. She saw, with increasing
amazement, that he was smiling. He had never smiled at her before, and
all at once he seemed singularly beautiful and sweet-faced to the girl.

"You are quite right, Renee," he said softly. "I am a pig. Only a pig.
I'll never change, except this time I realize my piggishness. Do you
think you can put up with me, now?"

And he kissed her white and sunken cheek tenderly, as he had never
kissed any one, not even his mother, before.

She burst into tears of exhaustion and relief, and felt something infinitely warm and lovely which she could not understand. She clung to
him, her face pressed to his, her tears running down his own cheek. And
he cried with her, as they stood there, their arms about each other.

CHAPTER CII

MAY, DURING her period of convalescence, thought of Ernest and Amy, and said to herself: I have tried to hate both of them, but I can't. I wish I could. But hate seems very petty in the face of life, like a child spitting at a mountain. She tried to recall some poem she had read somewhere: didn't it say something about there not needing to be a villain, that "passions spin the plot," and that we "are betrayed by what is false within"? But why false? A man surely is hardly responsible for the bend and shape and pattern of his character; at the best he can only disguise them, and that, even if the results are good, is hypocrisy. Ernest had been no hypocrite, and neither had Amy. Ernest had allowed his innate pattern to develop, with great destruction, however, to everyone and everything that had come near the borders of that pattern. But even his ability to allow the forming of the pattern had been part of his nature. It was very confusing; apparently the safe citizens, the upright, fine citizens, were only hypocrites deliberately distorting the innate shape of themselves. Civilization, then, was only a mass of twisted and tortured patterns, and it was only when war came or hate or greed, that the patterns straightened out convulsively and were their original shapes.

As she lay in her bed slowly recovering, May's tears washed out the acid outlines of her resentment and grief and hatred, and eventually she could feel sorry for Amy, who had also lost a son. May very well knew that Amy's children were alien to her, and this seemed a grief greater even than death. I have never understood my own children, she thought, but I have always loved them and they have loved me, even poor Joey, at the last. He really missed me when I went away, and Ernest would be surprised at his letters. But Amy's children have never loved her.

What is her life with Ernest? May thought, not without the old pain. What can she give him that I didn't? Some day he will learn that all devotion and love are the same, and it doesn't matter in the long run who gives them, so long as they are given. He is getting old; he will learn all this before very long. Even the memory of passion can become a weariness and a bore, and such a sentimental word as "affinity" can be something to remember with an embarrassed giggle.

May knew she could never be really happy again, that both her age and her losses and her experiences had made pure happiness impossible. But she was feeling something very like peace and contentment these

711

days. It was obvious to her after awhile that Renee and Godfrey were
in love.

Renee really knew a great deal about music, and her few gaps were
filled in by a passion for it. She gave Godfrey and his music all of her
fierce dark devotion. May's interest had been like a face determinedly
smiling, until the facial muscles had ached, but Renee needed no pretense. She flowed around Godfrey's tortuous personality like water,
content to follow the channels and the rushing cataracts. She made herself more quiet, more quiescent, following, yet retaining, her own identity. Never at any time did she irritate or annoy him or get in his way,
but when the occasion seemed necessary he could not turn her back nor
make her flow another way. She told May, quite seriously, that Godfrey
reminded her of her father, which convulsed May internally, for surely
no two men were less alike.

Just at this time the armaments industry was being investigated with
grim thoroughness by the French Government, and the papers were full
of the news. Ernest Barbour's name was frequently mentioned, and
once an old photograph of his, taken more than twenty years ago, appeared among other photographs of munitions manufacturers in the
papers. May cut out the dimmed print and put it away among her things.
She was not much interested in the investigation, but whenever she read
Ernest's name a thrill ran along her tired nerves and the old ache came
back. It never occurred to her that anything serious might happen to
him, for to her he seemed invincible. After awhile the investigations
began to dwindle, and his name no longer appeared.

In March, Godfrey and Renee were married at the American Embassy, very quietly. Only a few friends were there, and Renee, in vivid
blue velvet, with a white lace collar, and a blue hat wreathed in white
plumes, looked almost beautiful, so vivid and flaming were her dark
face and brilliant eyes. She had gained weight, and needed no artificial
padding to fill out her figure. The papers carried the news to America,
and two days later a cable arrived from Ernest expressing his pleasure
at the marriage, intimating he would like the young couple to come home
for a visit, on their honeymoon, and informing them that he had ordered
Cartier's to deliver a diamond tiara to Renee, and his Paris bank to
deliver an enormous check to Godfrey, as his gifts to them. May read
the cable, but her son and his young wife were already on the Riviera.
Ernest wastes no time on old animosities and old failures, she thought,
and perhaps that is the secret of his power. He always goes on from
where he is.

Now that she was alone again, the ancient sickness of mind, the old
longing and loneliness and sorrow, came back. It was spring in Paris,
but there was no pleasure in it for this woman getting old in a strange
country. She had lived here nearly four years but was still a stranger

without peace and without roots. She thought of America with poignancy and nostalgia, and even its faults seemed endearing to her. How did any one find it possible to forget the place where he had been born, to find any real sustaining comfort under alien skies, to learn all the nuances of alien tongues, to discover friends among alien faces? It was not possible, and the complete cosmopolitan was the complete alien. A man who found a home wherever he was never really had a home anywhere. He was like one of those Japanese plants without roots, that needed only air and a little water to grow in any land, but had no substance in itself, no strength, no roots to weld the soil and make it firm and a foundation on which to build an enduring home.

All May's roots were in the Sessions house, and in Windsor, where she had married and given birth, and had laid away her dead. All her substance, her flesh, was there. This ornate, carved, red-carpeted, gilded apartment on the Champs-Élysées was not home. These streets were not home. And as the days went on the nostalgia became an increasing throb and ache, like a growing abscess.

Then one dim green evening, two years later, when the sky was like pale polished silver, May opened her American newspaper to read that Amy Barbour, wife of Ernest Barbour, "the Armaments King," had died of typhoid fever, an epidemic which had raged, with intermissions, for years in the city of Windsor, Pennsylvania.

CHAPTER CIII

THE OLD butler did not open the white panelled door with the delicate fanlight above it. He had been replaced by a youngish man in new livery, who did not recognize this smartly dressed, plump but obviously foreign lady who was just paying off the driver of a station cab. The butler did not approve of strangers, and especially not of female strangers, and as the lady, white-haired and bright-eyed, with deep clefts in her cheeks where young dimples once had been, came into the hall, his courtesy did not decrease but his coldness grew.

"Good evening, Madam," he said frigidly, and inquiringly.

"Good evening," she replied, smiling a little. He was a trifle relieved. In spite of the foreign cut of the fashionable coat, the extra plume in the stylish hat, the scent of distinctly un-American perfume, the lady was obviously not a foreigner. Possibly a lady who travelled a great deal— "Mr. Barbour, Madam, is not—er—in the best of health lately, and after he returns home he invariably rests in his room until dinner time. He—er—has left standing orders that under no circumstances is he to be disturbed by any one or anything—except, perhaps, a fire. His own words, Madam."

"Well, I certainly am not a fire, am I?" responded the lady, with her kind and charming smile. "So, if you don't mind, I'll wait for him in the library," and without hesitation, as though she well knew her way about in that house, she walked across the hall toward the library. Amazed and apprehensive, the butler somehow got to the door before her and opened it with ceremony and anxiety. A low fire burned in the grate this early spring evening, but there was no other light. "Please don't light the lamps," said the lady. "I—I'd like to sit here awhile, in the darkness. You see, I—I know this house—quite well. I'll wait. Don't bother Mr. Barbour."

"But, Madam, you have not given me the name!" exclaimed the man, wild thoughts of female thieves, adventuresses and God knows what rioting through his mind. But she obviously knew her away about here; she spoke like a relative. He became suspicious: perhaps a relative that was not on the best of terms with the family, a poor relative. But those clothes!

"When Mr. Barbour comes downstairs, you might just send him in here, to me," said the lady. "He knows me very well. I want to—

surprise him. Just tell him a lady wishes to see him. I'm certain he won't blame you a bit!" and she smiled at him again, such a kind humorous smile, not the sort of cold convulsion of the lips with which other ladies spoke to him. All his apprehensions disappeared; she sat there by the fire, taking off her fine French gloves and loosening her furs. Her white hair glistened; the diamonds sparkled on her withered white fingers. An engraved watch was pinned by a jewelled butterfly to the shimmering black silk of her bodice. There was no doubt at all that she was a lady, and a great one, at that. The butler, feeling himself in some way drawn into a delightful conspiracy, bowed and retired. Whoever this lady was, Mr. Barbour could be only pleased to see her. Perhaps a sister, from England— Ladies were always up to these arch surprises, disturbing though they were to steadier male minds.

Left alone, the lady ceased smiling. She held out her hands to the fire in a distinctly automatic gesture. Over her shoulder, she looked slowly about the dark library. The fire evoked an arm of a chair here, the edge of a bookcase there, gilding the black and polished wood, picking out the scroll of a picture frame, glimmering on a glass door, displaying an ornament one moment only to let it fall back into shadow the next, advancing and receding over the thick dark crimson rug near the hearth. A clock, invisible in a black and distant corner, chimed with a deep softly sonorous note, and the fire crackled. The room was pervaded with a warm smell of old leather and bindings, sandlewood and furniture polish. Everything, except for the clock and the fire, was silent, not with an empty somber silence, but with the waiting, friendly, rich silence of home just before the dinner hour.

Home. The lady looked about the room, as one drinks after prolonged thirst. Home. It would always be home. Everything was the same. Not a thing had been moved or touched. The old elegance and security, the old polished beauty and dignity, were here as she remembered them. Surely nothing could be so cruel as to drive her out of this house again, her house, her home, from which she had been exiled but to which she had returned. She began to touch her eyes with the edge of her lace handkerchief. And now there was another sound in her ears, the quick painful beating of her heart, the pounding of her pulses.

She stood up and walked about the room, touching the mirror-like surface of the mahogany table with its brass feet, the back of a black leather chair with the imprint of bodies sunken into it, the crusted side of a vase, the rich heaviness of a curtain. The spring garden outside was filled with a dim white light, in which the new trees were blurred. A window stood a little ajar, and the lady could smell the pungent odor of newly thawed earth and new grass. She could see how the garden path turned toward the rear of the house: the sundial still stood there, and the arbor, and already there were frogs throbbing in the pool in the back.

All the sights and scents and touches and sounds of home! She leaned her wet cheek against the windowsill, the drawn curtain in her hand. If she just waited a minute or two, like this, she would hear Gertrude's high fluting voice above, the scrambling of Guy and Reginald in their bedroom and their affectionate quarrelsome voices; she would hear Joey's young surly rumble and the slam of his door; she would hear the faint tinkling of Godfrey's piano in the drawing room. She would hear Ernest's footsteps on the stairs, quiet, firm, slowly descending as though his foot ground on and then pushed away each stair. But surely a little quicker than that, a little firmer, than she could make this memory! A little surer, a little more determined. But she could not make the memory hurry or become firmer. Faster, faster, she thought with a sort of pain. Quicker, quicker. But the step was slow, almost as though it were a trifle uncertain.

Then, in reality, the door did open, and she saw a shadow in the dim doorway. Still at the window, still holding the curtain, she turned very slowly, almost as if her whole body had become numb. She was hidden by that curtain, hidden in the growing darkness. The shadow stood on the threshold, hesitatingly, then came into the room. "Is there someone here, waiting for me?" asked Ernest's voice, a little lower, a little slower and heavier than her memory of it.

"It is I, Ernest," she said in a faint voice. She dropped the curtain and advanced toward him. Waves of faintness rolled over her. The fire, aroused by the draft from the open door, burst into orange flame, illuminated the long dark room. It glimmered on Ernest's face, revealing it, and she saw that it was the face of an old man, now—old and hard and seamed and gray, and tired to death. But the chin was still firm as stone, and the sunken eyes, as they stared at her unbelievingly, were pale and glistening and implacable as ever.

As he stood there, gazing at her, his face wrinkling, his eyes blinking, she saw that he was almost gaunt, that his throat was withered and corded above the stiff winged collar and black cravat, that his shoulders were bony and lifted in the old man's posture under his black coat, that his hands, hanging at his sides, were clenched a little. But, even as she looked, the whole scene seemed to shift, and he was the young Ernest again, who had stood there in his youth, a stranger in the Sessions house, and behind him stood Gregory Sessions, with his Voltairean smile and his wicked eyes.

It was all a dream, all the years that had gone since the day she had first seen him, and they were back here together, young again, with children and grief and hatred and fear and pain all in the future, perhaps to be avoided. Yes, it was all a dream, even this.

"May," he said. His lips moved, and the name was hardly a sound on them.

"Yes, Ernest." She stood before him, and held out her hand. He took it. She could feel its cold dryness, and her fingers closed about it, warm firm fingers, leading him into the room.

"I've come home, Ernest. Your wife. I'll never go away again." And then, "Ernest! I've come home! Tell me you love me, just a little, a very little! Just a little will do, all the rest of my life!"

CHAPTER CIV

QUOTATION FROM *The Windsor Herald,* owned, controlled and managed by Barbour-Bouchard:

"On Tuesday evening, February 14, 1898, a reception will be held at the home of Mr. and Mrs. Ernest Barbour in honor of Mr. Barbour's seventy-first birthday. Among the illustrious guests who will be present are Mr. Jay Regan, whose late father was an intimate friend of Mr. Barbour, Mr. James Bellowes 'the Kerosene King,' Senators Geoffrey Walters and Burnsey Seaton, Mr. William Howard Taft, Governor Tom Rankin, former Governor William Trowbridge, Commodore George Vanderlip of New York, Mr. John Jacob Astor, Sir Oswald Temple-Temple, attached to the British Embassy, Count Ludwig Von Holsen, of the German Embassy, M. Etienne Beaugard, of the French Embassy, Prince Nicholas Kuropotkin, of the Russian Embassy, and Count Antony Romandi, of the Italian Embassy, Supreme Court Justice James Hilton, Secretary of War Burnside, Secretary of State Barnett.

.   .   .   .

"This is a momentous occasion for the city of Windsor, and a momentous occasion for Mr. Ernest Barbour, he having reached the age of seventy-one. It is needless to state the obvious fact that Windsor today might well be proud of Mr. Barbour, through whose genius, industry, sacrifices and true American spirit, it has become famous, and the cynosure of the eyes of the world. The story of Mr. Barbour's life is the story of America, colossal, courageous, bold, daring, determined, strong, unswerving, scornful of obstacles. Mr. Barbour stands among the industrial giants of this mighty age, individually unique, a figure for all posterity to admire.

"Ernest Barbour was only a young immigrant boy when in the year 1837 he arrived with his parents on these shores. The Barbour family came to Windsor because of the presence here of an uncle, Mr. George Barbour, who, with one Armand Bouchard, had started the embryo firm of Barbour-Bouchard. Mr. Joseph Barbour, father of Ernest, was admitted as a partner in the little gunpowder business, which at that time occupied a small wooden two-room building near the river. From this humble beginning, Mr. Ernest Barbour has built up the great Barbour-Bouchard Company, and its subsidiaries, among which are the Sessions

Steel Company, the Kinsolving Arms Company and the Amalgamated Chemical Company. Mr. Barbour is also a director of four major railroads, three coal companies, and three banks.

"There will also be a 'gathering of the clans' on this felicitous occasion. There will be present: Mr. Paul Barbour, Vice-President of Barbour-Bouchard, son-in-law of Mr. Ernest Barbour; Miss Alice Barbour, daughter of Mr. Paul Barbour and granddaughter of Mr. Ernest Barbour; Miss Elsa Barbour and Mrs. Percival Van Eyck, niece of Mr. Barbour; Mr. Percival Van Eyck of New York; Mr. Thomas Van Eyck, his son; Mr. Jules Bouchard, President of the Sessions Steel Company, and his wife, the former Adelaide Burgeon of this city, and their three sons, Pierre, Emile and Christopher; Mr. François Bouchard, the famous poet; Mr. Leon Bouchard, President of the Windsor Savings Bank, and his wife, the former Miss Antoinette Bouchard, niece of Mr. Ernest Barbour, and their children, Irene, Bertha, Georges, and Nicholas; Mr. Andre Bouchard, Vice-President of the Windsor Savings Bank, and his wife, the former Miss Beatrice Coley of this city, and their two children, Alexander and Alexa, who are twins; Major Norwood and Mrs. Norwood, and their two children, Chandler Norwood, General Manager of the Barbour-Bouchard Company, and Mrs. Henrik Van Ryn of New York; Mr. Henrik Van Ryn; Mrs. Chandler Norwood and daughter, Miss Ethel Norwood; Mr. Etienne Bouchard, the famous actor; Mr. Honore Bouchard, President of the Kinsolving Arms Company, and his wife, the former Miss Ann Richmond of New York, daughter of Mr. Bertram Richmond of the American Utilities Company, and their four sons, Francis, Jean, Henri and Peter.

"There is a possibility that General Edward Gordon will be present also, though the General is at the present time in Washington, discussing the Spanish situation with the President.

"Unfortunately, Mr. Godfrey Sessions, the famous composer, will be unable to attend the reception in honor of his father, Mr. Ernest Barbour. Mr. Sessions, it will be recalled, took his mother's maiden name for artistic reasons. He is at present in Vienna, where he is conducting a series of his symphonies and concertos before the Emperor Franz-Josef. Mr. Reginald Barbour, it is said, will also be unable to attend because of grave personal matters.

"After the reception, Mr. Barbour will lay the cornerstone of the new Martin Barbour Memorial Hospital, which will be one of the largest institutions of its kind in the State, and will be staffed by leading physicians of both Pennsylvania and New York. A fitting memorial, indeed, to the Barbour family! Mr. Barbour has interested himself in all branches of philanthropy, and this city owes its magnificent library, music hall, park, university, Home for the Indigent, stadium and orphanage to the Christian charity of this great man. Nor must we forget the Tuberculosis Sanitarium in the suburb of Lexington, and the Institute for the Study of Degenerative Diseases.

"Interviewed this morning by a representative of this newspaper, Mr. Barbour said, with his inimitable smile and graciousness: 'On this, my seventy-first birthday, I extend to all my fellow citizens of Windsor my blessings and my hope that they will carry forward the things I have only begun. If I can leave them nothing more than my philosophy that Hard Work, Industry and Vision, Sacrifice and Faith are the bedrock of all success and accomplishment, I shall have left them everything.'"

CHAPTER CV

ONE FINE DAY early in 1898, Jules Bouchard read and reread a telegram which he had just received from Washington.

"FIFTY PORTRAITS YOU DESIRED WILL BE DELIVERED AS ORDERED. JOHNSON AND I HAVE FINALLY SWUNG DECISION OF OUR PARTNERS FROM FIFTEEN TO FIFTY THOUGH CONSIDERABLE DIFFICULTY MIGHT BE ENCOUNTERED AT LAST MOMENT TO PREVENT YOU SECURING COPIES ANTICIPATED. YOUR AGENT WORKING HARD. MISTER DIAGO BUYING FIRST EDITIONS FROM OLD FRIEND WHO THANKS YOU FOR CUSTOMER. RUSH HIM FIRST EDITION DICKENS AT ONCE. HIS COPY VERY INFERIOR IT IS RUMORED."

Jules displayed a lively interest in this remarkable telegram, which might indeed have gained the attention of such an ardent bibliophile as the President of the Sessions Steel Company. It was signed: "Gibbons Rare Book and Miniature Company." Jules also was becoming a rather well-known connoisseur of art, especially in that branch pertaining to exquisite miniatures and portraits by the old masters. His library and his small gallery had already attracted considerable attention, and he had agents in all the capitals of Europe sedulously adding to his collections. Therefore, such a telegram, while gratifying, was not unusual. He received many such, including cables.

He still studied the telegram, his long thin brown hand, with its livid polished nails, fastidiously groping in a silver cigar box which he kept on his desk in the office. Finding by touch a long thin cigar, exquisitely banded and fragrant, he lit it with delicate firm gestures. The glow of the match showed his face, that Jesuitical face, long and lean, brown and seamed, with the brilliant black eyes under the full hooded lids. There were patches of white at his sunken veined temples, though the rest of his hair was as sleek and black as sealskin. His bony large nose, with its aristocratic high arch, jutted outwards, not arrogantly, but with something of an Indian austerity. A diamond sparkled in his dark-red satin cravat; another danced on the third finger of his left hand. His body, in the elegant black broadcloth he almost always affected, was lean and disciplined. At forty, Jules Bouchard was a fascinating man.

The more he read the telegram the more his interest and gratification increased. Finally, he lifted the telephone on his desk and called the bank. He was soon talking to Leon.

"I have very pleasant news about those books," he said. "Could you spare me the time to run over here and discuss them with me, or shall I go to your office? No time like the present, you know."

There was a pause, then Leon said: "Ah! But the Old Man is still away on his cruise. No use speaking of books until he gets back. Unless——"

"Exactly. I'll call our friend, also. You'll be here shortly? Good. You might call Honore. He's interested in first editions, too."

He then called the office of Barbour-Bouchard. Soon Paul was connected with him. Within the last few years a smooth social and business amiability had grown up, from necessity, between the two men. Nothing, therefore, could have been blander than Jules' voice. "Paul? It is almost six o'clock and I suppose you'll be leaving the office practically immediately. I've something of interest to tell you. Could you be here within twenty minutes? Good."

He rang for his secretary, a most efficient but silent young man, who came in with just the correct mixture of obsequiousness, worship and alertness. Jules smiled at him pleasantly. "George, I've got those Gainsborough miniatures! And those Dickens first editions! I told you I'd get them after all."

Mr. George Dickinson pursed his lips with respectful dubiousness. "There's been a lot of fraud lately in those things, Mr. Bouchard," he replied.

"Do you think they can deceive me?" demanded Jules with a joviality that just missed his eyes. "I consider myself quite the expert now, George."

"I hope you aren't going to be swindled, Mr. Bouchard."

Jules seemed a little amused. "I'm never swindled, George. You had your doubts about that Goya, too, but I proved you wrong."

"Which Goya, Mr. Bouchard?" asked Mr. Dickinson, with a smile that apologized for an apparent boldness. "The first or second?"

Jules laughed. "Now, George, is that Christian? Is that kind? At any rate, you ought to thank me for a very good copy of a Goya. Do you know, if we keep on this way, you'll have the world's very best collection of splendid frauds, many of them much better than the originals from which they were copied? I tell you, the old masters are quite frequently rotten. Why, that near-Corot I gave you is genius, pure genius! Corot himself would have acknowledged himself beaten."

Mr. Dickinson smiled thinly. "The difference, sir, of course, is only in the price."

"Price? Why, damn it, I paid as much for the fraud as though it had been an original. Don't be mercenary, George. Remember to appreciate art for art's sake, not for the tag it might carry. But I didn't call you in for an art discussion. I'm wondering if you'd drop by the house and tell

Mrs. Bouchard I'll not be home for dinner, and especially not for that reception she's been planning on taking me to. So, as she is exceedingly fond of you, I'm sending you as my proxy, both to dinner and the reception. I don't know what I'd do without you, George."

The young man colored with his delight, which was a little marred at the prospect of sitting again at the table with Jules' three exuberant young sons, Pierre, Emile and Christopher. He particularly detested ten-year-old Christopher, who had a cruel and disdainful face. However, he loved gentle fragile Mrs. Bouchard, who had poise, kindness and graciousness enough for a dozen women.

"Are you certain you'll not be needing me here tonight, sir?"

"Not at all. To tell you the truth, I'm expecting an agent from New York within an hour or so, with the miniatures. Then I'm going to have a bite with Mr. Honore. Don't tell Mrs. Bouchard that, however."

After his secretary had left the room, Jules returned again to the telegram. When engrossed, he had a habit of delicately smoothing his lips with the tip of his right index finger; despite the daintiness of the gesture, it had a touch of the deadly about it. A Jesuit who loved the feel of his own flesh as he contemplated a new method of exterminating heretics.

He thought, almost irrelevantly: Señor Dupuy De Lome was right: "A pot-house politician and caterer to the rabble." When it comes to seeking the main chance and procrastinating, our dear McKinley can outdo the English. But his bumptiousness has finally overcome his pseudo-British policies. Once a bar-politician, always a bar-politician.

He opened a drawer in his desk and drew out a silver flask of Napoleon, poured a small crystal glass full. He drank it slowly, savoring each drop. And looked at the telegram, smiling.

The telegram, de-coded, had nothing whatsoever to do with portraits or books. It read succinctly: FIFTY MILLION DOLLARS WILL BE PLACED BY CONGRESS AT PRESIDENT'S DISPOSAL FOR ARMAMENTS. WE HAVE INCREASED APPROPRIATION FROM FIFTEEN TO FIFTY MILLION AFTER LONG DEBATE. HOWEVER PEACE LOBBIES MIGHT PREVENT WAR WITH SPAIN AT LAST MOMENT. ARE DOING ALL WE CAN TO STOP THIS. SPAIN TODAY ORDERED ARMAMENTS FROM ROBSONS-STRONG. INFORMATION ON BEST AUTHORITY. SEND ROBSONS-STRONG INFORMATION ABOUT YOUR NEW MACHINE GUN WHICH WE HEAR IS BETTER THAN MAXIM PATENT THEY HOLD.

"Ah," said Jules. He wiped his lips with a fine monogrammed linen handkerchief. The door opened and Leon came in, strong, shortish, brown, almost burly these days, as he approached the forties. There was a bronze-like look about the rigidity of the folds of his broad face, and a bronze-statue appearance in the deliberate blankness of his eyes. He deposited his "bowler," cane and gloves on Jules' desk, and threw his velvet-collared overcoat over a chair.

"I was afraid you might not get here before Atlas-in-pantaloons arrived," said Jules. "Read this." He pushed the telegram across the desk to his brother. Leon read it. He put it down, and smiled with pleasure. "Fifty millions, eh? Not bad at all. And now, if the Boers can just be persuaded the British are robbers. which they are, of course— Is Honore coming? I couldn't get him, but left a message. I thought he might have rung you up."

"Not yet. I hope your message reaches him before he leaves for home. By the way, I've cabled the Old Man."

"Paul'll cut your throat for this!" Leon exclaimed in enjoyment.

"Probably, unless we hang him first. By the way, how is the matter of François and little Alice coming along?"

Leon pursed his rather thick lips. "Damn it, I'm sorry for the poor little girl. Not only is François seventeen years her senior, but he's an ass into the bargain."

"His poetry," suggested Jules, "is not too bad. Someone has compared it favorably with that of François Villon."

"Damn his poetry! That is really a very nice little girl, for all she is Paul's daughter. And I don't think Trudie would care much for her daughter marrying François."

Jules smoothed his lip with his finger. "You forget, Trudie loved Philippe, who was only one step, in his way, beyond François. At least, one can't imagine François being noble for his poetry or anything else, and dying, off on some island in a leper's hut, for the sake of it. Yes, Trudie loved Philippe, who was not even as worthwhile as François."

"What makes you think she cared for Philippe?"

Jules moved his silver cigar box an inch. "I know she did. Everyone knew it, except you, you dunderhead. And then when she heard he had died, she died, too. I'm not being romantic; I know. And I've listened very carefully to what our poor old Major has had to say about the last time Trudie came to our home and heard of Philippe's death. Poor old fluffy-mind: he betrayed something quite interesting, in his innocence, but I seem to be the only one who understood it."

"Understood what?" demanded Leon irritably, picking up the telegram again and scowling at it.

"That the Old Man left-handedly killed Philippe, and incidentally his own daughter. But all this is very old. What we are interested in just at present is François and Alice. This marriage has got to take place."

"You forget that Paul may decide to marry all of a sudden. Then he'll have children, perhaps sons. Where will we be then?"

"In a very good position. Paul's children won't be the Old Man's grandchildren. They'll be Martin Barbour's."

"If you think the Old Man is not aware of your scheming——"

"But he is!" Jules was smiling, his white teeth glittering. "He loves schemers. That was the trouble with all his own children: none of them were schemers, or realists. Weaklings, all of them. Had they schemed, had they returned his duplicity with worse duplicity, had they circumvented him, he would have taken them all to his heart. They could have had anything they had wanted: Trudie could have had her Philippe, Frey his music, Reggie his Amish wife, if they had schemed, and the Old Man would finally have laughed and forgiven them. But he hates simpletons——"

"And that's why he'll object to François, who is a simpleton."

"But, remember, we are behind François and little Alice-in-Wonderland. We'll forward the romance of these innocents. We'll do the scheming for them. Only last night little Alice visited us, and was all for blurting it out to her father and grandfather, about François. I persuaded her to keep her pretty little mouth shut. As for François, he never remembers anything from day to day anyway, and so there's no danger of a premature declaration from him. You know, sometimes I think he is a better egotist than any of us, even the Old Man. He never thinks of anything whatsoever but himself, and his damned sonnets."

"Did you read that one about *My Lady's Breast?*"

"God, yes! Little Alice, who has hardly any breast at all yet, was quite confused when he read it to her last night after dinner. But don't underestimate him: he's a damned good eater, for all his poetry, and there's always hope for a man who can demolish a roast the way he did. When his stomach's stuffed he becomes almost sensible and practical. That's why he could see my point when I suggested that he and Alice elope next week. I'll buy the tickets myself."

"Elope?" Leon stared, and his dark face flushed. "Look here, you're going too far, Jules! The Old Man will kick us so far that when we return the 'Bouchard' will be rubbed out of Barbour-Bouchard!"

Jules smiled. "Bouchard and Sons," he said in a musing voice. "I like it."

Leon snatched a cigar from the box, bit off the end, spat it out savagely. "Your scheme, Cardinal Richelieu, stinks. Putting aside the human sacrifice of a perfectly nice little girl, what do you think Paul will do about it?"

"He'll do whatever the Old Man says. You think it's a dangerous step. So do I. That bloody Englishman hates us because we're French, in spite of the fact that we're also his sister's children. But he loves intrigue and scheming and ruthlessness more than he hates us. And as I said before, he knows what we're up to, and has probably already warned Paul. So, don't let your conscience persuade you that we are taking gross advantage of someone or something."

"Well, there's Alice."

"She could marry worse than François. She's just the innocent, starry-eyed and idealistic type to marry an artist, any artist, even one that writes as foul poetry as does François. If she doesn't annex him, she'll be scampering off to some damned painter or musician or novelist who is being grossly misunderstood by the world. The maternal type, who also believes in Art, and 'simply adores it,' to use her own words. So, it's much better to keep the Barbour money in the family than to have it wasted on art galleries and artists. Don't pity the child too much. A pretty little piece, I admit, but an absolute little fool."

"You've forgotten Aunt May. I think her enthusiasm about François is well under control."

"But she hasn't forgotten Trudie, who wanted that ass of a Philippe. Stop worrying, Leon."

"I'm not worrying about Alice. But I don't want to lose what we've already got."

"We won't. Remember, we've bought back several nice blocks of stock in Barbour-Bouchard which the Old Man and Paul had been kind enough to present to certain amenable senators. We three own thirty-five percent of the stock in Barbour-Bouchard and fifty-one percent in the Kinsolving Arms Company, and forty percent in the Sessions Steel Company, not to mention respectable percentages in the Galby Lumber Mills, the United Utah Railroad, the Pennsylvania State Railroad, the Eastern States Railroad, the Pennsylvania Anthracite Company, the American Chemical Products Company, and a few nice blocks in the Bellowes Oil Company. Should we three, for instance—liquidate —Barbour-Bouchard might not recover."

The door opened and Honore entered with his peculiar sea-going gait and thrust-forward head. Though only thirty-eight, he appeared older than his cousins, possibly because his hair was prematurely gray all over, and his expression was somber even when he smiled. He resembled Leon more than any one else in all the family, but he had Eugene's reserved kindliness of eye and his father's own appearance of integrity and faint uneasiness in the presence of those who were blithely unscrupulous. His broad shoulders, always so powerful, had taken a great deal of flesh upon themselves, and he appeared much heavier than he really was.

"Ah," said Jules, at the entrance of his cousin.

"What are you two devils plotting now?" asked Honore, smiling at them, but the faint uneasiness becoming definite in his expression.

"Plotting? You wrong us, my dear Honore. We brought you here for a conference. We are expecting Paul. Read this telegram."

Honore, nervously lifting the tails of his coat, sat down; he read the telegram, his long, broad brown fingers stuffing his pipe meanwhile.

"Fifty millions, eh?" he said thoughtfully, looking at Jules. "More than we expected. But what if the war doesn't come off?"

"It will. Do you think we'd let fifty millions get away from us? You might as well give orders to hire a few hundred more men immediately."

"Just for a change," said Honore, "I'd like to believe that wars are really caused by injustice, and could possibly be righteous. But don't mind me: I said 'just for a change.' Sometimes I'm childish that way."

"Looking at it that way," Leon pointed out, "Spain has been rather rough on Cuba, you know. And England is a notorious bandit, so you could hardly call the annoyance of the Boers unjust. And Japan has been irritating Russia to a nasty and justified state, the dirty little yellow curs!"

"Well, we've helped their feelings along, don't forget."

Leon shrugged. Jules smiled at his cousin through slits of eyes.

"Cheer up, Honore." He opened his desk drawer and tossed a sheet of white vellum toward the other man. "I've just received a secret draft of the Czar's prospective letter to the European Powers."

Honore, sighing faintly, adjusted glasses, for he was nearsighted.

It purported to be a letter sent by Count Muraviev to the representatives of Russia at the different European courts.

"It is the supreme duty at the present time of all states to put some limit to these unnecessary armaments and to find some means of averting the calamities which threaten the whole world. Impressed by this feeling, his majesty, the emperor, has been pleased to command me to propose to all governments accredited to the imperial court, the meeting of a conference to discuss this grave problem. Such a conference, with God's help, would be a happy augury for the opening century. It would powerfully concentrate the efforts of all states which sincerely wish to see the triumph of the grand idea of universal peace over the elements of trouble and discord. It would, at the same time, bind their agreement by the principles of law and equity which support the security of states and welfare of peoples."

"This will be sent in August to all the Powers," said Jules, as Honore laid down the letter in silence. "We expect, thereafter, that in May, 1899, delegates will assemble at The Hague to discuss this. Three points will be discussed there, disarmament, humanitarian measures and arbitration."

"And what will our agents have to say at this conference?" asked Honore, his mouth twisting slightly.

Jules touched his lips delicately with his handkerchief. He regarded his cousin with a straightforward expression. "My dear Honore, our agents, like us, their employers, are realists, not pretty dreamers! Not like the Czar, for instance. They will very reasonably point out that disarmament is impracticable, especially for Russia, threatened by Japan, and France, threatened by Germany, and noble England, of course, threatened by perfidious foes in every quarter of the globe. They will point out that there is no satisfactory division between an armament for offensive purposes and a force for national defense. There will be no agreement, for the question of national defense is outside the field of international discussion, just as yet, anyway.

"However, our agents, being civilized men, will condemn the use of bullets that 'expand in the human body,' the throwing of projectiles or explosives 'from balloons or by other analogous means, for a period of five years,' and the making use of projectiles 'whose sole object is to diffuse asphyxiating or deleterious gases.'"

Honore stared into space, a grim smile on his mouth. "Yesterday," he said, "the Old Man wired his congratulations on my new invention, poison mustard gas, and has given orders that Barbour-Bouchard immediately put it on the market."

"Yes, I understand that," Jules replied, blandly. "And from this telegram from Washington, I understand your machine gun is much better than Maxim's."

"From whom I stole the idea," Honore pointed out, still smiling.

"But of course," came Jules' smooth voice. "We're all thieves. We all get ideas from each other. That is legitimate. Incidentally, Robsons & Strong are about to supply Maxims to the Boers. However, to get on about the Czar's letter: the part pertaining to arbitration. Now, I am a firm exponent of arbitration. Arbitration, by all means. I understand that the English delegate, Sir Julian Pauncefote, will introduce a proposal for the establishment of a permanent committee of arbitration. I understand this will be accepted——"

"And what then, becomes of us armaments manufacturers? Are we to beat our swords into plowshares, and so on?" Honore's smile had become drearily contemptuous, but he watched Jules alertly.

"Oh, by no means!" responded Jules, smiling in return. "As I said before, I am all for arbitration. Nothing in the world is as good for the munitions business as committees for arbitration!"

"I call that cheap cynicism," said Honore. "But go on. You can always be relied upon for some amusing deviltry."

"Our agents," went on Jules, "will be instructed to lend grave assent to the arbitration idea. And then they will point out in substance that to preserve peace one must prepare for war."

"In other words, to avert wars one must prepare for wars."

"You put it very cleverly, Honore. The Czar's little letter will cost us a pretty penny. Bribery has gone up. But I expect we will profit a great deal by the conference which will result. In the holy cause of peace every nation will look like an arsenal. We are about to become Merchants of Self-Defense."

"A rose by any other name——" said Leon, grinning.

"As for the poison gas business," Jules went on without a glance at his brother, "of course it is not to be used except in self-defense, or in the event of invasion."

"But self-defense covers a multitude of overt acts," said Honore.

"You become cleverer every day, Honore. By the way, are you coming any closer to the formula for the German slow-burning cocoa powder?"

"I think so. I'm using the microscope now on the German sample. But I understand the British are to buy the formula from the German manufacturer for thirty thousand pounds. The British would be very nasty about us stealing formulæ for which they pay a fortune to a traitor."

"Yes, nothing can be nastier and more righteous than a Britisher when someone steals something from him which he had stolen himself. But what about the formula?"

"I think I can change it slightly, so as to maintain its explosive qualities and yet make it a little different. However, we might not have to borrow: Robsons & Strong will probably furnish us with the original formula. Provided they can get it from the other manufacturer."

"True. Incidentally, we must prove to Robsons & Strong that our machine gun is superior to theirs. Then they could sell the Maxims to the Boers, before the war breaks out, and use our machine-gun patent themselves. I'll be interested to see how they turn out in practical experience. But we'll have a chance nearer at home."

"Promoting wars abroad may be all right, but Barbour-Bouchard has never yet betrayed its Government," said Honore stubbornly. "What the hell do we care for Cuba, anyway?" He reached for his overcoat and withdrew the evening paper. "Listen to this translation of a letter published in the foremost Spanish newspaper: 'America, under a hypocritical mask of concern and solicitude for Cuba, is preparing an imperialistic program, which has for its first act the seizing of Spanish colonies. It is then just a step to seizing control of South America, and instituting a holy war in Europe, which, when the smoke clears away, will reveal America as victor and merciless exploiter. America's gospel of peace is the ambush behind which she prepares for world-conquest.'" Honore tossed the paper aside. "Who is responsible for that little article, you or Robsons?" He helped himself to one of Jules' cigars. "How much did you pay Señor Dupuy De Lome, the Spanish minister at Washington, to write that naughty letter about McKinley?"

"Nothing at all, my dear Honore! You wrong De Lome by your insinuations."

"Hum. Perhaps. It's a habit of mine to 'wrong' everyone who comes in contact with you, Jules. But what are you going to do about Mr. Bryan, who thinks we are a stink in the nostrils of the righteous, and is doing some good work denouncing the imperialistic policy of the government? You can't assassinate him, you know, Jules. Assassination isn't being done these days in the best society."

"No one listens to Bryan, at least no one with sense," Jules laughed. "However, I've just had him endorsed by the Silver Republicans, and perhaps that'll divert his mind from us. He's ambitious, is our little back-country Messiah. But we'll never let him become President."

"Where do you get this 'editorial we'?" demanded Leon, who occasionally liked to spike his brother, for all his fondness. "You seem to forget that the Old Man is still very much alive. Or have you forgotten that?"

"Not at all. I never forget anything, dear Leon. I'm not forgetting, for instance, that the Old Man hasn't a year to live. You didn't know that? He's got a heart that's running on pure nerve now, and nothing else. Aunt May knows, that is why she dragged him away before Christmas on that cruise."

Leon could not help exchanging a swift glance with Honore. He knew that Honore preferred him to Jules, and he was candidly surprised at this. What did Honore expect of him? But just then Paul Barbour came in, his face flushed and heated-looking from hurry and annoyance.

Paul's big body had taken a great deal of fat upon itself. Being very tall, and weighing well over two hundred and twenty-five pounds, Paul dwarfed his smaller, slighter cousins. In the presence of his bulk, his fair complexion, blue eyes, and gray-streaked light chestnut hair, their darkness became gnome-like, their faces foreign and too subtle, their eyes secret and not to be trusted. He was the brutal and bellicose Saxon, forthright in his villainy and heavy savagery, and they were the sly Latins, supple of mind, swift of thought, crafty, smiling, cool and deadly. Yet, for all his bulk and visible power, the belligerency in his broad flushed face and choleric blue eye, his air of competence and blind power, he seemed less potent than they, less formidable, less to be feared and suspected. They sat about Jules' desk, looking up at him in courteous smiling silence, and something about them stopped him for a moment in the very act of removing his thick fur-lined coat. His expression, prepared to be contemptuous, sharpened a little, uneasily. The color spread to his heavy, clean-shaven jowls, tinged his neck. At forty-six, Paul was already showing the effects of over-eating.

"Well," he said, half enquiringly, half in irritation. "What is this weighty conference to which I have been invited? And why couldn't it have been at my office?"

A glance flicked between the brothers and Honore. But Jules was suavity itself.

"Please sit down, Paul. We all wished to have a talk with you, and as my office is the most central we decided to meet here. Will you have a cigar?"

"One of those poison strings you affect, Jules? No, thank you."

"You are very wise, Paul," said Honore, smiling at him. Paul smiled back, grudgingly. He feared and hated Jules, merely hated Leon, but sometimes almost liked Honore. He often said to Elsa that somehow a fellow might find it possible to trust Honore. However, he had less respect for Honore than he had for Jules and Leon. Mistakenly, he believed he might, if given the opportunity, browbeat and subjugate Honore, and therein lay his liking for him, and also a slight contempt.

He lit one of his own cigars, offered one to Honore, who accepted. Jules sat back in his chair, smiling amiably. He had lit the gas globes overhead, and they shone down on his sleek and bony skull. Leon, hunched forward so that his head seemed sunken between his broad square shoulders, looked at each of the other men with his narrowed eyes; his smile was a little sullen.

Jules very courteously handed Paul the telegram he had received, translated it for him. Paul read, and listened, and as he did so an unhealthy purplish flush overspread his cheeks, which seemed to swell with rage and offense.

"Why didn't I receive this information?" he demanded, his bellicose eye blazing upon Jules. "After all, Barbour-Bouchard is the parent organization, and the others are only subsidiaries. It was your duty to direct all information to be sent to our office. Besides, why haven't my agents been informed? And who the devil are your 'agents'?"

Jules was silent a moment; Leon hunched forward a little more, and Honore's brown pallor had colored as though his slow but steady temper were rising. Then Jules began to speak, smoothly as always, unfailingly polite:

"Your agents, my dear Paul, have apparently been asleep. I never thought much of them, myself, though you picked them personally. My agents and friends happen to be those I have cultivated over a period of years; it is not only a matter of money, and blocks of stock, but true friendship. My senators owe a great deal to me, and, naturally, they are active in my interests, and often exert themselves to prove their gratitude to me. And now that 'duty' business you speak of: we owe no duty to any one. Barbour-Bouchard, and all its 'subsidiaries,' are one unit, like one body, all parts coordinated for the common good. I needn't remind you of Honore's inventions, particularly the powders, which you are manufacturing on your own premises. Honore did not think of 'you' and 'we' when consigning the invention to the unit as a whole. I thought of all of us when I invented my steel. I do not quite like your imperialistic attitude." He paused, and his voice, though still silken, became full of sleek enmity: "You may be vice-president of Barbour-Bouchard, but I am president of the Sessions Steel Company, Leon is president of the Bank, and Honore is president of the Kinsolving Arms Company."

There was a long silence. Paul, turning his big head slowly on his short and powerful neck, looked at each of them in turn. He looked at those brown foreign faces, the alien eyes steady and fixed and without mercy, the subtle mouths. And then he turned back to Jules, and there was a nasty smile on his mouth.

"I see," he said significantly. "Threats, eh?"

"Threats?" expostulated Jules in a very hurt voice. "How preposterous you are, my dear Paul! Threats!"

Paul suddenly struck the desk with his big clenched fist. It made a meaty but heavy sound.

"Threats! That's what I said. Don't wriggle out of it, in your Frenchy way, Jules Bouchard! You are trying to remind me that my position might not be as secure as yours, that though I am vice-president of Barbour-Bouchard, I rate lower than you as a shareholder. You want to remind me that Honore and all of you own fifty-one percent in the Kinsolving Arms Company, thirty-five percent of the Barbour-Bouchard stock, forty percent in the Sessions Steel Company, and percentages, very nice percentages, in all the other subsidiaries. You want me not to forget these things, don't you?"

"Yes," said Leon brutally. "We want you not to forget. We want to remind you that we three act together, that all the Bouchards are behind us, and that behind you——"

"Is Ernest Barbour, president of Barbour-Bouchard," Paul interrupted, with a cunning smile at Leon.

"Allow me to correct you, Paul," said Jules, with a shake of his head. "Dear Uncle Ernest is not behind you. He is behind the winner. You win, and he'll back you; we win, and he'll back us. You know that, I can see by your face." He paused, and sighed. "Uncle Ernest is always the Britisher. And the British never back failures. They have a way of finding nobility and the highest motives in the top dog."

Paul's features had become congested with his rage and murderous hatred.

"You are counting on too much," he said in a voice shaken and hoarse. "I've been seeing this coming. You haven't been so subtle in your plotting. I've seen all along. And Uncle Ernest has seen it, you can wager on that."

"Of course he's seen it!" Jules laughed lightly. He beamed pleasantly on his infuriated cousin. "I quite agree with you there."

Paul's heart seemed to thicken in his chest, to stop his breath. His hands clenched and unclenched, and his throat swelled. Fear and impotence turned his body cold.

"I'll ask him," he said, and even to himself he sounded futile.

"Do," urged Jules. "And if I'm not mistaken, he'll laugh and admit it. Always the realist, dear Uncle Ernest."

Paul again struck the desk. "But if you think he'll back a lot of dirty, scheming, oily Frenchmen you're damned mistaken! He'll back you no more than he backed your pious imbecile of a brother, Philippe, when he wanted to marry Gertrude! He'll find a way to cheat you at the last moment, as he did your brother——"

He stopped, appalled, literally biting the stupid tongue that had betrayed him. He glared at the three unsmiling faces turned upon him, deadly, watching faces.

"Go on," said Jules softly, with a glance at Leon. "Go on. What did he do to Philippe?"

Paul tried to bluster. "You know very well that he finally brought Trudie to her senses, and made her realize what a foolish thing it would have been to marry Philippe." He felt very sick. Gertrude was dead eighteen years, but the mention of her name brought her before him, and he felt the old desperate stab of pain at the memory. Then, glancing up furtively at his cousins, he saw very clearly that any mercy, any cooperation he might have hoped for from them, was gone, and that they were now his enemies who would stop at nothing. This realization frightened him, drove away his grief, put him on enraged and loathing guard.

In the silence that followed, Leon began to stare broodingly at the floor, Honore appeared to be grimly depressed, and Jules very carefully fitted the tips of his delicate fingers together and then surveyed them with a sort of whimsical pleasure. He did not look at Paul when he spoke again.

"I have always considered you a man of sense and intelligence, Paul. You have done some remarkably splendid work in the last few years. Among other things, it was you who thought of sending a naval mission to South American countries and another to China, though the whole world laughed. Perhaps you didn't hear it laugh at the Yankee who refused to remember that these countries had declined similar offers from European Powers. Your ability not to hear laughter has always impressed me. I confess that I, myself, am very susceptible to laughter. Yes, you have done well. You haven't failed in anything you have undertaken. That is why we want you with us, instead of against us. You see, we wouldn't want to ruin you—entirely. After all, you are our cousin."

"And what the devil do you think you could do to me?" asked Paul contemptuously, but staring at Jules with a wary eye.

"It is inconceivable, of course," said Jules gently, "but we could liquidate. We could throw our stock upon the market. We could become another company, competitors. Honore owns the patents still, you know, as I hold mine. But, naturally, Uncle Ernest would not want us to do these things. He would make many—concessions—if we expressed ourselves as determined." He regarded Paul smilingly and blandly, his full eyes brilliant under their lids.

Fright possessed Paul, but his hatred was even greater.

"My daughter, Alice, is his granddaughter," he said.

"We have not forgotten that, and also that she is his heiress. Yes, we know that. You see, we are quite candid with you, Paul. In three years Alice will have reached her majority. Naturally, she will marry, and then there will be her husband, and her children— You might not even be president of Barbour-Bouchard, when the Old Man passes on to the heaven where all good pirates go. Now, we'd like to see you president. You deserve the position. But, if necessary, as you know, we can block you. And Uncle Ernest, on earth or off it, will watch us cut your throat with great amusement, in spite of the fact that he esteems you and likes you. But personal relationships and friendships were always less important to him than ruthlessness and ingenuity. I don't think he likes us very well, but he wouldn't lift a hand to keep us from ruining you. He's not capricious, even though he's a treacherous old dog.

"Now, then, he can't possibly live much longer. Everyone knows that. After his death, you can be president. It rests with us. So the question now is : are you with us or against us?"

Paul was breathing hoarsely, and the congestion in his face was alarming. He stared at Jules with an almost evil smile. "You are sure of yourself, aren't you? You mention that Alice is his heiress, and as a woman she won't take an active part in Barbour-Bouchard, and her husband probably will. But Uncle Ernest might leave everything to me, if I marry again, and have sons——"

"Who will not be his grandchildren, but the grandchildren of poor Uncle Martin, whom the Old Man didn't like at all," said Jules swiftly. He shook his head sadly. "No, I don't think you need have any hopes there. Alice will be his heiress. And knowing that, I'm certain that he is not at all without complacence when he remembers me, and Leon, and Honore. Honore, especially, is the son of the only man for whom he ever felt anything approaching real affection and friendship, and we are all, after all, the children of his sisters. While you are, in the last analysis, the son of the one man he despised above all others. The Old Man likes his joke, and if he liked it a little better he might try to hoodwink us by suddenly making you his heir. But he likes cleverness better than he does his joke, and splendid and competent and powerful though you are, Paul Barbour, you are no match for the three of us!

"But we appreciate you, and want you with us. We want you to be president when the Old Man dies."

"And what do you think will be his reaction if, and when, I repeat this whole interview to him?"

"He will admire us the more, be more amused, and think a great deal less of you, though none of all this is your fault, my friend."

Paul was silent. He chewed his lip. God, how true this was! Only he knew how true. Suddenly he would have given half his life to have been able to defy these plotters; for one moment he would have been willing to ruin himself for the exquisite joy of defying them. And then he knew that expediency and self-protection were dearer to him than defiance, more valuable than self-respect and honor.

He stood up, and Jules, Leon and Honore rose also, politely. Paul paused in the action of putting on his coat and surveyed Jules with contempt, hatred and menace.

"The president of Barbour-Bouchard isn't dead yet. And before he dies, I may have married Alice off to a man who might be able to outwit you."

He walked out without another word, without a reply to Jules' cordial "good night."

Leon put on his hat and picked up his coat.

"And what, if I may inquire, my subtle brother, have you gained or found out from this interview with our noble cousin?"

"Ah!" exclaimed Jules gently, raising his brows. "Numerous things! Ever so many important things, which were not mentioned! One was Alice, and her marriage to François, which must be pushed at once. And another, and by far the most important, that our Paul is a coward. And that, my children, is what I wished to find out definitely."

Honore shrugged, a little wearily. "I felt a trifle sorry for him. Jules, if you're going to hang a man, I don't see that it is necessary to apply the thumb-screws first. Hang him, cleanly, and have done with it. But you always did love thumb-screws."

He and Leon went to the door together. At the threshold Leon turned, saluted with mock respect, and grinned. "Good evening—padre," he said, and went out with his cousin.

CHAPTER CVI

BUT PAUL was not really a coward, after all. He knew things his cousins did not know about himself and Ernest Barbour. For the past few years he had felt himself stripped, exposed to bewildering elements, watched from ambush. Jules had said that Ernest was not capricious, but Paul believed he was. A cruel, coldly amused capriciousness.

Ernest had given him full right to believe that he would be his major heir. He remembered a certain day shortly after his marriage to Gertrude, when Ernest had called him into his office. He had told the young man that the day would arrive when he would have to manage Gertrude's share of his estate, Godfrey's share, Reginald's and Guy's. Administrator and executive, and president of Barbour-Bouchard! He had said "my assistant." "Eventually, take my place."

Now, Paul saw how nebulous, how cautious, all that had been. It Gertrude had lived, if they had had sons, if Godfrey and Reginald had remained in their father's favor, if Guy had not been killed, his, Paul's, position would have been secure beyond the slightest doubt. His sons would have inherited in direct line; he would have controlled the joint fortunes of Ernest's own sons. He would have had Gertrude's share. But he had no sons that would be grandsons of Ernest Barbour, and Gertrude, having died before her father, had no estate to leave her husband and her daughter. Frey would not receive anything beyond a pittance upon his father's death, and Reginald, with his dour, dark severity, had voluntarily removed himself from his family and wanted nothing from it. And would get nothing from it. Only a few years ago, Ernest, with a bland frankness that had terrified Paul, had informed his nephew that he intended to leave the greater part of his fortune to Alice, as would May. The balance would be distributed in small bequests to other relatives, including Paul, and the rest bequeathed to the various public philanthropic enterprises in which he was interested. (Charity! At his age! Paul had thought with disgust and disappointment, not for an instant deceived into believing that Ernest had changed his character over-night.)

Paul had little doubt that he would be elected president of Barbour-Bouchard when Ernest died, or retired. But it would be in reality a hollow title, for all its magnificent salary. At one time he had hoped that he might be able to buy the stock held by the Bouchards; remembering this hope now, as he was being driven home in his carriage, he laughed drearily at himself for his own naïveté. As well expect wolves to give up the sheep they have slaughtered as expect the Bouchards to give up Barbour-Bouchard stock and Sessions Steel stock, or stock in any other of the subsidiaries.

Paul had long suspected Jules and Leon and Honore, but the sudden realization of what he thought of as their rapacious perfidy came as a heavy blow. He told himself that had they not been sure of themselves they would not have been as candid as they had been. But in this, Paul deduced from his own character, not knowing that there could be such a thing as audacity. He thought their boldness came from a consciousness of security and knowledge which they were keeping to themselves; had he shown such boldness, he would have had such security and knowledge, first. He was no match for their subtleties, which Jules well knew. Paul, riding home, was assailed on all sides by maddening fear, impotence and rage. All at once, with a sensation of physical illness, he thought: *He* has told them something, he has confided something to them, he has encouraged them! He has betrayed me, done me in. But why? What have I done? I have done my best, which has been very good, as he himself has said. But since Trudie died, there has been a difference in his attitude toward me, a touch of malevolence, as though he believed in some way that it was my fault, that I should have made her love me and forget Philippe. But how could I? Who can do anything with women? I did my best, and I believe I was a good husband to Trudie. God knows I loved her, and still love her, and still can't forget her! If anything, her death, and Guy's death, and Joey's death, should have sealed my position with *him*. But they didn't. He has not been the same. Once, when I disagreed with him, he said angrily that I reminded him of my father. I'll never forget that day, and the look he gave me. But things had begun to change before that.

Not that he likes the Bouchards any better, except, perhaps, Honore. Still, that's just a sentimentality. But God help us when men like that get sentimental! However, he speaks admiringly of them, and calls them great rascals. He never calls me a great rascal, damn him! Whatever scurvy thing they do, he laughs, and says he could not have done it better, himself. Jules is quick-minded, and his schemes are preposterous and frequently theatrical. But damn it! they seem to work. They wouldn't have worked twenty years ago, but they work now. I can't understand it; things have changed. I don't know. But *he* doesn't seem to care that Jules is presumptuous, meddling in our own affairs; I can see through his specious proclamation that we are all one Unit, and should work together. Jules' business is the Sessions Steel Company, but he's all over, like a flea. A Jesuit flea. God, I don't know.

Jules was right. There was no mercy, kindness or loyalty in the man.

Let Paul weaken, let him show fear, let him blunder, and *he* would do him in, not with malice or anger, but just with an impersonal contempt. Paul would be no further use to him.

Twisting his cane in his gloved hands, Paul weltered in his miserable thoughts. Never had he felt so betrayed, in so precarious a position, surrounded by such enemies, of which not the least was his uncle.

The only hope Paul now had was that his uncle would continue to live and take an active part in the Company, and that in some way, not yet worked out, Paul would accomplish magnificent things beyond the really fine things he had already accomplished. But the greatest hope of all was a marriage for Alice, a marriage to a young man carefully chosen. But what young man? At one time she had seemed taken with a young chap from New York, a relative of Percival Van Eyck, extremely wealthy in his own right. He would have no objection, perhaps, to turning over to his father-in-law at the current market price, the stock of Barbour-Bouchard which belonged to his wife. Perhaps a pseudo-sale, or something of the sort. It could be managed, with a little manipulation. And then Paul had the most brilliant idea of all: Lucy's son, Thomas! A perfect match: Thomas was four or five years older than Alice, a millionaire in his own name, due to a fortune left him by his paternal grandmother. Thomas had seemed smitten by Alice last Christmas, and wrote to her at least twice a week even though she rarely answered any of his letters. Her objection to him seemed based on some notion of hers that he was "beefy" and "dull" and talked of "nothing but horses and Lillian Russell and his money." Only yesterday, when she had received a letter from him she had tossed it aside disdainfully with the remark: "That silly fat thing who thinks lobster a la Newburg the world's most exquisite emotion!" Paul, thinking rapidly, recalled that Alice held the opinion that Thomas had no "soul," whatever the hell *that* was, and that he was "gross, greedy, and thinking of food when he wasn't thinking of his stables or his dogs or telling an anecdote about Wilson Mizner or Diamond Jim Brady."

But Thomas was exactly what Paul needed. Rich, weak, self-indulgent, good-natured, easily hoodwinked, easily led, credulous, kind, loyal, anxious and almost piteously eager to please and help, full of admiration for his Uncle Paul, honest and simple—he was made to order! He was just what Alice needed, also, Paul thought. A darling little thing, but too ethereal of tastes. Paul knew his daughter well enough to guess that this ethereality was mostly childish affectation, though deadly serious. She had been convinced, in turn, that she was a literary genius, a composer, a musician, a painter and a sculptor. Now, it was all poetry. Almost every day she was stuffing sheets of the vile stuff into her muff and dashing over to Florabelle's house, where she usually found François at home and benignly willing to criticize. François, that feverish, dry-mouthed, brown-faced French monkey! Still a bachelor, still emaciated, still hysterical and effeminate, petulant and womanish-voiced, with his nervous fluttering hands, irritability, egotism and vanity! A poet, by God! But hardly the companion for an impressionable dear little idiot seventeen years his junior. However, the passion for poetry would go the way of the literature, the music and the painting, and there would be an end to the constant excited talk of François' "genius," and the dramatic gestures and the shining eyes. Paul was not worried about that; as yet he was blissfully unaware of Alice's real if temporary adoration of François, and the plot laid against his peace and paternal affection by the Bouchards.

No, he reflected, smiling fondly and with relief, Alice had no right to criticize her cousin Thomas. She was none too bright herself, for all her affectations and passionately declared love of "Art." Paul rightly suspected that his daughter had a fluffy mind, and was full of poses, innocent affectations and silly little mental snobberies. He also knew that she was a selfish little wretch, conceited, deliberately childish, silly, unfeeling, greedy for sensation and all prettinesses, opinionated and exigent. But he did not deplore these things; in a young creature like Alice, so lovely and sparkling and gay and small and exquisitely made, they were ornamentations, he thought. No one expected a pretty woman to have any brains; brains in a lovely daughter were really a detriment, especially to a scheming and ambitious father. He did not deplore at all his daughter's dabbling her little feet in the great ocean of the Arts; one expected these things in women, and he preferred her succeeding passions to the pursuits of other women, such as the cause of suffrage, tea-drinking, bridge-playing, gossiping and flirting, late hours and parties, extravagances and general foolishness. Women seemed to be in a ferment these days, restless and whining, belligerent and unpredictable, feverishly dashing about like cockroaches, their loud voices everywhere, their feverish faces in the public prints, their big plumed hats bobbing in places where twenty years ago it would have been preposterous for them to appear.

Yes, Alice, for all her scurryings and breathless eagerness and artistic phrases and affectations, was an "old-fashioned" girl, innocent and affectionate and altogether charming, not to say useless and vapid. Thomas was exactly the sort she should marry, and marry him she would.

But Paul knew that crudeness would be fatal. Like all shallow and senseless small creatures, Alice was obstinate; to tell her that she must marry Thomas, whom she affected to despise because he had no "soul" or "depths," would be fatal. Because she was weak, she had the strength of the weak, and nothing in heaven or earth could move her when she set her pretty pink mouth. Paul knew he must be adroit and careful; he must use guile, not reason or demands for obedience. He recalled Florabelle, and unwillingly admitted to himself that there was something very like his aunt in his daughter.

By the time the carriage was driving up the long wide curving sweep toward Robin's Nest, Paul's fears and apprehensions were appreciably allayed. He would outwit those damnable Bouchards after all! He was filled with a delightful exhilaration, a feeling of new strength and competence and power. He could give his mind, now, to the impending war and the appropriation of fifty million dollars to finance it. One of the things that Ernest had admired about Paul was his ability not to let personal matters and grudges interfere with prospects of profits, and in thinking of the war at this time he forgot Jules' arrogance and interference and the negligence of his own agents, and thought only of military contracts and Honore's new explosives and the new projectiles.

The winter twilight was engulfing Robin's Nest as Paul stepped out of his carriage. As always, he glanced up at the house, which he privately thought far superior to the Sessions house. He smiled, as usual, as his glance climbed from the lower stories to the wide eaves of the roof. It was his home; he had the Barbour love of security and steadfastness, the Barbour worship of strong and visible property. Here was a house to be proud of, sturdy and beautiful, artfully made to appear ancient and longstanding, ivied in the summer, sheltered by evergreens in the winter. A man could bring up his children here, and his grandchildren, and their children, and each year the house would grow more a part of the family tradition, more its home, more a background for all its history—its deaths and its lives, its comings and its goings, its joys and its sorrows. An invisible ivy would grow over it, and the trees of invisible memory would rise higher about it with each decade.

"Above all things, a man needs a house," he thought, with one of his unusual flashes of insight.

When Gertrude had been alive, there had been a polished cool graciousness about the interior of the house, a gleaming shadow over the floors and the walls, a quietness and almost airless dignity, long spacious vistas and glimpses of white marble, a certain chaste austerity which yet had been restful and finished. Elsa had changed very little in the house, yet in some mysterious way it had changed indeed, becoming somewhat stodgy in places, heavier, mellower of gleam, warmer, more stolid, but decidedly more home-like and comfortable. The same walls and floors and staircases and portraits and furniture and rugs and mirrors, but a deeper if less artistic humanity. Paul felt more at home in the atmosphere his sister had created; when Gertrude had been alive the air had always seemed slightly chilly, and a trifle too quiet.

He sent the perfect butler up to Elsa's private sitting room with the request that he would like to see his sister immediately. Miss Alice, he was informed, was visiting and had not yet returned. Yes, he believed she was at the home of her aunt, Mrs. Norwood. Paul frowned, surrendered his coat and hat and gloves and cane, and walked heavily into the library. He never read any of the books on the shelves in the great dim silent room, with its tremendous arched windows and mighty fireplace, but he liked the library. It gave him confidence, recharged his batteries of security. Elsa, stout, big, florid-faced, came into the room, and he kissed her warm firm cheek. Her hair, dressed in a huge pompadour, was streaked with gray. She wore a competent white starched shirtwaist and a thick black skirt with heavy rows of braid at the bottom. On her left breast was pinned a plain gold watch. Behind flashing glasses her eyes gleamed alertly.

"Dear, is it possible it is so late?" she exclaimed, snapping open the case of her watch and glancing at its white face. "Alice isn't home yet."

"So I understand. Whatever does she find down at the Norwoods'?"

"Heavens, I don't know, except that it must be her 'poetry.' She wrote something she called a sonnet this morning, and read it to me. Really quite horrible, all about the agony of frustrated love, and mystical attic rooms where she was weeping in loneliness and grief— Well, she's taken it to François, to correct and criticize."

"That miserable brown-skinned monkey! I don't know much about the publishing business, but it does seem to me that a man's stuff can't be good if he has to pay for its publication. I don't like Alice hanging out there with him all the time. It can't be healthy for a young girl to associate with an ego-maniac with a voice like a sick woman's and a disposition that would curdle milk. I'm beginning to worry about it."

"Tosh! Good heavens, Paul, you don't think there could ever be anything between that silly child and a man old enough to be her father! He's at least seventeen years older than she is. Don't be absurd!"

"Don't you be absurd, yourself, Elsa," he replied irately. "What I meant was that she should be in the society of young girls like herself, and boys. God, what ideas you do have!"

"Girls her own age?" Elsa laughed shortly. "You know what she thinks about them. 'Silly, stuffy, giggly, inconsequential, not concerned with the deeper things in life, no souls.' But what did you want to talk to me about? It must be important or you wouldn't have called me down before dinner."

"It is important. Sit down. Why is your face so red lately, Elsa? I don't believe you get enough exercise, and you eat too much. Now, please don't get huffy; it's just a piece of advice from one who's just as guilty as you are." He smiled disarmingly, and Elsa's annoyance subsided, though her glasses flashed. "Yes, it's important." And he sketched briefly for her the conversation he had had with his cousins. Elsa was his only confidante, the only creature in the world he could trust. "So, you see, I've got to work fast. If—Uncle Ernest is on his last legs, which I hardly believe in spite of that devil Jules, I've got to make plans and put them into action. I want you to take Alice to New York next week or so, for a long visit. Stay, of course, at Lucy's. Take Lucy into your confidence. She's already spoken of how nice it would be if Thomas and Alice were to marry. Tell her a little what I have told you. Push the business. Throw the children together, and keep Alice there until something serious develops. Damn it, buy Thomas a 'soul' if he must have it, and I don't care what it costs!" They laughed together for a few moments. "The boy's all right, and he's mad for Alice. She hasn't much imagination, and it will take very little to persuade her that Thomas is a philosopher, or something. Coach him in private, show him the way to her silly little heart. He'll be only too willing; it won't be the first time love's made a philosopher out of a pink-skinned hog. Well, he is, you know, Elsa, a perfectly sanitary, scrubbed, affectionate young hog, so don't be indignant. Take her shopping, buy her anything. Even women with 'souls' can't resist silk stockings and flounced petticoats and furs and jewels and French boots and gloves. I know! Alice likes to protect under-dogs, and after she is half persuaded Tommy has a soul, and he's touched her pity, you might disparage him, very artistically, of course. Nothing gross, or obvious. Lucy'll help. She's got brains. She might even engineer an elopement. Alice'll like that. Very romantic and dangerous and breathless, apt to arouse annoyance in stuffy old parents and aunts. Well, get her engaged, married if you can. It's so damned important that my life hinges on it."

Elsa thought over the plan for a few long minutes as she stared at the great log-fire that smouldered on the hearth.

"I think you're wrong about Uncle Ernest, Paul. You've never had reason to distrust him, you know. Why distrust him now? He's been marvelous to us, like a father, ever since Mother died. And he hasn't been the same since she died; gentler, more considerate, in spite of his marrying Aunt May again. His whole life is wrapped up in us and Alice. I think you've been letting your imagination run away with you. Why, he'd no more think of Jules Bouchard and all his cut-throat gang of cousins and brothers——"

Paul stood up in a sudden frenzy. His fleshy face flushed a darkish purple. "You talk like a fool and a woman, Elsa!" he exclaimed in a sort of rage. "I know what I know! I know what they're up to, all the Bouchards, from Jules to Andre and Etienne, and even that germ of a François! And even the Norwoods, Chandler and his senile old father! They'd all cut our throats. I've got reason to know this; I don't speak from imagination or suspicion. Please give me credit for knowing my own business, Elsa!"

Elsa's plump face became suffused with a rich dark scarlet. "Paul! How dare you talk to me that way! You forget yourself! I'm sure that

I'm no fool; I have a brain too, though you don't seem to realize it. I think you're wronging poor Uncle Ernest, who's so old and sick now, and has shown us every kindness and affection. But have it your own way!" She was panting a little, wounded and indignant. Paul looked down at her gloomily. She touched her eyes with a fine white linen handkerchief, then resumed resolutely: "Of course, I'll do what you wish. I've always thought Alice should marry Thomas, who's the nicest young fellow imaginable. He'll have ten or more millions some day, when Percy dies. Besides, it's very dull in Windsor in the spring, and I need some new clothes myself. We'll go next week." She stood up and went toward the door with offended dignity. Paul went after her and took her arm.

"All right, Elsa." He smiled. "I'm a little edgy. Probably I'm all wrong. I apologize. I haven't the slightest doubt that Uncle Ernest is a nice old lamb who is no longer concerned with business. I'm quite sure that he's all sweetness and light and will be properly indignant at the scheming of his precious French relatives." His mouth twisted acridly. "So, I'm forgiven? That's a nice girl." He patted the big plump shoulder that strained the sleeve of the starched shirtwaist.

Elsa, only half reconciled, went upstairs. Paul returned to the library fire. He chewed his lip as he stood on the hearth, with bent head. With Alice married to Thomas, and Ernest dead, and with the Van Eyck millions at his, Paul's, command, he would be able to block the needed credit for expansion to meet the demands which the Barbour-Bouchard Company expected to receive from the Government in its war with Spain, thus making the Bouchard pirates come to terms. Risky, desperate, a bold and audacious game, but he could do it! Paul winced a little at audacity, as usual, but now was the time for it. He would meet that omniscient Jules and would beat him on his own ground. He would risk ruin to ruin Jules. God, how he hated him! But he, Paul, would win. If only he dared consult Ernest, who would find a way! What a ghastly paradox that he dared not consult him!

But Ernest was still alive. He might live on, and on. Paul clenched his fists on the mantelpiece, began to beat the cold white stone slowly and heavily. "Christ!" he muttered, with a low and passionate intensity. "Let him die. Let him die. Holy Christ, let him die—at once!"

He stood there, shaking, for several minutes. Then he relaxed, all at once, and his knees trembled. His hands unclenched on the mantelpiece. His face was wet with sweat. He wiped it, with a sort of absent wonder that he should be so moved. The candles had been lit on the mantelpiece, and lifting his head, he stared at his own face in the dark gleaming mirror over the fireplace. It was haggard, livid, the face of a man who would kill, if necessary. For the fraction of a moment, he was appalled. Then he smiled, a little foolishly.

The dressing gong sounded through the warm stillness of the house.

CHAPTER CVII

PAUL LOVED his daughter, but that did not prevent him from knowing that she was a little fool. When he listened to her, he listened only to the sound of her light breathless small voice, so musical and pretty and child-like, but he rarely heard what she had to say. It was usually inconsequential and puerile, full of vanities and nothingnesses, sometimes tinged with a charming and innocent malice.

But tonight, at dinner, he listened to her prattle with a smile and secret intentness. He studied her with new calculation. On this little pretty thing's unsuspecting shoulders rested all the schemes, dreams and hopes of his life. What dainty little shoulders, what silly little shoulders!

She was so small and child-like, sitting there opposite him, the light of the hanging electric chandelier shining on her face. It shone on the dark-red pompadour which needed no "rats" to bolster up its heavy roll, and made coppery tendrils glitter about the tiny rosy ears. Alice had a small oval face with a dimple in the perfect, pointed white chin, a delicate petal tint in her transparent cheeks, a deep bright pink in her lovely, absolutely vapid little mouth. Her nose was like alabaster, clear and white, with slightly dilated nostrils, the Barbour nostrils. She had big dark-blue eyes, blazing and eager and perpetually excited, with dark-red lashes extravagantly sweeping and curled, and a low white forehead, which bulged like a very young child's. In fact, everything about her, from the slender bird-like throat, to the small but perfect breast and wee hands and absurd feet, was like a pretty child's. Even the lacy voile of her shirtwaist, with its inserts of cobweb lace and high boned collar and big velvet black bow at the neck and the jewelled watch on the left breast, and dark-blue serge skirt weighted with braid, could not detract from her infantile appearance. She looked like a little girl dressed up in her mother's mature clothing, and her habit of wrinkling her forehead and nose when she laughed or frowned added to the impression. Her expressions, though facile and quick and alive, were shallow, though not stupid. She had a thousand little affectations and poses and graces, chief among them being her devout belief that she was an artist, and intellectual.

She ate daintily, and mealtimes were usually nervy affairs of wrangles between herself and her Aunt Elsa about her meagre appetite. Elsa, who served the vegetables, refusing stoutly the assistance of the butler, was apt to heap Alice's plate with steaming mounds and to insist upon Paul giving the girl an extra slice of beef or chicken, and all the while Alice would keep up a plaintive monologue of protest, sometimes becoming quite tearful. Often they would both appeal to Paul, and he would be irascible or amused, depending on how he felt after his day.

But tonight Alice was too elated to notice the formidable piles on her gold-crusted plate. Her voice was shrill, as it was apt to become when she was excited, and her eyes danced and shone under her lashes with a polished blueness. It seems that François had deigned to approve of her sonnet, and had prophesied that she had finally found her "forte," which was poetry. Why, he had actually said that in some lines she had surpassed Elizabeth Browning!

"Imagine!" she exclaimed. "Elizabeth Browning!" She simpered, flashed her lighted glance from her aunt to her father. "Of course, that's all nonsense! But after François corrected it here and there, and gave me one or two suggestions, I had to admit to myself that it was really very good. I'm going to send it to the *Ladies' Home Friend,* and if they don't take it it'll just prove to me that François was right when he said that publishers weren't interested in good poetry."

Paul pursed his lips and pretended to be impressed as he sliced the capon. "You must read it to me, darling—after supper," he added hastily, as Alice showed symptoms of bounding from her chair and leaping upstairs after her sonnet. "You have quite a lot of poetry lying around, haven't you? Why don't you gather it together and take it to New York? Baxter & Company are always interested in good poetry, and I've got a little influence with them."

A curious mixture of expressions struggled on Alice's face; gratification at her father's unusual interest in her work, pleasure, excitement, hope, and then, a secretive and embarrassed look. All these were suddenly followed by an odd uneasiness and slight blush.

"I think it would be just as well if I *sent* them, Papa, dear," she said in a faint and hesitating voice.

"Why, don't you *want* to go to New York?" demanded Elsa in surprise, for Alice had a thousand times declared her fervent passion for that city and her loathing for "small-town" Windsor, where nothing ever happened and artists were unappreciated and suspect. Paul, too, put down his carving knife in surprise, and surveyed his daughter questioningly.

Alice's uneasiness and embarrassment visibly increased. She had never practiced deceit before, and it came hard to her, not because she was naturally honest and forthright, but because she had had little necessity heretofore to use deception. But she remembered cousin Jules' light warning that she must be "tactful" and keep her own counsel for a little while with regard to her love for François. So, while the struggle went on in her small, panicked mind, she could only stare helplessly at her father, the color brightening in her cheeks.

Paul frowned, puzzled. "Don't you want to go to New York?" he echoed his sister.

Alice tried to recover her composure. She began to stammer: "Why, I—I'd love to, but I just thought— I didn't see why it would be necessary. I—Mrs. Jessup's giving a party for Estelle this month, a—a spring party, and I promised, I mean, I'd like to go. And Beatrice is having her engagement reception——"

Paul was pleased, though still puzzled. "Well, I'm glad to see you taking an interest again in parties, like a normal little girl. You know, you've practically been in retirement since you got this poetry trash—I mean, this poetry passion, on the brain. However, suppose you and your Aunt Elsa go to New York after these heavy social engagements are over, eh?"

Alice was silent. She blinked childishly, her lashes slightly wet.

Elsa began to eat calmly, though an odd hammering began in her chest, and a terrible suspicion formed in her mind.

"To tell you the truth, pettie," she said smoothly, "I've just received a letter from your Aunt Lucy, and she isn't at all well, and has asked me to come to New York to see her. Naturally, I wouldn't want to go without you——"

Alice sighed. Then her face brightened just a trifle. "All right," she said grudgingly, "I'll go. Perhaps it would be best to see Baxter & Company, in person. You'll give me a letter of introduction, Papa? And besides," she added, brightening still more, "I do need some decent clothes. I'm in rags." She saw herself in fine new stylish clothes, beautiful for François. "For a week or so."

Dinner proceeded in peace until the wine was brought in. Alice giggled when the Sauterne was poured. "Jules says you don't know a thing about wines, Papa," she said, sparkling. "He says no bloody Britisher ever knew anything at all about food or wine, except boiled cabbage and beer."

Paul flushed. He did not speak until the three glasses were filled, Alice's being a very small one indeed. Then when the butler had retired, he said, quietly: "In the first place, Jules is quite mistaken: I am an American, not a Britisher. My mother came from an old and illustrious American family. Jules, himself, would always be a foreigner, no matter if he lived here a hundred years. And in the second place, I know considerable about wines."

Alice was not overawed. She giggled again. "Jules says, anyway, that Sauterne is the beginner's wine, and that any one who likes Trocken-

beerenauslese from the Rheinpfalz is a barbarian. He says that you don't
know a good Liebfraumilch from a bad one, if you even ever tasted
any——"

"You are being exceedingly impertinent, not to say ill-bred!" said
Elsa in a bad temper. "Almost as ill-bred as Jules, who is certainly no
gentleman! Whatever you can see in those Bouchards——!"

"Oh, I think Jules is so amusing, Aunt Elsa! And so handsome! What
a Mephistopheles he would make, in red satin and a sword! He's never
ill-natured, and that means so much. All the Bouchards are amusing;
they're so *alive,* Aunt Elsa! Not stodgy, like us."

"I must ask you to stop chattering like a little fool," said Paul, with an
enraged glare at his daughter. "You know absolutely nothing, for all
your prattle about culture. I must ask you not to be so thick with the
Bouchards: well, I don't mind Honore, who is a gentleman, and his
family, and Andre isn't so bad, and his children have breeding, but— Oh,
for God's sake, child, don't begin to weep! I didn't mean to hurt your
feelings but you are such a foolish little creature. The sooner you go to
New York the better——"

Alice wiped her eyes with childish anger. "I suppose you think that
horrible Thomas is better than the Bouchards! Well, he isn't! He's just
a lummox, a dolt, a lump of flesh without a mind— I declare, I simply
won't go to New York if I have to have him at my heels all the time."

Paul lost control of himself. His fingers clenched on his teaspoon,
and rage swelled his face.

"You'll go to New York whenever I say, my young madam!" he
shouted. "And you'll be a lady, and behave yourself, and treat your
cousin decently, and try to find something in him to admire, for, by
God——!"

"Paul!" exclaimed Elsa, flashing him an appalled warning. Paul subsided, breathing heavily, still flushed, still enraged. He drank his tea in
gulps.

Like so many people with facile and shallow minds, Alice had a sort
of quick insight and shrewdness. She knew instantly, now, why she was
to go to New York, and what was to be done to her there. She turned as
white as the tablecloth, and her beautiful dark-blue eyes dilated in fright
and horror. In a sort of sick fascination, she gazed fixedly at her father,
even her lips paling. Her life had been so sheltered, so cared for and so
careless, so gay and infantile, so without worry or distress of the slightest
sort, that this sudden realization wounded her all over, bruised her whole
mind.

She swallowed, her sick-child eyes dilating more and more until they
shone with a strained blue brilliance under the light. She visibly trembled.
Elsa, furious at Paul, loving her niece with all her heart, thought suddenly

of a crippled bird. And thinking of that bird, she remembered Godfrey, who had looked just like this, one terrible night, the last night she ever saw him, in the rooms where they had found him with that ghastly Frenchwoman. It was ages ago, but she remembered, and the tears ran into her throat. Swamped by the memory, she put her hand over Alice's, and smiled down at her with infinite love and tenderness.

"My lamb, if you don't want to go to New York, you needn't. And if you don't like Thomas I'll beat him off with my umbrella if he so much as looks at you! There now, eat your blanc mange and drink your tea. And don't forget," she added with a deeper smile and a touch on the young cheek, "you promised to read us your new sonnet."

Alice's color returned. She smiled uncertainly. Paul, realizing his mistake, demanded more tea in an irate voice. He met his sister's eyes; they were cold and hostile, and full of meaning.

They went into the living room where Paul, still trying not to look at his daughter, stirred the fire with unusual vigor, though the early spring evening had turned warmish. Alice languidly picked up a book, then tried to crochet, wandered to the piano where she strummed a few discordant bars, yawned, sighed, glanced furtively at her father, and then at the clock on the mantelpiece. She knew he was angry at her: it had been her intention to ask him to let her run over to her Aunt Florabelle's again, but she knew he was in no mood to consent. She yawned until her eyes were wet. Elsa, adjusting her spectacles, was reading the evening paper, Paul was reviewing some personal letters which had arrived at the house for him. He, too, wore spectacles while reading, and they made him seem older and heavier, less youthful, more middle-aged.

"What a dull, dull home I have!" thought Alice passionately. Then, as she always did when she was feeling sorry for herself, she thought: "Oh, how I do wish my poor dear Mama had lived! I'm sure she would not have been unreasonable, like Papa; she would have understood how I loathe Thomas. She looks so frail and sad in her photograph in my room, but so understanding." She thought of her grandmother, Amy, and the memory of her was sympathetic and beautiful; she had always been so sweet-smelling, so smiling, so serene. A certain other memory never failed to intrigue the girl: she remembered that her grandfather had wept at her grandmother's funeral, openly, as though no one else were there. The tears had dropped, one after another, over his cheeks, and had run over his cravat and his waistcoat. It seemed strange to see a man weep, especially one so old and gray as grandfather. She sat idly on the piano stool, thinking and remembering, swinging one slim little foot, her mouth dropped open slightly and vapidly. Then her expression quickened; words formed in her mind:

> "O you, so old and gray, why do you weep?
> Because the flesh you love has turned to dust?
> Because the lonely fire yourself must keep,
> And all your hopes are——"

The doorbell rang distantly. Alice scowled, the white transparent skin wrinkling over her nose and eyes. Some of Aunt Elsa's dull friends, no doubt, and perfectly stupid girls. The butler brought in a telegram on a silver tray. Paul took it and read it.

He glanced at Elsa swiftly. "Uncle Ernest and Aunt May are coming home. They landed this afternoon, and ought to be here tomorrow night."

Elsa put down her paper. "But they weren't expected for another month."

"True. But he's coming back on account of the impending war. Trust Uncle Ernest to smell powder a thousand miles away."

"Oh, is there going to be a war, really?" cried Alice, shining.

Paul looked at her irritably over his spectacles. "And if so, why does it concern you, miss? Of course there's going to be a war. We aren't going to allow Spain to torture Cuba much longer, I can tell you."

Another thought struck Alice. She tossed her head. "It ought to be good for business, then, Papa," she said.

Paul glared at her, stupefied for a moment. "What the devil do you know about my 'business,' Miss Impertinent?"

"Only that it's a nef—nef—nefarious one," responded Alice with defiance, but inwardly much frightened.

Utterly unable to speak, outraged, Paul turned demandingly to his sister. Elsa gazed at her niece, shocked.

"Whatever are you talking about, child?"

Alice tossed her head again, and showed her fright now. "Well, François said munitions are nef—nefarious, Aunt Elsa. He—he said munitions makers are mass-killers, and that some day we'll recognize that and drive them off the face of the earth. As a menace. A menace," she added, in a failing but still courageous voice.

"Well!" ejaculated Elsa, on an exhaling gush of breath. "I'm sure! François is certainly—certainly not very bright, I must say. Perhaps he doesn't realize that he lives in idleness on the proceeds of munitions. A menace! I never!"

"Go to bed," said Paul in a quiet and deadly voice. His face was pale.

Alice began to cry. "But, Papa, it's only half past nine——"

"Go to bed," he repeated, and there was something in his face and voice that terrified the girl. She got up and ran out of the room, completely demoralized.

When the door had shut behind the crying girl, Paul said to his sister in a tone of quiet violence: "You must keep her away from that house, Elsa. Do you hear me? I shall hold you responsible for this. If you can't be trusted I shall have to send her away to some school, some institution. I've seen something the last few minutes!"

Elsa, herself, was too shaken to be angered at her brother's words and tone. She sat, swallowing dryly, very pale.

"Get her to New York, if you have to drag her. Don't bring her back until it is all settled. Get her married there, if you can, if it takes a year. Today's Wednesday: get ready and take her Friday. In the meantime, don't let her out of your sight."

He got up and began to walk heavily about the room, his hands behind his back, his thoughts violent, full of hatred and fear.

He's coming back! he thought. He's coming back, and he'll live a thousand years!

CHAPTER CVIII

JULES BOUCHARD, it was generally conceded, had married "a great lady," of which there were deplorably few left these strident days He had been about twenty-six when he had married Miss Adelaide Burgeon, who was then four years his senior, being thirty. She was the only daughter of an old man, who had been born in Windsor but who had moved to Philadelphia when Adelaide had been a child. The family was impeccable, going far back to a noble gentleman who had arrived in Maryland with a fortune in the early part of the seventeenth century—a Catholic gentleman leaving a hostile Protestant England. Later, his descendants had come to Pennsylvania, that is, one or two of them who were adventurous and greedy and restless. They had built one of the first steel mills in Pittsburgh, made a vast amount of money, resumed their gentility and moved to Philadelphia. Miss Adelaide's father had had a quarrel with his relatives, had gone to Windsor and there married, in his middle age. Adelaide was the only result of that marriage. Her father had become homesick, eventually, and had returned to Philadelphia, only to come back to Windsor, there to remain until after his daughter's marriage, when he died. His fortune was reputed to be over four million dollars. In reality, it was scarcely one million, but as Jules said philosophically, "it did very nicely."

Old Mr. Land Burgeon had been "a great rascal." He had never engaged in business of any kind, but he was a brutal and savage old man, rapacious and merciless, snarling of speech, suspicious of the motives of everyone but his daughter, bad-tempered and insulting, irascible, and at times downright vicious. But no one questioned that he was a great gentleman, in spite of his roaring voice and bawdy insults. He had served two terms as Mayor of Windsor, and had been most merciless during the strikes. He carried a heavy cane, which he brandished and frequently used on the backs of servants and sometimes others. He hated practically everything, especially Jules Bouchard, when that astute young man had come a-wooing Adelaide.

"He's after your money, girl," he said to his daughter, sourly. "But then, who the devil would marry such a milk-face as you without money?" This, despite the fact that he had never loved any one but this meek, well-bred, delicate daughter of his, with the attenuated transparent face, big gray eyes and gentle voice. Mr. Burgeon had no reticences and the things he said to his daughter, in the presence of her friends, about her lack of bosom or narrowness of hips, often sent the poor girl off in an agony of shame, tears and red blushes. In fact, Mr. Burgeon was disappointed in his daughter: he liked lusty women, of vitality and laughter and flashing eyes, with bosoms "a man can lean his head on and not think he is up against the side of a barrel," and "with a backside a man can smack in a joke without cutting his hand on bones." He liked gaudy women, big women, full of zest and passion, witty women who could wink at a *double entendre*. Yet, chaste women, oddly. One of his chief and most ferocious complaints was that: "Either a woman is 'good' and has no blood in her damn skinny body, and no more zest than a slaughtered calf, or she is a whore, and has everything a man likes and needs to comfort him in the goddamn business of living!" He frequently became quite querulous because woman could not be a combination of Pallas Athene, Aphrodite and Diana.

Sometimes he would look at Adelaide as she moved softly and silently about the house; he would watch her, his hands folded on his cane, his chin on the backs of his hands, and he would scowl, noting how the folds of her skirts showed the ridges of her slight fleshless hips, and how the ripples of her bodices could not conceal the fact that she had practically no breasts. Finally, he would grunt savagely: "Well, at any rate, you'll bring me home no bastards!"

He lived with his daughter in the old family house, rather tumbledown and inconvenient, damp under trees that drowned and strangled it in summer in a welter of steaming green and covered it with a skeleton tangled mass in the winter. He pottered in his gardens, rumbled, bellowed, roared, visited seldom and then was so ill-natured that his hosts were terrified of him and endured him only because of his family name and money. He frightened off with ridicule, blunt questions, sarcasm, rudeness and bullying any possible suitors who might have come for Adelaide. But he could not frighten off Jules Bouchard.

"I don't know what he comes for!" he would say to Adelaide. "God knows, it isn't to seduce you! Not with the pretty little piece he has down there on Endicott Road, who's worth twice of you, my girl. So it must be he wants to marry you—for your money, or my money—though a devil like that could have a dozen women better than you."

He swore at Jules, cursed him, quarrelled with him, ordered him from the house dozens of times, shook his cane at him. But Jules only laughed, replied in kind, tormented the old man with his witticisms and thrusts, and usually ended up by playing whist with him. One night the old man said, after a successful game: "You can't pull the wool over my eyes, you damned scheming Frenchman. I hate you and always will, and I know what you're after."

Then one night Jules replied, smiling slightly: "If you know, my dear sir, what about it? Are you going to consent to Adelaide marrying me?"

The old man glared at him with his red-rimmed and choleric eyes, blasphemed, consigned him to the depths of various hells. Then, in a suddenly and curiously mild voice, he asked: "Why the devil do you want to marry Addie? She'll never give you brats, and God knows, she'll be no pleasure to sleep with." He peered at Jules cunningly: "It's the money, eh?"

"Possibly," replied Jules calmly.

"But you're no gentleman."

"Neither are you."

Mr. Land Burgeon laughed loudly, with pure enjoyment, and called Adelaide, who had been crocheting in another room, finding her deepest pleasure in the distant sound of Jules' voice, and waiting and living only for those moments when he would speak to her and hold her hand. She came into the room, blushing and smiling and trembling a little as her eyes met Jules'. She had long given up any hope of her father's consent to her marriage, and when she saw the old man, frowning formidably, with his thick lips thrust outward together as they always were when he was enraged, she felt her heart turn over painfully.

"Do you want to marry this scoundrel of a wily Frenchman?" he shouted at her. "This jackanapes with the priest's face?"

Poor Adelaide almost fainted in her tracks. She began to cry soundlessly, looking from Jules to her father.

"Then stop your damned snivelling and have him!" Mr. Burgeon roared. "But mark my words, not a penny of my money shall either of you have unless I get a grandson." He glowered at the paralyzed girl, glowered at Jules. "Bouchard! Butcher!" he muttered bitterly, and with contempt. "Well, the name's appropriate."

So Jules, who treated Adelaide with delicacy, gallantry and kindness, but certainly did not love her, was married to the daughter of Mr. Land Burgeon. And in spite of the old man's frequent and public announcements that his daughter didn't have "the insides" to bear children, bear children Adelaide did, and with great promptitude. In 1886 Armand arrived, in 1887, Emile, and in 1888, Christopher. "He pulled them out of his hat!" old Land exclaimed, with characteristic lack of reticence. "He never got them out of Addie!"

Jules had built a fine home in a very fashionable section of Windsor, a house all brick turrets and white balconies and porches. Jules liked gaiety about him, the flash of women's eyes, the smooth broadcloth backs of men, but he was careful to invite to his house only those of impeccable social standing, and in consequence his visitors were frequently dull. Most of them were Adelaide's friends, immaculate people, conservative people, unblemished and dimly polished people. Life at home was a succession of family dinners, correct, decorous dinners, dull and perfectly served, with heavy silver plate, Haviland china, silver soup tureens and urns, thick white napkins with monograms, decanters of sherry and Moselle. Adelaide was a splendid housekeeper, her servants excellently trained. Her voice was always soft, conciliating, pleasant and tender, her face shining with delicate sympathy and graciousness. Maternity had not rounded her figure in the least, but there was a well-bred vague maturity about her now. Her soft brown hair was drawn back smoothly and neatly from a central part, and even in 1898, when pompadours were the fashion, she wore a mass of shining brown braids coiled at the nape of her neck. There was no doubting the fact that Adelaide, with her neutral colored gowns and gentle words and quiet hands, was "a great lady." She adored Jules and her sons, and was sadly but silently aware of the fact that none of them, except, perhaps, the cruel-faced, thin-lipped Christopher, loved her.

She considered her husband's family bewildering. She was too kind to find any one of them atrocious or impossible. One or two of them terrified her, notably Ernest, who was always amiable to her, and Flora-belle. Having had little acquaintance with vulgarity and bad breeding, she did not recognize these things as such in her mother-in-law, and thought them merely incomprehensible and a little odd. She had been completely blind to them in her father, of whom she spoke as being "just a trifle blunt and outspoken, poor Papa!"

Her whole day was focussed toward the dinner hour, when Jules, dark-faced and polite, always courteous and attentive, sat at the head of the table, and she at the foot, with the boys on each side. Then she felt happy and secure, sheltered. She discussed letters received by her that day, a coming dinner, an invitation, an amusing story about a servant. Her father had been dead a number of years, and she missed him greatly. Never a night passed that she did not mention him, with a faint wet brightening of her sweet eyes. At night, at her table, presiding over the teapots and the cups, she looked almost beautiful, in an anæmic, colorless and gentle way, and Jules, glancing at her, would think he had done very well, with a "lady" for a wife, and her million dollars in his keeping.

She spoke tonight of "Aunt May," whom she loved and found familiar. A letter had arrived from Montreal, in which May had writ-ten that she and Ernest expected to return very shortly. Jules looked up, alertly. But all he said was, absently: "How nice for you, my dear! You and Aunt May are very congenial."

Armand was a bulky, almost beefy, boy, with a round red face and auburn hair, narrow cunning black eyes, and a pleasant smile. He seemed older than his twelve years, for he was big-, if shapeless-, bodied, and he had a mature, measured way of speaking. Eleven-year-old Emile was small, quick and athletic, and laughed easily. He was much less to be trusted than Armand, who had a certain private code of honor. Chris topher was the most like his father, but his skin was pale instead of brown, almost transparent, and he had "basilisk" eyes, gray and motionless and without passion. He was only ten, but his pale mouth was already fixed and settled in its fine cruelty. His nose resembled Jules', as did his low, persuasive voice. Small-boned, inclined to silence, brown-haired, exquisite, he had an air of delicacy extremely like his father's, yet also like his mother's. Jules called him a "bloodless young devil," and liked him the least of his sons. Without honor, himself, he preferred Armand, who had a certain honor, and disliked Christopher, who was most like himself.

"Jules, dear, I'm so sorry you were detained last night," said Adelaide, after a gentle warning glance at Emile, who was surreptitiously pinching Armand.

"So was I," said Emile. "I can't stand Dickinson. He's got hands that look and feel like cold boiled fish. And prim as an old maid, too. When he comes here to dine he's always looking at his watch, and just at three minutes to ten he always announces he's got to go. As if any one wanted him to stay."

"That's enough," replied Jules sharply, though he smiled inwardly. Adelaide murmured reprovingly at her son. "I'm sorry, darling," said Jules to his wife, "but I had considerable to detain me. But it was not necessary for you to stay home from Mrs. Sidway's reception."

"Oh, but I didn't want to go without you." Adelaide's voice was simple and clear. She gazed at her husband with all her innocent adoration in her eyes, and Jules gazed back, smiling fondly. He thought: There's a lot to be said for breeding, after all. Very convenient in a wife, for Adelaide can't possibly not know a little something about my "Merry Widow." He said: "I'm so sorry, Adelaide, but I must go off again immediately after dinner. I've heard from Andre that the old Major isn't very well. After all, he's in his eighties. It's pretty lonely for Mama there, too; she's getting old and there's no one at home but François, now, and you know what he is. Mama's sixty-five now, and too stout to get about much. She likes to see us occasionally."

"I'd go with you," said Adelaide contritely, "but I'm expecting Emma and Wilson tonight. They'll be disappointed not to find you in."

"Papa, may I have a bicycle?" asked Emile.

"Not until you learn to treat it better than you did the last," replied his father. "You've had four bicycles in two years, and I don't approve of carelessness and extravagance."

Armand, who was not very talkative, asked his father about the war. He listened to the reply with real interest and respectful attention. Jules enjoyed talking to the boy; he found him more intelligent than most adults. While he spoke, Armand watched him with his narrow, secret eyes. Emile, who was a sulker when he wasn't laughing, scowled at the silver epergne, muttered ill-temperedly at the maid when she offered him pudding. Christopher listened, as usual, to everything, and said nothing. When Jules' idle glance happened to touch him, the eyes of father and son met with a strange effect like that of a collision, followed by a recoil that resounded all through them. It was always this way, this deadly antagonism. Jules looked away, and fastened his attention courteously on his eldest son.

At the conclusion of the meal Jules rose to go, kissed his wife lightly, and promised to return as soon as possible.

"Give Mama Norwood a kiss for me," said Adclaide.

On the way to the hall and his coat and hat, Jules glanced with satisfaction into the rooms he passed. In an age that was stuffy and crowded with furniture and ornaments, Adelaide was far ahead of her time, for she had built her home of coolness, space, exquisitely grouped furniture of fine rosewood and slender mahogany, breadths of uncluttered polished floors, neutral-tinted walls and specially made plain rugs of dim and unobtrusive patterns. She relied on flowers and an occasional pastel in a plain frame, for ornamentation. Her taste was, like herself, impeccable.

It was a fine clear night, so Jules swung along lithely to his mother's house. Quaker Terraces was no longer fashionable; the houses were becoming dingy and shabby, the gardens and walks grubby. But old Florabelle would not leave the street; she had come here as Raoul's bride over forty years ago, and though she was in her late sixties, and the wife for many years now of Major Norwood and the mother of his children, every doorway and room, every inch of the garden, her very bedroom, shared with the Major, reminded her of her dead young lover and first husband. The furniture had been changed half a dozen times since Raoul's death, the walls painted and re-papered, but very often, even now, Florabelle would suddenly glance up with a half smile, for the years went back and she expected to see Raoul. When she spoke of him, even when in grief, she did not speak of him as dead, but as one living and loved, at a little distance. This steadfast love, this green loyalty, puzzled all her family, for the old, gross, cunning and petulant Florabelle was certainly a strange receptacle for the perfume of devotion.

Jules disliked the old house where he had been born. He had none of the French love for deep roots and walls that have stood for many years. He thought the house stuffy, dark, old-fashioned and decayed, as it was, and not having any sentimentality, he was not moved by the sight of the room where he had first breathed, nor the nursery where he had played as a child, nor the gardens in which he had raced. He loathed the bad taste of Florabelle's parlor, with its high narrow ceiling and long gloomy walls, and windows like dismal crevices. Here, he thought, was the very essence of a dying era, Victorianism, combined with a prodigious amount of bad taste. It was glitteringly clean, but crowded. Antimacassars, wax flowers under glass, overburdened marble mantelpieces draped in red velvet, whatnots groaning under collections of ivory and Dresden figurines, horsehair sofas and hideous walnut chairs and heavy tables, red velvet drapes on each side of Nottingham window curtains: all these made his eyes wince. On a white bearskin rug lay a yellow tomcat, bellicose and unfriendly.

Florabelle was extremely stout now; as she was short in stature, the fat of her made her look almost as broad as she was tall. Her breasts and belly had merged together in one solid mass under her black silk dress, which had a fussy arrangement of white lace at the throat. Her hair was white, but elaborately curled in a fashion dating from her youth. Under this mound of waves and curls was her face, triple-chinned, rosy, small-nosed, bright blue of eye, pouting with still red lip, still smooth and tinted of complexion. A pretty old fat face, and a vulgar, petulant one, shrewd but not intelligent, knowing and suspicious. Diamonds glittered everywhere on her, in her ears, at her throat, clustered on her fat white fingers. One leg was rather stiff these days, and she used a cane with a carved golden head. She read gay novels incessantly when she was not sewing or gossiping, and her interest in fashions, the affairs of her family and her neighbors, had not abated with the years. Neither had her malice decreased, nor her sympathy improved.

Florabelle's favorite was Jules, who had given her the least trouble of all her children. Moreover, he reminded her of his father. She liked to have him sit by her, and at these times she would keep her hand on his shoulder and lean toward him, smiling and listening, or scolding, her bright blue eyes glistening with malice or amusement or interest. She disliked Adelaide, whom she considered to have "no style."

Jules found his mother yawning over an article, in a paper, by Zola. Apparently Florabelle found that in this piece the writer was not living up to his usual reputation, for she seemed extremely bored. After she had kissed Jules, she exclaimed pettishly: "Whoever these days cares about the Dreyfus case! And something's always happening to the Jews, anyway. I haven't the slightest doubt they deserve it! People who are always in trouble, and having enemies and being run from place to place —well, I have no patience with them."

Jules examined the article, *J'accuse*, and put it down. "You're a good old barbarian, Mama," he said. He stared at the paper thoughtfully, where he had laid it on the table. "And a good old Britisher. Always kick the under dog. Under a realistic government, or philosophy, the under dog deserves kicking."

Major Norwood, in excellent health, sat on the opposite side of the fireplace, half dozing, half smiling. A mane of thick hair, snow-white and silken, lay on his shoulders, and his white mustache drooped almost to his chin. Age had only mellowed a temperament good-natured and kindly and honestly generous, if stupid, and he greeted everyone with an affectionate smile and deep interest, though he was apt to forget one immediately, and even to muddle his closest family relationships. But when it finally penetrated to the old man's consciousness that this was Jules, he became quite alert, and his innocent blue eyes began to shine under the shelf of his white eyebrows.

"My dear, dear Jules, how glad I am to see you! And how splendidly everything is going! I see that our stock has risen six points today. War rumors, eh?"

"I suppose so, Papa."

"I've wired my broker to buy three thousand shares for me tomorrow at the opening price."

Jules quickened, and frowned. "That was very foolish, Papa Norwood. You must let me send a wire cancelling it. You see, it is not at all certain that war will be declared, after all. I—I expect that the rumor will be pooh-poohed tomorrow night, and the stock will go down immediately. Suppose, for instance, that you put in your order to buy at eight or ten points lower than today's price?"

The Major was silent a moment, and his innocent eyes sharpened slowly as they fixed themselves on Jules' face. Then he nodded, and said, "Ah."

Jules smiled. By tomorrow night, he would be able to buy Barbour-Bouchard stock at ten points lower than today's price. He had seen to that very dexterously. Within a week it would be a third higher than it was today, and the Bouchards' net would draw in a pretty mess of fish.

Florabelle engaged Jules in a rapid-fire conversation, in which his part consisted of monosyllables. Among other things, she was annoyed, as usual, with François.

"I really don't know, Jules! A man of his age, sitting and mooning like a calf. It's enough to give me nerves all over. And so irritable it is impossible to have him in the room. Jules, did Adelaide buy you that cravat? Dear me, dear me, I always did say that poor girl had no taste, or was color-blind, or something. So drab and dreary. I declare, it is no contrast at all, all pale grays and dark gray brocade. No life. I like life. Now, a touch of red, or deep blue there, on the edge—but no, Adelaide must be satisfied, and so she picked out that cravat! Like a clergyman or an old gentleman. It would look much nicer on the Major, I'm sure. But what was I saying about François? Oh, yes, he gets duller every day. And it seems today that he expected that ridiculous child, Alice, to come, and she didn't. Such a silly, frivolous little piece, and besides, I never did like red hair. And Elsa has such atrocious taste, too, not like Adelaide's, which is so lifeless and dead, but too rich and heavy for such a small baggage. Do you know what she wore yesterday, and she not an ounce over ninety pounds? A sable cape! And a hat like a cartwheel on her head! You never saw anything so ridiculous! The child could hardly carry it all. And so saucy, too. When I suggested that her cape and hat certainly did not suit her, she became quite impertinent. I would have had my ears boxed soundly if I had answered my elders like that at her age. I really don't know what the world's coming to. Well! She had promised François to come today, and she didn't——"

Jules took her hand and held it firmly, as he always did when he wanted to stop her flow of talk and get her to concentrate.

"You say, she didn't come, after promising François?"

"Eh? Whatever! Why should you be so interested in that, Jules? Your eyes are like bright pinpoints. Well, she did promise. She told me she would be here for tea with me and François this afternoon. She always comes when she promises. But no doubt the chit had a cold or a headache, or something, and just couldn't come, and so I can't see why François should act like a caged lion—that's what the dear Major called it, didn't you, Major?—a caged lion. Walked back and forth and screamed at me, and when I said he'd probably have a fit, as he used to when he was a child, he was positively rude to me, wasn't he, Major?"

The Major started from a doze. "Eh? Oh, yes, my love. I believe he said: 'Shut up!' "

Florabelle whimpered. " 'Shut up!' To his mother! I tell you, I nearly swooned, Jules. I wish you would speak to him, indeed I do. And all because a child young enough to be his daughter didn't come to read her foolish poetry to him."

"Did Alice send a message to François?"

"No, Elsa called this afternoon, and was all sweetness, the big hulking creature. She said she and Paul thought Alice was bothering us too much lately, and was really quite considerate, and laughed a little about Alice, saying she was going to take her to New York for awhile. They are leaving the day after tomorrow, I believe. For a very extended stay. Elsa hinted that she and Paul were quite sure that Alice and her cousin Thomas Van Eyck were sweet on each other, and so——"

Jules stood up abruptly. "Where's François?"

"Why, he's upstairs in his room. Did you wish to see him, Jules? I'll send for him."

"Never mind, Mama. I'll go up myself and see him."

He almost ran from the hot bright room with its white bearskin rug. He found François sitting at his desk upstairs, brooding sullenly over several white sheets of paper. François turned his head as Jules knocked lightly and entered. He threw down his pen pettishly. "Well?" he asked rudely. "So it's you?"

Jules smiled amiably. "Yes, it's me. May I sit down? Thanks."

"I didn't say you could sit down," said François, glowering sus-

piciously. He was afraid of Jules, as well as disliking him. "But I suppose I can't throw you out."

"Hardly." Jules crossed his knees, lit one of his long thin cigars.
François coughed pointedly, looked excessively pained, then got up and
opened a window. He sat down again, surveyed Jules intently, his heavy
black eyebrows knotted together. He was very ill at ease. Jules always
made a little patch of nervous sweat break out between his shoulder-
blades, and he had the feeling that there was something dangerous in
the room with him. Even when they had been children it had been the
same. He covered his uneasiness, nervousness and suspicious fear by
exaggerated hostility and rudeness.

Jules, smoking elegantly, watched his brother. François was not
very tall, but he had a leanness and fleshlessness that made him appear
much taller than he was. He had a brown cadaverous face, with hollow
cheekbones, fiery but uncertain black eyes, long thin nose and chin, wide
hysterically tense mouth, and a shock of thick black hair which always seemed to need combing. His clothing seemed to be about to
blow off him, for his cravat slipped under one ear, his coat slipped off a
shoulder, his shoe-laces were perpetually untied, his waistcoat unbuttoned. He wore an expression of chronic petulance, impatience and
irritability, and his whole air, his jerky and high-pitched voice, testified to a passionate and arrogant egotism. He could never be in repose;
his legs were always twisting about chairs, his hands always plucking at
tablecloths, his nose and forehead mechanically wrinkling and smoothing themselves. There was something febrile and nerve-racking about
him.

He seemed more nervous than ever whenever Jules was about. As
Jules watched him, he could hardly contain his restlessness. He jerked his
head, tossed back his untidy hair, his nose and forehead wrinkled and
twitched. But all the time he fixed his sullen uncertain eyes upon his
brother and panted a little. His old feeling of adjacent danger increased
to the point of hysteria.

Jules coughed gently, and said with great smoothness: "You are looking tired, François. You need a rest, or change."

This was a sore spot with François, as Jules well knew. François,
overcome by this unexpected sympathy and gentleness from his feared
brother, flung out his hands impetuously. "Don't I know it! You are
right, Jules. I never thought you were so discerning and sympathetic.
Perhaps I've misjudged you. But I need a rest, or change. I—I feel I
am about to suffocate. It is deadly in this town of Windsor. It would
not be so bad if I had sufficient money of my own. But I haven't. You
know mother: she allows me a miserable one hundred dollars a month,
and swears I shall get no more until she dies and I receive my share of
father's estate. In the meantime, I starve! How can an artist endure such

a state of affairs? It strangles me—" He paused, and his strained eyes again fixed themselves with a pathetic expression of suspicion, pleading and trust upon Jules.

Jules studied the end of his cigar. "Yes," he said gently and thoughtfully. "I think I understand very well. I'm not going to pretend that I can feel completely what you say an artist must feel. But I can certainly understand what a man of your age must feel, being treated like a child. I've given the subject considerable thought lately."

Eagerness flashed like a light over simple François' face. "Jules! Can you help me? Will you speak to mother?"

Jules sighed. "As you have said, you know mother. François, I simply don't know what you can do! It is very terrible. That is why I have come to talk to you tonight. No one else will. Our family is not known for sympathy."

"Don't I know it!" exclaimed François bitterly. "Materialistic barbarians! Frey had to run away from them. Trudie, poor girl, ran away —into death, from them. Mother continually asks me: 'Why don't you do something practical—make money!' As if money were anything but the gruesome business of barter and exchange! The world thinks in terms of the bazaar, where everything is for sale, and nothing is sacred. Where beauty is valueless, unless it adorns something utilitarian, like— like——"

"A china chamber, for instance," suggested Jules.

François winced, but smiled. "Well, if one wants to be vulgar, yes. Yes! That is quite right. The world has a bed-chamber mind, and can see beauty only when it is as obvious and gross as painted pink roses and green leaves." He paused, then said with a return to his thin hostility, "But I still don't like that last Van Gogh of yours, Jules. Too—too——"

"Realistic, perhaps?"

"Realistic! What a horrible word! As though reality were to be cherished and admired and sought after, in all its ugliness! As though reality, so sordid and bleak and hideous and terrible, were something of value! That is the wonder and the joy and the salvation of beauty, that it masks and covers reality, and makes it endurable to our eyes."

Jules sighed lightly and examined his fingernails. "There is a lot in what you say, François, but living in a practical and a realistic world, one must give hostages, arrive at compromises. It is a paradox, but if one wishes to get what one wants, one must compromise. At first. But all this does not alter the basic fact that you, an intelligent man, who might be able to create if you had peace of mind, are treated ignominiously, like an imbecile child."

François regarded him with a sort of pathetic wonder. "I—I did not know you cared that much about me, Jules. You—you always seemed a trifle hard, and exigent, like our ghastly Uncle Ernest. I was wrong. I beg your pardon." He sighed, and to any one but Jules that sigh would have sounded very touching.

He looked at François gravely. "You are thirty-five, aren't you, François? Have you ever thought of marrying?"

François' face changed, colored, became for an instant almost radiant. Then it relapsed into heavy sullenness. He snatched at his discarded pen, thrust it viciously into the wood of his polished rosewood desk, then tossed it at the wall. "Married! My God! On one hundred dollars a month? Hah! What girl, what sweet little creature, even if she were an angel, and able to appreciate an artist, would marry a man with one hundred dollars a month? It would be a crime to ask her, and even if she consented, what man of honor——"

"True," cut in Jules deftly. "François, I must talk to you as man to man. Yesterday afternoon," he continued, lying smoothly and swiftly, "Paul Barbour came into my office when I was having a private conference with Honore and Leon, and began to shout at me like an enraged bull. It seems he suspected you and little Alice were plotting to get married. And he told me fully what he intended to do: he is going to send the child to New York and marry her off to her cousin, Thomas Van Eyck. Tomorrow, I believe."

While he had been speaking, François' face had turned a livid white, and blue lines had sprung out about his lips. All his pretentiousness disappeared; he sat there like a man stricken and anguished, as indeed he was.

"New York! Tomorrow! Alice!" His hands wrung together. "But he can't do that to my Alice! We love each other. She—she told me she didn't care what I had, she would marry me just the same. The—the years between us didn't matter, she said. All she wished to do was to serve me and my art—the darling! I can't believe this, Jules." He stood up, shaken with his distress. He looked down at his brother, pleadingly, desperately.

Jules shook his head sadly. "I'm afraid it is true. You know, François, I guessed some time ago that you cared for Alice. But it was Alice who inadvertently, poor child, betrayed the whole thing to me. This business will break her heart. If you care anything for her, you will contrive to take her away and marry her before she is sent to New York."

Francois flung out his arms in his desperation. "But how? I have only twenty dollars to my name at this minute! It is two weeks to the first, when Mother gives me my check for one hundred dollars. And how can I support my darling? Her father will cut her off, will give her nothing, if she marries me."

"You forget," said Jules gently, "Alice is her grandfather's heiress. Listen to me closely: Uncle Ernest won't cut her off. He'll admire her, and you, for going and getting what you both want. Paul isn't Crown

Prince any longer. I'm not speaking idly: I know. The old devil isn't going to live forever, and when you marry Alice, and he dies, you'll be the richest man in Windsor. Sit down, François, and try to listen carefully."

François sat down, trembling, but his face, turned to Jules, was full of excitement and hope and increasing joy. He leaned forward, eagerly, and put his quivering hand on his brother's knee. Jules laid his smooth cool brown hand on François' tremulous fingers, and pressed them affectionately.

"But you, as a man of honor, naturally, remember that before Uncle Ernest's death you will have a wife to support, and that, of course, you can't bring her here. Paul won't give her a cent, I agree with you. He'll probably have a stroke into the bargain, which wouldn't be bad at all. Now then: for years we've all tried to interest you in the company, but possibly you were correct when you said repeatedly that you were not fit for that work, that an artist would stifle in the atmosphere of business. A 'nefarious business' you called it, I believe?" he added with a smile. François blushed. "Well, never mind. It doesn't matter. You know your own feelings best. I am most certainly against any man entering a business for which he is constitutionally unfitted, and which will at once do violence to his conscience and his nature." (François looked a trifle foolish, and stammered incoherently: "Oh, damn it, I don't care whether it's nefarious or not! Money is money!")

"Quite true, François." Jules' smile was genial and indulgent. "Even if you are an artist, you can see things straight. That is the difference between a fool and a wise man. Now then: after Paul went away yesterday, Honore and Leon and I talked it all over. We were very indignant. We looked around for a solution, for we are all fond of little Alice, and naturally, of you. So eventually we arrived at a brilliant idea: Honore suggested that you be appointed a director of the Kinsolving Arms Company, at a salary of fifteen thousand dollars a year!"

Dazzled and excited though he was, François' face blanched with despair. "But I don't know anything about the Kinsolving Arms, Jules! What the hell could I do there? How could I earn fifteen thousand dollars a year? By sitting year after year in a stuffy drab office, where I'd smother, surrounded by machinery and tramping men, crushed under noise and smells—! My God, Jules! How could you be so cruel, offering me hope, then demanding my life in return for it?"

Jules listened to this hysterical outburst with an immovable expression, but his eyes, narrowed and hidden, glinted between their lids. A muscle twitched in his cheek, and his exquisitely kept hands clenched and moved as though they were strangling something loathesome and repulsive. But his voice was still gentle and indulgent, when François had finished.

"Of course, we understand all that, François. We're not offering you stones, or demanding anything. We are sincerely desirous of finding a solution for you and Alice. We want to help you. Now this directorship: all that will be required of you is to appear on the board of directors twice a year. For perhaps an hour or two. A mere honorary title. Do you understand? Nothing else will be required of you. Believe me, we are trying to help you."

François was almost beside himself with joy. He stood up, bent over Jules suddenly, and flung his arms about his brother's neck. "My God! My God!" he sobbed, standing upright after a convulsive moment. "What can I say? What can I do? What can I do! I can't believe it. It —it's like an answer to prayer, this deliverance. Like an awakening after hell. I've been sitting here, dying by inches, I tell you, Jules, planning suicide, weeping, tearing my hair, and you come like an archangel, like a deliverer— What can I do or say?"

"Well, sit down, and I'll tell you." Nothing could have been kinder than Jules' expression, nothing more affectionate. "We must be practical. Tomorrow, when Paul is at his office, you must go direct to Alice's home, and let nothing prevent you from seeing her. Not a dozen flunkeys, or that fat elephant, Elsa. Then, you must take the child away, just as she stands. Immediately. Before Elsa can telephone Paul. You will have a carriage waiting, and you will both immediately drive to some justice, or a minister, and marry. Secure the license before you go for the girl. Then, return here, and we'll take care of the rest."

"Jules, help me! Come with me tomorrow! You'll be able to get by Elsa, and reach Alice! Or just come with me, and sit in the carriage."

"I can't do that, François." Jules seemed pained. "It would never do for Paul to suspect that any of us, except you, had anything to do with this. Remember, we have business relationships to keep up, and so on. No, you must get up your courage and do it yourself. It won't be very hard." He stood up, drew out his wallet. "Here. Two fifty dollar bills. That ought to smooth your way nicely, tomorrow. And, just another thing: we'll all be interested. Telephone me when the deed is done, won't you?" He put his hand on François' bony and trembling shoulder. "Now, brace up. And, by the way, don't mention a word of this to our mother. You know Mama?"

"Don't I, though!" ejaculated François, laughing and sobbing together. He wrung Jules' hand. "God! You're an angel, Jules!"

CHAPTER CIX

RNEST BARBOUR, approaching seventy-two, did not like the last decade of the nineteenth century. It seemed to him that the decades of his youth had been gracious and graceful, more coordinated and stable, slower yet stronger and more significant. Now, everything was heat and flux and raucous voices and noise and ugliness.

It was a simple age, but also hideous, trying to relieve its own lack of beauty with flounces and ruffles. Even its corruption was naïve, its ugliness disarming. Life was a matter of whitewashed fences and rose gardens and box hedges and sleek horses, and big houses adorned by machine-made wooden fretwork and turrets, large feathered hats, plump beds, roast beef, watering places, twinkling victorias.

The age of advertising had begun: Hood's Sarsaparilla, Paine's Celery Compound, Lydia E. Pinkham's female wonder tonic, and Pearline, were beginning to make the nation conscious of its physical self. White's Yucatan Gum was setting the jaws of the younger generation to a bovine rhythm. Sailor hats, stuck on masses of pompadour with great sharp pins, adorned the heads of gay young women in heavy long-braided skirts and starched shirtwaists. (Ernest thought of the ribboned bell-like and dainty gowns of the women of his youth, from which slender waists, white bosoms and gleaming shoulders rose as from the calyx of a flower.) But today mutton-legged sleeves were outraging the masculine sense of beauty, and plumes obscured irate male views at the theatres. "Ta-ra-ra boom-de-ay," was tickling the feet of the young people, and everything was joyous; America had just emerged from the depression and panic of 1893 and was in an elated condition. Everyone was learnedly discussing the merits of Socialism and listening intently to a gentleman called Eugene Debs; from him, they turned with equal gravity to another and less intelligent prophet, one William Jennings Bryan, who was more picturesquely arrayed by nature and design than Debs and therefore more worthy of serious attention.

Never before had there appeared such heavy mustaches on the faces of elegant gentlemen, and never had beer been so carefully brewed and so copious. Saloons were rich in the luxury of mahogany bars and gleaming mirrors and mighty brass spittoons; the theatre resounded with sentimental dramas dripping with high motives and heroism. The new safety bicycles were everywhere and people were talking excitedly about the rumors of "flying machines," and the new gay slang expressions "You're off your trolley," "It's a good thing, push it along," "It's naughty but it's nice," were enlivening the language. Eleonora Duse stirred women with her stately gestures and passionate histrionics, and the ideal of female beauty was still Lillian Russell, the ideal of success, Diamond Jim Brady. Frontiers were disappearing farther and farther west. Gentlemen appeared at lawn parties in flannels and gaily striped blazers and caps with long visors, accompanying ladies with wasp waists, deep lace berthas, hats like aviaries or floral exhibits, and skirts that fell in cascades from prominent posteriors.

It was a raw, exuberant and vital age, full of stupidities and fatnesses and leannesses, but also excitements. America was feeling her power; through the smother of European foam she was lifting her strong young head, shouting coarsely but effectively. Suddenly conscious of herself, she blared her red-cheeked defiance across the seas. She drank her beer gustily, believed firmly, and at times, tearfully, in God and Country and Motherhood and the President and the Flag, called herself the refuge of the oppressed and invited the world to her table of thanksgiving. The world came, to laugh and stare and ridicule and envy.

Civil War veterans still marched in well-filled ranks. Speakers at reunions spoke of eternal peace. A certain German ruler spoke solemnly of German Kultur and wider understanding between nations, and science. France draped her statues of Alsace and Lorraine with black, and listened uneasily to the whispers of a man called Sazaroff, and other agents. English statesmen listened to the hosannas that were universally sung to peace, civilization, brotherhood, justice and faith, and cheered their ageing Queen, and in the meantime bought secret blocks of stock issued by one Robsons-Strong Company.

The America of Ernest Barbour's youth had been much like a more lavish and easier England, England expanded, become prosperous and rich. Castes had flourished, speech had been similar, mannerisms had been faithfully imported, morals had been borrowed. But this new America was something he did not know or care about, except that it bored him and exhausted him with feverish inanity and constant puerile laughter. He and his colleagues, for reasons of their own, had fomented contempt, distrust and ridicule for England, and having succeeded, he found what he had helped create distasteful.

He knew well enough that he was old, and dying. To be irritated as well, seemed to him insupportable. He realized, also, that there was no greater hell to be conceived than that of having a mind still unimpaired, an energy still avid, banked up in a body that trembled at exertion and grew exhausted, and memories that seemed to become more lurid and more intense as the present grew less significant. His mind, finding no satisfaction and value in the reality of the days, turned its back on time and began to thumb old pages. His sleep was a constant procession of vivid pictures which seemed utterly real and only then occurring; he never thought, when experiencing them: This is only a dream of what has gone and is dead.

Often he would dream of the dining room at the Sessions house, where he sat at the table and carved the joint or the roast. Dimly, he knew that May was there, and Godfrey and Reginald; they were faint if present shadows. But colorful, alive, shining with vitality, he saw the faces of Guy and Gertrude and Joey, young faces. He saw Gertrude with her sweet wild gestures, her cloud of dark hair, her swift, uncertain smile. Guy spoke, showing his glittering white teeth, the lamplight on his yellow hair. There was Joey, frowning heavily at his plate, but lifting his head alertly when his father spoke, watching his father's moving mouth. No one had seemed to care particularly about Joey, that heavy youth with the sullen voice and disagreeable features and rude mannerisms; but Ernest had cared, and had understood.

His three dead children, young again, alive again, sat at his table, and looked at him, smiling. Often he would wake up with a terrible start, thinking he had heard Gertrude's voice—Gertrude, who had been his darling. Sometimes he thought he could hear Guy's running light step, or Joey's rumbling tones. Then he would dream of Amy, sitting opposite him in candlelight, home again at the very table she had sat at when a child and a young girl, before her marriage to Martin. He could see the movement of her slim white hands, and the glitter of his own diamonds upon them, and her mouth, smiling and a little wry with experience. In his sleep, he would reach out to her, and hold May in his arms. This never failed to shock him into consciousness; for a few thundering singing moments in the dark, holding May, he would believe he held Amy. May, too, would wake up, and would know at once what had happened. She would press his face against her shoulder, or breast, and murmur to him, and soon he would fall asleep again. But May would not fall asleep, as she held him.

He was fonder than ever of May, and unspeakably grateful to her. Often he would say to her: "May, I don't know what I'd do without you, by God, I don't!" Then she would answer, smiling comfortably: "I don't, either."

Neither of them ever mentioned Gertrude or Guy or Joey, but only once or twice, in anguish, May had looked at Ernest and had cried silently: You have killed my children!

Finally, even Ernest knew that he was an old man and had very little longer to live. He had allowed May to take him on a long cruise, which lasted over four months. This so improved him that when he heard rumors of contention between America and Spain he abruptly transferred to a ship going to Europe and spent two months there, in spite of May's angry protests. Then he returned home.

He was very exhausted when he reached New York. May, hoping to get him to Windsor quietly, did not announce their arrival one stormy March morning. They drove to the Sessions house, and Ernest went to bed. The servants were busy downstairs; up here everything was warm red firelight against a background of a furious white blizzard. Ernest, who often, now, could not lie down and breathe with comfort, sat bolstered up in bed by a series of fat pillows. May sat beside him, holding his hand, smiling, talking with her old humor and laughter.

She looked at him, breathing on his pillows with difficulty. He had shrunken greatly the last year; even the broadness of his shoulders had thinned, become brittle. His throat was withered and corded, his face lined, gray and shrunken, the pale implacable eyes seeming much larger, almost protruding, in their sockets. His white hair was neatly combed, but still rose crestlike over his broad pale forehead, which was singularly free from wrinkles, except between the eyes, where the flesh was a deep irascible furrow. His ears were pallid lobes, his jawbone jutting and rigid. The hand May held was clammy and cool, and was a trifle tremulous.

He liked to hear May talk to him. Not even Amy, he thought, had had such a voice, rich and deep and humorous and quick. He hardly paid attention to what she was saying; he merely listened to the sound of her voice. He thought: May is an old woman. He studied her thick hair, which was like white silk, her lined, soft and withered cheeks, still delicately colored, her mouth, gleaming with the perfect porcelain of manufactured teeth, her plump collapsed bosom and heavy upper arms, the broad thighs that shimmered under black silk. But her eyes, sparkling and quick with intelligence, were the same, for all the discolored pockets under them and the fine wrinkles that webbed them. At seventy, May was a comely old woman, heavy with life and understanding.

He said: "May, I'm going to die soon."

Her smile slackened, but she answered vigorously: "Nonsense. You'll see ninety, at least."

His hand moved restlessly in hers. "Don't lie, May, either to yourself, or to me. I'm going to peg out. It's funny, though, to think that I've married you twice, and each time because I needed you." He smiled at her, not without irony. She waited, and her expression saddened. "The first time, I needed your money, and what you had. The second time, I needed you. Sometimes I think it was you I needed both times."

May swallowed, as though a ball had risen into her throat. She held his hand tightly, and her lashes became moist. "Ernest, dear, we've been married nearly fifty years, yet you've never said anything to me so wonderful as that before." She laughed shakily: "Yes, I said 'nearly fifty years,' for I don't consider that I wasn't still married to you— even when I wasn't!"

He regarded her curiously. "I haven't been a 'good' husband, May."

"I know that." She smiled a little. "I know that. But it didn't matter. I've always loved you."

He sighed, and turned his head away from her. He stared at the door, and his old sunken face became darker, grayer. May glanced at the door too, and knew, with a sinking of her heart, what he was looking for. He said: "I'd like to see Frey's and Renee's boy. I'm glad they named him Ernest. And I'd like to see Reginald's girls. Young women, now."

May thought, with a pressure like iron behind her eyes: Poor Ernest. How terribly he has failed!

Later on, toward evening, he told her to call Paul and Jules. May was distressed. Whatever did he wish to discuss business for, his first day home, and he so tired! Well, Paul, then, but why on earth, Jules? Jules!

"Jules," said Ernest quietly, "is the most dangerous enemy a man ever had. I don't know exactly if he is mine, but I can look at him, and see. He's no friend, even though I've done everything for him. I've got to see." He grinned faintly. "That damned Jesuit!" He told May that when she telephoned his nephews she was not to tell one that the other was coming. Waiting for them, after his light supper in bed, his face took on something of its old expectancy, its old vitality. His breathing became easier, and when the doctor called, he told his patient cheerfully that he'd soon be up and about, as well as ever.

Paul, affectionately indignant that he had not been told in advance of his uncle's homecoming, arrived first. Ernest listened ironically, allowed his hand to be shaken, replied casually to Paul's demands as to the state of his health. May, knitting near the fire, glanced repeatedly at Paul. "Where is little Alice?" she asked.

Paul sat down, but answered her question facing Ernest, as though his uncle had asked it. "I'm sending Alice to New York tomorrow night. I'd like her to marry Tom Van Eyck. Money there, and practically everything else, as you know, Uncle Ernest."

Ernest raised his white eyebrows. "Lucy's boy, eh? A lump. But a harmless young fellow. How does the child like the idea of marrying him?"

Paul hesitated, and seeing this, May exclaimed in alarm, dropping her knitting: "Paul, you aren't going to force her, are you? She's such a little creature, and—and—a little weak. She couldn't stand pressure. Paul, you aren't——"

Paul glanced at her with acute irritation and dislike, and for some reason his big face flushed. "Alice is a child, and doesn't know what she wants. I don't think you need worry that I'd make her do anything against her happiness, Aunt May. You don't think that, do you?"

May looked at him for a long moment. "I don't know," she said slowly, "I don't know." And turned her face toward Ernest, who was gazing at his own hands fixedly.

"Well, I know!" said Paul, more and more irritated.

There was a silence. The air of the room was heavy with the memory of Gertrude. Each one of the three was thinking of her.

"Is there some one else she—fancies?" asked Ernest at last in a casual voice.

Paul hesitated again. Then he waved his hand in an offhand manner. "No, of course not. But she's been hanging around Aunt Florabelle's house, reading and writing poetry with that ass of a François, and it's making her morbid, and giving her ideas that she's a genius, or something." He laughed shortly.

Ernest frowned. His manner became alert, almost menacing. "But François is at least seventeen years older than Alice. She surely can't fancy him?"

"Certainly not," replied Paul hurriedly.

May, disturbed and apprehensive, looked first at her husband and then at Paul. At that moment Jules was announced.

He came in, walking in his light buoyant manner, and greeted his uncle with the smoothest and most gracious respect. He inquired solicitously about his health. Ernest smiled. He always seemed to enjoy Jules, through whom he saw completely, and who always amused him. "You know you don't care a damn how I feel, Jules," he said. "Well, I don't hold it against you. Sit down and join us."

Paul's face was darkly colored. He did not know what to make of this. Evidently Ernest had been expecting Jules. Paul's heart began to thud painfully against the walls of his chest. What did all this mean? He nodded curtly to his cousin, and turned his back on him.

Ernest lost his casual manner now, and his amiable expression. He asked his wife to bring a sheaf of papers from his desk. He put his hands over them, and regarded his nephews piercingly. When he finally concentrated on Paul, his expression became more and more forbidding, and the old baleful light shot out from under his eyebrows.

"There are some things I want explained," he said harshly. "I hope you can explain them, Paul."

"Well, what are they?" Paul's voice was confident, even bellicose, but his face tightened a little. Jules, lighting a cigar, watched everyone intently. His eye glittered.

"You've been my sales manager in my absence," said Ernest quietly. "When I was in Europe, two months ago, I happened to meet and talk to Torsten Vilhelm Nordenfeldt. He wasn't much to be considered in the armaments business until he hired Sazaroff. You've heard of Sazaroff, I presume?" he added ironically.

Paul bit his lip, but said nothing. Jules smiled.

"Without Sazaroff, Nordenfeldt would have failed years ago. But Sazaroff is the best damned contact man any one could have. We haven't got any one like him. I wish to God we had! Wycherley, Hearns, Von Goebell, Pushkin: they are bloody idiots compared with him. Well, Nordenfeldt has offered, through Sazaroff, in the Mediterranean, some new inventions of his, base fuse, time fuse, light artillery guns, and something that'll revolutionize sea battles. And do you know what's happened? Sazaroff has sold practically every government he has approached! And what have we done, through our cursed agents? Sat on our backsides and watched ourselves being robbed!" A dark crimson congested his face, and May, full of fear, murmuring, rose and stood beside the bed. "We've got an eccentric screw breach, that Honore invented, that's ten times better than Nordenfeldt's. We've got better everything. We've got the French process secret of melinite, which Honore managed to secure for us. We could have sold directly, or through Robsons, to any of these governments, at a better price in the long run. But we didn't! Why?" He struck the paper violently with his hand.

Paul wet his lips. "I can't imagine. We've got our agents on the job. Sazaroff is a slimy devil, and got around things some way. I trust our agents. We can't get better men, Sazaroff or no Sazaroff. And besides, Sazaroff is on intimate terms with Georges Clemenceau. Thieves together. He's got a lot of contacts like that. It's something we can't get around."

"When I was younger, I got around them!" shouted Ernest in a strangled voice. "But now that I've let fools help in my affairs, we get beaten all over the damned map."

Paul was silent. May, terrified, put her hand on Ernest's forehead, but he jerked away from her savagely. Jules regarded the end of his cigar intently, and smiled gently.

"Robsons are fit to be tied," resumed Ernest, his passion rising more and more. "Nordenfeldt is tied up with that other English concern, and the business is going out of our hands. God, in all that mess over there, with French and British concerns fighting the Nickolayeff naval shipyards, and Turkish shipyards and naval ordnance in a filthy mess, we ought to have cleaned up in the hundred millions! But we didn't. And now, Russia is turning her back on Schultz-Poiret and dickering with Sazaroff——"

"You mean," interrupted Jules gently, " 'was' dickering."

Ernest turned to him, and his mouth fell open. "Eh? What is that?"

Jules pulled his chair closer. Paul's expression changed as he looked at his cousin. "It is regrettable," continued Jules meditatively, "that our

—I beg your pardon, Uncle Ernest—that your agents have been imbeciles. I always thought they were, but as I was not in a position to suggest, except as regards the Sessions Steel Company, I did not speak to you of them. However, I finally engaged agents of my own——"

"Your own?" exploded Ernest, with fury. "Your own!" Then, curiously, his fury subsided, and his face smoothed out. "Go on, Jules," he continued in an oddly mild voice, and turned his shoulder upon Paul.

"I know it was presumptuous, and I deservedly, no doubt, merit Paul's displeasure," Jules continued, with his gently deprecating air. Paul's hands slowly clenched. "But I felt, if things turned out rightly, that I would be forgiven. So I engaged three, much cleverer in many ways, than yours, and good matches for Sazaroff. One of them is the younger son of an English nobleman, whose father is a little niggardly. A very clever young man. He had some splendid connections in Russia and has done some excellent work for me—for us." Jules elegantly produced a sheet of newspaper. "I must explain one or two things: it is true that Sazaroff apparently beat M. Schultz with regard to Russian contracts. But M. Sazaroff is an accommodating and dexterous man. He can play both ends, not against the middle, but *for* the middle, meaning himself. When my English agent approached him in a reasonable manner, about three weeks ago, Sazaroff, being a gentleman, listened. Listened, and suggested. He had already bought land in Russia for a new factory, from which he was to get most of the profits, near the Donetz basin. A very fine idea, as that region has coal and iron in abundance. So, as a result of most reasonable conversations between my man and Sazaroff, Schultz-Poiret, who wanted to build a factory in the Ural Mountains, which was to be a French concern only, had to withdraw. Was forced to withdraw."

Paul's fleshy face became congested with murderous blood. "So that's how we lost out!" he cried, half rising in his seat.

But Ernest's expression remained calm and intent. His eyes had narrowed to mere slits. "Go on, Jules," he said, as though Paul had not spoken.

Jules smiled, as at the memory of a humorous episode. "There is a nice friendly spirit being cultivated these days between England and Russia. I rejoice to see it. Eventually, as we all know, England will need a powerful ally against Germany. I've always hated Germany, myself. It must be the French in me.

"At any rate, England and Russia are not going to let a little matter of war secrets interfere with their friendship. So now, I must read a little excerpt from the *Morning Times,* published only two weeks ago, with regard to Robsons-Strong and Russia: 'The English company is under contract to build and equip the Tzaritzine works and also for fifteen years to co-operate in the production of artillery and has agreed to place its entire knowledge of the technical side of the work, all patents, improvements, etc., at the disposal of the Russian company and be responsible for their correctness.' " He made a humorous gesture. "We hold twice as much stock in Robsons-Strong as we do in Schultz-Poiret."

There was a stupefied silence. Paul, his eyes bulging, glared insanely at his cousin. Ernest stared as if petrified. The blizzard hissed against the window and the curtains wavered in a draft.

Then Ernest burst into a mad shout of laughter, and struck the bony knee that rose under his counterpane. "You are a presumptuous dog, Jules! But I love you! Give me one of your poison cigars." And Jules knew, that beyond this, Ernest could pay a man no greater compliment.

Paul sat in rigid silence, his face was white as death, while Jules delicately lit the cigar his uncle held in his parched lips. May, sitting on the edge of the bed, sighed, fixed her anxious attention upon Ernest.

Ernest puffed and blinked in the smoke that rose from his cigar. He coughed once, or twice. He ignored Paul completely.

"Go on," he said to Jules, and when he looked at his nephew he seemed as inscrutable as a Buddha.

"It has been over six weeks, Uncle Ernest, since you were in Europe, and things have happened with which you are not informed as yet. When you left Windsor, you appointed Paul, Honore and myself, as your proxies. Things have moved very fast here, and Paul and I are willing to give you a brief synopsis tonight. Of course, various contracts and other matters must await your signature.

"I wish to tell you at this time of a certain private agent I have engaged, a cultured and well-connected agent from New York. He is special correspondent for the New York *Weekly News* as well as my own employee. His name is Mr. Rudolph Johnson; a relative of his, by the way, is one of the chief stockholders of the Nobel Dynamite Company. I sent him to South America, believing, at that time, that there was to be some disagreement between Chile and the Argentine, and while he contributed some splendid articles to the newspapers of both countries, he tried to sell our products to them. The Argentine, however, was a little cold to the idea, maintaining that it still desired peace with Chile—a very pusillanimous pack of statesmen it has! But Chile finally bought some of the new type warships from us, somewhat of the type we are preparing to sell to either Spain or America in the event of war, or rather, I should say, when the war comes, which I am confidently informed will be within the next six weeks.

"Then Johnson went to Siam and Japan. I have here a couple of letters from him:

" 'I shall try to see the Prime Minister with regard to the new battleship, as per your instructions. I think I can show the same model to the Emperor of China. I hope to see the Emperor before the outbreak of impending hostilities in the Orient, which ought to be exceedingly profitable, prominent European Powers being distinctly interested in that part of the world.'

"And another :

" 'I intend, very forcibly, to bring to the acute attention of Japan the great increase of the American Naval force. I think your other agents have inexcusably neglected this phase of the matter. I believe I can concentrate the attention of Japan on the American activity, pointing out, naturally, to her government that sudden armaments programs in one nation do not portend well for the peace of another. I shall present secret letters written by some of our Senators with imperialistic ambitions. The Japanese are a singularly suspicious people, which is natural to a people of intelligence and with a need for expansion. I, therefore, believe that after a short time they will be a lucrative customer and will proceed with naval and military preparations.' "

"Ah," muttered Ernest. He squinted intently through the smoke at Jules. Paul had gotten up and was now standing at the window, staring out, his hands thrust in his pockets. Ernest turned to him. "Aren't you interested, Paul?" he demanded satirically. "Or are we boring you?"

Paul came back to his chair. His face was swollen and suffused. He refused to look at Ernest and Jules, and sat down heavily, where he stared at the fire. None of them noticed how silent May had become, sitting on the edge of the bed, and how she wrung her handkerchief between her hands, and how filled with horror her eyes were.

"Where is Johnson now, Jules?" asked Ernest, after a little silence.

"In Spain." Jules smiled slightly. "However, I expect him home within the next two weeks. He has done some really excellent work there, especially in the newspapers. It seems there is a group of pacifists in the Spanish government, and the job Johnson has done holding them up to national scorn is something to admire !"

Paul grunted, and threw his cousin a vicious and gloating glance. "In spite of Honore, however, Robsons-Strong are supplying the Boers with Maxims, and not the pretty little piece of thieving we are putting out."

Jules made a suave and deprecating gesture, very foreign. "That is true, Paul. But perhaps you did not know that Robsons-Strong have purchased rights to our own gun, which will be used against the Boers, when the English people have been sufficiently aroused against them."

Ernest laughed again, loudly and shortly, and his peculiar laugh, as usual, lacked real mirth. Paul sank into silence again; his breath came unevenly. It was evident he was fighting some terrific battle in himself, and after one brief but piercing look at him, Ernest knew exactly what he was thinking.

"By the way," he said, "what do you think of the prospects now of Alfred Bassett's appointment as Assistant Secretary of War? God knows, we've spent a fortune on the man."

"I am certain of his appointment," replied Jules. "I received a letter to that effect from Washington only two days ago."

"I hope you're right," grunted Ernest. "If he isn't appointed our plans for a Spanish-American war will go up the flue. There's no chance of him becoming soft, after he's appointed, eh?"

"None at all! He's America's leading patriot, and his wife and daughter are both members of the Daughters of the American Revolution. And, by the way, Honore tells me that he has just received an immense order from Cuba for cartridges and rifles! That sounds exceedingly interesting, doesn't it?"

"There won't be any war with Spain!" shouted Paul with passionate suddenness. "She hasn't the money; her army and navy are rickety. She's not insane enough to risk a war with us! Damned Bassett or no damned Bassett!"

Jules replied, turning to his uncle, and smiling: "Sazaroff has just received some $25,000,000 worth of orders from Spain."

Paul glared at him, stupefied. Then he stuttered, purple with dismay and fury: "I don't believe it! It's one of your lies, Jules. I don't believe it! Where the hell would Spain get $25,000,000 from? Unless she could borrow it from outside. And who the devil would lend it to her?"

Jules spread out his hands, back up, and seemed to contemplate the smooth brownness of them with absent pleasure. "I'm not at liberty to say," he replied gently. Paul subsided, breathing audibly. He was livid now.

"The more I think of it, Jules, the more I am convinced that you are a presumptuous, if not an impudent dog," said Ernest amiably. "Your business was to attend to the Sessions Steel Company, principally. If Honore wished to have you meddling and smelling about the Kinsolving factories, that is his affair. But Barbour-Bouchard——"

"Pardon me, Uncle Ernest," replied Jules swiftly and with an effect of eagerness, "I believe, and I may be wrong, that we are all parts of a whole, that each one of us must be interested not only in his part but in all the others."

"But why didn't you tell Paul all this before now?"

Jules looked at his cousin, who was showing signs of awakening hope and pleased hatred. He turned back to his uncle.

"But," he protested, as though in bewilderment, "Paul already knew! I surely did not have to tell him matters concerning the business of which he is president!"

Ernest's sunken face took on an expression of pleased malice. *Touché*, he thought, regarding Jules with benign respect and amusement. He glanced at Paul, whose renewed color had already faded again, and in whose eyes stood confusion.

"Did you know all this, Paul?" he asked lightly.

Paul moistened his lips, which were the color of lead. "Yes. Certainly! Of course!" he replied hoarsely. "I think it is very impudent of Jules to make himself spokesman for me, but he is so damned glib, as you know, and likes to push himself." He shot his cousin an evil glance.

Jules smiled apologetically. "Forgive me, Paul. It is true that I am always too willing to review matters, and speak of them. I hope you will both realize that it is only excess of zeal."

Ernest permitted himself several moments of pure pleasure in watching Paul and Jules. Then he said to Jules: "But what have you done about our new submarine plans?"

May, who had still remained silent, now said coldly and firmly: "Ernest, you look exhausted! I must ask you to send Paul and Jules away, so you can rest. It is nearly ten o'clock." She regarded her nephews with dislike and bitterness.

Jules immediately rose with an expression of contrition. "Certainly! How thoughtless of us, Aunt May. Paul, may I offer you a lift?"

"No, thank you," replied Paul, with visible loathing. "I have my own carriage here."

Ernest, smiling faintly, looked from Paul to Jules. "Besides," he said, "I want to talk to Paul a minute or two longer. Alone. You'll excuse us, Jules?"

"Of course!" Jules' voice was all concern and graciousness. But a slight dark line appeared between his brilliant eyes, a line which Ernest regarded with an inward smile. Jules, after many expressions of hope for his uncle's improvement, and a gallant remark to May, and a bow to Paul, took his leave. The line between his eyes seemed permanently fixed.

Alone with Paul, Ernest did not speak for some moments. As for Paul, he was full of fear and sickness. He lit a cigarette with hands that visibly trembled. But when he looked furtively up at Ernest, he was agreeably surprised to see that the older man was regarding him with apparent kindness.

"Jules," said Ernest, "is a scraping French scoundrel. I detest the French. Always did." Paul listened with amazement, his heart beginning to throb.

"Tomorrow," continued Ernest placidly, "I'm going to make a new will. Alice will remain my heir, of course, but only if she does not marry, or has not already married, François Bouchard. I don't care who else she marries: the child must be happy, though I can't believe that dry-mouthed brown monkey could ever make her happy. But if she marries him, or has married him, you are to be my heir, Paul."

Paul's first expression was one of great joy, stupefaction and incredulity. He tried to speak, but his trembling lips could only move. He made a dumb and helpless gesture. Then all at once, the joy faded, was succeeded by expressions of absolute terror, realization, fear, despair and confusion. They raced over his face like wild and trampling horses, visibly grinding it, disintegrating it. He regarded Ernest with fiery eyes under a forehead that wrinkled convulsively. You fiend! he said inwardly. But aloud he said nothing.

After a few minutes, he left. His last words had been incoherent. He seemed to be under a terrible strain and distress.

Ernest, settling down comfortably under May's scolding ministrations, thought with amused pleasure: I've set him a pretty problem! It'll be interesting which he will sacrifice: his ambition to be my heir or his daughter's happiness. Greed or father-love. Which will win? Will he be soft enough to prevent Alice's marriage to a man who will destroy her life, or will he offer her up as a burnt offering to his ambitions?

But this was never to be known: what Paul would have done. For before he could change his will, before the next morning, in fact, Ernest Barbour suffered a stroke which totally paralyzed him.

CHAPTER CX

ALICE, IN TEARS, slipped her three fine cambric petticoats, bordered with thick hand-made embroidery, over her head. Over these she fastened and belted her gray woollen skirt. She looked at herself dismally in the mirror, a slender, slight young thing in a shirtwaist so white and starched that it glittered. She adjusted the velvet ribbon at the neck, patted her pompadour, glanced at her watch. Her cheeks were pale and wet. At ten o'clock she and her Aunt Elsa were leaving for New York.

That loathesome Thomas! she thought wretchedly. But they can't make me have him! Papa can't force me. I'm eighteen, going on nineteen. I love François, and I'm going to tell Papa, and it doesn't matter a snap whether they make me go to New York or not.

But in spite of her courageous thoughts, she went downstairs slowly and heavily, one step at a time. She passed the long pier mirror in its mahogany frame on the landing, and was interested by her reflection. There was no doubt of the fact that she looked tragic. Considerably cheered and consoled by this, she went down the remaining stairs at a brisker pace, in order to focus it on her father's attention before the smell of an exceedingly good breakfast could mar it. She decided, on reaching the folding mahogany doors of the dining room, that if anything, she resembled the young Juliet very closely.

But to her surprise, the dining room table, though set in perfect order and glistening with stiff white linen and bright silver, was empty. She glanced at her watch again; it was just eight o'clock. At that moment the grandfather clock in the hall chimed eight deep notes. Breakfast was invariably served at seven forty-five, and she was fifteen minutes late. For a second she thought that perhaps Paul and Elsa had eaten earlier, due to the journey to be taken, but a glance at the table plainly showed three places set.

The pantry door swung open and a maid entered with a plate of hot rolls under a napkin. She deftly removed two of the places set, leaving only one. Alice stared, her mouth dropping open.

"What's the matter with everybody, Louise?"

Louise appeared surprised. "Why, didn't you know, Miss Alice? Cook just told me. Seems like Mr. Ernest was taken bad in the night. The news came about six o'clock, and Mr. Paul and Miss Elsa went over to Mr. Ernest's at seven. Before breakfast. They haven't come back."

The misery was wiped off Alice's face completely, and her eyes sparkled. "Then I needn't go to New York!" she exclaimed, delighted. She suddenly remembered herself, and pulled down her mouth, though her eyes remained excited and anticipatory. "Is Grandpa dead yet?"

"I'm sure I don't know, Miss Alice." Louise's expression showed her disapproval of this shallow callousness. "But I reckon not. We'd've heard."

Alice sat down, more and more excited, and, the pressure on herself removed, ate a tremendous breakfast, an unusual event in itself. Her color was very high. Heavens, what an uproar there will be in the family, when Grandpa dies! What excitements, and solemnity and comings and goings and rustlings and carriages and flowers and tears and white linen handkerchiefs! She remembered herself again, and thought: Poor Grandpa.

When she had eaten, she became very restless. She wondered if she ought to dress and go over to her grandfather's house. Of course, there'd be no journey, or she would have had word. But perhaps he was just a little sick, and Aunt Elsa would soon be bustling in, demanding that the bags and trunks be brought down immediately, and calling for the carriage. If she, Alice, went to her grandfather's, Elsa might have a sudden rush of memory, and sweep Alice home. Whereas, if she kept still, and out of the way, there was a good chance of Elsa overlooking the matter of New York, especially if Grandpa stayed ill. Alice was fond of Ernest, but she sincerely hoped that he would remain ill enough for a week or two to delay this unpleasant journey.

She was about to slip upstairs to her room again, very softly, when the doorbell rang with what, to her strained ears, was a terrible row. She peered over the stairs as the butler went to answer it, hurrying from his pantry and buttoning his coat. When the opened door revealed François, she could hardly believe her eyes. Then, with a subdued cry of joy, she raced down the stairs and flung herself into his arms.

"Is Grandpa dead?" she screamed, pulling him by his coat into the hallway. The butler, severe and prim, retreated to his pantry, the door of which he left ajar, in order that he might listen.

François took the eager little hands off his coat and held them tightly. She saw at once that he was unusually grave, and a little pale.

"No, darling," he said, with a gentleness alien to him. "I've just heard. He's had a stroke. He'll probably recover, they say, if he doesn't have another."

Alice's facile features expressed her sudden dismay. "Then Aunt Elsa'll be home any moment and carry me off to New York!" she wailed.

François averted his head. "I suppose so," he said gloomily. All at once, he looked secretive and frightened, and pressed her hands so hard in his that she winced. Tears were already on her lashes.

"You know why they're taking you away, Alice?" He had dropped his voice to a whisper.

"Yes," she replied, also whispering, and glancing over her shoulder. She began to whimper, her mouth curving downwards, childishly. "But I won't marry him, François! I love you, and I'm going to tell Papa, just as soon as he gets back." The thought of her father's return made her shiver lightly. François put his arm about her and held her with a tense and trembling grip.

"You're such a little thing, Alice, and they'll make you do what they want. You're such a child. They'll take you away from me, and I'll never see you again, except as Tom Van Eyck's wife. They'll do to you what they did to your poor mother, poor Trudie."

Alice was instantly diverted. "What did they do, François?" She gazed at him with her big wet blue eyes, completely intrigued.

François hesitated. His mouth worked miserably. "She wanted to marry my brother, Philippe. You've heard of Philippe, Alice? Well, Uncle Ernest, curse him, wanted her to marry your father. He—he managed in some way to separate them, and Philippe became a priest and died on a leper island. And your mother married Paul. And then she heard that Philippe was dead, and she died, too, right away, after you were born." He clutched her desperately. "Alice, I can't let that happen to you, darling, not even if I have to carry you off, first."

"Oh—" breathed Alice, all exquisite excitement. "But how horribly cruel, how—how positively *inhuman*, François."

But the terror which François had been able to keep down for the last few minutes began to assail him again, and he glanced affrightedly at the street door behind him. He clutched her slight soft arm, and she winced again, absently.

"Alice, they'll do that to you, too. Alice, will you trust me, will you come with me?"

She stared, blinking. He pulled a paper from his pocket with hands that visibly shook. He thrust it under her nose, and she saw, to her stupefaction, that it was a marriage license. "Alice," he whispered hoarsely, "your father'll be back in a few minutes. They'll take you away. Trust me, darling. Come with me, now, and we'll be married at once."

She shrank, turning white. "But, François, I can't do that! Why, Papa'd never forgive me! He—he'd be so angry that he'd really whip me. I'd be so scared— I couldn't do that, François."

Desperate, he rattled the paper at her. "Alice, you must, or I'll go away, as Philippe did, and I—I'll die somewhere, all alone!" Terror had him now, like a wolf, and he forgot to whisper, speaking through trembling lips in a high shrill voice. "You said you loved me, but you'll let them send you away and marry you off to a young dolt! You said you loved me, but I can see now that you lied to me——"

Alice had recovered herself quickly. She was still pale, but she said with spirit and indignation: "I don't lie, François. At least, not about such things." She twisted her handkerchief in her hands, and was again frightened. "But what will Papa say?"

"Nothing. What can he say? You'll be my wife. Darling," and he pulled her despairingly to him, "come with me. I'll never ask you again, if you refuse. Don't let them kill me, and you."

Alice, after a moment's hesitation and miserable struggle, lifted up her face to his and kissed him. "I'll come, François dear, I'll come."

She slipped like a small shadow up to her room, put on her coat with cold numb fingers, pinned on her hat, caught up.her gloves and bag, and ran downstairs again. François already had the door open. He literally swept her outside, down the stone stairs, down the brick walk, into his waiting buggy. "Hurry, hurry!" he panted, glaring in his fear up and down the silent wintry road. The great scattered estates lay under a misty gray fog laced by bare branches. The sound of the racing buggy wheels was loud in the wet, blanketing stillness. Alice had begun to cry, first clinging to François, then shrinking away from him, her small face red and wet.

One hour later Jules arrived from Ernest's house at his office, in a great hurry. Ernest was "resting easily," and no change was expected for at least twenty-four hours. Jules had left him lying partly conscious on heaped pillows, breathing with a sound like rusty bellows.

Jules, with immense solicitude, had asked May exactly when the stroke had taken place, and when she informed him it had happened at three o'clock that morning, after Ernest had fallen asleep immediately on Paul's departure, he felt a great relaxing in him, so intense that a light sweat broke out over his forehead. No, May assured him, a slight frown of impatience on her haggard and ashen face, Ernest had seen no one at all after he and Paul had left. She began to weep, and Jules, still damp as to forehead, comforted her with such tenderness and sympathy that she was touched, even through her grief and terrible anxiety.

Jules, sitting at his desk, and smoothing his pale lip with his forefinger, thought exultantly: Then there has been no changing of the will. And if he lives twenty-four hours more, I certainly don't recognize the face of death!

The telephone rang. When he answered it, the receiver almost slipped in his damp hand. It was François, his voice as shrill and high and tight as a hysterical woman's. "I've had a hell of a time finding a telephone, Jules! But we're married! Alice and I were married half an hour ago! Married! We're going home now, to wait until the row blows over! Married, Jules! To my darling!" He coughed excitedly, while Jules wet lips suddenly dry. "We owe it all to you, Jules, God bless you!"

Exactly one hour later, Paul arrived, thrusting open doors, leaving a wind of chaos behind him, thrusting Jules' impeccable and protesting Mr. Dickinson aside with fury. He clutched his cane tightly, used it as a weapon to slam the door after him, in the face of the secretary. His own face was frightful. He stood before Jules, breathing with a horrible sound, gasping.

"Where is my daughter?" he demanded in a strangely quiet voice.

Jules raised his brows deprecatingly. "Your daughter, Paul? But how extraordinary of you to ask me! How should I know? I hope nothing has happened to the child."

Paul's mouth writhed, and he gasped for breath. "My daughter!" he cried hoarsely. "Where is my daughter?"

Jules stood up, and Paul looked on a face he had never seen before.

"Your daughter," said Jules softly, "is now—Alice Bouchard."

Paul's cane switched through the air like a blurred flash, and a welt, red and savage, sprang across Jules' cheek.

CHAPTER CXI

B

UT THE "change" in Ernest Barbour's condition came before twenty-four hours. Except for the nurses and servants, May was alone in the Sessions house when Ernest died.

To the last, even to the final moment, she had not really believed he would die. Could die. A world without Ernest Barbour was a world become two-dimensioned, life undermined, a cliff blown up and reduced to powder. It was reality become an empty nightmare. In all the years she had known him it had seemed incredible to her that he could ever die. His power had seemed less personal and circumscribed in himself, than universal. His ideas, his ambitions, his driving force, seemed to her, as they seemed to hundreds of others, things immortal, not to be destroyed by time or death. And yet, when he died, and lay there, with open eyes and slack mouth and hands that would never move again, he was, if at one with Cæsar, also one with the dead teamster who lay only four streets away from him and who had died at the same moment. Gregory Sessions had once said that democracy was the common denominator of the barnyard; but death was the ultimate cipher to which all life added up.

The night nurse had persuaded May to rest, repeating to her what the doctor had said. May had gone to her room, and had sat numbly by the low fire. She shivered at intervals, and there was a taste of lead in her mouth. She looked at the furniture in her room, and it all seemed strange and unreal to her. Even the deaths of her children had not given her this deadly agony.

She did not go to bed, though for a few moments she lay across the counterpane, her eyes fixed upon the wall pattern that appeared and disappeared in the lamplight and firelight. Then the mere supineness of her body made her mind more active, more twisted by fear and anguish, and she got up again.

At two o'clock there was a low tap on her door and the nurse thrust her head inside the room. "We've sent for the doctor again, Mrs. Barbour. Would you like to see Mr. Barbour, now?" Her face was grave.

May ran into her husband's room like a young girl. Before she reached the door she could hear his frightful breathing, which echoed through all the house. When she stood by his bedside, and looked at him by the light of the shaded lamp, she knew he was dying. Her first sensation was a stunned incredulity, leaving her so numb that she could feel nothing else for a little while.

A thaw had set in, and the mounds of snow outside were gray in the pale moonlight. But they were no grayer than Ernest's shrunken face, which seemed hardly larger than a young child's. His great broad forehead and thick shock of whitened hair looked grotesquely large, out of proportion, in contrast with that face. It was a mummy countenance, surmounted by the skull of a giant. From the ruin of his flesh his nose stood out, short and strong and distended, like the upturned prow of a ship that was swiftly sinking under water. His eyes were shut. May could see how he struggled for breath, for the cords twisted in his withered throat. His whole being was absorbed in one terrible fight for life-giving air; nothing else mattered to him except those short painful gulps; his hands were clenched on the counterpane, and upon his features was an intense concentration, as though he counted his breaths. Now all of the power of him, all the strength, the resistless force, was focussed on this small yet all-important point.

"Ernest!" cried May, overcome by her realization. She bent over him, speaking loudly: "Ernest, Ernest, darling! Look at me!"

A faint scowl of impatience touched that most awful concentration, as though she had inexcusably disturbed him in the midst of something portentous. But he did not open his eyes. The breathing went on. The nurse lifted his head a little, felt his pulse, fixing her eyes intently upon his face.

"The doctor will be here in a moment," she whispered. The pale wan moonlight striped the shadowy curtains, and there was silence outside and in the Sessions house.

May had put her hand over the icy bony fingers on the sheet. There was a sound of confusion in her brain, but she could feel nothing. She bent over Ernest again, and called him, urgently, out from the darkness and chaos where he fought in his colossal struggle to live. Perhaps she reached him, for his eyes slowly opened, bleared, tortured eyes, and he looked at her. His breathing became easier.

"Ernest, dearest," whispered May. "Dearest, don't you know me?"

He smiled at her, seemed, behind the webby curtain of his eyes, to recognize her.

"Amy," he said, and his voice was strong and quick again.

May still held his hand, but her face seemed to fall into ruin, to disintegrate.

"He knows you, Mrs. Barbour," said the nurse, pleased.

But May looked only at Ernest. His expression had become ineffably gentle, full of love and old passion. She had never seen this expression of his in all her married life with him. Only Amy had seen it. It was as if a scythe went slowly through all her body, laying it open, exposing it to agony and helplessness.

The icy fingers moved under hers, took possession of her hand. He held it strongly, with young possessiveness and power, as he had held Amy's hand. He was smiling, an indulgent but ironical smile. "I knew you had never really gone away, Amy," he said.

An iron spasm jerked May's face. She kissed his forehead, put her lips in his hair. "You know I could never have left you, really," she murmured. "You know I must always come back to you. It doesn't matter who else would leave you, Amy will always come back."

"Yes," he said, and smiled.

He seemed to sleep. His hand became colder and colder. Downstairs there was a subdued opening and shutting of the outside door, and quick heavy steps on the stairs. The doctor had arrived. He bent over Ernest, ignoring the old woman who half lay on the bed beside him, her lips in his hair. He glanced at the nurse, shook his head.

Ernest stirred feebly. He turned his head in the direction of the door. "I want to see the children," he said. "I want to see Trudie."

"Yes," said May, holding him. "Yes, dearest, they are coming."

His face brightened to a look of pleased expectancy.

He continued to stare at the door, waiting, watching, with pathetic impatience. Occasionally he would blink slowly, as he watched.

And then, finally, his eyes did not blink again, but stared, emptily, at the door.

On the other side of the world, in the sunlight, the Japanese at that moment, were firing a salute to their emperor. The great guns bellowed and vomited across sea-green water, shaking ocean and earth and heaven with thunder.

Barbour-Bouchard guns.

CHAPTER CXII

THE GUNS that had roared at the coming and the going of emperors were mere whispers compared to the thunder that followed Ernest Barbour's death. The British newspapers devoted pages to pictures and stories about him, boasting that he had been born in England, that descendants of his uncle, George Barbour, still lived there in Lancashire, on local farms or in Manchester itself. There were photographs of these descendants, and special correspondents were sent to interview them. With no exception at all, the relatives expressed their pious hopes for Ernest's situation among the dead, and eulogized him.

Great men in Europe and America were interviewed concerning him. Those connected with munitions were reserved and cautious, but politicians and financiers, senators and presidents, kings and emperors, were lavish in their expressions of grief, reverence and praise. Ernest's photographs, from young manhood to old age, appeared in hundreds of newspapers, his life story was printed in a dozen different languages. Wires hummed with the news of his death. Jay Regan, "the younger," was among the illustrious who thronged Windsor to attend his funeral. Condolences signed with famous names were delivered in yellow telegram sheafs to the widow, who never even glanced at them. In fact, very few looked at them, except reporters and inquisitive visitors. But Paul looked at them, with mingled gloom and pride. And strange to say, grief. As with most ruthless and sentimental people, death covered for him a multitude of sins, temporarily. However, beyond his uncle's death, he was not allowing himself to think much, or he would have become distracted.

But there was one man who raised a strong angry voice in the universal pæan of praise and sorrow, and this man was one Lord Kilby, a peer who had never bought an armaments share, and held a responsible Civil Service post:

"The world resounds with sentimental sorrow for the passing of this man whose tardy philanthropies cannot overweigh the universal agony and misery which he and his kind have inflicted on their fellow men. On every hand one hears expressions of regret and sees grave faces. Why?

"If Ernest Barbour had contributed a serum or a treatment for the cure of cancer, diabetes, syphilis or tuberculosis, which would have saved a million lives from premature death or living torture, his name would be known only to a few, and those he had benefited would have remained in ignorance even of his identity. Had he saved a life, the papers would have vouchsafed him a small paragraph on a back page. Had he lived in honor and kindness and integrity, there would have been only a small knot at his grave, and a half-foot headstone to mark where he lies.

"But this man manufactured death and ruin, built up an immense fortune on the bones of battlefields, suborned honor and the integrity of Governments, bought generals and politicians and journalists and kings with a cynicism that is inhuman, frightful to contemplate. All war widows and orphans, deprived old parents and crippled soldiers, owe their wretchedness to him and his kind. Every war that is brewing, and will be brewed in the ominous future, was born in his brain, for the sole purpose of increasing his wealth and his power. The civilizations that will die, the multitudes who will starve, the children who will perish in gutters and wallow in their blood, the homeless, the famine-stricken, the fleeing and the lost, the oppressed and the maimed, the wanderers who will fly in terror from land to land, seeking shelter, the ruined walls of cities and the blasted earth, the pestilences that will destroy and ravish, will all be, in that dark future, because he lived.

"If the foolish world has a prayer to be said on the passing of this man, it will be: 'Deliver us from this Evil.' "

Lord Kilby was known as an honorable and capable gentleman, and his words carried weight. They resulted in the forming of a Committee in London to "investigate" the armaments industry. But these innocent gentlemen soon collided with a most formidable array of their colleagues who owned large blocks of shares in this nefarious industry; they came suddenly face to face with the most relentless of countenances; at one time they brushed royalty and retreated in the utmost of decorous dismay. They arrived precipitately in a silent forest of mute and terrible enemies, all glaring at them with deadly eyes, all armed, all ferocious and watchful. The investigating Committee, in rather tremulous voices, announced that they had "found nothing of importance." And mopped their brows.

Ernest Barbour lay in state in the magnificent little church he had built in Windsor. All but his face was covered with a blanket of violets and lilies, roses and carnations. Burning crimson and deep blue light fell through the high narrow windows upon his features, so quiet and shrunken now. Old and dead though he was, never had he looked so implacable and relentless, for all the waxen folded hands and the closed eyes. All day long, for the three days he remained there, a long line of people from Windsor streamed by his coffin, whispering or awed, curious or sentimental. More than they came to see the dead man did they come to catch glimpses of men whose names were familiar in the newspapers they read. When the funeral services were held, on a clear pale March day, the church was packed to its doors, and a multitude gathered outside.

It was a dignified short service, for, as the minister said sorrowfully: "In his life he was simple and unpretentious. In his death let him remain so. In his life, he avoided all acclaim and notoriety, clung to the quiet ways and the gentle, unassuming manner of living. He believed that his memory would be his Monument, that the world would judge him for all the mighty things he had done, and think of him, in his private life, as a mere country gentleman. And that is how we remember him, less for his vast accomplishments, than for his tender interest in his fellow citizens in Windsor and his old-fashioned and steadfast faith in the Good, the True, and the Beautiful.

"And so, my dear sorrowing friends, let us remember, not the great man the world knew, but the Good Neighbor, the Friend, the simple local Citizen."

Jules Bouchard, sitting among his family, kept his head bowed. But a faint smile lay bleakly on his lips while the minister spoke.

Alice was there, terrified and pale and red-eyed, with her husband and her mother-in-law, and the old Major, who shuffled with his cane. Across the pews, across the dusty beams of light, she looked at her father, who would not look at her. Dear, poor Papa, how sad he seemed, how harassed, how pale! Aunt Elsa looked over once or twice, with great severity and bitterness, but the last look of all was soft and grieved. Alice could not bear that; she wept aloud.

The widow was there, swathed in black veils. She leaned her head on her hand, and never turned or moved during the entire service.

They carried him to the desolate cemetery, where the ground was still yellow with mud and the trees empty. They put him in the earth, and left him there. The cemetery had grown as the city had grown, and its outer edges were not far from the Sessions house. Now, through the leafless branches, the upper windows of the house looked across and down on the heaped grave. The house endured, but the man who had given everything for it, and destroyed everything for it, was nothing.

In another and lowlier section of the cemetery the teamster was already lying, his grave deserted except for a few sheaves of dead and blackened flowers.

CHAPTER CXIII

To the surprise of everyone, Ernest Barbour had left a considerable fortune to his son Godfrey, ten thousand dollars apiece to each of his granddaughters, Reginald's children, one hundred thousand dollars to Paul Barbour, the same to Elsa, ten thousand to Lucy Van Eyck, the same to his sister, Florabelle, and to May the income from a huge trust fund, which was to be returned to the bulk of the estate upon her death.

But his real heir, after various philanthropies were taken care of, was his granddaughter, Alice Bouchard. The size of the fortune was incredible; Alice was now one of the richest young women in America. The joint executors of the estate were Paul Barbour and Jules Bouchard.

Paul had hoped, to the last bitter moment, that his legacy would be materially larger than it was. He had expected at least five hundred thousand dollars. He had hoped that Ernest had indicated, at least in a suggestion, that he might be named as president of Barbour-Bouchard. But all he had now, was his hundred thousand dollars and his own private savings and fortune, which were very considerable—and the ominous realization that the Bouchards could now oust him entirely from Barbour-Bouchard and would probably do so.

When he heard that François had been named to the directorate of the Kinsolving Arms Company, he saw the plot in its entirety, and wondered incredulously why he had not seen it before Ernest's death. He became physically ill with anxiety, despair, bitterness and hatred and loss. Robin's Nest seemed unendurably desolate without Alice's high prattle and tapping heels and eager, breathless laugh. To come home, night after night, after a day of apprehension and hopelessness, to find Elsa, in mourning, waiting for him with red-rimmed eyes, was more than he could stand. In the four weeks following Ernest's death, he grayed perceptibly, and heavy lines dug themselves deeply on each side of his mouth.

He expected, each day, to receive a letter from the Bouchards, asking for his resignation. When it did not come, when he was not even invited to attend a business conference, his dismay and fear grew in proportion. It was the eve of the Spanish-American War, and, so far, all his conferences with Jules and Leon had been cold and formal conferences concerning the legacies. For three weeks Jules wore a scar on his cheek from Paul's cane, yet he never mentioned it nor explained it.

Then the strain overcame Paul, and in his desperate bitterness at what he thought was a cat-and-mouse game of Jules' he sent in his resignation as vice-president of Barbour-Bouchard. In this way, he thought wretchedly, he saved what little pride he had remaining to him: he could resign before being asked to resign. But he did not do this until he was convinced that his resignation would inevitably be demanded. He catered to self-pride only when it was absolutely necessary, when there was no escape into profit.

His resignation was sent in by messenger. It was all hopeless now; Jules could not be expected to forgive nor forget both the insult to his family and the assault upon his own person. It is a significant comment on Paul's character that he regretted both. He had been too "cocky" with regard to his own position, had had too much Anglo-American contempt for an alien race. He cursed himself a thousand times for not being wily and circumspect. Ernest, too, had been bold, but he had either had better luck or been surer of his position and what he might dare. He had been too much of an Englishman to be really audacious; his audacity had been an illusion.

Elsa was overwhelmed with the precariousness of her brother's position. Helplessly, she offered him her own legacy, and was hurt at Paul's short and violent laugh. "If it were a million dollars, it could not help me now," he replied.

Elsa drearily told him, that miserable evening after the resignation had been sent in, that May had finally declined their invitation to leave the Sessions house and live at Robin's Nest. "Imagine!" said Elsa, with lifeless scorn, "living in that great shabby old house all alone, with that antiquated furniture and the inconveniences, and the neighborhood what it has become, when she might be here with us, who would be only too glad to have her. Perhaps, too, she might help us. After all, Alice is her granddaughter, and she might have some influence with that terrible Jules. But Aunt May, for all her pleasant ways and tact, was always selfish. No wonder Uncle Ernest divorced her——"

The mention of Ernest's name threw Paul into a savage and hysterical frenzy. "Don't mention that devil's name to me again!" he shouted, clenching his fists and turning purple, to Elsa's stupefaction. "I forbid you to mention him! He ruined me, threw me down, made me a laughing stock, after all his fine promises and his hints and pretenses of affection. God! he led me to believe that he would leave me at least a million dollars, that I would be president of Barbour-Bouchard——" His voice almost became a sob; he panted hoarsely, and Elsa, to her horror and grief, saw that his eyes were wet. He went to the mantelpiece, leaned his arm upon it, and rested his forehead on his arm. She gazed at him, at his big broken body, his gray head, the gasps that heaved his broad shoulders. "Christ!" he went on in a high strained voice, as though he were on the verge of weeping, "I've given all my life to it, I've lived it, thought it, dreamed it, worked so damned hard at it! I've sacrificed everything to it, all my youth, my days and my nights. And for it all, I get a pittance—and the street!" His voice dwindled. "Curse him."

Elsa began to cry silently. "Don't talk like that, about the dead," she whimpered. "After all, Paul, dear, he did do a lot for us. We'd have much less if it had not been for him. Papa had squandered a great part of Mama's fortune on his silly charities and such, and Uncle Ernest redeemed a lot of it, paid you a large salary for years and years, made you a present of the mortgage on this house and estate, and left us two hundred thousand dollars. And though you are getting no comfort from it, he did leave your daughter millions of dollars. He was always so fond of her. I believe he cared even more for her than he cared for Trudie."

Paul did not answer. He stood there with his head bowed on his arm. A strange and unfamiliar slackness seemed suddenly to collapse his body, making it sag. That frightened Elsa more than anything else.

"I don't know what I'll do now," muttered Paul despairingly. "Where shall I go? What shall I do? I can't be idle. My life was in it. Without it, I'm cut in half; my life's amputated."

The library door opened, and Jules Bouchard entered with his swift soft step. He was hatless and coatless, and had evidently told the butler not to announce him. Paul, engrossed in his misery and grief, did not hear his almost soundless entry, but at Elsa's startled and astonished cry, he looked up heavily, his eyelids salt-bitten, his face blotched.

"Good evening," said Jules, coldly and imperturbably. "Good evening, Elsa. I hope I am not intruding upon you?" His rapid hidden eye saw everything; his expression was dark and inscrutable.

Elsa rose slowly. "Jules!" she murmured faintly. Then she colored and looked at her brother helplessly, wringing her hands with a gesture of unconscious fear and confusion. Paul, stupefied, could do nothing but stare, his arm still resting on the marble ledge.

Jules laid a slim black portfolio upon a table. "May I sit down, Elsa?" he asked. "Thank you. Please be seated, Elsa. No, it is not necessary for you to go," as Elsa started blindly for the door. She returned, slowly sank into her seat again, stared at Jules with a blank fascinated expression.

Jules looked up at Paul, who had not yet moved. His eyes narrowed and glinted, and upon his brown cheek there was still a suggestion of a welt.

"Your resignation was turned over to me tonight, Paul," he said quietly.

Now Paul turned a dusky purple. "And you've come to tell me it is accepted," he said hoarsely. His shoulders straightened, his hands formed into fists.

"You jump to conclusions," said Jules coldly, after a moment's silent scrutiny of his cousin. "Conclusions are almost invariably wrong. I have come here tonight because the matter is very serious. I have to come to ask you not to resign, and to bring you the information that we have voted only an hour ago that you be asked to accept the presidency of the Corporation."

Elsa cried out. She looked from Jules to Paul. The purple was fading from her brother's face; he was blinking incredulously, and visibly swallowing. His clenched fists opened, relaxed.

"At three times the salary you were receiving as vice-president," added Jules, and now he smiled, not a pleasant smile at all. Then, as Paul, unable to speak, remained silent, Jules went on: "I hope you will accept. We should regret it exceedingly if you refused. Frankly, we need you. It is entirely a business arrangement, and sentiment, or justice, has nothing whatsoever to do with it."

Paul groped for a chair, found it, sat down. He averted his head. Elsa, wringing her hands, hardly able to breathe, watched him.

Jules regarded the tip of his polished boot meditatively. His expression became gentler, thoughtful. "Not as a member of the Company, but as a man, I believe you were treated shabbily. Not for an instant did we doubt that you would be named president by our late lamented Uncle Ernest. It was a scurvy joke. But then, dear Uncle Ernest always had to have his little joke."

Paul slowly turned his head toward his cousin, and regarded him with astonishment and blank uncertainty. He wet his lips. He was utterly abased, but hope, shining, unbelieving, began to rise behind his eyes.

Jules smiled. "You will accept? Honore and Leon are anxiously waiting to hear from me."

"I accept," said Paul, in his hoarse and trembling voice. He caught his breath suddenly and loudly, as though an agony had been removed.

"Good. Very good indeed. Uncle Ernest had his joke, but we've got the last laugh." Nothing could have been friendlier than the tone and the smile that accompanied this. "We'll get along much better, now that we are alone," he added amiably. He drew Paul into the family circle of conspiracy and friendliness, and Paul, as if released from nightmare and torment and death, smiled in return, an odd wild smile. Elsa, smiling and weeping, beamed upon them both.

Jules withdrew some papers from the portfolio. "Here they are, Paul. Please sign them, after reading them."

Paul went through the motions of reading, but in reality the neatly typewritten pages were a blur to him. It was only toward the last that a significant item caught his attention. He glanced up at Jules, becoming pale and shaken again.

"It says: 'Bouchard and Sons.'"

"Yes," replied Jules unemotionally. "Bouchard and Sons." He fixed his hooded eyes intently on his cousin.

Paul, after a prolonged gaze, turned back to the papers. His pen hung motionless over them. They were no whiter than his face. Elsa put her handkerchief to her lips; her fallen lashes touched her cheeks. Then she heard a scratching. Paul was signing the papers. The pen fell from his fingers. Jules gathered them up swiftly and put them back into the portfolio.

"And now," he said, "let us briefly discuss business. Before long, I am reliably informed, we shall declare war against Spain. But not until we have finished armor-plating a few ships for Spain, and Robsons-Strong can make their own deliveries to her, and we can ship arms and explosives to Cuba. But this is now an old story. There are now Japan and Russia to consider, and the eternal Balkans, and an idea that has very recently been taking form with us and Robsons and Kronk and Schultz-Poiret and Bedors and Skeda and Sazaroff. It probably won't materialize for about ten years, but we need to start it at once if it is to happen as we wish it. In fact, I am informed that it has already begun in Germany, where they are talking of 'Der Tag——.' "

EPILOGUE

THERE IS a peculiar inconsistency in the minds of men, which allows for, and approves, the conduct of one group and opposes the same conduct in another group," said Jules to a reporter from the *New York Times,* during a heated official investigation concerning the business dealings of Bouchard and Sons during the Spanish-American War. "International trade of all sorts is conceded to be above national and racial prejudice, to be above war and blockades and private quarrels. It is the Esperanto of modern industrial life. With one inexplicable and notable exception: the armaments industry. This industry, so international, so necessarily without bias and local quarrels, suddenly, during war, is declared to be a circumscribed and solely national industry, and it is demanded of it, neutral and passionless though it is and must be, that it take sides. This attitude, stupid and arrogant, is a murderous attack on commercial life, a violation of the seller-customer relationship, which is the basis of free and prosperous international trade. Not only is this an assault upon the liberties of one group of men, liberties guaranteed by the Constitution, it is also tyranny of a distinctly dangerous type, auguring a dark future for other liberties of the people. You cannot burst one door of a house without laying the whole house open to pillage."

He spread out his hands simply. " 'If this be treason, make the most of it.' "

This interview was much admired, particularly among armaments makers and their stockholders all over the world. But the Government and the majority of the people were quite cynical about it, refusing to be impressed. One Senator said: "I would advise Mr. Bouchard to read the Constitution carefully before he undertakes to quote it so movingly another time. He is in the position of the devil quoting scripture. We admit that his grave warning against enemies of the people's liberties, and his anxiety about them, is very touching. But we would like at this time to point out, with the assistance of history, that the people will have very little need to worry about this, on the day that the armaments industry all over the world is outlawed, and the real enemies of the people are called out from behind their judicious and lofty masks, and shown to be who they are: the armaments makers."

At this time, Paul Barbour was indiscreet enough to make, as Jules Bouchard so trenchantly put it: "A complete damn fool of himself."

The particular moment when he accomplished this difficult feat was a delicate one.

He, too, gave an interview, which went the rounds of the world. He recalled the fact that Peter, to defend himself and the righteous, used a sword "with good effect." After this pious quotation, he went on:

"John has revealed to us a vision of the binding of Satan and the thousand years of peace which will follow. But there will be war before that time.

"War is a sickness of nations, the most fatal and the most dreadful of all pestilences. No one realizes this so completely as the armaments makers, who work hand in hand, admittedly, with science, for the production of more efficient weapons and gases of death. War, the sickness of men's minds, can only be cured by war, and the more dreadful it is, the more mercilessly it is waged, the more widespread, the greater will be the health of nations after the universal and bloody purge. War must be eradicated by the sword, by ruthlessness cultivated by the civilized nations against the uncivilized, the greedy-for-conquest.

"The armaments maker, by assisting in the elimination of the warlike and the barbarous, is the friend of peace, the destroyer of the sick. His guns and his explosives, his gases and his bullets, are the physicians that will heal the afflicted."

He added: "To ask peaceful and civilized nations to defend themselves with friendly words and conciliatory gestures is to ask a man to protect himself against a mad dog with a smile and an outstretched hand."

But Jules, usually so astute, was wrong this time. His French logic had no influence with the sentimental American mind, but Paul's speech, so sentimental, appealing as it did to simple ignorance and hoary, platitudinous beliefs, did more to placate public resentment than all of Jules' sophistry and bitter reason. Realizing this, Jules gave vent to an unprintable but succinct remark that was quoted, with enjoying laughter, among his kinsmen for years. It had something to do with Paul's bestowing an intimate salute upon the more secluded part of the public's anatomy. Thereafter, Paul was referred to, among the irreverent Bouchards, as "Cousin Ass."

All this was on the occasion of the discovery that the Spaniards were using "thousands of rifles resembling very closely the Kinsolving rifles issued to our own soldiers."

Another and renewed uproar occurred during the Russian-Japanese War, when it was discovered that the Kinsolving Arms Company had supplied the Japanese with 30,000,000 cartridges, tons of explosives, 200,000 gun slings and one hundred cannon. The simple Russian Government made a representation to Washington, and the people of California indignantly demanded another investigation. Paul, encouraged this time by Jules himself, made another speech, and everything subsided.

Bouchard and Sons now found that it was exceedingly profitable to bestow a lot of attention on re-purchasing, at a good price, explosives, guns and ammunition sold in the past to the great Powers, and reselling this old and sometimes obsolete equipment to poorer, smaller nations. Ernest had done some trade in this manner, but Bouchard and Sons enlarged on it, issuing catalogs, guaranteeing equipment, and advertising discreetly. In this edifying manner, a nation, eventually falling from first place, sometimes re-purchased goods it had formerly sold back to this remarkable Company after a first purchase. Jules Bouchard had discovered that the principle of the human circulatory system could be applied very nicely to the armaments industry. Bedors, Schultz-Poiret, Robsons-Strong, Kronk, and Sazaroff, expressing their private admiration, soon followed.

By 1905, Bouchard and Sons had greatly enlarged its fortunes, and Ernest himself might well have been amused, admiring and gratified.

An interval of comparative peace now came upon the world, though the Balkans rumbled as usual and there were minor disturbances. The Bouchards sold huge supplies of explosives to the United States Government for the purpose of railroad expansion and other peaceful improvements. Robsons-Strong yawned, after counting the profits of the Boer War, in which it had admirably demonstrated its patriotism by supplying both the British and the Boers with Maxim guns and other equipment. Bedors yawned, Schultz-Poiret yawned.

But Sazaroff did not yawn, neither did Kronk.

And eventually Schultz-Poiret stopped yawning, as did Bouchard and Sons, and Bedors and Robsons-Strong. For a pestilential whisper had come out of Germany, out of the Balkans, out of Russia. The Kronk plant at Essen was smoking nicely, and all at once the munition works of Schultz-Poiret at Le Creusot in Burgundy, began to smoke and show edifying activity, Robsons-Strong became mysteriously active, Skeda's eye brightened, Bedors wore a grave face, and Sazaroff moved about Europe with a speed and suppleness surprising in a man of his age.

The newspapers began to simmer. There was a report that a group of high British naval and military men were entertained at a large dinner by German government officials, and that one German proposed a toast to "Der Tag," the Day when Germans and Britons would be engaged in mortal combat. Guarded yet inflammatory articles against Germany appeared in the French papers; the same articles, almost word for word, appeared in the German newspapers against France. They were finely and subtly written, expressing vague but poignant suspicions, asking impersonal and rhetorical questions, insinuating abstract but ominous accusations. The Russian press also published similar articles, as did the British and the Austrian, the Bulgarian, the Greek and the Roumanian. Serbian papers uneasily whispered and looked apprehensively at Austria.

The strange thing about it all was that the group of men who wrote these articles were paid with a fine impartiality by Kronk and Schultz-Poiret, Skeda and Bedors and Bouchard and Sons.

In America, Jay Regan the Younger conferred with his associates, among whom were Jules Bouchard and his brother and cousins, as to the amounts which might be lent to Britain and to France, or possibly to Germany. Finally, after long debate, study of many papers, consultations with statesmen, bankers and politicians, a decision was reached.

An odd thing happened shortly afterwards. American histories, newspapers, orators and patriotic societies, suddenly ceased their baiting and ridicule of England. There was much unexpected talk about Hands across the Sea. Pleasant visits were arranged between prominent Britons and Americans. Anglo-American sentiment became warm and very close and understanding.

The wine in the vats began to ferment.